ERLE STANLEY GARDNER

SEVEN COMPLETE NOVELS

ERLE STANLEY GARDNER

SEVEN COMPLETE NOVELS

PERRY MASON

IN

THE CASE OF:

The Glamorous Ghost
The Terrified Typist
The Lucky Loser
The Screaming Woman
The Long-Legged Models
The Foot-Loose Doll
The Waylaid Wolf

AVENEL BOOKS • NEW YORK

This book was originally published as seven separate volumes.

The Case of the Glamorous Ghost copyright © MCMLV by Erle Stanley Gardner.

The Case of the Terrified Typist copyright ©MCMLVI by Erle Stanley Gardner.

The Case of the Lucky Loser copyright © MCMLVI by The Curtis Publishing Company, copyright © MCMLVII by Erle Stanley Gardner.

The Case of the Screaming Woman copyright © MCMLVII by Erle Stanley Gardner.

The Case of the Long Legged Models copyright © MCMLVII by The Curtis Publishing Company, copyright © MCMLVIII by Erle Stanley Gardner.

The Case of the Foot-Loose Doll copyright © MCMLVIII by The Curtis Publishing Company, copyright © MCMLVIII by Erle Stanley Gardner.

The Case of the Waylaid Wolf copyright © MCMLIX by The Curtis Publishing Company, copyright © MCMLIX by Erle Stanley Gardner.

This edition is published by Avenel Books,
distributed by Crown Publishers, Inc.,
by arrangement with William Morrow and Company.
a b c d e f g h
AVENEL 1979 EDITION
Manufactured in the United States of America

Library of Congress Cataloging in Publication Data

Gardner, Erle Stanley, 1889-1970.
    Erle Stanley Gardner, seven complete novels.

    CONTENTS: The foot-loose doll.—The glamorous ghost.—The long-legged models.—The lucky loser.—The screaming woman.—The terrified typist.—The waylaid wolf.
    1. Detective and mystery stories, American.
I. Title.
PZ3.G1714Er 1979 [PS3513.A6322]   813′.5′2   79-16338
ISBN 0-517-29363-3
ISBN 0-517-29364-1 lib. bdg.

CONTENTS

THE CASE OF
THE GLAMOROUS GHOST

FOREWORD

George Burgess Magrath has exerted a tremendous influence in the field of legal medicine and in the detection of crime.

Dr. Magrath's life is a splendid example of the manner in which a man's dynamic personality can spread out over the years, affecting the lives of others long after he is gone.

Many of my readers will remember what I have written about Frances G. Lee, the fabulous character who is mainly responsible for founding the Department of Legal Medicine at Harvard Medical School; a woman in her seventies who is respected by police officers everywhere, who is an authority in the field of homicide investigation and who has been appointed a captain in the New Hampshire State Police.

The fact that Captain Frances G. Lee became interested in legal medicine was due to the influence of Dr. Magrath. The fact that Captain Frances G. Lee invented her famous nutshell studies in unexplained death has been responsible for training hundreds of competent officers so that they can detect murders which otherwise might go not only undetected but unsuspected.

One of Dr. Magrath's greatest contributions to investigative science was his devotion to truth.

In every one of his field notebooks he wrote just inside the front cover a quotation from the writings of Dr. Paul Brouardel, the noted French doctor who was one of the first pioneers in legal medicine.

The quotation is as follows:

> "IF THE LAW HAS MADE YOU A WITNESS, REMAIN A MAN OF SCIENCE: YOU HAVE NO VICTIM TO AVENGE, NO GUILTY OR INNOCENT PERSON TO RUIN OR SAVE. YOU MUST BEAR TESTIMONY WITHIN THE LIMITS OF SCIENCE."

Dr. Magrath was a colorful personality. There was about him a flair for the dramatic. He was tall and heavy-set with superb shoulders and one of his greatest pleasures was rowing, or, more properly, sculling on the Charles River. He wore his hair long like Paderewski, his dress was informal, usually of soft tweeds, and his tie was invariably a dark Windsor.

There was about his personality something compelling that enabled him to dominate situations without apparently making the slightest effort to do so. He was in spirit a pioneer, blazing a trail in the investigative field, and he had all of the personality of the true pioneer. He was born on October 2nd, 1870. He died December 11th, 1938. During his lifetime he examined over twenty-thousand cases of unexplained deaths, and the present highly efficient science of homicide investigation is in large measure due to the trail blazed by Dr. Magrath. The blaze marks on that trail are Truth, Accuracy, Efficiency and Scientific Integrity. Today many feet follow along that trail, and the wayfarers either follow those same blaze marks or become hopelessly lost in the forest of prejudice.

The truly scientific investigator of homicide remains on the one trail that follows those same blazes which Dr. Magrath used for his own guidance.

And so I dedicate this book to the memory of:

GEORGE BURGESS MAGRATH, M.D.

Erle Stanley Gardner

CHAPTER ONE

I t was Della Street, Perry Mason's confidential secretary, who first called the lawyer's attention to the glamorous ghost.

"Why the grin?" Mason asked, as Della Street folded a newspaper and handed it to him.

"This should interest you."

"What is it?"

"A ghost that people saw last night out at Sierra Vista Park, a very glamorous ghost. A seductive ghost. It should make a case you'd be interested in."

Mason said, "You've already interested me."

He took the newspaper Della Street had handed him and read in headlines:

SEXY SPOOK STARTLES SPOONERS
GIRL GIVES CHASE WITH JACK HANDLE

The clipping had been written up in a light vein, a combination of news and humor.

The story as reported read:

> Last night was a night of witchery. The moon was full and fragrant wisps of breeze gently rustled the trees and greenery.
>
> George Belmont, 28, of 1532 West Woodwane Street and Diane Foley were sitting in their parked car, looking at the moon. Suddenly a beautiful wraith, apparently in the nude save for a fluttering diaphanous covering, drifted out of the shadows toward the car.
>
> According to George, the wraith was making the motions of a classical dance. Diane, outraged, described the same occurrence to police with far less imagery—a difference in viewpoint, no doubt.
>
> "We were sitting there talking," Diane told Officer Stanley of

the park patrol, "when a girl appeared in little or nothing and deliberately started vamping my boy friend. She wasn't dancing, she was giving the old come-on, and don't think I didn't know it."

"A seductive come-on?" Officer Stanley inquired.

"Call it seductive if you want to," Diane snorted. "It was just a wiggle as far as I'm concerned."

"And what did George do?"

"He said, 'Look at that,' and started to get out of the car. That was when I went into action."

"What did you do?"

"I grabbed up the first thing that was available and took after her, saying that I'd teach her better than to come prancing around without any clothes on, making passes at my boy friend."

According to police the "first thing that was available" was a jack handle which would certainly have inflicted what the law refers to as "grievous bodily injury," and, beyond any question, was within the classification of a deadly weapon.

The ghost, however, did not seem to realize its desperate plight. It was too busy getting out of there—but fast. Diane Foley, hampered by her more conventional garb, took after the ghost in a headlong pursuit which was punctuated from time to time with infuriated screams, arousing the attention of residents who bordered on the park and resulting in more than half a dozen calls to the police.

According to Diane the ghost did the screaming. According to neighbors Diane certainly was doing some screaming herself. As one man who telephoned the police said in a later report, "It sounded like a couple of coyotes out in the desert—and you know what that sounds like. One sounds like half a dozen. Two sound like . . . well, that was the way it sounded out there in the park. I certainly thought someone was getting murdered, or that at least it was a hand-to-hand hair-pulling match."

Be that as it may the "ghost," which George described as having a figure "simply out of this world," won the race and a breathless, indignant Diane, still carrying the jack handle, returned to the car.

Police, however, alerted by a dozen calls, converged on the neighborhood and soon were rewarded by picking up a young women walking demurely along clad in an opaque raincoat. In view of the cloudless night the raincoat seemed incongruous.

Interrogated by police, the young woman professed complete ignorance as to her name or address. Her mind, she said, was a blank.

Once at headquarters, it was soon discovered that her mind wasn't all that was blank. Under the raincoat, her only apparel was the remains of an expensive, gossamer slip, torn into the equivalent of Salome's seven veils.

Police felt they had apprehended the ghost, but the evidence was circumstantial. Diane was vague as to any identification and she refused to permit George to be called as a witness.

In view of the seeming amnesia the "ghost" is at present being held in the emergency hospital while police seek to learn her identity.

"Well," Mason said, "it would make a most interesting problem in identification. She should have committed some crime. It's too bad."

"Don't bewail your luck so soon," Della Street said. "I didn't call your attention to the article in the paper simply to send your thoughts woolgathering, but in my official capacity as your secretary.

"The half sister of this glamorous ghost is impatiently waiting in the outer office."

"The deuce!" Mason exclaimed. "What does she want?"

"Apparently the family wants you to represent the ghost. There seems to be a consensus of opinion that the ghost is up to her neck in a scrape of some kind and that you must get her out."

"What's the half sister's name, Della?"

"Mrs. William Kensington Jordan, and she seems to have the trappings of wealth and respectability."

Mason grinned. "Your build-up, Della, is excellent. By all means, let's see Mrs. William Jordan—but first tell me what she looks like."

"Neat, refined, well-groomed, nice clothes, neat ankles, expensive shoes..."

"How old?"

"Twenty-eight to thirty."

"Good-looking?"

Della Street hesitated a moment. "The lips are just a bit too thin. She tries to build them up with lipstick and...well, somehow it throws her face out of balance. A full mouth just doesn't go with that type of face. But she has nice, intelligent eyes."

"Well, let's take a look at her," Mason said. "I'm interested in the ghost."

"You would be," Della said dryly, heading for the outer office.

Mrs. Jordan, on being ushered into Mason's private office, stood for a moment in the doorway, regarding the lawyer with searching scrutiny. Della Street said, "This is Mr. Mason, Mrs. Jordan."

"Thank you," Mrs. Jordan snapped without moving her eyes in the slightest.

Mason smiled affably. "How do you do, Mrs. Jordan?"

She came forward and gave him her hand. "How do you do, Mr. Mason? It's a pleasure to meet you—and see that your looks measure up to your extraordinary reputation."

"Thank you," the lawyer said gravely, avoiding his secretary's amused eyes.

Mrs. Jordan's speech had that sharp, precise articulation which should go with thin lips, and her manner was incisive.

"Do sit down," Mason said, indicating the client's comfortable chair, "and tell me what you wanted to see me about."

"Have you read the paper?" Mrs. Jordan asked, seating herself, crossing her knees and carefully smoothing the skirt down over her legs.

Mason glanced at Della Street, nodded to Mrs. Jordan.

"Well," she said, "then you've read about this ghost, this exhibitionist in Sierra Vista Park who made a naked spectacle of herself in the moonlight."

Mason nodded. "I take it," he said, "from your description that you are not a believer in the supernatural."

"Not when Eleanor is concerned."

"And who is Eleanor?"

"The ghost. She's my half sister," she said.

"You have communicated that information to the authorities?" Mason asked.

"No."

"Why not?"

"I...I want to know where I stand first."

"Perhaps," Mason told her, "you'd better explain."

Mrs. Jordan made no attempt to disguise the bitterness in her voice.

"Eleanor," she said, "is an exhibitionist and an opportunist. She's also a liar."

"Evidently you have very little affection for your half sister."

"Don't misunderstand me, Mr. Mason. I hate the ground she walks on."

"I take it," Mason said, "that you have recognized the picture that was published in the newspaper, the picture of the young woman who has amne—"

"Amnesia my foot!" she interrupted. "She doesn't have any more amnesia than I do. She got in a jam once before and pulled that amnesia business to get herself out. She's done something that's a lulu this time and this is just her way of arousing sympathy and easing herself back into the family fold."

"I think," Mason said, "you'd better give me *all* the circumstances."

"About two weeks ago," Mrs. Jordan said, "Eleanor ran away with Douglas Hepner."

"And who's Douglas Hepner?"

"A drifter, a traveler, a fortune-hunter and an opportunist. He's as phony as a three-dollar bill."

"And you say your half sister ran away with him?"

"That's right."

"Marriage?" Mason asked.

"That's what *she* says."

"You were not at the ceremony?"

"Of course not. They simply took off. My husband, my father and I were away for the week end. When we returned we found a wire stating that they were happily married."

"Where was the wire from?"

"Yuma, Arizona."

"Lots of marriages are solemnized in Yuma," Mason said dryly. "People go there simply to get married."

"That's probably why they went there."

"To get married?"

"No, because Yuma has that reputation."

"You don't think they're actually married?"

"I don't know *what* to think, Mr. Mason. As far as Eleanor is concerned I've given up trying to think a long time ago."

"Well, suppose you tell me about her."

"My maiden name was Corbin. I'm Olga Corbin Jordan."

"Is your husband living?"

She nodded.

"You're living together?"

"Of course. Bill and I are very happy. I came here alone because he couldn't get away."

"But he knows you're coming?"

"Certainly. I don't have any secrets from Bill. Dad doesn't know all the details. I simply told him I was going to see a lawyer and that he wasn't to say a word to the police or to the newspapers until after he heard from me."

"You recognized your half sister's picture in the paper?"

. "Yes. It's a good likeness. Other people will recognize it too. That's why I was so impatient trying to get in to see you. We don't have much time."

"All right, just what do you want me to do?"

"Eleanor has been in four or five scrapes. Someone has always come to the rescue and got her out. Dad has always been most indulgent with her and ... well, I think she's the apple of his eye. She's spoiled and thinks she can wrap any man around her little finger. She's loaded with sex appeal, and does she use it!"

"Is she oversexed?" Mason asked.

"No, but the men whom she comes in contact with think *they're* oversexed. You've been around, Mr. Mason. You know that type of woman."

"How does she get along with women?"

"She doesn't deal with women. She makes her play for men and, believe me, she's clever at it. Of course, it's flattering—she makes them think they're wonderful—but when you have to live with that sort of thing day in and day out, week in and week out, when you know each new victim will be a sucker, you become disgusted with the whole thing."

"Particularly if you don't like her in the first place," Mason said dryly.

"Well, I don't like her," Olga Jordan blazed. "She's been a devastating influence on Dad ever since she was five years old."

"Is your mother living?"

She shook her head.

"You say Eleanor is your half sister?"

"I'll give you the highlights, Mr. Mason. I was born when Father was thirty years old. I'm twenty ... I'm thirty now. Dad is sixty. Mother died when I was five years old. Then when I was eight this Sally Levan came into Dad's life."

"She was Eleanor's mother?"

"That's right. And she had one definite, fixed idea in mind from the time she first met Dad. That was to throw her hooks into him and take him for all she could get. She raved about Dad and about how she loved every hair of his head. She wanted to raise a family and Eleanor was the result—not because she gave a hang about a family but she knew that as long as Dad had me she couldn't compete with that bond unless she had a child of her own who would be Dad's daughter and ... Oh, I was only eight years old at the time, and I know an eight-year-old child isn't supposed to notice those things, but, believe me, I saw it just as plain as day."

"She died?"

"Rather suddenly. Yes, she died. And I'll tell you, Mr. Mason, I've never made a point of being a hypocrite. I was eleven years old then, but I could see things just as clearly as I can see them now, and I was glad she died. I was glad then and I've been glad ever since."

"And thereafter you and Eleanor grew up together?"

"Thereafter I had the job of trying to be an older sister and a mother. Dad called me in and explained my responsibilities. I determined to do the best I could. I liked Eleanor at that time. I hated her mother, but I didn't have any feeling against Eleanor."

"That came later?" Mason asked.

"That came later."

"How much later?" Mason asked, glancing at Della Street.

"Not a lot later," Mrs. Jordan confessed. "By the time Eleanor was five years old you could see that she was her mother's child all over. She has beautiful large blue eyes, blonde hair that gives her an innocent sweet look—it's so fine and has such a sheen to it that it's almost like a halo, and she started cultivating that angelic look. She was just such a sweet, poor little motherless morsel that people fell all over themselves to help her.

"She used that technique until she learned about men—and then there was no stopping her."

"Go on," Mason said.

"Well, she would have caused Dad a lot of heartbreak if Dad had known about it. Dad never did know all the details. Bill and I helped cover things up. On occasion we lied our heads off. One time when we were on a vacation and Eleanor was supposed to have been with us, we backed up her alibi and lied like troopers."

"She wasn't with you?"

"No. Heaven knows where she was. But she told Dad she was going up to join us. We probably never would have learned anything about it if it hadn't been for the fact that we called up Dad to see how he was getting along and Dad asked how Eleanor was enjoying the trip. It took me just half a second to get the picture and for his sake I told him she was having the time of her life."

"Your father is fond of her?"

"Dad has been hypnotized by her, just as he was hypnotized by her mother. But I think Dad is beginning to get his eyes open just a little bit."

"And now you believe that she's this ghost who...?"

"I know it," she interrupted. "I could almost tell it even if it weren't for the picture in the paper. That technique is Eleanor's. It's just like her. She ran away with Douglas Hepner. Heaven knows what happened. Whatever it is you can expect the worst. All right, she had to come back to the family fold, but she's afraid of something. Something's happened so she has to make a plea for sympathy and sneak up on Dad's blind side.

"So she goes out in the moonlight, doing the dance of the seven veils and manages to get herself caught by the police—which, of course, she'd planned all along—and looks at them with those wide blue eyes of hers and says she doesn't know who she is, that she hasn't the faintest idea of the past. It's all a blank to her. So the police take her to the hospital, her picture is published in the paper and then the family is supposed to come rushing to her. There'll be a reunion. We'll get psychiatrists to get her memory back and in the midst of all that sympathy and sweet helplessness the thing that she's done that she's afraid of will come to light and she'll be forgiven."

Mason's eyes narrowed as he studied Mrs. Jordan. "Then why not go to the hospital and identify her," he asked, "and get it over with? If that's the game she's playing there's not much you can do about it. Why consult a lawyer?"

"I'm consulting you, Mr. Mason, partially because I'm tired of this whole business, and partially because I want to spare Dad as much as I can. I'm afraid—afraid of what Eleanor's done this time."

"Why?"

"This is...well, this is carrying things plenty far, even for Eleanor."

"And what do you want *me* to do?"

"I want you to go to the hospital with me. I want you to be there when I make the identification. I want you to take charge of things. You'll know how to handle the resulting publicity. You'll know how to handle reporters, and then I want you to sit down with Eleanor and I want you to *force* her to tell you *what* it is she's running away from, what it is that's happened, what has caused her to adopt this weird method of trying to arouse public sympathy and get herself reinstated with the family."

"And then?" Mason asked.

"And then," she said, "I want you to use every bit of resourcefulness at your command to try and square things, to try and clean the mess up so that...so that the newspapers don't get hold of things and so that Dad doesn't have too much of a shock."

"Is your father in good health?"

"Physically," she said, "he's straight as a ramrod, but he's in a peculiar position. Dad's in the wholesale jewelry business. He specializes in diamonds. People trust him. His word is as good as a written guarantee. If something should happen that would humiliate him, if there should be a big family scandal—well, it would crush him."

"And you think Eleanor may have...?"

"I think that whatever Eleanor's done this time," she interrupted, "it's *really* something. This isn't just an ordinary scrape. This is a dilly."

Mason hesitated. "I'm afraid, Mrs. Jordan," he said at length, "that you're letting your suspicions and your prejudices build up a set of circumstances in your mind that are purely imaginary. Why don't you wait until...?"

She shook her head impatiently. "There isn't time, Mr. Mason. Quite a few people know Eleanor. In all probability the hospital is receiving calls by this time, telling them who she is. We're going to have to work fast."

Mrs. Jordan opened her purse, took out a folded oblong of paper. "I know you're a busy and high-priced lawyer. I have made out a check payable to you for twenty-five hundred dollars, Mr. Mason. That is in the nature of a retainer."

Mason raised his eyebrows. "Usually," he said, "people go to an attorney and ask him how much..."

"I know," she said, "but this is different. This is an emergency."

Mason asked, "You want me to go to the hospital with you and then what?"

"I'll identify Eleanor, and then I want you to talk with her privately and alone after you've got rid of the reporters."

Mason said, "You will, of course, identify her as your half sister?"

"Naturally. And as far as the public is concerned the scene will be one of great affection and sympathy. Outwardly I'll do everything that the situation requires."

"Do you expect to have your father see her?"

"Not until after you've found out what has really happened."

"Do you think she'll tell me?"

"Probably not. You're going to have to talk with her and get clues. You'll need detectives. We will, of course, pay all expenses."

"What do you think Eleanor will do?" Mason asked.

"I can tell you *exactly* what she'll do. She'll look at us and turn her head away in bored indifference, a poor child who doesn't know who she is or anything about her past. And then I'll say, 'Eleanor, don't you know me?'

"She'll turn those big blue eyes on me as though I'm a total stranger and then suddenly the eyes will begin to widen. She'll blink. She'll do a double take. There'll be a ghost of a smile and then suddenly memory will come back with a rush and she'll exclaim, 'Olga! Olga, my *dar*ling' and throw her arms around me and cling to me like a drowning man clinging to a piece of driftwood."

"And then?" Mason asked.

"And then there'll be the terrific shock of readjustment. Memory will come pouring back to her in a flood. She'll pull out all the stops—and finally she'll wind up by remembering everything about her past life up until the moment she disappeared with Douglas Hepner, and from that time on her memory will be a complete blank. She simply won't know where she's been or what she's been doing during the past two weeks.

"She'll ask about Dad. She'll ask questions that show that in her poor little deranged mind she thinks it is still two weeks ago. It will come as a shock to her when I explain that there's a missing gap of two weeks."

"And she won't remember anything that happened? Even the show she put on in the park?"

"She'll look at newspaper reporters with shocked incredulity when they tell her about it."

"To carry through a situation of that sort is going to take a good deal of histrionic ability," Mason said. "Do you think she can do it and do it convincingly?"

"She'll fool everybody on earth," Mrs. Jordan said, "except one person."

"Who's that?"

"Me. I'm telling you that in advance, Mr. Mason, because she's going to fool *you!*"

Mason smiled. "Lawyers become somewhat cynical."

"She'll fool you," Olga Jordan asserted positively. "She'll fool you and when she finds out what you're there for, she'll hypnotize you. You'll be just like all the other men. You'll want to protect her. Don't misunderstand me. I *want* you to protect her and help her out of the scrape she's in because that's the only way you can help Dad and do a job protecting the family."

"When do we go to the hospital?" Mason asked.

"Now," she said, looking at her watch. "We haven't much time."

Mason nodded to Della Street. "I'll be out for an hour or an hour and a half, Della. Come on," he said to Mrs. Jordan, "let's get going."

CHAPTER TWO

The head nurse in the front office said, "Oh, yes, Mrs. Jordan. The police have been trying to reach you for the last hour. They're anxious to see if you can make an identification."

"There's a very great resemblance to my sister," Mrs. Jordan said. "I feel certain it is she."

"Yes. We've had several telephone calls since the picture was published in the paper from people who have told us they were sure it was Eleanor Corbin."

"Eleanor Hepner," Mrs. Jordan corrected firmly. "She was married about two weeks ago."

"Oh, I see. Well, would you mind going up, Mrs. Jordan? The doctor left word that you were to be admitted as soon as we could get in touch with you. He feels that the emotional shock of seeing you may do a good deal to restore the patient's memory. Of course, you understand in these cases we never know just what's going to happen. The nurse in charge will be with you. She has instructions from the doctor. You will have to follow her guidance.

"In case it should appear that your presence disturbs the patient then you'll have to withdraw. You will, of course, have to be very careful not to do anything that would tend to annoy or excite the patient unduly. But in case the emotional shock of seeing you *does* bring about recognition and breaks through the amnesia—well, then, of course, we'll have to be governed by circumstances."

"I understand," Mrs. Jordan said.

"And you'll co-operate with the nurse?"

"Certainly, but Mr. Mason is to be with me," Olga Jordan said.

The nurse hesitated. "There were no instructions about Mr. Mason, but..."

"Very definitely he must be with me," Olga Jordan said firmly, "in case she should recognize me and break through this amnesia. I noticed several reporters waiting around outside, and—well Mr. Mason has certain things to do in order to see that the publicity doesn't get out of hand and...there are certain things that he understands."

"Very well, we *have* been having a bad time with the reporters," the nurse said. "You will, of course, understand that you're to do the talking, Mrs. Jordan—that is, until we get a reaction. The nurse will advise you. Here she is now—Myrna, this is Mrs. Jordan, the sister of the patient in 981, that is, we *think* she's the sister. And this is Mr. Mason, the lawyer. Will you take them up, please, and see if Mrs. Jordan's presence brings about a recognition?"

The nurse nodded, turned with rubber-heeled efficiency and said, "This way, please."

She led the way, moving on silent feet, the starched skirt giving a faint rustle as she guided them to the elevator, up to the ninth floor, then down to room 981.

The nurse opened the door. "Go right in," she whispered. "Walk up to the bed. Stand beside her. Watch the expression on her face. If she shows any sign of recognition call out her name."

"I understand," Olga Jordan said, and she and Perry Mason moved on into the room.

The young woman who lay on the bed, attired in a hospital nightgown, was staring at the ceiling with vacant eyes. There was a helpless expression on her face that was pathetically appealing.

Olga Jordan moved over toward the bed.

The blue eyes detected motion within the room. They turned casually, making an appraisal of the newcomer, then as casually turned away.

Abruptly the eyes turned back again, studied Olga for a moment, started to turn away again, then with a start the eyes widened, the neck stiffened. The woman on the bed raised her head slightly.

"Eleanor," Olga Jordan said softly.

For a moment the eyes lighted with utter incredulity, then the girl blinked her lids a couple of times as though just waking up and snapped upright in bed.

"Olga!" she cried.

"Olga! My darling! Oh *dear, dear* Olga! I'm *so* glad to see you!"

She held out her arms.

Olga enclosed Eleanor in an embrace. "You poor darling," she said, "You poor, poor dear." Her voice was vibrant with sympathy.

Mason stood by the head of the bed. His eyes sought those of the nurse. The nurse smiled reassuringly, nodded at Mason, and moved quietly into the corner of the room where she could listen but wouldn't be readily visible to the patient.

"Oh Olga, it seems like it's ages since I've seen you and yet it couldn't have been...couldn't have been over an hour or two. Where am I, Olga? This room...?"

The blonde head turned from side to side. Abruptly she noticed Perry Mason. "Who's he?" she asked.

"That's Perry Mason, an attorney who's come to help you."

"An attorney? What do I want with an attorney to help *me*?"

"We thought you'd better have one."

"What for? I don't need a lawyer," Eleanor said, but she flashed a quick smile at Perry Mason. "But if I did need one," she said, "I'd want one just like you."

"Thank you," Mason said.

"Well, wherever I am and whatever it's all about," Eleanor said, "I'm going to get some clothes on right now and get out of here."

She flung back the covers on the bed, exposing shapely legs with creamy skin, then, realizing the position of the nightgown, hastily grabbed at the hem and pulled it down.

Olga pushed gently on the girl's shoulders.

"You'll have to stay here for a little while, Eleanor."

"Where's here and why do I have to stay?"

"It's a hospital, darling."

"A hospital!" Eleanor exclaimed.

Olga nodded.

"But what am *I* doing in a hospital? Why, Olga, it's absurd! I just left home. I...now wait a minute. Oh yes, there was that auto accident. What day is it?"

"Tuesday."

"Well, that's right," Eleanor said. "Yesterday was Monday. We left Monday night, the second."

"Where's Douglas?" Olga asked.

"Douglas? Good heavens, where *is* Doug? He was driving the car. What's happened? Is he hurt? Tell me, Olga. Don't try to break it to me gently! Where is he? Tell me."

"We don't know, darling," Olga said. "This is Tuesday, dear, but it's Tuesday the seventeenth, not Tuesday the third. We received a wire from Yuma, Arizona, and several post cards saying you had been married."

"Then they must have been sent *after* the accident, so Doug must have been all right."

"What accident, darling?"

"The one Monday night. The big white headlights came boring out of the darkness like two great big eyes trying to tear me apart, and then this awful..."

She broke off and hid her face with her hands.

Olga patted her shoulder, "There, there, dear, you mustn't worry. Don't try to remember anything."

"I'm all right," Eleanor said, "only I've got to find out what happened. If I've got a perfectly good husband running around loose somewhere, this doesn't fit in with my idea of a honeymoon. I guess I must have had a bump on the head in the auto accident."

She raised her hands to her head, moving the tips of her fingers through her blonde hair. She turned to Mason, regarded him with frank appraisal, said, "You're either going to have to get out of here or turn your back because I'm going to dress."

"Now wait just a moment," Mason said. "You must stay quiet. You've had a little trouble with your memory."

"I guess I got knocked out," Eleanor admitted, and then laughed. "But that's nothing. Lots of people get knocked out. Prize fighters get knocked out so often that they just bounce up and down like a rubber ball every time they hit the canvas. I guess I took a delayed bounce. What was the report on the accident? Who hit us?"

"We didn't know about any accident, darling," Olga said.

"Well, of all things. It certainly should have been reported. How did you happen to come here if you didn't know about the accident, Olga?"

"I saw your picture in the paper."

"My picture..."

"We were hoping perhaps you could tell us what had happened," Mason interposed.

"Well, all I know is that Doug and I were on our way to Yuma to get married.... Then I saw those headlights right in front of me and felt that terrible impact and... well, here I am in the hospital—at least you tell me it's a hospital."

Olga said, "Listen, Eleanor darling, no one knows what's happened. You've been out doing things on your own. No one knows what. You were picked up by the police last night, wandering around in a park with nothing on but a raincoat and a diaphanous slip..."

"I, in a park, without clothes! Well, I'll be damned!" Eleanor exclaimed, and then suddenly began to laugh.

Olga raised inquiring eyebrows.

"Well," Eleanor said, "I've heard the expression 'being knocked into the middle of next week.' but I guess that automobile accident knocked me into the middle of the week *after* next. So you're to be my mentor and guardian, Mr. Mason."

"I wouldn't go as far as that, but maybe I can help. Can you remember anything about the last two weeks?" Mason asked.

"I can't remember one single thing after we had the accident."

"The accident," Mason said, "was probably two weeks ago."

"Well, all I can remember is that I was lying here with my mind a blank and people gliding in and out and then I looked up and saw Olga and I felt a dizzy spinning sensation in my head and, all of a sudden, I woke up—and here I was—I mean here I am.

"I'm perfectly normal. I can remember everything that happened up until the moment that car came rushing toward us."

"Where was that?" Mason asked.

"Some place on the road to Yuma."

"You can't remember just where?"

"No. Now that you speak of it, things get fuzzy when I try to focus my mind on things that happened that night.... I get all dizzy.... I feel I'm slipping...."

"Don't try to recall anything, then," Mason said. "Just lie there and relax."

"Thank you, I feel a little tired all at once."

The door to the room swung open silently. A crisp-mannered, professional-looking man entered the room.

Mason stepped quickly between the bed and the new arrival.

"Who are you?" Mason demanded.

The man stared at Mason with surprise and some indignation. "Who are *you*? I am the doctor in charge of this case."

Mason turned to the nurse for confirmation. She nodded.

Mason grinned. "I'm the attorney in charge of this case. My name is Mason. I thought you might be a reporter."

"They've had a field day already with the police." The doctor turned to Eleanor. "You look as though you were feeling better."

"*Better?* I'm well! And I'm on my way."

"Doctor, Mrs. Hepner has regained her memory. She seems to be all right physically. We appreciate all you have done for her, but we want to get her out of here quickly and quietly."

"Now wait just a minute, Mr. Mason! This patient—"

"You undoubtedly know Dr. Ariel."

The doctor nodded.

"I'm going to call him immediately. We want Mrs. Hepner under his care—elsewhere."

"The police—"

"No charges have been filed against Mrs. Hepner, so the police have nothing to say about it. Mrs. Hepner will expect a bill for your services, Doctor, an *adequate* bill."

"And the reporters?" the doctor asked grimly.

Mason thought for a moment. "Tell them your patient has been identified and that she has been discharged from the hospital. That and nothing more. I can assure you that your co-operation will be appreciated."

The doctor studied Eleanor Hepner frowningly. Then he shrugged. "All right, if that's the way you want it."

He turned and opened the door into the corridor. "Nurse, I'd like to speak to you a moment."

The nurse followed him into the corridor and closed the door behind her.

"Olga, I *like* Mr. Mason," Eleanor sighed. "I'll take him any time."

Olga Jordan ignored her sister. "Mr. Mason, are you sure you know what you're doing?"

"I've got a pretty good idea," Mason said coolly. "Now, if you will hand me that telephone, please.... Thank you."

He called Dr. Claude Ariel, a client of his and explained the circumstances. He emphasized that in his opinion Eleanor should be kept quiet and that above all she should have no visitors.

"That's fine," Dr. Ariel said. "I'll call the hospital. I'm on the staff there. I'll also make arrangements to have the patient moved to a private sanitarium. I'll have that done by an ambulance. Now the sanitarium I would suggest is the Pine Haven Sanitarium up above Glendale. Do you have any preference?"

"No, the Pine Haven's fine with me," Mason said.

"All right, I'll get on the job. "I'll put on a special nurse I can trust right away, and I'll be there myself within half an hour. At that time I'll arrange for an ambulance to move the patient. I'll make all necessary arrangements at the sanitarium. There aren't any police charges against this patient, are there?"

"Not as yet," Mason said, "and I don't think there will be, but if there are, I'll put up bail and get her out, so you can go right ahead with your plans. Now it's very important that for the moment she receive no visitors."

"I understand," Dr. Ariel said. "You can trust me on that."

Mason thanked him and hung up.

Some ten minutes later there was a gentle tap on the door.

"Who is it?" Mason asked.

"I'm a special nurse. Dr. Ariel wanted me to take charge of the case and to see that the patient wasn't disturbed."

Mason opened the door. The nurse entered the room, promptly proceeded to close the door firmly. She smiled at Mason and said, "You believe in direct action, don't you?"

"It gets results," Mason said.

The nurse smiled at the blonde on the bed. "How are you feeling?" she asked.

"Better," Eleanor said cautiously. "I feel fine except when I try to recall certain events that took place."

"Then don't try to recall them," the nurse said.

Eleanor looked helplessly at Perry Mason and said, "I'd like to help you, Mr. Mason, I really would."

"That's all right," Mason said. "It may come back to you later."

"I remember," she said, "we were going to get married. We were driving to Yuma and...and there was Douglas' mother. He telephoned her and told her and...and I talked with her. She had a sweet voice and..."

"Where did you place the call from, do you know?" Mason asked.

"It was a service station somewhere where we stopped for gas."

"Where does his mother live?" Mason asked.

"Salt Lake City, but heavens, I don't know the address. And then we drove on and there were these headlights coming right toward me..." She put her hands over her face again and said through her fingers, "Mr. Mason, I have to hold on to myself. I get all dizzy when I start thinking of that. You don't mind, do you?"

The nurse looked at Mason and placed a finger across her lips.

Mason said, "No. Don't try to think about it at all."

"I can't help it. I just keep thinking up to that point and then my mind starts going round and round."

"The doctor will be here in a few minutes," Mason said. "He'll give you something to quiet you and then you'll go to a sanitarium where you can rest for a while."

Mason turned to Olga. "I think it'll be a good plan for us to leave now, Mrs. Jordan."

"I think so too," the nurse said. "The doctor has given orders that the patient is to have a sedative if she becomes at all restless."

"I don't want a sedative," Eleanor said. "I want to get out of here. I want to get my clothes on and find out what happened to Douglas."

Mason smiled understandingly. "You'd better rest and wait until after Dr. Ariel has had a good talk with you. Then he'll fix things so you can be discharged and..."

"But you said I'd have to go to a sanitarium. I don't want to go to a sanitarium. What do I want to go to a rest home for? A rest home is for people who are beginning to break up. I'm..."

Once more she threw the covers off the bed, kicked out a pair of smooth, well-shaped legs.

The nurse hurriedly interposed herself between the bed and Mason, pulled the covers up, said, "You mustn't do that. You must keep quiet. Just a few minutes longer and Dr. Ariel will be here."

"I don't want Dr. Ariel. I want Doug." Eleanor looked as though she would cry.

The nurse picked up a package she had carried with her into the room. There was the brief smell of alcohol, then Eleanor said, "Ouch, that hurts."

"Just hold still for a minute," the nurse said. "This is what the doctor ordered."

The nurse withdrew the hypodermic, turned to Mason and Olga, and nodded toward the door.

"She'll be all right now," the nurse said. "Dr. Ariel wants me to go along to the sanitarium as a special. I understand there are to be no visitors. You don't need to worry."

Mason took Olga Jordan's arm. "Let's go," he said.

Out in the corridor, Olga turned to Perry Mason. "Pretty good act, wasn't it?"

"Act or no act," Mason said, "let's get down to brass tacks and see what we have to do."

"Well," Olga said, "she's given you the information that she wants us to have. There's been an accident. She doesn't know where Douglas is. It's up to us to try and find him. We're also going to have to try and find out where the marriage took place. We're going to have to find out about Douglas Hepner's mother in Salt Lake City. And something seems to tell me we're going to have to move pretty fast because whatever it is that Eleanor has pulled this time it's really a lulu and when it catches up with her there's going to be quite a commotion. You're going to have to work fast, Mr. Mason."

"Fast work is going to mean a lot of expense," Mason said. "Are you prepared to pay for the necessary detective work...?"

"We're prepared to pay for anything within reason, Mr. Mason, but for heaven sakes get started and get to work on it fast."

"All right," Mason said. "What can you tell me about this man Hepner?"

"Not very much."

"When did you first meet him?"

"On that last trip to Europe, that is, on our way home from Europe. He was on the boat."

"Do you have any pictures?"

"Yes, I think I can find you some pictures. They're just snaps but..."

"That's all right," Mason said. "Get the snaps. Get them up to my office just as fast as you can. Now can you describe him?"

"Yes. He's tall—around six feet, I guess. He has dark hair and a snub nose, a ready smile and a magnetic personality."

"How old?"

"Twenty-seven or twenty-eight."

"He must have cut quite a swathe on the ship coming over from Europe," Mason said.

"You can say that again. You know how travel is these days. Men have to stay home and work. The women travel. Good-looking men are scarce as hen's teeth. Most of the men are the ones who have retired twenty years too late."

"You sound rather bitter," Mason said.

"I've done lots of traveling. Dad is in the wholesale jewelry business. We go to Europe quite often and..."

"Wait a minute," Mason said. "You're married. Does your father take you and your husband and...?"

"Oh, whenever Bill wants to go Dad takes him. But for the most part Bill likes to stay home and hang around the country club. He's quite a tennis and golf enthusiast and he likes horses. He doesn't care too much for Europe."

"You leave him and go with your father?"

"Yes. Dad needs us to act as traveling secretaries, to make appointments and keep track of his purchases and things of that sort."

"So Eleanor goes along?"

"I'll tell the world Eleanor goes along. She hasn't missed a trip to Europe in the last ten years. Don't be silly. Whenever there's any traveling little Eleanor is right along."

"Where did she meet Douglas Hepner?"

"On the ship."

"What does Hepner do?"

"Apparently nothing. He seems to be a gentleman of leisure. He's one of the most enigmatic individuals I ever knew. He simply won't talk about himself or his background. I think that's why Dad dislikes him. The man is as elusive as a Halloween apple in a barrel of water."

Mason said, "But he seems to be able to attract people and..."

"There's something strange about him. His personality seems to...well, it sort of holds its breath on you. Now that isn't what I'm trying to say. But... well, you get the idea he's playing poker with you. He's affable and polite and friendly, and all of a sudden you catch him looking at you as though he were sizing you up. Eleanor was crazy about him. We thought it was just a shipboard romance, and Lord knows she's had plenty of those."

"But it turned out to be serious?"

"Well, there again it's hard to tell just what *did* happen. No one could be certain whether they were serious or not right up until the minute they left for Yuma."

"How long ago was this cruise?"

"About three months ago."

"Eleanor and Douglas had a crush on shipboard?"

"Yes, but Douglas was in circulation. He was talking with everybody. That's one thing about the man. He's a great mixer when he wants to be, and he certainly got all over that ship."

"Then after you landed he kept up with Eleanor?"

"Well, for a while he didn't—I guess a month or so. And then all of a sudden he began to cultivate Eleanor and she was going out with him—nobody paid too much attention to it until it began to look as though she were serious about it."

"And what did your father say?"

"Dad never did like the man. He took an instinctive, intuitive dislike to him. And Dad's pretty hard to fool."

"But Hepner got Eleanor to go to Yuma and get married?"

"Apparently. Now there again, Mr. Mason, when it comes to telling you anything that Eleanor did or didn't do, all we know is that she left two weeks ago Monday night, that was the second. We got a wire from Yuma, Arizona, that was delivered early on the morning of the third, stating that she and Doug had been married, to please forgive her, that she was crazy about him and they were very happy. We got a couple of post cards, one sent from Yuma and one from Las Vegas, Nevada, and after that there was an interval of complete silence."

"So apparently from Yuma they went to Las Vegas."

"That's what her post card would indicate."

"And the postmarks on the cards?"

"They were from Yuma and from Las Vegas."

"Did you save those?"

"I'm sorry, we didn't. We saved the wire."

"All right," Mason said, "send up whatever snapshots you can find of Douglas Hepner, send up that wire and anything else you may have that you think will help. I'm going to get detectives on the job. We can trace that wire."

"You have confidence in this doctor you retained?" she asked.

"Absolutely," Mason said.

"He'll keep her out of circulation?"

Mason nodded. "Of course," he said, "newspapers will get part of the story. We don't know how much the first nurse overheard, and they may get at her."

"Oh, of course," Olga said, "that's the way Eleanor planned it. She was talking for publication. But the minute you started to pin her down she became afraid of you. She was afraid you'd cross-examine her and bring out the truth, so things began to get all fuzzy and she started getting dizzy, and she threw back the covers so you could see her nice legs."

"And you think all that was put on?" Mason asked.

She looked at him appraisingly. "My God, Mr. Mason, don't be naïve!"

CHAPTER THREE

From a pay station Mason called Paul Drake's office.

"Drake in?" he asked.

"Is this Mr. Mason?"

"That's right."

"Yes, he's here. I'll put him on the line."

A moment later Mason heard Drake's voice on the line.

"Hello, Paul," Mason said. "I have a job for you. It's an emergency."

"All your jobs are emergencies," Drake protested. "What is it this time?"

"Been reading the newspapers?"

"I always read the newspapers. It's part of my job."

"Have you read about the glamorous ghost of Sierra Vista Park?" Mason asked.

"You mean the nearly nude ghost that was traipsing around the park?"

"That's the one."

"Now there's the kind of an assignment a detective would like to have. If I'd had a pair of night binoculars and had been commissioned to sit out there in the moonlight and..."

"All right, Paul, here is where you go to work. The ghost is really Eleanor Hepner who was Eleanor Corbin. She left her home on the second of the month. Apparently she and Hepner went to Yuma, Arizona, and were married.

"Find out when and where. Get certified copies of the records.

"They were in an auto accident on the road. Get the facts on that. I want to know the name of the other party involved in the accident.

"After they were married, they went to Las Vegas. Cover the hotels and motels. Also I want you to find Hepner. He has a passport. Get what you can from the passport office. I'll have pictures up at your office within an hour.

"Get some men lined up. Trace Hepner and get a line on what he does, how much dough he has and where he got it.

"On the night of the second he placed a call to his mother in Salt Lake City. That call was put in from a phone booth at a service station on the road to Yuma where they stopped for gas. We don't know the place; however, figuring they started out with a full tank the place will probably be Indio or near Indio. Cover all calls from there to Salt Lake City on the night of the second.

"Find Hepner's mother. See if she knows where he is now. Find Hepner. See why he and Eleanor have split up. Get a pipeline into police headquarters, find out all they are finding out about Eleanor and see if they are intending to do anything.

"Don't waste time on Eleanor. She can't give us much help at the present time. For your information she's buried. I have her out of circulation."

"Okay," Drake said. "When do you want all this stuff, Perry?"

"Just as soon as you can possibly get it," the lawyer said and hung up.

CHAPTER FOUR

Olga Jordan was accompanied by her father when she brought the photographs and the telegram to Mason's office. She was more than twenty minutes late and started apologizing to Mason almost as soon as she had entered the office and introduced her father to him and Della Street.

"I'm terribly sorry, Mr. Mason. Usually I'm very prompt, but Father pointed out it would be ever so much better to get the negatives rather than merely bring you the photographic prints."

"That will help a lot," Mason said, his eyes on Olga's father.

Homer Corbin could have posed for pictures of a typical Southern colonel. He was a spare, erect man, with a white Vandyke beard carefully trimmed, bushy eyebrows and steel-gray, cold eyes in which the pupils seemed to be mere pinpoints.

"My daughter," he said, speaking with some dignity, "is a very estimable companion, a competent secretary and a rather poor photographer. However, these pictures give you a good idea of the man. I'm glad you're working on that angle, Mr. Mason. I think Douglas Hepner holds the key to whatever has happened."

"Sit down," Mason invited, and then to Corbin said, "You think something has happened, Mr. Corbin?"

Corbin said, "I believe it takes a great emotional shock to bring on amnesia."

"There has, of course, been a physical shock," Mason said. "As I understand it there was an automobile accident."

"Yes, yes, I know. Of course that could have happened, but Olga is rather shrewd, very observant and she is quite familiar with Eleanor's temperament. In fact Olga had to be something of a mother as well as an older sister to Eleanor."

"So she told me," Mason said.

"She very definitely feels that there is some emotional shock in the background, something that has brought on this attack of amnesia. If, of course, that is true, when we discover the event we are going to be faced with another problem, that is how to spare Eleanor from further suffering.

"Eleanor is very dear to me, Mr. Mason. I certainly trust that she hasn't married that bounder Hepner. If she has I feel that this amnesia can be turned to very great legal advantage. I feel that the ceremony can be annulled. Evidently, Mr. Mason, she remembers nothing after that automobile accident, therefore any marriage ceremony must have been performed while her mind was a blank."

"Except," Mason pointed out, "that she knew who she was after that accident and after the wedding ceremony. She sent you this telegram."

"That's true," the older man admitted, reluctantly.

"And some postal cards," Mason went on.

"Two postal cards—one from Yuma, one from Las Vegas."

"They were in her handwriting?"

Homer Corbin stroked his Vandyke, bringing his fingers down to the very point of the beard with a caressing motion. "Well there, Mr. Mason, we're confronted with a peculiar situation. I simply didn't notice the handwriting on the post cards, that is, I took it for granted it was Eleanor's handwriting. I may say that it bore a resemblance to her handwriting, but that, of course, is a far cry from being able to say definitely and positively, 'Yes, that is Eleanor's handwriting.'

"Now as far as the telegram is concerned that could have been sent by anyone. Personally I wouldn't put it a bit past this bounder Hepner to have taken advantage of Eleanor's befuddled mental condition, to have talked her into a marriage and then, in order to keep her family from finding out her real mental condition, sent a telegram in Eleanor's name and forged those postal cards. After all, the postal cards were rather brief and...they hardly seemed like Eleanor. There was a certain element of restraint in them and one doesn't usually associate Eleanor with restraint."

Olga started to say something, then changed her mind.

"Just what would have been his object in marrying your daughter?" Mason asked.

"I think the man is a bounder, a cad, a fortune-hunter."

"I take it that Eleanor has good financial prospects?"

Corbin fastened his cold eyes on Mason and then shifted them slightly toward Olga and then back to Mason. "On my death Eleanor will inherit a very substantial sum of money. Both of my children will be very well fixed as far as this world's goods are concerned."

"All right," Mason said, "let's take a look at the photographs."

"I have here some prints that I tore rather hastily from my photograph book," Olga said, "I've circled Doug Hepner. Here he is standing with Eleanor and another girl. Here he is in a group. Here he is talking with Eleanor at the ship's rail. This probably is the best one of all. Eleanor took this with my camera. It shows him alone, standing by the rail, about the only time I ever saw him on the ship when he didn't have some woman making a pass at him.

"Now here are the negatives. You can find the negatives that go with these pictures....You will get to work at once, Mr. Mason?"

"*Get* to work?" Mason exclaimed. "Good Lord, I've *been* working for an hour and a half. The Drake Detective Agency has men out. We're trying to trace the automobile accident. We're trying to trace that telephone call that Eleanor says Douglas Hepner put through to his mother in Salt Lake City..."

"But you don't know where the call was placed," Olga said.

"I'm assuming that they started out with a full tank," Mason said. "Probably they stopped for gas either at Banning or at Indio, possibly Brawley. We're checking all three places. We're also checking all reports of accidents on the night of the second. We're checking car registrations and ... perhaps you know what kind of a car he was driving."

"He had an air-conditioned Oldsmobile," she said, "one of the big ones. He was very proud of it."

The unlisted telephone on Mason's desk rang sharply.

Since only Della Street and Paul Drake had the number of that telephone Mason motioned to Della Street to hand him the phone and said, "Here's Paul Drake on the line now. He may have something to report."

Mason picked up the telephone, said, "Hello, Paul," and heard Drake's voice saying, "We struck pay dirt on the phone call, Perry."

"Go ahead," Mason said. "My clients are in the office now. I'd like to get the information."

"Well," Drake said, "your hunch was right. It came through from Indio. It was put in at nine-thirty-five on the evening of August second. It was a person-to-person call put in by Douglas Hepner to Sadie Hepner at Salt Lake City. The number is Wabash 983226."

"Have you made any investigation at the other end?" Mason asked.

"No time yet," Drake said. "I thought I'd pass it on to you and see what you wanted to do."

"I'll call you back," Mason said.

He hung up the telephone, turned to Homer Corbin, and said, "We've traced Hepner's mother in Salt Lake City. Now if you want to work fast on this I suggest that I call her and tell her I'm interested in locating her son. If time isn't so essential I can get detectives at Salt Lake to find out something about the woman and we can make a more indirect approach."

Olga and her father exchanged significant glances. It was Olga who answered Mason's question. "I think you'd better put through the call," she said.

Mason said, "Della, put through a call, a person-to-person call. We want to talk with Mrs. Sadie Hepner at Wabash 983226, and you'd better monitor the conversation when the call comes through."

Della Street picked up the telephone. "Give me an outside line, Gertie."

She put through the call, asking the operator to rush it as it was quite important, while the little group sat in tense silence.

Abruptly Della Street nodded to Perry Mason.

Mason picked up the phone.

"Here's your party," the operator said.

"Hello," Mason said.

A richly mellow, feminine voice at the other end of the line said, "Yes, hello."

"Mrs. Hepner?" Mason asked.

"Yes. This is Mrs. Hepner."

"Mrs. Hepner, this is Perry Mason. I am very anxious to get in touch with your son, Douglas Hepner. I wonder if you can tell me where he could be reached?"

"Have you tried Las Vegas?" the voice asked.

"Is he there?" Mason asked.

"He telephoned from Barstow when he was on his way to Las Vegas two or three nights ago—now wait a minute, it was ... I can give you the exact date ... it was the thirteenth, the evening of the thirteenth."

"And he was on his way to Las Vegas?"

"Yes, he said that he thought he might get up to see me but he evidently couldn't make it."

"You don't know where he was staying in Las Vegas or what he was doing or...or whom he was with?"

"No, I'm sure I can't help you on that, Mr. Mason. May I ask what your interest is?"

"Could you," Mason asked, avoiding the question, "tell me if your son is married or single?"

"Why, he's unmarried."

"I believe there was an Eleanor Corbin who..."

"Oh yes, Eleanor Corbin," the voice said. "Yes, he called me up...oh, it must have been two weeks ago. He was with Eleanor Corbin at the time and he said something that led me to believe his intentions might be serious, but when he called up from Barstow he was with another girl whom he introduced to me over the phone as Suzanne. May I ask why you're interested in locating him, Mr. Mason, and how it happens that you're calling me?"

"I'm trying to find him," Mason said, "and I don't have any other way of reaching him."

"How did you get my address?"

"I happened to know that you were his mother and that he kept in close touch with you."

"And how did you know that, Mr. Mason?"

"Through friends."

"What is your occupation, Mr. Mason? Are you a reporter?"

"No, definitely not."

"What *is* your occupation?"

"I'm an attorney."

"Are you representing my son?"

"No. However, I'm interested in..."

"I think perhaps, Mr. Mason, I will have to refer you to my son for any further answers to questions. I'm sorry, perhaps I've been a bit indiscreet. I thought you were a friend of Doug's. Good-by."

The telephone clicked at the other end of the line.

Mason said to Della Street, "Jump down the hall to Drake's office, get him to put Salt Lake detectives on Mrs. Hepner. Find out everything they can about her. Get some elderly woman operative who has a sympathetic approach to get in touch with her and win her confidence, start her talking."

Della Street grabbed her shorthand book. "Shall I repeat the conversation to Paul Drake?"

Mason nodded. "Give him all of it."

"*We'd* like to know what it was," Olga Jordan said as the door closed behind Della Street.

Mason repeated his conversation with Mrs. Hepner. When he reached the references to Suzanne, Olga and her father exchanged glances.

"Now then," Mason said, "do you know anyone whose first name is Suzanne? Think back over the passenger list. Think carefully. See if you can remember anyone on the ship with that first name. She would probably be some young, attractive woman who showed an interest in Hepner, a rather..."

Abruptly Olga Jordan snapped her fingers.

"You have it?" Mason asked.

She turned to her father. "Suzanne Granger!" she exclaimed.

Her father's bushy eyebrows drew together, his eyelids lowered as he considered the problem, then he said slowly, "Yes, it *could* well have been Miss Granger."

"Who is Suzanne Granger?" Mason asked.

"As far as we know she's just a name—that is, we met her, of course. Eleanor knew her better than we did. She was in that crowd that played around together—they usually put the ship's bar to bed every night after the dancing and...I think she lives here in the city."

"Any chance you can get her address?" Mason asked.

"I...now wait a minute. Eleanor has an address book that she jots down names in and keeps track of people she meets....I'm wondering if she took that book with her or whether it's in her desk. I can see if Bill's home. He could..."

Olga reached toward the telephone.

Mason handed it to her, said, "Just tell the girl at the switchboard to give you an outside line."

"An outside line, please," Olga said into the telephone, then her fingers flew rapidly over the dial.

After a moment she said, "Hello. Hello, Bill. Bill, this is Olga. Bill, this is important. Don't stop to ask questions. Run up to Eleanor's room. Look in her desk. See if you can find her address book. See if you can find Suzanne Granger's address. If you don't find it there, see if she didn't save the passenger list on the ship home—there were some autographs and addresses on it."

Mason said to the father, "We can find it from passport information if we have to, or we may locate it from a directory, but this may be faster."

He picked up the other phone, said to the girl at the switchboard, "Gertie, look through the telephone directory. See if a Suzanne Granger has a listed telephone."

Mason held on to the phone while Gertie was looking up the information and Olga held on to the other phone while she was waiting for her husband to look through Eleanor's address book.

A few moments later Gertie relayed the information to Perry Mason. "I don't find any Suzanne Granger listed, Mr. Mason. There's an S. Granger and an S.A. Granger and an S.D. Granger and..."

"I have it," Olga interrupted triumphantly from the other telephone.

"Never mind," Mason said. "Skip it, Gertie."

He hung up.

Olga said, "It was on the passenger list. Suzanne Granger autographed it and her address is on there—the Belinda Apartments."

Into the telephone she said, "Thanks, Bill. We're at Mr. Mason's office. We'll be home shortly. Better wait."

She hung up.

"Well," Olga said, "this gives us a definite lead. Of course it's rather a delicate matter, Mr. Mason. You can't come right out and ask a young woman if she spent a week end with the husband of your client who is suffering from amnesia."

"Mr. Mason will know how to handle it, Olga," Homer Corbin said. "As a lawyer he will understand that we can't any of us afford to lay ourselves open to an action for defamation of character."

"That, of course, is the danger in a matter of this kind," Mason said. "I think I'll handle this personally."

"I wish you would," Corbin said. He got to his feet. "Come, Olga," he said, "I think we've done everything we can here. You have the negatives, Mr. Mason, you have the telegram and you have the information about Suzanne. You'll know what to do with all of that.

"There is only one other matter that I thought I might call to your attention. When she left the house on the second, Eleanor had some rather expensive and very distinctive luggage.

"We do quite a bit of traveling and as you are probably aware, on these larger steamers the problem of getting luggage through Customs is rather complicated. There is usually a considerable delay finding and collecting all one's luggage in one place because luggage usually looks very much alike. So I had some distinctive luggage made for the two girls and myself. Olga's luggage has a pattern of orange and white checkers. Eleanor's is red and white. Eleanor has two suitcases and an overnight bag. I feel certain that anyone who saw those cases would remember them because of their unique color design. When you start trying to trace Eleanor's movements in Yuma and in Las Vegas you might remember that point about the luggage."

"Thanks," Mason said. "That could be very valuable. Her luggage was simply in alternate squares of red and white?"

"Completely checkerboarded," Corbin said. "It is very conspicuous. It was purposely designed to be conspicuous."

"Thanks," Mason said. "Now I think I'll see what I can do with Miss Granger."

"You will, of course, be circumspect," Corbin cautioned. In the doorway he turned. "Spare no expense, Mr. Mason. Employ all the assistance that you need. Do anything that you think is required under the circumstances."

Mason nodded.

Corbin walked two steps through the door, then turned, retraced his steps and said, "That is, spare no *reasonable* expense, Mr. Mason." With that he turned and marched from the office.

CHAPTER FIVE

The Belinda Apartments had an air of substance and dignity. It made no outward attempt to compete with the more ornate apartments in the neighborhood.

The clerk on duty regarded Mason and Della Street superciliously.

"Suzanne Granger," Mason said.

"Your name, please."

"Mason."

"The initials?"

"The first name is Perry."

If the name meant anything to him, the clerk gave no sign.

"Miss Granger is not in at present."

"When will she be in?"

"I'm sorry. I can't give you that information."

"Do you know if she's in the city?"

"I'm sorry, sir. I can't help you."

"I suppose," Mason said, "you would place a message in her mailbox?"
"Of course."

Mason extended his hand. The clerk, with punctilious formality, took a sheet of paper and an envelope from under the desk and handed them to Mason.

Mason took a fountain pen from his pocket, hesitated a moment, then wrote:

> Della:
> There's something a little fishy about this. It's a little *too* cold,
> a little *too* formal. His face froze when I mentioned my name.
> I'm going to write a note. You stand where you can watch the
> girl at the switchboard. See if you can pick up anything.

Mason pushed the note over toward Della Street, then suddenly said, "Wait a minute, I think I'll set forth my business in detail. May I have another sheet of paper, please?"

The clerk silently handed him another sheet of paper.

Mason went over to a writing desk and seated himself. Della Street remained for a moment by the reception counter, then sliding her elbow along the edge of the counter, she moved slowly and apparently aimlessly toward the switchboard.

The clerk retired behind a glassed-in partition to a private office.

Mason waited for some three minutes, moving his pen as though writing on the paper. In the end he wrote simply:

> Miss Granger:
> I think it will be to your advantage to get in touch with me as
> soon as possible after you return to your apartment.

Mason signed his name, folded the note, sealed it in the envelope, and taking it to the desk, wrote on the outside, "Miss Suzanne Granger."

Della Street said in a low voice, "He stepped into the office and called apartment 360. He's still talking on that call. You can see the line is still plugged in."

The clerk looked out through the glass-enclosed office, almost immediately hung up the telephone, came out and extended his hand for the note.

Mason, with his pen poised over the envelope, said, "What's the apartment number?"

For a moment the clerk hesitated but Mason's poised pen had about it an air of compelling urgency. The clerk's cold, slightly protruding eyes looked down at the point of the pen for a moment, then he said, "Apartment 358—although that's not at all necessary. Miss Granger will get the message."

Mason wrote down the apartment under her name, handed the envelope to the clerk," Will you see that she gets this as soon as she comes in?"

Mason took Della Street's arm, escorted her across the lobby to the street.

"Now what?" she asked. "Suzanne Granger in 358, and he telephones to 360! What goes on?"

"That," Mason told her, "is something we'll have to find out. We don't *know* that Suzanne lives in 358."

"If you could find some way to drop a firecracker down the collar of that stuffed shirt at the desk it would suit me fine."

Mason nodded. "I have a feeling, Della, that several people are conspiring to give us a run-around. Let's just walk around the block."

"Walk?"

"That's right," he said, holding her elbow and starting out briskly. "We'll leave the car parked where it is and see what we can find. After all, there must be some way of getting service to these apartments, taking things in and out and...Here's an alley. Let's turn down here."

They walked down the alley, came to the back of the apartment house and saw a wide door paneled by thick glass backed by steel mesh. Mason and Della Street entered and saw a sign, "*Service Elevators.*"

Mason pressed the button and a slow, lumbering elevator came up from the basement.

An assistant janitor looked at them inquiringly.

Mason said indignantly to Della Street, "The idea of treating us like garbage and telling us to go back to the service elevator."

Della Street said angrily, "Well, some day we'll get even with him."

They entered the service elevator. Mason snapped, "Third floor....I take it *you've* no objection to garbage."

"What's the matter?" the janitor asked.

"Nothing," Mason said irritably, as though spoiling for a fight. "I'm a vulgar tradesman, that's all. The front elevators it seems are reserved for guests."

"Well, don't take it out on me. I have my troubles too," the janitor said, pulling the control and sending the elevator slowly upward to the third floor. "Lots of people don't like the guy you're thinking about."

Mason and Della Street got out, oriented themselves by studying the sequence of several apartment numbers and walked down to apartment 360.

Mason pressed the buzzer to the right of the door.

A woman in her early thirties, dressed to go out, opened the door, started to say something, then stepped back in open-mouthed surprise.

"You!" she exclaimed.

"Exactly," Mason said and volunteered no other information, but simply stood there.

"Why, I...I...what are you doing here?"

"Maybe the clerk at the desk got his signals mixed."

She had a look of such apparent consternation on her face that after a moment Mason said, "Or perhaps you did."

"What do you want?"

Mason did not reply to her question. "You seem to know who I am," he observed.

"I recognized you from your pictures. You're Perry Mason, the lawyer, and this is your secretary, Miss Street."

Mason remained perfectly silent.

"Well, you are, aren't you?" she asked.

"Yes. I want to talk to you."

She looked at him frowningly. Then Mason and Della Street entered the apartment.

Mason noticed that there were morning newspapers on the floor, that someone had neatly snipped the account of the park ghost from the paper. There was no sign of what had been done with the clipping, but the newspaper lying on the floor bore mute testimony to someone's interest in the case.

"Are you sure *you* are not the one who is confused, Mr. Mason, that you haven't got me mixed up with someone else? I'm certain you have never even heard of me. My name is Ethel Belan."

Mason caught Della Street's eye and gave her a warning glance. "Sit down,

Della," he said, and settled himself comfortably in one of the overstuffed chairs.

"No, I'm not confused, Miss Belan. It is you I want to talk to. I'm representing the young woman you've been reading about," Mason said, indicating the mutilated newspaper on the floor.

Ethel Belan started to say something, then apparently changed her mind and was silent.

"Nice apartment you have here," Mason said.

"Thank you."

"You get a view out over Sierra Vista Park from those front windows?"

"Yes, it's nice having a park right across the street."

"Double apartment?" Mason asked, looking around.

"Yes."

"Someone share it with you?"

Ethel Belan looked around the apartment as though looking for something that would give her an inspiration as to how to handle the situation. Her eyes rested momentarily on the telephone, then moved toward the window. "I took a lease on it some time ago. I had a very congenial young woman living with me but she was transferred to a position back East and I... well, I haven't as yet found anyone to share the apartment. I think it pays to go easy in matters of that sort."

Mason nodded. "Do you smoke?" he asked Ethel Belan, taking his cigarette case from his pocket.

"No, thank you. I don't smoke."

"May I?"

"Of course."

Mason lit a cigarette, settled back in the chair.

Ethel Belan said pointedly, "I was just going out."

Again Mason nodded, smoking in silence.

"Mr. Mason, may I ask just *what* it is you want?"

Mason seemed somewhat surprised. "Don't you know?"

"I... I'd prefer to have you tell me. I..."

Mason studied the smoke eddying upward from his cigarette. "In representing a client one has to exercise a certain amount of caution. It is very easy to make a statement which can perhaps be misconstrued and then the situation becomes complicated. It's much better to let the other party make the statements and then either agree or disagree."

"Well, Mr. Mason, I've got nothing in the world to talk to you about. I realize, of course, that you're a highly successful and reputable lawyer, but..."

Mason's eyes bored steadily into hers. "Was that your raincoat Eleanor was wearing?"

The question took her completely by surprise.

"Why," she said, "I... oh, so *that's* what brought you here! You traced the raincoat!"

Mason gave himself over to contemplation of the smoke spiraling upward from his cigarette.

"Mr. Mason, did Eleanor *send* you here or did you come here because of the raincoat?"

Mason abruptly turned to Ethel Belan. "We want to get her things," he said.

"Why... I..."

"I brought my secretary along," Mason said, "in case there should be any packing to be done."

"Well, I...what gave you the idea that I had any of Eleanor's things here, Mr. Mason?"

Mason shook his head.

"I understand her mind was a complete blank as to where she had been and what had happened for the last two weeks," Ethel Belan said.

Mason's smile was as enigmatic as that of the sphinx.

"Very well," Ethel Belan said abruptly, "I guess it's all right. You're a reputable attorney and you wouldn't be here asking for her things unless she'd sent you for them. This way, please."

She led the way into one of the two bedrooms, opened a closet door and said, "All of those things on the hangers are hers. That's her suitcase in the closet, that's her two-suiter there, and..."

"And her overnight bag, I take it," Mason said, indicating the red and white overnight bag.

"Exactly."

Mason said quite casually to Della Street, "You'll try packing them up as well as you can, Della?"

Della Street nodded.

"We may as well go out and sit down," Mason said. "Della Street will pack the things."

"I...I have an appointment, Mr. Mason. I...I'll wait here and close up as soon as Miss Street has them packed. Perhaps I can help."

Mason nodded.

The two women took clothes from the hangers, put them in the suitcases. Ethel Belan opened a drawer and took out handkerchiefs, lingerie and nylon stockings which she handed to Della. Della Street packed them silently.

"Well, I guess that's all," Ethel Belan said.

"We will, of course, trust your discretion in the matter," Mason said significantly.

Ethel Belan hesitated a moment, then said, "Actually, Mr. Mason, there was another week's rent due."

"Oh, yes," Mason said, taking his wallet from his pocket. "How much was it?"

"Eighty-five dollars."

Mason hesitated perceptibly.

"Of course," Ethel Belan said rapidly, "that's not exactly half of what I'm paying for the apartment but that was the price that was agreed upon."

"I understand," Mason said, counting out a fifty, three tens and a five.

He handed the currency to Ethel Belan.

"I'm wondering," he said, "since I'm acting in a representative capacity and will necessarily have to submit an expense account, if you'd mind...?"

"Not at all," she said.

She took a piece of paper and wrote:

> Received of Perry Mason, attorney for Eleanor Corbin, eighty-
> five dollars. Rent from August 16th to August 23rd.

She signed it, and Mason gravely pocketed the receipt, said, "If you can carry the overnight bag, Della, I'll carry the other two."

Ethel Belan's curiosity suddenly got the better of her. "I don't understand how you...how you got up here," she said.

"After the clerk phoned you," Mason said, "we felt that we could hardly count on his co-operation."

"But didn't...you didn't ask for *me!*"

Mason smiled. "An attorney has to be discreet. He has to be *very* discreet, Miss Belan."

"I see," she said gravely. "I hope you can be as discreet about my connection with this as you are about other things, Mr. Mason. I have a rather responsible position in a downtown department store. This happens to be my afternoon off. I...you just happened to catch me at home."

"Exactly," Mason said, "and I think it might be well if you didn't mention our visit to anyone."

"How are you going to get the baggage out?"

"We'll arrange for that," Mason said. "Come on, Della. Can you wait about five minutes before you go out, Miss Belan?"

She glanced at her watch. "I'm sorry, I can't. I've got to leave. I'll ride down in the...oh, I understand, you must have come up the freight elevator."

Mason nodded.

"Well then," she said, "I...oh, I see, and you'll be taking the baggage out the same way...well, thanks a lot, Mr. Mason."

She gave him her hand and a cordial smile, shook hands more perfunctorily with Della Street and ushered them out of the apartment.

She went at once toward the passenger elevator. Mason and Della Street walked around the corridor to the freight elevator.

"Think she'll tell the clerk?" Della Street asked.

"Darned if I know," Mason said, "but we have the baggage now. It's evidently Eleanor's baggage and we'll keep it."

Della let out a long sigh. "Lord! My head is still whirling. I was never so surprised in my life to discover that Ethel wasn't Suzanne Granger, or rather—well, you know what I mean. And as for the bluff *you* pulled! I almost gasped out loud when I heard you ask her so casually if that was her raincoat."

"Evidently it was," Mason said. "You see it's the dry season here and when Eleanor packed she certainly didn't put in a raincoat, that is, not a heavy, opaque raincoat like the one she was wearing when the police picked her up. If she'd had a raincoat in her suitcase it would have been one of those transparent plastic types that can be folded into a small, compact bundle."

"But why in the world would Eleanor have wanted to take off her clothes there in the apartment, put on a raincoat, go over to the park and start dancing around in the moonlight, and why would Ethel Belan have given her the raincoat and..."

"Let's not overlook one point," Mason said. "She may not have given Eleanor the raincoat. Eleanor may simply have appropriated that. It was evidently Ethel Belan's raincoat, that's all. She didn't tell us anything else."

"Yes, that's right," Della Street said.

"Of course," Mason pointed out, "she acted on the assumption that we knew. Now notice that this receipt covers rent from the sixteenth to the twenty-third. It's the seventeenth now. You can see that Ethel Belan has an eye on the financial end of things, and since the rental was by the week we can assume that the rental started either on the second or the ninth of this month."

"But Eleanor left home on the evening of the second."

"That's right," Mason said, "so probably rental started on the ninth, which leaves her whereabouts from the second to the ninth as a problem."

"And did you notice that Ethel Belan referred to her as Eleanor Corbin, not as Eleanor Hepner?"

"Very definitely," Mason said.

"And what in the world was she doing in that apartment from the ninth to the sixteenth...?"

The freight elevator lumbered to a stop. The door rumbled open.

Mason stood aside for Della to enter, then, carrying the two suitcases, carefully holding them so it could not be told whether they were empty or packed, said to the elevator man, "A job of baggage repair and he sends us to the tradesmen's entrance! The elevators are reserved for *guests*!"

"I know, I know," the janitor sympathized. "They do funny things here. If you'd given the bellboy a dollar to take them down you could have gone down the front way, but..."

"*We* should give a bellboy a dollar!" Mason exclaimed. "A dollar for what? A dollar to carry suitcases across the lobby to an automobile...?"

The elevator rattled and swayed on downward, and came to a stop at the ground floor. Mason and Della Street emerged into the corridor, then through the heavy doors into the alley.

Mason said to Della Street, "You walk around and get the car, Della. Drive around here to the alley and pick me up. I'll wait with the baggage."

"Why not you get the car and I'll..."

"Someone," Mason said with a grin, "might try to take the baggage away from you."

Mason stood by the three pieces of baggage, all decorated in red and white checkerboards, watching Della Street's trim figure as she hurried down the alley, then turned into the street. Some three minutes later she was back with the car. Mason loaded the baggage into the trunk. Della Street slid over from the driver's seat and Mason got in behind the wheel.

"Where to?" she asked.

"How about your apartment?" Mason asked. "This luggage is rather conspicuous and the office may have some people who would notice. It will probably be described in the press later on."

Della Street nodded.

Mason drove the car through the afternoon traffic, stopped at an intersection and motioned to a boy who was selling newspapers.

Della Street skimmed through the early evening edition while Mason continued to drive the car.

"Well!" she exclaimed.

"Good coverage?" Mason asked.

"I'll say. The newspapermen seem to have taken particular delight in letting you realize that you're persona non grata."

"How come?"

"Evidently they felt that you wanted to avoid publicity so they gave you plenty. Of course it's a nice story. Heiress identified by wealthy family. High-priced attorney retained to control publicity and represent the young woman in any action that may be filed. Chief, when you come right down to it, the family certainly did a strange thing, didn't they?"

Mason nodded.

"Coming in with a retainer of that sort—good Lord, that's the type of retainer you'd expect in a murder case."

Again Mason nodded.

"And this talk about protecting the family from publicity—when you stop to think of it, it was inevitable that the things they did would *make* publicity, ten times as much publicity as they'd have otherwise received."

Again Mason nodded.

"Well, you're a big help I must say," Della Street said.

"I was simply agreeing with you."

"Well, it just hit me all of a sudden how peculiar it was for people to come to you and ask you to handle the publicity and...well, they said they wanted things minimized, but what has happened has just transformed a small story into a big story.

"Perry Mason, the famous criminal attorney, retained by the family, fires the doctor, spirits the patient to a private sanitarium in an ambulance that uses its siren to go through signals at sixty miles an hour so it can't be followed. Nobody knows where the patient is. The wealthy family, the background, the trips to Europe, picture of the father. Story about an elopement with Douglas Hepner. Good Lord, Chief, it's completely incongruous. The very things that they told you they were doing to control publicity have resulted in smearing the thing all over the front page."

Again Mason nodded.

"I take it," she said, "your thinking is in advance of mine and may I ask when this idea which has now hit me with such terrific impact first occurred to you?"

"When they handed me the twenty-five-hundred-dollar check," Mason said.

"Well," she told him, "I certainly swung late on that one! Why in the world do you suppose they did anything like that?"

"Because, as Olga Jordan so aptly expressed it, judging from the scrapes Eleanor has been in before, this one is a lulu."

"Well," she said, "it'll be interesting to interview Suzanne Granger and see what her connection is. I take it she's a third point in a triangle."

"Could be," Mason said.

Della Street, piqued at the lawyer's reticence, settled back against the cushions and remained silent until they reached her apartment house.

"Want me to call a bellboy?" she asked.

"No," Mason said, "I'll go up with you. In that way people will think you've been out on a case and you're just coming back with your suitcases. Hang it, I wish these things weren't so conspicuous."

"We're pretty likely to find the lobby completely deserted," Della Street said, "and, after all, we dash around on cases so much that people take us more or less for granted."

They parked the car. Mason opened the trunk and said, "You take the overnight bag, I'll take the other two, Della."

They entered the apartment, found the lobby deserted, and went to Della Street's apartment.

"What should I do with these things?" she asked. "Unpack them and put the clothes on hangers, or just leave them...?"

"Leave them packed," Mason said. "I take it you checked through the articles as you were packing them, Della?"

"Just the clothes you'd expect," Della said. "Some of them hadn't even been unpacked. She had an assortment of dresses, underwear, lots of stockings. I presume her more personal things are in the overnight bag."

"Let's just take a look in there," Mason said. "We'd better see what we have."

"Suppose it's locked?" Della Street asked, regarding the formidable catches.

"If it is," Mason said, "we'll get a locksmith and unlock it. I want to see what's in there."

Della Street tried the catches. They snapped up and she pulled back the lid. "Oh-oh!" she exclaimed. "What a *beautiful* bag!"

The interior had been carefully designed to hold an array of creams and lotions around the edges in special containers. The inside of the lid held a beautiful beveled mirror, and a small margin between the mirror and the edge of the lid was fitted with loops containing a complete manicure outfit. The space in the center of the bag held some folded stockings, some lingerie and a nightgown.

Della Street held the nightgown up against her shoulders. "Well, well, well," she said.

It was one of the new short nightgowns, not much longer than a pajama top.

"Brevity," Mason said, "is supposed to be the soul of wit."

"You couldn't ask for anything wittier than this then," Della Street said.

"Well, we live and learn," Mason told her, grinning. "Personally I guess I'm getting a bit out of date."

"*You* are!" she exclaimed. "How do you suppose this makes *me* feel?"

Abruptly she laughed to hide her confusion, folded the garments, put them back in the overnight bag. She casually unscrewed the lid from one of the jars and said, "Eleanor evidently gives a great deal of thought to her skin."

"Some skin," Mason said. "You should have seen her in the hospital when she threw back the covers and started to get up."

"Good-looking?"

Mason smiled reminiscently.

"I suppose," Della Street said somewhat bitterly, "she was all unconscious of your presence and just threw back the covers. A girl who is accustomed to wearing nightgowns that short should be a little discreet about tossing covers back."

"While brevity," Mason said, "may be the soul of the wit, it isn't supposed to have anything to do with discretion."

Della Street placed an exploring middle finger into the jar of cream, said, "Well, I'll see how this expensive cream works on the skin of a working girl and..."

Abruptly she stopped.

"What is it?" Mason asked.

"Something in here," she said, "something hard."

Her middle finger brought out a blob of cream.

"It has a hard interior, Chief. It feels like glass or..."

Della Street reached for a package of cleansing tissue, rubbed the object in the tissue and then opened the paper.

"Good Lord!" Mason exclaimed.

The facets of a beautifully cut diamond coruscated in glittering brilliance.

"Anything else?" Mason asked after a moment.

Again Della Street dipped her finger into the cream jar. Again she came up with a hard object. This time the cleansing tissue removed the cream and disclosed the beautiful deep green of an emerald.

"I don't know much about gems," Della Street said, "but those certainly look to me like the cream of the crop."

"No pun intended, I take it," Mason said.

She looked blank for a moment, then smiled and said, "Well, let's see what else is in the cream—or shall we?"

Mason nodded.

By the time Della Street had thoroughly explored the jar of cream they had a collection of fifteen diamonds, three emeralds and two rubies.

"There are," she pointed out, "quite a few jars in here in addition to various bottles and..."

"We'll take a look," Mason said.

"And what do you suppose Eleanor will say when she finds out that we have taken liberties with her overnight bag?"

"We'll find out what she says," Mason told her, "but we'll look."

"She may not like it."

"I'm her attorney."

"*She* didn't say so—only the family said so."

Mason was thoughtful for a moment. "That's right," he agreed.

"But do we go ahead?"

"Quite definitely we go ahead, Della."

Twenty minutes later Della Street surveyed the glittering assortment of gems.

"Good Lord, Chief, there's a fortune here. What do we do with them?"

Mason said, "We count them. We make as much of an inventory as we can. We wrap them individually in cleansing tissue so we don't mar them in any way."

"And then what?" Della Street said.

"Then," Mason said, "we put them in a safe place."

"And what's your suggestion of a safe place?"

Mason's eyes narrowed. "Now," he said, "you have asked a highly pertinent question."

"The office safe?"

Mason shook his head.

"A safe-deposit box?"

"That's a little awkward."

"What do you mean?"

"We don't know what these gems are. They may be her personal property. They may have been stolen. They may have been smuggled. They may represent very concrete and perhaps very damaging evidence."

"And under those circumstances, what?"

"Under those circumstances," Mason said, "I find myself in a peculiar situation. I am, of course, charged with protecting the interests of my client, Eleanor Corbin or Eleanor Hepner, as the case may be."

"And the good name of the Corbin family," Della Street pointed out. "That, I believe, was considered of paramount importance when the retainer was given."

Mason nodded.

"And so?" she asked.

"So," Mason said, "I'm going to telephone Paul Drake. He'll send an armed detective down here to act as a bodyguard for you. The detective will escort you to one of the best hotels in the city. Pick the one that you like the best and where you'd like to stay if you had an unlimited expense account."

She raised her eyebrows.

"You will," Mason said, "register under your true name so that there will be no question of concealment. You will have your luggage with you, and immediately after you have registered and been shown to a room you will go down to the office and tell the clerk that you have some valuables you want to leave in the hotel safe. In those large hotels they have very fine safes and safe-deposit boxes. They'll give you a box. You'll put the package of gems in the box. The clerk will lock up the box and hand you the key."

"And then what?"

"Then," Mason said, "you will start leading a double life. You will come to work as usual during the daytime, but during the late afternoons and evenings you will be the glamorous and mysterious Miss Street who flutters around the hotel as a paying guest, putting on that tight elastic bathing suit of yours, dipping into the pool, being sedate and reserved but not at all forbidding. And in case any amiable and attractive young chap starts making wolf calls you will be archly amused. You will let him buy you a drink and a dinner and Paul Drake's operatives, who will be keeping you under surveillance, will promptly proceed to find out all about the young man's background and whether he's merely acting the part of a wolf with thoroughly dishonorable intentions, or whether his interest is aroused by things other than your face, figure and personality."

"And the key to the hotel lock box?" she asked.

"The key, just as soon as you get it," Mason said, "will be given to me and I'll see that it is put in a safe place so that in case any slick pickpocket should go through your purse while you're dancing or drinking he would find nothing more than the expense money—which is to be furnished by the Corbins."

"You make it sound very exciting and attractive," Della Street said.

"In that case," Mason told her, "we'll make immediate arrangements for the bodyguard."

Mason stepped to the phone, called Paul Drake's number.

"Perry Mason talking. Put Paul on the line, will you? Is he there? ... Fine, thanks."

A moment later, when Paul Drake came on the line, Mason said, "Paul, I want a bodyguard. I want someone who is dependable, tough and wide-awake, someone who knows his way around."

"Okay."

"How soon can I have him?"

"Half or three-quarters of an hour if you're in a hurry."

"I'm in a hurry."

"Where do you want him?"

"Della Street's apartment."

"Okay. Who do you want him to bodyguard?"

"Della."

"The devil!"

"I want someone who packs a rod and knows how to use it," Mason said. "Then Della is going to a high-class hotel. I want her kept unostentatiously under surveillance at the hotel."

"Now wait a minute," Drake said, "you said a high class hotel?"

"The best."

"We can't do it unless it happens to be a place where I know the house detective, and even then..."

"What do you mean, you can't do it?" Mason interrupted.

"It isn't being done, that's all. You can't hang around a place like that keeping a woman as good-looking as Della under surveillance without their knowing about it and then they bring you in and..."

"Can't you have people register as guests and...?"

"Oh sure, if you want to go that strong. That thing runs into money at a good hotel, but if you want to have them register as guests there's nothing to it."

"Okay," Mason said, "have them register as guests. Have one fellow who is young, who can act as an escort in case it becomes advisable, and one fellow who is old and grizzled and tough and is more interested in the financial section than figures in a bathing suit, someone who will not be hypnotized by the smooth sheen of a nylon stocking, but who will keep his eye on surroundings. And get more men if you have to."

"What's the idea?" Drake asked.

"I can't tell you right now. How are you coming with your homework?"

"Look," Drake said, "things are happening. Did you see the papers?"

"Della told me we'd attracted quite a bit of publicity."

"That's only half of it," Drake said. "Now look, Perry, I'm damned if I can find where Eleanor ever married this Hepner guy. It was supposed to have taken place at Yuma, Arizona. We've combed through the records, we've even figured they might have been married under assumed names, and we've checked all of the marriages that were performed on the second and third of August. We've managed to account for everyone. Furthermore we've gone over details in every automobile accident that took place anywhere along the road to Yuma on the night of the second and we can't find anything. We can't get a trace of Douglas Hepner any—"

"What about his mother in Salt Lake?" Mason asked.

"Now there is *really* something."

"What?"

"The so-called mother," Drake said, "turns out to be a beautiful brunette babe about twenty-seven years old with lots of this and that and these and those, who lives in a swank apartment when she's there but who flits around like a robin in the springtime. She catches planes on short notice. She goes hither and yon, and..."

"And she poses as Douglas Hepner's mother?" Mason asked.

"Apparently only over the telephone. The registration is Mrs. Sadie Hepner on the apartment."

"Good Lord," Mason said, "another wife?"

"We can't tell."

"What does she say?"

"She doesn't say. Apparently she hung up the telephone after talking with you, and got the hell out of there. In fact it's very possible that she was in the process of packing up when you phoned her. She returned this morning from some mysterious mission, packed up and left the place within about fifteen minutes of the time you called her. She took a flock of suitcases with her, got into her nice, shiny Lincoln automobile, told the garage attendant she was headed for Denver and took off. She had gone by the time my operatives got to her apartment.

"We traced her as far as the garage and ran up against a blank wall. Do you want us to try to pick up her trail along the road?"

"Sure. Try Denver, San Francisco and here."

"It's like a needle in a haystack. We may be able to pick up her trail from her license number when she checks in at one of the California checking stations—but suppose she really is headed for Denver?"

"If she said Denver she probably meant California. Give it a try, Paul. What about the wire from Yuma?"

"That wire was phoned in from a pay station. No one knows any more about it than that. Hundreds of wires all reading about the same way flow through the Yuma telegraph office."

"Keep running down any lead you uncover," Mason told him.

"Well," Drake said, "things are being stirred up. I've got men in Las Vegas. We've managed to get some pretty good pictures from those negatives and I rushed a man over to Las Vegas by plane. He'll be inquiring around there. We're also looking for marriage records in Las Vegas. I should have some more stuff for you late tonight."

"Stay with it," Mason said. "Put men on the job."

"Of course," Drake pointed out, "it would help if you'd give me some kind of an inkling what you're working on and what you're looking for."

"I'm looking for information."

"So I gathered," Drake told him dryly.

CHAPTER SIX

It was nearly ten o'clock when Perry Mason dropped into Paul Drake's office.

The detective was seated at his desk in his shirt sleeves, sipping coffee and holding a phone to his ear.

He nodded as Mason came in, put down the coffee cup, said, "I've just struck something important out in Las Vegas, Perry. My gosh, I've got an army of operatives on the job. I've told every one of them to phone in the minute he finds anything that may be at all significant. No marriage records in Las Vegas, Nevada. Guess I told you. Can't remember just what I've reported and what I haven't. Things have been coming too fast. My man over in Las Vegas says it's a hundred and fifteen and... Hello, hello... Hello, yes... He did, eh?... All right, keep trying... All right."

Drake hung up the phone, sighed wearily, said, "What's the idea with Della?"

"Della," Mason said, "is putting on the dog. She's joined the ranks of the idle rich, and is looking around."

"So I gathered. Is she still a working gal?"

"Daytimes she's a working gal," Mason said. "Nighttimes she stays at the hotel and your men watch her."

"Bait for a trap?" Drake asked.

"Could be. What's the dope on Doug Hepner?"

"That's a funny thing," Drake said.

"What is?"

Drake pushed the coffee cup to one side.

Drake said, "I flew one of my operatives over to Las Vegas, Nevada. He had a bunch of pictures of Hepner. We had some pretty good enlargements and..."

"You told me all that," Mason interrupted impatiently.

"I know, but I wanted you to get the picture. My man picked up some of my associates in Las Vegas and got them all started working. Gosh, Perry, do you have any idea of the number of people who pour through Las Vegas, Nevada, in the course of a week?"

"I suppose it's a lot," Mason said. "What are you leading up to? Do you want to show me some particularly brilliant piece of detective work?"

"Hell, no," Drake said. "On the off-chance that this man Hepner had done some gambling and that might be the answer, we took his photograph and dropped around to a couple of dealers that we knew. Understand, Perry, there wasn't one chance in a thousand, not one chance in a million that anything like that would have paid off, but we took a chance at it just to see what would happen."

"All right, what happened?"

"One of these dealers knew the guy."

"Douglas Hepner?"

"Yes. He hadn't seen the guy for a year, but he knew him, knew all about him, knew what he was doing."

"Shoot," Mason said.

"He used to be a gambler, a professional. He free-lanced on poker games for a while. He acted as shill for a house. He ran roulette and twenty-one games, and was pretty fair. He was dependable, sharp, quick, likable, had a nice voice and personality and..."

"How long ago?"

"Oh, that was three, four years ago."

"Come on," Mason said impatiently, "get down to the present. What's he doing now?"

"Believe it or not, collecting rewards."

"Collecting rewards?" Mason echoed.

"That's right."

"Who from?"

"The United States Government."

"How come?"

Drake said, "You know what happens when people go to Europe."

"Sure. They send home post cards. They bring home souvenirs. They..."

"And one woman out of three does a little smuggling—sometimes it doesn't amount to much, sometimes it's a lot."

"Go ahead," Mason said.

"The United States Customs pays a reward for information that leads to the recovery of smuggled goods. Suppose Mrs. Rearbumper smuggles in a ten-thousand-dollar diamond. She's just as safe as can be unless she happens to have bought that diamond where some spotter on the other side tipped off the Government."

Mason nodded.

"If, however, the Government gets a tip-off, they go through all of Mrs. Rearbumper's things. They find the diamond. They confiscate the diamond. They fine her. And then if she wants her diamond back she has to buy it back. There's a nice little bit of sugar for the Government and the Government naturally likes to preserve its sources of information, so it pays off."

"I see," Mason said dryly.

"Now then, that's why I was trying to give you this background of Douglas Hepner. Two years or so ago he went to Europe. He thought he'd do a little gambling on the boat. He found that that was a pretty tough nut to crack. The big steamship companies don't like to have professional gamblers take money from the passengers. So Hepner, with his nice manners, his knowledge of the world, his suave approach, started using his eyes and ears. He made friends on the trip over. He kept up with his friends in Europe. He posed as having quite a bit of information about values, particularly in regard to jewelry—and I guess he does know quite a bit about diamonds.

"The result was that within thirty days he knew of a big chunk of gems that had been purchased with no intention on the part of the purchaser of paying any duty to Uncle Sam.

"Hepner's trip paid off. Thereafter he started taking more and more trips."

"And he met Eleanor Corbin on a boat coming back from Europe three months ago," Mason said.

"Exactly," Drake told him.

"Do you suppose Eleanor did a little smuggling?"

"Eleanor is quite capable of doing a lot of smuggling," Drake said. "Eleanor has been in a couple of scrapes. She's a hot wire."

"The point is, did someone turn in information on her and did she get caught smuggling?"

"She didn't get *caught* smuggling," Drake said.

"More and more interesting," Mason pointed out.

"She became very friendly with Douglas Hepner. Now do you suppose Douglas Hepner was merely cultivating her as a contact, or do you suppose Douglas Hepner knew about some jewelry she was bringing into this country and was persuaded by one means or another not to say anything?"

"You open up very interesting vistas," Mason said. "How am I going to find Douglas Hepner?"

"That, of course, is the sixty-four-dollar question," Drake said. "Lots of people are asking that question right at the moment."

"Who, for instance?"

"Newspaper reporters. They'd like to make a nice story out of this. It has some choice angles. A bride who can't remember anything about her wedding night or her honeymoon. That's a nice angle. On the other hand, the daughter of a wealthy family who says she's married to Douglas Hepner, and Douglas Hepner says she isn't. She's sporting a wedding ring and a loss of memory. Nice stuff.

"Or take it from the angle of a girl who goes bye-bye for a week end with a good-looking guy she met on shipboard. A nice juicy little scandal here. Lots of people slip out over week ends. They often wonder what would happen if they got caught. So when they read about someone who does get caught it gives the story a lot of impact."

"This smuggling angle gives the whole situation a new slant, Paul."

"It opens up complications," Drake said. "A man who goes in for that line of work is, of course, interested in the twenty percent. He forms friendships for the purpose of getting information. He becomes sort of a sublimated stool pigeon, no matter how lofty he thinks his motives are. He cultivates middle-aged women who think he's a wonderful dancing partner.... They become great friends. She tells him about picking up a present for her sister. It was wonderfully cheap and if she can only get it in without paying duty on it, it will be a lot cheaper. She asks him what he thinks. Of course he advises her to go right ahead and then goes back and enters down the name and the approximate amount in a little notebook.

"Well then, of course, once you start figuring on the twenty percent, another beautiful angle opens up."

"Blackmail?" Mason asked.

"Blackmail," Drake said. "Mrs. Rearbumper simply couldn't stand it to be branded as a criminal. That would be terrible. That would put her right out of circulation in the set to which she belongs."

"There is," Mason said, "also a wonderful opportunity for high-grading. Let's suppose that John K. Bigshot, a big gem importer, has worked out a pretty good system of smuggling in a lot of gems at a clip. The Customs men don't catch him but Douglas Hepner catches him. The gems are concealed in a crutch that's been skillfully hollowed out, or in a wooden leg that..."

"Sure," Drake said, "there are lots of possibilities."

"Some of them more possible than others," Mason told him.

"Uh-huh."

"So," Mason said, "suppose Hepner is about to inform the Government in order to collect a twenty percent reward on a bunch of smuggled gems. Suppose word of that gets out. People have different reactions. Some people would want to run to him and pay him off. Some would try to skip the country and wait until things blew over. Some would try first one way and then another to silence him. If he couldn't be silenced and the game happened to be important enough, the shipment big enough, or the information Hepner had vital enough, well..." Mason shrugged his shoulders.

Again the phone on Drake's desk rang.

Drake picked it up, said, "Okay, let me have that..."

The other phone rang.

Mason said, "Hang on just a moment. I'll see what this is."

Drake said, "Hello...that's right. Drake speaking..."

He was silent for a matter of some twenty seconds, listening to what was coming in over the telephone, then he said, "This is important. Keep me posted on everything. Good-by."

Drake slammed up that phone, barked into the other one, "Matter of major emergency. If I don't call you in fifteen minutes call me back in fifteen."

Drake slammed the phone into its cradle, turned to Mason. A faint flush of excitement was stealing over the detective's cheeks.

"Know something?"

"What?"

"The police just discovered a man's body in Sierra Vista Park. The body was located within a couple of hundred yards of where Eleanor was tripping around in a thin slip and sweet smile."

"What about the body?" Mason interrupted.

"That's darn near all I know and apparently it's darn near all the police know. The body has a very neat bullet hole in the back of the head. Apparently the bullet didn't go through the skull."

"How long ago did it happen?"

"Anywhere from twenty-four to thirty-six hours," Drake said.

"Did police find the body?"

"A necking couple left the car and went smooching into the dark shadows. The body was lying in a thick patch of brush. There was a trail through there and the body was just off the trail."

"It's Hepner?" Mason asked.

"So far there's been no identification. It's just a body with a bullet hole in the back of the head."

Mason grabbed for one of the telephones, said to the girl on Drake's exchange, "Get me outside, fast."

Mason dialed a number, said, "This is Perry Mason. I have to talk with Dr. Ariel. Get me through just as soon as you can. This is a major emergency."

Thirty seconds later Dr. Ariel was on the line.

Mason said, "I'm very much concerned about our mental patient, Doctor."

"Eleanor Hepner?"

"That's right."

"Her progress is very satisfactory."

"As I understand it, in treating a person of that sort it's necessary to avoid any mental shock. Any emotional upset could have disastrous results."

"Well, of course," Dr. Ariel said cautiously, "the patient is rather a peculiar individual. She seems to be well-oriented, with a good sense of humor and..."

"As I understand it," Mason said, "an emotional shock could send such a patient off the deep end."

"Well, I wouldn't worry too much. You..."

"As I understand it, an emotional shock could be disastrous."

Dr. Ariel thought for a moment, said, "Excuse me, I'm a little dumb tonight. It could be, yes."

"It's to be avoided?"

"Well, it certainly isn't what the doctors call 'indicated.'"

"I have a feeling," Mason said, "that she may be pestered by lots of people."

"No one knows where she is, Perry."

"They don't now, but it might be possible for them to find out."

"You mean newspaper reporters?"

"Perhaps—and others."

"You mean relatives?"

"I was thinking of newspaper reporters—and others."

"You don't mean the police, Perry?"

"Well, of course, one never knows."

"Forget it," Dr. Ariel said. "The police have nothing against her. She was wandering around in the moonlight but she wasn't entirely in the nude. They couldn't even get her on indecent exposure. They can't get an identification, and anyhow, the police have wiped the slate clean."

"That's an interesting expression," Mason said. "You wipe the slate clean. Why do you do that?"

"To get rid of what's written on it," Dr. Ariel said, puzzled.

"No. It's because a slate is meant to be written on," Mason corrected. "You wipe it clean so you can write something else on it. I think our patient should be transferred to some place where no one can find her and disturb her."

Dr. Ariel thought for a moment, then said, "Well, of course, these things are a little tricky. No one can predict just what's going to happen."

"I think we should guard against *any* eventuality," Mason insisted.

"Okay," Dr. Ariel said. "I'll get busy."

"I feel she should be where *no one* can disturb her," Mason went on.

"I got you the first time," Dr. Ariel said. "That is, after I finally tumbled. It's going to take a little doing, but I think it can be done."

"At once," Mason said.

"Oh sure," Dr. Ariel told him. "This is an emergency. Got any news for me?"

"No."

"You mean no news?"

"I mean not for you," Mason said. "You'd better get busy. I'm very much concerned about the health of my client and your patient."

"So am I, now that you mention it," Dr. Ariel said. "Thanks for calling, Perry. Good-by."

Mason hung up the phone, turned to Paul Drake. "Paul, you've got a pipeline into police headquarters—"

"A couple of newspaper reporters are willing to do a little work on the side after they phone the story in to the newspaper—and, of course, lots of times newspapers know things that they don't publish."

"Use all your contacts," Mason said. "Spend money as necessary. Find out everything about the body. Find out if it could have been suicide. What kind of a weapon was used. Where the weapon is. How long the body was dead. Check the identification. Find out where Hepner resided. Locate his automobile. Check back on his movements...."

"The police will be doing all that," Drake said. "We can't compete with the police."

"I didn't ask you to," Mason said. "I told you to get that information. I don't give a damn *how* you get it or who gets it first. I want it."

"Okay," Drake said wearily. "And I was just going home. Where will you be, Perry?"

Mason said, "I'll be where no one can find me until after Eleanor has been moved and after the body has been identified. That means I'll be out of circulation until tomorrow morning. I'll then show up at the office as usual. In the meantime, don't waste time trying to reach me because you can't do it."

CHAPTER SEVEN

Mason glanced at his watch as he left Paul Drake's office. It was eighteen minutes past ten.

Mason drove to a service station, had his car filled with gasoline, and while the attendant was washing the windshield, called the Belinda Apartments.

"I know it's late," he told the girl at the switchboard, "but I'd like to talk with Suzanne in 358—that is Miss Granger. I told her earlier in the day that I'd call her."

"Just a moment, I'll connect you,"

A few moments later Mason heard a calm, feminine voice saying, "Yes ...hello."

"I'm sorry to disturb you at this late hour," Mason said, "but this is about Douglas Hepner."

"Hepner," she said. "Hepner...Oh yes. And who are you, please?"

"I wanted to ask you some questions."

"And who are you?"

"The name," he said, "is Mason, Perry Mason, an attorney. I left a note in your box."

"Oh yes."

"Did you get it?"

"Certainly."

Mason said, "I thought you should have an opportunity for rehearsal."

"To rehearse what, Mr. Mason?"

"Your story."

"What story?"

"The story you're going to have to tell the police and newspaper reporters later on. You can try it out on me and I can question you and point out any contradictions."

"Mr. Mason, are you trying to threaten me?"

"Not at all."

"Why should *I* be telling a story to the police?"

"You're going to be questioned."

"About Douglas Hepner?"

"Yes."

"Where are you now?"

"Not too far from your apartment house."

She hesitated a moment, then laughed. "You know, Mr. Mason, you interest me. I've read a lot about you and your technique of cross-examination. On second thought, I think it would be rather fun to have you fasten your penetrating eyes on me and try to get me rattled. By all means come out."

"I'll be out right away," Mason told her and hung up the phone.

At the Belinda Apartments Mason smiled reassuringly at the clerk at the desk, a different one from the person he and Della Street had encountered earlier in the day.

"Miss Granger," Mason said, "in 358. She's expecting me."

"Yes, she phoned," the clerk said. "Go right up, Mr. Mason."

Mason went to 358, pressed the buzzer. The door was opened almost instantly by an attractive young woman, who regarded the lawyer with challenging gray eyes.

"I want to congratulate you, Mr. Mason," she said. "Won't you come in?"

Mason entered the apartment.

"Congratulate me on what?"

She indicated a chair.

"On the line you used."

"What?"

"That one about asking if I didn't want to rehearse my story before I was questioned by others."

"Oh," Mason said, noncommittally.

"It's rather effective. Do you use it often?"

"It's one of my favorites," Mason conceded. "It *usually* gets results."

"It's provocative. It's just a little alarming and yet one can't say that it constitutes a definite threat."

"I'm glad you appreciate it," Mason said.

She offered him a cigarette.

"I'll have one of my own, if you don't mind," Mason said, taking out his cigarette case and lighter.

She took a cigarette, leaned forward for Mason's light, took a deep drag, settled back and blew out a cloud of smoke.

"Well, Mr. Mason, do you prefer to engage in a little preliminary sparring while we size each other up, or will you try for a quick knockout?"

"It depends on the adversary."

"You'd better spar then."

"Perhaps we'd better be frank. Suppose you tell your story and then I'll question you on it."

"I don't like that procedure. Suppose *you* ask questions."

"Very well. You knew Douglas Hepner?"

"Yes."

"How long had you known him?"

"I met him three or four months ago on a ship coming from Europe."

"You were friendly with him?"

"On shipboard?"

"Both on shipboard and afterward."

"Let's put it this way. I was friendly with him on shipboard and I was friendly with him afterward, but there was an interval during which I didn't even see the man. Then I happened to run into him one day in an art store, and of course, we renewed our association. He bought me a drink as I remember it and asked for a dinner date. I was engaged that night but I believe I went to dinner with him the following night. Now would you mind telling me why you're asking these questions, Mr. Mason, and why you intimate that the police will be interested."

"I'm representing a young woman who is suffering from temporary amnesia."

"So I understand. A woman who claims to be Mrs. Douglas Hepner. How interesting! Did you think that perhaps I could help her prove her point, make an honest woman out of her, so to speak? You had quite a write-up in the evening papers, Mr. Mason."

"So I've been told," Mason said dryly. "Now I'd like to find out something about your dates. You saw Douglas Hepner recently?"

"Oh yes."

"How recently?"

"Why I believe...I believe the evening of the fifteenth was the last time I saw him."

"Did he tell you he was married?"

"He certainly did not."

"Did he tell you that he was *not* married?"

"Not in so many words, but he...I gathered that he...well, I don't think I care to discuss that matter, Mr. Mason. You'd better ask those questions of Mr. Hepner. I presume that he'll be somewhat surprised when he reads the papers and finds he's supposed to be married to this young woman who has lost her memory."

"You saw quite a good deal of Hepner after that first dinner date?"

"I saw something of him, yes."

"He was here at the apartment?"

"Yes."

"Could you," Mason asked, "tell me just how that happened?"

Her eyes were mocking. "Why, certainly, Mr. Mason. I invited him in. I pay rent on this apartment, you know."

"How many times was he here?"

"I didn't keep a record."

"Have you any recollection?"

"Only generally. It would take some time for me to go back and check that recollection."

"Would you care to do that?"

"Not now, Mr. Mason."

"Did you know his family?"

"His family? Why, no."

"Is that so," Mason said, his voice showing surprise. "I talked with his mother over the telephone and she told me that she had talked with someone in Barstow who claimed to be...However, perhaps there was a misunderstanding."

"So *that's* your knockout punch," she said, her eyes levelly regarding his. "I was wondering when you'd quit sparring and try for a knockout. All right, I went to Las Vegas with Douglas Hepner. So what? I'm over the age of consent and under the age of indifference. I felt like doing a little gambling and Doug was going to Las Vegas. He invited me to go and I went. So what?"

"So nothing," Mason said.

"And," she went on, "Doug stopped at what should have been the most romantic moment to call his mother in Salt Lake City. It was a new revelation of the Hepner character as far as I was concerned. Frankly, it wasn't anything that I cared for in particular. Parental devotion is always commendable but there are times and circumstances. I had made no promises going to Las Vegas. We were simply going for the trip, but a man in Hepner's position should have been at least speculating as to the possibilities of developments. He should have been making guarded approaches—not definitely burning his bridges behind him, but nevertheless making approaches.

"Instead he stopped at Barstow for gasoline, telephoned his mother in Salt Lake City and told her he was with a very interesting young woman, that he couldn't definitely say that his intentions were serious because he didn't know what *my* intentions were, but that he wanted her to meet me over the telephone, and then without any previous warning he put me on the line."

"And what did you say?" Mason asked.

"I was completely flabbergasted. I wasn't expecting to be called to the telephone, I wasn't expecting to hear Doug Hepner discuss his matrimonial intentions with his mother and then call me to carry on a polite conversation."

"He told her who you were?"

"Told her who I was, gave her my name, my address, a description of my build—rather a flattering description, by the way. He certainly noticed things about height, size, weight, measurements. I felt as though I were being discussed for a beauty contest."

"And you say he gave her your address?" Mason prompted.

"Just about every darned thing about me. And then he put me on the line."

"And what did you say?"

"I said, 'Hello, Mrs. Hepner. I'm very glad to meet you,' and so forth, and she said, 'My son tells me you're on the way to Las Vegas with him,' and I felt angry and embarrassed. I made up my mind right then and there that as far as Doug Hepner was concerned he could take me to Las Vegas and buy me dinner and I'd do a little gambling and he could pay the rent on two motel units, count them, Mr. Mason, *two*!" She held up two fingers.

"In other words, the approach," Mason said, "was unexpected and ineffective."

"Call it that if you want. *I* had a very good time."

"Can you remember the date?"

"I have very definite occasion to remember the date."

Mason raised his eyebrows.

"While I was gone," she said, "my apartment was broken into and acts of vandalism were committed, but I...well, I didn't complain to the police. I know who did it and why it was done."

"Vandalism?" Mason asked.

She nodded, her eyes angry at the recollection.

"What happened?" Mason asked.

"I'm an artist. I'm not a creative artist. My hobby is studying certain phases of European art. I'm something of a bungling amateur. I probably never will make any great contributions to the artistic world. But nevertheless I like to study early pigmentation, the use of color and lighting effects. I think that a great deal more can be learned about schools of painting through lighting effects than is generally realized.

"Now you want to talk about romance and evidence and amnesia and if I get started talking about European painting you're going to be bored."

"You mentioned certain acts of vandalism."

"I travel quite a bit. I go to Europe sometimes two or three times a year. I'm writing a book which may never amount to much and yet, on the other hand, it may achieve some recognition in art circles. I have great hopes for it. In any event, I'm trying to get my research work handled in such a manner that the book will at least be recognized as being authoritative.

"I have made a great number of copies of various masterpieces, not the entire paintings but the particular parts that I consider significant in connection with my theories. For instance, it may be just a trick of lighting, the manner in which the shadow is depicted on the interior of a hand which is painted so the palm is away from the painter and in shadow.

"On the original painting this hand may be quite small, but I enlarge it so it will cover the entire page in a book. I flatter myself that I am able to make very good copies. At least I use infinite pains."

"And the vandalism?" Mason asked, interested.

"Someone got in my apartment and deliberately ruined several hundred dollars' worth of painting materials."

"May I ask how?"

"Someone cut the bottoms off the tubes of my paints with a pair of scissors, then squeezed all of the paint out. Some of it was put on a palette. Some of it on my washbowl. Some of it was smeared over my bathtub—the bathtub looked like a rainbow having St. Vitus's dance."

"You didn't call the police?"

"Not as yet," she said, "but I know who did it."

"May I ask who?"

"You may well ask who," she said angrily. "Your client did it! While I don't care for publicity and don't want to drag her into court I feel like wringing her damn neck!"

"Eleanor Hepner did that?" Mason asked incredulously.

"Eleanor Corbin!"

"How do you know that...?"

The phone rang.

She said, "Pardon me a moment," picked up the telephone, said, "Yes... hello...oh yes...."

She was silent for several seconds listening to the voice at the other end of the telephone wire, then she said, "Are you sure?...Have they made...you think it is?"

Again she was silent for several moments, then said, "I have a guest now...thanks...good-by," and hung up the telephone.

She didn't return immediately, but sat there at the telephone, looking down at the instrument. Then she sighed, walked back to Mason and said, "Well, Mr. Mason, I guess that's all. You've had your field day and you've learned about the Las Vegas trip."

Abruptly she blinked back tears.

"I'd like to know just what caused you to suspect..."

"I dare say you would, Mr. Mason, but I'm finished. I have no further comment."

She got up, walked across to the hall door and held it open.

"Really," Mason said, "I have tried to be considerate, Miss Granger. You're going to have to tell this story at least to the police and..."

"You used that approach, Mr. Mason," she said. "It got you the interview. It's been used once and I no longer find it amusing or challenging. Good night."

Mason arose from his chair, but didn't at once leave the apartment.

"Is it," he asked, "in order for me to inquire if I have said something that offended you?"

She said suddenly, "Will you get the hell out of here, Mr. Mason? I want to b-b-b-bawl, and I don't want to have you sitting there looking at me while I do it."

"In other words," Mason said, not unkindly, "the telephone call was to advise you that they have found and identified Douglas Hepner's body."

She drew herself up, said, "So you knew that he was dead when you came here to interview me! You knew...Mr. Mason! I think I can hate you for that!"

Mason took a good long look at her face and then walked through the open door, out into the corridor.

The door slammed behind him.

CHAPTER EIGHT

Mason was already at the office when Della Street unlocked the office door and, humming a little tune, entered the room, stopping in surprise as she saw Mason at his desk.

"Hello, Della," Mason said. "How's everything coming?"

"What are you doing here?" she asked.

"Checking up on things," Mason said. "There have been...well, developments."

"Such as what?"

"The papers haven't said anything about it as yet," Mason said, "but the body that was found in Sierra Vista Park has been identified as that of Douglas Hepner."

"He's dead?"

"That's right. Shot in the back of the head with a revolver. There's a wound of entrance but no wound of exit, which means the police will be able to recover the bullet and that means that with proper ballistics examination they can determine what gun fired the bullet—provided, of course, they can find the gun. What happened with you, Della?"

"Well," she said, "I had an interesting evening."

"Any approaches?"

"Lots of them."

"Significant?"

"I don't think so. I think they represented merely the usual wolf on the prowl. Of course in a high-class hotel of that sort the approach is rather guarded, discreet and refined, but it has the same ultimate objective as it would have anywhere else."

"What happened?"

"Oh, I was asked very discreetly if I cared to dance. One of them even made a circumspect approach via the waiter with a note stating that I looked lonely and that if I cared to dance the gentlemen two tables over would be very anxious to dance with me."

"Gentle*men?*" Mason asked.

"Two of them."

"What did you do?"

"I danced."

"What did they do?"

"They danced. They made exploratory remarks."

"Passes?"

"Not passes. Exploratory verbal excursions for the purpose of testing my defenses."

"And how were your defenses?"

"Adequate, but not impregnable. I didn't give them the impression that they were storming a Maginot Line. I let them feel that the territory might be invaded, conquered and occupied but definitely not as the result of one skirmish. In other words, I was sophisticated, amused and —I didn't slam any doors. I take it that was what you wanted."

"That was what I wanted at the time," Mason said, "but I don't know now."

"Why?"

"Because I'm afraid there are certain developments that are going to make for complications."

"Such as what?"

"Eleanor Hepner, or Eleanor Corbin as the case may be, had been out of circulation for some two weeks. She was discovered wandering around in the park without adequate covering. Her skin is very light, very creamy..."

"Ah yes, her skin," Della murmured. "I've heard you refer to it several times."

Mason grinned. "It's worth referring to, Della. The point is that if she had been wandering around for any length of time without clothing her skin would very definitely have shown a redness, an irritation, in short, it would have been sunburned, and..."

"And, of course," Della Street said, "as a good detective you observed those things."

"One learns by observation."

"So I gather. But go on, tell me more about that delightful creamy skin."

"Well," Mason said, "it wasn't the least bit sunburned. It hadn't been exposed to wind, air, or anything other than..."

"The soft lights of a bedroom," Della Street interrupted acidly.

Mason went on without noticing the interruption. "Therefore I knew she must have been staying near where she was picked up in the Sierra Vista Park. So, as you know, I made a bluff and got Ethel Belan to admit the girl had been there, but, of course, we didn't learn why. Perhaps Ethel Belan didn't know why. Now I'm afraid I do know why."

"Why?"

"Suzanne Granger. And that makes it look very much as though Eleanor actually hadn't been married."

"In what way?"

"If she had been married," Mason said, "it is difficult to believe that her husband would have deserted her during the honeymoon and started playing around with Suzanne Granger. If, on the other hand, she had gone away on a week-end trip, become infatuated, and if Hepner hadn't been equally infatuated but had perhaps become somewhat bored..."

"With that skin? With those beautiful legs?" Della Street asked.

"A man who travels as much as Hepner might well become surfeited with such things."

"I see. *You* don't travel. Do you mean *he* became bored with Eleanor's charms?"

"It could be."

"My, my," Della Street said, "I'd never have thought it possible from your description."

"And so," Mason said, "Eleanor goes to live with Ethel Belan where she can keep an eye on Suzanne. Then Suzanne goes to Las Vegas for a week end with Douglas Hepner, and while she is gone Eleanor gets into the Granger apartment and commits many acts of vandalism, the type of thing that a woman who is exceedingly catty and exceedingly jealous would do to hurt another woman."

"Such as what?"

"Such as cutting the bottoms off a lot of tubes of expensive oil paints, squeezing out the contents all over the place."

"Did she do that?"

"Suzanne Granger thinks she did."

"Did she tell you why?"

"No. Our conversation was interrupted."

"Well, that's interesting," Della Street said. "Just where does that leave us?"

"It may leave us in a beautiful situation," Mason said. "It sketches Eleanor Hepner..."

"Or Eleanor Corbin," Della corrected.

"Or Eleanor Corbin," Mason admitted, "in a very unfavorable light. And then, of course, one wonders."

"Wonders what?"

"Suzanne Granger," Mason said, "is an artist. She's a student of painting and of painting technique. She's very much interested in the old masters. She's writing a book on lighting effects and so forth. She hopes the book..."

"How old?"

"Twenty-four, -five or -six."

"That means seven, eight or nine," Della Street said. "Good-looking?"

"Very."

"What about *her* skin?"

"I noticed only her face and hands."

"Well," Della Street said, "I'm glad to see *some* of your contacts are conservative."

"I think," Mason said, "you're missing the point."

"I don't think I missed it with Eleanor."

"One doesn't," Mason said, grinning.

"Go on."

"The point is," Mason said, "that Suzanne Granger positively believes that Eleanor got into her apartment while she was in Las Vegas, cut the bottoms off the tubes of paint and..."

"Yes, yes, you told me that," Della Street said. "Pardon me if I seem a little out of character as the docile secretary this morning, but remember that I was Little Miss Richbitch last night, and I've been bandying repartee with predatory males."

Mason grinned. "It's all right, Della. I like it. The point is, suppose it hadn't been sabotage."

"What do you mean?"

"Suppose Eleanor had a definite objective in mind?"

"Cutting the bottoms off tubes of oil paints, squeezing the contents around the apartment?" Della Street asked. "What in the world would she be doing if...?"

"You don't get the sketch," Mason said. "You're accepting Suzanne Granger's story at face value."

"You don't believe Eleanor did it?"

"I'm not commenting about that at the present time," Mason said, "but here's Suzanne Granger, young, attractive, very much on her toes, writing a serious book which requires a lot of research work, trotting off to Europe two or three times a year, visiting studios, carrying a huge number of tubes of paint.

"She has probably built up a character with Customs officials so that they recognize her as a very serious young woman engaged in copying masterpieces. They say, 'How do you do, Miss Granger? How are you today? And did you buy anything while you were abroad?' and she says, 'Just the usual assortment of lingerie and a little perfume which I have here in this suitcase.'

"So then the Customs officials open the suitcase, riffle their hands down through the folded feminine garments, check the perfume, say, 'Thank you very much, Miss Granger,' close the suitcase, put on the Customs sticker and Suzanne motions for the porter."

"And all the while," Della Street asked, "concealed within those tubes of paint are various and sundry gems?"

"Now," Mason said, "you're beginning to get the idea. There is, of course, a sequence there that a cold, cynical, skeptical mind can't overlook. On the one hand we have Suzanne Granger, a very serious-minded but attractive young woman who is interested in gathering material for a scholarly book on art. We also have her going to Las Vegas with Douglas Hepner, who seems to have been exceedingly inept in his approach."

"He got her to go, didn't he?"

"He got her to go, Della, but there again is the pattern. He paused at Barstow to buy gasoline. He was seized with the impulse to telephone his very dear mother in Salt Lake. He telephoned Mother and told her that he was with a Suzanne Granger, that Suzanne Granger was headed for Las Vegas to spend a week end with him."

"What a *nice* approach," Della Street said. "How happy Suzanne must have felt!"

"Exactly," Mason said. "And since we now know that Douglas Hepner's mother was an attractive brunette with a good figure and a mysterious personality, and since we now know that while Suzanne Granger was gone someone got in her apartment and clipped the bottoms off the tubes of paint and squeezed out all the paint, and since we now know that concealed within the lotions and creams of Eleanor was a small fortune in jewels, and since we now know that Suzanne Granger didn't notify the police of what had happened ...well, there we have the elements of something to think about."

"Darned if we don't," Della Street admitted.

"It begins to look like a pattern."

"And what an *interesting* pattern!" Della said.

"Exactly," Mason said. "Imagine how a young woman must feel. She starts out with Douglas Hepner. The air is surcharged with romance. They're headed out away from the city, away from the conventional environment, away from association with those who know them. They're going to venture forth as strangers, a young man and a young woman, driving in the same automobile. They're going to be away for one, two or perhaps three days.

"Probably there's been nothing crude in his approach. So far everything is perfectly proper. They are, of course, unchaperoned, but after all a man isn't supposed to take a chaperone in this day and age if the young woman happens to be over the age of consent, free, unattached, sophisticated...And then Douglas Hepner stops for gasoline. He says casually, 'I have a call to make. Come on over.'

"Naturally the young woman walks over. She wants to know whether he's calling ahead for reservations and if so what type of reservations he's asking for. She doesn't intend to have him take too much for granted. She wants to have the privilege of reaching a decision rather than have it taken for granted.

"And dear little Douglas calls up 'Mother' and says, 'Mother dear, I just wanted to talk with you. At a time like this a man's thoughts quite naturally turn to his mother. I'm headed out for a week end and I have a cute little trick with me. Her name is so-and-so. She's five foot four, weighs a hundred and twelve pounds, has a bust measurement of thirty-four inches, a waist measurement of twenty-six, and a hip measurement of thirty-six, calf thirteen and a half, thigh nineteen inches. Her address is Apartment 358, The Belinda Apartments, Los Angeles, and you really should get acquainted with her because some day you'll be meeting her, and here she is on the phone, Mother.'"

Della Street made a little face. "I can imagine how *that* would leave a young woman feeling."

"We know how it left Suzanne Granger feeling," Mason said.

"In other words, Mr. Hepner paid for two hotel rooms."

"Two units in a motel," Mason corrected.

"And when Suzanne Granger returned she found her apartment had been broken into and...Chief, that was the same approach he used with Eleanor."

Mason nodded.

"So what do you suppose Eleanor found had happened when she returned?"

"She didn't return," Mason said, "not to her residence anyway."

"How very, very interesting," Della said, "and so someone puts a bullet in the back of Mr. Hepner's head. One can well imagine that if Douglas Hepner's romantic adventures followed such a delightful pattern the end was almost inevitable."

Mason said, "All right, Della, your reasoning is sound but the way you put it carries the taint of your stay at a high-class hotel as a single, unattached woman. Let's get into our working clothes and..."

She picked up a file of unanswered mail. "And you can dictate some of these letters," she said.

Mason winced.

"I've culled out everything except the important stuff, so..."

"Well," Mason said, "I suppose..."

They were interrupted by Paul Drake's code knock on the door.

"Let Paul in, Della," Mason said.

She said, "Saved by the bell—but you're going to have to get those letters out of the way some time today, Chief. They're things that are important, things I've been holding here until I'm ashamed to hold them any longer."

She opened the office door, said, "Hi, Paul."

Drake grinned at Della Street and said, "Two operatives submitted reports on your activities last night, young lady. I gather that you were in circulation."

"I was being more circulated against than circulating," Della Street said.

"What's the idea, Perry?" Paul Drake asked. "Come to think it over, I don't want to know."

"It might be a good idea if you didn't," Mason admitted. "What about the body? Has it been positively identified?"

"Yes, it's Hepner. He met his death as a result of one shot with a .38 caliber bullet. Now then, Perry, I'm bringing you bad news."

"How bad?"

"That depends," Drake said. "You know all of the cards in the suit. You know pretty much who is holding them. I don't even know what's trumps. I give you the information. It's a one-way street. Now I *think* I'm bringing you bad news."

"Go ahead," Mason said. "What is it?"

"This Ethel Belan who has apartment 360 at the Belinda Apartments has cracked."

"How bad?"

"All the way."

"To whom?"

"Police."

"I didn't think she'd have the moral stamina to stick it out," Mason said. "What does she know?"

"Now there," Drake said, "you're getting into the top classification of super-secret police archives. Whatever it is, it's causing them to smile and lick their chops like a cat who has just managed to overturn a cream bottle and has its belly full."

"Any chance of talking with her?"

"Just as much chance of talking with her as there is standing on the back porch and shouting a message to the man in the moon. The police have her tied up so tight you can't get within a mile of the hotel where she's staying. They got her to throw some things in a bag. Then they whisked her out of the apartment, rushed her to a hotel where she's in a suite of rooms guarded by a policewoman. Those rooms are at one end of a corridor. The suite of rooms opposite is taken by two deputy district attorneys who are interrogating her in relays. That end of the corridor is blocked off by a police guard. Plain-clothes detectives are scurrying in and out like rats looting a grain bin.

"I'm merely reporting this, since you apparently anticipated it."

"What do you mean I anticipated it?"

"You got Della in the same hotel hours before the police moved in. Della's room is even on the same floor as the suite where they're holding Ethel Belan. *I* don't want to know anything. I'm merely telling you what you know already, but I want to tell you so no one can make a point later on that I didn't tell you."

Drake exchanged glances with Della Street.

"Well," Drake went on, "whatever Ethel Belan has told them is damned important and they're really going to town."

"You don't have any idea what it is?"

"Not the slightest, and, what's more, I'm not to be allowed to have any idea what it is. The D.A. is going to move for an indictment with the grand jury and then he's going to press for an immediate trial."

"He won't file a complaint?"

"No complaint, no information, no preliminary hearing, no chance for you to cross-examine witnesses until you get to court in front of a jury," Drake said. "By that time they'll have it sewed up. They're really going to town on this one, Perry."

Mason thought that over for a minute. "What else?" he asked.

"It seems that Eleanor Corbin had a permit for a .38 caliber revolver. No one can find that revolver. She had it with her a few days before she left home. Presumably she was carrying it with her when she left. Police don't know where it is now."

Mason thought that over.

"Of course, you've got her out of circulation now," Drake said, "but when the grand jury returns an indictment and the police notify you and the doctors in charge, and the general public through the newspapers, that she's under indictment for first-degree murder, she then becomes a fugitive from justice and anyone who conceals her is headed for the hoosegow.

"Temporarily you've outsmarted them and they're conceding that you've won one trick. But by two-thirty or three o'clock this afternoon she'll be a fugitive and then they'll be only too glad to have you conceal her."

Mason's eyes narrowed in thought. "Go on, Paul."

"Now then, police have found Hepner's automobile. It's been pretty badly smashed. Evidently it was in some sort of head-on collision, but police can't find out where the collision took place, they can't find out where the car came from or anything about it."

"That's strange," Mason said. "Why can't they trace that auto accident?"

"Apparently there's no report of it."

"Where did they find the car?"

"In a garage. It was brought in by a tow car late Sunday night. It was left for repairs. The garage people were told that Hepner would be in within twenty-four hours to check it over and that he wanted it repaired and put in shape."

"What about the tow car? Can't they trace that?"

"No one ever got the license on the tow car. Why should they? It was just an ordinary tow car. It came in and dumped the wrecked car and went on its way."

"That's a garage here in town?"

"That's right. The All Night and Day Emergency Repair Company."

"The police talked with them?"

"The police talked with them and my men talked with them," Drake said. "They're very close-mouthed. Personally, I think they *may* know something they're not telling. What they tell is a straightforward story. This wrecking car came in towing Hepner's Oldsmobile. The front end was all caved in. The rear wheels were okay. They'd hoisted the front end up with a derrick and towed it in.

"It was just another job as far as the garage was concerned. They had the car. They didn't intend to spend any money on it until they'd talked with the owner. They just dumped the wreck out in the back along with a lot of other wrecked vehicles. They didn't even check it over carefully to find out how badly it was injured or whether it was worthwhile repairing. In other words, they did exactly nothing. They let it sit there. They knew that the automobile was worth enough for junk to more than cover any storage bill that would pile up. They were waiting for Hepner. Hepner didn't show up."

"I suppose the police have examined the car," Mason said.

"Have the police examined the car!" Drake exclaimed. "I'll say they *are* examining the car! They're examining it with a microscope. They're working against time and trying to get the findings ready for the grand jury by two o'clock this afternoon.

"They've found out that the car with which Hepner's automobile had a collision was painted black. From a chemical analysis of the paint they think it was probably a truck. Police are looking for that truck. They're combing every garage in town."

"Anything else?" Mason asked.

"That seems to be the size of it so far," Drake said. "I'm sorry we don't have more to report, Perry, but we've had lots of people finding out lots of nothing. If you want to find out that marriage licenses *haven't* been issued for two people, or that two people *didn't* stay at a hotel on a certain date as man and wife, you have to comb the records, and use up a lot more manpower than if you struck pay dirt.

"In other words, if they *did* register you may find the register the second or third place you look. But if they didn't register you have to cover the whole doggone outfit."

"I know, I know," Mason interposed.

"I've been up all night," Drake said. "I can stick it out for another twelve or fifteen hours and then I'm going to have to cave in and get some sleep.

"You're in a jam, Perry. Whatever you're going to do you're going to have to do between now and two-thirty or three o'clock. At that time you're going to get a telephone call from your friend, the district attorney, telling you there's an indictment for your client, Eleanor Corbin, alias Eleanor Hepner, and will you please see that she is surrendered; that if she is not surrendered will you please tell them where she is; and if you withhold information you'll be obstructing the interests of justice, compounding a felony and all that sort of legal stuff."

"And if the district attorney can't get hold of me?" Mason asked.

"In that event, by five o'clock the newspapers will proclaim to the world that there's a felony warrant out, that the girl is a fugitive from justice, and your doctor will be put in a spot that he won't want to occupy and you won't want to put him in."

Mason nodded.

"So," Drake said, "what do I do?"

Mason said, "Stay on the job until they issue the indictment, Paul, and then go home and get some sleep. Keep getting what information you can. Have your correspondents in Las Vegas start covering motels. Also see if Suzanne Granger and Douglas Hepner registered under their own names in two separate motel units on the night of the thirteenth—that would be Friday."

"Well, well, Friday the thirteenth," Drake said. "*Two* separate units?"

"That's right."

"He got her to go to Las Vegas with him and then they had two units in a motel," Drake said. "Do I get it right?"

"That's the story," Mason told him. "I want it verified."

"Want to bet that it can't be verified?"

"I have a hunch," Mason said, "that you're going to find it happened exactly that way—that they occupied two separate units."

"I don't want to be crude," Drake said, glancing surreptitiously at Della Street, "but my curiosity is aroused."

Della said, "Mr. Hepner was inept, Paul."

"How soon can you have the information?" Mason asked.

"Perhaps by two o'clock," Drake said. "If you're right we may have it sooner. It's just like I told you, when you're looking..."

"I understand," Mason told him. "Get busy."

"Okay," Drake said and left the office.

Della Street looked inquiringly at Mason. "Now what?" she asked.

"We're in a fix," Mason said. "Your hotel is crawling with detectives. The minute you show up they'll pounce on you. They'll make a double check, they'll find out about the 'valuables' in the hotel safe. They'll want to look. They'll get a court order if they have to. They may not have to."

"That would seem to leave us high and dry," she said.

"And you have your clothes there?"

"*All* my best clothes."

Mason thought for a moment, said, "It's a problem we'll have to solve later, Della. Right now we're metering minutes. See if you can get Dr. Ariel on the phone."

Della Street put through the call. It took her two or three minutes before she was finally able to locate the doctor.

"Hello, Doctor," Mason said. "I'm sorry to have to disturb you. I..."

"I was just getting ready to operate," Dr. Ariel said. "What's the trouble now?"

"That patient," Mason said. "You put her some place where she couldn't be found?"

"That's right."

"We're going to have to find her."

"How come?"

"She's going to be indicted for first-degree murder by two-thirty or three o'clock this afternoon. By that time she'll technically become a fugitive from justice. In case you should happen to read a paper and know that she was wanted and didn't communicate information..."

"I very seldom read the evening papers," Dr. Ariel interrupted. "Was that what was bothering you?"

"No," Mason said. "I think the going will be pretty tough on this one, Doctor. I don't want you to take a chance."

"I'll do anything I can, Perry."

"No, I think we're going to have to surrender Mrs. Hepner and I think you should be the one to do it. When the papers come out just call up the police and tell them that Mrs. Hepner is under your care, that you feel that it is only fair to let the police know where she is, that you think she should not be subjected to any shock and that you want to warn the police that she is under medical psychiatric care and so forth."

"When?"

"As soon as you read about it in the newspapers. In the meantime where is she?"

"The Oak and Pines Rest Home."

"Thanks a lot, Doctor. Remember, as soon as the paper comes out ring up the police—better have someone with you listening to the conversation. If you have a good office nurse you can trust, get her to call the police, tell them that Eleanor Hepner is a patient of yours and that you felt you should communicate her whereabouts to the police although she is under medical attention and all that. Get it?"

"I get it."

"Okay," Mason said. "Good-by."

Mason hung up, glanced at his watch.

Della Street tossed the file of important mail back on the desk and said, "I take it you can now attend to the mail."

"I think not, Della."

"I thought not."

Mason grinned. "You have a few things to do."

"What?"

"You have to call up your hotel, tell the clerk that you're expecting to go to Mexico City with friends on a plane, that you want to keep your room while you're gone, that you don't want to have any misunderstanding about the bill and that you'll mail two hundred and fifty dollars on account."

"And the two hundred and fifty dollars?" Della Street asked.

"You draw it out of the account as a business expense," Mason said. "You charge it to the Corbins. We certainly were unfortunate in our choice of hotels. Now you can't go back there and you don't dare to check out."

"Well," Della Street said somewhat wistfully, "that terminates my very interesting night life. I am going to be missed this evening. Some guests are going to be making discreet inquiries."

"When they find you have gone to Mexico City with friends," Mason said, "they won't fly to Mexico City after you, will they, Della?"

"Oh no, but they'll reproach themselves for not having been a little more persistent in their approach last night. Going to Mexico City 'with friends' has interesting connotations in the mind of the young predatory male who is busily engaged in planning a campaign."

"Yes, I see your point. However, at the moment there's no help for it."

"Isn't it fortunate," Della Street said, "that Eleanor has such a considerate family. Here she finds herself with an attorney all ready to represent her on a murder charge, a lawyer who was retained even before the corpse was discovered."

"It is," Mason said, "a singularly interesting coincidence."

CHAPTER NINE

Della Street brought Perry Mason the morning newpapers. Mason tilted back in his swivel chair, opened the newspapers and studied them.

"Paul Drake phoned," she said. "His men found that Suzanne Granger and Douglas Hepner did have two motel units in Las Vegas just as she told you they did. The date was Friday the thirteenth."

Mason pursed his lips. "Well, we know what we have to work with now," he said.

"She takes a nice photograph," Della Street pointed out the picture in the newspaper, showing Eleanor flanked by a police matron on one side, a detective on the other.

"Yes, Olga evidently got some other clothes out of her closet."

"She wears them well," Della Street commented.

"Nice figure," Mason said.

"And the creamy skin, remember?"

"Oh yes," Mason said, smiling. "How could I ever forget?"

"So she still can't remember what happened," Della Street said.

"That's it," Mason told her. "It's all spread out in choice newspaper jargon. Beautiful heiress—the lost week end—is she a kissless bride or did she settle for a week end at Las Vegas?—'My mind is a perfect blank ever since that horrible accident,' heiress tells officers, choking back sobs."

"What do they say about the gun?" Della asked.

"She did have a gun once. It's been missing for some time. She had occasion to look for it when she was packing to run away with Hepner—not that she wanted to take the gun but in going through the articles in the drawer where she usually kept the gun she had occasion to notice that it was missing. And she hasn't the faintest idea where her luggage is now."

"I wonder if the police know?" Della Street asked.

Mason said, "According to Paul Drake, Ethel Belan has 'told all.'"

"Do you suppose she has?"

"The police haven't as yet asked any questions about luggage."

"And Ethel Belan must have told them..."

The telephone rang.

Della Street picked it up, said, "Hello... Yes, Gertie.... Put her on."

Della Street turned to Perry Mason and said, "A personal call for me, Chief. Some woman says it's very important."

Della Street turned back to the telephone. "Hello, yes... I see. Go ahead. Give me the details...."

Della Street hung on to the telephone for nearly a minute, making rapid shorthand notes. Then she put down the pen, said, "All right, Mrs. Fremont. There was nothing else you could have done. It's all right. Yes, thank you very much and thank you for letting me know."

Della Street hung up, turned to Perry Mason and said, "Well, Ethel Belan talked all right."

Mason raised his eyebrows in silent interrogation.

"That was Mrs. Fremont, manager of the apartment house. Lieutenant Tragg showed up there with a search warrant issued by a court granting permission to search my apartment to look for three articles of red and white checkered baggage, the property of Eleanor Corbin, alias Eleanor Hepner, who is accused of murder. They delivered a copy of the search warrant to the manager, demanded a passkey, entered my apartment and found the articles. They left a receipt for the three articles with the manager."

"Very considerate," Mason said, "very nice. All in accordance with the law in such cases made and provided."

"Well?" Della Street asked.

Mason shrugged his shoulders.

"And what about the gems?" Della asked.

"There," Mason said, "you have a question."

"Well, what's the answer?"

"I don't know."

"If you don't, who does?"

"Probably no one."

"Chief, if those gems are evidence, isn't it illegal for you to withhold that evidence?"

"Evidence of what?" Mason asked.

"Well, evidence of... I don't know—evidence of smuggling perhaps."

"What makes you think the stones were smuggled?"

"How about murder?"

"What makes you think the stones have anything to do with the murder? I have a duty to my client. If the police can tie those gems in with a murder case and make them important evidence that's different, but those gems are in my possession as an attorney. They may be evidence of something else. They might be evidence of blackmail. How do I know? I certainly am not going to take it on myself to assume that they're connected in any way with the death of Douglas Hepner and turn them over to the police, who will promptly call in the newspaper reporters. It'll be bad enough the way it is. They'll go through those bags and inventory the stuff that's in there. They'll have a cute little model demonstrate Eleanor's nighty. You can figure out what's going to happen."

"And you intend to sit tight with those gems?"

"As things now stand I intend to sit tight."

"Suppose they catch you?"

"I'll cross that bridge when I come to it, too."

"Chief, Paul Drake says that the police are absolutely jubilant over this case, that Hamilton Burger, the district attorney, is walking on air, that they're prepared to lower the boom on you on this one."

"So what?"

"Can't you duck it?"

Mason shook his head. "Not now. I'm stuck with it."

"I wish you wouldn't hang on to those gems."

"What do you want me to do? Call up the police?"

"No."

"What?"

"You can talk with your client and ask her about them and find out..."

"My client says she can't remember what happened," Mason interposed.

"Your client is a damn liar!" Della Street said. "You know it, she knows it, and she knows you know it."

"But," Mason said, "if she should change her story now and say that she *could* remember and tell me about those gems, give me some story about where they came from and tell me what I was to do with them, *then* the probabilities are I'd be charged with notice that the gems were evidence of something. As it is, I don't know anything about them."

"Well," Della Street said, "I suppose it had to happen sooner or later, but I hate to think of Hamilton Burger being so smugly triumphant."

"So do I," Mason told her. "But don't forget he hasn't won his case yet. He's trying to jockey things so he can get an immediate trial and that's going to suit me fine."

"Wouldn't it be better for you to wait and see what develops?"

Mason shook his head. "Hamilton Burger isn't a fast thinker and he isn't a thorough thinker. If he rushes into court he's pretty apt to have a weak spot in his armor somewhere. If I give him time that battery of assistants he keeps up there will put him in an impregnable position. As matters now stand we'll let him start charging forward with the arc light of publicity full upon his portly figure."

"You think he may stumble?" Della Street asked.

"Well," Mason said, "I'll put it this way—he *could*."

CHAPTER TEN

Perry Mason surveyed the crowded courtroom, taking mental inventory of the situation.

Behind him and slightly to one side sat his client, officially described as Eleanor Corbin, alias Eleanor Hepner.

In the front row of the courtroom was her father, Homer Corbin, a quietly dressed, well-groomed individual whose very appearance lent an air of respectability to the defendant's case.

But Homer Corbin was in the wholesale jewelry business. The decedent, Douglas Hepner, had been a freelance Government informer who made it his business to track down illicit shipments of jewels and turn that information over to the Government. Did the district attorney know that?

If Homer Corbin should take the stand to testify to the good character of his daughter, or to testify to any event leading up to the crime, Mason could visualize Hamilton Burger, the district attorney, asking:

"And did you know, Mr. Corbin, that the decedent, Douglas Hepner, was engaged in the business of detecting smuggled shipments of jewelry, reporting those shipments to the Customs authorities, and receiving a twenty-percent reward therefor; that that was the way he made his living?"

Hamilton Burger would slightly incline his head as if anxious to miss no syllable of the answer, then he would say:

"And I believe, Mr. Corbin, that *you* first met the decedent on a ship returning from Europe?"

Then the district attorney would step back a few paces, smile at the harassed witness and say almost casually:

"I believe, Mr. Corbin, that you are in the wholesale jewelry business and that your trip to Europe was a business trip, was it not?"

The insinuation would be there, implanted in the minds of the jury. None of those questions would be objectionable from a legal standpoint. They would merely sketch the background of the witness, his possible bias, his occupation, his knowledge of the decedent, but the cumulative impact would be deadly.

Seated beside her father was Olga Jordan, a thin-mouthed, clever woman, who somehow managed to give the impression of putting on a false front. Not only was it the manner in which she tried to disguise the thin line of her lips with heavy lipstick, but it was something about her manner itself, the alert, intent way with which she regarded everything that took place as though searching for an opportunity to turn every event to her own personal advantage.

Beside his wife, Bill Jordan, a sunburned playboy, was not likely to create a good impression with the jury. He was too young to have retired, too bronzed by sun-swept hours on the golf course to appeal to a jury of men and women who had worked and worked hard during their entire lifetime.

Those were the only people on whom Mason could count to counteract whatever case the district attorney was about to present, and try as he might Mason had no inkling of the ace that the district attorney had in the hole.

The testimony given before the grand jury and on which the indictment had been based showed that the defendant, Eleanor Corbin, had been friendly with

Douglas Hepner, that she had left her home with Douglas Hepner, that she had sent a telegram from Yuma stating that they were married, that two weeks later the body of Douglas Hepner had been found, that he had been shot in the back of the head with a .38 caliber bullet, that the defendant owned a .38 caliber revolver, that the defendant had stated to Ethel Belan she considered Douglas Hepner her boy friend and that Suzanne Granger had insinuated herself into the picture; that the defendant had stated that she would kill Douglas Hepner if he tried to throw her overboard, that at the time the defendant made that statement she had in her possession and exhibited a .38 caliber revolver, that the defendant was then living with Ethel Belan who had an apartment adjoining that of Suzanne Granger, a young woman who had attracted the attention of Douglas Hepner and who was going out with him.

This created a web of circumstantial evidence which had been sufficient to bring about an indictment at the hands of a friendly grand jury. It would hardly be sufficient to warrant a conviction before a trial jury. Therefore Mason knew that Hamilton Burger undoubtedly had some evidence which would, in his mind, be determinative, but neither Perry Mason nor the Drake Detective Agency had been able to find out what that evidence was.

And so Perry Mason found himself for once in his life entering upon a trial of a case where he knew that he would inevitably be confronted with evidence which would be disastrous to the defendant, where he had been unable to learn from the defendant the true story of what had happened, where he must rely entirely on his powers of observation and cross-examination, where he would have to get the facts of the case from the mouths of hostile witnesses.

Hamilton Burger, the district attorney, flushed and triumphant in the face of apparent victory, made an opening statement to the jury. After outlining a few preliminary facts by way of background, he said:

"We expect to show you, ladies and gentlemen, that the defendant in this case, actuated by jealousy, armed herself with a .38 caliber revolver; that she made financial arrangements with Ethel Belan to share apartment 360 so that she could spy upon Suzanne Granger who lived in apartment 358; that the purpose of so doing was to catch the man who she claimed was her husband, Douglas Hepner, the decedent, in a compromising position with Suzanne Granger; that she threatened that if she couldn't have Douglas Hepner no one else would ever have him.

"And so, ladies and gentlemen of the jury, we find Douglas Hepner, the decedent, dead, with a bullet from the defendant's gun in his brain, and the defendant making elaborate preparations to have it appear she was mentally irresponsible, that she had amnesia, what we might term a synthetic amnesia, carefully cultivated to shield her from being forced to answer embarrassing questions, an amnesia which psychiatrists will testify is completely simulated."

"Just a moment, Your Honor," Mason said. "I dislike to interrupt the district attorney's opening statement, but the defense will challenge the testimony of any psychiatrist who attempts to qualify as a mind reader. The science of psychiatry is not so far advanced that any man can tell with certainty..."

Hamilton Burger interrupted with affable good nature. "That is conceded, ladies and gentlemen of the jury. I withdraw any statement I made about the psychiatrist. We'll put the psychiatrists on the stand. We'll qualify them. We'll let them testify. We'll let counsel for the defense object and we'll let the Court rule on the admissibility of the evidence. But for the present time I withdraw any reference I have made to any psychiatric testimony.

"And that, ladies and gentlemen, is in a general way the picture that we expect to develop before you. Since some of the evidence may be controversial, and since we want to expedite matters, I won't go into all of the details at this time."

And, using Perry Mason's interruption as an excuse to keep his case outlined in broad generalities, Hamilton Burger thanked the jurors and sat down.

Mason turned to Paul Drake. "Notice, Paul, that he said the bullet in the head of Douglas Hepner had been fired from the defendant's gun."

"Did he say that?" Drake whispered.

Mason nodded. "He slipped it in almost casually."

Judge Moran said, "Does the defendant wish to make any statement at this time?"

"No, Your Honor," Mason said. "We will reserve our opening statement until later. Perhaps we may dispense with it entirely. I think the jurors understand fully that it is incumbent upon the prosecution to prove the guilt of the defendant beyond all reasonable doubt, and if the prosecution fails to do this we will rely upon that failure and will put on no evidence at all."

"Is that an opening statement?" Hamilton Burger asked.

"No," Mason said, "it is a statement to the Court."

"You mean you aren't going to put on any evidence for the defense?"

"Not unless you put on sufficient evidence to raise an issue. The law presumes the defendant innocent."

Judge Moran said, "That will do, gentlemen. I don't want any colloquy between counsel. Please address your remarks to the Court. Mr Prosecutor, the defendant has waived an opening statement at this time. Put on your first witness."

Hamilton Burger bowed and smiled. Nothing could affect his glowing good humor.

"My first witness," he said, "is Raymond Orla."

Raymond Orla took the oath and disclosed that he was a deputy coroner, that he had been called to Sierra Vista Park when the body of Douglas Hepner had been discovered at about 9:15 P.M. on the night of August seventeenth. He had taken charge of proceedings there at the scene and had had photographs taken. He identified various photographs as showing the position of the body and the location where it had been found. He had made an examination of the body, had not moved it until after photographs had been taken; then the body had been taken to the coroner's laboratory where the clothes had been removed and an autopsy had been performed. Photographs had been taken of the body during the several stages of the autopsy and he had these photographs.

Hamilton Burger announced that the photographs of the autopsy would be subject to inspection by counsel but he thought they were too gruesome to be submitted to the jury who presumably were not as accustomed as counsel to seeing photographs of a body during a post-mortem examination.

Orla testified that there was a bullet hole in the back of the head of the decedent, that aside from a few bruises there were no other injuries or marks of violence, that the autopsy surgeon had recovered the bullet from the head.

"That's all," Hamilton Burger said suavely. "I don't know whether counsel has any desire to cross-examine."

"Oh, just one or two questions," Mason said breezily. "What happened to the clothes the decedent was wearing?"

"They were folded and placed in a locker at the coroner's office. They are still there."

"And those clothes are subject to inspection by counsel for the defense at any time," Hamilton Burger interposed. "I'll instruct the witness to arrange for such an inspection at any hour of the day or night."

And the district attorney even made a little bow as though acknowledging applause for his fairness.

"What about the personal possessions? What things were in the man's pockets?" Mason inquired of the witness, ignoring the district attorney's interpolation.

"I have a list," Orla said.

He whipped a notebook from his pocket. "The following articles were in the possession of the decedent: One notebook, a driving license, one fountain pen, one leather key container containing four keys, one handkerchief, one dollar and ninety-six cents in small change, one silver cigarette case, six cigarettes."

"And that's all?" Mason asked.

"Yes, sir. That's all."

"Where are those articles?"

"At the coroner's office."

"I want them introduced in evidence," Mason said.

"Come, come," Hamilton Burger said. "These articles are purely incidental. They have no bearing on the case."

"How do *you* know they don't have any bearing on the case?" Mason said.

"Well, if you want them introduced in evidence, go ahead and introduce them as part of your case. They're not part of mine."

"Your Honor," Mason said, "I would like to have these articles introduced in evidence. I feel that they may be significant, particularly the notebook."

"The notebook was entirely blank," Orla said.

"You mean there was nothing in it?"

"Absolutely nothing. The pages were entirely blank. The notebook was a leather notebook which contained a compartment for a driving license and a filler which was detachable. Evidently an old filler had been taken out shortly prior to the death of the decedent and a new filler put in. There was not so much as the scratch of a pen on the new filler."

"What about the driving license?" Mason asked.

"It was in the notebook, in a transparent cellophane window compartment designed for such purpose."

"If the Court please," Mason said, "I would like to have these articles introduced. I am perfectly willing to stipulate that they may be considered a part of my case, but I would like to have them introduced now."

Hamilton Burger said, "Your Honor, I feel that the People should be permitted to go ahead and put on its case. The defense can then put on its case. I don't think we should have the cases put on piecemeal."

"Under those circumstances," Mason said, "as part of my cross-examination I am going to insist that these articles be introduced in evidence."

"You can't do that as a part of cross-examination."

"I can ask this witness to bring the articles into court," Mason said.

"Come, come," Judge Moran said. "I don't see any point to be gained in becoming technical over these articles. They were in the possession of the decedent, Mr. Witness?"

"That's right. Yes, sir."

"They were in his pockets?"

"Yes, sir."

"And you personally removed them from his pockets?"

"I did. Yes, sir."

"Those articles may be placed in the custody of the Court and marked 'Defendant's Exhibits for Identification.' At this time the articles will be marked for identification only and defense counsel can cross-examine the witness on any of those articles that he wishes. Later on, if defendant wishes, those articles may be received in evidence."

"Thank you, Your Honor," Mason said. "And the defense would like a set of the photographs showing the autopsy of the decedent."

"I have a set of photographs for defense counsel," Hamilton Burger said, presenting a whole sheaf of 8 x 10 glossy photographs with a courtesy so elaborate that it was again obviously designed to impress the jury with his complete fairness.

"Thank you," Mason said. "No further questions."

Dr. Julius Oberon was called as a witness. He gave his qualifications as a forensic pathologist and coroner's physician. He stated that he had performed the autopsy on the body of the decedent, that he had recovered a .38 caliber bullet from the head of the decedent, that the discharge of the bullet into the man's head had resulted in almost instant death. He pointed out the location of the wound of entrance, described generally the damage to the brain, stated that there were no other injuries which could have caused death, and that in his opinion the victim on which he performed the autopsy had been dead for approximately twenty-four to thirty-six hours. He could not fix the time of death any closer than that.

"And what did you do with this bullet after you removed it from the head of the decedent?" Hamilton Burger asked.

"I turned it over to a ballistics expert."

"You may cross-examine," Hamilton Burger said.

Mason glanced at the doctor, who was settling himself firmly in the witness chair as though bracing himself to resist a verbal attack.

"You say death was virtually instantaneous, Doctor?"

"Yes, sir."

"On what do you base that opinion?"

"The nature of the wound, the damage to the brain."

"That wound would have produced complete, instantaneous unconsciousness?"

"Yes, sir."

"But not necessarily death?"

"What do you mean?"

"Aren't you familiar, Doctor, with cases where there is extensive hemorrhage from a head wound, in other words, haven't you had many cases in your own experience where the brain tissue has been damaged and there has been extensive hemorrhage?"

"Yes, indeed. I have seen cases of massive hemorrhage."

"What causes such cases, Doctor?"

"Why, the blood in the body drains out through the damaged blood vessels."

"It is pumped out by the heart, isn't it?"

"Yes, sir."

"So that in those cases, while the person may be completely unconscious, there is nevertheless life for some considerable period of time, a life which manifests itself through the activity of the heart pumping blood into the blood vessels?"

"Yes, sir, that is right."

"Was that the case in this instance, Doctor?"

"Definitely not. There was very little bleeding."

"Did you notice any blood clot on the ground near the head of the decedent?"

"Yes, sir. There was *some* external bleeding, not much."

"And some internal?"

"Yes, sir, but the bleeding was not extensive."

"And predicating your opinion on that lack of bleeding you decided that death was virtually instantaneous, is that right?"

"Not on the lack of bleeding alone, but on the position of the wound and the extent of the brain damage."

"You have seen similar wounds with equally extensive damage where there had been considerable hemorrhage and where the decedent had therefore lived for some time although completely unconscious?"

"Yes, sir."

"Now then, Doctor, did you take into consideration the possibility that the decedent might have been killed at some other place and the body transported to the place where it was found?"

"I did. Yes, sir."

"Did you negate such a possibility?"

"In my own mind, yes."

"May I ask for your process of reasoning, Doctor?"

"The nature and extent of the wound, the damage to the brain, the nature of the hemorrhage, the position of the blood clot, the absence of vertical blood smears, the position of the body—things of that sort."

Mason said, "It is then your opinion, Doctor, that someone stood behind the decedent, shot him in the back of the head with a .38 caliber revolver, and that death was instantaneous, or virtually instantaneous?"

"That is correct, except as to one matter."

"What is that?"

"The decedent may have been seated at the time of his death. I am inclined to think he was. From the position in which the body was found I am inclined to think the decedent was seated on the grass with his legs doubled to the right, his left hand resting on the ground. In that case since the course of the bullet wound was not downward, the person who shot him was also seated on the ground somewhat behind him. Or was so stooped or crouched that the gun was on a level with the back of the decedent's head."

"Thank you," Mason said. "That is all, Doctor."

"No further questions on redirect," Hamilton Burger said. "I now wish to call Merton C. Bosler to the stand."

Mason, watching Hamilton Burger, saw the district attorney glance at the clock as though carefully timing the course of events.

Merton C. Bosler qualified himself as a ballistics expert. He had, he said, been present at the time the autopsy was performed, he had seen Dr. Oberon remove the fatal bullet from the skull of the decedent, he had seen Dr. Oberon mark that bullet. The bullet had then been turned over to him as a ballistics expert.

In fifteen minutes, led by Hamilton Burger's skillful questioning, Merton C. Bosler proved conclusively that the bullet he produced was correctly identified and that it had been discharged through the barrel of a .38 caliber Smith & Wesson revolver. The bullet and a series of enlarged photographs were received in evidence. The jurors in turn examined the fatal bullet gravely as though by so doing they were able to determine the issues in the case.

"Now then," Hamilton Burger continued, "did you make any search of the vicinity where the body was found for the purpose of determining whether any weapon was lying nearby?"

"I assisted in such a search."

"Did you find such a weapon nearby?"

"Not at the time."

"Now then," Hamilton Burger said triumphantly, "did you subsequently make a search using any mechanical or electronic device?"

"I did. Yes, sir."

"What device?"

"I used what is known as a mine detector."

"And what is that?"

"That is an electronic device so designed that when it is moved over the surface of the ground it will give a peculiar squeal when it is moved over a metallic object."

"And what did you find?"

"Well, we found several metallic objects which were not significant. We found an old rusted penknife. We found the metallic lever key which had been used to open a can of sardines with the tin top of the sardine can still around it, and..."

"Yes, yes," Hamilton Burger interrupted. "Never mind these insignificant objects. What else, if anything, did you find that you consider a significant object?"

"We found a .38 caliber Smith & Wesson revolver with one discharged shell. The number of the revolver was C-48809."

"Indeed," Hamilton Burger said triumphantly. "And did you make any ballistics tests with that weapon?"

"I did. Yes, sir."

"Did you fire test bullets through that weapon?"

"Yes, sir."

"And what was the result of that test?"

"The result was that the two sets of individual characteristics—those on the fatal bullet and those on the one fired in the laboratory—exactly matched."

"Did you photograph that matching?"

"I did."

"Will you produce that photograph, please?"

The witness produced a big 8 x 10 photograph. It was placed in evidence and carefully explained to the jury.

"Where did you find this weapon?"

"The weapon was buried about eight inches beneath the ground. It had been thrust into a hole which had evidently been made by some burrowing animal and then the hole had been plugged up with dirt. Over the surface of the ground dry leaves and twigs had been scattered so that it was virtually impossible to notice any disturbance of the ground."

"But you located this with a mine detector, and then did what?"

"Then we carefully examined the ground, carefully moved away the dry leaves and twigs and were then able to observe the place where earth had been pushed into the hole. We removed this earth and found the weapon in the hole."

"And where was this with relation to the place where the body of the decedent was discovered?"

"Fifty-six feet in a northeasterly direction."

"Someone was with you at the time?"

"Oh yes, sir. There were several people."

"Among them was a surveyor?"

"Yes, sir."

"A man who drove a stake at the place where the weapon was discovered and oriented it with the place where the body had been found?"

"That is right. Yes, sir."

"Do you know that surveyor's name?"

"Yes, sir. It was Stephen Escalante."

"Now then, Mr. Bosler, did you subsequently make any examination of the records of firearm purchases on file in this county?"

"I did. Yes, sir."

"And did you find any record of a Smith & Wesson revolver, number C-48809, having been sold in this county?"

"I did. Yes, sir."

"And according to the records, who purchased that weapon?"

"Eleanor Corbin."

"The defendant in this action?"

"Yes, sir."

"And her signature appears upon that record?"

"It does. Yes, sir."

"That is a public record in this county, made such by law?"

"Yes, sir."

"You have a photostatic copy of that record?"

"I do. Yes, sir."

Hamilton Burger was exceedingly unctuous.

"Your Honor, it is approaching the hour for the evening adjournment. I will ask to have this photostatic copy of the record introduced at this time. I have not as yet shown that the signature on this firearms sale registration is the signature of the defendant, Eleanor Corbin, but I expect to produce evidence tomorrow morning, that is, evidence of a handwriting expert, showing that the signature is that of the defendant. However, I believe that the evidence is sufficient in view of the nature of this record to have this photostatic copy introduced in evidence at this time."

"No objection," Mason said, smilingly unconcerned, and giving no sign that this testimony had not been fully anticipated by the defendant. "We will stipulate that this page of the firearms register book may go into evidence, that is, the photostatic copy may, and in order to save the district attorney trouble we will stipulate that the signature appearing on there is actually the signature of the defendant in this case."

Burger showed surprise. "You'll stipulate to that?" he asked.

"Why, certainly," Mason said, smiling affably.

"Very well," Judge Moran ruled. "The photostatic copy will be received in evidence with its appropriate numbers, Mr. Clerk, and court will adjourn until ten o'clock tomorrow morning."

As the crowd started shuffling from the courtroom, Della Street and Paul Drake headed through the rail toward Perry Mason.

Mason turned to Eleanor. "Was that your gun?" he asked.

"That is my gun."

"And how did it get there, where it was found?"

"Mr. Mason, I give you my word of honor, I cross my heart and hope to die, I have absolutely no recollection. I carried that gun for personal protection. There had been so many instances of women being molested and . . . well, I didn't live exactly a quiet life and quite often I had to carry jewelry from my father's place of business to my home. The police themselves suggested that I should carry that gun. It's one of those weapons with a two-inch barrel that is designed to fit in a pocket or in a woman's purse."

"And when you left home on this so-called honeymoon of yours you had that gun with you?"

"Yes, I carried it with me. I may as well admit it now. I'm trapped."

"And you *didn't* have it with you when you were apprehended by the police?"

"Quite obviously, Mr. Mason," she said, smiling slightly, "I didn't have it with me. I had very little with me. I believe my garments were described in the press as 'a fluttering diaphanous covering.'"

"Dammit," Mason said angrily, "don't joke about it. That gun is going to convict you of murder. You left home with Douglas Hepner. He was murdered and he was murdered with your gun."

"But it was two weeks after I'd left home with him. A lot can happen in two weeks."

"It doesn't make any difference what else happened," Mason said angrily. "He was killed on the sixteenth and he was killed with your gun, within a hundred yards of the place where you were seen running around practically naked in the moonlight."

"You're angry with me, aren't you?"

"I just wish you'd tell me what happened," Mason said, "so I'd have a chance to save you from the death penalty or from life imprisonment. If you shot him you could at least give me an opportunity to plead self-defense or justifiable homicide or..."

"I'm afraid," she said, "you forget that the bullet was squarely in the back of the man's head. That would seem to negate any theory of self-defense."

A policewoman beckoned for the defendant.

Mason, still angry, said, "I hope you'll do something to recover your memory before ten o'clock tomorrow morning, because if you don't..." He broke off as he saw a newspaper reporter coming toward him.

The newspaper reporter pushed forward. "Mr. Mason, I wonder if you'd care to make any statement?"

Mason smiled genially. "No statement at the present time," he said, "other than that the defendant is absolutely innocent."

"Is it true that she has no recollection of what happened on the night of the murder?"

"Amnesia," Mason said, "is a subject for the experts. I am not an expert. You might ask one of the psychiatrists about retrograde amnesia from mental shock. That's all I can tell you at the present time."

"Your defense will include amnesia?"

"My defense," Mason said, smiling, "is not being announced at the present time for reasons which should be quite obvious. However, you may quote me as stating that before this case is finished Hamilton Burger is going to be greatly surprised."

And, smiling confidently, Mason picked up the papers from the table in front of him, put them in the brief case and snapped the brief case shut.

Mason cupped his hand around Della Street's elbow, nodded to Paul Drake, said in a low voice, "Let's get out of here where we can talk," and led the way across the courtroom through the court reporter's room, down the corridor and into a witness room.

Mason kicked the door shut, said, "Well, there it is out in the open."

"What can you do against a combination like that?" Drake asked.

Mason shrugged his shoulders.

Drake said, "You can see now why Burger was so anxious to get to trial. Good Lord, Perry, you can't beat a case like that."

Mason pushed back his coat, put his thumbs in the armholes of his vest, started pacing the floor. "I wish that girl would tell me the truth," he said.

"She isn't telling you the truth because she can't," Drake said. "She killed him. There isn't one chance in a million that she didn't kill him."

"Chief," Della Street said, "isn't there some way of combating this question of the ownership of the gun? Of course, it's her gun. It was registered to her. But suppose somebody stole it."

"That, of course," Mason said, "is the only defense we have, but you're overlooking the trap that Hamilton Burger is setting for me."

"What's that?"

"He wants me to work some line of cross-examination that will bring out that very point," Mason said. "Then he's going to bring his star witness to the stand."

"Who's that?"

"Ethel Belan."

"What will she swear to?"

"Heaven knows," Mason said, "but probably it will be to the effect that she saw Eleanor Corbin with that gun in her possession within a few hours of the time of the murder. Lord knows what she's going to testify to, but it's something devastating, you can bet your bottom dollar on that. Otherwise Burger would never have put her up at an expensive hotel, given her a bodyguard, kept her in isolation, away from everyone who might tip us off to what her story was going to be."

"That's so," Drake agreed morosely. "How about making a deal with the D.A., Perry?"

"On what?"

"Copping a plea of guilty, taking life imprisonment and saving your client from the death penalty. After all, with her looks and a little luck she'll get out with some of her life left to live."

Mason shook his head. "I can't do that."

"Why?"

"Because she won't tell me that she actually killed the guy. I can't put an innocent woman up against the horror of life imprisonment on a deal of that sort.

"Figure what it means, Paul. She's young. She's attractive. She's got a good figure. She likes to show it. She has been free as the air. She travels around to Europe and South America. She eats in the best restaurants. She has been on top of the world.

"Now put her in the drab confines of a prison life, take away all initiative, all glamour, all variety. It's condemning her to a monotonous procession of days, one day just like another. Lights out at a certain time each night. Up at a certain time each morning. Drab, tasteless breakfast according to a regular schedule. Time slips through her fingers and goes down the drain. She lives on prison grub. It's a diet that will keep her nourished but it consists of starches in place of proteins. She gets fat. Her tissues become water-logged. She loses her figure. She lets her shoulders sag in a dejected droop. And then after fifteen or perhaps twenty years she gets out. What's she going to do? She's no longer attractive to me. She's no longer filled with that devil-may-care spontaneity which now gives her her charm. Her life has gone. She has the stigma of prison surrounding her. She..."

"She'd ten thousand times rather walk into the execution chamber," Della Street said, "and so would I."

"There we are," Mason said.

"Well, we have to do *something*," Drake said. "We can't sit back and take this lying down."

"Of course we're going to do something," Mason flared. "I'm just trying to get things organized in my own mind. We've got to find out something about this case that the prosecution doesn't know. We've got to find it out fast and then we've got to prove what actually *did* happen."

"What actually did happen," Drake said. "is that your client killed Hepner. She got jealous because he started two-timing her and she shot him. Why the hell can't she be normal? Why can't she get on the witness stand, cross her legs, show the jury a lot of cheesecake and tell about that night when Douglas taunted her with the fact that he had betrayed her virtue and wasn't going to do anything about it, how she thought she could scare him into marrying her if she took the gun from her purse, intending just to frighten him, and then he taunted her some more and all of a sudden everything went black. And then the next thing she remembers is his body inert and silent in death. And so she lost her mind and went tearing around in the moonlight, putting on the dance of the seven veils."

"It's a goofy defense," Della Street said, "but at least it's a defense, and with her figure and her charm she could get by with it—at least enough so that some of the old goats on the jury would be hypnotized by her nylon stockings and hold out for acquittal. They'd finally compromise on manslaughter."

"You overlook the fact," Mason said, "that a lawyer is an officer of the court. He represents justice. He represents right. I'm not supposed to use my brains and try to stand between a guilty defendant and the law of the land. I'm supposed to see that my clients are protected, that their interests are protected.

"Now then, Paul, let's look at this thing from a logical standpoint. Let's not let ourselves get stampeded and let's not let ourselves get hypnotized. What have you got in your pockets?"

"Me? My pockets?" Drake asked.

Mason nodded.

"A bunch of junk," Drake said.

"Take it out," Mason said. "Put it on the table."

Drake looked at him in surprise.

"Go ahead," Mason said.

Silently Drake started pulling things out of his pockets.

"Well, I'll be darned," Della Street said, watching the collection pile up on the table. "And then you men talk about the stuff that goes in a woman's purse!"

Drake put down pencil, fountain pen, notebook, knife, cigarette case, lighter, keychain, handkerchiefs, wallet, small change, driving license, a couple of opened letters, an airplane time schedule, a package of chewing gum.

Mason surveyed the collection thoughtfully.

"All right," Drake said, "what have I proved?"

"That," Mason told him, "is something that I wish I knew, but you sure have proven something."

"I don't get it," Drake said.

"Contrast what you have in your pockets, which is probably an average collection of the stuff carried by a busy man, and think of the things which the coroner said were in the pockets of Douglas Hepner."

"Well, of course," Drake said, "I..."

"Let's look at it this way. Hepner smoked. He had his cigarettes in a cigarette case. Where were his matches? Where was his knife? Nearly every man carries a penknife of some sort. He had a small amount of chicken feed in his pocket but no bills. He had a driving license but no membership cards in anything. No clubs, no addresses, nothing of that sort."

Drake frowned thoughtfully for a moment. "By gosh," he said, "when you come right down to it, Perry, that *was* a very meager assortment of junk."

"Of course it was," Mason said. "Where did Hepner live?"

"Now there," Drake said, "is something that bothers the hell out of the police. Ostensibly he lived at the Dixiecrat Apartments. He had an apartment there but it wasn't really lived in. There was maid service and the maid said there would be days at a time, sometimes a couple of weeks at a stretch, when the beds wouldn't have been slept in, when the linen wouldn't have been used in the bathroom. There was never any food in the icebox. He didn't send out his laundry from there, and..."

Mason snapped his fingers.

"What?" Drake asked.

"That's it," Mason said. "The laundry! Come on, Paul!"

"Where?"

"Over to the coroner's office," Mason said. "We were invited to inspect the clothes that the decedent was wearing when the body was found. Let's check for a laundry mark. It's a cinch Hepner didn't do his own laundry."

"Okay," Drake said. "We may have something there, but...oh shucks, Perry, if there'd been a laundry mark on those clothes the police would have checked it long before this."

"How do we know they haven't?" Mason said.

"Well, if they have you'll learn about it in due time."

"I want to learn about things before they're thrown at me in court," Mason said. "Just suppose that that client of mine *is* telling the truth. Suppose she *can't* remember what happened. Suppose that she's being railroaded on a murder charge and can't..."

"The chances of that are just about one in fifty million," Drake said. "The D.A. has had her examined by psychiatrists. They're satisfied she's faking. The minute she gets on the witness stand and claims that she can't remember what happened, the D.A. is going to start throwing a cross-examination at her that will leave her wilted like a hot lettuce leaf. Then he's going to throw on a battery of psychiatrists and just about prove that she's lying."

"All right," Mason said, "if she's lying, I can't let her get on the witness stand and put herself in that position, but I have to prove to myself that she is lying. Do you have any ultraviolet light in your office, Paul?"

"Yes, I've got a little hand lamp that plugs into an AC current and has two types of filter—a long-length violet and..."

"Get it," Mason said. "Bring it along. Lots of laundries these days are using fluorescent ink as a laundry mark. That may give us a clue. What about those keys? There were four keys on the key container. Did the police ever find out what locks they fitted?"

"One of them was to that apartment in the Dixiecrat apartment house. I don't know about the others."

"Okay," Mason said. "Take along a block of wax, Paul. While I'm keeping the

attention of the authorities focused on something else, make a wax impression
of every one of the keys on that key container."

"Are you supposed to have those?" Drake asked dubiously.

"Any law against it?" Mason asked.

"Hell, I don't know, Perry. You know the law."

"Then do what I tell you to. I want an impression of those keys. We've got
work to do. We're beginning to find out what we're up against now, and we can
gamble that tomorrow Hamilton Burger is going to throw a mountain at us.
He'll bury us under an avalanche."

"Ethel Belan?" Drake asked.

Mason nodded. "It's a safe bet that her testimony is really going to throw a
harpoon into us.

"Burger has timed this whole thing. Tonight he'll have us worrying about the
gun, frantically trying to dig up evidence that will make the jury think it was
stolen.

"Then when we're all ready to stake our case on that he'll have Ethel Belan
jerk the rug out from under us.

"Then Hamilton Burger is going to smile sweetly and say, 'The prosecution
rests,' and toss the case into my lap.

"If I put Eleanor on the witness stand they're going to tear her to pieces. If I
don't, she's going to get convicted. Either way it goes we're hooked. Come on,
let's go."

CHAPTER ELEVEN

A somewhat bored attendant at the coroner's office, said, "I'll have to call either
the D.A. or the police."

"You won't catch the D.A. at this hour," Mason said. "There was a
stipulation made in court this afternoon that we could inspect the clothing of
Douglas Hepner."

"Oh, I guess it's all right," the attendant said. "There's no reason why you
shouldn't. Didn't Raymond Orla testify up there today?"

"That's right."

"Well, I've got a night number. I can get him. He'll be getting home just
about this time. You wait here."

The attendant entered another office, carefully closing the door behind him,
then, after some five minutes, came back and nodded. "It's okay," he said. "Orla
said the D.A. said you could look at them. Right this way."

He led the way down a long corridor, into a room where there were
numbered lockers. He took a key from his pocket, opened a locker and said,
"There you are. These are the clothes."

"There were some articles of personal property," Mason said. "A fountain
pen, notebook, things of that sort."

"Those will be in this little lock box here."

The attendant opened the lock box, placed them all on a table. "I'll have to
sort of stick around," he apologized.

"Certainly," Mason said, glancing significantly at Della Street.

"My, what a job you must have here," Della Street said, moving over to inspect some of the other lockers. "You have to keep all of these straight." She laughed. "As a secretary I can appreciate the problem you have."

The attendant began to warm up. He moved over to Della Street's side. "Well, it's quite a job," he admitted. "Of course, you see, things keep changing here. We'll have cases come in and...some of them aren't here twenty-four hours. Some of them where there's a court action on are here for weeks. Now over here is our temporary side. Things here run from twenty-four to seventy-two hours. And in this other room over here we keep the bodies. On this temporary side the numbers on the lockers and the numbers on the lockers containing the bodies are both the same so that we can give a body a key number—take a tag and tie it on his big toe.

"I presume this is all pretty gruesome to you. Most women get the creeps. You can see that tier of files in there looks like oversized filing drawers. Each one of them has a body, kept under just the right amount of refrigeration."

"No, it doesn't frighten me," Della Street said, her voice showing interest. "I'm a realist. I know that death is one logical end of the life stream, just as birth is at the other end. And I know that a certain percentage of deaths are sudden and unexplained. It's up to you people to keep the records straight."

She moved over toward the other room and the attendant, after pausing to glance momentarily over his shoulder, followed her, explaining as he went.

Mason examined the garments. "This is a tailor-made suit, Paul," he said, "but the label has been carefully cut out. Suppose the police did it?"

"I doubt it," Drake said. "You never can tell. It's been cut out all right."

Mason said, "Take this underwear, Paul. Hold the coat over it. Now get your ultraviolet light going."

Paul Drake held the coat over the underwear, making something of a tent of it, then flashed the ultraviolet light on the underwear.

Almost immediately a number flared into brilliance.

"This is it," Mason said excitedly. "Get this, Paul."

Mason smoothed out the underwear. Drake held the light.

The number N-4464 flared up brilliantly.

"Quick," Mason said. "Get that light away, Paul. I don't want the attendant to report to the police what we've been doing and give the police any ideas."

"What about the suit?" Drake asked.

"We won't bother with it now," Mason said. "While Della has him over there get the wax impression of those keys. I'll hold the coat up as though I'm looking through the lining and hold it between you and the attendant."

The attendant, looking back at them, had turned and started moving back toward the table. Della Street held him back with one last question. Mason held up the coat on its wire hanger, apparently inspecting the lining.

Della Street veered over toward a locker. "What's this?"

The attendant, suddenly suspicious, broke away, hurried forward. Mason turned the garment on the hanger, apparently completely oblivious of the fact that anyone else was in the room, yet managing to hold the coat in front of the attendant very much as a toreador holds the cape in front of the bull.

"What are you guys doing?" the attendant asked.

Mason said accusingly, "They've cut the label out of this coat. We're going to have to see that label."

"Who's cut it out?" the attendant demanded.

"How should I know?" Mason said. "It's in your custody."

"Well, it wasn't cut out after it came here."

"It wasn't?" Mason asked in surprise. "Didn't the police do it?"

"Heck, I don't know. We just keep the stuff, that's all. But no one here cut any labels out."

"You mean to say you don't cut out the labels in order to check...?"

"We don't touch a thing. You'll have to take that business up with the police. All we're supposed to do is keep the stuff. I have orders to let you look at it, that is, the D.A. said you could look at it, and that's that. As far as I'm concerned, go ahead and look. What's that guy doing over there?"

Drake straightened, holding the key container in his hand. "I've been studying these keys," he said, "trying to find out whether there's any identifying number on them."

The attendant laughed. "That's one thing the police sure worked on. They went over those keys with a magnifying glass. There aren't any numbers on them."

"Oh well," Drake said, tossing the keys back on the table. "I guess there's no need for me to look at them then. How about it Perry? Have you seen everything you want?"

"I suppose so," Mason said grudgingly. "What about his shoes?"

"I can tell you something about the shoes," the attendant said. "Of course I don't want to be quoted."

"It's confidential if you say it's confidential," Mason told him.

"Well, the shoes were sold by a downtown department store as you can see. Police checked. It was a cash purchase. The guy didn't have any credit there. The shoes were part of a shipment received about three months ago. Police thought they had something for a while but it turned out to be a blind alley."

"Just what were they looking for?" Mason asked.

"Looking for anything they could find. There was something mysterious about the guy's apartment. He wasn't there much of the time. The police are trying to find out where he spent his time."

"Probably in travel," Mason said casually.

"That's the way of it," the attendant said. "It's probably the explanation. The guy was on the move all the time. Well, you folks finished?"

"We're finished."

The attendant returned the articles to the lock box and the filing cabinet, locked the filing cabinet, smiled at Della Street and said, "It was a pleasure. Anything else I can do for you fellows?"

"Not at the moment," Mason told him. "Well, let's go and eat. I just wanted to check on that stuff," he explained to the attendant. "You know how it is. You can hear someone describe a suit of clothes or something but it's hard to tell..."

"Yeah, I know," the attendant said. "I guess you've got the picture now."

"I think I have," Mason said.

"Well, good night."

They moved into the fresh air of outdoors, away from the stuffy smell of corpses, pathological specimens and the odor of death.

"Well?" Drake asked.

"You've got your work cut out for you, Paul," Mason said. "You've got to get that laundry mark traced and you've got to do it fast."

"Have a heart, Perry, I'm hungry. We can't get the thing until..."

"You've got to get it," Mason said. "In the first place the police have most of these laundry marks filed, that is, the general code and..."

"And you know how anxious *they'll* be to help us," Drake said.

"Try the sheriff's office," Mason said. "Dig out some of your contacts. Get hold of the secretary of the laundry association."

Drake groaned. "I can see that I'm going to have a night of it."

"You may get it faster than you think," Mason told him. "Those laundry marks are important. Hamilton Burger was too sure of himself on this case. He thinks he's got a cinch case and has just made a superficial investigation. Some of the police would have known about that laundry number. A lot of laundries are using that ultraviolet device now. They can stamp on a big, easily read number without defacing the garment. Now get busy, Paul. Did you get the wax impression of the keys?"

"I sure did. Just had time to get the last impression when the attendant came back. Thought for a moment he'd caught me."

"It wouldn't have made any difference if he had," Mason said. "We're entitled to inspect those keys, and in order to inspect them we can photograph them or do anything else."

Della Street said, "I can take charge of having the keys made, Paul. There's a locksmith who has his shop near my apartment. He frequently works late, and if he isn't working I know where to find him. I pass the time of day with him every once in a while. You go ahead and chase down the laundry mark. Chief, you go to the office and I'll take the car and go down and get the keys made."

"Okay," Mason said, "but remember he has to keep his mouth shut."

"I think you can trust him all right," Della said. "He's a great fan of yours, follows all of your cases in the newspapers, and if he thought he was doing something to help he'd be tickled to death."

"Well, he can do something all right," Mason said, "and let's hope it will help. Paul, you get busy on that laundry number. Della, as soon as you get the keys made come back to the office and we'll wait for Paul and see if he gets any results."

Mason drove back to the office. Drake started work at once on the telephone. Della Street took the car and went out to get keys made.

Mason latchkeyed the door of his private office, switched on the lights, and started pacing the floor, taking mental inventory.

Fifteen minutes lengthened into twenty, became a full half hour.

The unlisted telephone rang sharply. Mason picked it up. Drake's voice came over the wire. "Think I'm getting some place, Perry. I managed to locate the secretary of the laundry association. He doesn't have any idea what I'm working on. The number is a code. The 64 means that it's the Utility Twenty-four-hour Laundry Service, and the N-44 is the individual mark. The secretary tells me that the name of the patron whose laundry mark is registered probably begins with an N and that he's forty-fourth on the list. He's given me the name of the manager of the laundry and I'm trying to locate him now. I hope I'll have something for you within a short time. When do we eat?"

"When we get this thing buttoned up."

"Look, Perry, I can have a hamburger sent up from downstairs. It's not much, but a hamburger and a good mug of coffee will help a lot."

"When Della gets back," Mason said. "If we haven't had a break by that time we'll have something sent in while you're working."

"Okay," Drake said. "I just thought I'd let you know that we're striking pay dirt. But why would the thing be listed under N? Do you suppose Hepner was using an alias?"

"He could have," Mason said. "There's something pretty damn mysterious about Hepner's whole background."

"Okay," Drake said. "I'll let you know."

Another ten minutes passed, then Della Street came in jingling a bunch of keys.

"Okay?" Mason asked.

"Okay, Chief. I had two of each made so that in case we were fortunate enough to find the locks they fitted we would have two strings to our bow. Sometimes in making up keys from a wax impression some little imperfection or other will throw them off. I have a file here. The key man gave it to me and suggested that if the keys didn't work we start filing the edges, just touching them up a bit."

"And he's going to keep quiet about it?" Mason asked.

"He's having the time of his life," Della Street said. "He told me to pass the word on to you that any time he could help you in any way on a case to just let him know and that you could trust him to be the soul of discretion."

"Well, that helps," Mason said, grinning. "You and the locksmith seem to think that once we find the locks that these keys fit we're going to walk right in."

"Well," Della Street asked, "what's the object of having keys if you aren't going to use them?"

"That, of course," Mason said, "is a question. Let's go on down to Drake's office and see how he's coming. He thought maybe he'd have something for us in a short time and suggested that we might celebrate by having hamburgers and coffee sent up to the office."

"I could use some of that," Della Street said. "Let's go."

They switched off the lights, walked down the corridor to Drake's office. The night telephone operator motioned for them to go on in.

"Paul's on the phone," she said. "He's been on the phone almost constantly. Go on in. I won't need to announce you."

Mason held open the wooden gate and Della Street preceded him down the long, narrow corridor, flanked by the doors of small offices on each side where Drake's operatives interviewed witnesses, prepared reports and at times conducted polygraph tests.

Drake was talking on the telephone, making notes, as Mason and Della Street entered. He waved his hand at them, nodded his head exultantly and said, "Just a minute, let me get that down. Now, let's see. That's Frank Ormsby Newberg at the Titterington Apartments on Elmwood Place.... Can you tell us how long he's been a customer?...I see...kept the same laundry mark, eh?...All right, thanks....No, no, this is just a routine check trying to trace a lost suitcase. Question of whether or not there's a twenty-five dollar limit on liability for loss of a suitcase and trying to prove identity of garments. Nothing except a routine matter and I'm sorry I bothered you after office hours but I'm working against rather a tight schedule....That's right. This is the Drake Detective Agency....Sure, look me up. Perhaps *we* can give *you* a helping hand some time. Okay, good-by."

Drake hung up the telephone, said, "Well, we have it. Frank Ormsby Newberg, Titterington Apartments, Elmwood Place."

"Okay," Mason said, "let's go."

"Eats?" Drake asked.

Mason shook his head, glanced at his wrist watch, said, "Not yet."

"It would only take a minute to..."

"We don't know how many minutes we have left," Mason said. "You can't tell what we're going to run into. We're working against time and against the police. That attendant at the coroner's laboratory *may* not have been as preoccupied as he seemed."

CHAPTER TWELVE

The Titterington Apartments turned out to be a narrow-fronted, three-story, brick building, more than a hundred feet deep, with no clerk on duty. The names of the tenants of the apartments were listed in a long directory to the right of the locked front door. There was a speaking tube by each name and a call button.

"Old-fashioned joint," Paul Drake said. "What do we do?"

Mason found the name of Frank Ormsby Newberg listed opposite apartment 220, and pressed the button.

There was no answer.

Mason waited a while, then pressed the button the second time.

Mason turned to Della Street.

Wordlessly she handed him the set of four keys.

Mason tried the first one in the front door. Nothing happened.

The second one fitted smoothly in the lock and clicked back the bolt.

Mason held the key between his thumb and forefinger, said, "This looks like the key. Let's go."

Drake said, "Are we apt to get into trouble over this, Perry?"

"Of course," Mason said, "but all I'm doing at the moment is trying to find out if the keys fit."

"Are you going into the apartment?"

"That," Mason said, "depends."

There was a little cubbyhole lobby in the front of the building and a sign reading "Manager—Apt. 101," with an arrow pointing to the apartment.

Mason led the way down the corridor to the lighted elevator shaft. The automatic elevator wheezed upward to the second floor. Apartment 220 was designated by a number on the door in a poorly lit corridor. There was a fairly good-sized crack at the bottom of the door and no light came through from this crack although other apartment doors on the same floor showed well-defined ribbons of light.

There was a doorbell to the right of the door. Mason pressed this and could hear a buzzer sounding on the inside of the apartment.

Drake said, "Perry, this thing gives me the creeps. Let's go talk with the manager. Let's keep our noses clean."

"Before I talk with the manager," Mason said, "I want to be sure what I'm talking about."

"I don't want to go in," Drake said.

"You don't mind if we demonstrate that the key fits, do you?"

"I don't like any part of this," Drake said.

"I don't like it myself," Mason told him, "but I'm trying to find evidence."

They stood there waiting.

The corridor was poorly ventilated. There was a warm aroma of cooking odors mingled with the feel of human tenancy. Down the corridor someone was listening to a television show and the words were plainly audible through the thin door of the apartment.

"An old dump made over," Drake said.

Mason nodded, then gently inserted the key which had opened the front door, and which he had been holding in his thumb and forefinger.

"I'm just going to try this," he said.

The lawyer twisted the key. Nothing happened.

He moved the key slightly back and forth in the lock, exerted pressure, but the key refused to turn.

Della Street said, "How about the file, Chief? The locksmith said perhaps we'd have to dress off a high spot."

Mason withdrew the key, looked at it for a moment, then tried another key on the key container. That key didn't even fit the lock. Nor did a third key. But the fourth key slid smoothly into the lock.

Again Mason twisted the key and this time the bolt on the door slid quietly back.

"Oh-oh!" Drake said.

Mason, placing a handkerchief over the palm of his hand and the tips of his fingers, gently turned the knob and opened the apartment door.

"Now this," Drake said, "is where I came in. I don't want any part of this."

Mason stood in the doorway for a second or two, then reached in and groped for the light switch. He found it and pressed the light button.

The interior of the apartment looked as though it had been visited by a cyclone. Drawers had been pulled out, cupboards had been opened, dishes had been piled on the floor, clothing was stacked in a heap, papers had been strewn about indiscriminately.

"I guess someone beat us to it," Della Street said.

The elevator door clanged open. Someone started down the corridor.

"Inside," Mason said, and led the way into the apartment.

Della Street followed him immediately. Drake hesitated, then reluctantly entered.

Mason kicked the door shut.

"Don't touch anything," the lawyer warned.

"Now look, Perry," Paul Drake said. "We're sitting in on a game. We don't know what's trumps. The only thing we know for sure is that *we* don't have *any.*"

As they stood there waiting they could hear steps in the corridor and voices.

Paul Drake whispered, "Perry, this is carrying things too far. If anything should happen and we were seen and recognized as we go out..."

Della Street put her fingers to her lips. "Shhhhh, Paul!"

The voices came closer.

Abruptly they could recognize the voice of Sergeant Holcomb of Homicide Squad saying, "Now as I understand it, Madam, you think you recognized his picture."

The steps paused in front of the door.

"That's right," a woman's voice said. "I'm satisfied from the picture in the paper that he's the one who rented this apartment, under the name of Frank Ormsby Newberg."

"Well," Sergeant Holcomb said, "an identification from a picture is a tricky thing. We'll see if there's anybody home."

The buzzer sounded.

Paul Drake looked desperately around him. "There must be a back way out somewhere," he whispered.

"We haven't time to find it," Mason whispered in reply. "They have a passkey. Della, do you have a notebook?"

She nodded.

"Get it out," Mason said.

The buzzer sounded again.

Mason said, "Start writing, Della, anything."

Della Street started writing shorthand in the small notebook which she took from her purse.

Knuckles pounded on the door, then Sergeant Holcomb said, "All right, we'll try the passkey."

Mason turned the knob, swung the door open and said, "Well, well. Good evening, Sergeant Holcomb. This *is* a surprise!"

Holcomb's face registered dismayed incredulity.

"What the devil?" he exclaimed as soon as he could find his voice.

Mason said smoothly, "I'm taking inventory."

"*You* are? What the devil right have *you* got to be *here* and what are you taking an inventory of?"

"The assets of the estate, of course," Mason said.

Holcomb stood, groping for words that refused to come.

Mason said, "My client, Eleanor Hepner, is the widow of Douglas Hepner. We are, of course, at the moment engaged in a murder trial but that doesn't affect the estate. As soon as she's acquitted she'll be entitled to inherit all of the property as the surviving widow. In the meantime she's entitled to letters of administration and naturally, as her attorney, I'm taking an inventory."

Mason turned to Della Street and said, "Five dress shirts. One, two, three, four, five, six, seven athletic shorts. One, two, three, four..."

"Hey, wait a minute," Sergeant Holcomb bellowed. "What is this? Are you trying to tell me that Frank Ormsby Newberg is an alias of Douglas Hepner?"

"But of course," Mason said. "Didn't you know that?"

"How the devil would we have known it?" Sergeant Holcomb asked. "If it hadn't been for this woman calling the police and insisting that she recognized Douglas Hepner's picture in the paper as that of the tenant of one of her apartments who hadn't shown up for a while, we'd never had got a lead on this apartment."

"Well, well," Mason said indulgently. "Why didn't you simply ask me?"

"Ask *you!*" Holcomb exclaimed.

"Why, certainly," Mason said.

"How did you get in here?" Holcomb demanded.

"With the key," Mason said.

"What key?"

Mason's voice had the quiet patience of an indulgent parent trying to explain a very simple problem to a very dull child. "I have told you, Sergeant, that my client, Eleanor Hepner, or Eleanor Corbin as she is mentioned in the indictment, is the surviving widow of Douglas Hepner. Quite naturally she'd have the key to the apartment where she spent her honeymoon, wouldn't she?"

The woman who was evidently the manager of the apartment house said, "Well, he never told me anything about being married."

Mason smiled at her. "I understand. Rather mysterious, wasn't he?"

"He certainly was," she said. "He'd come here and keep the most irregular hours, then he'd disapppear and you wouldn't see him for a while. Then he'd be back and...it drove us crazy trying to get in a weekly cleaning of the apartment."

"Yes, I can well understand," Mason said. "Eleanor told me that...however, I think perhaps under the circumstances I'd better wait until she tells her story on the witness stand."

Sergeant Holcomb, completely nonplused, said, "Perhaps you can tell me what this is all about. How did it happen this apartment is wrecked like this? You didn't pull all this stuff out taking inventory."

"Evidently," Mason said, "someone has been in here, someone who was searching for something. As soon as we had completed our inventory I was going to suggest that the police had better try taking some fingerprints. As you'll perhaps notice, Sergeant, we're not touching anything but are simply standing here in the middle of the floor making an inventory of the things that are readily visible. Now, Della, there are some men's suits in the closet. Try not to leave any fingerprints on the door. Open the door with your foot. That's right. Three business suits, one tuxedo, five pairs of shoes, and...yes, that's a suitcase in the back of the closet there, and..."

"Hey, wait a minute," Holcomb said. "All this stuff is evidence."

"Evidence of what?" Mason asked.

"I don't know, but it's sure evidence. Someone has been in here."

"Elemental, my dear Sergeant," Mason said.

"Dammit, I can get along without any of your humor, Mason. You're willing to admit that Frank Ormsby Newberg was Douglas Hepner?"

"But, of course," Mason said as though this were one of the most obvious facts in the entire case.

"Well, we've been trying to find out where he lived. We were satisfied there was some sort of a hideout like this."

"You could have simplified matters a lot if you'd asked me," Mason said.

"You evidently just got here yourself," Holcomb said.

"That's right. I've been busy, Sergeant."

"Well, we want to investigate this. I'm getting in touch with Headquarters. We're going to have some fingerprint men down here. We're going to go through this thing with a fine-toothed comb looking for evidence. We don't want *anybody* in here messing things up."

Mason hesitated for a moment. "Well," he said at last, "I don't think there's any objection on the part of the widow to that, Sergeant, except that I want you to take great precautions to see that the personal property is conserved. There is, of course, as you know, a mother involved in the case and it may be the mother will make accusations against the widow and..."

"If you know where the mother is," Holcomb said, "you can tell us. *We* can't find her."

"Neither could we," Mason said. "She seems to have disappeared. Now wouldn't you consider that as a suspicious circumstance, Sergeant?"

Sergeant Holcomb, gradually recovering his poise, said, "We don't need any wisecracks from you, Mason. Do you know where the mother is?"

"No."

"You have the key to this apartment?"

"That's right."

"I want it."

Mason shook his head. "No. The manager can let you in with the passkey. The key that I have I want to return to...well, you can understand my position, Sergeant."

"I'm not sure that I can," Holcomb said. "There's something fishy as hell about this whole business."

"There certainly is," Mason agreed good-naturedly. "Someone has been in here searching for something. I had assumed it was the police until you told me that this whole thing came as a surprise to you. Of course, Sergeant, I'm willing to take your word. I won't question *your* statement for a minute, although there are times when you seem to be a little reluctant to return the courtesy."

Sergeant Holcomb turned to Della Street. "How long have you folks been here?"

Mason said patiently, "For a little while. I've been busy in court and I've been busy with the preparation for trial. I haven't had an opportunity to look into the civil aspects of the case because of the criminal charge that has been pending against my client. I do, however, expect to file an application for letters of administration and..."

"Now listen," Holcomb interrupted. "You don't need to go over that again. I asked a question of your secretary."

"I'm trying to give you the information you wanted," Mason said.

"Oh hell, what's the use!" Holcomb exclaimed disgustedly. "Get out of here. I'm telephoning Headquarters for some fingerprint men. Now get the hell out of here and don't come back until I tell you you can."

"That's a rather highhanded attitude," Mason said, "in view of the fact that..."

"Come on. Out!" Holcomb said. "Just get the hell out of here."

He turned to the manager of the apartment house, a rather fleshy woman, in the late forties, who was standing in the doorwy with eyes and ears that missed nothing. "We're going to seal up this apartment," he said. "We're going to see that no unauthorized person enters it. Now if you'll just step out in the corridor we'll get these three people out of here, then I'll be the last to leave the apartment. You can give me the duplicate key and I'll telephone Headquarters."

The woman stepped out into the corridor.

"Go on," Holcomb said to Mason. "Out."

Paul Drake moved out into the corridor with alacrity. Della Street followed, and Mason brought up the rear, saying, "You can make a note, Della, that the taking of inventory was interrupted by the arrival of the police who wished to investigate an apparent burglary. Make a note of the date and the exact time. And now," Mason said urbanely to Sergeant Holcomb, "we'll hold the police responsible. I take it that you'll notify me when you've finished with your investigation so we can continue with our inventory. Good night, Sergeant." And Mason, nodding to Della Street, led the way down the corridor to the elevator.

As they entered the cage and closed the door, Drake leaned back, supporting himself in a corner of the elevator, and, taking a handkerchief from his pocket, made elaborate motions of wiping his brow.

"You can do the damnedest things, Perry," he said.

Della Street, voice apprehensive, said, "*Now* how are you going to explain the fact that Eleanor, who has previously told the police she can't remember a thing about where she spent the time or what happened after she started on her honeymoon, has disclosed to you the apartment where Douglas Hepner lived and given you a key to that apartment?"

Mason said, "I'll cross that bridge when I come to it."

"The hell of it is," Drake groaned, "there isn't any bridge. There's only a chasm, and when you come to it you're going to have to jump."

CHAPTER THIRTEEN

As court convened the next morning an unusual situation was commented on by courtroom attachés.

Usually a trial in which Perry Mason appeared would fill every seat in the courtroom. Now there was but a sprinkling of spectators, a sinister indication of the fact that in the mind of the public the case against Eleanor Hepner was so dead open-and-shut that the contest was too one-sided to be dramatic and that even the ingenuity of Perry Mason couldn't keep the case from being a run-of-the-mill conviction.

Hamilton Burger, the district attorney, noticed the vacant rows of seats with annoyance. Cases where he had met humiliating defeat at the hands of Perry Mason had made newspaper headlines and had resulted in packed courtrooms. Now that he was in a position to win a case hands down it appeared he would have but a small audience.

Hamilton Burger said, "Your Honor, I now wish to call Ethel Belan to the stand."

"Very well," Judge Moran said. "Come forward and be sworn, Miss Belan."

Ethel Belan, carefully groomed for her appearance on the stand, her manner radiating self-confidence and an eager desire to match wits with Perry Mason, held up her hand, was sworn, took the witness stand, answered the usual preliminary questions as to occupation and residence, then glanced expectantly at Hamilton Burger.

Burger, with the manner of a magician about to perform a trick which will leave the audience speechless, said, "You live in apartment 360 at the Belinda Apartments, Miss Belan?"

"That is right. Yes, sir."

"Who has the adjoining apartment on the south?"

"Miss Suzanne Granger has apartment 358."

"You are acquainted with Miss Granger?"

"Oh, yes."

"How long has she lived in that apartment?"

"Some two years, to my knowledge."

"And how long have you lived there in apartment 360?"

"Just a little over two years."

"Are you acquainted with the defendant, Eleanor Corbin?"

"I am. Yes, sir."

"When did you first meet her?"

"On the ninth of August."

"Of this year?"

"Yes."

"And how did you happen to meet the defendant?"

"She came to see me. She said she had a proposition to make to me."

"And did she make such a proposition?"

"Yes."

"This was in writing or in a conversation?"

"In a conversation."

"Where did that conversation take place?"

"In my apartment."

"And who was present at that conversation?"

"Just the defendant and me."

"And what did the defendant say at that time, as nearly as you can give us her exact words?"

"The defendant told me that she was interested in Suzanne Granger in the adjoining apartment."

"Did she say why?"

"She said Miss Granger had stolen her boy friend."

"Did she use the word husband or the expression boy friend?"

"She said boy friend."

"Did she give you the name of the boy friend?"

"Yes, sir."

"What was that name?"

"Douglas Hepner."

"And what was the proposition the defendant made to you?"

"She wanted to come and live with me in my apartment. She wanted to see whether Douglas Hepner was actually calling on Suzanne Granger. She said that Douglas Hepner had told her it was purely a business relationship, that she felt certain he was two-timing her with Suzanne Granger, that she wanted to find out. She offered to pay me two hundred dollars as a bonus and a rental of eight-five dollars a week for two weeks."

"And what did you do in relation to this proposition that she made?"

"Naturally I jumped at the chance. The apartment had been rather expensive, my roommate had left and I was a little lonely. I had a roommate for some eighteen months, then she left and I have been carrying the apartment alone because I wanted to find someone who was completely congenial. That hadn't been as easy as I had hoped. This offer was one I could hardly afford to reject."

"So the defendant moved in with you?"

"That is right."

"Now I have here a sketch map of the arrangement of your apartment and the arrangement of the adjoining apartment, that of Suzanne Granger. I am going to ask you if this correctly shows your apartment?"

"It shows the arrangement of my apartment, but I have never been in Miss Granger's apartment."

"That's right. I am going to identify it as Miss Granger's apartment by another witness. I am asking you only to tell us whether this correctly shows the arrangement of your apartment."

"It does. Yes, sir."

"It represents a correct delineation of the general plan of your apartment?"

"Yes, sir."

"Now did the defendant designate any particular place where she was to stay in the apartment?"

"She did indeed. My bedroom was the one with the larger closet. It was next to the bedroom occupied by Miss Granger in 358. The defendant insisted that I should move my bedroom to the other one with the smaller closet so she could move in this bedroom which was next to the Granger apartment."

"Now then," Hamilton Burger said, rising from his chair with ponderous grace, and with something of a verbal flourish in his voice, "I show you People's Exhibit G, a .38 caliber Smith & Wesson revolver, number C-48809, and ask you if you have ever seen that gun before?"

"Just a moment, Your Honor," Mason said. "That question is objected to as leading and suggestive."

"It can be answered yes or no," Hamilton Burger said.

"Certainly it can," Mason said, "but you have indicated the answer that you desire. If you want to ask this witness about *any* gun, go ahead and ask the witness, but don't shove the weapon in her face, don't designate it, don't describe it by number. If she saw a .38 caliber revolver, let her testify to that fact."

"Oh, it's so obvious, Your Honor," Hamilton Burger said. "This objection is merely for the purpose of..."

"Technically the objection is well taken," Judge Moran said.

"Very well," Hamilton Burger said, tossing the revolver back on the clerk's desk with a gesture of disgust. "Did the defendant have any weapon in her possession?"

"Yes, sir."

"What?"

"A .38 caliber revolver."

"Can you describe that revolver?"

"It had a short barrel. It was blued steel. It looked just like that revolver you picked up just now."

Burger turned and let the jury see his triumphant grin as he looked at Perry Mason.

"Did she show you that revolver?"

"I saw it in her overnight bag."

"I am coming to that," Hamilton Burger said. "What luggage did the defendant have with her when she moved in?"

"She had an overnight bag, a suitcase and a two-suiter. They were all very distinctive, a red and white checkerboard pattern."

"And what became of this luggage?"

"She telephoned me about it."

"Who did?"

"The defendant."

"You talked with her on the phone?"

"Yes, sir."

"Did you recognize her voice?"

"Yes, sir."

"Did you call her by name?"

"Yes, sir."

"Did she call you by name?"

"Yes, sir."

"What was the date of this conversation?"

"The Seventeenth of August."

"And what did she say?"

"She said, 'Ethel, you're going to have to stand back of me. I'm pretending I have amnesia. Don't say anything to anyone about my staying with you. Don't communicate with the police or newspaper reporters. Just sit tight. I'll send for my luggage when I think it's safe to do so.'"

"You're certain about that conversation?" Hamilton Burger asked.

"Why, of course. Yes, sir."

"And the defendant said she was feigning amnesia?"

"Yes, sir."

"And this was on the seventeenth?"

"Yes, sir."

"At what time?"

"About eight-thirty in the morning."

"Now then," Hamilton Burger said, his manner showing that this was the dramatic highlight of the entire case, "did you ask the defendant why the necessity for all this secrecy, why she was feigning amnesia?"

"Yes, sir."

"And did the defendant answer you?"

"Yes, sir."

"Did the defendant make any explanation, give any reason that would account for her conduct?"

"Yes, sir."

"And what was that reason?"

"The defendant said, and I can give you her exact words because they seared themselves into my memory, she said, 'Ethel, I'm in a scrape, and I've got to protect myself.' "

Hamilton Burger stood facing the jury, his hands slightly outspread, prolonging the dramatic effect of that moment by a significant silence.

Judge Moran, finally realizing the tactics of the district attorney, his voice showing irritation, said, "Well, proceed with your questioning, Mr. District Attorney, unless you have finished with the witness, and if you have, kindly advise counsel for the defense so he may cross-examine."

"No, Your Honor," Hamilton Burger said, still facing the jury, "I am by no means finished with this witness. I was merely collecting my thoughts as to further questions."

"Well, get them collected and proceed," Judge Moran said testily.

"Yes, Your Honor."

Hamilton Burger turned to the witness. "At the time she told you this, the body of Douglas Hepner had not been discovered. Is that right?"

"Objected to as calling for a conclusion of the witness, as argumentative, as leading and suggestive," Mason said.

"Sustained," Judge Moran snapped.

Burger tried another tack. "Now what did you do with the luggage belonging to the defendant and which you said you had in your possession?"

"That was given to her attorney."

"By her attorney you mean Perry Mason, the lawyer seated here at the defendant's counsel table?"

"Yes, sir."

"And when did you give that baggage to him?"

"On the seventeenth day of August. In the afternoon."

"And how did you happen to give it to him?"

"Well, he came to see me. He was accompanied by his secretary, Della Street. He knew that the defendant had been staying with me and from what he said I gathered that ... well, he wanted the luggage and I let him have it."

"And that luggage which you gave Perry Mason was the same which the defendant had left with you?"

"It was."

Hamilton Burger said, "I now hand you an overnight bag bearing the initials E.C. and ask you if you have ever seen that bag before?"

"Yes, sir."

"Where did you see it before?"

"In my apartment."

"When?"

"When Eleanor brought it to my apartment and again when I gave it to Perry Mason."

"Do you wish the Court and the jury to understand that this is one of the articles of baggage that you gave Mr. Perry Mason?"

"It is. Yes, sir."

"And it is the same bag that the defendant brought to your apartment?"

"Yes, sir."

"I show you a suitcase. Do you recognize it?"

"Yes, sir, that is the suitcase she brought with her to the apartment and one of the articles I gave Mr. Mason."

"And this two-suiter?"

"The same."

"I ask they be introduced in evidence, Your Honor."

"Any objection?" Judge Moran asked of Mason.

"Not to the bags, Your Honor. The contents have not been identified."

"The bags are now empty," Burger said with a smile. "I anticipated this objection by the defense."

"Then I have no objection to the bags being received in evidence," Mason said. "I feel certain they are the same bags the witness gave me."

Burger whirled suddenly to Perry Mason and said, "And now you may cross-examine, sir."

The district attorney walked over to the plaintiff's counsel table and flung himself into his seat, grinning at the smiling faces of two assistant district attorneys who flanked him on each side.

"Did you," Mason asked the district attorney, "intend to introduce that diagram in evidence?"

"I did."

"You mentioned that there was another witness who would identify it as to the Granger apartment."

"That is true."

"If you have that witness here," Mason said, "I would suggest that I defer my cross-examination of this witness until you have put this other witness on the stand, identified this diagram, and then I will be in a position to cross-examine the witness intelligently as to the position of the various rooms in the apartment."

"Very well," Hamilton Burger said. "Call Webley Richey. You may step down from the witness stand for a moment, Miss Belan. The testimony of Mr. Richey will be quite brief, and then you may resume the witness stand for cross-examination."

"Yes, sir," the witness said.

"Sit right here inside the rail," Judge Moran instructed. "Mr. Mason will want to proceed with his cross-examination as soon as Mr. Richey has been asked a few questions, which I take it, Mr. District Attorney, are in the nature of routine."

"That is right."

"Come forward and be sworn, Mr. Richey," Judge Moran said.

Mason, turning to look at the witness who was coming forward, said under his breath to Della Street, who was seated slightly behind him and to the right of the defendant, "Well, well, well, see who's here. The supercilious clerk who high-hatted us."

Richey came forward, was sworn, and gave his name, age, address and occupation to the court reporter, then looked up expectantly at the district attorney.

Hamilton Burger, his voice indicating to the jury that this was merely a matter of red tape brought about because of the annoying persistence of the defendant's counsel, said, "Now as I understand it your name is Webley Richey and you are employed as a clerk at the Belinda Apartments."

"Yes, sir."

"How long have you been so employed?"

"Something over two years."

"Are you familiar with the apartments on the third floor?"

"I am. Yes, sir."

"Do you know the tenant of apartment 358, Miss Suzanne Granger?"

"I do. Yes, sir."

"And Ethel Belan, the witness who has just testified?"

"Yes, sir."

"Are you familiar with the floor plan of the various apartments occupied by Suzanne Granger and by Ethel Belan?"

"I am. Yes, sir."

"I show you a diagram and ask you whether or not that diagram correctly designates the position of the various rooms in apartment 358 and in apartment 360?"

The witness glanced at the diagram and said, "It does. Yes, sir. The two apartments are identical except that the closet in one of the bedrooms in 360 is three and a half feet shorter than the other closets shown on this sketch map, otherwise the apartments are identical in plan."

"This map is a floor plan. Is it made to scale?"

"It is. Yes, sir."

"Who made it?"

"I did."

"At whose request?"

"At yours, sir."

"And it is a full, true and accurate descriptive diagram?"

"It is. Yes, sir."

"I ask that it be introduced in evidence," Hamilton Burger said. "That's all."

"Oh, just a moment," Mason said. "I have a few questions on cross-examination."

"But there can't be any objection to the diagram," Hamilton Burger said.

"I just want to find out a few things about the witness's background," Mason retorted.

"Very well, cross-examine," Judge Moran said, his voice indicating that he would consider any lengthy cross-examination an imposition on the time of the Court and the jury.

Richey faced Mason with the same supercilious, somewhat patronizing manner which he had displayed when he was behind the desk at the Belinda Apartments.

"Do you remember when you first saw me in August of this year?" Mason asked.

"Yes, sir. Very well."

"I asked for Miss Suzanne Granger, did I not?"

"Yes, sir."

"And you told me that she was out and could not be reached?"

"That is correct."

"I told you who I was and I told you I wanted to leave a message for her?"

"Yes, sir."

"Oh, just a moment, Your Honor," Hamilton Burger said. "This is hardly proper cross-examination. This witness was produced only for the purpose of testifying to a floor plan of an apartment. That floor plan is quite obviously correct. Counsel has made no objection to it. This cross-examination is incompetent, irrelevant and immaterial. It calls for matters not covered on the direct examination, and it is entirely out of order. It is simply consuming time."

"So it would seem," Judge Moran said. "I am inclined to agree with the prosecution, Mr. Mason."

"The object of this cross-examination," Mason said, "is simply to show bias on the part of the witness."

"But what good will that do since apparently there is no question as to the accuracy of the..."

Judge Moran caught himself just in time to keep from commenting on the evidence. He said somewhat testily, "Very well. Technically I believe you're within your rights, Counselor. Proceed. The objection is overruled."

"Let me ask this one question," Mason said. "As soon as I asked for Suzanne Granger didn't you step into a private, glass-enclosed office, pick up a telephone and ring the apartment of Ethel Belan?"

Mason was unprepared for the expression of consternation which appeared on Richey's face.

"I...I have occasion to call many of the apartments."

Mason, suddenly realizing he had struck pay dirt, pressed on quickly. "I'm asking you did you or did you not at that particular time retire to your private office and call the apartment of Ethel Belan?"

"I...after all, Mr. Mason, I can't be expected to remember every apartment that I call. I..."

"I am asking you," Mason thundered, "whether or not at that particular time you did not retire to a glass-enclosed, private office and call the apartment of Ethel Belan? You can answer that question yes or no."

"Provided, of course, he remembers the occasion and what he did on that occasion," Hamilton Burger said, rushing to the witness's rescue.

"I can't remember," Richey said, flashing a grateful glance at the district attorney.

Mason smiled. "You might have remembered," he asked the witness, "if it hadn't been for the prompting by the district attorney?"

"Your Honor," Hamilton Burger protested, "I object to that question. It's not proper cross-examination."

"Well, I think the witness may answer it," Judge Moran said. "The jury, of course, saw the demeanor of the witness, heard the question and answer. You may answer that question, Mr. Richey."

"I...I can't remember calling Ethel Belan's apartment."

"You can't remember ever calling Ethel Belan's apartment?" Mason asked.

"Oh, yes. Naturally I call many of the apartments. I guess I have called many of the apartments many times."

"Then what do you mean by saying you can't remember?"

"I can't remember calling it on that particular occasion."

"Do you remember stepping into the glass-enclosed office?"

"No."

"Do you remember your conversation with me?"

"Yes."

"Do you remember what you did immediately following that conversation?"

"No."

"I will ask you," Mason said, "if at any time on that day you talked with Ethel Belan on the telephone and told her that Mr. Perry Mason, an attorney, was in the building and that he was asking for Suzanne Granger? Now you can remember if you did that. Answer yes or no. Did you or didn't you?"

"I...I don't think I did."

"Or did you use words having substantially that same meaning or effect?"

"I...I...I simply can't remember, Mr. Mason."

"Thank you," Mason said. "That's all. I will stipulate the diagram may be received in evidence. Now, as I understand it, Miss Belan is to take the stand for cross-examination."

Richey left the stand. Ethel Belan returned to the stand, settled herself and glanced at Perry Mason as much as to say, "All right. Come on. See what you can do with *me*."

"You're absolutely certain that the defendant had a revolver while she was in your apartment?"

"Absolutely certain."

"That it was a blued-steel revolver?"

"Yes."

"That it was a .38 caliber revolver?"

"Yes."

"In how many calibers are revolvers manufactured?" Mason asked.

"Why, I...I'm not an expert on guns. I don't know."

"What is the meaning of .38 caliber?" Mason asked. "What does it have reference to?"

"It's the way they describe a gun."

"Certainly it's the way they describe a gun," Mason said, "but what does it relate to? What does caliber mean?"

"It has something to do with the weight of the shells, doesn't it?"

"With the weight of the bullet?"

"Yes."

"In other words, a long, slender bullet would have a higher caliber than a short, thicker bullet if it weighed more?"

"Oh, Your Honor," Hamilton Burger said, "I object to this as an attempt to mislead the witness. This is not proper cross-examination. The witness has not qualified as an expert, and..."

"The objection is overruled," Judge Moran snapped. "This witness has described the revolver in the possession of the defendant as a .38 caliber revolver. Counsel is certainly entitled to find out what she means by .38 caliber."

"Go ahead," Mason said. "Answer the question."

"Why, if the bullet, if the long, slender bullet weighs more, why, it is a bigger caliber, that is, I think it is."

"That's what you mean by caliber?" Mason said.

"Yes, sir."

"So when you described the .38 caliber revolver, you referred to a revolver shooting a bullet of a certain weight. Is that right?"

"Oh, Your Honor, this is certainly assuming facts not in evidence," Hamilton Burger said. "It is not proper cross-examination. It is an attempt to mislead the witness."

"Overruled," Judge Moran snapped. "Answer the question."

The witness glanced dubiously at the district attorney, then after some hesitancy, said, "Yes, sir. I believe so. Yes, sir."

"When you used the words .38 caliber you were describing only the weight of the bullet?"

"Yes, sir."

"Did you mean that the bullet weighed 38 grains?"

"I believe that is it. Yes, sir."

"You don't know whether the gun was a .38 caliber, a .32 caliber, or a .44 caliber, do you?"

"Well, it was described to me as a .38 caliber revolver," the witness said, obviously becoming confused.

"So you simply repeated the words that had been used to you. Is that right?"

"Yes, sir."

"And when you said it was a .38 caliber revolver you didn't know whether it was a .38 caliber revolver or a .32 caliber revolver or a .44 caliber revolver, did you?"

"Well, the district attorney told me..."

"Not what someone told you but what you know of your own knowledge," Mason said. "Do you know?"

"Well, I guess, if you want to come right down to it, I'm a little hazy about what caliber means."

"Then you don't know whether the defendant had a .38 caliber revolver, a .32 caliber revolver or a .44 caliber revolver, do you?"

"Well, if you want to put it that way, I don't," the witness snapped.

Mason said, "That's the way I want to put it. And now we'll see if your recollection is any better than that of Webley Richey. Do you remember the occasion when Mr. Richey telephoned you and said that Perry Mason, the lawyer, was in the building, asking questions, that he was inquiring for Suzanne Granger but that there was a possibility he might be very suspicious of the facts, but that he, Richey, had got rid of Mason and you wouldn't be bothered with him? Now those may not be the exact words, but I will express it as having been in words to that effect purely for the purpose of identifying the conversation. Do you remember the occasion of that conversation?"

She tilted her head back. Her chin came up. For a moment her eyes were defiant. Then, as she met the steady gaze of Mason's eyes, saw the granite-hard lines of his face, she wavered, lowered her eyes and said, "Yes, I remember it."

"Do you remember the date and the hour?"

"It was on the seventeenth day of August, sometime in the afternoon. I don't remember exactly what time."

"But you can place the time with reference to the time when I called on you," Mason said. "It was immediately before, wasn't it?"

"That depends on what you mean by immediately."

"If you want to quibble," Mason said, "we'll say that it was within approximately ten or fifteen minutes of the time I called on you."

"Well...oh, all right, have it your own way."

"It isn't my way, or your way, or Richey's way," Mason said. "It's a question of what is the truth. That's what the judge and the jury want to know."

"Well, he called me and said something along those lines. Yes."

"What is the connection between you and Richey?" Mason asked.

"Your Honor, I object to that as incompetent, irrelevant and immaterial, not proper cross-examination."

Judge Moran hesitated for a moment, then said, "The objection is sustained."

Mason, looking surprised and hurt so that the jury would be sure to note the expression on his face, sat down and turned to Della Street.

"I want to quit this cross-examination at a point where the jurors feel that my hands are being tied by Hamilton Burger's objections and the Court's rulings. I want them to feel that there is something important in this case that is being withheld from them, some sinister something in the background. I think this is a good time to quit. I'm whispering to you now so they'll think I'm conferring with you on a point where we have a lot at stake."

Della Street nodded.

"Now shake your head gravely," Mason said.

She did as he instructed.

Mason sighed, made a little gesture of weary dismissal with his hands, said, "Well, of course, Your Honor, this is a part of the case which the defendant considered vital."

He glanced down at Della Street again, shrugged his shoulders, said, "Very well, if that is the ruling of the Court I have no further questions."

"The Court doesn't intend to close any doors," Judge Moran said, suddenly suspicious that Mason had jockeyed him into a position where there was error in the record. "You are at liberty to reframe the question."

"Did you tell Webley Richey all about your agreement with the defendant?" Mason asked.

"Objected to as calling for hearsay evidence, as not proper cross-examination, as calling for matter which is incompetent, irrelevant and immaterial," Burger said.

"I will permit the question on the ground that it may be preliminary as to the bias of the witness," Judge Moran ruled.

"Answer the question," Mason said.

"Well, in a way, yes."

"And did he advise you?"

"Same objection," Burger snapped.

Judge Moran's fingertips moved slowly along the angle of his jaw. "What a third person may have told this witness is something else. You may answer the question yes or no—only as to whether he did advise you."

"Yes."

"What did he tell you?"

"Objected to, Your Honor. This is plainly hearsay, incompetent..."

"I think so. The objection is sustained," Judge Moran said.

"Did you ask for and receive his advice prior to the date when the defendant was first taken into custody?"

Burger said doggedly, "I object on the ground that it is incompetent, irrelevant and immaterial, that the question is vague and indefinite and it is not proper cross-examination."

Judge Moran debated the matter in his own mind. "Can you reframe your question, Mr. Mason?"

"No, Your Honor."

Judge Moran glanced somewhat dubiously at the district attorney.

"I feel that my objection is well taken, Your Honor," Hamilton Burger said.

"I think it is quite obvious that counsel is merely on a fishing expedition. If there is any agreement in connection with the testimony in this case, any agreement in connection with the facts in this case, he can so specify."

"My question is broad enough to include all of those things," Mason said.

"Too broad," Hamilton Burger retorted. "It covers everything. I contend, Your Honor, that the question is not proper cross-examination. I am quite willing to accept a ruling to that effect for the record."

"Very well," Judge Moran ruled. "The Court will sustain the objection."

"That's all," Mason said.

"That's all," Hamilton Burger snapped.

The witness started to leave the stand, then Burger, with every appearance of sudden recollection, said, "Oh, no, it isn't either. There's one other matter. I should have brought this out on my direct examination. I beg the pardon of Court and counsel. I overlooked the matter. One of my assistants has just called my attention to the oversight."

"Very well, you may ask your question," Judge Moran ruled.

Hamilton Burger faced the witness. "Did you at any time see the defendant in the possession of any articles other than this revolver—articles of some extraordinary value?"

"Yes."

"What?"

"She had a large number of precious stones."

Hamilton Burger appeared excited. "Precious stones, did you say?"

"That's right."

The jurors were now sitting forward on their chairs, watching the witness with fascination.

"Where were you when you saw these?" Burger asked.

"I had started to go into her bedroom. The door was slightly ajar. The hinges had been well oiled. She didn't hear me."

"And what was she doing?"

"She had a pile of gem stones on some paper tissues on the bed. She was kneeling by the bed. Her back was to me. She was counting the gems."

"How many gems?"

"Quite a number."

"Did she know you had seen her?"

"No, sir. I backed out as soon as I realized I was intruding. I gently closed the door and she never realized..."

"Never mind what she did or didn't realize," Burger interrupted. "You're not a mind reader. You saw those stones?"

"Yes, sir."

"You don't know what became of those gems?"

"No, sir."

"But you did see them in the defendant's possession?"

"Yes, sir."

"And for all you know these stones could have been contained in the luggage you delivered to Perry Mason?"

"Objected to as argumentative, assuming a fact not in evidence, leading and suggestive and utterly incompetent, irrelevant and immaterial," Mason said.

"Sustained."

"Cross-examine," Hamilton Burger snapped.

Mason hesitated a long moment, said to Della Street, "There's a trap here,

Della, but I'm going to have to face it. He's making it appear I am afraid to have the facts brought out about those gems, that *I'm* keeping things from the jury. Well, here we go."

Mason slowly rose from his seat at the counsel table, walked over to the corner of the table and stood looking at the witness.

"You stood in the door of the room?" he asked.

"Yes."

"And saw these gems on the bed?"

"Yes."

"A distance of how many feet?"

"Perhaps ten feet."

"You saw they were gems?"

"Yes, sir."

"What kind?"

"Diamonds and emeralds and a few rubies."

"How many real gems have you ever owned in your life?" Mason asked.

"I...well, I have some chip diamonds."

"Were these chip diamonds?"

"No."

"How many full-cut diamonds have you ever owned?"

The witness averted her eyes.

"How many?" Mason asked.

"None," she confessed.

"How many genuine rubies have you ever owned?"

"One. That is, it was given to me. I...I supposed it was genuine."

"How long did you have it in your possession?"

"I still have it."

"When was it given to you?"

"Ten years ago."

"Is it genuine?"

"I have assumed that it is. I tell you, Mr. Mason, that it was given to me and so I don't know. I have assumed it is a genuine ruby."

"How about these rubies on the bed," Mason asked, "were they genuine rubies, costume jewelry or imitations?"

"They were rubies."

"Genuine?"

"Yes, sir. At least that is my impression. I am testifying now to the best of my ability."

"Exactly," Mason said. "And you have gone over your testimony many times with the district attorney?"

"I have told him what happened. I haven't gone over my testimony."

"You have told him what you expected to testify to?"

"Well, in a way."

"You have told him *everything* that happened, haven't you?"

"Yes."

"And you have told him that those were genuine rubies?"

"Yes."

"You were within ten feet of them?"

"Yes."

"No closer than that?"

"No, I suppose not."

"How long were you standing in the door?"

"Perhaps for ten seconds."

"Now this ruby that you own. How is that mounted? Is it in a ring?"

"Yes."

"The ruby is perhaps your birthstone?"

"Yes."

"And there is a certain sentimental attachment in connection with that particular ruby?"

"Yes."

"And you have worn it and looked at it many times?"

"Yes."

"Within a matter of inches from your eyes?"

"Yes."

"And yet," Mason said, "you still don't know whether *that* ruby is genuine. Yet you want this jury to believe that you could stand ten feet away and look at an assortment of gems for not more than ten seconds and unhesitatingly testify that each and every one of the gems was genuine. Is that right?"

"Well, I...of course, when you put it that way it sounds absurd."

"It sounds absurd because it is absurd," Mason said. "You aren't an expert on gems."

"No, but you can tell whether gems are genuine or not."

"How?"

"Well, you know instinctively. You can tell from the way they sparkle."

"But you didn't know instinctively about this ruby that you've possessed for ten years. You simply assume it's genuine. You don't know whether it's a synthetic ruby or an imitation ruby or what it is."

"Well, I...it was different from the rubies that I saw there."

"In what way?"

"Those rubies had more fire."

"Then you assume that this gem you have been familiar with for ten years is not genuine, that it is an imitation of some sort, a synthetic?"

"I don't know."

"How many gems were there on the bed?"

"I would say, oh, perhaps fifty."

"There could have been more?"

"There certainly could. There might have been as many as seventy-five."

"If you had seventy-five gems to inspect in ten seconds you must have inspected them at the rate of better than seven a second. Isn't that true?"

"I suppose so."

"You know, do you not, that it takes an expert jeweler many seconds of examination with a magnifying glass to tell whether a gem is genuine or not?"

"Well, I suppose so."

"Yet you, without any knowledge of gems, without ever having possessed genuine gems, with the exception of one ruby that you don't know is genuine, want to put yourself in the position of swearing absolutely that you looked at from fifty to seventy-five stones ten feet away in a period of ten seconds, and are willing to pronounce each and every one of them genuine?"

"I didn't say that. I can't pronounce each and every one of them genuine."

"How many of them were spurious?"

"I don't know."

"What percentage of them was spurious?"

"I don't know."

"How many of them were genuine?"

"I don't know."

"Was one of them genuine?"

"Yes, of course."

"Were two of them genuine?"

"I tell you I don't know."

"Exactly," Mason said. "You don't know whether any of them was genuine or not, do you?"

"I think they were."

"You knew instinctively, is that right?"

"Yes."

"You simply saw them as a glittering pile of gems?"

"Yes."

"That's all," Mason said, smiling at the jury.

Hamilton Burger came forward, a triumphant smirk on his face.

"Now assuming for the sake of this question that Douglas Hepner was killed on the sixteenth of August at about five o'clock in the afternoon, did you see these gems before or after his death?"

"Objected to as incompetent, irrelevant and immaterial, argumentative evidence," Mason said angrily. "I assign the asking of that question as prejudicial misconduct and ask the Court to advise the jury to disregard it."

Judge Moran's face was stern. "The objection is sustained. The jury will disregard the question."

"Very well," Hamilton Burger said. "*When* did you see these gems?"

"On the sixteenth of August."

"At what time?"

"At about six o'clock in the evening."

"That's all."

"No further questions," Mason said.

"That's all," Hamilton Burger said. "We will now call Miss Suzanne Granger to the stand."

Suzanne Granger came forward and was sworn.

"You are the Suzanne Granger who occupies apartment 358 in the Belinda Apartments?"

"Yes, sir."

"Is that Mrs. or Miss Granger?"

"Miss."

"You are living alone in an apartment there?"

"Yes."

"You have been to Europe on several occasions?"

"I am interested in art. I spend what time and what money I can afford in European museums studying pigmentation, the work of the old masters, and gathering data which I do not care to reveal in advance of the book I am writing on the subject."

"You recently returned from Europe?"

"I did."

"And while you were on shipboard did you meet Douglas Hepner?"

"That is right."

"Now you became friendly with Douglas Hepner?"

"There was a shipboard friendship, yes."

"And then what happened?"

"Then I didn't see Douglas for...oh, a few weeks and then I happened to run into him and he asked me for a date and..."

"Now when was this that he asked you for a date?"

"That was during the latter part of July."

"And then what?"

"I went out to dinner with him two or three times and he told me..."

"Now I don't think we're entitled to have his conversation introduced in evidence," Hamilton Burger said with a great show of legal virtue, "but I think you can testify as to the relationship which developed."

"Well, he became friendly to the extent of confiding in me."

"You were out with him several times?"

"That's right."

"And at times he returned with you to your apartment?"

"Naturally he saw me home."

"And came into your apartment for a nightcap?"

"That's right. I invited him in as a matter of common courtesy and he always accepted."

"Now then," Hamilton Burger said, "we are somewhat handicapped by not being able to show the conversations which took place, but I will ask you if on occasion Douglas Hepner discussed the defendant, Eleanor Corbin, with you?"

"Indeed he did."

"Now, of course," Hamilton Burger said, "I feel that we are not entitled to bring those conversations into evidence except that I will ask you if at any time during any of those conversations he ever referred to Eleanor Corbin as his wife?"

"Indeed he did not. In fact, on the contrary he..."

"Never mind, never mind," Hamilton Burger said, holding up his hand, palm outward, as though he were a traffic officer flagging down oncoming traffic. "I want to keep the examination within strictly legal limits. Since it was claimed that the defendant was his wife I am simply asking you whether he ever referred to her as his wife. You have said he did not. That answers the question. Now then, I am going to ask you about something that *is* proper. Did you ever have a conversation with the defendant about Douglas Hepner?"

"I did. Yes, sir."

"And when was that?"

"That was about the fifteenth of August."

"And what was said?"

"I...well, Douglas had been calling on me and then when he left I noticed that the door of apartment 360 opened just a crack so that the defendant could watch him as he walked down the hall and..."

"How did you know it was the defendant who was watching?"

"Because...well, because I knew she had moved in with Ethel Belan for the purpose of spying..."

"Never mind the purpose," Burger interrupted, "that's a conclusion of the witness. Your Honor, I ask that the witness be instructed to confine her answers to the question and not volunteer information."

"Very well," the witness said with hostility. "I knew that the defendant had moved in with Ethel Belan. I knew that on almost every occasion that Douglas left my apartment the door would open. Since there would have been no way of knowing exactly when he was going unless she had some means of listening in on conversations I knew what was happening."

"And on this particular occasion what happened?"

"As soon as Douglas had entered the elevator and before she had a chance to close the door I walked over and pushed the door open."

"And who was standing on the other side of the door?"

"Eleanor Corbin."

"You mean the defendant in this action?"

"Yes, sir."

"That is the woman sitting beside Mr. Perry Mason, there at the defense counsel table?"

"Yes."

"Go ahead, tell us what happened."

"I told the defendant she was making a fool of herself. I said, 'You can't hold a man that way. You're just a jealous, frustrated fool, and furthermore I want you to quit listening to what goes on in my apartment. I'm not going to have you or anyone else listening in on my private conversations. I think there's a law against that, and if I have to I'm going to do something about it.' "

"And what did the defendant say?"

"The defendant became furious. She told me that I was a tramp, that I was trying to steal Douglas away from her, that like all men he was an opportunist and that I was deliberately providing an opportunity."

"Did she say anything at that time about being married to Douglas Hepner?"

"She said she wanted to marry him. She said that if she couldn't have him nobody would have him."

"Did she make any threats?"

"Oh, I don't remember all that she said. Yes, of course, she made threats. She treatened to kill both him and me. She said that she would kill Douglas if I tried to take him away from her—something to the effect that if she couldn't have him no one else could."

"Was anyone else present at that conversation?"

"Just the two of us were actually present at the time."

"Did the defendant say anything about how she proposed to carry out her threats?"

"Yes, indeed. She opened her purse. She showed me a revolver and said she was a desperate woman and that it wasn't safe to trifle with her, or words to that effect."

"What did she have in her purse?"

"A revolver."

"I call your attention to Plaintiff's Exhibit G and ask you if you have ever seen that revolver before?"

"I don't know. I've seen one that looks very much like it."

"Where?"

"In the defendant's handbag."

"And what happened after this conversation?"

"I turned around and went back into my apartment."

"I think," Hamilton Burger said, "you may now cross-examine this witness, Mr. Mason."

And Burger went back and seated himself at his counsel table, smiling to himself, his face radiating complete self-satisfaction.

Mason said, "You instituted this conversation, did you, Miss Granger?"

"You mean I took the initiative in bringing it about?"

"Yes."

"I most certainly did. I was tired of being spied upon and I intended to put a stop to it."

"Did anyone else hear this conversation? Was Miss Belan present?"

"Miss Belan was away. The defendant was alone in the apartment."

"In other words," Mason said, smiling easily, "it's only your word against hers. You..."

"I am not accustomed to having my word doubted," Suzanne Granger said indignantly.

"The point, however, is that no one else heard this conversation," Mason said.

"In that you are wrong," she retorted acidly. "I was the only other person present but Mr. Richey overheard the conversation and later remonstrated with me about it. He said that this was a high-class apartment house and people didn't have brawls..."

"Never mind what someone else said to you," Mason said. "That is hearsay. I am asking you if anyone else was present at that conversation."

"Mr. Richey was in an adjoining apartment. The door was open and he heard the entire conversation."

"That's all," Mason said.

"Just a minute," Hamilton Burger said. "You didn't tell me about Mr. Richey having heard the conversation."

"You didn't ask me."

"After all," Mason said, "it's a conclusion as far as this witness is concerned. *She* doesn't know that Richey heard the conversation."

"Well, he certainly came to me afterward and remonstrated with me about..."

"There, there, that will do," Hamilton Burger said. 'Your Honor, this opens up a very interesting phase of this case that I hadn't known about before. Why didn't you tell me, Miss Granger?"

"Tell you about what?"

"About the fact that someone else was present at this conversation?"

"He wasn't present. He only heard it. And besides I'm not accustomed to having my word doubted."

"But this is a court of law," Hamilton Burger said.

She gave her head a little toss and said, "I told you what happened and I told the truth."

"Very well," Hamilton Burger said. "That's all."

The district attorney glanced at the clock, said, "Your Honor, I know it is early but I think the prosecution will rest its case within the next few minutes after court reconvenes. However, there are certain points I would like to check over with my associates to make certain that I have introduced all of the evidence that I desire to produce at this time. I think the Court will agree that the case is moving very expeditiously and, of course, the Court will realize that a prosecutor is always faced with a problem at such a time as to what evidence is legitimately a part of his case in chief and what should be saved for rebuttal. I feel, therefore, that I am justified in asking the Court to recess at this time until two o'clock this afternoon so that I may check over my evidence. I feel certain that the prosecution will rest its case not later than two-thirty."

"Very well," Judge Moran ruled. "Court will take a recess until two o'clock this afternoon, predicated on the statement of the district attorney that he expects to rest his case by two-thirty."

Mason turned to the policewoman who was approaching to take charge of the defendant. "I want to talk with the defendant a little while," he said. "I would like to go into the witness room."

"Very well, Mr. Mason," she said. "It's early, so I can give you fifteen or twenty minutes."

"I think that will be enough," Mason said.

He nodded to Della Street, and said to Eleanor, "Please step this way, Mrs. Hepner."

Eleanor followed him into the witness room.

Mason kicked the door closed.

"All right," he said, "this is it."

"What is?"

"Quit stalling," Mason said. "They've jerked the rug out from under you. Now I'm not a magician. This is the time when I have to know what happened. The district attorney is going to rest his case at two-thirty this afternoon. He has a perfect case of first-degree murder. If you don't go on the stand you're licked. If you do go on the stand and testify to this amnesia business they'll rip you wide open. If you admit that telephone conversation with Ethel Belan you're a gone goose. It shows your amnesia is just a dodge.

"If you deny that conversation the district attorney probably has switchboard records from the hospital to show that you called Ethel Belan's number. You must have slipped the call through while the nurse was out of the room.

"He also has a bunch of psychiatrists who have examined you and will swear your loss of memory is merely a defensive pose. Now then, I have to know the facts.

"You've lied to me. It's probably too late to do anything now, but at least I have to know the truth."

She avoided his eyes. "Why did he want an adjournment at this time?" she asked.

"Because," he said, "he wants to check with Richey and see if Richey overheard that conversation. If Richey did and if his recollection coincides with that of Suzanne Granger's he's going to put Richey on the stand. Otherwise, he'll fumble around with a few platitudes and state that after checking with his associates he feels that they have introduced all of the evidence they care to in chief and that the balance of evidence will be saved for rebuttal, that therefore the prosecution rests its case."

"You think I'm not telling the truth about not being able to remember, don't you, Mr. Mason?"

Mason shrugged his shoulders and said, "It's your funeral, and," he added, "I mean that literally. It will be your funeral. They can return a verdict that will mean you're strapped into the little steel chair in a small, glass-windowed cubbyhole. Then everyone will withdraw. The door will clang shut and you'll hear the clank of an iron gate as the cyanide pellets are dropped into the acid. Then you'll hear a little hissing and..."

"Don't!" she screamed. "Don't do that to me. Good God, don't you suppose I've sweated through this thing in a nightmare night after night?"

"I'm telling you now," Mason said, "because this is the last time. This is the last opportunity anyone has to help you. Now then, you go ahead. It's your move."

Eleanor glanced at Della Street. Her glance was that of a trapped animal.

"Want a cigarette?" Della asked.

Eleanor nodded.

Della gave her a cigarette and lit it for her. Eleanor took in a deep breath. She exhaled a cloud of smoke, said, "It's so damn bad, Mr. Mason, that if I tell it to you you'll walk out on me."

"Tell it to me," Mason said.

"It's the truth," she said.

"What is?"

"What they've been saying."

"The story the witnesses have been telling?"

She nodded.

"You killed him?" Mason asked.

"I didn't kill him, but what good is it going to do for me to say so?"

"Suppose," Mason said kindly, "you start at the beginning and tell me the truth, but condense it into a capsule because we aren't going to have much time. I'll ask you questions about the parts I want you to elaborate."

She said, "I've always been rather wild. I've been in a few scrapes in my time. My father is conservative. He values his good name, his standing in the community and things of that sort.

"Coming over from Europe I met Douglas Hepner. Father didn't like him. One thing led to another. Father told me that if I married Doug Hepner I was finished as far as any financial connection with the family was concerned. He had been paying me a rather generous allowance but he'd threatened to stop it several times, and this time he really meant business."

"Go on," Mason said. "What happened?"

"Doug and I were in love—not so much on shipboard, that was one of those shipboard affairs. He was pretty much in demand as a dancing partner and...well, I thought it was a shipboard crush, but it wasn't. It was the real thing as far as I'm concerned and I supposed it was with him."

"Go on," Mason said.

"All right, it began to be serious and we talked a lot about getting married. Dad told me that if I married Doug I might just as well wash my hands of the family."

"Did Hepner tell you what his occupation was—how he made a living?"

"Yes."

"When?"

"The last few weeks—when we were talking about getting married. He told me a lot of things about himself. He'd been a rolling stone. He was an adventurer and an opportunist. He'd gone in for this stuff that he called being a free-lance detective. He was finding out about smuggled stones and getting a reward."

"Go on," Mason said.

"Well, this Suzanne Granger—I hate that woman."

"Never mind that," Mason said. "You haven't time for that. Go on, tell me what happened."

"Well, anyhow, Doug got the idea that Suzanne Granger was the head of a huge smuggling ring. Don't ask me how he got the idea because I don't know. I don't know what evidence he had."

"Did he work hand in glove with the Customs people?" Mason asked. "Perhaps they tipped him off."

"No, I don't think so. The Customs people had absolutely no suspicion of Suzanne Granger. They let her breeze through Customs with as much deference as though she'd been a visiting potentate. She's one of those queenly, aristocratic women who always want to be better than the other person, want to get the other person on the defensive."

Mason said, "Try and forget how much you hate her and give me the facts and give them to me fast."

"Well, Doug said that if he could break up that smuggling ring Suzanne was in he could make enough from the reward to buy an interest in an importing company. He knew of one he could pick up cheap from a friend of his, and with his knowledge and connections he could build it up to something really big."

"He thought Suzanne Granger was a smuggler?"

"Either she was the big smuggler or she had the contact. I think he thought she was the big smuggler."

"So what did he do?"

"He told me that he'd have to be free to date Suzanne. He said he wouldn't get too involved with her, he'd just date her and sound her out so he could get access to her apartment. He told me that he was going to have associates search her apartment. In order to do that he had to be sure. He wanted to be where he could listen to what went on in her apartment. He had a listening device, some sort of a microphone with electronic amplification that he could press against the wall of the bedroom in Ethel's apartment and hear everything that went on in Suzanne Granger's apartment.

"So he and I worked out this plan. I was to pose as a jealous, frustrated woman. I made a deal with Ethel Belan to get into her apartment.

"Well, somehow something happened and Suzanne Granger learned that I was in the adjoining apartment. I don't know how, but Doug knew. I guess she must have told Doug I was in there snooping."

"So then what?"

"So then Doug told me to plan on leaving the apartment for long periods of time. In that way Suzanne Granger would think the coast was clear and she would go on making her plans to dispose of the smuggled stones.

"The man who runs the freight elevator hates the snobs in the front office and Doug bribed him. In that way Doug could ride up in the freight elevator without anyone knowing about it.

"So what would happen, Ethel would leave and go to work. She works as some sort of a buyer in a department store. After she'd gone I'd put on my things and go out in the hallway, making a lot of noise, then I'd take the elevator down and walk right past the desk. I was there as a guest, not as a tenant, but I'd contrive to let the girl at the switchboard know I expected to be out all day. Then I'd go out and usually stay out."

"And Douglas would move in?"

She nodded. "He'd go up in the freight elevator and take over."

"But he *could* have gone to Suzanne Granger's apartment."

"If he wanted to he could have."

"And for all you know, he did."

"Well, if he'd been doing that why would he have asked me to get in Ethel Belan's apartment in the first place?"

Mason thought that over.

"He had a key?" he asked.

"Of course he had a key. I gave him my key long enough to have a duplicate key made. If you'll examine the keys that he had on him at the time of his death I'm certain you'll find that one of the keys fits Ethel Belan's apartment."

"The police don't know that?" Mason asked.

"Apparently so far the police don't know it."

"And, of course, Ethel Belan had no idea that Doug was using her apartment as a listening post to monitor what went on in Suzanne Granger's apartment."

"No, of course not, that's why Douglas was supposed to be hot and heavy after Suzanne, and I was supposed to be there eating my heart out and listening and trying to catch them out.

"We had to play it that way because Ethel's a rattlebrained little biddy who would have spilled the beans if she'd had any inkling of what was going on.

"Even as it was, Ethel Belan began to be a little suspicious. She thought that Doug had been visiting me in the apartment while she was out and wondered if my jealousy wasn't an act trying to cover up something. She talked a little bit to Suzanne Granger and Doug got terribly afraid that Suzanne was smart enough to put two and two together.

"So Doug told me to arrange a scene where I was to goad Suzanne into saying something to me, then I was to open my purse and show her my gun and make threats against everybody and everything and put on the act of a jealous woman, the neurotic type who can be dangerous.

"Well, I did that and it worked. I don't know just what happened because within half an hour of the time we had that scene Doug doubled back to the apartment and put the listening device on and listened and seemed to be tickled to death with what he heard. He told me that he thought he knew the answer. He told me to let him have my gun and go out and that he'd get in touch with me later on."

"And you gave him your gun?"

"Of course," she said. "I'd give him anything he asked for."

"You weren't married, were you?"

"We were going to be married as soon as..."

"But you *weren't* married!"

"Doug said we'd have to wait, but on that trip to Yuma and Las Vegas we traveled as man and wife."

"Why did you say you were married?"

"Doug said it was like a common law marriage and he told me to wire the family from Yuma. We didn't want any fuss."

"And the car wreck?" Mason asked.

"That was a fib. I made that up."

"But his car was smashed."

"I know. That's where I got the idea of the wreck. I had to have something to use for an excuse to account for my loss of memory."

"When did his car get smashed?"

"Sunday evening—the night before he died. A big truck rounded a curve and came straight for him. It's a wonder Doug wasn't killed. That's what the truck driver was trying to do.

"You see, this is a regular smuggling gang and...well, they play dirty. I wanted Doug to quit then because it showed they were after him. That's when I give him the gun. He promised he would if he couldn't crack the case within a couple more days, but he thought he was on the point of making a big stake that would get us started in this new business."

"You gave him your gun when he asked for it and what did you do?"

"I went out."

"And when did you come back?"

She lowered her eyes. "Later."

"How much later?"

"Quite a bit later."

"Was Doug there when you came back?"

"No."

"Was Ethel Belan?"

"No, she was away for the week end and wasn't coming back until Monday."

"Now what about those gems?" Mason asked. "How did you get them?"

"Mr. Mason, you've got to believe me. That story about the gems is absolutely completely cockeyed. I never had any gems. I never saw any gems. She's lying when she says she saw me with those gems."

Mason's eyes were cold. "You didn't conceal them anywhere in your baggage?"

"Don't be silly, Mr. Mason. I'm telling you the truth now."

"You've told me that before."

"On my word of honor."

"You've said that before too."

"You just have to believe me."

"I can't believe you," Mason said. "There's too much corroborative evidence against you. I've got to fight this case through. They've got you dead to rights. They've caught you in a whole series of lies. They have proven that Doug Hepner was killed with your gun, that within a very short time prior to his death you had stated that he was your boy friend, that Suzanne Granger was stealing him, that if you couldn't have him nobody else could, and that you'd kill him rather than give him up."

"I know," she said, "but I've tried to tell you...that was what Doug told me to say, that was an act I was putting on at his request."

"There's only one person who can save you from the death cell by corroborating your story on that," Mason said.

"Who's that?"

"Doug Hepner, and he's dead. If you're telling the truth you put yourself in the power of fate when you told that story, and if you're not telling the truth..."

"But I am, Mr. Mason. I'm telling you the absolute truth."

"You're lying about those gems."

"I'm not, Mr. Mason."

"But suppose they should find those gems—perhaps in your baggage?"

"Well, I guess I'd be on my way to the gas chamber. It would be the final corroboration of Ethel Belan's story that would...it would make people think that Doug had recovered gems and I'd stolen them from Doug and...well, it would just be a mess that nobody could get out of."

"You're in a mess now," Mason said, "and I don't see how anyone can get you out of it."

"Can't I tell them the truth? Can't I tell them that Doug told me to put on that act? Can't I tell them that Doug was sort of a detective for the Customs officials? Can't we bring on the Customs officials to corroborate that? Can't we at least insinuate that Suzanne Granger was a smuggler?

"I understand that while she was gone on a trip to Las Vegas her apartment was broken into and all the tubes of paint were cut open. Couldn't she have had gems in the tubes of paint?"

"She could have," Mason said. "Who accompanied Suzanne to Las Vegas?"

"That's something I don't know."

"But if we do that," Mason said, "and if we should by any strange chance get anyone on the jury to believe us, then that story told by Ethel Belan about you having that assortment of gems in your possession would make it appear that *you* were the one who had gone into the apartment and cut open the tubes of paint, that *you* were the one who had recovered the gems, that *you* had tried to hold out on Douglas Hepner, and that had resulted in a fight and that you had killed Hepner."

"But she's lying about the gems."

"All right, let's pass that for a moment," Mason said wearily. "Now I want the real story of why you were running around in the park in the moonlight, making come hither gestures to masculine motorists..."

"But I wasn't, Mr. Mason. I was appealing for help. I was trying to get the *woman* to follow me."

"It didn't look that way," Mason said. "When the woman followed you, you started screaming and..."

"She didn't follow me, she was chasing me. She was chasing me with a jack handle."

"Well, why did you want her to follow you?" Mason asked.

"I wanted her to find Doug's body."

"You what?" Mason asked, his voice showing his utter incredulity.

"I wanted her to find Doug's body. I was going to lead her to it."

"You knew that Doug was there, dead?"

"Yes, of course."

"How did you know that?"

"Because Doug and I had a rendezvous there in the park. Whenever anything happened and we got signals mixed or we wanted to communicate with each other we'd meet there at that place in the park.

"When I went there this night, Doug was lying there dead and my gun was right there beside him."

"Go on," Mason said, glancing hopelessly at Della Street.

"Well," she said, "of course it was a terrific shock to me, but... well, instantly I saw the spot I was in, Mr. Mason. I had been trapped into making that statement to Suzanne only the day before—understand, when I say I was trapped, I mean that events had trapped me. I don't mean that Doug had anything to do with it.

"But there I was. I'd sworn that I was going to kill Doug and that if I couldn't have him no one else would and all of that stuff and I'd exhibited my gun—and, of course, it *was* my gun. I'd had it in my possession and then I'd given it to Doug when he asked for it. Someone must have followed him there to the park where he went to meet me, overpowered him, pulled the gun out of his pocket and shot him in the back of the head.

"There was his body lying there, with my gun beside it. I simply didn't know what to do."

"I can well imagine," Mason said dryly. "Now tell us what you did do, and for once try telling the truth."

"I picked up the gun and carried it over to where I could bury it. I was terribly afraid that they'd pick me up while I had the gun in my possession. I knew that every minute, every second that I had that gun in my possession I was in a very, very vulnerable position.

"I finally found a place where I could bury it where a ground squirrel or something had dug down in the ground. I shoved it way down in this hole and then kicked dirt in on top of it and put dry leaves and sticks over the top of the ground so I didn't think there was one chance in a million anyone could find it."

"And then?" Mason asked.

"Then I knew that I was in a spot. I didn't know what to do and I was in a panic. When you get in a panic like that you just can't think clearly."

"What did you think you were trying to do?"

"Well, I felt that if I should be found out there in the park without any clothes on, I could tell a story about having been out there with Doug and having been assaulted by a strange man who killed Doug and attempted to rape me, that I fought my way clear and was wandering around in a semi-dazed condition."

"Go on," Mason said.

"So I rushed back to the apartment," she said, "took my clothes and literally tore them off of me. Then I borrowed one of Ethel's raincoats and walked over to the park. I kicked up a bunch of ground as though there'd been a struggle and left the clothes scattered around. Then I hid the raincoat and went out across the park until I saw a car that was parked. Then I came toward it, making motions to the woman. I felt that I should act as though I were too modest to come out where the man could see me. I was appealing for feminine help and ... well, you know what happened. The woman started after me with a jack handle thinking I was being promiscuous and trying to vamp her boy friend. I ran, and I guess I was screaming, and managed to get away from her.

"Then I realized I was in a devil of a mess. I couldn't make the same approach again and I thought I'd just better go back to the apartment and try something else. So I picked up my clothes and wadded them into a small bundle and stuffed them down another ground squirrel hole and put earth on them and..."

"Where are they now?" Mason asked.

"As far as I know they're in that same ground squirrel hole."

"Then what?"

"Then I picked up this raincoat where I'd hidden it, where I felt certain it wouldn't be found, put it on and started back to Ethel's apartment and ... well, that's when fate started taking a hand in the game. That's when everything I did went wrong. Police picked me up and I just didn't know what to say. I certainly was in a position where I needed time to stall.

"I'd been in a jam once before and had pulled this business about a loss of memory and a friendly doctor had helped me along with it and I'd got by very nicely. I felt that that would establish something in the way of a precedent, that I could show I had these attacks of amnesia and ... well, that's what I did."

Mason said, "Eleanor, do you expect anyone on earth to believe that story?"

She avoided his eyes for a moment, then looked at him.

"No," she admitted, "not now."

"If you get on the stand and try to tell that story to the jury," Mason said, "the district attorney will rip you up with cross-examination, he'll show that you've lied before, time and time again, he'll show the utter, weird improbability of that story, and he'll convict you of first-degree murder."

"As I see it," she said, looking him squarely in the eyes, "it's all a question of whether we can shake Ethel Belan's story about me having those gems. If I had them then, of course, people will think that I recovered the gems while Suzanne Granger was in Las Vegas, and that because I was having a fight with Doug or something of that sort I tried to keep them all and Doug and I quarreled."

"Exactly," Mason said dryly. "On rebuttal or cross-examination it's going to come out what Doug Hepner actually did for a living. The district attorney has been holding back on that. If you take the stand he'll crucify you with it on cross-examination. If you don't take the stand he'll bring it out if I put on any evidence at all."

"But if you don't put on any evidence at all then he can't bring it out, can he?"

"If I don't put on any evidence at all," Mason said, "he won't need to."

"Well, I've told you the truth. That's all I can do."

"This is your last chance to tell the whole truth."

"I've told it."

Mason got to his feet. "Come on, Della," he said.

At the door he nodded to the policewoman. "That's all."

CHAPTER FOURTEEN

Mason, Della Street and Paul Drake sat huddled in the restaurant booth, engaged in low-voiced conversation

"What are you going to do?" Drake asked.

"I'm damned if I know," Mason said, "but I've got to do something and I've got to do it fast. The way things stand right now there isn't a whisper of a chance."

The waiter came and presented the check. "Everything all right?" he asked.

"Everything was fine," Mason said.

"To look at you you'd never know you were going to have to go into court and let Hamilton Burger cut your throat," Paul Drake said.

"And it didn't affect your appetite any," Della Street observed.

"I didn't dare to let it affect my appetite," Mason said. "Food makes energy. I didn't eat heavy food but I ate food that will furnish me with a little fuel to last through the afternoon—and it's going to be *some* afternoon."

"Can't you let Eleanor go on the stand and tell her story no matter how utterly incredible it sounds?" Paul Drake asked.

Mason shook his head.

"Well then, couldn't you work a razzle-dazzle that would sound plausible? Couldn't you sketch Suzanne Granger as a sinister character? Couldn't you cast her in the role of a smuggler who had paint tubes full of gems?

"Suppose Eleanor got those gems? Then Suzanne would do anything to get them back. Suppose Eleanor gave them to Doug Hepner? Well, there you have motive and opportunity. Hell's bells, Perry, give this Granger dame a working over on cross-examination, sneer at her, question her great love of art, insinuate she's a smuggler. Ask her why she didn't report this vandalism to the police. Give her hell."

Mason shook his head.

"Why not?" Drake asked.

"Because," Mason said, "it isn't the truth."

"Don't be naive," Drake said. "A lot of criminal lawyers I know don't pay much attention to the truth. Often when the truth would get a client stuck a good lawyer has to resort to something else."

"I'm afraid of anything that isn't the truth." Mason said. "My client tells me a story that's almost impossible to believe, but it's her story. If I, as her attorney, adhere to that story I at least am being true to the ideals of my profession. I may think it's a lie, but I don't know it's a lie.

"If, however, I think up some synthetic story, then I *know* it's false and I'm afraid of anything that's false. A lawyer should seek the truth."

"But your client's story, from what I gather about it, *can't* be true," Drake said.

"Then," Mason said, "it's up to me to seek out the truth."

"But the reason she's lying is that the truth is something she can't face."

"You mean she killed him?"

"It could be that. Or it may be she's trapped by a whole series of events so that the truth would betray her."

"If she killed him, that's her funeral. If she didn't then only the truth can save her. Her fear of the truth is that a jury won't believe it. It's my duty to uncover the truth and then see that the jury knows it is the truth and believes it."

"Yes," Drake said sarcastically. "It's up to you to try to cast Ethel Belan in the role of a liar and Suzanne Granger in the role of a smuggler, with Eleanor taking the part of a pure maiden who is being persecuted. Look where that leaves you."

"There's something about the way Eleanor does things that destroys all confidence in her. The Granger woman radiates truth and integrity on the witness stand. She's proud and aristocratic. She scorns subterfuge and her record is as clean as a hound's tooth.

"On the other hand, there's Eleanor who pulled all this stuff of flashing guns around, who lied about being married, who made statements that she was going to kill the man she loved so that nobody else could have him in case she couldn't have him, and betraying herself every time she opened her mouth. Then the minute she goes on the stand and admits that she knew Doug had been killed with her own gun and...well, there you are."

Paul Drake looked at his watch. "Well, Perry," he said, "I guess we're going to have to shuffle on up to the execution chamber. I certainly hate to see Hamilton Burger hand you one, but this is the time he's really done it."

"A made-to-order case," Mason admitted. "No wonder Hamilton Burger was so damned happy. He's been laying for this for years. This is the time he has everything his way."

"But what *are* you going to do, Chief?" Della Street asked.

"I don't know," Mason admitted. "Eleanor is my client and I'm going to do the best I can for her. Burger has been putting in the noon hour talking with Webley Richey. If Miss Granger's story isn't true, naturally Richey won't be in a position to corroborate it. Therefore, Burger will rest his case right after he walks into court. If it develops that he's got a corroborating witness he'll put Richey on the stand."

"But you can't cross-examine Richey on that conversation for more than a minute or two," Drake said.

"I've got to find a loophole somewhere," Mason said. "Our only hope is that Burger rests his case without recalling Richey. If he does that I'll know something's wrong with Suzanne Granger's story. If he recalls Richey I'll know Eleanor's case is hopeless. Richey is the barometer."

They entered the Hall of Justice, were whisked upward in an elevator and walked into the courtroom.

It was quite evident that Eleanor had been crying during the noon hour. Her swollen, red-rimmed eyes were definitely no help as far as Mason's task was concerned.

Della Street, sizing up the grim, hard faces of the jurors as they gazed in unsympathetic appraisal at the defendant, leaned toward Perry Mason and said, "Gosh, Chief, I feel like bawling myself. Look at the faces on the jurors."

"I know," Mason said.

A smiling Hamilton Burger, flanked by his assistant district attorneys, made something of a triumphant entry into the courtroom, and a few moments later Judge Moran took the bench and court was called to order.

"Are the People ready to proceed?" Judge Moran asked.

"This tells the story," Mason whispered.

Hamilton Burger got to his feet. "Your Honor," he said, "we have one more witness, a witness whom I didn't realize could corroborate the story of Miss Granger until Miss Granger's statement on the stand took me completely by surprise. Because I hadn't anticipated such a situation, I hadn't asked Miss Granger or Mr. Richey about the conversation. Miss Granger had told me as she had stated on the stand, that just she and the defendant were present at the time of this conversation and I had let it go at that. I simply hadn't thought to ask her if some other person who hadn't been present might nevertheless have overheard the conversation.

"I mention this in order to show the Court and counsel my good faith in the matter.

"Mr. Webley Richey, will you come forward, please? You have already been sworn. Just take your position there on the witness stand, please."

Richey walked forward with studied dignity. He seated himself on the witness stand, glanced patronizingly at Perry Mason, then raised his eyebrows in silent interrogation as he looked at Hamilton Burger. His manner said louder than words that he was graciously granting permission to the district attorney to question him.

"Did you," Hamilton Burger asked, "hear a conversation on or about the fifteenth day of August of this year between the defendant and Suzanne Granger?"

"I did. Yes, sir."

"Where did that conversation take place?"

"At the door of apartment 360."

"And who was present at that conversation?"

"Just Miss Granger and the defendant."

"Tell us what was said," Hamilton Burger said.

"Just a moment," Mason said. "I would like to ask a preliminary question."

"I don't think you're entitled to," Hamilton Burger said. "You can object if you want to."

"Very well," Mason said. "I object on the ground that the question calls for a conclusion of the witness. If the Court please the witness has testified that only two people were present. Therefore he wasn't present."

"But he certainly can testify to what he heard," Judge Moran ruled.

"Provided he can identify the voices," Mason said, "but there has as yet been no proper foundation laid."

"Oh, very well," Hamilton Burger said. "You know the defendant, do you, Mr. Richey?"

"I do. Yes, sir."

"Have you talked with her?"

"Well...on occasion."

"Do you know her voice?"

"Well...yes. I know her voice very well."

"And was she one of the persons who participated in the conversation?"

"Yes, sir."

"And how about the other person?"

"That was Miss Granger."

"Do you know her voice?"

"Very well."

"Go on. Tell us what was said."

"Well, Miss Granger said that she didn't propose to have anyone spying on her, that she didn't like it, that she was independent, paid her own bills and intended to live her own life and she wasn't going to have anyone keeping watch on her."

"And what did the defendant say to that?"

"The defendant said that she was trying to steal her boy friend."

"Boy friend or husband?" Hamilton Burger asked.

"Boy friend."

"Go ahead."

"And the defendant said that she wasn't going to stand idly by and let anyone steal her boy friend, that if Suzanne Granger interfered she would shoot Suzanne Granger, and if she couldn't get her boy friend back by any other means she certainly would see to it that no one else had him."

"Did she say how she proposed to see that no one else had him?"

"She said that she would kill him."

"And did she at that time exhibit a weapon?"

"Well, of course," Richey said, "I couldn't see what was going on. I could only hear. But I gathered from the conversation that she was showing a weapon to Miss Granger. She said something about, 'You can see that I'm prepared to make good my promise,' or something of that sort."

"You may inquire," Hamilton Burger said smugly.

Mason glanced at the clock. Somehow he had to think up a strategy by which this rather routine corroborating witness could become a pivotal controversial figure so that the case would drag on until the next day.

"Subsequently," Mason asked, "you remonstrated with the parties about this scene?"

"I spoke to Miss Granger about it, yes."

"That was in your official capacity?"

"Certainly."

"You were the clerk on duty at the apartment house and as such felt that you had the duty of maintaining order and the dignity of the apartment?"

"Absolutely."

"And in that capacity you spoke to Miss Granger, I believe remonstrated was the word she used?"

"Yes, sir."

"And what did you say?"

"I told her that the Belinda Apartments was a high-class apartment house, that we didn't believe in having brawls."

"What did you say to the defendant?"

"I didn't talk to her. She went out right after the altercation with Miss Granger."

"Why didn't you talk to her later?"

"Well, I...officially, you understand, I hadn't been advised the defendant was a tenant. She was there as a guest of a tenant. Actually she had made financial arrangements with Miss Belan to share her apartment, but that was supposed to be confidential. No one was supposed to know that Miss Belan had a subtenant in the apartment. The defendant was supposed to be a guest. In that way it wasn't necessary for her to register."

"I see. Who told you about the arrangements?"

"Miss Belan."

"Not the defendant?"

"No."

"Then you had never talked with the defendant personally?"

"I saw her from time to time."

"But you hadn't talked with her?"

"I tried to take no official notice of the fact that she was a paying tenant in the house."

"Then you hadn't talked with her?"

"Not in that sense of the word."

"Then how," Mason asked, "could you be familiar with the sound of her voice?"

The witness hesitated. "I...I had heard it."

"How had you heard it?"

"Why, by hearing her speak."

"When had you heard her speak?"

"I don't know—from time to time, I guess."

"Over the telephone?"

"Yes, over the telephone."

"Do you sometimes monitor the switchboard?"

"Well, I...sometimes I check on calls."

"You don't actually manipulate the switchboard yourself?"

"No."

"Do you know how to do so?"

"I'm afraid I do not."

"Then when you say you monitor calls does that mean you listen in on calls?"

The witness became embarrassed. "I wouldn't use that term, Mr. Mason. It sometimes is necessary to make decisions in regard to the lines."

"What do you mean by that?"

"If, for instance, a person has placed a long-distance call and then is engaged in some rather trivial telephone conversation when the long-distance call comes in, I have to give the operator a signal as to whether the local conversation should be interrupted so that the long-distance call can come across the board."

"I see. That takes a certain amount of judgment?"

"A very great deal of discretion."

"It means that you have to know the habits of the people?"

"Oh yes, definitely."

"I mean their telephone habits."

"Yes, sir."

"And have some idea as to the importance of the long-distance call?"

"Well, yes."

"And the only way you can get that is by monitoring the conversations from time to time?"

"Well, I wouldn't say that."

"How else would you get the information?"

"I wouldn't know. Perhaps intuitively."

"You do monitor conversations, don't you?"

"I have."

"You make a habit of it, don't you?"

"Definitely not."

"When you're not busy with something else?"

"Well, sometimes I listen in on the line, that is, I . . . well, I have monitored conversations when I felt there was some reason for it."

"And the switchboard is so constructed that any conversation can be monitored from your office. In other words, your phone can be plugged in on any line going across the switchboard?"

"Well, of course, the switchboard is one of those . . ."

"Answer the question," Mason said. "Isn't it a fact that the switchboard is so constructed that your telephone can be plugged in on any line so that you can monitor any conversation that's going through the switchboard?"

"Well, you see . . ."

"I want an answer to that question," Mason thundered. "Is that a fact?"

"Yes."

"Well now," Mason said, smiling, "was there any reason why you couldn't have answered that question directly? Were you ashamed of what you did in monitoring the conversations?"

"No, definitely not."

"I'm sorry if I got that impression from your continued evasions," Mason said.

Hamilton Burger jumped to his feet. "That remark is uncalled for, Your Honor. The witness didn't continually evade the question."

Mason smiled at the judge. "I won't argue the point, Your Honor. I'll leave it entirely to the jury."

"But I don't like that insinuation in the record," Hamilton Burger protested.

"I didn't think you would."

Judge Moran said, "Come, come, gentlemen. We'll have no more personalities. Go on with your cross-examination, Mr. Mason."

"Now according to your version of this conversation," Mason said, "Miss Granger was a perfect lady. She made no threats."

"No, sir."

"*She* didn't pull a gun on the defendant?"

"Definitely not."

"*She* didn't threaten to shoot the defendant?"

"No, sir."

"*She* didn't threaten to shoot Douglas Hepner?"

"Definitely not."

"*She* comported herself in a respectable manner throughout?"

"Yes, sir."

"Then why did you deem it necessary to remonstrate with *her*?"

"I . . . well, of course, she was the one who initiated proceedings. It was she who opened the door and told the defendant she didn't propose to have anyone spying on her."

"You were there, you said, in an adjoining apartment?"

"Yes, sir."

"How could you hear so clearly what was being said?"

"The door of the apartment was open."

"And you were there in your official capacity?"

"Yes, sir."

"Then why didn't you step out into the hallway and put a stop to the altercation then and there?"

The witness hesitated.

"Go on," Mason said. "Why didn't you? What was holding you back?"

"Well, of course, in many years of employment in high-class apartment houses one learns a certain amount of discretion. When one interferes in a quarrel between two angry women..."

"*Two* angry women?" Mason asked.

"Well, yes, sir."

"I thought you said it was one angry woman and one dignified one? Were both women angry?"

"Well, I think Miss Granger was angry when she started the conversation."

"She pushed the door open and confronted the defendant?"

"Well, I...I don't know about pushing the door open. I couldn't see. I could only hear."

"And she was angry?"

"I think her feelings were outraged."

Mason said, "You draw a very nice line of distinction, Mr. Richey. One woman was angry and the other woman's feelings were outraged. Yet when you said you didn't interfere you said that you didn't want to get mixed up in an altercation between *two* angry women."

"Oh, have it your way," Richey said. "I'm not going to quibble with you, Mr. Mason."

"You're not quibbling with me," Mason said. "I'm trying to get the exact picture of what happened."

"After all, is it that important?" Hamilton Burger asked somewhat sneeringly.

"It's important because it shows the attitude of this witness," Mason said.

"An absolutely unbiased, impartial witness," Hamilton Burger retorted with feeling.

"Is that so?" Mason said. "Now, Mr. Richey, you have testified that you were in an adjoining apartment at the time?"

"Yes, sir."

"And the door was open?"

"Yes, sir."

"That is, the door from the apartment to the corridor?"

"Yes, sir."

"And you could hear the sounds of the altercation?"

"Yes, sir."

"What apartment were you in?" Mason asked, getting to his feet and raising his voice. "Tell us, what apartment were you in?"

"Why, I...I was in an adjoining apartment."

"Adjoining what?"

"Adjoining...well, it was a nearby apartment."

Mason said, "You've used the word adjoining a dozen different times. Now was it an adjoining apartment or wasn't it?"

"It was a nearby apartment."

"Was it an adjoining apartment?"

"At this time, Mr. Mason, it would be difficult for me to tell you what apartment I was in."

"So you can remember the conversation almost verbatim," Mason said, "and yet you can't remember what apartment you were in."

"Well, I haven't given that matter much thought."

"Let's give it some thought now. What apartment were you in?"

"I...I'm sure I can't...it would be very difficult..."

"Was it an adjoining apartment?"

"Adjoining what?"

"You've used the word," Mason said. "What did you mean by it?"

"Well, I...I don't know what I meant by it."

"In other words, you were using words without knowing their meaning?"

"I know the meaning of the word adjoining."

"And you used that word?"

"Yes, sir."

"All right, what did you mean when you used it?"

"Well, there, of course...I wasn't thinking."

"You're under oath?"

"Of course."

"You knew you were testifying under oath?"

"Yes, sir."

"And yet when you said adjoining and knew the meaning of the word you didn't think of the meaning at the time you used it?"

"Well, that's not expressing it very fairly."

"Express it in your words then," Mason said. "Express it fairly."

"Oh, Your Honor," Hamilton Burger said, "this is browbeating the witness."

"I'm not browbeating him," Mason said. "Here's a witness who has an air of supercilious superiority. Here's a witness who has testified a dozen times that he was in an adjoining apartment. Now I'm trying to find out whether he actually was in an adjoining apartment."

"Well, of course, if you want to be technical about it, there could actually be only two adjoining apartments, one on each side," Richey blurted.

"That's exactly what I'm trying to get at," Mason said. "You understand the meaning of the word adjoining?"

"Yes, sir."

"What is it?"

"It means immediately contiguous to."

"All right. Were you in an apartment that was immediately contiguous to apartment 360?"

"It would be difficult for me to tell you at this time, Mr. Mason."

"I think, if the Court please, that question has been asked and answered half a dozen times," Hamilton Burger said. "The witness has stated he can't remember."

"He didn't state any such thing," Mason said. "He said that it would be difficult for him to tell me. *Were* you in one of the adjoining apartments?"

"Well, I...I may have been."

"You said so a dozen times, didn't you?"

"I don't know how many times."

"You used the word adjoining?"

"I believe I did. I used it without thinking."

"Were you testifying without thinking?"

"No, I simply used the word without thinking."

"Exactly," Mason said. "You were betraying yourself by the use of the word. There was only one adjoining apartment that had the door open and that was apartment 358. That was the apartment of Suzanne Granger. She had gone out, in fact she had stormed out when she found the defendant watching Douglas Hepner's departure down the elevator. She stormed out and left the door open. You therefore heard the conversation. You were in Suzanne Granger's apartment, weren't you?"

"I...I can't remember."

"You can't remember whether you were in the apartment of Suzanne Granger at the time this conversation took place?"

"I...I...well...come to think of it, I remember now that I was."

"Oh, you were in there?"

"Yes, sir."

"On official business?"

"I was in there in connection with my employment. Yes, sir."

"And you were there in that apartment when Suzanne Granger stormed out of the apartment and left the door open?"

"Yes, sir."

"Now when Douglas Hepner departed he had left by that door and gone to the elevator, had he not?"

"Yes, sir."

"And Suzanne Granger had stepped to the door and was watching to see if the door of apartment 360 opened a crack. Isn't that right?"

"I don't know what was in her mind."

"But she did step to the door, didn't she?"

"Yes, sir."

"And then while you were standing there you heard the clang of the elevator door as Douglas Hepner went down?"

"Yes, sir."

"And then saw Suzanne Granger storm out into the corridor?"

"Well, I don't know what you mean by storming. She went out into the corridor."

"Hurriedly?"

"Yes."

"Angrily?"

"Yes."

"And you stood there in the apartment behind this open door and heard the conversation?"

"Yes, sir."

"Now why," Mason said, pointing his finger at Richey, "why did you try to conceal the fact that you were in Suzanne Granger's apartment?"

"I didn't. I said I was in an adjoining apartment."

"Then when you said you were in an adjoining apartment you meant that you were in the apartment adjoining that of Ethel Belan, in other words in Suzanne Granger's apartment?"

"Certainly."

"Then why did you tell us it would be difficult for you to tell me what apartment you were in?"

"Well, I didn't want to come out and mention it in so many words."

"Didn't you try to convey the effect that you couldn't remember what apartment you were in?"

"Certainly not. I said that it would be difficult for me to tell you. I was very careful in choosing my language."

"Yet you noticed that the learned district attorney became confused by your language and stated to the Court that you had testified half a dozen times that you couldn't remember. Didn't you hear him say that?"

"Yes, sir."

"And you didn't try to straighten him out or tell him that it wasn't that you couldn't remember but simply that it would be difficult for you to say?"

"Well, I...I feel that the district attorney can take care of himself."

"You don't have to do his thinking for him, is that it?"

"Well, you can put it that way if you want."

"And then, later on, you did say you couldn't remember and then said you had remembered, isn't that right?"

"I may have. I was confused."

"Actually you did remember?"

"I remembered until I became confused and then I forgot. When I remembered I told you so. When I said it would be difficult for me to tell you, I meant just that."

"Yet at one time you said you couldn't remember?"

"I may have."

"That was a lie?"

"Not a lie. I was confused."

"You said you couldn't remember?"

"You got me so rattled I didn't know what I was saying."

"Now why was it difficult for you to tell us that you were in Suzanne Granger's apartment?"

"Because I suddenly realized that under the circumstances it might be...it might be embarrassing."

"To whom?"

"To Miss Granger."

"So you were willing to quibble and avoid answering the question in order to spare Suzanne Granger's feelings?"

"I try to be a gentleman."

"Was there any reason why you shouldn't have been in Suzanne Granger's apartment?"

"Not in my official capacity, no."

"And you were there in your official capacity?"

"Yes, sir."

"What were you doing?"

"I...I was discussing a matter with Miss Granger."

"A matter which had to do with her position as a tenant and your position as the clerk?"

"It was in my official capacity. Yes, sir."

"What were you discussing?"

"Oh, if the Court please," Hamilton Burger said, "I object to that. It's incompetent, irrelevant and immaterial. It's not proper cross-examination."

"On the other hand," Mason said, "it goes to the very gist of the motivation and the bias of this witness. It is an important question."

Judge Moran frowned thoughtfully. "Under certain circumstances," he said,

"I would think that it would be rather remote, but in view of the situation that has developed with the examination of this witness it...I think I will overrule the objection."

"What were you discussing?" Mason said.

"I can't remember."

"Now this time you don't mean that it would be difficult for you to say, you mean that you can't remember?"

"I mean that I can't remember."

"You remember the conversation that took place between Miss Granger and the defendant?"

"Yes, sir."

"You remember that almost word for word?"

"I remember what was said. Yes, sir."

"But you can't remember the conversation which took place immediately before that, the conversation on an official matter between you and Miss Granger?"

"No, sir, I can't."

"Then how do you know it was on an official matter?" Mason asked.

"Because otherwise I wouldn't have been there."

"You're certain of that?"

"Definitely."

"You have never been in the apartment of Suzanne Granger except upon an official matter?"

The witness hesitated, glanced appealingly at Hamilton Burger.

"Oh, Your Honor," Hamilton Burger said, "now we are getting far afield. This is an attempt to discredit the witness, to besmirch the reputation of another witness and..."

"This shows the bias of the witness," Mason said, "and I furthermore fail to see how the fact that he was in the apartment of Miss Granger on a matter other than official business is going to besmirch her reputation."

"Of course," Judge Moran said thoughtfully, "this cross-examination has taken a most peculiar turn."

"The reason it has taken a most peculiar turn," Hamilton Burger said, "is very simple. The defendant, in desperation, is sparring for time. He's trying to introduce every possible technicality that he can in order to try and appraise the case which has been made by the People so that he will know what sort of a defense to put on."

"I think that remark is uncalled for," Judge Moran said. "The jury will disregard that. Any remark made by counsel for either side is not to be taken as evidence. And I consider, Mr. District Attorney, that in your position you should realize that a statement of that sort in front of the jury might well become prejudicial misconduct."

"I'm sorry, Your Honor, I withdraw the statement. I made it in the heat of...well, of exasperation."

"Now then," Judge Moran said, "I want to repeat that this cross-examination has taken a peculiar turn. Yet it is a logical turn in view of the testimony of the witness. I don't care to comment on that testimony because that is not my function. I am here to rule on legal questions. However, I think that under the circumstances I will give the defense the utmost latitude in cross-examination. The objection is overruled."

"Were you ever there on matters other than business?" Mason asked.

"Well, I may have dropped in from time to time just to pass the time of day."

"If," Mason said, "some tenant of a neighboring apartment, not an adjoining apartment but a neighboring apartment, should say that you had been in there dozens of times, would that testimony be incorrect?"

"Now just a minute, Your Honor," Hamilton Burger said, "I object to that question as argumentative, as not proper cross-examination, as assuming facts not in evidence."

"It's argumentative," Judge Moran said. "The objection is sustained."

"Were you in there dozens of times?" Mason asked.

The witness, plainly rattled, shifted his position on the witness stand, cleared his throat, reached for a handkerchief, blew his nose.

"Any time you've finished with your stalling," Mason said, "just answer the question."

"I...it depends on what you mean by dozens of times."

"In what way?" Mason asked.

"How many dozens?"

"I'll leave it to you," Mason said. "How many dozens of times have you been in there on matters that were not official?"

"I...I can't remember."

"Five dozen times?"

"Oh, I don't think so."

"Four dozen times?"

"Hardly."

"Three dozen times?"

"Well...perhaps."

"Then what did you mean by telling us that you wouldn't have been in there except on an official matter?"

The witness hesitated for a moment, then with his face suddenly lighting in a triumphant leer, he said, "I mean on the day in question, Mr. Mason. Your question related to a conversation on the fifteenth day of August of this year, and I told you I wouldn't have been in there at that time except on an official matter."

"You mean on that day?"

"Yes, sir."

"And what was there about that day that was different from the three dozen odd times that you had been in there when it wasn't on official business?"

"Well, I...I didn't say it was three dozen."

"I thought you did."

"I said it might have been three dozen."

"All right," Mason said. "What was different about this fifteenth day of August of this year? Was there anything different?"

"Well...there had been events which made the day unusual."

"Now how long had you been in that apartment at the time of the conversation?" Mason asked.

"For a...well, there again I...I can't remember."

"You didn't enter *after* Hepner entered?" Mason said.

"No, sir."

"Then you must have been in there *before* Hepner entered?"

"Yes, sir."

"Did you see Douglas Hepner in there?"

"I...I heard him."

"That's what I thought," Mason said. "Let's be frank about this now."

Mason reached over to the counsel table, grabbed up a sheaf of documents, turned the pages rapidly as though looking for some statement that he had, then, apparently finding it, marched forward to confront the witness and said, "You were hidden in that apartment listening to what Douglas Hepner said, weren't you?"

The witness twisted and turned uncomfortably.

Mason glanced at the paper as though reading, then looked back at the witness and said, "Now you're under oath. Let's have it straight. Were you concealed in that apartment, listening, or not?"

"Yes, sir. I was."

"That's better," Mason said, folding the papers and tossing them back on the counsel table with a dramatic gesture. "Now why were you in there listening?"

"Because I felt that matters had reached a point where...where I should know what was going on."

"Between Miss Granger and Douglas Hepner?"

"Well, I wanted to know what was going on. I wanted to know what all the facts actually were. I wanted to know what the defendant was doing up there and how far..."

Suzanne Granger jumped to her feet, her face flaming with indignation, and shouted, "This man is lying. He wasn't in my apartment. He..."

"Just a moment, just a moment," Hamilton Burger exclaimed angrily, turning to face Suzanne Granger.

"Be seated, Miss Granger," Judge Moran said not unkindly. "We can't tolerate a disturbance in the court. The witness is testifying."

"He's testifying to falsehoods, Your Honor."

Judge Moran said, more sternly this time, "There is no occasion for you to comment on the testimony of the witness. If you have anything to say concerning it you can talk to the district attorney or, for that matter, you're at liberty to talk to counsel for the defense, but we can't have proceedings interrupted in this manner. If you can't control yourself I will have to eject you. Now do you understand?"

"I understand, but I don't feel called upon to sit here and listen to statements that reflect upon my good name. The witness told *me* he was in an adjoining apartment. That was my testimony this morning and..."

"You won't engage in an argument with the Court in front of the jury," Judge Moran ruled. "Now, Miss Granger, sit down."

She seated herself.

"Now remain quiet," Judge Moran said. "If you want to communicate with counsel for either side you may do so during the recess. We will have no more interruptions."

Judge Moran turned to Perry Mason. "Go on with your cross-examination, Mr. Mason."

"Is it possible," Mason asked, "that you were in Miss Granger's apartment without her knowledge?"

"I...I..."

"Just a moment," Hamilton Burger said, lunging to his feet. "This witness can't testify to what Miss Granger knows or what she didn't know. That question calls for a conclusion of the witness."

"Sustained," Judge Moran said, smiling slightly.

"Is it possible," Mason said, "that *you* took precautions to see that Miss Granger *didn't* know that you were in her apartment?"

"I...I...I can hardly say."

"You mean you can't remember, or that it's difficult for you to say?"

"Well, I...of course I can't say as to what she knew."

"How did you get in that apartment?"

"I used a master key."

"Was Miss Granger in the apartment when you entered?"

"No, sir."

"Miss Granger came in later?"

"Yes, sir."

"Was Mr. Hepner in there when you entered?"

"No, sir."

"Mr. Hepner came in later?"

"Yes, sir."

"Did you go there to meet Miss Granger?"

"No, sir."

"Did you go at Miss Granger's request?"

"No, sir."

"Why did you go there?"

"I went there to...to make an investigation."

"An investigation of what?"

"Miss Granger had reported that there had been acts of sabotage committed in her apartment."

"What sort of sabotage?" Mason asked.

"Objected to as incompetent, irrelevant and immaterial, and not proper cross-examination," Hamilton Burger said.

"Overruled," Judge Moran snapped. "I'm going to give counsel latitude to find out the true situation here. It's been brought in on direct evidence and I think counsel is entitled to clarify it fully on cross-examination. Answer the question."

"Well, Miss Granger reported that while she was away on a week-end trip someone had broken into the apartment and had...well, had clipped the ends off the tubes of her oil paints and then had squeezed all of the oil paints out on the..."

"Oh, if the Court please," Hamilton Burger said, "that is very plainly hearsay. I submit that any statement as to what had happened made by Miss Granger to this witness and not under oath is hearsay and that this is not proper cross-examination."

Judge Moran hesitated. "I think we are trying to determine what was said in a conversation," he said, "not to establish a fact by evidence of that conversation. However...I will ask the witness a few questions."

Judge Moran swung around so as to look at Richey's profile. "Look up here, Mr. Richey."

Richey reluctantly raised his eyes to meet those of the magistrate.

"Did you personally go up to the apartment to inspect this act of sabotage?"

"Yes, sir."

"Did you personally see the paints from these tubes of oil paint spread around the apartment?"

"Yes, sir. They were spread all over the bathtub and the washbowl and...it was quite a mess."

"How many tubes of paint?" Judge Moran asked.

"Heavens, I don't know. There must have been...well, there were dozens of them. It was a terrible mess."

"Who cleaned up the apartment?"

"The janitor."

"Was this reported to the police?"

"I don't believe so."

"Why?"

Hamilton Burger said, "Just a moment, Your Honor. I'm trying to protect the record here so that we don't drag in a lot of extraneous matters and get lost in a maze of confusing side issues. After all, it seems to me that it has no bearing on the case which we are now trying as to whether an act of sabotage was committed in the apartment of the witness, Suzanne Granger, or not.

"I don't wish to be placed in the embarrassing position of objecting to the Court's question, but I do wish to point out to the Court that there is a limit of pertinency and relevancy."

"Yes, I suppose so," Judge Moran ruled, somewhat reluctantly. "I guess perhaps we *are* getting this inquiry rather far afield, but it is impossible not to believe that there is some connection...however, I won't comment on the evidence. I think perhaps that it is better if the Court withdraws that last question."

"On the other hand, Your Honor," Mason said, "I feel that the defense should be permitted to explore this matter. I feel that there is a very definite connection between what happened in the apartment of Miss Granger and what was happening in the apartment of Ethel Belan, and, since the prosecution has been permitted to show what happened in Ethel Belan's apartment, it seems to me that the defense should be permitted to explore the unusual and bizarre circumstances which it is now apparent were taking place in the apartment of Suzanne Granger."

Suzanne Granger started to get to her feet.

"Just a moment," Judge Moran snapped. "Now Miss Granger, be seated and remain seated. Don't open your mouth. Don't address the Court. Don't say a word. You either remain in that seat and keep silent or I'll have a bailiff eject you. Do you understand that?"

She subsided in tight-lipped indignation.

"Very well," Judge Moran said. "Now let's try and get this situation straightened out. I think under the circumstances the Court will refrain from asking further questions. Mr. Mason, you were cross-examining the witness. You ask your questions. The district attorney can object to those questions and the Court will rule on the objections."

Hamilton Burger, badly flustered, glanced at the clock and the confused witness, and realized that his carefully planned schedule of procedure was going awry.

"Your Honor," he said, "I feel that the Court can rule at this time as to this entire matter, that questions concerning it are improper and..."

"I don't," Judge Moran snapped. "Go ahead with your examination, Mr. Mason."

Mason said to the witness, "Now let's get this straight. You went to the apartment of Suzanne Granger. You let yourself in with your passkey. Was that in an official capacity?"

"I considered it so. Yes."

"You wanted to make certain inspections?"

"Yes."

"And this was on the fifteenth?"

"Yes."

"That was Sunday?"

"Yes."

"There had previously been an act of sabotage reported in the apartment, an act of vandalism?"

"Yes."

"At what time was this reported?"

"At about one o'clock in the afternoon."

"Of that same day?"

"Yes."

"That act was reported to you?"

"Yes."

"By whom?"

"By Miss Granger."

"And what had she said?"

"She said that she had been on a week-end trip in Las Vegas and..."

"Did she say with whom she had made that trip?"

"I object. Incompetent, irrelevant, immaterial, not proper cross-examination," Hamilton Burger shouted.

"Sustained," Judge Moran said. "I think this entire conversation may be improper."

"Then I object to it."

"The objection is sustained."

"You went to Miss Granger's apartment on the fifteenth?"

"Yes, sir."

"You let yourself in with a passkey?"

"Yes, sir."

"Was that the first time you had gone to that apartment that day?"

"No, sir."

"When had you been there earlier?"

"When Miss Granger took me up to the apartment to show me what had happened during her absence."

"That was when you saw the tubes of paint cut open and the paint smeared on the bathtub?"

"Yes, sir."

"Now can you describe generally the condition of the apartment at that time?"

"Oh, Your Honor," Hamilton Burger said, "this thing is getting all out of hand. We have a murder case. The People are about ready to rest their case. It's a clean-cut case. In fact, I may say it's a dead open-and-shut case. Now we've gone far afield with acts of vandalism that..."

"However, in view of the fact that this witness was called to the stand to corroborate a conversation taking place between Miss Granger and the defendant on that day," Judge Moran said, "I think counsel is entitled to explore the rather unusual fact that this witness was apparently by his own admission concealed in the Granger apartment without the knowledge of the tenant."

"I think the Court shouldn't comment on the evidence," Hamilton Burger said.

"I'm not commenting on it," Judge Moran said. "I'm simply telling you what the witness testified to. Your objection is overruled. Go on with your examination, Mr. Mason."

"Answer the question," Mason said. "Describe the condition of the apartment."

"Well, it was a wreck."

"What do you mean by that?"

"A search had been made."

"What sort of a search?"

"A very thorough search. Things had been dumped from the drawers and..."

"I object," Hamilton Burger said. "The witness isn't entitled to state that a search had been made. That's a conclusion."

"It's too late for an objection now," Judge Moran ruled, his manner plainly showing his interest in this entire line of testimony. "The witness has answered the question. Now go ahead. Let's get this situation clarified if we can."

"You were called in there by Suzanne Granger as the official representative of the apartment house?"

"Yes, sir."

"And you ordered it cleaned up."

"Yes, sir."

"Did you summon the police?"

"No, sir."

"Did Miss Granger summon the police?"

"Objected to as calling for a conclusion of the witness," Hamilton Burger said.

"Sustained."

"Did Miss Granger say anything to you about not calling the police?"

"Same objection."

"Overruled."

"Yes, sir, she did."

"What did she say?"

"I asked her if we should call the police and she said no, that she knew who was responsible for the damage and that she didn't care to have the police called."

"So then you summoned the janitor?"

"Yes, sir."

"And ordered the janitor to clean up the mess?"

"That is, to clean up the bathtubs and the washbowl. It was something of a job. He had to use turpentine and then, of course, the maids came in and cleaned off the turpentine, the washbowl and the bathtub."

"Then you left?"

"I had left before the maids came in."

"And then after the maids and the janitor left, and while Miss Granger was out, you sneaked back to the apartment?"

"I went back to the apartment."

"Miss Granger was not there?"

"I have told you several times she wasn't there."

"You knew she wasn't there?"

"Well, I...I had seen her go out."

"And when you went back there what did you do?"

"I started looking around."

"Checking the damage?"

"Yes, sir."

"But the damage had all been cleaned up by that time, hadn't it?"

"Well, I guess it had."

"Then why did you go there?"

"To see that the damage had been cleaned up."

"And then Miss Granger returned?"

"Yes, sir."

"Did you let her know that you were in the apartment?"

"No, sir, I didn't."

"What did you do?"

"When I heard her returning I slipped into a closet."

"And remained there?"

"Yes, sir."

"And what did Miss Granger do?"

"She was in something of a hurry. She hurriedly disrobed and took a shower. Then she stood in front of a dressing table..."

"*Stood* in front of a dressing table?"

"Yes, sir."

"Then you must have been watching?"

"I had opened the door of the closet a crack."

"So you could see?"

"Yes."

"Why did you do that?"

"I had been trapped in there and I wanted an opportunity to escape."

"So you were watching Miss Granger standing there in front of the dressing table so that you could find an opportunity to escape?"

"Yes."

"How was she clothed?"

"She was just out of the shower."

"You mean she was in the nude?"

"I...I believe so, sir."

"What do you mean, you believe so? You were watching, weren't you?"

"Well, yes."

"Was she clothed?"

"No."

"And you were watching simply in order to find a favorable opportunity to make your escape?"

"Yes, sir."

"Well, why didn't you make your escape while she was in the shower?"

"I...I was confused at the time."

"Yes, so it would seem," Mason commented dryly.

"It was an embarrassing situation."

"And you become confused when you're embarrassed?"

"Quite naturally, yes."

"And you're embarrassed now?"

"In a way."

"Then are you confused?"

"That doesn't follow. I'm telling the truth."

"That," Mason said, "is all."

Hamilton Burger heaved a very audible sigh of relief.

"That's all, Mr. Richey. You may leave the stand. That, Your Honor, is the People's case."

"Just a moment," Mason said. "I desire to ask some additional questions on cross-examination of some of the People's witnesses."

"I object," Hamilton Burger said. "The defense had every opportunity to cross-examine every witness."

"But," Mason said, "the district attorney was given an opportunity to put the witness Richey back on the stand for the second time after previously calling the witness and not asking him about this conversation."

"That's because the prosecution was taken by surprise, Your Honor," Hamilton Burger said.

"And so was the defense," Mason said. "I feel that under the circumstances I'm entitled to ask some more questions of Miss Granger on cross-examination. I also have some further questions to ask of Dr. Oberon."

Hamilton Burger, fighting desperately to keep control of the situation, said, "The prosecution has no objection to further questions on cross-examination of Dr. Oberon, but the prosecution definitely objects to any cross-examination of Miss Granger at this time."

"Well," Judge Moran said, "if you have no objection to further cross-examination of Dr. Oberon, let's let him resume the stand and then the Court will reserve its ruling on the matter of further cross-examination of Miss Granger."

"It will take a few minutes to get Dr. Oberon here," Hamilton Burger said.

"Very well, the Court will take a five-minute recess," Judge Moran said.

The judge had hardly left the bench when Suzanne Granger, bristling defiance, came striding down the aisle.

Hamilton Burger rushed toward her.

"Now, Miss Granger," he said, "just a moment. Let's be reasonable, please."

Mason raised his voice. "Did you wish to talk with me, Miss Granger?"

She hesitated, looking at Perry Mason, then at Hamilton Burger.

"No, no," Burger protested. "You're the People's witness. Now we'll give you every opportunity to get the facts straight, Miss Granger. Just be calm, please."

Mason moved down the aisle. "If Hamilton Burger is going to put you on the stand so you can tell the true story of what happened I won't have to do it, Miss Granger, but otherwise if you want to protect your reputation I'll be only too glad to..."

An officer interposed himself between Mason and the witness.

Hamilton Burger swung Suzanne Granger away from Mason and toward the witness room. Another officer helped block Mason's way.

Mason turned to Paul Drake and winked. He walked dejectedly back to the counsel table where a policewoman was keeping the defendant in custody.

He leaned over and whispered in Eleanor's ear, "What's this all about? Why was Richey in that apartment?"

"I don't know. I think he's in love with her," she whispered.

Mason grinned. "You think then that he was jealous of Douglas Hepner?"

"Doug," she said with dignity, "was not making love to Suzanne Granger. He was simply trying to get information. He was dating her and taking her out, but that's all."

"That's what you think," Mason said.

"That's what Doug told me and Doug wouldn't lie—not to me."

Mason returned once more to where Paul Drake was standing.

"Paul," he said, "cover the door of the witness room where Burger took Suzanne Granger. I want to see if the conversation is friendly. I want to get the expression on her face when she comes out."

"I'll see what I can do," Drake said, "but I can't get near the door. They've got a bunch of gorillas covering the district attorney and he isn't in the happiest of moods this afternoon."

"I know, but get out in the corridor if you have to. Look around. See what happens when she comes out. See whether they are smiling and friendly, or how they act."

Drake nodded and left the courtroom.

A few minutes later Dr. Oberon, carrying a brief case, came hurrying into the courtroom. The bailiff called for the jury and Judge Moran returned to the bench.

"Where's the prosecutor?" Judge Moran asked.

One of the deputy district attorneys looked toward the door of the witness room. His manner was somewhat harassed, somewhat anxious.

"The district attorney," he said, "has been detained momentarily but as I understand it this is a situation where counsel for the defense desires to ask additional questions on cross-examination of Dr. Oberon. In the absence of the district attorney my associate and I will represent the prosecution."

"Very well," Judge Moran said. "I take it there is no objection to this further cross-examination of Dr. Oberon."

"None whatever," the deputy said with smug virtue. "If there is any fact in the case that Dr. Oberon has testified to which the defense wishes cleared up we will be only too glad to co-operate to the extent of our ability."

"Thank you," Mason said affably. "That attitude is appreciated and I trust you will be equally broad-minded in regard to clearing up any situation with Miss Granger."

The deputy district attorney, suddenly taken aback, blurted, "Well, I don't know about that...you'll have to ask the chief...that question is in Mr. Burger's province."

Judge Moran smiled slightly. "We'll cross the bridge when we come to it, Mr. Mason. You may now proceed with further cross-examination of Dr. Oberon."

Mason faced Dr. Oberon.

"Doctor, as I understand it, you have stated that the cause of death was a .38 caliber bullet which lodged in the brain?"

"That is correct. Yes, sir."

"Did you examine the body to determine if there was any contributing cause of death?"

"What do you mean?"

"I direct your attention to a photograph which was taken at the time of the autopsy. It shows the right arm of the decedent, and I call your attention to two little spots on that right arm."

"Yes, sir."

"Why was that photograph taken?"

"Because of the spots."

"You directed that that photograph be taken?"

"Yes, sir."

"And why?"

"Well, the spots were...I thought we should have the photograph. I believe that every evidence of any abnormality should be photographed in an autopsy, particularly in cases of homicide."

"And what was abnormal about these blemishes?"

"Well, they are some sort of puncture."

"In other words, Doctor, you thought they might have been made by a hypodermic needle, didn't you?"

"Well, there was always that possibility."

"And why didn't you mention that in your direct testimony, Doctor?"

"Well, I wasn't asked about it, either on direct or cross-examination."

"But why didn't you mention it?"

"I didn't feel called upon to mention it unless I was asked."

"But you considered it highly significant?"

"I considered it significant."

"How significant?"

"I took a picture of the arm, that is, I asked to have a picture taken of the punctures."

"That are in the right arm?"

"Yes, sir."

"A right-handed man administering a hypodermic would be inclined to puncture the left arm, would he not?"

"Either the left arm or the left leg."

"You thought these were the marks of a hypodermic?"

"They could have been."

Burger came tiptoeing into the courtroom and took his seat at the counsel table between the two deputies. His face was flushed and angry.

"And did you test the body for morphia?" Mason asked, when the district attorney had settled himself.

"No."

"Did you test it for any drugs?"

"No. I determined the cause of death."

"Was there anything in the evidence that made you feel that at the time the bullet was fired the decedent might have been under the influence of drugs?"

"Objected to as incompetent, irrelevant and immaterial, not proper cross-examination," Hamilton Burger said.

"Overruled," Judge Moran snapped, his eyes on the doctor.

"Well...I...no, I can't say that."

"The body was subsequently embalmed?"

"I believe so, yes."

"And buried?"

"Yes."

"Doctor, would embalming destroy the evidence of poison?"

"Of some poisons, very definitely. Cyanide of potassium would be completely neutralized by the embalming."

"What about morphia?"

"Morphine is an alkaloid. It would be possible to get evidence in the system for a period of...well, several weeks."

"If the body should be exhumed at the present time and there was morphine present, could that be determined?"

"Let's see, when was the murder?...I think there might be a good chance, yes."

Mason turned to the Court. "Your Honor," he said, "I ask that this body be exhumed. I believe that at the time of death Douglas Hepner was under the influence of morphine which had been given to him by persons who had taken him a prisoner."

"You have some grounds for this assertion?" Judge Moran asked.

"Many grounds," Mason said. "Look at the contents of the man's pockets. Whatever money he had in the form of currency had been taken. All of the pages of a notebook on which there was any writing had been removed and a new filler placed in the cover. The man had cigarettes in a silver case but there were no matches and no lighter. In other words nothing with which he could set a fire. He had no knife. I believe that Douglas Hepner was held a captive before his death."

"Now just a minute, just a minute," Hamilton Burger said angrily, getting to his feet. "Here's another grandstand play unsupported by evidence, a mere statement of counsel that is injected for the purpose of drawing a red herring across the trail of murder. These are things that can't be proven."

"They certainly can't be proven if we bury the evidence," Mason said.

"Of course," Judge Moran pointed out, "even if it should appear that the decedent had been given injections of morphine, that wouldn't establish the point you are trying to make."

"It would fit in with evidence which I hope to produce to establish that point," Mason said.

"An order of exhumation should only be made under most extraordinary circumstances," Judge Moran said. He turned to Dr. Oberon. "Doctor, you noticed these punctures of the skin?"

"Yes, sir."

"And what made you think they were hypodermic punctures?"

"The appearance of the arm and the punctures. I thought they might well have been made by a hypodermic which had been administered... well, rather shortly before death."

"Then why didn't you try to determine what drug had been administered?"

"I... I was instructed not to."

"By whom?"

"I rang up the district attorney and told him what I had found. He asked me what was the cause of death and I told him it was a .38 caliber bullet which had been fired into the back of the head. He said, 'All right, you've got your cause of death. What more do you want?' and hung up."

There was a moment of silence.

"I was merely trying to keep from confusing the issues," Hamilton Burger said, "because I know only too well how easy it is for a shrewd defense attorney to pick up some piece of purely extraneous evidence and torture it into..."

"Nevertheless," Judge Moran interrupted, "under the circumstances the autopsy surgeon should have followed up that lead. Let me ask you a few more questions, Doctor. Were there any marks indicating that this man customarily used drugs? In other words, were there any old puncture marks or . . .?"

"No, sir, there were not. I looked the body over very carefully. With the confirmed addict we usually find quite a few such puncture marks and frequently there is a species of tattooing. The hypodermic needle will be disinfected by means of flame from a match. A certain amount of soot or carbon will be deposited on the needle and injected into the skin, leaving very definite tattoo marks. There were just these two marks in the right arm and there had been minor extravasation."

Judge Moran stroked his chin thoughtfully.

"I think perhaps the jury should be excused during this argument," Hamilton Burger said.

"The defense is entitled to... the Court is going to take an adjournment and give this matter further consideration. I dislike to adjourn at this hour in the afternoon but I'm going to continue this matter until ten o'clock tomorrow morning. It is quite apparent that the case has progressed up to this point with unusual rapidity. For certain reasons which I need not comment on now, counsel for the defense is placed in a position where he must rely on every Constitutional right which is given his client."

"I don't think the Court needs to comment on that," Hamilton Burger said acidly.

"I don't either," Judge Moran said. "I'm simply pointing out certain elemental matters. The Court feels it might be well to take a recess until tomorrow morning at ten o'clock unless there is an objection on the part of counsel. Is there any objection?"

"There is no such objection," Mason said. "The defense makes a motion for such continuance."

"The prosecution objects," Hamilton Burger said. "It is quite obvious that up to a point the defense let the case develop rapidly until it had seen the entire hand of the prosecution. It is equally evident that thereupon the defense started a whole series of stalling tactics. This whole question of asking to have a body exhumed because of a couple of pin pricks is absurd. There's no question what caused death. It was caused by a bullet fired from the defendant's gun after the defendant had threatened to kill the decedent."

Judge Moran listened patiently, then said, "The defense is entitled to know every factor in the case. Apparently what might have been a material factor was not investigated at the time of autopsy because the prosecution wished to keep the issues from being confused.

"What might confuse the issues in the mind of the prosecution might well be a very significant matter to the defense.... You're making a motion for a recess, Mr. Mason?"

"Yes, Your Honor."

"The motion is granted," Judge Moran snapped.

There was a considerable measure of excitement manifest in the demeanor of the few spectators who were watching the trial as Judge Moran left the bench.

The jurors, filing from the courtroom, glanced at the defendant, and now there was more curiosity, a certain measure of sympathetic interest in their glances.

Hamilton Burger, cramming papers down into his brief case with an unnecessary vigor that indicated suppressed anger, spoke briefly to his assistants, and strode from the room.

Della Street came up to grasp Mason's arm.

"You've got them guessing, Chief," she said.

Mason nodded.

A policewoman touched Eleanor on the shoulder, escorted her from the courtroom. Paul Drake came forward.

"What happened?" Mason asked.

Drake shrugged his shoulders. "I couldn't get near the place but I managed to see Suzanne Granger when she came out. She went right to the elevators and left the building. She was white-faced, she was so mad. You can see what effect the interview had on Burger. He's looking for an opportunity to commit a murder himself. What do you suppose happened, Perry?"

"There's only one thing that could have happened," Mason said. "Somehow Suzanne Granger's story contradicts that of Richey. You say that Suzanne Granger went to the elevators?"

"That's right."

Mason grinned. "That means Burger told her to go home, not to stay around the courtroom. We'll serve her with a subpoena as a defense witness. He won't be expecting that. This adjournment took him by surprise."

"How did you find out about these puncture wounds?" Drake asked.

Mason grinned. "In checking over the pictures of the body at the autopsy, I noticed that there was an enlarged picture of the right forearm. It was a picture that had no business being in the collection according to the theory of the prosecution. There was no apparent reason for taking it.

"I couldn't imagine why on earth that picture had been taken. Then I realized that the autopsy surgeon must have directed the taking of this picture because he wanted to protect himself.

"At first I couldn't see what it was. There were, of course, these small spots, but they could have been blemishes on the photograph. Yet there undoubtedly had been something that caused the autopsy surgeon to direct that picture to be taken. So I took a chance. It was, of course, a last desperate chance. The minute I'm forced to put on my defense I'm licked. My only hope is to find some weakness in the prosecution's case."

"How much chance do you have of doing that?" Della Street asked.

Mason shook his head. "A darn slim chance," he admitted, "but it's the chance I'm taking."

CHAPTER FIFTEEN

Mason, who had for hours been pacing back and forth in his office, said to Della Street, "Della, there has to be an answer. There's something that doesn't fit. Somewhere in here there's a key clue that..."

Suddenly Mason broke off and snapped his fingers. "I've got it! It was right under my nose all the time. I should have had it sooner. I muffed it."

"Muffed what?" Della Street asked.

"The keys."

"What about them?"

"Remember," Mason said, "that when we entered the Titterington Apartments I tried different keys until I found one that opened the front door?"

She nodded.

"And," Mason went on excitedly, "we went up to the apartment that Hepner had maintained under the name of Newberg. I tried *that* key on the door. It slipped into the lock all right but it didn't work the latch. I thought then I was on the wrong scent, but I tried the other keys just as a matter of routine and one of them opened the door."

"I don't see what that proves," she said.

"On that type of apartment," Mason said, "the front door has a lock that can be worked by any key to any apartment in the house. Hang it, Della, that other key is the thing we've been looking for."

"The key clue, eh?" Della Street asked with a wan smile.

"Damned if it isn't," Mason said. "Stick around, Della. Ride herd on the office. Keep in touch with Paul Drake. If you don't hear from me by nine-thirty, go on home."

She laughed. "Try and make me. I'm going to wait here now until...Chief, can't I go with you?"

He shook his head. "I need you to hold down the office and for all I know you may have to bail me out of jail."

Mason grabbed his hat and hurried out of the door.

Mason picked up his car and drove to the Titterington Apartments.

He rang the bell marked "Manager."

The same woman came to the door who had accompanied Sergeant Holcomb when Mason, Della Street and Paul Drake had been discovered in the apartment rented by Frank Ormsby Newberg.

Mason said, "I'm not sure if you remember me but..."

"Certainly I remember you, Mr. Mason."

"I want some information."

"I'm sorry, Mr. Mason, but as far as that Newberg apartment is concerned I can't..."

"Not about the Newberg apartment," Mason said. "I want to compare a key that I have with duplicate keys of the apartments."

"Why?"

"I can't tell you. I'm working on a lead."

She shook her head.

Mason took a twenty-dollar bill from his pocket and said, "I'm not going to *take* any of your keys. I simply want to *check* the keys of the different apartments."

"Why?"

"I'm trying to find out something about the way these keys are made."

"Well," she said, "I guess...no one told me you couldn't do that, although they warned me against you. They said you were pretty tricky."

Mason laughed. "The police always adopt a dim view of anyone trying to make an independent investigation. The police theory isn't *always* right."

She debated the matter with herself for a moment, then said, "I'd have to watch you, Mr. Mason, to see what you're doing."

"Certainly," Mason said.

She opened the door of a key cupboard and at the same time took the twenty-dollar bill which Mason extended toward her.

Mason took a key from his pocket, started comparing it with the other keys.

"Is this a key to an apartment here in the house?" she asked.

Mason said, "I'm trying to determine whether another key might open some apartment here."

"Well, it certainly wouldn't. These locks are the best."

Mason, hurrying through his comparison of the keys, suddenly found a key that was identical with the key he held in his hand.

He held the key only long enough to make sure they were the same, noted the number of 281, then replaced the apartment house key on its hook without giving any sign. He went on comparing his key with the others until at last he came to the end of the board.

Slowly he shook his head.

"I could have saved you twenty dollars and a trip down here, Mr. Mason. All you needed to have done was to have telephoned me and asked me if some other key would have fitted one of these apartments. We're very careful about them. We've had some trouble and..."

"Well, I just had to make sure," Mason said, ruefully.

"How are things coming with your case?" she asked.

"So-so."

The manager shook her head slowly from side to side. "I'm afraid that girl's guilty."

"Of course," Mason said, "the fact that Hepner had an apartment here under the name of Frank Ormsby Newberg introduces an element of mystery into the case. I'd like to find out something about it."

"So would I," she said.

"Did he have any friends here in the building?"

She shook her head.

"Do you have many vacancies?"

"Very, very few."

"Let's take a couple of them at random," Mason said. "For instance, here's apartment 380. How long has the tenant been in there?"

"Some five or six years."

"260?"

"About two years."

"281," Mason said.

"Well, that, of course, is exceptional."

"Why?"

"That girl came here because she had a relative who was very ill and she had to be here off and on. She moved here from Colorado some place. It was temporary. Her relative died a week ago and she's moving out for good."

"Oh, I believe I read of the case. She's a blonde?"

"No, a brunette. About twenty-seven. Rather quiet but with a very nice appearance, well-dressed, good figure. She impresses you."

Mason frowned. "I wonder if I've seen her. What's her name?"

"Sadie Payson."

"I don't believe I am familiar with the name," Mason said. "How about 201?"

"That's a man. He's been with us six or seven years."

"You evidently have a bunch of steady, reliable tenants."

"That's the kind of a place I try to run, Mr. Mason."

"How long have you been manager?"

"For ten years. I've made it a point to weed out my tenants carefully, to get those who are steady and dependable. It's a lot better to have rentals coming in regularly than to have trouble with collections and having people moving in and out."

"That, of course, is true. But I don't see how you can weed them out."

"Well, I flatter myself I'm a pretty good judge of character."

"What about this man that you knew as Newberg?"

"That's one of the reasons I was suspicious when I saw his picture in the paper. He didn't fit in somehow. He was like a phony diamond. It's nice-looking and it glitters and it sparkles, but you just have the feeling all the time that there's something wrong."

"And that's the way you felt about Newberg?"

"Yes—after he'd moved in and been here for a while. When I first met him I felt that he was just the type I wanted. He told me he was studying to be an engineer and that he'd be away on field trips quite a bit.

"Well, it wasn't long before I realized the man wasn't really *living* in the apartment. He was just using it for some reason or other. You can tell when an apartment's being lived in. There's a feel about the place.

"Of course, Mr. Newberg would come and stay a few days. He'd sleep there lots of times, but you couldn't feel right about him. He paid the rent right on the dot so there was no way I could question him or ask him to move."

"Women?" Mason asked.

"Definitely not. I watched him on that. Of course a man's apartment is his home and ordinarily I don't snoop, but in this case if he'd been at all promiscuous... well, good heavens, here I am rambling on, and I had orders not to talk to you or give you any information about Newberg."

"Nothing wrong with what you're telling me," Mason said. "I really should hire you to sit with me in court and help me pick jurors. I see that you can judge character quickly and accurately."

"Well, after you've seen enough of people you can spot the ones that aren't on the up-and-up—at least I know I can."

"Thanks a lot," Mason told her. "I'd like to visit with you and talk about people, but since the police told you not to talk to me I'll be on my way."

He went out, walked twice around the block, came back ten minutes later and pressed the button opposite the name of Sadie M. Payson.

There was no answer.

Mason opened the front door with his key and went up to the second floor. He walked down to 281, rang the doorbell, and, when he received no answer, inserted the key in the lock, twisted it and found that the lock worked back smoothly.

The lawyer withdrew the key, stood in front of the door, hesitating.

Abruptly a woman's voice on the other side of the door said, "Who's there?"

Mason said, "I'm the new tenant."

"The new tenant! What in the world are you talking about? I'm not out yet."

"I'm the new tenant," Mason said. "I have the key. I'm sorry if I'm disturbing you but..."

The door was flung open. An indignant brunette, pulling up a zipper on a housecoat, regarded him with flashing eyes. "Well, I certainly like that! And I certainly admire your crust! I'm not leaving until midnight. I haven't moved out and I haven't surrendered my key and the rent's paid until the first."

"I'm sorry," Mason said, "but it's imperative that I get some measurements of the apartment."

She stood there in the doorway, bristling with indignation. Behind her, Mason saw two suitcases, open on a bed, being packed. There was a traveling bag on a chair. She was evidently wearing only the housecoat and slippers. She said, "Why, if you'd have come walking in here you'd have caught me... undressed."

"But you didn't answer the door."

"Of course I didn't answer the door. I didn't want to be disturbed. I've just had a bath and I'm getting my things packed and then I'm going to the airport. The manager had no right renting you this apartment."

"I'm sorry," Mason said. "I understood you were leaving and I have to have measurements for some of the things I'm buying."

"I'm leaving at midnight. I haven't checked out, and the rent's paid."

"Well," Mason said, with his best smile, "I guess there's no harm done."

"No harm done because I threw on a housecoat when I heard your key in the lock! Haven't I seen you somewhere before? Your face..."

"Yes?" Mason asked as she broke off abruptly.

"You're Mason," she said, "Perry Mason! I've seen your face in the papers. That's why you looked familiar! You're the one who's defending that woman. You..."

She started to slam the door.

Mason pushed his way into the apartment.

The woman in the housecoat fell back toward the rear of the apartment.

Mason kicked the door shut.

"Get out," she said. "Get out or I'll..." Her voice trailed away into silence.

"Call the police?" Mason asked.

She whirled abruptly toward one of the suitcases, came up with a gun that glittered in her hand.

"I'll do something more effective than that, Mr. Mason."

"And *then* what will you tell the police?" Mason asked.

"I'll tell them I..."

She started groping for the zipper on the housecoat. "I'll tell them that you tried to attack me—and I'll make it stick."

Mason stepped forward. "Before you do anything like that," he said, "permit me to give you this document."

"What...what's that?"

"That," Mason said, "is a subpoena to appear in court tomorrow and testify on behalf of the defense in the case of the People of the State of California versus Eleanor Corbin alias Eleanor Hepner."

Her eyes showed dismay, then determination. Her hand found the zipper on the housecoat, jerked it half down. She ripped a jagged tear in the cloth. Mason, lunging forward, grabbed the hand that held the gun, pushed the arm back and up, twisted the gun from her grasp and put it in his pocket.

She flung herself at him and Mason threw her over onto the bed.

"Now," he said, "sit down and quit acting like a fool. I may be the best friend you have in the world."

"You," she exclaimed, "the best friend! I like *that*!"

"I may be the best friend you have in the world," Mason repeated. "Look at the spot you're in. You posed as Douglas Hepner's mother, living in Salt Lake. You worked with him on a racket that started out as a freelance detective business, getting twenty percent of smuggled gems, and developed into blackmail.

"Then Douglas Hepner is found dead with a bullet in the back of his head and you are on the point of taking a midnight plane out of the country."

"So what? What if I am? This is a free country. I can do as I damn please."

"Sure you can," Mason said, "and, by doing it, put a rope right around that pretty little neck of yours. If I were as unscrupulous as you seem to think I am, I'd like nothing better than to let you get on the plane and then drag you into the case and accuse you of the murder. That would save Eleanor from a first-degree murder rap."

"He was killed with her gun," the woman said.

"Sure he was," Mason said, "and she'd given him her gun as protection. Somebody had been jabbing him with a hypodermic needle and he was under the influence of morphia when he died. He was probably so groggy he only had a faint idea of what he was doing. Under those circumstances it would have been easy for anyone to have taken the gun from his pocket and shot him in the back of the head."

"You say he was under the influence of morphine?"

"I think he was. He'd been jabbed with a hypodermic."

"That," she said, "explains it."

"Explains what?"

"I don't have to tell you," she said. "I'm just getting things straight in my own mind."

"No," Mason told her, "you do have to tell me. I've served a subpoena on you.

You're either going to talk to me now in private or you're going to talk on the witness stand in public—with newspaper reporters making notes of everything you say."

"You can't bluff me."

"Somewhere," Mason said, "you have a family—a mother, a father, perhaps you've been married and separated and have a child. You don't want those people to get that picture of you. You..."

She blinked back tears. "Damn you," she said.

"I'm simply pointing things out to you," Mason said.

"You don't have to drag my family into it."

"You'd be the one who was dragging your family into it," the lawyer told her. "You and Doug Hepner were working a racket. I don't know how much of it was handled for the reward, how much of it was blackmail, but you had a system of signals. When Doug wanted someone blackmailed he'd make himself agreeable until he had them hooked for a week-end trip somewhere. Then he'd telephone you and give you the name and address. You'd show up and be Hepner's wife, sort of a complicated badger game. You'd threaten to name the woman as corespondent and..."

"No, no," she said, "it was nothing like that. I didn't sink that low."

"All right," Mason told her, "what was it?"

She struck a match and lit a cigarette with trembling hands. "I got teamed up with Doug when I went to Europe as a secretary for one of the Governmental agencies. I served a trick over there and came back. I thought I was smart. I smuggled in a little jewelry—not too much, just what I could afford. It got past the Customs all right but it didn't get past Hepner."

"How did he know about it?" Mason asked.

"I suppose I talked too much. I talked to another girl who had been with me over there. She was my closest friend, but she fell head over heels in love with Hepner on the boat, and babbled everything she knew.

"Well, one thing led to another and I became Doug's partner."

"Also his mistress?" Mason asked.

"What do you think?"

"Go ahead," Mason said.

"Doug was clever, unbelievably clever. He had a magnetic personality and he could insinuate his way into anyone's good graces. We worked a great racket. He'd travel back and forth to Europe. He'd get enough information lined up to keep going for quite a while in between trips."

"On smuggling?" Mason asked.

"The smuggling was the small end of it," she said. "The blackmail was the big end. Doug would get a line on gems that had been smuggled. He'd turn in enough to the Customs for his twenty-percent take to give himself a standing and an apparent occupation. The rest of the time it was blackmail."

"Who did the blackmail?"

"I did."

"Go on."

"I had an apartment in Salt Lake. Over the telephone I'd pose as Doug's mother. When he had someone ready to be picked he'd get them out on a week-end trip. Obviously I had to know just as soon as they got started. Well, Doug would telephone me, but he did it in such a way that he always put the girl on a spot. He'd call me as his mother. He'd introduce the girl over the telephone and would say something out of a clear sky that indicated he was intending to marry the girl.

"You know how that would make a girl feel. She was starting out on a week-end trip and then it would appear that the guy's intentions were honorable and he was thinking of marrying her...well, that was my cue. While Doug and the girl were away I'd take the first plane and get into the girl's apartment. I'd really go through it and, believe me, I know how to search. If there was anything in the apartment I found it. If it was valuable I appropriated it. The girl couldn't afford to make a complaint, but if it was run-of-the-mine stuff then I'd show up later on as a Customs agent. I'd state that I was very sorry but that we had traced the gems and that it was going to be necessary to swear out a warrant for arrest and things of that sort.

"Quite naturally the girl would turn to Doug for advice and he'd act as intermediary and finally suggest that I could be bought off. Well, you know what that meant. There wasn't any end to it."

"But what about Eleanor?" Mason asked. "Had she or her family been smuggling?"

"If they had, I didn't find anything when I searched their apartment."

"I don't get it. Doug seems to have been in love with Eleanor and was planning to marry her. And he has you search her apartment?"

"You don't get the sketch. Doug wasn't really in love with Eleanor and never had any intention of marrying her. But he was working on something big, something that was really terrific. He was on the trail of a regular professional smuggling ring. And he needed her help. He was just stringing her along."

"Did he know who was in it?"

"Certainly we knew who was in it."

"Who?"

"Suzanne Granger."

"Go on," Mason said. "Tell me the rest of it."

"Well, Doug needed somebody that he could use, someone who had a definite background. It was a deal that he couldn't use me on, or at least he *said* he couldn't."

"You doubted that?"

She said, "There had been many women in Doug Hepner's life. Eleanor was just another leaf on the tree, and when the leaves begin to fall you don't count each individual leaf. You simply rake them up in a pile and cart them away or burn them."

"You're bitter," Mason said.

"Of course I'm bitter."

"At Eleanor?"

"It wasn't her fault. Doug started playing her in the routine way, or at least that's what he made me think. He started out with her on a week end when her whole family was to be away, telephoned from Indio and..."

"And you went to search their place?"

"Yes. I had to watch my chance. I got in and searched the whole place. I drew a blank. I went back to Salt Lake. I didn't hear from Doug for a week. Then he got in touch with me. He said he had been working on a big deal.

"I don't think he'd really fallen for Eleanor. He was on something big and he was playing square on the financial end. He was going to give me my cut. At least I *think* he was."

"Go on," Mason said.

"Well, Doug said he could use Eleanor, that she could pose as a jealous neurotic. He thought that he could get her into the apartment next to Suzanne Granger."

"And then?"

"Then Doug made his usual play for Suzanne. He got her to go to Las Vegas with him over a week end. He telephoned me from Barstow. I was on a plane within an hour of the time he telephoned. I went through that girl's apartment and, believe me, I went through it. I thought, of course, she might be using her tubes of paint as a means of smuggling."

"What did you find?"

"Not a thing."

Mason said, "It came out in testimony today that Ethel Belan saw Eleanor with a whole bunch of gems—at least that's what she claimed."

She said, "I'm going to tell you something, Mr. Mason. No one else knows this. On the morning of the sixteenth Doug telephoned me. He was excited. He said, 'They almost got me last night, but I've got the thing licked. It was a different setup from what I thought it was and it was so clever it had me fooled for a while. You'd never have guessed their hiding place. But I've got the stones now and if I can ever get out of here without being killed we're going to be sitting pretty. This is a professional smuggling ring and your cut on this is going to run into big money.' "

"He was excited?"

"Yes."

"And he was evidently in the apartment house?"

"He must have been right in Suzanne Granger's apartment."

"And when was this?"

"About ten o'clock in the morning of the sixteenth."

"But you'd searched Suzanne Granger's apartment."

"I'd searched it Saturday and, believe me, I'd made a good job."

"How did you get in?"

She said, "I've developed a technique for that."

"And what about this apartment you're in now?"

"This is my hideout here. I posed as a woman who was nursing a sick relative who wasn't expected to live. I had a key to Doug's apartment and he had a key to mine. Of course I didn't dare use hotels."

"His apartment was searched," Mason said hastily.

"That's what bothers me—and it frightens me."

"You didn't search it?"

"Heavens no. If he'd had the gems he'd have come to my apartment with them the first thing. I waited here for him all day and that night. When I finally found out his apartment had been searched I dashed back to Salt Lake, packed up everything in the apartment and waited to see if he'd call me there."

"That's when your call came in. I thought you were one of the gang teamed up with Suzanne Granger, so I played it straight and told you just what Suzanne could have told you. Then I hung up, threw my suitcases into my car and got out of there."

"Didn't you think it was dangerous to come here?"

"At first. Then I realized no one knew of this place. The rent was paid for three months so I decided to stay on. There was always the chance I'd get some clue as to what Doug had done with those gems. If I could be on the spot and get them I'd be sitting pretty. Otherwise..." She broke off with a little shrug of her shoulders.

"Do you know who killed him?"

"Eleanor killed him. I think she found out when he got the gems...I don't *know*. All I *know* is that Doug had the gems before he was killed."

"And he was dealing with a professional smuggling ring?"

"Yes. One that operated on a big scale."

"And Eleanor wasn't in it?"

"Heavens no. Eleanor was helping him. She had set the stage for spying on Suzanne Granger."

"And you knew that Doug Hepner had coached her to take the part of a jealous mistress, a woman who had used that approach to get herself into Ethel Belan's apartment? You knew she had instructions to threaten to kill Doug Hepner to keep anyone else from having him?"

She hesitated. "If I say that will it help the girl?"

"It may result in her acquittal."

"And if I don't admit that it may mean she gets convicted?"

"Yes."

She paused, took a deep breath. "I don't know that she isn't guilty. I don't have to say a thing."

Mason said, "There'll be a terrific battle over whether I can get your testimony into the evidence. I think the judge will let it in. In any event, if you'll tell the truth, I'll try. The district attorney will claim it's hearsay, not part of the *res gestae* and too remote.

"However, before I can lay my plans I'll have to know where you stand and I'd have to know the facts."

"I'd have to take the witness stand?"

"Yes."

She shook her head. "I can't do it. You called the turn. I have a child—a daughter, eight years old. I don't want newspaper notoriety. I can't be cross-examined about my past."

Mason said, "You can't let Eleanor walk into the gas chamber for a crime she didn't commit."

She shook her head. "I'm not going to help you, Mr. Mason."

Mason's face was as granite.

"You're going to help me," he said. "You don't have any choice in the matter. That's why I served that subpoena on you."

She said bitterly, "You have lots of consideration for that Eleanor Corbin, who has a fortune back of her, but think of me. I'm leaving here with just what you see on the bed."

Mason said, "I'm sorry. The honest part of your business was one thing. The blackmail was something else. You're going to have to begin over."

"On what?" she asked bitterly. "On what's inside of this housecoat! That's the only asset I have in the world, except a bus ticket to New Mexico, thirty dollars in cash, and..."

"I thought you were taking a midnight plane," Mason said.

Her laugh was bitter. "My days of plane travel are over. I'm going by bus, but I didn't think I had to tell the apartment manager that."

"All right," Mason said, "now listen. I'm not making any promises but if we can get this case solved it *might* be that we could recover the gems that Doug Hepner told you about. It might be that we could break up that smuggling ring."

"And then you'd grab..."

"No," Mason told her, "that's what I'm trying to tell you. That would be your cut."

She studied him with thoughtful eyes. "You're dealing with a tough bunch," she said.

Mason said, "My secretary, Della Street, is going to come and get you. You're going to a place where you'll be safe. Tomorrow morning you're going on the witness stand. If we recover those gems you get the reward. Then you promise me that you're going to turn your back on blackmail and rackets and are going to be the kind of a mother that your child can be proud of."

She regarded him steadily for a moment, then got up and put her hand in his. "Is that *all* you want?" she asked.

"That's all I want," Mason told her.

CHAPTER SIXTEEN

Della Street was waiting for Mason when he entered the courtroom. She handed him a chamois skin bag containing the gems that had been taken from Eleanor's cold cream.

"Everything okay?" Mason asked.

"Okay, Chief," she said. "Sadie's waiting down in the car. One of Paul Drake's men is with her. When you want her, step to the window and flip your handkerchief. Drake's man will be watching. He'll bring her up."

Judge Moran took the bench and the bailiff pounded the court to order.

Judge Moran said, "The Court has decided that under the present circumstances there is no reason for ordering the exhumation of the body of the decedent. However, the Court wishes to state that it is the duty of the coroner's physician not only to determine the cause of death but to discover any contributing causes. Apparently there is no independent reason to believe that the puncture marks in the arm of the decedent were made by a hypodermic. So far we have merely a conjecture on the part of the autopsy surgeon. The present ruling of the court is that an exhumation will not be ordered. If there should be any new evidence indicating independently the presence of morphia, or that the decedent had been held a prisoner against his will, the Court will again consider the matter.

"Now as I understand it, counsel for the defense wished to ask additional questions on cross-examination of the witness Suzanne Granger."

"If the Court please," Hamilton Burger said, "we are prepared to resist such a request on the part of the defendant's counsel. We have some authorities..."

"What sort of authorities?" Judge Moran asked.

"Authorities indicating that in a criminal action the defendant cannot cross-examine piecemeal, that he must conclude his cross-examination of a witness before the witness is excused from the stand."

"You don't need to cite authorities to that point," Judge Moran said. "The Court is quite familiar with them. However, Mr. District Attorney, in your search of the law did you also find a series of authorities holding that the trial judge is completely in charge of the order of proof and the examination of witnesses and is obligated to exercise his authority in the interests of justice?"

"Well, of course, Your Honor," Hamilton Burger conceded, "that is a general rule. However, in this case..."

"In this case," Judge Moran said firmly, "you put the witness Richey on the stand. You didn't ask him about overhearing the conversation which Suzanne

Granger had with the defendant. That matter was brought out afterward. Thereupon you put on the witness Richey for the second time. The Court granted you permission to do that. The Court feels that defendant's request to interrogate Miss Granger in regard to the matters testified to by Richey is a reasonable request under the peculiar circumstances of this case—I repeat, Mr. District Attorney, *under the peculiar circumstances of this case.* The Court, therefore, orders Miss Granger to take the stand."

Suzanne Granger arose, started toward the witness stand and said, "I am very anxious, Your Honor, to take the witness stand. The district attorney refused to..."

"Never mind that," Judge Moran said. "You will take the witness stand. You have already been sworn. You are to be cross-examined by counsel for the defense. You will not volunteer any information. You will wait until questions are asked and then you will answer those questions, confining your answers to the subject matter called for by the question. In that way we will give the prosecution an opportunity to object to any improper questions."

Mason said, "You have heard Mr. Richey's testimony?"

"I did."

"You returned to your apartment on the fifteenth of August and found that it had been searched and that acts of vandalism had been committed?"

"Yes, sir."

"You complained to the management?"

"I spoke to Mr. Richey about it."

"And what happened?"

"He went to the apartment, surveyed the damage, ordered the janitor and the maids to clean up. He asked me if I wished to notify the police. I told him I did not."

"Why?"

"Because I was satisfied that it was the work of..."

"Now just a moment," Hamilton Burger said. "I object, Your Honor, that this is not proper cross-examination, that the question is incompetent, irrelevant and immaterial, that the reason the witness did not want to call the police is entirely outside the issues of this case, and that if she had in her own mind an idea as to what had happened or why it happened the prosecution is certainly not bound by some *thought* the witness may have. The witness can be examined as to *facts* and not as to *thoughts.*"

"I want to show bias and prejudice against the defendant in the case," Mason said.

"Very well, reframe your question," Judge Moran said. "The objection to the present question is sustained."

"Did you," Mason asked, "state to Mr. Richey that the vandalism was the work of Eleanor Hepner, or Eleanor Corbin as the case may be, who was spying on you in the adjoining apartment?"

"Same objection," Hamilton Burger said.

"Overruled," Judge Moran said. "Answer the question."

"I did."

"Was there any evidence, any fact, any proof that caused you to believe she had done this?"

"No evidence, no fact, no proof. It was my intuition if you want to call it that. Now I also want to state that..."

"Don't volunteer any information," Judge Moran said. "Wait until you are questioned."

She tightened her lips.

"Now then," Mason said, "later on you returned to your apartment?"

"I did."

"And Mr. Hepner called on you that evening?"

"Yes."

"Prior to the time Mr. Hepner called did you take a shower?"

"I took a tub bath."

"Was it possible for anyone to have been concealed in your closet?"

"Definitely it was not. I looked in the closet. I unpacked a suitcase. I took some clothes out of the suitcase and hung them in the closet. There was no one there."

"Thank you," Mason said, "that is all."

Hamilton Burger conferred in whispers with his associates, then said, "That is all."

"Very well, you may leave the stand," Judge Moran said, his manner showing that he was very puzzled.

"The prosecution rests. That's the People's case," Hamilton Burger said.

Perry Mason got to his feet. "Now, Your Honor," he said, "at this time the defense wishes to make an opening statement to the jury as to what it expects to prove."

"Very well," Judge Moran said.

The courtroom, which was now filled with spectators, broke into whispers and was quieted by the bailiff.

Perry Mason quietly stepped forward to stand in front of the jury.

"Ladies and gentlemen of the jury," he said, "we expect to produce evidence to show that Douglas Hepner was engaged in a very unusual occupation, that he made his living by means of collecting rewards as a free-lance detective.

"We expect to show that Douglas Hepner had been a gambler, that he had learned that the United States pays informers twenty percent of the value of merchandise smuggled into this country if an informer produces evidence resulting in the recovery and confiscation of the merchandise so smuggled.

"That was Douglas Hepner's occupation.

"Douglas Hepner knew the defendant—well. They had discussed marriage many times. But Eleanor Corbin wanted him to quit that business and he had promised to buy an interest in an importing business after their marriage and cease his so-called free-lance detecting.

"However, Douglas Hepner, at the time of his death, was working on one last case on which he wanted the defendant to help him. We propose to show that Douglas Hepner was on the trail of a ring of smugglers who were professional smugglers, who were making a profession of bringing gems into this country illegally.

"We propose to show that in order to break up this ring, thereby getting a last reward which he would use as a stake to buy his way into this importing business, Douglas Hepner enlisted the aid of the defendant Eleanor; that he deliberately cast her in the part of a jealous, neurotic mistress who was to secure a room in apartment 360 because Douglas Hepner thought Suzanne Granger was a part of the smuggling ring.

"Suzanne Granger was making frequent trips to Europe. She was doing a considerable amount of painting and she carried back and forth many tubes of paint, tubes which would make an ideal place of concealment for gems if she had been so minded."

Suzanne Granger jumped up, started to say something and was immediately silenced by a bailiff whom Judge Moran had placed at her side.

"Just a moment, Mr. Mason," Judge Moran said. He turned to the courtroom. "Miss Granger," he said, "you have repeatedly created a disturbance. The Court has placed a bailiff beside you. The Court intends to see that you conduct yourself in an orderly manner and do not interrupt proceedings of this court. Any further attempt at an interruption will be treated by the Court as a contempt. Do you understand?"

"Am I not going to be given an opportunity to...?"

"Not at this time, not in this manner and not at this place," Judge Moran said. "Remain seated and be quiet. Now, Mr. Mason, go on with your opening statement."

"We expect to show," Mason said, "that Douglas Hepner was mistaken about one thing, and that was the identity of the woman who acted as custodian of the smuggled gems and the location of the smuggled gems. We expect to show that the actual custody of the gems was in a place and was carried out in a manner far more ingenious and subtle.

"We expect to show that the defendant, Eleanor, carried out the instructions of Douglas Hepner; that she duly secured lodgings with Ethel Belan as has already been established by the evidence of witnesses.

"We expect to prove that at the last minute Douglas Hepner discovered the real secret of the smuggling ring; that Douglas Hepner had one other female accomplice, a woman who had been working with him for some period of time; that Douglas Hepner actually recovered a small fortune in gems and that he thereupon communicated with this woman and told her that his life was in danger.

"We expect to show that Douglas Hepner left the Belinda Apartments surreptitiously using the freight elevator, that he proceeded to a hideout apartment he maintained under a pseudonym; that he was followed by the conspirators who believed he had these gems in his possession. We expect to show that his enemies trapped Douglas Hepner in his apartment, doped him with a large injection of morphia, that he thereupon was held prisoner while a determined effort was made by the heads of the smuggling ring to recover the gems. That they not only searched him but ransacked his apartment; that he was held prisoner all day, and was given a second injection of morphine shortly before his death. That when they failed to recover the gems they killed Douglas Hepner under such circumstances that the crime would naturally be framed on the defendant Eleanor, hoping thereby to make it appear that any story she might tell would be a self-serving declaration subject to suspicion and regarded with skepticism by the district attorney."

Hamilton Burger, smiling scornfully, whispered to one of his assistants, then leaned back and shook with silent laughter.

"And," Perry Mason went on, "the proof of this is that Douglas Hepner *did* recover those gems and that the defense now has those gems in its possession and knows the identity of the smugglers."

Mason suddenly took a piece of chamois skin from his pocket, spread it on the counsel table, picked up the chamois bag Della Street had given him and poured a cascade of glittering gems onto the chamois skin.

Hamilton Burger jumped up. "What's this? What's this?" he asked, striding forward.

The jurors craned their necks.

"We expect," Mason went on, "to introduce these gems in evidence and..."

"Your Honor, Your Honor," Hamilton Burger shouted. "I object. Counsel can't produce his exhibits before the jury at this time. He can only tell the jury what he expects to prove."

"That's what I'm doing," Mason said. "I expect to prove to the jury that Douglas Hepner had recovered these gems."

"Those are the gems Ethel Belan described," Hamilton Burger said. "Those were in the possession of the defendant. The mere fact that the defendant produces them now..."

Judge Moran interrupted sternly. "Counsel for the prosecution can argue the prosecuter's case to the jury at the proper time. It will not be argued now."

"I object to this evidence being produced in front of the jury."

Mason said, "I am merely showing the jury what I expect to prove, Your Honor, and I may state at this time that Douglas Hepner had made one very simple mistake. Knowing that Webley Richey, one of the clerks in the apartment house, was a member of the smuggling ring, he naturally assumed that Suzanne Granger, with her frequent trips to Europe, was part of the ring. The true, diabolically clever scheme didn't occur to him at first. When it did occur to him he found the gems. He found them in a hiding place so ingeniously constructed that it was extremely difficult to detect. However, in entering that hiding place he set off a burglar alarm and when he did that he knew he was trapped. There had already been one attempt on his life and he knew that if he were caught leaving the apartment house with the gems in his possession it would be sure death.

"So he locked the door of the apartment. He telephoned his assistant to report what he had found, and he then concealed the gems in the one place where he thought he had any faint chance of keeping them secreted. He had to do all this in a matter of seconds.

"Then he unlocked the apartment door and stepped into the hall, expecting to be seized and searched, expecting to have to battle for his life.

"To his surprise no one was there. He was not molested. Knowing he didn't have the gems on him gave him a surge of confidence. He raced for the freight elevator and pressed the button.

"It seemed ages before the lumbering freight elevator came up and stopped. Everything seemed to be clear. He sneaked out the rear entrance of the apartment house and sought sanctuary in his hideout apartment. I do not think Douglas Hepner even knew he was being trailed, or once in his apartment he would not have responded to that knock on the door. Obviously he expected someone else, for he opened the door—and then Douglas Hepner knew he had gambled and lost. Hands grabbed him, arms held him, a hypodermic needle jabbed him."

"Oh, Your Honor," Hamilton Burger interrupted. "All of this is plainly improper. Counsel only has the right to outline the evidence he expects to put on. He is building up a suspense story here that sounds like a movie scenario. He can't *prove* this. He's talking about the thoughts and emotions of a dead man. He's outlining hearsay. He's rationalizing..."

"I think the objection is well taken," Judge Moran interposed. "Defense counsel has unquestioned oratorical ability. He is now telling a story, not reciting what he proposes to prove."

"But I do propose to prove it, Your Honor," Perry Mason protested. "I expect to put on witnesses who will establish the facts and these other matters are fair inferences to be drawn from those facts."

"Just *how* do you expect to prove these things?" Judge Moran asked.

Perry Mason said, "I have waiting downstairs a surprise witness who will prove these things. I need only to step to this window and wave my handkerchief and this witness will be on her way up."

Hamilton Burger, livid with anger, said, "Your Honor, I must object to this statement. There is perhaps no law that counsel should not be dramatic, but counsel must at least be truthful."

Mason stepped to the courtroom window, waved a handkerchief, said, "If I may have a moment's indulgence, Your Honor, I have given the signal which will bring my witness here."

Hamilton Burger said, "Your Honor, I also wish to object to any proof concerning any statement that Douglas Hepner may have made to any persons about his life being in danger or about having recovered any gems. Unless that was a dying declaration it would be hearsay, it would have no part in this case."

Mason turned to face the Court. "Your Honor, this *was* a dying declaration. That is why the morphia becomes important. Hepner specifically told this witness that he doubted if he could leave the apartment house alive. It was also a part of the *res gestae*."

Hamilton Burger, so angry he could hardly talk, said, "Your Honor, that is simply an attempt to put the cart before the horse and then try to show that there must have been a horse or the cart wouldn't have been there. Here we have drama deliberately concocted. Counsel seeks to capture the interest of the jury by going to the window and waving a handkerchief. Why all this cloak-and-dagger business?"

"Because," Mason said, "in the event this witness had been seen in the building she might have been killed before she could testify. I propose to show that Webley Richey and Ethel Belan were partners in a smuggling ring of enormous proportions and..."

"Ethel Belan!" Burger exclaimed.

"Exactly," Mason said. "Why did you think one of her closets was three and a half feet shorter than any other closet in the building?"

"Here we go again," Burger shouted. "Counsel makes an opening statement that sounds like a dime novel, then he starts smearing the prosecution's witnesses. Let him cease this talk and put on his proof if he has any."

"That's what I'm trying to do," Mason said, "and I notice my surprise witness has just entered the courtroom. Miss Payson, please come forward and be sworn."

Sadie Payson marched up to the witness stand, held up her hand and was sworn.

After the first preliminary questions and answers, Mason said, "You knew Douglas Hepner in his lifetime?"

"Yes."

"What was your relationship to him?"

"I was associated with him in business."

"What sort of a business?"

"Recovering smuggled gems."

"Do you know when Douglas Hepner died?"

"On the sixteenth of August."

"At what hour?"

"I know when the autopsy surgeon says he died."

"Some time before that had you had a conversation with Douglas Hepner?"

"I had."

"Did he tell you that he expected to die?"

"Now just a moment," Hamilton Burger said, "I object to that question as leading and suggestive. It also calls for hearsay evidence."

Mason said, "It is part of the *res gestae,* Your Honor, and it is a dying declaration."

Judge Moran said, "It would seem to require that more foundation be laid before it can be described as either. At the present stage of the evidence I am inclined to sustain the objection. However, I would like to have you lay as complete a foundation as possible before the Court is called upon to rule finally on the matter."

Mason turned to face the witness. He picked up a sheet of paper which he had dropped over the pile of gems in the chamois skin on the counsel table.

As he picked up the paper, Sadie Payson's eyes caught the glitter of the gems.

"Oh, you *did* find them!" she exclaimed. "You *did* find them! Those are the ones Doug telephoned about! He told me he had them. He told me they..."

"Order, order!" shouted the bailiff.

"The witness will be silent," Judge Moran thundered.

But there could be no mistaking the spontaneous nature of the exclamation Sadie Payson had given. No amount of rehearsal could have accounted for that joyful exclamation.

Judge Moran said, "Court is going to take a ten-minute recess. The Court would like to see counsel for both sides in chambers. Mr. Mason, I would suggest that those gems should not be left lying there on the counsel table. If you wish to mark them for identification you may deliver them to the clerk for safekeeping.

"Court will take a ten-minute recess."

CHAPTER SEVENTEEN

In the Judge's chambers, Hamilton Burger, shaking with rage, pointed his finger at Perry Mason.

"That was a cheap trick to get the witness to exhibit emotion in front of the jury! It was a deliberate attempt to get testimony before the jury which Perry Mason knew the Court should exclude. That paper had been carefully put over the gems and was deliberately removed. This whole presentation turns a court of law into a carnival side show!"

"That whole thing was perfectly proper," Mason said. "Douglas Hepner recovered those gems the day before his death. He was drugged and held a prisoner. They tried to find out what he had done with the gems. Actually what he had done with them was very simple. He had recovered the gems and he was going to try to leave the apartment house. He had tripped a burglar alarm when he found the hiding place of the gems. He knew that the chances of his escape were slim. Eleanor's overnight case was lying there on the dressing table. It was open. He stepped over to that overnight case, unscrewed the tops of several cream jars, forced gems down inside the jars, then hurried from the apartment house as though trying to make his escape."

"You're not grandstanding in front of a jury now," Hamilton Burger said. "I want to see some proof."

Mason glanced at his watch. "You will," he said, "within a few minutes. Fortunately the Customs officials are a lot more open-minded. They have secured a search warrant and are at the moment searching Ethel Belan's apartment. I am quite satisfied that they will find that her closet has been very skillfully subdivided so that the back part of it represents a place where smuggled goods can be deposited. If you'll notice this map, which was drawn to scale, you'll note that the closet in Ethel Belan's apartment is approximately three and a half feet shorter than the closet in the Granger apartment. Yet there is no structural reason why the closets shouldn't have been of the same length.

"And if you want to keep your face from being red in public, you'd better get Ethel Belan and Webley Richey into custody before this thing breaks wide open and before they've made good their escape. I deliberately made my opening statement in the way I did so they'd know the jig was up and try to escape. That would clinch the case against them and..."

Hamilton Burger bellowed, "I don't have to take advice from you. I don't have to..."

The telephone on Judge Moran's desk tinkled into noise.

"Just a moment, gentlemen," the somewhat bewildered jurist said, and picked up the telephone.

He said, "Hello," listened for a few moments, then said, "I'll call you back."

He hung up the telephone and turned to the district attorney. "It seems," he said, "that Mr. Mason left word with the Customs officials to telephone me as soon as the search warrant had been served. They found a concealed partition in the back of Ethel Belan's closet. There were no gems there but there is an estimated two hundred and fifty thousand dollars' worth of illegal narcotics.

"I think, Mr. District Attorney, that you might do well to reconsider the entire situation before going back into court."

Hamilton Burger's expression was that of a man whose entire world is collapsing around him.

Judge Moran turned to Perry Mason. "I feel you should be congratulated, Mr. Mason, on your apparent solution of this case, although I deplore the dramatic manner in which you presented the facts."

"I *had* to present them in that manner," Mason said, "otherwise Ethel Belan and Webley Richey wouldn't have tried to escape. As it was, when I produced those gems they felt certain I had them dead-to-rights.

"And don't congratulate me on being astute. I should have noticed the significance of one closet being three feet and a half shorter than the others, and should have appreciated the fact that there were only two apartments Webley Richey could have been in where he could have heard that conversation. He was trapped by having remonstrated with Suzanne Granger about it and counting on her not telling the district attorney about it.

"If he hadn't overheard that conversation while concealed in Suzanne Granger's apartment there was only one other place where he could have been concealed and overheard what was said and that was in Ethel Belan's apartment. But he couldn't have been concealed in there unless he had been in some sort of a specially constructed place of concealment because the defendant had entered the apartment shortly after he did and she didn't see him.

"Just because I have a client who is flighty, who became panic-stricken and resorted to falsehood, I almost failed to look at the evidence with a coldly analytical eye."

Judge Moran glanced at Perry Mason. There was grudging admiration in his eyes. "Some very clever reasoning, Counselor," he said, "but I still deplore your dramatic use of my courtroom."

The judge turned to Hamilton Burger. "I think, Mr. District Attorney, it's your move. The Court will give you another ten minutes to make it."

Hamilton Burger started to say something, changed his mind, heaved himself up out of the chair, turned, and without a word lunged from the judge's chambers. A moment later the door slammed.

Judge Moran looked at Perry Mason. A faint smile softened the jurist's face. "I deplore your procedure, Mason," he said, "but I'm damned if I don't admire the effectiveness of your technique."

THE CASE OF
THE TERRIFIED TYPIST

FOREWORD

It is so trite to say that truth is stranger than fiction that one dislikes to use the expression, yet there is absolutely no other way of describing the strange situation that took place in Texas, where within the framework of the law a principality was created that was completely foreign to all of our American traditions.

All of this started out innocently enough. A large section of Texas was peopled by Spanish-speaking citizens and an American acquired a position of leadership and started advising these people how to mark their ballots. Apparently he had their best interests at heart and received their virtually unanimous support.

The community became known as the Principality of Duval and the man who gave the instructions to the voters was known as the "Duke of Duval."

Later on this situation developed to a point where successors to the Duke of Duval used their power to establish what was in effect a principality within a state. That principality became steeped in hatreds and ruled by fear, and fear ruled with an iron hand.

The state seemed powerless. The whole machinery of government in Duval was in the hands of one person.

Then my friend the Honorable John Ben Shepperd became the attorney general of the State of Texas.

Shepperd went into Duval and started fighting.

It was a knockdown drag-out fight. The story of what happened is so lurid, so utterly inconceivable that it staggers the imagination.

John Ben Shepperd won that fight. It took courage, honesty, competence, resourcefulness and guts.

When I first knew John Ben Shepperd, he was the attorney general of Texas. I am honored that he made me an honorary special assistant attorney general of Texas, and my commission as such hangs in my office today.

Texans don't do things the way other people do. If a Texan likes you, he is for you a hundred per cent. If he doesn't like you, he may or may not be polite, but his formal politeness will be as frigid as a blizzard wind in the Texas Panhandle.

Texas is a big, raw, blustering state with a highly developed sense of the dramatic, a spirit of the Old West still rampant, and is peopled by citizens who think only in terms of the superlative. This causes many people to doubt the sincerity of the Texan. The trouble is some of these critics simply don't understand the Texan language and the Texan thought. When a Texan uses superlatives, he is completely sincere. He thinks in superlatives. He expresses himself in superlatives.

On one of my recent trips to Texas, I was the speaker at a noonday banquet. My big plate tried in vain to hold a Texas-size steak which overflowed it at the edges.

As soon as that banquet was over, the chief of police rushed me out to his automobile and with red light and screaming siren, we started for the airport.

At the airport my friend the late Jim West, one of Texas' rugged multimillionaires, had his plane waiting and as soon as he heard the siren screaming in the distance, he started warming up the motors. By the time the police car speeded onto the airport's runway and stopped within a few feet of the airplane, the motors were warmed up and ready for a take-off.

I was rushed up into the interior of the plane, the door slammed, the motors roared and the plane was in the air.

An hour and a half later, almost an hour of which had been spent in flying over Jim West's ranch, we came down at the ranch house. A servant put a gallon flagon in my hand. It was filled with cold, frothy beer. It was a hot summer day and I drank copiously of the beer. As fast as I lowered the flagon an inch or so, someone would reach over my shoulder with a couple more cans of ice-cold beer and keep it up to the brim.

Shortly afterward we had a "little old barbecue." I was given a steak that was so big it had to be served on a platter.

When we had finished that repast, Jim West announced that his nearest neighbor, who lived thirty-odd miles away, wanted to meet our group and we were transferred in specially made Jeeps to the ranch of Dolph Briscoe.

Briscoe greeted us with typical Texas hospitality. He invited us in for a "snack."

The snack consisted of—you guessed it. And Dolph Briscoe was properly apologetic.

"That steer," he said in his Texas drawl, "played me false. I tried to make him weigh a ton, but after he got up to nineteen hundred and sixty pounds he just wouldn't put on any more fat, and in order to have the meat properly aged for you folks when you got here, I had to kill him when he was just forty pounds short of a ton. I'm not going to lie to you folks, that there's a Texas steer but he's forty pounds short of a ton."

Now that's Texas. If you don't understand it, it seems weird and bizarre. If you understand it, you love it and you love the Texans, and your understanding has to be based on the fact that the underlying keynote of the Texan is sincerity. If he likes you, he wants to do everything he can for you.

There is the old story of the Texan who went out to lunch with his friend. After lunch the friend stopped in at a Cadillac agency to look over a new car he was thinking of buying.

When he finally made up his mind to buy the car, the Texan whipped out his checkbook. "Here," he said, "this one is on me. You paid for the lunch."

That story is probably an exaggeration, but it is nevertheless typical.

My friend John Ben Shepperd is a Texan. When he embarked upon a career of law enforcement as attorney general of Texas, he went all the way. Entirely at his own expense he published a newsletter roundup of crime and justice for the Lone Star State. He tried to see that all law enforcement officers knew what the law was.

As my friend the Honorable Park Street, a prominent trial attorney of San Antonio and for years an associate of mine on the Court of Last Resort, expressed it, "Many a criminal is caught in Texas by a cowboy-booted constable or sheriff whose standard equipment includes a .45 revolver and a blue-backed *Peace Officer's Handbook*, written by John Ben Shepperd."

"Crime," drawls John Ben Shepperd, "is not sluggish or unintelligent. It plays infinite variations on its own theme, developing new forms and methods. Like the hare and the tortoise, it outruns us unless we plod relentlessly along carrying the law forward on our backs."

From time to time, I made talks on law enforcement in Texas while John Ben Shepperd was the attorney general of the state.

From the time my group arrived at the borders of Texas, we would be met by assistant attorneys general, airplanes and prominent citizens. We would be whisked from place to place at breath-taking schedule, yet the whole itinerary would be carefully planned to the last detail: Planes would be waiting for us at dawn, would take off on schedule and arrive on schedule for breakfast appointments and conferences. Lunches would be at points several hundred miles distant and we would be back in Austin for dinner. The pace was relentless and terrific. Yet the assistants assured me that this was the tempo at which John Ben Shepperd conducted his office.

Heaven knows how many honors were conferred upon him. I do know that he was the deserving recipient of three honorary Doctor of Laws degrees, and I also know that one of the honors he valued at the top of the list was a simple plaque presented to him by United Mothers and Wives of Duval County. It says, "To John Ben Shepperd, who purchased with courage and Christian integrity the right of our children to grow up uncorrupted and unafraid."

And so I dedicate this book to my friend—

THE HONORABLE JOHN BEN SHEPPERD

—Erle Stanley Gardner

CHAPTER ONE

Perry Mason eyed the brief which Jackson, his law clerk, had submitted for his approval.

Della Street, sitting across the desk from the lawyer, correctly interpreted the expression on Mason's face.

"What was wrong with it?" she asked.

"Quite a few things," Mason said. "In the first place, I've had to shorten it from ninety-six pages to thirty-two."

"Good heavens," Della said. "Jackson told me he had already shortened it twice and he couldn't take out another word."

Mason grinned. "How are we fixed for typists, Della?"

"Stella is down with the flu and Annie is simply snowed under an avalanche of work."

"Then we'll have to get an outside typist," Mason told her. "This brief has to be ready for the printer tomorrow."

"All right. I'll call the agency and have a typist sent up right away," Della Street promised.

"In the meantime," Mason told her, "I'm going over this thing once again and see if I can't take out another four or five pages. Briefs shouldn't be written to impress the client. They should be concise, and above all, the writer should see that the Court has a clear grasp of the *facts* in the case before there is any argument about the *law*. The judges know the law. If they don't, they have clerks who can look it up."

Mason picked up a thick blue pencil, held it poised in his hand, and once more started reading through the sheaf of pages, which already showed signs of heavy editing. Della Street went to the outer office to telephone for a typist.

When she returned Mason looked up. "Get one?"

"The agency doesn't have one at the moment. That is, those they have are rather mediocre. I told them you wanted one who is fast, accurate and willing; that you didn't want to have to read this thing through again and find a lot of typographical errors."

Mason nodded, went on with his editing. "When can we expect one, Della?"

"They promised to have someone who would finish it by two-thirty tomorrow afternoon. But they said it might be a while before they could locate just the girl they wanted. I told them there were thirty-two pages."

"Twenty-nine and a half," Mason corrected, smilingly. "I've just cut out another two and a half pages."

Mason was just finishing his final editing half an hour later when Gertie, the office receptionist, opened the door and said, "The typist is here, Mr. Mason."

Mason nodded and stretched back in his chair. Della started to pick up the brief, but hesitated as Gertie came in and carefully closed the door behind her.

"What's the trouble, Gertie?"

"What did you say to frighten her, Mr. Mason?"

Mason glanced at Della Street.

"Heavens," Della said, "I didn't talk with *her* at all. We just rang up Miss Mosher at the agency."

"Well," Gertie said, lowering her voice, "this girl's scared to death."

Mason flashed a quick smile at Della Street. Gertie's tendency to romanticize and dramatize every situation was so well known that it was something of an office joke.

"What did *you* do to frighten her, Gertie?"

"*Me!* What did *I* do? Nothing! I was answering a call at the switchboard. When I turned around, this girl was standing there by the reception desk. I hadn't heard her come in. She tried to say something, but she could hardly talk. She just stood there. I didn't think so much of it at the time, but afterward, when I got to thinking it over, I realized that she was sort of holding on to the desk. I'll bet her knees were weak and she—"

"Never mind what you thought," Mason interrupted, puzzled. "Let's find out what happened, Gertie. What did you tell her?"

"I just said, 'I guess you're the new typist,' and she nodded. I said, 'Well, you sit over at that desk and I'll get the work for you.'"

"And what did she do?"

"She went over to the chair and sat down at the desk."

Mason said, "All right, Gertie. Thanks for telling us."

"She's absolutely terrified," Gertie insisted.

"Well, that's fine," Mason said. "Some girls are that way when they're starting on a new job. As I remember, Gertie, *you* had *your* troubles when you first came here, didn't you?"

"Troubles!" Gertie exclaimed. "Mr. Mason, after I got in the office and realized I'd forgotten to take the gum out of my mouth, I was just absolutely gone. I turned to jelly. I didn't know what to do. I—"

"Well, get back to the board," Mason told her. "I think I can hear it buzzing from here."

"Oh Lord, yes," Gertie said. "I can hear it now myself."

She jerked open the door and made a dash for the switchboard in the outer office.

Mason handed Della Street the brief and said, "Go out and get her started, Della."

When Della Street came back at the end of ten minutes Mason asked, "How's our terrified typist, Della?"

Della Street said, "If that's a terrified typist, let's call Miss Mosher and tell her to frighten all of them before sending them out."

"Good?" Mason asked.

"Listen." Della Street said.

She eased open the door to the outer office. The sound of clattering typewriter keys came through in a steady staccato.

"Sounds like hail on a tin roof," Mason said.

Della Street closed the door. "I've never seen anything like it. That girl pulled the typewriter over to her, ratcheted in the paper, looked at the copy, put her hands over the keyboard and that typewriter literally exploded into action. And yet, somehow, Chief, I think Gertie *was* right. I think she became frightened at the idea of coming up here. It may be that she knows something about you, or your fame has caused her to become self-conscious. After all," Della Street added dryly, "you're not entirely unknown, you know."

"Well," Mason said, "let's get at that pile of mail and skim off a few of the important letters. At that rate the brief will be done in plenty of time."

Della Street nodded.

"You have her at the desk by the door to the law library?"

"That seemed to be the only place to put her, Chief. I fixed up the desk there when I knew we were going to need an extra typist. You know how Stella is about anyone using *her* typewriter. She thinks a strange typist throws it all out of kilter."

Mason nodded, said, "If this girl is good, Della, you might arrange to keep her on for a week or two. We can keep her busy, can't we?"

"I'll say."

"Better ring up Miss Mosher and tell her."

Della Street hesitated. "Would it be all right if we waited until we've had a chance to study her work? She's fast, all right, but we'd better be sure she's accurate."

Mason nodded, said, "Good idea, Della. Let's wait and see."

CHAPTER TWO

Della Street placed a sheaf of papers on Mason's desk. "Those are the first ten pages of the brief, Chief."

Mason looked at the typewritten sheets, gave a low whistle and said, "Now *that's* what I call typing!"

Della Street picked up one of the pages, tilted it so that the light reflected from the smooth surface, "I've tried this with two or three sheets," she said, "and I can't see where there's been a single erasure. She has a wonderful touch and she certainly is hammering it out."

Mason said, "Ring up Miss Mosher. Find out something about this girl. What's her name, Della?"

"Mae Wallis."

"Get Miss Mosher on the line."

Della Street picked up the telephone, said to Gertie at the switchboard, "Mr. Mason wants Miss Mosher at the secretarial agency, Gertie. . . . Never mind, I'll hold the line."

A moment later Della Street said: "Hello, Miss Mosher? . . . Oh, she is? . . . Well, I'm calling about the typist she sent up to Mr. Mason's office. This is

Della Street, Mr. Mason's secretary.... Are you sure? ... Well, she must have left a note somewhere.... Yes, yes ... well, I'm sorry.... No, we don't want *two* girls.... No, no. Miss Mosher sent one up—a Mae Wallis. I'm trying to find out whether she'll be available for steady work during the next week.... Please ask Miss Mosher to call when she comes in."

Della Street hung up the phone, turned to Perry Mason. "Miss Mosher is out. The girl she left in charge doesn't know about anyone having been sent up. She found a note on the desk to get us a typist. It was a memo Miss Mosher had left before she went out. The names of three girls were on it, and this assistant has been trying to locate the girls. One of them was laid up with flu, another one was on a job, and she was trying to locate the third when I called in." .

"That's not like Miss Mosher," Mason said. "She's usually very efficient. When she sent this girl up, she should have destroyed the memo. Oh, well, it doesn't make any difference."

"Miss Mosher's due back in about an hour," Della Street said. "I left word for her to call when she comes in."

Again Mason tackled the work on his desk, stopping to see a client who had a three-thirty appointment, then returning to dictation.

At four-thirty Della Street went out to the outer office, came back and said, "She's still going like a house afire, Chief. She's really pounding them out."

Mason said, "That copy had been pretty badly hashed up and blue-penciled with strike-outs and interlineations."

"It doesn't seem to bother her a bit," Della Street said. "There's lightning in that girl's finger tips. She—"

The telephone on Della Street's desk shrilled insistently. Della Street, with her hand on the receiver, finished the sentence, "... certainly knows how to play a tune on a keyboard."

She picked up the receiver, said, "Hello.... Oh, yes, Miss Mosher. We were calling about the typist you sent up.... What? ... You didn't? ... Mae Wallis? ... She *said* she came from your agency. She said you sent her.... Why, yes, that's what I understood she said.... Well, I'm sorry, Miss Mosher. There's been some mistake—but this girl's certainly competent.... Why, yes she's got the work almost finished. I'm terribly sorry, I'll speak with her and—Are you going to be there for a while? ... Well, I'll speak with her and call you back. But that's what she said ... yes, from your agency.... All right, let me call you back."

Della Street dropped the phone into its cradle.

"Mystery?" Mason asked.

"I'll say. Miss Mosher says *she* hasn't sent anyone up. She's had a hard time getting girls lined up, particularly ones with qualifications to suit you."

"Well, she got one this time," Mason said, fingering through the brief. "Or at least *someone* got her."

"So what do we do?" Della Street asked.

"By all means, find out where she came from. Are you sure she said Miss Mosher sent her?"

"That's what Gertie said."

"Are you," Mason asked, "going *entirely* on what Gertie said?"

Della Street nodded.

"You didn't talk it over with Miss Wallis?"

"No. She was out there waiting to go to work. While I was talking with you, she found where the paper and carbons were kept in the desk. She'd ratcheted them into the machine, and just held out her hand for the copy. She asked if I wanted an original and three carbons. I said that we only used an original and two for stuff that was going to the printer. She said she had one extra carbon in the machine, but that she wouldn't bother to take it out. She said that she'd only make an original and two on the next. Then she put the papers down on the desk, held her fingers poised over the keyboard for a second, then started banging out copy."

"Permit me," Mason said, "to call your attention to something which clearly demonstrates the fallacy of human testimony. You were doubtless sincere in telling Miss Mosher that Mae Wallis said she had been sent up from her agency, but if you will recall Gertie's exact words, you will remember that she said the girl seemed frightened and self-conscious, so Gertie asked her if she was the new typist. The girl nodded, and Gertie showed her to the desk. At no time did Gertie say to us that she asked her if Miss Mosher had sent her."

"Well," Della Street said, "I had the distinct impression—"

"Certainly you did," Mason said. "So did I. Only long years of cross-examining witnesses have trained me to listen carefully to what a person actually says. I am quite certain that Gertie never told us she had specifically asked this girl if she came from Miss Mosher's agency."

"Well, where *could* she have come from?"

"Let's get her in and ask her," Mason said. "And let's not let her get away, Della. I'd like to catch up on some of this back work tomorrow, and this girl is really a wonder."

Della Street nodded, left her desk, went to the outer office, returned in a moment and made motions of powdering her nose.

"Did you leave word?" Mason asked.

"Yes, I told Gertie to send her in as soon as she came back."

"How's the brief coming?"

Della Street said, "She's well along with it. The work's on her desk. It hasn't been separated yet. The originals and carbons are together. She certainly does neat work, doesn't she?"

Mason nodded, tilted back in his swivel chair, lit a cigarette and said: "Well, we'll wait until she shows up and see what she has to say for herself, Della. When you stop to think about this, it presents an intriguing problem."

After Mason had smoked a leisurely cigarette Della Street once more went to the outer office and again returned.

Mason frowned, said, "She's probably one of those high-strung girls who use up a lot of nervous energy banging away at the typewriter and then go for a complete rest, smoking a cigarette or..."

"Or?" Della Street asked, as Mason paused.

"...or taking a drink. Now, wait a minute, Della. Although there's nothing particularly confidential about that brief, if we keep her on here for four or five days, she's going to be doing some stuff that *is* confidential. Suppose you slip down to the powder room, Della, and see if perhaps our demon typist has a little flask in her purse and is now engaged in chewing on a clove."

"Also," Della Street said, "I'll take a whiff to see if I smell any marijuana smoke."

"Know it when you smell it?" Mason asked, smiling.

"Of course," she retorted. "I wouldn't be working for one of the greatest trial attorneys in the country without having learned at least to recognize some of the more common forms of law violation."

"All right," Mason said. "Go on down and tell her that we want to see her, Della. Try and chat with her informally for a minute and size her up a bit. You didn't talk with her very much, did you?"

"Just got her name, and that's about all. I remember asking her how she spelled her first name, and she told me M-A-E."

Mason nodded. Della Street left the room and was back within a couple of minutes.

"She isn't there, Chief."

"Well, where the devil *is* she?" Mason asked.

Della Street shrugged her shoulders. "She just got up and went out."

"Say anything to Gertie about where she was going?"

"Not a word. She just got up and walked out, and Gertie assumed she was going to the washroom."

"Now that's strange," Mason said. "Isn't that room kept locked?"

Della Street nodded.

"She should have asked for a key," Mason said. "Even if she didn't know it was locked, she'd have asked Gertie how to find it. How about her hat and coat?"

"Apparently she wasn't wearing any. She has her purse with her."

"Run out and pick up the last of the work she was doing, will you, Della? Let's take a look at it."

Della Street went out and returned with the typed pages. Mason looked them over.

"She has a few pages to go," Della Street said.

Mason pursed his lips, said, "It shouldn't take her long, Della, I certainly cut the insides out of those last few pages. That's where Jackson was waxing eloquent, bombarding the Court with a peroration on liberties, constitutional rights and due process of law."

"He was so proud of that," Della Street said. "You didn't take it *all* out, did you?"

"I took out most of it," Mason said. "An appellate court isn't interested in eloquence. It's interested in the law and the facts to which it is going to apply the law.

"Good Lord, Della, do you realize that if the appellate judges tried to read every line of all of the briefs that are submitted to them, they could work for twelve hours each day without doing one other thing, and still couldn't read the briefs?"

"Good heavens, no! Aren't they supposed to read them?"

"Theoretically, yes," Mason said. "But actually, it's a practical impossibility."

"So what do they do?"

"Most of them look through the briefs, get the law points, skip the impassioned pleas, then turn the briefs over to their law clerks.

"It's my experience that a man does a lot better when he sets forth an absolutely impartial, thoroughly honest statement of facts, including those that are unfavorable to his side as well as those that are favorable, thus giving the appellate court the courtesy of assuming the judge knows the law.

"The attorney can be of help in letting the judge know the case to which the law is to be applied and the facts in the case. But if the judge didn't know what the law was, he wouldn't have been placed on the appellate bench in the first place. Della, what the devil *do* you suppose happened to that girl?"

"She must be in the building somewhere."

"What makes you think so?"

"Well, there again—well, it's just one of those presumptions. She certainly is coming back for her money. She put in a whale of an afternoon's work."

"She should have stayed to finish the brief," Mason said. "It wouldn't have taken her over another forty or fifty minutes, at the rate she was working."

"Chief," Della Street said, "you seem to be acting on the assumption that she's walked out and left us."

"It's a feeling I have."

Della Street said, "She probably went down to the cigar counter to buy some cigarettes."

"In which event, she'd have been back long before this."

"Yes, I suppose so. But...but, Chief, she's bound to collect the money for the work she's done."

Mason carefully arranged the pages of the brief. "Well, she's helped us out of quite a hole." He broke off as a series of peculiarly spaced knocks sounded on the corridor door of his private office.

"That will be Paul Drake," Mason said. "I wonder what brings *him* around. Let him in, Della."

Della Street opened the door. Paul Drake, head of the Drake Detective Agency, with offices down the corridor by the elevator, grinned at them and said, "What were *you* people doing during all of the excitement?"

"Excitement?" Mason asked.

"Cops crawling all over the building," Drake said. "And you two sitting here engaged in the prosaic activities of running a humdrum law office."

"Darned if we weren't," Mason said. "Sit down, Paul. Have a cigarette. Tell us what it's all about. We've been putting in our time writing briefs."

"You would," Drake told him, sliding down into the big overstuffed chair reserved for clients, and lighting a cigarette.

"What's the trouble?" Mason asked.

"Police chasing some dame up here on this floor," Drake said. "Didn't they search your office?"

Mason flashed a swift, warning glance at Della Street.

"Not that I know of."

"They must have."

Mason said to Della Street, "See if Gertie's gone home, Della."

Della Street opened the door to the outer office, said, "She's just going home, Chief."

"Can you catch her?"

"Sure. She's just at the door." Della Street raised her voice, "Oh, Gertie! Can you look in here for a minute?"

Gertie, ready to leave for the evening, came to stand in the doorway of the office. "What is it, Mr. Mason?"

"Any officers in here this afternoon?" Mason asked.

"Oh, yes," Gertie said. "There was some sort of a burglary down the corridor."

Again Mason caught Della's eye.

"What did they want?" Mason asked.

"Wanted to know if everyone in the office was accounted for, whether you had anyone in with you, and whether we had seen anything of a girl burglar."

"And what did you tell them?" Mason asked, keeping his voice entirely without expression.

"I told them you were alone, except for Miss Street, your confidential secretary. That we only had the regular employees here in the office and a relief typist from our regular agency who was working on a brief."

"And then what?"

"Then they left. Why?"

"Oh, nothing," Mason said. "I was just wondering, that's all."

"Should I have notified you? I know you don't like to be disturbed when you're working on correspondence."

"No, it's all right," Mason said. "I just wanted to get it straight, Gertie. That's all. Good night, and have a good time."

"How did you know I have a date?" Gertie asked.

"I saw it in your eyes," Mason said, grinning. "Good night, Gertie."

"Good night," she said.

"Well," Drake said, "there you are. If you'd happened to have had some woman client in your private office, the police would have insisted on talking to you and on getting a look at the client."

"You mean they searched the floor?" Mason asked.

"They really went through the joint," Drake told him. "You see, the office where the trouble occurred is right across from the women's restroom. One of the stenographers, opening the restroom door, saw this young woman whose back was toward her fumbling with the lock on the office door, trying first one key then another.

"The stenographer became suspicious. She stood there watching. About the fourth or fifth key, the girl managed to get into the office."

"What office was it?" Mason asked.

"The South African Gem Importing and Exploration Company."

"Go on, Paul."

"Well, this stenographer was a pretty smart babe. She telephoned the manager of the building and then she went out to stand by the elevators to see if this girl would come out and take an elevator. If she did that, the stenographer had made up her mind she'd try to follow."

"That could have been dangerous," Mason said.

"I know, but this is one very spunky gal."

"She could have recognized the woman?"

"Not the woman. But she knew the way the woman was dressed. You know the way women are, Perry. She hadn't seen the woman's face, but she knew the exact color and cut of her skirt and jacket, the shade of her stockings and shoes; the way she had her hair done, the color of her hair, and all that."

"I see," Mason said, glancing surreptitiously at Della Street. "That description was, of course, given to the police?"

"Oh, yes."

"And they didn't find her?"

"No, they didn't find a thing. But the manager of the building gave them a passkey to get into the office of the gem importing company. The place looked as if a cyclone had struck it. Evidently, this girl had made a very hurried search. Drawers had been pulled out, papers dumped out on the floor, a chair had been overturned, a typewriter stand upset, with the typewriter lying on its side on the floor."

"No sign of the girl?"

"No sign of anyone. The two partners who own the business, chaps named Jefferson and Irving, came in right on the heels of the police. They had been out to lunch, and they were amazed to find how much destruction had taken place during their brief absence."

Mason said, "The girl probably ran down the stairs to another floor and took the elevator from there."

Drake shook his head. "The building manager got this stenographer who had given the description, and they went down to stand at the elevators. They watched everyone who went out. When the police showed up—and believe me, that was only a matter of a minute or two; these radio cars are right on the job—well, when the police showed up, the manager of the building briefed them on what had happened. So the police went up and the girl and the manager continued to stand at the elevators. The police weren't conspicuous about it, but they dropped in at every office on the floor, just checking up."

"And I suppose the restrooms," Mason said.

"Oh, sure. They sent a couple of girls into the restrooms right away. That was the first place they looked."

"Well," Mason said, "we seem to be doing all right, Paul. If I don't go out and get tangled up in crime, crime comes to me—at least indirectly. So Jefferson and Irving came in right after the police arrived, is that right?"

"That's right."

"And the manager of the building was down there at the elevators, waiting for this girl to come out?"

"That's right."

Mason said, "He knew, of course, the office that the girl was burglarizing?"

"Of course. He told the police what office it was and all about it. He even gave them a passkey so they could get in."

"And then he waited down there at the elevators with the stenographer who had seen this woman burglarizing the office?"

"That's right."

"A lot of elaborate precautions to catch a sneak thief."

"Well, I'm not supposed to talk about clients, Perry, and I wouldn't to anyone else, but as you know, I represent the owners of the building. It seems this gem importing company is expecting half a million dollars' worth of diamonds before long."

"The deuce!"

"That's right. You know the way they do things these days—insure 'em and ship 'em by mail."

"The strange thing," Mason said thoughtfully, "is that if Irving and Jefferson came in right on the heels of the police, with the manager of the building standing down there at the elevators, he didn't stop them and tell them that they'd find police in their office and—

"What's the matter?" Mason asked, as Drake suddenly sat bolt upright.

Drake made the motion of hitting himself on the head.

"What are you trying to do?" Mason asked.

"Knock some brains into my thick skull," Drake said. "Good Lord, Perry! The manager of the building was telling me all about this, and that point never occurred to me. Let me use the phone."

Drake moved over to the phone, called the office of the manager and said, "Paul Drake talking. I was thinking about this trouble down at the gem importing company. According to police, Irving and Jefferson, the two partners who run the place, came in while they were searching."

The receiver made squawking noises.

"Well," Drake said, "*you* were standing down at the foot of the elevators with this stenographer. Why didn't you tell them that police were in their office—"

Drake was interrupted by another series of squawking noises from the receiver. After a moment the detective said, "Want me to look into it, or do you want to?...Okay. Call me back, will you? I'm up here in Perry Mason's office at the moment.... Well, wait a minute. The switchboard is disconnected for the night, I guess. I'll catch that call at my—"

"Hold, it, Paul," Della Street interrupted. "I'll connect this line with the switchboard, so you can get a call back on this number."

"Okay," Drake said into the telephone. "Mason's secretary will fix the line, so this telephone will be connected on the main trunk line. Just give me a buzz when you find out about it, will you?"

Drake hung up the telephone, went back to the client's chair, grinned at Mason and said, "You'll pardon me for taking all the credit for your idea, Perry, but this is my bread and butter. I couldn't tell him the idea never occurred to me until I got to talking with you, could I?"

"No credit," Mason said. "The thing is obvious."

"Of course it's obvious," Drake said. "That's why I'm kicking myself for not thinking of it right at the start. The trouble was, we were so interested in finding out how this girl vanished into thin air that I for one completely overlooked wondering how it happened that the manager didn't stop Jefferson and his partner and tell them what was happening."

"The manager was probably excited," Mason said.

"I'll tell the world he was excited. Do you know him?"

"Not the new one. I've talked with him on the phone, and Della Street's talked with him. I haven't met him."

"He's an excitable chap. One of those hair-triggered guys who does everything right now. At that, he did a pretty good job of sewing up the building."

Mason nodded. "They certainly went to a lot of trouble trying to catch one lone female prowler."

The telephone rang.

"That's probably for you," Della Street said, nodding to Paul Drake.

Drake picked up the telephone, said, "Hello.... Yes, this is Paul Drake.... Oh, I see. Well, of course, that could have happened, all right. Funny you didn't see them.... I see. Well, thanks a lot. I just thought we ought to check on that angle.... Oh, that's all right. There's no reason why that *should* have occurred to you.... Not at all. I'd been intending to ask you about it, but it slipped my mind. I thought I'd better check up on it before knocking off for the night.... Okay. Thanks. We'll see what we can find out."

Drake hung up, grinned at Mason and said, "Now the guy thinks I was working overtime, cudgeling my brain on his problem."

"What about the two partners?" Mason asked. "What's the answer?"

"Why, they evidently walked right by him and got in the elevator. Of course, the manager and the stenographer were watching the people who were getting *out* of the elevators. At that time, right after lunch, there's quite a bit of traffic in the elevators.

"The manager just finished talking with Jefferson on the phone. Jefferson said *he* saw the manager and this girl standing there and started to ask him a question about something pertaining to the building. Then he saw from the way the man was standing that he was evidently waiting for someone, so the two partners just went on past and got in the elevator just as it was starting up."

Mason said, "That sounds plausible, all right. What do you know about Jefferson and Irving? Anything?"

"Not too much. The South African Gem Importing and Exploration

Company decided to open an office here. Their business is mostly wholesale diamonds. They have their main office in Johannesburg, but there's a branch office in Paris.

"This deal was made through the Paris office. They wrote the manager of the building, received a floor plan and rental schedules, signed a lease and paid six months' rent in advance.

"They sent Duane Jefferson out from South Africa. He's to be in charge. Walter Irving came from the Paris office. He's the assistant."

"Are they doing business?"

"Not yet. They're just getting started. I understand they're waiting for a high-class burglarproof safe to be installed. They've advertised for office help and have purchased some office furniture."

"Did those two chaps bring any stock of diamonds with them?" Mason asked.

"Nope. Unfortunately, things aren't done that way any more, which has cost us private detectives a lot of business. Gems are sent by insured mail now. A half a million dollars' worth of stones are sent just as you'd send a package of soiled clothes. The shipper pays a fee for adequate insurance and deducts it as a business cost. If gems are lost, the insurance company writes out its check. It's an infallible, foolproof system."

"I see," Mason said thoughtfully. "In that case, what the devil was this girl after?"

"That's the sixty-four dollar question."

"It was an empty office—as far as gems go?"

"That's right. Later on, when the first shipment of gems arrives, they'll have burglar alarms all over the place, an impregnable safe and all the trimmings. Right now it's an empty shell.

"Gosh, Perry, it used to be that a messenger would carry a shipment of jewels, and private detective agencies would be given jobs as bodyguards, special watchmen and all of that. Now, some postal employee who doesn't even carry a gun comes down the corridor with a package worth half a million, says, 'Sign here,' and the birds sign their name, toss the package in the safe and that's all there is to it.

"It's all done on a basis of percentages. The insurance business is tough competition. How'd you like it if an insurance company would insure your clients against any loss from any type of litigation? Then your clients would pay premiums, deduct them as a business cost, and—"

"The trouble with that, Paul," Mason said, "is that when they come to lock a guy in the gas chamber it would take an awful big insurance check to make him feel indifferent."

Drake grinned. "Dammed if it wouldn't," he agreed.

CHAPTER THREE

When Paul Drake had left the office Mason turned to Della Street.

"Well, what do *you* think, Della?"

Della Street said, "I'm afraid it could be—it was about the same time and...well, sometimes I think we don't pay enough attention to Gertie because she *does* exaggerate. Perhaps this girl really was frightened, just as Gertie said, and...well, it could have been."

"Then she must have come in here," Mason said, "because she knew her escape was cut off. There was no other place for her to go. She had to enter some office. So she came in here blind and was trying to think of some problem that would enable her to ask for a consultation with me, when Gertie let the cat out of the bag that we were expecting a typist."

Della Street nodded.

"Go out and look around," Mason said. "I'm going out and do a little scouting myself."

"What do you want me to do?" Della Street asked.

"Look over the typewriter she was using. Look over the typewriter desk. Then go down to the restroom and look around. See if you can find anything."

"Heavens, the police have been all through the restroom."

"Look around, anyhow, Della. See if she hid anything. There's always the chance she might have had something in her possession that was pretty hot and she decided to cache it someplace and come back for it later. I'll go down and get some cigarettes."

Mason walked down the corridor and rang for an elevator, went down to the foyer and over to the cigar stand. The girl behind the counter, a tall blonde with frosty blue eyes, smiled impersonally.

"Hello," Mason said.

At the personal approach the eyes became even more coldly cautious. "Good afternoon," the girl said.

"I am looking for a little information," Mason said.

"We sell cigars and cigarettes, chewing gum, candy, newspapers and magazines."

Mason laughed. "Well, don't get me wrong."

"And don't get *me* wrong."

"I'm a tenant in the building," Mason said, "and have been for some time. You're new here, aren't you?"

"Yes, I bought the cigar stand from Mr. Carson. I—Oh, I place you now! You're Perry Mason, the famous lawyer! Excuse me, Mr. Mason. I thought you were...well, you know a lot of people think that just because a girl is running a cigar counter she wraps herself up with every package of cigarettes she sells."

Mason smiled. "Pardon *me*. I should have introduced myself first."

"What can I do for you, Mr. Mason?"

"Probably nothing," Mason said. "I wanted a little information, but if you're new here, I'm afraid you won't know the tenants in the building well enough to help me."

"I'm afraid that's right, Mr. Mason. I don't have too good a memory for names and faces. I'm trying to get to know the regular customers. It's quite a job."

Mason said, "There are a couple of relative newcomers here in the building. One of them is named Jefferson, the other Irving."

"Oh, you mean the ones that have that gem importing company?"

"Those are the ones. Know them?"

"I do *now*. We had a lot of excitement here this afternoon, although I didn't know anything about it. It seems their office was broken into and—"

"They were pointed out to you?"

"Yes. One of them—Mr. Jefferson, I believe it was—stopped here for a package of cigarettes and was telling me all about it."

"But you didn't know them before?"

"You mean by sight?"

Mason nodded.

She shook her head. "I'm sorry, I can't help you, Mr. Mason."

"Well, that's all right," Mason told her.

"Why do you ask, Mr. Mason? Are you interested in the case?"

Mason smiled. "Indirectly," he said.

"You're *so* mysterious. I may not have recognized you when you walked up, but I have heard so much about you that I feel I know you very well indeed. What's an indirect interest, Mr. Mason?"

"Nothing worth talking about."

"Well, remember that I'm rather centrally located down here. If I can ever pick up any information for you, all you have to do is to let me know. I'll be glad to co-operate in any way that I can. Perhaps I can't be so efficient now, since I am relatively new here, but I'll get people spotted and . . . well, just remember, if there's *anything* I can do, I'll be glad to."

"Thanks," Mason told her.

"Did you want me to talk with Mr. Jefferson some more? He was quite friendly and chatted away with me while I was waiting on him. I didn't encourage him, but I have a feeling . . . well, you know how those things are, Mr. Mason."

Mason grinned. "You mean that he's lonely and he likes your looks?"

Her laugh showed that she was flustered. "Well, I didn't exactly say that."

"But you feel he could be encouraged?"

"Do you want me to try?"

"Would you like to?"

"Whatever you say, Mr. Mason."

The lawyer handed her a folded twenty dollar bill. "Try and find out just where the manager of the building was when Jefferson and Irving came back from lunch."

"Thank *you*, Mr. Mason. I feel guilty taking this money, because now that you mention the manager of the building I know the answer."

"What is it?"

"They came in while the manager and a young woman were standing watching the elevators. One of the men started to approach the manager as though he wanted to ask him a question, but he saw the manager was preoccupied watching the elevators, so he veered off.

"I didn't think anything about it at the time, but it comes back to me now that those were the two men who were pointed out to me later. I hope that's the information you wanted, Mr. Mason."

"It is, thanks."

"Thank *you*, Mr. Mason. If there's ever anything I can do for you I'd be glad to, and it isn't going to cost you a twenty every time either."

"Thanks," Mason said, "but I never want something for nothing."

"*You* wouldn't," she said, giving him her most dazzling smile.

Mason rode back up in the elevator.

Della Street, in a state of subdued excitement, was waiting to pounce on him as soon as he opened the door of his private office.

"Good heavens!" she said. "We're mixed in it up to our eyebrows."

"Go on," Mason said. "What are we mixed in?"

Della Street produced a small, square tin box.

"What," Mason asked, "do you have there?"

"A great big hunk of semi-dried chewing gum."

"And where did you get it?"

"It was plastered on the underside of the desk where Mae Wallis had been working."

"Let's take a look, Della."

Della Street slid open the lid of the box and showed Mason the chewing gum. "This is just the way it was plastered to the underside of the desk," she said.

"And what did you do?"

"Took an old safety razor blade and cut it off. You can see there is an impression of fingers where she pushed the gum up against the desk."

Mason looked at Della Street somewhat quizzically. "Well," he said, "you *are* becoming the demon detective, Della. So now we have a couple of fingerprints?"

"Exactly."

"Well," Mason told her, "we're hardly going to the police with them, Della."

"No, I suppose not."

"So in that case, since we aren't particularly anxious to co-operate with the police, it would have been just as well if you had destroyed the fingerprints in removing the gum, Della."

"Wait," she told him. "You haven't seen anything yet. You observe that that's a terrific wad of gum, Chief. A girl could hardly have had all that in her mouth at one time."

"You think it was put there in installments?" Mason asked.

"I think it was put there for a purpose," Della Street said. "I thought so as soon as I saw it."

"What purpose?" Mason asked.

Della Street turned the box over on Mason's desk so that the wad of gum fell out on the blotter. "This," she said, "is the side that was against the desk."

Mason looked at the coruscations which gleamed through a few places in the chewing gum. "Good Lord, Della!" he said. "How many are there?"

"I don't know," Della said. "I didn't want to touch it. This is just the way it came from the desk. You can see parts of two really large-sized diamonds there."

Mason studied the wad of chewing gum.

"Now then," he said thoughtfully, "this becomes evidence, Della. We're going to have to be careful that nothing happens to it."

She nodded.

"I take it the gum is hard enough so it will keep all right?" Mason asked.

"It's a little soft on the inside, but now that the air's getting to the top, the gum is hardening rapidly.

Mason took the small tin box, replaced the gum and studied it, tilting the box backwards and forwards so as to get a good view of both the top and bottom sides of the chewing gum. "Two of those fingerprints are remarkably good latents, Della," he said. "The third one isn't so good. It looks more like the side of the finger. But those two impressions are perfect."

Della Street nodded.

"Probably the thumb and the forefinger. Which side of the desk was it on, Della?"

"Over on the right-hand side of the desk."

"Then those are probably the impressions of the right thumb and forefinger."

"So what do we do?" Della Street asked. "Do we now call in the police?"

Mason hesitated a moment, said, "I want to know a little more about what's cooking, Della. You didn't find anything in the restroom?"

Della Street said, "I became a scavenger. I dug down into the container that they use for soiled paper towels—you know, they have a big metal box with a wedge-shaped cover on top that swings back and forth and you can shove towels in from each side."

Mason nodded. "Find anything, Della?"

"Someone had used the receptacle to dispose of a lot of love letters, and the disposal must either have been very, very hasty, or else the girl certainly took no precautions to keep anyone who might be interested from getting quite an eyeful. The letters hadn't even been torn through."

"Let's take a look at them," Mason said.

Della Street said, "They were all in one bunch, and I salvaged the whole outfit. Gosh, I'm glad the rush hour is over. I would have felt pretty self-conscious if someone had come in and caught me digging down in that used towel container!"

Mason's nod showed that he was preoccupied as he examined the letters.

"What do you make of them?" Della Street asked.

"Well," Mason said thoughtfully, "either, as you suggested, the person who left them there was in very much of a hurry, or this was a plant and the person wanted to be certain that the letters would be noticed and could be read without any difficulty. In other words, it's almost too good. A girl trying to dispose of letters would hardly have been so careless about dropping them into the used-towel receptacle in one piece—unless it was a plant of some kind."

"But how about a man?" Della Street asked. "Apparently, the letters were sent to a man and—"

"And they were found in the *ladies'* restroom."

"Yes, that's so."

Mason studied one of the letters. "Now, these are rather peculiar, Della. They are written in a whimsical vein. Listen to this:

> " 'My dearest Prince Charming,
> " 'When you rode up on your charger the other night, there were a lot of things I wanted to say to you, but I couldn't think of them until after you had left.
> " 'Somehow the glittering armor and that formidable helmet made you seem so virtuous and righteous that I felt a distant creature from another more sordid world.... You perhaps don't know it, Prince Charming, but you made quite a handsome spectacle, sitting there with the visor of your helmet raised, your horse with his head down, his flanks heaving and sweating from

the exertion of carrying you on that mission to rescue the damsel
in distress, the setting sun reflecting from your polished
armor . . .'"

Mason paused, glanced up at Della Street, and said, "What the devil!"

"Take a look at the signature," Della Street said.

Mason turned over two pages and looked at the signature—"Your faithful
and devoted Mae."

"You will notice the spelling," Della Street said. "It's M-A-E."

Mason pursed his lips thoughtfully, said, "Now, all we need, Della, is a
murder to put us in a thoroughly untenable position."

"What position?"

"That of withholding important evidence from the police."

"You're not going to tell them anything about Mae Wallis?"

Mason shook his head. "I don't dare to, Della. They wouldn't make even the
slightest effort to believe me. You can see the position I'd be in. I'd be trying to
explain that while the police were making a search of the building in order to
find the woman who had broken into the offices of the South African Gem
Importing and Exploration Company, I was sitting innocently in my office; that
I had no idea that I should have mentioned the typist who dropped in from
nowhere at exactly the right time, who seemed completely terrified, who was
supposed to have been sent from Miss Mosher's agency, even though, at the
time, I *knew* that she hadn't been sent from Miss Mosher's agency."

"Yes," Della Street said, smiling. "With your connections and reputation, I
can see that the police would be at least skeptical."

"Very, very skeptical," Mason said. "And since it's bad for the police to
develop habits of skepticism, Della, we'll see that they aren't placed in an
embarrassing position."

CHAPTER FOUR

It was three days later when Perry Mason unlocked the door of his private
office and found Della Street waiting for him, his desk carefully cleaned and for
once the pile of mail far to one side.

"Chief," Della Street said in a voice of low urgency, "I've been trying to get
you. Sit down and let me talk with you before anyone knows you're in."

Mason hung up his hat in the hat closet, seated himself at the desk, glanced at
Della Street quizzically and said, "You're certainly worked up. What gives?"

"We have our murder case."

"What do you mean 'our murder case'?"

"Remember what you said about the diamonds? That we only needed a
murder case to make the thing perfect?"

Mason came bolt upright in his chair. "What is it, Della? Give me the low-
down."

"No one seems to know what it's all about, but Duane Jefferson of the South
African Gem Importing and Exploration Company has been arrested for
murder. Walter Irving, the other member of the company, is out there in the

outer office waiting for you. There's a cablegram from the South African Gem Importing and Exploration Company sent from South Africa, advising you that they are instructing their local representative to pay you two thousand American dollars as a retainer. They want you to represent Duane Jefferson."

"Murder?" Mason said. "Who the devil is the corpse, Della?"

"I don't know. I don't know very much about it. All I know is about the cablegram that came and the fact that Walter Irving has been in three times to see you. He asked that I notify him just as soon as you arrived, and this last time he decided that he wouldn't even take chances on the delay incident to a telephone call but was going to wait. He wants to see you the minute you come in."

"Send him in, Della. Let's find out what this is all about. Where's that tin box?"

"In the safe."

Mason said, "Where's the desk Mae Wallis was using when she was here?"

"I moved it back into the far corner of the law library."

"Who moved it?"

"I had the janitor and one of his assistants take it in for us."

"How are you on chewing gum, Della?"

"Pretty good. Why?"

Mason said, "Chew some gum, then use it to plaster that wad with the diamonds in it back on the desk in exactly the same place you found it."

"But there'll be a difference in freshness, Chief. That other gum is dry and hard now, and the new gum that I chew will be moist and—"

"And it will dry out if there's a long enough interval," Mason interrupted.

"How long will the inteval be?"

"That," Mason told her, "will depend entirely on luck. Send Walter Irving in, Della, and let's see what this is all about."

Della Street nodded and started for the outer office.

"And fix that gum up *right away*," Mason reminded her.

"While Irving is in here?"

Mason nodded.

Della Street went to the outer office and returned with Walter Irving, a well-dressed, heavy-set man who had evidently prepared for the interview by visiting a barber shop. His hair was freshly trimmed, his nails were polished, his face had the smooth pink-and-white appearance which comes from a shave and a massage.

He was about forty-five years old, with reddish-brown, expressionless eyes, and the manner of a man who would show no surprise or emotion if half of the building should suddenly cave in.

"Good morning, Mr. Mason. I guess you don't know me. I've seen you in the elevator and you've been pointed out to me as being the smartest criminal lawyer in the state."

"Thank you," Mason said, shaking hands, and then added dryly, " 'Criminal lawyer' is a popular expression. I prefer to regard myself as a 'trial lawyer.' "

"Well, that's fine," Irving said. "You received a cablegram from my company in South Africa, didn't you?"

"That's right."

"They've authorized me to pay you a retainer for representing my associate, Duane Jefferson."

"That cablegram is a complete mystery to me," Mason said. "What's it all about?"

"I'll come to that in a moment," Irving told him. "I want to get first things first."

"What do you mean?"

"Your fees."

"What about them?"

Irving raised steady eyes to Mason. "Things are different in South Africa."

"Just what are you getting at?"

"Just this," Irving said. "I'm here to protect the interests of my employers, the South African Gem Importing and Exploration Company. It's a big, wealthy company. They want me to turn over a two-thousand-dollar retainer to you. They'd leave it to your discretion as to the balance of the fee. I won't do business that way. On this side of the water, criminal attorneys are inclined to grab all they can get. They—Oh, hell, Mr. Mason, what's the use of beating around the bush? My company has an idea that it's dealing with a barrister in a wig and gown. It doesn't have the faintest idea of how to deal with a criminal lawyer."

"Do you?" Mason asked.

"If I don't I'm sure as hell going to try and find out. I'm protecting my company. How much is it going to cost?"

"You mean the total fee?"

"The total fee."

Mason said, "Tell me about the case, just the general facts and I'll answer your question."

"The facts are utterly cockeyed. Police raided our office. Why, I don't know. They found some diamonds. Those diamonds had been planted. Neither Jefferson nor I had ever seen them before. Our company is just opening up its office here. Some people don't like that."

"What were the diamonds worth?"

"Something like a hundred thousand dollars retail."

"How does murder enter into it?"

"That I don't know."

"Don't you even know who was murdered?"

"A man named Baxter. He's a smuggler."

"Were these his diamonds—the ones the police found in your office?"

"How the hell would *I* know?"

Mason regarded the man for a few seconds, then said, "How the hell would *I* know?"

Irving grinned. "I'm a little touchy this morning."

"So am I. Suppose you start talking."

"All I can tell you for sure is that there's some kind of a frame-up involved. Jefferson never killed anyone. I've known him for years. My gosh, Mr. Mason, look at it this way. Here's a large, exceedingly reputable, ultraconservative company in South Africa. This company has known Duane Jefferson for years. As soon as they hear that he's been arrested, they're willing to put up whatever amount is required in order to secure the very best available representation.

"Mind you, they don't suggest they'll advance Jefferson money to retain counsel. The company itself instructed me to retain the best available counsel for Jefferson."

"And you suggested me?" Mason asked.

"No. I would have, but somebody beat me to it. I got a cablegram authorizing me to draw a check on our local account in an amount of two thousand dollars and turn that money over to you so you could start taking the necessary legal steps immediately. Now if my company pays your fees, who will your client be?"

"Duane Jefferson."

"Suppose Jefferson tries to get you to do something that isn't in his best interests. What would you do—follow his instructions, or do what was best for him?" ·

"Why do you ask that question?"

"Duane is trying to protect some woman. He'd let himself get convicted before he'd expose her. He thinks she's wonderful. *I* think she's a clever, two-timing schemer who is out to frame him."

"Who is she?"

"I wish I knew. If I did, I'd have detectives on her trail within the next hour. The trouble is I don't know. I only know there *is* such a woman. She lost her head over Duane. He'll protect her."

"Married?"

"I don't think so. I don't know."

"What about the murder case?"

"It ties in with smuggling. Duane Jefferson sold a batch of diamonds to Munroe Baxter. That was through the South African office. Baxter asked Jefferson to arrange to have the diamonds cut, polished and delivered to our Paris office. Our Paris office didn't know the history of the transaction. It simply made delivery to Baxter on instructions of the South African office. Usually we try to know something about the people with whom we are dealing. Baxter juggled the deal between our two offices in such a way that each office thought the other one had done the investigating.

"Baxter had worked out one hell of a slick scheme. He had faked a perfect background of respectability."

"How did you find out about the smuggling?" Mason asked.

"His female accomplice broke down and confessed."

"Who is she?"

"A girl named Yvonne Manco."

"Tell me about it," Mason said.

"Didn't you read the account about a fellow jumping overboard from a cruise ship and committing suicide a while back?"

"Yes, I did," Mason said. "Wasn't *that* man's name Munroe Baxter?"

"Exactly."

"I knew I'd heard the name somewhere as soon as you mentioned it. How does the murder angle enter into it?"

Irving said, "Here's the general sketch. Yvonne Manco is a very beautiful young woman who sailed on a cruise ship around the world. She was the queen of the cruise. The ship touched at Naples, and when Yvonne started down the gangplank, she was met by Munroe Baxter, a man who had the appearance of a Frenchman, but the name, citizenship and passport of a United States citizen. You must understand all of these things fully in order to appreciate the sequence of events."

"Go ahead," Mason said.

"Apparently, Munroe Baxter had at one time been in love with Yvonne Manco. According to the story that was given to the passengers, they had been going together and then the affair had broken up through a misunderstanding."

"Whoever wrote that script did a beautiful job, Mr. Mason."

"It was a script?" Mason asked.

"Hell, yes. It was as phony as a three dollar bill."

"What happened?"

"The passengers naturally were interested. They saw this man burst through the crowd. They saw him embrace Yvonne Manco. They saw her faint in his arms. There was a beautiful romance, the spice of scandal, a page out of this beautiful young woman's past. It was touching; it was pathetic—and, naturally, it caused an enormous amount of gossip."

Mason nodded.

"The ship was in Naples for two days. It sailed, and when it sailed Munroe Baxter was pleading with Yvonne Manco to marry him. He was the last man off the ship; then he stood on the pier and wept copiously, shedding crocodile tears."

"Go on," Mason said, interested.

"The ship sailed out into the Mediterranean. It stopped in Genoa. Munroe Baxter met the ship at the dock. Again Yvonne Manco swooned in his arms, again she refused to marry him, again the ship sailed.

"Then came the pay-off. As the ship was off Gibraltar a helicopter hovered overhead. A man descended a rope ladder, dangled precariously from the last rung. The helicopter hovered over the deck of the ship, and Munroe Baxter dropped to the deck by the swimming pool, where Yvonne Manco was disporting herself in the sunlight in a seductive bathing suit."

"Romantic," Mason said.

"And opportune," Irving said dryly. "No one could resist such an impetuous, dramatic courtship. The passengers virtually forced Yvonne to give her consent. The captain married them on the high seas that night. The passengers turned the ship upside down in celebration. It was wonderful stuff."

"Yes, I can imagine," Mason said.

"And, of course," Irving went on, "since Baxter boarded the ship in that dramatic manner, without so much as a toothbrush or an extra handkerchief, how would the customs people suspect that Munroe Baxter was smuggling three hundred thousand dollars' worth of diamonds in a chamois-skin belt around his waist?"

"In the face of all that beautiful romance, who would have thought that Yvonne Manco had been Munroe Baxter's mistress for a couple of years, that she was his accomplice in a smuggling plot and that this courtship was all a dramatic hoax?"

"I see," Mason said.

Irving went on, "The stage was all set. Munroe Baxter, in the eyes of the passengers, was a crazy Frenchman, a United States citizen, of course, but one who had acquired all the excitability of the French.

"So, when the ship approached port and Yvonne Manco, dressed to the hilt, danced three times with the goodlooking assistant purser, it was only natural that Munroe Baxter should stage a violent scene, threaten to kill himself, break into tears, dash to his stateroom and subsequently leap overboard after a frenzied scene in which Yvonne Manco threatened to divorce him."

"Yes," Mason said, "I remember the newspapers made quite a play of the story."

"It was made to order for press coverage," Irving said. "And who would have thought that the excitable Munroe Baxter carried with him three hundred thousand dollars in diamonds when he jumped overboard, that he was a powerful swimmer who could easily swim to a launch which was opportunely waiting at a pre-arranged spot, and that later on he and the lovely Yvonne were to share the proceeds of a carefully written, superbly directed scenario, performed very cleverly for the sole purpose of fooling the customs men?"

"And it didn't?" Mason asked.

"Oh, but it did! Everything went like clockwork, except for one thing—Munroe Baxter didn't reappear to join Yvonne Manco. She went to the secluded motel which was to be their rendezvous. She waited and waited and waited and waited."

"Perhaps Baxter decided that a whole loaf was better than half a loaf," Mason said.

Irving shook his head. "It seems the lovely Yvonne Manco went to the accomplice who was waiting in the launch. At first, the accomplice told her that Baxter had never showed up. He told her that Baxter must have been seized by cramps while he was swimming underwater."

"Did this take place within the territorial waters of the United States?" Mason asked.

"Right at the approach to Los Angeles Harbor."

"In daylight?"

"No, just before daylight. You see, it was a cruise ship and it was gliding in at the earliest possible hour so the passengers could have a maximum time ashore for sightseeing."

"All right, Baxter was supposed to have drowned," Mason said. "What happened?"

"Well, Yvonne Manco had a horrible suspicion. She thought that the accomplice in the launch might have held Baxter's head underwater and might have taken the money belt."

"Probably, she wouldn't have said anything at all, if it hadn't been for the fact that customs agents were also putting two and two together. They called on the lovely Yvonne Manco to question her about her 'husband' after it appeared that she and her 'husband' had sailed on another cruise ship as man and wife some eighteen months earlier."

"And Yvonne Manco broke down and told them the whole story?" Mason asked.

"Told them the whole story, including the part that it had been Duane Jefferson who had been involved in the sale of the jewels. So police became very much interested in Duane Jefferson, and yesterday afternoon, on an affidavit of Yvonne Manco, a search warrant was issued and police searched the office."

"And recovered a hundred thousand dollars in gems?" Mason asked.

"Recovered a goodly assortment of diamonds," Irving said. "Let us say, perhaps a third of the value of the smuggled shipment."

"And the remaining two-thirds?"

Irving shrugged his shoulders.

"And the identification?" Mason asked.

Again Irving shrugged his shoulders.

"And where were these gems found?"

"Where someone had very cleverly planted them. You may remember the little flurry of excitement when an intruder was discovered in the office—the police asked us to check and see if anything had been taken. It never occurred to us to check *and see if anything had been planted.*"

"Where were the diamonds found?"

"In a package fastened to the back of a desk drawer with adhesive tape."

"And what does Duane Jefferson have to say about this?"

"What could he say?" Irving asked. "It was all news to him, just as it was to me."

"You can vouch for these facts?" Mason asked.

"I'll vouch for them. But I can't vouch for Duane's romantic, crazy notions of protecting this girl."

"She was the same girl who entered the office?"

"I think she was. Duane would have a fit and never speak to me again if he knew I ever entertained such a thought. You have to handle him with kid gloves where women are concerned. But if it comes to a showdown, *you're* going to have to drag this girl into it, and Duane Jefferson will cease to co-operate with you as soon as you mention her very existence."

Mason thought the matter over.

"Well?" Irving asked.

"Make out your check for two thousand dollars," Mason told him. "That will be on account of a five-thousand-dollar fee."

"What do you mean—a five-thousand-dollar fee?"

"It won't be more than that."

"Including detectives?"

"No. You will have to pay expenses. I'm fixing fees."

"Damn it," Irving exploded. "If that bunch in the home office hadn't mentioned a two-thousand-dollar retainer, I could have got you to handle the whole case for two thousand."

Mason sat quietly facing Irving.

"Well, it's done now, and there's nothing I can do about it," Irving said, taking from his wallet a check already made out to the lawyer. He slid the check across the desk to Perry Mason.

Mason said to Della Street, "Make a receipt, Della, and put on the receipt that this is a retainer on behalf of Duane Jefferson."

"What's the idea?" Irving asked.

"Simply to show that I'm not responsible to you or your company but only to my client."

Irving thought that over.

"Any objections?" Mason asked.

"No. I presume you're intimating that you'd even turn against me if it suited Duane's interests for you to do so."

"I'm more than intimating. I'm telling you."

Irving grinned. "That's okay by me. I'll go further. If at any time things start getting hot, you can count on me to do anything needed to back your play. I'd even consent to play the part of a missing witness."

Mason shook his head. "Don't try to call the plays. Let me do that."

Irving extended his hand. "I just want you to understand my position, Mason."

"And be sure *you* understand *mine*," Mason said.

CHAPTER FIVE

Mason looked at Della Street as Walter Irving left the office.

"Well?" Della Street asked.

Mason said, "I just about had to take the case in self-defense, Della."

"Why?"

"Otherwise, we'd be sitting on top of information in a murder case, we wouldn't have any client whom we would be protecting, and the situation could become rather rugged."

"And as it is now?" she asked.

"Now," he told her, "we have a client whom we can be protecting. An attorney representing a client in a murder case is under no obligation to go to the police and set forth his surmises, suspicions, and conclusions, particularly if he has reason to believe that such a course would be against the best interests of his client."

"But how about the positive evidence?" Della Street asked.

"Evidence of what?"

"Evidence that we harbored a young woman who had gone into that office and planted diamonds."

"We don't *know* she planted diamonds."

"Who had gone into the office then."

"We don't *know* she was the same woman."

"It's a reasonable assumption."

"Suppose she was merely a typist who happened to be in the building. We go to the police with a lot of suspicions, and the police give the story to the newspapers, then she sues for defamation of character."

"I see," Della Street said demurely. "I'm afraid it's hopeless to try and convince you."

"It is."

"And now may I ask you a question, Counselor?"

"What?"

"Do you suppose that it was pure coincidence that you are the attorney retained to represent the interests of Duane Jefferson?"

Mason stroked his chin thoughtfully.

"Well?" she prompted.

"I've thought of that," Mason admitted. "Of course, the fact that I am known as a trial attorney, that I have offices on the same floor of the same building would mean that Irving had had a chance to hear about me and, by the same token, a chance to notify his home office that I would be available."

"But he said he didn't do that. He said somebody beat him to it and he got the cable to turn over the two thousand dollars to you."

Mason nodded.

"Well?" Della Street asked.

"No comment," Mason said.

"So what do we do now?"

"Now," Mason said, "our position is very, very clear, Della. I suggest that you go down to the camera store, tell them that I want to buy a fingerprint camera, and you also might get a studio camera with a ground-glass focusing arrangement. Pick up some lights and we'll see if we can get a photograph of those latent fingerprints on the gum."

"And then?" she asked.

"Then," Mason said, "we'll enlarge the film so that it shows only the fingerprints and not the gum."

"And then?"

"By that time," Mason said, "I hope we have managed to locate the girl who made the fingerprints and find out about things for ourselves. While you're getting the cameras I'll go down to Paul Drake's office and have a chat with him."

"Chief," Della Street asked somewhat apprehensively, "isn't this rather risky?"

Mason's grin was infectious. "Sure it is."

"Hadn't you better forget about other things and protect yourself?"

Mason shook his head. "We're protecting a client, Della. Give me a description of that girl—the best one you can give."

"Well," Della Street said, "I'd place her age at twenty-six or twenty-seven, her height at five feet three inches, her weight at about a hundred and sixteen pounds. She had reddish-brown hair and her eyes were also a reddish-brown— about the same color as her hair, very expressive. She was good-looking, trim and well proportioned."

"Good figure?" Mason asked.

"Perfect."

"How was she dressed?"

"I can remember that quite well, Chief, because she looked stunning. I remember thinking at the time that she looked more like a client than a gal from an employment agency.

"She wore a beautifully tailored grey flannel suit, navy blue kid shoes. Umm, let me see...yes, I remember now. There was fine white stitching across the toes of the shoes. She carried a matching envelope purse and white gloves. Now let me think. I am quite sure she didn't wear a hat. As I recall, she had a tortoise-shell band on, and there wasn't a hair out of place.

"She didn't take her jacket off while she was working, so I can't be certain, but I think she had on a pale blue cashmere sweater. She opened just the top button of her jacket, so I can't say for sure about this."

Mason smiled. "You women never miss a thing about another woman, do you, Della? I would say that was remembering *very* well. Would you type it out for me—the description? Use a plain sheet of paper, not my letterhead."

Mason waited until Della Street had finished typing the description, then said, "Okay, Della, go down and get the cameras. Get lots of film, lights, a tripod, and anything we may need. Don't let on what we want to use them for."

"The fingerprint camera—isn't that a giveaway?"

"Tell the proprietor I'm going to have to cross-examine a witness and I want to find out all about how a fingerprint camera works."

Della Street nodded.

Mason took the typed description and walked down the hall to Paul Drake's office. He nodded to the girl at the switchboard. "Paul Drake in?"

"Yes, Mr. Mason. Shall I say you're here?"

"Anybody with him?"

"No."

"Tell him I'm on my way," Mason said, opening the gate in the partition and walking down the long glassed-in runway off which there were numerous cubby-hole offices. He came to the slightly more commodious office marked "Paul Drake, Private," pushed open the door and entered.

"Hi," Drake said. "I was waiting to hear from you."

Mason raised his eyebrows.

"Don't look so innocent," Drake said. "The officials of the South African Gem Importing and Exploration Company have been checking up on you by long-distance telephone. They called the manager of the building and asked him about you."

"Did they ask him about me by name," Mason asked, "or did they ask him to recommend some attorney?"

"No, they had your name. They wanted to know all about you."

"What did he tell them?"

Drake grinned and said, "Your rent's paid up, isn't it?"

"What the devil is this all about, do you know, Paul?"

"All I know is it's a murder rap," Drake said, "and the way the police are acting, someone must have caved in with a confession."

"Sure," Mason said, "a confession that would pass the buck to someone else and take the heat off the person making the so-called confession."

"Could be," Drake said. "What do we do?"

"We get busy."

"On what?"

"First," Mason told him, "I want to find a girl."

"Okay, what do I have to go on?"

Mason handed him Della Street's typewritten description.

"Fine," Drake said, "I can go downstairs, stand on the street corner during the lunch hour and pick you out a hundred girls of that description in ten minutes."

"Take another look," Mason invited. "She's a lot better than average."

"If it was average I could make it a thousand," Drake said.

"All right," Mason said. "We're going to have to narrow it down."

"How?"

"This girl," Mason said, "is an expert typist. She probably holds down a very good secretarial job somewhere."

"Unless, of course, she *was* an exceedingly fine secretary and then got married," Drake said.

Mason nodded, conceding the point without changing his position. "She also has legal experience," he said.

"How do you know?"

"That's something I'm not at liberty to tell you."

"All right, what do I do?"

Mason said, "Paul, you're going to have to open up a dummy office. You're going to telephone the Association of Legal Secretaries; you're going to put an ad in the bar journal and the newspapers; you're goint to ask for a young, attractive typist. Now, I don't *know* that this girl takes shorthand. Therefore, you're going to have to state that a knowledge of shorthand is desirable but not necessary. You're going to offer a salary of two hundred dollars a week—"

"My Lord!" Drake said. "You'll be deluged, Perry. You might just as well ask the whole city to come trooping into your office."

"Wait a minute," Mason told him. "You don't have the sketch yet."

"Well, I certainly hope I don't!"

"Your ad will provide that the girl must pass a typing test in order to get the job. She must be able to copy rapidly and perfectly and at a very high rate of speed—fix a top rate of words per minute.

"Now, the type of girl we want will already have a job somewhere. We've got to get a job that sounds sufficiently attractive so she'll come in to take a look. Therefore, we can't expect her in during office hours. So mention that the office will be open noons and until seven o'clock in the evening."

"And you want me to rent a furnished office?" Drake asked.

"That right."

Drake said lugubriously: You'd better make arrangements to replace the carpet when you leave. The one that's there will be worn threadbare by the horde of applicants—How the devil will I know if the right girl comes in?"

"That's what I'm coming to," Mason said. "You're going to start looking these applicants over. You won't find many that can type at the rate specified. Be absolutely hard-boiled with the qualifications. Have a good secretary sitting there, weeding them out. Don't pay any attention to anyone who has to reach for an eraser. The girl I want can make that keyboard sound like a machine-gun."

"Okay, then what?"

"When you get girls who qualify on the typing end of the job," Mason said, "give them a personal interview. Look them over carefully to see how they check with this description and tell them you want to see their driving licenses. A girl like that is bound to have a car. That's where the catch comes in."

"How come?"

Mason said. "Sometime this afternoon I'm going to send you over a right thumbprint—that is, a photograph of a thumbprint—perhaps not the best fingerprinting in the world but at least you'll be able to identify it. When you look at their driving licenses, make it a point to be called into another room for something. Get up and excuse yourself. You can say that there's another applicant in there that you have to talk to briefly, or that you have to answer a phone or something. Carry the girl's driving license in there with you, give the thumbprint a quick check. You can eliminate most of them at a glance. Some of them you may have to study a little bit. But if you get the right one, you'll be able to recognize the thumbprint pretty quickly."

"What do I do then?"

"Make a note of the name and address on the driving license. In that way, she won't be able to give you a phony name. And call me at once."

"Anything else?" Drake asked.

"This is what I think," Mason said, "but it's just a hunch. I *think* the girl's first name will be Mae. When you find a girl who answers that general description and can type like a house afire, whose first name is Mae, start checking carefully."

"When will you have that thumbprint?"

"Sometime this afternoon. Her driving license will have the imprint of her right thumb on it."

"Can you tell me what this is all about?" Drake asked.

Mason grinned and shook his head. "It's better if you don't know, Paul."

"One of those things, eh?" Drake asked, his voice showing a singular lack of enthusiasm.

"No," Mason told him, "it isn't. It's just that I'm taking an ounce of prevention."

"With you," Drake told him, "I prefer a *pound* of prevention. If things go wrong, I know there won't be more than an ounce of cure."

CHAPTER SIX

Mason sat in the vistors' room at the jail and looked across at Duane Jefferson.

His client was a tall, composed individual who seemed reserved, unexcited, and somehow very British.

Mason tried to jar the man out of his extraordinary complacency.

"You're charged with murder," he said.

Duane Jefferson observed him coolly. "I would hardly be here otherwise, would I?"

"What do you know about this thing?"

"Virtually nothing. I knew the man, Baxter, in his lifetime—that is, I assume it was the same one."

"How did you know him?"

"He represented himself as a big wholesale dealer. He showed up at the South African office and wanted to buy diamonds. It is against the policy of the company to sell diamonds in the rough, unless, of course, they are industrial diamonds."

"Baxter wanted them in the rough?"

"That's right."

"And he was advised he couldn't have them?"

"Well, of course, we were tactful about it, Mr. Mason. Mr. Baxter gave promise of being an excellent customer, and he was dealing on a cash basis."

"So what was done?"

"We showed him some diamonds that were cut and polished. He didn't want those. He said that the deal he was putting across called for buying diamonds in the rough and carrying them through each step of cutting and polishing. He said he wanted to be able to tell his customers he had personally selected the diamonds just as they came from the fields."

"Why?"

"He didn't say."

"And he wasn't asked?"

"In a British-managed company," Jefferson said, "we try to keep personal questions to a minimum. We don't pry, Mr. Mason."

"So what was done finally?"

"It was arranged that he would select the diamonds, that we would send them to our Paris office, that there they would be cut and polished, and, after they were cut and polished, delivery would be made to Mr. Baxter."

"What were the diamonds worth?"

"Wholesale or retail?"

"Wholesale."

"Very much less than their retail price."

"How much less?"

"I can't tell you."

"Why not?"

"That information is a very closely guarded trade secret, Mr. Mason."

"But I'm your attorney."

"Quite."

"Look here," Mason said, "are you British?"

"No."

"American?"

"Yes."

"How long have you been working for a British company?"

"Five or six years."

"You have become quite British."

"There are certain mannerisms, Mr. Mason, which the trade comes to expect of the representatives of a company such as ours."

"And there are certain mannerisms which an American jury expects to find in an American citizen," Mason told him.

"If a jury should feel you'd cultivated a British manner, you might have reason to regret your accent and cool, impersonal detachment."

Jefferson's lip seemed to curl slightly. "I would have nothing but contempt for a jury that would let personal considerations such as those influence its judgment."

"That would break the jurors' hearts," Mason told him.

Jefferson said, "We may as well understand each other at the outset, Mr. Mason. I govern my actions according to principle. I would rather die than yield in a matter of principle."

"All right," Mason said. "Have it your own way. It's your funeral. Did you see Baxter again?"

"No, sir, I didn't. After that, arrangements were completed through the Paris office."

"Irving?" Mason asked.

"I don't think it was Irving, Mr. Mason. I think it was one of the other representatives."

"You read about the arrival of the cruise ship and Baxter's supposed suicide?"

"I did, indeed, Mr. Mason."

"And did you make any comment to the authorities?"

"Certainly not."

"You knew he was carrying a small fortune in diamonds?"

"I assumed that a small fortune in diamonds had been delivered to him through our Paris office. I had no means, of course, of knowing what he had done with them."

"You didn't make any suggestions to the authorities?"

"Certainly not. Our business dealings are highly confidential."

"But you did discuss his death with your partner, Irving?"

"Not a partner, Mr. Mason. A representative of the company, a personal friend but—"

"All right, your associate," Mason corrected.

"Yes, I discussed it with him."

"Did he have any ideas?"

"None. Except that there were certain suspicious circumstances in connection with the entire situation."

"It occurred to you that the whole thing might have been part of a smuggling plot?"

"I prefer not to amplify that statement, Mr. Mason. I can simply say that there were certain suspicious circumstances in connection with the entire transaction."

"And you discussed those with Irving?"

"As a representative of the company talking to an associate, I did. I would prefer, however, not to go into detail as to what I said. You must remember,

Mr. Mason, that I am here not in an individual but a representative capacity."

"You may be in this country in a representative capacity," Mason said, "but don't ever forget that you're here in this jail in a purely individual capacity."

"Oh, quite," Jefferson said.

"I understand police found diamonds in your office," Mason went on.

Jefferson nodded.

"Where did those diamonds come from?"

"Mr. Mason, I haven't the faintest idea. I am in my office approximately six hours out of the twenty-four. I believe the building provides a scrubwoman with a master key. The janitor also has a master key. People come and go through that office. Police even told me that there was someone trying to break into the office, or that someone had broken into the office."

"A girl," Mason said.

"I understand it was a young woman, yes."

"Do you have any idea who this woman was?"

"No. Certainly not!"

"Do you know any young women here in the city?"

Jefferson hesitated.

"Do you?" Mason prodded.

Jefferson met his eyes. "No."

"You're acquainted with *no* young woman?"

"No."

"Would you perhaps be trying to shield someone?"

"Why should I try to shield someone?"

"I am not asking you why at the moment. I am asking you if you are."

"No."

"You understand it could be a very serious matter if you should try to falsify any of the facts?"

"Isn't it a rule of law in this country," Jefferson countered, "that the prosecution must prove the defendant guilty beyond all reasonable doubt?"

Mason nodded.

"They can't do it," Jefferson said confidently.

"You may not have another chance to tell me your story," Mason warned.

"I've told it."

"There is no girl?"

"No."

"Weren't you writing to some young woman here before you left South Africa?"

Again there was a perceptible hesitancy, then Jefferson looked him in the eyes and said: "No."

"Police told you there was some young woman who broke into your office?"

"Someone who opened the door with a key."

"Had you given your key to any woman?"

"No. Certainly not."

Mason said: "Look here, if there's anyone you want protected, tell me the whole story. I'll try to protect that person as far as possible. After all, I'm representing you. I'm trying to do what is for your best interests. Now, don't put yourself in such a position that you're going to have to try to deceive your attorney. Do you understand what that can lead to?"

"I understand."

"And you are protecting no one?"

"No one."

"The district attorney's office feels that it has some evidence against you, otherwise it wouldn't be proceeding in a case of this kind."

"I suppose a district attorney can be mistaken as well as anyone else."

"Better sometimes," Mason said. "You're not being very helpful."

"What help can I give, Mr. Mason? Suppose *you* should walk into your office tomorrow morning and find the police there. Suppose they told you that they had uncovered stolen property in your office. Suppose I should ask you to tell me the entire story. What could you tell me?"

"I'd try to answer your questions."

"I have answered your questions, Mr. Mason."

"I have reason to believe there's some young woman here in the city whom you know."

"There is no one."

Mason got to his feet. "Well," he told the young man, "it's up to you."

"On the contrary, Mr. Mason. I think you'll find that it's up to *you*."

"You're probably right, at that," Mason told him, and signaled the guard that the interview was over.

CHAPTER SEVEN

Mason unlocked the door of his private office. Della Street looked up from her work. "How did it go, Chief?"

Mason made a gesture of throwing something away.

"Not talking?" Della Street asked.

"Talking," Mason said, "but doesn't make sense. He's protecting some woman."

"Why?"

"That," Mason said, "is something we're going to have to find out. Get the cameras, Della?"

"Yes. Cameras, lights, films, tripod—everything."

"We're going into the photographic business," Mason said. "Tell Gertie we don't want to be disturbed, no matter what happens."

Della Street started to pick up the connecting telephone to the outer office, then hesitated. "Gertie is going to make something out of *this*!" she said.

Mason frowned thoughtfully. "You have a point there," he said.

"With her romantic disposition, she will get ideas in her head that you'll never get out with a club."

"All right," Mason decided. "Don't let her know I'm in. We'll just go into the law library and—do you think you could help me lift that desk over on its side, Della?"

"I can try."

"Good. We'll just go into the library, close and lock the door."

"Suppose Gertie should want me for something? Can't we tell her what we're doing so she can—"

Mason shook his head. "I don't want *anyone* to know about this, Della."

Della went through the motions of throwing something in the waste-basket. "There goes my good name," she said.

"You'll need to stay only to help me get the desk over on its side, and you can fix up the lighting. We'll lock the door from the law library to the outer office and leave the door to this office open. You can hear the phone if Gertie rings."

"That's all right," Della Street said, "but suppose she comes in for something?"

"Well, if the door's open," Mason said, "she'll see that we're photographing something."

"Her curiosity is as bad as her romanticism," Della said.

"Does she talk?" Mason asked.

"I wish I knew the answer to that one, Chief. She must talk to that boy friend of hers. You couldn't keep Gertie quiet with a muzzle. I doubt that she talks to anyone else."

"Okay," Mason said, "we'll take a chance. Come on, Della. Let's get that desk on its side and get the floodlights rigged up."

"Here's a chart," Della Street said, "giving all the exposure factors. I told the man at the camera store we wanted to copy some documents. You have to change your exposure factor when you do real close-up photography. He suggested that we use film packs with the camera where you focus on the ground glass. The fingerprint camera is supposed to be a self-contained unit, with lights and every—"

"I understand," Mason interrupted. "I want to get the wad of chewing gum photographed in place on the bottom of the desk, then I want to get close-ups showing the fingerprints. We can get the photographer to enlarge the fingerprints from these photographs in case the fingerprint camera doesn't do a good job."

"The fingerprint camera seems to be pretty near—" She paused suddenly.

Mason laughed. "Foolproof?"

"Well," Della Street said, "that's what the man at the camera store said."

"All right," Mason told her, "let's go. We'll take photographs at different exposures. You have plenty of film packs?"

"Heavens, yes! I figured you'd want to be sure you had the job done, and I got enough film so you can take all the pictures you want at all kinds of different exposures."

"That's fine," Mason told her.

Della Street took one end of the typewriter desk, Mason the other. "We'll have to move it out from the wall," Mason said. "Now tilt it back, Della. It'll be heavy just before it gets to the floor. You think you can—?"

"Good heavens, yes, Chief. It's not heavy."

"The drawers are full of stationery, and that typewriter—We could take some of the things out and lighten it."

"No, no, let's go. It's all right."

They eased the desk back to the floor.

"All right," Mason said, "give me a hand with the lights and the tripod. We'll get this camera set up and focused."

"I have a magnifying glass," Della Street said. "They seem to think that on the critical focusing necessary for close-ups it will help."

"Good girl," Mason told her. "Let's see what we can do. We'll want an unbalanced cross-lighting, and since light varies inversely as the square of the distance, we'll space these lights accordingly."

Mason first took a series of pictures with the fingerprint camera, then got the lights plugged in and adjusted, the studio camera placed on the tripod and properly focused. He used a tape measure to determine the position of the lights, then slipped a film pack into the camera and regarded the wad of chewing gum thoughtfully.

"That's going to be fine," Della Street said. "How did you know about using unbalanced cross-lighting to bring out the ridges?"

"Cross-examining photographers," Mason said, "plus a study of books on photography. A lawyer has to know a little something about everything. Don't you notice *Photographic Evidence* by Scott over there?" Mason indicated the book bound in red leather.

"That's right," she said. "I remember seeing you studying that from time to time. You used some of his stuff in that automobile case, didn't you?"

"Uh huh," Mason said. "It's surprising how much there is to know about photography. Now, Della, I'm going to start with this lens at *f11*, taking a photograph at a twenty-fifth of a second. Then we'll take one at a tenth of a second, then one at a second. Then I'll use the cable release and we'll take one at two seconds. Then we'll try *f16*, run through the exposures all over again, then take another batch at *f22*."

"All right," Della Street said. "I'll keep notes of the different exposures."

Mason started taking the pictures, pulling the tabs out of the film pack, tearing them off, dropping them into the waste-basket.

"Oh oh," Della Street said. "There's the phone. That's Gertie calling."

She made a dash for Mason's private office. Mason continued taking pictures.

Della Street was back after a moment. "Walter Irving wants you to call just as soon as you come in."

Mason nodded.

"Gertie asked if you were in yet, and I lied like a trooper," Della Street said.

"Okay, Della. Walter Irving didn't say what he wanted, did he?"

"He said he wanted to know if you'd been able to get any information out of Duane Jefferson about the woman in the case."

Mason said, "As soon as we get finished here, Della, tell Paul Drake I want to put a shadow on Irving."

"You suspect him?"

"Not exactly. The policy of this office is to protect our client and to hell with the rest of them."

"What's the client doing?"

"Sitting tight. Says he knows nothing about the girl who broke into the office, that he doesn't know any girl here, hasn't been corresponding with anyone, and all that."

"You think he has?"

"That wasn't just a casual visit that Mae Wallis paid to their office."

"You've decided she was the girl?"

"Oh, not officially. I'd deny it to the police. But where did the diamonds in the chewing gum come from?"

"Chief, why would *she* plant a hundred thousand dollars' worth of diamonds and then keep a couple of diamonds with her and conceal them in a wad of chewing gum?"

"I can give you *an* answer," Mason said, "but it may not be *the* answer."

"What is it?"

"Suppose she had been given some gems to plant. She must have had them wrapped in tissue paper in her purse. She had to work in a hurry and probably became somewhat alarmed. Something happened to make her suspicious. She realized that she had been detected."

"What makes you say that?"

"Because she roughed up the office, making it appear she was looking *for* something. Otherwise she'd have slipped in, planted the diamonds and left."

"Then you think the diamonds that she put in the chewing gum were ones she had overlooked when she was making the plant?"

"I said it was *an* answer. After she got established as a typist in our office, she had a breathing spell. She opened her purse to make sure she hadn't overlooked anything, and found several of the diamonds. She knew that police were on the job and that there was a good chance she might be picked up, questioned, and perhaps searched. So she fastened the diamonds to the underside of the desk."

"I keep thinking those 'Prince Charming' letters have something to do with it, Chief."

Mason nodded. "So do I. Perhaps she planted the diamonds in the office and at the same time deliberately planted the letters in the restroom."

"She could have done that, all right," Della Street admitted. "There's the phone again."

She gathered her skirts and again sprinted for Mason's private office. Mason continued to take photographs while she answered the phone and returned.

"What is it?" Mason asked.

"I have to announce," she said, "that Gertie is just a little suspicious."

"Yes?" Mason asked.

"Yes. She wants to know why it's taking me so long to answer the phone."

"What did you tell her?"

"Told her I was doing some copy work and I didn't want to stop in the middle of a sentence."

Mason snapped out the floodlights. "All right, Della. We'll quit. We have enough pictures. Tell Paul Drake I want shadows put on Walter Irving."

CHAPTER EIGHT

A few mornings later Mason was scanning the papers on his desk. "Well, I see that the grand jury has now filed an indictment, charging Duane Jefferson with first-degree murder."

"Why the indictment?" Della Street asked.

"The district attorney can proceed against a defendant in either of two ways. He can file a complaint or have someone swear to a complaint. Then the Court holds a preliminary hearing. At that time the defendant can cross-examine the witnesses. If the Court makes an order binding the defendant over, the district attorney then files an information and the case is brought on to trial before a jury.

"However, the district attorney can, if he wishes, present witnesses to the grand jury. The grand jury then returns an indictment, and the transcript of the testimony of the witnesses is delivered to the defendant. In that case, there is no opportunity for counsel for the defense to cross-examine the witnesses until they get to court."

"Now, in this case against Duane Jefferson, the main witness before the grand jury seems to have been Yvonne Manco, who tells a great story about how her lover-boy, Munroe Baxter, was rubbed out by some nasty people who wanted to steal the diamonds he was smuggling. Then there is the testimony of a police officer that a large portion of those diamonds was found in the office occupied by Duane Jefferson."

"Is that testimony sufficient to support an indictment?" Della Street asked.

Mason grinned and said, "It certainly wouldn't be sufficient standing by itself to bring about a conviction in a court of law."

"Do you intend to question the sufficiency of the evidence?"

"Lord, no," Mason said. "For some reason the district attorney is breaking his neck to get prompt trial, and I'm going to co-operate by every means in my power."

"Wouldn't it be better to stall the thing along a bit until—?"

Mason shook his head.

"Why not, Chief?"

"Well, the rumor is that the district attorney has a surprise witness he's going to throw at us. He's so intent on that he may overlook the fact that there isn't any real *corpus delicti.*"

"What do you mean?"

"The body of Munroe Baxter has never been found," Mason said.

"Does it have to be?"

"Not necessarily. The words *corpus delicti*, contrary to popular belief, don't mean the 'body of the victim.' They mean the 'body of the crime.' But it *is* necessary to show that a murder was committed. That can be shown by independent evidence, but of course the *best* evidence is the body of the victim."

"So you're going to have an immediate trial?"

"Just as soon as we can get an open date on the calendar," Mason said. "And with the district attorney and the defense both trying to get the earliest possible trial date, that shouldn't be too difficult. How's Paul Drake coming with his office setup?"

"Chief, you should see that. It's wonderful! There's this ad in all of the papers, advertising for a legally trained secretary who can type like a house afire. The salary to start—to start, mind you—is two hundred dollars a week. It is intimated that the attorney is engaged in cases of international importance and that there may be an opportunity to travel, to meet important personalities. It's a secretary's dream."

"And the office where he's screening applicants?" Mason asked.

"All fitted out with desks, typewriters, law books, plush carpets and an air of quiet dignity which makes it seem that even the janitor must be drawing a salary about equal to that of the ordinary corporation president."

"I hope he hasn't overdone it," Mason said. "I'd better take a look."

"No, it isn't overdone. I can assure you of that. The air of conservatism and respectability envelops the place like a curtain of smog, permeating every nook and cranny of the office. You should see them—stenographers who are applicants come in chewing gum, giggling and willing to take a chance that lightning may strike despite their lack of qualifications. They stand for a few seconds in that office, then quietly remove their gum, look around at the furniture and start talking in whispers."

"How does he weed out the incompetents?" Mason asked.

"There's a battery of typewriters; girls are asked to sit at the typewriters, write out their names and addresses and list their qualifications.

"Of course, a good typist can tell the minute a girl's hands touch the keyboard whether she is really skillful, fairly competent, or just mediocre. Only the girls who can really play a tune on the keyboard get past the first receptionist."

"Well," Mason said, "it's—"

The private, unlisted phone jangled sharply.

"Good Lord," Della Street said, "that must be Paul now. He's the only other one who has that number."

Mason grabbed for the phone. "That means he's got information so hot he doesn't dare to go through the outer switchboard. Hello...hello, Paul."

Drake's voice came over the wire. He was talking rapidly but in the hushed tones of one who is trying to keep his voice from being heard in an adjoining room.

"Hello, Perry. Hello, Perry. This is Paul."

"Yes Paul, go ahead."

"I have your girl."

"You're certain?"

"Yes."

"Who is she?"

"Her name is Mae W. Jordan. She lives at Seven-Nine-Two Cabachon Street. She's employed at the present time in a law office. She doesn't want to give the name. She would have to give two weeks' notice. She wants the job very badly, and, boy, can that girl tickle the typewriter! And it's wonderful typing."

"What does the *W* stand for?" Mason asked. "Wallis?"

"I don't know yet. I'm just giving you a quick flash that we have the girl."

"You know it's the same one?"

"Yes. The thumbprints match. I'm holding her driving license right at the moment."

"How about the address?" Mason asked.

"And the address is okay. It's Seven-Nine-Two Cabachon Street, the same address that's given on her driving license."

"Okay," Mason said. "Now here's what you do, Paul. Tell her that you *think* she can do the job; that you'll have to arrange an appointment with Mr. Big himself for six o'clock tonight. Tell her to return then. Got that?"

"I've got it," Drake said. "Shall I tell her anything else about the job?"

"No," Mason said. "Try and find out what you can. Be interested but not *too* curious."

"You want me to put a shadow on her?"

"Not if you're certain of the address," Mason said.

"Think we should try to find out about the law office where she's working?"

"No," Mason said. "With her name and address we can get everything we need. This girl is smart and sharp, and she may be mixed up in a murder, Paul. She's undoubtedly connected in some way with a diamond-smuggling operation. Too many questions will—"

"I get it," Drake interruped. "Okay, Perry, I'll fix an appointment for six o'clock and call you back in fifteen or twenty minutes."

"Do better than that," Mason said. "As soon as you've finished with this girl, jump in your car and come up here. There's no use waiting around there any longer. We've found what we were looking for. You can close the office tomorrow. Take your ads out of the papers and tell all other applicants that the job has been filled. Let's start cutting down the expense."

"Okay," Drake said.

Mason hung up the phone and grinned at Della Street. "Well, we have our typist, Della. She's Mae W. Jordan of Seven-Nine-Two Cabachon Street. Make a note of that—and keep the note where no one else can find it."

CHAPTER NINE

Paul Drake was grinning with the satisfaction of a job well done as he eased himself into the big overstuffed chair in Perry Mason's office.

"Well, we did it, Perry, but it certainly was starting from scratch and working on slender clues."

Mason flashed Della Street a glance. "It was a nice job, Paul."

"What gave you your lead in the first place?" Drake asked.

"Oh," Mason said with a gesture of dismissal, "it was just a hunch."

"But you had a damn good thumbprint," Drake said.

"Purely fortuitous," Mason observed.

"Well, if you don't want to tell me, I don't suppose you will," Drake said. "I see they've indicted Jefferson."

"That's right."

"The district attorney says there are certain factors in the situation which demand a speedy trial in order to keep evidence from being dissipated."

"Uh huh," Mason said noncommittally."

"You going to stall around and try for delay?"

"Why should I?"

"Well, ordinarily when the D.A. wants something, the attorney for the defense has different ideas."

"This isn't an ordinary case, Paul."

"No, I suppose not."

"What have you found out about Irving?" Mason asked.

Drake pulled a notebook from his pocket. "Full name, Walter Stockton Irving. Been with the Paris branch of the South African Gem Importing and Exploration Company for about seven years. Likes life on the Continent, the broader standards of morality, the more leisurely pace of life. Quite a race horse fan."

"The deuce he is!"

"That's right. Of course, over there it isn't quite the way it is here."

"A gambler?"

"Well, not exactly. He'll get down to Monte Carlo once in a while and do a little plunging, but mostly he likes to get out with a pair of binoculars and a babe on his arm, swinging a cane, enjoying the prerogatives of being a quote gentleman unquote."

"Now that," Mason said, "interests me a lot, Paul."

"I thought it would."

"What's he doing with his time here?"

"Simply waiting for the branch to get ready for business. He's leading a subdued life. Doubtless the murder charge pending against Jefferson is holding him back slightly. He seems to have made one contact."

"Who?" Mason asked.

"A French babe. Marline Chaumont."

"Where?"

"A bungalow out on Ponce de Leon Drive. the number is 8257."

"Does Marline Chaumont live there alone?"

"No. She has a brother she's taking care of."

"What's wrong with the brother?"

"Apparently he's a mental case. He was released from a hospital, so that his sister could take care of him. However, elaborate precautions are being taken to keep the neighbors from knowing anything about it. One of the neighbors suspects, but that's as far as it goes at the present time."

"Violent?" Mason asked.

"No, not at this time. Just harmless. You've heard of prefrontal lobotomy?"

"Yes, sure. That's the treatment they formerly used on the hopelessly violent insane and on criminals. I understand they've more or less discontinued it."

"Turns a man into a vegetable more or less, doesn't it?"

"Well, you can't get doctors to agree on it," Mason said. "But I think it now has generally been discontinued."

"That's the operation this chap had. He's sort of a zombie. I can't find out too much about him. Anyhow, Marline knew your man Irving over in Paris. Probably when Marline is freed of responsibilities and gets dolled up in glad rags she's quite a number."

"How about now?" Mason asked.

"Now she's the devoted sister. That's one thing about those French, Perry. They go to town when they're on the loose, but when they assume responsibilities they *really* assume them."

"How long has she been here?" Mason asked.

"She's been in this country for a year, according to her statements to tradesmen. But we haven't been able to check up. She's new in the neighborhood. She moved into her house there when she knew that her brother was coming home. She was living in an apartment up to that time. An apartment house would be a poor place to have a mental case. Marline knew it, so she got this bungalow."

"Living there alone with her brother?"

"A housekeeper comes in part of the day."

"And Irving has been going there?"

"Uh huh. Twice to my knowledge."

"Trying to get Marline to go out?"

"What he's *trying* to get is a question. Marline seems to be very devoted to her brother and very domesticated. The first time my operative shadowed Irving to the place it was in the afternoon. When Marline came to the door there was an affectionate greeting. Irving went inside, stayed for about an hour, and when he left, seemed to be trying to persuade Marline to come with him. He stood in the doorway talking to her. She smiled but kept shaking her head.

"So Irving went away. He was back that night, went inside the house, and apparently Marline sold him on the idea of brother sitting because Marline went out and was gone for an hour or two."

"How did she go?"

"By bus."

"She doesn't have a car?"

"Apparently not."

"Where did she go?"

"Gosh, Perry! You didn't tell me you wanted me to shadow *her*. Do you want me to?"

"No," Mason said, "I guess not, Paul. But the thing interests me. What's happened since?"

"Well, apparently Irving recognized the futility of trying to woo Marline away from her responsibilities, or else the trouble Jefferson is in is weighing heavily on his shoulders. He's keeping pretty much to himself in his apartment now."

"What apartment?" Mason asked.

"The Alta Loma Apartments."

"Pick up anything about the case, Paul?"

"The D.A. is supposed to be loaded for bear on this one. He's so darned anxious to get at you, he's running around in circles. He's told a couple of friendly reporters that this is the sort of case he's been looking for and waiting for. Perry, are you all right on this case?"

"What do you mean, 'all right'?"

"Are *you* in the clear?"

"Sure."

"You haven't been cutting any corners?"

Mason shook his head.

"The D.A. is acting as though he had you where he wanted you. He's like a kid with a new toy for Christmas—a whole Christmas tree full of new toys."

"I'm glad he's happy," Mason said. "What about this Mae Jordan, Paul?"

"I didn't get a lot more than I told you over the phone, except that she's promised to be there at six tonight."

"She's working?"

"That's right."

"What kind of an impression does she make, Paul?"

"Clean-cut and competent," Drake said. "She has a nice voice, nice personality, very neat in her appearance, knows what she's doing every minute of the time, and she certainly can type. Her shorthand is just about as fast as you'd find anywhere."

"She's happy in her job?"

"Apparently not. I don't know what it's all about, but she wants to get away from her present environment."

"Perhaps a thwarted love affair?"

"Could be."

"Sounds like it," Mason said.

"Well, you can find out tonight," Drake told him.

"When we get her into that office tonight, Paul," Mason said, "don't mention my name. Don't make *any* introductions. Simply state that I am the man for whom she will be working."

"Will she recognize you?" Drake asked.

"I don't think I've ever seen her," Mason said, glancing at Della Street.

"That doesn't necessarily mean anything. Your pictures get in the paper a lot."

"Well, if she recognizes me it won't make any difference," Mason said, "because outside of the first few questions, Paul, I'm not going to be talking to her about a job."

"You mean that she'll know the thing was a plant as soon as you walk in?"

"Well, I hope not quite *that* soon," Mason said. "But she'll know it shortly after I start questioning her. As long as she talks I'm going to let her talk."

"That won't be long," Drake said. "She answers questions, but she doesn't volunteer any information."

"All right," Mason said. "I'll see you a little before six tonight, Paul."

"Now remember," Drake warned, "there may be a little trouble."

"How come?"

"This girl has got her mind all set on a job where she can travel. She wants to get away from everything. The minute you let her know that you were simply locating her as a witness, she's going to resent it."

"What do you think she'll do?" Mason asked.

"She may do anything."

"I'd like that, Paul."

"You would?"

"Yes," Mason said. "I'd like to know just what she does when she's good and angry. Don't kid yourself about this girl, Paul. She's mixed up in something pretty sinister."

"How deep is she mixed up in it?"

"Probably up to her eyebrows," Mason said. "This Marline Chaumont knew Walter Irving in Paris?"

"Apparently so. She was sure glad to see him. When he rang the bell and she came to the door, she took one look, then make a flying leap into his arms. She was all French."

"And Irving doesn't go there any more?"

Drake shook his head.

"What would she do if I went out to talk with her this afternoon?"

"She might talk. She might not."

"Would she tell Irving I'd been there?"

"Probably."

"Well, I'll have to take that chance, Paul. I'm going to call on Marline Chaumont."

"May I suggest that you take me?" Della Street asked.

"As a chaperon or for the purpose of keeping notes on what is said?" Mason asked.

"I can be very effective in both capacities," Della Street observed demurely.

"It's that French background," Drake said, grinning. "It scares the devil out of them, Perry."

CHAPTER TEN

Perry Mason drove slowly along Ponce de Leon Drive.

"That's it," Della Street said. "The one on the left, the white bungalow with the green trim."

"Mason drove the car past the house, sizing it up, went to the next intersection, made a *U* turn, and drove back.

"What are you going to tell her?" Della Street asked.

"It'll depend on how she impresses me."

"And on how we impress her?"

"I suppose so."

"Isn't this somewhat dangerous, Chief?"

"In what way?"

"She'll be almost certain to tell Irving."

"Tell him what?"

"That you were out checking up on him."

"I'll tell him that myself."

"And then he'll know that you've had people shadowing him."

"If he's known Miss Chaumont in Paris, he won't know just *how* we checked up. I'd like to throw a scare into Mr. Walter Irving. He's too damned sure of himself."

Mason walked up the three steps to the front porch and pushed the bell button.

After a moment the door was opened a cautious three inches. A brass guard chain stretched taut across the opening.

Mason smiled at the pair of bright black eyes which surveyed him from the interior of the house. "We're looking for a Miss Chaumont."

"I am Miss Chaumont."

"Of Paris?"

"*Mais oui.* I have lived in Paris, yes. Now I live here."

"Would you mind if I asked you a few questions?"

"About what?"

"About Paris?"

"I would love to have you ask me questions about Paris."

"It's rather awkward, standing out here and talking through the door," Mason said.

"Monsieur can hear me?"

"Oh, yes."

"And I can hear you."

Mason smiled at her. Now that his eyes were becoming accustomed to the half-light he could see the oval of the face and a portion of a trim figure.

"Were you familiar with the South African Gem Importing and Exploration Company in Paris?"

"Why do you ask me that question?"

"Because I am interested."

"And who are you?"

"My name is Perry Mason. I am a lawyer."

"Oh, *you* are Perry Mason?"

"That's right."

"I have read about you."

"That's interesting."

"What do you want, Mr. Mason?"

"To know if you knew of the company in Paris."

"I have known of the company, yes."

"And you knew some of the people who worked for that company?"

"But of course, Monsieur. One does not become, as you say, familiar with a company, *non.* One can only become familiar with people, with some of the people, yes? With the company, *non.*"

"Did you know Walter Irving while you were in Paris?"

"Of course. He was my friend. He is here now."

"You went out with him occasionally in Paris?"

"But yes. Is that wrong?"

"No, no," Mason said. "I am simply trying to get the background. Did you know Duane Jefferson?"

"Duane Jefferson is from the South African office. Him I do not know."

"Did you know anyone from the South African office?"

"Twice, when people would come to visit in Paris, they asked me to help...well, what you call, entertain. I put on a daring dress. I act wicked with the eyes. I make of them...what you call the visiting fireman, *non?*"

"And who introduced you to these men?"

"My friend, Walter."

"Walter Irving?"

"That is right."

"I would like to find out something about Mr. Irving."

"He is nice. Did he tell you I am here?"

"No. I located you through people who work for me. They have an office in Paris."

"And the Paris office locates me here? Monsieur, it is impossible!"

Mason smiled. "I am here."

"And *I* am here. But...well, a man of your position, Monsieur Mason, one does not—how you call it?—contradict."

"What sort of a fellow is Walter Irving?"

"Walter Irving has many friends. He is very nice. He has—how you say?— the too big heart. That big heart, she is always getting him in trouble. He gives you too much...the shirt off his back. When he trusts, he trusts, that one. Sometime people, they take advantage of him. You are his friend, Monsieur Mason?"

"I would like to know about him."

"This woman with you is your wife?"

"My secretary."

"Oh, a thousand pardons. You seem...well, you seem as one."

"We have worked together for a long time."

"I see. Could I say something to you as the friend of Walter Irving?"

"Why not?"

"This Duane Jefferson," she said. "Watch him."

"What do you mean?"

"I mean he is the one to watch. He is sharp. He is very smooth. He...he is filled with crazy ideas in his head."

"What do you know about him?"

"*Know*, Monsieur? I *know* but little. But a woman has intuition. A woman can tell. Walter, I know very well. He is big. He is honest. He is like a dog. He trusts. But Walter likes what you call the show-off, the grandstand. He likes many clothes and to show off the good-looking woman on his arm. He likes crowds. He likes—"

She broke off and laughed. "He is simple, that one, for one who is so smart otherwise. He cares about a girl, that she should make people turn to look when he walks with her. So when I go out with Walter I put on a dress that...well, your secretary will know. The curves, yes?"

Della Street nodded.

She laughed very lightly. "Then Walter is very happy. I think, Monsieur Mason, that this Jefferson—"

"But I thought you didn't know Jefferson?"

"I hear people talk, and I listen. At times I have very big ears. And now, Monsieur Mason, you will pardon me, no? I have a brother who is sick in his upstairs. He will get better if he can be kept very quiet and have no excitement. You are nice people, and I would invite you in, but the excitement, no."

"Thank you very much," Mason said. "Does Walter Irving know you are here in the city?"

"Know I am here? Of course he knows. He has located me. He is very eager, that Walter Irving. And he is nice company. If I did not have my brother, I would put on clothes that show the curves and go with him to the night clubs. That he would love. That also I would like. However, I have responsibilities. I have to stay home. But, Monsieur Mason, please…you listen to Marline Chaumont. This Duane Jefferson, he is very cold, very polished, and treacherous like a snake."

"And if you see Walter Irving, you will tell him we were here?"

"You wish me not to?"

"I don't know," Mason said. "I am simply checking."

"I will make you the bargain, Monsieur Mason. You do not tell Walter Irving what I said about Duane Jefferson, and I do not say to Walter Irving anything that you are here. We keep this a little secret between us, no?

"But, Monsieur Mason, please, if this Duane Jefferson has done things that are wrong, you see that he does not pull my friend Walter down with him?"

"You think Jefferson did something wrong?"

"I have heard people talk."

"But his company gives him an excellent reputation. His company feels the utmost confidence in his honor and his integrity."

"I have told you, Monsieur Mason, that companies cannot feel; only the people in the companies. And later on, when the case comes to trial, Monsieur Mason, I shall read the papers with much interest. But you watch closely this Duane Jefferson. Perhaps he will tell you a story that is very fine as stories go when you do not question, but when he gets on the witness stand and finds that he cannot use the cold English manner to hide behind, then perhaps he gets mad, and when he gets mad, poof! Look out!"

"He has a temper?" Mason asked.

"That, Monsieur Mason, I do not know, but I have heard what others say. He is bad when he gets mad. His manner is a mask."

"I thank you," Mason said.

She hesitated a moment, then archly blew him a kiss with the tips of her fingers. The door closed gently but firmly.

CHAPTER ELEVEN

Perry Mason and Paul Drake left the elevators, walked down the corridor of the big office building.

"Here's the suite," Drake said, pausing in front of a door which had on its frosted glass only the single word "Enter" and the number 555.

Drake opened the door

"Well," Mason said, looking around, "you certainly fixed up a place here, Paul."

"Rental of desks and chairs," Drake said. "Rental of typewriters. The rest of it all came with the furnished office."

"I didn't know you could rent places like this," Mason said.

"This building caters to an international clientele," Drake explained.

"Occasionally they need a large furnished office for directors' meetings, conferences, and things of that sort. The last time this was rented, which was last week, a big Mexican company had it for a trade conference.

"They expect to lose money on this office, of course, but the international goodwill and the convenience to tenants in the building who have big meetings from time to time are supposed to more than offset the loss. Come on in here, Perry."

Drake led the way into a private office.

"This where the interviews take place?" Mason asked.

"That's right."

"This girl will be here at six o'clock?"

"Right on the dot. I have an idea that girl prides herself on being prompt and efficient."

"That's the way I had her sized up," Mason said.

"You aren't ready to tell me yet how you got a line on her?"

"No."

"Or what she has to do with the case?"

Mason said, "She *may* be the girl who made the surreptitious entry into the offices of the South African Gem Importing and Exploration Company."

"I surmised that," Drake said. "It's almost the same description that the police had."

"You have a tape recorder connected?" Mason asked.

"This room is bugged with three microphones," Drake told him. "There's a tape recorder in that closet."

"And what about a receptionist?" Mason asked.

"My receptionist is coming in to—" He broke off as a buzzer sounded. "That means someone's coming in."

Drake got up, went out into the big reception room, came back in a moment with a very attractive young woman.

"Meet Nora Pitts, Perry. She's one of my operatives, working as a receptionist here, and she really knows the ropes."

Miss Pitts, blushing and somewhat flustered, came forward to give Perry Mason her hand.

"I'd been hoping I'd meet you on one of these jobs, Mr. Mason," she said. "Mr. Drake keeps me on for the office type of work. Usually I'm on stake-outs. I was beginning to be afraid I was just *never* going to meet you."

"You shouldn't hold out on me like this, Paul," Mason said to the detective.

Drake grinned, looked at his wrist watch, said: "You understand the setup, Nora?"

She nodded.

"Do you know Della Street, my secretary?" Mason asked.

"I know her by sight, yes."

"Well," Mason said, "after this girl has been in here for a few minutes, Miss Street is going to come in. I told her to be here promptly at fifteen minutes past six."

Nora was listening now, her personal reaction at meeting Mason completely subdued by professional concentration.

"What do I do?" she asked.

"I think that this girl will be here by six o'clock, or at least a couple of minutes past six," Mason said. "You send her in as soon as she arrives. I'll start talking with her and questioning her. Della Street will be in at six-fifteen on the dot.

We'll hear the buzzer in the office when the door opens and know that she's here, so there'll be no need for you to notify us. Just have Della sit down and wait. I'll buzz for her when I want her sent in."

"Okay," she said.

"You got it, Nora?" Drake asked.

She nodded. "Of course."

Drake looked at his watch. "Well, it's seven minutes to six. She may come in early. Let's go."

Nora Pitts, with a quick smile at Mason, went back to the reception room.

In the office Drake settled down for a smoke, and Mason joined him with a cigarette.

"The newspapers indicate your client is a cold fish," Drake said.

Mason said irritably, "The guy is trying to protect some girl, and we're not going to get his story out of him until after we've got the story out of this girl."

"And you think Mae Jordan is the girl?"

"I don't know. Could be."

"Suppose she is?"

"Then we'll break her down and get her story."

"What do you propose to do then?"

"We'll get a tape recording," Mason said. "Then I'll go down to the jail, tell Jefferson what I have, and tell him to come clean."

"Then what?"

"Then I'll have his story."

"How's the district attorney going to identify those diamonds, Perry?"

"I don't know much about this case, Paul, but I do know a lot about the district attorney. He's been laying for me for years.

"This time he thinks he has me. He must have a pretty good case. But I'm gambling there's a legal point he's overlooked."

"What's the point?"

"The *corpus delicti.*"

"You think he can't prove it?"

"How's he going to prove a murder?" Mason asked. "They've never found Munroe Baxter's body. Now then, I can show the jury, by Hamilton Burger's own witnesses, that Munroe Baxter was a clever actor who planned to fake a suicide in order to smuggle in gems. Why wouldn't he fake a murder in order to keep from splitting the profit with his female accomplice?

"I'll tell the jury that it's almost certain Baxter has some new babe he's stuck on, some oo-la-la dish who is ready, able and willing to take Yvonne Manco's place as his female accomplice.

"What would be more likely than that Baxter would pretend he had been murdered, so that Yvonne Manco wouldn't be looking for him with fire in her eye?"

"Well, of course, when you put it that way," Drake said, "I can see the possibilities."

"All right," Mason grinned, "that's the way I'm going to put it to the jury. Hamilton Burger isn't going to have the smooth, easy sailing he's anticipating. He'll surprise me. I'll concede he must have something that will hit me hard, but after that, we're going to get down to fundamentals. He can hurt me, but I don't think he can do any more than that. I can blast his case out of court."

They smoked in silence for a few minutes, then Mason said, "What time have you got, Paul? I have five minutes *past* six."

"I have six minutes past, myself," Drake said. "What do you suppose has happened?"

"Do you think she's changed her mind?" Mason asked.

"Hell, no! She was too eager."

Mason began to pace the floor, looking from time to time at his watch. Promptly at six-fifteen the buzzer sounded.

Mason opened the door to the reception room, said: "Hello, Della. Come in."

Della Street entered the private office. "No typist?" she asked.

"No typist," Mason said.

"Suppose it's simply a case of her being delayed or—"

Mason shook his head. "That girl wasn't delayed. She has become suspicious."

"Not while she was here," Drake said positively. "When she left the place, her eyes were shining. She—"

"Sure," Mason said. "But she's smart. She went to the Better Business Bureau or a credit agency and got somebody to call up the office of this building and find out who was renting this office."

"Oh-oh!" Drake exclaimed.

"You mean you left a back trail?" Mason asked.

"I had to, Perry. If she went at it that way, she could have found out this office was being rented by the Drake Detective Agency."

Mason grabbed for his hat. "Come on, Paul. Let's go."

"Want me?" Della Street asked.

Mason hesitated, then said, "You may as well come on, and we'll buy you a dinner afterward."

Mason paused in the big reception office only long enough to tell Nora Pitts to stay on the job until Drake phoned.

"If that girl comes in, hold her," Drake said. "Keep her here and phone the office."

They got in Mason's car. Mason drove to the address on Cabachon Street, which was a narrow-fronted, two-story apartment house.

"Apartment two-eighteen," Drake said.

Mason repeatedly jabbed the button. When there was no answer he rang the bell for the manager.

The door latch clicked open. Drake held the door open. They went in. The manager, a big-boned woman in her sixties, came out to look them over. She studied the group with a cold, practiced eye. "We have no short-term rentals," she said.

Drake said, "I'm an investigator. We're looking for information. We're trying to locate Mae Jordan."

"Oh, yes," the woman said. "Well, Miss Jordan left."

"What do you mean she left?"

"Well, she told me she'd be away for a while and asked me if I'd feed her canary."

"She was going somewhere?"

"I guess so. She seemed in a terrific hurry. She dashed into the apartment and packed a couple of suitcases."

"Was she alone?" Mason asked.

"No. Two men were with her."

"Two men?"

"That's right."

"Did she introduce them?"

"No."

"They went up to the apartment with her?"

"Yes."

"And came down with her?"

"Yes. Each one of them was carrying a suitcase."

"And Miss Jordan didn't tell you how long she'd be gone?"

"No."

"How did she come here? Was it in a car or a taxicab?"

"I didn't see her come, but she left in a private car with these two men. Why? Is there anything wrong?"

Mason exchanged glances with Paul Drake.

"What time was this?" Mason asked.

"About...oh, let's see...It's been a little over an hour and a half, I guess."

"Thank you," Mason said, and led the way back to the car.

"Well?" Drake asked.

"Start your men going, Paul," Mason said. "Find out where Mae Jordan worked. Get the dope on her. Dig up everything you can. I want that girl."

"What are you going to do with her when you get her?" Drake asked.

"I'm going to slap her with a subpoena, put her on the witness stand, and tear her insides out," Mason said grimly. "How long will it take you to find out where Walter Irving is right now?"

"I'll know as soon as my operatives phone in the next report. I've got two men on the job. Generally, they phone in about once an hour."

"When you locate him, let me know," Mason said. "I'll be in my office."

Della Street smiled at Paul Drake. "Dinner," she said, "has been postponed."

CHAPTER TWELVE

Mason had been in his office less than ten minutes when the unlisted phone rang. Della Street glanced inquiringly at Mason. The lawyer said, "I'll take it, Della," and picked up the phone.

"Hello, Paul, What is it?"

Drake said, "One of my operatives reported Irving is on his way to this building, and he's hopping mad."

"To *this* building?"

"That's right."

"That leaves three objectives," Mason said. "His office, your office, or mine. If he comes to your office, send him in here."

"If he comes to your office, will you want help?"

"I'll handle it," Mason said.

"My operative says he's really breathing fire. He got a phone call in the middle of dinner. He never even went back to the table. Just dashed out, grabbed a cab, and gave the address of this building."

"Okay," Mason said. "We'll see what develops."

Mason hung up the telephone and said to Della Street, "Irving is on his way here."

"To see you?"

"Probably."

"So what do we do?"

"Wait for him. The party may be rough."

Five minutes later angry knuckles banged on the door of Mason's private office. "That will be Irving," Mason said. "I'll let him in myself, Della."

Mason got up, strode across the office and jerked the door open.

"Good evening," he said coldly, his face granite hard.

"What the hell are you trying to do?" Irving asked furiously. "Upset the apple cart?"

Mason said, "There are ladies present. Watch your language unless you want to get thrown out."

"Who's going to throw me out?"

"I am."

"You and who else?"

"Just me."

Irving sized him up for a moment. "You're one hell of a lawyer, I'll say that for you."

"All right, " Mason told him. "Come in. Sit down. Tell me what's on your mind. And the next time you try to hold out anything on me, you'll be a lot sorrier than you are right now."

"I wasn't holding out on you. I—"

"All right," Mason told him. "Tell me *your* troubles, and then *I'll* tell *you* something."

"You went out to call on Marline Chaumont."

"Of course I did."

"You shouldn't have done it."

"Then why didn't you tell me so?"

"To tell you the truth, I didn't think you could possibly find out anything about her. I still don't know how you did it."

"Well, what's wrong with going to see her?" Mason asked.

"You've kicked your case out of the window, that's all that's wrong with it."

"Go on. Tell me the rest of it."

"I'd been nursing that angle of the case until I could get the evidence we needed. She was pulling this gag of having an invalid brother on her hands so she—"

"That's a gag?" Mason interrupted.

"Don't be any simpler than you have to be," Irving snapped.

"What about her brother?" Mason asked.

"Her brother!" Irving stormed. "Her brother! You poor, simple-minded boob! Her so-called brother is Munroe Baxter."

"Go on," Mason said. "Keep talking."

"Isn't that fact enough to show you what you've done?"

"The fact would be. Your statement isn't."

"Well, I'm telling you."

"You've told me. I don't want your guesses or surmises. I want facts."

"Marline is a smart little babe. She's French. She's chic, and she's a fast thinker. She's been playing around with Munroe Baxter. He likes her better than Yvonne Manco. He was beginning to get tired of Yvonne.

"So when Munroe Baxter took the nose dive, he just kept on diving and came up into the arms of Marline Chaumont. She had a home all prepared for him as the invalid brother who was weak in the upper story."

"Any proof?" Mason asked.

"I was getting proof."

"You've seen Marline?"

"Of course I've seen her. After I got to thinking things over, I made it a point to see her."

"And did you see her brother?"

"I tried to," Irving said, "but she was too smart for me. She had him locked in a back bedroom, and she had the only key. She wanted to go to the all-night bank and transact some business. I told her I'd stay with her brother. She took me up on it.

"After she was gone, I prowled the house. The back bedroom was locked. I think she'd given him a sedative or something. I could hear him gently snoring. I knocked on the door and tried to wake him up. I wanted to look at him."

"You think he's Munroe Baxter?"

"I know he's Munroe Baxter."

"How do you know it?"

"I don't have to go into that with you."

"The hell you don't!"

Irving shrugged his shoulders. "You've started messing up the case now. Go ahead and finish it."

"All right, I will," Mason said. "I'll put that house under surveillance. I'll—"

"You and your house under surveillance!" Irving exclaimed scornfully. "Marline and her 'brother' got out of there within thirty minutes after you left the place. That house is as cold and dead as a last-year's bird's nest. In case you want to bet I'll give you ten to one you can't find a fingerprint in the whole damn place."

"Where did they go?" Mason asked.

Irving shrugged his shoulders. "Search me. I went out there. The place was empty. I became suspicious and got a private detective agency to get on the job and find out what had happened. I was eating dinner tonight when the detective phoned. Neighbors had seen a car drive up. A man and a woman got out. A neighbor was looking through the curtains. She recognized you from your pictures. The description of the girl with you checked with that of your secretary here, Miss Street.

"Half an hour after you left, a taxi drove up, Marline sent out four big suitcases and a handbag. Then she and the taxi driver helped a man out to the car. The man was stumbling around as though he was drunk or drugged or both."

"And then?" Mason asked.

"The cab drove away."

"All right," Mason said. "We'll trace that cab."

Irving laughed scornfully. "You must think you're dealing with a bunch of dumb bunnies, Mason."

"Perhaps I am," Mason said.

"Go on and try to trace that couple," he said. "Then you'll find out what a mess you've made of things."

Irving got to his feet.

"How long had you known all this?" Mason asked, his voice ominously calm.

"Not long. I looked Marline up when I came here. She knows everyone in the Paris office. She was our party girl. She always helped in entertaining buyers.

"She's smart. She got wise to the Baxter deal and she put the heat on Baxter.

"As soon as I went out to Marline's place to call on her, I knew something was wrong. She went into a panic at the sight of me. She tried to cover up by being all honey and syrup, but she overdid it. She had to invite me in, but she told me this story about her brother. Then she kept me waiting while she locked him up and knocked him out with a hypo. That evening she left me alone so I could prowl the house. Baxter was dead to the world. She's a smart one, that girl.

"I was getting ready to really bust this case wide open, and then you had to stick your clumsy hand right in the middle of all the machinery."

Irving started for the door.

"Wait a minute," Mason said. "You're not finished yet. You know something more about all—"

"Sure I do," Irving said. "And make no mistake, Mason. What I know I keep to myself from now on. In case you're interested, I'm cabling the company to kiss their two-thousand-dollar retainer good-bye and to hire a lawyer who at least has *some* sense."

Irving strode out into the corridor.

Della Street watched the closing door. When it had clicked shut she started for the telephone.

Mason motioned her away. "Remember, it's all taken care of, Della," he said. "Paul Drake has two men shadowing him. We'll know where he goes when he leaves here."

"That's fine," she said. "In that case, you can take me to dinner now."

CHAPTER THIRTEEN

Della Street laid the decoded cablegram on Mason's desk as the lawyer entered the office.

"What's this, Della?" Mason asked, hanging up his hat.

"Cablegram from the South African Gem Importing and Exploration Company."

"Am I fired?"

"Definitely not."

"What does it say?" Mason asked.

"It says you are to continue with the case and to protect the interests of Duane Jefferson, that the company investigated you before you were retained, that it has confidence in you, and that its official representative in the area, and the only one in a position to give orders representing the company, is Duane Jefferson."

"Well," Mason said, "that's something." He took the decoded telegram and studied it. "It sounds as though they didn't have too much confidence in Walter Irving."

"Of course," she told him, "we don't know what Irving cabled the company."

"We know what he told us he was cabling the company."

"Where does all this leave him?" Della Street asked.

"Out on a limb," Mason said, grinning, and then added, "It also leaves us out on a limb. If we don't get some line on Mae Jordan and Marline Chaumont, we're behind the eight ball."

"Couldn't you get a continuance under the circumstances until—"
Mason shook his head.

"Why not, Chief?"

"For several reasons," Mason said. "One of them is that I assured the district attorney I'd go to trial on the first date we could squeeze in on the trial calendar. The other is that I still think we have more to gain than to lose by getting to trial before the district attorney has had an opportunity to think over the real problem."

"Do you suppose this so-called brother of Marline Chaumont is really Munroe Baxter?"

Mason looked at his watch, said, "Paul Drake should have the answer to that by this time. Get him on the phone, Della. Ask him to come in."

Ten minutes later Paul Drake was laying it on the line.

"This guy Irving is all wet, Perry. Marline Chaumont showed up at the state hospital. She identified herself as the sister of Pierre Chaumont. Pierre had been there for a year. He'd become violent. They'd operated on his brain. After that, he was like a pet dog. He was there because there was no other place for him to be. Authorities were very glad to release Pierre to his sister, Marline. The chance that he is Munroe Baxter is so negligible you can dismiss it.

"In the first place, Marline showed up and got him out of the state hospital more than a month before Baxter's boat was due. At the time Marline was getting him out of the hospital, Munroe Baxter was in Paris."

"Is his real name Pierre Chaumont?"

"The authorities are satisfied it is."

"Who satisfied them?"

"I don't know; Marline I guess. The guy was going under another name. He'd been a vicious criminal, a psychopath. He consented to having this lobotomy performed, and they did it. It apparently cured him of his homicidal tendencies, but it left him like a zombie. As I understand it, he's in sort of a hypnotic trance. Tell the guy anything, and he does it."

"You checked with the hospital?"

"With everyone. The doctor isn't very happy about the outcome. He said he had hoped for better results, but the guy was a total loss the way he was and anything is an improvement. They were damn glad to get rid of him at the hospital."

"Yes, I can imagine. What else, Paul?"

"Now here's some news that's going to jolt you, Perry."

"Go ahead and jolt."

Mae Jordan was picked up by investigators from the district attorney's office."

"The hell!" Mason exclaimed.

Drake nodded.

"What are they trying to do? Get a confession of some sort out of her?"

"Nobody knows. Two men showed up at the law office where she works yesterday afternNon. Is took me a while to get the name of that law office, but I finally got it. It's one of the most substantial, conservative firms in town, and it created quite a furor when these two men walked in, identified themselves and said they wanted Mae Jordan.

"They had a talk with her in a private office, then came out and hunted up old man Honcut, who's the senior member of the firm Honcut, Gridley and Billings. They told him that for Mae's own safety they were going to have to keep her out of circulation for a while. She had about three weeks for vacation coming, and they told Honcut she could come right back after the trial."

"She went willingly?" Mason asked.

"Apparently so."

Mason thought that over. "How did they find her, Paul?"

"Simplest thing in the world. They searched Jefferson when they booked him. There was a name and address book. It was all in code. They cracked the code and ran down the names. When they came to this Jordan girl she talked."

"She tried to talk herself out by talking Duane Jefferson in," Mason said grimly. "When that young woman gets on the stand she's going to have a cross-examination she'll remember for a long, long time. What about Irving, Paul? Where did he go after he left here?"

"Now there," Drake said, "I have some more bad news for you."

Mason's face darkened. "That was damn important, Paul. I told you—"

"I know what you *told* me, Perry. Now *I'm* going to tell *you* something about the shadowing business that I've told you a dozen times before and I'll probably tell you a dozen times again. If a smart man knows he's being tailed and doesn't want to be shadowed, there's not much you can do about it. If he's smart, he can give you the slip every time, unless you have four or five operatives all equipped with some means of intercommunication."

"But Irving didn't *know* he was being tailed."

"What makes you think he didn't?"

"Well," Mason said, "he didn't act like it when he came up here to the office."

"He sure acted like it when he left," Drake said. "What did you tell him?"

"Nothing to arouse his suspicions. Specifically, what did he do, Paul?"

"He proceeded to ditch the shadows."

"How?"

"To begin with, he got a taxi. He must have told the taxi driver there was a car following him that he wanted to ditch. The cab driver played it smart. He'd slide up to the traffic signals just as they were changing, then go on through. My man naturally tried to keep up with him, relying on making an explanation to any traffic cop who might stop him.

"Well, a traffic cop stopped him and it happened he was a cop who didn't feel kindly toward private detectives. He got tough, held my man, and gave him a ticket. By that time, Irving was long since gone.

"Usually a cop will give you a break on a deal like that if you have your credentials right handy, show them to him and tell him you're shadowing the car ahead. This chap deliberately held my man up until Irving got away. Not that I think it would have made any difference. Irving knew that he was being tailed, and he'd made up his mind he was going to ditch the tail. When a smart man gets an idea like that in his head, there's nothing you can do about it except roll with the punch and take it."

"So what did you do, Paul?"

"Did the usual things. Put men on his apartment house to pick him up when he got back. Did everything."

"And he hasn't been back?"

Drake shook his head.

"All right. What about the others?"

"Marline Chaumont," Drake said. "You thought it would be easy to locate her."

"You mean you've drawn a blank all the way along the line?" Mason interposed impatiently.

"I found out about Mae Jordan," Drake said.

"And that's all?"

"That's all."

"All right. What about Marline Chaumont? Give me the bad news in bunches."

"It took me a devil of a time to find the taxicab driver who went out to the house," Drake said. "I finally located him. He remembered the occasion well. He took the woman, the man, four suitcases and a handbag to the airport."

"And then what?" Mason asked.

"Then we drew a blank. We can't find where she left the airport."

"You mean a woman with a man who is hardly able to navigate by himself, with four big suitcases and a handbag, can vanish from the airport?" Mason asked.

"That's right," Drake said. "Just try it sometime, Perry."

"Try what?"

"Covering all of the taxicab drivers who go to the air terminal. Try and get them to tell you whether they picked up a man, a woman, four suitcases and a handbag. People are coming in by plane every few minutes. The place is a regular madhouse."

Mason thought it over. "All right, Paul," he said. "Irving told me we'd get no place, but I thought the four suitcases would do it."

"So did I when you first told me about it," Drake said.

"They went directly to the airport?"

"That's right."

"Paul, they must have gone *somewhere.*"

"Sure they went somewhere," Drake said. "I can tell you where they *didn't* go."

"All right. Where didn't they go?"

"They didn't take any plane that left at about that time of day."

"How do you know?"

"I checked it by the excess baggage. The taxi driver says the suitcases were heavy. They must have weighed forty pounds each. I checked the departures on the planes."

"You checked them by name, of course?"

Drake's look was withering. "Don't be silly, Perry. That was the first thing. That was simple. Then I checked with the ticket sellers to see if there was a record of tickets sold at that time of day with that amount of excess baggage. There wasn't. Then I checked with the gate men to see if they remembered some woman going through the gate who would need help in getting a man aboard the plane. There was none. I also checked on wheel chairs. No dice. So then I concluded she'd gone to the airport, unloaded, paid off the cab, and had picked up another cab at the airport to come back."

"And you couldn't find that cab?"

"My men are still working on it. But that's like going to some babe wearing a skirt reaching to her knees, a tight sweater, and asking her if she remembered anybody whistling at her yesterday as she walked down the street."

After a moment Mason grinned. "All right, Paul. We're drawing a blank. Now why the devil would the district attorney have Mae Jordan picked up?"

"Because he wanted to question her."

"Then why wouldn't he have let her go after he questioned her?"

"Because he hasn't finished questioning her."

Mason shook his head. "You overlook what happened. She went up to her room, packed—got two suitcases. The district attorney is keeping her in what amounts to custody."

"Why?"

Mason grinned. "Now wait a minute, Paul. That's the question that I asked you. Of course, the only answer is that he wants her as a material witness. But if he does that, it means that she must have told a story that has pulled the wool completely over his eyes, and he fell for it hook, line, and sinker."

"You don't think she's a mateial witness?" Drake asked.

Mason thought the situation over for a minute, then a slow smile spread over his features. "She would be, if she told the truth. I don't think ther's any better news that I could have and."

"Why?"

"Because if the district attorney doesn't put her on the stand as a witness, I'll claim that he sabotaged my case by spiriting away *my* witnesses. If he does put her on the stand, I'll make him the sickest district attorney west of Chicago."

"You're going to play into his hands by going to an immediate trial?" Drake asked.

Mason grinned. "Paul, did you ever see a good tug of war?"

Drake thought for a moment, then said, "They used to put them on in the country towns on the Fourth of July."

"And did you ever see the firemen having a tug of war with the police department?"

"I may have. I can't remember. Why?"

"And," Mason went on, "about the time the fire department was all dug in and huffing and puffing, there would be a secret signal from the police department and everybody would give the firemen a lot of slack and they'd go over backwards, and then the police department would give a big yo-heave-ho and pull the whole aggregation right over the dividing line on the seat of their pants."

Drake grinned. "Seems to me I remember something like that, now that you speak of it."

"Well," Mason said, "that is what is known as playing into the hands of the district attorney, Paul. We're going to give him lots of slack. Now, answering your question more specifically—yes, I'm going to an immediate trial. I'm going to go to trial while the D.A. is hypnotized by Mae Jordan's story and before he finds out I know some of the things I know and that he doesn't know."

CHAPTER FOURTEEN

The selection of the jury was completed at ten-thirty on the second day of the trial. Judge Hartley settled back on the bench, anticipating a long, bitterly contested trial.

"Gentlemen," he said, "the jury has been selected and sworn. The prosecution will proceed with its opening statement."

At that moment, Hamilton Burger, the district attorney, who had left the selection of the jury to subordinates, dramatically strode into the courtroom to take charge of the trial personally.

The district attorney bowed to the judge and, almost without pausing, passed the counsel table to stand facing the jury.

"Good morning, ladies and gentlemen of the jury," he said. "I am the district attorney of this county. We expect to show you that the defendant in this case is an employee of the South African Gem Importing and Exploration Company; that through his employment he had reason to know that a man named Munroe Baxter had in his possession a large number of diamonds valued at more than three hundred thousand dollars on the retail market; that the defendant knew Munroe Baxter intended to smuggle those diamonds into this country, and that the defendant murdered Munroe Baxter and took possession of those diamonds. We will introduce witnesses to show premeditation, deliberation and the cunning execution of a diabolical scheme of murder. We will show that a goodly proportion of the diamonds smuggled into the country by Munroe Baxter were found in the possession of the defendant. On the strength of that evidence we shall ask for a verdict of first-degree murder."

And Hamilton Burger, bowing to the jury, turned and stalked back to the counsel table.

Court attachés looked at each other in surprise. It was the shortest opening statement Hamilton Burger had ever made, and no one missed its significance. Hamilton Burger had carefully refrained from disclosing his hand or giving the defense the faintest inkling of how he intended to prove his case.

"My first witness," Hamilton Burger said, "will be Yvonne Manco."

"Come forward, Yvonne Manco," the bailiff called.

Yvonne Manco had evidently been carefully instructed. She came forward, trying her best to look demure. Her neckline was high and her skirt was fully as long as the current styles dictated, but the attempt to make her look at all conservative was as unsuccessful as would have been an attempt to disguise a racing sports car as a family sedan.

Yvonne gave her name and address to the court reporter, then looked innocently at the district attorney—after having flashed a sidelong glance of appraisal at the men of the jury.

Under questioning of the district attorney, Yvonne told the story of her relationship with Munroe Baxter, of the carefully laid plot to smuggle the gems, of the tour aboard the cruise ship, the spurious "whirlwind courtship."

She told of the plot to arrange the fake suicide, her deliberate flirtation with the assistant purser, the scene on the ship, and then finally that early morning plunge into the waters of the bay. She disclosed that she had carried a small compressed air tank in her baggage and that when Baxter went overboard, he was prepared to swim for a long distance under water.

Hamilton Burger brought out a series of maps and photographs of the cruise ship. He had the witness identify the approximate place where the leap had taken place, both from the deck of the steamer and from its location in the bay.

"You may cross-examine," he said to Perry Mason.

Mason smiled at the witness, who promptly returned his smile, shifted her position slightly and crossed her legs, so that two of the masculine members of the jury hitched forward in their chairs for a better look, while the chins of two of the less attractive women on the jury were conspicuously elevated.

"You go by the name of Yvonne Manco?" Mason asked.

"Yes."

"You have another name?"

"No."

"You were really married to Munroe Baxter, were you not?"

"Yes, but now that I am a widow I choose to keep my maiden name of Yvonne Manco."

"I see," Mason said. "You don't want to bear the name of your husband?"

"It is not that," she said. "Yvonne Manco is my professional name."

"What profession?" Mason asked.

There was a moment's silence, then Hamilton Burger was on his feet. "Your Honor, I object. I object to the manner in which the question is asked. I object to the question. Incompetent, irrelevant, and immaterial."

Judge Hartley stroked his chin thoughtfully. "Well," he said, "under the circumstances I'm going to sustain the objection. However, in view of the answer of the witness—However, the objection is sustained."

"You were, however, married to Munroe Baxter?"

"Yes."

"On shipboard?"

"Yes."

"Before that?"

"No."

"There had been no previous ceremony?"

"No."

"Are you familiar with what is referred to as a common law marriage?"

"Yes."

"Had you ever gone by the name of Mrs. Baxter?"

"Yes."

"Prior to this cruise?"

"Yes."

"As a part of this plot which you and Munroe Baxter hatched up, he was to pretend to be dead. Is that right?"

"Yes."

"With whom did the idea originate? You or Munroe Baxter?"

"With him."

"He was to pretend to jump overboard and be dead, so he could smuggle in some diamonds?"

"Yes. I have told you this."

"In other words," Mason said, "if at any time it should be to his advantage, he was quite willing to pretend to be dead."

"Objected to as calling for the conclusion of the witness as already asked and answered," Hamilton Burger said.

"Sustained," Judge Hartley said.

Mason, having made his point, smiled at the jury. "You knew that you were engaging in a smuggling transaction?" he asked the witness.

"But of course. I am not stupid."

"Exactly," Mason said. "And after this investigation started, you had some contact with the district attorney?"

"Naturally."

"And was it not through the offices of the district attorney that arrangements were made so you could testify in this case, yet be held harmless and not be prosecuted for smuggling?"

"Well, of course—"

"Just a minute, just a minute," Hamilton Burger interrupted. "I want to interpose an objection to that question, Your Honor."

"Go ahead," Judge Hartley ruled.

"It is incompetent, irrelevant and immaterial. It is not proper cross-examination."

"Overruled," Judge Hartley said. "Answer the question."

"Well, of course there was no definite agreement. That would have been...unwise."

"Who told you it would be unwise?"

"It was agreed by all that it would be unwise."

"By all, whom do you mean? Whom do you include?"

"Well, the customs people, the district attorney, the detectives, the police, my own lawyer."

"I see," Mason said. "They told you that it would be unwise to have a definite agreement to this effect, but nevertheless they gave you every assurance that if you testified as they wished, you would not be prosecuted on a smuggling charge?"

"Your Honor, I object to the words 'as they wished,' " Hamilton Burger said. "That calls for a conclusion of the witness."

Judge Hartley looked down at the witness.

Mason said, "I'll put it this way, was there any conversation as to what you were to testify to?"

"The truth."

"Who told you that?"

"Mr. Burger, the district attorney."

"And was there some assurance given you that if you testified, you would be given immunity from the smuggling?"

"If I testified to the *truth*? Yes."

"Before this assurance was given you, you had told these people what the truth was?"

"Yes."

"And that was the same story you have told on the witness stand here?"

"Certainly."

"So that when the district attorney told you to tell the truth, you understood that he meant the same story you have just told here?"

"Yes."

"So then, the assurance that was given you was that if you would tell the story you have now told on the witness stand, you would be given immunity from smuggling."

"That was my understanding."

"So," Mason said, "simply by telling this story you are given immunity from smuggling?"

"Well, not— It was not that...not that crude," she said.

The courtroom broke into laughter.

"That," Mason said, "is all."

Hamilton Burger was plainly irritated as the witness left the stand. "My next witness will be Jack Gilly," he said.

Jack Gilly was a slender, shifty-eyed man with high cheekbones, a long, sharp nose, a high forehead, and a pointed chin. He moved with a silence that was almost furtive as he glided up to the witness stand, held up his hand, was sworn, gave his name and address to the court reporter, seated himself, and looked expectantly at the district attorney.

"What's your occupation?" Hamilton Burger asked.

"At the moment?" he asked.

"Well, do you have the same occupation now you had six months ago?"

"Yes."

"What is it?"

"I rent fishing boats."

"Where?"

"At the harbor here."

"Were you acquainted with Munroe Baxter during his lifetime?"

"Just a moment before you answer that question," Mason said to the witness. He turned to Judge Hartley. "I object, Your Honor, on the ground that the question assumes a fact not in evidence. As far as the evidence before this court at the present time is concerned, Munroe Baxter is still alive."

"May I be heard on that, Your Honor?" Hamilton Burger asked.

"Well," Judge Hartley said, hesitating, "it would certainly seem that the logical way to present this case would be first to— However, I'll hear you, Mr. District Attorney."

"If the Court please," Hamilton Burger said, "Munroe Baxter jumped overboard in deep water. He was never seen alive afterward. I have witnesses from the passengers and the crew who will testify that Munroe Baxter ran to the rear of the ship, jumped overboard and vanished in the water. The ship called for a launch to come alongside, the waters were searched and searched carefully. Munroe Baxter never came up."

"Well," Judge Hartley said, "you can't expect this Court to rule on evidence predicated upon an assumption as to what you intend to prove by other witnesses. Moreover, your own witness has testified that this was all part of a scheme on the part of Munroe Baxter to—"

"Yes, yes, I know," Hamilton Burger interrupted. "But schemes can go astray. Many unforeseen things can enter into the picture. Jumping from the deck of a ship is a perilous procedure."

Judge Hartley said, "Counsel will kindly refrain from interrupting the Court. I was about to say, Mr. District Attorney, that the testimony of your own witness indicates this was all part of a planned scheme by which Munroe Baxter intended to appear to commit suicide. In view of the fact that there is a presumption that a man remains alive until he is shown to be dead, the Court feels the objection is well taken."

"Very well, Your Honor, I will reframe the question," Hamilton Burger said. "Mr. Gilly, did you know Munroe Baxter?"

"Yes."

"How well did you know him?"

"I had met him several times."

"Were you acquainted with Yvonne Manco, who has just testified?"

"Yes."

"Directing your attention to the sixth day of June of this year, what was your occupation at that time?"

"I was renting boats?"

"And to the fifth day of June, what was your occupation?"

"I was renting boats."

"Did you rent a boat on the fifth of June at an hour nearing seven o'clock in the evening?"

"Yes, sir."

"To whom did you rent that boat?"

"Frankly, I don't know."

"It was to some man you had never seen before?"

"Yes."

"Did the man tell you what he wanted?"

"He said that he had been directed to me because I was—"

"Just a moment," Mason interrupted. "I object to any conversation which did not take place in the presence of the defendant and which is not connected up with the defendant."

"I propose to connect this up with the defendant," Hamilton Burger said.

"Then the connection should be shown before the conversation," Mason said. Judge Hartley nodded. "The objection is sustained."

"Very well. You rented a boat to this man who was a stranger to you?"

"Yes, sir."

"From what this man said, however, you had reason to rent him the boat?"

"Yes."

"Was money paid you for the boat?"

"Yes."

"And when did the man start out in the boat, that is, when did he take delivery of it?"

"At about five o'clock the next morning."

"What were the circumstances surrounding the delivery of the boat?"

"He stood on the dock with me. I had a pair of powerful night glasses. When I saw the cruise ship coming in the harbor, I said to this man that I could see the cruise ship, and he jumped in the boat and took off."

"Did he start the motor?"

"The motor had been started an hour previously so it would be warm and so everything would be in readiness."

"And what did the man do?"

"He guided the boat away from my dock and out into the channel."

"Just a moment," Mason said. "Your Honor, I move to strike all of this evidence out on the ground that it has not been connected with the defendant in any way."

"I am going to connect it up," Hamilton Burger said, "within the next few questions."

"The Court will reserve a ruling," Judge Hartley said. "It seems to me that these questions are largely preliminary."

"What did *you* do after the boat was rented?" Hamilton Burger asked the witness.

"Well," Gilly said, "I was curious. I wanted to see—"

"Never mind your thoughts or emotions," Hamilton Burger said. "What did you *do*?"

"I walked back to where my car was parked, got in the car and drove out to a place I knew on the waterfront where I could get out on the dock and watch what was going on."

"What do you mean by your words, 'what was going on'?"

"Watch the boat I had rented."

"And what did you see?"

"I saw the cruise ship coming slowly into the harbor."

"And what else did you see?"

"I saw Munroe Baxter jump overboard."

"You know it was Munroe Baxter?"

"Well, I— Of course, I knew it from what happened."

"But did you recognize him?"

"Well... it looked like Baxter, but at that distance and in that light I couldn't *swear* to it."

"*Don't* swear to it then," Hamilton Burger snapped. "You saw a man jump overboard?"

"Yes."

"Did that man look like anyone you knew?"

"Yes."

"Who?"

"Munroe Baxter."

"That is, as I understand your testimony, he looked like Munroe Baxter, but you can't definitely swear that it *was* Munroe Baxter. Is that right?"

"That's right."

"Then what happened?"

"I saw people running around on the deck of the cruise ship. I heard voices evidently hailing a launch, and a launch came and cruised around the ship."

"What else happened?"

"I kept my binoculars trained on the boat I rented."

"What did you see?"

"There were two men in the boat."

"*Two* men?" Hamilton Burger asked.

"Yes, sir."

"Where did the other man come from, do you know?"

"No, sir. I don't. But I am assuming that he was picked up on one of the docks while I was getting my car."

"That may go out," Hamilton Burger said. "You don't know of your own knowledge where this man came from?"

"No, sir."

"You know only that by the time you reached the point of vantage from which you could see the boat, there were two men in the boat?"

"Yes, sir."

"All right, then what happened?"

"The boat sat there for some time. The second man appeared to be fishing. He was holding a heavy bamboo rod and a line over the side of the boat."

"And then what happened?"

"After quite a while I saw the fishing pole suddenly jerk, as though something very heavy had taken hold of the line."

"And then what?"

"Then I could see a black body partially submerged in the water, apparently hanging onto the fish line."

"And then what did you see?"

"One of the men leaned over the side of the boat. He appeared to be talking—"

"Never mind what he appeared to be doing. What did he do?"

"He leaned over the side of the boat."

"Then what?"

"Then he reached down to the dark object in the water."

"Then what?"

"Then I saw him raise his right arm and lower it rapidly several times. There was a knife in his hand. He was plunging the knife down into the dark thing in the water."

"Then what?"

"Then both men fumbled around with the thing that was in the water; then one of the men lifted a heavy weight of some kind over the side of the boat and tied it to the thing that was in the water."

"Then what?"

"Then they started the motor in the boat, slowly towing the weighted object in the water. I ran back to my automobile, got into it and drove back to my boat pier."

"And what happened then?"

"Then after a couple of hours the man who had rented the boat brought it back."

"Was anyone with him at the time?"

'No, sir, he was alone."

"What did you do?"

"I asked him if he had picked anyone up and he—"

"I object to any conversation which was not in the presence of the defendant," Mason said.

"Just a moment," Hamilton Burger said. "I will withdraw the question until I connect it up. Now, Mr. Gilly, did you recognize the other man who was in the boat with this stranger?"

"Not at the time. I had never seen him before."

"Did you see him subsequently?"

"Yes, sir."

"Who was that man?"

"The defendant."

"You are referring now to Duane Jefferson, the defendant who is seated here in the courtroom?"

"Yes, sir."

"Are you positive of your identification?"

"Just a moment," Mason said. "That's objected to as an attempt on the part of counsel to cross-examine his own witness."

"Overruled," Judge Hartley said. "Answer the question."

"Yes, sir, I am positive."

"You were watching through binoculars?"

"Yes, sir."

"What is the power of those binoculars?"

"Seven by fifty."

"Are they a good pair of binoculars?"

"Yes, sir."

"With coated lenses?"

"Yes, sir."

"You could see the boat clearly enough to distinguish the features of the people who were in the boat?"

"Yes, sir."

"Now then, after the boat was returned to you, did you notice any stains on the boat?"

"Yes, sir."

"What were those stains?"

"Bloodstains that—"

"No, no," Hamilton Burger said. "Just describe the stains. You don't know whether they were blood."

"I know they *looked* like blood."

"Just describe the stains, please." Hamilton Burger insisted, striving to appear virtuous and impartial.

"They were reddish stains, dark reddish stains."

"Where were they?"

"On the outside of the boat, just below the gunwale, and over on the inside of the boat where there had been a spattering or spurting."

"When did you first notice those stains?"

"Just after the boat had been returned to me."

"Were they fresh at that time?"

"Objected to as calling for a conclusion of the witness and no proper foundation laid," Mason said.

"The objection is sustained," Judge Hartley ruled.

"Well, how did they appear to you?"

"Same objection."

"Same ruling."

"Look here," Hamilton Burger said, "you have been engaged in the fishing business and in fishing for recreation for some time?"

"Yes, sir."

"During that time you have had occasion to see a lot of blood on boats?"

"Yes, sir."

"And have you been able to judge the relative freshness of the stains by the color of that blood?"

"Yes, sir."

"That's fish blood the witness is being asked about?" Mason interposed.

"Well...yes," Hamilton Burger conceded.

"And may I ask the prosecutor if it is his contention that these stains on the boat the witness has described were fish blood?"

"Those were stains of human blood!" Hamilton Burger snapped.

"I submit," Mason said, "that a witness cannot be qualified as an expert on human bloodstains by showing that he has had experience with fish blood."

"The principle is the same," Hamilton Burger said. "The blood assumes the same different shades of color in drying."

"Do I understand the district attorney is now testifying as an expert?" Mason asked.

Judge Hartley smiled. "I think the Court will have to agree with defense counsel, Mr. District Attorney. There must first be a showing as to whether there is a similarity in the appearance of fish blood and human blood *if* you are now trying to qualify this witness as an expert."

"Oh, well," Hamilton Burger said, "I'll get at it in another way by another witness. You are positive as to your identification of this defendant, Mr. Gilly?"

"Yes, sir."

"And he was in the boat at the time you saw this thing—whatever it was— stabbed with a knife?"

"Yes, sir."

"Were these stains you have mentioned on the boat when you rented it?"

"No."

"They were there when the boat was returned?"

"Yes."

"Where is this boat now?" Hamilton Burger asked.

"In the possession of the police."

"When was it taken by the police?"

"About ten days later."

"You mean the sixteenth of June?"

"I believe it was the fifteenth."

"Did you find anything else in the boat, Mr. Gilly?"

"Yes, sir."

"What?"

"A sheath knife with the name 'Duane' engraved on the hilt on one side and the initials 'M.J.' on the other side."

"Where is that knife?"

"The police took it."

"When?"

"At the time they took the boat."

"Would you know that knife if you saw it again?"

"Yes."

Hamilton Burger unwrapped some tissue paper, produced a keen-bladed hunting knife, took it to the witness. "Have you ever seen this knife before?"

"Yes. That's the knife I found in the boat."

"Is it now in the same condition it was then?"

"No, sir. It was blood—I mean, it was stained with something red then, more than it is now."

"Yes, yes, some of those stains were removed at the crime laboratory for analysis," Hamilton Burger said suavely. "You may cross-examine the witness, Mr. Mason. And I now ask the clerk to mark this knife for identification."

Mason smiled at Gilly. "Ever been convicted of a felony, Mr. Gilly?" Mason asked, his voice radiating good feeling.

Hamilton Burger jumped to his feet, apparently preparing to make an objection, then slowly settled back in his chair.

Gilly shifted his watery eyes from Mason's face to the floor.

"Yes, sir."

"How many times?" Mason asked.

"Twice."

"For what?"

"Once for larceny."

"And what was it for the second time?" Mason asked.

"Perjury," Gilly said.

Mason's smile was affable. "How far were you from the boat when you were watching it through your binoculars?"

"About...oh, a couple of good city blocks."

"How was the light?"

"It was just after daylight."

"There was fog?"

"Not fog. A sort of mist."

"A cold mist?"

"Yes. It was chilly."

"What did you use to wipe off the lenses of the binoculars—or did you wipe them?"

"I don't think I wiped them."

"And you saw one of these men fishing?"

"Yes, sir. The defendant held the fishing rod."

"And apparently he caught something?"

"A big body caught hold of the line."

"Have you seen people catch big fish before?"

"Yes, sir."

"And sometimes when they have caught sharks you have seen them cut the sharks loose from the line or stab them to death before taking them off the hook?"

"This wasn't a shark."

"I'm asking you a question," Mason said. "Have you seen that?"

"Yes."

"Now, did this thing that was on the fishing line ever come entirely out of the water?"

"No, sir."

"Enough out of the water so you could see what it was?"

"It was almost all underwater all the time."

"You had never seen this man who rented the boat from you before he showed up to rent the boat?"

"No, sir."

"And you never saw him again?"

"No, sir."

"Do you know this knife wasn't in the boat when you rented it?"

"Yes."

"When did you first see it?"

"The afternoon of the sixth of June."

"Where?"

"In my boat."

"You had not noticed it before?"

"No."

"Yet you had looked in the boat?"

"Yes."

"And from the time the boat was returned to you until you found the knife, that boat was where anyone could have approached and dropped this knife into it, or tossed it to the bottom of the boat?"

"Well, I guess so. Anyone could have if he'd been snooping around down there."

"And how much rental did this mysterious man give you for the boat?"

"That's objected to as incompetent, irrelevant, and immaterial and not proper cross-examination," Hamilton Burger said.

"Well," Mason said, smiling, "I'll get at it in another way. Do you have an established rental rate for that boat, Mr. Gilly?"

"Yes, sir."

"How much is it?"

"A dollar to a dollar and a half an hour."

"Now then, did this stranger pay you the regular rental rate for the boat?"

"We made a special deal."

"You got *more* than your regular rental rate?"

"Yes, sir."

"How much more?"

"Objected to as not proper cross-examination, calling for facts not in evidence, and incompetent, irrelevant, and immaterial," Hamilton Burger said.

"Overruled," Judge Hartley said.

"How much rental?" Mason asked.

"I can't recall offhand. I think it was fifty dollars." Gilly said, his eyes refusing to meet those of Mason.

"Was that the figure that you asked, or the figure that the man offered?"

"The figure that I asked."

"Are you sure it was fifty dollars?"

"I can't remember too well. He gave me a bonus. I can't recall how much it was."

"Was it more than fifty dollars?"

"It could have been. I didn't count it. I just took the bills he gave me and put them in the locked box where I keep my money."

"You keep your money in the form of cash?"

"Some of it."

"Did you ever count this bonus?"

"I can't remember doing so."

"It could have been more than fifty dollars?"

"I guess so. I don't know."

"Could it have been as much as a thousand dollars?"

"Oh, that's absurd!" Hamilton Burger protested to the Court.

"Overruled," Judge Hartley snapped.

"Was it?" Mason asked.

"I don't know."

"Did you enter it on your books?"

"I don't keep books."

"You don't know then how much cash is in this locked box where you keep your money?"

"Not to the penny."

"To the dollar?"

"No."

"To the hundred dollars?"

"No."

"Have you more than five hundred dollars in that box right now?"

"I don't know."

"More than five thousand dollars?"

"I can't tell."

"You may have?"

"Yes."

"Now, when were you convicted of perjury," Mason asked, "was that your first offense or the second?"

"The second."

Mason smiled. "That's all Mr. Gilly."

Judge Hartley glanced at the clock. "It appears that it is now time for the noon adjournment. Court will recess until two o'clock. During this time the jurors will not form or express any opinion as to the merits of the case, but will wait until the case is finally submitted before doing so. Nor will the jurors discuss the case among themselves or permit it to be discussed in their presence. The defendant is remanded to custody. Court will recess until two o'clock."

Paul Drake and Della Street, who had been occupying seats which had been reserved for them in the front of the courtroom, came toward Perry Mason.

Mason caught Paul Drake's eye, motioned them back. He turned to his client. "By the way," Mason said, "where *were* you on the night of the fifth and the morning of the sixth of June?"

"In my apartment, in bed and asleep."

"Can you prove it?" Mason asked.

Jefferson said scornfully, "Don't be absurd! I am unmarried, Mr. Mason. I sleep alone. There was no occasion for me to try and show where I was at that time, and there is none now. No one is going to pay any attention to the word of a perjurer and a crook who never saw me in his life before. Who is this scum of the waterfront? This whole thing is preposterous!"

"I'd be inclined to think so, too," Mason told him,"if it wasn't for that air of quiet confidence on the part of the district attorney. Therefore, it becomes very important for me to know exactly where you were on the night of the fifth and the morning of the sixth."

"Well," Jefferson said, "on the night of the fifth...that is, on the evening of the fifth I—I see no reason to go into that. On the sixth...from midnight on the fifth until eight-thirty on the morning of the sixth I was in my apartment. By nine o'clock on the morning of the sixth I was in my office, and I can *prove* where I was from a little after seven on the morning of the sixth."

"By whom?"

"By my associate, Walter Irving. He joined me for breakfast at seven in my apartment, and after that we went to the office."

"What about that knife?" Mason asked.

"It's mine. It was stolen from a suitcase in my apartment."

"Where did you get it?"

"It was a gift."

"From whom?"

"That has nothing to do with the case, Mr. Mason."

"Who gave it to you?"

"It's none of your business."

"I *have* to know who gave it to you, Jefferson."

"I am conducting my own affairs, Mr. Mason."

"I'm conducting your case."

"Go right ahead. Just don't ask me questions about women, that's all. I don't discuss my female friends with anyone."

"Is there anything you're ashamed of in connection with that gift?"

"Certainly not."

"Then tell me who gave it to you."

"It would be embarrassing to discuss any woman with you, Mr. Mason. That might bring about a situation where you'd feel I was perjuring myself about my relationship with women...when I get on the stand and answer questions put by the district attorney."

Mason studied Jefferson's face carefully. "Look here," he said. "Lots of times a weak case on the part of the prosecution is bolstered because the defendant breaks down under cross-examination. Now, I hope this case is never going to reach a point where it will become necessary to put on any defense. But if it does, I've got to be *certain* you're not lying to me."

Jefferson looked at Mason coldly. "I *never* lie to *anyone*," he said, and then turning away from Mason signaled to the officer that he was ready to be taken back to jail.

Della Street and Paul Drake fell in step with Mason as the lawyer started down the aisle.

"What do you make of it?" Mason asked.

"There sure is something fishy about this whole thing," Drake said. "It stinks. It has all the earmarks of a frame-up. How can Burger think people of that sort can put across a deal like this on a man like Duane Jefferson?"

"That," Mason said, "is the thing we're going to have to find out. Anything new?"

"Walter Irving's back."

"The deuce he is! Where has he been?"

"No one knows. He showed up about ten-thirty this morning. He was in court."

"Where?"

"Sitting in a back row, taking everything in."

Mason said, "There's something here that is completely and thoroughly contradictory. The whole case is cockeyed."

"The police have something up their sleeves," Drake said. "They have some terrific surprise. I can't find out what it is. Do you notice that Hamilton Burger seems to remain thoroughly elated?"

"That's the thing that gets me," Mason said. "Burger puts on these witnesses and acts as though he's just laying a preliminary foundation. He doesn't seem to take too much interest in their stories, or whether I attack their characters or their credibility. He's playing along for something big."

"What about Irving?" Drake asked. "Are you going to be in touch with him?"

"Irving and I aren't on friendly terms. The last time he walked out of my office he was mad as a bucking bronco. He cabled his company, trying to get me fired. You haven't found out anything about Marline Chaumont or her brother?"

"I haven't found out where they are," Drake said, "but I think I've found out how they gave me the slip."

"How?" Mason asked. "I'm interested in that."

"It's so damn simple that it makes me mad I didn't get onto it sooner."

"What?"

Drake said, "Marline Chaumont simply took her suitcases and had a porter deposit them in storage lockers. Then she took her brother out to an airport limousine, as though they were *incoming* passengers. She gave a porter the keys for two of the lockers, so two suitcases were brought out. She went in the limousine to a downtown hotel. She and her brother got out and completely vanished."

"Then, of course, she went back and got the other suitcases?" Mason asked.

"Presumably," Drake said, "she got a taxicab after she had her brother safely put away, went out to the airport, picked up the other two suitcases out of the storage lockers, and then rejoined her brother."

Mason said, "We've got to find her, Paul."

"I'm trying, Perry."

"Can't you check hotel registrations? Can't you—?"

"Look, Perry," Drake said, "I've checked every hotel registration that was made at about that time. I've checked with rental agencies for houses that were rented. I've checked with the utilities for connections that were put in at about that time. I've done everything I can think of. I've had girls telephoning the apartment houses to see if anyone made application for apartments. I've even checked the motels to see who registered on that date. I've done everything I can think of."

Mason paused thoughtfully. "Have you checked the car rental agencies, Paul?"

"What do you mean?"

"I mean the drive-yourself automobiles where a person rents an automobile, drives it himself, pays so much a day and so much a mile?"

The expression on Drake's face showed mixed emotions. "She wouldn't— Gosh, no! Good Lord, Perry! Maybe I overlooked a bet!"

Mason said, "Why couldn't she get a drive-yourself automobile, put her stuff in it, go to one of the outlying cities, rent a house there, then drive back with the automobile and—"

"I'd say it was one chance in ten thousand," Drake said, "but I'm not going to overlook it. It's all that's left."

"Okay," Mason said. "Try checking that idea for size, Paul."

CHAPTER FIFTEEN

Promptly at two o'clock court reconvened and Judge Hartley said, "Call your next witness, Mr. District Attorney."

Hamilton Burger hesitated a moment, then said, "I will call Mae Wallis Jordan."

Mae Jordan, quiet, demure, taking slow, steady steps, as though steeling herself to a task which she had long anticipated with extreme distaste, walked to the witness stand, was sworn, gave her name and address to the court reporter, and seated herself.

Hamilton Burger's voice fairly dripped sympathy. "You are acquainted with the defendant, Duane Jefferson, Miss Jordan?" he asked.

"Yes, sir."

"When did you first get acquainted with him?"

"Do you mean, when did I first see him?"

"When did you first get in touch with him," Hamilton Burger asked, "and how?"

"I first saw him after he came to the city here, but I have been corresponding with him for some time."

"When was the date that you first *saw* him? Do you know?"

"I know very well. He arrived by train. I was there to meet the train."

"On what date?"

"May seventeenth."

"Of this year?"

"Yes, sir."

"Now then, you had had some previous correspondence with the defendant?"

"Yes."

"How had that corrrespondence started?"

"It started as a...as a joke. As a gag."

"In what way?"

"I am interested in photography. In a photographic magazine there was an offer to exchange colored stereo photographs of Africa for stereo photographs of the southwestern desert. I was interested and wrote to the box number in question."

"In South Africa?"

"Well, it was in care of the magazine, but it turned out that the magazine forwarded the mail to the person who had placed the ad in the magazine. That person was—"

"Just a moment," Mason interrupted. "We object to the witness testifying as to her conclusion. *She* doesn't know who put the ad in the magazine. Only the records of the magazine can show that."

"We will show them," Hamilton Burger said cheerfully. "However, Miss Jordan, we'll just skip that at the moment. What happened?"

"Well, I entered into correspondence with the defendant."

"What was the nature of that correspondence generally?" Hamilton Burger asked. And then, turning to Mason, said, "Of course, I can understand that this may be objected to as not being the best evidence, but I am trying to expedite matters."

Mason, smiling, said, "I am always suspicious of one who tries to expedite matters by introducing secondary evidence. The letters themselves would be the best evidence."

"I only want to show the *general* nature of the correspondence," Hamilton Burger said.

"Objected to as not being the best evidence," Mason said, "and that the question calls for a conclusion of the witness."

"Sustained," Judge Hartley said.

"You received letters from South Africa?" Hamilton Burger asked, his voice showing a slight amount of irritation.

"Yes."

"Those letters were signed how?"

"Well... in various ways."

"What's that?" Hamilton Burger asked, startled. "I thought that—"

"Never mind what the district attorney thought," Mason said. "Let's have the *facts.*"

"How were those letters signed?" Hamilton Burger asked.

"Some of them were signed with the name of the defendant, the first ones were."

"And where are those letters now?"

"They are gone."

"Where?"

"I destroyed them."

"Describe the contents of those letters," Hamilton Burger said unctuously. "Having proved, Your Honor, that the best evidence is no longer available, I am seeking to show by secondary evidence—"

"There are no objections," Judge Hartley said.

"I was going to state," Mason said, "that I would like to ask some questions on cross-examination as to the nature and contents of the letters and the time and manner of their destruction, in order to see whether I wished to object."

"Make your objection first, and then you may ask the questions," Judge Hartley said.

"I object, Your Honor, on the ground that no proper foundation for the introduction of secondary testimony has been laid and on the further ground that it now appears that at least some of these letters did not even bear the name of the defendant. In connection with that objection, I would like to ask a few questions."

"Go ahead," Hamilton Burger invited, smiling slightly.

Mason said, "You said that those letters were signed in various ways. What did you mean by that?"

"Well—" she said, and hesitated.

"Go on," Mason said.

"Well," she said, "some of the letters were signed with various... well, gag names."

"Such as what?" Mason asked.

"Daddy Longlegs was one," she said.

There was a ripple of mirth in the courtroom, which subsided as Judge Hartley frowned.

"And others?"

"Various names. You see we...we exchanged photographs...gag pictures."

"What do you mean by gag pictures?" Mason asked.

"Well, I am a camera fan, and the defendant is, too, and...we started corresponding formally at first, and then the correspondence became more personal. I...he asked me for a picture, and I...for a joke I—"

"Go ahead," Mason said. "What did you do?"

"I had taken a photograph of a very trim spinster who was no longer young, a rather interesting face, however, because it showed a great deal of character. I had a photograph of myself in a bathing suit and I...I made a trick enlargement, so that the face of the trim spinster was put on my body, and I sent it to him. I thought that if he was simply being flirtatious, that would stop him."

"Was it a joke, or was it intended to deceive him?" Mason asked.

She flushed and said, "That first picture was intended to deceive him. It was done so cunningly that it would be impossible for him to know that it was a composite picture—at least, I thought it would be impossible."

"And you asked him to send you a picture in return?"

"I did."

"And did you receive a picture?"

"Yes."

"What was it?"

"It was the face of a giraffe wearing glasses, grafted on the photograph of a huge figure of a heavily muscled man. Evidently, the figure of a wrestler or a weightlifter."

"And in that way," Mason asked, "you knew that he had realized your picture was a composite?"

"Yes."

"And what happened after that?"

"We exchanged various gag pictures. Each one trying to be a little more extreme than the other."

"And the letters?" Mason asked.

"The letters were signed with various names which would sort of fit in with the type of photograph."

"You so signed your letters to him?"

"Yes."

"And he so signed his letters to you?"

"Yes."

Mason made his voice elaborately casual. "He would sign letters to you, I suppose, as 'Your Prince,' or 'Sir Galahad,' or something like that?"

"Yes."

"Prince Charming?"

She gave a quick start. "Yes," she said. "As a matter of fact, at the last he signed *all* of his letters 'Prince Charming.'"

"Where are those letters now?" Mason asked.

"I destroyed his letters."

"And where are the letters that you wrote to him, if you know?"

"I...I destroyed them."

Hamilton Burger grinned. "Go right ahead, Mr. Mason. You're doing fine."

"How did you get ahold of them?" Mason asked.

"I...I went to his office."

"While he was there?" Mason asked.

"I—When I got the letters, he was there, yes."

Mason smiled at the district attorney. "Oh, I think, Your Honor, I have pursued this line of inquiry far enough. I will relinquish the right to any further questioning on the subject of the letters. I insist upon my objection, however. The witness can't swear that these letters ever came from this defendant. They were signed 'Prince Charming' and other names she said were gag names. That's her conclusion."

Judge Hartley turned toward the witness. "These letters were in response to letters mailed by you?"

"Yes, Your Honor."

"And how did you address the letters you mailed?"

"To 'Duane Jefferson, care of the South African Gem Importing and Exploration Company.'"

"At its South African address?"

"Yes, Your Honor."

"You deposited those letters in regular mail channels?"

"Yes, Your Honor."

"And received these letters in reply?"

"Yes, Your Honor."

"The letters showed they were in reply to those mailed by you?"

"Yes, Your Honor."

"And you burned them?"

"Yes, Your Honor."

"The objection is overruled," Judge Hartley said. "You may introduce secondary evidence of their contents, Mr. District Attorney."

Hamilton Burger bowed slightly, turned to the witness. "Tell us what was in those letters which were destroyed," he said.

"Well, the defendant adopted the position that he was lonely and far from the people he knew, that he didn't have any girl friends, and...oh, it was all a gag. It's *so* difficult to explain."

"Go ahead; do the best you can," Hamilton Burger said.

"We adopted the attitude of...well, we pretended it was a lonely hearts correspondence. He would write and tell me how very wealthy and virtuous he was and what a good husband he would make, and I would write and tell him how beautiful I was and how—Oh, it's just simply out of the question to try and explain it in cold blood this way!"

"Out of context, so to speak?" Hamilton Burger asked.

"Yes," she said. "That's just it. You have to understand the mood and the background, otherwise you wouldn't be able to get the picture at all. The letters, standing by themselves, would appear to be hopelessly foolish, utterly asinine. That was why I felt I had to have them back in my possession."

"Go ahead," Hamilton Burger said. "What did you do?"

"Well, finally Duane Jefferson wrote me one serious letter. He told me that his company had decided to open a branch office in the United States, that it was to be located here, and that he was to be in charge of it and that he was looking forward to seeing me."

"And what did you do?"

"All of a sudden I was in a terrific panic. It was one thing to carry on a joking correspondence with a man who was thousands of miles away and quite another thing suddenly to meet that man face to face. I was flustered and embarrassed."

"Go on. What did you do?"

"Well, of course, when he arrived—he wired me what train he was coming on, and I was there to meet him and—that was when things began to go wrong."

"In what way?"

"He gave me a sort of brush-off, and *he* wasn't the type of person *I* had anticipated. Of course," she went on hastily, "I know what a little fool I was to get a preconceived notion of a man I'd never seen, but I had built up a very great regard for him. I considered him as a friend and I was terribly disappointed."

"Then what?" Hamilton Burger asked.

"Then I called two or three times on the telephone and talked with him, and I went out with him one night."

"And what happened?"

She all but shuddered. "The man was utterly impossible," she said, glaring down at the defendant. "He was patronizing in a cheap, tawdry way. His manner showed that he had completely mistaken the tone of my correspondence. He regarded me as...he treated me as if I were a...he showed no respect, no consideration. He had none of the finer feelings."

"And what did *you* do?"

"I told him I wanted my letters back."

"And what did he do?"

She glared at Duane Jefferson. "He told me I could *buy* them back."

"So what did you do?"

"I determined to get those letters back. They were mine, anyway."

"So what did you do?"

"On June fourteenth I went to the office at a time when I knew neither the defendant nor Mr. Irving would normally be there."

"And what did you do?" Hamilton Burger asked.

"I entered the office."

"For what purpose?"

"For the sole purpose of finding the letters I had written."

"You had reason to believe those letters were in the office?"

"Yes. He told me they were in his desk and that I could come and get them at any time after I had complied with his terms."

"What happened?"

"I couldn't find the letters. I looked and I looked, and I pulled open the drawers of the desk and then—"

"Go on," Hamilton Burger said.

"And the door opened," she said.

"And who was in the doorway?"

"The defendant, Duane Jefferson."

"Alone?"

"No. His associate, Walter Irving, was with him."

"What happened?"

"The defendant used vile language. He called me names that I have never been called before."

"And then what?"

"He made a grab for me and—"

"And what did you do?"

"I backed up and tipped over a chair and fell over. Then Mr. Irving grabbed

my ankles and held me. The defendant accused me of snooping and I told him I
was there only to get my letters."

"Then what?"

"Then he stood for a moment looking at me in apparent surprise, and then
said to Mr. Irving, 'Damned if I don't believe she's right!'"

"Then what?"

"Then the phone rang and Irving picked up the receiver, listened for a
minute and said, 'Good God! The police!'"

"Go on," Hamilton Burger said.

"So the defendant ran over to a filing cabinet, jerked it open, pulled out a
whole package of my letters tied up with string and said, 'Here, you little fool!
Here are your letters. Take them and get out! The police are looking for you.
Someone saw you break into the place, and the police have been notified. Now,
see what a damn fool you are!'"

"What happened?"

"He started pushing me toward the door. Then Mr. Irving pushed something
into my hand and said, 'Here, take these. They'll be a reward for keeping your
big mouth shut.'"

"And what did you do?"

"As soon as they pushed me out of the door, I made a dash for the women's
restroom."

"Go on," Hamilton Burger said.

"And just as I opened the door of the restroom, I saw the defendant and
Walter Irving run out of their office and dash to the men's room."

"Then what?"

"I didn't wait to see any more. I dashed into the restroom and unfastened the
string on the package of letters I had been given, looked through the contents
to see that they were mine, and destroyed them."

"*How* did you destroy them?"

"I put them in the wastepaper receptacle with the used towels, where they
would be picked up and incinerated."

"And then what did you do?"

"Then," she said, "I was trapped. I knew the police were coming. I—"

"Go ahead," Hamilton Burger said.

"I had to do something to get out of there."

"And *what* did you do?" Hamilton Burger said, a smile on his face.

"I felt that perhaps the exits might be watched, that I must have been seen by
someone who had given the police a good description, so I...I looked around
for someplace to go, and I saw a door which had the sign on it saying, 'Perry
Mason, Attorney at Law, Enter.' I'd heard of Perry Mason, of course, and I
thought perhaps I could hand him a line, telling him I wanted a divorce or
something of that sort, or that I'd been in an automobile accident...just make
up a good story, anything to hold his interest. That would enable me to be in his
office when the police arrived. I felt I could hold his interest long enough to
avoid the police. I wanted to stay there just long enough so I could get out after
the police had given up the search. I realize now that it was a crazy idea, but it
was the only available avenue of escape. As it happened, Fate played into my
hands."

"In what way?"

"It seemed Mr. Mason's secretaries were expecting a typist. They'd
telephoned some agency and a typist was supposed to be on her way up. I stood,
hesitating, in the doorway for a moment, and the receptionist took me for the

typist. She asked me if I was the typist, so of course I told her yes and went to work."

"And," Hamilton Burger said smugly, "you worked in the office of Perry Mason that afternoon?"

"I worked there for some little time, yes."

"And then what?"

"When the coast was clear I made my escape."

"When was that?"

"Well, I was working on a document. I was afraid that if it was finished, Mr. Mason would ring up the secretarial agency to find out what the bill was. I just didn't know what to do. So when there was a good break, I slipped down to the restroom, then to the elevator and went home."

"You have mentioned something that was pushed into your hand. Do you know what that consisted of?"

"Yes."

"What?"

"Diamonds. Two diamonds."

"When did you find out about them?"

"After I'd been working for a few minutes. I'd slipped what had been given me into my handbag. So when I had a good chance I looked. I found two small packets of tissue paper. I removed the paper and found two diamonds.

"I got in a panic. I suddenly realized that if these men should claim the intruder had stolen diamonds from their office, I'd be framed. I wouldn't have any possible defense anyone would believe. So I just had to get rid of these diamonds. I realized right away I'd walked into a trap."

"What did you do?"

"I stuck the diamonds to the underside of the desk, where I was working in Mr. Mason's office."

"How did you stick them to this desk?"

"With chewing gum."

"How much chewing gum?"

"A perfectly terrific amount. I had about twelve sticks in my purse, and I chewed them all up and got a big wad of gum. Then I put the diamonds in the gum and pushed them up against the underside of the desk."

"Where are those diamonds now?"

"As far as *I* know, they're still there."

"Your Honor," Hamilton Burger said, "if the Court please, I suggest that an officer of this court be dispatched to the office of Perry Mason, with instructions to look at the place described by this witness and bring back the wad of chewing gum containing those two diamonds."

Judge Hartley looked at Mason questioningly.

Mason smiled at the judge. "*I* certainly would have no objection, Your Honor."

"Very well," Judge Hartley ruled. "It will be the order of the Court that an officer of this court proceed to take those diamonds and impound them."

"And may they be sent for *immediately*, Your Honor," Hamilton Burger asked, "before... well, before something happens to them?"

"And what would happen to them?" Judge Hartley asked.

"Well, now that it is known," Hamilton Burger said, "now that the testimony has come out... I... well, I would dislike to have anything happen to the evidence."

"So would I," Mason said heartily. "I join the prosecutor's request. I suggest that one of the deputy district attorneys instruct an officer to proceed at once to my office."

"Can you designate the desk that was used by this young lady?" Hamilton Burger asked.

"The desk in question was one that was placed in the law library. It can be found there."

"Very well," the judge ruled. "You may take care of that matter, Mr. District Attorney. Now, go on with your questioning."

Hamilton Burger walked over to the clerk's desk, picked up the knife which had been marked for identification. "I show you a dagger with an eight-inch blade, one side of the hilt being engraved with the word 'Duane,' the other side with the initials 'M.J.' I will ask you if you are familiar with that knife."

"I am. It is a knife which I sent the defendant at his South African address as a Christmas present last Christmas. I told him he could use it to protect... protect my honor."

The witness began to cry.

"I think," Hamilton Burger said suavely, "that those are all of the questions I have of this witness. You may cross-examine, Mr. Mason."

Mason waited patiently until Mae Jordan had dried her eyes and looked up at him. "You are, I believe, a very fast and accurate typist?"

"I try to be competent."

"And you worked in my office on the afternoon in question?"

"Yes."

"Do you know anything about gems?"

"Not particularly."

"Do you know the difference between a real diamond and an imitation diamond?"

"It didn't take an expert to tell those stones. Those were very high-grade stones. I recognized what they were as soon as I saw them."

"Had you bought those stones from the defendant?" Mason asked.

"What do you mean, had I bought those stones?"

"Did you pay him anything? Give him any consideration?"

"Certainly not," she snapped.

"Did you pay Mr. Irving for those stones?"

"No."

"Then you knew those stones did not belong to you?" Mason asked.

"They were given to me."

"Oh, then you thought they were yours?"

"I felt certain I'd walked into a trap. I felt those men would say I'd gone to their office and stolen those diamonds. It would be my word against theirs. I knew they hadn't given me two very valuable diamonds just to keep quiet about having exchanged letters."

"You say *they* gave you the diamonds. Did you receive them from Jefferson or from Irving?"

"From Mr. Irving."

Mason studied the defiant witness for a moment. "You started corresponding with the defendant while he was in South Africa?"

"Yes."

"And wrote him love letters?"

"They were not love letters."

"Did they contain matters which you wouldn't want this jury to see?"

"They were foolish letters, Mr. Mason. Please don't try to put anything in them that wasn't in them."

"I am asking you," Mason said, "as to the nature of the letters."

"They were *very foolish* letters."

"Would you say they were indiscreet?"

"I would say they were indiscreet."

"You wanted them back?"

"I felt...well...foolish about the whole thing."

"So you wanted the letters back?"

"Yes, very badly."

"And, in order to get them back, you were willing to commit a crime?"

"I wanted the letters back."

"Please answer the question. You were willing to commit a crime in order to get the letters back?"

"I don't know that it's a crime to enter an office to get things that belong to me."

"Did you believe it was illegal to use a skeleton key to enter property belonging to another person, so that you could take certain things?"

"I was trying to get possession of property that belonged to me."

"Did you believe that it was illegal to use a skeleton key to open that door?"

"I...I didn't consult a lawyer to find out about my rights."

"Where did you get the key which opened the door?"

"I haven't said I had a key."

"You've admitted you entered the office at a time when you knew both Jefferson and Irving would not be there."

"What if I did? I went to get my own property."

"If you had a key which opened the door of that office, where did you get it?"

"Where does one ordinarily get keys?"

"From a locksmith?"

"Perhaps."

"Did you get a key to that office from a locksmith?"

"I will answer no questions about keys."

"And suppose the Court should instruct you that you had to answer such questions?"

"I would refuse on the grounds that any testimony from me relating to the manner in which I entered that office would tend to incriminate me, and therefore I would not have to answer the question."

"I see," Mason said. "But you have already admitted that you entered the office illegally. Therefore, an attempt to exercise your constitutional prerogative would be too late."

"Now, if the Court please," Hamilton Burger said, "I would like to be heard on this point. I have given this question very careful thought. The Court will note that the witness simply stated that she entered the office at a time when the defendant and his associate were absent. She has not stated *how* she entered the office. As far as her testimony is concerned, the door could well have been unlocked; and, inasmuch as this is a public office, where it is expected the public will enter in order to transact business, there would have been nothing illegal about an entrance made in the event the door had been unlocked. Therefore, the witness is in a position, if she so desires, to refuse to testify as to the manner in which she entered that office, on the ground that it might tend to incriminate her."

Judge Hartley frowned. "That's rather an unusual position for a witness called on behalf of the prosecution, Mr. District Attorney."

"It's an unusual case, Your Honor."

"Do you wish to be heard on that point, Mr. Mason?" Judge Hartley asked.

Mason smiled and said, "I would like to ask the witness a few more questions."

"I object to any more cross-examination on this point," Hamilton Burger said, his voice showing exasperation and a trace of apprehension. "The witness has made her position plain. Counsel doesn't dare to cross-examine her about the pertinent facts in the case, so he continually harps upon the one point where this young woman, yielding to her emotions, has put herself in an embarrassing position. He keeps prolonging this moment, as a cat plays with a mouse, hoping thereby to prejudice the jury against this witness. The witness has made her position plain. She refuses to answer questions on this phase of the matter."

Mason smiled. "I have been accused of prolonging this phase of the examination in an attempt to prejudice the jury. I don't want to prejudice the jury. I'd like to get information which the jurors want.

"When the district attorney was prolonging the examination of Mr. Gilly in an attempt to prejudice the jury against the defendant, you didn't hear me screaming. What's sauce for the goose should be sauce for the gander."

Judge Hartley smiled. "The objection is overruled. Go ahead with your questions."

"Will you tell us the name of the person who furnished you with the key that enabled you to get into the office of the South African Gem Importing and Exploration Company?"

"No."

"Why not?"

"Because, if I answered that question, it would tend to incriminate me, and therefore I shall refuse to answer."

"You have discussed this phase of your testimony with the district attorney?"

"Oh, Your Honor," Hamilton Burger said, "this is the same old gambit so frequently pursued by defense attorneys. I will stipulate that this witness has discussed her testimony with me. I would not have put her on the stand unless I knew that her testimony would be pertinent and relevant. The only way I could know what it was, was to talk with her."

Mason kept his eyes on the witness. "You have discussed this phase of your testimony with the district attorney?"

"Yes."

"And have discussed with him what would happen in case you were asked a question concerning the name of the person who furnished you the keys?"

"Yes."

"And told him you would refuse to testify on the ground that it would incriminate you?"

"Yes."

"Did you make that statement to the district attorney, or did he suggest to you that you could refuse to answer the question on that ground?"

"Well, I...I...of course I know my rights."

"But you have just stated," Mason said, "that you didn't know that it was a crime for you to enter an office to get property that belonged to you."

"Well, I...I think there's a nice legal point there. As I now understand it, a public office...that is, a place that is intended to be open to the public is

different from a private residence. And where property belongs to me—"
Mason smiled. "Then you are *now* taking the position, Miss Jordan, that it was
no crime for you to enter that office?"

"No."

"Oh, you are *now* taking the position that it *was* a crime for you to enter that
office?"

"I now understand that under the circumstances it—I refuse to answer that
question on the ground that the answer may incriminate me."

"In other words, the district attorney suggested to you that you should
consider it was a crime, and therefore you could refuse to answer certain
questions when I asked them?"

"We discussed it."

"And the suggestion came from the district attorney that it would be well
under the circumstances for you to refuse to answer certain questions which I
might ask on cross-examination. Is that right?"

"There were certain questions I told him I wouldn't answer."

"And he suggested that you could avoid answering them by claiming
immunity on the ground that you couldn't be forced to incriminate yourself?"

"Well, in a way, yes."

"Now then," Mason said, "you had two diamonds with you when you left that
office?"

"Yes."

"They didn't belong to you?"

"They were given to me."

"By whom?"

"By Mr. Irving, who told me to take them."

"Did he say *why* you were to take them?"

"He said to take them and keep my big mouth shut."

"And you took them?"

"Yes."

"And you kept your mouth shut?"

"I don't know what you mean by that."

"You didn't tell anyone about the diamonds?"

"Not at that time."

"You knew they were valuable?"

"I'm not simple, Mr. Mason."

"Exactly," Mason said. "You knew they were diamonds and you knew they
were valuable?"

"Certainly."

"And you took them?"

"Yes."

"And what did you do with them?"

"I've told you what I did with them. I fastened them to the underside of the
desk in your office."

"Why?" Mason asked.

"Because I wanted a place to keep them."

"You could have put them in your purse. You could have put them in your
pocket," Mason said

"I...I didn't want to. I didn't want to have to explain how I came by the
diamonds."

"To whom?"

"To anybody who might question me."

"To the police?"

"To *anyone* who might question me, Mr. Mason. I felt I had walked into a trap and that I was going to be accused of having stolen two diamonds."

"But you had been given those diamonds?"

"Yes, but I didn't think anyone would believe me when I told them so."

"Then you don't expect the jury to believe your story now?"

"Objected to," Hamilton Burger snapped. "Argumentative."

"Sustained," Judge Hartley said.

"Isn't it a fact," Mason asked, "that someone who gave you a key to the office which you entered illegally and unlawfully, also gave you a package of diamonds which you were to plant in that office in a place where they would subsequently be found by the police?"

"No!"

"Isn't it a fact that you carried those diamonds into the building wrapped up in tissue paper, that you put those diamonds in a package and concealed them in the office, that you were forced to leave hurriedly because you learned the police had been tipped off, and after you got in my office and started to work, you checked through your purse in order to make certain that you had disposed of all of the diamonds and to your horror found that two of the diamonds you were supposed to have planted in that office had been left in your purse, and that, therefore, in a panic, you tried to get rid of those diamonds by the means you have described?"

"Just a moment!" Hamilton Burger shouted. "I object to this on the ground that it assumes facts not in evidence, that it is not proper cross-examination, that there is no foundation for the assumption that—"

"The objection is overruled," Judge Hartley snapped.

"Isn't it a fact," Mason asked, "that you did what I have just outlined?"

"Absolutely not. I took no diamonds with me when I went to that office. I had no diamonds in my possession when I went in."

"But you don't dare to tell us who gave you a key to that office?"

"I refuse to answer questions about that."

"Thank you," Mason said. "I have no further questions."

Mae Jordan left the stand. The jurors watched her with some skepticism.

Hamilton Burger called other witnesses who established technical background—the exact position of the cruise ship in the harbor when Baxter jumped overboard, passengers who had seen Baxter jump and the owner of a launch which had been cruising in the vicinity. He also introduced police experts who had examined the bloodstains on Gilly's boat and bloodstains on the knife and pronounced them to be human blood.

Mason had no cross-examination except for the expert who had examined the bloodstains.

"*When* did you make your examination?" Mason asked.

"June nineteenth."

"At a time when the bloodstains were at least ten days to two weeks old?"

"So I should judge."

"On the boat?"

"Yes."

"On the knife?"

"Yes."

"They could have been older?"

"Yes."

"They could have been a month old?"

"Well, they could have been."

"The only way you have of knowing when those bloodstains got on the boat was from a statement made to you by Jack Gilly?"

"Yes."

"And did you know Jack Gilly had previously been convicted of perjury?" The witness squirmed.

"Objected to as incompetent, irrelevant, and immaterial and not proper cross-examination," Hamilton Burger said.

"Sustained," Judge Hartley snapped. "Counsel can confine his cross-examination to the bloodstains, the nature of the tests, and the professional competency of the witness."

"That's all," Mason said. "I have no more questions."

Max Dutton, Hamilton Burger's last witness of the afternoon, was distinctly a surprise witness. Dutton testified that he lived in Brussels; he had come by airplane to testify at the request of the district attorney. He was, he testified, an expert on gems. He used a system of making models of gems so that it would be possible to identify any particular stone of sufficient value to make it worthwhile. He made microscopic measurements of the dimensions, of the angles, of the facets, and of the locations of any flaws. The witness testified he maintained permanent records of his identifications, which facilitated appraisals, insurance recoveries and the identification of stolen stones.

He had, he said, been employed by Munroe Baxter during his lifetime; Munroe Baxter had given him some gems and asked him to arrange for the identification of the larger stones, so that they could be readily identified if necessary.

The witness tried to state what Munroe Baxter had told him—the manner in which he had received the stones—but on objection by Perry Mason the objection was sustained by the Court. However, Hamilton Burger was able to show that the stones came to the witness in a box bearing the imprint of the Paris office of the South African Gem Importing and Exploration Company.

The witness testified that he had selected the larger stones and had made complete charts of those stones, so that they could be identified. He further stated that he had examined a package of stones which had been given him by the police and which he understood had been recovered from the desk of the defendant, and that ten of those stones had proved to be identical to the stones he had so carefully charted.

"Cross-examine," Hamilton Burger said.

"This system that you have worked out for identifying stones takes into consideration every possible identifying mark on the stones?" Mason asked.

"It does."

"It would, therefore, enable anyone to duplicate those stones, would it not?"

"No, sir, it would not. You might cut a stone to size; you might get the angle of the facets exactly the same. But the flaws in the stone would not be in the proper position with relation to the facets."

"It would, however, be possible to make a duplication in the event you could find a stone that had certain flaws?"

"That is very much like asking whether it would be possible to duplicate fingerprints, provided you could find a person who had exactly identical ridges and whorls," the witness said.

"Do you then wish to testify under oath that your system of identifying stones is as accurate as the identification of individuals through the science of fingerprinting?" Mason asked.

The witness hesitated a moment, then said, "Not quite."

"That's all," Mason announced, smiling. "No further questions."

The court took its evening adjournment.

As Mason gathered his papers together Walter Irving pushed his way through the crowd that was leaving the courtroom. He came up to Mason's table. His grin was somewhat sheepish.

"I guess perhaps I owe you an apology," he said.

"You don't owe me anything," Mason told him. "And make no mistake about it, I don't owe you anything."

"You don't owe me anything," Irving said, "but I'm going to make an apology anyway. And I'm further going to tell you that that Jordan girl is a brazen-faced liar. I *think* she broke into that office to plant those diamonds; but regardless of her purpose in getting into the office, there was never any scene such as she testified to. We didn't get back from lunch until after she had done what she wanted to do in that office and had skipped out. We can prove that, and that one fact makes that Jordan girl a damn liar.

"And what's more, I didn't give that Jordan girl any diamonds," Irving said. "I didn't tell her to keep her mouth shut. Now that I've seen her, I remember having seen her at the train. She met Duane and tried to force herself on him. As far as I know, that's the only time in my life I've ever set eyes on her. That girl is playing some deep game, and she's not playing it for herself, Mr. Mason. There's something behind it, something very sinister and something being engineered by powerful interests that have made a dupe of your district attorney."

"I hope so," Mason said. "Where have you been, incidentally?"

"I've been in Mexico. I admit, I underestimated your abilities, but I was trying to give you an opportunity to direct suspicion to me in case you wanted to."

"Well, I haven't wanted to," Mason said, and then added significantly, "yet."

Irving grinned at him. "That's the spirit, Counselor. You can always make a pass at me and confuse the issues as far as the jury is concerned, even if you don't want to be friendly with me. Remember that I'm available as a suspect."

Mason looked into his eyes. "Don't think I'll ever forget it."

Irving's grin was one of pure delight. His reddish-brown eyes met the cold, hard gaze of the lawyer with steady affability. 'Now you're cooking with gas! Any time you want me, I'll be available, and I can, of course, give Duane a complete alibi for the morning of the sixth. We had breakfast together a little after seven, got to the office shortly before nine, and he was with me all morning."

"How about the evening of the fifth?" Mason asked.

Irving's eyes shifted.

"Well?" Mason asked.

"Duane was out somewhere."

"Where?"

"With some woman."

"Who?"

Irving shrugged his shoulders.

Mason said, "You can see what's happening here. If the district attorney makes enough of a case so that I have to put the defendant on the stand, there is every possibility that Duane Jefferson's manner, his aloofness, his refusal to answer certain questions, will prejudice his case with the jury."

"I know," Irving said. "I know exactly what you're up against. Before you ever put him on the stand, Mr. Mason, let me talk with him and I'll hammer some sense into his head, even if it does result in his undying enmity forever afterwards. In short, I want you to know that you can count on me all the way through."

"Yes," Mason said, "I understand you sent a most co-operative cablegram to your company in South Africa?"

Irving kept grinning and his eyes remained steady. "That's right," he said. "I asked the company to fire you. I'm sending another one tonight, which will be a lot different. You haven't found Marline Chaumont yet, have you?"

"No," Mason admitted.

Irving lost his grin. "I told you you wouldn't. That's where you loused the case up, Mason. Aside from that, you're doing fine."

And, as though completely assured of Mason's goodwill, Walter Irving turned and sauntered out of the courtroom.

CHAPTER SIXTEEN

Back in his office that evening, Mason paced the floor. "Hang it, Paul!" he said to the detective. "Why is Hamilton Burger so completely confident?"

"Well, you jarred him a couple of times this afternoon," Drake said. "He was so mad he was quivering like a bowl of jelly."

"I know he was mad, Paul. He was angry, he was irritated, he was annoyed, but he was still sure of himself.

"Hamilton Burger hates me. He'd love to get me out on a limb over a very deep pool and then saw off the limb. He wouldn't even mind if he got slightly wet from the resulting splash. Now, there's something in this case that we don't know about."

"Well," Drake said, "as far as this case is concerned, what does he have, Perry?"

"So far he doesn't have anything," Mason said. "That's what worries me. Why should he have that much assurance over a case which means nothing. He has a woman adventuress and a smuggler; he has a man who concededly planned to fake a suicide. The man was a strong swimmer. He had an air tank under his clothes. He did exactly what he had planned he was going to do, to wit, jump over the side of the ship and disappear, so that people would think he was dead.

"Then Hamilton Burger brings on the scum of the earth, the sweepings of the waterfront. He uses a man who deliberately rented a boat to be used in an illegal activity, a man who has been twice convicted of felony. His last conviction was for perjury. The jury isn't going to believe that man."

"And what about the girl?" Della Street asked.

"That's different," Mason said. "That girl made a good impression on the jury. Apparently, she was hired to take those gems to the office and plant them. The jury doesn't know that. Those jurors are taking her at face value."

"Figure value," Paul Drake corrected. "Why did you let her off so easy, Perry?"

"Because every time she answered a question she was getting closer to the jury. Those jurors like her, Paul. I'm going to ask to recall her for further cross-examination. When I do that, I want to have the lowdown on her. You're going to put out operatives who will dig up the dirt on her. I want to know everything about her, all about her past, her friends, and before I question her again, I want to know where she got that key which opened the office."

Drake merely nodded.

"Well," Mason said impatiently, "aren't you going to get busy, Paul?"

The detective sat grinning. "I am busy, Perry. I've been busy. This is once I read your mind. I knew what you'd want. The minute that girl got off the stand, I started a whole bunch of men working. I left this unlisted number of yours with my confidential secretary. She may call any minute with some hot stuff."

Mason smiled. "Give yourself a merit badge, Paul. Hang it, there's nothing that gets a lawyer down worse than having to cross-examine a demure girl who has hypnotized the jury. I can't keep shooting blind, Paul. The next time I start sniping at her, I've got to have ammunition that will score dead-center hits.

"Now, here's something else you'll have to do."

"What's that, Perry?"

"Find Munroe Baxter."

"You don't think he's dead?"

"I'm beginning to think Walter Irving was right. I think the supposedly half-witted brother of Marline Chaumont may well be Baxter, despite those hospital records. In a deal of this magnitude we may find a big loophole. If this fellow in the mental hospital was so much of a zombie, what was to prevent Marline Chaumont from identifying him as her brother, getting him out, then farming him out and substituting Munroe Baxter? What are we doing about finding her, Paul?"

"Well, we're making headway, thanks to you," Drake said. "I'm kicking myself for being a stupid fool. You were right about those car rentals, and I sure overlooked a bet there. Two of those car rentals have agencies right there at the airport. In order to rent a car, you have to show your driving license. That means you have to give your right name."

"You mean Marline Chaumont rented a car under her own name?"

"That's right. Showed her driving license, rented the automobile and took it out."

"Her brother was with her?"

"Not at that time. She left the airport by limousine as an incoming passenger, went uptown with her brother and two suitcases, then came back, rented a car, picked up the other two suitcases, drove out, picked up her brother, and then went someplace."

"Where?" Mason asked.

"Now, that's something I wish I knew. However, we stand a chance of finding out. The car rental is predicated on the mileage driven, as well as on a per diem charge. The mileage indicator on the car when Marline Chaumont brought it back showed it had been driven sixty-two miles."

Mason thought a moment, then snapped his fingers.

"What now?" Drake asked.

"She went out to one of the suburban cities," Mason said. "She's rented a place in one of those suburbs. Now then, she'll want to rent another car, and again she'll have to use her driving license. She was afraid to keep that car she had rented at the airport because she thought we might be checking there."

"We would have been checking within a matter of hours if I'd been on my toes," Drake said ruefully.

"All right," Mason said, "she rented a car there. She was afraid we might trace her, get the license number of the car, have it posted as a hot car and pick her up. So she got rid of that car just as soon as she could. Then she went to one of the outlying towns where they have a car rental agency and signed up for another car. She's had to do it under her own name because of the license angle. Get your men busy, Paul, and cover *all* of the car rental agencies in those outlying towns."

Paul Drake wormed his way out of the chair to stand erect, stretch, say, "Gosh, I'm all in myself. I don't see how you stand a pace like this, Perry."

He went over, picked up the unlisted telephone, said, "Let me call my office and get people started on some of this."

Drake dialed the number, said, "Hello. This is Paul. I want a bunch of men put out to cover all of the outlying towns. I want to check every car rental agency for a car rented by Marline Chaumont.... That's right. Everything.

"Now you can—How's that? ... Wait a minute now," Drake said. 'Give that to me slow. I want to make some notes. Who made the report? ... All right, bring it down here at once. I'm in Mason's office—and get those men started."

Drake hung up the telephone and said, "We've got something, Perry."

"What?"

"We've found out the ace that Hamilton Burger is holding up his sleeve."

"You're sure?"

"Dead sure. One of the detectives who worked on the case knows the angle. He tipped a newspaper reporter off to come and see you get torn to ribbons tomorrow, and the reporter pumped him enough to find out what it was. That reporter is very friendly with one of my men, and we got a tip-off."

"What is it?" Mason asked.

"We'll have all the dope in a minute. They're bringing the report down here," Drake said. "It concerns the woman that Duane Jefferson is trying to protect."

Mason said,"Now, we're getting somewhere, Paul. If I know that information, I don't care what Hamilton Burger thinks he's going to do with it. I'll out-general him somehow."

They waited anxiously until knuckles tapped on the door. Drake opened the door, took an envelope from his secretary, said,"You're getting operatives out checking those car rentals?"

"That's already being done, Mr. Drake. I put Davis in charge of it, and he's on the telephone right now."

"Fine," Drake said. "Let's take a look. I'll give you the dope, Perry."

Drake opened the envelope, pulled out the sheets of flimsy, looked through them hastily, then whistled.

"All right," Mason said, "give."

Drake said, "The night of June fifth Jefferson was down at a nightspot with a woman. It was the woman's car. The parking attendant parked the car and some customer scratched a fender. The attendant got records of license numbers and all that. The woman got in a panic, gave the parking attendant twenty bucks, and told him to forget the whole thing.

"Naturally, the attendant had the answer as soon as that happened. She was a married woman. There's no doubt the guy with her was Duane Jefferson."

"Who was she?" Mason asked.

"A woman by the name of Nan Ormsby."

"Okay,"Mason said. "Perhaps I can use this. It'll depend on how far the affair has gone."

Drake, who had continued reading the report, suddenly gave another whistle.

"What now?" Mason asked.

"Hold everything," Drake said. "You have as juror number eleven Alonzo Martin Liggett?"

"What about him?" Mason asked.

"He's a close friend of Dan Ormsby. Ormsby is in partnership with his wife. They have a place called 'Nan and Dan, Realtors.' Nan Ormsby has been having trouble with her husband. She wants a settlement. He doesn't want the kind of a settlement she wants. He hasn't been able to get anything on her yet.

"Now, with a juror who is friendly to Dan Ormsby, you can see what'll happen."

"Good Lord!" Mason said. "If Hamilton Burger uses that lever—"

"Remember, this tip comes straight from Hamilton Burger's office," Drake said.

Mason sat in frowning concentration.

"How bad is it?" Drake asked.

"It's a perfect setup for the D.A.," Mason said. "If he can force me to put my client on the stand, he can go to town. The jury isn't going to like Duane Jefferson's pseudo-British manner, his snobbishness. You know how they feel about people who get tied up with the British and then become more English than the English, and that's what Jefferson has done. He's cultivated all those mannerisms. So Hamilton Burger will start boring into him—he was breaking up a home, he was out with a married woman—and there's Dan Ormsby's friend sitting on the jury."

"Any way you can beat that, Perry?" Drake asked.

"Two ways," Mason said, "and I don't like either one. I can either base all of my fight on trying to prove that there's been no *corpus delicti*, and keep the case from going to the jury, or, if the judge doesn't agree with me on that, I'll put the defendant on the stand, but confine my direct examination to where he was at five o'clock on the morning of the sixth and roar like the devil if the district attorney tries to examine him as to the night of the fifth. Since I wouldn't have asked him anything about the night of the fifth—only the morning of the sixth—I can claim the D.A. can't examine him as to anything on the night of the fifth."

"He'll have to make a general denial that he committed the crime?" Drake asked.

Mason nodded.

"Won't that open up the question of where he was on the night of the fifth when the boat was being rented?"

"The prosecution's case shows that the defendant wasn't seen until the morning of the sixth, after the boat had been rented—that is, that's the prosecution's case so far. We have the testimony of Jack Gilly to that effect."

"Well," Drake said, "I'll go down to my office and start things going. I'll have my men on the job working all night. You'd better get some sleep, Perry."

Mason's nod showed his preoccupation with other thoughts. "I've got to get this thing straight, Paul. I have a sixth sense that's warning me. I guess it's the way Hamilton Burger has been acting. This is one case where I've got to watch every time I put my foot down that I'm not stepping right in the middle of a trap."

"Well," Drake said, "you pace the floor and I'll cover the country, Perry. Between us, we may be in a better position tomorrow morning."

Mason said, "I should have known. Burger has been triumphant, yet his case is a matter of patchwork. It wasn't the strength of his own case that made him triumphant, but the weakness of my case."

"And now that you know, can you detour the pitfalls?" Drake asked.

"I can try," Mason said grimly.

CHAPTER SEVENTEEN

Judge Hartley called court to order promptly at ten.

Hamilton Burger said, "I have a couple more questions to ask Mr. Max Dutton, the gem expert."

"Just a moment," Mason said. "If the Court please, I wish to make a motion. I feel that perhaps this motion should be made without the presence of the jury."

Judge Hartley frowned. "I am expecting a motion at the conclusion of the prosecution's case," he said. "Can you not let your motion wait until that time, Mr. Mason? I would like to proceed with the case as rapidly as possible."

"One of my motions can wait," Mason said. "The other one, I think, can properly be made in the presence of the jury. That is a motion to exclude all of the evidence of Mae Jordan on the ground that there is nothing in her testimony which in any way connects the defendant with any crime."

"If the Court please," Hamilton Burger said, "the witness, Dutton, will testify that one of the diamonds which was found on the underside of the desk in Perry Mason's office was one of the identical diamonds which was in the Munroe Baxter collection."

Mason said, "That doesn't connect the defendant, Duane Jefferson, with anything. Jefferson didn't give her those diamonds. Even if we are to take her testimony at face value, even if we are to concede for the sake of this motion that she took those diamonds out of the office instead of going to the office to plant diamonds, the prosecution can't bind the defendant by anything that Walter Irving did."

"It was done in his presence," Hamilton Burger said, "and as a part of a joint enterprise."

"You haven't proven either one of those points," Mason said.

Judge Hartley stroked his chin. "I am inclined to think this motion may be well taken, Mr. District Attorney. The Court has been giving this matter a great deal of thought."

"If the Court please," Hamilton Burger pleaded desperately, "I have a good case here. I have shown that these diamonds were in the possession of Munroe Baxter when he left the ship. These diamonds next show up in the possession of the defendant—"

"Not in the possession of the defendant," Mason corrected.

"In an office to which he had a key," Hamilton Burger snapped.

"The janitor had a key. The scrubwoman had a key. Walter Irving had a key."

"Exactly," Judge Hartley said. "You have to show some act of domination over those diamonds by the defendant before he can be connected with the case. That's a fundamental part of the case."

"But, Your Honor, we *have* shown that act of domination. Two of those diamonds were given to the witness Jordan to compensate her for keeping silent about her letters. We have shown that Munroe Baxter came up and took hold of that towing line which was attached to the heavy fishing rod; that the defendant stabbed him, took the belt containing the diamonds, weighted the body, then towed it away to a point where it could be dropped to the bottom."

Judge Hartley shook his head. "That is a different matter from the motion as to the testimony of Mae Jordan. However, if we are to give every credence to all of the prosecution's testimony and all inferences therefrom, as we must do in considering such a motion, there is probably an inference which will be sufficient to defeat the motion. I'll let the motion be made at this time, and reserve a ruling. Go ahead with your case, Mr. District Attorney."

Hamilton Burger put Max Dutton back on the stand. Dutton testified that one of the gems which had been recovered from the blob of chewing gum that had been found fastened to the underside of Mason's desk was a part of the Baxter collection.

"No questions," Mason said when Hamilton Burger turned Dutton over for cross-examination.

"That," Hamilton Burger announced dramatically and unexpectedly, "finishes the People's case."

Mason said, "At this time, Your Honor, I would like to make a motion without the presence of the jury."

"The jurors will be excused for fifteen minutes," Judge Hartley said, "during which time you will remember the previous admonition of the Court."

When the jurors had filed out of court the judge nodded to Perry Mason. "Proceed with your motion."

"I move that the Court direct and instruct the jury to return a verdict of acquittal," Mason said, " on the ground that no case has been made out which would sustain a conviction, on the ground that there is no evidence tending to show a homicide, no evidence of the *corpus delicti*, and no evidence connecting the defendant with the case."

Judge Hartley said, "I am going to rule against the defense in this case, Mr. Mason. I don't want to preclude you from argument, but the Court has given this matter very careful consideration. Knowing that such a motion would be made, I want to point out to you that while, as a usual thing, proof of the *corpus delicti* includes finding the body, under the law of California that is not necessary. *Corpus delicti* means the body of the crime, not the body of the victim.

"Proof of *corpus delicti* only shows that a crime has been committed. After the crime has been committed, then it is possible to connect the defendant with that crime by proper proof.

"The *corpus delicti*, or the crime itself, like any other fact to be established in court, can be proved by circumstantial as well as direct evidence. There can be reasonable inferences deduced from the factual evidence presented.

"Now then, we have evidence which, I admit, is not very robust, which shows that Munroe Baxter, the purported victim, was carrying certain diamonds in his possession. Presumably he would not have parted from those diamonds without a struggle. Those diamonds were subsequently found under circumstances which at least support an inference that they were under the domination and in the possession of the defendant.

"One of the strongest pieces of evidence in this case is the finding of the bloodstained knife in the boat. I am free to admit that if I were a juror I would not be greatly impressed by the testimony of the witness Gilly, and yet a man who has been convicted of a felony, a man who has been convicted of perjury may well tell the truth.

"We have in this state the case of *People* v. *Cullen*, 37 California 2nd, 614, 234 Pacific 2nd, 1, holding that it is not essential that the body of the victim actually be found in order to support a homicide conviction.

"One of the most interesting cases ever to come before the bar of any country is the case of *Rex* v. *James Camb*. That was, of course, a British case, decided on Monday, April twenty-sixth, nineteen hundred and forty-eight, before the Lord Chief Justice of England.

"That is the famous *Durban Castle* case in which James Camb, a steward aboard the ship, went to the cabin of a young woman passenger. He was recognized in that cabin. The young woman disappeared and was never seen again. There was no evidence, other than circumstantial evidence, of the *corpus delicti*, save the testimony of the defendant himself admitting that he had pushed the body through the porthole but claiming that the woman was dead at the time, that she had died from natural causes and he had merely disposed of the body in that way.

"In this case we have, of course, no admission of that sort. But we do have a showing that the defendant sat in a boat, that some huge body, too big in the normal course of things to be a fish, attached itself to the heavy fishing tackle which the defendant was dangling overboard; that the defendant or the defendant's companion thereupon reached down and stabbed with a knife. A knife was subsequently found in the boat and the knife was smeared with human blood. It was the defendant's knife. I think, under the circumstances, there is enough of a case here to force the defense to meet the charge, and I think that if the jury should convict upon this evidence, the conviction would stand up."

Hamilton Burger smiled and said, "I think that if the Court will bear with us, the Court will presently see that a case of murder has been abundantly proved."

Judge Hartley looked almost suspiciously at the district attorney for a moment, then tightened his lips and said, "Very well. Call the jury."

Mason turned to his client. "This is it, Jefferson," he said. "You're going to have to go on the stand. You have not seen fit to confide in me as your lawyer. You have left me in a position where I have had to undertake the defense of your case with very little assistance from you.

"I think I can prove the witness Mae Jordan lied when she said that you came into the office while she was still there. I have the girl at the cigar counter who will testify that you men did not come in until *after* the manager of the building was standing down at the elevators. I think once we can prove that she lied in one thing, we can prove that she is to be distrusted in her entire testimony. But that young woman has made a very favorable impression on the jury."

Jefferson merely bowed in a coldly formal way. "Very well," he said.

"You have a few seconds now," Mason said. "Do you want to tell me the things that I should know?"

"Certainly," Jefferson said. "I am innocent. That is all you need to know."

"Why the devil won't you confide in me?" Mason asked.

"Because there are certain things that I am not going to tell anyone."

"In case you are interested," Mason said, "I know where you were on the night of June fifth, and furthermore, the district attorney knows it, too."

For a moment Duane Jefferson stiffened, then he turned his face away and said indifferently, "I will answer no questions about the night of June fifth."

"You won't," Mason said, "because I'm not going to ask them on direct examination. Now just remember this one thing: I'm going to ask you where you were during the early morning hours of June sixth. You be *damn* careful that your answer doesn't ever get back of the time limit I am setting. Otherwise, the District Attorney is going to rip you to shreds. Your examination is going to be very, very brief."

"I understand."

"It will be in the nature of a gesture."

"Yes, sir, I understand."

The jury filed into court and took their seats.

"Are you prepared to go on with your case, Mr. Mason?" Judge Hartley asked.

Mason said, "Yes, Your Honor. I won't even bother the Court and the jury by wasting time with an opening statement. I am going to rip this tissue of lies and insinuations wide open. My first witness will be Ann Riddle."

Ann Riddle, the tall, blonde girl who operated the cigar stand, came forward.

"Do you remember the occasion of the fourteenth of June of this year?"

"Yes, sir."

"Where were you at that time?"

"I was at the cigar stand in the building where you have your offices."

"Where the South African Gem Importing and Exploration Company also has its offices?"

"Yes, sir."

"You operate the cigar stand in that building?"

"Yes, sir."

"Do you remember an occasion when the manager of the building came down to stand at the elevator with a young woman?"

"Yes, sir."

"Did you see the defendant at that time?"

"Yes, sir. The defendant and Mr. Irving, his associate, were returning from lunch. They—"

"Now just a minute," Mason said. "You don't *know* they were returning from lunch."

"No, sir."

"All right, please confine your statements to what happened."

"Well, they were entering the building. The manager was standing there. One of the men—I think it was Mr. Irving, but I can't remember for sure— started to walk over to the manager of the building, then saw that he was intent upon something else, so he turned away. The two men entered the elevator."

"This was after the alarm had been given about the burglary?" Mason asked.

"Yes, sir."

"You may inquire," Mason said to Hamilton Burger.

Hamilton Burger smiled. "I have no questions."

"I will call the defendant, Duane Jefferson, to the stand," Mason said.

Duane Jefferson, cool and calm, got up and walked slowly to the witness stand. For a moment he didn't look at the jury, then when he did deign to glance at them, it was with an air of superiority bordering on contempt. "The damn fool!" Mason whispered under his breath.

Hamilton Burger tilted back in his swivel chair, he interlaced his fingers back of his head, winked at one of his deputies, and a broad smile suffused his face.

"Did you kill Munroe Baxter?" Mason asked.

"No, sir."

"Did you know that those diamonds were in your office?"

"No sir."

"Where were you on the morning of the sixth of June? I'll put it this way, where were you from 2:00 A.M. on the sixth of June to noon of that day?"

"During the times mentioned I was in my apartment, sleeping, until a little after seven. Then I had breakfast with my associate, Walter Irving. After breakfast we went to the office."

"Cross-examine," Mason snapped viciously at Hamilton Burger.

Hamilton Burger said, "I will be very brief. I have only a couple of questions, Mr. Jefferson. Have *you* ever been convicted of a felony?"

"I—" Suddenly Jefferson seemed to collapse in the witness chair.

"Have you?" Hamilton Burger thundered.

"I made one mistake in my life," Jefferson said. "I have tried to live it down. I thought I had."

"Did you, indeed?" Hamilton Burger said scornfully. "Where were you convicted, Mr. Jefferson?"

"In New York."

"You served time in Sing Sing?"

"Yes."

"Under the name of Duane Jefferson?"

"No, sir."

"Under what name?"

"Under the name of James Kincaid."

"Exactly," Hamilton Burger said. "You were convicted of larceny by trick and device."

"Yes."

"You posed as an English heir, did you not? And you told—"

"Objected to," Mason said. "Counsel has no right to amplify the admission."

"Sustained."

"Were you, at one time, known as 'Gentleman Jim,' a nickname of the underworld?"

"Objected to," Mason said.

"Sustained."

Hamilton Burger said scornfully, "I will ask no further questions."

As one in a daze, the defendant stumbled from the stand.

Mason said, his lips a hard, white line, "Mr. Walter Irving take the stand."

The bailiff called, "Walter Irving."

When there was no response, the call was taken up in the corridors.

Paul Drake came forward, beckoned to Mason. "He's skipped, Perry. He was sitting near the door. He took it on the lam the minute Burger asked Jefferson about his record. Good Lord! What a mess! What a lousy mess!"

Judge Hartley said not unkindly, "Mr. Irving doesn't seem to be present, Mr. Mason. Was he under subpoena?"

"Yes, Your Honor."

"Do you wish the Court to issue a bench warrant?"

"No, Your Honor," Mason said. "Perhaps Mr. Irving had his reasons for leaving."

"I daresay he did," Hamilton Burger said sarcastically.

"That's the defendant's case," Mason said. "We rest."

It was impossible for Hamilton Burger to keep the gloating triumph out of his voice. "I will," he said, "call only three witnesses on rebuttal. The first is Mrs. Agnes Elmer."

Mrs. Agnes Elmer gave her name and address. She was, she explained, the manager of the apartment house where the defendant, Duane Jefferson, had rented an apartment shortly after his arrival in the city.

"Directing your attention to the early morning of June sixth," Hamilton Burger said, "do you know whether Duane Jefferson was in his apartment?"

"I do."

"Was he in that apartment?"

"He was not."

"Was his bed slept in that night?"

"It was not."

"Cross-examine," Hamilton Burger said.

Mason, recognizing that the short, direct examination was intended to bait a trap into which he must walk on cross-examination, flexed his arms slowly, as though stretching with weariness, said, "How do you fix the date, Mrs. Elmer?"

"A party rang up shortly before midnight on the fifth," Mrs. Elmer said. "It was a woman's voice. She told me it was absolutely imperative that she get in touch with Mr. Jefferson. She said Mr. Jefferson had got her in—"

"Just a minute," Mason interrupted. "I object, Your Honor, to this witness relating any conversations which occurred outside of the presence of the defendant."

"Oh, Your Honor," Hamilton Burger said. "This is plainly admissible. Counsel asked this question himself. He asked her how she fixed the date. She's telling him."

Judge Hartley said, "There may be some technical merit to your contention, Mr. District Attorney, but this is a court of justice, not a place for a legal sparring match. The whole nature of your examination shows you had carefully baited this as a trap for the cross-examiner. I'm going to sustain the objection. You can make your own case by your own witness.

"Now, the Court is going to ask the witness if there is any other way you can fix the date, any way, that is, depending on your own actions."

"Well," the witness said, "I know it was the sixth because that was the day I went to the dentist. I had a terrific toothache that night and couldn't sleep."

"And how do you fix the date that you went to the dentist?" Mason asked.

"From the dentist's appointment book."

"So you don't know of your own knowledge what date you went to the dentist, only the date that is shown in the dentist's book?"

"That's right."

"And the entry of that date in the dentist's book was not made in your own handwriting. In other words, you have used a conversation with the dentist to refresh your memory."

"Well, I asked him what date I came in, and he consulted his records and told me."

"Exactly," Mason said. "But you don't know of your own knowledge how he kept his records."

"Well, he's supposed to keep them—"

Mason smiled. "But *you* have no independent recollection of anything except that it was the night that you had the toothache, is that right?"

"Well, if you'd had that toothache—"

"I'm asking you if that's the only way you can fix the date, that it was the night you had the toothache?"

"Yes."

"And then, at the request of the district attorney, you tried to verify the date?"

"Yes."

"When did the district attorney request that you do that?"

"I don't know. It was late in the month sometime."

"And did you go to the dentist's office, or did you telephone him?"

"I telephoned him."

"And asked him the date when you had your appointment?"

"Yes."

"Aside from that, you wouldn't have been able to tell whether it had been the sixth, the seventh, or the eighth?"

"I suppose not."

"So you have refreshed your recollection by taking the word of someone else. In other words, the testimony you are now giving as to the date is purely hearsay evidence?"

"Oh, Your Honor," Hamilton Burger said, "I think this witness has the right to refresh her recollection by—"

Judge Hartley shook his head. "The witness has testified that she can't remember the date except by fixing it in connection with other circumstances, and those other circumstances which she is using to refresh her recollection depend upon the unsworn testimony of another. Quite plainly hearsay testimony, Mr. District Attorney."

Hamilton Burger bowed. "Very well, Your Honor."

"That's all," Mason said.

"Call Josephine Carter," Burger said.

Josephine Carter was sworn, testified she was a switchboard operator at the apartment house where the defendant had his apartment, that she worked from 10:00 P.M. on the night of the fifth of June until 6:00 A.M. on the morning of June sixth.

"Did you ring the defendant's phone that night?"

"Yes."

"When?"

"Shortly before midnight. I was told it was an emergency and I—"

"Never mind what you were *told*. What did you *do*?"

"I rang the phone."

"Did you get an answer?"

"No. The party who was calling left a message and asked me to keep calling to see that Mr. Jefferson got that message as soon as he came in."

"How often did you continue to ring?"

"Every hour."

"Until when?"

"When I went off duty at six in the morning."

"Did you ever get an answer?"

"No."

"From your desk at the switchboard can you watch the corridor to the elevator, and did you thereafter watch to see if the defendant came in?"

"Yes. I kept watch so as to call to him when he came in."

"He didn't come in while you were on duty?"

"No."

"You're certain?"

"Postive."

"Cross-examine," Burger snapped at Mason.

"How did you know the phone was ringing?" Mason asked smilingly.

"Why I depressed the key."

"Phones get out of order occasionally?"

"Yes."

"Is there any check signal on the board by which you can tell if the phone is ringing?"

"You get a peculiar sound when the phone rings, sort of a hum."

"And if the phone doesn't ring, do you get that hum?"

"I...we haven't been troubled that way."

"Do you know of your own knowledge that you fail to get that hum when the phone is not ringing?"

"That's the way the board is supposed to work."

"I'm asking you if you know of your own knowledge?"

"Well, Mr. Mason, I have never been in an apartment where the phone was not ringing and at the same time been downstairs at the switchboard trying to ring that telephone."

"Exactly," Mason said. "That's the point I was trying to make, Miss Carter. That's all."

"Just a moment," Hamilton Burger said. "I have one question on redirect. Did you keep an eye on the persons who went in and out, to see if Mr. Jefferson came in?"

"I did."

"Is your desk so located that you could have seen him when he came in?"

"Yes. Everyone who enters the apartment has to walk down a corridor, and I can see through a glass door into that corridor."

"That's all," Burger said, smiling.

"I have one or two questions on recross-examination," Mason said. "I'll only bother you for a moment, Miss Carter. You have now stated that you kept looking up whenever anyone came in, to see if the defendant came in."

"Yes, sir."

"And you could have seen him if he had come in?"

"Yes, sir. Very easily. From my station at the switchboard I can watch people who come down the corridor."

"So you want the Court and the jury to understand that you are certain the defendant didn't come in during the time you were on duty?"

"Well, he didn't come in from the time I first rang his telephone until I quit ringing it at six o'clock, when I went off duty."

"And what time did you first ring his telephone?"

"It was before midnight, perhaps eleven o'clock, perhaps a little after eleven."

"And then what?"

"Then I rang two or three times between the time of the first call and one o'clock, and then after 1:00 A.M. I made it a point to ring every hour on the hour."

"Just short rings or—"

"No, I rang several long rings each time."

"And after your first ring around midnight you were satisfied the defendant was not in his apartment?"

"Yes, sir."

"And because you were watching the corridor you were satisfied that he couldn't have entered the house and gone to his apartment without your seeing him?"

"Yes, sir."

"Then why," Mason asked, "if you *knew* he wasn't in his apartment and *knew* that he hadn't come in, did you keep on ringing the telephone at hourly intervals?"

The witness looked at Mason, started to say something, stopped, blinked her eyes, said, "Why, I...I...I don't know. I just did it."

"In other words," Mason said, "you *thought* there was a possibility he might have come in without your seeing him?"

"Well, of course, that *could* have happened."

"Then when you just now told the district attorney that it would have been impossible for the defendant to have come in without your seeing him, you were mistaken?"

"I...well, I...I had talked it over with the district attorney and...well, I thought that's what I was supposed to say."

"Exactly," Mason said, smiling. "Thank you."

Josephine Carter looked at Hamilton Burger to see if there were any more questions, but Hamilton Burger was making a great show of pawing through some papers. "That's all," he snapped gruffly.

Josephine Carter left the witness stand.

"I will now call Ruth Dickey," Hamilton Burger said.

Ruth Dickey came forward, was sworn, and testified that she was and had been on the fourteenth of June an elevator operator in the building where the South African Gem Importing and Exploration Company had its offices.

"Did you see Duane Jefferson, the defendant in this case, on the fourteenth of June a little after noon?"

"Yes, sir."

"When?"

"Well, he and Mr. Irving, his associate, rode down in the elevator with me about ten minutes past twelve. The defendant said he was going to lunch."

"When did they come back?"

"They came back about five minutes to one and rode up in the elevator with me."

"Did anything unusual happen on that day?"

"Yes, sir."

"What?"

"The manager of the building and one of the stenographers got into the elevator with me, and the manager asked me to run right down to the street floor because it was an emergency."

"Was this before or after the defendant and Irving had gone up with you?"

"After."

"You're certain?"

"Yes."

"About how long after?"

"At least five minutes."

"How well do you know the defendant?" Hamilton Burger asked.

"I have talked with him off and on."

"Have you ever been out with him socially?"

She lowered her eyes. "Yes."

"Now, did the defendant make any statements to you with reference to his relationship with Ann Riddle, the young woman who operates the cigar stand?"

"Yes. He said that he and his partner had set her up in business, that she was a lookout for them, but that no one else knew the connection. He said if I'd be nice to him, he could do something for me, too."

"You may cross-examine," Hamilton Burger said.

"You have had other young men take you out from time to time?" Mason asked.

"Well, yes."

"And quite frequently you have had them make rather wild promises about what they could do about setting you up in business if you would only be nice to them?"

She laughed. "I'll say," she said. "You'd be surprised about what some of them say."

"I dare say I would," Mason said. "That's all. Thank you, Miss Dickey."

"That's all our rebuttal," Hamilton Burger said.

Judge Hartley's voice was sympathetic. "I know that it is customary to have a recess before arguments start, but I would like very much to get this case finished today. I think that we can at least start the argument, unless there is some reason for making a motion for a continuance."

Mason, tight-lipped, shook his head. "Let's go ahead with it," he said.

"Very well, Mr. District Attorney, you may make your opening argument."

CHAPTER EIGHTEEN

Hamilton Burger's argument to the jury was relatively short. It was completed within an hour after court reconvened following the noon recess. It was a masterpiece of forensic eloquence, of savage triumph, of a bitter, vindictive attack on the defendant and by implication on his attorney.

Mason's argument, which followed, stressed the point that while perjurers and waterfront scum had made an attack on his client, no one had yet shown that Munroe Baxter was murdered. Munroe Baxter, Mason insisted, could show up alive and well at any time, without having contradicted the testimony of any witness.

Hamilton Burger's closing argument was directed to the fact that the Court would instruct the jury that *corpus delicti* could be shown by circumstantial evidence, as well as by direct evidence. It was an argument which took only fifteen minutes.

The Court read instructions to the jurors, who retired to the jury room for their deliberations.

Mason, in the courtroom, his face a cold, hard mask, thoughtfully paced the floor.

Della Street, sitting at the counsel table, gave him her silent sympathy. Paul Drake, who had for once been too depressed even to try to eat, sat with his head in his hands.

Mason glanced at the clock, sighed wearily, ceased his pacing and dropped into a chair.

"Any chance, Perry?" Paul Drake asked.

Mason shook his head. "Not with the evidence in this shape. My client is a dead duck. Any luck with this car rental?"

"No luck at all, Perry. We've covered every car rental agency here and in outlying towns where they have branches."

Mason was thoughtful for a moment. "What about Walter Irving?"

"Irving has flown the coop," Drake said. "He left the courtroom, climbed into a taxicab and vanished. This time my men knew what he was going to try to do, and they were harder to shake. But within an hour he had ditched the shadows. It was a hectic hour."

"How did he do it?"

"It was very simple," Drake said. "Evidently it was part of a prearranged scheme. He had chartered a helicopter that was waiting for him at one of the outlying airports. He drove out there, got in the helicopter and took off."

"Can't you find out what happened? Don't they have to file some sort of a flight plan or—"

"Oh, we know what happened well enough," Drake said. "He chartered the helicopter to take him to the International Airport. Halfway there, he changed his mind and talked the helicopter into landing at the Santa Monica Airport. A rented car was waiting there."

"He's gone?"

"Gone slick and clean. We'll probably pick up his trail later on, but it isn't going to be easy, and by that time it won't do any good."

Mason thought for a moment. Suddenly he sat bolt upright. "Paul," he said, "we've overlooked a bet!"

"What?"

"A person renting a car has to show his driving license?"

"That's right."

"You've been looking for car rentals in the name of Marline Chaumont?"

"That's right."

"All right," Mason said. "Start your men looking for car rentals in the name of Walter Irving. Call your men on the phone. Start a network of them making a search. I want that information, and I want it now."

Drake, seemingly glad to be able to leave the depressing atmosphere of the courtroom, said, "Okay, I'll start right away, Perry."

Shortly before five o'clock a buzzer announced that the jury had reached its verdict. The jury was brought into court and the verdict was read by the foreman.

"We, the jury impaneled to try the above-entitled case, find the defendant guilty of murder in the first degree."

There was no recommendation for life imprisonment or leniency.

Judge Hartley's eyes were sympathetic as he looked at Perry Mason. "Can we agree upon having the Court fix a time for pronouncing sentence?" he asked.

"I would like an early date for hearing a motion for a new trial," Mason said. "I will stipulate that Friday will be satisfactory for presenting a motion for new trial and fixing sentence. We will waive the question of time."

"How about the district attorney's office?" Judge Hartley asked. "Will Friday be satisfactory?"

The deputy district attorney, who sat at the counsel table, said, "Well, Your Honor, I think it will be all right. Mr. Burger is in conference with the press at the moment. He—"

"He asked you to represent the district attorney's office?" Judge Hartley asked.

"Yes, Your Honor."

"Represent it then," Judge Hartley said shortly. "Is Friday satisfactory?"

"Yes, Your Honor."

"Friday morning at ten o'clock," Judge Hartley said. "Court is adjourned. The defendant is remanded to custody."

Reporters, who usually swarmed about Perry Mason asking for a statement, were now closeted with Hamilton Burger. The few spectators who had been interested enough to await the verdict got up and went home. Mason picked up his brief case. Della Street tucked her hand through his arm, gave him a reassuring squeeze. "You warned him, Chief," she said. "Not once, but a dozen times. He had it coming."

Mason merely nodded. Paul Drake, hurrying down the corridor, said, "I've got something, Perry."

"Did you hear the verdict?" Mason asked.

Paul Drake's eyes refused to meet Mason's. "I heard it."

"What have you got?" Mason asked.

"Walter Irving rented an automobile the day that Marline Chaumont disappeared from the airport. Last night he rented another one."

"I thought so," Mason said. "Has he turned back the first automobile?"

"No."

"He keeps the rental paid?"

"Yes."

"We can't get him on the ground of embezzling the automobile, so we can have police looking for it as a 'hot' car?"

"Apparently not."

Mason turned to Della Street. "Della, you have a shorthand book in your purse?"

She nodded.

"All right," Mason said to Paul Drake, "let's go, Paul."

"Where?" Drake asked.

"To see Ann Riddle, the girl who bought the cigar counter in our building," Mason said. "We may be able to get to her before she, too, flies the coop. Hamilton Burger is too busy with the press, decorating himself with floral wreaths, to do much thinking now."

Drake, his voice sympathetic, said, "Gosh, Perry, it's...I can imagine how you feel...having a client convicted of first-degree murder. It's the first time you've ever had a client convicted in a murder case."

Mason turned to Paul Drake, his eyes were cold and hard. "My client," he said, "hasn't been convicted of anything."

For a moment Drake acted as if his ears had betrayed him, then, at something he saw in Mason's face, he refrained from asking questions.

"Get the address of that girl who bought the cigar stand," Mason said, "and let's go."

CHAPTER NINETEEN

Mason, his face implacably determined, scorned the chair offered him by the frightened blonde.

"You can talk now," he said, "or you can talk later. Whichever you want. If you talk now it may do you some good. If you talk later you're going to be convicted as an accessory in a murder case. Make up your mind."

"I've nothing to say."

Mason said, "Irving and Jefferson went into the building *before* the excitement. When they entered their office, Mae Jordan was there. They caught her. The phone rang. They were warned that the police had been notified that a girl was breaking into the office and that the police were coming up; that the girl who had seen the woman breaking in and the manager of the building were waiting at the elevators. There was only one person who could have given them that information. That was you."

"You have no right to say that."

"I've said it," Mason said, "and I'm saying it again. The next time I say it, it's going to be in open court.

"By tomorrow morning at ten o'clock we'll have torn into your past and will have found out all about the connection between you and Irving. By that time it'll be too late for you to do anything. You've committed perjury. We're putting a tail on you. Now start talking."

Under the impact of Mason's gaze she at first averted her eyes, then restlessly shifted her position in the chair.

"Start talking," Mason said.

"I don't have to answer to you. You're not the police. You—"

"Start talking."

"All right," she said. "I was paid to keep a watch on things, to telephone them if anything suspicious happened. There's nothing unlawful about that."

"It goes deeper than that," Mason said. "You were in on the whole thing. It was their money that put you in the cigar store. What's your connection with this thing?"

"You can't prove any of that. That's a false and slanderous statement. Duane Jefferson never told that little tramp anything like that. If he did, it was false."

"Start talking," Mason said.

She hesitated, then stubbornly shook her head.

Mason motioned to Della Street. "Go over to the telephone, Della. Ring up Homicide Squad. Get Lieutenant Tragg on the line. Tell him I want to talk with him."

Della Street started for the telephone.

"Now wait a minute," the blonde said hurriedly. "You can't—"

"Can't what?" Mason asked as her voice trailed into silence.

"Can't make anything stick on me. You haven't got any proof."

"I'm getting it," Mason told her. "Paul Drake here is an expert detective. He has men on the job right now, men who are concentrating on what you and Irving were doing."

"All right. Suppose my gentleman friend *did* loan me the money to buy a cigar stand. There's nothing wrong with that. I'm over the age of consent. I can do what I damn please."

Mason said, "This is your last chance. Walter Irving is putting out a lot of false clues, shaking off any possible pursuit. Then he'll go to Marline Chaumont. She's in one of the outlying towns. When she and Irving get together, something's going to happen. He must have given you an address where you could reach him in case of any emergency. That will be Marline's hide-out. Where is it?"

She shook her head.

Mason nodded to Della Street. Della Street started putting through the call.

Abruptly the blonde began to cry.

"I want Homicide Department, please," Della Street said into the phone.

The blonde said, "It's in Santa Ana."

"Where?" Mason asked.

She fumbled with her purse, took out an address, handed it to Mason. Mason nodded, and Della Street hung up the telephone.

"Come on," Mason said.

"What do you mean, come on?" the girl said.

"You heard me," Mason told her. "We're not leaving you behind to make any telephone calls. This is too critical for us to botch it up now."

"You can't *make* me go!"

"I can't make you go with *me*, but I can damn sure see that you're locked up in the police station. The only bad thing is that will cost about fifteen minutes. Which do you want?"

She said, "Stop looking at me like that. You frighten me. You—"

"I'm putting it to you cold turkey," Mason said. "Do you want to take a murder rap or not?"

"I—" She hesitated.

"Get your things on," Mason said.

Ann Riddle moved toward the closet.

"Watch her, Della," Mason said. "We don't want her to pick up any weapons."

Ann Riddle put on a light coat, picked up her purse. Paul Drake looked in the purse and made sure there was no weapon in it.

The four of them went down in the elevator, wordlessly got in Mason's car. Mason tooled the car out to the freeway, gathered speed.

CHAPTER TWENTY

The house was in a quiet residential district. A light was on in the living room. A car was parked in the garage. A wet strip on the sidewalk showed that the lawn had recently been sprinkled.

Mason parked the car, jerked open the door, strode up the steps to the porch. Della Street hurried along behind him. Paul Drake kept a hand on the arm of Ann Riddle.

Mason rang the bell.

The door opened half an inch. "Who is it?" a woman's voice asked.

Mason pushed his weight against the door so suddenly that the door was pushed inward.

Marline Chaumont, staggering back, regarded Mason with frightened eyes. "You!" she said.

"We came to get your brother," Mason said.

"My brother is—how you call it?—sick in the upstairs. He has flies in his belfry. He cannot be disturbed. He is asleep."

"Wake him up," Mason said.

"But you cannot do this. My brother he—You are not the law, *non*?"

"No," Mason said. "But we'll have the law here in about five minutes."

Marline Chaumont's face contorted into a spasm of anger. "You!" she spat at the blonde. "You had to pull a double cross!"

"I didn't," Ann Riddle said. "I only—"

"I know what you did, you double-crosser!" Marline Chaumont said. "I spit on you. You stool squab!"

"Never mind that," Mason said. "Where's the man you claim is your brother?"

"But he *is* my brother!"

"Phooey," Mason told her.

"He was taken from the hospital—"

"The man who was taken from the state hospital," Mason said, "isn't related to you any more than I am. You used him only as a prop. I don't know what you've done with him. Put him in a private institution somewhere, I suppose. I want the man who's taken his place, and I want him now."

"You are crazy in the head yourself," Marline Chaumont said. "You have no right to—"

"Take care of her, Paul," Mason said, and started marching down the hall toward the back of the house.

"You'll be killed!" she screamed. "You cannot do this. You—"

Mason tried the doors one at a time. The third door opened into a bedroom. A man, thin and emaciated, was lying on the bed, his hands handcuffed at the wrists.

A big, burly individual who had been reading a magazine got slowly to his feet. "What the hell!" he thundered.

Mason sized him up. "You look like an ex-cop to me," he said.

"What's it to you?" the man asked.

"Probably retired," Mason said. "Hung out your shingle as a private detective. Didn't do so well. Then this job came along."

"Say, what're you talking about?"

"I don't know what story they told *you*," Mason said, "and I don't know whether you're in on it or not, but whatever they told you, the jig's up. I'm Perry Mason, the lawyer."

The man who was handcuffed on the bed turned to Perry Mason. His eyes, dulled with sedatives, seemed to be having some difficulty getting in focus.

"Who are you?" he asked in the thick voice of a sleep talker.

Mason said, "I've come to take you out of here."

The bodyguard said, "This man's a mental case. He's inclined to be violent. He can't be released and he has delusions—"

"I know," Mason said. "His real name is Pierre Chaumont. He keeps thinking he's someone else. He has a delusion that his real name is—"

"Say, how do you know all this?" the bodyguard asked.

Mason said, "They gave you a steady job. A woman handed you a lot of soft soap, and you probably think she's one of the sweetest, most wonderful women on earth. It's time you woke up. As for this man on the bed, he's going with me right now. First we're going to the best doctor we can find, and then...well, then we'll get ready to keep a date on Friday morning at ten o'clock.

"You can either be in jail at that time or a free man. Make a choice now. We're separating the men from the boys. If you're in on this thing all the way, you're in a murder case. If you were just hired to act as a guard for a man who is supposed to be a mental case, that's something else. You have your opportunity to make your decision right now. There's a detective downstairs and police are on their way out. They'll be here within a matter of minutes. They'll want to know where you stand. I'm giving you your chance right now, and it's your *last* chance."

The big guard blinked his eyes slowly. "You say this man *isn't* a mental case?"

"Of course he isn't."

"I've seen the papers. He was taken from a state hospital."

"Some other guy was taken from a state hospital," Mason said, "and then they switched patients. This isn't a debating society. Make up your mind."

"You're Perry Mason, the lawyer?"

"That's right."

"Got any identification on you?"

Mason handed the man his card, showed him his driving license.

The guard sighed. "Okay," he said. "You win."

CHAPTER TWENTY-ONE

The Bailiff called court to order.

Hamilton Burger, his face wearing a look of smug satisfaction, beamed about the courtroom.

Judge Hartley said, "This is the time fixed for hearing a motion for new trial and for pronouncing judgment in the case of *People* v. *Duane Jefferson*. Do you wish to be heard, Mr. Mason?"

"Yes, Your Honor," Perry Mason said. "I move for a new trial of the case on the ground that the trial took place in the absence of the defendant."

"What?" Hamilton Burger shouted. "The defendant was present in court every minute of the time! The records so show."

"Will you stand up, Mr. Duane Jefferson?" Mason asked.

The man beside Mason stood up. Another man seated near the middle of the courtroom also stood up. Judge Hartley looked at the man in the courtroom.

"Come forward," Mason said.

"Just a minute," Judge Hartley said. "What's the meaning of this, Mr. Mason?"

"I asked Mr. Jefferson to stand up."

"He's standing up," Hamilton Burger said.

"Exactly," Mason said.

"Who's this other man?" the Court asked. "Is he a witness?"

"He's Duane Jefferson," Mason said.

"Now, just a minute, just a minute," Hamilton Burger said. "What's all this about, what kind of a flim-flam is counsel trying to work here? Let's get this thing straight. Here's the defendant standing here within the bar."

"And here's Duane Jefferson coming forward," Mason said. "I am moving for a new trial on the ground that the entire trial of Duane Jefferson for first-degree murder took place in his absence."

"Now just a moment, just a moment!" Hamilton Burger shouted. "I might have known there would be something like this. Counsel can't confuse the issues. It doesn't make any difference now whether this man is Duane Jefferson or whether he's John Doe. He's the man who committed the murder. He's the man who was seen committing the murder. He's the man who was tried for the murder. If he went under the name of Duane Jefferson, that isn't going to stop him from being sentenced for the murder."

"But," Mason said, "some of your evidence was directed against my client, Duane Jefferson."

"*Your* client?" Hamilton Burger said. "That's your client standing next to you."

Mason smiled and shook his head. "*This* is my client," he said, beckoning to the man standing at the gate of the bar to come forward once more. "This is Duane Jefferson. He's the one I was retained to represent by the South African Gem Importing and Exploration Company."

"Well, he's not the one you defended," Hamilton Burger said. "You can't get out of the mess this way."

Mason smiled and said, "I'm defending him now."

"Go ahead and defend him. He isn't accused of anything!"

"And I'm moving for a new trial on the ground that the trial took place in the absence of the defendant."

"This is the defendant standing right here!" Hamilton Burger insisted. "The trial took place in *his* presence. *He's* the one who was convicted. I don't care what you do with this other man, regardless of what his name is."

"Oh, but you introduced evidence consisting of articles belonging to the real Duane Jefferson," Mason said. "That dagger, for instance. The contents of the letters."

"What do you mean?"

"Mae W. Jordan told all about the letters she had received from Duane Jefferson, about the contents of those letters. I moved to strike out her testimony. The motion was denied. The testimony went to the jury about the Daddy Longlegs letters, about the Prince Charming letters, about the gag photographs, about the getting acquainted, and about the dagger."

"Now, just a moment," Judge Hartley said. "The Court will bear with you for a moment in this matter, Mr. Mason, but the Court is going to resort to stern measures if it appears this is some dramatic presentation of a technicality which you are using to dramatize the issues."

"I'm trying to clarify the issues," Mason said. "What happened is very simple. Duane Jefferson, who is standing there by the mahogany swinging gate which leads to the interior of the bar, is a trusted employee of the South African Gem Importing and Exploration Company. He was sent to this country in the company of Walter Irving of the Paris office to open a branch office. They were to receive half a million dollars' worth of diamonds in the mail.

"Walter Irving, who had been gambling heavily, was deeply involved and knew that very shortly after he had left Paris there would be an audit of the books and his defalcations would be discovered.

"This man, James Kincaid, was groomed to take the place of Duane Jefferson. After the shipment of gems was received, James Kincaid would take the gems and disappear. Walter Irving would duly report an embezzlement by Jefferson and thereafter Jefferson's body would be discovered under such circumstances that it would appear he had committed suicide.

"The trouble was that they couldn't let well enough alone. They knew that Munroe Baxter was smuggling diamonds into the country, and they decided to kill Baxter and get the gems. Actually, Walter Irving had been working with Baxter in connection with the smuggling and for a fee had arranged for the stones to be delivered to Baxter under such circumstances that they could be smuggled into this country.

"The spurious Duane Jefferson didn't need to be clever about it, because he intended to have the shipment of stones in his possession and the real Duane Jefferson's body found, long before the police could make an investigation. However, because of a tax situation, the shipment of gems was delayed, and naturally they couldn't afford to have the spurious Jefferson disappear until the shipment had been received, so that Walter Irving could then report the defalcation to the company. Therefore, the real Duane Jefferson had to be kept alive."

"Your Honor, Your Honor!" Hamilton Burger shouted. "This is simply another one of those wild-eyed, dramatic grandstands for which counsel is so noted. This time his client has been convicted of first-degree murder, and I intend to see to it personally that his client pays the supreme penalty."

Mason pointed to the man standing in the aisle. "This is my client," he said. "This is the man I was retained to represent. I intend to show that his trial took place in his absence. Come forward and be sworn, Mr. Jefferson."

"Your Honor, I object!" Hamilton Burger shouted. "I object to any such procedure. I insist that this defendant is the only defendant before the Court."

Judge Hartley said, "Now, just a moment. I want to get to the bottom of this thing, and I want to find out exactly what counsel's contention is before I start making any rulings. Court will take an adjournment for fifteen minutes while we try to get at the bottom of this thing. I will ask counsel for both sides to meet me in chambers. The defendant, in the meantime, is in custody. He will remain in custody."

Mason grinned.

The tall, gaunt man standing in the aisle turned back toward the audience. Mae Jordan moved toward him. "Hello, Prince Charming," she ventured somewhat dubiously. Jefferson's eyes lit up.

"Hello, Lady Guinevere," he said in a low voice. "I was told you'd be here."

"Prince...Prince Charming!"

Mason said, "I'll leave him in your custody, Miss Jordan." Then Mason marched into the judge's chambers.

CHAPTER TWENTY-TWO

"Well?" Judge Hartley said.

"It was quite a plot," Mason explained. "Actually, it was hatched in Paris as soon as Walter Irving knew he was going to be sent over to assist Duane Jefferson in opening the new office. A girl named Marline Chaumont, who had been a Paris party girl for the company and who knew her way around, was in on it. James Kincaid was in on it. They would have gotten away with the whole scheme, if it hadn't been for the fact that they were too eager. They knew that Baxter was planning to smuggle in three hundred thousand dollars' worth of diamonds. Gilly was to have taken the fishing boat out and made the delivery. They persuaded Gilly that Baxter had changed his mind at the last minute because of Gilly's record. He wanted these other men to take the boat out. Gilly was lying when he testified about his rental for the boat. He received twenty-five hundred dollars. That was the agreed price. Marline Chaumont has given me a sworn statement."

"Now just a minute," Judge Hartley said. "Are you now making this statement about the client you're representing in court?"

"I'm not representing him in court," Mason said. "I'm representing the real Duane Jefferson. That's the one I was retained to represent. I would suggest, however, that the Court give this other man an opportunity to get counsel of his own, or appoint counsel to represent him. He, too, is entitled to a new trial."

"He can't get a new trial," Hamilton Burger roared, "even if what you say is true. You defended him and you lost the case."

Mason smiled coldly at Hamilton Burger. "You might have made that stick," he said, "if it hadn't been for the testimony of Mae Jordan about all of her correspondence with Duane Jefferson. That correspondence was with the real Duane Jefferson, not with the man you are trying for murder. You can't convict Duane Jefferson of anything, because he wasn't present during his trial. You can't make the present conviction stick against the defendant now in court, because you used evidence that related to the real Duane Jefferson, not to him.

"What you should have done was to have checked your identification of the man you had under arrest. You were so damned anxious to get something on me that when you found from his fingerprints that he had a record, you let your enthusiasm run away with you.

"You let Mae Jordan testify to a lot of things that had happened between her and the real Duane Jefferson. It never occurred to you to make certain that the man she sent the knife to was the same man you were trying for murder.

"The spurious Jefferson and Irving drugged the real Jefferson shortly after they left Chicago on the train. They stole all of his papers, stole the Jordan letters, stole the knife. It will be up to you to prove that at the next trial—and I'm not going to help you. You can go get the evidence yourself. However, I have Marline Chaumont in my office and I have a sworn statement made by her, which I now hand to the Court, with a copy for the district attorney.

"Just one suggestion, though. If you ever want to tie this case up, you'd better find out who that man was who was in the boat with Kincaid, because it certainly wasn't Irving.

"And now may I ask the Court to relieve me of any responsibility in the matter of the defendant, James Kincaid, who is out there in the courtroom. He tricked me into appearing in court for him by: artifice, fraud, and by misrepresenting his identity. My only client is Duane Jefferson."

"I think," Judge Hartley said, "I want to talk with this Duane Jefferson. I suppose you can establish his identity beyond any question, Mr. Mason?"

"His fingerprints were taken in connection with his military service," Mason said.

"That should be good enough evidence," Judge Hartley agreed, smiling. "I'd like to have a talk with him now."

Mason got up, walked to the door of chambers, looked out at the courtroom, and turned back to smile at the judge. "I guess I'll have to interrupt him," Mason said. "He and the witness Mae Jordan are jabbering away like a house afire. There seems to be a sort of common understanding between them. I guess it's because they're both interested in photography."

Judge Hartley's smile had broadened. "Perhaps, Mr. Mason," he suggested tentatively, "Miss Jordan is telling Mr. Jefferson where she got that key."

THE CASE OF
THE LUCKY LOSER

FOREWORD

Nearly a year ago my good friend John Ben Shepperd, the Attorney General of the State of Texas, told me, "The next big development in law enforcement must come from the people rather than from the police."

General Shepperd wasn't content with merely predicting such a development. He discussed it with several influential businessmen in Texas, and soon these businessmen began to take action.

J. Marion West of Houston, Texas, affectionately known as "Silver Dollar" West, is an attorney at law, a cattleman, an oil operator, and is widely respected for his knowledge of police science. He spends a large portion of his time assisting local police officers in the Houston area.

I have for some years been associated with Park Street, who is a member of "The Court of Last Resort," a San Antonio attorney with driving energy, and a boundless enthusiasm for his work. Park Street has as his lifetime ambition a desire to improve the administration of justice.

Jackson B. Love, of Llano, Texas, is an ex-Texas Ranger who has had considerable experience as a peace officer. He owns and operates a large ranch, has exceptionally sound business judgment, is quite an historian, and collects books dealing with the frontier period of the West.

W. R. (Billy Bob) Crim, of Kilgore, Texas, a man with extensive oil interests in Kilgore, Longview and Dallas, is vitally interested in state police work and is an authority on weapons.

Frederick O. Detweiler, president of Chance Vought Aircraft, Incorporated, Dallas, Texas, is representative of the modern executive, with broad interests, a razor-keen mind and a background of knowledge ranging from economics to public relations. He is one of the prominent businessmen of Texas and is known and loved all over the state for his intense interest in better law enforcement.

Dr. Merton M. Minter is a prominent physician of San Antonio, a man loved and respected by those who know him. Recently he began to take an active interest in law enforcement. A member of the Board of Regents of the

University of Texas, he is particularly interested in the educational aspects of crime prevention and law enforcement.

These people got together with Attorney General John Ben Shepperd and decided to organize the Texas Law Enforcement Foundation, of which my good friend Park Street is Chairman and J. Marion (Jim) West is Vice-chairman.

When Texas does anything, it does it in a big way, and this Law Enforcement Foundation is no exception.

Col. Homer Garrison, Jr., Director of the Texas Department of Public Safety, and as such, head of the famed Texas Rangers, a man who is acclaimed everywhere as one of the outstanding figures in the field of executive law enforcement, is Chairman of the Advisory Council of the Foundation.

I consider myself greatly honored in that I have been appointed a special adviser of this Foundation.

The Texas Law Enforcement Foundation isn't a "Crime Commission." Its primary purpose is to acquaint citizens everywhere with their civic responsibilities in the field of law enforcement. The Foundation wants the average citizen to have a better understanding of the causes of crime, of how crime can be prevented, of the responsibilities of the police officer, the latent dangers of juvenile delinquency, the purpose and problems of penology, and the responsibilities of the organized bar and of lawyers generally.

If the average citizen can't learn more about the problems with which the various law enforcement agencies have to contend, the citizen can't play his part in the job of curtailing crime.

As of this writing, organized crime is making an alarming bid for power. Juvenile delinquency is but little understood and is on the increase.

On many fronts we are trying to combat atomic age crime methods with horse-and-buggy thinking.

Efficient law enforcement can't function in a civic vacuum. The police force depends on the training, integrity and loyalty of its members for efficiency, and on public understanding and co-operation for its very life.

It is well known that if the average community had half as much loyalty to its police as the police have to the community we would have far less crime.

Because I consider the work of this law enforcement foundation so important, I have departed from my usual custom of dedicating books to outstanding figures in the field of legal medicine, and I dedicate this book to those citizens of Texas who, at great personal and financial sacrifice, have been responsible for bringing into existence a new concept of law enforcement.

Erle Stanley Gardner

CHAPTER ONE

Della Street, Perry Mason's confidential secretary, picked up the telephone and said, "Hello."

The well-modulated youthful voice of a woman asked, "How much does Mr. Mason charge for a day in court?"

Della Street's voice reflected cautious appraisal of the situation. "That would depend very much on the type of case, what he was supposed to do and—"

"He won't be supposed to do anything except listen."

"You mean you wouldn't want him to take part in the trial?"

"No. Just listen to what goes on in the courtroom and draw conclusions."

"Who is this talking, please?"

"Would you like the name that will appear on your books?"

"Certainly."

"Cash."

"What?"

"Cash."

"I think you'd better talk to Mr. Mason," Della Street said. "I'll try to arrange an appointment."

"There isn't time for that. The case in which I am interested starts at ten o'clock this morning."

"Just a moment, please. Hold the wire," Della Street said.

She entered Mason's private office.

Perry Mason looked up from the mail he was reading.

Della Street said, "Chief, you'll have to handle this personally. A youthful sounding woman wants to retain you to sit in court today just to listen to a case. She's on the phone now."

"What's her name?"

"She says it's Cash."

Mason grinned, picked up his telephone. Della Street got on the other line, put through the connection.

"Yes?" Mason said crisply. "This is Perry Mason."

The woman's voice was silky. "There's a criminal case on trial in Department Twenty-Three of the Superior Court entitled People versus Balfour. I would like to know how much it's going to cost me to have you attend court during the day, listen to the proceedings, and then give me your conclusions."

"And your name?" Mason asked.

"As I told your secretary, the name is Cash—just the way the entry will appear on your books."

Mason looked at his watch. "It is now nine twenty-five. I have two appointments this morning and one this afternoon. I would have to cancel those appointments, and I would only do that to handle a matter of the greatest importance."

"This *is* a matter of the greatest importance."

"My charges would be predicated upon that fact, upon the necessity of breaking three appointments and—"

"Just what would your charges be?" she asked.

"Five hundred dollars," Mason snapped.

The voice suddenly lost its silky assurance. "Oh!...I...I'm sorry. I had no idea....We'll just have to forget it, I guess. I'm sorry."

Mason, moved by the consternation in the young woman's voice, said, "More than you expected?"

"Y...y...yes."

"How much more?"

"I...I...I work on a salary and...well, I—"

"You see," Mason explained, "I have to pay salaries, taxes, office rental, and I have a law library to keep up. And a day of my time—What sort of work do *you* do?"

"I'm a secretary."

"And you want me just to listen to this case?"

"I did...I guess I...I mean, my ideas were all out of line."

"What had you expected to pay?"

"I had hoped you'd say a hundred dollars. I could have gone for a hundred and fifty...Well, I'm sorry."

"Why did you want me to listen? Are you interested in the case?"

"Not directly, no."

"Do you have a car?"

"No."

"Any money in the bank?"

"Yes."

"How much?"

"A little over six hundred."

"All right," Mason said. "You've aroused my curiosity. If you'll pay me a hundred dollars I'll go up and listen."

"Oh, Mr. Mason!...Oh...thanks! I'll send a messenger right up. You see, you mustn't ever know who I am....I can't explain. The money will be delivered at once."

"Exactly what is it you want me to do?" Mason asked.

"Please don't let *anyone* know that you have been retained in this case. I would prefer that you go as a spectator and that you do not sit in the bar reserved for attorneys."

"Suppose I can't find a seat?" Mason asked.

"I've thought of that," she said. "When you enter the courtroom, pause to look around. A woman will be seated in the left-hand aisle seat, fourth row back. She is a red-haired woman about...well, she's in her forties. Next to her will be a younger woman with dark chestnut hair, and next to her will be a seat on which will be piled a couple of coats. The younger woman will pick up the coats and you may occupy that seat. Let's hope you aren't recognized. Please *don't* carry a brief case."

There was a very decisive click at the other end of the line.

Mason turned to Della Street.

"When that messenger comes in with the hundred dollars, Della, be sure that he takes a receipt, and tell him to deliver that receipt to the person who gave him the money. I'm on my way to court."

CHAPTER TWO

Perry Mason reached the courtroom of Department Twenty-Three just as Judge Mervin Spencer Cadwell was entering from his chambers.

The bailiff pounded his gavel. "Everybody rise," he shouted.

Mason took advantage of the momentary confusion to slip down the center aisle to the fourth row of seats.

The bailiff called court to order. Judge Cadwell seated himself. The bailiff banged the gavel. The spectators dropped back to their seats, and Mason unostentatiously stepped across in front of the two women.

The younger woman deftly picked up two coats which were on the adjoining seat. Mason sat down, glancing surreptitiously at the women as he did so.

The women were both looking straight ahead, apparently paying not the slightest attention to him.

Judge Cadwell said, "People of the State of California versus Theodore Balfour. Is it stipulated by counsel that the jurors are all present and the defendant is in court?"

"So stipulated, Your Honor."

"Proceed."

"I believe the witness George Dempster was on the stand," the prosecutor said.

"That's right," Judge Cadwell said. "Mr. Dempster, will you please return to the stand."

George Dempster, a big-boned, slow-moving man in his thirties, took the witness stand.

"Now, you testified yesterday that you found certain pieces of glass near the body on the highway?" the prosecutor asked.

"That is right, yes, sir."

"And did you have occasion to examine the headlights on the automobile which you located in the Balfour garage?"

"I did, yes, sir."

"What was the condition of those headlights?"

"The right headlight was broken."

"When did you make your examination?"

"About seven-fifteen on the morning of the twentieth."

"Did you ask permission from anyone to make this examination?"

"No, sir, not to examine the car itself."

"Why not?"

"Well, we wanted to check before we committed ourselves."

"So what did you do?"

"We went out to the Balfour residence. There was a four-car garage in back. There was no sign of life in the house, but someone was moving around in an apartment over the garage. As we drove in, this person looked out of the window and then came down the stairs. He identified himself as a servant who had one of the apartments over the garage. I told him that we were officers and we wanted to look around in the garage, that we were looking for some evidence of a crime. I asked him if he had any objection. He said certainly not, so we opened the garage door and went in."

"Now, directing your attention to a certain automobile bearing license number GMB 665, I will ask you if you found anything unusual about that car?"

"Yes, sir, I did."

"What did you find?"

"I found a broken right front headlight, a very slight dent on the right side of the front of the car, and I found a few spatters of blood on the bumper."

"What did you do next?"

"I told the servant we would have to impound the car and that we wanted to question the person who'd been driving it. I asked him who owned it, and he said Mr. Guthrie Balfour owned it, but that his nephew, Ted Balfour, had been driving—"

"Move to strike," the defense attorney snapped. "Hearsay, incompetent, irrelevant, immaterial. They can't prove who drove the car by hearsay."

"Motion granted," Judge Cadwell said. "The prosecution knows it can't use evidence of that sort."

"I'm sorry, Your Honor," the prosecutor said. "I was about to stipulate that part of the answer could go out. We had not intended to prove who was driving in this way. The witness should understand that.

"Now just tell the Court and the jury what you did after that, Mr. Dempster."

"We got young Mr. Balfour up out of bed."

"Now, when you refer to young Mr. Balfour, you are referring to the defendant in this case?"

"That's right. Yes, sir."

"Did you have a conversation with him?"

"Yes, sir."

"At what time?"

"Well, by the time we had this conversation it was right around eight o'clock."

"You got him up out of bed?"

"Somebody awakened him, he put on a bathrobe and came out. We told him who we were and what we wanted, and he said he wouldn't talk with us until he was dressed and had had his coffee."

"What did you do?"

"Well, we tried to get something out of him. We tried to be nice about it. We didn't want to throw our weight around, but he kept saying he wouldn't talk until he'd had his coffee."

"Where did this conversation take place?"

"At the Guthrie Balfour residence."

"And who was present at that conversation?"

"Another police officer who had gone out with me, a Mr. Dawson."

"He is here in court?"

"Yes, sir."

"Who else was present?"

"The defendant."

"Anyone else?"

"No, sir."

"Where did that conversation take place?"

"In the house."

"I mean specifically where in the house?"

"In a small office, sort of a study that opened off from the defendant's bedroom. The butler or somebody had brought up some coffee, cream and sugar and the morning paper, and we drank coffee—"

"You say '*we* drank coffee'?"

"That's right. The butler brought in three cups and saucers, cream, sugar, and a big electric percolator. We all three had coffee."

"Now, just what did you say to the defendant and what did he say to you?"

Mortimer Dean Howland, the attorney representing Balfour, was on his feet. "I object, Your Honor. No proper foundation has been laid."

Judge Cadwell pursed his lips, looked down at the witness, then at the prosecutor.

"And," Howland went on, "I feel that I should be entitled to cross-examine this witness before any admission, confession, or declaration by the defendant is received in evidence."

"We're not laying the foundation for a confession, Your Honor," the prosecutor said.

"That's precisely my objection," the defense attorney remarked.

Judge Cadwell gave the matter careful consideration.

Mason took advantage of the opportunity to study the young woman on his right. Having saved a seat for him, she must have known he was to be there. Having known that, the chances were she was the woman who had sent him the retainer.

"What's the case?" Mason asked her in a whisper.

She looked at him coldly, elevated her chin and turned away.

It was the man on Mason's left who tersely said, "Hit and run, manslaughter."

Judge Cadwell said, "I will accept the prosecutor's assurance that no confession is called for by this question and overrule the objection. The witness will answer the question."

The witness said, "He said he'd been seeing his uncle and his uncle's wife off on a train, that he'd then gone to a party,where he'd had a few drinks and—"

"Just a moment, Your Honor, just a moment," the defense attorney interrupted. "It now appears that the statement by the prosecutor was incorrect, that they *are* attempting to establish a confession or an admission and—"

"I'm going to ask the prosecutor about this," Judge Cadwell interrupted sternly.

The prosecutor was on his feet. "Please, Your Honor. If you will listen to the answer, you will understand my position."

"There is an admission?" Judge Cadwell asked.

"Certainly, Your Honor, but an admission does not rank in the same category with a confession."

"They are attempting to show that he confessed to being drunk," the defense attorney said.

"I'll let the witness finish his answer," Judge Cadwell said. "Go on."

"The defendant said that he'd had a few drinks at this party and had become ill. He thought at least one of the drinks had been loaded. He said he passed out and remembered nothing until he came to in his automobile, that—"

"Your Honor, Your Honor!" the defense attorney protested. "This now has the very definite earmarks of—"

"Sit down," Judge Cadwell said. "Let the witness finish his answer. If the answer is as I think it's going to be, I am then going to call on the prosecutor for an explanation. The Court doesn't like this. The Court feels that an attempt has been made to impose on the Court."

"If you will only hear the answer out," the prosecutor pleaded.

"That's exactly what I'm going to do."

"Go ahead," the prosecutor said to the witness.

The witness continued. "He said that for a brief instant he came to his senses in his car, that some woman was driving."

"Some *woman?*" Judge Cadwell exclaimed.

"Yes, Your Honor."

"Then *he* wasn't driving?"

"That's right, Your Honor," the prosecutor said. "I trust the Court will now see the reason for my statement."

"Very well," Judge Cadwell said. He turned to the witness. "Go on. What else did the defendant say?"

"He said that he partially revived for a moment, that he remembered being very sick, that the next thing he remembered he was home and in bed, that he had a terrific thirst, that the hour was four thirty-five in the morning, that he was conscious but very thick-headed."

"Did you ask him who the woman was who was driving the car?" the prosecutor asked the witness.

"I did."

"What did he say?"

"He said he couldn't remember, that he couldn't be certain."

"Which did he say—that he couldn't remember or he couldn't be certain?"

"He said both."

"What did you ask him?"

"I asked him several questions after that, but I had no more answers. He wanted to know what had happened. I told him that we were investigating a death, a hit-and-run case, and that there was some evidence his car had been involved. So then he said if that was the case he would say nothing more until he had consulted with his attorney."

"You may cross-examine," the prosecutor said.

Mortimer Dean Howland, attorney for Balfour, was known for his hammer-and-tongs, browbeating cross-examination.

He lowered his bushy eyebrows, thrust out his jaw, glared for a moment at the witness, said, "You went out to that house to get a confession from the defendant, didn't you?"

"I did nothing of the sort."

"You *did* go out to the house?"

"Certainly."

"And you *did* try to get a confession from the defendant?"

"Yes, in a way."

"So then you did go out to that house to try and get a confession from the defendant—either by one way or another!"

"I went out to look at the defendant's automobile."

"*Why* did you decide to go out to look at the defendant's automobile?"

"Because of something I had been told."

The lawyer hesitated, then, fearing to open that legal door, abruptly changed his tactics. "When you *first* saw the defendant, you wakened him from a sound sleep, didn't you?"

"*I* didn't. The servant did."

"You knew that he had been ill?"

"He looked as though he'd had a hard night. That was all I knew until he told me he'd been sick. I thought that he—"

"Never mind what you thought!" Howland shouted.

"I thought that's what you asked for," the witness said calmly.

There was a ripple of merriment throughout the courtroom.

"Just concentrate on my questions!" Howland shouted. "You could tell that the defendant was not in good health?"

"I could tell that he wasn't fresh as a daisy. He looked like a man with a terrific hangover."

"I didn't ask you that. I asked you if you couldn't tell that he wasn't in good health."

"He wasn't in good spirits, but he sure looked as though he *had* been in spirits."

"That will do," Howland said. "Don't try to be facetious. A man's liberty is at stake here. Simply answer the questions. You knew that he wasn't his normal self?"

"I don't know what he's like when he's normal."

"You knew that he had been aroused from sleep?"

"I assumed that he had."

"You knew that he didn't look well?"

"That's right."

"How did he look?"

"He looked terrible. He looked like a man with a hangover."

"You've seen men with hangovers?"

"Lots of them."

"Have *you* ever had a hangover?"

"Your Honor, I object to that," the prosecutor said.

Howland said, "Then I move to strike out the answer of the witness that the defendant had a hangover on the ground that it is a conclusion of the witness, that the answer is merely an opinion, and that the witness is not properly qualified to give that opinion."

"I'll withdraw the objection," the prosecutor said.

"Have *you* ever had a hangover?"

"No."

"You have *never* had a hangover?"

"No."

"You're not a drinking man?"

"I'm not a teetotaler. I take a drink once in a while. I can't ever remember being intoxicated. I can't ever remember having had a hangover."

"Then how do you know what a man with a hangover looks like?"

"I have seen men with hangovers."

"What is a hangover?"

"The aftermath of an intoxicated condition. I may say it's the immediate aftermath of an intoxicated condition when the alcohol has not entirely left the system."

"You're now talking like a doctor."

"You asked me for my definition of a hangover."

"Oh, that's all," Howland said, making a gesture of throwing up his hands as though tired of arguing, and turned his back on the witness.

The witness started to leave the stand.

"Just a moment," Howland said suddenly, whirling and leveling an extended forefinger. "One more queston. Did the defendant tell you what time it was that he passed out?"

"He *said* about ten o'clock."

"Oh, he said about ten o'clock, did he?"

"Yes, sir."

"You didn't tell us that before."

"I wasn't asked."

"You were asked to tell what the defendant told you, weren't you?"

"Yes."

"Then why did you try to conceal this statement about its being near ten o'clock?"

"I...well, I didn't pay much attention to that."

"Why not?"

"Frankly, I didn't believe it."

"Did you believe his story about some woman driving his car?"

"No."

"Yet you paid attention to that part of his statement?"

"Well, yes. That was different."

"In what way?"

"Well, that was an admission."

"You mean an admission adverse to the interest of the defendant?"

"Certainly."

"Oh! So you went there prepared to remember any admissions the defendant might make and to forget anything he might say that was in his favor, is that it?"

"I didn't forget this. I simply didn't mention it because I wasn't asked the specific question which would call for it."

"What time were you called to investigate the hit-and-run accident?"

"About two o'clock in the morning."

"The body was lying on the highway?"

"Yes, sir."

"How long had it been there?"

"I don't know of my own knowledge."

"Do you know when it was reported to the police?"

"Yes."

"When?"

"About fifteen minutes before we got there."

"That was a well-traveled highway?"

"It was a surfaced road. There was some traffic over it."

"The body couldn't have been there on such a well-traveled road more than ten or fifteen minutes without someone having reported it?"

"I don't know."

"It's a well-traveled road?"

"Yes."

"And the defendant was driven home at about ten o'clock?"

"That's what he said."

"And he was ill?"

"That's what he said."

"And went to bed?"

"That's what he said."

The lawyer hesitated. "And went to sleep?"

"He didn't say that. He said his mind was a blank until he came to around four-thirty in the morning."

"He didn't say his mind was a blank, did he?"

"He said he couldn't remember."

"Didn't he say that the next thing he knew he came to in bed?"

"He said the next thing he *remembered* he was in bed, and it was then four thirty-five in the morning."

"But some of what the defendant told you you didn't remember—everything he said that was in his favor."

"I told you I did remember it."

"And neglected to tell us."

"All right. Have it that way if you want it that way."

"Oh, that's all," Howland said. "In view of your very apparent bias, I don't care to ask you any more questions."

The witness glared angrily and left the stand.

The prosecutor said, "No redirect examination. Call Myrtle Anne Haley."

The redheaded woman who was seated on the aisle two seats over from Perry Mason got up, walked to the witness stand, held up her right hand, and was sworn.

Mason stole a surreptitious glance at the young woman sitting next to him.

She held her chin in the air, giving him only her profile to look at. Her expression held the icy disdain that a young woman reserves for someone who is trying to pick her up and is being offensive about it.

CHAPTER THREE

Myrtle Anne Haley took the oath, gave her name and address to the court reporter, and settled herself in the witness chair with the manner of one who knows her testimony is going to be decisive.

The prosecutor said, "I call your attention to the road map which has been previously identified and introduced in evidence as People's Exhibit A, Mrs. Haley."

"Yes, sir."

"Do you understand that map? That is, are you familiar with the territory which it portrays?"

"Yes, sir."

"I call your attention to a section of Sycamore Road as shown on that map and which lies between Chestnut Street and State Highway. Do you understand that that map delineates such a section of road?"

"Yes, sir."

"Have you ever driven over that road?"

"Many times."

"Where do you live?"

"On the other side of State Highway on Sycamore Road."

"Can you show us on this map? Just make a cross on the map and circle the cross."

The witness made a cross on the map and enclosed it in a circle.

The prosecutor said, "I will call your attention to the night of the nineteenth and the morning of the twentieth of September of this year. Did you have occasion to use the highway at that time?"

"On the morning of the twentieth—early in the morning—yes, sir."

"At what time?"

"Between twelve-thirty and one-thirty."

"In the morning?"

"Yes, sir."

"In which direction were you driving?"

"Going west on Sycamore Road. I was approaching Chestnut Street from the east."

"And did you notice anything unusual at that time?"

"Yes, sir. A car ahead of me which was being driven in a very erratic manner."

"Can you tell me more about the erratic manner in which the car was being driven?"

"Well, it was weaving about the road, crossing the center line and going clear over to the left. Then it would go back to the right and at times would run clear off the highway on the right side."

"Could you identify that car?"

"Yes. I wrote down the license number."

"Then what?"

"Then I followed along behind; that at this wide place in the road about four-fifths of the way to State Highway I shot on by."

"You say you *shot* on by?"

"Well, I went by fast when I had a chance. I didn't want the driver to swerve into me."

"I move to strike everything about why she passed the car," Howland said.

"That will go out," Judge Cadwell said.

"After you got by the car what did you do?"

"I went home and went to bed."

"I mean immediately after you got by the car. Did you do anything?"

"I looked in the rearview mirror."

"And what did you see, if anything?"

"I saw the car swerve over to the left, then back to the right, and all of a sudden I saw something black cross in front of the headlights, and then for a moment the right headlight seemed to go out."

"You say it *seemed* to go out?"

"After that it came on again."

"And that was on Sycamore Road at a point between Chestnut Street and State Highway?"

"Yes, sir."

"That is the point at which you saw the light blink off and then on?"

"Yes, sir."

"At a time when you were looking in your rearview mirror?"

"Yes, sir."

"And did you know what caused that headlight to seem to go out?"

"I didn't at the time, but I do now."

"What was it?"

"Objected to as calling for a conclusion of the witness," Howland said. "The question is argumentative."

"The objection is sustained," Judge Cadwell said. "The witness can testify to what she saw."

"But, Your Honor," the prosecutor said, "the witness certainly has the right to interpret what she sees."

Judge Cadwell shook his head. "The witness will testify to what she saw. The jury will make the interpretation."

The prosecutor paused for a minute, then said, "Very well. Cross-examine."

"You took down the license number of this automobile?" Howland asked.

"That's right."

"In a notebook?"

"Yes."

"Where did you get that notebook?"

"From my purse."

"You were driving the car?"

"Yes."

"Was anyone with you?"

"No."

"You took the notebook from your purse?"

"Yes."

"And a pencil?"

"Not a pencil. A fountain pen."

"And marked down the license number of the automobile?"

"Yes."

"What was that license number?"

"GMB 665."

"You have that notebook with you?"

"Yes, sir."

"I would like to see it, please."

The prosecutor smiled at the jury. "Not the slightest objection," he said. "We're very glad to let you inspect it."

Howland walked up to the witness stand, took the notebook the witness gave him, thumbed through the pages, said, "This seems to be a notebook in which you kept a lot of data, various and sundry entries."

"I don't carry anything in memory which I can trust to paper."

"Now then," Howland said, "this number, GMB 665, is the last entry in the book."

"That's right."

"That entry was made on September twentieth?"

"About twelve-thirty to one-thirty on the morning of September twentieth," the witness stated positively.

"Why haven't you made any entries after that?"

"Because, after I read about the accident, I reported to the police, the police took the book, and it was then given back to me with the statement that I should take good care of it because it would be evidence."

"I see," Howland said with elaborate politeness. "And how long did the police have the book?"

"They had the book for...I don't know...quite a while."

"And when was it given back to you?"

"Well, after the police had it, the district attorney had it."

"Oh, the police gave it to the district attorney, did they?"

"I don't know. I know the prosecutor was the one who gave it to me."

"When?"

"This morning."

"This *morning?*" Howland said, his voice showing a combination of incredulity and skeptical sarcasm. "And *why* did the prosecutor give it back to you this morning?"

"So I could have it on the witness stand."

"Oh, so you would be able to say that you had the notebook with you?"

"I don't know. I suppose that was it."

"Now then, did you remember the license number?"

"Certainly I did. Just as I told you. It's GMB 665."

"When did you last see that license number?"

"When I handed you the book just a moment ago."

"And when before that?"

"This morning."

"At what time this morning?"

"About nine o'clock this morning."

"And how long did you spend looking at that number at about nine o'clock this morning?"

"I...I don't know. I don't know as it makes any difference."

"Were you looking at it for half an hour?"

"Certainly not."

"For fifteen minutes?"

"No."

"For ten minutes?"

"I may have been."

"In other words, you were memorizing that number this morning, weren't you?"

"Well, what's wrong with that?"

"How do you know that's the same number?"

"Because that's my handwriting, that's the number just as I wrote it down."

"Could you see the license number of the car ahead while you were writing this?"

"Certainly."

"All the time you were writing?"

"Yes."

"Isn't it a fact that you looked at the license number, then stopped your car, got out your notebook, and—"

"Certainly not! It's just as I told you. I took out my notebook while I was driving and wrote down the number."

"You are right-handed?"

"Yes."

"You had one hand on the wheel?"

"My left hand."

"And were writing with your right hand?"

"Yes."

"Do you have a fountain pen or a ball-point pen?"

"It a plain fountain pen."

"The top screws off?"

"Yes."

"And you unscrewed that with one hand?"

"Certainly."

"You can do that with one hand?"

"Of course. You hold the pen . . . that is, the barrel of the pen with the last two fingers, then use the thumb and forefinger to unscrew the cap."

"Then what did you do?"

"I put the notebook down on my lap, wrote the number, then put the cap back on the pen and put the notebook and fountain pen back in my purse."

"How far were you from the automobile when you were writing down this number?"

"Not very far."

"Did you see the number all the time?"

"Yes."

"Plainly?"

"Yes."

"Did you write this number in the dark?"

"No."

"No, apparently not. The number is neatly written. You must have had some light when you wrote it."

"I did. I switched on the dome light so I could see what I was writing."

"Now then," Howland said, "if you had to memorize that number this morning *after* the prosecutor had given you your notebook, you didn't know what that number was *before* he gave you the notebook, did you?"

"Well . . . you can't expect a person to remember a number all that time."

"So you didn't know what it was this morning?"

"After I'd seen the book."

"But not before that?"

"Well . . . no."

Howland hesitated for a moment. "After you had written down this number you drove on home?"

"Yes."

"Did you call the police?"

"Certainly. I told you I did."

"When?"

"Later."

"After you had read in the newspaper about this accident?"

"Yes."

"That is, about the body having been found on this road?"

"Yes."

"You didn't call the police before that?"

"No."

"Why did you write down this license number?"

Her eyes glittered with triumph. "Because I knew that the person who was driving the automobile was too drunk to have any business being behind the wheel of a car."

"You knew that when you wrote down the license number?"

"Yes."

"Then why did you write it down?"

"So I'd know what it was."

"So you could testify against the driver?"

"So I could do my duty as a citizen."

"You mean call the police?"

"Well, I thought it was my duty to make a note of the license number in case the driver got in any trouble."

"Oh, so you could testify?"

"So I could tell the police about it, yes."

"But you *didn't* tell the police until after you'd read in the paper about a body having been found?"

"That's right."

"Even after you saw this mysterious blackout of the right headlight you didn't call the police?"

"No."

"You didn't think there was any reason to call the police?"

"Not until after I'd read in the paper about the body."

"Then you *didn't* think there had been an accident when you got home, did you?"

"Well, I knew something had happened. I kept wondering what could have caused that blackout of that headlight."

"You didn't think there had been an accident?"

"I knew something had happened."

"Did you or did you not think there had been an accident?"

"Yes, I realized there must have been an accident."

"When did you realize this?"

"Right after I got home."

"And you had taken this number so you could call the police in the event of an accident?"

"I took the number because I thought it was my duty to take it...yes."

"Then why didn't you call the police?"

"I think this has been asked and answered several times. Your Honor," the prosecutor said. "I dislike to curtail counsel in his cross-examination, but this certainly has been gone over repeatedly in the same way and in the same manner."

"I think so," Judge Cadwell said.

"I submit, Your Honor, that her actions contradict her words, that her reasons contradict her actions."

"You may have ample opportunity to argue the case to the jury. I believe the fact which you wished to establish by this cross-examination has been established," Judge Cadwell said.

"That's all," Howland said, shrugging his shoulders and waving his hand as though brushing the testimony to one side.

"That's all, Mrs. Haley," the prosecutor said.

Mrs. Haley swept from the witness stand, marched down the aisle, seated herself on the aisle seat.

She turned to the young seated beside Perry Mason. "Was I all right?" Mrs. Haley asked in a whisper.

The young woman nodded.

Judge Cadwell looked at the clock, and adjourned court until two o'clock that afternoon.

CHAPTER FOUR

During the afternoon session the prosecution tied up a few loose ends and put on a series of technical witnesses. By three-thirty the case was ready for argument.

The prosecutor made a brief, concise argument, asked for a conviction, and sat down.

Mortimer Dean Howland, a criminal attorney of the old school, indulged in a barrage of sarcasm directed at the testimony of Myrtle Anne Haley, whom he characterized as "the psychic driver," a "woman who could drive without even looking at the road."

"Notice the driving activities of this woman," Howland said. "When she first comes to our notice she is driving without looking at the road because she is getting her fountain pen and her notebook out of her purse. Then she is opening the notebook and making a note of the license number.

"Look at where she made this notation, ladies and gentlemen of the jury. She didn't open the notebook at random and scribble the license number on *any* page she happened to come to. She carefully turned to the page which contained the last notebook entry; then she neatly wrote the license number of the automobile.

"Look at this exhibit," Howland said, going over and picking up the notebook. "Look at the manner in which this number is written. Could you have written a license number so neatly if your eyes had been on the road while you were driving a car? Certainly not! Neither could this paragon of blind driving, this Myrtle Anne Haley. She was writing down this number with her eyes on the page of the notebook, not on the road.

"You'll remember that I asked her on cross-examination if she had sufficient light to write by, and do you remember what she said? She said she turned on the dome light of the automobile, so that she would have plenty of light.

"*Why* did she need plenty of light? Because she was watching what she was writing, not where her car was going.

"If her eyes had been on the road, she wouldn't have needed any light in the interior of the automobile. In fact, that light would have detracted from her ability to look ahead down the road. The reason she needed light, ladies and gentlemen, was because she was driving along, looking down at the page of the notebook as she wrote.

"She was driving at an even faster rate of speed than the car ahead because she admits she *shot* past that car. *But,* ladies and gentlemen, she didn't have her eyes on the road.

"I'm willing to admit that some unfortunate person was struck by an automobile on that stretch of road. Who was more likely to have struck that person? The driver of the car ahead, or some woman who admits to you under oath that she was speeding along that road not looking where she went, with her eyes on the page of a notebook?

"And who was driving this automobile, the license number of which Myrtle Anne Haley was so careful to write down? The prosecution asked her all about the license number, but *it never asked her who was driving the car!* It never

asked her even if a *man* was driving the car. For all we know, if she had been
asked she may have said that a woman was driving the car."

"Your Honor." the prosecutor said, "I dislike to interrupt, but if the
prosecution failed to cover that point, we ask to reopen the case at this time and
ask additional questions of the witness, Myrtle Anne Haley."

"Is there any objection?" Judge Cadwell asked.

"Certainly there's an objection, Your Honor. That's an old trick, an attempt
to interrupt the argument of counsel for the defense and put on more
testimony. It is an attempt to distract the attention of the jury and disrupt the
orderly course of trial."

"The motion is denied," Judge Cadwell said.

Howland turned to the jury, spread his hands apart and smiled. "You see,
ladies and gentlemen, the sort of thing we have been up against in this case. I
don't think I need to argue any more. I feel I can safely leave the matter to your
discretion. I know that you will return the only fair verdict, the only just verdict,
the only verdict that will enable you to feel that you have conscientiously
discharged your sworn duty—a verdict of NOT GUILTY!"

Howland returned to his chair.

The prosecutor made a closing argument, the judge read instructions to the
jury, and the jury retired.

Mason arose with the other spectators as court was adjourned, but Mortimer
Dean Howland pushed his way to Mason's side. "Well, well, well, Counselor.
What brings *you* here?"

"Picking up some pointers on how to try a case."

Howland smiled, but his eyes, gimleted in hard appraisal, burned under
bushy eyebrows as they searched Mason's face.

"*You* don't need any pointers, Counselor. I thought I had glimpsed you in the
crowd this morning, and then I was quite certain that you sat through the entire
afternoon session. Are you interested in the case?"

"It's an interesting case."

"I mean are you interested professionally?"

"Oh, of course professionally," Mason said with expansive indefiniteness. "I
don't know any of the parties. By the way, who was the person who was killed?"

"The body has never been identified," Howland said. "Fingerprints were sent
to the FBI, but there was no file. The person was evidently a drifter of some
sort. The head had been thrown to the highway with a terrific impact. The skull
was smashed like an eggshell. Then both wheels had gone completely over the
head. The features were unrecognizable."

"What about the clothing?"

"Good clothing, but the labels had been carefully removed. We thought, of
course, that meant the decedent might have had a criminal record. But, as I say,
there were no fingerprints on file."

"Was this license number written in the notebook *immediately* under the
other entries on the last page?" Mason asked.

"Come take a look," Howland invited, placing a fraternal hand on Mason's
shoulder. "I'd like to have you take a look at that and tell me what *you* think."

Howland led the way to the clerk's desk. "Let's look at that exhibit," he said,
"...the notebook."

The clerk handed him the notebook.

Mason studied the small, neat figures near the bottom of the page.

"You couldn't do that without a light to save your life," Howland said. "That woman wasn't watching the road while she was writing down the figures."

"I take it that you know the right headlight on *her* car wasn't smashed," Mason said.

"We know lots of things," Howland observed, winking. "We also know that it's an easy matter to get a headlight repaired. What's your opinion of the case, Mason? What do you think the jurors will do?"

"They may not do anything."

Howland's voice was cautious. "You think it will be a hung jury?"

"It could be."

Howland lowered his voice to a whisper. "Confidentially," he said, "that's what I was trying for. It's the best I can hope to expect."

CHAPTER FIVE

Mason sat at his desk, thoughtfully smoking. Della Street had cleaned up her secretarial desk, started for the door, returned for something which she had apparently forgotten, then she opened the drawers in her desk one after another, taking out papers, rearranging them.

Mason grinned. "Why don't you just break down and wait, Della?"

"Heavens! Was I that obvious?"

Mason nodded.

She laughed nervously. "Well, I *will* wait for a few minutes."

"The phone's plugged in through the switchboard?"

"Yes. Gertie's gone home. She left the main trunk line plugged through to your phone. In case this woman—"

Della Street broke off as the telephone rang.

Mason nodded to Della Street. "Since you're here, better get on the extension phone with your notebook and take notes."

Mason said, "Hello."

The feminine voice which had discussed the matter of a retainer with him earlier in the day sounded eager. "Is this Mr. Mason?"

"Yes."

"Did you get up to court today?"

"Certainly."

"And what did you think?"

"Think of what?"

"Of the case."

"I think probably it will be a hung jury."

"No, no! Of the witness."

"Which witness?"

"The redheaded woman, of course."

"You mean Mrs. Myrtle Anne Haley?"

"Yes."

"I can't tell you."

"You can't tell me?" the voice said, sharp with suspicion. "Why that's what you went up there for. You—"

"I can't discuss my opinion of Mrs. Haley's testimony with a stranger," Mason interrupted firmly.

"A stranger? Why, I'm your client. I—"

"How do I know you're my client?"

"You should be able to recognize my voice."

Mason said, "Voices sound very much alike sometimes. I would dislike very much to have someone claim I had made a libelous statement which wasn't a privileged communication."

There was silence at the other end of the line, then the woman's voice said, "Well, how *could* I identify myself?"

"Through a receipt that I gave the messenger who delivered the hundred dollars to me. When you produce that receipt, I'll know that I'm dealing with the person who made the payment."

"But, Mr. Mason, can't you see? I can't afford to have you know who I am. This whole business of using the messenger was to keep you from finding out."

"Well, I can't give my opinion of testimony unless I'm *certain* my statement is a privileged communication."

"Is your opinion that bad?"

"I am merely enunciating a principle."

"I...I already have that receipt, Mr. Mason. The messenger gave it to me."

"Then come on up," Mason said.

There was a long moment of silence.

"I took all these precautions so I wouldn't have to disclose my identity," the voice complained.

"I am taking all these precautions so as to be certain I'm talking to my client," Mason said.

"Will you be there?"

"I'll wait ten minutes. Will that be sufficient?"

"Yes."

"Very well. Come directly to the side door," Mason said.

"I think you're horrid!" she exclaimed. "I didn't want it like this." She slammed the receiver at her end of the telephone.

Mason turned to Della Street, who had been monitoring the conversation. "I take it, Miss Street, that you have decided you're not in a hurry to get home. You'd like to wait."

"Try putting me out of the office," she laughed. "It would take a team of elephants to drag me out."

She took the cover off her typewriter, arranged shorthand notebooks, hung up her hat in the coat closet.

Again the telephone rang.

Mason frowned. "We should have cut out the switchboard as soon as we had our call, Della. Go cut it out now...Well, wait a minute. See who's calling."

Della Street picked up the telephone, said, "Hello," then, "Who's calling, please?...Where?...Well, just a moment. I think he's gone home for the evening. I don't think he's available. I'll see."

She cupped her hand over the mouthpiece of the telephone and said, "A Mr. Guthrie Balfour is calling from Chihuahua City in Mexico. He says it's exceedingly important."

"Balfour?" Mason said. "That will be the uncle of young Ted Balfour, the defendant in this case. Looks like we're getting dragged into a vortex of events, Della. Tell long-distance you've located me and have her put her party on."

Della Street relayed the message into the telephone and a moment later nodded to Mason.

Mason picked up the telephone.

A man's voice at the other end of the line, sounding rather distant and faint, was nevertheless filled with overtones of urgency.

"Is this Perry Mason, the lawyer?"

"That's right," Mason said.

The voice sharpened with excitement. "Mr. Mason, this is Guthrie Balfour. I have just returned from the Tarahumare Indian country and I must get back to my base camp. I've received disquieting news in the mail here at Chihuahua. It seems my nephew, Theodore Balfour, is accused of a hit-and-run death.

"You must know of me, Mr. Mason. I'm quite certain you know of the vast industrial empire of the Balfour Allied Associates. We have investments all over the world—"

"I've heard of you," Mason interrupted. "The case involving your nephew was tried today."

The voice sounded suddenly dispirited and dejected. "What was the verdict?"

"As far as I know, the jury is still out."

"It's too late to do anything now?"

"I think perhaps it will be a hung jury. Why do you ask?"

"Mr. Mason, this is important! This is important as the devil! My nephew *must not* be convicted of anything."

"He can probably get probation in case he's convicted," Mason said. "There are certain facts about the case that make it very peculiar. There are certain discrepancies—"

"Of course there are discrepancies! Can't you understand? The whole thing is a frame-up. It's brought for a specific purpose. Mr. Mason, I can't get away. I'm down here on an archeological expedition of the greatest importance. I'm encountering certain difficulties, certain hazards, but I'm playing for big stakes. I...Look, Mr. Mason, I'll tell you what I'll do. I'll put my wife aboard the night plane tonight. She should be able to make connections at El Paso and be in your office the first thing in the morning. What time do you get to your office?"

"Sometime between nine and ten."

"Please, Mr. Mason, give my wife an appointment at nine o'clock in the morning. I'll see that you're amply compensated. I'll see that you—"

"The attorney representing your nephew," Mason interrupted, "is Mortimer Dean Howland."

"Howland!" the voice said. "That browbeating, loudmouthed bag of wind. He's nothing but a medium-grade criminal attorney, with a booming voice. This case is going to take brains, Mr. Mason. This...I can't explain. Will you give my wife an appointment for tomorrow morning at nine o'clock?"

"All right," Mason said. "I may not be free to do what you want me to do, however."

"Why?"

"I have some other connections which may bring about a conflict," Mason said. "I can't tell you definitely, but...well, anyway, I'll talk with your wife."

"Tomorrow at nine."

"That's right."

"Thank you so much."

Mason hung up. "Well," he said to Della Street, "we seem to be getting deeper and deeper into the frying pan."

"Right in the hot fat," Della obseved. "I—" She broke off as a nervous knock sounded on the door of Mason's private office.

Della crossed over and opened the door.

The young woman who had been seated next to Perry Mason in the courtroom entered the office.

"Well, good evening," Mason said. "You weren't very cordial to me earlier in the day."

"Of course not!"

"You wouldn't even give me the time of day."

"I... Mr. Mason, you... you've jockeyed me into a position... well, a position in which I didn't want to be placed."

"That's too bad," the lawyer said. "I was afraid *you* were going to put *me* in a position in which *I* didn't want to be placed."

"Well, you know who I am now."

"Sit down," Mason said. "By the way, just who are you...other than Cash?"

"My name is Marilyn Keith, but please don't make any further inquiries."

"Just what is your relationship to Myrtle Anne Haley?"

"Look here, Mr. Mason, you're cross-examining me. That's not what I wanted. I wanted certain information from you. I didn't want you even to know who I am."

"Why?"

"That's neither here nor there."

Mason said, "You're here and it's here. Now what's this all about?"

"I simply *have* to know the real truth—and that gets back to Myrtle Haley's testimony."

"Do you know the man who was killed?"

"No."

"Yet," Mason said, "you have parted with a hundred dollars of your money, money which, I take it, was withdrawn from a rainy-day fund, to retain me to listen to the case in court so you could ask me how I felt about the testimony of Myrtle Anne Haley?"

"That's right. Only the money came from...well, it was to have been my vacation fund."

"Vacation?"

"Mine comes next month," she said. "I let the other girls take theirs during the summer. I had intended to go to Acapulco...I will, anyway, but...well, naturally I hated to draw against my vacation fund. However, that's all in the past now."

"You have the receipt?" Mason asked.

She opened her purse, took from it the receipt which Della Street had given the messenger, and handed it to him.

Mason looked the young woman in the eyes. "I think Myrtle Haley was lying."

For a moment there was a flicker of expression on her face, then she regained her self-control. "Lying deliberately?"

Mason nodded. "Don't repeat my opinion to anyone else. To you this is a privileged communication. If you repeat what I said to anyone, however, you could get into trouble."

"Can you...can you give me any reasons for your conclusions, Mr. Mason?"

"She wrote down the license number of the automobile," Mason said. "She wrote it down in her notebook in exactly the right place and—"

"Yes, of course. I heard the argument of the defense attorney," Marilyn interrupted. "It sounds logical. But on the other hand, suppose Myrtle *did* take her eyes off the road? That would only have been for a minute. She didn't have her eyes off the road *all* the time she was writing. She just glanced down at the notebook to make certain she had the right place and—"

Mason picked up a pencil and a piece of paper. "Write down the figure six," he instructed Marilyn Keith.

She wrote as he directed.

"Now," Mason said, "get up and walk around the room and write another six while you're walking."

She followed his instructions.

"Compare the two figures," Mason told her.

"I don't see any difference."

"Bring them over here," Mason said, "and I'll show you some difference."

She started over toward the desk.

"Wait a minute," Mason said. Write another figure six while you're walking over here."

· She did so, handed him the pad of paper with the three sixes on it.

"This is the six that you wrote while you were sitting down," Mason said. "You'll notice that the end of the line on the loop of the six comes back and joins the down stroke. Now, look at the two figures that you made while you were walking. In one of them the loop of the six stops approximately a thirty-second of an inch before it comes to the down stroke, and on the second one the end of the loop goes completely through the down stroke and protrudes for probably a thirty-second of an inch on the other side.

"You try to write the figure six when you're riding in an automobile and you'll do one of two things. You'll either stop the end of the loop before you come to the down stroke or you'll go all the way through it. It's only when you're sitting perfectly still that you can bring the end of the six directly to the down stroke and then stop.

"Now, if you'll notice the figure GMB 665 that Myrtle Anne Haley *claims* she wrote while she was in a moving automobile, with one hand on the steering wheel, the other hand holding a fountain pen, writing in a notebook which was balanced on her lap, you'll note that both of the figures are perfect. The loops join the down strokes, so that the loops are perfectly closed. The chances that that could have been done twice in succession by someone who was in a moving automobile going over the road at a good rate of speed under the circumstances described by Myrtle Anne Haley, are just about one in a million."

"Why didn't the defense attorney bring that out?" she asked.

"Perhaps it didn't occur to him," Mason said. "Perhaps he didn't think he needed to."

She was silent for several seconds, then asked, "Is there anything else?"

"Lots of things," Mason said. "In addition to a sort of sixth sense which warns a lawyer when a witness is lying, there is the question of distance.

"If Mrs. Haley passed that car at the point she says she did, and then looked in the rearview mirror as she says she did, she must have been crossing State Highway when she saw the light go out. She'd hardly have been looking in her rearview mirror while she was crossing State Highway."

"Yes, I can see that," the young woman admitted. "That is, I can see it now that you've pointed it out."

Mason said, "Something caused you to become suspicious of Myrtle Haley's testimony in the first place. Do you want to tell me about it?"

She shook her head. "I can't."

"Well," Mason said, "you asked me for my opinion. You paid me a hundred dollars to sit in court and form that opinion. I have now given it to you."

She thought things over for a moment, then suddenly got up to give him her hand. "Thank you, Mr. Mason. You're...you're everything that I expected."

"Don't you think you'd better give me your address now?" Mason said. "One that we can put on the books?"

"Mr. Mason, I can't! If anyone knew about my having been to you, I'd be ruined. Believe me, there are interests involved that are big and powerful and ruthless. I only hope I haven't gone so far as to get you in trouble."

Mason studied her anxious features. "Is there any reason as far as you are concerned why I can't interest myself in any phase of the case?"

"Why do you ask that question?"

"I may have been approached by another potential client."

She thought that over. "Surely not Myrtle Haley!"

"No," Mason said. "I would be disqualified as far as she is concerned."

"Well, who is it?" she asked.

"I'm not free to tell you that. However, if there is any reason why I shouldn't represent *anyone* who is connected with the case in any way, please tell me."

She said, "I would love to know the real truth in this case. If you become connected with it you'll dig out that truth...and I don't care who retains you. As far as I'm concerned, you are free to go ahead in any way, Mr. Mason." She crossed to the door in one quick movement. "Good night," she said, and closed the door behind her.

Mason turned to Della Street. "Well?" he asked.

"She doesn't lie very well," Della said.

"Meaning what?"

"She didn't dig into her vacation money just to get your opinion of Myrtle's testimony."

"Then why *did* she do it?"

"*I think,*" Della Street said, "she's in love, and I *know* she's frightened."

CHAPTER SIX

Perry Mason latchkeyed the door of his private office, hung up his hat.

Della Street, who was there before him, asked, "Have you seen the morning papers?" She indicated the papers on Mason's desk.

He shook his head.

"There was a hung jury in the case of People versus Ted Balfour. They were divided evenly—six for acquittal and six for conviction."

"So what happened?" Mason asked.

"Apparently, Howland made a deal with the prosecutor. The Court discharged the jury and asked counsel to agree on a new trial date.

"At that time Howland got up, said that he thought the case was costing the state altogether too much money in view of the issues involved. He stated that he would be willing to stipulate the case could be submitted to Judge Cadwell, sitting without a jury, on the same evidence which had been introduced in the jury trial.

"The prosecutor agreed to that. Judge Cadwell promptly announced that under those circumstances he would find the defendant guilty as charged, and Howland thereupon made a motion for suspended sentence. The prosecutor said that under the circumstances and in view of the money that the defendant had saved the state, he would not oppose such a motion, provided the defendant paid a fine. He said he would consent that the matter be heard immediately.

"Judge Cadwell stated that in view of the stipulation by the prosecutor, he would give the defendant a suspended jail sentence and impose a fine of five hundred dollars."

"Well, that's interesting," Mason said. "It certainly disposed of the case of People versus Balfour in a hurry. We haven't heard anything from our client of yesterday, have we, Della?"

"No, but our client of today is waiting in the office."

"You mean Mrs. Balfour?"

"That's right."

"How does she impress you, Della? Does she show signs of having been up all night?"

Della Street shook her head. "Fresh as a daisy. Groomed tastefully and expensively. Wearing clothes that didn't come out of a suitcase. She really set out to make an impression on Mr. Perry Mason.

"Apparently she chartered a plane out of Chihuahua, flew to El Paso in time to make connections with one of the luxury planes, arrived home, grabbed a little shut-eye and then this morning started making herself very, very presentable."

"Good-looking?" Mason asked.

"A dish."

"How old?"

"She's in that deadly dangerous age between twenty-seven and thirty-two. That's about as close as I can place her."

"Features?" Mason asked.

"She has," Della Street said, "large brown expressive eyes, a mouth that smiles to show beautiful pearly teeth—in short, she's a regular millionaire's second wife, an expensive plaything. And even so, Mr. Guthrie Balfour must have done a lot of window-shopping before he had this package wrapped up."

"A thoroughly devoted wife," Mason said, smiling.

"Very, very devoted," Della Street said. "Not to Mr. Guthrie Balfour, but to *Mrs.* Guthrie Balfour. There's a woman who's exceedingly loyal to herself."

"Well, get her in," Mason said. "Let's have a look at her. Now, she's a second wife, so really she's no relation to young Ted Balfour."

"That's right. You'll think I'm catty," Della Street observed, "but I'll tell you something, Mr. Perry Mason."

"What?"

"You're going to fall for her like a ton of bricks. She's just the type to impress you."

"But not you?" Mason asked.

Della Street's answer was to flash him a single glance.

"Well, bring her in," Mason said, smiling. "After this build-up, I'm bound to be disappointed."

"You won't be," she told him.

Della Street ushered Mrs. Guthrie Balfour into Mason's private office.

Mason arose, bowed, said, "Good morning, Mrs. Balfour. I'm afraid you've had rather a hard trip."

Her smile was radiant. "Not at all, Mr. Mason. In the first place, I was here at home by one-thirty this morning. In the second place, traveling on air-conditioned planes and sitting in sponge rubber reclining seats is the height of luxury compared to the things an archeologist's wife has to contend with."

"Do sit down," Mason said. "Your husband seemed very much disturbed about the case against his nephew."

"That's putting it mildly."

"Well," Mason said, "apparently, the young man's attorney worked out a deal with the prosecutor. Did you read the morning paper?"

"Heavens, no! Was there something in there about the case?"

"Yes," Mason said. "Perhaps you'd like to read it for yourself."

He folded the paper and handed it to her.

While she was reading the paper, Mason studied her carefully.

Suddenly Mrs. Balfour uttered an exclamation of annoyance, crumpled the paper, threw it to the floor, jumped from the chair, and stamped a high-heeled shoe on the paper. Then abruptly she caught herself.

"Oh, I'm sorry," she said. "I didn't realize."

She stepped carefully off the paper, disentangling her high heels, raising her skirts as she did so, so that she disclosed a neat pair of legs. Then, dropping to her knees, she started smoothing the newspaper out.

"I'm so sorry, Mr. Mason," she sad contritely. "My temper got the best of me... that awful temper of mine."

"Don't bother about the paper," Mason said, glancing at Della Street. "There are plenty more down on the newsstand. Please don't give it another thought."

"No, no... I'm sorry. I... let me do penance, please, Mr. Mason."

She carefully smoothed out the paper, then arose with supple grace.

"What was there about the article that annoyed you?" Mason asked.

"The fool!" she said. "The absolute fool! Oh, they should never have let that braggart, that loudmouthed egoist handle the case—not for a minute."

"Mortimer Dean Howland?" Mason asked.

"Mortimer Dean Howland," she said, spitting out the words contemptuously. "Look what he's done."

"Apparently," Mason said, "he's made a pretty good deal. In all probability, Mrs. Balfour, while the jury was out, Howland approached the prosecutor, suggested the possibility of a hung jury, and the prosecutor probably didn't care too much about retrying the case. So it was agreed that if there was a hung jury, the case could be submitted to Judge Cadwell on the evidence which had been introduced, which was, of course, equivalent to pleading the defendant guilty, only it saved him the stigma of such a plea.

"The prosecutor, for his side of the bargain, agreed that he would stipulate the judge could pass a suspended sentence and the case would be cleaned up. Of course, the trouble with a stipulation of that sort is that on occasion the judge won't ride along, but takes the bit in his teeth and insists on pronouncing sentence. Judge Cadwell, however, is known for his consideration of the practical problems of the practicing attorney. He virtually always rides along with a stipulation of that sort."

Mrs. Balfour followed Mason's explanation with intense interest, her large brown eyes showing the extent of her concentration.

When Mason had finished she said simply, "There are some things that Ted Balfour doesn't know about. Therefore, his attorney could hardly be expected to know them. But they are vital."

"What, for instance?" Mason asked.

"Addison Balfour," she explained.

"What about him?" Mason asked.

"He's the wealthiest member of the family, and he's terribly prejudiced."

"I thought your husband was the wealthy one," Mason ventured.

"No. Guthrie is pretty well heeled, I guess. I don't know. I've never inquired into his financial status. Under the circumstances, my motives might have been misunderstood," she said, and laughed, a light, nervous laugh.

"Go on," Mason said.

"Addison Balfour is dying and knows it. Eighteen months ago the doctors gave him six months to live. Addison is really a remarkable character. He's wealthy, eccentric, strong-minded, obstinate, and completely unpredictable. One thing I do know—if *he* ever learns that Ted Balfour has been convicted of killing a man with an automobile, Addison will disinherit Ted immediately."

"Ted is mentioned in his will?"

"I have reason to believe so. I think Ted is to receive a large chunk of property, but Addison is very much prejudiced against what he calls the helterskelter attitude of the younger generation.

"You see, Ted took his military service. He's finished college and is now taking a six-months' breathing spell before he plunges into the business of Balfour Industries.

"Ted had some money which was left him outright by his father. Addison didn't approve of that at all. There is also a fortune left Ted in trust. Ted bought one of these high-powered sports cars that will glide along the highway at one hundred and fifty miles an hour, and Addison had a fit when he learned of that.

"You see, my husband is childless, Addison is childless, and Ted represents the only one who can carry on the Balfour name and the Balfour traditions. Therefore, he's an important member of the family."

"Ted wasn't driving his sports car the night of the accident?" Mason asked.

"No, he was driving one of the big cars."

"There are several?"

"Yes."

"The same make?"

"No. My husband is restless. He's restless mentally as well as physically. Most people will buy one make of car. If they like it, they'll have all their cars of that make. Guthrie is completely different. If he buys a Cadillac today, he'll buy a Buick tomorrow, and an Olds the next day. Then he'll get a Lincoln for his next car, and so on down the line. I've only been married to him for two years, but I guess I've driven half a dozen makes of cars in that time."

"I see," Mason said. "Now, just what did you have in mind?"

"In the first place," she said, "this man Howland must go. Do you have any idea how it happened that Ted went to him in the first place?"

Mason shook his head.

"You see, my husband and I left for Mexico the day of the accident. This happened the night we left. Ted was very careful that we didn't hear anything about it. We've been back in the wild barranca country. We came to Chihuahua for mail and supplies and there was a letter there from the trustee of Ted's trust fund. Guthrie called you immediately after he'd read that letter. He simply had to return to base camp, and from there he's going out on a very dangerous but exciting expedition into very primitive country."

"You went by train?"

"Yes. My husband doesn't like airplanes. He says they're nothing but buses with wings. He likes to get in an air-conditioned train, get single occupancy of a drawing room, stretch out, relax and do his thinking. He says he does some of his best thinking and nearly all of his best sleeping on a train."

"Well," Mason said, "the case has been concluded. There's nothing for me or anyone else to do now."

"That's not the way my husband feels about it. Despite the court's decision, he'll want you to check on the evidence of the witnesses."

"What good would that do?"

"You could get the stipulation set aside and get a new trial."

"That would be difficult."

"Couldn't you do it if you could prove one of the main witnesses was lying?"

"Perhaps. Do you think one of the main witnesses was lying?"

"I'd want to have you investigate that and tell me."

"I couldn't do anything as long as Howland was representing Ted."

"He's finished now."

"Does he know that?"

"He will."

Mason said, "There's one other matter you should know about."

"What?"

"Without discussing details," Mason said, "I was retained to sit in court yesterday and listen to the evidence in the case."

"By whom?"

"I am not at liberty to disclose that. I'm not certain I know."

"But for heaven's sake, why should anyone ask you simply to sit in court and listen?"

"That," Mason said, "is something I've been asking myself. The point is that I *did* it. Now I don't want to have any misunderstandings about this. I have had one client who asked me to sit in court and listen."

"And you sat in court and listened?"

"Yes."

"What did you think of the case?"

"There again," Mason said, "is something I have to discuss cautiously. I came to the conclusion that one of the principal witnesses might not be telling the truth."

"A witness for the prosecution?"

"Yes. The defense put on no case."

"Well, is that going to disqualify you from doing what we want?"

"Not unless you think it does. It complicates the situation in that Howland will think I deliberately watched the trial in order to steal his client."

"Do you care what Howland thinks?"

"In a way, yes."

"But it's not going to be too important?"

"Not *too* important. I would like to have the matter adjusted so that Howland can understand the situation."

"You leave Howland to me," she said. "I'm going to talk with him, and when I get done telling him a few things, he'll know how my husband and I feel."

"After all," Mason said, "Ted is apparently the one who retained him, and Ted is over twenty-one and able to do as he pleases."

"Well, I am going to talk with Ted, too."

"Do so," Mason said. "Get in touch with me after you have clarified the situation. I don't want to touch it while Howland is in the picture."

Mrs. Balfour whipped out a checkbook. 'You are retained as of right now," she said.

She took a fountain pen, wrote out a check for a thousand dollars, signed it *Guthrie Balfour, per Dorla Balfour,* and handed it to Mason.

"I don't get it," the lawyer said. "Here's a case that's all tried and finished and now you come along with a retainer."

"Your work will lie in convincing Addison that Ted wasn't really involved in that case," she said. "And there'll be plenty of work and responsibility, don't think there won't be.

"For one thing, you're going to have to reopen the case. Frankly, Mr. Mason, while Addison may blame Ted, he'll be furious at Guthrie for letting any such situation develop. He thinks Guthrie puts in too much time on these expeditions.

"Just wait until you see what you're up against, and you'll understand what I mean.

"And now I must go see Ted, let Howland know he's fired and... well, I'm going to let *you* deal with Addison. When you see him, remember *we've* retained you to protect Ted's interests.

"Will you hold some time open for me later on today?" she asked.

Mason nodded.

"You'll hear from me," she promised and walked out.

When the door had clicked shut, Mason turned to Della Street. "Well?"

Della Street motioned toward the crumpled newspaper. "An impulsive woman," she said.

"A very interesting woman," Mason said. "She's using her mind all the time. Did you notice the way she was concentrating when I was explaining what had happened in the case?"

"I noticed the way she was looking at you while you were talking," Della Street said.

"Her face was the picture of concentration. She is using her head all the time."

"I also noticed the way she walked out the door," Della Street said. "She may have been using her mind when she was looking at you, but she was using her hips when she knew you were looking at her."

Mason said, "You were also looking."

"Oh, she *knew* I'd be looking," Della Street said, "but the act was strictly for your benefit."

CHAPTER SEVEN

It was ten-thirty when Mason's unlisted phone rang. Since only Della Street and Paul Drake, head of the Drake Detective Agency, had the number of that telephone, Mason reached across the desk for it. "I'll answer it," he said to Della, and then, picking up the receiver, said, "Hello, Paul."

Paul Drake's voice came over the wire with the toneless efficiency of an announcer giving statistical reports on an election night.

"You're interested in the Ted Balfour case, Perry," he said. "There have been developments in that case you ought to know about."

"In the first place, how did you know I am interested?" Mason asked.

"You were in court yesterday following the case."

"Who told you?"

"I get around," Drake said. "Listen. There's something funny in that case. It may have been a complete frame-up."

"Yes?" Mason asked. "What makes you think so?"

"The body's been identified," Drake said.

"And what does that have to do with it?" Mason asked.

"Quite a good deal."

"Give me the dope. Who is the man?"

"A fellow by the name of Jackson Eagan. At least that's the name he gave when he registered at the Sleepy Hollow Motel. It's also the name he gave when he rented a car from a drive-yourself agency earlier that day."

"Go on," Mason said.

"The people who rented the car made a recovery of the car within a day or two. It had been left standing in front of the motel. The management reported it; the car people assumed it was just one of those things that happen every so often when a man signs up for a car, then changes his mind about something and simply goes away without notifying the agency. Since the car people had a deposit of fifty dollars, they simply deducted rental for three days, set the balance in a credit fund, and said nothing about it. Therefore, the police didn't know that Jackson Eagan was missing. The motel people didn't care because Eagan had paid his rent in advance. So if it hadn't been for a fluke, police would never have discovered the identity of the body. The features were pretty well damaged, you remember."

"What was the fluke?" Mason asked.

"When the body was found there was nothing in the pockets except some odds and ends that offered no chance for an identification, some small coins and one key. The police didn't pay much attention to the key until someone in the police department happened to notice a code number on the key. This man was in the traffic squad and he said the code number was that of a car rental agency. So the police investigated, and sure enough, this key was for the car that had been parked in front of the motel for a couple of days."

"When did they find out all this?" Mason asked.

"Yesterday morning, while the case was being tried. They didn't get the dope to the prosecutor until after the arguments had started, but police knew about it as early as eight o'clock. The reason it didn't reach the prosecutor was on account of red tape in the D.A.'s office. The guy who handles that stuff decided it wouldn't make any difference in the trial, so he let it ride."

"That's most interesting," Mason said. "It may account for the sudden desire on the part of a lot of people to retain my services."

"Okay. I thought you'd be interested," Drake said.

"Keep an ear to the ground, Paul," Mason said, hung up the telephone and repeated the conversation to Della Street.

"Where does that leave you, Chief?" she asked.

"Where I always am," Mason said, "right in the middle. There's something phony about this whole business. That Haley woman was reciting a whole synthetic lie there on the witness stand, and people don't lie like that unless there's a reason."

"And," Della Street said, "young women like Marilyn Keith don't give up their vacation to Acapulco unless there's a reason."

"Nor women like Mrs. Guthrie Balfour literally force retainers on reluctant attorneys," Mason said. "Stick around, Della. I think you'll see some action."

Della Street smiled sweetly at her employer. "I'm sticking," she announced simply.

CHAPTER EIGHT

By one forty-five Mrs. Balfour was back in Mason's office.

"I've seen Ted," she said.

Mason nodded.

"It's just as I surmised. Ted was given a loaded drink. He passed out. I don't know who had it in for him or why, but I can tell you one thing."

"What?"

"He wasn't the one who was driving his car," she asserted. "A young woman drove him home—a cute trick with dark chestnut hair, a nice figure, good legs, and a very sympathetic shoulder. I think I can find out who she was by checking the list of party guests. It was a party given by Florence Ingle."

"How do you know about the girl?" Mason asked.

"A friend of mine saw her driving Ted's car, with Ted passed out and leaning on her shoulder. He'd seen her at the parking space getting into Ted's car. She had Ted move over and she took the wheel. If anyone hit a pedestrian with the car Ted had that evening, it was that girl."

"At what time was this?" Mason asked.

"Sometime between ten and eleven."

"And after Ted got home what happened?" Mason asked.

"Now as to that," she said, "you'll have to find the young woman who was driving and ask her. There were no servants in the house. Remember, Guthrie and I had taken the train. Before that there'd been a farewell party at Florence Ingle's. I'd told all of our servants to take the night off. There was no one at our house."

"Ted was in his bedroom the next morning?" Mason asked.

"Apparently he was. He told me he became conscious at four-thirty-five in the morning. Someone had taken him upstairs, undressed him, and put him to bed."

"Or he undressed himself and put himself to bed," Mason said.

"He was in no condition to do that."

"Any idea who this girl was?" Mason asked.

"Not yet. Ted either doesn't know or won't tell. Apparently, she was some trollop from the wrong side of the tracks."

Mason's frown showed annoyance.

"All right, all right," she said. "I'm out of order. I'm not a snob. Remember, Mr. Mason, I came from the wrong side of the tracks myself, and I made it, but I'm just telling you it's a long, hard climb. And also remember, Mr. Mason, you're working for me."

"The hell I am," Mason said. "You're paying the bill, but I'm working for my client."

"Now don't get stuffy," she said, flashing her teeth in a mollifying smile. "I had Ted write a check covering Howland's fees in full and I explained to Mr. Howland that as far as Mr. Guthrie Balfour and I were concerned, we preferred to have all further legal matters in connection with the case handled by Mr. Perry Mason."

"And what did Howland say then?"

"Howland threw back his head, laughed and said, 'If it's a fair question, Mrs. Balfour, when did you get back from Mexico?' and I told him that I didn't know whether it was a fair question or not, but there was no secret about it and I got back from Mexico on a plane which arrived half an hour past midnight, and then he laughed again and said that if I had arrived twenty-four hours sooner he felt certain he wouldn't have had the opportunity to represent Ted as long as he did."

"He was a little put out about it?" Mason asked.

"On the contrary, he was in rare good humor. He said that he had completed his representation of Ted Balfour, that the case was closed, and that if Mr. Mason knew as much about the case as he did, Mason would realize the over-all strategy had been brilliant."

"Did he say in what respect?"

"No, but he gave me a letter for you."

"Indeed," Mason said.

She unfolded the letter and extended it across the desk. The letter was addressed to Perry Mason and read:

> My dear Counselor,
>   I now begin to see a great light. I trust your time in court was well spent, but don't worry. There are no hard feelings. You take on from here and more power to you. I consider myself completely relieved of all responsibilities in the case of the People versus Ted Balfour, and I am satisfied, not only with the compensation I have received, but with the outcome of my strategy. From here on, the Balfour family is all yours. They consider me a little crude and I consider them highly unappreciative in all ways except insofar as financial appreciation is concerned. I can assure you that those matters have been completely taken care of, so consider yourself free to gild the lily or paint the rose in any way you may see fit, remembering only that it's advisable to take the temperature of the water before you start rocking the boat.
>   With all good wishes,
>   Mortimer Dean Howland

"A very interesting letter," Mason said, handing it to Mrs. Balfour.

"Isn't it?" she remarked dryly after having read it. She returned it to Perry Mason.

"*Now,* what do you want me to do?" Mason asked.

"The first thing I want you to do," she said, "is to go and see Addison Balfour. He's in bed. He'll never get out of bed. You'll have to go to him."

"Will he see me?"

"He'll see you. I've already telephoned for an appointment."

"When?" Mason asked.

"I telephoned about thirty minutes ago. The hour of the appointment, however, is to be left to you. Mr. Addison Balfour will be *very* happy to see the great Perry Mason."

Mason turned to Della Street. "Ring up Addison Balfour's secretary," he said, "and see if I can have an appointment for three o'clock."

CHAPTER NINE

Some two years earlier, when the doctors had told Addison Balfour that he had better "take it easy for a while," the manufacturing magnate had moved his private office into his residence.

Later on, when the doctors had told him frankly that he had but six months to live at the outside, Addison Balfour had moved his office into his bedroom.

Despite the sentence of death which had been pronounced upon him, he continued to be the same old irascible, unpredictable fighter. Disease had ravaged his body, but the belligerency of the man's mind remained unimpaired.

Mason gave his name to the servant who answered the door.

"Oh, yes, Mr. Mason. You are to go right up. Mr. Balfour is expecting you. The stairs to the left, please."

Mason climbed the wide flight of oak stairs, walked down the second floor toward a sign which said "Office," and entered through an open door, from behind which came the sound of pounding typewriters.

Two stenographers were busily engaged in hammering keyboards. A telephone operator sat at the back of a room, supervising a switchboard.

At a desk facing the door sat Marilyn Keith.

"Good afternoon," Mason said calmly and impersonally as though he had never before seen her. "I am Mr. Mason. I have an appointment with Mr. Addison Balfour."

"Just a moment, Mr. Mason. I'll tell Mr. Balfour you're here."

She glided from the room through an open doorway and in a moment returned.

"Mr. Balfour will see you now, Mr. Mason," she said in the manner of one reciting a prepared speech which had been repeated so many times and under such circumstances that the repetition had made the words almost without meaning. "You will understand, Mr. Mason, that Mr. Addison Balfour is not at all well. He is, for the moment, confined to his bed. Mr. Balfour dislikes to discuss his illness with anyone. You will, therefore, please try to act as though the situation were entirely normal and you were seeing Mr. Balfour in his office. However, you will remember he is ill and try to conclude the interview as soon as possible.

"You may go in now."

She ushered Mason through the open door, along a vestibule, then swung open a heavy oaken door which moved on well-oiled hinges.

The man who was propped up in bed might have been made of colorless wax. His high cheekbones, the gaunt face, the sunken eyes, all bore the unmistakable stamp of illness. But the set of his jaw, the thin, determined line of his mouth showed the spirit of an indomitable fighter.

Balfour's voice was not strong. "Come in, Mr. Mason," he said in a monotone, as though he lacked the physical strength to put even the faintest expression in his words. "Sit down here by the bed. What's all this about Ted getting convicted?"

Mason said, "The attorney who was representing your nephew appeared to think that the interests of expediency would best be served by making a deal with the district attorney's office."

"Who the hell wants to serve the interests of expediency?" Balfour asked in his colorless, expressionless voice.

"Apparently your nephew's attorney thought that would be best under the circumstances."

"What do you think?"

"I don't know."

"Find out."

"I intend to."

"Come back when you find out."

"Very well," Mason said, getting up.

"Wait a minute. Don't go yet. *I* want to tell *you* something. Lean closer. Listen. Don't interrupt."

Mason leaned forward so that his ear was but a few inches from the thin, colorless lips.

"I told Dorla—that's Guthrie's wife—that I'd disinherit Ted if he got in any trouble with that automobile. That was just a bluff.

"Ted's a Balfour. He has the Balfour name. He's going to carry it on. It would be unthinkable to have the Balfour Allied Associates carried on by anyone who wasn't a Balfour. I want Ted to marry. I want him to have children. I want him to leave the business to a man-child who has the name of Balfour and the characteristics of a Balfour. Do you understand?"

Mason nodded.

"But," Addison went on, "I want to be sure that Ted knows the duties and responsibilities of a Balfour and of the head of a damn big business."

Again Mason nodded.

Addison Balfour waited for a few seconds as though mustering his strength.

Addison Balfour breathed deeply, exhaled in a tremulous sigh, took in his breath once more and said, "Balfours don't compromise, Mr. Mason. Balfours fight."

Mason waited.

"Lots of times you win a case by a compromise," Balfour said. "It's a good thing. You may come out better in some isolated matter by compromise than by fighting a thing through to the last bitter ditch.

"That's a damn poor way to go through life.

"Once people know that you'll compromise when the going gets tough, they see to it that the going gets tough. People aren't dumb. Businessmen get to know the caliber of the businessmen they are dealing with. Balfours don't compromise.

"We won't fight unless we're in the right. When we start fighting, we carry the fight through to the end.

"You understand what I mean, Mason?"

Mason nodded.

"We don't want the reputation of being compromisers," Balfour continued. "We want the reputation of being implacable fighters. I want Ted to learn that lesson.

"I'd told Guthrie's wife that I'd disinherit Ted if he ever got convicted of any serious accident with that automobile. Scared her to death. She has her eye out for the cash. What do you think of her, Mason?"

"I'm hardly in a position to discuss her," Mason said.

"Why not?"

"She's somewhat in the position of a client."

"The hell she is! Ted Balfour is your client. What makes you say she's a client? She didn't retain you, did she?"

"For Ted Balfour."

"She did that because Guthrie told her to. How was the check signed?"

"Your brother's name, Guthrie Balfour, per Dorla Balfour."

"That's what I thought. She wouldn't give you a thin dime out of her money. Heaven knows how much she's got! She's milked Guthrie for plenty. That's all right. That's Guthrie's business.

"Don't be misled about money, Mason. You can't eat money. You can't wear money. All you can do with money is spend it. That's what it's for.

"Guthrie wanted a good-looker. He had money. He bought one. The trouble is, people aren't merchandise. You can pay for them, but that doesn't mean you've got 'em. Personally, I wouldn't trust that woman as far as I could throw this bed, and that isn't very damn far, Mason. Do you understand me?"

"I understand the point you're making."

"Remember it!" Balfour said. "Now, I want young Ted to fight. I don't want him to start out by compromising. When I read the paper this morning I was furious. I was going to send for you myself, but Dorla telephoned my secretary and told her she'd made arrangements to have you step into the picture. What are you going to do, Mason?"

"I don't know."

"Get in there and fight like hell! Don't worry about money. You have a retainer?"

"A retainer," Mason said, "which at first blush seemed more than adequate."

"How does it seem now?"

"Adequate."

"Something happened?"

"The case has taken on certain unusual aspects."

"All right," Balfour said. "You're in the saddle. Start riding the horse. Pick up the reins. Don't let anybody tell you what to do. You're not like most of these criminal lawyers. You don't want just to get a client off. You try to dig out the truth. I like that. That's what I want.

"Now remember this: If a Balfour is wrong, he apologizes and makes restitution. If he's right, he fights. Now you start fighting.

"I don't want you to tell Dorla that I'm not going to disinherit Ted. I don't want you to tell Ted. I want Ted to sweat a little blood. Ted's going to have to get in the business pretty quick, and he's going to have to become a Balfour. He isn't a Balfour now. He's just a kid. He's young. He's inexperienced. He hasn't been tempered by fire.

"This experience is going to do him good. It's going to teach him that he has to fight. It's going to teach him that he can't go through life playing around on his dad's money. Scare the hell out of him if you want to, but make him fight.

"Now I'll tell you one other thing, Mason. Don't trust Dorla."

Mason remained silent.

"Well?" Addison Balfour snapped.

"I heard you," Mason said.

"All right, I'm telling you. Don't trust Dorla. Dorla's a snob. Ever notice how it happens that people who have real background and breeding are considerate, tolerant, and broad-minded, while people who haven't anything except money that they didn't earn themselves are intolerant? That's Dorla. She's got about the nicest figure I've ever seen on a woman. And I've seen lots of them.

"Don't underestimate her, Mason. She's smart. She's chain lightning! She's got her eye on a big slice of money, and Guthrie hasn't waked up yet. That's all right. Let him sleep. He's paid for a dream. As long as he's enjoying the dream, why grab him by the shoulder and bring him back to the grim realities of existence?

"Guthrie isn't really married to Dorla. He's married to the woman he visualizes beneath Dorla's beautiful exterior. It's not the real woman. It's a dream woman, a sort of man-made spouse that he's conjured up out of his own mind.

"When Guthrie wakes up he'll marry Florence Ingle and really be happy. Right now he's a sleepwalker. He's in a dream. Don't try to wake him up.

"I'm a dying man. I can't bring up Ted. After Ted's family died Guthrie and his wife took over. Then Guthrie's wife died and he bought beauty on the auction block. He thought that was what he wanted.

"He knows I'll raise hell if he neglects Ted's bringing up. Dorla isn't a good influence on Ted. She isn't a good influence on anyone. But she's smart! Damned smart!

"If she has to get out from under, she'll trap you to save her own skin. Don't think she can't do it.

"Guthrie gave you a retainer. Don't bother about sending him bills. Send bills to the Balfour Allied Associates. I'll instruct the treasurer to let you have any amount you need. I know you by reputation well enough to know you won't stick me. You should know me by reputation well enough to know that if you overcharge me it'll be the biggest mistake you ever made in your life. That's all now, Mason. I'm going to sleep. Tell my secretary not to disturb me for thirty minutes, no matter what happens. Don't try to shake hands. I get tired. Close the door when you go out. Good-by."

Addison's head dropped back against the pillow. The colorless eyelids fluttered shut over the faded blue eyes.

Mason tiptoed from the room.

Marilyn Keith was waiting for him on the other side of the vestibule door. "Will you step this way, please, Mr. Mason?"

Mason followed her into another office and gave her Balfour's message. Marilyn indicated a telephone and a desk. "We have strict instructions not to put through any phone messages to anyone who is in conference with Mr. Balfour," she said. "But Miss Street telephoned and said you must call at once upon a matter of the greatest urgency."

"Did she leave any other message?" Mason asked.

Marilyn Keith shook her head.

Mason dialed the number of the unlisted telephone in his office.

When he heard Della Street's voice on the line he said, "Okay, Della, what cooks?"

"Paul's here," she said. "He wants to talk with you. Are you where you can talk?"

"Fairly well," Mason said.

"Alone?"

"No."

"Better be careful about what comments you make, then," she said. "Here's Paul. I'll explain to him that you'll have to be rather guarded."

A moment later Paul Drake's voice came on the line. "Hello, Perry."

"Hi," Mason said, without mentioning Drake's name.

"Things are happening fast in that Balfour case."

"What?"

"They secured an order for the exhumation of the corpse."

"Go ahead."

"That was done secretly at an early hour this morning."

"Keep talking."

"When police checked at the motel, back-tracking the car, they learned something that started them really moving in a hurry. Apparently someone in the motel had heard a shot on the night of the nineteenth. They dug the body up. The coroner opened the skull, something which had never been done before."

"It hadn't?"

"No. The head had been pretty well smashed up and the coroner evidently didn't go into it."

"Okay, what happened?"

"When they opened the head," Paul Drake said, "they found that it wasn't a hit-and-run accident at all."

"What do you mean?"

"The man had been killed," Drake said, "by a small-caliber, high-powered bullet."

"They're certain?"

"Hell, yes! The bullet's still in there. The hole was concealed beneath the hair and the coroner missed it the first time. Of course, Perry, they though they were dealing with a hig-and-run death and that the victim was a drifter who had been walking along the road. The whole thing indicated a ne'er-do-well who happened to get in front of a car being driven by an intoxicated driver."

"And now?"

"Hells bells!" Paul Drake said. "Do I have to draw you a diagram? Now it's first-degree murder."

"Okay," Mason said. "Start working."

"What do you want, Perry?"

"Everything," Mason said. "I'll discuss it with you when I see you. In the meantime, get started."

"What's the limit?" Draked asked.

"There isn't any."

"Okay. I'm starting."

Mason hung up and turned to Marilyn Keith. "Well?" he asked.

"Have you told anyone about me?"

"Not by name."

"Don't."

"I'm in the case now."

"I know."

"It may be more of a case than it seemed at first."

"I know."

"I'm representing Ted."

"Yes, of course."

"You know what that means?"

"What?"

"I may have to show who was really driving the car."

She thought that over for a minute, then raised her chin. "Go right ahead, Mr. Mason. You do anything that will help Ted."

"This case may have a lot more to it than you think," Mason told her. "Do you want to tell me anything?"

"I drove the car," she said.

"Was that the reason you came to me?"

"No."

"Why?"

"On account of Ted. Oh, please, Mr. Mason, don't let anything happen to him. I don't only mean about the car; I mean—lots of things."

"Such as what?" Mason asked.

"Ted's being exposed to influences that aren't good."

"Why aren't they good?"

"I can't tell you all of it," she said. "Mr. Addison Balfour is a wonderful man, but he's an old man. He's a sick man. He's a grim man. He looks at life as a battle. He was never married. He regrets that fact now, not because he realizes that he missed a lot of love, but only because he has no son to carry on the Balfour business.

"He wants to make Ted a second Addison Balfour. He wants to make him a grim, uncompromising, unyielding fighter.

"Ted's young. His vision, his ideals are younger and clearer than those of Addison Balfour. He sees the beauties of life. He can enjoy a sunset or the soft spring sunlight on green hills. He sees and loves beauty everywhere. It would be a tragic mistake to make him into a grim, fighting machine like Addison Balfour."

"Any other influences?" Mason asked.

"Yes."

"What?"

"The influence of beauty," she said.

"I thought you said you wanted him to appreciate beauty."

"Real beauty, not the spurious kind."

"Who's the spurious beauty?" Mason asked.

"Dorla."

"You mean to say she's married to his uncle and has her eyes on the nephew?"

"She has big eyes," Marilyn Keith said. "Oh, Mr. Mason, I *do* so hope you can handle this thing in such a way that ... well, give Ted an opportunity to develop his own individuality in his own way. There'll be lots of time later on for him to become as grim as Addison Balfour, and a lot of time later on for him to become disillusioned about women.

"And if Guthrie Balfour should think that Ted and Dorla ... Mr. Mason, you're a lawyer. You know the world."

"What you have outlined," Mason said, "or rather, what you have hinted at, sounds like quite a combination."

"That," she said, "is a masterpiece of understatement. You haven't met Banner Boles yet."

"Who's he?"

"He's the trouble shooter for the Balfour interests. He's deadly and clever, and whenever he's called in he starts manipulating facts and twisting things around so you don't know where you're at. Oh, Mr. Mason, I'm terribly afraid!"

"For yourself?"

"No, for Ted."

"You may not be in the clear on this thing," Mason said, his voice kindly, "and now that I'm representing Ted, I may have to drag you in."

"Drag me in if it will help Ted."

"Does he know you drove him home?"

"He's never intimated it if he does."

"What happened?"

"He was out in the parking space back of Florence Ingle's place. He wasn't drunk. He was sick. I knew he couldn't drive in that condition. I saw him trying to back the car. He was barely able to sit up."

"Did you speak to him?"

"I just said, 'Move over,' and I got behind the steering wheel and drove him home."

"What happened?"

"The last part of that trip he was falling over against me, and I'd have to push his weight away so I could drive the car. He'd fall against the wheel. I guess I was going all over the road there on Sycamore Road, but I didn't hit anyone, Mr. Mason. That is, I don't *think* I did. I kept my eyes on the road. I tried to, but he would lurch against me and grab the wheel. I should have stopped, but I wasn't driving fast."

"You put him to bed?"

"I had a terrible time. I finally got him to stagger up to his room. I took his shoes off. I tried to find a servant, but there didn't seem to be anyone at home."

"What time was this?"

"A lot earlier than Myrtle Haley said it was."

Mason was thoughtful. "How did you get home? If you called a cab we may be able to find the driver and establish the time element by—"

"I didn't call a cab, Mr. Mason. I was afraid that might be embarrassing to Ted—a young woman leaving the house alone, the servants all away. I walked to the highway and thumbed a ride. I told the man who picked me up a story of having to walk home."

Mason looked at her sharply.

"There was no reason why any young woman couldn't have called a cab from that house at ten-thirty or eleven at night."

"Don't you see?" she pleaded. "I'm not just any young woman. I'm Addison Balfour's confidential secretary. I know the contents of his will. If he thought I had any interest in Ted...or that I had been in Ted's room—Oh, Mr. Mason, please have confidence in me and *please* protect my secret!

"I have to go now. I don't want the girls in the office to get suspicious. I'm supposed to be letting you use the phone. The switchboard operator will know how long it's been since you hung up. Good-by now."

Mason left Addison Balfour's residence, stopped at the first telephone booth, called Paul Drake, said, "I can talk now, Paul. Here's your first job. Find out where Ted Balfour is. Get him out of circulation. Keep him out of circulation. Get in touch with me as soon as you have him and—"

"Whoa, whoa," Drake said. "Back up. You're not playing tiddlywinks. This is for high stakes, and it's for keeps."

"What do you mean?" Mason asked.

"Hell!" Drake said. "The police had Ted in custody within fifteen minutes of the time the autopsy surgeon picked up the telephone and made his first preliminary report about the bullet."

"Where are they keeping him?" Mason asked.

"That's something no one knows," Drake said.

"How about the press, Paul?"

"Figure it out for yourself, Perry. Here's the only heir to the Balfour fortune charged with a murder rap which was dressed up to look like a hit-and-run accident. What would you do if you were a city editor?"

"Okay," Mason said wearily. "Get your men working. I'm on my way to the office."

CHAPTER TEN

Mason hurried to his office and started mapping out a plan of campaign before he had even hung up his hat.

"Paul," he said to the detective, "I want to find out everything I can about Jackson Eagan."

"Who doesn't?" Drake said. "If they'd been on the job, police would have spotted this as murder right at the start. I've seen photographs of the body, Perry. You don't smash up a man's head like that in a hit and run. That man had been tied to a car somehow and his face had literally been dragged over the road. His head was then smashed in with a sledge hammer or something. It was done so the authorities would never think to look for a bullet.

"It worked, too. They thought the guy had been hit, his head dashed to the pavement and then his clothes had caught on the front bumper and he'd been dragged for a while."

"Couldn't it have been that way?" Mason asked.

"Not with the bullet in the guy's brain," Drake said.

"All right," Mason told him, "let's use our heads. The police are concentrating on Ted Balfour. They're trying to get admissions from him. They're trying to check what he was doing on the night of the nineteenth of September. They'll be putting all sorts of pressure on him to make him disclose the identity of the girl whom he remembers as having driven the car.

"There's just a chance that by using our heads we may have just a few minutes' head start on the police on some of these other angles that they won't think of at the moment.

"Now, these car rental agencies won't rent a car unless they see a driver's license, and they usually make a note on the contract of the number of the driver's license. Have operatives cover the car rental agency, take a look at the contract covering the Jackson Eagan car on that date. See if we can get the number of the driver's license from the contract.

"There's a chance we can beat the police to it in another direction. The police won't be able to get in the Balfour house until they get a search warrant or permission from Ted Balfour. Quite frequently you can tell a lot by going through a man's room. They'll be searching his clothes for bloodstains. They'll be looking for a revolver. They'll be doing all of the usual things within a matter of minutes, if they aren't doing it already.

"Della, get Mrs. Guthrie Balfour on the phone for me. Paul, get your men started covering all these other angles."

Drake nodded, said, "I'll go down to my office, so I won't be tying up your telephone system, Perry. I'll have men on the job within a matter of seconds."

"Get going," Mason said.

In the meantime, Della Street's busy fingers had been whirring the dial of the unlisted telephone which was used in times of emergency to get quick connections. A moment later she nodded to Perry Mason and said, "I have Mrs. Balfour on the line."

Mason's voice showed relief. "That's a break," he said. "I was afraid she might be out."

Mason picked up the telephone, said, "Hello, Mrs. Balfour."

"Yes, Mr. Mason, what is it?"

"There have been some very important and very disturbing developments in the matter which you discussed with me."

"There have?" she asked, apprehension in her voice.

"That's right."

"You mean...you mean that the matter has been—Why I thought—"

"It doesn't have anything to do with that matter, but a development from it," Mason said. "The police are now investigating a murder."

"A murder!"

"That's right. I don't want to discuss it on the phone."

"How can I see you?"

Mason said, "Wait there. Don't go out under any circumstances. I'm coming over as soon as I can get there."

Mason slammed up the telephone, said to Della Street, "Come on, Della. Bring a notebook and some pencils. Let's go!"

Mason's long legs striding rapidly down the corridor forced Della Street into a half run in order to keep up. They descended in the elevator, hurried over to Mason's car in the parking lot, and swung into traffic.

"Do you know the way?" Della Street asked.

"Fortunately I do," Mason said. "We go out the State Highway. The scene of the accident was only about a mile from the Balfour estate, and maps were introduced in the case yesterday. You see, the prosecution was trying to prove that Ted Balfour would normally have used this route along Sycamore Street to the State Highway, then turned up State Highway until he came to the next intersection, which would have been the best way to the Balfour estate."

"If there was a murder," Della Street said, "how can they prove that Ted Balfour was in on it?"

"That's what they're *trying* to do right now," Mason said. "They have a pretty good case of circumstantial evidence, indicating that Balfour's *car* was mixed up in it, but they can't prove Balfour was mixed up in it, at least, not from any evidence they had yesterday."

"So what happens?"

"So," Mason said, "*we* try to find and appraise evidence before the police think to look for it."

"Isn't it illegal to tamper with evidence in a case of this sort?"

"We're not going to tamper with evidence," Mason said. "We're going to *look* at it. Once the police get hold of it, they'll put it away and we won't be able to find out anything until we get to court. But if we get a look at it first, we'll know generally what we're up against."

"You think some evidence may be out there?" Della Street asked.

"I don't know," Mason told her. "I hope not. Let's look at it this way, Della: the man was shot. The body was mutilated to conceal the gunshot wound and prevent identification. Then it was taken out and placed by the side of the road. They waited for the tipsy driver to come along and then they threw the body out in front of the car."

"Why do you say 'they'?" Della Street asked.

"Because one man wouldn't be juggling a body around like that."

"Then Ted Balfour may have simply been the means to an end?"

"Exactly."

"But how did they know that a tipsy driver *would* be coming along that road?"

"That's the point," Mason said. "Somebody loaded Balfour's drink. He probably wasn't only intoxicated; he was doped."

"Then how do you account for his testimony that a girl was driving the car?" Della Street asked.

"That was probably a coincidence. It *may* not be the truth."

"That was Ted's story," Della Street said.

"Exactly. Myrtle Anne Haley swore that she was following a car that was weaving all over the road. The prosecutor didn't ask her who was driving the car, whether it was a man or a woman, whether there was one person in the driver's seat, or whether there were two."

"And all those head injuries," Della Street asked, "were simply for the purpose of preventing the corpse from being identified?"

"Probably for the primary purpose of concealing the fact that there was a bullet hole in the head."

"Would Ted Balfour have been mixed up in anything like that?"

"He could have been. We don't know. We don't know the true situation. Myrtle Haley is lying at least about some things. But that doesn't mean *all* of her testimony is false. I think she wrote down that license number sometime after she got home. I think she wrote it down in good light and while she was seated at a table. But her testimony may well be true that she was following a car which was weaving all over the road."

"Then Ted must have been driving it?"

"Don't overlook one other possibility," Mason said. "Ted may have been sent home and put to bed in an intoxicated condition, and then someone took the automobile out of the garage, started weaving all over the road as though driving in an intoxicated condition, waited until he was certain some car behind him would spot him and probably get the license number, then the dead body of Jackson Eagan was thrown in front of the automobile."

"But why?" Della Street asked.

"That," Mason said, "is what we're going to try to find out."

On two occasions after that Della Street started to say something, but each time, glancing up at the lawyer's face, she saw the expression of extreme concentration which she knew so well, and remained silent.

Mason slowed at the intersection, turned from State Highway, ran for about two hundred yards over a surfaced road, and turned to the right between huge stone pillars marking the driveway entrance in a stucco wall which enclosed the front part of the Balfour estate.

The tires crunched along the graveled driveway, and almost as soon as Mason had brought his car to a stop, the front door was thrown open by Mrs. Guthrie Balfour.

Mason, followed by Della Street, hurried up the steps.

"What is it?" she asked.

"Have the police been here yet?" Mason asked.

"Heavens, no!"

"They're coming," Mason said. "We're fighting minutes. Let's take a look in Ted's room."

"But why, Mr. Mason?"

"Do you know a Jackson Eagan?"

"Jackson Eagan," she repeated. "No, I don't believe so."

"Ever hear of him?" Mason asked.

She shook her head, leading the way up a flight of steps. "No," she said over her shoulder, "I'm quite certain I haven't heard of any Jackson Eagan. Why?"

"Jackson Eagan," Mason said, "is the corpse. He registered at the Sleepy Hollow Motel. He was murdered."

"How?"

"A bullet in the head."

"Are they certain?"

"The bullet was still there when the body was exhumed."

"Oh," she said shortly.

She fairly flew up the wide oaken staircase, then hurried down a wide corridor and flung open the door of a spacious corner bedroom. "This is Ted's room," she said.

Mason regarded the framed pictures on the wall—some of them Army pictures, some of them college pictures, a couple of gaudy pin-ups. There were pictures of girls fastened to the sides of the big mirror.

In one corner of the room was a gun cabinet with glass doors. Another locker contained an assortment of golf clubs and two tennis rackets in presses.

Mason tried the door of the gun cabinet. It was locked.

"Got a key to this?" he asked her.

She shook her head. "I don't know much about this room, Mr. Mason. If it's locked, Ted would have the only key."

Mason studied the lock for a moment, then opened his penknife and started pushing with the point against the latch of a spring lock, biting the point of the knife into the brass, and moving the lock back as far as he could.

"I've got to have something to hold this lock," he said after a moment.

"How about a nail file?" Della Street asked, producing a nail file from her purse.

"That should do it," Mason said.

He continued prying the latch back with his knife, holding it in position with the point of the nail file until he could get another purchase on the lock with the knife point. After a few moments the latch clicked back and the door swung open.

Mason hurriedly inspected the small-caliber rifles, paying no attention to the shotguns or the high-powered rifles.

"Well?" she asked, as Mason smelled the barrels.

"None of them seems to have been freshly fired," Mason said. "Of course, they could have been cleaned."

He opened a drawer in the cabinet, disclosing half a dozen revolvers. He pounced on a .22 automatic, smelled the end of the barrel thoughtfully.

"Well?" Mrs. Balfour asked.

Mason said, "This could be it."

He replaced the .22, pushed the drawer shut, closed the glass doors of the cabinet. The spring lock latched into place.

Mason opened the door to the tile bathroom, looked inside, opened the door of the medicine cabinet, opened the door of the closet, and regarded the long array of suits.

"There had been a going-away party in honor of your husband and you the night of September nineteenth?" Mason asked.

She nodded.

"That's when Ted Balfour got—"

"Became indisposed," she interrupted firmly.

"Became indisposed," Mason said. "Do you know what clothes he was wearing that night?"

She shook her head. "I can't remember."

"Was it informal or black tie?"

"No, it was informal. You see, my husband was leaving on a train for Mexico."

"You accompanied him?"

"Yes. He had intended to go alone and have me ride with him only as far as the Pasadena-Alhambra station. But at the last minute he changed his mind and asked me to go all the way. I didn't have a thing to wear. I . . . well, I was a little put out."

Della Street said, "Good heavens! I can imagine you would be annoyed, starting out without . . . You mean, you didn't have a *thing?*"

"Not even a toothbrush," she said. "I had a compact in my handbag and fortunately I had a very small tube of cream that I use to keep my skin soft when the weather is hot and dry. Aside from that, I just had the clothes I was standing in. Of course, it wasn't too bad. I was able to pick up an outfit at El Paso, and then I got some more clothes at Chihuahua.

"My husband is an ardent enthusiast when it comes to his particular hobby. He had received some information on new discoveries to be made in the Tarahumare country in Mexico. Those Tarahumare Indians are very primitive and they live in a wild country, a region of so-called barrancas, which are like our Grand Canyon, only there are hundreds and hundreds of miles of canyon—"

"What's this?" Mason asked, pouncing on a heavy, square package at the far end of the closet.

"Heavens! I don't know. It looks like some kind of an instrument."

"It's a tape recorder," Mason said, "and here's something else that apparently goes with it. Does Ted go in for Hi-fi?"

She shook her head. "Not unless it something new with him. He's not much on music. He goes in more and more for outdoor sports. He wanted to go with my husband on this trip, and Guthrie almost decided to take him, but because of Addison's condition and because my husband felt that Addison wouldn't like having Ted go on the expedition, it was decided Ted should remain here. I now wish to heaven we'd taken him!"

"Ted didn't like the decision?"

"He was very disappointed, Mr. Mason."

"All right," Mason said. "Let's be brutally frank. Do you have an alibi for the night of the nineteenth?"

"Heavens, yes, the best in the world. I was on the train with my husband."

"Well," Mason said, "you may be asked—"

He broke off as chimes sounded through the house.

Mason said, "That may be the police. Are there back stairs?"

She nodded.

Mason said, "We'll go down the back way. Della, you get my car, drive it around to the garage. I'll get in the car in the garage. Don't tell the officers anything about the stuff I've taken, Mrs. Balfour. You'd better go and talk with them yourself."

Mrs. Balfour flashed him a smile. "We have the utmost confidence in you, Mr. Mason. The whole family does." She glided out of the room.

"Still using her hips," Della Street said.

"Never mind that," Mason told her. "Grab that other package. I'll take this."

"Chief, are we supposed to do this?"

"It depends on how you look at it," Mason told her. "Come on. Let's get down the back stairs. I'll walk over to the garage. Della, you walk around the front of the house very innocently and very leisurely. If there's an officer sitting in the car out in front, flash him a smile. If the car is empty, as I hope will be the case, you can be in a little more of a hurry than you would otherwise. Drive back to the garage, pick me up and we'll get out of here."

Mason carried the heavy tape recorder down the back stairs. Della Street carried the smaller package.

They made an exit through the kitchen, down the steps of the service porch. Mason hurried out toward the garage. Della Street swung to the left around the house, her feet crunching gravel as she walked with a quick, brisk step.

"More casually," Mason cautioned.

She nodded and slowed down.

Mason turned toward the garage, entered and waited until he saw the car, with Della Street at the wheel, come sweeping around the driveway.

"Police?" Mason asked.

She nodded. "It's a police car. Red spotlight. Intercommunicating system and—"

"Anyone in it?"

"No."

Mason grinned. "That's a break."

He opened the rear door of the car, put the tape recorder and the other square package on the back floor, slammed the door shut, jumped in beside Della and said, "Let's go!"

Della Street swung the car in a swift circle, poured gas into the motor as she swept down the curving driveway.

"Okay," Mason cautioned. "Take it easier now as we come out on this road. Don't try to make a left turn. We may run into more police cars. Turn right and then make another right turn a mile or so down here. That'll be Chestnut Street and that will bring us to Sycamore Road. We can get back on that."

Della made a right turn as she left the driveway.

Perry Mason, looking back through the rear window of the car, suddenly whirled his head, settled down in the seat.

"Something?" Della Street asked.

"Two police cars just turning in from the State Highway," Mason said. "Apparently we made it in the nick of time."

CHAPTER ELEVEN

Back in his office Mason found a jubilant Paul Drake.

"We're ahead of the police all the way, Perry."

"How come?"

"That car Jackson Eagan rented," Drake said, "there was a driver's license number on the records."

"What was it?"

"License number Z490553," Drake said.

"Able to trace it?"

"There again we had success. I got in touch with my correspondent in Sacramento. He rushed a man down to the motor vehicle department. That is the number of a driver's license issued to Jackson Eagan, who lives in Chico, a city about two hundred miles north of San Francisco in the Sacramento Valley."

"You have the address?"

"I have the address," Drake said. "I have the guy's physical description from the driver's license and our correspondent in Chico is checking on Jackson Eagan right now."

"What's the description?" Mason asked.

Drake read off his notes: "Male, age 35, height 5'10", weight 175 pounds, hair dark, eyes blue."

"That helps," Mason said. "Now tell me, Paul, what the devil is this?"

Mason removed the cover from the tape recorder.

"That's a darn good grade of a high-fidelity tape recorder," Drake said. "It has variable speeds. It will work at one and seven-eighths inches a second, or at three and three-quarter inches a second. At one and seven-eighths inches a second it will run for three hours on one side of a spool of long-playing tape."

"You understand how this particular model works?" Mason asked.

"Perfectly. We use them in our work right along. This is a high-grade model."

"All right," Mason said, "let's see what's recorded on this tape."

"It's the latest long-playing tape," Drake said, plugging in the machine. "You get an hour on one of these spools at three and three-quarter inches to the second, or an hour and a half if you use the long-playing tape. At one and seven-eighths inches per second you get three hours on one side of the tape."

"What's the reason for the difference in speed?" Mason asked.

"Simply a question of fidelity. You use seven and a half inches for music, three and three-quarter inches for the human voice where you want fidelity, but you can get a very satisfactory recording at one and seven-eighths."

"Okay," Mason said. "Let's see what's on the tape."

"I guess the machine's warmed up enough now," Drake said.

He threw a switch.

The spool of tape began to revolve slowly, the tape being taken up on the other spool, feeding through the listening head on the machine.

"Seems to be nothing," Drake said after a moment.

"Keep on," Mason said. "Let's be certain."

They sat watching the tape slowly move through the head of the machine for some three of four minutes.

Drake shook head. "Nothing on it, Perry."

Mason regarded the machine in frowning contemplation.

"Of course," Drake said, "there might be something on the other side. This is a half-track recording. You record on one side of the tape, then reverse the spools and record on the other half of the tape. That is, the recording track is divided into two segments and—"

"Reverse it," Mason said. "Let's see if there's something on the other track."

Drake stopped the machine, reversed the spool. Again the tape fed through the head of the machine, again there was nothing until suddenly a woman's voice coming from the machine said, "...fed up with the whole thing myself. You can stand only so much of this gilded—" There followed complete silence.

Drake manipulated the controls on the machine. There was no further sound.

"Well?" Mason asked.

Drake shook his head. "I don't get it."

"Let's take a look at this other box," Mason said. "What's that?"

Drake opened the box. His eyes suddenly glistened with appreciation. "This," he said, "is *really* something."

"All right, what is it?"

"A wall snooper," Drake said.

"What's that, Paul?"

"A very sensitive mike with an electric boosting device. You fasten it to a wall and sounds of conversation in the next room that you can't even hear come in on this mike, are amplified and go on the tape. Then you can plug in earphones, and as the tape goes through a second head, you can hear what's been recorded.

"That's the reason for what we heard on the tape, Perry. The device had been used for a snooping job, then the tape had been fed through the erasing head. They quit erasing on the last few inches of the second half-track and a few words were left."

Mason thought that over. "Why would Ted Balfour have been doing a snooping job, Paul?"

"Perhaps a gag," Drake said. "Perhaps a girl friend. It could be any one of a hundred things, Perry."

Mason nodded. "It could even be that he was checking up on his uncle's new model wife," he said.

"And the job wound up in murder?" Drake asked.

"Or the job wound up by his having a murder wished on him," Mason observed.

Knuckles tapped on the exit door of Mason's private office.

"That's my secretary," Drake said, listening to the rhythm of the code knock.

Della Street opened the door.

"Please give this to Mr. Drake," the secretary said, handing Della a sheet of paper on which there was a typewritten message.

Della Street handed it across to Paul Drake.

"Well, I'll be damned," Drake said.

"What is it?" Mason asked.

"Telegram from my correspondent in Chico. Listen to this:

"JACKSON EAGAN WELL-KNOWN TRAVEL WRITER RESIDING THIS CITY. MOVED AWAY. HAD TROUBLE TRACING, BUT FINALLY FOUND RESIDED BRIEFLY AT MERCED THEN WENT TO YUCATAN,

WHERE HE DIED TWO YEARS AGO. BODY SHIPPED HOME FOR BURIAL. CLOSED COFFIN. WIRE INSTRUCTIONS.'"

Drake ran his fingers through his hair. "Well, Perry, now we've had everything. Here's a case where the corpse died twice."

Mason nodded to Della Street. "Get out blanks for a petition for habeas corpus," he said. "We're going to file a habeas corpus for Ted Balfour. I have a hunch that it's up to me to work out a legal gambit which will keep the real facts in this case from ever being brought out."

"How the hell are you going to do that?" Drake asked.

Mason grinned. "There's a chance, Paul."

"One chance in a million," Drake said.

"Make it one in five," Mason told him. "And let's hope it works, Paul, because I have a feeling that the true facts in this case are so loaded with explosive they could touch off a chain reaction."

CHAPTER TWELVE

Judge Cadwell assumed his seat on the bench, glanced down at the courtroom and said, "Now, this is on habeas corpus in the case of Theodore Balfour. A petition was filed, a writ of habeas corpus issued, and this is the hearing on the habeas corpus. I assume that the writ was applied for in connection with the usual practice by which an attorney who is denied the right to communicate with a client applies for a writ of habeas corpus to force the hand of the prosecutor."

Roger Farris, the deputy district attorney, arose and said, "That is correct, Your Honor. We have now filed a complaint on the defendant, accusing him of the crime of murder of one Jackson Eagan, who was then and there a human being, the murder committed with premeditation and malice aforethought, making the crime first-degree murder.

"The prosecution has no objection to Mr. Perry Mason, as attorney for the defendant, interviewing the defendant at all seasonable and reasonable times."

"I take it then," Judge Cadwell said, glancing down at Perry Mason, "it may be stipulated that the writ can be vacated and the defendant remanded to the custody of the sheriff."

"No, Your Honor," Mason said.

"What?" Judge Cadwell rasped.

"No such stipulation," Mason said.

"Well, the Court will make that ruling anyway," Judge Cadwell snapped. "It would certainly seem that if this man is charged with murder—Now, wait a minute. The Court will not accept the statement of the prosecutor to that effect. You had better be sworn as a witness, Mr. Prosecutor, unless the facts appear in the return to the writ on file in this court."

"They do, Your Honor. The facts are undisputed. Even if they weren't, the Court could take judicial cognizance of its own records."

"Very well," Judge Cadwell said.

"May I be heard?" Mason asked.

"I don't see what you have to be heard about, Mr. Mason. You surely don't contend that where a petitioner has been formally charged with the crime of first-degree murder and has been duly booked on that crime that he is entitled to be released on habeas corpus, do you?"

"In this case, Your Honor, yes."

"What's the idea?" Judge Cadwell asked. "Are you being facetious with the Court, Mr. Mason?"

"No, Your Honor."

"Well, state your position."

"The Constitution," Mason said, "provides that no man shall be twice put in jeopardy for the same offense. Your Honor quite recently reviewed the evidence in the case of People versus Balfour and found him guilty of involuntary manslaughter."

"That was committed with an automobile," Judge Cadwell said. "As I understand it, this is an entirely different case."

"It may be an entirely different case," Mason said, "but the prosecution is barred because this man has already been tried and convicted of the crime of killing this same Jackson Eagan."

"Now just a minute," Judge Cadwell said as the prosecutor jumped to his feet. "Let me handle this, Mr. Prosecutor.

"Mr. Mason, do you contend that because the People mistakenly assumed that this was a hit-and-run case and prosecuted the defendant under such a charge, the People are now barred from prosecuting him for first-degree murder—a murder which, so far as the record in the present case discloses, was perpetrated with a lethal weapon? I take it that is a correct statement, is it not, Mr. Prosecutor?"

"It is, Your Honor," Roger Farris said. "It is our contention that Jackson Eagan was killed with a bullet which penetrated his brain and caused almost instant death. We may state that the evidence supporting our position is completely overwhelming. The bullet went into the head but did not emerge from the head. The bullet was found in the brain when the body was exhumed and that bullet has been compared by ballistics experts with a weapon found in the bedroom of Theodore Balfour, the defendant herein, a weapon which was the property of the defendant. The fatal bullet was discharged from that weapon.

"It was quite apparent what happened. An attempt was made to dispose of the victim by having it appear that the man had died as the result of a hit-and-run accident.

"We are perfectly willing, if Mr. Mason wishes, to move to dismiss the former charge of involuntary manslaughter against Mr. Balfour so that he can be prosecuted on a charge of first-degree murder."

"I don't request any such thing," Mason said. "The defendant has been tried, convicted, and sentenced for the death of Jackson Eagan."

"Now just a minute," Judge Cadwell said. "The Court is very much concerned with this point raised by Mr. Mason. The Court feels that point is without merit. A man who has been tried for involuntary manslaughter committed with a car cannot claim that such a prosecution is a bar to a prosecution for first-degree murder committed with a gun."

"Why not?" Mason asked.

"Why not!" Judge Cadwell shouted. "Because it's absurd. It's ridiculous on the face of it."

"Would the Court like to hear authorities?" Mason asked.

"The Court would very much like to hear authorities," Judge Cadwell said, "if you have any that bear upon any such case as this."

"Very well," Mason said. "The general rule is that where a person is indicted for murder, the charge includes manslaughter. In other words, if a man is charged with first-degree murder it is perfectly permissible for a jury to find him guilty of manslaughter."

"That is elemental," Judge Cadwell said. "You certainly don't need to cite authorities on any such elemental law point, Mr. Mason."

"I don't intend to," Mason said. "It therefore follows that if a man is tried for first-degree murder and is acquitted, he cannot subsequently be prosecuted for manslaughter involving the same victim."

"That also is elemental," Judge Cadwell said. "The Court doesn't want to waste its time or the time of counsel listening to any authorities on such elemental points."

"Then perhaps," Mason said, "Your Honor would be interested in the Case of People versus McDaniels, 137 Cal. 192 69 Pacific 1006 92 American State Reports 81 59 L.R.A. 578, in which it was held that while an acquittal for a higher offense is a bar to any prosecution for a lower offense necessarily contained in the charge, the converse is also true, and that conviction for a lower offense necessarily included in the higher is a bar to subsequent prosecution for the higher.

"The Court should also study the Case of People versus Krupa, 64 C.A. 2nd 592 149 Pacific 2nd 416, and the Case of People versus Tenner, 67 California Appelate 2nd 360 154 Pacific 2nd page 9, wherein it was held that while Penal Code Section 1023 in terms applies where the prosecution for the higher offense is first, the same rule applies where the prosecution for the lesser offense comes first.

"It was also held in the Case of People versus Ny Sam Chung, 94 Cal. 304 29 Pacific 642 28 American State Reports 129, that a prosecution for a minor offense is a bar to the same act subsequently charged as a higher crime."

Judge Cadwell regarded Mason with frowning contemplation for a moment, then turned to the prosecutor. "Are the people prepared on this point?" he asked.

Roger Farris shook his head. "Your Honor," he said, "I am not prepared upon this point because, frankly, it never occurred to me. If it had occurred to me, I would have instantly dismissed it from my mind as being too utterly absurd to warrant any serious consideration."

Judge Cadwell nodded. "The Court feels that the point must be without merit," he said. "Even if it has some merit, the Court would much rather commit error in deciding the case according to justice and the equities, rather than permit what might be a deliberate murder to be condoned because of a pure technicality."

"I would like to suggest to the Court," Mason said, "that it would be interesting to know the theory of the prosecution. Is it the theory of the prosecution that if the jury in this case should return a verdict of guilty of manslaughter, and the Court should sentence the defendant to prison, the prosecution could then file another charge of murder against the defendant and secure a second punishment?"

"Certainly not!" Farris snapped.

"If you had prosecuted this man for murder originally," Mason said, "and the jury had returned a verdict of not guilty, would it be your position that you could again prosecute him on a charge of involuntary manslaughter?"

"That would depend," Farris said, suddenly becoming cautious. "It would depend upon the facts."

"Exactly, Mason said, grinning. "Once a defendant has been placed on trial, jeopardy has attached. Once the defendant has been convicted and sentenced, he has paid the penalty demanded by law. If the prosecution, as a result of poor judgment, poor investigative work, or poor thinking, charges the man with a lesser offense than it subsequently thinks it might be able to prove, the prior case is nevertheless a bar to a prosecution for a higher offense at a later date."

Judge Cadwell said, "The Court is going to take a sixty-minute recess. The Court wants to look up some of these authorities. This is a most unusual situation, a most astounding situation. I may state that as soon as I heard the contention of the defendant, I felt that the absurdity of that contention was so great that it amounted to sheer legal frivolity. But now that I think the matter over and appreciate the force of the defendant's contention, it appears that there may well be merit to it.

"Looking at it from a broad standpoint, the defendant was charged with unlawful acts causing the death of Jackson Eagan. To be certain, those acts were of an entirely different nature from the acts now complained of, but they brought about the same result, to wit, the unlawful death of Jackson Eagan.

"The defendant was prosecuted on that charge and he was convicted. Is it possible, Mr. Prosecutor, that this whole situation was an elaborate setup by the defendant in order to escape the penalties of premeditated murder?"

"I don't know, Your Honor," Farris said. "I certainly wouldn't want to make a definite charge, but here is a situation where legal ingenuity of a high order seems to have been used to trap the prosecution into a most unusual situation. Looking back on the evidence in that hit-and-run case, it would seem almost a suspicious circumstance that the witness, Myrtle Anne Haley, so promptly and obligingly wrote down the license number of the car of the defendant, Ted Balfour.

"The situation is all the more significant when one remembers that the witness in question is employed by a subsidiary of the Balfour Allied Associates. Frankly, our office was amazed when she came forward as such a willing informant."

Judge Cadwell pursed his lips, looked down at Perry Mason thoughtfully. "There *is* some evidence here of legal ingenuity of a high order," he said. "However, present counsel did not try that hit-and-run case."

"But present counsel did sit in court after the case got under way," Farris pointed out. "He did not sit in the bar, but sat as a spectator—a very interested spectator."

Judge Cadwell looked once more at Perry Mason.

"I object to these innuendoes, Your Honor," Mason said. "If the prosecution can prove any such preconceived plan or conspiracy on the part of the defendant to mislead the authorities and bring about a trial for a lesser charge, the situation will be different; but it would have to amount to a fraud on the Court brought about with the connivance of the defendant, and there would have to be *proof* to establish that point."

"The Court will take a sixty-minute recess," Judge Cadwell said. "The Court wants to look into these things. This is a most unusual situation, a very unusual situation. The Court is very reluctant to think that any interpretation of the law could be such that a defense of once in jeopardy could, under circumstances such as these, prevent a prosecution for first-degree murder."

"And may the Court make an order that I be permitted to communicate with the defendant during the recess?" Mason asked. "The defendant was arrested and has been held incommunicado so far as any worthwhile communication with counsel, with family or friends is concerned."

"Very well," Judge Cadwell ruled. "The sheriff will take such precautions as he may see fit, but during the recess of the Court Mr. Mason will be permitted to communicate with his client as much as he may desire."

"I can put the defendant in the witness room," the deputy said, "and Mr. Mason can communicate with him there."

"Very well," Judge Cadwell said. "I don't care how you do it, but it must be a communication under such circumstances that the defendant can disclose any defense he may have to the charge and have an opportunity to receive confidential advice from his attorney. That means that no attempt should be made to audit the conversation in any manner.

"Court will take a recess for one hour."

Mason motioned to Ted Balfour. "Step this way, if you please, Mr. Balfour."

Roger Farris, his face showing his consternation, hurried to the law library in a panic of apprehension.

CHAPTER THIRTEEN

Balfour, a tall, wavy-haired young man who seemed ill at ease, seated himself across the table from Perry Mason. "Is there any chance you can get me out of this mess without my having to go on the witness stand?"

Mason nodded.

"That would be wonderful, Mr. Mason."

Mason studied the young man. He saw a big-boned, flat-waisted individual whose slow-speaking, almost lethargic manner seemed somehow to serve as a most effective mask behind which the real personality was concealed from the public gaze.

Mason said, "Suppose you tell me the truth about what happened on the night of September nineteenth and the early morning of September twentieth."

Balfour passed a hand over his forehead. "Lord, how I wish I knew!" he said.

"Start talking and tell me everything you do know," Mason said impatiently. "You're not dealing with the police now. I'm your lawyer and I have to know what we're up against."

Ted Balfour shifted his position. He cleared his throat, ran an awkward hand through his thick, wavy, dark hair.

"Go on," Mason snapped. "Quit stalling for time. Start talking!"

"Well," Ted Balfour said, "Uncle Guthrie was going to Mexico. He was going into the Tarahumare country. He's been down there before, sort of scratching the surface, as he expressed it. This time he wanted to get down in some of the barrancas that were so inaccessible that it was reasonable to suppose no other white man had ever been in there."

"Such country exists?"

"Down in that part of Mexico it does."

"All right. What happened?"

"Well, Dorla was going to ride as far as Pasadena with him, just to make sure that he got on the train and had his tickets and everything and that there were no last-minute instructions. She was to get off at the Alhambra-Pasadena station, but at the last minute Uncle Guthrie decided he wanted her with him and told her she'd better go along."

"How long has she been married to your uncle?"

"A little over two years."

"How long have you been home from the Army?"

"A little over four months."

"You have seen a good deal of her?"

"Well, naturally, we're all living in the same house."

"She's friendly?"

"Yes."

"At any time has she seemed to be overly friendly?"

"What do you mean by that?" Balfour asked, straightening up with a certain show of indignation.

"Figure it out," Mason told him. "It's a simple question, and any show of righteous indignation on your part will be a damn good indication to me that there's something wrong."

Ted Balfour seemed to wilt in the chair.

"Go on," Mason said, "answer the question. Was there any indication of overfriendliness?"

Balfour took a deep breath. "I don't know."

"What the hell do you mean, you don't know?" Mason blazed. "Come clean!"

"Uncle Guthrie and Uncle Addison wouldn't like your questions or your manner, if you don't mind my saying so, Mr. Mason."

"To hell with your uncles!" Mason said. "I'm trying to keep *you* from going to the gas chamber for first-degree murder. As your attorney, I have to know the facts. I want to know what I'm up against."

"The gas chamber!" Ted Balfour exclaimed.

"Sure. What did you think they did with murderers? Did you think they slapped their wrists or cut off their allowances for a month?"

"But I... I didn't do a thing. I don't know anything about this man, Jackson Eagan. I never met him. I surely didn't kill him or anyone else."

Mason's eyes bored into those of the young man. "Did Dorla become too friendly?"

Ted Balfour sighed. "Honest, Mr. Mason, I can't answer that question."

"What do you mean, you can't answer it?"

"Frankly, I don't know."

"Why don't you know?"

"Well, at times I'd think... well... it's hard to explain what I mean. She sometimes seems to sort of presume on the relationship, and I'd think she... and then again, it would be... It's something I just don't know."

"What did she do?"

"Well, she'd run in and out."

"Of your room?"

"Yes. It would be different if she were really my aunt. But she's not related at all, and...well, there's not any way of really describing what I mean."

"You never tried to find out? You never made a pass?"

"Heavens, no! I always treated her just as an aunt, but she'd run in and out, and occasionally I'd see her—One night when Uncle Guthrie was away and she thought she heard a noise downstairs, she came to my room to ask me if I'd heard it. It was bright moonlight and she had on a thin, filmy nightgown...and she said she was frightened."

"What did you do?"

"I told her she was nervous and to go back to bed and lock her bedroom door. I said even if someone were downstairs he couldn't bother her if she kept her door bolted, and all the stuff was insured."

"Did your uncle ever get jealous?"

"Of me?"

"Yes."

"Heavens, no!"

"Is he happy?"

"I've never asked him. He's never confided in me. He's pretty much occupied with his hobby."

"Look here," Mason said. "Was your uncle *ever* jealous of anyone?"

"Not that I know. He kept his feelings pretty much to himself."

"Did he ever ask you to check on Dorla in any way?"

"Gosh, no! He wouldn't have done that."

"Suppose he had been jealous. Suppose he thought she was two-timing him?"

"That would be different."

"All right," Mason said. "You have a tape recording machine with a special microphone that's built to flatten up against a wall. Why did you have that and who told you to get it?"

Ted Balfour looked at him blankly.

"Go on," Mason said. "Where did you get it?"

"I never got it, Mr. Mason. I don't have it."

"Don't be silly," Mason told him. "You have it. It was in your closet. I took it out. Now tell me, how did it get there?"

"Somebody must have put it there. It wasn't mine."

"You know I'm your lawyer?"

"Yes."

"And I'm trying to help you?"

"Yes."

"No matter what you've done, you tell me what it is and I'll do my best to help you. I'll see that you get the best deal you can get, no matter what it is. You understand that?"

"Yes, sir."

"But you mustn't lie to me."

"Yes, sir."

"All right. Have you been lying?"

"No, sir."

"You've told me the truth?"

"Yes, sir."

Mason said, "Let's go back to the night of the nineteenth. Now what happened?"

"My uncle was leaving for Mexico. Dorla was going with him as far as

Pasadena. Then Uncle Guthrie changed his mind at the last minute and took Dorla with him. He's funny that way. He has a restless mind. He'll be all enthused about something or some idea, and then he'll change. He'll have a car and like it first rate and then something will happen and he'll trade it in on a new model, usually of a different make."

"Would he feel that way about women?"

"I guess so, but Aunt Martha died, so he didn't have to trade anything in. I mean, Dorla was a new model. She appealed to him as soon as he saw her."

"I'll bet she did," Mason said.

Ted Balfour seemed apologetic. "I guess that after Aunt Martha died the family sort of expected Uncle Guthrie would marry Florence Ingle. She's a mighty fine woman and they've been friends. But Dorla came along and ... well, that's the way it was."

"You don't call her 'Aunt Dorla'?"

"No."

"Why?"

"She doesn't want me to. She says it makes her seem ... she used a funny word."

"What was it?"

"De-sexified."

"So at the last minute and because of something that may have happened on the train, your uncle decided he wouldn't let her stay behind in the same house with you?"

"Oh, it wasn't that! He just decided to take her with him."

"And she didn't have any clothes with her?"

"No, sir. She purchased things in El Paso."

"Did you go to the station to see your uncle and Dorla off?"

"Yes, sir."

"Who else went?"

"Three or four of his intimate friends."

"How about Marilyn Keith, Addison Balfour's secretary, was she there?"

"She showed up at the last minute with a message Uncle Addison asked her to deliver. She wasn't there to see him off exactly, but to give him the message."

"Then what happened?"

"Well, there'd been something of a going-away party before."

"Where was this party held?"

"At Florence Ingle's place."

"Is she interested in archeology?"

"I guess so. She's interested in things my uncle is interested in."

"She knew your uncle for some time before he married Dorla?"

"Oh, yes."

"And your uncle's close friends felt he might marry this Florence Ingle?"

"That's what I've heard."

"How does Florence like Dorla?"

"All right, I guess. She's always very sweet to her."

"Ted, look at me. Look me in the eyes. Now tell me, how does she like Dorla?"

Ted took a deep breath. "She hates Dorla's guts."

"That's better. Now, Florence Ingle gave this party?"

"Yes."

"And you put your uncle and Dorla aboard the train; that is, some of you did?"

"Yes."

"You left the party to do that?"

"Yes."

"Where did they take the train?"

"At the Arcade station."

"And then you went back to the party?"

"Yes."

"Dorla was to get off the train at the Alhambra-Pasadena station?"

"Yes, sir."

"And how was she to get back?"

"By taxicab. She was to go back to the house...you know, her house."

"You went back to the Florence Ingle party?"

"Yes."

"Now, did Marilyn Keith go back there?"

"Yes, she did. Mrs. Ingle invited her to come along, and she did."

"Did you talk with her?"

"Mrs. Ingle?"

"No, Marilyn Keith."

"Some...not much. She's a very sweet girl and very intelligent."

"All this was after dinner?"

"Yes, sir."

"About what time was it when you got back there?"

"I'd say about...oh, I don't know. I guess it was around eight-thirty or nine o'clock when we got back to Florence Ingle's house."

"And how late did you stay?"

"I remember there was some dancing and a little talk and the party began to break up pretty early."

"How many people were there?"

"Not too many. Around eighteen or twenty, I guess."

"And you were not driving your sports car?"

"No, I was driving the big car."

"Why?"

"Because I was taking Uncle to the train and his baggage was in the car."

"All right. What happened after you went back to the party?"

"I had two or three drinks, not many. But along about ten o'clock I had a Scotch and soda, and I think that almost immediately after I drank that I knew something was wrong with me."

"In what way?"

"I began to see double and...well, I was sick."

"What did you do?"

"I wanted to get out in the open air. I went out and sat in the car for a while and then I don't know...the next thing I knew I came to in the car. I haven't told anyone else, but Marilyn Keith was driving."

"Did you talk with her?"

"I asked her what had happened, and she told me to keep quiet and I'd be all right."

"Then what?"

"I remember being terribly weak. I put my head over on her shoulder and passed out."

"Then what?"

"The next thing I knew I was in bed. It was four thirty-five."

"You looked at your watch?"

"Yes."

"Were you undressed?"

"Yes."

"In pajamas?"

"Yes."

"Do you remember undressing?"

"No."

"Did you go out again after Marilyn Keith took you home?"

"Mr. Mason, I wish I knew. I haven't told anybody else this, but I just don't know. I must have."

"Why do you say you must have?"

"Because I had the key to the car."

"What do you mean?"

"It was in my trousers pocket."

"Isn't that where you usually keep it?"

"That's where *I* usually keep the key to my car. Whenever I run the car in, I take the key out and put it in my trousers pocket; but I don't think Marilyn Keith would have put it there."

"You don't leave the cars with keys in them in the garage?"

"No. Everyone in the family has his own key to each of the cars."

"How well do you know Marilyn Keith?"

"I've seen her a few times in my uncle's office. That's all."

"Ever been out with her?"

"No."

"Do you like her?"

"I do now. I'd never noticed her very much before. She's Uncle Addison's secretary. She'd always smile at me and tell me to go right in whenever I went up to visit Uncle Addison. I never noticed her as a woman or thought about her in that way. Then at the party I got talking with her socially and I realized she was really beautiful. Later on, when I got sick...I can't describe it, Mr. Mason. Something happened. I was leaning on her—I must have been an awful nuisance—and she was so sweet about it, so competent, so considerate. She was sweet."

"She put you to bed?"

"She took me up to my room."

"You suddenly realized you liked her?"

"Yes."

"A little more about Florence Ingle—was she married when your uncle first knew her?"

"Yes."

"What happened to her husband?"

"He was killed."

"Where?"

"In a plane crash."

"A transport plane?"

"No, a private plane. He was doing some kind of prospecting."

"So Mrs. Ingle became a widow, and how long was that before your aunt died?"

"Oh, six months or so, I guess."

"And after that Florence Ingle resumed her friendship with your uncle?"

"Yes."

"Then Dorla came along and whisked your uncle right out from under Mrs. Ingle's nose?"

"I guess so. I wouldn't want to say."

"Is there anything else that you think I should know?"

"Just one thing."

"What?"

"The speedometer on the big car."

"What about it?"

"There was too much mileage on it."

"When?"

"The next morning."

"Why did you notice that?"

"Because I noticed the mileage when we were at the station. The car had to be serviced and I was going to get it serviced. It had turned up an even ten thousand miles as I was driving to the station, and my uncle remarked about it and said that I was to get it serviced. There shouldn't have been over another twenty or twenty-five miles on it at the most."

"But there was more on it?"

"I'll say there was."

"How much more?"

"As nearly as I could work it out, about twenty-five miles too much."

"Did you tell anyone about this?"

"No, sir."

"Did you tell Howland about it?"

"No, sir."

"Tell Howland about any of this stuff we've been discussing?"

"No, sir. Howland told me that he didn't want me to tell him anything until he asked me. He said that he liked to fight his cases by picking flaws in the prosecution's case, that if it came to a showdown, where he had to put me on the witness stand, he'd ask me some questions, but he didn't want to know the answers until that became necessary."

"So you didn't tell him anything?"

"No, sir. I told him I hadn't hit anyone with the car, and that's all."

"But because you had the key in the pocket of your clothes, and because there was that extra mileage on the car, you think it was taken out again?"

"Yes sir, because the key was in my *trousers* pocket."

"But how do you know Marilyn Keith drove you straight home? How do you know that she didn't go out somewhere with you in the car and try to wait until you got sobered up somewhat before she took you home, then decided it was no use and drove you back?"

"I don't know, of course."

"All right," Mason said. "You've given me the information I want. Now sit tight."

"What's going to happen, Mr. Mason? Is the judge going to turn me loose?"

"I don't think so."

"Mr. Mason, do you think I...do you think I *could* have killed that man? Could have killed anyone?"

"I don't know," Mason said. "Someone got a gun out of your cabinet, killed a man, put in fresh shells, and replaced the gun."

Ted Balfour said, "I can't understand it. I...I *hope* I didn't go out again."

"If you had, you certainly wouldn't have taken the gun."

The young man's silence caught Mason's attention.

"Would you?" he snapped?"

"I don't know."

"What about that gun?" Mason said. "Did you have it with you?"

"It was in the glove compartment of the car."

"The hell it was!"

Balfour nodded.

"Now you tell me *why* you had that gun in the glove compartment," Mason said.

"I was afraid."

"Of what?"

"I'd been doing some gambling...cards. I got in too deep. I was in debt. I'd been threatened. They were going to send a collector. You know what that is, Mr. Mason...when the boys send a collector. The first time he just beats you up. After that...well, you have to pay."

Mason regarded the young man with eyes that showed sheer exasperation. "Why the hell didn't you tell me about this before?"

"I was ashamed."

"Did you tell the police about having the .22 in the car?"

Balfour shook his head.

"About the gambling?"

"No."

"Did you tell them about the mileage on the speedometer or about having the key to the car in your pocket?"

"No, sir, I didn't."

"When did you take the gun out of the glove compartment and put it back in the gun cabinet?"

"I don't know. I wish I did. That's another reason I feel certain I must have taken the car out again after Marilyn Keith took me home. Next morning, the gun was in the gun case in the drawer where it belongs. Marilyn certainly wouldn't have taken the gun out of the glove compartment. Even if she had, she wouldn't know where I keep it. It had been put right back in its regular place in the gun cabinet."

Mason frowned. "You could be in one hell of a fix on this case."

"I know."

"All right," Mason said. "Sit tight. Don't talk with anyone. Don't answer any questions the police may ask you. They probably won't try to get any more information out of you. If they do, refer them to me. Tell them I'm your lawyer and that you're not talking."

"And you don't think the judge will turn me loose on this technicality?"

Mason shook his head. "He's struggling between his concept of the law and his conscience. He won't turn you loose."

"Why did you raise the point?"

"To throw a scare into the prosecutor," Mason said. "They know now they have a monkey wrench in the machinery which may strip a few gears at any time. You're just going to have to stand up and take it from now on, Ted."

"I'll stand up and take it, Mr. Mason, but I sure would like to know what happened. I—Gosh! I can't believe that...well, I just *couldn't* have killed the man, that's all."

"Sit tight," Mason said. "Don't talk with newspaper reporters, don't talk with police, don't talk with anyone unless I'm present. I'll be seeing you."

Thirty minutes later Judge Cadwell returned to court and proceeded with the habeas corpus hearing.

"Surprisingly enough, this technical point seems to have some merit," the judge ruled. "It comes as a shock to the Court to think that a defendant could place himself behind such a barricade of legal technicality.

"However, regardless of the letter of the law, there are two points to be considered: I can't dismiss the possibility that this whole situation has been deliberately engineered so there will be a technical defense to a murder charge. The other point is that I feel a higher court should pass on this matter. If I grant the habeas corpus, the defendant will simply go free. If I hold the defendant for trial by denying the writ, the matter can be taken to a higher court on a plea of once in jeopardy.

"Since a plea of once in jeopardy will pesumably be made at the time of the trial of the case, it will be among the issues raised at that trial. This court does not intend to pass on the validity of such a plea of once in jeopardy at this time, except insofar as it applies to this writ of habeas corpus. The Court denies the habeas corpus. The prisoner is remanded to the custody of the sheriff."

Mason's face was expressionless as he left the courtroom. Paul Drake buttonholed him in the corridor.

"You wanted the dope on that tape recorder," Drake said. "I got the serial number, wired the manufacturer, the manufacturer gave me the name of the distributor, the distributor checked his records to the retailer. I finally got what we wanted."

"Okay," Mason said. "Who bought it?"

"A woman by the name of Florence Ingle living out in the Wilshire district. Does that name mean anything to you?"

"It means a lot," Mason said. "Where is Mrs. Ingle now?"

"I thought you'd ask that question," Drake said. "The answer gave us one hell of a job."

"Where is she?"

"She took a plane. Ostensibly she went on to Miami, then to Atlantic City, but the person who went on to Atlantic City wasn't Mrs. Ingle at all. She registered at hotels under the name of Florence Ingle, but it wasn't the same woman."

"Got a description?" Mason asked.

"Florence Ingle is about thirty-eight, well groomed, small-boned, good figure, rich, a good golfer, brunette, large dark eyes, five feet two, a hundred and seventeen pounds, very gracious, runs to diamond jewelry and is lonely in an aristocratic way. She's rather a tragic figure.

"The woman who impersonated Florence Ingle was something like her, but was heavier and didn't know her way around in the high-class places. She was tight-lipped, self-conscious, overdid everything trying to act the part of a wealthy woman. In the course of time she vanished absolutely and utterly, without leaving a trail. She left a lot of baggage in the hotel, but the bill was paid in full, so the hotel is storing the baggage."

"Never mind all the build-up," Mason said. "Did your men find out where Florence Ingle is now?"

"Yes. It was a hell of a job, Perry. I want you to understand that—"

"I know, I know," Mason said. "Where is she?"

"Staying at the Mission Inn at Riverside, California, under the name of Florence Landis, which was her maiden name. She's posing as a wealthy widow from the East."

"Now," Mason said, "we're beginning to get somewhere."

CHAPTER FOURTEEN

Perry Mason stood at the cigar counter for a few minutes. He lit a cigarette, sauntered across to the outdoor tables by the swimming pool, started toward the entrance of the hotel, thought better of it, stretched, yawned, walked back toward the pool, seated himself in a chair, stretched his long legs out in front of him, and crossed his ankles.

The attractive brunette in the sunsuit who was seated next to him flashed a surreptitious glance from behind her dark glasses at the granite-hard profile. For several seconds she appraised him, then looked away and regarded the swimmers at the pool.

"Would you prefer to talk here or in your room, Mrs. Ingle?" Mason asked in a conversational voice, without even turning to glance at her.

She jumped as though the chair had been wired to give her an electric shock, started to get up, then collapsed back in the chair. "My name," she said, "is Florence Landis."

"That's the name you registered under," Mason said. "It was your maiden name. Your real name is Florence Ingle. You're supposed to be on a vacation in Atlantic City. Do you want to talk here or in your room?"

"I have nothing to talk about."

"I think you have," Mason said. "I'm Perry Mason."

"What do you want to know?"

"I'm representing Ted Balfour. I want to know what you know and I want to know *all* you know."

"I know nothing that would help Ted."

"Then why the run-around?"

"Because, Mr. Mason, what I know would hurt your client. I don't want to do anything to hurt Ted. I'm trying to keep out of the way. Please, *please* don't press me! If you do, you'll be sorry."

Mason said, "I'm sorry, but I have to know what you know."

"I've warned you, Mr. Mason."

Mason said, "You can talk to me. You don't have to talk to the prosecution."

"What makes you think I know anything?"

"When a witness runs away I want to know what she's running from and why."

"All right," she said, "I'll tell you what it's all about. Ted Balfour killed that man and then tried to make it look like an automobile accident."

"What makes you think so?"

"Because Ted was in a jam. Ted had an allowance and he couldn't afford to exceed it. He got up against it for money and started playing for high stakes, and then he started plunging. He didn't have the money, but his credit was good and . . . well, it's the old story. His cards didn't come in and Ted was left in a terrific predicament.

"If either one of his uncles had known what he was doing, he would have been disinherited—at least Ted thought so. They had him pretty well scared. Personally, I'm convinced that while they might try to frighten the boy, they never would have gone so far as to disinherit him."

"Go on," Mason said. "I take it Ted came to you?"

"Ted came to me."

"What did he tell you?"

"He told me he had to have twenty thousand dollars. He told me that if he didn't get it, it was going to be just too bad."

"What made him think so?"

"He had a letter that he showed me."

"A letter from whom?"

"He knew who had written the letter, all right, but it was unsigned."

"Who had written it?"

"The syndicate."

"Go on," Mason said.

"The letter told him that they didn't like welchers. They said that if he didn't get the money, their collector would call."

"Twenty thousand dollars is a lot of money," Mason said.

"He never would have got in that deep if they hadn't played him for a sucker. They let him get in deeper than he could pay and then saw that he was dealt the second-best hands."

"And then when they had him hooked, they lowered the boom? Is that right?"

"That's right."

"Did you come through with the twenty thousand?"

"No, I didn't. I wish I had now. I thought Ted had to be taught a lesson. I felt that if he got the money from me, it wouldn't be any time at all until he'd start trying to get the money to pay me back by betting sure things. I felt it was time for Ted to grow up. Oh, Mr. Mason, if you only knew how I've regretted that decision!

"Ted was sick over the whole thing. He told me he had a .22 automatic in the glove compartment of his car and he intended to use it. He said that he wasn't going to be waylaid and beaten up and then simply tell the police he didn't have any idea who did it. He said that he was good for the money but that it would take him a while to get it together. There was a trust which had been left him by his parents and he thought he could explain the situation to the trustee, but the trustee was on vacation and he had to have a little more time."

"All right," Mason said, "what happened?"

"The dead man must have been the collector," she said. "Don't you see? Ted killed him and then tried to make it look as though the man had been killed in a hit-and-run accident."

Mason studied her thoughtfully for moment, then said, "You told that readily enough."

"It's the truth."

"I'm sure it is. I merely said, you told it to me readily enough."

"I had to. You've trapped me. I don't know how you found me here, but since you found me, I had to tell you what I know, no matter whom it hurts."

"All right," Mason said. "So far, so good. Now tell me the real reason you went to such pains to keep from being questioned."

"I've told you everything I know."

"What about the tape recorder?"

"What tape recorder?"

"The one you bought—the wall snooper."

"I don't know what you're talking about."

"Come on," Mason said. "Come clean!"

"Mr. Mason, you can't talk to me like that! You must think I'm someone whom you can push around. Your very manner is insulting. I am a truthful woman, and I am not a woman who is accustomed to being pushed around by—"

Mason reached in the inside pocket of his lightweight business suit, pulled out a folded paper, and dropped it in her lap.

"What's that?" she asked.

"Your copy of a subpoena in the case of People versus Balfour. Here's the original, with the signature of the clerk and the seal of the Court. Be there at the time of trial; otherwise be subject to proceedings in contempt of court."

Mason arose, said, "I'm sorry I had to do that, but you brought it on yourself, Mrs. Ingle. Good-by now."

Mason had taken two steps before her voice caught up with him. "Wait, wait, for heaven's sake, Mr. Mason, wait!"

Mason paused, looked back over his shoulder.

"I'll... I'll tell you the truth. You can't do this to me, Mr. Mason. You can't! You mustn't!"

"Mustn't do what?"

"Mustn't subpoena me in that case."

"Why?"

"Because if you put me on the stand I... it will... it will be terrible."

"Go ahead," Mason said. "Keep talking."

She stood looking at his stern features, her own face white and frightened. "I don't dare to," she said. "I simply don't dare tell anyone."

"Why not?"

"It's... it won't help you, Mr. Mason. It will... it will be terrible!"

"All right," Mason said, "you have your subpoena. Be there in court."

"But you can't put me on the stand. If I told about what Ted Balfour had asked me to do, if I told about his needing the money and the collector—"

"No one would believe you," Mason interrupted. "I've served a subpoena on you. You're trying to get out of circulation. That subpoena is going to smoke you out in the open. The only reason for it is that I want the true story. If you know something that's causing you to take all these precautions, I want to find out what it is."

She looked at him as though she might be about to faint, then, with difficulty composing herself, she said, "Come into the bar where we can talk without my making a spectacle of myself."

"You'll tell me the truth?" Mason asked.

She nodded.

"Let's go," Mason told her, leading the way to the bar.

"Well?" Mason said after the waiter had gone.

"Mr. Mason, I'm protecting someone."

"I was satisfied you were," Mason said.

"Someone whom I love."

"Guthrie Balfour?" Mason asked.

For a moment it appeared she would deny it. Then she tearfully nodded.

"All right," Mason said. "Let's have the truth this time."

"I'm not a good liar, Mr. Mason," she said. "I never had occasion to do much lying."

"I know," Mason said sympathetically.

She had taken off the dark glasses. The eyes that looked at the lawyer were circled with the weariness of sleepless nights and filled with dismay.

"Go on," Mason said. "What happened?"

She said, "Mr. Mason, that Dorla Balfour is a scheming, wicked woman who has almost a hypnotic influence over Guthrie Balfour. She's not his type at all. He's wasting himself on her, and yet somehow...well, somehow I wonder if she doesn't have some terrific hold on him, something that he can't escape."

"What makes you think so?" Mason asked.

"She's twisting him around her thumb."

"Go on."

"I'll tell you the real story, Mr. Mason, the whole story. Please listen and don't interrupt. It's a thoroughly incredible story and I'm not proud of my part in it, but...well, it will explain a lot of things."

"Go ahead," Mason said.

"Dorla Balfour was and is a little tramp. She was taking Guthrie for everything she could take him for, and, believe me, the minute Guthrie Balfour got out of town, she was getting herself in circulation without missing a minute."

Mason nodded.

"Guthrie had begun to wake up," she said. "He wanted a divorce, but he didn't want to get stuck for a lot of alimony. Dorla wouldn't mind a bit if he'd divorce her, but she has her grasping little hand out for a big slice of alimony. She'd go to the best lawyers in the country and she'd make herself just as much of a legal nuisance as is possible. She'd tie up Guthrie's property. She'd get restraining orders. She'd drag him into court on orders to show cause, and she'd...well, she'd raise the devil."

"Meaning that she'd drag your name into it?" Mason asked.

Mrs. Ingle lowered her eyes.

"Yes or no?" Mason asked.

"Yes," she said in a low voice. "Only there was nothing...nothing except sympathy."

"But you couldn't prove that?" Mason asked.

"She could make nasty insinuations and get notoriety for both of us."

"Okay," Mason said, "now we're doing better. Let's have the story."

"Well, Guthrie was leaving for Chihuahua City; that is, that's what he told her. Actually, he got on the train at Los Angeles and then left it at the Alhambra-Pasadena station."

"*He* left it?" Mason asked.

She nodded.

"Why, that's what Dorla was supposed to have done," Mason said.

"I know," she said. "That was all part of the plan he had worked out. When the train stopped at the Pasadena station, he kissed her good-by and got back aboard the train. The vestibule doors slammed and the train started out. Guthrie sent the porter back on an errand, opened the car door on the other side of the car, and swung to the ground as the train was gathering speed. By the time the train had gone on past, Dorla was in a taxicab."

"And Guthrie?" Mason asked.

"Guthrie jumped in a car he'd rented earlier in the day from a drive-yourself rental agency. He'd parked the car at the station. He followed Dorla."

"Then, when the train pulled out, neither Guthrie nor Dorla was aboard?"

"That's right."

"Go ahead. What happened then?"

"Guthrie followed Dorla. Oh, Mr. Mason, I'd pleaded with him not to do it. I asked him a dozen times to get some private detective agency on the job. That's their business. But Guthrie had to do this himself. I think he was so utterly fascinated by Dorla that he wouldn't believe anything against her unless he saw it with his own eyes.

"I think he knew the truth, but I think he knew himself well enough to feel she'd be able to talk him out of it unless he saw her himself and had the proof. He wanted proof without any outsiders for witnesses. That's why he asked me to get him that tape recorder. He wanted to record what was happening after she...well, you know, after she met the man."

"Go on," Mason said. "What did Dorla do?"

"Drove to the Sleepy Hollow Motel."

"So then what?"

"She met her boy friend there. They had a passionate reunion."

"Where was Guthrie?"

"He'd managed to get into the unit that adjoined the one where Dorla's boy friend was staying. He'd put the microphone up to the wall and he had a tape recording of the whole business."

"You were there with him?"

"Good heavens, no! That would have ruined everything he was trying to do."

"That's what I thought, but how do you know all this?"

"He phoned me."

"From Chihuahua?"

"No. Please let me tell it in my own way."

"Go ahead."

"After a while Dorla went out. She said she had to go home and let Ted know she was seeking her virtuous couch. She said that she'd pick up a suitcase and be back later on in the evening."

"Then what?"

"That's where Guthrie made the mistake of his life," she said. "He thought that he might be able to go into the motel next door, face this man who was registered under the name of Jackson Eagan and put it up to him cold turkey. He thought that this man might get frightened and sign a statement. It was a crazy thing to do."

"What happened?"

"This man, Eagan, was in a dimly lit motel bedroom. The minute Guthrie walked in Eagan snapped on a powerful flashlight and the beam hit Guthrie right in the face, completely blinding him. Eagan, on the other hand, could see his visitor. He obviously recognized Guthrie, felt certain the irate husband was about to invoke the unwritten law, and threw a chair. He followed it up by hitting the blinded Guthrie with everything he had.

"Guthrie tried to frighten this man by bringing out this gun of Ted's that he'd taken from the glove compartment of the car without Ted's knowing it.

"The two men started fighting for the gun. In the struggle the gun went off and Eagan fell to the floor. Guthrie knew from the way he hit the floor he was dead. And all at once Guthrie realized the full implications of the situation. He was afraid someone might have heard the shot and phoned for the police, so he jumped in his car and drove away fast."

"Then what?"

"Then," she said, "Guthrie had this idea. He realized that nobody, except me, knew that he had left the train. He called me from the telephone in his house. He told me everything that had happened. He said that he was going to take the company plane, fly to Phoenix and pick up the train there. He said he'd wire for Dorla to join him at Tucson, and in that way Dorla would have to give him an alibi. He asked me to take a commercial plane to Phoenix and fly his plane back. He said that he would leave a note with the attendant so that I could get the plane, and if I'd do that, well, no one would ever be the wiser."

"And so?" Mason asked.

"So I did that. I went down to Phoenix the next day. His plane was there and so was the note so that I could get it without any trouble. I flew it back, picked up his rented car where he'd left it at the hangar, and returned it to the rental agency."

"And Dorla joined him?"

"Dorla must have joined him. Only to hear her tell it, she never got off the train. I know that's a lie because I know from Guthrie what really happened. You can see the whole thing, Mr. Mason. He called on her to give him an alibi. He didn't tell her what happened. He didn't need to. When she got her suitcase and returned to the motel, she found her lover boy, Eagan, lying there dead.

"Now, under those circumstances, I know exactly what she'd have done, and it's just what she did. She telephoned for Banner Boles, the ace trouble shooter for Balfour Allied Associates. Boles realized at once that it would be better to have a drunk-driving charge against Ted and try to beat that rap than to have a murder charge against Guthrie. He's unbelievably resourceful and clever.

"So he fixed the whole deal up and Dorla flew to Tucson and picked up the train. Guthrie asked her to swear she'd been on the train all the time. That was right down her alley. Now she has a murder rap on him and she'll bleed him white. There won't be any divorce until she is all ready for it, with a new husband picked out, and she'll strip Balfour of everything he has left when she's ready to cut loose from him."

"That's all of it?" Mason asked.

"That's all of it," she said. "Now you see why I had to get out of circulation. It was all right for a while. It looked like a hit and run. Of course, Ted was mixed up in it, but everyone knew that Ted could get a suspended sentence if he was found guilty."

"And what did you hear from Guthrie after he went to Mexico?" Mason said.

"Only this," she said, fighting to keep her lips straight as she opened her handbag and took out a crumpled wire.

She passed the wire over to Mason. Mason unfolded the yellow paper and read:

"SAY NOTHING OF WHAT HAS HAPPENED. DORLA AND I HAVE REACHED FULL AGREEMENT AND BELIEVE EVERYTHING WILL COME OUT ALL RIGHT IN THE FUTURE.

GUTHRIE"

"That," Mason said, "was sent from Chihuahua City?"

She nodded.

"And since that time?"

"Since that time I haven't heard a word. Dorla has been with him, and heaven knows *what* she's done."

Mason said, "Would Guthrie Balfour sit back and see Ted convicted of murder?"

"No, of course not, not of murder. He'll come forward if he has to. After all, Mr. Mason, it *was* self-defense."

"He'd have a hell of a time proving that now."

"Well, now you know the facts. What are *you* going to do?"

"There's only one thing I can do," Mason said.

"What?"

"I'm representing Ted Balfour."

"You mean you'll blow the whole case wide open?"

"I'll blow the top clean off," Mason said, "if I have to."

She looked at him with angry eyes. "I played fair with you, Mr. Mason."

"I'm playing fair with my client," Mason told her. "That's the only fair play I know."

"Do you think I'm a complete, utter fool?" she asked. "You couldn't drag that story out of me on the witness stand no matter *what* you did. I told you so you'd know, so you'd understand what to do. Can't you understand? You're working for the Balfours. They're wealthy. You can have any amount you need as a fee, only fix this thing up so that ... well, work it out on a basis of legal technicalities so the facts never need to come out."

Mason got to his feet. "You already have my answer."

"What do you mean?" she asked.

"The paper you folded and put in your purse—your subpoena to appear as a witness on behalf of the defendant."

CHAPTER FIFTEEN

As Perry Mason entered the office, Della Street said, "We have troubles."

"What?" Mason asked.

"I don't know. But Addison Balfour telephoned."

"Personally?"

"Personally."

"And talked with you?"

"That's right."

"What did he want?"

"He said that this wasn't the simple case it seemed, that the whole Balfour empire was threatened, that he was going to leave it up to you to work out the best deal possible. He said his right-hand man, Banner Boles, would be in touch with you within a short time, that Boles knew his way around and knew how to handle things."

"And did he say what the trouble was?"

"No."

"Or what Banner Boles wanted to see me about?"

"No. It was just to tell you that there was trouble and Boles would be seeing you."

"Okay," Mason said, "I'll see him."

"How did you come out with Florence Ingle?"

"I had a nice talk with her," Mason said.

"You don't seem very happy about it."

"I'm not."

The phone rang. Della Street answered it, said, "Yes, just a moment, Mr. Boles; I'm quite certain he'll talk with you." She cupped her hand over the mouthpiece, nodded toward the telephone, and said to Perry Mason, "This is Banner Boles on the line now."

Mason picked up the extension phone on his desk, said, "Yes, hello. This is Perry Mason talking."

"Banner Boles, Mr. Mason," a hearty voice at the other end of the line said.

"How are you, Mr. Boles?"

"Did Addison Balfour telephone you about me?"

"I understand he talked with my office," Mason said. "I'm just getting in myself."

"Well, I want to see you."

"So I understand. Come on up."

There was a moment's silence at the other end of the line, then Boles said, "This is rather a delicate matter, Mr. Mason."

"All right, we'll talk it over."

"Not in your office, I'm afraid."

"Why not?" Mason asked.

"I don't go to any man's office with the sort of stuff we're going to talk about."

"Why not?"

"How do I know it isn't bugged?"

"By me?" Mason asked.

"By anybody."

"All right," Mason said. "Where *do* you want to talk?"

"On neutral grounds," Boles said laughingly, the good nature of his voice robbing the words of any offense. "Tell you what I'll do, Mr. Mason. I'll come up to your office. As soon as I come in, you leave with me. We'll go downstairs. We'll walk as long as you suggest. Then we'll stop and take the first taxicab that comes by. We'll talk in the taxi."

"All right," Mason said. "Have it your own way."

He hung up the telephone, said to Della Street, "One of those things."

"He's coming in?"

"Coming in," Mason said. "And wants to go out where we can talk in privacy."

"Chief, I'm afraid there's a chance they'll try to frame you if you don't do what they want in this thing. These people are big and they play for keeps."

"I've had the same thought," Mason said, pacing the floor.

"You learned something from that Ingle woman, didn't you?"

"Yes."

"What?"

"Let me think it over a while," Mason said, and continued pacing the floor. Abruptly he stopped, said to Della Street, "I want to know everything there is to know about Jackson Eagan."

"But he's dead."

"I know he's dead. But I want to know everything about him. All we have is the information from his driver's license and that telegram from Paul's contact. I want to know what he looked like, where he lived, who his friends were, how it happened he died, where the body's buried, who attended the funeral. I want to know everything."

"He died in Yucatan, Mexico," Della said.

Mason said, "I want Drake to find out who identified the body. I want to find out everything about the guy, and I want a copy of that driving license of Eagan's. I want to check his thumbprint on the driver's license with that of the dead man."

Della Street nodded, went over to the typewriter, typed out a list of the things Mason wanted. The lawyer continued to pace the floor.

Della said, "I'll take this down the corridor to Paul Drake personally."

"Have one of the girls take it down," Mason said. "I want you waiting here. When Boles comes in I want you to go out and size him up before I have a talk with him."

"Okay, I'll send one of the girls down right away." Della Street went out to the outer office and was back in a moment, saying, "I sent Gertie down to Drake's office. Your man, Boles, came in while I was out there in the outer office. I told him I'd tell you he was here."

"What does he look like?" Mason asked.

"He's rather tall...oh, perhaps an inch and a half or two inches under six feet. He's very good-looking, one of those profile guys who holds his chin up high. He has black, wavy hair and very intense blue eyes. He's well dressed and has an air of assurance. You can see he's quite a diplomat."

"Yes," Mason said, "a trouble shooter for the Balfour enterprises would have to be a smart cookie.

"Let's have a look at him, Della. Is he carrying a brief case?"

She shook her head.

"All right, tell him to come in."

Della Street went out and escorted Boles to the office. Boles came forward with a cordial smile, gripped Mason's hand in a hearty handshake, said, "I'm sorry to make a damned nuisance out of myself, Counselor, but you know how it is. Having the sort of job I do makes things rather difficult at times. Shall we take a walk?"

"Yes," Mason said, "we'll go out if you want, but I can assure you it's all right to talk here."

"No, no, let's take a walk."

"I see you're not carrying a brief case."

Boles threw back his head and laughed. You're a smart guy, Mason. I wouldn't pull anything as crude as that on you. I'll admit I have used a concealed tape recorder in a brief case, but I wouldn't try it with a man of your caliber. Moreover, when I play with men like you, I play fair. I wouldn't want you to try to record my conversation and I'll be damned if I'll try to record yours."

"Fair enough," Mason said. He turned to Della Street. "Della, I'll be back about...hang that watch! What time is it, Boles?"

Boles instantly shot out this hand, looked at his wrist watch, said, "Ten minutes to three."

"You're way off," Mason told him.

"No, I'm not. It's exactly ten minutes to three."

"Your watch says twelve-thirty," Mason told him.

Boles laughed. "You're wrong."

"Let's take a look," Mason observed.

"I tell you you're wrong," Boles said, suddenly losing his smile.

Mason said, "I either take a look at your wrist watch, or we don't talk."

"Oh, all right," Boles said, unstrapping the wrist watch, pulling loose two wires and dropping it in his pocket. "I should have know better than to try it."

"Any other microphones?" Mason asked. "How about behind your necktie?"

"Take a look," Boles invited.

Mason felt behind the necktie, patted the inside pocket of the coat, reached inside, pulled out the small, compact wire recorder, and said, "Let's take the battery out of this and then I'll feel better."

"We'll do better than that," Boles said. "*You* carry the thing in *your* pocket. I'll keep the microphone that's made to look like a wrist watch."

"All right," Mason told him. "Let's go."

They walked silently down the corridor to the elevator, rode down the elevator to the street.

"Which way do you want to go?" Boles asked.

"Suit yourself," Mason told him.

"No, you pick the direction."

"All right. We'll go up this street here."

They walked up the street for a couple of blocks. Abruptly Mason stopped. "All right," he said, "let's catch the first cab that comes along."

They waited for two or three minutes, then found a cruising cab, climbed inside, and settled back against the cushions.

"Where to?" the driver asked.

"Straight down the street," Mason told him, "then turn out of traffic some place. We're closing this window to your compartment because we want to talk."

"Any particular destination?" the cabdriver asked.

"No. Just drive around until we tell you to turn back."

"I'm going to keep out of the traffic jams then, if you don't mind."

"Okay by us," Mason told him.

The cabdriver pushed the sliding window into place, which shut off the back of the car.

Mason turned to Boles. "All right," he said, "let have it."

Boles said, "I'm the grease in the works of Balfour enterprises. That means I get in lots of tight spots."

Mason nodded.

"Guthrie Balfour telephoned. He wanted me to fly down and join him in Chihuahua."

Again Mason nodded.

"Now what I'm going to tell you," Boles said, "has to be absolutely confidential. You can't tell anyone anything about it."

"In talking to me," Mason said, "you are talking to a lawyer who is representing a client. I'll make no promises, bind myself to nothing."

"Remember this," Boles said ominously. "You're being paid by the Balfour enterprises."

"It doesn't make any difference who pays me," Mason said. "I'm representing a client."

Boles regarded him thoughtfully for a moment.

"Does that change the situation?" Mason asked.

"I'm going to tell you certain things," Boles said. "If you're smart, you'll play the game my way. If you try to play it any other way, you may get hurt."

"All right," Mason said. "What's the story?"

Boles said, "You're not to let Mrs. Guthrie Balfour know anything about this conversation."

"She isn't my client," Mason said, "but I make no promises."

"All right," Boles said, "here we go. You want to get some dope on Jackson Eagan, don't you?"

"I'm trying to, yes."

"Here you are," Boles said, reaching in his pocket. "Here's Jackson Eagan's driving license. Here's the carbon copy of the contract that he had with the drive-yourself car agency that rented him the automobile. Here's the receipt for the unit at the Sleepy Hollow Motel. Here's a wallet with some identification cards, some club cards and around two hundred and seventy-five dollars in currency. Here's a key ring containing a bunch of keys. Here's a very valuable wrist watch with a broken crystal. The watch isn't running. It is stopped at one thirty-two."

Boles took the collection from his pocket, handed it across to Mason.

"What about these?" Mason asked.

"Put them in your pocket," Boles said.

Mason hesitated a moment, then dropped the assortment into his pocket. "Where did they come from?" he asked.

"Where do you think?" Boles asked.

Mason flashed a quick glance at the cabdriver, saw the driver was paying no attention to anything except the traffic ahead, then turned to Boles. "I'm listening."

"Balfour Allied Associates is a big corporation," Boles said. "The stock, however, is held entirely by members of the family. On the other hand, the members of the family have virtually no property except that stock. It's the policy of the Balfour empire to throw everything into the corporation. The members of the family draw substantial salaries. In addition to that, all of their traveling expenses, a good part of their living expenses, and many incidentals are furnished by the company under one excuse or the other, such as entertainment of customers, office rental for homework on Saturdays and Sundays and that sort of stuff."

"Go ahead," Mason said.

"You're a lawyer," Boles went on. "You can see what a setup of that kind means. If anything happened and an outsider got a judgment of any sort against one of the Balfours, an execution would be levied on the stock of the individual Balfour. In that way, unless the company made a settlement, there would be a stockholder who was an outsider. No one wants that."

"To whom are you referring?" Mason asked.

"Dorla Balfour," Boles said shortly.

"What about her?"

"Addison Balfour is the business brains of the company," Boles said. "Guthrie doesn't do very much in connection with the property management. Theodore, who was Ted Balfour's father, was pretty much of a right-hand man for Addison, but Guthrie is a total loss as far as the business is concerned.

"Naturally, when Guthrie remarried and picked up a girl like Dorla, Addison regarded the entire transaction with considerable consternation. He attended the wedding, offered his congratulations, kissed the bride, then very quietly started building up a slush fund in the form of cash which he could use to make a property settlement with Dorla when the time came."

"Go on," Mason said.

"However," Boles said, "Dorla couldn't even wait to play the game cleverly. She started playing around. I won't go into details. Naturally, Addison, while he had hardly dared hope for this, was prepared for it. He told me to keep an eye on her.

"I was ready to get the goods on her which would have taken Guthrie off the hook, when Guthrie somehow or other became suspicious and like a damn fool tried to pick up his own evidence.

"If he'd only come to me, I could have shown him photostats of motel registers where she and this Jackson Eagan had registered together dozens of times.

"However, Guthrie wanted to get the evidence his own way. He was going to be smart—the damn fool!

"Guthrie started out on this trip to Mexico. He told Dorla he wanted her to ride on the train as far as the Pasadena-Alhambra station. That was so she'd know that he was on the train and would get careless."

"It worked?" Mason asked, his voice carefully masked.

"Admirably. She got off one side of the train; Guthrie opened a vestibule door on the other side of the train, dropped off on the blind side, waited until the train had pulled out, walked over to the car that he had rented, and followed Dorla.

"Dorla was in a hurry. She couldn't wait to get to the Sleepy Hollow Motel, where this steady boy friend, Jackson Eagan, was registered. She went in with him, there was an ardent reunion, and then after a while Dorla came out. She went home to get some things.

"Guthrie had come prepared for all eventualities. But as it happened, fate played into his hands. The motel unit next to the one occupied by Jackson was empty. Guthrie had a tape recorder with a very sensitive microphone that fastens up against the wall. He put the mike up against the wall and settled back to listen.

"That microphone picked up sounds which were inaudible to the ear, but he could plug a pair of earphones in and listen as the tape went over a secondary head, which enabled him to listen to everything that was on the tape."

Mason nodded again.

"He listened to plenty," Boles said. "Then Dorla left in Jackson Eagan's car to get her suitcase.

"Well, that's when Guthrie Balfour did the most foolish thing of all.

"He had all the evidence he needed on the tape recorder. But, like a bungling amateur, he thought he could confront Jackson Eagan, take the part of the outraged husband, and get Eagan to sign some sort of a confession.

"So Guthrie opened the door and went into the dimly lit motel. Eagan aimed a flashlight at his face, recognized him and they started fighting. Guthrie had the .22 automatic he had taken from the glove compartment of Ted's car. There was a struggle. The gun went off and Eagan fell to the floor with a bullet in his head.

"Guthrie got in a panic. He dashed out of the place and ran to the telephone booth that was in front of the office. He called the trouble number. That's where I came in.

"That telephone has right of way over anything. I answered the phone.

Guthrie told me he was at the Sleepy Hollow Motel, that he'd had trouble and that it was *very* serious.

"I told him to wait and I'd get out there right away. Guthrie was scared stiff. He could hardly talk on the phone. He seemed to be in pretty much of a daze.

"I got out there in nothing flat. Guthrie was seated in his rented car and was shaking like a leaf. I finally got out of him what had happened."

"So what did you do?" Mason asked.

"I did the only thing there was to do," Boles said. "Guthrie was supposed to be on a train to El Paso, en route to Chihuahua. Nobody knew he'd gotten off that train. I told him to take the company plane, fly to Phoenix, and get aboard the train. I told him that I'd arrange to come down later on and pick up the plane. I told him I'd take care of everything and not to bother."

"So what did he do?"

"Started off to get the plane, just as I told him."

"He could fly it himself?"

"Sure, he could fly it himself. He had a key to the hangar. He takes off from a private landing field at the suburban factory. There was absolutely nothing to stand in his way. It was a cinch."

"What did you do?"

"What do you think I did?" Boles said. "I took the body out. I tied it on my car and dragged the face off it. I banged it around so the head was smashed up like an eggshell, took it out and dumped it on the highway, so it would look like a hit and run. Fortunately, the gun was a small-caliber gun, there hadn't been any hemorrhage, and what bleeding had taken place had been on the rug in the motel unit. I took that rug, put it in the car, and subsequently burned it up. I took the rug out of the unit Balfour had been occupying and put it in the unit Eagan had occupied.

"Before I'd got very far with what I was doing, Dorla came back."

"What did you tell her?"

"I did what any good trouble shooter should have done under the circumstances," Boles said. "I told her that I'd been the one who was shadowing her, that I knew all about what she was doing, that I had the dope on her, that I had a tape recording that showed her guilty of infidelity. I told her that I had a written statement from Jackson Eagan, but that after I got the written statement out of him he jumped me and I had to shoot him in self-defense.

"I told Dorla to help me plant the body and make it look like a hit and run and then that she was to take the first plane to Tucson, and get aboard the train Guthrie was on. She was to tell Guthrie she was in a jam, that she'd been driving while intoxicated and had hit a man with the family car, that it was up to him to protect her, that he was to swear he'd talked her into staying on the train with him, and that she'd been on the train all the time. He was to take her down to Mexico with him and he was to give her an alibi.

"In that way, I had Dorla mixed into the thing up to her pretty little eyebrows. I had her really believing that Guthrie had been on the train all the time and that *I* was the only one who knew anything about what had been going on."

"Then she helped you get the car Ted had been driving?" Mason asked.

"Sure. We planted the guy in the right place and then I had Dorla wait until after Ted came home with the car. Fortunately he was pretty pie-eyed. Marilyn Keith took him upstairs and, I guess, put him to bed. Then she came down, and I'll sure hand it to that kid! She was plucky. She didn't even leave a back trail by calling for a taxicab. She walked out to State Highway and took a chance on hitchhiking a ride home. For an attractive girl like that, that was quite some chance. That's a lot of devotion to her job. I'm going to see that that girl gets a real raise in pay as soon as this thing is over."

"Go on," Mason said. "Then what happened?"

"After that, it was all just a matter of cleaning up details," Boles said. "Dorla took the car out, smashed into the guy. We left a few clues scattered around. Then she took the car back and parked it. I called the cops next morning and gave them an anonymous tip on the Balfour car.

"Now that's where Dorla double-crossed me. She's a smart little trollop. I had it planned so the evidence would point to *her* as the one who had driven the car and hit the man.

"She played it smart. Before she took the plane to Tucson, she sneaked into Ted's room and planted the car key in Ted's pocket. Ted was dead to the world. The Keith girl had left him with all his clothes on except his shoes. She'd taken those off. Dorla undressed him, put his pajamas on, and fixed it so he thought he'd gone out a second time and that the accident probably had happened then.

"Now then, Mason, that gives you an idea what you're up against."

"One other question," Mason said. "What about the witness, Myrtle Anne Haley?"

"A complete phony," Boles said. "I had a body to account for and we wanted to be certain that Dorla was where she could be charged with the hit and run—unless she got Guthrie to back her on her fake alibi. That would put Dorla completely in our power. But the time element became confused, Ted talked too much to the investigating officers, and Dorla did too good a job getting Guthrie to back up her phony alibi. So that left Ted holding the bag. I hadn't planned it that way but Ted *shouldn't* have had any trouble beating the case. Then that damn fool, Howland, loused everything up.

"I got this witness, this Myrtle Anne Haley who is working for the Balfour enterprises. I told her what she had to swear to—The dumb cluck got it pretty well mixed up. I've used her before. She's loyal, even if she isn't smart. For a thousand bucks she'll play along with anything.

"I admit I made a mistake with Howland. I didn't pay him by the day. I paid him by the job. So Howland saw an opportunity to wipe it all off the books by making a deal with the prosecution under which Ted would get a suspended sentence.

"Now then, there's the story. I've dumped it in your lap."

"What do you expect *me* to do with it?" Mason asked.

"You've made a good start already," Boles said. "That's one hell of a clever point you made with that once-in-jeopardy business. You go ahead and pull that prior conviction stuff for all it's worth. Never let them get to trial on the merits. Keep hammering home that point of being once in jeopardy. I think it's a hell of a good point. So does a lawyer whom I've consulted. He says you're tops and you've got a point there that will keep them from ever bringing out the evidence they have. He says you're a genius."

"I may not be able to work it that way," Mason said coldly.

"What do you mean?"

"Suppose I put in a plea of once in jeopady and the judge overrules it? Then the district attorney goes to trial."

"Exactly," Boles said. "And at that time you don't take any part in the trial at all. You simply sit back and let them handle it all their own way. You refuse to cross-examine witnesses. You refuse to put on any witnesses of your own. You refuse to argue anything except this plea of once in jeopardy. Then, if the jury returns a verdict of guilty, you're in a position to go before the supreme court on that once-in-jeopardy point. You will have aroused the sympathy of the Supreme Court because you didn't put on any evidence and didn't make any defense."

"Are you," Mason asked, "telling me how to conduct the case?"

There was a moment's silence. Boles' blue eyes became hard as steel. "You're damn right I am. We're paying the bill."

"You may be paying the bill," Mason told him, "but I'm representing a client. Suppose the Supreme Court doesn't set aside the verdict on my once-in-jeopardy theory? Then young Balfour is convicted of murder."

"A damn sight better to have Ted Balfour convicted of second-degree murder than to have the whole Balfour family rocked by a family scandal and a verdict of first-degree murder. Ted isn't important. Guthrie Balfour is. However, we could easily make out a case of self-defense for Ted where we couldn't for Guthrie."

Mason said, "My responsibility is to my client."

"Look, " Boles said coldly, "your obligation is to do what I tell you to do. We're paying the freight. I'm master-minding this thing. You try to double-cross me and I'll make you the sickest individual in the state of California. And don't ever forget I can do it.

"You're supposed to be smart and to know your way around. If you had half of the things to contend with that I've had to take in my stride, you'd realize you didn't know anything. Don't think this is the first killing I've had to square. And some of the things have been pretty damn nasty."

"All right," Mason said. "Now I know your position and you know mine. I'll also tell you something to remember: I don't suborn perjury and I don't go for all this crooked business. I rely on the truth. The truth is a better weapon than all these crooked schemes of yours."

Boles said, "You're kicking a chance at a hundred-thousand-dollar fee out the window and you're leaving yourself wide open."

"To hell with the fee," Mason said. "I'm protecting my client. I'll do what I think is for his best interests."

Boles reached forward and tapped on the window of the cab.

The driver turned around.

"Stop right here. Let me out," Boles said.

Boles turned to Mason. "Under the circumstances, you can pay for the cab."

Mason whipped a paper from his pocket and shoved it in Boles' hand as the cab lurched to a stop.

"What's this?" Boles asked.

"A subpoena ordering you to attend court as a witness for the defense," Mason said.

For a moment Boles' jaw sagged open in incredulous surprise, then he said, "Why you dirty son-of-a-bitch!"

Boles slammed the cab door shut with a vigor which rattled the glass.

"Turn around," Mason instructed the cabdriver. "Go back to the place where you picked us up."

CHAPTER SIXTEEN

Perry Mason regarded the letter which Della Street placed on his desk on top of the morning mail.

"You say that came registered mail, special delivery?"

She nodded. "They don't lose any time, do they?"

Mason read aloud:

"Dear Sir:

"You are hereby notified that, effective immediately, you are relieved of all duties in connection with the defense of Theodore Balfour, Jr., in the case of People versus Balfour. From now on the defendant will be represented by Mortimer Dean Howland as his attorney. You will please submit any expenses which you have incurred to date, together with the necessary vouchers showing the nature and extent of those expenses. From the date of receipt of this communication, you will incur no more expenses on behalf of the Balfour Allied Associates, and any such bills as you may submit for your personal compensation to date in connection with said case will be predicated upon a per diem basis. Otherwise, those bills will be contested. We will allow you a maximum of two hundred and fifty dollars per day for your time.

"Very truly yours,
"Balfour Allied Associates
"per Addison Balfour.

"Makes it nice and official, doesn't it?" Mason said.

"What about Ted Balfour? Do you have to withdraw simply because—"

"Not because Addison Balfour says so," Mason observed. "But put yourself in Ted's place. Boles goes to him and tells him that I won't co-operate and that the Balfour Allied Associates have lost confidence in me, that they're not putting up any more money for his defense as long as I'm connected with the case in any way, that if Mortimer Dean Howland represents him they will go the limit. What would *you* do under those circumstances?"

"Well, what are you going to do?"

"I'm damned if I know," Mason said thoughtfully. "If I go to young Balfour and tell him the truth, Howland will claim that I'm guilty of unprofessional conduct in trying to solicit employment.

"The probabilities are that if I even try to see Balfour, I'll be advised that Balfour has stated I am no longer representing him and therefore I have no visitor's privileges?"

"So what are you going to do?"

"So," Mason said, "I'm going to put it up to Ted Balfour. At least, I'm going to try to see him."

"And what are you going to tell him?"

"I'm going to shoot the works."

The telephone on Della Street's desk rang. She picked it up, said, "Just a minute," turned to Mason and said, "Your first client is back. Marilyn Keith. Says she has to see you at once on a matter of the greatest urgency."

"Show her in," Mason said.

Marilyn Keith had quite evidently been crying, but her chin was high and she didn't try to avoid Mason's probing eyes.

Her quick eyes flashed at the pile of mail on Mason's desk. "I see you received your notification," she said.

Mason nodded.

She said, "Mr. Mason, I'm sorry that you had a difference of opinion with Banner Boles. He's... well, he's very, very powerful and he's very, very clever."

Mason merely nodded.

"I know, of course, what it's all about," she said, indicating the notification on the desk. "Mr. Addison Balfour dictated that to me and had me take it to the main post office, so that you'd get it first thing this morning."

Mason said, "Let's be frank, Miss Keith. You're working for the Balfour Allied Associates. A situation has developed where the interests of Ted Balfour may have become adverse to those of your employer. I don't want you to—"

"Oh, forget it!" she blazed. "Don't be so damn stupid!"

Mason raised his eyebrows.

"For your official information," she said, "I am no longer employed by the Balfour Allied Associates."

"What happened?"

She said, "I have been accused of betraying my employer, of being disloyal, and of using confidential information which I received in the course of my employment for my personal advantage."

"Mind telling what happened?" Mason asked, the lines of his face softening somewhat. "And do sit down. I only have a minute, but I'm anxious to hear what you have to say."

She said, "I went up to the jail to call on Ted Balfour."

"You did!" Mason exclaimed.

She nodded.

"And what did you tell him?"

"I told him that the Balfour Allied Associates were cutting off all their aid as long as he had you for a lawyer, that if he accepted Mortimer Dean Howland as his lawyer and discharged you, the Balfour Allied Associates would put up all of the money that was necessary to fight his case all the way through the courts on the theory that you had raised; to wit, that he had once been placed in jeopardy and therefore couldn't be tried again.

"I also told him that, while I didn't know the details, I knew that the Balfour Allied Associates were prepared to toss him to the wolves in order to save their own skins. I told him that if he insisted on keeping you as his attorney, I was satisfied that you would loyally represent his interests to the best of your ability."

"And what did he do?"

"Well," she said, "he wanted to keep you if there was any way of paying you."

"He told you that?"

"Yes."

"So what did you do?"

She opened her purse, said, "I made out a check to you in an amount of five hundred and twenty-five dollars. That's every cent I have in the world, Mr. Mason, and I don't know when you're going to get any more. I know that's not the type of fee you get in a murder case. It's just on account."

Mason took the check, studied it for a moment.

"I'll get another job somewhere," she said bravely, "and I'll set aside a regular percentage of my paycheck. I'll give you a promissory note, Mr. Mason, and—"

Mason said, "You're not likely to get another job with the Balfour Allied Associates making charges that you used confidential information for your own personal gain."

She fought back tears. "I'm not foolish enough to try it here," she said. "I'm going to some other city and I'm not going to tell them anything about having been with Balfour Allied Associates."

Mason stood thoughtfully regarding her.

"Will you do it, Mr. Mason? Will you, *please?* Oh, will you *please* represent Ted?"

"He wants me to?" Mason asked.

"Very much," she said. "It's an uphill battle, but you'll be honest. And you'll have a terrific fight. You have no idea of the ruthless power of the Balfour Allied Associates, or the manner in which Banner Boles uses that power.

"Boles was educated as an attorney, although he never practiced. He's been a lobbyist and he knows his way around. You give that man unlimited money and all the power of the Balfour Allied Associates back of him, and anything that he can't buy out of his way he'll club out of his way."

"Do you think Ted will want me after Boles has been to see him?"

"That's why I had to see you now," she said. "You go and see Ted. Go and see him right now. Tell him that you're going to stay with him. But please, Mr. Mason, please don't tell him that *I* am paying anything. Oh, I know it's pitifully inadequate. But if you only can...if you only will..."

Mason picked up her check, tore it in half, tore the halves into quarters, dropped the pieces in the wastebasket, walked over and put his arm around her shoulder. "You poor kid," he said. "Forget it. I'll go and see Ted Balfour and tell him that I'll stand by him. You save your money for a cushion until you can get another job. You'll need it."

She looked up at him for a moment, then lost all semblance of maintaining her poise. Her head came forward on the lawyer's shoulder and her body was shaken by sobs.

Della Street tactfully eased out of the room.

CHAPTER SEVENTEEN

Judge Cadwell said, "Gentlemen, the jury has been sworn. The defendant is in court. The jurors are all present.

"I may state that, while I do not consider myself prejudiced so that I am disqualified from trying the issues in this case, I was hoping that it would be assigned to another judge. I have, of course, already become familiar with the legal point raised by the defense in connection with habeas corpus.

"It appears that the facts supporting the plea of once in jeopardy are completely within the knowledge of the Court. There is no dispute as to those facts. There is therefore no issue to go to the jury in connection with a plea of once in jeopardy. It becomes a matter for the Court to pass upon as a matter of law. The Court therefore decides that there is no merit to the plea of once in jeopardy.

"The Court makes this ruling with some hesitancy because it is aware that the point is a close one. However, this Court simply can't conceive that it is the purpose of the law to clothe a defendant with immunity simply because, through a misinterpretation of facts or a paucity of facts, prosecution was originally had upon another theory, or for a lesser offense. Yet the Court is forced to admit that the authorities seem to indicate such is the case.

"In view of the undisputed facts in the case the point is one which can be taken to the appellate courts and passed upon by them. Therefore, the real interests of the defendant will in no wise be curtailed by this ruling of the Court. I overrule the plea of once in jeopardy and the prosecution will proceed with its case."

Roger Farris made a brief opening statement to the jury and then started putting on witnesses.

The autopsy surgeon in the coroner's office testified to having performed an autopsy on a body which had at first been certified out as a hit-and-run case. Afterwards, the body had been exhumed when it appeared that there were certain discrepancies in the evidence. At that time a more detailed examination of the skull had been made, and it was found that death had resulted from a bullet wound. The course and nature of the bullet wound was described and the bullet, which had been recovered from the wound, was introduced in evidence.

Mason offered no questions on cross-examination.

A .22 automatic was produced and identified by manufacturer's number. The sales record showed that the weapon had been sold to the defendant Ted Balfour.

Again there was no cross-examination.

Roger Farris put a witness on the stand who qualified as an expert on firearms and firearms identification. He testified that he had fired test bullets from the automatic and had compared them with the fatal bullet which had been introduced in evidence, and that the markings on the bullet showed beyond doubt that the fatal bullet had been fired from the automatic which had been received in evidence.

Again Mason did not cross-examine.

Judge Cadwell frowned down at Mason. "Now let me understand the position of counsel," he said. "Is it the position of counsel that, because the Court has overruled the plea of once in jeopardy, counsel intends to take no part in this trial? Because, if such is to be the position of counsel, I feel that the Court should warn counsel that counsel is here for the purpose of representing the interests of the defendant, and that, as an officer of the Court, it is the duty of counsel to see that the defendant is represented."

"I understand the Court's position," Mason said. "I am not cross-examining these witnesses, because I have no questions to ask of them. I intend to participate actively in this trial."

"Very well," Judge Cadwell said frowning. "The Court needs only to point out, Mr. Mason, the importance of these witnesses. However, the Court will make no comment on the testimony. Proceed with the case."

"Now then, Your Honor," Roger Farris said, "it appears that Myrtle Anne Haley, who was a witness for the People at the previous trial of this action when the defendant was indicted for negligent homicide, is at the moment unavailable. We propose to show that we have made every effort to locate her. Being unable to do so, in view of the fact that the parties to this action are the same as the parties in the other action, to wit, the People of the State of California as plaintiff and Theodore Balfour, Jr., as defendant, we wish to read her testimony into the record. I understand there is no objection."

"Any objection?" Judge Cadwell asked.

Mason smiled. "Not in the least, Your Honor. I am glad to have this done if counsel will first prove the witness is unavailable. This action on the part of counsel, using the identical evidence used in the other trial shows the solidity of our plea of once in jeopardy."

"The actions aren't the same," Farris said. "The parties are the same, that's all."

"Judge Cadwell stroked his chin. "Of course," he said, "that does tend to give force to the defendant's plea of once in jeopardy. However, the Court has ruled on that, and that ruling will stand. Make your showing, Mr. Prosecutor. Counsel will be advised that any objection which counsel wishes to take to any question as contained in the transcript may be made at this time and the Court will then rule on that objection."

"Farris produced an investigator for the district attorney's office who testified that Myrtle Anne Haley had moved from her residence and had left no forwarding address, that he had talked with all of her friends and acquaintances but no one knew where she had gone, that he had made every effort to find her and serve a subpoena on her without avail. She had been employed by a subsidiary of the Balfour Allied Associates and she had left abruptly without even calling for her last paycheck. The intimation was strongly that pressure brought to bear by the Balfour company had caused this prime witness for the prosecution to absent herself.

Cross-examination?" Judge Cadwell asked Mason.

Mason shook his head. "No cross-examination."

"Very well," Judge Cadwell said, "I will grant the motion of the prosecution that the testimony of Myrtle Anne Haley may be read in the record, after that testimony is properly authenticated, there being no objection."

The court reporter was thereupon duly sworn and read the transcript of Myrtle Anne Haley's testimony.

With the manner of a magician bringing a startling trick to a breath-taking conclusion, Roger Farris called out in a ringing voice, "Will Mr. Banner Boles take the stand?"

Banner Boles came forward, held up his hand, was sworn, gave his name, age, residence, and occupation, and settled himself comfortably in the witness stand.

"Are you acquainted with the defendant, Theodore Balfour, Jr.?" Farris asked.

"Yes, sir. Certainly."

"How long have you known him?"

"For some ten years."

"What were you doing on the nineteenth of September of this year?"

"I was working for the Balfour Allied Associates."

"Specifically what duties did you perform that night?"

"Mr. Guthrie Balfour was leaving for El Paso. From there he was going to Mexico. It was part of my assignment to see that he got safely aboard the train."

"Somewhat in the nature of a bodyguard?"

"Well, more in the nature of a general trouble shooter."

"You saw him on the train for El Paso?"

"I did."

"Who else?"

"His wife, Dorla Balfour."

"She boarded the same train with him?"

"Yes, sir."

"Where had you been prior to the time you went to the depot?"

"There had been a little social gathering, something in the nature of a going-away party at the home of Mrs. Florence Ingle who is a friend of the Balfours."

"And you had been at that party?"

"I had, yes, sir."

"And what happened after you escorted Mr. and Mrs. Guthrie Balfour to the train?"

"I went back to my office."

"You have an office uptown?"

"Yes, sir."

"It is not at the Balfour Allied Associates?"

"I have an office there too, but I have an uptown office which is kept open twenty-four hours a day."

"For what purpose, may I ask?"

"People call me when something comes up and there is any trouble."

"And were you called on the evening of the nineteenth?"

"No, sir."

"You were not?"

"No, sir."

"I thought—Oh, I beg your pardon, it was early in the morning of the twentieth. Were you called then?"

"Yes, sir."

"Who called you?"

"The defendant."

"You are referring to the defendant, Theodore Balfour, Jr.?"

"Yes, sir."

"Do you know where he was calling you from?"

"I only know where he said he was calling me from."

"And where was that?"

"It was a telephone booth at a service station at the intersection of Sycamore Road and State Highway. The service station was closed but he was calling from the booth."

"And what did he say?"

"He asked me to join him at once. He said he was in trouble."

"What did you do?"

"I jumped in my car and got out there as quick as I could."

"How long did it take?"

"About twenty minutes, I guess."

"Did you give the defendant any instructions before you left?"

"I told him to wait there until I arrived."

"Was he there when you arrived?"

"No, sir. He was not."

"Where was he?"

"Well, I cruised around for a while trying to find—"

"Never mind that. Tell us where you finally found the defendant."

"I found him at home."

"That is, at the residence of Mr. and Mrs. Guthrie Balfour?"

"Yes, sir."

"That was where he was living?"

"Yes, sir."

"And what did you do?"

"I didn't want to get everybody up. I wanted to find out if the defendant was home."

"In your capacity with the organization, do you have keys for the residences of the executives of the Balfour Allied Associates?"

"I have pass keys I can use if there is an emergency."

"And did you use one of those keys?"

"Yes, sir."

"Where did you go first?"

"First I looked in the garage to see if the car the defendant had been driving was in the garage."

"You found that it was in the garage?"

"Yes, sir."

"What was its condition?"

"Well, I used my flashlight and walked around the car looking for signs of trouble because, from the tone of voice in which the defendant had telephoned me, I thought he had been—"

"Never mind what you *thought*," Farris interrupted sharply. "Just tell what you *did*."

"I looked the car over."

"What did you find?"

"I found that the right front headlight was smashed, that there was a dent in the right fender, and there were a few flecks of blood on the front bumper near the right-hand side; that is, I assumed the spots were blood. They were red spots which had crusted and looked like blood."

"So then what did you do?"

"So then I switched off my flashlight, closed the garage door, went to the house, inserted my key in the front door, opened the front door, and walked upstairs."

"And where did you go?"

"To the room occupied by the defendant."

"You had been in that room before?"

"Oh, yes."

"You knew where it was?"

"Yes, sir."

"And what did you do?"

"I tapped on the door and said, 'This is Banner, Ted. Let me in.'"

"Did you receive any response?"

"No, sir."

"What did you do?"

"I went inside the room."

"And what did you find?"

"I found the defendant very drunk, in what I would call an alcoholic stupor, lying fully clothed on the bed."

"What about his shoes? Were they on or off?"

"They were on."

"What time was this?"

"This was about two o'clock in the morning. I had left the service station at one-fifty, and I guess it took me about five minutes to look through the garage and study the automobile."

"Now, when you say, 'the automobile,' what automobile do you mean?"

"I mean the automobile photographs of which have been introduced in evidence, the one having license number GMB 665."

"Did you have any conversation with the defendant there in his room at that time?"

"Yes, sir."

"Who else was present?"

"No one."

"Just the two of you?"

"Yes, sir."

"What did you do?"

"I had quite a time getting the defendant so he could wake up and talk."

"What did you do?"

"I took off his coat. I took off his overshirt. I took off his undershirt. I got towels, soaked them in cold water, and put them on his abdomen and on his neck. I sat him up in bed and shook him. I put cold compresses on his eyes and on the back of his neck, and finally he became conscious, or wakened, or whatever you want to call it."

"He recognized you?"

"Oh, yes."

"And what was the conversation you had with him at that time as nearly as you can remember?"

"Well, I asked him what he wanted, and he told me he had been in a jam but he had finally figured how to get out of it all by himself."

"What did he tell you?"

"He told me that he had been gambling at cards pretty heavy, that he had run out of cash and had been using the credit that he had with a certain syndicate, that he had sustained losses and that those losses had piled up and the syndicate had called on him to pay."

"He told you all this?"

"Yes, sir."

"How did he speak?"

"His voice was thick. He was quite intoxicated, but I got it out of him a bit at a time."

"Go ahead. Then what did he tell you?"

"He told me that he had received a couple of telephone calls from the syndicate saying he had to pay up or else. After that he said he had received an anonymous, unsigned letter saying that if he didn't pay up they were going to send their 'collector.'"

"Did he tell you what he thought the threat meant when they said that they were going to send their collector?"

"Yes, sir."

"What did he say?"

"He said that that meant someone to beat him up. He said that they got pretty tough with fellows that didn't pay, that the first time they beat them up, and the second time they took them for a one-way ride."

"Go on," Farris said, glancing triumphantly at the jurors who were sitting on the edges of their chairs, leaning forward, drinking in Boles' words with rapt attention. "What else did he say?"

"Well, he said that he had tried to raise twenty thousand dollars, that he didn't dare to go to Addison Balfour, that he had hoped an opportunity would present itself to speak to Guthrie Balfour before he took off for Mexico, but that, in the crush of the party, there had been no opportunity. He knew that he would have to approach the subject very tactfully. Otherwise, he would be rebuffed.

"He stated that he had some money that was in a trust fund which had been left him by his parents, and that he had been trying to reach the trustee in order to get some money from him, but that the trustee was out of town on a vacation, that he was hoping he could stall the matter along until the return of the trustee."

"Did he say anything else?"

"He said that he had talked to one of his father's friends, a Florence Ingle."

"That was the woman who had given the party?"

"Yes."

"Did he say when he had talked with her?"

"He said that night. He said that he had asked her for twenty thousand dollars but that she had been unable or unwilling to give it to him."

"Then what did he say?"

"He said that he drank more than was good for him, that he was rather intoxicated by somewhere around ten o'clock, that a young woman had driven his car home for him, and had put the car in the garage."

"Did he tell you the name of the young woman?"

"He *said* that he didn't know the young woman's identity. But I thought he did. However, I didn't—"

"Never mind what you *thought!*" Farris shouted. "You're familiar with the rules of examination, Mr. Boles. Kindly refrain from giving any of your conclusions. Tell us only what the defendant said to you and what you said to the defendant."

"Yes, sir."

"Now, what did the defendant say to you about having been brought home?"

"Well, the defendant said he had been brought home by this young woman, that she had taken his shoes off, that he had stretched out on the bed, that he had been pretty drunk and that he had gone to the bathroom and been sick, that after that he felt a little better. He suddenly remembered that the trustee who handled his trust fund sometimes came back early from a vacation, and checked in at a motel on the outskirts of town, that this man was an elderly man with poor eyesight who disliked to drive at night, and that, when he returned from a trip and it was late, he would stay at a motel on the outskirts of town rather than drive in. He said he decided to drive out and see if the trustee had returned."

"And then what?"

"So he put on his shoes, let himself out of the house, and went to the garage. He said, however, that because of the threats which had been made and because of the late hour, he had opened his gun cabinet and had taken a .22 automatic which he had put in his pocket."

"Go on. What else did he say?"

"He said that, when he reached the garage, he thought he saw a shadowy figure; that, because he had been drinking, he finally decided it was just his imagination; that he opened the garage door and stepped inside; and that, just as he had his hand on the handle of the car door, someone put his hand on his shoulder from behind and said, 'Okay, buddy, I'm the collector.'"

"Go on," Farris said. "What else?"

"He said he was frozen with terror for the moment and that then the man who had said he was a collector hit him a hard blow in the chest, a blow that slammed him back against the wall of the garage; that the man had then said, 'That's a sample! Now get in the car. You and I are going for a little ride. I'm going to teach you not to welch on bets.'"

"Go on," Farris said. "What else?"

"And then the defendant told me that almost without thinking and in actual fear of his life he had jerked out the .22 automatic and had fired from the hip; that he was an exceptionally good shot; and that he had shot directly at the man's head. The man staggered back, half-sprawled against the front seat. He was not dead, but was unconscious.

"The defendant said that he knew he had to do something at once; that he had lifted this man into the front seat of the automobile; that he closed the car door; that he jumped in the other side, and drove, anxious only to get away from the house for fear that someone might have heard the shot. He said he drove down to the State Highway; that he turned left and stopped at the closed service station on Sycamore; that he called me from the phone booth there and asked me to come at once. He wanted me to tell him what could be done and how he could arrange for medical attention for the man in the car.

"He then told me that after he had hung up and returned to the car, he discovered the man was no longer breathing; that he put his hand on his wrist and there was no pulse; that the man had died while he was telephoning.

"He said that changed the situation materially; that he had then tried to call me again, but that my assistant who answered the telephone assured him I had already left."

"Go on," Farris said, "what else did he tell you? Did he tell you what he did after that?"

"Yes, sir."

"What was it?"

"He said that he felt that the problem was simplified because he had only a dead man to deal with. He said that the shock had sobered him up pretty much, that he searched the body and took everything in the line of papers that the man might have—all means of identification; that he took the man's wallet; that he even took his handkerchief, so it would not be possible to trace a laundry mark; that he took his key ring, his pocketknife, all of his personal belongings."

"Then what?"

"He said that he ran the car out Sycamore Road and then got out and placed the body on the front bumper; that he drove as fast as he could and then suddenly slammed on the brakes; that the body rolled off the bumper and skidded and rolled for some considerable distance along the highway; that he then deliberately ran over the head, then turned the car around and ran over the head again; that he ran over the head several times, so as to be sure that not only would the features be unrecognizable but that it would prevent the bullet hole from showing."

"Did he tell you anything about a bullet being in the head?"

"He told me that he thought the bullet had gone clean through the head and was in the garage somewhere."

"Go on," Farris said.

"Well, the defendant asked me to take charge of things from there on. I told him that there was nothing much I could do; that he had already done everything; that I felt the best thing to do was to go and find the body and report the matter to the police, stating that he had acted in self-defense and in fear of his life; that this man had assaulted him first."

"So what was done?"

"I told him to wait there, that I would go and find the body. He described exactly where he had left it."

"And what happened?"

"I found I was too late. By the time I got there a police car was there and I felt that, under the circumstances, I didn't want to assume the responsibility of notifying the police. I thought that I would wait until I had an opportunity to think the matter over."

"To discuss the matter with your superiors?" Farris said sharply.

"Well, I wanted time to think it over."

"You realized that you should have reported this?"

"Yes, sir."

"And you didn't do so?"

"No, sir."

"Why?"

"Because I am paid to see that matters are handled smoothly. I didn't want to hash this thing up. I wanted to see one of my friends on the police force and see if I could find some way of making a report that would not be publicized. I knew that if I reported to the police officers who were there with the body, there would be publicity, that the defendant would be picked up and lodged in jail, and I felt that—well, I felt that wasn't the best way for a trouble shooter to handle an affair of that sort."

"So what did you finally do?"

"I went back and helped Ted Balfour get undressed and into his pajamas. He wanted some more to drink and I didn't stop him in the least. In fact, I encouraged him to drink, hoping that he might forget about the whole business."

"And then?"

"And then I took from him the papers he had taken from the body and went home and went to bed."

"And then?" Farris asked.

"And then I slept late the next morning. When I awakened I learned that police had already interrogated the defendant; that in some way they had learned his automobile had been involved in the matter; and that he was going to be prosecuted for an involuntary homicide with a car."

"So what did you do?"

"I did nothing."

Farris, with the manner of a television director who has brought his show to a conclusion right on the exact second, looked up at the clock and said, "Your Honor, it seems to be the hour for the noon adjournment. While I think I have now concluded my direct examination of this witness, it might be well to have the noon recess at this time, because I would like to go over the testimony in my mind and see if perhaps I have left out a question."

"Just a minute," the judge said, "The Court has one question before we adjourn. Mr. Boles, you have stated you took those papers from the defendant?"

"Yes, sir."

"What did you do with them?"

"I held them for a while."

"Where are they now?"

"To the best of my knowledge, they are in the possession of Mr. Perry Mason."

"What?" Judge Cadwell exclaimed, coming bolt upright on the bench.

"Yes, Your Honor."

"You gave those papers to Perry Mason?"

"Yes, sir."

"Has Mr. Mason communicated with the district attorney's office in any way concerning those papers?" Judge Cadwell asked Roger Farris.

"No, Your Honor."

"When did you give Mr. Mason those papers?" Judge Cadwell asked.

"I don't have the exact date. I gave them to him after he had become associated, that is, after he had taken over the defense of Ted Balfour. During the first case the attorney representing the defendant was Mortimer Dean Howland."

"You said nothing to Mr. Howland about those papers?"

"No, sir."

"Did you say anything to anyone at any time about having those papers other than to Mr. Mason?"

"No, sir."

"And you gave those papers to Mr. Mason?"

"Yes, sir."

"Mr. Mason!" Judge Cadwell said.

"Yes, Your Honor."

"The Court..." Judge Cadwell's voice trailed off into silence. "The Court is about to take the noon recess," he said. "Immediately after the discharge of the jury, I would like to have counsel for both sides approach the bench. The Court will admonish the jury not to form or express any opinion in this case until it is finally submitted to the jury for decision. The jurors will not discuss the case with others or permit it to be discussed in their presence. Court will now take a recess until two o'clock.

"Mr. Mason and Mr. Farris, will you please come forward?"

Mason and Farris approached the bench, Farris trying to keep his face in a mask of grave, judicial concern as befitted one who is called upon to be present at a time when a brother attorney is subjected to a tongue lashing. Judge Cadwell waited until the jurors had filed from the courtroom. Then he said, "Mr. Mason, is this true?"

"I doubt it, Your Honor," Mason said.

"You what?" Judge Cadwell snapped.

"I doubt it."

"I mean about the papers."

"Some papers were given to me, yes."

"By Mr. Boles?"

"Yes, Your Honor."

"And did he tell you those were papers that he had taken from the defendant or that had been given him by the defendant?"

"No, sir."

"What were those papers?"

"I have them here, Your Honor."

"Mason produced a sealed Manila envelope and handed it to the judge.

Judge Cadwell ripped open the envelope, started looking through the papers. "Mr. Mason," he said, "this is a very grave matter."

"Yes, Your Honor."

"The papers in this envelope are matters of evidence. They constitute most important bits of evidence in the case."

"Evidence of what?" Mason asked.

"Evidence corroborating Boles' story, for one thing," Judge Cadwell snapped.

Mason said, "If Your Honor please, that's like the man who tells about shooting a deer at three hundred yards and says that the deer fell right by a certain oak tree, that if you don't believe him, he'll point out the oak tree, because it's still standing there and that will substantiate his story."

"You question Mr. Boles' story?"

"Very much," Mason said.

"But you certainly can't question the fact that this evidence is most important evidence. This is evidence which should have been in the hands of the authorities."

"Evidence of what, Your Honor?"

"Here is the driving license of Jackson Eagan."

"Yes, Your Honor."

"Do you mean to say that is not important?"

"I fail to see why," Mason said.

"That would serve as an identification. An attempt has been made by the police to have this corpse identified. So far no identification has been made other than a tentative identification of Jackson Eagan."

"But Jackson Eagan is dead," Mason said. "He died two years before this case ever came up."

"How do you know he died?" Judge Cadwell said.

"Here is a contract that was signed, apparently by the decedent, a contract for the rental of that automobile. Do you claim these matters are not important, Mr. Mason?"

"No, sir."

"You certainly understand that they are matters of evidence?"

"Yes, Your Honor."

"As an officer of this Court, as an attorney at law, it is your duty to submit any matter of evidence, any physical matter which you have in your possession to the authorities. To suppress willfully or conceal any evidence of this sort is not only a violation of law but is a violation of your duties as an attorney."

Mason met the judge's eyes. "I'll meet that charge, Your Honor, when it is properly made, at the proper time and at the proper place."

Judge Cadwell's face turned a deep purple. "You are intimating that I have no right to bring this matter up?"

"I am stating, Your Honor, that I will meet that charge at the proper time and in the proper place."

"I don't know whether this constitutes a contempt of Court or not," Judge Cadwell said, "but it certainly constitutes a breach of your professional duty."

"That's Your Honor's opinion," Mason said. "If you wish to hold me for contempt I'll get a writ of habeas corpus and meet the contempt charge. If you wish to cite me for unprofessional conduct, I will meet that charge at the proper time and in the proper place.

"In the meantime, may I suggest to the Court that a defendant is on trial in this Court, that any intimation on the part of the Court that his counsel has been guilty of any breach of ethics might well be held against the defendant by the jury, and that it is the duty of the Court to refrain from expressing any opinion as to the action of counsel in this matter."

Judge Cadwell took a deep breath. "Mr. Mason," he said, "I am going to do everything I can to see that the rights of the defendant are not prejudiced by the conduct of his counsel. However, I can assure you that, as far as this Court is concerned, I feel that you have forfeited the right to the respect of the Court. Quite apparently you, as an attorney, have endeavored to condone a felony and you have suppressed evidence. As far as the witness Boles is concerned, I assume that he has endeavored to make atonement by going to the authorities and telling his story, but apparently you have done nothing."

"I have done nothing," Mason said, "except try to protect the rights of my client, and I'm going to try to protect them to the best of my ability."

"Well, you certainly have a different idea of the professional duties of an attorney than I do," Judge Cadwell snapped. "That is all. I'll think the matter over during the noon adjournment. I may decide to take some action when Court has reconvened."

CHAPTER EIGHTEEN

Perry Mason, Della Street, Marilyn Keith, and Paul Drake sat in a booth in the little restaurant where Mason usually ate lunch when he had a case in court.

"Well," Paul Drake asked, "just where does that leave us, Perry?"

"Out on the end of a limb," Mason admitted. "It's perjury, and it's the damnedest, most clever perjury I've ever encountered."

"He's clever," Marilyn Keith said, "frighteningly so, and he's powerful."

Mason nodded. "He's had legal training. He's been a lobbyist. He doubtless knows every trick of cross-examination that I do. It's his word against mine and he's manufactured a story that seems to have all sorts of factual corroboration."

"What about his withholding evidence?" Drake asked.

"Sure," Mason said. "He admits it. So what? The district attorney won't do a thing to him. He won't even slap his wrists. He'll tell him he *should* have surrendered the evidence to the district attorney's office, and not to do it again, but that's all.

"The devil of it is," Mason went on, "that it puts the defendant in such a hell of a position. It's a clever story. It has aroused a certain amount of sympathy for Ted Balfour on the part of the jurors. If Ted goes on the stand and tells approximately that same story, says that he relied on the advice of the older man, some members on that jury are going to vote for acquittal. They'll finally reach some kind of a compromise verdict."

"How good is your point about this once-in-jeopardy business?" Drake asked.

"Damn good," Mason said. "In the right kind of a case, the Supreme Court is pretty apt to go all the way."

"Well, it would make a terrific case," Drake said, "if we could only get a little more evidence about the collector coming to call."

Mason said, "The worst of it is, the story sounds so plausible that I'm almost believing it myself."

"Is there anything you can do?" Marilyn Keith asked him.

"I have one weapon," Mason said. "It's a powerful weapon. But sometimes it's hard to wield it because you don't know just where to grab hold of it."

"What weapon is that?" Della Street asked.

"The truth," Mason said.

They ate for a while in silence.

"You'll cross-examine him?" Paul Drake asked.

"I'll cross-examine him. It won't do any good."

"If his story had been true—well, what about it, Perry, what about concealing evidence?"

"As I told Judge Cadwell, I'll cross that bridge when I come to it," Mason said. "Right now I'm trying to think of the best way to protect young Balfour. Of course no matter what anyone says, that driving license of Jackson Eagan doesn't prove a thing. It shows a thumbprint on the driving license and it's not the thumbprint of the corpse." Mason took from his pocket a set of ten fingerprints. "These are the fingerprints of the corpse. This is the thumbprint on the driving license of Jackson Eagan. You can see that they don't compare at all."

"Jackson Eagan was buried," Paul Drake said. "But no one really identified the body. The body had been shipped from Yucatan, Mexico. The story was that it had been identified down there by the widow."

"Just what were the circumstances?" Mason asked.

"Eagan was a writer. He was on a trip getting local color. No one knows exactly how he died. Probably heart failure, or something of that sort. A party of archeologists stumbled on his body. They notified the authorities. The body was taken in to Merida in Yucatan, and the widow was notified by telegram. She flew down to identify the body and bring it home for the funeral. Naturally under the circumstances, the funeral was held with a closed coffin."

Mason said thoughtfully, "Just supposing the widow wanted her freedom and perhaps wanted to collect some insurance. It was quite a temptation for her to swear that the body was that of her husband."

"Of course we get back to that thumbprint," Drake said, "but when you look at the signature on this contract to rent the car, the signatures certainly tally."

"They certainly seem to be the same signature," Mason said. "Paul, how about the application for a driving license signed by Guthrie Balfour? Did you get that?"

Drake said, "I wired for a certified copy of Guthrie Balfour's last application for a driving license. It should be here any minute. I was hoping it would come in this morning. I feel certain that it must arrive in the late morning mail. One of my operatives will bring it up to court as soon as it comes in."

"I want it as soon as I can get it," Mason said.

"Do you have any plans for this afternoon's session?" Drake asked.

Mason shook his head, said, "Something like this catches you flatfooted. I had anticipated that they would try to make things tough for me, but I didn't think I'd have someone get on the stand and commit deliberate perjury like that.

"Paul, the number of that taxicab in which we took the ride was 647. I want to try and find the driver of the cab. I doubt if he'd remember anything that would be of help, but at least we can check. He should remember the occasion, even if he can't identify Boles."

"I'll have my men round him up," Drake said.

"Well," Mason announced, "I'll just have to go back there and take it on the chin. I've absorbed lots of punishment before and I guess I can take a little more."

"Of course you have the advantage of knowing what actually happened," Della Street said. "Eagan was shot by Guthrie Balfour. He telephoned Florence Ingle and admitted that."

"Well, why not use that?" Marilyn Keith asked. "Why not just go ahead on that basis and—?"

Mason smiled and shook his head. "No can do."

"Why not?"

"Because Guthrie Balfour told her over the telephone that he had killed this man. He said the killing was accidental, that the gun had gone off in a struggle."

"Can't you use that?"

"No."

"Why not?"

"Because that's hearsay. If we had Guthrie Balfour here, we could put him on the stand and question him, and, if he told a different story, we could then put Florence Ingle on the stand and impeach him by having Florence tell what he had said. But the law won't let a witness simply testify to what someone else has said over the telephone."

"It let Banner Boles testify to what Ted said over the telephone!" Marilyn exclaimed indignantly.

"Sure," Mason said, "because Ted's the defendant. You can always show any adverse statement that has been made by a defendant, but, unfortunately for us, Guthrie Balfour isn't a defendant. The technical rules of evidence prevent us getting at what we want."

"And what does Guthrie Balfour say about it?" Marilyn asked.

"Nobody knows," Mason said. "Guthrie headed back to his base camp. How about your men? Any luck, Paul?"

Drake shook his head. "Guthrie Balfour was in Chihuahua very briefly. He headed back for the Tarahumare country somewhere. He was only in Chihuahua long enough to telephone you and put his wife on a plane to come in and see you. Then he was off again. And my best guess, Perry, is that this expedition of his may have started out as a little archeological exploration, but it has now developed into a game of hide-and-seek. I don't think he intends to have anybody catch up with him until after this case is all over. Of course, in justice to him, you have to remember that as far as he's concerned it's still only a hit-and-run case. He feels nothing very much can happen to Ted—a fine or a suspended sentence."

Mason signed the luncheon check, said, "Well, we may just as well go back and face the music. We may not like the tune but we'll dance to it."

CHAPTER NINETEEN

After court had been reconvened at two o'clock, Roger Farris said, "I have no more questions of this witness. You may cross-examine, Mr. Mason."

Mason said, "Do you remember an occasion a short time ago when you telephoned me at my office, Mr. Boles?"

"Perfectly," Boles said affably.

"You came up to my office and said you had something to tell me?"

"Yes, sir."

"And I asked you to talk to me in my office and you said you'd prefer not to do so?"

"Yes, sir, that's quite right."

"And we went out and rode around in a taxicab together?"

"Yes, sir."

"You remember that, do you?"

"Certainly, sir. I not only remember it, but I took the precaution of jotting down the number of the taxicab so that the driver could bear me out in case you tried to confuse me on cross-examination or tried to deny that I gave you these papers."

"You gave them to me while we were in the taxicab?"

"That's right."

"And what did you tell me when you gave me the papers?"

"The same story that I have told on the witness stand today."

"At that time, didn't you tell me that Mr. Guthrie Balfour had told you that *he* had done the shooting and that the dead man had been someone who was in the Sleepy Hollow Motel?"

Boles looked at Mason with absolute, utter incredulity. "Do you mean that *I* told you *that?*" he asked.

"Didn't you?" Mason asked.

"Good heavens, no!" Boles said. "Don't be absurd, Mr. Mason. Why in the world should I tell you that? Why Guthrie Balfour was...why he was on his way to Mexico. I put him on the train personally."

"What about the company airplane? Wasn't that subsequently picked up in Phoenix?"

"Either Phoenix or Tucson, I think," Boles said. "But that was at a later date. One of the company employees flew down there on a matter of some importance and then I believe left the plane, as he took a commercial airline on East. I don't know, but I can look up the company records, in case you're interested, Mr. Mason. I'm quite satisfied the company records will show that to be the case."

"I dare say," Mason said drily.

There was a moment's pause.

"Did you go out to the Sleepy Hollow Motel on the evening of the nineteenth or the twentieth?" Mason asked.

Boles shook his head, and said, "I wasn't anywhere near there. No one knew anything about this car at the Sleepy Hollow Motel until I believe the police picked it up, by tracing a key. I don't know about those things. I think the police could tell you, Mr. Mason."

"When did you last see Guthrie Balfour?" Mason asked.

"When he took the train at the Arcade Station."

"And you haven't seen him since?"

"No, sir."

"Or heard from him?"

"Yes, sir. I've heard from him."

"When did you hear from him?"

"I believe that was the day that Mr. Balfour was tried the first time before the first jury. I believe that's the date but I'm not certain. Mr. Guthrie Balfour had been back in the mountains somewhere. He came in briefly for supplies and learned of the defendant's arrest. He telephoned me and told me that he had just talked with you on the telephone, and that his wife Dorla was flying up to get in touch with you."

There was an air of complete candor about the witness which carried conviction.

"You recognized his voice?"

"Of course."

"That's all for the moment," Mason said. "I may wish to recall this witness."

"You may step down," Judge Cadwell said. "Call your next witness, Mr. Prosecutor."

"Florence Ingle," the prosecutor announced.

Florence Ingle came forward, was sworn, gave her name and address.

"You have been subpoenaed as a witness for the defense?" Farris asked.

"Yes, sir."

"I will ask you whether you saw the defendant on the evening of September nineteenth?"

"I did," she answered in a low voice.

"What was his condition?"

"When?"

"At the time you last saw him?"

"At the time I last saw him he had quite evidently been drinking."

"Did he tell you anything at that time about being in debt?"

"Yes, sir. It was a little before that time...the evening of September nineteenth."

"What was the conversation please? But first let me ask you, who was present at that time?"

"Quite a number of people were present at the house, but they were not present when we had the conversation; that is, they were not where they could hear the conversation."

"Just the two of you were present?"

"Yes, sir."

"And what did the defendant tell you?"

"He asked if he could borrow twenty thousand dollars. He told me that he was in debt, that he had run up some gambling debts and that the persons with whom he had been dealing telephoned him and threatened to send a collector unless he made immediate payment."

"Did he say anything about what he thought the collector wanted?"

"Yes, he said those collectors got pretty rough the first time, that sometimes they took people on a one-way ride, but that they beat up anyone who welched on a bet."

"And did he tell you what he intended to do if a collector tried to beat him up?"

"He said he was going to defend himself."

"Did he say how?"

"He said, 'With a gun.'"

"You may inquire," Farris said.

"Did you have any talk with Guthrie Balfour, the defendant's uncle, on that day?" Mason asked.

"Objected to as incompetent, irrelevant, and immaterial, not proper cross-examination" Farris said.

"I would like to have an answer to the question, Your Honor. I think that there is an entire transaction here which should be viewed as a unit."

"Certainly not as a unit," Farris said. "We have no objection to Mr. Mason asking this witness about any conversation she may have had with the defendant in this case. We have no objection to Mr. Mason asking about any matters which were brought up in connection with the conversation on which the witness was questioned on her direct examination, but we certainly do not intend to permit any evidence as to some conversation she may have had with the uncle of the defendant which was not within the presence of the defendant and which, for all we know, has absolutely nothing to do with the issues involved in this case.

"If there is any such conversation and if it is pertinent, it is part of the defendant's case. This witness is subpoenaed as a witness for the defense. Counsel can examine her as much as he wants to about any conversation with Mr. Guthrie Balfour when he calls her as his own witness. At that time we will of course object to any conversation which took place without the presence of the defendant or which has no bearing upon the present case.

"If a person could prove a point by any such procedure as this, there would be no point in swearing a witness. Anyone could get on the stand and tell about some conversation had with some person who was not under oath."

"I think that's quite right, Mr. Mason," Judge Cadwell said. "The Court wishes to be perfectly fair and impartial in the matter, but you can't show any evidence of a conversation with some person who is not a party to the proceedings, and you can't frame such a question as part of your cross-examination. The Court will permit you the most searching cross-examination as to this particular conversation the witness has testified to. The objection is sustained."

"No further questions," Mason said.

"We will call Mrs. Guthrie Balfour to the stand," Farris said.

While Mrs. Balfour was walking forward, Paul Drake stepped up to the bar and caught Mason's eye. He handed Mason a paper and whispered, "This is a certified photostatic copy of Guthrie Balfour's application for a driving license."

Mason nodded, spread out the paper, glanced at it, looked at it again, then folded the paper.

Dorla Balfour was making quite an impression on the jury. The trim lines of her figure, the expressive brown eyes, the vivacious yet subdued manner with which she indicated that her natural vitality was being suppressed out of deference to the solemnity of the occasion, made the jurors prepare to like her right from the start.

She gave her name and address to the court reporter, adjusted herself in the witness chair with a pert little wiggle, raised her lashes, looked at the deputy district attorney, then at the jury, then lowered her lashes demurely.

At that moment there was a commotion in the courtroom, and Hamilton Burger, the big grizzly bear of a district attorney, came striding purposefully into the courtroom.

It needed only a glance at the smug triumph of his countenance to realize that word of Perry Mason's discomfiture had been relayed to him, and he had entered the case personally in order to be in at the kill.

Too many times he had seen Mason, by the use of startling ingenuity, squeeze his way out of some seemingly impossible situation. Now he had waited until he was certain Mason had shot all the arrows from his quiver before entering court. It was apparent to everyone that Dorla Balfour would be the last witness, and then Mason would be forced to make a decision. Either he would put the defendant on the stand, or he would not. If he put the defendant on the stand and the defendant's story coincided with that of Banner Boles, the defendant might have a good chance of showing self-defense. But in that case, Mason would run the risk of an admission of unprofessional conduct and be branded for withholding evidence Boles had given him. If the defendant's story should differ from Boles' testimony, there was not one chance in a hundred the jury would believe it.

Farris, apparently trying to appear in the best possible light before his chief, said, "Mrs. Balfour, do you remember the evening of the nineteenth of September of this year?"

"Very well," she said.

"Did you have any conversation with the defendant on that day?"

"I did, yes, sir."

"When?"

"In the evening."

"Where?"

"At a party given by Mrs. Ingle for my husband."

"That was in the nature of a going-away party?"

"Yes, sir."

"Your husband took the train that night?"

"Yes, sir."

"And did you take the train?"

"Yes, sir, I was to have accompanied my husband as far as the station at Pasadena. However, at the last minute he asked me to go all the way with him."

"Well, never mind that," the prosecutor said. "I'm just trying to fix the time and place of the conversation. Now who was present at this conversation?"

"The one I had with the defendant?"

"Yes."

"Just the defendant and I were present. That is, there were other people in the group but he took me to one side."

"And what did he say to you?"

"He told me that he had incurred some gambling debts; that they were debts on which he didn't dare to welch; that he had been plunging because he had got in pretty deep and he had to make good or he was threatened with personal danger. He said that they had told him a collector was coming, that these collectors were sort of a goon squad who would beat him up and—well, that he *had* to have some money."

"Did he ask you for money?"

"Not me. But he asked me if, while I was on the train, I couldn't intercede for him with my husband and get my husband to let him have twenty thousand dollars."

"You may inquire," Farris said.

"And you did intercede with your husband?" Mason asked.

"Not then. I did later on."

"How much later on?"

"Well, Mr. Mason, you understand I was supposed to get off the train at Pasadena, and then Guthrie asked me to go on with him all the way. He said that he felt uneasy, that he felt that something perhaps was going to happen. He asked me to accompany him."

"And you did?" Mason asked.

"Objected to as incompetent, irrelevant, and immaterial. Not proper cross-examination in that it has nothing to do with the conversation concerning which this witness has testified. We are perfectly willing to let Mr. Mason explore all of the facts in connection with that conversation, but any conversation which subsequently took place between this witness and her husband would be incompetent, irrelevant, and immaterial. It would be hearsay, and we object to it."

"Sustained," Judge Cadwell said.

"Didn't you actually get off the train at Pasadena?" Mason asked.

"Objected to as incompetent, irrelevant, and immaterial. Not proper cross-examination."

"I will permit the question," Judge Cadwell said. "I am going to give the defense every opportunity for a searching cross-examination. The question of what this witness may have said to her husband is one thing, but any of the circumstances surrounding the conversation that was had on this occasion may be gone into. Answer the question."

"Certainly not," she said.

"Didn't you go to the Sleepy Hollow Motel on that evening?"

"Oh, Your Honor," Roger Farris protested. "The vice of this is now perfectly apparent. This is an attempt to befuddle the issues in this case. It is also a dastardly attack on this witness. It makes no difference what she did. She has testified only to her conversation."

"She testified that she went on the train with her husband," Judge Cadwell said. "The Court wishes to give the defense every latitude. I think I will permit an answer to this question."

"Did you go to the Sleepy Hollow Motel?" Mason asked.

"Certainly not," She flared at him. "And you have no right to ask such a question, Mr. Mason. You know perfectly good and well that I didn't do any such thing."

"Do you remember an occasion when your husband telephoned me from Chihuahua?" Mason asked.

"Certainly," she said.

"You were with him at that time?"

"Yes."

"And that is when you returned from Chihuahua?"

"Yes."

"That was the occasion when the defendant was on trial for manslaughter?"

"It was the day after the trial; that is, it was the day of the trial, but after the trial had been concluded."

"And you did catch a plane from Chihuahua?"

"I chartered a plane from Chihuahua and was taken to El Paso. I caught a plane at El Paso and came here. Yes."

"And you saw me the next morning?"

"Yes."

"And you were with your husband when he telephoned?"

"Oh, Your Honor," Farris said, "here we go, on and on and on. This is the vice of opening the door on cross-examination. I don't know what counsel is expecting to prove. I do know that we would like to confine the issues in this case to a simple question of fact. I object to this question on the ground that it is not proper cross-examination, that it's incompetent, irrelevant, and immaterial."

"I am going to permit the answer to this one question," Judge Cadwell said. "I think myself this is going far afield, but it may have a bearing on possible bias on the part of the witness.

"The question, Mrs. Balfour, is whether you were with your husband at the time he telephoned Mr. Mason on that date."

"I was. Yes, sir."

"And," Mason went on, "were you subsequently with him when he telephoned to Mr. Banner Boles?"

"I am not going to object to this question," Roger Farris said, "on the sole and specific understanding that it is not to be used to open a door for a long involved line of extraneous questions. I don't think counsel is entitled to go on a fishing expedition."

"The Court feels that this line of questioning has certainly gone far enough," Judge Cadwell said. "The Court wishes to give the defense every opportunity for a cross-examination. Answer the question, Mrs. Balfour. Were you with your husband when he telephoned Mr. Banner Boles?"

"Yes, sir."

"Well then," Mason said, getting to his feet, "perhaps, Mrs. Balfour, you wouldn't mind turning to the jury and explaining to them how it could possibly be that you journeyed on the train to El Paso with a corpse, that you spent some time in Chihuahua with a corpse, that you were with a corpse when he telephoned Mr. Banner Boles?"

"What in the world do you mean?" she snapped, before the stupefied Roger Farris could even so much as interpose an objection.

"Simply this," Mason said, snapping open the paper he was holding. "The right thumbprint of your husband Guthrie Balfour which is shown on this certified copy of an application for a driver's license is an exact copy of the right thumbprint of the dead man, as disclosed by the coroner's record. The man who was found with this bullet in his brain, the man who was supposedly the victim of this hit-and-run episode, that man was your husband, Guthrie Balfour. Now perhaps you can explain how it happened that you spent this time with a dead man?"

"It can't be," she said vehemently. "I was with my husband. I—"

"Let me see that thumbprint," Judge Cadwell snapped.

"And let me take a look at the exhibit showing the fingerprints of the dead man," Judge Cadwell said.

For a long moment he compared the two prints.

"Would the prosecution like to look at this evidence?" Judge Cadwell asked.

"No, Your Honor," Hamilton Burger said smiling. "We are too familiar with counsel's dramatic tricks to be impressed by them."

"You'd better be impressed by this one," Judge Cadwell said, "because unless there's some mistake in the exhibit it is quite apparent that the prints are the same."

"Then it is quite apparent that there has been some trickery in connection with the exhibits," Hamilton Burger said.

"Now if the Court please," Mason went on, "I am suddenly impressed by certain signatures on the record of the Sleepy Hollow Motel, which I have had photostated. It is evident that one of these signatures, that of Jackson Eagan, is similar to the signature on the driver's license issued to Jackson Eagan. However, I would like time to have a handwriting expert compare the signature of the man who signed his name 'Jackson Eagan' with the handwriting of Banner Boles. I think, if the Court please, I begin to see the pattern of what must have happened on the night of September nineteenth."

"Now just a moment, just a moment," Hamilton Burger shouted. "I object to any such statement by counsel. I object to such a motion. I object to the Court permitting any such statement in front of a jury. I charge counsel with misconduct because of that remark, and I ask the Court to admonish the jury to disregard it."

Judge Cadwell turned to the openmouthed jurors. "The jurors will not be influenced by any remarks made by counsel for either side," he said. "The Court, however, of its own motion, is going to take an adjournment for an hour, during which time certain records will be examined. I am particularly anxious to have a qualified fingerprint expert examine this unquestioned similarity between a thumbprint of Guthrie Balfour on this application for a driving license, and the right thumbprint of the dead man who is the decedent in this case. Court will take a one-hour recess, during which time the jurors are not to converse with anyone about this case, not to discuss it among yourselves, and not to form or express any opinion. Court will take a recess."

Judge Cadwell banged down his gavel, rose from the bench, and said, "I'd like to see counsel for both sides in chambers."

CHAPTER TWENTY

In Judge Cadwell's chambers an irate Hamilton Burger said, "What I want to find out first is why Perry Mason withheld and concealed this evidence."

"Well, what *I* want to find out," Judge Cadwell said, "is Mr. Mason's theory of what happened in this case."

"With all due respect to Your Honor," Hamilton Burger said, "I think Mr. Mason's explanation should come first. I don't think he is entitled to appear here in good standing until he has purged himself of this charge."

"With all due respect to your opinion," Judge Cadwell snapped, "this is a first-degree murder case. Mr. Mason seems to have a theory which accounts for this startling fingerprint evidence. I want to hear that theory."

Mason grinned at the discomfited district attorney and said, "I think it's quite simple, Your Honor. The rented car which was found at the Sleepy Hollow Motel was a car which had apparently been rented by Jackson Eagan, despite the fact that the records show that Jackson Eagan has been dead for some two years.

"That car actually was rented by Banner Boles. Obviously Boles must have been in Mexico when the body of Jackson Eagan was discovered. He took charge of Eagan's papers. He knew that Eagan would have no further use for his driving license. He noticed that the physical description fitted his own physical description. Occasionally, when he was working on a job where he didn't want to use his own name, or when he wanted to go on a philandering expedition, he knew that by renting a car and using the Eagan name, with the Eagan driving license as a means of identification, there was no way his real identity could be traced.

"I could have proved that Guthrie Balfour got off the train to follow his wife if the rules of evidence had permitted me to show a conversation Guthrie Balfour had with Florence Ingle. I couldn't show that in court, but I can tell Your Honor that that's what happened.

"Dorla Balfour was having an affair with none other than Banner Boles of Balfour Allied Associates."

"Oh, bosh!" Hamilton Burger snapped.

Judge Cadwell frowned. "We'll let Mr. Mason finish, Mr. Burger. Then you may have your turn."

Mason said, "Florence Ingle had a conversation over the telephone with Guthrie Balfour. He was ready to divorce Dorla, he wanted to get evidence on her, so he wouldn't have to pay excessive alimony. She got off the train, as planned, at Pasadena and Guthrie Balfour got off the train as he had planned it all along, getting off on the other side of the train. He hurried to a car which he had rented earlier in the day and left there at the station so he could jump in it and drive off. He followed his wife to the place of rendezvous. He secured an adjoining cabin, set up a very sensitive microphone which recorded everything that took place in the adjoining cabin on tape. Then Dorla went home to get her suitcase and planned to return to spend the night.

"The tape recorder recorded all of the words that were spoken in the other cabin, but because of the extreme sensitivity of the microphone there was a certain distortion and Guthrie Balfour still didn't know the identity of the man who was dating his wife. After Dorla left, he determined to enter the cabin, act the part of the outraged husband, and get a statement.

"He entered the cabin. The lights were low. Banner Boles, who occupied that cabin, was waiting for Dorla to return. To his surprise and consternation, he saw the husband, who was not only the man whose home he had invaded, but who was one of the men he worked for.

"He knew that Guthrie Balfour hadn't as yet recognized him, and he didn't dare to give Balfour the chance. He dazzled Balfour by directing the beam of a powerful flashlight in the man's eyes. Then, having blinded Balfour, he threw a chair and launched an attack, hoping that he could knock Balfour out and make his escape from the cabin before his identity could be discovered.

"Balfour drew his gun, and in the struggle the gun went off. That was when Banner Boles, acting with the rare presence of mind which has made him such a skillful trouble-shooter, sank face down on the floor, pretended to be mortally wounded, then lay still.

"In a panic, Guthrie Balfour ran out, jumped into his rented car and drove home. He didn't know what to do. He knew that his shot was going to result in a scandal. He wanted to avoid that at all costs. Then it occurred to him that no one really knew he had got off the train, except the man whom he had every reason to believe was lying dead in the Sleepy Hollow Motel.

"In the meantime, Banner Boles got to his feet, ran to the telephone booth, and put through a call to Dorla at her home telling her exactly what had happened."

"You know this for a fact?" Judge Cadwell asked.

"I know most of the facts. I am making one or two factual deductions from the things I know."

"Using a crystal ball," Hamilton Burger sneered.

"So," Mason went on, "Guthrie Balfour planned to take the company plane to Phoenix, board the train there, and pretend that nothing had happened. He rang up Florence Ingle and asked her to go to Phoenix on a commercial plane and fly the company plane back. He felt that he could trust Florence Ingle. She was the only one in whom he confided. However, he overlooked the fact that Dorla Balfour was at home, that she had been warned that her perfidy had been discovered, that her house of cards was about to come tumbling down. She concealed herself. As soon as she heard his voice, she tiptoed to a point of vantage where she could hear what he was saying. While she was listening to that phone conversation, she suddenly knew a way by which she could extricate herself from her predicament.

"So Dorla waited until her husband had hung up, then rushed to him in apparent surprise and said, 'Why, Guthrie, I thought you were on the train. What happened?'

"Balfour had probably placed Ted's gun on the stand by the telephone. Dorla, still acting the part of the surprised but faithful wife, with her left arm around her husband, picked up the gun and probably said, 'Why dear, what's this?'

"Then she took the gun and shot him in the head without warning.

"Then she telephoned Banner Boles at whatever place he had told her he'd be waiting, and asked him to come at once. So he grabbed a cab and joined Dorla. Then he took charge. Between them they got the idea of banging the body around so that the features would be unrecognizable, making it appear to be a hit-and-run accident and framing Ted with the whole thing, knowing that in case that didn't work they could use Florence Ingle to make it appear Guthrie Balfour was the murderer and that he had resorted to flight.

"So Boles returned the car that he had rented in the name of Jackson Eagan and left it there at the motel. He hoped the hit-and-run theory would work and the corpse would remain unidentified, but if things didn't work another anonymous tip to the police would bring Jackson Eagan into the picture. Boles wanted to have a complete supply of red herrings available in case his scheme encountered difficulties anywhere.

"Thereafter, as things worked out, it was relatively simple. Banner Boles returned to the Florence Ingle party. He managed to drug a drink so that Ted Balfour hardly knew what he was doing. Boles intended to take charge of Ted at that point, but Marilyn Keith saw Ted in an apparently intoxicated condition, so she drove him home and put him to bed.

"However, after she had gone home, the conspirators got the car Ted had been driving, took it out and ran it over Guthrie Balfour's body, smashed up the headlight, left enough clues so that the police would be certain to investigate, and then, in order to be certain, arranged that there would be a witness, a Myrtle Anne Haley, who would tie in the accident directly with Ted Balfour. They arranged to have an anonymous tip send the police out to look at Ted's car.

"It only remained for the conspirators to take the company plane, fly it to Phoenix and get aboard the train, using the railroad ticket which they had taken from Balfour's body. Since Dorla had overheard her husband's conversation with Florence Ingle, she knew that Florence Ingle would go to Phoenix and bring the plane back, feeling certain that she was helping Guthrie Balfour in his deception.

"Of course, the planning in this was part of the master-minding of Banner Boles. That's been his job for years—to think fast in situations where another man would be panic-stricken, to mix up the evidence so that it would be interpreted about any way he wanted to have it interpreted. This was probably one of the high lights of his career.

"He crossed the border, taking out a tourist card as Guthrie Balfour. He was very careful not to telephone anyone who could detect the deception. For instance, he never telephoned Florence Ingle to thank her for what she had done or to tell her that everything had worked out according to schedule. He didn't dare to do that because she would have recognized that the voice was not that of Guthrie Balfour. On the other hand, since *I* didn't know Guthrie Balfour and had never talked with him, Boles was able to ring me up, disguise his voice slightly, tell me that he was Guthrie Balfour and that he was sending his wife to see me."

"That's all very interesting," Judge Cadwell said. "How are you going to prove it?"

"*I'm* not going to prove it," Mason said, "but I think that the police can prove it if they will go to the unit in the Sleepy Hollow Motel which was occupied by Banner Boles when he registered under the name of Jackson Eagan, and I think they'll find there's a small bullet hole in the floor which has hitherto been unnoticed. I think that if the police dig in there, they'll find another bullet discharged from that gun belonging to Ted Balfour."

"Very, very interesting," Judge Cadwell said. "I take it, Mr. District Attorney, that you will put the necessary machinery in motion to see that this case is investigated at once."

"If Mr. Mason is entirely finished," Hamilton Burger said angrily, "I'll now ask the Court to remember that I'm to have my inning. I want to ask Mr. Mason how it happened he was in possession of this evidence which he was concealing from the police."

"I wasn't concealing it from the police," Mason said. "I was waiting for an opportunity to present it in such a manner that a murderer could be apprehended.

"For your information, when we were in that taxicab Banner Boles confessed the whole thing to me, except, of course, that he didn't admit that he was the Beau Brummell who had been making love to Dorla Balfour. He offered me a fee of more than a hundred thousand dollars to see that the facts didn't come out in court. Under the circumstances, I was entitled to hold the evidence until the moment when a disclosure would bring the real criminal to justice. I wasn't concealing any evidence. I was waiting to produce it at the right time.

"However, Banner Boles got on the stand, committed perjury, and forced my hand. I had to surrender the evidence before I was ready."

"Your word against that of Banner Boles," Hamilton Burger said.

"Exactly," Mason told him, smiling. "My word against that of a perjurer and accessory to a murder."

"How are you going to prove that?" Hamilton Burger snapped. "You've come up here with a cockeyed theory, but how are you going to prove it?"

"*You* can prove it if you get busy and recover that extra bullet," Mason said. "And you can prove it if you ask him how it happened that, under oath, he swore to a conversation with a man whose fingerprints show that he had been dead for some time before the conversation took place. You can also prove it by getting in touch with the Mexican government and finding the tourist card that was issued to Guthrie Balfour. You'll find that that was in the handwriting of Banner Boles and you'll find that when Banner Boles left Mexico, he surrendered that tourist card properly countersigned."

Judge Cadwell smiled at the district attorney. "I think, Mr. District Attorney," he said, "most of the logic, as well as *all* of the equities, are in favor of Perry Mason's position."

CHAPTER TWENTY-ONE

Perry Mason, Della Street, Marilyn Keith, Paul Drake, and Ted Balfour gathered for a brief, jubilant session in the witness room adjacent to Judge Cadwell's courtroom.

"Remember now," Mason cautioned Ted Balfour, "at the moment you are jubilant because you have been released. But your uncle has been murdered. You had an affection for him. You're going to be interviewed by the press. You're going to be photographed, and you're going through quite an ordeal."

Balfour nodded.

"And then," Mason said, "you're going to have to get in touch with your Uncle Addison Balfour and explain to him what happened, and you're going to have to see that Marilyn Keith is reinstated."

"You leave that to me," Balfour said. "I'm going to have a talk with him within thirty minutes of the time I leave this courthouse."

A knock sounded on the door. Mason frowned. "I'd hoped the newspaper reporters wouldn't find us here. I didn't want to face them until we were ready. Well, we'll have to take it now. I don't want them to think we're hiding."

Mason flung the door open.

However, it wasn't a newspaper reporter who stood on the threshold, but the bailiff of Judge Cadwell's court who had arranged, in the first place, to have the witness room made available for the conference.

"I don't like to disturb you, Mr. Mason," he said, "but it's a most important telephone call."

"Just a moment," Mason told the others. "You wait here. I'll be right back."

"There's a phone in this next room," the bailiff said.

"Better come along, Paul," Mason said. "This may be something you'll have to work on. You, too, Della."

Della Street and Paul Drake hurried out to stand by Mason's shoulder as Mason picked up the receiver.

"Hello," Mason said.

A thin, reedy voice came over the line. "Mr. Mason, I guess you recognize my voice. I'm Addison Balfour. Please don't interrupt. I haven't much strength.

"I'm sorry that I was deceived about you. I shouldn't have listened to others. I should have known that a man doesn't build up the reputation you have built up unless he has what it takes.

"I'm all broken up about Guthrie but there's no help for that now. We all have to go sometime.

"You have done a remarkable piece of work. You have, incidentally, saved the Balfour Allied Associates from a great scandal, as well as a great financial loss."

"You know what went on in court?" Mason asked.

"Certainly I know," Addison Balfour snapped. "I also know what went on in the judge's chambers. I may be sick, but I'm not mentally incapacitated. I've had reports coming in every half-hour. Don't think I'm a damn fool just because I acted like one when I let Banner Boles talk me into firing you, so he could try to get Mortimer Dean Howland to take over Ted's defense.

"You send your bill to the Balfour Allied Associates for a hundred and fifty thousand dollars for legal services, and you tell that secretary of mine to get the hell back here on the job. I'm going to make a very substantial cash settlement with her to compensate her for the defamation of character connected with her temporary discharge. As for my nephew, you can tell him to stop worrying about his gambling debt now. I think he's learned his lesson.

"And if you want to cheer up a dying old man, you people will get out here as soon as you can and tell me that I'm forgiven. That's all. Good-by."

Addison Balfour hung up the phone at the other end of the line.

Mason turned to find the anxious faces of both Paul Drake and Della Street.

"Who was it?" Della Street asked.

"Addison Balfour," Mason told her. "He's anxious to make amends. He wants us out there as soon as possible."

"Well, then we'd better get out there as soon as possible," Paul Drake said. "In fact, it would be a swell thing from a standpoint of public relations if the newspaper reporters had to interview us *after* we got out there."

"We won't be able to leave the building undetected," Mason said. "We can tell the reporters that we're going out there, but we're going to be interviewed within a few minutes, Paul."

Mason pushed open the door to the witness room, then suddenly stepped back and gently closed the door.

"We'll wait a minute or two before we go in," he said, grinning. "I think the two people in there are discussing something that's damned important—to them."

THE CASE OF
THE SCREAMING WOMAN

FOREWORD

The more I study murder cases in real life the more I am impressed with the work being done by the leaders in the field of legal medicine.

Take my friend Dr. A. W. Freireich, for instance. He is a warm, friendly man. We all know him affectionately as "Abe," but formally he is A. W. Freireich, M.D., a Diplomate of the American Board of Internal Medicine, a Fellow of the American College of Physicians, Director of the Division of Internal Medicine at Meadowbrook Hospital in Nassau County, New York, Assistant Professor of Clinical Medicine at the New York University Post-Graduate School, Past President of the American Academy of Forensic Sciences.

More specifically, if you take an overdose of barbiturates (sleeping pills), sink into a coma and are at the point of knocking on the pearly gates, you will be brought back to the grim realities of mundane life (if they get to you in time) because Dr. Freireich had the daring, the imagination and the background of knowledge to administer the first intravenous injection of benzedrine sulphate to a dying girl of nineteen. The treatment brought her back to consciousness and established a new technique for combatting barbiturate poisoning.

In murder cases, it was Dr. Freireich who analyzed the small bottle of whisky from which Judd Gray tried to drink when he was being brought back from Syracuse by the New York City Police. The fact that this whisky had been loaded with mercury went a long way toward implicating Ruth Snyder in that famous case.

Many times when ingenious defense counsel had thought up ideas intended to influence jurors into finding murderers completely blameless, the presence of Dr. Freireich on the witness stand or seated at the side of the prosecuting attorney effectively hampered the verbal embellishments so necessary in making such ideas seem plausible.

In one case, the theory of the defense was that the murderer had been suffering from lead poisoning. Since he had been drinking heavily the night before it was claimed this caused an acidosis which brought about the release of lead from its storage place in the bones, giving the defendant "acute mania."

This was most plausibly presented to the jury. Dr. Freireich, however, was able to show that the defendant didn't have lead poisoning in the first place, thereby dealing the theory and the defendant's hopes of acquittal a body blow.

In another case the murderer had cut the throat of the five-year-old child of a neighbor and sought to escape punishment by claiming a condition of "hypoglycemia" but overlooked an essential fact of bodily chemistry which Dr. Freireich was able to point out to the prosecuting attorney. The result was to establish the fallacy of the defense reasoning to the satisfaction of the jury which promptly returned a verdict of first degree murder.

However, the main thing about Abe Freireich which appeals to all who know him is the warm, human friendliness of the man. He is never upstage. He never surrenders to petty jealousies and one never hears any criticism coming from his lips. Despite his vast knowledge he tries to create the impression that he is after all a very ordinary individual. At such meetings as those of the American Academy of Forensic Sciences, he is known for his warm handclasp and friendly grin. And when a mystery writer needs some bit of medical knowledge which is hard to find in textbooks, Abe Freireich will sit down and patiently explain the obscure bits of poison lore which have somehow eluded the "authorities on the subject."

So I dedicate this book to my friend:

A. W. FREIREICH, M.D., F.A.C.P.

Erle Stanley Gardner

CHAPTER ONE

Della Street, Perry Mason's confidential secretary, entered Mason's private office, walked over to the lawyer's desk and said, "You always like something out of the ordinary, Chief. This time I have a lulu!"

"Unusual?" Mason asked, looking up from the papers on his desk.

"Unique," she said.

"Give," Mason told her.

"A Mrs. John Kirby telephoned," Della Street said, "and wanted to retain you to cross-examine her husband."

"A divorce case?" Mason asked.

"No, she and her husband are good friends."

"Yet she wants me to cross-examine him?"

"That's right."

"About what?"

"About where he was last night."

Mason frowned. "Della, I'm not a lie detector. I'm not a psychoanalyst. I don't handle cases involving domestic relations."

"That's what I told Mrs. Kirby," Della Street said.

"She told me she only wanted her husband's interests protected. She said she wanted you to listen to his story, puncture his self-assurance, and rip him to pieces."

"To what purpose?"

"She didn't say. I told her to call back in five minutes, and—This is probably the call," Della Street said as the telephone on her secretarial desk rang noisily.

"I'll talk with her," Mason decided.

Della Street picked up the receiver, said, "Hello. Yes, Mrs. Kirby.... Yes, Mr. Mason will talk with you."

She nodded to Mason who picked up the phone on his desk, said, "Hello, this is Mr. Mason talking."

Mrs. Kirby's voice was well modulated, and entirely different from the strident, emotionally surcharged tones Mason had expected to hear.

"I'd like to have you cross-examine my husband," she said.

"About what?" Mason asked.

"About where he was last night."

"Why?"

"So he'll realize his story won't stand up."

"So you can reproach him, or get a divorce, or—?"

"Good heavens, Mr. Mason! Don't misunderstand me. I'm a very devoted wife. I love my husband. That's why I'm calling you. He told me a story. I don't want him to tell that story to anyone else."

"Why not?" Mason asked.

"He might get stuck with it."

"What's wrong with it?"

"You'll know when you hear it."

"And you want me to cross-examine him?"

"Yes."

"Why?"

"So he'll realize his story is absurd. I'm hoping he'll then tell you what actually did happen."

"And then?" Mason asked.

"Then," she said, "you can help him. He won't tell you the truth on the first visit, but after you point out the weak spots, he'll leave your office determined to plug up those weak spots. Then, between us I'm hoping we can straighten things out."

"Why?"

"So we can help him."

"Can't you tell him that you know he's lying and—?"

"No, no, Mr. Mason! Please! It has to be done my way. My husband's a sales expert. He can make people believe black is white, and he's not averse to trying if he gets in trouble.

"He's in trouble now, but he doesn't know it. In order to keep our marriage happy I have to be the devoted, credulous wife. Please, Mr. Mason!"

"But how are you going to get him to come in to see me?"

"Leave that to me."

"Very well," Mason said. "But understand one thing, Mrs. Kirby, I don't want you to interrupt, I don't want you to—"

"Oh good heavens!" she interposed, "*I* won't be there."

"Very well," Mason said. "Send him in at two o'clock this afternoon."

"Thank you," she cooed. "Good-by, Mr. Mason."

Mason hung up the telephone and glanced at Della Street. "Well," he said, "there's a welcome interruption to an otherwise humdrum day. You certainly described that one, Della!"

She raised an inquiring eyebrow.

"Unique!" Mason told her.

CHAPTER TWO

At one-fifty-five, Mason pushed aside the list of citations on which he had been working and said to Della Street, "That's enough of routine for one day, Della. Let's have a cigarette and see if John Kirby is on time."

Mason settled back in his swivel chair, lit a cigarette, laced his fingers behind his head and smoked for a moment in silence.

The telephone on Della Street's desk rang, and Della Street said, "Yes, Gertie, what is it?" listened for a moment, then said, "Just a moment and I'll see.

"Mr. John Northrup Kirby is here for a two o'clock appointment with Mr. Mason," she said.

Mason looked at his watch. "Two minutes early, Della. John Kirby may lie to his wife, but he keeps his appointments. Tell Gertie to get his address and phone number, then to send him in."

Della Street relayed the instructions to the receptionist, then rose and went to wait at the door of Mason's private office.

"Hello, Mr. Kirby," she said after a few moments, "I'm Della Street, Mr. Mason's confidential secretary. Step right this way, please."

She stood to one side, and a big, bluff man with a jovial grin came breezing into the office, said, "Well, well, well, how are you, Mr. Mason? I've heard so much about you and about your cases. It's a real pleasure!"

Mason extended his hand which was promptly gripped by strong, stubby fingers.

"Sit down, Mr. Kirby," Mason said.

Kirby was in his early forties, a thick-necked individual with heavily colored cheeks, thin dark hair, and the breezy positive manner of a man whose personality is never at rest for a moment but is always vigorously asserting itself.

"Well, Mr. Mason, I suppose you wonder why I'm here."

Kirby let his expansive smile include Della Street.

"The truth of it is," Kirby went on, "I'm wondering myself what the devil I'm doing here. My wife told me I should see a lawyer. I finally agreed to run up and have a talk with you just to keep peace in the family. So she made this appointment for two o'clock. But when you come right down to it, Mr. Mason, there's just no reason on earth why I *should* see a lawyer."

"Except to keep peace in the family," Mason said.

"That, of course." Kirby grinned. "After a while that becomes mighty damned important. Well, Mr. Mason, I know you're busy. I know you're terribly busy. I'll begin right at the start. It was something that happened last night and I just can't understand why my wife should feel— However, there's no use going into that. I'll just begin at the beginning and tell you exactly what happened."

"Go ahead," Mason said. "Do that."

"Well, we had a sales meeting last night. I'm president of the Kirby Oilwell Supply Company, Mr. Mason, and we have these get-togethers every once in a while when we bring up the problems of sales resistance and things of that sort."

"And something happened at this sales meeting?" Mason asked. "Something that caused you to—?"

"No, no, no! Not at the meeting, Mr. Mason, it was after the meeting."

"I see. Go ahead."

"Well, we had this meeting out at a roadhouse. Yesterday was Monday and this place is usually closed Mondays, so there was no regular trade to bother with. We made arrangements to have an exclusive on the place, charter the whole shebang just for our gang."

Mason nodded his understanding.

"I was driving home, Mr. Mason. The reason I mention this roadhouse is that it was quite a ways out and I was driving back home when I saw this girl on the road."

"Driving?" Mason asked.

"Walking, Mr. Mason, carrying a one-gallon, red gasoline can. Well, of course you know what that means, and I stopped instantly. Some poor girl who had run out of gas and had to walk to a service station and was coming back to her car."

Mason nodded.

"I'll admit that right after I came to a stop, Mr. Mason, I had a qualm, a little misgiving. I understand that holdup men sometimes use a girl for bait, but this girl was walking right along, not standing in one place. She seemed to be minding her own business, and she looked like a real little lady, a very nice refined young woman."

"How old?" Mason asked.

"Oh, twenty-two or so. Something like that. Young, good-looking, well dressed, the kind of a girl who would be driving a good car."

"Go on," Mason said. "You picked her up. What happened?"

"Well, I picked her up. She had this one-gallon can of gasoline. I asked her where she was going, and she said just about a quarter of a mile farther, that her car had run out of gas, and she'd had to walk back to the gas station."

"Go on," Mason said.

"Well, I just sort of crawled along looking for this car of hers, and we covered half a mile and there was no car. Then we covered a mile and there was no car. I asked her how come, and she said she couldn't understand it, and then we came to a gasoline station. Well, of course she knew that she'd left her car between where I picked her up and *that* gasoline station, so we turned around and went back.

"I drove back to where I *thought* I'd picked her up. Then, so there'd be no chance of a mistake, I kept right on until I came to the service station where she'd bought the gas. Then I turned around, took the extreme right-hand side of the road and just barely crawled along. I kept my headlights on high so they showed every bit of the side of the road."

"No car?" Mason asked.

"No car."

"So then what did you do?" Mason asked.

"Then I questioned the girl. She told me she'd taken the keys out of the car and put them under the rubber floor mat. Then she'd walked back to this service station, told them her story, got a gallon can of gasoline, and had started back to the car. She said the tank was just absolutely bone dry, that the car wouldn't go another foot without gas.

"Well, of course, Mr. Mason, there was no question about it by that time. Someone had stolen the car—either someone who had siphoned off gas and put it in the tank and driven off, or someone who had simply put a tow chain on the car and gone off with it."

"You notified the police of course?" Mason asked.

Kirby shifted his position. "Now there's the reason that my wife thought I'd better talk to a lawyer. I didn't."

"Why not?"

"She didn't want me to."

"Why?"

"Now there's something she wouldn't tell me, Mr. Mason. But here was this young woman—one of the most pathetic situations I've ever encountered. She didn't have a dime to her name. She—"

"How about a purse?" Mason asked.

"She'd left the purse in the car. She said there wasn't a great deal of money in the purse. She'd taken out a dollar bill, enough to pay for the gas and had put that in her stocking. She said she didn't want to carry the purse in one hand and the gasoline can in the other as she walked back—"

"She walked back, not ahead?"

"That's right, Mr. Mason. She said she remembered having passed a gasoline station not more than a half or three-quarters of a mile back. It had been a Shell station and she was carrying a Standard Oil credit card. She liked to buy all of her gasoline on that credit card and, while she knew her tank was low, she thought she had enough for another eight or ten miles. She thought she could get into town easily, and she was looking for a Standard station. Then the motor started to cough and sputter, and the car ran completely out of gas. She used the last of her momentum to pull over to the side of the road."

"She got it completely off the highway?"

"Got it completely off the highway. There was a place where she could get clean over onto a turnout by the side of the road."

"And then what happened?"

"Then she walked on back to the service station."

"Didn't she catch a ride?"

"No, it was only half a mile or so, and she was a little frightened about riding with strangers."

"Yet she rode with you all right?"

"She explained that. She said that when she walked up to the gasoline station she was walking on the side of the road, out on the gravel, but after she got the can of gasoline—it was only a gallon can but it began to get heavy, so then she started walking on the pavement. She said that she was getting a little weary and—well, something about my appearance seemed to reassure her. She told me that I seemed like what she called a 'Good Joe'—a nice compliment from a young woman like that. Believe me, she had class stamped all over her."

"What eventually happened?" Mason asked.

"Well, I naturally didn't know what the devil to do. Here was this girl who had just had her car stolen, no purse, no driving license, credit card, social security number—"

"You got this girl's name?" Mason asked.

"Oh, yes, we got quite friendly. Now don't misunderstand me, Mr. Mason, but I'm just trying to tell this thing the way it happened."

"What was her name?"

"Lois Wagner."

"She was a working girl? Married? Single? What?"

"Well, I gathered she'd been married and divorced. She was a little reticent about telling me her personal history, and under the circumstances I didn't feel like pressing an inquiry. You understand, Mr. Mason, it doesn't take very long to drive a couple of miles looking for a car, and...oh, I suppose she was in the car with me for perhaps ten or fifteen minutes in all. I told her that she certainly should notify the police and give a description of the car, and she said, no, she didn't want to do that. So then I asked her what she was going to do, and she said frankly she had no idea. I asked her if she had any friends in the city, and she said she didn't know a soul. So I said, 'Now, look here, young lady. I'm not going to have you wandering around at night.' She pointed out that she didn't have any money, and I told her nevertheless I wasn't going to turn her loose to wander along the road."

"I see," Mason said dryly.

"Of course, Mr. Mason, I detect a certain note of skepticism in your voice, and I admit I felt the same way. I just had the feeling along toward the last that it was some sort of a game where she was bait or a decoy and—Well, I'm in a business where I have to do a lot of entertaining here and there, and I never know when I'm going to be traveling around, so I always carry quite a large sum of money with me."

"What do you mean, a large sum of money?" Mason asked.

"Well, I keep a thousand dollar bill concealed in the back of my card case, and then I have a wallet that usually has around seven hundred and fifty to fifteen hundred dollars in it. I try to carry four or five hundred-dollar bills all the time."

"I see," Mason said. "And you had money with you last night?"

"Oh yes."

"About how much?"

"Oh, I'd say around two thousand dollars. Well, anyway, I took this girl to a motel and told the proprietor I wanted a room for her, and—well, damn it! He wouldn't let me have one."

"Why not?"

"Suspicious, I suppose. Of course the idea of a single girl coming in that way with an older man and—damn it! He had a sign out that said '*Vacancy*' just as plain as could be, yet he had the crust to tell me that he didn't have any vacancies, that everything he had, had been reserved in advance."

"So what did you do?"

"Well, I explained to Miss Wagner that—it was a rather embarrassing situation."

"Go on," Mason said.

"So she suggested that perhaps if I'd register as husband and wife then we could get a room all right and she could stay in the room and I could go on. She was a very, very good sport about it. Of course she felt all broken up over the theft of the car and the loss of her purse and her personal baggage and all that, but she seemed most considerate and understanding, and she was afraid she was delaying me, afraid that she was making a terrific nuisance out of herself."

"What time was this?" Mason asked

"Along about midnight. The sales meeting broke up a little after eleven, and oh, I suppose it was right around midnight."

"All right," Mason said, "so she suggested that you register as husband and wife, and what did you do?"

"Well, I went on to the next motel we came to. That was the Beauty Rest Motel. I drove in and said I wanted accommodations, and the manager just gave us a quick look and said, 'Twenty dollars,' so I registered."

"How did you register?" Mason asked. "Under your own name?"

"No, sir, I didn't, Mr. Mason. You see her name was Wagner, so I registered as Mr. and Mrs. John Wagner, and well, I'd forgotten to find out what city she was from, so I put down the first thing that came in my mind—San Francisco, California—and gave the first address that popped into my head. And then the registration blank provided for the license number of the automobile and the make of the automobile. Well, of course, I put down the make and I put down the first three letters of my license number and the first digit. Then I got smart and put down two phony numbers for the last two.

"By that time I was doubting the wisdom of what I was doing."

"I can well understand that," Mason said.

"Well, it was all right, Mr. Mason. I didn't know for a minute, but I thought perhaps there was going to be a catch in it somewhere, but there wasn't. I put up the money for the cabin, the manager took us down and showed us the cabin, and I parked the car and told Miss Wagner good night. I told her I wished she'd let me call the police, about the car, but she said there were reasons that she couldn't explain, and she simply didn't want the police brought in on the case. So I gave her ten dollars, told her good night, and went on home."

"What time did you get home?"

"Sometime around one o'clock or so. I didn't look at my watch."

"And your wife?"

"My wife was in bed."

"She woke up when you came in?"

"Oh yes, she woke up and asked a few questions about the meeting."

"You told her about Miss Wagner?"

"Not last night, no. I didn't tell her that until this morning. My wife is a frightfully good sport, Mr Mason. She's been around salesmen and sales meetings and all that, and she's broad-minded and tolerant and she was laughing a little about the way we call these meetings to discuss new numbers in the catalogue and always wind up with the same old strip tease. She asked me if the meeting wasn't a little later than usual. So then I told her about this girl and she became very sympathetic. She said I should have brought her to the house, and insisted that I go back to the Beauty Rest Motel and see if we couldn't do something for her."

"You went back?"

"Yes. My wife went with me. We drove right up to the unit that had been rented to us, Unit Number 5, and the key was in the door. I went inside. The bed had been slept in, but there wasn't any sign of the young woman."

"Then what?"

"That's all there is, Mr. Mason. That's the story. She simply got up early, left the key in the door, and took off.

"My wife is afraid I may have let myself in for something. Of course charging me twenty dollars for a motel room for two people shows the manager of the motel was suspicious when we registered. I couldn't help that. I wanted to get on home, so I paid the twenty bucks. I'd have paid twenty-five if he'd said twenty-five."

"And so?" Mason asked.

Kirby spread his hands apart in an eloquent gesture. "That's it, Mr. Mason. That's the whole story."

"Well, that's a very interesting story," Mason said. "It's rather an unusual adventure! By the way, does your wife believe the story?"

"Why, of course she does. Why shouldn't she?"

"You didn't notice any skepticism on her part?"

"Of course not. Why the devil should she be skeptical? What is there that doesn't sound right? It's the truth."

"She wanted you to see a lawyer?"

"Only so I could be protected in case there was any—well, in case it was sort of a frame-up. After all, this girl may show up later on and try to make trouble over that husband-and-wife registration.

"Not that she could really do anything. My wife has absolute confidence in me, Mr. Mason. She knows I'm telling the truth."

Mason glanced at Della Street. "When you first noticed this woman she was carrying a red gasoline can?"

"That's right."

"A one-gallon can?"

"Yes sir."

"The kind that are issued by service stations to people who have run out of gas?"

"Yes, sir."

"How was she dressed?"

"Oh, I don't know, Mr. Mason. I don't think a man notices a woman's clothes very much. She had some kind of a gray outfit. I remember a gray skirt, and I think brown shoes and stockings."

"Flat-heeled shoes?"

"No, sir. Very nicely cut shoes."

"High-heeled?"

"Fairly high heels. Nice alligator shoes."

"Now when you got to the motel," Mason said, "you quite naturally didn't leave the gallon can of gasoline with her?"

"No, sir, I didn't. I— That would have been rather absurd to have put a girl off at a motel without a purse, or a toothbrush, or anything, and left her a gallon can of gasoline."

Kirby laughed nervously.

"Then," Mason said, "the gallon can of gasoline must still be in your car?"

"Well, yes. Of course. I guess it is."

"Where is your car now?"

"Down in the parking lot."

Mason said, "I'll go down with you, and we'll take a look at that gasoline can. Perhaps that will tell us something."

"Well," Kirby said, running his hand over the thin hair which swept back from his forehead, "come to think of it, Mr. Mason, I don't remember seeing that gasoline can in the car this morning."

"You don't!"

"No."

"Do you keep your car in a garage at your house?"

"Yes, sir."

"A double garage?"

"A three-car garage."

"Do you have a chauffeur or anyone who works on the cars?"

"No, sir, not regularly."

"Then who could possibly have taken the can out of the car?"

"Mr. Mason, I don't know, I...to tell you the truth, I just don't know what did happen to that can of gasoline."

Mason said, "I'd better look up the automobile registration and find out about the car that's registered in the name of Lois Wagner. We'll check back and find out what dealer sold her the car, and in that way we can get a description of the car and—"

"Now wait a minute, Mr. Mason," Kirby interrupted, "you're going pretty fast on this thing."

"You're consulting me as an attorney," Mason pointed out.

Kirby cleared his throat, ran a finger around the inside of his collar. "It looks to me as though you're trying to break down my story."

"Break it down," Mason exclaimed. "Why there's nothing wrong with the story, is there?"

"Certainly not!" Kirby said stiffly. "Only you're making it sound as though I was trying to... to make an alibi in a murder case, or something. Good heavens, is that clock right?"

"Yes."

"Then I'm way off! My watch must be running half an hour behind. I have another appointment, a *very* important appointment, and I'm late for it."

Mason said, "If your watch is off, Kirby, you must have come half an hour early for your appointment with me."

"Well... yes... I wanted to be sure to be here. Well, thanks a lot, Mr. Mason. I'll call you later on. I'm terribly sorry! I'll be seeing you."

He was out of his chair and through the door all in one motion.

Della Street looked at Perry Mason.

"Well?" the lawyer asked.

"He is now on his way to buy a one-gallon gasoline can," Della Street said. "And then he'll have to paint it red and batter it up a bit."

Mason grinned. "By this time he realized his story won't stand up, Della."

Della Street frowned, said, "I've heard that name somewhere before. Something that keeps trying to register in my mind. I— Good heavens!"

Mason raised his eyebrows.

Della Street's eyes widened. "Chief!" she exclaimed. "It all fits in."

"All right," Mason said. "What is it, Della?"

Excitement made Della Street's words tread on each other's heels as she said, "Chief, driving in this morning I had the radio on in my car. I was listening to the news and the weather forecast and there was an item of local news about a Dr. P. Lockridge Babb, living out some place on Sunland Drive, who was assaulted last night, knocked unconscious and is lying in a critical condition at the hospital this morning.

"Neighbors heard a woman screaming, heard the sound of blows and saw a young woman running out of the house. As I remember it, the description was almost identical with this girl that Mr. Kirby picked up."

"That description doesn't mean much, Della," Mason said. "Neighbors could describe almost any young girl as having the same general appearance."

"I know, Chief. But now I know where I heard the name of Kirby. Police thought the assailant was someone who had made an appointment late at night with Dr. Babb. They felt the young woman was probably a narcotics user, and, after she had entered Dr. Babb's office, she slugged him with a heavy glass beaker, grabbed his supply of narcotics and ran out.

"So the police looked through Dr. Babb's appointment book acting on the theory that he wouldn't have let anyone in at that late hour at night unless there had been an appointment."

"How late?" Mason asked, his eyes hard with interest.

"Around eleven-thirty."

"All right. Go ahead," Mason said. "What about the appointment book?"

"There were two names on it. I've forgotten the other name, but I remember that one of them was Kirby. I wouldn't have remembered that if it hadn't been for hearing it this morning, and then again this afternoon. It's been ringing a bell with me all day—that there was something I should know about this client of ours."

Mason pursed his lips, drummed silently with the tips of his fingers on the surface of his desk. "Probably there's nothing to it, Della, but run down the hall to the Drake Detective Agency, and get Paul Drake to find out something about this Dr. Babb business. Look up the location. If the location is right, the time is right, the description is right and the name is right, it *may* be that we have a client who's in a serious predicament.

"Try and get John Kirby on the telephone. Ring his office and leave word that I want him to call just as soon as he comes in. Try and get Mrs. Kirby on the phone and tell her I want to get in touch with her husband. Let's check on this thing.

"Now be careful not to get Paul Drake all steamed up. Tell him it's just a routine matter we're checking, not a case in which we have a particular interest. Just ask him to get busy on the telephone, find out what the facts are, and then report to me. Get one or the other of the Kirbys on the phone just as soon as you've started Paul Drake working."

Della Street nodded and left the office.

Ten minutes later Mason was advised that John Kirby wasn't at his office, that the residence phone didn't answer and there was, therefore, no way of reaching Mrs. Kirby. Paul Drake had been contacted and would report as soon as he could get the facts.

CHAPTER THREE

It was nearly four o'clock when Della Street relayed Paul Drake's report to Perry Mason.

"Dr. P. Lockridge Babb, also known as Dr. Phineas L. Babb, is sixty-two years old, a semiretired physician and surgeon, living at 19647 Sunland Drive.

"That location is within a few blocks of the Beauty Rest Motel where John Kirby took the young woman.

"About eleven-thirty last night, one of Dr. Babb's neighbors heard a woman screaming and the sound of blows. The sounds came from the doctor's house. Evidently there was quite a commotion. A general handy man and assistant who lives in back of the house over the garage was taking a shower at the time. The sound of the screams was loud enough for him to hear over the sound of the shower.

"He threw a towel around himself and ran down the stairs from his apartment to see what was wrong.

"The neighbors on the east, whose name is Dunkirk, heard the commotion and saw this girl run out of the house. They notified the police. Police got there almost within a matter of seconds. A radio car was in the neighborhood when the report was received.

"The officers found Dr. Babb lying unconscious on the floor. A heavy glass beaker had evidently been used as a weapon. It was lying broken into halves a short distance away.

"The Dunkirks saw this girl running out of the house. She's described as young, dark brown hair, dressed in just about the same way as the girl Kirby picked up. The interesting thing is that Mrs. Dunkirk, who saw her, is certain that the girl was not carrying a purse. Her hands were empty as if she'd been in a struggle and had dashed out leaving her purse behind.

"I've been trying to get Mr. Kirby every few minutes. His office says he isn't in, and they don't know where he is. The number at the Kirby residence still doesn't answer. I've been calling there every ten or fifteen minutes.

"Police found the appointment book kept by Dr. Babb in his office. It shows that during the evening he had appointments with two persons: one by the name of Kirby, one by the name of Logan. No initials are listed in the book.

"Dr. Babb is in a critical condition. He's still unconscious."

Mason asked, "Was there any sequence on these names, Della?"

"It's hard to tell," she said. "The appointment book is one that has a separate page for each day of the year. Then these pages are divided into hours and half-hours.

"If these times as shown on the printed page mean anything, then Logan's appointment was for eleven, Kirby's for eleven-thirty.

"Police are inclined to believe Dr. Babb paid no attention to the printed subdivisions showing time. There had been several appointments for the afternoon apparently simply grouped as a unit. Then there were these two appointments for the evening."

Mason digested that information, then sat for a moment in frowning concentration.

Abruptly he pushed back his chair and got to his feet.

"Grab some shorthand notebooks and plenty of pencils, Della. It may or may not be a wild goose chase, but if we're going to have Kirby for a client, we'll at least give him *some* protection."

CHAPTER FOUR

It was still some two hours before sunset when Perry Mason and Della Street drove past the address on Sunland Drive.

Dr. Babb's bungalow was set back from the street at the foot of a steep hill. Behind the bungalow was a two-car garage, with an apartment over the garage.

"The Dunkirks must live in that house up on the hill fronting on this other street. Can you see the name of that street, Della?"

"Rubart Terrace," Della Street said, peering at the road sign.

"All right," Mason said, "let's go talk with the Dunkirks. Then we'll have a chat with this handy man who evidently lives in that apartment over the garage."

Mason turned his car up the steep incline at Rubart Terrace, parked his car with some difficulty on account of the steep grade. He and Della Street climbed steps to the porch of the Dunkirk house.

A man answered Mason's ring.

"I'm Mr. Mason," the lawyer said with his most affable smile, "and this is Miss Street. Are you Mr. Dunkirk?"

"That's right," the man said without showing either hostility or cordiality, standing there in the door waiting for Mason to go on. He was a man in his early fifties, with sandy hair, bushy eyebrows, gray eyes, sloping shoulders and a stubby, sandy mustache.

"I believe it was your wife who telephoned the police?" Mason asked.

"That's right."

"Is she in?"

"Yes."

Mason gave the man his best smile. "We'd like to talk with her."

"What about?"

"About what she saw and heard."

"She's told the police."

"I understand," Mason said.

The man in the doorway let the conversation fall to a flat stop. The sound of a piano banging away at an old-time piece of jazz music came from the house.

Mason stood expectantly waiting.

From behind the man in the shadows of the hallway a woman's voice, sharp with excitement, said, "Is that Perry Mason, the lawyer?"

"How do you do," Mason called across the man's shoulders to the invisible woman in the shadows. "Yes, I'm Perry Mason."

"Well, for heaven's sakes!" the woman exclaimed. "The idea of you coming here! Why, I never expected to see *you* calling at *my* house. I saw you in court once. Motley, get away from that door. Come in, Mr. Mason. Come in."

Mrs. Dunkirk was heavier than her husband, probably a good ten years younger, a full-curved blonde who seemed to be gregariously inclined and who instantly took charge of the situation.

"You folks come right in. What did you say this young woman's name was?"

"Miss Street," Mason said, "my secretary."

"Oh yes, Miss Street, how are you? I'm certainly glad to meet you, and I guess you've already met my husband. He's a little resentful of all the interruptions we've had to put up with last night and today. Now come right in and sit down. I heard you say you wanted to talk about what happened last night."

"That's right," Mason said.

"What's your interest in it, Mr. Mason?"

Mason smiled and said, "A client of mine is somewhat concerned about Dr. Babb. You see he's a friend of the doctor's. They're trying to get things all lined up—"

"Oh, I see," she interrupted. "Well, after all, there isn't very much I can tell. Perhaps you folks would like to sit right down here by the window. That's where I was sitting last night when all this happened."

"You certainly have a nice view from this window," Mason said as she led the way to chairs.

Yes, we just live around that window. Motley simply can't get away from it. He likes to sit and look out over the valley. He'll spend half the time here with his binoculars, watching birds and people and...just browsing."

Dunkirk said, "You make me sound lazy. I worked hard, Mr. Mason, until I was able to retire a couple of years ago, and I don't aim to do any great amount of work any more. We've got enough to live on as long as we keep our expenses budgeted and don't spend our money traveling around."

His wife laughed nervously. "That intended for me, Mr. Mason. I've been trying to get him to take a trip down through Mexico and then South America. He isn't much for traveling."

"When you're traveling, you're spending money," Dunkirk said.

Mrs. Dunkirk, trying to keep what was evidently a sore point with her husband out of the conversation, said, "Well, you want to know what happened. We were sitting right here, my husband and I, and we'd been sitting in the dark talking for a while. Motley had some pictures he wanted to develop. He's fixed up a darkroom in the basement. He went down and started puttering around with his pictures. I sat here waiting for him to come back.

"When Motley is in the darkroom and comes up in between operations, he doesn't like to have his eyes dazzled with bright light and then go back to his photography. So we sit here with the lights out, and because the lights are out we have the drapes pulled back. It's beautiful up here at night, Mr. Mason. You see Rubart Terrace climbs up quite steeply, and we can look right out over the top of Dr. Babb's house and garage. We can see strings of lights from the valley, and watch the lights of cars on the boulevard. I suppose we'll get tired of it after a while, but right now I prefer it to television. It's a moving panorama."

"I take it you haven't been here very long?" Mason said.

"Not long enough to take the view for granted as yet. I hope we never do. I think it's the most beautiful place we've ever lived in, and very healthful, too. We're up here above the valley, and the smog—we haven't had any smog at all, well, that is, not to speak of."

Dunkirk said tonelessly, "We haven't been here long enough to tell."

"Motley's cautious." She smiled at Mason. "Well, I am willing to take Dr. Babb's word for it as far as I'm concerned. Dr. Babb says this location is relatively free of smog and he's been here for more than ten years."

"You've been visiting back and forth with Dr. Babb since you moved here?" Mason asked.

"Oh yes. You see Motley knew Dr. Babb before we moved in. It was because of Dr. Babb that we got this place. He told us it was for sale and he thought it was a good buy."

Motley Dunkirk said, "Dr. Babb treated me eight years ago and did a good job of it. He's a good doctor."

Mason picked up the pair of powerful binoculars which were lying on a coffee table and held them to his eyes. "These are remarkably fine binoculars," he exclaimed.

"Aren't they?" Motley said. "I think I'm pretty much of an expert on binoculars, and this is the best glass I've ever seen. They have an exceptionally wide field and very sharp definition. Look at that cat down there in Dr. Babb's yard, Mr. Mason. What's that he's playing with?"

Mason turned the glasses on the cat. "Dr. Babb's cat?" he asked.

"No, it belongs to the people next door, the ones who live on the west of Dr. Babb, Mr. and Mrs. Grover Olney. We don't know very much about them. They're not inclined to be neighborly. I guess they're all right, but they keep very much to themselves."

"The cat seems to have a goldfish," Mason said.

"Well now, what do you know?" Mrs. Dunkirk said. "That's the first time that cat has caught one of those goldfish, but heaven knows it's put in enough time sitting there by the pool."

"The cat spends some time there?"

"Yes. The cat's quite a hunter. It's fascinated by the goldfish. It sits there by the side of the sunken garden for hours. Notice the way Dr. Babb laid that out. I think it's very artistic."

"Dr. Babb didn't lay it out," Motley Dunkirk corrected. "It's that handy man of his, Donald."

"That's right, Don Derby," Mrs. Dunkirk said. "He's quite a worker. He's always puttering around with something, like when he took out the strip of lawn that was in there. It really was too small to be a lawn, so he made a beautiful sunken garden with a pool for the goldfish and a little artificial stream running between ornamental rock walls. Notice the various colored rocks there, Mr. Mason. They came from all over the country. Whenever Don can get away for a few days, he brings home a collection of rocks. He likes to go out in the desert and prospect."

"For minerals?" Mason asked.

"Not minerals. Just rocks. I don't think he'd know one mineral from another, but I'm satisfied some of those rocks really have value. Some of them are just as heavy as lead. Particularly the batch he brought home from that last trip. When was that, Motley? About a month ago?"

"I believe so," her husband said.

"Well," Mrs. Dunkirk said, "I know that you want to know what happened, Mr. Mason, and good gracious, I know what a busy man you are! I read about your cases. they certainly seem to be spectacular."

Mason smiled courteously.

"He *makes* them spectacular," Dunkirk said.

Mrs. Dunkirk said, "Now just don't interrupt me, Motley, and I'll go right ahead and tell them the story."

Della Street opened her notebook, held a pencil poised over the page.

"Police asked me particularly about fixing the time," Mrs. Dunkirk said. "It's pretty difficult to fix something like that right down to the minute. I have to sort of piece things together. The light over Dr. Babb's porch was on. I'd been sitting here for a while with Motley. He'd put through one batch of pictures and there was another batch he was very anxious to get developed. He went down to the darkroom. That must have been right around eleven-fifteen. I decided I'd make a cup of chocolate. I went to the kitchen and made the chocolate, and came back to sit by the window, sipping the chocolate and soaking up the view. That was eleven-thirty as nearly as I can make an estimate."

She ceased talking for a moment and the piano music changed from jazz to classical.

Mrs. Dunkirk said by way of explanation, "That's my niece Gertrude. She's going to be with us for a few weeks. Young people these days are quite a handful. She has to be doing something all the time.

"She's going to be terribly upset about that cat and the goldfish. She loves those fish—spends a good part of her time sitting over there by the goldfish pool, hand feeding the goldfish. In just a few days she's managed to tame them."

"How old is your niece?" Mason asked

"Sixteen."

"Did she see anything last night?"

"Heavens, no! She was playing away on that piano."

"She plays very well, although there's a certain—well a mechanical rhythm to her playing."

Mrs. Dunkirk laughed. "Of course there is. It's a player piano. That's one of Motley's most treasured possessions, a genuine antique. It was one of the old kind that works with bellows and strips of perforated paper but Motley has fixed it up with an electric motor. He has a whole library of the old pieces. Land sakes! Sometimes I think Gertrude's going to wear that piano out. She was in there last night playing it until after midnight."

"Could we talk with her?" Mason asked.

There was a sudden embarrassed silence; then Motley Dunkirk said, "I don't think it would be advisable. She didn't see anything."

"She's very shy," Mrs. Dunkirk said.

"And easily upset, intensely nervous," Motley went on.

Again there was a brief silence.

Mrs. Dunkirk said, "Well, now, let's see. Where was I? I was telling you about this girl. Oh yes.

"I saw this young woman come walking up the street. You know, it was rather late for a young woman to be walking around unescorted, and—well, I noticed her. I wondered who she was. I didn't think she was anyone who lived here in the neighborhood. I didn't have anything else to do or anything to watch, so I picked up this pair of binoculars from the coffee table—we always keep them right there where they're handy—and looked at her.

"And then she turned in at Dr. Babb's house, and I could see her very plainly as she stood under the porch light. She had on a gray plaid jacket with a bluish-green ruffled blouse, and brown shoes. She was wearing a gray skirt. She had dark brown hair. I couldn't see the color of her eyes. She didn't wear a hat, and—"

"Just a minute," Mason asked. "Was she carrying a handbag or a purse or anything when she went in?"

"Now that's something I can't remember clearly, but I don't think she was carrying a thing. I won't say for certain but that's what I think. I do know she wasn't carrying a thing when she ran out."

"Go on," Mason said.

"Well, this young woman went in there, and it wasn't very long after that before I heard this terrific banging. At first I couldn't imagine where it was coming from. I called down to my husband to see if everything was all right, but he was shut in the darkroom and couldn't hear me. I hurried to the front door. Just then the woman started screaming. She screamed twice. I waited until the screaming had stopped for a few seconds; then I ran and telephoned for the police. By that time, of course, I knew the sounds were coming from Dr. Babb's house. I told the police I wanted to report that a woman was screaming and glass was smashing and I could hear blows."

"And then?" Mason asked.

"Then," she said, "I hung up the phone and went back to the front door."

"Not the window?" Mason asked.

"Heavens, no, Mr. Mason! I was standing there in the front door. I wanted to hear and see what was happening and to get away from the noise of that piano."

"Was the porch light on? Here, I mean."

"No, the porch light was out but the hall light was on. It was dark in the living room. There was just a small amount of light coming from the street light up there on Rubart Terrace. The porch light was still on over at Dr. Babb's house."

"All right, what happened?" Mason asked.

"I saw that young woman come running out of that front door just as fast as she could leg it."

"It was the same young woman?" Mason asked.

"Absolutely the same."

"And what happened?"

"She ran away down the street. I started down to Dr. Babb's house so I'd be there when the police arrived and that was when I saw Motley coming up the stairs."

Her husband said sharply, "I told you not to say anything about that, Elvira."

She said, smiling at Mason, "Motley just doesn't ever want to get tied up in anything as a witness."

"Coming up what stairs?" Mason asked.

"Up the cement stairs," she said. "You see, Mr. Mason, there's that flight of stairs from Dr. Babb's place up to Rubart Terrace, and then there are stairs from the lower part of our lot down to the street. Motley heard the scream and started down to see if he could be of any help, and then decided there wasn't anything he could do, so he turned around and came back."

"Donald had run down from his place over the garage," Motley said by way of explanation. "There was no need for me to go on the rest of the way down after he arrived. You see I had that batch of pictures right in the critical stage. I'd started to go down—oh, I don't know, I guess I was about a quarter way down the steps. That must have been while she was telephoning, and then I looked up and I saw Donald Derby, the handy man, down there, with a towel wrapped around him banging on the back door, so I turned around and hurried back up to get to my pictures."

Mrs. Dunkirk laughed. "Donald had been taking a shower. He heard the screams and didn't even wait to dress. That was just before the police showed up.

"There certainly was lots of excitement. I knew that since I'd been the one who telephoned I should be there to tell the officers about this girl, so they wouldn't lose any time. So I ran down the cement walk to Rubart Terrace, ran down to Sunland Drive, and over to the house and I got there just a short time after the police arrived. I told them about the girl, and after a minute or so one of the officers started right out in the police car looking for her, leaving the other man in charge of the premises."

"And where was the handy man?" Mason asked.

"They sent him back up to his place to dress. You see, he lives over the garage there, and he certainly has a remarkably nice apartment. It's just as comfortable as can be."

"Has he been with Dr. Babb for some time?"

"He's been with Dr. Babb ever since I got acquainted with the doctor," Motley Dunkirk said.

"You didn't talk with the police?" Mason asked him.

Dunkirk shook his head. "I was back in my darkroom by the time the police arrived, and, as far as I'm concerned, I want to keep out of it. I was a witness once, and I was never so disgusted in my life. They had me come to court four times, and every time there'd be a continuance. Then, when I finally got on the witness stand and told what I knew, the lawyer on the other side browbeat me and shouted at me and shook his finger in my face and as good as called me a liar every time I opened my mouth. I got so mad I could hardly talk. I went home and was so sick I went to bed.

"And the judge sat up there on the bench and didn't do a thing about it. He didn't say a word to that lawyer. Everybody acted bored about the whole thing."

"What kind of a case was it?" Mason asked.

"Just a little, two-bit automobile accident case," Motley Dunkirk said. "I get mad every time I think about it."

"Mrs. Dunkirk said, "Motley dashed back up the steps and dove right into his darkroom. He kept at work on the pictures. I talked with the police, and because I talked with them, and because I'd been the one who had seen what had happened, they didn't bother to come over here or ask if my husband had seen anything."

"Well," Motley said, "as far as I'm concerned, the woman who ran out of the *front* door didn't have a thing to do with it. It was the other woman who is responsible for whatever happened."

"*Another* woman?" Mason asked.

"That's right. The woman who ran out the back way."

"I never did see her," Mrs. Dunkirk explained to the lawyer. "She must have gone out when I was telephoning the police, or when I was getting the front door open. I didn't see her at all. Only Motley saw her."

Mason's voice showed sharp interest. "You saw another person?" he asked Motley Dunkirk.

"That's right," Motley told him. "This person was a woman and she came out the back door. And I have an idea she came out the back door about the time my wife was telephoning to the police."

Mason frowned. "This doesn't give us a very good basis for a time schedule," he said.

"We just can't figure it out," Motley said. "I've been trying to compare notes with Elvira and it's hard to get things straight. You see when I got part way down those steps I couldn't see the front of the house. My wife, up on the porch and at the window here, could see both the front and the back of the house, but she went to the telephone. Then right after that she ran down the street to get to the front of Dr. Babb's house, and after she did that she couldn't see the back of the house.

"I wear bifocal lenses and stairs bother me, so I had my head down watching those steps, but I'd stop and look up once in a while, and I certainly saw this woman."

"You mean the woman who left by the front door and—?"

"No, no," Motley said impatiently. "I mean the woman who left by the back door."

"Tell me about her," Mason said.

"Well, the way I figure it, this woman was the one who must have knocked Dr. Babb out. That's the *only* way I can figure it."

"Can you describe her?" Mason asked.

"Nope. She was a woman and that's all I can say. She was wearing a coat—it came about to her knees, I guess."

"A hat?"

"I couldn't see, or else I can't remember. I just had a glimpse of her, Mr. Mason. The back door swung open and this woman came out on the run."

"Where did she go?"

"She took off around the house, running the other way so the house was between us. I only saw her for a second."

Mason fought to keep his face expressionless. "Then the police don't know anything about this woman you saw running out of the house?"

"That's right, Mr. Mason, they don't. You see they never did come over here. Elvira went over to Dr. Babb's house to talk with them. At that time she knew nothing about this other woman. She didn't tell them about seeing me on the steps. She just said I'd been down in my darkroom. You see, the way our house is built on a side hill, our so-called basement is built into the bank at the back but is sort of a ground floor on the street side. That's the way they do with this type of hillside construction in this country."

Mrs. Dunkirk said to Mason, "I'm worried about Motley not saying anything about what he saw. Don't you think he should report what he saw to the police?"

Mason looked over to make certain that Della Street's busy pencil was recording his words. "I certainly *do* think that your husband should advise the police. I think it is his *duty* to do so."

Dunkirk's laugh was dry and mirthless. "Anytime the police want to know what I saw they can come and ask me, and I'll tell them. I'm not looking for any trouble. I'm certainly not going out of my way to get my name mixed up in anything. As far as I'm concerned, I think Elvira has done too much talking already.

"Now I'm going back downstairs. I got some pictures washing down there. Might surprise you, Mr. Mason, but I won a first prize in a contest given by one of the photographic magazines this month, and I've got one of my pictures hung in a camera exhibition in New York right now."

"Good for you!" Mason exclaimed.

Mrs. Dunkirk's smile was maternal. "He's just like a kid with a new toy," she said, "but I think it's good for a man to have a hobby after he retires."

"It certainly is," Mason agreed, glancing at his watch, "and now I've got to be on my way. This was a most interesting interview. Is the hired man over there now?"

"I believe he is. The police are letting him use the apartment over the garage, but they've sealed up Dr. Babb's house. No one can get in."

Mason frowned. "Do they expect Dr. Babb to die?"

"I don't know. They won't tell a body a thing."

"Well, we'll talk with the handy man," Mason said.

Mason and Della Street shook hands with the Dunkirks and descended the steps to Mason's car. The lawyer carefully backed out onto Rubart Terrace and eased the car into Sunland Drive, then parked again almost in front of Dr. Babb's house.

"How about this other woman?" Della Street asked.

"No one knows about her except Mr. and Mrs. Dunkirk, you and me, Della. And I'm certain your notes disclose that I advised Mr. Dunkirk to communicate his information to the police."

"I have a verbatim transcript of the conversation."

Mason grinned.

"Are you going to tell your clients?"

"I'll have to think it over, Della. Let's go talk with the handy man."

The lawyer, accompanied by Della Street walked up the cement driveway past Dr. Babb's house, around to the back, and climbed the steps to the apartment over the garage.

Mason pressed his finger against a bell button to the right of the door, and after a moment the door was opened by a wiry, lean-waisted individual apparently in the late fifties.

"Hello," he said, "how's Dr. Babb?"

"I don't know," Mason told him.

The man's face showed disappointment.

"You're asking about what happened last night, aren't you? I saw you folks go up to call on the Dunkirks."

"That's right," Mason explained. "But I haven't seen Dr. Babb and haven't heard anything new about his condition. He was still unconscious the last I heard."

"Well, come in if you want," the man said. "What do you want?"

"We only wanted to ask you a few questions."

"Well, come on in."

Mason and Della Street entered a small two-room apartment. The door automatically clicked shut as their host explained, "I'm sorry you have to come in through the kitchen. I told Doc he'd built the whole thing backwards, but that's the way Doc planned it and that's the way it is."

"My name's Mason," the lawyer said as the handy man led the way through the kitchen to the other room of the apartment, a combination sitting room and bedroom.

Apparently the name meant nothing to the handy man. "I'm glad to know you, Mr. Mason," he said. "Just call me Donald, or Don. Everybody does. Have a seat, Mrs. Mason."

Mason shook his head and smiled. "This is Miss Street, my secretary."

"Oh! I'm sorry! No hard feelings. Sit down both of you. I'll sit on the bed. You folks sit in the chairs there. Now what was it you wanted to know?"

"Just what happened?" Mason said.

Derby shook his head. "I've been through it so darn many times," he said wearily. "All right. Here's what happened. I was taking a shower in there, and I heard—"

"Had you been here all evening?" Mason asked.

"Me? No, I'd been over with Doc. Doc works pretty late hours."

"Do you have regular hours?"

"I work when Doc works. I come over here when he tells me to go over to my place. He's apt to open that back door and call to me any time. He just whoo-hoos and I go over."

"Dr. Babb had a couple of appointments for last evening?"

"That's what they tell me. I didn't know. The police got his appointment book. They say there are two names in it: Kirby and Logan. Neither one of them means anything to me, but that's neither here nor there—although I've heard that name Logan somewhere before, been trying to think of it all day but can't quite make it. Never did hear the name of Kirby.

"Anyway Doc had got everything out of the way that was bothering him last night, so he sent me over here. Told me he wouldn't be needing me any more."

"What time?" Mason asked.

"I suppose that was about eleven o'clock."

"And you undressed and took a shower?"

"Not right away. I puttered around for a while with a few little things and got sheets changed on my bed. I'd left in a hurry yesterday morning, and had left the bed just the way I climbed out of it."

"Why the hurry?" Mason asked.

"Doc had something he wanted. Forgotten now what it was. He stepped to the back door and let out a yell for me. That's the way he is; when he wants something he wants it. I was up all right, and had had my breakfast, but I hadn't straightened up around here. It was the day I change the sheets on my bed. I like to keep things shipshape and tidy."

"All right," Mason said. "You got into the shower. What happened?"

"I heard something that was shrill and sharp, and then suddenly I realized it must be a woman screaming. I shut off the water and ran over to the window, soaking wet. I was just in time to see the back door swinging shut. Doc had opened that back door to call to me all right, but he'd either changed his mind or somebody had jerked him back—probably stuck a gun in his ribs. I was just in time to see the door as it swung shut.

"Well, I knew Doc wanted me and I reckoned he wanted me right away. I knew something was wrong down there, so I dashed over and grabbed the towel and wrapped it around my middle."

"You saw the door swinging shut?"

"That's right. There's an automatic closing dodad on it. It would have shut the minute Doc stepped back inside the house."

"Did you see anyone come out?"

"Nope. I don't think any person could have gone out. I think Doc pulled the door open to yell for me to come over and someone must have stuck a gun on him and jerked him back. Anyhow that's what I *think* happened."

"Could he have called for you and you not have heard it because of the water running in the shower?" Mason asked.

"Nope, I don't think so. When Doc hollers he lets out one hell of a bellow. I'd have heard him. I heard that woman scream even with the water running in the shower, and she was inside Doc's house."

"How do you know that?" Mason asked. "Couldn't it have been a woman standing at the open door and screaming? She could have gone back inside the house just as you reached the window."

The handy man thought that over. He rubbed his hand along his jaw. "Gosh yes!" he said at length. "When you put it that way, I guess she could. I'd been wondering about that door. If Doc had got it open, he'd have bellowed, and I'd have heard him."

"What did you do?"

"I grabbed a towel, ran down the stairs and banged on the back door for Doc to let me in. There wasn't a sound from inside the house. Everything was just as quiet as could be. That scared me. I started around to the front of the house, and stopped just long enough to tap on the side window, and that's when this police officer who had moved around from the front of the house and saw me standing there wanted to know what the hell I was doing and who I was."

"And then?" Mason asked.

"The other officer had gone in through the front door. It was open."

"You mean unlocked?"

"No, I mean partially opened. Anyhow that's what the officer said."

"Does Dr. Babb keep narcotics over there?" Mason asked.

"I wouldn't know. I suppose he does. Come to think of it I guess he has to."

"Do you have keys to the house over there?" Mason asked.

"Not me. Doc says this is my house and that's his. When he wants me over there he calls me. If he doesn't call me I don't come. That suits me all right. He can mind his business, and I'll mind mine. I'm working for him, and I try to do as I'm told and keep my nose clean."

"All right," Mason told him, "now I suppose you've talked with Mr. and Mrs. Dunkirk?"

"I've talked with her. I haven't talked with him."

"You heard her description of the young woman who was seen running out of the house?"

"Uh-huh."

"I am wondering," Mason said, "if perhaps this same young woman hadn't called on the doctor on other occasions."

"Perhaps, I wouldn't know. He didn't have many patients. He's sort of retired. I try to keep out of the way when there's a patient over there, unless Doc wants something. I help out once in a while whenever he needs a helper.

"Doc's a close-mouthed cuss. That suits me all right. He's trying to retire, you know. Say, wait a minute! I've got an idea. There may not be anything to it, but there's just a chance. I think this woman's name *was* Logan. She sure had class. She was over—let me see—it'd be Friday, Friday morning."

"Go on," Mason said.

"Well, now look," Donald said. "I was working out there on the goldfish pool you can see right down there out of the window when this girl drove in, in this nice, shiny Ford and asked me if Dr. Babb was home.

"Well, Dr. Babb doesn't pay me to give out information, and I said she'd have to go to the front door and find out. But she just laughed and honked the horn a couple of times, and pretty soon the back door opened and Dr. Babb came out and was glad to see her, and she got out of the car and went in.

"Now this dame was real class. She had chestnut-colored hair, and she had lots of this and that and these and those. At first I didn't like her so much because of the high and mighty way she'd acted when she asked me if Dr. Babb was in, but she sure made a hit with me after she came out. She stood around and wanted to know all about the goldfish and really made sort of a play to butter me up. I couldn't figure what she had in mind, but it was nice.

"She'd been driving this new car of hers with one of the temporary pasteboard license numbers pasted on the inside of the rear window. She told me she'd just got her regular license plates. She said she was going to put 'em on, and it seemed the most natural thing in the world for me to volunteer to do it for her.

"Shucks! It wasn't anything that took over a few minutes and I was glad to do it, but she sure made a production out of getting me lined up so I'd do the job.

"Now *her* name was Logan. I remember she told me her last name. I can't think of the first name to save my life, but I do remember the license number on the plates. It was AAL 279.

"Now maybe that'll help. I don't know."

Mason glanced at Della Street. "Did the police ask you anything about whether you knew anyone by the name of Logan?"

"Sure they did. But I didn't tell them this because I hadn't thought of it at the time. It's just this minute popped into my head, and I still don't know whether it means anything or not, but I'm sure now that her name was Logan."

"It could be the same girl." Mason said. "How did it happen she drove her car into the driveway and stopped out here in front of the garage?"

"Hanged if I know."

"Had she ever been here before?"

"Not that I know of, but she certainly seemed to know Doc all right. I'd been away for four days earlier in the week and she could have been around here during that time all right."

"There's a young woman across the street," Mason said, "a niece of the Dunkirks. Do you know her?"

"You mean Gertrude?"

"Yes. Do you know her?"

Donald laughed a short mirthless laugh. "Sure I know her. She's over here off and on watching the goldfish, playing with the cat. Poor kid, I guess she has nothing else to do.

"She's a funny kid. If I'd been Doc I'd have sent her peddling papers, but he sure puts up with her, feels sorry for her. She's hanging around all the time, and she'll go through that back door. If somebody opens that back door she'll dart in before it closes and be inside the house before a man can wink his eye.

"She acts like she has a case on Doc—wants to be around him all the time. She told me that Doc's the only one who really understands her. She has spells of being moody, that girl. I saw her a while back when she didn't know I was watching her. She was sitting there by the goldfish pool crying, not hard crying, just sort of weeping.

"I guess Doc's putting up with her on account of the Dunkirks. They're old friends of his. *They* say the girl is sixteen. For my money she's about fifteen. She's big and well formed, but you can tell the way she acts she's just a big, overgrown kid."

"Well," Mason said, getting to his feet, "I just wanted to drop in and talk with you. You've told me what I wanted to know."

Donald touched the lawyer's sleeve. "You don't know anything about how Doc's getting along?"

"No. I suppose you could telephone the hospital and—"

"I can't telephone from here," Donald said. "The house over there was sealed up by the police. They've put special padlocks on the doors. They told me I could keep on living up here, but I know Doc wouldn't want me to go away under the circumstances. He'd want me to keep an eye on the place."

"You don't have a telephone in this house?" Mason asked.

Donald shook his head.

"Well," Mason told him, shaking hands, "we may be seeing you again. I'll try to find out how Dr. Babb is coming along, in case we drop in again."

"Do that," Donald said, "and come in any time. A fellow gets sort of lonesome just sticking around here doing nothing except reading and listening to the radio. And thanks a lot for dropping in, folks."

He escorted them to the door, and insisted on shaking hands with both the lawyer and his secretary.

"And now?" Della Street asked, as they descended the stairs from the garage.

"Now," Mason said, "we'll telephone Paul Drake."

They found a phone booth at a service station six blocks down on the main highway.

Mason dialed Drake's number. "Paul," he said, "I want a name and address from an automobile license and I want it quick."

"What's the number?"

"AAL 279," Mason said.

"Okay," Drake said, "give me three or four seconds to relay the request to one of my operatives and he'll get busy. Hang on for a minute, Perry, I've got something to say to you."

Mason held on to the telephone for some ten seconds; then Drake was back.

"Okay, Perry, I've got that in the works. Call me again in ten minutes and I'll have the information."

"All right, Paul, what was it you said you wanted to tell me?"

"You sent Della down to pick up information about a narcotics robbery, chap by the name of Dr. Babb?"

"That's right," Mason said. "What do you have on it, Paul? Anything?"

"The guy died about thirty minutes ago. They said that he recovered consciousness enough to answer questions. There's a rumor he gave the police information but that's all I know. They're not releasing any further information."

Mason thought that over for a minute.

"Okay, Paul, thanks," he said. "I'll call you in ten minutes."

Mason sprinted for the car.

"What is it?" Della Street asked.

"It is now a case of murder," Mason said, "and we may be just *one* jump ahead of the police. Paul said to call him in ten minutes and he'll have the address of the license number AAL 279."

"Where are we going now?"

"Over toward Kirby's house. If the automobile license pays off, we'll be that much nearer the center of the city. If it doesn't we'll swing over to Kirby's and see what we can find out there."

Mason drove for ten minutes, then stopped the car in front of a phone booth. "Give Paul a ring, Della."

Della Street entered the booth, telephoned Paul Drake and came hurrying out. "The name is Norma Logan. The car is a very late model secondhand Ford, and the address is Mananas Apartments."

"Atta girl! Mason said. "The Kirbys can wait, Della. Let's go!"

CHAPTER FIVE

The directory by the side of the door of the Mananas Apartments showed that Miss Norma Logan lived in apartment 280.

Mason and Della Street took an automatic elevator to the second floor, found the apartment and rang.

The door was opened by a strikingly beautiful young woman with blue eyes and chestnut hair. From the interior of the apartment came the faint aroma of cooking.

"Yes?" she asked, in a voice that was pleasing to the ears.

"I'm Perry Mason, an attorney," the lawyer said.

For a moment she glanced away from him, then looked back.

"Yes?" she said again.

"You're Norma Logan?"

"Yes."

"This is my secretary, Miss Street, Miss Logan."

Norma Logan acknowledged the introduction with an inclination of her head and the faintest of smiles.

"May we come in?" Mason asked.

"I'm sorry. I'm just cooking dinner, and then I have to dress. I have a date tonight."

"We want to talk with you," Mason said.

"I'm sorry."

"About Dr. Babb," Mason said.

Again the eyes flickered away from Mason's, only to return. "Dr. Babb?" she asked, and shook her head. "I'm afraid I don't know any Dr. Babb."

"You did," Mason told her.

Again she shook her head.

"And about John Kirby," Mason told her.

"Kirby?" She repeated the name as though trying to test the sound on her ears. "I'm sorry, Mr. Mason, are you quite certain you have the right Miss Logan?"

"You're Norma Logan?"

"Yes."

"Then I'm quite certain."

"Well *I'm* quite certain there's some mistake. I don't know any Dr. Babb and I don't know of any Kirby. Kirby? I've heard the name somewhere but I certainly can't place any Kirby at the moment."

"Do you have a Ford you recently purchased?"

"Yes, if that makes any difference. And now I'm very sorry, Mr. Mason, but I have no time to stand here and discuss these matters. There's been some mistake and since I'm in very much of a hurry, I'm going to have to ask you to excuse me."

She started to swing the door.

Mason pushed his weight against it. For a moment, she struggled to get the door closed. Then she jumped back. "All right," she said angrily, "do you want me to start screaming?"

Mason, followed by Della Street, walked through the door.

"Close it, Della," Mason said.

Della Street closed the door.

"This is an outrage," Norma Logan blazed. "I'm going to scream . . . or I'll call the manager. I'll call the police. You have no right to do this."

"I think you'd better call the police," Mason said. "I think they're the ones who are interested and since they're going to have to be called in sooner or later let's have them in now."

She looked at him, white-faced, indignant and apparently badly shaken. "What in the world are you talking about?"

Mason said, "I hate to bring bad news, but Dr. Babb died about an hour ago."

"I don't care if a hundred Dr. Babbs died," she blazed at him. "I don't know any Dr. Babb. What are you talking about?"

"And Mr. Kirby can't be found," Mason said. "I think the police will probably be taking a great deal of interest in some of these developments."

"So what?"

"Aren't you sorry Dr. Babb died?" Mason asked.

"I would be if I—" Suddenly she collapsed in a chair and burst into tears.

Mason sat down on the davenport.

Della Street promptly seated herself at a small table, took out her shorthand notebook and pencil.

"Now suppose you tell me what happened," Mason said, "but before you do so let's have one thing understood. I can't act as your attorney, and anything you tell me won't be confidential and it won't be privileged. I am representing someone else."

She raised frightened, tear-filled eyes. "There's been some terrible mistake, Mr. Mason. I *do* know a John Kirby, but I *don't* know Dr. Babb."

"Where were you last night?" Mason asked.

"I was driving my new automobile out in the northwest part of town. I thought I had plenty of gasoline, but I didn't. I ran out of gas and had to walk back to the service station."

"Go on," Mason told her in an expressionless voice.

"I got a gallon can of gasoline and started walking toward my car. A man by the name of Kirby picked me up. I had never seen him before, and I don't ever expect to see him again. He drove me to where my car had been parked. When we got there the car was gone. Someone had evidently siphoned gasoline into my car and driven it away.

"Mr. Kirby was a perfect gentleman. He took me to a motel, registered me, and then went home without... well, you know, without any passes or any fresh talk. He was just a wonderful gentleman."

"How very fortunate!" Mason said dryly. "And then what happened?"

"Then early this morning...I...well, I was worried and frightened, and I couldn't sleep, so I got up about daylight and walked down to the highway. A milkman, making early morning deliveries, picked me up and carried me in to where I could get a taxicab. I came home, and about noon I received a call from a roadhouse—the Purple Swan. They said my car was parked in the driveway where it was an obstruction, and would I please do something about it. I made sure it was my car."

"How did they get your name?" Mason asked.

"From the registration certificate."

"So you went out there and retrieved the car?"

"Yes."

"What was the name of the motel where you stayed?"

"I can't remember."

"Do you remember its location?"

"Yes, I'd know it if I saw it again."

"Well," Mason said, "let's check back a little. You're absolutely certain you don't know any Dr. Babb?"

"I'm positive."

"You never did know of him?"

"I never heard of him in my life."

"How long have you had your license plates and registration certificate on your new Ford automobile?"

"Not very long. Just a few days."

"Who put the license plates on the car for you?"

"Does that make any difference?"

"It might."

"I had it done."

"Who did it?"

"A friend who happened to be handy with tools."

"A handy man?" Mason asked.

"I suppose so. Why? What difference does it make?"

"It makes a lot of difference," Mason said, "because he happened to remember the license number. You see it was last Friday, and you were out at Dr. Babb's place. You didn't stop in front of the house, but drove your car right up the driveway and around to the back of the house. You stopped in front of the goldfish pool. You may remember the handy man was there. You used a little flattery, turned on the personality and got him to put on the license plates for you."

Her wide, pathetic eyes showed that she knew she was trapped.

"Now then," Mason said, "Dr. Babb is dead. He has been murdered. You were seen running out of the house. You have a short time before the police get here. I don't know how long. It may be a matter of minutes, it may be a matter of days, but they'll find you. You don't have to tell me your story. If you want to, I'll be glad to listen, but I'm representing someone else."

"I know whom you're representing," she said. "You're representing John Kirby. He told me if anything happened and you *should* be able to find me that I was to back up his story about the gasoline and the stolen automobile."

"When did he tell you that?" Mason asked.

"About half an hour ago."

"He was here?"

"No. He called me on the phone."

Mason's eyes narrowed. He glanced over to where Della Street's busy pencil was flying over the page of the shorthand notebook.

"Better tell me the whole story," he said wearily.

She said, "I'm Ronnie's half-sister."

"Who's Ronnie?" Mason asked.

"Ronson Kirby."

"Go on," Mason told her.

"He's the cause of it all."

"Any relation to John Kirby?"

"Don't you know?" she said. "He's the son."

"Go on."

She said, "Dr. Babb was running just the opposite of an abortion mill. He was running a baby mill."

Mason waited for her to go on.

"I uncovered it because I was interested in Ronnie. Otherwise I would never have had the faintest inkling of what was going on. Dr. Babb was awfully clever. He had two little private hospitals. One of them was a hospital where rich society women went, ostensibly to be confined.

"The other hospital was where unfortunate women went to be delivered of children they didn't want.

"Instead of going through the red tape of adoption proceedings and conforming to all of the laws in regard to adoption, Dr. Babb would simply fill out a birth certificate and sign it as the attending physician. That made the baby the legitimate child of the foster parents as far as the records were concerned.

"Dr. Babb had quite a business, and he handled it so discreetly that no one ever suspected. He even had printed instructions to be followed by the persons who were going to get the children.

"Unfortunate young women who found themselves in trouble could go to Dr. Babb. He would arrange to place them in homes where they could work for their board and room until the last six weeks. Then they went to his private hospital and waited. When the child was born, the mother got a thousand dollars and knew that she would never see the child again. Dr. Babb promised her it would have a good home. That was all he would say.

"For most of the women that was enough. An unfortunate girl could tell her friends she was going away to visit distant relatives. A few months later she could return with new clothes and a story of having had a swell job she finally quit because of being homesick.

"Dr. Babb was very, very clever. Very few of the girls even knew his name. He had another doctor, an assistant who ran the hospital where the babies were actually delivered."

"Know his name?"

"No."

"Go on."

"Well, in the meantime, the foster mother was waiting at the other hospital. She had been there for some ten days after having practiced an elaborate deception on her friends.

"Dr. Babb covered everything very carefully with his printed instructions. His service cost a lot of money. He wouldn't touch a case for under ten thousand dollars."

Mason regarded Norma Logan thoughtfully. "You knew that Dr. Babb was dead?" he asked.

"Yes."

"Before I told you?"

"Yes."

"Who told you?"

"Mr. Kirby."

"When?"

"When he phoned a short time ago."

"Look," Mason told her, "I am representing the guy. I've got to find him. I've got to find him immediately. Seconds are precious. He didn't go near his office all afternoon. His house phone doesn't answer. Now where can I reach him?"

She shook her head. "I can't help you on that. He...he's keeping out of sight."

"Why?"

"So the situation will crystallize before he's called on to face the police."

Mason started pacing the floor. Abruptly he whirled once more to face Norma Logan. "All right. Let's hear about Ronnie, and how you came to know John Kirby, and what really happened last night."

"My father," she said, "was one of the most wonderful men in the world. He was an adventurer, impractical, but dashing and magnetic.

"I hardly remember my mother at all. After she died, I was my daddy's girl. We had wonderful times together. Sometimes he was in the chips and we'd travel, and sometimes he was broke and we'd get by on nothing.

"Then about eight years ago, Dad married again. About a year after the marriage he was completely wiped out. He trusted a partner who took him to the cleaners good and proper. Dad simply couldn't understand that. He was getting older and he couldn't understand that either. He still had the same spirit of romantic daring and adventure, but—well, he wasn't young any more.

"He went on an expedition to South America, up in the jungles. That expedition was going to make him rich again. After a few weeks we received a report he had died. He left his second wife pregnant, and penniless. I was a green seventeen-year-old kid who knew a little shorthand, and I tried to stand by. I promised my stepmother that I'd get a job and support her. What a laugh that was: I couldn't do more than provide myself with the bare essentials.

"My stepmother heard of Dr. Babb's so-called service. And so I had a half-brother whom I never saw. My stepmother died a few months later, brokenhearted and disillusioned. She was terribly in love with my father up to the day she died. Dad had that way about him. When women fell in love with him, they just never got over it. I think they all recognized his short-comings, but his fascination, his charm, and his gallantry, his romantic way of looking at life made him a perpetual prince charming.

"I had the name of Dr. Babb. I knew Ronnie had been placed somewhere. I couldn't find any records, however. Then a short time ago, while putting together the few facts I had, I suddenly realized how Dr. Babb must have worked the whole thing. So I went back and consulted the records. I knew Ronnie's birthday. I looked up the birth records as of that day, and then looked up each birth certificate. As it happened it was a day when there was only one birth certificate signed by Dr. Babb. That was the birth of a son to John and Joan Kirby.

"For a while, I thought I'd try and look up the Kirbys without letting them know who I was just so I could get a look at my half-brother. I felt certain he'd look like Dad. If he does, if he has that fine, magnetic charm, that devil-may-care gallantry, the world will be his oyster. I was terribly anxious to look him up. Then I thought I hadn't better."

"What *did* you do?" Mason asked.

"I went to Dr. Babb," she said. "I told him who I was and what I wanted."

"I wanted to be assured that Ronnie was happy and was in a good home."

"And what happened?"

"Dr. Babb was terribly upset that I'd found him, but when I explained how I felt, he was greatly relieved. It seems this doctor who was his assistant had fallen on evil ways. He was a narcotic addict and he wanted money.

"When Dr. Babb knew I'd found out about Ronnie by investigative work he was very co-operative. He assured me Ronnie was very happy. He promised that he would get in touch with me if at any time he felt there was anything that was going to interfere with Ronnie's happiness. On the strength of that assurance, I decided that I'd just keep in the background and not try to see Ronnie or get acquainted."

"And then?" Mason asked.

"Then last Friday Dr. Babb telephoned. He said that I wasn't to get alarmed but that someone was trying to blackmail him. He said someone had found out what had been going on in the Kirby case, but lacked the definite evidence."

"Now, wait a minute," Mason said. "Did he say 'in the Kirby case' or was it in all his cases, and that he was calling you because of your interest in the Kirby case?"

"No, he said it was someone who was only interested in the Kirby case."

"All right. What did you do?"

"I went out and saw him, and then yesterday afternoon I telephoned John Kirby at his office. I told him I had to see him on a matter of the greatest importance, that it had something to do with the welfare of his son."

"What happened?"

"I couldn't get Kirby until afternoon. He was very much disturbed. He told me that he was having a sales meeting at a roadhouse called the Purple Swan, that he would be tied up until after eleven o'clock, but that if I'd meet him there at eleven o'clock, he'd be very glad to see me."

"You met him there?"

"Yes."

"And then what?"

"I told him what had happened. We decided to go and see Dr. Babb."

"You telephoned Dr. Babb?"

"No."

"What did you do?"

"We just drove by the place, and saw that there was a light on in the house. Mr. Kirby felt that it would be better for me to go first and find out if the coast was clear. He was afraid that someone else might be there, and he didn't want any other person to see him in that house. He said that no one could *prove* anything, and for that reason, he wasn't going to have any personal contact with Dr. Babb that anyone could establish."

"So what did you do?"

"Mr. Kirby parked his car on one of the side streets. I got out and went to the house. I started to ring the bell, and then decided to try the front door, the one which led into the reception room. It was unlocked. I opened the door and went on in."

"And then?" Mason asked.

"I'm going to tell you the truth now, Mr. Mason."

"That's what I want."

"Well, I sat down and within a short time, I guess less than a minute, I heard this terrific commotion from one of the inner rooms. There must have been a struggle going on. I could hear trampling feet and I thought I heard a blow and I distinctly heard a thud. Something that jarred the entire house. And then I heard a woman screaming."

"You *heard* a woman screaming?" Mason exclaimed.

"That's right."

"You didn't scream yourself?"

She shook her head.

"What did you do?" Mason asked.

"I ran to the door."

"The front door?"

"No, no! The door to the inner office where the commotion was taking place."

"What happened?"

"I opened that door and a body—I suppose it was that of Dr. Babb—was lying on the floor. A woman who had her back to me was standing over him, bending down."

"Did you ever see her face?"

"Yes, as she straightened I had a look at her profile."

"Can you describe her?"

"She was somewhere in the early thirties. She was well groomed, had a slightly upturned nose, dark hair and eyebrows, a mature sort of woman, but not heavy, not fat."

"Then what happened?"

"She ran toward the back of the house."

"And then?" Mason asked.

She said, "Mr. Mason, I did something that probably I shouldn't have done, but if I had it to do over again, I'd do it."

"What?"

"I stole Dr. Babb's confidential records."

"What do you mean, his confidential records?"

"The only one that he kept, the only master book that showed where his babies had gone."

"How did you know he had it?"

"I spied on him, Mr. Mason. He looked up some information about Ronnie, about his birthday and so forth, and—well, he thought I was in the reception room. Actually I had gone into one of the dressing rooms and had the door open a crack. I was peeping out because I wanted to know where he kept this information I knew he was going to look up.

"Dr. Babb was pretty smart. He kept most of his records in nicely bound, expensive books, but there was one book in a cheap, pasteboard cover with a spiral binding that didn't look like anything particularly important and that was the one he looked at when he was finding out about Ronnie. He didn't even keep that book in the safe. He kept it in a little secret drawer in his desk."

"What did you do?"

"When I saw this woman, I was satisfied she was after this record because his safe door was open and books and documents had been tumbled out on the floor. I felt certain that when she dashed out the back door, she had probably taken *some* book with her that she *thought* was the record book she wanted. I knew that the police would come and—well, I knew that if this record book ever fell into the hands of the police there'd be the devil to pay. I was thinking not only of Ronnie but of all of the other children who were like Ronnie.

"You can understand what it means, Mr. Mason, when a child has been raised to think he's in the security of a home with natural parents and then suddenly finds out that he's an adopted child, and—And then of course there's the question of what the authorities would do. Here are heaven knows how many children with birth certificates that aren't worth the paper they're written on. And if anyone actually had the true facts— Of course, the difficulty would be in getting the true facts. But with the master records to go by, detectives could trace down those facts, and—well, you can see what would happen."

"So you got this book?" Mason prompted.

"I got it, Mr. Mason. I stuck it down my dress and ran out of that house just as fast as I could go. I knew that there had been enough commotion so that the neighbors would call the police. I felt there was nothing I could do for Dr. Babb and nothing I could do by staying there and being found there."

"Just what did you do?"

"I ran back to Mr. Kirby's car. I told him that I had to get to a place of concealment fast. I saw the woman who lives up on the hill above Dr. Babb's house standing in the doorway of her house as I ran out. The porch light was on at Dr. Babb's house and I'm satisfied she had a good look at me."

"So what happened?"

"Mr. Kirby started driving away from there. A police car went tearing past us before we'd gone half a block. I told Mr. Kirby we might run into a roadblock. No one was looking for a man, but they might very well be looking for a woman of my description."

"So you decided to stop at a motel?" Mason asked.

"We didn't then, but as we drove along we saw this motel with a sign saying, 'Vacancy,' and Mr. Kirby ran the car in there. I told him to register as husband and wife. That was the only way we could have any safety and get a unit. So he registered as husband and wife and we moved in. After a few minutes Mr. Kirby drove away by himself."

"Then what?"

"Then he returned about four or five o'clock in the morning, picked me up, drove me back to the Purple Swan where I'd left my car, and I got in it and drove home."

"And he told you what to say in case you were questioned?"

"Yes, then and later. He said I was to tell that story about the automobile and having run out of gas, but he said no one would ever question me because they couldn't ever find out who I was. He said that if the going should get tough and *he* had to bolster up *his* story, he'd suddenly remember something about me that would enable detectives to locate me at this address, and then I could substantiate his story."

"Did you tell him about the book?" Mason asked.

She said, "I've told no one about the book."

"Where is it?" Mason asked.

"I have it."

Mason shook his head. "I've found you. Police can find you. This isn't an assault any more. It's a murder case. You're going to be charged with murder."

"*I* am?" she asked incredulously."

"Sure. What the hell did you think?"

"But Mr. Mason, the woman who killed him was the one who screamed, the one who was in the inside office."

"Look," Mason told her. "Don't be naïve. You went to Dr. Babb's house. You were concerned about the security of Ronson Kirby. At least that's *your* story. As far as the police are concerned, they may feel that you were hired by John Kirby to go get that book. I don't know. I have your word for it, that's all. "*You* say that there was another woman in there, a woman who screamed."

"Well, that's what happened. The neighbors heard her scream."

"The neighbors heard a woman scream," Mason said, "but the police will act on the assumption that you went there for the definite purpose of stealing this book, that Dr. Babb had left the front door open, that you entered the reception room and opened the door to the inner office. Dr. Babb was probably in another part of the house. You saw your opportunity. You slipped in and tried to steal this book. Dr. Babb came in and caught you at it. There was a struggle. You cracked him over the head with a beaker, probably only intending to knock him out or keep him from grabbing you. But you hit him too hard. That's when you screamed. Then you grabbed the book and ran out."

"But, Mr. Mason, I'm telling you the truth. There *was* another woman in there."

"Perhaps there was. But *you're* lying to me."

"What do you mean?"

"You said that you and Kirby went to see Dr. Babb cold turkey, that you didn't telephone or have any appointment."

"We didn't."

"Then," Mason said, "how does it happen that Dr. Babb's appointment book showed that he had a late evening appointment with both of you? Your names are both in his book."

She looked at Mason with wide, startled eyes. "Did Kirby telephone him?" Mason asked.

"He...he must have."

"All right," Mason told her. "You're hotter than a stove lid as far as the police are concerned. I found you and they're going to find you. Give me that notebook and then get out of here."

"Where shall I go?"

"That's up to you," Mason said. "But for a while at least don't be where the police can pick you up.

"And I'll tell you something else because it's my duty to tell you as a lawyer. If you get out of here, that can be evidence against you. It can be evidence of flight, but I'll give you one ray of hope. I happen to know that there *was* another woman in the house and I'm going to try my damnedest to find out who she was. I don't have a single solitary thing to work on right now except perhaps a question of fingerprints which the police may uncover."

"How much time do I have?" she asked.

Mason shrugged his shoulders. "Perhaps two seconds. Perhaps two weeks. If

Kirby phones again, tell him to ring the Drake Detective Agency in my building and leave word where I can reach him. Tell him the message will be relayed to me at any hour of the day or night, and tell him it's damned important."

"And you don't think I should tell that story he told me to?"

"I can't advise you. I can only tell you to get a lawyer of your own, and do it at once. In the meantime, I want that book."

"Why?"

"To make certain it doesn't get into the hands of the police or into the hands of a blackmailer."

"I can't give it to you."

"Why?"

"I...I don't know. I trust you, but I *know* it's safe with me."

"No, it isn't," Mason said. "You're hotter than a firecracker. You're going to be picked up. Police will search you and go through your car."

She looked at him a moment, then turned to Della Street. "Will you come with me a moment, Miss Street? I want to talk with you woman to woman."

Della Street flashed a swift glance at Mason, then said, "All right. Where do you want me to go?"

Norma Logan opened the bathroom door. She and Della went inside. The door was locked. After a few moments, the lock clicked back and the door opened.

Norma Logan said, "I'm not going to give it to you, Mr. Mason. You are in a way just as hot as I am. I've talked with Miss Street. We've thought of a safe place for that book."

Mason glanced at Della. She met his eyes, gave a brief nod of her head.

"Have you told Kirby anything about this book?" Mason asked.

She shook her head. "I didn't know how far I could trust Mr. Kirby."

"All right," Mason said. "Don't tell him. Don't tell anybody."

"If I should be questioned by the police, should I tell them the story Mr. Kirby told me to tell?"

"There," Mason said, "I'm not in a position to advise you. Understand definitely that I'm not your lawyer. I'm representing John Kirby. I'd suggest that you consult a lawyer *at once*, that you tell him what happened, and that you take his advice. I'm on my way. Come on, Della."

Della Street waited until they were in the automobile leaving the Mananas Apartments.

"May I ask a question, Chief?" she said at length.

"Sure, go ahead."

"That woman isn't your client?"

"Definitely not."

"Yet you asked her for that notebook."

"Yes."

"Why?"

"Because," Mason said, "from what she told me I knew that that notebook was too dangerous to leave kicking around. In the first place, I'm representing John Kirby. I realize now what was bothering him when he came in to see me this afternoon. I'm trying to protect his son."

"Is it ethical?" Della Street asked.

"Hell, no!" Mason said, "it isn't ethical. That notebook is stolen property, Della. If I take it into my possession, I become an accessory after the fact. I'd be violating the Penal Code. I'd have possession of stolen property, and I haven't the faintest intention of letting that property get to the police."

"And if I should have that book, where would it leave you professionally?"

"Behind the eight ball if I *knew* you had it."

"He drove for a while in silence, then said somewhat savagely, "Ethics are rules of conduct that are made to preserve the dignity and the integrity of the profession. I'm inclined to conform to the spirit of the rules of ethics rather than the letter."

"But what about the courts?"

"They'll conform to the letter rather than the spirit. If the police ever find out that girl had that notebook and that it came under my control, and that information should get to Hamilton Burger, the district attorney, who hates the very ground I walk on, he'll have the opportunity he's been waiting for. He'll charge me with receiving stolen property. He'll throw the Penal Code at me."

"And then what will *you* do?"

"Then," Mason said, "I'll truthfully say that I don't *know* where the book is. I know one thing, Della, I'm not going to rip the veil off the past, and throw heaven knows how many children to the wolves.

"That's the worst of the law. It has to conform to the letter. It can't cut corners. If the law finds out that these children were illegally placed in homes, the law will *have* to declare them the wards of the state. Then the parents can only try to get the children by adoption proceedings. A lot of children who have had all the security of thinking that they are in their own natural homes with their own natural parents will learn the truth. The case will get a lot of newspaper publicity, some of the mothers will come forward, blackmailers will move in, there'll be hell to pay."

"And *you're* willing to risk your reputation and *your* liberty to keep that from happening?"

Mason grinned at her. "You're darned right I am. I'm a lawyer. It may sound corny, but my life is dedicated to improving the administration of justice. I'm loyal to my clients. I'm trying to represent John Kirby and his son. But don't start hanging any crepe on the office door as yet. I have a certain amount of human ingenuity, considerable legal agility, and I'm going to use them both.

"And," he added, after a moment, "I don't *know* where the book is now."

"What about Kirby?" Della Street asked. "Are you going to try to find him?"

"How can I?" He's gone to cover at least for the moment. It was a fool thing to do, but he's done it. If he gets in touch with Norma Logan, she'll deliver my message that he's to call Paul Drake. Drake will see that he gets in touch with me. I'll tell Drake to have an operative watch Kirby's house and tell Kirby to call me if he or his wife returns home. I'll meet Paul Drake at seven-forty-five tomorrow morning in case I don't hear from Kirby before that. There's no use for us to sit up and beat our brains out. We'll need a night's sleep. Tomorrow's pretty apt to be one hell of a day."

"You can say that again," Della Street murmured.

CHAPTER SIX

Seven-forty-five o'clock in the morning found Perry Mason at Paul Drake's office. The detective was a few minutes late.

"Hi, Perry," Paul said. "What's the great idea?"

"Trying to do an honest day's work," Mason said grinning. "What's the idea of being ten minutes late?"

Drake looked at his watch. "It's only eight and a half minutes. I've been digging out material."

"What?"

"I've been putting two and two together."

"How come?" Mason asked.

Drake settled himself in the creaking swivel chair behind the battered desk. Tall, dull-eyed, unemotional, he had carefully studied the art of blending into his environment and flattening himself into insignificance.

"On that Dr. Babb case," he said. "Police got a good description of a young woman who ran out the front door of that house."

Mason lit a cigarette.

"They wondered how it happened the girl was able to disappear so completely, because the police were on the job almost within a matter of seconds. They called other police cars, and threw out a pretty good net."

"A girl can go a long ways in a short time in an automobile," Mason said.

"*Provided* she has the automobile," Drake said, "and *provided* it's parked reasonably near to the scene of operations. In this particular instance police are working on the theory that the girl was on foot."

"Go ahead," Mason said.

"In which event," Drake said, "she must have got off the streets in a hurry. So just as a matter of routine, the police started checking a motel that was in the neighborhood, the Beauty Rest Motel."

"Find anything?" Mason asked noncommittally.

"Not what they were looking for at the time, but they found something that ties in."

"What?"

"They were asking if some young, unattached woman, answering a certain description, had registered in the motel at about eleven-forty to eleven-forty-five Monday evening. They were asking about unescorted women.

"The manager told them that, while there had been no unescorted young women of that description, a couple had registered at the time mentioned, under rather suspicious circumstances. They had registered as husband and wife. The so-called husband, however, had left the motel, leaving the woman there alone, and the time of his departure was such that the manager became a little suspicious. He said the man wasn't in the unit more than a few minutes."

"Uh-huh," Mason said.

"When the police checked the room where Dr. Babb had been assaulted, they naturally dusted for fingerprints. They didn't find any fingerprints on the glass beaker that had been used as a weapon, but they *did* find some fingerprints that weren't those of Dr. Babb or of his handy man. From the manner in which one of the fingerprints had been superimposed on a print which the police felt certain had been made by Dr. Babb a short time before the assault, police had the idea they might have the fingerprint of the assailant."

"So what did they do?"

"Went to Unit 5 in the Beauty Rest Motel," Drake said, "and took fingerprints. They got the fingerprints of this same woman."

"That makes it interesting, doesn't it?" Mason said.

"Very," Drake said.

"Now then, the police picked up Dr. Babb's appointment book. It showed he had three or four appointments for the afternoon, and two for the evening. They were listed as Kirby and Logan."

"No first names or initials?"

"No first names or initials," Drake said.

"Go on," Mason told him. "Anything else?"

"So naturally," Drake said, "the police became very much interested in the identity of the man who had driven this young woman to the Beauty Rest Motel. He had registered under a name which proved to be phony and an address which was fictitious, but he had given the make and license number of his automobile.

"That license number also turned out to be phony, but apparently it's phony only as to two numbers. The manager of the motel *thought* he had checked the number given on the registration card with the license number of the automobile. He says that he knows that he checked the first three letters which are JYJ. The next digit is listed on the registration card as a one and the manager feels certain that it was a one. The discrepancy in the license number, therefore, must lie with the last two digits, and that narrows the search to ninety-nine cars. Since the police know the make of the car they are looking for, it's going to take them only a very short time to get the data they want."

"Uh-huh," Mason observed.

"So," Drake told him, "knowing that you're very anxious to get in touch with Kirby, knowing that the name Kirby was on Dr. Babb's appointment book— well, I've been putting two and two together. That's all."

"Find out anything?" Mason asked.

"Not yet. No one has shown up at the Kirby residence. It was dark all night. The garage doors are closed and locked. Of course, Perry, if the police should pick up Kirby and if they should find the fingerprints of this young woman in Kirby's car, it would quite naturally put Kirby in one hell of a spot. He'd have to tell who the young woman was. He'd have to explain why he registered the way he did. In view of the fact that the case is now a murder—well, there'd be hell to pay."

"And you think that police are hot on the trail?" Mason asked.

"You bet they're hot on the trail," Drake said. "They'll—"

He broke off as a telephone rang shrilly. "Here it starts," Drake said grinning. "The life of a detective. Glamorous in fiction, but for the most part sitting at the end of a telephone correlating information. Stick around, Perry."

Drake picked up the receiver, said "Hello.... Yeah, this is Drake.... Oh-oh, where are you? Okay, hold on for instructions."

Drake turned to Perry Mason. "That's my operative out at the Kirby house," he said. "The Kirbys showed up about ten minutes ago. My man had to drive down to a service station to telephone. He wants to know whether you want him to go back and keep the place under surveillance, or—"

"Tell him to come on in," Mason said, "and not to hang around the house. If there's any chance police may show up, I don't want them to collar your man and shake him down to find out what he's doing there."

"Okay," Drake said. He turned to the telephone and said, "Come on in, Bill.... Yeah, that's right. To the office."

Drake hung up.

Mason reached for the phone, said to Drake's switchboard operator, "I want the residence of John Kirby. I want to talk with Kirby personally. The number is Bayside 9-6 something or other. I'm not sure of the last three numbers. Get him for me, will you? Okay, I'll hold the line."

Mason waited on the line, and after some thirty seconds heard the voice of Drake's telephone operator, "Mr. Kirby is on the line, Mr. Mason."

Mason said, "Okay, thanks." The line clicked.

"Hello," Kirby said.

"This is Perry Mason, Kirby," the lawyer said.

"Oh yes, Mason."

"Where the hell have you been?" Mason asked.

"What do you mean, where the hell have I been?" Kirby asked indignantly. "I've been out on a short business trip. I had my wife and son with me. Why? What's it all about?"

Mason said, "It's too long to tell you over the phone and too dangerous. You wait there for me. I'm coming out. Under no circumstances leave the place until I arrive."

"But what in the world are you—?"

"There isn't any time to explain," Mason said, "and don't act so damned innocent."

Mason slammed up the phone. "I'm on my way, Paul," he said. "No, wait a minute. Let me call Della."

Mason held onto the telephone, clicked the connection, said to Drake's exchange operator, "How about getting Della Street for me? You have her number."

"Right away, Mr. Mason," she said.

A moment later Della Street's voice came over the phone.

"Had breakfast?" Mason asked.

"Just leaving for the office," she answered.

"Stick around," Mason told her. "I'm going out to Kirby's. I'll drive by your apartment and pick you up. You have notebooks and pencils?"

"Uh-huh, I'll be waiting down in front with my brief case all loaded. I'll be there in exactly ten minutes and wait until you come."

"Good girl!" Mason told her.

Mason hung up, said to Drake, "Your operator has the number of Kirby's residence. Call me out there if anything vitally important happens. Otherwise, wait until I call you. I should be back in my office by ten o'clock."

Mason hurried to the elevator, picked up his car in the parking lot, and drove past the building where Della Street had her apartment exactly twelve minutes from the time he had left Drake's office. Della Street was standing by the curb, trim and efficient, a leather brief case held in her gloved hand.

Mason slid the car to a stop, held the door open.

"What's new, Chief?" she asked.

"Quite a bit," Mason said. "You're looking fine this morning."

"Thanks."

"Its a real pleasure to have someone like you, Della. I wish I could tell you what it means."

"You can't?" she asked swinging her legs into the car and slamming the door shut.

"Not in words."

"Well, you can always try," she said smiling. "Ears are very receptive to words of that sort, no matter how inadequate they may be."

Mason grinned. "All right," he said. "It's nice to have you around. It's nice to know that I can trust you in a pinch, that you know me well enough to know exactly what I want you to do in any given set of circumstances. It's nice to have your loyalty, your dependability, and...and you're easy on the eyes."

"Well," she said, "*those* words weren't very inadequate. Thanks, Chief."

Mason was silent for a moment, then said, "Kirby was out all last night. Apparently on a business trip. I would be more inclined to be credulous and considerate if we didn't know that he'd called Norma Logan."

"I take it that, when we meet Mr. Kirby this time," Della Street said, "he is going to hear a little lecture about the fallacy of lying to his lawyer."

"If we have time," Mason said, "we're *really* going to rake that bird over the coals."

"And then what?"

"Then," Mason said, "I want to find out whether I'm representing him as his lawyer. After all, he only came to the office to tell me a story and that's the last opportunity I've had to check with him. Everything else I've done on my own. I'm putting in a lot of time, and running up quite a bill for detectives."

"Wouldn't it have been better to have waited until you were sure?" she said.

"From a dollars and cents basis, yes," Mason said, "but somehow, Della, I'm not built that way. I want to protect a client and, knowing that while I was sitting around twiddling my thumbs waiting for a formal notice of employment and a retainer the case might have been blown wide open, I preferred to take a gamble."

"Part of the service you give clients," Della said.

"Part of the service I *try* to give clients," Mason told her. "Of course, you lose out sometimes, but in the long run it winds up on the credit side of the ledger."

Again they drove in silence until Mason said, "That street is right along here someplace, Della. Take a look at the names on the street signs, will you? Oh-oh, here it is right here."

Mason made a right-hand turn and drove for three blocks.

"That'll be the house over there on the left, Della."

"*Some* house!" she said.

Mason said, "I presume Mr. John Kirby has done right well for himself. We'll soon find out a little more about Mr. John Kirby and a *lot* more about the case."

Mason parked the car in front of the house and he and Della Street hurried up the long strip of cement sidewalk which led to the front porch.

Mason pushed his thumb against the mother-of-pearl bell button. They heard chimes in the interior of the house but no sounds of activity from within.

Mason frowned, looked at his watch. "Hang it," he said, "seconds are precious and they fool around answering the door."

"Do they know you're coming?" Della asked.

"Yes, I told Kirby to be here and—" Mason jabbed savagely at the button, ringing the chimes in steady sequence.

"Well," Della Street said at length, "it doesn't seem to be just a question of waiting to answer the bell. It would seem to be there's no one home."

Mason said, "If he took it on himself to take a powder—"

"What about Mrs. Kirby?"

"I didn't talk with her personally," Mason said, "but she's home. The three of them were away all night. They showed up half an hour ago."

"Who's the third?"

"Ronson."

"Oh yes. They'd all been away together?"

"That's right."

"So what do we do?" Della Street asked. "Just wait or go back to the office?"

"I don't want to do either," Mason told her. "If we go back to the office, we'll lose valuable time. I want to get in touch with Kirby. He wants me to realize that he's a big executive and can do his own thinking. He thinks I know nothing whatever about Dr. Babb and that I'm hounding him for more details about that story he told us of picking up the hitchhiker on the highway. Let's take a look in the garage, Della."

Mason left the porch, led the way around across the lawn to the three-car garage. He tried one of the doors and found it securely locked. The next door was locked and so was the third.

"Well," Mason said, "I guess we'd better wait until someone shows up. Let's go sit in the car and wait at least a few minutes, Della."

They started walking back down the driveway. Suddenly Mason turned at a noise behind him.

The garage doors had swung upward, and the interior of the garage showed one vacant stall, two stalls with cars parked in them.

"What in the world?" Della Street gasped. "How did those doors open?"

Mason whirled, "Come on, Della," he said, and started walking rapidly toward the garage.

"What is it?" she asked. "Did someone see us there and—"

"A ray of black light," Mason said. "It's fixed so that, when they swing one of their cars in the driveway, the garage doors all open. Probably they stay open for a matter of sixty seconds or something of that sort and then close."

"But, Chief," Della Street said, "doesn't that make the garage vulnerable to any prowler or—?"

"They can undoubtedly turn a switch on the inside of the house and shut this mechanism off," Mason told her. "The fact that it's been left on indicates they intend to be back within a short time. Probably Kirby wanted to go somewhere and felt he could get back before I arrived. Come on, Della. Let's go in before the doors close."

They entered the garage and Mason started looking around.

"Now this big Olds with the license plate JYJ 112 is undoubtedly the car Kirby was driving night before last," Mason said. "Then they have a sports car over there, and the vacant stall is where—" He broke off as the three doors of the garage swung silently downward and clicked in place.

"Evidently," Mason said, "we trip another timing mechanism as we go through the door of the garage."

"And now we're locked in?" Della Street asked.

Mason looked around the garage and said, "No, that door leads to the house. Let's see if it's unlocked."

Della Street, who was nearer to the door, turned the knob. "It's unlocked," she said. She opened it and said, "It opens into a passageway which seems to go right into the house."

"All right," Mason told her. "I'm interested in this car Kirby was driving last night. Let's take a look at it."

Mason looked at the outside of the car for a moment, then opened the door. "Oh-oh."

"What?" Della Street asked.

"A gallon can of gasoline," Mason said holding it up."

"Well, well, well," Della Street observed. "*Now* he has the props to back up his story."

Mason pressed his thumb against the catch of the glove compartment, opened it, looked inside and pulled out a small printed slip of paper, then began to chuckle.

"What is it?" Della Street asked.

"Our friend Kirby is unspeakably naïve," Mason said. "He not only bought this gasoline can from a service station but he got a sales slip with it and then forgot and left the sales slip in the glove compartment of his automobile."

"When's it dated?" Della Street asked.

"It's dated yesterday," Mason told her. "He probably went out right after his interview with me and purchased an authentic, slightly battered, red gasoline can."

"What are you going to do?"

"I'll just put this sale slip in my pocket. I'll leave the gasoline can where it is. Then later on when Kirby tells us, all smiles, that the gasoline can was in his automobile all the time but was down back of the front seat and he just hadn't noticed it, I'll ask him what became of the *other* gasoline can, and he'll want to know, of course with a show of indignation, what other gasoline can I'm talking about, and then I'll flash this sales slip on him and say, 'The one you bought yesterday at the Chevron station at Figueroa and Atcheson streets, of course.'"

"He'll wonder how you found out about it," Della Street said.

"Let him," Mason told her. "It won't do him any harm to do a little speculating."

Della Street thoughtfully regarded the automobile. "Do you suppose he'll think his wife is mixed up in it, that she went through the glove compartment, and—"

"That's right," Mason said. "You have a point there, Della. I'll have to—" He broke off in midsentence at the sound of a metallic click. Without other warning, the three doors of the garage swung upward, disclosing a dark blue sedan in the driveway.

A good-looking young woman at the wheel of the sedan piloted it expertly through the open doors of the garage, opened the car door and slid part way out before she noticed Perry Mason and Della Street.

With an exclamation of embarrassed surprise, she grabbed at her skirt which had been dragging behind her on the seat, whipped it down and said, "Who are you, and what are *you* doing in *here?*"

The mechanism sent the garage doors swinging silently downward.

"Permit me to introduce myself. I'm Perry Mason."

"*You* are!"

"Yes. You're Mrs. Kirby?"

"Yes."

"This is Miss Street, my confidential secretary. We came out here to talk with your husband, and minutes are precious."

"Well, why aren't you in the house talking with him?"

"Because," Mason said, "no one seems to answer the doorbell. We walked around to see if the garage might be open. It wasn't. Then we walked back toward my car, which is parked in front, intending to wait there, and the garage doors obligingly flew open."

"She suddenly laughed. The sharp edge of irritation left her voice. "Well, at least our garage was hospitable if my husband wasn't," she said.

"I'm afraid he isn't home," Mason said.

"Oh yes he is. His car's here. He told me you'd phoned that you were on your way out and that he was waiting for you. I left to take Ronnie to school."

"Your husband didn't answer the doorbell," Mason said.

"He may have been in the bathroom. We'll go dig him out. Why are you out here, Mr. Mason? Has there been some development?"

"There are lots of developments," the lawyer said grimly. "I tried to get you people on the telephone all yesterday afternoon and evening."

"We went with John on a business trip. Is it anything serious?"

"Very serious. You can listen in when I talk with your husband, Mrs. Kirby."

"That's fine," she told him. "We'll get him. Come on in."

She opened the door from the garage into the passageway which led to a reception hallway in the house.

"Only your husband home?" Mason asked.

"It's the servants' day off," she explained. "We keep a cook and a housekeeper, and I let them both off on the same day. Wednesdays John and I usually dine out and Ronnie spends the afternoon and evening with a young friend. They take care of Ronnie during Wednesday when our servants are off and we take care of their youngster Thursdays when their servants are off. It makes a very nice arrangement. Come on in and sit down. I'll get John for you."

She indicated seats in a spacious living room and called, "John! Oh, John!" There was no answer.

"Sit down and be comfortable, folks," she invited, "or look around. John is undoubtedly upstairs. He may be in the shower. I'll find him."

"Abruptly lowering her voice she said to Mason, "John's story about that girl in the jacket with the mother-of-pearl buttons, the alligator shoes, do you believe there really was such a girl?"

"Yes," Mason said.

Her face showed surprise. "You believe his story, then, about—?"

"No," Mason interrupted, "I don't believe his story. I have to get to him and tip him off to certain things about that story. Will you get him please?"

"Right away," she promised. "He's upstairs somewhere."

She ran up the stairs and Mason walked across to the bookcases and inspected the volumes. Della Street looked at some of the paintings, then settled herself in a chair.

From time to time they heard steps upstairs, and twice they heard Mrs. Kirby calling her husband.

At length she came downstairs. "Mr. Mason, I'm afraid something's gone wrong somewhere."

"Why?" Mason asked.

"John isn't here."

"Where would he have gone?"

"No place. His car's in the garage."

"You've looked the place over?" Mason asked sharply.

"I've looked the place over—that is, I looked in all the bathrooms and bedrooms and every place I could think of, and I've called. Of course," she said, her face suddenly white and strained, "I didn't look in the closets."

"Your husband may have been taken away against his will, or he may have decided he was up against something he didn't want to face. Look in the closets."

She took one quick look at his face, then flew upstairs.

"We'll look around downstairs," Mason called up to her.

Mason and Della Street looked through the dining room the downstairs bedrooms, the maids' rooms, the basement, the pantry, opening closet doors, giving the place a thorough search. When they returned, Mrs. Kirby was in the living room.

"He simply isn't in the house," she said.

"All right," Mason told her. "There's only one answer to that."

"What?"

"He was taken away."

"What do you mean?"

"By the police."

She looked at him with wide, startled eyes. "Mr. Mason, what in the world *are* you talking about?"

"There isn't any time to tell you now," Mason said. "I want you to answer two or three questions and answer them fast. If the police question your husband, will he tell them the same story that he told me yesterday afternoon?"

"I suppose so. I know that you jarred his self-complacency when you pointed out certain discrepancies in that story, but—well, you have to understand John's character to understand his reactions. He'd try to bolster up the weak points in the story, and . . . I know he intended to see you again today and he felt that he could convince you of the truth of what he had told you yesterday."

Mason said, "If the police should start tripping him up, would he have sense enough to tell them he wasn't going to answer any more questions until he had talked with me, or would he go ahead and try to explain?"

"I'm afraid he'd try to explain, Mr. Mason. You see he's been a salesman all his life. He's accustomed to meeting the objections of a prospect and explaining them away. If the police give him a chance he'll talk and keep talking."

"That's what I was afraid of," Mason said. "Come on, Della."

"Where are you going?" she asked.

Mason said, "In view of your husband's prominence, I don't think they'll book him right away. I think they'll take him to the district attorney's office. That's where I'm going."

"But why in the world should they take him to the district attorney's office?" Mrs. Kirby asked. "What on earth are they going to question him about?"

Mason and Della Street started for the door. "Murder," Mason called back over his shoulder.

CHAPTER SEVEN

Mason piloted his car through traffic, conscious of the fact that the police already had a head start which was lengthening with each delay.

By the time Mason reached the district attorney's office, it was after nine-thirty.

"Is Mr. Hamilton Burger, the district attorney, in?" Mason asked.

"Yes."

"Tell him Perry Mason wishes to see him, please."

"I'm sorry. Mr. Burger left word that he isn't to be disturbed under any circumstances. I'm not permitted to call him on the phone or to interrupt in any way. He's in a very important conference."

Mason said, "I have a client in here."

"Who?" she asked.

"Mr. John Northrup Kirby. I demand to see him at once."

"You will have to ask Mr. Burger about that."

"Then tell him I'm here."

"I can't. He's not to be disturbed."

Mason said, "He's talking with John Kirby. I'm Kirby's counsel. I demand that I be permitted to see Mr. Kirby."

"I have no authority in the matter."

"You're in charge here, aren't you?"

"I'm only an employee."

"Then try to have me thrown out," Mason said, pushing past the woman's desk through a swinging door and down a long corridor toward Hamilton Burger's private office.

A startled deputy, evidently alerted by telephone, flung open a door, debouched into the corridor. "You can't come in here," he said.

"I'm in here," Mason told him.

The deputy hurried to the lawyer's side.

"Get out."

"Put me out."

The deputy hesitated. Mason pushed his way to the door of Hamilton Burger's office, tried the knob. The door was locked. Mason banged his fist against the panels of the door.

Hamilton Burger's voice could be heard from the interior of the office. He was evidently talking on the phone and his voice was sharp with irritation.

Mason again banged his fist on the panels.

Abruptly the door was thrown open and Hamilton Burger, the big, grizzly bear of a district attorney who made no secret of his dislike for Perry Mason, stood glowering in the doorway.

"Don't bang on my door," he shouted. "I'll have you arrested."

"Go ahead," Mason invited. "I'm here to protect the rights of my client."

"And who's your client?"

"John Northrup Kirby," Mason said, raising his voice.

"Is he accused of crime?"

"I don't know," Mason said, "but he's my client. I'm here to protect his rights. I want to be present while he is being interviewed."

"We can't stand for that, Mason."

"Why not?" Mason asked.

"We're investigating a murder."

"Is Kirby implicated?"

"It's a little early to tell yet."

"Under those circumstances," Mason said, "the purpose of my request becomes even more apparent."

Mason looked at his wrist watch, noted the time and jotted that time down in a notebook. "I've made a formal demand on you," he said.

"Now wait a minute," Burger said, "you're not going to trap me with any technicality. Mr. Kirby, as far as I'm concerned, is merely a material witness, except of course the fact that he has retained a high-priced criminal attorney such as you indicates there's something in the background I don't know about."

"There can be lots of things in the background *you* don't know about," Mason said, "but the fact remains anyone has a right to retain me in connection with any matter he damn pleases, and I have a right to talk with my client."

"Your client was not brought here under process," Hamilton Burger said. "He came here voluntarily."

Mason kept his voice up. "Then he can leave here voluntarily. Come on Kirby."

"We haven't finished questioning him," Burger said.

"I think you have," Mason said.

John Kirby came to stand behind Burger.

"I trust you realize," Burger said, "that any such attitude as this makes Mr. Kirby more of a suspect than a witness. I have been protecting him from all publicity in the case as a witness. As a suspect I can give him no such protection."

He turned to Kirby. "I trust you will appreciate the situation, Mr. Kirby. You have registered at a motel with a young woman as husband and wife. We have no desire to pillory you with publicity as long as you cooperate. I suggest you carefully consider the facts in the situation."

"Come on, Kirby, let's go!" Mason said.

"Can't this wait?" Kirby asked Mason. "Mr. Burger has been most considerate and—"

"Hell, no! It can't wait," Mason told him. "Get going if you want me to represent you."

Kirby hesitated.

"Make up your mind," Mason told him.

Kirby eased out into the hallway, his manner hesitant.

"All right, Mason," Burger said. "There's your client. Look him over. No bruises. No marks of a rubber hose. No torture. No pressure. No violence. How did we treat you, Kirby?"

"With every consideration," Kirby said.

Hamilton Burger grinned. "Your lawyer evidently doesn't have as much confidence in your story as you want us to have. He seems to feel that you need protection, that you need to be advised as to what he refers to as 'your rights.'"

Kirby's face flushed. "I didn't ask Mr. Mason to be here. I—"

"Never mind, Kirby," Mason said. "Don't let him lead you on. I'll explain to you in the car. Let's go!"

"Perhaps Kirby would like to have you explain right here and now," Hamilton Burger said. "Come in, Mason, and we'll talk things over. We may be able to get the whole matter cleared up."

"I'll talk to my client in private, if you don't mind," Mason said. "Come on, Kirby."

Hamilton Burger stood in the doorway grinning as Mason escorted his client to the elevator.

"What the devil!" Kirby said angrily. "That is the one touch I didn't want, Mason. Can't you understand the position in which you put me by busting in there? Good heavens, Mason! I'm not a child! I am a businessman. I'm accustomed to carrying on rather large and important business transactions, and if I do say so myself, I know my way around."

"I see," Mason said. "Perhaps you'd better wait and talk in the car."

Kirby drew himself up angrily. "I think I can talk any place I damn please, Mason. I'm trying to point out to you that, while I may call on you for advice as to the law, I don't need anyone to do my thinking for me."

"Exactly," Mason said. "You can tell me about it after we get in the car."

Kirby rode down in the elevator and strode alongside Mason to the parking place where Della Street was seated in the rear of the car.

"How do you do, Miss Street," he said gruffy.

"Get up in front," Mason told Kirby. "I'll drive you home."

"You don't need to," Kirby told him. "I can get a cab. It may be a lot cheaper in the long run, a hell of a lot cheaper. I don't know why you feel you have to chaperon me, Mason. I'm fully capable of taking care of myself."

"You told the district attorney about what happened Monday night?" Mason asked.

"Is there any reason why I shouldn't?"

"It's a hell of a story!" Mason said.

"I'm not accustomed to having my word doubted, Mr. Mason," Kirby said, getting into the car.

Mason started the motor.

"How did you know Dr. Babb had died?" Mason asked.

"Who's Dr. Babb?"

"The doctor you dealt with when you conspired to violate the laws in regard to adoption. The doctor whom you paid to list Ronson in the Vital Statistics as the son of you and your wife."

"I don't know what you're talking about," Kirby said sullenly.

"You may not know what I'm talking about now," Mason said, "but you sure as hell knew all about it last night when you called Norma Logan and told her Dr. Babb had died and instructed her to back up your story about having run out of gas on the highway, having her car stolen and abandoned by somebody out at the Purple Swan."

"Here again, I don't know what you're talking about," Kirby said. "The name Logan means nothing to me, and I certainly didn't ask anyone to back up my story. It is, of course, possible that you know something I don't, and that the young woman whom I picked up *did* have the name of Logan."

"You told that story to the district attorney?"

"Certainly."

"Just as you told it to me?"

"Yes. Why would I have changed it?"

"Well," Mason said, "that's done it. That puts the fat in the fire."

"What do you mean, the fat in the fire, Mason? Those people were courtesy itself. They were very, very considerate. They even refused to give out any tip to the newspapers so that I wouldn't be hounded by the press. They put it up to me that if I'd co-operate with them, they'd co-operate with me, and they're certainly doing a job!"

"Yes, I can imagine," Mason said, working his way through traffic and getting on the approach to the freeway.

"And, by the way," Kirby went on, "that gasoline can was in my car all the time, just as you surmised."

"I see," Mason said.

"I found it as soon as I went back down to my car. However, I had this other appointment and I couldn't telephone you at the time, but I decided to let you know as soon as I could. And then the police showed up at my house and asked me if I'd mind having a talk with the district attorney about some information I seem to possess. How do they find out those things? I put down the first part of my license number correctly because I felt the manager would probably remember that, but the last two figures I juggled completely."

"Did you tell the officers about the gasoline can?"

"Certainly."

"About it being in your car?"

"Of course."

"Did they ask you to produce it?"

"They did better than that. A few minutes ago they put out a call over the police radio and had a police car drive by the house and pick it up."

"Then probably they have it by this time," Mason said.

"And you don't need to be so stuffy about it," Kirby blazed.

"I just wanted to keep you in the clear," Mason said.

"Well, I'm in the clear," Kirby snapped. "You can trust my discretion in some things, Mr. Mason. I don't need you to hold my hand every time someone asks me a question."

Mason said, "I was afraid that you might give the officers permission to search your car and garage."

"Well, why not?" Kirby asked. "They would like very much to get fingerprints of this young woman, and there's no reason why I shouldn't help them. They already have her fingerprints from the unit in the motel. I don't know why they're so worked up about her. They wouldn't tell me that. They did ask me if I'd ever heard of a Dr. Babb."

"What did you tell them?"

"The truth. I don't think I ever heard of him in my life."

"You told the D.A. that?"

"Certainly."

"Said you'd never heard of him?"

"I said the name meant absolutely nothing to me. That's the truth, it doesn't. Now what's wrong with cooperating with the police in this thing? Why shouldn't I let them search my car if they want to? Why shouldn't I let them question and search to their heart's content?"

"Quite all right, if you feel that way," Mason told him. "Of course, when they search the car they'll dig into the glove compartment and look through any papers that might be there and—Well, when I heard you were at the D.A.'s office I just thought I'd better get in touch with you."

Kirby suddenly straightened up in the seat, his forehead puckered into a frown.

"What's the matter?" Mason asked.

"Nothing!" Kirby said shortly. "I...I was just thinking. What'll they do about fingerprinting the car, Mason? Will they fingerprint it there in the garage?"

Mason said, "Probably they'll send a tow car around to pick up the front end and take it up to the police laboratory. I take it they asked you if you'd have any objection?"

"That's right."

"You told them you had no objection?"

"Of course. How long will it take them to get the tow car there?"

"Not very long."

"Hang it! Mason," Kirby said, "you're driving at a snail's pace! I've lost enough time over this thing as it is. I'd like to get home."

"Why?"

"Because I'm a busy man. You've been talking about that glove compartment. Come to think of it, there *may* be some business papers in there that I wouldn't want to have the public know about. I have competitors who would like to find out some of my business secrets."

Mason said, "That's one of the reasons I wanted to get in touch with you before you'd given them permission to go out and pick up your car."

"Well, you were just a little bit late," Kirby said angrily.

"That's right," Mason said, "through no fault of mine. If you'd insisted on waiting for me when they asked you to go to the district attorney's office, I could have gone with you. You knew I was on my way to your house."

"Step on it!" Kirby said impatiently.

"And in case this is bothering you," Mason said, reaching in his pocket, "I took the precaution of removing the sales slip which was given you by the service station when you bought that one-gallon can of gasoline, Kirby."

Kirby snatched at the receipt, then looked at Mason with stormy, suspicious eyes. "And what are you going to do with that information?" he asked.

"Nothing," Mason said. "With some clients, of course, I'd have to coach them what to do, but since you are a businessman and are accustomed to fast thinking, reaching important decisions and all that, I won't have to say a word."

"As a matter of fact," Kirby blurted after a short silence, "that sales slip doesn't mean what you think it means."

"I see," Mason said.

Kirby settled back against the cushions, his eyes narrowed in thought.

Mason said, "For once tell me the truth, Kirby. Did you have an appointment with Dr. Babb Monday night, either with or without this Logan girl?"

"No."

"Is that the truth?"

"Yes."

"It may be important."

"All right, suppose it is. I've told you the truth. Now shut up and let me think. I've got to correlate certain events in my own mind."

CHAPTER EIGHT

Mrs. Kirby was standing in front of the house as they drove up.

She ran to her husband as Mason turned the car into the driveway.

"John!" she said, "is everything all right?"

John Kirby gave her the genial smile of a successful salesman who is firmly convinced of his own ability to cope with any situation which may arise. "Everything's under control," he said.

She flashed Mason a grateful glance. "You were in time!"

Her husband said, "Mason hurried up there, Joan, but actually there was no need of all the fireworks. I covered the situation with the D.A. and we're buddies. We're just like that."

John Kirby held up his hand with the first and second fingers crossed.

"John," she asked anxiously, "*what* did you tell him?"

"Why, I told them the truth of course. *I* don't have anything to conceal. I picked up a woman and took her to a motel. I registered as husband and wife because that was the only way I could get her a room, but I just registered and then went on. I didn't hang around at all."

"Did they ask you about this woman in some detail?" Mason inquired.

"Why of course, they wanted to know all about her. They have an idea that she's mixed up in an attack on some doctor. They may be able to prove it, too. They found her fingerprints in the motel, and also found some of her fingerprints in this doctor's house."

"You know that this was a murder, John?" she asked. "You knew that this Dr. Babb had died? I heard it on the radio just now."

"They didn't tell me that," her husband said, "but I realized they were investigating something they thought pretty serious, something a little more grave than just an ordinary theft of narcotics. Anyhow I came clean. I told them exactly what had happened. They came and got my car?"

"Yes."

"How did they take it? Did they drive it?"

"No, they towed it," she said. "They were very careful not to touch the interior of the car at all. They wanted to get fingerprints."

"Well, it's all right," Kirby assured her. "I gave them permission. I told them I had another car which we could use. After all, dear, there's no use getting excited about all this."

"Now look," Mason said to Kirby, "you're not kidding anyone except yourself. On Monday night shortly after eleven-thirty, someone committed an assault on Dr. Babb. You'd had some previous dealings with Dr. Babb. A girl was seen running out of Dr. Babb's office. Neighbors can identify her if they see her again. You took that girl to the Beauty Rest Motel and registered with her as husband and wife. The evidence in the case pointed to you but because you're a prominent man the police weren't going to proceed against you until after you had crucified yourself by admitting that you took the girl to that motel.

"Police have checked Dr. Babb's office and found the girl's fingerprints. They checked the Unit Number 5 in the motel and found more of those same fingerprints. By the time they have checked your car and found her fingerprints in your car, they'll be ready to act, regardless of how prominent you may be. They'll have enough evidence against you to hold you as an accessory.

"I've played along with you, hoping that you'd tell me the truth and I wouldn't have to take you to pieces in order to get the true story.

"I don't know how much of this your wife knows, but it's time she knew the whole business. Dr. Babb had a service by which he juggled the birth records so black-market babies could be carried on the birth records as legitimate children. You and your wife subscribed to that service. Ronson was a black-market baby. He still is, despite the fact that the birth certificate registers him as your son.

"The police have been playing with you as a cat plays with a mouse. The reason Hamilton Burger, the district attorney, was so cordial to you is that he felt certain he had you in a trap. He was tickled to death. Not only does he want to solve the case and have the credit of getting a conviction, but he's not at all averse to all the publicity that will go with convicting a wealthy man of murder.

"The young woman whom you took out to Dr. Babb's office was Norma Logan. Actually she's a half-sister of Ronson. She's been interested in him. She knows all about the kind of service Dr. Babb was giving in connection with the black-market babies.

"Now then, I've been given the run-around long enough. Let's have the truth and have it fast, and then I'll tell you what you're up against."

John Kirby looked at Mason with an expression of utter consternation on his face.

"John," his wife said, "did you do that?"

"I drove the girl out to Dr. Babb's place," he said in a low voice, "but you don't need to worry, dear. That girl didn't do anything illegal. She's in the clear and, despite Mr. Mason's gloomy predictions, she's going to stay in the clear. They may be able to prove she went out to Dr. Babb's office, but that's *all* they can prove, and don't forget it."

Mason stood regarding Kirby with angry eyes, feet spread apart, hands jammed in his trousers pockets.

He said, "You've engaged in the most expensive past-time known to litigants, that of lying to your lawyer. If you had told me the truth yesterday afternoon, I might have been able to have saved you from a lot of things that are going to happen."

"What's going to happen?" Kirby asked. "I'm in trouble on this thing, Mason, but not in the kind of trouble you think, and not in as deep as you think. Remember this, I'm rather a prominent man in this city. I have influential friends and contacts. I can pull a lot of political wires if I have to."

"Sure you can," Mason said. "That's why they pulled this cat-and-mouse business with you and decided to wait until they had you absolutely hooked before they moved against you.

"It may be they'll be ready to move against you as soon as they find Norma Logan's fingerprints in your car. It may be they'll wait until they've picked up Norma Logan and heard her story."

"They won't hear her story," Kirby said.

"Don't kid yourself," Mason told him. "They'll make her talk."

Kirby shook his head. "If they pick her up, she'll be like a clam, if not for my sake, at least for Ronnie's sake."

"No, she won't," Mason said, "because you've jerked the rug out from under her. You told her to corroborate your story about your picking her up. When she tells that story she's sunk. The police will then have the deadwood on her. They can then convict her of murder. They can convict you of being an accessory."

Kirby ran his hands through his hair. "Damn it!" he said. "This thing is— How the devil did they learn she was registered at that motel?"

"They learned it the same way they're going to learn a lot of other things," Mason said. "Through good, hard work. Now then, what do you want me to do? Do you want me to represent you, or do you want me to walk out and send you a bill for what I've done to date?"

"Good heavens, no! Don't leave us!" Mrs. Kirby interposed. "Mr. Mason, you *must* represent John and you *must* try to do something to keep all of this about Ronnie from coming out in the papers.

"Ronnie's a sensitive, sweet youngster. He thinks that we are his natural parents, and he has all of the feeling of security which come from that feeling. If he ever finds out that he's adopted—Well, you either tell a child that he's adopted when he's old enough to start talking things over or you never tell him. To let him have the feeling that he's with his natural parents and then give him that emotional shock is simply terrible."

Mason said, "You could have thought of that, you know, six years ago when you tried to outwit the law."

"Well, quite a few people are in the same boat," John Kirby said. "I found out about Dr. Babb from a friend who's—Well, he's the president of a bank. I can tell you one thing—if any of this hits the newspapers, there will be so much influence brought to bear on the district attorney that he'll wish he'd never started this thing."

"Phooey!" Mason said. "It'll give the district attorney an opportunity for a self-righteous crusade. It'll give him the chance to pose as a fearless public official who hews to the line and lets the chips fall as they will.

"Now then, I want to know one thing, Kirby. Can you keep your mouth shut? When the police come back to arrest you, can you tell them that you've told them your story and you don't intend to discuss it any more?"

"I can if you think that's the thing to do," Kirby said, "but I still think—"

"I know you do," Mason told him, "and I haven't time to argue it with you or discuss it. I'm busy. I'm going to have to do things to protect your son's interest."

Mrs. Kirby said quietly, "Go ahead and protect them, Mr. Mason, and send us the bill. As far as Ronnie is concerned, we'll do anything we can."

"All right," Mason said, turning to her, "now I talked with this Norma Logan. I told her that I wasn't in a position to advise her. I told her to see an attorney. I hope she's done so. I think the attorney will tell her not to talk, not even to give the officers the time of day until we know more about the facts in this case, and about how much they have against her.

"Now then," he said, turning back to Kirby, "I'm going to ask you this question once more, and I'm going to tell you now that the whole safety and happiness of your son may depend upon it. Did you make an appointment with Dr. Babb for Monday night?"

"No, I didn't."

"Your name was on his appointment book. How did it get there?"

"I didn't make any appointment."

Mrs. Kirby said hurriedly, "But the name Logan was also on there, Mr. Mason. Couldn't this girl, this Logan girl have made it?"

"That's what I'm trying to get at," Mason said. "Somebody's lying. She tells me she didn't make an appointment. I want to know if you did."

Kirby met his eyes. "Mason," he said, "I've been a fool. I've tried to lie to you when I should have told you the truth. But I'll tell you the truth on this. I did *not* make any appointment with Dr. Babb. I didn't have any contact with Dr. Babb. I talked only with Norma Logan. I was afraid to talk with Dr. Babb because...because I thought it might be blackmail. And I'm not too certain even yet that it isn't blackmail."

"Neither am I," Mason said. "That's why I'm feeling my way. When the officers come out to pick you up and tell you you're under arrest for murder, tell them you've make your statement and you're not going to say another word."

"You seem to think they're going to come out and arrest me," Kirby said.

"I know damn well they are," Mason said. "Come on, Della. Let's go."

Mason jerked open the door of his car, said to Mrs. Kirby, "Don't leave the house. I want you to stay here where I can get in touch with you. They may come and place your husband under arrest any time or they may wait awhile. Keep me advised.

"As for you, Kirby, I want to know where you are every minute of the day. I suppose you'll go to your office. It would look better if you did. When you get to your office, telephone me. If for any reason you leave your office, telephone me. I want to be in touch with you at all times."

"When is the critical period?" Kirby asked. "When will—?"

"As soon as they've processed your car for fingerprints. If they find that girl's fingerprints in your car, they'll be ready to take action. That action will consist in picking you up and shaking you down to find out the girl's identity and her address. If you break down and give them that, they may simply hold you as a witness until they've built up more of a case against the girl. But in the end the result will be the same. They'll charge her with murder and hold you as being an accessory."

"Then you feel I shouldn't tell them anything about the girl?"

"Shorten that sentence," Mason said. "I feel that you shouldn't tell them anything."

Mason slammed the car door, stepped on the throttle, and shot out from the curb.

"Well," Della Street said, "at least now we know what we're up against."

"I'm not so certain we do," Mason said.

"What do you mean?"

"The girl's jacket," Mason said grimly.

"What do you mean? What jacket?"

"Norma Logan's jacket," Mason explained.

"What about it?"

"The mother-of-pearl buttons," Mason said. "You heard Mrs. Kirby describe the girl and the mother-of-pearl buttons on the jacket. How did *she* know about those buttons?"

"Why from her husband, of course," Della Street said.

Mason said, "Then her husband told her something he didn't tell us. He didn't describe the buttons at any time when he was talking to us."

Della Street started to say something, then suddenly caught herself. An expression of complete dismay spread over her features. "Good Lord!" she exclaimed.

"Exactly," Mason commented.

"What are you going to do?"

"We'll wait until the police have arrested John Kirby," Mason said. "Then, when there's no opportunity for him to coach her, we'll have her up in the office and then we may find out what actually did happen."

"Chief," Della Street said, her voice showing her worry, "you're taking too many chances in this thing. That notebook which Norma Logan found and took, the story of the woman who ran out of the house, the mother-of-pearl buttons—Chief, I wish you'd never become involved in this case."

"So do I," Mason said, "but it's too late for that now."

CHAPTER NINE

At eleven-thirty, Mason's phone rang. Della Street picked up the receiver, said, "Yes, who is it, Gertie?...I'm quite sure Mr. Mason will want to talk with her. Put her on."

Della Street nodded to Mason. "Mrs. Kirby," she said.

Mason picked up the telephone.

Mrs. Kirby, her voice sounding almost hysterical, said, "It's happened, Mr.

Mason. Police came and took John into custody. They said they were picking him up on suspicion of being an accessory to murder."

"All right," Mason told her. "That's that. Do you think he'll follow my instructions and keep quiet?"

"I certainly hope he will. He knows now that the happiness of Ronnie is at stake as well as...well I *hope* he'll keep quiet."

"You're not certain?"

"I'm not certain, Mr. Mason. Remember that my husband has been trained to try and explain, to convince, to persuade. If they're clever—"

"They will be," Mason interrupted. "Get in your car and get up to my office just as quick as you can. I'll be waiting. How long will it take you?"

"Twenty or twenty-five minutes."

"Try to make it less than that," Mason said.

Mason hung up the telephone, said, "Well, Della, we're in it now."

Della Street, her eyes showing her worry, lowered her voice. "Chief, that book—Wouldn't it be better to destroy it?"

He shook his head. "Not now. Later on, perhaps.

"Now then, Della, get on the telephone. Cancel any appointments I have for today, and rush Mrs. Kirby in here just as soon as she comes to the office."

Mason pushed back his chair, got to his feet, walked over to the window, jammed his hands down in his trousers pockets and stood looking down at traffic in the street, his concentration such that he was entirely oblivious of everything about him.

Twenty minutes later Della Street opened the door and said, "Mrs. Kirby."

"Bring her in."

"She's here," Della said.

Mrs. Kirby moved past Della on into the office.

"Sit down," Mason said.

She said, "Oh, Mr. Mason, it was terrible! They came out and arrested John. I believe they'd have placed him in handcuffs if—"

"Sit down!"

She eased herself down into the client's chair.

"Now talk," Mason told her.

"What do you mean?"

Mason said, "You knew about Dr. Babb. You participated in the conspiracy at the time Ronnie was supposed to have been born to you."

"I was in on the scheme. I went to Dr. Babb's maternity hospital, so-called, and I did what he told me to about making announcements to my most intimate friends. And, well—there was a period of about six weeks when I kept absolutely out of circulation, when I saw no one. If that's what you call participating I participated."

"When did you first know that there was going to be trouble about this thing?"

"About what?"

"About Ronnie."

"Not until after—well not until after you pointed out the holes in my husband's story."

Mason said, "Your husband came home from a sales meeting. The next morning he told you this cock-and-bull story about having picked up a young woman carrying a gasoline can and you immediately got frightened, rang me up and asked me to cross-examine your husband."

"Why, yes, of course. What's wrong with that?"

"Everything," Mason said.

"I don't think I know what you mean."

"The hell you don't," Mason told her. "You knew there was trouble over Ronnie. You knew it probably before your husband did. You told me about a girl who was in Dr. Babb's office. You said she was wearing a jacket with mother-of-pearl buttons."

"Well, she was."

"How do *you* know?"

"My husband told me."

"No, he didn't. He didn't know anything at all about what kind of buttons were on that jacket. He didn't know much about her clothes. He described them the way a man would describe a woman. You described that jacket the way a woman would describe it.

"Now then, Dr. Babb had an appointment late at night with someone by the name of Kirby. Your husband says he wasn't the one. There are two people in the family by the name of Kirby. Tell me about your appointment with Dr. Babb and try telling me the truth!"

She sat speechless, looking at him in wide-eyed consternation.

"You were out there," Mason said. "How did you happen to be out there?"

"I...I was the one who had the appointment."

"That's better," Mason told her. "Now start talking, and for once try to tell me the truth."

She said, "I don't know whether it was my conscience, or a premonition of impending evil, but I always had the feeling that something was going to happen to Ronnie because of Dr. Babb. My husband would laugh at me and tell me the thing was absolutely foolproof and bulletproof and not to worry, but I always had that feeling. Then Monday I saw a letter addressed to my husband with Dr. Babb's imprint in the upper left-hand corner."

"Where did you see that letter?" Mason asked.

"At the house. My husband gets most of his mail at the office, but some of the personal things, some of the advertisements and circulars and things of that sort come to the house. He usually doesn't pay too much attention to that mail, and sometimes lets it go for a day or so without looking at it."

"All right," Mason said. "I take it you steamed the envelope open."

"I tore the envelope open. It was addressed to my husband and Dr. Babb said that a certain matter which he thought had been concluded a good many years ago had developed ramifications which he thought should be discussed. He suggested that my husband get in touch with him."

"And later on you gave that letter to your husband?"

"I did nothing of the sort. I burnt that letter in the stove."

"You didn't tell your husband anything about it?"

"No."

Mason eyed her thoughtfully. "So then you telephoned Dr. Babb asking for an appointment? Why didn't you tell your husband and let him do that?"

"Because I was afraid he'd try to put too much sugarcoating on a bitter pill. I simply had to know the truth."

"So Dr. Babb gave you an appointment?"

"Yes."

"When?"

"He said to come around eleven-thirty that night."

"That was Monday?"

"Yes."

"You didn't tell your husband about that appointment?"

"No."

"Why?"

"Because I didn't want to alarm him. I knew he was going to be at that sales meeting and—well you know how sales meetings are, Mr. Mason. They talk a little business, then put on some so-called entertainment, which you can put in quotes—I guess it entertains the salesmen all right. They get a terrific bang out of it. I felt that I could see Dr. Babb and get home before my husband arrived. Even if I didn't he wouldn't think anything of it because I quite frequently go out when he's tied up with his sales meetings."

"All right," Mason said, "now suppose you tell me exactly what happened out there at Dr. Babb's house."

"I parked my car a block or so from Dr. Babb's office. I walked to his house and went in through the outer door to the reception room."

"That door was unlocked?"

"Yes. But an electric buzzer evidently sounds when you go in because Dr. Babb came to the door leading from the reception room into the inner offices."

"What happened?"

"He said I was early, that I'd have to wait a few minutes. So he let me sit in the waiting room. He said he was in the middle of another matter, that he'd see me as soon as possible.

"So I sat down to wait, and I became terribly nervous. It suddenly dawned on me that the mere fact of my presence in Dr. Babb's office was most incriminating. Suppose he was under investigation by the police, suppose someone who knew me should come in. So I worked myself into a nervous frenzy. I simply couldn't afford to be left there in his waiting room.

"There was a rest room at the end of the office. I explored it and found it had two doors. One of them led into the inner office, and one of them to the outer office.

"I went in that room and kept the door to the outer office unlatched. It was open just a crack so I could see out."

"What happened?"

"Then after a few minutes the outer door opened and this girl came in."

"The girl your husband described?"

"Yes."

"You had a good look at her?"

"Yes."

"Then what happened?"

"Then all of a sudden there was a commotion from the inner office. I could hear blows and the sound of crashing glass."

"What did you do?"

"I opened the door into the inner office. Dr. Babb was lying on the floor. A man who had his back to me was going through the contents of the safe; that is, he was bent over in front of the safe and was throwing books and papers out."

"What did you do?"

"All I could do was scream."

"You screamed?"

"At the top of my lungs. I'm afraid I became completely hysterical."

"And what did the man do?"

"He bolted out to the back of the house."

"You saw his face?"

She shook her head.

"Then what?"

"I realized the man had fled through a back door. My screams had frightened him more than he'd frightened me. So I went to bend over Dr. Babb, and then I thought of this girl in the waiting room. I knew that girl was still in the outer office; at least I thought she was. I didn't want her to see me, so I ran out through the back way, the way the man had gone. I must have been right on his heels."

"Did you see any trace of the man after you got outside?"

"I didn't see anyone. The door from the office led into a sort of operating room. There was a door from the operating room that was open and I ran through that and saw a door which I thought led out to the back yard. It did. I ran through that door.

"I ran out, then steadied myself, took a deep breath, and tried to get myself together. I walked as quietly as possible around the far side of the house, around the yard of the house next door, and then to my car. I drove away from there and went, I guess, about ten or fifteen blocks and then I went all to pieces. I parked the car in at the curb and sat there and cried and shook and cried and finally got hold of myself and drove on home."

"Then what?"

"I undressed and went to bed, and a little while later John came in. I pretended that I was drugged with sleep. I asked him a few questions about the sales meeting and pretended to fall asleep. Actually I was as wide awake as I've ever been in my life, only I forced myself to lie still."

"And your husband?" Mason asked.

"My husband went to bed in his room—"

"You have separate rooms?" Mason asked.

"Yes, separate rooms, with a connecting dressing room and a connecting bath. We leave the door open all the time, but my husband comes in late quite frequently and I'm a light sleeper. He tries not to disturb me."

"Did he go out again?"

"Yes."

"When?"

"It must have been around three o'clock in the morning."

"How long was he gone?"

"About an hour and a half."

"You heard him take the car out of the garage?"

"Yes."

"You didn't ask him anything about that?"

"No."

"What did you do?"

"Well, the next morning I was so nervous I could hardly eat, but I asked my husband about the sales meeting and then he went on and told me this story about the young woman he'd picked up, and I fell for it at first. I thought he was telling the truth. I told him he mustn't leave a young woman like that marooned without any money no matter who she was, that we should drive out there and pick her up, give her some breakfast, and find out what we could do."

"He agreed to do that?"

"Very reluctantly. He kept trying to tell me that it wasn't the thing to do, but I insisted it was, so he finally drove me out there. I don't know just when I began to realize that he was lying, Mr. Mason. In the first place, I knew from the way he acted in going out there that he didn't expect to find that woman there at the motel. So then I began to think about how he had gone out around three or four o'clock in the morning, and I felt certain he'd gone back to pick her up.

"However, I didn't say anything. I let him talk, but I kept thinking, and of course I was terribly concerned about Dr. Babb. I kept the radio on while we were driving and a news program came on and I heard about what had happened and heard that the police had taken an appointment book which had the names of Logan and Kirby in it.

"I knew of course, Mr. Mason, that it was my name they were talking about, that I was the Kirby, but I could see from the expression on John's face that *he* thought *he* was the one."

"Go on," Mason said, "what did you do?"

"I turned to John and asked him. I said, 'John, were you out there at Dr. Babb's last night? Isn't he the same one who helped us with Ronnie?'"

"And what did he say?" Mason asked.

"Then was when I really knew that my husband was lying and knew that we were in bad trouble. He was very glib and very persuasive, the way he is when he's trying to sell someone a bill of goods."

"Then what?" Mason asked.

"Then I didn't know what to do, but I kept thinking things over, and then I telephoned you, and after you said you'd see my husband at two o'clock, I rang him up at the office and told him that I wanted him to go and tell his story to you. I told him that we didn't know but what this girl was some sort of blackmailer, and if he would tell his story to you it would lay a foundation so that, in case she did subsequently try any blackmail, we could count on your sympathetic cooperation."

"Did you have any trouble persuading him?"

"Some, but not too much. Now that's the story, Mr. Mason. Now I've come clean with you and now you know what we're up against."

Mason's fingertips drummed noiselessly on the blotter of his desk.

She said, "I'm sorry, Mr. Mason, I should have told you all this right at the start. I would have done so if it hadn't been for Ronnie. It's difficult to tell you how I feel about him. I have not only a love for him but a desire to protect him. I'd do anything for him. I'd kill if I had to, to protect him.

"Ronnie is one of the dearest children you have ever seen. He's so poised, has such charm and character—there's something about him even at the age of six that is...it's hard to descibe. It's a very definite quality, a sort of gallantry. When you see him, you'll understand.

"Mr. Mason, we simply must keep him from having the emotional shock that is going to take place if he finds out about his...about his adoption."

"Yes," Mason said, "and then when you add to that the shock of having both of his parents mixed up in a murder case, yes, it's one hell of a mess you've dumped in my lap, Mrs. Kirby."

"Well, at least," she said, "I have come clean. I've put all the cards on the table."

"Yes," Mason told her dryly, "now that the police have trumped all your aces, you put your twos and threes in my hand and ask me to carry on the game."

CHAPTER TEN

After Mrs. Kirby left the office, Della Street pulled up a chair and sat down across the desk from Perry Mason.

"Chief, I'm worried."

"Who isn't?" Mason said.

"Where does all of this leave you?"

"In the middle of a legal quicksand. In the first place, I'm not entirely certain whom I'm representing. Ostensibly I'm representing John Kirby. But the thing that he wants me to do above all else is protect Ronnie.

"Now then if we put on the evidence we have, we can get John Kirby out of the mess—at least I hope we can, but in doing that we get Mrs. Kirby right into the middle of a murder charge."

"Are you going to tell Mr. Kirby about his wife being out there?"

"There again," Mason said, "we run up against a problem. It's my duty to tell my client what I know. However, there are some aspects of this case I'm going to have to think over."

"Chief, what worries me is that book."

Mason got up and began pacing the floor, thinking, frowning. Abruptly he stopped pacing, turned to Della Street. "You have that book?"

"I've never told you so in so many words."

"Tell me now. Do you have it?"

"Yes."

"Get it."

"It will take a little time."

"Go get it."

"Now?"

"Now."

Della Street left the office, returned in some five minutes, handed Mason a small cardboard-backed, spiral-bound notebook.

"Now I'm more frightened than ever."

Mason slid the book into the side pocket of his coat. "Forget it, Della, I'll carry the ball from now on."

Della Street said, "You have that book and it's stolen property. Norma Logan isn't your client. The things she's told you aren't confidential communications. You can't justify yourself on the ground of protecting a client—you've taken evidence into your possession, you're concealing that evidence, and the fact that it's stolen property means that you're technically guilty of receiving stolen property. You know what Hamilton Burger, the district attorney, will do if he ever gets an inkling of that."

Mason nodded.

"And," Della Street went on, "it seems to me inevitable that he's going to find out about it."

Mason said, "When an attorney's doing what he thinks is right, Della, he is entitled to take advantage of every technicality in the law. I've told you that I have a certain amount of legal ingenuity, and a certain amount of human ingenuity. I'm going to exercise them both."

"And you're not going to surrender that book to the police?"

"Not in a hundred years," Mason said.

"Then that leaves you in a vulnerable position."

Mason again got up and started pacing the floor. "That appointment book, Della; Dr. Babb wrote the name 'Kirby' in it. It didn't stand for John Kirby but for Joan Kirby.

"He also wrote the name Logan. I've been assuming that meant John Kirby and Norma Logan had a joint appointment. We now know that they didn't.

"Hang it, Della, do you suppose the name Logan didn't mean Norma but meant the boy's father?"

"Good heavens!" Della Street exclaimed.

Mason continued pacing the floor.

"But the father's been dead for six years, Chief."

Mason said, "Get Paul Drake on the phone, Della. Tell him to look up the whole Logan family tree. Let's not jump at any more erroneous conclusions."

Della Street put through the call, relayed Mason's instructions to the detective, then hung up the phone, looked anxiously at Mason.

"Chief, couldn't you go to some good criminal attorney about that book, and—?"

"Why?" Mason asked.

"He could advise you not to turn the book over to the police. Then you'd be acting under legal advice and—"

The phone rang. Della Street scooped up the telephone, listened for a moment, said, "Just a moment, Gertie," then turned to Mason.

"Carver Kinsey is in the office and says he has to see you immediately on a matter of importance."

"Carver Kinsey," Mason said musingly. "To give the devil his full title Carver Moorehead Kinsey, one of the slickest criminal attorneys at the bar. Now what the devil do you suppose *he* wants?"

"I don't know," Della Street said, "but look, Chief, couldn't you at least consult with him, couldn't you ask him to advise you? If you could get some attorney to advise you that it was all right for you to keep that book, then you'd technically be acting under the advice of counsel, and—" She broke off as Mason smiled and shook his head.

"He wouldn't advise me to keep the book, Della."

"Why not?" she asked.

"Because," Mason said, "he knows he couldn't get away with it. He also knows that the bar association is watching him very, very closely. There's one lawyer who is *really* shifty."

"Crooked?" Della Street asked.

"They've never caught him at it," Mason said, "not with anything they could prove, but he's smart and clever and slick. Tell him to come in, Della."

Della went out and escorted Carver Kinsey back to the inner office.

Kinsey was a short, slender individual, who was inordinately proud of his clothes. He kept himself tailored to the minute, and had his hair trimmed every third day. His nails were glistening, his hands were as soft as his eyes were hard.

As someone had expressed it, Kinsey was always trying to improve the appearance of the package, because he knew that the goods inside were rotten.

"Good afternoon, Counselor," Kinsey said.

"How are you, Kinsey?" Mason said, shaking hands. "What brings you up here?"

"Oh, just a little visit," Kinsey said. "I was in the building, so I thought I'd drop in and say hello. After all, we don't see each other too often, but I follow your cases with the greatest interest. In fact, Mason, you might say this is the visit of a disciple to the old maestro. I thought perhaps if I spent a few minutes with you, some of your brilliance and resourcefulness might rub off on me, and I need it. Would it be all right if we dispense with the presence of Miss Street for a few minutes?"

Mason smiled and shook his head. "Miss Street is my right hand. I am too busy to explain all of the ramifications of everything to her, so I let her sit in on all of the conferences and in that way she knows as much about the business as I do. You don't need to worry about her discretion."

"I'm not worrying about her discretion, but I'm worried about that pencil she has a habit of picking up, and that shorthand notebook that gets filled with verbatim transcriptions of conversations."

"Are you going to say something you don't want to be taken down?" Mason asked.

"Yes."

"You aren't going to say anything that you would repudiate afterwards, are you?"

Kinsey met Mason's eyes. "Yes."

Mason smiled. "Well, there's nothing like frankness. Put your pencil away and come over here and sit down where Mr. Kinsey can watch you, Della."

"I'd prefer to have no witnesses," Kinsey said.

"Under those circumstances," Mason told him, "you virtually double my desire to have a witness present."

"Oh, all right," Kinsey surrendered. "I want to talk with you about that Babb case."

"What about it?" Mason asked, his face instantly becoming an expressionless granite-hard mask.

"I'm representing Norma Logan. You told her to go to an attorney. She came to me. Thanks for sending me the business."

"I didn't send her to you," Mason said. "I simply told her to see an attorney. I felt under the circumstances I shouldn't even make any recommendation."

"Well, thanks anyway, Counselor. I got the business."

"Lucrative?" Mason asked.

Kinsey met his eyes. "It's going to be."

"Go on," Mason said.

Kinsey said, "I'm not going to pull any punches with you, Mason, and I'm not going to beat around the bush. I'm an attorney. I'm representing Norma Logan. She doesn't have any money to pay me. I'm in a spot where I've got to cut a corner. I don't do that for chicken feed. I want money."

"And how do you feel you are going to get money?" Mason asked.

"*You're* going to give it to me."

"*I* am?"

"You are. Of course, you'll get it from your client, but I need money."

"How much money?"

Kinsey said, "Let's put the cards on the table, Mason. Your client is a wealthy oil man. He's fighting for his life in a murder case. At the proper time my client Norma Logan can clear him. She can show that he was waiting outside, and that some woman was the one who perpetrated the crime."

"Provided a jury believes her."

"By the time I get done coaching her, even the district attorney will believe her."

"Let's hope so," Mason observed.

"However, that isn't the main thing," Kinsey said. "There's the matter of a notebook which was delivered to Miss Street, Mason."

"Who says so?"

"My client."

"What about the notebook?"

"That notebook is a remarkable record, Mason. An attorney who had that notebook could call on some of the wealthiest families in this city. He could let them know that he had the notebook. He could let them know that they could trust his discretion. Almost overnight he'd find himself in an enviable position. He'd have clients of wealth and respectability. He could quit this rat race of criminal law and move in on oil business, big corporation work. In short, he'd have the world by the tail on a downhill pull.

"That notebook is a legal gold mine, Mason, and there's enough in it for both of us."

"I don't know what you're talking about," Mason said.

"Oh, don't play dumb," Kinsey told him, "and don't be afraid to incriminate yourself. Here, I haven't got any concealed recording devices on me. Take a look."

Kinsey opened his coat, spread his arms wide.

Mason made no move to get up from behind his desk where he was seated. "You and I look at things from a different viewpoint, Kinsey," he said.

"I know, I know," Kinsey said. "You're one of these lucky guys. You defend a client and get him off because he's innocent. I defend a client and get him off because I knock a hole in the prosecution's case somewhere, or get a hung jury. They accuse me of suborning perjury, of bribing jurors and suppressing evidence. You're lucky and smart as hell. *You* can afford to pull all this ethical stuff. *I* can't. I'm in a rat race, and it's going to catch up with me sooner or later. One of these days I'll be disbarred and because of the income tax I can't salt away enough to see me through. This situation that has developed now is the answer to everything. This is a dream come true. You know it and I know it.

"We don't have to pull any blackmail. All we have to do is to let John Doe the big banker and Richard Roe the financier know that we know their son and daughter were respectively the products of Dr. Babb's ingenious scheme for short-cutting adoption proceedings.

"We don't ask for any money. We simply tell these people that we know, that we are, however, very sympathetic and will do what we can to protect their interests.

"They don't pay us any money for blackmail. These people control corporations that are using attorneys all the time. They spend thousands of dollars for lawyers' fees.

"They begin to call on us in connection with their corporation work. We join their clubs. We get in on the ground floor of investments. We become wealthy, respected and influential. The district attorney, who now hates us with an undying hatred, will begin to fawn on us and cultivate our friendship. We'll represent political influence, campaign contributions and political advancement. The Governor will consult us when there's a vacancy on the bench. We'll move into the hallowed inner circles of influence. We'll reek with respectability. We'll get out of this slimy practice of criminal law."

Mason said, "That may be the way you look at it, Kinsey. It's not the way I look at it. The practice of criminal law isn't slimy unless you make it slimy. It isn't a rat race unless you run with the rats. The law gives every person accused of crime an opportunity to be confronted with the witnesses against him, the chance to cross-examine those witnesses, to present his case to a jury. The law clothes him with constitutional rights and safeguards against wrongful conviction, and—"

"Oh, save it!" Kinsey interrupted angrily. "Save it for a jury or a meeting of the bar association. Don't peddle that stuff to me. You've been lucky. You've been shrewd. You've been able to pick innocent clients and get them off by dramatic bits of last-minute legal melodrama.

"But don't kid yourself. Despite the fact that you've represented innocent clients, you've made powerful enemies. The district attorney is after you the same as he's after me. He'd like nothing better than to disbar you and I hold in my hand the means by which he *can* disbar you. Let's be frank, Mason. Let's face the facts."

"What do you mean?" Mason asked.

"You know what I mean. You've received stolen property. All I need to do is to put my client on the stand at the right time. All I need to do is to give a tip to the right people and I can become the fair-haired child while you're finally caught in a legal cul-de-sac."

"You intend to do that?" Mason asked.

"I intend to get money," Kinsey said. "I intend to have a fee. I'm not going to pull the legal chestnuts out of the fire for a rich oil man and have nothing in return except a few pennies from a secretary, or a mortgage on a Ford automobile which isn't paid for.

"I'm playing around with the big money in this thing, and I intend to get some."

"And then?" Mason asked.

"And then," Kinsey said, "I intend to get possession of that notebook. I intend to get the information that is going to make us both rich. I'm not going to hog it. I'm going to share it with you. There's enough there for both of us. Dr. Babb is dead. He left behind that notebook which contained secrets that are worth more than a million dollars, not in blackmail but in legal fees."

"It sounds very much like blackmail to me," Mason said.

"Don't be naïve," Kinsey told him. "There's no one who could touch us with a ten-foot pole on a situation of that sort. We'd be collecting legal fees from clients who annually pay out hundreds of thousands of dollars in legal fees."

"Specifically what do you want now?" Mason asked.

"Now," Kinsey said, "I want a retainer."

"How much of a retainer?"

"Let's not beat around the bush, Mason. I'm not in this business for my health. I want twenty-five thousand dollars *cash*."

"And what do you propose to do in return for that cash?"

"I propose to represent Norma Logan."

"In what way?"

"I propose to handle her case in such a way that she won't be involved in anything, and if your man Kirby comes through with the money like a little gentleman, I intend to handle Norma Logan's case in such a way that it won't embarrass John Kirby and it won't bring out any information about Ronson Kirby that is going to cause any heartache."

"And if you don't get the money?" Mason asked.

"Don't be silly, Mason. You act as though you were trying to get me out on a legal limb. I'm not making any threats. I'm not making any promises. I'm simply telling you that I'm representing Norma Logan, that under the circumstances of this case it will be advisable for John Kirby to give me a retainer of twenty-five thousand dollars now."

"And later?" Mason asked.

"Later," Kinsey said, "you and I will share the information in that notebook."

Mason said, "I'll pass your request on to my client."

"Oh, come off your high horse," Kinsey told him. "Don't pull that dignified stuff. Get on the telephone. Ring up—"

"My client is in custody," Mason said.

"Of course he's in custody. I'm telling you to ring up his wife. She can make out a check for twenty-five thousand dollars without even knowing the money's gone."

"What makes you think so?" Mason asked. "What's your source of information?"

"Kirby himself told my client that he and his wife had a joint checking account of over a hundred thousand dollars, that whenever the balance got below that point his cashier simply diverted enough from the incoming oil royalties to keep the amount at a hundred thousand dollars."

"I'd have to talk with my client," Mason said.

"Well," Kinsey said angrily, "how long is it going to take you to talk with your client?"

"I can't tell."

"All right, what about that notebook?"

"On the notebook," Mason said, "I can give you a definite answer now."

"What is it?"

"If," Mason said, "there exists any such notebook as you have mentioned, and if circumstances developed which placed that notebook in the possession of my secretary or myself, I would exercise every precaution, every bit of ingenuity I could summon to see that neither *you* nor anyone else ever got possession of that notebook or any of the information it contained."

Kinsey jumped to his feet, his face flushed. He hammered the corner of Mason's desk. "Don't think you can adopt that holier-than-thou attitude! Don't think you're so utterly irreproachable! You're in a situation right now where you're violating the ethics of the profession and the law of this state. I can lower the boom on you any time I want to and if you don't snap out of it I'm going to do that very thing."

"You don't need to pound the desk," Mason said. "You don't need to raise your voice and you don't need to waste any more of your valuable time. You've told me your story and there's the door."

"What are you going to do about letting your client pay me a fee?" Kinsey asked.

"I'm going to give *that* matter careful consideration. I'm going to try to do what is for the best interests of my client. Right at the moment, I'm inclined to think that it would be both unwise and unethical for him to contribute a dime to Norma Logan's lawyer. If that should ever come out, it would be a fact which the district attorney could use in attempting to show a conspiracy, a joint purpose in their negotiations with Dr. Babb, whatever those negotiations were. That might tend to crucify my client."

"You damn fool!" Kinsey said. "No one is going to know about it. I told you I wanted the twenty-five thousand dollars in *cash*. I assumed that you were smart enough so you'd see that the payment couldn't ever be traced."

"And once my client did that," Mason said, "you would have a strangle hold over him that—"

"What's the difference?" Kinsey interrupted. "I've got one anyway. I know all about his son."

"You may know," Mason said, "but you've no proof. As far as the records are concerned, Ronson Kirby was born in legal wedlock to John Kirby and his wife Joan Kirby."

"You try to adopt that attitude," Kinsey threatened, "and I'll jerk the rug out from under you. I'll handle this thing in such a way that you'll be the sorriest individual who ever stepped into a courtroom. I'll feather my nest one way or another in this thing, and don't think I won't do it legally.

"I'm charged with protecting the best interests of my client, Norma Logan. If I can protect them through you and through Kirby, I'd say that that was the way to give her the protection she needs. If I can't get you to listen to me, I can damn well get immunity for Norma Logan by having her tell her full story to the district attorney. Her *full* story, mind you, Mason!"

"I heard you the first time," Mason said.

"And your answer?"

"I gave it to you some time ago."

"You have to put my proposition up to Kirby. *You* can't take the responsibility of turning it down," Kinsey said.

"I'll think it over," Mason told him, "and I'm going to put it up to Kirby. Then I'm going to *advise* him that, if he falls for any such scheme as that, he'll have cause to regret it as long as he lives."

Kinsey turned without a word, jerked open the door, and went out.

Della Street looked at Mason's granite-hard features. "Oh, Chief!" she said. "*Why* did this have to happen? I...I could cry!"

"Crying won't help," Mason said, pushing back his chair and starting to pace the office floor. "Crying won't do a damn bit of good."

"What will do good?" Della Street asked.

"I'm damned if I know," Mason said. "Not at this stage of the game anyway."

"But *what* are you going to do?"

"I'm going right ahead. I'm going to insist that the prosecution go ahead with the preliminary hearing in the case of the People versus Kirby. I'm going to cross-examine witnesses to the best of my ability, and if Carver Kinsey wants to go to the district attorney and purchase immunity for Norma Logan, I'm going to...I'm going to—" A grim smile crossed Mason's face. "Frankly, Della, I don't know what I *am* going to do."

CHAPTER ELEVEN

Even a few hours of incarceration had served to melt the aura of self-assurance which had surrounded John Kirby.

The man who sat on the other side of the glass partition and conferred with Mason through a built-in microphone in the heavy plate glass was an entirely different individual from the John Kirby who had breezed into Mason's office to tell him the story of the young woman with the gasoline can whom he had encountered on the road late Monday night.

Mason finished his recital of Carver Kinsey's offer, saying, however, nothing about the notebook.

"He wants twenty-five thousand dollars cash?" Kirby asked.

"That's right."

"And if he gets that he'll see that this Logan girl is a friendly witness?"

"He didn't say that. He gave me to understand such would be the case."

"And if he doesn't get it, she'll go to the district attorney?"

Mason nodded.

"I think we'd better give it to him," Kirby said. "I hate to do it, but...I'm fairly well heeled, Mason. I can afford it, and I *can't* afford to take chances."

Mason told him, "I don't think you can afford to do it."

"Why not?"

"I don't think you can afford to get mixed up with that crowd or follow that line of ethics."

"We're not playing with ethics now, Mason. We're facing grim reality. We're facing murder charges. We're facing absolute disaster. We're facing the almost-inevitable certainty that our relations with Dr. Babb are going to be publicized."

Mason nodded, said, "This isn't blackmail. It's legal, but it comes pretty close to blackmail. The more I think of it, the more I'm against it. I advise you not to do it."

"I think we should."

"Then get another lawyer," Mason told him.

Kirby flushed. "Damn you, Mason! You don't leave a man much choice in the matter."

"You have your choice," Mason told him. "Either let me handle the case my way or get some other lawyer."

"Do you always play a no-limit game?" Kirby asked irritably.

"The games I sit in are always no-limit games," Mason told him.

"Well, just what *do* you intend to do?"

"I intend to move for an immediate preliminary hearing. I think we can get it."

"Don't they usually try for delay in cases of this sort?"

"I suppose so," Mason said, "but I think the thing to do is to hit this thing while it's hot. If we have any chance, I want to take that chance before all of this information about Dr. Babb and your son is publicized. If we can't win, let's find out how bad the situation is."

"Suppose it's one where we don't stand *any* chance?"

"You always stand a chance," Mason told him, "provided you're telling me the truth. You never went inside of that house?"

"Absolutely not. What's more they can't prove that I did. All they can prove is that I was connected in some way with a young woman who did go in that house. And I don't think they can actually *prove* that she committed the murder."

Mason said, "They don't as yet have the case they want. They have a series of suspicious circumstances and they may be able to marshal enough evidence to get a judge to bind you over for trial. But they don't have the evidence they need to convict you in front of a jury."

"Isn't that all the more reason why we should try to do business with Carver Kinsey?"

"That," Mason said, "is all the more reason why we should *not* do business with Carver Kinsey."

"I've got a lot at stake," Kirby reminded him.

Mason's smile was enigmatical. "*You've* got a lot at stake! You should be in *my* shoes for a while."

"Well," Kirby said resignedly, "I'm not in your shoes, but I am in your hands, Mason. Do what you think best."

"You want me to continue to represent you?"

"Very definitely."

"All right," Mason told him, catching the eye of the guard and signifying that the interview was over, "I'm going to push for an immediate preliminary hearing."

CHAPTER TWELVE

Sims Ballantine, the trial deputy, who had recently been handling many of the more important preliminary hearings, got to his feet when Judge Conway Cameron called the case of the People versus John Northrup Kirby.

"May the Court please," Ballantine said, "we are ready to proceed with the hearing. I will state very frankly to the Court that I don't know what the evidence in this case will show."

"You mean you haven't discussed the case with the police or the witnesses?" Judge Cameron asked.

"Yes, Your Honor, with *some* of the witnesses."

"Not with others?" Judge Cameron asked.

"We don't as yet know who some of the others are, Your Honor. I'll state very frankly that I would much prefer to have a continuance in this case. If we can have such a continuance it is possible that some matters which are in doubt at the present moment can be clarified. I feel that it may well be advantageous to the defendant to have a continuance."

"And the defense?" Judge Cameron asked, looking at Perry Mason.

"The defendant wishes the prosecution either to proceed with the preliminary hearing or dismiss the case," Mason said.

"Very well," Judge Cameron ruled, "we'll proceed with the preliminary."

He turned to Ballantine. "Do I understand it to be the position of the district attorney's office that it may not have sufficient evidence in its possession at this time to ask for an order binding the defendant over?"

"No, Your Honor, that is not our position," Ballantine said. "We *do* have sufficient evidence on which to ask the Court to bind the defendant over. Whether we have enough evidence at the present time to get a conviction in front of a jury in the superior court is another question. I am stating my position frankly to the Court."

"The Court appreciates frankness," Judge Cameron said. "The Court also would call to the attention of counsel that while there is a rigid rule as to the defendant's rights when a postponement is asked, it is always possible for the district attorney to dismiss the complaint without prejudice and transfer the entire matter to the grand jury where all of the witnesses can be heard before any action is taken."

"I understand, Your Honor, but action has already been taken in this case. A complaint has been filed, and the prosecution feels that to dismiss the complaint at this time might have an adverse effect."

"Very well," Judge Cameron ruled, "but don't think you're going to take this Court on any fishing expedition. If you're not certain of your case, dismiss it, back up and go before the grand jury. That's my suggestion."

"We're certain we can present a strong enough case to bind the defendant over," Ballantine said.

"Then go ahead and put it on," Judge Cameron said sharply. "You understand the rule of law and the Court understands it."

"Joseph Hesper," Ballantine said.

Hesper came forward, took the oath, testified that he was a police officer, that he had been on duty in Radio Car Number 157 on the 5th of the month, that at 11:34 a call had been received stating that there apparently was a disturbance at 19647 Sunland Drive, that he and his partner, George Franklin, had hurried to the house, that they were within a few blocks of the place at the time the call was received, that they followed the best police procedure in dealing with calls of that nature. They took care not to alarm the suspect, they shut off the car motor, as well as shutting off the car headlights when they were a block away. They coasted up to the house, using the hand brake so that they would not give a telltale flash with the red warning brake. As the car was braked to a stop with the hand brake, the witness Hesper had said, "I'll take the front, George, you take the back."

Whereupon in accordance with a routine worked out in such cases, Franklin had dashed around to the back door while the witness had gone to the front door, had started to ring the bell button, then had noticed that the front door was slightly ajar. He had pushed it open, called out that he was a police officer, had received no answer and had entered the house; then as he moved through the rooms and entered the inner office he had found broken glass from a heavy beaker on the floor and a man lying partially on his right side with his right arm outstretched, his left arm doubled, the left hand underneath his breast. There were fragments of broken glass lying about, and the witness had bent over and felt for a pulse. He found that there was a faint, thready pulse, and at that moment he heard his partner, George Franklin, calling out that he had found a man tapping on a window at the back of the house. The witness had thereupon gone to the back door, opened the door, and let in his partner, who was at that time accompanied by one Donald Derby, who, it turned out, was Dr. Babb's handy man. Hesper testified that Derby had a soggy bath towel wrapped around his middle and was shivering as he had just emerged from a shower. The witness had questioned Derby briefly, ordered him to return to his rooms and then had notified headquarters asking for an ambulance and a fingerprint man.

The witness went on to state that a neighbor, a Mrs. Dunkirk who lived next door, had pounded on the front door, seeking admission; that he had gone to the door and had talked with this witness, then had again telephoned headquarters asking for assistance from any radio cars which might be available in nearby territory.

"Cross-examine," Ballantine said.

"You followed your usual routine of police procedure?" Mason asked.

"Yes, sir."

"You checked both the front and the back of the house?"

"Yes, sir."

"Then, after calling for the ambulance and asking for a fingerprint man to be sent out, you called again asking for more cars?"

"Yes."

"Why?"

"Because I wanted to pick up a young woman who had been seen running from the house."

"Who saw her?"

"Mrs. Dunkirk."

"Did she describe this young woman?"

"Yes."

"What did she say?"

"Now just a minute," Ballantine interrupted. "We don't want hearsay testimony here. Never mind what she told you."

"I have no objection," Mason said.

"I do," Ballantine said. "Let's not get this record cluttered up with a lot of hearsay. Then pretty quick defense counsel will be wanting to impeach the witness on a lot of immaterial evidence."

"Then you can make an objection," Mason said, "and it will be well taken."

"I'm making it now," Ballantine said.

Judge Cameron smiled. "It's well taken," he said.

"You did, however, talk with this neighbor and from something that you learned from her you did take some action?"

"Yes, sir."

"What?"

"I left my partner George Franklin in charge of the place while I started cruising around the vicinity looking for this young woman."

"Did you talk with neighbors on both the east and west?"

"I talked with the neighbor on the east first, that is she came over to talk with me, and immediately after that took off looking for this young woman. I didn't talk with the neighbor on the west until sometime later, after I'd given up the search as fruitless. Those people weren't home at the time the assault took place."

"Can you tell us exactly what you did to see that the evidence in the house wasn't contaminated?"

"Certainly. We closed up the house absolutely and we were very careful to touch nothing, to see that no slightest bit of evidence was disturbed. The house is still sealed."

"Was the handy man in the house with you where he could touch things?" Mason asked.

Hesper seemed rather scornful. "The handy man was never permitted in the house. I interrogated him through the back door; then I sent him back to get his clothes on and ordered him to remain in his quarters. It would have been contrary to proper procedure to have permitted *any* person to enter the house before the fingerprint men had tried to find what they could. My partner did the best he could until reinforcements arrived."

"When was that?"

"The ambulance arrived within about fifteen minutes. However, other police cars closed in on the district and joined in the search for the young woman who we felt might still be in the neighborhood."

"How long did that search continue?"

"I would say about ten minutes. By that time we had become satisfied she had eluded us and the other cars went back to their beats. My partner and I turned the Babb case over to the fingerprint men and technicians."

"Then what?"

"Then we started checking the time element. The handy man felt positive Dr. Babb had gone to the back door to call him, had opened the back door, and had then been jerked back by his assailant."

"Now just a minute," Judge Cameron interrupted. "We're getting into a lot of hearsay evidence here. Probably some of it is pertinent, because the question was a very broad general question which called for a statement as to how the witness had gone about checking the time element. Nevertheless this is plainly hearsay."

"But Your Honor," Ballantine protested, "the cross-examiner himself has called for this hearsay evidence. The question very definitely opens the door."

"We're not objecting, Your Honor," Mason said. "We want to know exactly what was done. After all, this is merely a preliminary examination and we feel that Your Honor can disregard evidence which is improper."

"Well, it's a whole lot better not to introduce it in the first place," Judge Cameron said. "However, in the interests of expediting matters, I'll let the witness proceed. Go ahead with the testimony."

"Well," Hesper said, "I'll put it this way. Assuming that last scream heard by Mrs. Dunkirk took place just before the police were notified, and assuming this handy man stood at the window for four seconds—and we were able to estimate that time both by having him re-enact what he had done and by checking the size of the little pool of water which had dripped from him while he was standing in front of the window—we estimated the time interval which had elapsed between screams and the time Derby saw the back door close, as well as the time which elapsed from the closing of the back door until we arrived at the house.

"We followed the wet footprints on the linoleum in Derby's house from the shower to the front window, from the window to where he had gone to grab the towel, and down the stairs. We could, in other words, follow the handy man's route, step for step.

"By making a comparative test with our shoes on, we found that the elapsed time would be between ten and twelve seconds from the time Derby left the bath until he arrived at the back door of the house. However, he was barefoot and when we took our shoes and socks off and made another test we found that we were slowed down materially. This was particularly true at the place where we started down the outside steps from the garage. We were also slowed down materially in crossing the yard. We estimated the barefoot time, if I may so describe it, as being between fifteen and eighteen seconds, and he probably was in the yard about fifteen seconds before we arrived."

"You considered that time element important?" Mason asked.

"Everything is important in connection with good investigative work," the witness said.

"Did you consider the possibility that there might have been some other person in the house who went *out* the back door?" Mason asked.

"We tried to consider *every* possibility."

"Was there something that led you to believe someone other than this young woman you have described had been in the house?"

The witness, suddenly cautious, said, "Well, I'll put it this way. There could have been."

"Could have been what?"

"There could have been some other person in the house."

"Were there any *facts* which indicated some other person had been in the house?"

The witness glanced at the deputy district attorney, shifted his position in the witness chair and said, "No, I won't say there were any *facts*."

"Were any fingerprints found on the back doorknob on the inside of the door, indicating some person had made a hurried exit?" Mason asked.

"If he knows," Ballantine said.

"Yes," Judge Cameron said, "if you know."

"I don't know. I wasn't present when the knob was tested for prints," the witness said, obviously relieved.

Mason studied the witness for a few seconds, said, "Now I believe you testified that your partner was out at the back, calling for you to open up?"

"Yes."

"And did you open up the back door?"

Again the witness shifted his position.

"Yes, sir."

"And in so doing, superimposed your own fingerprints upon any other which might have been on the doorknob?"

"That calls for a conclusion of the witness, Your Honor," Ballantine objected. "The question is argumentative, it calls for a conclusion of the witness."

Mason said, "This witness has been testifying, Your Honor, as to the best police procedure. He's obviously an expert in that field. I think it's proper cross-examination."

"I'll permit him to answer this question," Judge Cameron said. "It probably calls for a conclusion, but—well, after all, the situation is obvious."

The embarrassment of the witness became apparent. "Well, yes," he admitted. "I probably *should* have told George Franklin to bring his man around to the front door. However, there was a certain element of urgency in his request that I open the back door, and I did it without thinking."

"And thereby left *your* fingerprints on that knob when you did it?"

"Naturally."

"And thereby obliterated the prints of any other person who might have emerged from that door previously?"

"Objected to as argumentative," Ballantine said.

"The objection is sustained," Judge Cameron ruled. "I think we have explored the possibilities of the situation so that it is quite apparent what happened."

"That's all," Mason said.

Ballantine's next witness was Harvey Nelson, who qualified as a fingerprint expert and testified that he had processed Dr. Babb's house for fingerprints, that he had uncovered several latents of a type which he described as promising, that some of those fingerprints—many of them, in fact—were the prints of Dr. Babb, that some of them were the prints of the handy man. But there were, in addition to those, several latent prints which had been developed sufficiently to be identifiable, but as yet they had not been traced to the fingers which had made them.

Ballantine introduced certain particular fingerprints in evidence, and then asked the witness if he had found any other place where those same fingerprints had been made.

Nelson stated that he had found two separate localities where the prints had been made.

"Where?" Ballantine asked.

"One in the automobile belonging to the defendant, the other in Unit 5 of the Beauty Rest Motel."

Ballantine unrolled a map. "I have here a map diagram of the premises. We can have it properly identified, or if counsel wishes, it can be stipulated into evidence."

"I'll stipulate it may go in subject to the right to challenge it if it should subsequently turn out to be incorrect in any detail," Mason said.

"Very well," Ballantine said. "Now will you show the location of Dr. Babb's house and the location of the Beauty Rest Motel on this map?"

The witness did so.

"Assuming that the map is drawn to accurate scale," Ballantine said, "what is the approximate distance in an air line between the two?"

"About seven hundred feet in an air line. Of course, in going by road it is necessary to make some right angle turns, and the distance is somewhat greater."

"How far by road?"

"About twelve hundred feet."

"While you were in Dr. Babb's house developing latent fingerprints, did you observe any particular objects there?"

"Several."

"Did you observe an appointment book?"

"I did."

"Where was that appointment book?"

"On a desk in the corner of the office which I have referred to in my notes as a consultation office. It is not the little room where Dr. Babb was found, but it is a room where there is a desk, some chairs and several bookcases filled with medical books. Therefore, in my notes I referred to it as the consultation office."

"Did you mark this book in some way so that you could identify it?"

"I did."

"I show you a book and ask you if that book contains a mark of identification made by you?"

"It does."

"Will you tell the Court what that book is?"

"That book is the so-called appointment book which I found in the room I have referred to as the consultation office."

"I ask that the book be received in evidence," Ballantine said, "and we'll call the Court's attention to the appointments for the fifth day of this month."

"No objection," Mason said. "I suggest that the appointments be read into evidence."

"Very well."

"There are several appointments during the day," Ballantine said, "but in the evening there are two appointments listed: Logan and Kirby."

"Only those two?" Judge Cameron asked.

"Yes, Your Honor."

"Are there initials or addresses or any other means of identification than the name itself?"

"No, Your Honor, simply the names. If the Court will notice the appointment book, the Court will see that all of the appointments are made in that way. Simply the last name. No initials, no address."

"Very well," Judge Cameron said. "It may be received in evidence."

"Now then, Mr. Nelson, did you subsequently call on Dr. Babb at the hospital prior to his death?"

"I did. Yes, sir."

"On how many occasions?"

"Three occasions."

"What did you do on the first occasion?"

"I took his fingerprints so that I could have some means of comparing the latent fingerprints by eliminating those that had been made by Dr. Babb."

"And on the second occasion?"

"I heard that Dr. Babb was regaining consciousness. I tried to ask him some questions."

"Did he answer?"

"He did not."

"The third occasion?"

"The third occasion was shortly prior to his death."

"What was his condition at that time?"

"Objected to," Mason said, "on the ground that no proper foundation has been laid. This witness is an expert on fingerprnts but not on medicine."

"Well, I will ask you this question," Ballantine said. "What was his apparent condition with reference to being conscious?"

"He was conscious, he could answer questions, but for some reason it was impossible for him to carry on a conversation. He could answer questions yes and no, and he gave us one name."

"What name was that?"

"The name of John Kirby."

"And how did he happen to give you that name?"

"I asked him if he knew who had struck him, and he said, 'Yes.' I asked him to give me the name and he finally gave me the name of 'John Kirby.'"

"You may inquire," Ballantine said to Perry Mason.

Mason said to the witness, "You stated that he finally gave you the name."

"Yes, sir."

"What names did he give you prior to that time?"

"He didn't give any."

"What happened?"

"We seemed to have some difficulty getting through to him. I would ask him a question several times, and he'd lie there looking blank; then finally the question would reach him and he'd answer yes or no."

"You couldn't tell whether he understood the question?"

"Only by his answers."

"And his answers being only yes or no," Mason said, "there was, I take it, the chance that he only knew you were asking him questions and in trying to answer he used the only two words he was able to use, so there was perhaps a fifty-fifty chance he may have used them incorrectly."

"I don't think so," the witness said.

"I'm asking you about the facts," Mason said.

"Oh, if the Court please," Ballantine said, "this whole examination is argumentative. The question is argumentative. He hasn't qualified this man as a medical expert, nor has he permitted him to qualify himself so that questions of this sort could be answered."

"Nevertheless," Judge Cameron said, "the witness was permitted to testify as to the man's general condition as it was apparent to a layman. I think the question is in order.

"The witness may answer giving his opinion not as an expert but as a layman."

"I think that when he answered the question he was giving the information called for in the question," the witness said. "I reached that conclusion from the nature of his answers. I think we had some trouble reaching him with the questions, but when we did, I think he could answer them and I think he did answer them."

"Now you say that he *finally* gave you the name of John Kirby?" Mason said.

"Yes, sir."

"And that prior to that time he had not given you any name?"

"Yes, sir, that is correct."

"In other words, you asked him several times who did it?"

"We asked him several times if he knew who did it."

"And what happened then?"

"Several times the question went unanswered. Finally in response to the question after it had been repeated some seven or eight times he said, 'Yes.'"

"And then you asked him who did it?"

"Yes."

"And he answered?"

"Yes."

"That question?"

"Yes."

"The first question?"

"No, it wasn't the first question. It was a repetition of the first question."

"How many times was it repeated?"

"Oh, perhaps seven or eight."

"It may have been more than eight?"

"It could have been."

"It might have been as many as twelve?"

"I didn't count the number of times we repeated the question. I was trying to get through to him."

"You asked him over and over who did it?"

"Yes."

"And then waited after each question for an answer?"

"Yes."

"And there was silence?"

"That's right."

"And then finally about the tenth time, or perhaps the thirteenth or fourteenth time, when you asked the question, you got an answer?"

"I don't think it could have been the fourteenth time. I don't think we repeated the question fourteen times. My best recollection is that we might have repeated it about seven or eight times."

"And he finally made a statement which you thought was an answer?"

"He stated the name John Kirby very plainly, very distinctly."

"Wasn't there a certain slurring of speech?"

"Well...not to the extent that it wasn't possible to recognize the name. I will say that when his answers were given, they were clear. There was a certain amount of slurring but not any real mumbling."

"Did you at that time know the defendant in the case?"

"No, sir. We didn't get on his trail until after we had made an exhaustive check of car registrations getting the various combinations of letters and figures. We had several cars to check, but as soon as we had this name we found a car that fit the description registered in the name of Kirby, so we got busy almost immediately checking the defendant."

"And then you processed his car for fingerprints?"

"Right."

"And found latent fingerprints of this same person who had been in the unit of the motel and in the house of Dr. Babb?"

"Yes, sir."

"That's all," Mason announced.

"I will call Milton Rexford as my next witness," Ballantine said.

Rexford, a tall, somewhat stooped individual in his early forties, slouched his way to the witness stand, held up his right hand, took the oath, and stood for a moment looking around the courtroom through pale gray eyes. Then he settled himself in the witness chair, gave his full name as Milton Hazen Rexford, and stated that his residence was on Malacca Avenue.

Ballantine introduced a map showing the territory in question and the witness marked a cross on the map to show the place where he lived.

Malacca Avenue was depicted on the map as the street turning off from Sunland on the opposite side from Rubart Terrace, and a half block down the street.

"I wish to direct your attention to the evening of the fifth of this month," Ballantine said to the witness. "That would be Monday evening. Do you remember that evening?"

"Yes."

"Directing your attention to a time shortly before eleven-thirty, what were you doing?"

"I was getting ready for bed."

"You were in the bedroom of your house?"

"Yes."

"Does that bedroom front on Malacca Avenue?"

"Yes."

"Were the lights on in your bedroom?"

"No, sir."

"Why not?"

"Because my wife was already in bed. She'd pulled back the drapes and opened the window so she'd get fresh air. I didn't want to turn on the room lights and shine 'em in her eyes, so I was undressing there by the open window with the lights out."

"Did you see an automobile at that time?"

"I did."

"Where?"

"Well, a good-looking automobile came to a stop right in front of my house. I couldn't figure who was coming to see me at that hour of the night, and—"

"Never mind your mental reactions or your conclusions. Just tell us what you saw," Ballantine said.

"Well, I took a good look at the license number before the man turned the lights off."

"Did you see the license number?"

"Yes."

"Do you remember it?"

"I certainly do."

"What was it?"

"JYJ 112."

"Did you see the man who was driving the car?"

"That's right."

"Who was that man?"

"There he sits!" the witness said, raising a long thin arm and pointing with a bony forefinger directly at John Kirby.

"You are now indicating John Northrup Kirby, the defendant in this action?"

"That's right!"

"What did he do after he parked the car?"

"He switched off the lights, and then he just sat there for a second or two, and then some young woman opened the car door and got out."

"Can you describe this woman?"

"I didn't see her so plain. I didn't see her face. She was a woman, that's all I know."

"Can you tell how she was dressed?"

"Sort of light clothes. I mean kind of light-colored, sort of tannish maybe."

"What did she do?"

"She walked up the street toward Dr. Babb's place."

"Then what did you see?"

"Well, I guess it was about maybe, oh . . . six, seven or eight minutes, and all of a sudden here this young woman came down the hill, lickety-split. She jumped in the car and said something to the man, and the lights on the car came on, and believe me, that car went away from there fast!"

"How did it go?"

"Made a U-turn, right slap-bang around, and went off down Malacca Avenue."

"You are certain of your identification that it was the defendant who was driving the car?"

"Absolutely certain."

"When did you next see the defendant?"

"Wednesday."

"Where?"

"At the jail."

"Did you see him by himself, or were other persons present?"

"There was what you call a line-up," Rexford said. "A bunch of people, maybe five or six, all standing up."

"And you identified the defendant at that time?"

"That's right."

"Picked him out of the line?"

"Uh-huh."

"Cross-examine!" Ballantine snapped at Perry Mason.

"You sat there by the bedroom window looking out at the car?" Mason asked.

"That's right."

"And you saw a woman run back to the car?"

"That's right."

"You said she was running fast?"

"That's right."

"I believe you said, 'lickety-split'?"

"Uh-huh."

"That means fast, does it?"

"I always figured it did."

"And what did she do?"

"She whipped the door open, jumped in the car, said something to the man, and away they went!"

"The bedroom window was open?"

"That's right."

"Could you hear what she said to the man?"

"Not at that distance."

"Was the car door open or closed when she said something to him?"

"It was closed."

"You couldn't hear the words?"

"No."

"Could you hear voices through the closed car door?"

"No."

"Then how did you know she said something to him?"

"Well, what made him go chasing away like that if she didn't say something to him?"

"Did you see her turn her head toward the man and speak to him?"

"No, the car was dark. But a moment later, the lights on the car came on and I could see the two of them in there when the car went around in a U-turn. Believe me, he sure whipped that car around!"

"The only time you saw the man in front of your house he was seated behind the steering wheel of an automobile, wasn't he?"

"That's right."

"When you identified him in the line-up, you didn't identify him sitting down. You identified him standing up."

"Uh-huh."

"You could see the rear license number when the car came to a stop?"

"Yes, sir."

"Then the car wasn't directly in front of your bedroom window when it came to a stop, but must have been some distance up the street. Otherwise you wouldn't have been able to have seen the rear license plate?"

"That's right."

"So the person who was in the driver's seat wasn't where you could see his profile. You were looking at the back of his head, weren't you?"

"Well, kind of quartering, I guess."

"The man who was behind the steering wheel was on the side away from the curb?"

"Right."

"The right side of the car was the side nearest your house. The left side was the side toward the street?"

"Uh-huh."

"Was the man wearing a hat?"

"I believe he was."

"Aren't you certain?"

"Well, it's kind of hard to tell. It wasn't easy to see."

"When the lights were turned off in that car, it was rather dark in the interior of the automobile?"

"Right."

"There's a street light up on Sunland Drive?"

"There's a street light, but it didn't shine inside the car so much. It was hard to tell whether the driver had a hat on or not."

"Couldn't you tell when the lights of the car were on?"

"I suppose I could. I just can't remember whether he had a hat on or whether he didn't."

"You did look at the license plate on the automobile?"

"Absolutely."

"And you're sure of the license number?"

"Positive."

"How long was it after the car came to a stop before the lights were turned off?"

"Oh, no time at all. Just maybe a second or so."

"And during that time you were wondering who was stopping in front of your place?"

"That's right."

"You thought perhaps it was someone who might be coming to see you?"

"Right."

"So you paid particular attention to the license number?"

"I already said I did."

"You were looking at that while the lights were on?"

"Yes."

"Do you want us to understand that you were looking at the license plate all the time the lights were on?"

"Right."

"So you weren't looking at the man who was driving the car?"

"Well, I looked at him afterwards."

"That was *after* the car lights had been turned off?"

"Right."

"So you later identified the defendant while he was standing up in a line-up, yet the only time you had previously seen him he had been seated in an automobile where you only had a quartering view of his head under such lighting conditions that you couldn't tell whether he had a hat on. Is that right?"

"Objection, argumentative," Ballantine said.

"Overruled!"

The witness fidgeted in the chair.

"Is that right?" Mason asked.

"I guess so."

"No further questions," Mason said.

"That's all," Ballantine said. "No further questions."

"Donald Rufus Derby," Ballantine said.

The handy man came forward and was sworn. He testified that he had been taking a shower, that he had heard a woman scream, that he had shut off the water in the shower bath, dashed to the window overlooking Dr. Babb's house, had seen the back door closing, had hurried to the towel rack, thrown a towel around his middle, and dashed down the stairs.

By the time he had crossed the cement apron in front of the garage and reached the back door of the house, the door was closed and the spring lock in place. He had pounded on the door with his knuckles, and had received no answer and had heard no sound from the inside of the house. He had then gone around to the side window and was tapping on that side window when an officer had grabbed him from behind.

He had thereupon explained the situation to the officer who had held him for a few moments while the other officer opened the back door. The witness had then been sent back to his apartment to get some clothes on and wait until the officers had finished with their inspection of the premises. They had then examined him in some detail, and had conducted tests to determine the time element.

"Cross-examine," Ballantine said to Perry Mason.

"You reached the window just in time to see the back door of Dr. Babb's house closing?" Mason asked.

"Yes, sir."

"Did you see anyone running out of the back door?"

"No, sir."

"Did you see anyone at all down there in the yard?"

"No, sir."

"If someone had run out of the back door just before you got to the window, could you have seen that person?"

"I've been thinking it over," the witness said. "I don't think anybody could have got out that door and got around the house and out of my sight before the door closed. My own idea is that Doc Babb was trying to call me and—"

"Never mind your ideas," Ballantine interrupted sharply. "Simply listen to the questions and answer them."

"No further questions," Mason said.

Judge Cameron said, "Just a moment, gentlemen. I'm sorry that we were late in starting this hearing. However, there was another matter on the calendar which had to be disposed of. I notice that it is now the hour for the afternoon adjournment. Court will take a recess until tomorrow morning at ten o'clock. The defendant is remanded to custody."

CHAPTER THIRTEEN

Della Street was waiting for Perry Mason in the office.

"How did the case go?" she asked anxiously.

"So-so," Mason said. "They have a witness who saw Kirby drive up, park his car, and let Norma Logan out. He saw Norma Logan take off in the direction of Dr. Babb's house, and then after a few minutes come running back lickety-split, jump in the car, say something to Kirby and Kirby took off in a hurry."

"Oh-oh," Della said in dismay.

"That means," Mason explained, "that they have a pretty good prima-facie case *provided* they can show that Norma Logan hit Dr. Babb on the head. And that they *can't* show.

"The handy man *thinks* Dr. Babb got as far as the back door and opened it to call to him, but we know that Derby saw the back door closing just after some unidentified man, closely followed by Joan Kirby, had dashed out.

"Now then, under those circumstances, I can call Motley Dunkirk to the witness stand, prove that he saw some woman running out of that back door, and knock their case against Norma Logan into a cocked hat.

"That starts the police on a brand new investigative tangent, but gets Joan Kirby involved in the killing."

"Do you think they can find out this woman was Joan Kirby?" Della Street asked.

"I'm wondering if I dare take a gamble on that. However, I think they'll find out all right. Did we hear anything from Carver Kinsey, Della?"

"Not a peep."

"Well," Mason said, "He's sitting tight. he hasn't gone to the district attorney as yet."

"How do you know?"

"How do I know?" Mason asked grinning. "I know because Sims Ballantine, the trial deputy, was conducting the hearing. The minute Carver Kinsey breathes a word to the police or the district attorney you'll see Hamilton Burger come striding into the courtroom, and when he does that will mean the fat is in the fire."

"But Norma Logan doesn't know that it was Mrs. Kirby who was in the house," Della Street said.

"Not by name," Mason said. "But she can give a pretty good description.

"So far the case hasn't attracted too much newspaper attention. A prominent businessman is accused of murder, but the developments have been taking place with such rapidity that the public hasn't had its interest whipped up to a point where sob sisters will start interviewing the wife, where newspaper artists will start making sketches, and all of that.

"When that happens Norma Logan is going to see photographs of the wife, she'll see artists' sketches, and above all she'll talk to Carver Kinsey. Kinsey will note the name 'Kirby' in the appointment book, will suddenly put two and two together, and then he'll *really* be in a position to make demands."

"Then what will happen?"

"I'm darned if I know," Mason admitted. "What about Paul Drake? Did he get anything on the Logan family?"

"He sure did. I have it all right here. He looked up Norma Logan's birth certificate, found out the name of her father, and has had men working getting all the information he could.

"There's no question about the father having gone up into the upper Amazon, and he was never heard of after that.

"But here's something, Chief, that's significant: the uncle, that is, the father's brother, is Steve Logan."

"Who's Steve Logan?" Mason asked.

"The big used-car dealer," she said. "Remember all the television advertisements with the slogan, 'Stick by Steve,' 'Buy a used car from Steve Logan, run it for a year, trade it in on another used car, and have the cheapest mileage transportation in the country.'"

"Oh yes, I place him now," Mason said. "Steve Logan, the one who sticks by his customers; you stick by Steve and Steve sticks by you. So he's Norma Logan's uncle?"

"That's right, and Dr. Babb was one of Steve's customers. Dr. Babb had gone into semiretirement. He was trying to keep costs down wherever he could, and he had been buying cars from Steve Logan for three years. He'd pick up a pretty good used car, drive it for a year, go back to Steve and turn it in. I guess there's something to that slogan all right, because apparently Steve made him pretty good deals."

"How did Paul find out all this?" Mason asked.

"I don't know. He had a lot of men out, but I know he traced the registration on Dr. Babb's automobile to find out about Dr. Babb and knew he purchased it through Steve Logan."

"I see," Mason said frowning. "That may complicate the situation, Della. There's a good chance that the Logan appointment on Dr. Babb's books for Monday night was an appointment with Steve Logan. How does Norma get along with her uncle? Does anybody know?"

"That nice shiny car she had was purchased through him," Della Street said.

Mason said, "I think we want to talk with Paul. I—"

He broke off as Paul Drake's code knock sounded on the door.

Mason opened the door and Drake came in.

"Hi, Perry, how's the case going?"

"Sixes and sevens," Mason said. "Della was telling me about your report on Steve Logan, Paul."

"Well, I've got something else," Drake said, "and this may help you."

"What?"

"Logan was out at Dr. Babb's place Monday afternoon."

"Steve Logan?" Mason asked sharply.

"That's right."

"Doing what? Do you know?"

"Sure I know," Drake said, "there's no great secret about it. He was getting specifications on the little garden out there in back, particularly on the goldfish pool."

"Why?"

"Because he likes it. He wants to put in something similar in his show windows. It's his idea that people will walk right by an inanimate display but will always stop to look at something that's moving. He feels that a goldfish display will attract people if the display is made sufficiently attractive."

"How did you find all this out?" Mason asked.

"Just fooling around and asking questions in the neighborhood. The neighbors on the west told me about this one. No one's bothered to talk with them very much because they were out at the time the assault took place. They came back from a movie and arrived just about the time the ambulance did. The name is Olney. Mr. and Mrs. Grover Olney.

"However, these people are acquainted with Steve Logan by sight, and they saw him out there taking measurements in the back yard, getting a plan of the goldfish pool and the way the water runs into it.

"You see, water has to be aerated to keep goldfish happy and healthy and this handy man out there has built up quite an ingenious little pathway for the water to follow with little miniature waterfalls, and all of that, and then it flows into this big goldfish pool, is drained out, pumped back into the channel and down through the waterfalls again. The whole thing is handled with a little electric motor."

"Does it run all the time?" Mason asked.

"No," Drake said, "Dr. Babb used to shut it off when he went to bed, then turn it on in the morning. The sound of running water interfered with his sleep. He didn't like it."

Mason said, "That's interesting. I guess no one has ever thought to find out whether the motor had been shut off or not on Monday night."

"Apparently it was shut off," Drake said. "Incidentally, Perry, there's one other person who is interested in goldfish and that's Gertrude, the niece who's visiting the Dunkirks up on the hill.

"Mrs. Dunkirk you know was the one who saw the woman running out of the house."

"Okay," Mason said, "what have you found out about Gertrude, Paul?"

"Gertrude is a problem. I can find out more about her if you want. She's been in some sort of scrape and she's planning to stay with the Dunkirks for three months. While she's staying there, she's keeping out of circulation.

"There's something funny about that whole business. She is nervous, restless, and while she doesn't go out any and mingle with the other young people, she's sixteen, unmarried and—well, it's a hell of a thing to say, Perry, but these neighbors on the west gave her a good once-over and *they* think she's going to have a baby."

Mason and Della Street exchanged glances.

"And she hangs around Dr. Babb's back yard and the goldfish pool?" Mason asked.

"Yes, she got acquainted with Dr. Babb and—I suppose you knew the Dunkirks knew Babb before they moved into the neighborhood."

"I know," Mason said. "Where was Gertrude during the commotion out there Monday night, Paul?"

"Playing the piano like mad," Drake said. "Neighbors farther up the hill who didn't even hear the screams heard the piano banging away."

Mason became thoughtful. "I wonder," he said, "if—"

Knuckles pounded on the corridor door to Mason's private office.

Mason frowned. "See who it is, Della. Tell whoever it is that I'm engaged in the trial of a case, that the office is closed and I can't see anyone."

Della Street opened the door a crack, said, "Mr. Mason is engaged in the trial of a case and...oh, hello, Mr. Kinsey."

Carver Kinsey pushed the door open with the easy assurance of one who is completely immune to rebuffs.

"Hello, Drake," he said. "How's the old sleuth coming? Hi, Mason! How's the case?"

"So-so," Mason said.

Kinsey made himself at home, drew up a chair, took out a cigarette, lit it, blew out the match with a smoky exhalation, grinned at Mason and said, "Let's talk some more."

"Drake quickly sized up the situation, said, "Well, Perry, I'll keep busy on this angle and see if I can find out anything else."

"Stay with it," Mason told him.

Drake left the office.

Kinsey said, "Well, Mason, I'm at the place where I have to have a showdown."

"As far as I'm concerned, you've already had it," Mason said.

Kinsey said, "You're playing a deep game, Mason. I don't know what it is but I want you to know that I don't intend to let you off the hook.

"Norma tells me there's no question that Babb was murdered by some woman who must have been in the inner office when she arrived, some woman who ran out of the back door.

"There's an automatic door-closing device on that back door. The handy man saw the door closing. He doesn't think that anyone could have run out but he has to admit it's a possibility. Of course, he thinks Dr. Babb was going to the back door to call up to him to come down. Naturally he would think that, what with all the screaming and stuff."

Mason stretched and yawned.

"Therefore," Kinsey went on, "you have a lead-pipe cinch. You only need to produce Norma Logan, put her on the stand, have her tell her story, and the case against John Kirby goes out the window."

"Provided they believe her," Mason said.

"I've got her coached," Kinsey said. "They'll believe her. She'll tell her story embellished by cheesecake, tears and corroboration."

"What corroboration?" Mason asked.

Kinsey grinned. "Leave it to me."

"And so?" Mason asked.

"And so," Kinsey said, "we've reached the end of the trial, Mason. I want the information that's in that book. I'll share it with you. You can keep whatever fee you receive for getting the case against Kirby thrown out of court."

"You're *so* good to me," Mason said.

"Damned if I'm not," Kinsey retorted. "Actually the book belongs to my client," Kinsey went on. "I could hold the whole thing as my client's property."

"Where did your client get it?" Mason asked.

Kinsey grinned. "She stole it, if you come right down to it. But you know something, Mason?"

"What?"

"She *could* be in error on that. It *could* happen that she found the book on the sidewalk where someone who had run out of Dr. Babb's house ahead of her could have dropped it. Having found the book that way, it wouldn't be stolen property, and she wouldn't be obligated to return it to anyone unless there was a positive and complete identification, which under the circumstances can't be made."

Mason shook his head. "I'm not buying any part of that, Kinsey."

Kinsey's face darkened. "You might consider your own position in this thing, Mason. Right now you're not only concealing evidence, but you have stolen property in your possession. Certain people that I know of would like very much to work things up on that basis."

"Would they indeed?" Mason asked. "If, as you now suggest, your client found the book on the sidewalk I wouldn't be guilty of anything in holding the book."

"My, but you're bright!" Kinsey said. "You get the idea very rapidly. I haven't suggested as yet to my client that she might have found the book on the sidewalk, but I have impressed upon her that she's going to go to prison for a long, long time unless she does *exactly* as I tell her."

Mason said, "I get your idea, Kinsey. I got it the first time. I gave you your answer the first time. Now Della Street and I are going to dinner. Would you mind getting the hell out of the office?"

Kinsey got to his feet. "You know, Mason," he said, "you always did underestimate me."

"Possibly," Mason said.

"You think that I'm afraid to make a move," Kinsey said. "You think that I don't dare to approach the district attorney because the district attorney hates me almost as much as he hates you.

"I'm going to tell you something, Mason. I'm a damn sight smarter than you give me credit for being. By the time I get done with this thing, I'm going to be sitting on top of the heap."

"Go ahead and sit on it," Mason said, getting to his feet, "but get the hell out of here before I throw you out."

"Okay, okay," Kinsey said, bowing and smiling at Della Street. "I'll be seeing you one of these days, Mason."

Kinsey opened the door and vanished.

Della Street's anxious eyes appraised Perry Mason. "Chief," she said, "I'm shivering in my shoes."

Mason's eyes were slitted with concentration. "Forget it, Della," he said. "We don't have any other choice in the matter. We can't do business with anyone like that. Hang it! Della, this thing all ties together."

"What?"

"The Dunkirks' niece is wild. She got into trouble. The parents were frantic, so the Dunkirks told them about Dr. Babb. Dr. Babb had gone into semiretirement, but for his friends the Dunkirks he was willing to go into business once more.

"So Gertrude came to stay with her aunt and uncle. Circumstances are such that she had to keep pretty much to herself. The whole thing begins to add up."

"I know," Della Street said, "but what's going to happen tomorrow morning? What's going to happen if Hamilton Burger should walk into court and accuse you of having stolen property in your possession and what would happen if Norma Logan has been so thoroughly hypnotized by this shyster lawyer that she goes on the stand and backs up his story?"

"That," Mason said, "is a bridge we'll cross when we come to it. So far Kinsey has been bluffing. He wants that notebook. If he goes to Hamilton Burger— well, he might make a trade with Burger. Burger *might* agree to turn over the book to him in return for getting something he can use against me. But there's one thing none of them have taken into consideration, Della."

"What's that?" she asked.

"The technical rules of evidence," Mason said.

CHAPTER FOURTEEN

Perry Mason had paced the floor of his apartment for some two hours before retiring, then, after he had gone to bed, had tossed and turned for another hour before sleep finally came to him.

That sleep was interrupted at about three in the morning by the strident, insistent ringing of the telephone bell. The number of that unlisted telephone was known to only three people in the world: Perry Mason, Della Street, and Paul Drake, the detective.

Mason groped for the light switch, fumbled with the telephone, said sleepily, "Hello."

Della Street's voice, sharp with urgency, said, "Chief, something's happened!"

The note in her voice snapped Mason to instant wakefulness.

"All right, Della, what is it?"

"Officers pounded on my door a few minutes ago."

"Go on," Mason told her.

"I put on a robe, got up and demanded to know who it was. They told me it was the law. Finally I opened the door. They pushed a subpoena into my hands. A *subpoena duces tecum,* calling for a cardboard-backed notebook which was the property of Dr. P. L. Babb. I'm ordered to appear in Judge Cameron's court at ten o'clock and to have the notebook with me. What do I do?"

Mason said, "Turn out your lights, go back to bed, and go to sleep."

"Heavens, Chief! I couldn't sleep now. I'm...I'm frightened. That means Kinsey has gone to the district attorney."

"All right," Mason said, "let me handle it. Take a glass of hot milk, go to bed, and forget it."

"Is it all right?" she asked anxiously.

"It's all right," Mason assured her. "Sit tight, Della. Get a good sleep. Don't be worried."

Mason had hardly hung up the telephone before the buzzer of his apartment sounded. The buzzer was supplemented by pounding knuckles on the door.

Mason opened the door.

A uniformed officer pushed a paper into his hands. "A *subpoena duces tecum,*" he said. "Case of People versus Kirby, Judge Cameron's court, ten o'clock today. G'-by."

"Thank you, officer," Mason said.

"Don't mention it," the officer told him. "Sorry I had to get you up, but those were orders."

"Quite all right," Mason said closing the door.

The lawyer sat on the edge of the bed, tapped a cigarette on his thumbnail, snapped a match into flame, lit the cigarette, inhaled deeply, then regarded the carpet with frowning concentration.

Again the telephone rang.

Mason picked it up. "Hello, Paul," he said.

Paul Drake's voice showed surprise. "How did you know it wasn't Della?"

"She just called."

"I see. Did they serve her?"

"Uh-huh."

Drake said, "My man called me just a few minutes ago. I wanted to warn you so you could keep out of the way and get Della into hiding if you wanted to. That Logan girl has told the D.A. one hell of a story."

"What happened?" Mason asked.

"Well, of course, I'm getting if from an underground pipeline," Drake said. "I don't have any details, but here are the general facts: Carver Kinsey is attorney for Norma Logan. Now get this, Perry, she was the mysterious girl who was seen running out of Dr. Babb's house at the time of the murder.

"Kinsey went to the D.A. about eight o'clock last night. He sold Hamilton Burger a bill of goods. Burger is reported to have made a deal with Kinsey by which Norma Logan will be let off the hook if she gets on the stand and tells her story.

"All hell is going to break in that case at ten o'clock this morning and you're going to be in the center of it.

"Now then, is there anything I can do?"

"I don't think so, Paul."

"I sure hope you know what you're doing," Drake said.

"So do I," Mason told him. "Thanks for calling, Paul."

Mason hung up, dressed, started pacing the floor.

CHAPTER FIFTEEN

Word had passed like wildfire that fireworks were scheduled to go off in Judge Cameron's court, and the courtroom was jam-packed with interested spectators and newspaper reporters.

Judge Cameron surveyed the crowd with uncordial appraisal. His manner plainly indicated that he wondered what sudden, unexpected turn of events had caused this surge of interest.

It was also apparent that Hamilton Burger, the district attorney, had now taken personal charge of the case.

As Judge Cameron called the court to order, Hamilton Burger said, "Your Honor, the prosecution desires to call Miss Della Street to the stand. Miss Street is a hostile witness. She is the secretary of Mr. Perry Mason who is representing the defendant."

Judge Cameron said sharply, "You can't do that, Mr. Prosecutor. Any communication made by a client to an attorney is confidential and the same rule holds good for the confidential secretary of an attorney."

"I'm not trying to get testimony concerning a communication, Your Honor. I am trying to recover stolen goods."

"Stolen goods!" Judge Cameron exclaimed.

"Stolen goods!" Hamilton Burger repeated. "We propose to show that certain personal property of Dr. Babb was stolen from his office and that this property was turned over to Miss Street. We have had a *subpoena duces tecum* served upon both Miss Street and Mr. Mason."

Judge Cameron rubbed his hand over the top of his head. "This is most unusual," he said. "It is a most unusual procedure."

"It is a most unusual situation," Hamilton Burger retorted. "I have some authorities if the Court would care to listen to those citations. A privileged communication relates only to disclosures which a client makes to an attorney for the purpose of securing advice as to his legal rights. It does not stretch so far as to give an attorney immunity from responsibility when he participates in concealing evidence, committing a crime, or receiving stolen property.

"In fact, there are exceptions to the rule in regard to confidential communications made to an attorney. There is a long line of authorities on the subject and I am prepared to quote a list of citations supporting what I am trying to do."

Judge Cameron said, "Well, let us proceed in an orderly fashion. You may call Miss Street to the stand, and then ask her certain questions. Specific objections may then be made to those specific questions, and the Court will make specific rulings on each objection. Is Miss Street in court?"

Della Street arose.

"Come forward and be sworn, Miss Street," Judge Cameron said, not unkindly.

Della Street walked forward, held up her hand, was sworn, gave her name and address to the court reporter, and seated herself on the witness stand.

"Miss Street," Hamilton Burger said, "you are employed by Perry Mason?"

"Yes, sir."

"And have been so employed by him for some time?"

"Yes, sir."

"In the capacity of confidential secretary?"

"Yes, sir."

"Are you acquainted with Norma Logan?"

"I have met her."

"Did you see her on Tuesday the sixth of this month during the early part of the evening?"

"Yes, sir."

"Who was with you at that time?"

"Mr. Mason."

"You had a conversation with Miss Logan?"

"Yes, sir."

"To your knowledge is this Miss Logan a client of Perry Mason?"

"Not to my knowledge."

"Did Mr. Mason go to her in search of information rather than in answer to a request from her?"

"Yes."

"Now then," Hamilton Burger went on triumphantly, "in that conversation which took place that night, did Miss Logan tell you that she had stolen a certain notebook from the premises occupied by Dr. Babb on the evening of Monday, the fifth of this month? Answer that question yes or no."

"Just a moment," Mason said. "We object to that question, if the Court please, on the ground that it calls for a privileged communication."

Hamilton Burger arose ponderously. "Now, Your Honor, I am prepared to submit authorities on that point. In the first place, Mr. Perry Mason was there just as any other citizen would be there. He was representing the defendant, John Northrup Kirby. That was the reason he went there. He was trying to get evidence for Kirby. He was *not* representing Norma Logan in any way. He was not acting as *her* attorney. Any communication which was made to him by Norma Logan was not a communication made to her attorney. *She* had not retained him. *She* does not look upon him as her attorney; in fact, he could not be her attorney because of the fact that he is representing the defendant Kirby in this case, and there would be a conflict of interest as between Kirby and Norma Logan.

"If the Court please, we are now prepared to show exactly what happened on the night of the fifth. We are prepared to prove that the defendant in this case is an accessory before, as well as after, the fact to murder, that he transported Norma Logan to the scene of the crime, that he waited for her return, that he then took her in his automobile and hurried her to a motel where he registered under a fictitious name as husband and wife, that thereafter he concocted a story about finding a woman who was carrying a gasoline can to a car which had become stalled, and which subsequently apparently was stolen.

"He told this story in order to account for the fingerprints of Norma Logan in his car. Subsequently in order to substantiate that purely synthetic story still further, he produced a red gasoline can which he said was the gasoline can the young woman had been carrying.

"If the Court please, we are now prepared to show that that gasoline can was a fabricated piece of evidence *and that the fingerprints of Mr. Perry Mason appear on that gasoline can.*"

Judge Cameron looked at Perry Mason. "Do you desire to be heard, Mr. Mason?"

"On what charge?" Mason asked. "Am I being charged with planting evidence in this case in the form of a gasoline can?"

"You certainly are," Hamilton Burger roared, "and when I take the matter up with the grievance committee of the bar association, you'll be charged formally."

"Because my fingerprints were on the can?" Mason asked.

"You know what I'm talking about," Hamilton Burger said.

"Did you personally examine that gasoline can?" Mason asked.

"I certainly did!" Hamilton Burger retorted. "I know what I'm talking about in this case. I personally saw that gasoline can. I personally examined it. I had it in my personal possession. It is in my personal possession now!"

"Then," Mason said urbanely, "doubtless *your* fingerprints are on it, and, if that is the sole criterion of guilt, I can prefer charges against you before the grievance committee of the bar association."

Hamilton Burger's face purpled.

Judge Cameron flashed a quick smile, then rapped for order. "It would seem that the gasoline can is entirely outside the issues we are here to try at the present time. At least, it is outside the scope of this question.

"Is it your contention, Mr. Mason, that you were representing Norma Logan in any way, or that you are now representing her?"

"No, Your Honor."

"Then it would seem that the question is not subject to objection on the ground that it calls for privileged communication."

Mason said, "The question is further objected to, Your Honor, on the ground that it is argumentative, calls for a conclusion of the witness and calls for hearsay testimony."

Judge Cameron turned to the court reporter. "Will you read the question, please?"

The court reporter read the question: "'Now then, in that conversation which took place that night, did Miss Logan tell you that she had stolen a certain notebook from the premises occupied by Dr. Babb on the evening of Monday, the fifth of this month?'"

Judge Cameron said, "As the question is phrased, the objection will be sustained."

Hamilton Burger took a deep breath. "Did Norma Logan give you a pasteboard-backed notebook that night, Miss Street? You may answer that question yes or no."

"Now just a moment," Mason said. "That question is objected to on the ground that it is incompetent, irrelevant and immaterial if the Court please. Unless the district attorney *first* shows that this notebook has some bearing on the issues in the case at present being tried before the Court, it is completely irrelevant. Miss Street may have received a hundred things last Tuesday night from a hundred different people."

"The objection is sustained," Judge Cameron said.

"Oh, Your Honor!" Hamilton Burger said. "This is grasping at straws. This is taking advantage of every technicality in the book. This is—"

"The Court has ruled, Mr. Prosecutor," Judge Cameron said. "The objection is based upon technical grounds, but nevertheless the objection is well taken."

"Well," Hamilton Burger blurted, "Norma Logan told you at that time she had stolen this notebook from Dr. Babb's office, didn't she?"

"Objected to," Mason said, "on the ground that the question calls for hearsay testimony."

Judge Cameron smiled. "Quite obviously the objection is well taken."

Hamilton Burger said, "If the Court please, I want that notebook produced. I can assure the Court, as prosecutor in this case, that that notebook is highly pertinent to the issues involved. I can assure the Court that the issues which Mr. Perry Mason is avoiding with all of the legal agility at his command are issues which are pertinent and vital to the determination of this case."

"Well, keep your temper and don't shout at the Court," Judge Cameron snapped. "Go ahead and ask your questions."

"Will you produce that notebook?" Hamilton Burger thundered at Della Street.

"What notebook?" she asked.

"The notebook Norma Logan gave you Tuesday night," Hamilton Burger roared.

"Objected to," Perry Mason said, "as assuming a fact not in evidence. The Court has already ruled that any evidence as to anything received by Miss Street last Tuesday night is incompetent, irrelevant and immaterial, unless the prosecutor *first* shows it is connected with the issues involved in this case."

"I have assured the Court that it is! I have assured the Court on my honor as an attorney," Hamilton Burger shouted.

"I don't want your assurance," Mason said. "I'm representing the defendant John Kirby. The Constitution provides that he has the right to be confronted with the witnesses against him, and that he has the right to cross-examine those witnesses. If you want to have it appear in the record that this notebook is vital to the issues involved in this case, take the oath and get on the stand, and I'll cross-examine *you*, and prove that all *you* know about it is based on hearsay evidence."

Hamilton Burger started to say something, then found he had nothing to say. He glared at Perry Mason, then bent over to have a whispered conference with Sims Ballantine.

Abruptly Burger straightened, pointed his finger at Della Street, and said, "Did you have reason to believe, Miss Street, that a notebook you received last Tuesday night was connected with the murder of Dr. Phineas L. Babb, and pertinent evidence in the case of the People versus John Northrup Kirby?"

"Objected to," Mason said, "as calling for a conclusion of the witness, as argumentative and indirectly as calling for hearsay evidence."

Judge Cameron said, "Mr. Prosecutor, the Court is going to sustain the objection. Quite obviously you are going at the matter backwards. If it is your contention that this witness received any property from one Norma Logan, and that that property had in turn been stolen from the house of Dr. Babb, and was evidence in connection with this case, you're first going to have to show that in fact such a notebook has been stolen, that it is pertinent, and *then* you can ask this witness questions concerning it. But quite obviously you can't lay the entire foundation by examining this witness in this manner.

"Now the Court can appreciate that the circumstances are such that you may find them personally and officially exasperating, but nevertheless there's only one logical, orderly way to go about this thing, and in view of the objections which have been made by counsel, I am constrained to point out to you that you are adopting the wrong course."

"I'm going to fight it out on this line, if it takes all morning," Hamilton Burger shouted.

"Very well," Judge Cameron snapped.

"Last Tuesday night," Hamilton Burger said to Della Street, "you received property which you had reason to believe was evidence in this case, and you concealed that evidence, didn't you? Answer that question yes or no."

"Objected to," Mason said, "on the ground that it calls for a conclusion of the witness. The defendant in this case is not bound by what Miss Street may have *thought* she was receiving, provided she did receive anything. The defense in this case can only be bound by pertinent evidence which is introduced in an orderly manner, and shown to be connected with the case."

"The objection is sustained," Judge Cameron said.

"Well, Miss Logan gave you *something* Tuesday night, didn't she?"

"Objected to as incompetent, irrelevant and immaterial," Mason said. "It makes no difference what this witness may have received unless it was something that pertained to the present case."

"Sustained," Judge Cameron said.

Again Hamilton Burger had a whispered conference with his assistant.

Ballantine was gesticulating, explaining, while Hamilton Burger, flushed with anger, was quite evidently loath to follow the advice his assistant was giving him.

Judge Cameron said, "I think it is only fair to point out to you, Mr. District Attorney, that the Court has explained to you that there is no way you can prove this article to which you are referring is pertinent to the issues involved in this case unless this witness knows it of her own knowledge. You can't prove that by hearsay. It would certainly seem to me that the first step in a logical, orderly presentation would be to call Miss Logan as a witness."

"Very well," Hamilton Burger yielded with poor grace. "Step down, Miss Street. I'll call Norma Logan to the stand."

The courtroom buzzed with whispers, and Hamilton Burger, plainly exasperated to the point of apoplexy, slowly seated himself at the counsel table reserved for the prosecution.

Mason beckoned to Mrs. Kirby and, when she came forward, said, "Mrs. Kirby, I want you to sit here beside your husband."

Mrs. Kirby eased herself down into the chair which Mason drew up beside him.

"Will anyone object?" she asked.

"We'll wait and see," Mason whispered. "Now then, while I have you both together, I want you to know that I've put up with a lot in this case. I was retained do what was necessary to protect the best interests of your son. I'm going to do it. I'm going to play the cards my own way. I'm—"

Mason stopped abruptly as Norma Logan came forward and raised her right hand. She took the oath and, quite evidently badly shaken, seated herself in the witness chair.

Hamilton Burger himself arose to conduct the examination. "You were acquainted with Dr. Babb during his lifetime?"

"Yes."

"On the night of Monday, the fifth of this month, did you go to the house of Dr. Babb?"

"Yes."

"Who took you there?"

"Mr. Kirby. He waited for me in his car."

"By Mr. Kirby, you mean the defendant in this case?"

"Yes, sir."

"And what did you do?"

"I went to Dr. Babb's office and entered and then took a seat in the waiting room."

"While you were at Dr. Babb's house, did you take any article of personal property without the permission of Dr. Babb?"

"Objected to," Mason said, "as incompetent, irrelevant and immaterial."

"I think you'll have to connect it up," Judge Cameron said. "I think a better foundation should be established."

"Very well," Hamilton Burger said. "I will ask you if you had occasion to enter the consultation office of Dr. Babb while you were there?"

"I did."

"And what was the occasion?"

"I heard a commotion and—" Suddenly the witness straightened on the witness stand. Her eyes became large and round. She raised a trembling forefinger, pointed it at Mrs. Kirby, and shouted, "That's the woman! *That's the woman!*"

"Now, just a moment! Just a moment!" Judge Cameron said. "What's all this about?"

"That's the woman! That's the woman who murdered Dr. Babb!" the witness screamed, still pointing at Mrs. Kirby.

Hamilton Burger, in a frenzy of excitement, pushed forward to stand by the witness. "You mean *that's* the woman you saw in the room?"

"Yes, yes! The woman who was bending over Dr. Babb. That's the one who was in there!"

"Now, just a moment! Just a moment!" Hamilton Burger said. "I want to get this straight." He turned to the Court and said, "If the Court please, a situation has now developed that is totally unexpected. I would like to have permission of the Court to withdraw this witness temporarily until I can confer with her."

"Not before I've cross-examined her in connection with the statement she has just made," Mason said.

"Quite obviously," Hamilton Burger insisted, "this witness is emotionally upset. She is in no condition to be examined at the present time."

Mason said, "If the Court please, the prosecution's own witness has now identified another person as being the one who murdered Dr. Babb. This exonerates the defendant, John Northrup Kirby."

"Unless they acted together and in unison," Judge Cameron said. "Does the prosecution contend such is the case?"

"Very frankly," Hamilton Burger said, "the prosecution doesn't know."

"Well, if *you* don't know, you can't expect *us* to know," Judge Cameron said. "If you aren't satisfied there was a conspiracy or a joint undertaking, you're hardly in a position to ask the Court to bind the defendant over, in view of the statement which now comes from the lips of your own witness that Mrs. Kirby was the one who committed the murder."

"And," Perry Mason interpolated, "the witness has also testified that, at the time the murder was committed, the defendant in this case was sitting in a car some distance from the scene of the murder waiting for this witness to rejoin him."

"I don't think she has testified in quite that detail," Judge Cameron said, "but that would seem to be the effect of her testimony."

"Your Honor, if the Court please, *please,* Your Honor," Hamilton Burger said, "I want to withdraw the witness until she can become more composed. I would like to find out myself what this is all about."

"I can go on," Norma Logan said. "I was just upset. That's all. I haven't had any sleep and...and the shock of seeing that woman—"

"Just a moment," Judge Cameron said. "The Court will handle this. Just where did you see this woman, Miss Logan?"

"I went to Dr. Babb's office. I sat in the waiting room. I heard a commotion and the sound of a blow and a body falling, and then I heard a woman screaming. I ran to the door of the inner office and saw Dr. Babb lying on the floor. I saw this woman bending over him."

"What did you do?" Judge Cameron asked.

"I stood there for a moment."

"Did she see you?"

"No, I'm satisfied she did not. She bent over Dr. Babb. The safe door was open and papers were scattered around over the floor. Then she dashed toward the back of the house."

"And then?" Judge Cameron asked.

"Then," she said, "I entered the room. I bent over Dr. Babb. I found he was still alive. I...I knew of one book in Dr. Babb's desk that I wanted. I took that book and ran with it."

"Where did you go?" Judge Cameron asked.

"I dashed down the street to where Mr. Kirby was waiting in his car."

"By Mr. Kirby you are referring to the defendant in this case?"

"Yes."

"And what did you do?"

"I got in the car and drove away with him. I told him what had happened and he took me down to a motel."

Judge Cameron said to the district attorney, "It would certainly seem, under the circumstances, Mr. District Attorney, that unless you are now prepared to prove some joint action on the part of husband and wife, your proof in this case shows that Mr. Kirby, the present defendant, must be innocent. As to whether his wife is guilty, that's another question. His wife is not formally before the Court at this time. She is not charged with anything."

Carver Kinsey, who had been sitting just inside the space reserved for attorneys, got up from his chair, hurried to Hamilton Burger's side and engaged in a whispered conference.

Hamilton Burger listened attentively, finally nodded, faced the judge.

"If the Court please," he said, "I'm trying to get this matter cleaned up, but since we now have the witness on the stand, I want to ask her one question. What did you do with that book which you took from Dr. Babb's office, Miss Logan?"

"Objected to as incompetent, irrelevant and immaterial," Perry Mason said. "It now appears from the prosecution's own witness that this defendant John Kirby must be innocent of any criminal act, except perhaps that of helping to conceal a witness. In view of the fact that he is not connected with the death of

Dr. Babb, what this witness did with any property she might have taken from the home of Dr. Babb is absolutely immaterial as far as *this* defendant is concerned."

Judge Cameron frowned.

"If the Court please," Hamilton Burger said, "I want to be heard on this. Here is an important piece of evidence. Here is a piece of evidence which, in all probability, constituted the motivation for the murder of Dr. Babb. If that piece of evidence was delivered to the attorney for the defense or to his secretary, and has been willfully suppressed, that in itself is a breach of professional ethics and receiving that property, knowing that it had been stolen from the home of Dr. Babb, amounts to concealing stolen property, which is a felony."

"The Court will give Mr. Mason a chance to be heard," Judge Cameron said. "It would seem that the position of the district attorney is well taken."

"Suppose it is," Mason said, "what does it prove? It may prove a case against me, if that is the attitude the district attorney wants to take. But *I* am not on trial in this case. It certainly doesn't tend to prove anything against my client. It can't even prove anything against Mrs. Kirby. According to the testimony of the witness, Mrs. Kirby had already left the premises when this witness entered the private office and took the notebook from the desk. Mrs. Kirby can't be held responsible for something this witness did *after* she had left the premises, and certainly Mr. Kirby cannot be charged with any responsibility."

"I'm not charging Kirby with responsibility," Hamilton Burger bellowed. "I'm charging *you* with responsibility. I'm charging you with receiving stolen property."

"Go ahead and arrest me then," Perry Mason said.

"By heavens, I will!" Hamilton Burger shouted. "I now have the evidence. I'm going to sign a complaint personally charging you with receiving stolen property."

"Go ahead," Mason challenged.

"Now just a moment," Judge Cameron said. "We're going to keep this proceeding orderly. What are you going to do with the case against this defendant John Northrup Kirby, Mr. District Attorney?"

Hamilton Burger said, "I'm going to dismiss it. I—No, wait a moment, Your Honor, I'm going to get one matter straight before I do. I want to withdraw this witness from the stand and recall the witness Harvey Nelson who previously testified about Dr. Babb's dying statements. I think I know now what happened and I think I am prepared to clean up a corrupt mess which has existed at this bar for some time. Every case which Mr. Mason has handled has been presented with a dramatic fanfare of legal trumpets which has doubtless gratified Mr. Mason and surrounded him with the glitter of dazzling notoriety, but—"

"Now just a moment, Mr. Prosecutor," Judge Cameron interrupted. "We're not going to engage in personal abuse of counsel at this time. Address your remarks to the Court and refrain from inflammatory statements of this sort."

"Very well, if the Court please," Hamilton Burger said savagely, "I'll confine myself to the issues in the present case. I think we have witnessed a very cleverly played, in fact, a diabolically concocted scheme of—"

"Never mind that!" Judge Cameron said. "Specifically why are you addressing the Court?"

"I want to recall the witness Harvey Nelson."

"There seems to be no objection," Judge Cameron said. "Go ahead and recall him, and kindly refrain from these inflammatory statements. I may call your attention, Mr. Burger, to the fact that while certain aspects of the present case are what you might term flamboyantly dramatic, the entire drama has been the result of your own questions and your own conduct."

"All right," Hamilton Burger said. "I was tricked into a situation where this defendant and his counsel have received a temporary advantage, but I can assure the Court it will be short-lived."

"The Court has no interest in that matter whatever," Judge Cameron said. "The Court is interested in seeing that justice is done in an orderly manner. Therefore, if your remarks are addressed to the Court they are out of order, and if they were addressed to the representatives of the press, they were uncalled for. The Court has warned you on this matter, Mr. Prosecutor, and the Court does not intend to repeat that warning. The Court would suggest that you control yourself and either present this case or dismiss it."

"Call Harvey Nelson," Hamilton Burger said.

Nelson, who had been waiting at the swinging gate to the inner bar of the courtroom, pushed his way through and approached the witness stand.

"You've already been sworn," Hamilton Burger said. "Sit down there. Now Mr. Nelson, you made some comments about a statement made by Dr. Babb prior to his death when you asked him in the presence of witnesses if he knew who his assailant was and the doctor said he did and then mentioned a name."

"That's right," Nelson said.

"Now, in view of developments," Hamilton Burger said, "it occurs to me that the name *John* Kirby and the name *Joan* Kirby are sufficiently similar in sound so there could well have been a confusion in your mind. Is it possible that what the doctor actually said was Joan Kirby instead of John Kirby?"

"Just a moment," Mason said. "I object to the question on the ground that it is leading and suggestive, on the ground that it is an attempt to coach his witness while he is on the stand, that it is an attempt to put testimony in the mouth of the witness, that it is viciously leading, that it—"

"You don't need to go any further," Judge Cameron said. "The objection is sustained."

Hamilton Burger frowned. "I want to get this before the Court at this time," he said, "so that—"

"Before the *Court?*" Judge Cameron asked.

"Well, if the Court please, it's only fair to the public to understand the situation here."

"The Court has previously advised you, Mr. Burger, that you should present your testimony in an orderly manner and without regard to the press. Now the objection has been sustained. There's nothing before the Court. Do you want to ask another question, or have you finished?"

Hamilton Burger turned to engage in another whispered conference with Ballantine, then said, "I'll go at it in another way, Your Honor." He turned to the witness. "Mr. Nelson, you stated that the dying man made a statement to you as to the identity of his assailant."

"Yes, sir."

"Was that statement preserved in any way?"

"Yes, sir. It was."

"In what way?"

"On a tape recorder."

"And how was that done?"

"The microphone of a tape recorder was within a few inches of the lips of the dying man. The entire conversation was recorded on that tape recorder."

"Do you have that tape in your possession?"

"I do, but it is not with me at the moment."

"Can you get it?"

"Yes."

"And that tape shows exactly what was said?"

"It does."

"Then that tape is the best evidence, Your Honor," Hamilton Burger said, "and I have a right to have it played."

"I don't know whether it's the best evidence or not," Judge Cameron said, "but...is there any objection from the defense?"

"I would like to ask a question on cross-examination," Mason said.

"Very well, go ahead."

"You didn't tell us about this tape recording before."

"I wasn't asked."

"You deliberately refrained from mentioning it?"

"I didn't intend to mention it unless I was asked."

"Did someone give you instructions not to mention it unless you were asked?"

"Oh, Your Honor," Hamilton Burger said, "this is the same old seven and six, the same type of cross-examination, the same—"

"The district attorney will make specific objections and address his comments to the Court and refrain from criticizing counsel on the other side," Judge Cameron said. "The question is certainly well taken because it indicates the bias of the witness. The objection is overruled. Answer the question."

"Did someone tell you that?" Mason asked.

"Yes."

"Who?"

"Mr. Ballantine."

"By Mr. Ballantine, you mean the deputy district attorney here?"

"Yes."

"And what did he tell you?"

"He told me not to say anything about that tape recording unless I was interrogated concerning it. I have been interrogated on it now."

"All right," Mason said smiling. "Go and get the tape recording. We'll be very glad to hear it."

"This is going to take a few minutes, if the Court please," Hamilton Burger said. "May we have a thirty-minute recess?"

"Very well," Judge Cameron said. "The Court will take a thirty-minute recess. Now the Court is not entirely clear as to the admissibility of a tape recording made under such circumstances."

"It's the best evidence," Hamilton Burger said. "It records the sound itself."

"Is there any objection from the defense?" Judge Cameron asked Mason.

"None, Your Honor."

"Of course," Judge Cameron said, "in the present state of proof it now appears that the prosecution's own evidence indicates the innocence of the defendant."

"I know, I know, Your Honor. I'm just going at this thing...I want to go at it in my own way," Hamilton Burger said.

"The Court would like to point out that a proceeding before the grand jury is the proper manner in which to find out what happened in a case where the district attorney isn't certain. It is not the province of this Court to supervise a fishing expedition in trying to determine what actually did or did not happen."

"Yes, Your Honor," Hamilton Burger said, "if the Court will grant a thirty-minute recess and bear with me for a few moments, I think we can clear the matter up."

"Very well," Judge Cameron said, his manner showing an obvious dislike for tactics that quite plainly were designed to see that the inevitable dismissal of the case against John Kirby left the district attorney in the best possible light so far as newspaper publicity was concerned.

When the Judge had left the bench, John Kirby looked at his wife incredulously. "Joan, were you out there?" he asked.

"Yes," she whispered.

"But why in the name of reason—? How did you—?"

"That will do," Mason said. "People are watching you. Just curtail your conversation. You're leaving things in my hands."

Kirby said grimly, "If you have that book, Mason, they'll get Ronnie. They'll get him and they'll get you. Damn it! They—"

"Take it easy," Mason interrupted. "I'm mapping the strategy in this case and I'll take care of myself."

CHAPTER SIXTEEN

The scene in the courtroom was highly dramatic when Judge Cameron again took the bench at the end of the thirty-minute recess.

Harvey Nelson had set up a tape-recording device with an extension loud-speaker.

"Do you have the tape recording you have testified to?" Hamilton Burger asked the witness.

"I do."

"Will you please play that tape recording?"

Amidst tense, expectant silence, the machine gave forth a high-pitched hum. Suddenly from the loud-speaker came a voice so true to life that it startled the spectators. The amplified volume filled the courtroom.

"Dr. Babb, can you hear me? Can you hear me, Doctor? Dr. Babb, can you hear me?"

"Yes."

"Dr. Babb, do you know who hit you?"

"Dr. Babb, can you tell us the name of the person who hit you?"

There were several more repetitions of the question, then the answer, "Yes."

"Please give us the name. Doctor, please give us the name."

Again the question was repeated several times, and then in a slightly slurred tone of voice came the answer.

"That's all," Hamilton Burger said. "Shut off the machine."

Burger turned triumphantly to the Court. "It is quite plain, now that we listen to it, that the name Dr. Babb gave is that of *Joan* Kirby, and not *John* Kirby."

"Please play that tape recording again," Judge Cameron said.

The witness played it once more.

"Of course," Judge Cameron pointed out, "in a matter of this sort, the imagination plays a part. The Court quite distinctly hears the name Kirby. Whether the first name is *John* or *Joan* is a question. The Court is very much inclined to think that the name is *John* Kirby rather than *Joan* Kirby."

"If the Court please," Hamilton Burger said, "making allowances for the fact that this man was injured, that there is a slight impediment in his speech, I think it is quite apparent that the name is Joan Kirby."

"Well," Judge Camerson said, "what's before the Court at this time?"

"I wanted to get this evidence into the record."

"I'm quite certain you did," Judge Cameron snapped. "But the case which you are *now* trying is the case of the People versus John Northrup Kirby. Now you are introducing evidence which you claim shows the dying man gave the name of the defendant's wife."

"I have not as yet excluded the possibility of a joint effort," Hamilton Burger said lamely.

"Well, you haven't any evidence which indicates it," Judge Cameron said. "Do you have any further questions of this witness?"

"No."

"Any cross-examination?" Judge Cameron asked Mason.

"No, Your Honor, I am assuming that the district attorney wishes to introduce this tape recording into evidence."

"Well, now, wait a minute," Hamilton Burger said. "We let the Court listen to the tape. I see no reason to have it introduced in evidence."

"That's the only way you can keep a record," Mason said. "The court reporter can't transcribe the sounds that came from the tape recorder."

"He certainly can," Hamilton Burger said. "The name Joan Kirby is there as plain as can be."

"A few minutes ago, you were claiming it was the name John Kirby," Mason said.

Hamilton Burger showed his embarrassment.

"The Court thinks the tape should be introduced in evidence. It can subsequently be withdrawn, if necessary; but if it's part of the record, it should be in evidence," Judge Cameron said.

"Very well, Your Honor."

"Do you have any cross-examination of this witness?" Judge Cameron asked Mason.

"No, Your Honor."

"Call your next witness," Judge Cameron said to Hamilton Burger.

"If the Court please," Burger said, "I don't know whether we wish to dismiss this case against John Kirby or not. I would prefer to have a short time to think it over. Could we take a recess until two o'clock this afternoon?"

"Any objection on the part of the defense?" Judge Cameron asked.

Mason said, "I would like to recall one witness for further cross-examination if there is going to be continuance."

"Who is the witness?" Judge Cameron asked.

"The handy man who assisted Dr. Babb."

"Very well," Judge Cameron ruled. "The Court will refrain temporarily from ruling on the motion for a recess. Will the witness come forward please?"

The handy man came forward, took the witness stand.

Mason said, "I wanted to ask you one more question in view of the testimony of the witness Norma Logan that a woman ran out the back door. I believe there is an automatic door-closing device on the back door of Dr. Babb's house?"

"Yes, sir."

"Directing your attention to the place where you live over the garage, as I remember it there is a similar closing device and spring lock on your door. Is that correct?"

"Yes, sir."

"Now, then," Mason said, "when you left your apartment over the garage attired only in a towel, and dashed down to Dr. Babb's house, you found the back door of Dr. Babb's house closed and locked?"

"Yes, sir."

"You were attired only in a towel?"

"Yes, sir."

"And you have testified that the officers ordered you to go back to your quarters and wait there?"

"Yes, sir."

"Which you did?"

"Yes, sir."

Mason smiled. "Now," he said, "kindly tell the Court how it happened that, if you went down there attired only in a bath towel, if there is an automatic door-closing device on your door which causes it to swing shut, and if there is a spring lock on that door, how were you able to get back into your apartment? Who opened the door for you? Where did you have your key?"

"And furthermore, Mr. Derby, I am going to ask you if, when the tape recording was played, and if, when you heard the voice of the dead man name the person who assaulted him, you didn't half get out of your chair with the intention of running from the courtroom because *you*, knowing Dr. Babb's voice better than anyone in the courtroom, heard him distinctly say that the name of his assailant was not John Kirby or Joan Kirby, but was Don Derby?"

Mason sat down.

Donald Derby started to say something; then found he had nothing to say. His face showed his utter consternation.

"And now," Mason went on with a little bow to the completely astounded district attorney, "I have no objection whatever to taking a recess until two o'clock this afternoon.

"In the meantime, I would suggest that, if you make a careful search of the clothes in the closet of Dr. Babb's house, you will find a suit of clothes in there which fits this witness but which wouldn't have fitted Dr. Babb. I think you will find a pair of shoes in there which wouldn't have fitted Dr. Babb. I think you will find socks, underwear and a shirt thrown into a corner of the closet or concealed in a bureau drawer.

"And by the time you have completed that investigation, you won't need to worry about pressing charges against Mrs. Joan Kirby, and in case you're still intending to file a complaint against me, charging me with receiving stolen property, you had better check with the public administrator, who will tell you that I told him I was holding subject to his orders a notebook which I was informed had been taken from the house of Dr. Phineas L. Babb."

"You gave that book to the public administrator?" Hamilton Burger exclaimed incredulously.

"I am holding it subject to his order," Mason said, "and since Dr. Babb left no heirs, the public administrator is for the moment the real custodian of all the property. Therefore, instead of *receiving* stolen property, I have *recovered* stolen property, and am holding it for its rightful owner.

"Since you have seen fit to team up the resources of your office with the ideas of Mr. Carver Kinsey, I thought both of you would be interested to learn that the public administrator has signified a willingness to co-operate with me."

Burger took a deep breath. "You wouldn't have gone near the public administrator if it hadn't been for a *subpoena duces tecum* having been served on you and your secretary."

"Then," Mason said, "if you were trying so desperately to trap me you should have refrained from serving the *subpoena duces tecum,* Mr. District Attorney."

Judge Cameron looked from one to the other, then looked to where Donald Derby was sitting in the witness chair. "Mr. Derby," Judge Cameron said, "can you answer that question propounded by counsel?"

"I don't have to," Derby said defiantly. "If they want to proceed against me, let them try and prove a case."

Judge Cameron turned to the district attorney. "Under the circumstances," he said, "the Court will take a recess until two o'clock this afternoon. I would suggest, Mr. Disrict Attorney, that you take immediate steps to see that this matter is investigated, and this time I trust that it will be *competently* investigated."

CHAPTER SEVENTEEN

Perry Mason and Della Street regarded the curly-headed six-year-old child who stood quietly beside the chair occupied by Mrs. Kirby in Mason's office.

"I thought you'd like to see the one for whom you did all of this work," she said.

"Hello, Ronnie," Mason said.

"Will you shake hands with Mr. Mason, Ronnie?"

Ronnie came forward, shook hands gravely with Perry Mason and bowed courteously to Della Street.

"Oh, you darling!" Della Street said, taking him suddenly into her arms.

When she released him, Ronnie backed away, apparently somewhat embarrassed by the effusive greeting, but still determined to be polite.

The door from the outer office opened, and John Kirby came in. "They told me you were in here and that I could come in," he said, "so here I am, checkbook in hand. Mason, can you ever forgive us for leaving you so much in the dark? We should have trusted you."

"It's always advisable to trust an attorney," Mason said dryly. "If you leave him in the dark he may kick something over."

"Well, Mr. Mason found his way through the dark all right," Mrs. Kirby said, "and when he turned on the light it certainly was a brilliant, dazzling light. The only thing is, I can't see why the police didn't know Dr. Babb said Don Derby instead of John Kirby."

"They were chasing too many red herrings," Mason said. "Motley Dunkirk could have given them the key clue. In view of the fact that the man in Dr. Babb's office made a dash for the back door shortly after you screamed, it would appear that this man, whoever he was, should have been *seen* leaving the place.

"Mrs. Dunkirk was watching the door for some seconds *after* the screams. She saw no one. She went to the telephone to call the police some seconds after the screams had ceased. Her husband saw you emerge from the door. If the man ran when you started to scream, he must have left the building at a time when Mrs. Dunkirk would have seen him.

"That brought up the interesting possibility that he hadn't ever left the house, that he had deliberately concealed himself, hoping that you would run out of the back door just as you did, so that he could then return to the safe and get the book he wanted before the police arrived.

"Derby naturally assumed that you were going to call the police. He knew that he had relatively only a few seconds within which to accomplish his mission. Instead of running out of the back door when you screamed, he dashed into Dr. Babb's bedroom, closed the door and hurriedly divested himself of his wearing apparel. He had the foresight to take the key to his apartment out of his pocket before he hung his suit on a hanger in Dr. Babb's closet, kicked off his shoes and socks, threw his underwear into a corner of the closet, and then dashed out to get the notebook that he wanted, a notebook with which he intended to make a fortune out of blackmail."

Della Street extended her hand to Ronnie. "Suppose we go look the offices over, Ronnie, while Mother and Daddy talk business with Mr. Mason? Do you want to?"

"Sure," Ronnie said smiling. "I like you. I'd like to go with you."

"Heartbreaker!" Della Street said as she gave him her hand and led him into the law library.

"Thanks to Paul Drake's excellent work in interviewing Steve Logan we can put together exactly what happened," Mason said.

"Steve Logan looked Dr. Babb up when the doctor started buying cars. For one thing, Steve was making a routine credit check, but over and beyond that Steve Logan knew that when his brother's second wife had been confined she had consulted Dr. Babb.

"Steve felt Dr. Babb was running some sort of a service and he wanted to know more about it. So he cultivated the handy man, talked with the doctor, and finally was ready to demand a showdown.

"The reason Dr. Babb didn't want to see Mrs. Kirby until late on that Monday night was that he already had an eleven o'clock appointment with Steve Logan. He wanted to try to find out just how much Logan was surmising. Also Dr. Babb intended to try to influence Steve Logan through Steve's niece, Norma, if he had to.

"So Steve Logan came to keep his appointment Monday night. Dr. Babb was talking with him, and when Mrs. Kirby came in several minutes before the time of her appointment, Dr. Babb was greatly concerned. He didn't want Steve Logan and Mrs. Kirby to meet. Norma had traced Ronnie to the Kirby's. Her uncle had only traced Ronnie to the doctor.

"Shortly before eleven o'clock, Dr. Babb had told Derby there would be nothing more for Derby to do that night and told Derby to go on up to his apartment. Derby pretended to do so, but instead of that had concealed himself in a closet in the inner office. He either knew something was in the wind and he had the idea of cutting himself in on a piece of cake, or else Steve Logan had bribed Derby to find out where Dr. Babb kept his records of babies whom he had placed in homes.

"Steve wouldn't admit that to Paul Drake, but I rather have an idea that was the main reason for Derby's interest.

"After Steve Logan had left via the back door so Mrs. Kirby wouldn't see him, Dr. Babb just happened to open the closet door, discovered Derby, and so knew what was going on.

"Derby, knowing then that he was in for it, tried to get the records he wanted by simply overpowering Dr. Babb and grabbing them. Derby knew that once Dr. Babb had discovered his duplicity his job had gone out the window.

"Derby slugged his employer, and hit him too hard. He had turned to the safe when he heard Mrs. Kirby's screams. Alarmed and anxious to frame an alibi as well as to get one more chance at finding the book he wanted, he dashed toward the back door, but instead of leaving by that door, he detoured into Dr. Babb's bedroom, undressed and, hurriedly removing the key to his apartment from his clothes, grabbed a towel, wrapped it around his middle and made one more swift search for the book he wanted, a book which Norma Logan had already taken while Derby was undressing.

"He only had a few seconds. Then satisfied he couldn't find the book, he dashed out the back door and plunged into the goldfish pool so he would be all wet when the officers arrived. He barely made it.

"The officers, falling for his scheme, sent him up to his apartment to dress. Once up there he turned on the shower, made the wet footprints on the linoleum which the officers subsequently checked, then dried himself and dressed."

"But how did you first surmise all this?" John Kirby asked.

Mason said, "The key clue was the fact that a neighbor's cat was playing with a dead goldfish. The cat had never been able to catch a goldfish until that day.

"I wondered how the cat had managed to be so successful that one time, and then later on I suddenly realized that the cat hadn't caught the goldfish at all. Someone had jumped into the goldfish pool; that had caused a sudden overflow of water from the pool, and the fish had been swept out of the pool on the crest of this wave of water.

"It had flopped around on the ground until it had died, and there the cat found it the next day."

Kirby looked worried. "With all of this information floating around now, can you still protect our secret?"

"I think I can," Mason said, "if you'll just stop lying to me. We've come this far all right. I have some tricks left up my sleeve that I can use if I have to. Steve Logan made a statement to Paul Drake, but he's consulted a lawyer now and isn't saying a word at the moment."

"How can we ever apologize to you for not taking you into our confidence in the first place?" Kirby asked contritely.

"That," Mason said, "can be taken care of only by check. And," he added grimly, "don't think for a minute it won't be on the bill."

THE CASE OF
THE LONG-LEGGED MODELS

FOREWORD

For some time I have been intending to dedicate a book with a suitable foreword to Michael Anthony Luongo, a quietly competent, exceedingly thorough expert in the field of legal medicine.

I first met Dr. Luongo several years ago when I attended a seminar on homicide investigation given under the auspices of Captain Frances G. Lee of New Hampshire in the Harvard Medical School.

At that time I was impressed with Dr. Luongo's complete intellectual honesty, his sincerity, his self-effacing devotion to his profession.

Dr. Luongo is still a comparatively young man, yet he is a senior member of the Department of Legal Medicine in the Harvard Medical School. For many years he has been a teacher in the Harvard seminars on homicide investigation. He is an associate pathologist for the Massachusetts State Police, and a forensic pathologist certified by the American Board of Pathology.

One of Dr. Luongo's outstanding traits is his desire for truth and his refusal to be stampeded into jumping to conclusions. It is a well-known fact in police circles that when officers are enthusiastically building up a case against some defendant, Dr. Luongo is quite likely to take the other side of the argument just to make certain the police don't get off on the wrong foot.

At such times, I am told, he presents the opposing case with a brilliance that would be a credit to any of the skilled defense attorneys who have national reputations.

One thing is certain: By the time Dr. Luongo has permitted himself to reach a conclusion, it is the result of logic, scientific reasoning, keen perception and honest appraisal of the facts.

For some years I have been watching Dr. Luongo progress in his chosen profession, earning the respect of those who work with him, and building a nationwide reputation for intellectual integrity and fairness.

Men like Dr. Luongo are pioneering a new field of forensic medicine where the expert witness, instead of being a partisan advocate for the side which has called him, appears as an absolutely impartial scientist with high ideals, representing neither the prosecution nor the defense but only Truth and Justice.

And so I dedicate this book to my friend:

MICHAEL ANTHONY LUONGO, M.D.

Erle Stanley Gardner

CHAPTER ONE

Perry Mason, feeling Della Street's eyes on him, looked up from his lawbook to regard the trim, efficient figure in the doorway.

"What is it, Della?"

"What is the status of an unmarried woman who is quote, keeping company, unquote, with an unmarried male?"

Mason cocked a quizzical eyebrow. "There is no *legal* status, Della. Why do you ask?"

"Because," she said, "a Miss Stephanie Falkner is waiting in the outer office. She says she has been quote keeping company unquote with Homer Garvin."

"Homer Horatio Garvin?" Mason asked. "Our client?"

"Not with Homer Garvin, Sr.," she said, "but with Homer Garvin, Jr."

"Oh yes, Junior," Mason said. "He is in the automobile business, I believe. And what seems to be Miss Falkner's trouble?"

"She wants to see you about a personal matter and hopes her Garvin contact will open the door to your interest in her problem."

"What's the problem, Della?"

"She inherited a gambling place at Las Vegas, Nevada. Her problem seems to concern that."

Mason slapped his hand on the desk. "Put a dollar on number twenty-six, Della."

Della Street made motions of spinning a roulette wheel, then of tossing an ivory ball into the perimeter of the wheel. She leaned forward as though watching the ball with complete fascination.

Mason also leaned forward, eyes intent on the same spot at which Della Street was looking.

Della suddenly straightened up with a smile. "I'm sorry, Chief, you lost. Number three came up."

She reached over to the corner of the desk and picked up Mason's imaginary dollar.

Mason made a grimace. "I'm a poor loser."

"What about Miss Falkner?" Della Street asked.

"Let's call Garvin, Sr. and find out the exact status of this woman. How old is she?"

"Twenty-three or twenty-four."

"Blonde or brunette?"

"Brunette."

"Curves?"

"Yes."

"Looks?"

"Yes."

"Let's talk with Garvin before we get our feet wet."

Della Street moved over to her secretarial desk, asked the switchboard operator for an outside line, dialed the number, waited a moment, then said, "Mr. Garvin, please. Tell him Miss Street is calling.... Yes.... Tell him Della Street.... He'll recognize the name.... Yes, Della Street.... I'm secretary to Mr. Perry Mason, the lawyer. Will you *please* put the call through to Mr. Garvin? It's rather important."

There was a moment of silence while Della Street listened to the party at the other end of the line.

"Well, where can I reach him on long distance?"

Again there was an interval of silence.

"I see," Della Street said. "Please tell him that I called, and ask him to call me whenever he gets in touch with you."

Della Street hung up the telephone. "That was Miss Eva Elliott, his very important secretary. She says that Mr. Garvin is out of town and she can't give me any number where he can be reached."

"Eva Elliott!" Mason said. "What's happened to Marie Arden? Oh, I know. She got married."

"About a year ago," Della Street reminded him. "You sent her an electric coffee urn, a waffle iron, and an electric stewpan as a wedding present."

"A year?" Perry Mason asked.

"I think so," Della Street said. "I can look up the bill on the wedding presents."

"No," Mason said, "never mind. Come to think of it, we haven't had any business dealings with Garvin since that new secretary came in."

"Perhaps you aren't even his attorney any more," Della Street said.

"Now wouldn't that be embarrassing," Mason told her. "I guess I'd better talk with Miss Falkner and see what she has to say. Bring her in, Della."

Della Street withdrew, returned a few moments later and said, "Miss Falkner, Mr. Mason."

Stephanie Falkner. a long-legged brunette with gray eyes, walked calmly across the office, gave Perry Mason a cool hand, and murmured, "This is a real pleasure, Mr. Mason."

The unhurried, well-timed precision of her motions indicated professional training.

"Please be seated," Mason said.

"Now before you tell me anything, Miss Falkner, please understand that I have done Mr. Garvin's legal business for years. There isn't a great deal of it because he's a shrewd businessman, and he keeps out of trouble. So he rarely has any occasion to consult an attorney. But I consider him one of my regular clients and, in addition to that, I am his friend."

"That's why I'm here," she said, leaning back in the overstuffed, comfortable chair and crossing her knees.

"Therefore," Mason went on, "before I could even consider handling any matter which you might want to consult with me about, I would want to take it up with Mr. Garvin, make a complete disclosure to him, and then make certain there would be no possibility of conflicting interests. Would that be satisfactory?"

"Not only would that be entirely satisfactory but I am here because you are Mr. Garvin's lawyer. I want you to get in touch with him."

"All right," Mason said, "with that understanding, go ahead."

She said, "I inherited an interest in a place at Las Vegas."

"What sort of place?"

"A motel and casino."

"Some of those are fabulously large and..."

"Not this one," she interrupted. "It's rather modest, but it has a nice location and I believe it is capable of expansion."

"How much of an interest did you inherit?" Mason asked.

"There's a tight little corporation. My father was president. I inherited forty per cent of the stock. The other sixty per cent is divided among four individuals."

"When did your father die?" Mason asked.

For a moment her face became wooden, then she said tonelessly, "Six months ago. He was murdered."

"Murdered!" Mason exclaimed.

"Yes," she said. "You may have read about it..."

"Good heavens!" Mason exclaimed. "Was your father Glenn Falkner?"

She nodded.

Mason frowned. "The murder has, I believe, never been solved."

"Murders don't solve themselves," she said, bitterly.

Mason said, "I don't want to ask you to discuss anything that is distasteful to you or..."

"Why not?" she asked. "Life is filled with distasteful tasks. I made up my mind to suppress my feelings before I came in."

"All right," Mason said, "go ahead. Tell me about it."

"My mother died when I was four. That was the beginning of a seven-year cycle of bad luck. At least that's what Dad thought. He was horribly superstitious. I guess all gamblers are.

"Dad had been well fixed. He was cleaned out in the depression. He was out of money and out of work. He took whatever he could get. He started work in a speak-easy restaurant. The man who owned the place died. Dad bought out the heirs. He had the place built up when Prohibition was repealed.

"However, there's no use boring you with the story of Dad's hard luck. He had plenty. He also had some good luck. Dad was a gambler. He wasn't a bootlegger but he was willing to operate a speak-easy restaurant. He was a plunger by nature, by inclination and by occupation.

"There are some things gamblers are good at, some things gamblers are bad at. Gamblers learn to control their emotions. Gamblers learn to be good losers. Gamblers become poker-faced and undemonstrative, and gamblers can hardly make a good home for girls, either teen-aged or younger. Gambling takes place at night.

"So I didn't see much of my father. He kept me in boarding schools, and every time it would be the same story. Dad wanted me to have the best, but the best boarding schools don't cater to the daughters of gamblers. So Dad would pose as an investor. The daughters of persons who gamble on the stock market are very, very eligible. The daughters of men who gamble across the table are very, very ineligible.

"It never occurred to Dad that it would be better and less cruel to put me in a school where I could sail under my true colors, where the standards weren't so strict. He wanted me to have the best, so I met a lot of social snobs. I would last for a year, then somehow or other it would come out that Dad was a gambler and I'd have to leave.

"I absorbed some of my father's philosophy. I became undemonstrative. I didn't dare form friendships because I didn't want to sail under false colors.

"So, as soon as I was old enough, I finished my education and went out on my own. I became a professional model. I made good money at it.

"Dad drifted into Las Vegas. In the course of time, he acquired some property, put a small motel on it, expanded as much as he could, and then wanted me to come and live with him.

"It was no go. He'd sleep until noon, get in about three o'clock in the morning. Property kept going up in value. A group of people got an option on some adjoining property. They wanted an option on Dad's property. The idea was they were going to move our small units off the property, consolidate the two, put up a huge, expensive hotel with swimming pool, gambling, night-club entertainment and all the rest.

"Dad was willing to sell out, but not for the price they offered. Dad learned he was dealing with a syndicate, found out what they had in mind, and held out for a good price.

"The syndicate was furious. When they couldn't handle things any other way, they began to make threats. Dad laughed at them.

"That's where Dad made his fatal mistake."

"The syndicate killed him?" Mason asked.

She shrugged her shoulders. Her face was expressionless. "I don't know. No one knows. Dad was murdered. That put fear into the hearts of the other stockholders. They wanted to sell for just about anything. From a business point of view, Dad's murder couldn't have been improved upon as far as the syndicate was concerned."

"Go on," Mason said, "what happened?"

"I inherited forty per cent of the stock. The remaining sixty per cent was owned by four people, each of whom had fifteen per cent. While I was still numbed by the news of Dad's death, a man got busy buying up stock. Three of the other stockholder's were only too willing to sell out for whatever the syndicate wanted to pay them.

"Before Dad's death I had met Homer Garvin, Jr. We were keeping company. I saw something of his father. Immediately after the murder, Junior's father asked me to tell him what I knew about my dad's death. I told him.

"Garvin, Sr. knew even before I did that the other stockholders would be willing to sell for just about anything they could get. He tried to beat this mysterious stock purchaser to it, but was too late. Mr. Garvin got to only one of the stockholders on time. He bought his holdings.

"That's the story to date. Mr. Garvin has fifteen per cent of the stock. I have forty per cent. Now a group calling itself a *new* syndicate wants to buy all the stock."

"What do you want?" Mason asked.

She said, "I want to sell. However, I'm not going to let them murder Dad and then take my stock for some nominal consideration. Dad gave his life. I'm going to see that these people don't benefit by his murder.

"Now then, a man whom I will refer to as Mr. X is here in town. I don't know whether he represents the so-called new syndicate or not. I know the man personally. I met him when I was doing model work in Las Vegas.

"All I know is that someone visited three of the other stockholders when they were frightened stiff, offered cash for their stock, paid the cash, had the certificates endorsed then faded from the picture.

"That was all I knew until a few days ago. Then Mr. X sent in the endorsed certificates to be registered in his name.

"Then he phoned me, told me he was interested in buying my holdings as well as those of Mr. Garvin, and asked me to meet him tomorrow night at eight-thirty.

"I'd like to get in touch with Mr. Garvin and see if he wants to pool our interests. I don't want to sell unless he sells at the same time. Otherwise they'd have control and freeze him out.

"Mr. Garvin is out of town. He left yesterday. I can't find out where he is. His secretary hates the ground I walk on. She wouldn't even give me the time of day."

"How about Junior?" Mason asked. "Can't he find out where his father is?"

"Junior is east attending a meeting."

Mason said, "Mr. Garvin might not like the idea of you dealing with this man. He may suggest that I have the personal contact."

"I know," she said. "But with me it's a matter of family pride. I'm going to carry on where Dad left off."

"You'd like to see your father's murderer brought to justice?"

"Naturally. That's the second reason I came to see you."

"Go on," Mason said.

"You know what happens with these gangster murders," she said. "The police huff and they puff, and they mouth great threats to all gangsters. They righteously resolve in great headlines that this city will never tolerate gangsterism, that this murder will be solved.

"They've never solved a gangster killing yet that I ever heard of—except once when they convicted the wrong man."

"So what do you want me to do?" Mason asked.

"After this stock sale goes through, I want to retain you to do something about my father's murder. I want you to get a private detective to start looking into the case, to unearth clues that can be turned over to the police.

"Then I want you to sort of chaperon the case, to act as liaison man between the private detective and the police, to use your brains to interpret the evidence."

Mason shook his head. "You don't need to retain an attorney to see that the police solve a murder case."

"What have they done so far?"

"I don't know."

"Neither does anyone else."

"Could this Mr. X have been implicated in the murder? He seems to have profited by it."

"Certainly he could."

"Then you should let Garvin conduct the negotiations."

"When Mr. Garvin got this stock," she said, "he thought he was buying something to give me as a wedding present. He thought I was to be his daughter-in-law. Now that situation has changed...radically."

"Where can I get in touch with you?" Mason asked.

"You can't," she said. "I'll be in touch with you tomorrow morning. Will ten o'clock be all right?"

Mason glanced at Della Street, said, "Very well. Ten tomorrow morning."

She included Della Street in her smile, said, "I take it I can get out through this exit door to the corridor?"

Mason nodded.

Stephanie Falkner glided to the door, opened it, turned, said in a calm, cool voice to Perry Mason, "Until tomorrow. And *please* reach Mr. Garvin in the meantime."

Mason turned to Della Street as the exit door closed behind the young woman. "I don't think I'd like to play poker with that young woman, Della."

"Well," she asked, "what do you think you *are* playing?"

"I'm damned if I know," Mason told her. "I'm going down and talk to that new secretary of Garvin's. Perhaps I can pry some information out of her."

"Chief, if she makes that sale, if Homer Garvin says it's all right, would you try to do what she asks and act as liaison man in this murder case?"

"I don't know, Della. It would depend. I don't think she needs to retain a lawyer for that."

"Chief, I'm frightened. The pit of my stomach is telling my brain to try to keep you out of this mess."

Mason smiled. "Well, I'll go see Eva Elliott. Perhaps I can learn something from her. We'll cross the other bridges when we come to them."

CHAPTER TWO

Eva Elliott, a tall, blue-eyed blonde with penciled eyebrows, was seated at her secretarial desk. She had moved this desk to the opposite side of the office from that occupied by her predecessor. It was in a corner which framed her blonde beauty against the dark mahogany paneling. Drapes on the windows had been carefully arranged so that the lighting made the corner seem to be part of a stage set.

As Mason opened the door the phone rang.

Eva Elliott flashed him a smile, picked up the telephone, held it close to her lips, and talked for a few minutes in a low voice. Mason was barely able to hear the words.

"No, I can't tell you when he'll be in. I'm sorry. Yes, he's out of town. May I take a message?

"Thank you. Good-bye."

She hung up the receiver, turned to face Mason.

"I'm Perry Mason," the lawyer explained.

Her eyes widened. "Oh, Mr. Mason, the lawyer!"

"That's right."

"Oh yes, Mr. Mason. I have a note for Mr. Garvin to get in touch with you just as soon as he comes in. Your secretary called, you know."

"Thanks," Mason said. "I see you've moved your desk."

"No, I haven't moved it, Mr. Mason."

"Marie had it over..."

"Oh," she said, "*I* moved it from where *Marie* had it. The light was all wrong."

"What do you hear from her?" Mason asked.

"She has been in twice," Eva Elliott said somewhat frigidly.

"What's her name now?" Mason asked. "I always think of her as Marie Arden."

"She married a man by the name of Lawton Barlow."

"Oh, yes," Mason said. "I remember. Tell me, Miss Elliott, where is Mr. Garvin?"

"He's away on a business trip."

"When did he leave?"

"I—He wasn't in the office all yesterday afternoon."

Mason regarded her with thoughtfully studious eyes. "Something unusual about it?" he asked.

"Nothing unusual at all, Mr. Mason. Mr. Garvin, as you know, makes a great many business trips. He has a lot of diversified investments and he has properties that are widely scattered."

"I see," Mason said. "I take it that you know I do all of his legal business?"

"I've heard him speak of you."

"I'd like very much to get in touch with him."

"Mr. Mason, may I ask if this is something which has to do with Miss Falkner?"

Mason's face became expressionless. "Why?" he asked.

"All right," she said. "I'll put my cards on the table. I—Mr. Mason, it's very important that we not be interrupted. Would you mind if I lock the office door? Then would you step into Mr. Garvin's private office with me? We won't be disturbed there."

"Certainly," Mason said.

She arose from behind the desk, walked with long-legged grace across to lock the door, then opened a door marked "Private." Mason followed her into Garvin's sumptuously furnished private office.

She turned to face Mason, her hands and hips pressing against the edge of Garvin's desk. Her pose was that of a movie star holding her chin up so as to present the best camera angle.

"Mr. Garvin is going to be furious with me if he knows I have said anything about it to you. However, you are a good judge of character and you don't need to have me point out that Stephanie Falkner is a very shrewd, very scheming, very selfish individual.

"Stephanie Falkner, as you probably know, was very friendly with Homer Garvin, Jr. Now Junior is carrying the torch for another girl, so Stephanie seems to be cultivating the father. Mr. Garvin is taking an interest in her. I don't know *exactly* what her game is now, but I *do* know that it is something intended to be for the advantage of Stephanie Falkner.

"I don't want to play cat's-paw for her and I know you don't. So please don't take any story she tells at face value.

"Now I'd be fired if either of the Garvins knew that I had told you any of this. But I have a loyalty to them that is not going to be stifled by the dictates of expediency.

"Now then, Mr. Mason, are you going to accept this confidence in the spirit in which it is offered, or are you going to tell Mr. Garvin what I said?"

Mason smiled at her. "I'm going to accept it in the spirit in which it was offered."

"Thank you," she said, and with a swift gesture moved out from the edge of the desk to extend both of her hands to Perry Mason. "I think you're *wonderful!*"

Mason left Garvin's office, and telephoned Della Street.

"Della," he said, "do we have the address of Marie Arden, who is now Mrs. Lawton Barlow?"

"I think so," she said. "Just a minute. You want her phone number or her address?"

"Her address," Mason said.

"Going calling?" she asked.

"Uh-huh."

Della Street gave him the address and said, "Give her my love."

"I will," Mason said.

He hailed a cab, gave the driver the address he had copied down in his notebook, then settled back against the cushions, narrowed his eyes in thoughtful concentration, and lit a cigarette.

At length the cab driver slowed, turned down a side street, and pulled in at the curb.

"This is the number," the cab driver said.

Mason asked him to wait and walked up to the house. Before he could ring the bell the door was flung open.

"Gosh! Mr. Mason, but I'm glad to see *you!*" Marie Barlow exclaimed.

"You're looking fine," Mason said.

She laughed. "Don't kid me. The baby's due in nine weeks. I'm an elephant. I'm letting all the housework go and the place is a mess. Forgive the appearances. Sit down in that chair. It's the most comfortable. Can I buy you a drink?"

"No, thanks," Mason said. "I'm trying to get some information about Homer Garvin."

"About what?"

"To find out where I can reach him for one thing."

"He's away?"

"Yes."

"Have you talked with Eva Elliott?"

"I've talked with her."

"And you didn't get what you wanted?"

"I got virtually nothing." Mason said.

Marie Barlow laughed. "Well, then you'll know the way *I* feel when I go up to the office. I tried it a couple of times and then decided to forget it."

"Did you see Homer?"

"Neither time. I know he was busy once. The other time, I don't think he was busy but she just wouldn't ring."

"What's the idea?"

"I don't know. Of course I was with Homer for twelve years. You get pretty close to a business and pretty close to a boss in that time. After Homer's wife died, he really went all to pieces for a while. He was beginning to get back on his feet when I decided to take the matrimonial plunge. Believe me, Mr. Mason, I put it off for over three months just because I was afraid the job of having to reorganize the office on top of everything else would have a bad effect on Homer Garvin.

"Actually he found out I was putting it off. Of course when I came out with that sparkler on my finger he wanted to know when the event was going to take place. One thing led to another and he began to suspect that I was holding off on his account. So he told me to go ahead and get married before he fired me. Gosh, Mr. Mason! He's a wonderful guy!"

"Was Stephanie Falkner in the picture while you were there?"

She shook her head. "She came later. Eva Elliott was Junior's light of love at the time but he was beginning to cool off. He goes overboard for long-legged models with poise and curves.

"I believe Stephanie was just coming into the picture. Junior got his dad to put Eva Elliott in the office at a whale of a salary. She's ornamental, unscrupulous and conceited. I'm a cat and I don't like her. Her sole secretarial training consists of a course in typing and in watching glamorous secretaries on the screen and on television."

"Then how can she handle Garvin's business?" Mason asked.

Marie said with feeling, "That's what *I'd* like to know."

Mason said, "I think Garvin may be in Las Vegas. Where would he be staying?"

She thought for a minute and said, "Nine chances out of ten it would be the Double-O Motel. That's one of the newer places. But surely Eva Elliott *must* know where he is."

"She said not."

Marie shook her head. "That was one thing about Homer. He would never be out of touch with the office; even when he didn't want anyone else to know where he was he'd be in touch with me all the time so that I could reach him in case anything of real importance broke at this end."

"Well, Eva Elliott seemed completely in the dark," Mason said. "Of course it may have been an act."

"May have been an act is right," Marie said laughing. "But don't let me prejudice you, Mr. Mason. You know how it is after a girl gets married. She gets a whole new life of her own. If anybody had ever told me that I'd let myself get out of touch with Mr. Garvin this way, I'd have said he was crazy. But—well, I offered to stay there for a while helping Eva Elliott take over, but she wanted to be on her own, so I left and thought she'd be telephoning for help within the first twenty-four hours. She didn't. I've never heard a squawk out of her.

"So I went in a few days later, said I was uptown shopping, and just dropped in to have a talk with Homer and see if I could help. The atmosphere was formal and icy. She said Mr. Garvin was in a conference.

"Then the next time I went in was about two months later. She was frigidly polite. I hung around there for ten or fifteen minutes chatting. She didn't ring Mr. Garvin's phone to tell him I was there and naturally I didn't want to make an issue of it. So I left. I felt that after all he could get in touch with me if he wanted me."

"Did he?" Mason asked.

She blinked her eyes rapidly, shook her head.

There was silence for several seconds. Suddenly she said. "Gosh! Mr. Mason, there must have been a hundred problems that came up on which they needed my help. I can understand why Eva Elliott didn't call me. She's a theatrical, stage-struck show horse, but for the life of me I can't understand why Homer didn't call up and ask me for information that I had at my finger tips. Eva Elliott would have had to dig that stuff out of the files, and even if she could have found it, she wouldn't have known what to do with it."

"You never called Garvin on the phone?"

"No, I didn't. I—Well, I think it was up to him to have called me. I'm not going to put myself in the position of having that new secretary of his turn me down more than twice."

"Well," Mason said, "give *me* a ring once in a while, and run and say hello when you get in circulation again. Della and I will both be glad to see you."

"I most certainly will, Mr. Mason. Gosh! It was good to see you. Just like old times!"

She stood in the doorway watching him wistfully as he walked down to the taxicab, and was still standing there as the cab made a U-turn and started back toward Mason's office.

CHAPTER THREE

"Find out anything?" Della Street asked, as Mason latch-keyed the door of his private office.

"Uh-huh. I don't know just how definite it is, but there's certainly something sticky in the atmosphere around Garvin's office. Just how long has it been since we've heard from him, Della?"

"I can look up the charge books, and..."

"Do that, will you?"

Della Street went out to the outer office and was back within a matter of minutes. "It's been something over a year."

"In other words, he hasn't been in touch with me since he employed his new secretary," Mason said.

"He probably hasn't had any reason to get in touch with you."

Mason pursed his lips. "A lot of changes seem to have taken place in Garvin coincidental with hiring that new secretary.

"All right, Della, we'll take a chance. It may be that he's having someone else do his legal work. Ring the Double-O Motel at Las Vegas and ask if Homer H. Garvin is there. Tell him that it's Perry Mason calling. Be sure they get the name of the person calling."

"Right away," Della promised. "I'll start Gertie working on the call."

Della Street walked out to the switchboard, gave her instructions to Gertie and came back to Mason's office.

The phone rang. Mason nodded to Della Street. She picked up the receiver, said, "Hello....Yes, he is....Just a moment, Mr. Garvin."

"On the line," she said.

Mason picked up his telephone. "Hello, Homer, this is Perry."

The voice that came over the line sounded guarded. "Oh yes. Hello, Perry."

"Are you where you can talk?" Mason asked.

"Only to a very limited extent," Garvin said.

Mason said, "I have had a visit from a tall brunette with gray eyes who has a forty per cent interest in a company in which you're interested. She's been approached by certain interests that have something to do with..."

"Hold it!" Garvin said. "Don't go any further. I'll call you back. Where can I reach you in...in an hour?"

"I'll wait here at the office," Mason said.

"Wait there for an hour, and I'll give you a ring. Good-bye."

Garvin hung up the telephone.

"Well," Mason said, "that gives me an hour to work on this brief. That'll be after five. Ask Gertie if she'd mind staying for..."

"Gertie has a date tonight," Della Street said. "I'll be glad to stay, Chief."

Mason said, "There's so much darn mystery about this....Oh well, Garvin probably was talking from a phone in the lobby or something of that sort. We'll hold everything until we hear from him."

Mason plunged back into the lawbooks, his powers of concentration such that the other matter was absolutely dismissed from his mind. He was to all intents and purposes oblivious of the passing time.

Della Street saw that the office closed at five o'clock, then went out and sat at the switchboard until twenty minutes past five when the Garvin call came through.

Mason picked up the receiver, heard the long distance operator say, "Your party is on the line," then heard the sound of coins being dropped in the coin box.

"What the thunder?" Mason said as soon as he heard Garvin's voice on the line. "Why didn't you call collect? You have an account here, you know."

"I know," Garvin said. "Can you tell me generally what this is all about, Perry? Be careful not to mention names."

"Well, the young woman that I spoke to you about has received an offer. A mysterious Mr. X, who may be a representative of interests having headquarters where you are now, is going to talk with her tomorrow.

"She felt that it might be well for you and her to take concerted action. Any separate action would simply result in leaving the other party out on the end of a limb."

"I see," Garvin said.

"I hope I didn't disturb you," Mason went on. "I had the devil of a time locating you."

"That's all right....How did you locate me, Perry?"

"Through Marie Arden—Marie Barlow."

"But I didn't tell *her* where I was."

"She knew where you would be staying in Las Vegas."

"Well, why the devil didn't you call my office? Why go get some secretary who hasn't been with me for a year and..."

"Hold everything!" Mason said. "I talked with your secretary, Eva Elliott. She couldn't give me any information."

"She what!"

"Couldn't tell me where you were."

"What the hell are you talking about?" Garvin said. "I've been in touch with Eva. I always keep in touch with the office."

"Well, perhaps your call came through after I talked with her," Mason said.

"I was down there about...oh, I don't know...around two-thirty or two-forty-five, and she said she couldn't tell me a thing."

"I talked with her at eleven-thirty and again at one-forty-five in the afternoon."

"Well, she may have felt I wasn't entitled to the information," Mason said. "Don't get worked up about it."

"Worked up about it!" Garvin exclaimed. "Why, I—Oh well, I guess you're right, Mason. Now look, can you get the name of the party with whom this woman is dealing?"

"So far she's referred to him as a mysterious Mr. X."

"I've an idea who this fellow is," Garvin said. "He's tried to keep under cover. He's dangerous.

"Now here's what I want you to do, Mason. I want that woman protected. Tell her that you're representing my fifteen per cent until I can get on the job personally. Find out who this party is who has been in touch with her, get his name and address, and the minute you get them, communicate them to me. Simply ring up the Double-O here and, if I'm not in, ask for Lucille. Give her the name and address."

"Just ask for Lucille?"

"That's right."

"Do you want to fix a price on your stock?" Mason asked.

"Not now," Garvin said. "I want to find out exactly how much money the other side is willing to pay. This person probably won't make any offer, but I want you to let him know that you're in the picture and that I'm in the picture. If he thinks he's dealing with only one person and that person is a woman, you can't tell what will happen.

"Now look, Mason, I have only a minute to talk. There's another party coming to meet me, and— Oh-oh, I'm sorry. That's all. Take care of yourself. Good-bye."

The phone clicked at the other end of the line.

CHAPTER FOUR

Stephanie Falkner showed up on the stroke of ten for her appointment.

Mason regarded her thoughtfully. "I've heard from Homer Garvin."

"Where is he?"

"He called me, Mason said, "from a pay station telephone. He was in Las Vegas when he telephoned. He wants me to act as his representative. He wants me to call on this party whom you refer to as Mr. X. He wants me to size the man up and feel him out. He doesn't want to put any price on his stock until after I have explored the situation."

"I see," she said thoughtfully.

"Is that all right with you?" Mason asked.

"It's not what I had in mind, but anything Mr. Garvin wants is all right with me."

"Would you care to tell me who Mr. X is and where I can find him?"

She hesitated a moment, said, "His name is George Casselman. I am to meet him at Apartment 211 at the Ambrose Apartments at eight-thirty tonight, and to save you the trouble of looking up the address, it's 948 Christine Drive.

"Please remember to tell Mr. Garvin for me that I will be guided by his wishes in the matter. I will keep my appointment but only for the purpose of holding the situation open.

"Thank you very much for having been so patient with me and for seeing me, Mr. Mason, and good morning."

She arose, smiled, turned her back abruptly and walked out.

Della Street said to Perry Mason, "I'd be willing to bet that her abrupt departure was because there's something she was afraid you were going to ask her if she waited.

"Let me go out and talk with Gertie. Gertie gets some wild ideas at times, but she notices things while clients are waiting in the outer office and there are times when Gertie is almost psychic."

Della Street left to talk with the receptionist, was back in a matter of seconds with a newspaper.

"No wonder!" she said.

"What?"

"Homer Garvin, Jr. returned home on an afternoon plane yesterday. He brought his bride with him. He was married in Chicago."

"Oh-oh," Mason said.

"Leave it to Gertie," Della Street said. "She's an incurable romanticist. She faithfully reads the society columns and all about the weddings. Would you like to look at a picture of Homer Garvin and his bride taken at the plane?"

Mason regarded the picture thoughtfully.

"A good-looking girl," he said at length. "Anything about her background?"

"She has been a publicity model at one of the Las Vegas resorts," Della Street said. "Young Garvin met her there a couple of months ago."

"He works fast," Mason said.

"Or she does," Della Street pointed out.

"Well," Mason said, "that can account for a lot of things. Ring up the Double-O Motel in Las Vegas, Della. See if you can get Homer Garvin. If you can't, ask for Lucille and relay the message that the name Mr. Garvin wanted is that of George Casselman, that the address is 948 Christine Drive in the Ambrose Apartments, Apartment 211."

Della Street nodded, left the office and was back in ten minutes.

"I couldn't get him, Chief, but I did talk with Lucille and left the message with her."

"Did you get her last name or find out anything about her?"

"From the way she answered the phone I have a idea she's the manager of the motel. I simply asked for Lucille and the woman who had answered said that she was Lucille. I told her my name and she asked if I had a message for Mr. Garvin. So I gave her Casselman's name and address."

Mason lit a cigarette and frowned thoughtfully.

"So what do you do, if anything?" Della Street asked.

Mason said, "Under the circumstances, I think I am free to call on Mr. Casselman this evening before Stephanie Falkner gets there. I suppose further that a wedding present is in order for Homer Garvin, Jr. You had better organize yourself into a shopping department, Della ... something around fifty dollars."

"Will Casselman talk with you?" Della Street asked.

"I don't know," Mason said, "but if he's in, *I'll* talk with *him!*"

CHAPTER FIVE

Promptly at eight o'clock Mason parked his car across the street from the Ambrose Apartments and walked over to the entrance.

To the right of the door was a long row of push buttons. To the right of each push button was a name and an apartment number, and to the right of the card was the end of an old-fashioned speaking tube.

Apartment 211 had the name Casselman opposite it.

Mason pressed the call button.

Almost immediately there was an answer. "Who is it?"

"Mr. Mason."

"What do you want?"

"I want to see you."

"What about?"

"About some stock."

A moment later the buzzer which released the electric catch on the front door sounded.

Mason pushed the front door open, climbed a flight of stairs to the second floor, walked down a corridor to where a figure was standing in a lighted doorway.

"You're Mason?" the man asked.

"Yes. Casselman?"

"That's right."

"I wanted to talk with you about some stock. I'm representing Homer Garvin. Does the name mean anything to you?"

The man who had been silhouetted in the lighted doorway suddenly stepped back. The light from the inside illuminated sharp, thin features. The man was slender, alert and about thirty-five years of age. He was smiling broadly.

"Yes, yes, Mr. Mason. It means a good deal to me. Won't you come in, *please?*"

Casselman flashed a glance at a wrist watch. "May I ask how you located me here?"

Mason said curtly, "I'm a lawyer," as though that explained everything.

"Oh yes, I see. The question still remains that—Good heavens! You aren't *Perry* Mason?"

"That's right."

"Well, well! This is indeed a pleasure."

Casselman extended his hand. Mason shook hands. Casselman's fingers were wiry and strong.

"Sit down, Mr. Mason. Sit down. Can I get you a drink?"

"No, thanks," Mason said, "I haven't much time."

Again Casselman looked at his watch. "I'm rather pressed for time myself, Counselor. I have another appointment. Shall we get down to business?"

Mason nodded, sat down and took a cigarette from his case.

"I take it you're familiar with the outstanding stock in the corporation?"

"That's right.

"I control forty-five per cent of the stock. Your client has fifteen per cent and Stephanie Falkner has forty per cent."

"Uh-huh," Mason said, exhaling a cloud of cigarette smoke, crossing his long legs, and settling back in the chair comfortably.

"These Nevada corporations are different from some of the others," Casselman said. "Gambling is legalized in Nevada, and of course that makes a difference."

"Naturally," Mason said.

"Gambling attracts gamblers," Casselman said.

"Exactly," Mason observed.

"And since gambling is not legalized in other states, the activities of gamblers are quite frequently associated with illegalities."

"Naturally."

"That is something many people don't appreciate in dealing with situations of this sort."

"I appreciate it."

"Let's get down to brass tacks. What will Garvin take for his stock?"

"What will you give?"

"I am prepared to make one final definite offer."

"What is it?"

"I'll give thirty thousand dollars for that fifteen per cent of the stock."

"It's worth more."

"That's a matter of opinion. You are entitled to yours, I am entitled to mine. It's worth thirty thousand to me only because it would represent the controlling interest."

"I'll pass the offer on to my client, but I don't think it's going to be satisfactory."

"Well, that's as high as we'll go and I can point out one other thing to you, Mr. Mason."

"What?"

"If by any chance we should get control of the corporation, that offer will of course be withdrawn. Once we get control we'll buy out Garvin at our own price."

"I don't think so," Mason said.

"Why not?"

"Because I don't think you realize how much trouble a minority stockholder can be in a corporation of this nature."

"Perhaps you don't realize the type of person you'd be dealing with," Casselman said.

"That's entirely possible," Mason told him. "Perhaps the others don't realize the type of person they'd be dealing with."

Casselman said, "Now, look, Mason, let's keep this on a business basis. Let's not get personal. You might get hurt."

Mason said, "I'm not a damned bit afraid of getting hurt. I don't frighten easily. Glenn Falkner was murdered. You went out and bought up three blocks of stock because the stockholders were frightened. Garvin isn't frightened and I'm not frightened."

"I don't want any trouble, Mason," Casselman said at length.

"Then don't ask for it," Mason told him. "For your information, Garvin won't sell you his stock so you can get control of the corporation and then buy out the Falkner stock at your own price. We'll offer you Garvin's holdings as a part of a unit transaction with Stephanie Falkner."

Casselman said suddenly, "All right. I'll give her the same price. If you can..."

Abruptly the telephone rang. Casselman jumped nervously, said, "Excuse me a moment." He walked into another room, picked up the telephone, and Mason heard him say, "Hello.... You can't.... Not now!" There was a moment's silence, then Casselman said something in a low voice which Mason could not hear. After that he said, "Okay, give me two minutes," and hung up without saying good-bye.

Casselman returned to the room, plainly uneasy and impatient, and said, "Mr. Mason, I'm going to have to ask you to excuse me. I have an appointment at eight-thirty, and a very important matter has come up which I have to dispose of between now and then."

"Very well," Mason said, moving toward the door. "How about giving me your telephone number?"

"I'm sorry. It's an unlisted number."

Mason stood with his hand on the knob, waiting.

Casselman said hurriedly, "All right, it's Belding 6-9754."

"Thank you," Mason said, and moved out into the corridor. Casselman made no move to shake hands but hurriedly pulled the door closed. Mason noticed the door did not have a spring lock.

Mason left the apartment house, then sat in his car waiting. After a few minutes he saw Homer Garvin, Sr. drive up, jump from his car and hurry to the door of the apartment house.

Mason started to press his horn button, then something in Garvin's manner caused him to change his mind. He sat watching, an interested spectator.

Garvin opened the outer door of the apartment house with a key and went in.

Three or four minutes later Garvin came back out, got in his car and had some trouble extricating himself from his parking place because of another car which had moved in ahead of him.

Mason pressed the button on his horn twice but Garvin, wrestling with the steering wheel, seemed too preoccupied to hear Mason's signal.

It was just as Garvin moved out of the parking place that Stephanie Falkner drove up. She evidently saw Garvin as he drove out ahead of her car but did nothing to attract his attention. She did not see Mason but parked her car and went at once to the door of the apartment house.

Just as she was on the point of pressing Casselman's bell, the door opened and a rather portly woman in her late forties emerged, then obligingly paused to hold the door open for Stephanie.

During the interval Mason had been waiting, only Homer Garvin and Stephanie Falkner had passed through the front door of the apartment house, and except for Garvin, the portly woman had been the only one to leave.

Mason waited a minute or two longer, then started his car and slowly circled the block.

It was quite dark. The only street illumination came from the lights at the corner. As Mason reached the front of the house again, he saw that Stephanie Falkner's car was still parked in the place where she had left it.

The fourth time, Mason was halfway around when he saw the figure of a woman running down the service stairs at the back of the apartment house.

The lawyer slowed his car.

The woman ran to the alley, emerged on the lighted street and reluctantly slowed her pace to a walk.

Mason brought his car to a stop "Want a ride, Miss Falkner?"

She jumped back with a short half-scream, then caught herself.

"Oh, you startled me!"

"I'm sorry. I didn't mean to. Everything all right?"

"Yes, of course."

"Get in. I'll drive you to your car. Did you get an offer?"

"Yes."

"How much?"

"Thirty thousand. He said it was all he could pay."

"Cash?"

"Yes. How long have *you* been out here?"

"Oh, for a while."

"What are you doing?"

"I saw Casselman."

"*You* did?"

"Uh-huh."

"He didn't say anything about it. Did he make you an offer?"

"Yes."

"How much?"

"I'd prefer to have Homer Garvin tell you about that. As a lawyer I'm in a position to get information but not to give out any."

"I see," she said.

"Did you accept his offer?" Mason asked, slowing his car to a crawl.

"Certainly not. I told you I wouldn't. I told him I'd call back and let him know."

"Get along all right?" Mason asked.

"Certainly."

"Any threats?"

"Of course not."

"Any trouble?"

"Certainly not."

"Then why didn't you come out the front door?"

She caught her breath sharply. "Where were you?"

"Out back."

She said, "I—He was talking over the telephone, and . . . well, I wanted to hear what he was saying. I sneaked out into the kitchen. It sounded as though the conversation might go on for a long time, then all of a sudden he hung up. I was trapped. He went back to the front room and, of course, saw I wasn't there. So I sneaked out the back door and ran down the steps. In that way he won't know I was listening. Later on I'll tell him I got tired waiting and went out the front door while he was talking."

"To whom was he talking?" Mason asked.

"I don't know. The conversation wasn't long enough for me to find out."

Mason regarded her sharply. "You had *some* compelling reason for trying to listen in on that conversation?"

She looked at him for a moment, then said, "Yes. I heard him use the name Garvin, and at first I thought it was ... well, it might have been Homer Garvin calling."

"Was it?"

"No. Apparently it was a woman."

"You don't know who this person was?"

"No."

"Any idea?"

"It could have been Junior's new wife. He was married in Chicago."

"Could you gather from his tone whether it was a business deal or perhaps something involving a romantic attachment?"

"No."

"Yet you heard some of the conversation?"

"Not enough to do any good."

"You could hear the tone of his voice?"

"Yes."

"And couldn't tell anything from that what the conversation was about?"

"No."

Mason regarded her thoughtfully.

"Well, here's my car," she said. "I'm living at the Lodestar Apartments. You can call me there after you get in touch with Mr. Garvin."

There was a definite note of dismissal in her voice. She jumped out of Mason's car, slid in behind the wheel of her car, turned the ignition key. The motor throbbed to life.

"I probably don't sound like it," she said, "but I'm very grateful to you." The car eased away from the curb.

Mason drove back to his office.

"Did you see Casselman?" Della Street asked.

Mason nodded.

"How is he? Dangerous?"

"If you had your back turned."

She said, "Homer Garvin phoned to say he'd be up here in about half an hour. He said he had just got in from Las Vegas."

"When did he phone, Della?"

"Five minutes ago."

Mason said, "Don't let me forget to congratulate him on his new daughter-in-law, Della."

Della Street laughed. "There was a certain urgency about his voice," Della Street said. "I think perhaps he has other matters on his mind."

They worked on letters until there was a tap at the door of Mason's office. Della Street opened the door. Homer Garvin who, Mason's records showed, was fifty-one years old yet who looked no older than forty, said, "Hello, Della," surveyed her with pin-pointed gray eyes and patted her shoulder. Then he came across to shake hands with Mason, looked at his watch and said, "We're going to have to work fast, Perry. Have you seen Casselman?"

"Yes."

"What did he offer?"

"Thirty thousand dollars for the fifteen per cent interest you own."

"What did he offer Stephanie?"

"Thirty thousand dollars for the forty per cent interest."

"That can't be right, Mason! He surely wouldn't offer the same price for fifteen per cent as for forty per cent."

"Both represent a controlling interest."

"Why...that just isn't right. He—Let's go see Stephanie. I have something to tell her. What did you think of Casselman, Mason?"

"He's a cold-blooded crook, but I think he'd wilt in a face-to-face fight."

Garvin said, "From information I have now acquired, I have every reason to believe he's the man who murdered Glenn Falkner, Stephanie's father."

"Evidence you can take to the police?" Mason asked sharply.

"I think so, Perry. A few hours before his death, Glenn Falkner told a friend of his he had a business matter to discuss with Casselman. I have finally managed to track down the car Casselman was driving at the time of Glenn Falkner's death. Casselman sold it within three days after the murder. He traded it in on a new car.

"Now you'll remember Glenn Falkner was riding in a car with somebody at the time he was murdered. The car was seen to come down the street at pretty good speed. The door on the right-hand side was flung open, and a body was pushed out of the car. It hung half in and half out of the car for about half a block, then hit the pavement with a thud and rolled over and over. The car sped away.

"Horrified pedestrians ran up to the man and found that he was dead as a mackerel. He had been shot once in the head, twice through the body. One of the bullets was still in the body.

"The car Casselman was driving at that time, or at least the car that he owned at that time, had been pretty carefully cleaned up, but by looking with a magnifying glass I could still find several small spots down between the opening of the door and the side of the front seat. There is also a dent in the metal of the door frame which in all probability was made by a bullet.

"I got a detective over there in Las Vegas to make some tests for me. He's a pretty good detective and understands something about scientific investigation. There's a test for blood they can make with luminol, that brings out blood spots and causes them to glow in the dark. He treated this car with luminol and got a very strong blood reaction from folds in the leather upholstery in the front seat, from a spot down underneath the seat cushion, and from the spots I had found between the side of the seat and the door."

"Of course," Mason said, "that's very interesting. It is a clue. It's what we might call a suspicious circumstance. However, it's not proof."

"I know. When I confront Casselman with that proof he's going to start explaining. *Then* I may get proof."

"When *you* confront him with it?" Mason said.

"That's right."

"You'd better let the police do that."

Garvin flipped back the lapel of his coat. "I'm not afraid of the cheap crook. I'd shoot the guy like a dog if he so much as lifted a finger against us."

Mason said sharply, "Do you have a license to carry that?"

"Don't be silly," Garvin said. " I have something better than a license. I'm a deputy sheriff. I'm supposed to carry arms. I have several revolvers and I'm not foolish enough ever to be without one. If anybody ever tries to hold me up, he's going to have his hands full."

Mason regarded Garvin thoughtfully. "Where do you keep those other guns?"

"Various places. Junior has one, there's always one in my safe. I own a sporting-goods store among my other investments. I *always* carry a gun. I'm never without one, day or night.

"It makes me sick to open the papers and read about thugs beating their victims to death, old women being robbed and clubbed.

"Someday one of those guys will tackle me and then there will be fireworks. Kill a few of those people off and it will be a good thing all around.

"The way it is now, the honest citizen is disarmed by law. The crook carries a gun as a matter of habit. Arm the law-abiding citizens, kill off some of these crooks and we'd have a lot better law enforcement."

Mason shook his head. "Police who have studied the situation don't agree with you, Homer."

"Sure," Garvin said, "but their way isn't working out so well, either."

Della Street caught Perry Mason's eye.

Mason got her signal, turned to Homer Garvin.

"By the way," he said, "I see you're to be congratulated on a new daughter-in-law."

Garvin sighed. "Yes," he said. "I haven't seen her yet. I talked with her on the telephone and gave the couple my blessing."

"She's a nice-looking girl," Della Street said.

"Leave it to Junior! He picks them nice-looking.... The trouble with him is that he's restless, no emotional stability. A year or so ago it was all Eva Elliott. He wanted to marry her. Then that blew up. I felt sorry for Eva and gave her a job in the office when Marie left. By that time, Junior was rushing Stephanie Falkner.

"You may not know it but that's how I became interested in this Falkner corporation. Six months ago I thought that Stephanie Falkner was going to be one of the family—and, hang it, I wish she had been. There's a fine, level-headed girl! She could have been a balance wheel for Junior.

"Well, I hope he settles down now. That was what he needed—to get married and settle down. He's too darned impulsive.

"Mason, what the devil *are* we going to do about this situation with Casselman?"

"Let's go have a talk with Stephanie Falkner," Mason said.

"Do you suppose it's too late?" Garvin asked.

"We can find out," Mason told him. "Della, ring the Lodestar Apartments, and see if Stephanie can talk with me. You don't need to tell her that Mr. Garvin is with me. Simply tell her that we'd like to come over."

"You want me along?" Della Street asked.

Mason nodded. "There might be a stock-pooling agreement to write up."

Della Street went out to put through the telephone call.

"Gosh! What a pleasure it is to have a real, dependable secretary," Garvin said. "I can't begin to tell you how I miss Marie Arden."

"Marie Barlow now," Mason said.

Garvin frowned. "There should be a law against secretaries committing matrimony," he said. "Hang it, Mason! Do you know she's never been in to see me since she got married? I just can't understand it."

"What makes you think she hasn't been in to see you?" Mason asked.

"She hasn't, that's all. I've never heard a word from her, not even a telephone call."

Mason said, "For your information, Homer, she was in twice to see you. She got such a cold shoulder from your new secretary that she made up her mind she wasn't wanted."

"You mean Eva Elliott kept *her* from coming in to see me?" Garvin asked incredulously.

"That's right. She told her you were busy. She didn't even offer to ring your telephone."

"Why...why—Well, that makes me feel a lot better."

"Better?" Mason asked.

"Yes," Garvin said. "I fired Eva Elliott tonight. I got back and asked her what the devil she meant by not telling you where I was. She told me that I'd told her not to tell anyone and that she was simply following instructions.

"That girl is completely show crazy. She wants to dramatize everything she does in terms of what some actress has done on film somewhere. Believe me, Mason, she makes it a point to go to every movie she can find that features a secretary. She tunes in on every television program where there is a secretary playing a part. She studies the Hollywood concept of secretarial efficiency and then goes into the office and tries to act that part. It's a case of a poor actress trying to take the part of a good actress who in turn is trying to follow the concept of a Hollywood director as to what a good secretary should be like. I got good and tired of it. I..."

Della Street returned from the switchboard, said, "Miss Falkner says to come right over."

"Come on," Mason said, "let's go."

CHAPTER SIX

Stephanie Falkner opened the door, said, "Hello, Mr. Mason. Hello, Miss Street...*Homer!*"

Garvin said, "I tagged along, Stephanie."

She gave him both of her hands. "Congratulations! Have you seen her?"

"Not yet," Garvin said. "I'm just back from Las Vegas and I've been busy."

"You'll love her, Homer. I was in Las Vegas when she was a hostess and prop bathing girl at one of the pools. She's a darling....Come on in! I'll rustle up some chairs. I was just getting ready to call it a day."

She ushered them into the simple apartment, said, "Can I buy you folks a drink?"

"No, thanks," Garvin said. "We're here on business."

"Oh." Her face fell.

Garvin said, "I'm going to give it to you straight from the shoulder, Stephanie. It's about your father. I'm going to put it right on the line."

"Go ahead."

"I've been in Las Vegas, checking some angles I have up there. I have some sources of information."

"Go on."

He said, "I haven't anything that I can go to the authorities with as yet, but George Casselman was the man who killed your father."

"I see," she said, her face suddenly wooden, and she added, "I wish I'd known that a little earlier this evening."

"All right," Garvin said, "let's put it on a business basis. I picked up stock in that motel corporation to help you when I thought you were going to be one of the family.

"It isn't efficient for that little motel to continue to operate as it's now operating. The property has become too valuable. Taxes are too high. Yet you can't do anything with that property as it is. There's no chance of getting the property on the north, and the property on the south is controlled by this syndicate that wants to get the motel property in order to put up a reasonably big building which can pay off. It's time for you to sell out."

"Yes," she said, "I think it's time for me to sell out and pull up my roots here."

Garvin said, "I think Casselman is a chiseler. I doubt if he actually represents the syndicate. I think he's an independent operator, but of course the syndicate would be glad to do business with him if he had the property.

"It's my plan to go direct to the syndicate and find out what their best offer is. In order to do that I want to be in a position to close out the deal. Now then tell me, what do you actually want for your stock?"

"I was offered thirty thousand dollars by Casselman," she said. "I'll take it if I can't do better, but I don't think that's enough."

"What would you take and be satisfied?"

"Anything over thirty thousand."

"All right," Garvin said, "give me a ten-day option to sell your stock at eighty thousand dollars, and if I can get anything above that, we'll split the profits. You take half and I take half. I'll put my stock in at the same time, at the same price ratio, and we'll make a deal with the syndicate. We'll split anything above that figure fifty-fifty."

"Fair enough," she said. "Only you can't get eighty thousand for my stock."

"You have a typewriter here, Stephanie?"

She nodded.

"Then, let's draw up a document. Mason, you can dictate it and we'll sign it right now."

"I can do it at my office in the morning," Mason said.

"I'd like to get the thing cleaned up tonight."

"All right," Mason told him and motioned to Della Street.

Stephanie Falkner found stationery and carbon paper. Della Street sat at the typewriter and typed as Mason dictated a short form of agreement.

When he had finished, she ratcheted the paper out of the typewriter, handed one copy to Mason, one to Stephanie Falkner, one to Garvin.

"Okay?" Garvin asked Stephanie after he had read it.

"Okay," she said.

"Let's sign."

They signed the agreement.

"Well," Mason said, "I guess that covers everything we can do tonight. You'll be in touch with me in the morning, Homer?"

"Probably," Garvin said.

"And how about you, Miss Falkner? I can reach you here?"

"If anything turns up, yes."

Garvin hesitated.

Della Street flashed Mason a glance, said, "Well, I'm a working girl. I should be getting home."

"I'll drive you home," Mason said.

Garvin hesitated a moment, then said to Stephanie Falkner, "Now I'll take that drink, Stephanie."

Stephanie Falkner saw them to the door, stood watching them down the corridor; then, as they entered the elevator, closed the door gently.

"Now," Mason said, "why should she keep insisting Casselman only offered her thirty thousand dollars for forty per cent of the stock when he offered me that same amount for fifteen per cent of the stock, and offered to buy it all at the same rate?"

"Any ideas?" Della Street asked.

"No," Mason said, "but I'm certain that if it hadn't been for that phone call, he was going to make me a firm offer of eighty thousand for her stock and thirty thousand for Garvin's stock."

"Then the phone call caused him to change his mind?"

"Something did," Mason said.

"Someone who saw him?"

"No one entered the apartment house except—Oh well, let's let things wait until tomorrow. We may know a lot more when we see Garvin again."

CHAPTER SEVEN

Mason swung his car into the parking lot the next morning, nodded to the attendant, pulled into his regular parking stall, walked over to the sidewalk, and was just turning into the foyer of the building where he had his office, when he became conscious of Della Street at his side.

"Hi, Chief," she said in a low voice. "Thought I'd catch you before you'd get to the office. Want to keep walking?"

Mason glanced at her in surprise. "What's wrong, Della?"

"Perhaps a lot."

"Shall we go back to the car?"

"No, let's just walk."

They fell into step, moving along in a stream of early morning pedestrian traffic which was pounding its way along the sidewalk.

"What gives?" Mason asked.

Della Street said, "Lt. Tragg was in the office looking for you. I wouldn't doubt but what he's waiting in the foyer of the building to collar you as soon as you show up. I tried to ring you at your apartment, but you'd left."

"What does Tragg want?" Mason asked.

She said, "George Casselman has become a corpse. A maid opened the door of his apartment and found him dead on the floor, a big bullet hole in the front of his chest."

"When?" Mason asked.

"Apparently about eight o'clock this morning. The news just came over the radio as I was..."

"No, no," Mason said, "when was the time of death?"

"No information on that as yet."

"Why does Tragg want to see *me?*"

"I'm just putting two and two together and making eight."

"Good girl!" Mason said. "I have one very important thing to do. Let's catch a cab and see if we can find out something important before we have to answer a lot of questions."

Mason swung over to the curb, waited impatiently as the long line of morning traffic went streaming past.

Finally he caught a vacant cab and said, "Lodestar Apartments."

Della Street glanced at him. "We don't telephone first?"

Mason shook his head.

"Surely, Chief, you don't think...?"

"Exactly," Mason said. "I'm not doing any thinking yet. I want information, then I'll start thinking.

"For your confidential, private, and exclusive information, Homer Garvin called on George Casselman around eight-fifteen yesterday evening. He didn't see fit to tell me about that visit, so I said nothing to anyone.

"Also, for your confidential information and as food for thought, if when Stephanie Falkner called on Casselman at eight-thirty last night she found she was interviewing a corpse, and had subsequently been asked what she had been offered for her stock, she'd have had to make up a fictitious figure.

"That *might* account for the discrepancy between what Casselman offered me for Garvin's stock and what she said she had been offered for hers."

"Oh-oh!" Della Street exclaimed. "I never thought of it in that light, Chief. I guess I'm a little dumb this morning."

"Nothing dumb about the way you stood down there on the sidewalk waiting to catch me as I left the parking lot. You did a smooth job. I didn't pick you out. That's an art, blending with a crowd."

She laughed. "Actually I was in the shoeshine stand. I had the shine boy shine my shoes, and then had him give me another shine. I was on my third shine when you showed up. I felt that I'd be conspicuous if I stood around on the sidewalk, and I didn't know whether Tragg had any men on the job or not."

"Good girl!" Mason said.

They were silent until the driver drew up in front of the Lodestar Apartments.

"Better wait," Mason told him. "We'll be back within a few minutes and then we're going other places."

"Okay, I'll hold it," the driver said.

Mason and Della Street entered the apartment house. Mason nodded to the man at the desk and walked across to the elevators so casually that no one asked him where he was going.

They took the elevator to the third floor, walked down to Stephanie Falkner's apartment.

Mason tapped gently on the door.

Stephanie Falkner called through the closed door. "Who is it?"

"Mr. Mason."

"Are you alone?"

"Miss Street's with me."

The bolt clicked on the door. Stephanie Falkner, dressed in a housecoat and slippers, said, "Everything's in a mess. I'm a slow starter in the mornings. I've just had breakfast and haven't cleaned up. Can I fix you some coffee?"

"No, thanks," Mason said. "We just wanted to get a little information."

"I presume it's rather important to bring you out at this time in the morning."

"It could be," Mason said.

"All right, what's the information?"

"When we left here last night, Homer Garvin was here?"

She nodded.

"How long did he stay here?"

For a moment her face broke into an expression of anger. "None of your damn business!" she flared.

Mason said, "I'm sorry. We're making it our business. For your information, George Casselman turned up very, very dead in his apartment this morning."

Her gray eyes surveyed Mason's face, then shifted to Della Street's face. "Sit down," she said.

The folding bed had not as yet been made, and she seated herself on the edge of the bed.

Mason looked at the rumpled pillows on the bed, suddenly jumped to his feet, walked to the bed, jerked one of the pillows aside, and disclosed a snub-nosed revolver.

"What's this?"

"What do you think it is? A toothbrush?"

Mason stood looking down at the revolver.

"Unless I'm greatly mistaken," he said, "this is very similar to the revolver which Homer Garvin had in his shoulder holster last night."

She said nothing.

Mason leaned over and picked up the revolver.

"In case you want to know," she said after a moment, "Homer was concerned about my personal safety. He was going to try to do something with the syndicate and—well, you know what the syndicate did once before."

"So he left his gun here with you for your protection?"

"That's right."

Mason looked the weapon over, smelled the barrel, frowned, swung open the cylinder, and said, "You seem to have one empty cartridge in the gun, Miss Falkner."

"*I* don't have any empty cartridges in any gun," she said. "It is not *my* gun. I tell you Mr. Garvin left it here last night for my protection. I didn't want it and I don't want it."

"But you did put it under your pillow?"

"Where would *you* put it?" she asked sarcastically.

Mason abruptly arose from his chair, put the gun back under the pillow where he had found it.

"Now what?" she asked.

Mason said, "I am not representing you. I am not your attorney. I am not a police officer, and I have no right to question you, but I want to know if you went out last night after we left you."

She said, "I haven't been out of this apartment since the last time you saw me."

Mason nodded to Della Street.

"All right," Stephanie said, "George Casselman has been murdered. He's the man who killed my father. What do you expect me to do? Break down and have hysterics?

"Look," she went on, "You're a lawyer. You're clever. You know the ropes. You're representing Homer Garvin. You aren't representing me. You'd do anything in your power to save your client. You'd throw me to the wolves so Homer Garvin could get away."

"That's rather an inaccurate description of my attitude," Mason said, "but we'll let it go at that. Come on, Della."

Mason walked out.

"Now where?" Della Street asked as the door of the apartment closed behind them.

"Now," Mason said, "we go hunt up Homer Garvin and we hunt him up fast. We hope we get there before the police do."

"Do they have any line on him?" Della Street asked.

"They will if Stephanie Falkner tells them about the gun."

"And will she tell them about the gun?"

"That," Mason said, "is something on which I don't care to speculate."

"Do you think she will?"

"She will if she's smart. Think what it would mean *if* that should turn out to be the murder weapon."

"Shouldn't you have taken it?"

Mason held the elevator door open for Della Street. "Not on your life," he said. "It's too hot for me to handle."

They went down in the elevator, crossed the lobby, entered the cab, and Mason gave the address of Homer Garvin's office.

"Think he'll be there?" Della Street asked.

"He'll either be there or we'll find out where we can locate him," Mason said. "This time we won't take any back talk from a blonde secretary who's trying to make a production out of everything she does."

The cab deposited them at the building where Garvin had his office. "Keep on holding it," Mason said. "We shouldn't be long."

He and Della Street were whisked up in an express elevator.

Mason walked down the corridor to the door which said: "HOMER H. GARVIN, INVESTMENTS. ENTER."

The lawyer twisted the knob, pushed the door, and recoiled in surprise. The door was locked.

Mason looked at his watch. "Hang it! Garvin should be here or one of his secretaries should be in. She..."

"Remember," Della Street said, "he told us that he'd fired her last night. Perhaps there was a scene, and she has decided he's not entitled to two weeks' notice, or he's decided he doesn't want her hanging around."

"Well, there should be *someone* here," Mason said. He knocked on the door of the office, then walked around the corridor to the door marked, "HOMER H. GARVIN, PRIVATE," and knocked on that door.

"Guess there's no one home," Mason said. "Let's go down to the lobby and get busy on the telephone, Della."

"I don't know the phone number of his apartment, and it's an unlisted telephone, Chief."

"That's all right. We'll get it from Gertie."

Mason and Della Street went down to the lobby of the building where there was a row of telephone booths. Della Street got Gertie on the phone, got the number of Garvin's apartment, dialed, waited, and said, "No answer."

"All right," Mason said to Della Street, "try Homer Garvin, Jr."

"He's on a honeymoon," Della Street said.

"Not in the used-car business," Mason told her. "He had his honeymoon in Chicago. Say you want to talk with him personally. Don't tell anyone who it is unless you have to. Say it's about a car you want to buy, and you want to talk with him personally."

Della Street nodded, put through the call, spent a few moments arguing with a salesman, then opened the door of the booth to say, "He's coming on the line."

"Okay," Mason said, "let me take it."

Della Street glided out of the booth. Mason slipped in to take her place. A brisk voice came over the receiver. "Yes, hello. This is Garvin talking."

"Perry Mason, Homer."

"Oh yes. How are you, Counselor?"

"Fine! Congratulations!"

"Well, thanks. Thanks a million!" he said. "It was ... it was rather sudden— but after all, that's the way I do things."

"Going to be out there for a few minutes?" Mason asked.

"Sure, I'm on the job all morning. What can I do for you?"

"We're coming out," Mason said. "I want to talk with you."

"Got a car to trade?" Garvin asked.

"It's a little more personal than that."

"Okay, I'll be here."

Mason hung up the phone, nodded to Della Street, and they returned to the taxi. Mason gave the address of the block where Garvin had his used-car market.

The cab driver slowed down as he came to the address. "Someplace here you wanted?" he asked. "This is a used-car lot."

"That's the place," Mason said. "Right in there."

"Okay." The driver turned in through an archway over which crimson letters some six feet high spelled out: "GIVE-AWAY GARVIN."

The car purred into the lot. Cars were parked in a row under a shed on the edge of which were various messages: "IF THEY DON'T MOVE WITHIN THIRTY DAYS, I MOVE THEM!—GARVIN."...."YOU CAN'T GO WRONG, BECAUSE I WON'T LET YOU!—GARVIN."...."IF I BUY IT, IT'S GOOD! IF I SELL IT, I MAKE IT GOOD.—GARVIN."

"Any place in particular?" the driver asked.

"To the office," Mason said.

The office building was a one-story rambling affair. Several salesmen were on duty, talking with customers or looking for prospects.

Mason told the cab to wait, smiled at the salesmen, said, "I'm looking for the skipper," and entered the office.

Homer Garvin, Jr. was twenty-seven years of age, unusually tall, with dark hair, dark restless eyes, and quick, nervous gestures. He was wearing an expensively tailored suit, and was talking over the telphone as Mason entered the office.

"All right. All right," Garvin said into the telephone, looking up at Mason as he did so. "My lawyer's here. I've got to talk over this thing with him. I'll have to call you back.... No, I can't say when.... I may be busy.... Good-bye."

Garvin slammed down the receiver, pushed back the swivel chair, jumped to his feet, and came toward Mason with outstretched hand.

"Well, well, well! How are you, Counselor? I haven't seen you for quite a while!"

"It has been a long time," Mason said. "Congratulations!"

Young Garvin bowed modestly. "She's a wonderful girl, Counselor. I don't know how I managed to hypnotize her. I guess it's just good old salesmanship paying off. How are you, Miss Street? You're certainly looking fine."

"Thank you."

Mason said, "We wanted to get in touch with your dad, Junior, and his office is closed."

"The office closed!" Junior exclaimed. "Why the office should be open. Eva Elliott should be there."

"I have an idea she's no longer with your dad. Do you know where he is?"

"Why no! I haven't—The truth of the matter is I haven't seen Dad since we got back....To tell you the truth, Mr. Mason, there's just a trace of a misunderstanding, a little friction. Dad will come around all right, but he thought I was playing fast and loose, and—well, you know how it is. It's hard for the older generation to understand us younger people. I venture to say my Dad had the same trouble with *his* father.

"We're living at a much more rapid pace than we ever did before, and—well, things are different, that's all. Now you take the way I run my business. I have to operate at high speed. I have to keep moving. I'm like a man skating on thin ice, and it affects the way I live, the way I feel, the way I think. But times are different from what they were a few years ago."

"You're talking about friction with your father over business matters?" Mason asked.

"No, a difference over personal affairs," Garvin said. "I'm sorry I can't help you, Mr. Mason. How about looking at a car while you're down here? I've got just exactly the sort of a car for you. Good, big, powerful, air-conditioned automobile that is in virtually new condition. You can make enough of a saving on it so you could count on economical transportation."

"I'm afraid not," Mason said. "How about Eva Elliott, your father's secretary? If she isn't at the office, where would she be?"

"You'd have to catch her at her apartment, I guess."

"Do you know where she lives?"

"Sure. Wait a minute. I have it here."

Young Garvin opened a drawer in the desk, took out a little, black notebook, thumbed through the pages, said, "She lives in the Monadnock Apartments, Apartment 317, and her telephone number is Pacific 7-2481. But she'll be at the office. She may have stepped out for a little while, but she's there. She's always there. She's very dependable, that girl. I recommended her to Dad, and she's making a wonderful secretary. Thoroughly efficient, up on her toes all the time. And she's sure a pretty girl. Walk in that office and see her sitting there with the back lighting on her blonde hair, and it's a pretty picture."

"Well, I'll go take a look at the picture," Mason said. "If your father gets in touch with you, tell him that I want to see him on a matter of some urgency."

"I'll do that," Garvin promised. "How about a car for you, Miss Street? We've got some dandies here, and I'd be in a position to give you folks the real low-down. I'd not only give you a bedrock price, but I'd give you all the history of the automobile. You see, I'm making a specialty these days of one-owner cars. Every car you see on this lot has only had one owner."

"Some other time," Della Street smiled. "Right now I'm a working girl."

"Well, remember the address. Here, take one of my cards. You have to use transportation, and that's quite a big item in a working girl's overhead. I can cut your transportation costs right down to the bone."

"Thank you," Della said. "I'll be in sometime."

"Well, do that."

Junior escorted them out to the taxicab, looked at the cab with some disfavor, said, "Just the mileage that you're paying on this cab would— Oh well, never mind. I'll tell Dad if he gets in touch with me, Counselor."

The cab driver slammed the door and drove out of the used-car lot.

Della Street looked at Perry Mason and suddenly burst out laughing. Mason shook his head. "Well, he's always trying."

"Where to now?" the cab driver asked.

"Monadnock Apartments," Mason said. "You know where that is?"

The driver nodded, eased the cab out into the traffic. "About a ten-minute run," he said.

"Okay," Mason told him.

Della Street said, "Now the trouble Junior had with his father must have started when he telephoned him from Chicago and told him that he was married, or that he was just about to get married."

Mason nodded.

"Do you suppose it was because his dad had suspected he was doing wrong by Stephanie Falkner?"

"It's hard to tell *what* caused the trouble," Mason said, "but evidently there's a bit of feeling. It will be interesting to see what Eva Elliott has to say about the marriage."

"There's just a possibility," Della Street said, "that Eva Elliott doesn't feel very cordial toward you."

"I would say that was a masterly understatement," Mason said.

"And," Della Street went on, "it's only etiquette to call and ask if it's all right to come up. A young woman quite frequently doesn't look her best in the morning."

"And if she says she doesn't want to see us, then what do we do?"

Della Street thought that over. "Well," she said, "that could prove embarrassing."

"Exactly," Mason told her. "So we'll get up to the apartment as best we can, and then see what happens."

The Monadock Apartments proved to be one which had an outer door and a push-button system, with communication from the apartments.

Mason found a key on his ring which fitted the outer door, and he and Della Street went to Apartment 317.

Mason knocked on the door of the apartment, one sharp knock, a pause, four short knocks, a pause, then two short knocks.

Almost instantly the door was thrown open. Eva Elliott, dressed for the street, said, "Well, you have a crust to—" She stopped short as she saw Mason and Della Street on the threshold.

"Oh," she said. "I thought it was someone else."

"I want to talk with you a minute," Mason said. "May we come in? This is Miss Street, my secretary."

"I don't have much time this morning. I'm going out. I have an appointment and ..."

"It will only take a few minutes."

She yielded the point with poor grace. "Well, come on in."

Mason and Della Street entered the apartment.

"You're not with Mr. Garvin any more?" Mason asked.

"Thanks to you," she said, but without bitterness, "I am not."

Mason raised his eyebrows. "Thanks to me?"

"Mr. Garvin said that I should have told you where he was."

"You knew?" Mason asked.

"I knew, but he told me not to tell anyone. In my vocabulary, Mr. Mason, *anyone* means *anyone*."

"I see."

"What would it mean to you?"

"Well," Mason said smiling, *"almost* anyone. Do I gather that there are some hard feelings?"

She said, "If you ask me, I think the whole Garvin family stinks. I did think that only the son was a rotter, but I guess it's a question of 'like father like son, and vice versa."

Mason said, "I dislike to see you lose your job on account of some misunderstanding, particularly one that had something to do with my calling on you."

"Don't give it a thought," she said. "I'm a lot better off than I would be sitting in that stuffy, old office wasting my time. I've got places to go and things to do, and it's about time I started."

"Would you mind telling me about it?" Mason asked.

She said, "Mr. Garvin got back from Las Vegas. He had a chip on his shoulder and I knew it the minute he walked into the office. He had telephoned and asked me to wait until he arrived. He said I could have dinner and put it on the expense account. Not a word about overtime. Just a dinner on the expense account. And I have to watch my figure. I ate pineapple and cottage cheese salad when I'd like to have a big steak and everything that goes with it, but you can't have poise and avoirdupois at the same time. The plan I've laid out for *my* life calls for grace, a certain amount of poise and not too much avoirdupois."

"Go on," Mason said.

"Well, as you're probably aware, Mr. Garvin has that private office of his fitted up so it's almost an apartment. There's a nice tile shower and dressing room. He has a little closet that is fixed up with an electric plate so he can warm up coffee and fix himself a snack whenever he doesn't want to go out. He has a bar with an electric icebox. In fact, he sometimes uses the place as an apartment. I've known times, when he's expecting an important long distance call, that he'd stay right there in his office for twenty-four hours at a time.

"Well, he came back from Las Vegas and I could see that he was terribly worked up about something. I hoped he'd get it off his chest and leave me at least part of the evening free, but not him. He is just as selfish as his son. He told me he was all dirty and sticky from the trip, and he was going to take a shower. So he popped into his dressing room and took a shower, and left me cooling my heels out there in the outer office until he came out all nicely fixed up with a clean suit out of his closet, and *then* he proceeded to jump on me."

"And you?" Mason asked.

She said, "I told him I didn't have to take that from anybody. I told him that when he gave me instructions I followed them, and that, as far as I was concerned, he could take his job and give it to somebody else."

"And what did he say?"

"He said that suited him all right, and I went out of the office."

"What time was this?" Mason asked.

"He got in early enough, about eight-forty-five I guess, and he kept me waiting while he was getting all cool and comfortable so he could pick on me....I just kept getting madder and madder."

"Now wait a minute. What time did this interview take place?"

"I guess it was a little after nine."

"And he told you he'd just got in from Las Vegas?"

"That's what he said."

"Did he drive in from Las Vegas or fly?"

"I don't know. He had his car with him but that doesn't mean anything because he keeps four or five cars, and then whenever he wants he'll pick up other cars from his son's used-car lot."

"How long had he been in Las Vegas?"

"Two days."

"May I ask what *you* intend to do now?"

"What I intend to do now," she said, "is do what I should have done a long time ago: devote myself to my stage career."

"I didn't know you'd been on the stage."

"Well, I...I didn't say I'd *been* on the stage, but I've had *training* for the stage. I'm being interviewed this morning for a bit part and I'm going to have to go right now, Mr. Mason. I'm sorry. I don't have any hard feelings against you but I think I've received a raw deal."

"You're finished at the office?" Mason asked.

"Am I finished? I hope to tell the world I'm finished....Now I don't like to have to throw you out, but out you go. You've taken up too much of my time already.

"Why don't you ask Mr. Garvin what happened? *He'll* tell you."

"I wanted to get your side of it."

"If I gave you my side," she said, "you'd be here all morning. His low-down son rushed me off my feet, and then when he began to get tired of me he wished me off on his dad as a secretary. Then the first thing I knew Junior was making a whirlwind campaign for Stephanie Falkner. Then he goes to Chicago and marries some babe he's hardly had a chance to know. She's some cutie from Las Vegas who came drifting into his used-car lot—just by chance. He sold her a used car and *she* certainly sold *him* a bill of goods!

"Believe me, he won't have her six months before he's trading her in on another model. That man doesn't know what he wants....Now come on. I'm awfully sorry but you're going to have to leave. Be a sport and get out of here."

"You have a car?" Mason asked.

"I'm getting a cab."

"Going out to..."

"I'm going out to Hollywood, in case you're interested."

Mason said, "I have a cab waiting downstairs. You can ride with us as far as my office. That's right on your way and will save you getting a cab here."

She looked him over and said, "Well, darned if you aren't human after all. That's a deal. Come on. Let's go."

She bustled out of the apartment, closed and locked the door, hurried to the elevator, and almost ran to the cab.

They drove to Mason's office. Mason said to the cab driver, "Add a trip to Hollywood to what you have on the meter already, and tell me how much."

The cab driver made an estimate.

"Here's the fare and the tip," Mason said. "Deliver the young lady where she wants to go."

The cab driver touched his cap. Mason and Della Street got out of the cab and had no more than crossed the sidewalk when Lt. Tragg of the Metropolitan Homicide Squad fell into step beside them.

"Well, well," he said. "So you've been out early-birding this morning. Catch any worms?"

"Oh, we don't call this early," Mason said.

"It isn't.... I thought *you* were in the office, Miss Street."

"I was," Della Street said.

"You folks get around. You certainly do," Tragg told them. "Well, let's go up where we can talk."

"About what?" Mason asked.

"Oh, about murder," Tragg said. "It's as good a subject as any, and it happens to be a subject in which we're both interested, you on one side, I on the other."

They walked silently across to the elevator, rode up to Mason's floor, walked down the corridor. Mason unlocked the door of his private office, offered Tragg a cigarette, seated himself, held a flame to the tip of the officer's cigarette, nodded surreptitiously to Della Street, and settled back in his chair.

"Well?" Mason asked.

"George Casselman," Lt. Tragg said.

"What about him?"

"Dead."

"How did he die?"

"A contact shot with a .38 caliber revolver."

"When?"

"Sometime last night."

"Where?"

"In the apartment where I understand you saw him sometime around eight o'clock."

"Indeed," Mason said. "How did you get that information?"

"That," Tragg told him grinning, "is a professional secret. I'm keeping the extent of my information to myself. In that way you won't know how much I know or how little I know. It gives me all the advantage in asking questions."

"Assuming that I would be inclined to depart from the truth in my answers," Mason said.

"That's what I'm assuming," Tragg told him. "Not that you'd lie, Mason, but you have a diabolically clever way of giving answers that don't answer. Now you saw Casselman last night. What did you see him about?"

"A business deal."

"What sort of a business deal?"

"One that involved a client's affairs."

"There you go again," Tragg said. "I want to know what you were discussing."

"My client's affairs are always kept private," Mason said. "There's a code of legal ethics dealing with the matter."

"Makes it very convenient for you in a murder case, doesn't it?"

"At times," Mason admitted.

Tragg studied him thoughtfully. "Now Casselman had some other appointments last night."

"Did he?"

"Do you know with whom?"

"I know other people were going to see him—that is, Casselman was expecting them."

"Who were they?"

"I'm afraid I can't help you there, Lieutenant."

"What do you mean, you can't help me?"

"I mean just that. I can't help you."

"That could mean a lot of things. Either that you don't know or that you can't tell."

"There's still a third possibility," Mason said. "Hearsay evidence is no good in a court of law. When I say that I can't *help* you, it might mean that I had only some hearsay evidence, and that would be of no help at all."

"You see what I mean?" Tragg said, turning to Della Street. "What kind of an answer is that?"

Tragg turned back to the lawyer.

"Now I wanted to see you this morning before you'd had a chance to talk with any of your clients," Tragg said. "I'm sorry that didn't work out. I think perhaps Miss Street's efficiency may have had something to do with that. However, Mason, we police aren't entirely dumb. After I found out that you didn't arrive at the office at your usual time and that Miss Street had stepped out on a matter of some urgency, I put two and two together and so I waited. When you drove up in the taxicab, you were getting just a little careless. You should have paid off the cab a block from the office and walked the rest of the way. As it is now, I have the number of the cab, and as soon as I call the dispatcher, the cab driver will be asked to report to us. Then we'll know just where you went with the cab and gradually we'll piece that cab trip together and perhaps find some very interesting stuff."

"Doubtless you will," Mason said. "I'm glad you called my attention to a mistake in my technique, Tragg."

"Don't mention it," Tragg said. "I knew from the expression on your face, that as soon as you saw me you were mentally kicking yourself for not walking that last block.

"I suppose you'd have done it anyway if it hadn't been for this cute blonde in the car with you. She'd have thought it a little strange if you'd stopped the cab a block from your office.

"Now then, that brings up the next pertinent question: Who was this blonde and why didn't she get out when you got out?"

"The blonde," Mason said, "was named Eva Elliott. She lives in Apartment 317 at the Monadnock Apartments. Her telephone number is Pacific 7-2481. She was formerly employed as a secretary for Homer Horatio Garvin, a client of mine, and was on her way to Hollywood to try out for a bit part. The young woman is more than mildly interested in a theatrical career."

"Well," Tragg said, "thanks for the information. I can cross that off."

"What do you mean, you can cross that off?"

"It doesn't have very much connection with the murder," Tragg said, "or you wouldn't have told me all of that. Now where else did you go with the cab?"

"That," Mason said, "is a matter I don't think I'm in a position to discuss at the moment."

"I see, I see," Tragg said. "Now this Eva Elliott had been secretary to Homer Garvin?"

"That's right."

"And Homer Garvin is a client of yours?"

"Yes."

"When did he last consult you?"

"I take care of all his legal business, I believe," Mason said. "Sometimes I will have quite a bit of work for him, and then at other times things will go along for months at a time without my hearing from him."

Tragg turned again to Della Street. "Just listen to this fellow, Miss Street. Lots of interrogators would get side-tracked and forget what the question was about by the time they'd digested an answer like that. Now, let's see, didn't my question have to do with when Garvin had *last* consulted your employer? I'm afraid you'll have to help me from getting lost in a maze of words, Miss Street."

"As it happened," Mason said, "I was the one who was trying to get in touch with Garvin. I was trying to get in touch with him Monday afternoon and I am still trying to get in touch with him."

Tragg thought that over, then said, "You were trying to get in touch with him Monday afternoon?"

"That's right."

"And you're still trying to get in touch with him?"

"Right."

"Now," Tragg said, "would you go further and say that you had not seen Garvin between the time you first tried to get in touch with him Monday and the present time when you are still trying to get in touch with him?"

Mason grinned.

Tragg shook his head. "A man has to watch you all the time, Mason. It's not what you say, but what you don't say. Now for your information, I know that Homer Garvin saw George Casselman last night."

"That *he* saw George Casselman last night?" Mason exclaimed.

Tragg nodded. "Now then, let me ask you a personal question."

"What?"

"Did you go to Casselman's apartment last night, then wait out by the back stairs, pick up a young woman and take her away in your car?

"A witness thinks you did. The light wasn't too good, but this witness saw you well enough to recognize you."

"Indeed."

"Now then, could it be possible that some young woman pushed a gun up against Casselman's breadbasket, pulled the trigger, then rang you on the telephone and said, 'Oh, Mr. Mason, come at once. Something terrible has happened!'? Could it further be possible that you asked her what had happened, and she told you that she and Casselman had had a difference of opinion, that in order to frighten him she had pulled out a gun, that Casselman grabbed her and struggled for the gun, and in the struggle, much to her surprise, she heard the roar of an explosion and then Casselman fell back on the floor?

"And under those circumstances, could it have been possible that you suggested to her that it would be highly inadvisable to go out the front door, but that you would come to the service entrance and escort her out the back door and down to your automobile, and that in the meantime she was to say nothing about what had happened?"

Mason gave that matter thoughtful consideration. "You mean that I would advise her to say nothing to the police about what had happened?"

"I'm considering that as a possibility."

"Not to report the body?"

"Exactly."

"Wouldn't that be rather unprofessional on my part?"

"It depends on how you look at it," Tragg said. "A legal code of ethics can be interpreted in many different ways. It's a well-known fact that your interpretation of a code of ethics is all in favor of your client. You wouldn't want your client to do anything that would incriminate her, no matter what the law on the subject might be."

Mason deliberated for a moment. "I take it you mean that my obligation not to betray a client would control all of the other rules of ethics?"

"Something like that."

"It's an interesting possibility," Mason admitted.

"You haven't answered the question."

"Then I'll answer it now. The answer is no."

"You wouldn't kid me?"

"No."

"When did you first learn Casselman was dead?"

"Miss Street heard it on the radio this morning."

"And told you?"

"Yes."

"When?"

"Early."

"How early?"

"I can't say."

"And you went right out to start a cover-up?"

"I went right out to try to get in touch with a client."

"Garvin?"

"Yes."

"Why?"

"I wanted to tell him Casselman was dead. I thought it might change some of his plans."

"See Garvin?"

"No."

"Talk with him?"

"No."

"Well thanks, Mason. I wanted to ask. I was instructed to interview you."

"I'm always glad to co-operate with the police," Mason said.

Tragg drew his extended forefinger across his throat. "If everyone co-operated like you do, Mason, the D.A. wouldn't have a thing to worry about."

"No?"

"No, we'd never catch anyone, so he wouldn't have to try any cases.... Well, I thought I'd give you an opportunity to come clean."

"Thanks."

"You *have* had an opportunity to come clean, you know. By the same sign, if you've tried to gum up the works, you've done it after knowing what we're looking for. That's bad.

"Now we're looking for Garvin. If you get in touch with him, tell him to call Homicide and ask for me. Tell him it's rather important."

Tragg got up from his chair, stretched, yawned, said, "Thanks a lot for all the help you've given me, Mason. Not conscious help of course, but unconscious help. I can assure you it's been considerable.

"By the way, just checking through the records, we note that Homer Garvin had himself appointed a deputy sheriff so he could carry a gun—a special deputy.... You know the pitch—personal protection. Large sums of money late at night, and all that sort of thing. He's quite an operator, I understand. Carries quite a bit of cash with him.... You wouldn't happen to know where Garvin's gun is now, would you?"

"What gun?"

"The one Mr. Garvin usually carries with him."

"Wouldn't it be in Mr. Garvin's possession?"

"I don't know. I'm sure I don't know," Tragg said. "But," he announced purposefully, "we intend to find out and you can gamble on that, Mr. Mason.

Well, good morning. I won't detain you any longer. I know that you're busy.
And after all, now that I've been here you'll probably have some telephoning to
do."

"You haven't tapped the line, have you?" Mason asked.

"No, no, no," Tragg said. "We wouldn't go that far. Well, I'll be seeing you,
Counselor. Bye now."

Tragg left the office.

Mason said to Della Street, "Get Marie Barlow on the phone, Della."

"Marie Barlow...? Oh, Marie Arden. I can't get used to her married name."

Della Street called the switchboard and a moment later said, "Here's Marie
on the phone."

"Marie," Mason said, "this may be rather important. A lot of things have
happened since I saw you last. Garvin may call you. If he does, I want you to tell
him to get in touch with me at once, and tell him that he had better be a little
careful how he does it because police are looking for him."

"Good heavens! The police!"

"That's right."

"What makes you think he'll get in touch with me?"

"Because I told him last night that you had been in to see him twice. It was
news to him. His secretary had given him to understand that you'd never even
asked for him."

"What! Why that little, two-timing—Why that..."

"Careful," Mason said, "don't get your blood pressure up. For your
information, Eva Elliott was fired last night and is no longer with Mr. Garvin."

"Well, good for the boss!" Marie exclaimed. "Who's running the office?"

"So far no one," Mason told her.

"Look, Mr. Mason," she said, "I'm going back."

"What do you mean?"

"I mean I'm going back and open up that office for Mr. Garvin, and I'm going
to stay on the job until he can get another secretary."

"You can't do that," Mason told her.

"Why can't I do it? I still have my old key to the office. I know the ropes. I
know the clients. And while a lot of water has run under the bridge since I have
been there, I know enough about his investments and his manner of operation
so I can keep from lousing anything up.

"With my figure the way it is, I won't be any ornament to the office the way
Eva Elliott *tried* to be, but at least I can be efficient and I'll answer the phone
and see that he gets messages and see that the people who want to get in touch
with him can get in touch with him."

"That might not be advisable," Mason said.

"What do you mean?"

"Some people," Mason said.

She laughed. "I'll use my discretion."

"The situation may be a little different from what you anticipate. Some of the
people who want to get in touch with him may be clothed with authority."

She thought that over for a moment, then said, "Thanks for the tip, Mr.
Mason. My husband has the car. I'm calling a taxicab. If you get in touch with
Mr. Garvin, tell him I'm on the job, and that all he'll owe me will be taxicab fare
back and forth."

"Okay," Mason said. "It may be a good idea."

He hung up the telephone, turned to Della Street. "I'm going out, Della. This
time I'm going in my car, not in a taxicab."

"Want a witness?" she asked.

"No, I think you can do more good right at the moment by staying on the job here and—" He broke off as the phone rang.

Della Street picked up her secretarial phone, said, "Who is it, Gertie? Yes, I'm quite sure Mr. Mason wants to talk with him.... Homer Garvin on the line," she said.

Mason grabbed the phone. "Hello, Homer. Where are you?"

Garvin said, "Listen closely, Mason. I may not have time for anything except a few words."

"Shoot!" Mason told him.

Garvin said, "There's a possibility Stephanie Falkner fired the shot that killed Casselman while she was acting in self-defense. I want you to get on the job and protect her."

"All right," Mason said. "If those are your instructions, that's fine, but where the devil are you and what—?"

"I'm being a red herring," Garvin interrupted.

"What do you mean?"

"I'm drawing the police off on a false scent. I'm going to try to keep on being a red herring. If I can get the police to accuse *me* of the crime, it will take a lot of the sting out of it when they finally back up and go after Stephanie."

"Wait a minute," Mason cautioned. "That's dangerous. You may not be in the clear yourself."

"I don't want to be in the clear."

"Flight," Mason said, "can be taken as an indication of guilt and can be received in evidence as such."

"All right then, I'll resort to flight."

"You can't do that," Mason protested. "You can't pile up evidence against yourself. *You* may wind up behind the eight ball in this thing."

"That's all right. You take care of Stephanie. I'll take care of myself. Your first duty is to Stephanie. Do whatever you can to protect her, regardless of where the chips fall."

"Even if you become involved?"

"Even if I become involved."

"What's the idea?" Mason asked. "Just because your son was going with Stephanie Falkner and—?"

"Because," Garvin interrupted, "I love the girl. I guess I always have. I had been afraid to admit it even to myself. I'm telling you that in confidence, Mason, and if you blab that to anyone, even to Della Street, I'll break your damn neck. You wanted to know why. Now I've told you why."

Mason paused thoughtfully.

"You on the line?" Garvin demanded.

"I'm on the line," Mason said. "Here's a piece of news for you. I talked with Eva Elliott. She's out of your life for good and all. She won't even go near the office. The place is closed up tighter than a drum."

"We can't have that," Garvin said. "I've got a dozen deals pending and— You'll have to get me someone, Mason."

"I already have," Mason said. "I talked with Marie Barlow on the phone. I told her Eva Elliott had been fired and that there was no one in the office. She's grabbing a taxicab and going up. She has her old key. She says she'll at least keep things in line."

"That," Garvin said, "is a load off my mind. Bless the girl. You said she was going to have a baby?"

"In about nine weeks."

"Tell her to stick it out as long as she can," Garvin said. "You may not hear from me for a while, Perry. I may be hard to find."

"Damn it!" Mason said. "You can't do that. You..."

There was a click at the other end of the line. The phone went dead.

Della Street raised her eyebrows in silent inquiry.

Mason said, "He *may* be stringing me along. He *says* he's playing red herring. I'm to represent Stephanie Falkner and try to keep her from getting involved."

"I heard your end of the conversation," Della Street said. "What was it he said when you asked him if he felt he owed that duty just because his son jilted her?"

Mason grinned and said, "He told me that if I told anyone, even you, the answer to that, he'd break my damn neck.... I'm going out, Della. I'll be back in about an hour. If anybody wants me, you haven't the faintest idea where I am."

"Could I make a guess?"

"Certainly."

"You're going to Homer Garvin's office and make certain there is no incriminating evidence for the police to find."

"That," Mason told her, "is an idea. It's a very good idea. The only trouble is there are two things wrong with it."

"What?"

"First," Mason said, "as an attorney I couldn't remove any evidence. That would be a crime. Second, I have something a lot more important to do.

"You must learn, Della, that an attorney cannot conceal evidence and he can't destroy evidence.

"You must also learn that an attorney with imagination and an abiding belief in the innocence of the client he's representing can do a great deal. We have two things to be thankful for."

"What?"

"First, that we know in advance the police are going to trace the route taken by that taxicab, and second, the fact that Homer Garvin's wife insisted their first child be named Homer, Jr."

"That," Della Street said, wrinkling her forehead, "is just half as clear as mud."

"I'll be back in an hour," Mason said, and walked out.

CHAPTER EIGHT

Mason drove his car into the used-car lot operated by Homer Garvin, Jr. He noticed that several salesmen were busy pointing out the good features of cars to prospective customers and was able to open the door of his car and get halfway to Garvin's office before a salesman buttonholed him.

"Want to make a deal on that car?" the salesman asked.

Mason shook his head. "I want to see Garvin."

Mason opened the door of the office with the salesman at his heels. "That car of yours looks clean. We could make you a good deal on it, particularly if it's a one-owner car," the salesman said.

Mason paid no attention either to the salesman or to Garvin's secretary, but crossed the office and jerked open the door marked, "Private."

Homer Garvin looked up from his desk in surprise.

"Pardon the informality," Mason said, "but this is important. I want to talk with you where we can be undisturbed. How the hell do I get rid of this salesman who is yapping at my heels?"

"There's only one way that I know of," Garvin said. "Buy one of our cars."

Mason turned to the salesman. "This is a private conference. I'm not here trading automobiles."

"Did you come in a cab or in your own car?" Garvin asked Mason.

"My own car."

Garvin nodded to the salesman. "Take his car out for a little spin, Jim. See what sort of shape it's in. Then check with our appraiser and see the best offer we can make. Mason is entitled to a top offer on his car and a discount on anything we have on the lot."

"Go ahead," Mason said, "if that will take the heat off. But we're going places, Homer. If you have a man take my car out, you'll have to furnish the transportation."

"That's exactly what I was hoping," Garvin said. He turned to the salesman. "Take one of the appraisers with you and put the car through its paces.

"All right, Mr. Mason, what can I do for you?"

Mason waited until the door had closed. "You got a gun?" he asked the young man.

"What's the idea?" Garvin asked.

"I want to know if you have a gun," Mason said. "I assume that you have. I know that you keep large quantities of cash on the lot here, and..."

"I've got a gun," Garvin said.

"Got a permit?"

"Sure, I've got a permit. Good Lord! Mr. Mason, you don't think I'm going to sit out here running a joint like this and be a pushover for any stick-up man that comes in, do you? I..."

"Let me see the gun you have in your desk," Mason said.

Garvin regarded him curiously for a moment, then pulled open the upper right-hand desk drawer, took out a gun and slid it across the desk to Mason.

Mason picked up the gun, threw it down a couple of times in order to get the balance of the weapon, said, "This is a mighty good gun, Homer. It's a duplicate of one your dad carries."

"I wouldn't have anything except the best, Mr. Mason. Dad gave me that. It's just like..."

Mason pulled the trigger.

The roar of an explosion filled the little office. The bullet plowed a furrow across the polished mahogany of Garvin's desk, glanced off the desk and imbedded itself in the wall.

"Hey! You damned fool!" Garvin shouted. "*Put it down!*"

Mason looked at the weapon in stupefied surprise.

The door of the private office burst open. A frightened secretary stood on the threshold. A broad-shouldered salesman advanced belligerently on Mason.

"Drop it!" he shouted. "Drop it before I break your jaw!"

Mason, still holding the gun, backed away. "Lord!" he said. "I didn't know it was loaded."

Garvin motioned the others back. "It's all right," he said. "It's Perry Mason, the lawyer."

"It isn't a stick-up?" the man asked.

Garvin shook his head.

Mason glanced ruefully at the desk. "My gosh!" he said, "I was just giving the trigger a little try and—That's certainly a smooth mechanism."

"Of course, it's a smooth mechanism," Garvin said. "That's the reason I keep it here. It's well oiled. It's a beautiful gun. It's built like a watch. It has the smoothest action I can find on the market. And because I keep it for protection, I keep it loaded. There's very little percentage in clicking an empty gun at a bandit who is trying to hold you up."

Mason slid the gun back to Garvin. "I guess I've got no business handling these things," he said.

Garvin said drily, "You seem to know a lot more about them in court than you do when you're visiting clients."

Mason turned to the secretary and the salesman. "I'm sorry. I guess I've made a commotion. I owe your boss a new desk."

"And close the door," Garvin said, "when you go out."

The secretary held the door open. The broad-shouldered salesman backed out rather reluctantly. The good-looking secretary closed the door.

"All right," Garvin said. "Now what? If you were anybody but Perry Mason, that act would have been convincing."

Mason grinned. "Put the gun in your pocket and come along."

"With the gun?"

"With the gun. You may need it."

"All right, I'll put another shell in before—"

"No, no. Just the way it is," Mason told him.

"All right, where do we go?"

"We take a little ride."

Garvin picked up a phone, said, "Get Ralph for me.... Ralph, I'm going out on a personal demonstration. Get me that x-60 job we took in yesterday. Have it out in front right away.... That's right! When I say 'right away' I mean *right away!*"

Garvin surveyed the damaged desk. "Makes quite a groove," he said. "That was a swell-looking desk, but I didn't know the veneer on it was so thin. May I ask what's the idea, Mr. Mason?"

"The general idea," Mason said, "is that I want you to demonstrate this x-60 job you're talking about."

"You're going to love it," Garvin said. "It's a sports job and it has more horses under the hood than you can use under ordinary conditions. But when you're out on the highway, and you want to pass somebody, you pass him. You pass him right now, without any long, drawn-out agony while you're driving along the road two abreast. You get back in your lane of traffic before anybody has a chance to come around a curve and smack you head-on, and—"

"I don't pass people on an approach to curves," Mason said.

"You may think you don't," Garvin said, "and you may try not to. But when you're driving over a strange road, unless you're fully familiar with the grades, you'll find that sooner or later you'll be going on what you think is a level road, but actually it's a pretty good grade. The topography of the country is such that you'll be fooled. You'll try to pass someone on what looks like a sufficiently adequate space of open road, and—"

"Save it!" Mason told him. "Let's take a look at this x-60 job of yours."

"Right this way," Garvin said.

He led the way out through the outer office. The secretary, standing by the water cooler, a glass of water in her hand, her face still pale, looked at Mason as one regards a creature from another planet.

Garvin held the door open, said, "Get right in. Get in behind the wheel of that car, Mr. Mason."

Mason hesitated at the sight of the sports automobile which was drawn up in front of the place.

"Ever driven one of them?" Garvin asked.

"No."

"Get in, try it and overcome both your prejudices and your ignorance at the same time. Greatest little job on earth! Compact! Efficient! Snappy! Distinctive! That's the kind of job you *should* be driving, Mr. Mason."

"Hang it!" Mason said. "In a car like that I'd stand out like a sore thumb. I'd go to call on a client and a hundred motorists driving by would see the car parked in front of the place and would say, 'Why, that's Mr. Mason's car. He must be in there calling on a client.'"

Young Garvin grinned. "Would that be bad?" he asked.

"That," Mason said, "would be fatal."

"Not the way we understand publicity in the used-car business," Garvin said. "The canons of professional ethics prevent you from advertising but there's nothing that says people can't talk about you. Slide in behind the wheel, Mr. Mason. Go ahead. . . . I did what you wanted and it's cost me a desk. This isn't going to cost you a cent—unless you buy it."

Mason slid in behind the wheel.

"Turn the key all the way to the right," Garvin instructed, walking around the car and climbing in beside Mason.

Mason turned the key to the right. The motor gave one quick throb, then subsided into subdued pulsations which seemed as smooth as the ticking of a watch.

"Slide it into gear," Garvin said, "and push down the throttle. *Easy!*"

Mason put the car into gear, pressed the throttle slightly and the car shot ahead as though it had been launched from a catapult.

"I said, 'Easy!'" Garvin warned.

Mason spun the wheel just in time to catch a break in traffic and glide out onto the highway.

"You're riding a polo pony now," Garvin warned. "The slightest touch on that wheel, the slightest touch on the throttle brings action."

"I'll say it brings action," Mason said.

"You'll get to like it," Garvin told him.

"If I live long enough," Mason said dubiously.

"May I ask where we're going?" Garvin inquired.

"For a ride," Mason told him. "I am testing out your x-60 job."

"Suits me," Garvin said. "Take a couple of corners where there isn't any traffic. Get accustomed to the feel of that steering wheel and, for heaven's sake, go easy on the throttle."

"Hang it, Garvin!" Mason said. "This car is ten years too young for me."

"On the contrary," Garvin said "a car of this sort should never be sold to anyone younger than you are. This car should only be operated by someone who has the judgment and wisdom which comes from mature experience."

Mason looked at him in surprise. "Are those your real sentiments about sports cars?" he asked.

"Hell, no!" Garvin said. "That's good salesmanship. Where are we going?"

"Places," Mason said.

"Well, get this baby out on the freeway where we can roll it along a little bit. I want you to see what acceleration is."

"No," Mason said, "I'm getting along all right. I'm studying."

"The car?"

"Hell, no!" Mason said. "I'm studying salesmanship."

Homer Garvin laughed.

Mason drove for several minutes then swung the car into a side street.

Garvin said suddenly, "Hey! Wait a minute! What's happening here?"

Mason braked the car to a stop in front of the Lodestar Apartments.

"We have a job to do."

"Now just a—Wa-i-i-i-i-i-t a minute!" Garvin said. "I don't know what *you* have in mind, but the answer is no."

"Come on," Mason told him.

"I'm a married man," Garvin told him.

"How does it feel?" Mason asked him.

"I don't know yet. It's a thoroughly enjoyable experience so far, but... I can see where it has advantages and disadvantages. However, I do have the most wonderful girl in the world, and I'm not going to do anything to jeopardize her happiness or mine."

"I wouldn't want you to," Mason said. "Come on along."

"What do you have in mind? Are you going to ask me to make some sort of a statement or..."

Mason said, "I want you to keep your mouth shut. I want you to listen. If you feel like it you can nod your head."

"And if I don't feel like it?"

"Just stand there and take it."

Garvin said, "Mason, I hope you know what you're doing."

"I hope I do too," Mason told him, "and we haven't much time to do it. Now let's get started."

Mason led the way into the apartment house, up to Stephanie Falkner's apartment. The lawyer tapped on the door of the apartment. There was a rustle of motion from the other side of the door, then the door opened a crack.

"Who is it?" Stephanie Falkner asked.

She saw Mason and said, "Oh, Mr. Mason!" She threw the door open, then her eyes widened as she saw Homer Garvin, Jr. standing just behind Mason.

"Now get this straight, Stephanie," Homer Garvin said. "Whatever this is all about, it's Mr. Mason's idea. None of it is mine."

"Shut up," Mason told him. "Come in. Keep quiet!"

Stephanie Falkner fell back. Mason escorted Garvin into the apartment, kicked the door shut behind him.

"Congratulations, Homer!" Stephanie said.

"Shut up, both of you," Mason snapped. "We don't have much time. Stephanie, Homer Garvin has been concerned about your safety. Despite his recent marriage, you remain a very dear friend. In view of what happened to your father and because he has learned through me that negotiations are again pending with what is probably the same syndicate, he feels that you should have something for your protection."

"For *her* protection!" Garvin asked.

"Shut up," Mason said. "Give her the gun."

Garvin hesitated a moment, then reached in his pocket and pulled out the gun.

"Take it, Stephanie," Mason said.

"What do I do with it?"

"You might try putting it under the pillow," Mason told her.

Garvin said, "One shot has been fired. Mr. Mason—"

"Quiet!" Mason said. "You told me you didn't intend to say anything and now you want to do all the talking."

"Stephanie, Homer Garvin is very much concerned about your safety. He wants you to have a weapon so that you can protect yourself. There is no secret about this. There's no reason for any deception. If anyone asks you where you got the gun, you can tell them that it is a gun you received from Homer Garvin, and conversely if anyone asks you where the gun is you got from Homer Garvin, there is no reason why you shouldn't hand over this gun.

"You will note that one shot has been discharged from this weapon. That was the condition of the weapon when it was given to you. You have no idea as to who discharged the cartridge, where or when. If anyone wants to know the answer to those questions, it will be necessary for them to check with Homer Garvin.

"Thank you very much for your courteous attention and I think it was a splendid gesture on the part of Mr. Garvin to see that you were protected.

"That's all. Come on, Homer."

Mason opened the door of the apartment. Stephanie Falkner regarded them with puzzled eyes. The gun lay on the table in the middle of the room.

Homer Garvin said, "I'd have told you about it before you read it in the papers, Stephanie, only I—"

"You don't have to explain, Homer," she said. "I understand perhaps a lot more than you think. I understand your restless nature, your ceaseless attempt to make over your environment. After all, there's no reason why we can't be friends."

Homer pushed past Mason, stepped forward and extended his hand. The two shook hands.

Mason, holding the door of the apartment open, said, "Homer Garvin, if you don't get out of here, I'll call a taxi and ride back in that."

"That does it, honey," Homer Garvin said. "I'm selling the sucker a car."

"More power to you," Stephanie Falkner said. And then added, "You may need it."

Garvin stepped into the hall, and Mason shut the door of the apartment.

They took the elevator to the ground floor and were starting across the lobby when Mason suddenly grabbed Garvin's arm and said, "This way, please."

Mason led Garvin over to the seats by a table covered with reading matter. He grabbed a magazine, pushed Garvin down on the seat, shoved the magazine in his hands, picked up a newspaper and sat down beside him.

The door of the apartment house opened.

Lt. Tragg of the Homicide Squad, accompanied by Sgt. Holcomb and the taxi driver who had driven Mason earlier in the morning, approached the desk. They talked briefly with the attendant, then entered the elevator.

"All right," Mason said, "let's go, and let's hope they didn't notice that sports car out front."

"What the hell do you mean, didn't notice it?" Garvin said. "That's like suggesting a banker doesn't notice the steam calliope in a circus parade as it goes by during a directors' meeting."

"That," Mason said, "is what I'm afraid of. If you're going to do business with me on an automobile, you'll have to get something dark, quiet, and conservative."

"I have just the thing for you," Garvin said.

"What is it?"

"A secondhand hearse. It's only had one owner."

CHAPTER NINE

At two-fifteen the telephone in Mason's private office rang and Della Street said, "Marie Barlow is on the phone, says it's rather urgent."

Mason nodded, took the telephone, said, "Hello, Marie. This is Perry Mason."

"Oh, Mr. Mason, I'm so glad I caught you. Two officers of the Homicide Squad are here, Lt. Tragg and Sgt. Holcomb. They have a search warrant authorizing them to search Mr. Garvin's office for bloodstains, bloodstained garments, or other evidentiary matters in connection with the perpetration of a homicide in connection with the death of one George Casselman. What do I do?"

"Dust off the chairs," Mason said. "Invite them to make themselves at home. Tell them to search all they damn please. Have them give you an inventory of anything they take from the office. Give Sgt. Holcomb my compliments, and ask them to try to refrain from leaving any burning cigarettes on the office tables and desks so they leave burnt smudges."

"*That* should do it," she said.

"That will do it," Mason told her. "Telephone me when they leave."

Mason hung up the phone, said to Della Street, "Well, here's where the trouble starts. I'm going down the hall to see Paul Drake. Call me there if anything breaks."

Mason walked down the corridor, pushed open the door of the entrance office on which a sign read "DRAKE DETECTIVE AGENCY." He said to the receptionist, "Paul in?"

She nodded.

"Busy?"

"No, Mr. Mason. Go right on down. Want me to announce you?"

"No need unless there's someone with him."

"He's alone."

Mason pushed open the gate which led to a corridor flanked by small, cubbyhole offices each just big enough to interview a witness in privacy or where an operative could prepare a typewritten report.

Drake's office was down at the end of the corridor and was slightly larger, having room for a desk and a couple of extra chairs. Four telephones were arranged in a row on the desk.

Drake was checking a report as Mason pushed open the door.

"Hi, Paul."

"Hi, Perry."

"Want a job?"

"Sure."

"George Casselman."

"He was murdered last night," Drake said.

"You keep up on your murders, don't you?"

"So do you, if I may say so."

Mason grinned. "I'm particularly interested in the time of death, any suspects the police may have, any information they may uncover, anything you can get on the background of Casselman.

"I'd suggest you grub around in Las Vegas, because I think he has a Las Vegas background. I don't know how long he's been living in the apartment where the body was found. I want to get everything. The works."

"I can give you some information right now," Drake said. "Casselman was a penny-ante racketeer."

"Gambler?" Mason asked.

"Not so much gambler as petty rackets."

"Okay," Mason said. "See what you can find out. I can give you one tip."

"What?"

"You remember a man who was killed here a few months ago, fellow by the name of Falkner—Glenn Falkner?"

"Oh yes, gangster killing, wasn't it?"

"It was not," Mason said. "That is, I don't think it was, although the police have listed it as a gangster killing, and as a result not too much was ever done on it.

"Because Casselman had some connections in gambling circles and Glenn Falkner did too, police have made a check on Stephanie Falkner, the daughter of the man who was murdered a few months ago."

"You representing her?" Drake asked.

"I'm looking out for her interests, Paul."

"Okay, I'll get busy. What is this? Big, medium-sized, or small job?"

"Whatever is necessary to get the information. Start out easy and finish up hard."

Drake reached for a telephone. "Okay, Perry, I'll start some men on it right now. I have a man down in the pressroom at headquarters who gets stuff as fast as it's available for the papers."

"Have him keep an ear cocked," Mason said, "and shoot the information down to the office as soon as you get it."

"Okay," Drake said, "I'm started."

Mason walked back to his own office, heard steps in the corridor behind him, turned and saw Stephanie Falkner hurrying down the corridor.

"Well," Mason said, "what brings you here?"

"Oh, Mr. Mason, I'm *so* glad I found you. May I see you a moment?"

"Come on in this way," Mason said, fitting a latchkey to the door of his private office.

He opened the door, said, "We have company, Della," and ushered Stephanie Falkner into the office.

"What's new?" he asked.

"The police came to my apartment within a few minutes after you left. The gun was still on the table. I forgot about it for the moment and then tried to hide it by throwing a scarf over it when they came in. I'm afraid I was a little clumsy."

"What happened?" Mason asked.

"They grabbed the gun. They smelled it, broke it open, wanted to know where I got it."

"And what did you tell them?"

"I told them Homer Garvin had given it to me for protection, that he thought perhaps my life was in danger."

"You didn't tell them whether it was Senior or Junior?" Mason asked.

"Was I supposed to?"

"I wouldn't know," Mason said.

"Well, from the manner in which the whole situation developed, I... well, I just told them so much and then didn't tell them any more. They asked me about when I had last seen Mr. Garvin."

"And what did you tell them?"

"Told them that I had seen him that morning. That seemed to excite them a lot and they put through a couple of phone calls, then left in a hurry."

"No further questioning?"

"No further questioning."

"All right," Mason said, "they'll question you again. When they do, I want you to do something."

"What?"

"Tell them that you won't answer any more questions unless I am present."

"But Mr. Mason, isn't that equivalent to...? Well, doesn't that...I mean, isn't that virtually an admission of guilt?"

"They may think it is," Mason said, "but we're playing for big stakes in a no-limit game. Don't answer any more questions. Don't even give them the time of day. Don't tell them what the weather is, or where you were born. Think you can do that?"

"I can, if you want me to."

"I do. Garvin asked me to protect your interests."

"Mr. Mason, I—There's one thing I thought I should tell you. Homer Garvin came back last night..."

"Now do you mean Senior or Junior?"

"The father."

"All right," Mason said, "he came back. What happened?"

"He said he couldn't sleep. He wanted to talk to me. We had a nice long talk."

"What time did he leave?"

"That's the thing that—Well, it was around midnight when he left."

"That's fine," Mason said. "Don't answer any questions. Just don't be too available."

"What do you mean by that?"

Mason nodded to Della Street, said, "Do you like this dress on her, Della?"

"Very much indeed," Della Street said.

"I don't," Mason said. "I don't think it's photogenic. I don't think she'll take good pictures in that dress.... How long would it take to pick out a dress which would have good striking black and white lines that would photograph well? Something with a deep V in front and white lines that emphasize the figure?"

"It might not take long," Della Street said, then at the expression on Mason's face, hastily said, "Again it might take quite a while to get *exactly* what *you* have in mind."

"You see," Mason said to Stephanie Falkner, "you're going shopping."

"When?"

"Now. Got any money?"

"Yes."

"Then shop. Make yourself conspicuous when you shop. Try on a lot of dresses. Be difficult. Have it so the salesgirls will be sure to remember you."

"Then what?"

"Then," Mason said, "keep in touch with me by telephone. If you want to reach me at any time and the office is closed, telephone the Drake Detective Agency, tell them who you are, and leave a message. I want to know where I can get in touch with you at all times."

"The Drake Detective Agency?"

"That's right. That's the one down the hall. Give her one of Paul Drake's cards, Della."

"And I'm not to talk with the police?"

"Not with the police. Not with the newspaper reporters. Not with anyone unless I am present. Don't absolutely refuse to talk, simply refuse to talk with anyone unless I am present. Can you do that?"

"Yes."

"Where's the other gun?"

"It's in a place where no one will ever find it."

"You're sure?"

"I'm absolutely positive."

"All right," Mason told her, "get started on your shopping tour. That will probably keep you pretty well occupied until the stores have all closed."

Stephanie Falkner went out. Della Street eyed Perry Mason quizzically. "It's a crime to conceal evidence?" she asked.

"Oh, definitely," Mason said. "But it's no crime to advise a client not to talk. And it's a breach of ethics for a lawyer to fail to protect the best interests of his client."

Della Street studied the expression on his face for a moment, then burst out laughing.

CHAPTER TEN

The telephone on Della Street's desk rang sharply.

Mason picked up the instrument, said, "Yes, Gertie, what is it? Della's out. Oh, Marie Barlow? Put her on."

Marie Barlow's voice said, "Hello."

"How's everything coming?" Mason asked.

"All right."

"The search finished?"

"Yes."

"Did they take anything?"

"Not a thing. They prowled around, seemed terribly disappointed, and left."

"It may be a trap," Mason warned. "How's the office?"

"I've never seen such an unholy mess in all my life!"

"What do you mean, a mess?"

"I mean a mess. I don't think this girl had the faintest idea about how the business was handled, or how the files were kept. I have already found duplicate files. I have found correspondence filed in the wrong places. I can't find any system to the way she handled bills payable."

"Such as what?" Mason asked.

"Take that apartment house out on Seaforth Avenue, for instance, the one that Mr. Garvin bought just before I left. There have been electrical repair bills on it for over three thousand dollars, and that's just too darn much."

"Perhaps television was installed in the different apartments," Mason said.

"Well, I'm checking on it, but after the way I left things, it's certainly an Alice in Wonderland situation now."

"Okay," Mason told her, "straighten things out the best you can. Keep in touch with me. And tell Garvin I want to see him if he calls in."

"Should I tell him about the search warrant if he calls in over a public telephone?"

"Sure," Mason said. "Give him all the information you have."

"I was thinking that he might be calling on a party line of some sort, or there might be a leak over a public telephone."

"There's apt to be a leak over any telephone," Mason told her. "You have to take that chance."

"Okay," she said, "I'll get busy trying to straighten out the mess up here."

Mason had hardly hung up the telephone when he heard Paul Drake's code knock on the corridor door of his private office. He swept open the door, said, "Come on in, Paul."

Drake said, "Thanks, Perry," moved over to the client's chair, sat conventionally for a moment while he was fishing a notebook out of his pocket, then whirled around so that he was sitting crosswise in the chair, one rounded leather arm propped against the small of his back, the other furnishing a rest for his long legs.

"Now this is a hell of a mess, Perry!" he said.

"What?"

Drake said, "I'm afraid you're in for some unpleasant publicity, Perry."

"What's the matter?" Mason asked, raising his eyebrows.

"You know the columnist Jack Crowe who runs the daily column in the paper entitled, 'Crowe's Caws'?"

Mason nodded.

"Well," Drake said, "somebody down at young Garvin's secondhand-car lot came up with a story about you handling a gun that you didn't think was loaded, and blowing a furrow all the way across the top of young Garvin's desk."

Mason looked sheepish. "Good heavens, Paul! Don't tell me *that's* going to get in the papers?"

"Not going to get in the papers!" Drake said. "A choice item like that? Hell! You couldn't have pulled that job under more auspicious circumstances as far as publicity is concerned, if you had been trying to..."

Drake stopped abruptly.

"What's the matter?" Mason asked.

Drake regarded Mason thoughtfully. "That was a hell of a statement I just made," he said. "It's given me a little food for thought."

"What statement?"

"That if you had been trying to get publicity you couldn't have done it under more auspicious circumstances. You're getting the publicity all right.... I couldn't believe the story when I first heard it. I'm beginning to believe it now."

"I was careless," Mason admitted.

"Well," Drake said, "just for your information, Crowe got the tip, and he's printing a humorous article about the lawyer who is so full of technical information about firearms that he can make the ballistics experts look foolish on the witness stand, pulling the didn't-know-it-was-loaded line the minute he gets his hands on a firearm."

"That would be very, very embarrassing," Mason admitted.

"That's what I thought when I first heard it," Drake commented thoughtfully.

"You're changing your mind now?" Mason asked.

Drake's eyes took on a faraway look as he gazed over toward the windows in unblinking concentration. Abruptly he jackknifed himself up out of the chair.

"What makes you think you can get away with this stuff, Perry?"

"I don't," Mason said.

"Then what's the idea of trying it?"

"It gives the columnists something nice to write about. Having gone that far, Crowe will follow up on the story the next day."

"Well," Drake said, "my face is a little red, Perry. I thought I had a hot tip and—Perry, are you certain you haven't violated the law?"

Mason grinned. "I guess perhaps I have, Paul, but by the time the smoke blows away, discharging a firearm within the city limits is the only thing they can actually hook me on."

CHAPTER ELEVEN

When Mason entered his office on Thursday morning, Della Street had a copy of the morning newspaper placed on his desk. The paper was folded over so as to leave the column entitled, "Crowe's Caws" in the most visible position.

Mason had just started to read the column when Della Street came in from the outer office.

"Hi, Della," Mason said. "I gather that I am the subject of a little publicity."

"*Quite* a little publicity," she said.

Mason read:

> "Perry Mason, the spectacular trial attorney, whose cases have such a tendency to explode into courtroom pyrotechnics, and who has won many a courtroom battle by proving that his technical knowledge of forensic ballistics is at least the equal of that of the expert whom he is cross-examining, proved to be not

quite so adept when it came to handling firearms on a practical basis.

"Seems Stephanie Falkner, the attractive young woman whose father was murdered some time back in a case which so far has never been solved, received some threats which caused Perry Mason considerable concern. Homer Garvin, the high-powered used-car salesman, and Stephanie had at one time been quite ga-ga. It is to be presumed that Garvin's recent marriage terminated the romance, but apparently not the friendship.

"When the noted lawyer called to Homer Garvin's attention the fact that Stephanie might be in danger, Garvin promptly produced a gun and suggested that Miss Falkner be given an adequate means of protection.

"Perry Mason was all in favor of the deal, and picked up the gun to test the balance, and decide whether the mechanism functioned perfectly.

"It functioned.

"The result was considerable excitement in the offices of the used-car dealer, a long deep furrow ploughed in the veneered desk, and a rather red face on the noted attorney.

"Inasmuch as Mason's face rarely becomes red, the occasion was considered epochal by an interested but somewhat apprehensive audience. However, all's well that ends well, and, since police have been wondering whether the gun which they found in Stephanie Falkner's apartment with one exploded shell in the mechanism had been used in connection with a homicide, it gives this column great pleasure to point out that they need look no farther than Homer Garvin's desk to find the bullet that is missing.

"It was reported that the used-car dealer had been planning on having a new desk installed immediately, but as salesmen piloted in a procession of potential customers to view the damages, and the customers somehow affixed their signatures on dotted lines before leaving the place, Garvin has decided to feature the 'wounded' desk as his main attraction—sort of a *corpus deskus.*"

Mason had just finished reading the account in the paper when the telephone on Della Street's desk jangled.

Della Street answered the telephone, and nodded to Perry Mason. "It's Paul Drake. He's coming right down."

"Hear anything from Homer Garvin?" Mason asked her after she had hung up.

"Senior or Junior?"

"Either."

"Junior telephoned. He's tickled to death with the publicity. He's sold five cars to prospective purchasers who originally came in to survey the damage in the desk."

"He'd better give me a commission," Mason said. "Hear anything from Stephanie Falkner?"

"Not a word."

"That's a little strange, Della."

"She may be a late sleeper," Della Street said.

Mason frowned. "Give her a ring. Wake her up."

Della Street picked up the phone, said, "Ring the Lodestar Apartments, Gertie. We want to talk with Stephanie Falkner."

While she was waiting, Paul Drake's knuckles tapped the code knock on the door.

Mason got up to let him in, and Della Street said, "She doesn't seem to answer, Chief."

"Tell Gertie to keep trying," Mason said. "Hi, Paul, what's new?"

Drake said, "George Casselman had a criminal record. He served time, once for pimping, once for extortion. He was killed sometime between seven and eleven-thirty o'clock Tuesday night by a .38 caliber bullet which was fired from a gun that was held against Casselman's chest. It made what is described in medical circles as a contact wound. You know what a contact wound is.

"The muzzle of the gun is held directly against the body into which the shot is fired. The bullet not only enters the body, but a lot of explosive gases from the gun also enter and cause quite a bit of internal damage."

"Anyone hear the shot?" Mason asked.

"Apparently not. In cases of contact wounds, the sound of the shot may not be much louder than that of an inflated paper bag being smashed."

"Then no one heard it?"

"No one heard it."

"What else, Paul?"

Before Drake could answer, the telephone on Della Street's desk rang again.

Della Street picked up the telephone, said, "Hello," in a subdued voice, then said, "Yes, he's here," turned to Paul Drake and said, "For you, Paul. It's your office. They say it's most important."

Drake moved over to the telephone, said, "Hi, this is Paul," waited a moment, then said, "The devil...!" There was a long silence. Then, "They're sure...? Okay."

Drake hung up the phone and stood for a moment in puzzled perplexity.

"Well," Mason said impatiently.

"This," Paul said, "is the best-kept secret of the day. Police knew about it yesterday and managed to keep it buttoned up."

"Well, what is it?"

"Bullets fired from the gun police found in Stephanie Falkner's apartment match the fatal bullet that killed George Casselman."

"Which gun?" Mason asked sharply.

"Which?" Drake asked in surprise. "Why, there's only one, the one Garvin gave her."

Mason's eyes narrowed.

Drake said, "This means that *you* had the fatal gun in *your* possession and that you discharged one shell into the desk at Homer Garvin's office in the used-car lot. Quite naturally, police felt at first that you were engaged in some sort of a hocus-pocus trying to confuse the issue somehow. They picked young Garvin up and are giving him a shakedown. Their original idea was that you must have planted the murder weapon in his desk."

"They've changed their minds now?" Mason asked tonelessly.

"They're changing their minds," Drake said. "At the moment they have a brand-new suspect, in the person of Mrs. Homer Garvin, Jr. It seems she was employed as a resident hostess, bathing beauty and ornamental model at one of the Las Vegas hotels out on the Strip. She knew Casselman. No one seems to know how well. They found Casselman's unlisted number written down on a memo pad by her telephone.

"Casselman was a blackmailer. The young woman just got married. Figure that one out and you have a perfect sequence.

"That, in the words of the police, makes your clumsy attempt to fake a didn't-know-it-was-loaded accident at Garvin's used-car lot a diabolically clever attempt to mix up the ballistics experts.

"Police don't like that. The ruse almost worked. They're examining all the evidence carefully. The D.A. would love to book you. If he could catch you tampering with evidence, he'd turn the department upside down trying to get a conviction."

Mason nodded to Della Street. "Tell Gertie to get Junior on the telephone. He probably won't be in, but have Gertie leave word for him to call."

Mason pushed back the chair from his desk, got up and began pacing the floor. Abruptly he turned, said to the detective, "Paul, I want to know what's going on. I want all the information you can get on what the police are doing. They probably have both Stephanie Falkner and Garvin, Jr. Thank heavens Senior is across the state line! They'll have to unwind some red tape before they can drag him in. There's something fishy about this whole business."

Drake said, "Watch yourself, Perry. Keep in the clear on this thing. Police are going to want to know how it was that you had such unerring insight as to go out to Garvin's used-car lot, ask for a gun, fire a bullet into Garvin's desk, and then take the gun up and leave it with Stephanie Falkner in a place where police would be sure to find it."

"You aren't telling me anything," Mason said, "but there's a lot back of all this that *you* don't know. Get busy and start finding things out."

Drake nodded, left the office.

Mason continued pacing the floor for a while, then whirled to face Della Street. "There's only one answer, Della."

"What?" she asked.

"Homer Garvin, Sr.," Mason said, "must have a key to the office at Junior's used-car lot. Garvin, Sr. had possession of the murder gun. He knew that Garvin, Jr. kept a gun in his desk. So Garvin, Sr. went out and substituted guns. He put the murder gun, which must have been reloaded, in Junior's desk where police would never think of looking, then took Junior's gun out of the desk. He fired one shot through that gun, then took it up and left it in Stephanie Falkner's apartment. His idea was that the police would find the gun with the empty shell, think that Stephanie had killed Casselman, and then be forced to abandon that theory because they would find that the gun she had hadn't been used in the crime. That's why he was so anxious to have me do everything I could for Stephanie."

"Go on from there," Della Street said.

"So that's where I inadvertently nullified everything he had done," Mason said. "Feeling certain that the police would pick up Stephanie Falkner for questioning and feeling that, by that time, they could well have found out Garvin, Sr. had given her a gun, or that they would search for a gun, I conceived the idea of having Garvin, Jr. also give her a gun. In that way, if the police found the one gun, they would hardly keep on searching for another gun. And if they knew Garvin, Sr. had left a gun with her and demanded she produce it, she could have produced the gun that Garvin, Jr. left and so mixed the case all up.

"As it happens, by one of those peculiar coincidences which sometimes occur in real life, my brilliant idea backfired. I went out and got the very gun that Garvin, Sr. was trying to keep from ever being associated with Stephanie Falkner. I took *that* gun to Stephanie Falkner's apartment and left it right where police would be sure to find it."

"Where does that leave you?" Della Street asked apprehensively.

"I'm darned if I know where it leaves *me*, Della. The police can't say I was concealing evidence. I went out and dug up the very bit of evidence they wanted so badly, and placed it in the possession of the woman they probably had pegged as their number one suspect.

"At the moment I'm not concerned where it leaves *me*, but where it leaves my *clients*."

"And," Della Street asked, "*who* do you suppose fired the fatal bullet from the gun in question into the body of George Casselman?"

"Now there," Mason said, "you raise quite a question.

"In the minds of the police, Junior's new wife now becomes a prime suspect, or perhaps Junior himself. Police won't credit me with good faith. They'll naturally think I was trying to take the heat off Junior and his wife by implicating Stephanie Falkner.

"I have an idea that Junior and his wife are going to be very, very angry. They'll feel I went out there with the murder weapon, that I asked Junior for his gun, that I did a little sleight-of-hand substitution, and under cover of the confusion resulting from the apparently accidental discharge of the weapon, managed to substitute the murder gun in place of the one Junior had given me. Junior thereupon walked into my trap, took the gun up to Stephanie Falkner and left it with her.

"I can also imagine that when Garvin, Sr. reads the papers *he's* going to be cursing me for a clumsy lout."

"And the police?" Della Street asked.

"The police will naturally assume that whatever I did was designed to confuse the issues. They will now be able to prove that *I* had the fatal gun in *my* possession. Once having reached tht point, they'll drag me into it as deep as they can drag."

"Can they *prove* it was the fatal gun?"

"They can now."

"How?"

"By that bullet which was fired into Junior Garvin's desk. If it wasn't for that bullet, they'd have one hell of a time *proving* that I ever had the fatal gun.

"Once they recover that bullet, which eyewitnesses can testify was fired by me, they can show it came from the fatal gun. Remember, Della, I went out there to see Casselman. It's not too utterly improbable that the D.A. may try to claim I committed the murder."

"Then if it wasn't for the bullet you fired into Junior's desk, they couldn't absolutely *prove* that the gun you had in your possession was the fatal gun?"

"They could prove it by inference," Mason said, "but that's all."

"Chief, couldn't I get Paul Drake to go out there and get that bullet? If police don't think of it in time and that bullet has disappeared...?"

Mason shook his head.

"Why not?"

"Because, Della, Paul Drake has a license. He doesn't dare to cut corners. They'd take his license away. The minute you suggested anything like that to Paul Drake he'd be in a panic."

Della Street thought the situation over. "Just where *did* that bullet go, Chief?"

Mason said, "I fired the gun at the desk on an angle, hoping that the bullet would glance up into the wall."

"Did it?"

"I think it did."

"And just *why* did you fire it?" she asked.

Mason grinned. "So that the gun the police found in Stephanie Falkner's apartment would have one discharged cartridge case in the cylinder. Then in case the police should have been looking for a gun with one discharged cartridge, they'd quit looking as soon as they found this gun I'd had Junior leave there."

"So what do we do now?" Della Street asked.

"Right now," Mason said, "we can't do anything except wait."

"That," Della Street said, "is the most difficult thing I know of. I'm afraid my nerves are giving out. I'm going to skip down and get something for my head. I'll be right back."

"What's the matter?" Mason asked sharply.

She averted her eyes. "I didn't sleep much last night. I kept thinking about Stephanie Falkner and Garvin, Jr. I don't know why—I guess I'm just getting..."

Mason said, "You're overworked, Della. You're putting in altogether too much time at the office and taking too many responsibilities. You can't keep on supervising the work that goes out of here, handling mail, apportioning work to the stenographers, and checking the work they do, running the office, and at the same time trying to keep up with me on these cases."

"Well, it *is* something of a strain," she admitted, "but it's never bothered me before. It was just last night, I...I just couldn't sleep. I guess it was the romantic angle. Imagine how Stephanie must have felt when she picked up the paper and found Garvin, Jr. had married without telling her. And Garvin, Sr. was so anxious to have her in the family.

"I went to sleep and then woke up crying. I...I couldn't get back to sleep."

Mason said, "Della, get out of here. Jump in your car. Go on out to your apartment and forget about this whole business. You take a sleeping pill and get to bed. I'll call you if any emergency comes up. Tomorrow may be a hectic day but nothing much is going to happen today because police won't dare to make any definite move with things all mixed up the way they are now. Police will try to unscramble the mess before they do anything."

"And when they make a move, they'll make it against you?" she asked.

"They will if they have a chance," Mason said. "Hamilton Burger, the district attorney, will see to that and Sgt. Holcomb would back him up in it.

"Hang it!" he said irritably, "it shows how circumstances can betray you and how coincidences can make a mess. You go on home, Della."

"You'll promise to call me if anything urgent develops?"

"Cross my heart," Mason said.

"Well," she surrendered, "I think I will. I feel like a wet dishrag."

"You may be coming down with something," Mason said. "You'd better see a doctor before—"

"No," she said, "I just feel that if I could get some sleep it would be all I needed. I should have taken a sleeping pill last night, but I waited so long that I knew if I took one I wouldn't be much good today."

"You go take a sedative right now, and go to bed," Mason said. "What's more, watch yourself. If you develop any fever, call a doctor. I'm inclined to agree with you. I think all you need is a good rest, but make sure."

"All right," she told him, "and you remember, you're to call me if anything urgent develops."

Mason nodded and resumed pacing the floor

CHAPTER TWELVE

Homer Garvin, Sr. called just before noon.

"Good work, Perry!" he said.

"What are you talking about?" Mason asked.

"You should know," Garvin said.

"Where are you?"

"Las Vegas, Nevada."

"I'm afraid," Mason said, "there have been some developments that you don't know about, Homer, some complications that..."

"I know all about them," Garvin said. "That's why I'm calling. I'm over here in Nevada, but I'm keeping in touch with developments. I have my own sources of information."

Mason said, "Did you know about the police picking up your son and his wife for questioning? Did you know about the gun I accidentally discharged and which turned out...?"

"I know *all* about it," Garvin said. "You're doing all right, Mason. Now remember this: it's your duty to protect Stephanie Falkner at all costs."

"What about your son and his wife?"

"Do what you can," Garvin said, "but don't bother about them. Police can't make any case against either one of them, and they'll drop them like hot potatoes when they finish their investigative work."

"Do you want me to represent them?" Mason asked.

"Go ahead. Represent everybody," Garvin said, "but primarily you're representing Stephanie Falkner."

"And what about you?"

"I'll take care of myself. But I want to know something about my rights."

"What about them?"

"Garvin said, "I'm over here at the Double-O Motel. I'm registered under my own name. I haven't resorted to flight. I can prove that I have business here. I expect police to locate me at any moment.

"Here's what I'd *like* to do, Mason. I'd like to simply sit tight and refuse to answer any question on the grounds that I have no information that would be of value and that I do not intend to volunteer any statement until my attorney can be with me."

Mason said, "That might put you in an embarrassing position as far as the public is concerned. It wouldn't endear you to the police, and they'd pin something on you if they had a chance."

"Let them pin," Garvin said.

"You know," Mason told him, "there's *some* evidence in this case that points toward you."

"There'll be more before I get done," Garvin told him. "You represent Stephanie. *She's* the one who is going to need the representation. Do you understand?"

"I think so."

Garvin said, "Do anything you can to keep police from building up a case against her. I'll take care of myself. Now here's what I want to do. I want to refuse to make any statement to the police. I don't have to talk, do I?"

"Not if you tell them you won't make any statement except in the presence of your attorney."

"And you're my attorney," Garvin said. "Also I take it it's very inconvenient if not impossible for you to come to Las Vegas, Nevada."

"I have very urgent matters in my office here at the moment," Mason said.

"That's what I thought," Garvin said. "I'm willing to make a statement, but only in the event that you are present at the time. Now then, I want to know what will happen if they try to get tough with me."

"You're out of the state," Mason said. "They can charge you with murder, and try to extradite you."

"I take it," Garvin said, "that, since I'm out of the state, they won't be in such a hurry to try to arrest me on a definite charge."

"They'll want to feel they have a pretty good case before they do anything," Mason said.

"That's what I thought."

"But they *may* feel they have a pretty good case," Mason warned.

"In which event, we'll sit tight and make them prove it beyond all reasonable doubt."

"Don't waive extradition," Mason warned.

"I won't waive anything except my hands."

"I'm afraid police are interrogating Stephanie Falkner right now."

"Sure, they are. They're also interrogating my son and his bride. You know, Mason, the more trails they have to follow, the more confused they'll get. I don't know just how you did what you did, but you did a wonderful job. Now if you want to get in touch with me, just ring the Double-O Motel and leave any message you want with Lucille."

"Okay," Mason told him, "and if you should call me and I'm not in, or if you want to call me at night, get in touch with the Drake Detective Agency. You're going to have a bill to pay on this, Homer."

"I don't expect something for nothing," Garvin said.

"I'm keeping some private detectives on the job. I just want to be sure that..."

"You do anything you see fit," Garvin interrupted. "Spend as much money as you want. I've never kicked about your charges yet, and I'm not going to begin now. But whatever you do, be sure to protect Stephanie Falkner. Good-bye."

Mason was just dropping the receiver into its cradle when he heard the sound of a key at the lock of the door to his private office.

Mason whirled just as the door opened, and Della Street stood in the doorway.

"Now what?" Mason said. "I told you to go home and rest, Della, to take a sleeping pill and..."

"I didn't need one, Chief," she said. "I got some headache medicine downstairs. I went home and relaxed and felt a lot better....I got to thinking about what Mr. Garvin had said to us about buying cars."

"Go on," Mason said, suddenly straightening in the chair.

"Well," Della Street said, "after all, there *is* a terrific depreciation in buying new cars, and if you know someone who is in the used-car business and who will give you a good deal..."

"Della," Mason interrupted, "do you mean to say that instead of sleeping you went out to Junior Garvin's used-car lot and..."

"But I wasn't sick, Chief. I simply had a headache and I hadn't slept well last night, but the headache medicine quieted my nerves and made me feel all right."

"Go on," Mason said, "what did you do?"

"Well, I just kept thinking about what Garvin had told us. You see, my car didn't seem to be running right. I stopped by the used-car lot. After all, it's right on my way to the office. Well, only a few blocks out of the way."

"All right," Mason said, "what *did* you do?"

"Junior Garvin wasn't there," she said, "but I met one of the *nicest* salesmen, and he knew that Junior Garvin was your friend. I told him that Junior had offered to make either or both of us a good deal. He had a car there that was just a dream of a car."

"You bought it?" Mason asked.

"Well," she said, "I'm giving it serious consideration. I tried to telephone you to ask you what you thought about it, but there was something wrong with the line. I couldn't seem to get a connection."

Before Mason could say anything, Paul Drake's code knock sounded on the door of the office.

"Let Paul in, Della," Mason said.

Della Street opened the door.

"Hi, Della," Drake said. "Well, Perry, you'd better get ready to receive official visitors."

"Why?" Mason asked.

"Police are biting their fingernails, tearing their hair, and raising hell generally," Drake said, "but I have one tip that may help you. That's why I dashed in, to tip you off to something that may help."

"What?"

"Police overlooked a bet. It didn't occur to them to go down and dig the bullet out of the desk at young Garvin's place until just a few minutes ago. Sgt. Holcomb went down there with the ballistics experts, and *what* do you think they found?"

"What?" Mason asked.

"Some souvenir hunter had made off with the bullet. It had struck the desk at an angle, glanced into the wall, and hit a steel girder. Somebody had made just a little hole in the plaster and lifted the bullet out as neatly as could be."

Mason frowned for a moment, then whirled to face Della Street.

"Can you imagine that!" Della exclaimed. "Now who in the world could have done that, Paul?"

"Some souvenir hunter," Drake said. And then added, "It may louse up the whole case."

"I don't see just how," Della Street said, her manner demure, her eyes innocent.

"It makes one link in a chain of proof turn up missing." Drake explained. "Police don't like that. Also they're mad because it will now appear they were caught napping."

"How did you get the information, Paul?" Mason asked.

"It came in a roundabout way," Drake said evasively.

"All right," Mason said. "Give."

"Well, this columnist Crowe ran that paragraph in his column, and naturally it attracted a lot of interest. So it was only natural that he'd want to keep in touch with things and get a follow-up if possible."

Mason nodded.

"Well," Drake went on, "he's quite friendly with the head salesman at Junior Garvin's place. So when the police came out there searching for the bullet and found that someone had beat them to it, this salesman learned about it and of course relayed the information on to Crowe. Crowe is running quite a paragraph on it tomorrow morning, although of course the police don't know that. I have a confidential source of information in Crowe's office. I'd advised this source of information that I was interested in any follow-up material and I received this tip on the phone just a few minutes ago."

"All right," Mason said, "thanks a lot, Paul. Keep on the job and let me know. Put out as many men as you need to give this case a thorough coverage."

"Within reasonable limits?" Drake asked.

"Within no limits at all," Mason said. "I want the facts."

"Okay," Drake said, "I'll keep digging."

"And thanks for that tip, Paul. It may be very, very important."

"That's okay," Drake said, obviously pleased. "I'll keep you posted, Perry." He left the office.

As the door clicked shut behind him, Mason turned to Della Street.

"All right, Della," he said, "now let's have the *real* story. You..."

The door from the outer office was pushed open and Sgt. Holcomb came in unannounced.

"Well," he said, "a little conference, eh?"

"A little *private* conference," Mason said.

"That's all right," Sgt. Holcomb grinned. "Go right on talking. I instructed Gertie out there not to announce me. I told her I'd just come right on in."

"Nothing like making yourself at home," Mason said.

"That's right," Holcomb agreed, standing by the door leaning his back against the wall. "I represent the majesty of the law. The law doesn't sit outside and wait in anybody's outer office. When we have to see somebody, we see them."

"Don't you even announce the fact that you are coming?" Mason asked.

"Some of the officers do," Holcomb said. "I don't. I don't believe in tipping a man off. I like to watch his face during the first second or two after he sees me walk in."

"And did you learn anything from *my* face?" Mason asked.

"I think I did. I know damn well you didn't want to see me. That's one thing."

"Well, since you're here, you may as well sit down. Take your hat off, and let's see what we can do for you."

"I'm comfortable the way I am," Holcomb said.

"All right, what do you want?"

"You know what I want."

"I'm not a mind reader, Sergeant, so I don't intend to waste my time speculating on what it is you want. Previous experience has shown me you are quite able to express your ideas, your wants, your likes and your dislikes. Now start talking."

"You're the one to start talking," Sgt. Holcomb said. "You went down to Homer Garvin's used-car lot and fired a gun into Garvin's desk."

"An accidental discharge of a firearm, my dear Sergeant," Mason said. "I intend to reimburse Mr. Garvin for the desk. No one was hurt, and I fail to see why it should arouse any interest on the part of the police."

"The interest on the part of the police," Sgt. Holcomb said with elaborate sarcasm, "comes from what you doubtless consider purely a minor matter: the fact that this gun was the murder weapon which was used to kill George Casselman in the Ambrose Apartments the night before."

"Are you certain?" Mason asked.

"Of course, I'm certain! Now then I want to know where you got that gun?"

"The gun," Mason said, "was given to me by Homer Garvin, Jr. I asked him if he had a gun, and he said he did. He said that he had one that he used to protect himself against holdups. In the used-car business they sometimes take in quite a bit of money in the form of cash. Garvin, I believe, has a permit to carry the weapon. He said that he did. That, however, is something which you are in a position to look up much more easily than I am."

"So Garvin gave you that gun?" Holcomb asked.

"He handed me the gun, or rather he showed it to me. I reached out, picked it up, and tried the balance of it. I threw it down, the way a man will in trying out the balance of a gun, and I guess in doing so I must have inadvertently pulled the trigger. In any event, Garvin didn't tell me that it was loaded."

"You thought he'd be protecting himself with an empty gun?" Sgt. Holcomb asked.

"I don't know that I gave the matter any thought at all. I wouldn't tell you that I actually did intend to snap the trigger, nor on the other hand would I go so far as to say that I didn't intend to snap the trigger. I was testing the balance of the gun, and it went off."

"And what happened after that?" Holcomb asked.

"Stephanie Falkner is a client of mine. She was, I felt, in some danger. Her father had been murdered, and the murderer is still at large as far as we know. I suggested to young Garvin it might be a good idea for him to take the gun and leave it with her for a short time. You see, he and Stephanie Falkner had been quite good friends before his marriage."

"So I understand," Holcomb said drily. "Now then, Mason, you know damn well that the gun you got from Garvin wasn't the murder weapon that killed George Casselman."

"I'm glad to hear you say so, Sergeant. I didn't think it was, either. But since the police have so dogmatically asserted that it *was* the weapon, I didn't feel in a position to contradict them."

"You know what I mean," Sgt. Holcomb said. "You substituted weapons. You had the murder weapon in your possession. You had received it from a client. You had that gun concealed on you when you went down to call on Garvin. You asked Garvin if he had a gun. He told you he did. He put the gun out on the desk. You fired Garvin's gun so as to divert attention from yourself and in the resulting confusion switched guns."

"Then," Mason said, "it is now your contention that Garvin's gun was *not* the murder weapon."

"That's what I think."

"And you think that I had the murder weapon with me and that I substituted it for Garvin's gun?"

"That's right."

"Well," Mason said, "you can quite soon test the accuracy of your conclusions by taking the number of the murder weapon and tracing it on the firearms registration."

"We've done that," Sgt. Holcomb said. "The gun was purchased by Homer Garvin, Sr., the old man."

"Then how did Garvin, Jr. get it?"

"His father has a sporting-goods store among his other investments. He took three identical guns, snub-nosed, two-inch barrel, detective guns, kept two for himself and gave one to his son."

"Kept *two* for himself?" Mason asked.

"That's what the boy tells us."

"Then the firearms register shows the gun that I received from young Garvin was a gun that had been given him by his father. Is that right?"

"The firearms register shows that the gun with which the murder was committed was one of three weapons purchased by Homer Garvin, Sr. Now we know damn well that the gun you got from young Garvin *wasn't* the gun that was used in committing the murder."

"How do you know?" Mason asked.

"Because young Garvin is able to account for the possession of that gun every minute of the time during the evening on which the murder was committed."

"Then it couldn't have been the murder gun."

"That's what I'm telling you," Sgt. Holcomb said.

"Well, make up your mind," Mason told him. "First, you claim it was the murder gun, then you claim it wasn't the murder gun."

"You know what I mean. You substituted the murder gun. You knew that the murder gun was a gun which had been purchased by Homer Garvin's father. He had given it to Stephanie Falkner. She went out and killed George Casselman with it. She called on you for help. You took the murder gun to young Garvin's place of business, got his gun, fired it into the desk, and then in the resulting confusion you switched weapons and got him to take the murder weapon up to Stephanie Falkner."

"Can you tell me any reason why I should take the murder weapon and leave *it* for police to find?" Mason asked.

Sgt. Holcomb stroked the angle of his jaw. "I don't know why you did all this stuff, but you sure as hell did it. Now then, I'm telling you something else, wise guy. You aren't in the clear on this thing yourself."

"No?" Mason asked.

"No," Holcomb said. "The best medical evidence we can get indicates that Casselman *could* have met his death at the time *you* were calling on him."

"Meaning that I committed the murder?" Mason asked.

"Meaning that you *could have* committed the murder. I'll say this for you, Mason, I don't think you would have gone up there and murdered him in cold blood, but if he had made some threats, if he had started reaching for a gun, you could damn well have poked that gun in his guts and pulled the trigger."

Mason smilingly shook his head. "You'll have to do better than that,

Sergeant. You'll have to get something more than mere speculation to make a case. George Casselman was alive and well when I left him. I do know that he was expecting some mysterious visitor."

"Stephanie Falkner," Sgt. Holcomb said.

"Not Stephanie, Sergeant. Her appointment was later. This was someone who telephoned and was coming right up."

"How do you know?"

"Casselman asked me to leave. He said he was expecting someone. He said there were complications."

"And you left?"

"Yes."

"And then went around to the back of the apartment so you could wait until a mysterious young woman came running down the service stairs and then you picked her up."

"Did I do that?" Mason asked.

"You did exactly that," Sgt. Holcomb said, "and that mysterious young woman, whoever she was, was the murderer. You're trying to protect her. You knew that she was going to call on Casselman. She came running down the stairs and told you she'd killed Casselman. She shoved the murder weapon into your hand and asked you what she should do. You told her not to worry, that you'd dispose of the murder weapon in such a way that you'd mix the facts in the case all up."

"Well," Mason said, "it's an interesting theory. I think you're going to have a lot of trouble trying to prove it, Sergeant, because it happens to be incorrect."

"We've *got* the proof," Sgt. Holcomb said.

"Indeed," Mason said.

"We have witnesses who saw you waiting out there in back, who saw you picking up this young woman and driving away with her. We have witnesses to the fact that you had the murder weapon in your possession, that you fired a shot from the murder weapon into the desk out there at Garvin's used-car lot."

"And how are you going to prove it was the murder weapon?" Mason asked.

"By the bullet, you dope! Our ballistics expert can tell whether the bullet you fired out there came from the murder weapon. If it did, then it's a fair inference that you got the murder weapon from this young woman who ran down the back stairs from Casselman's apartment. On the other hand, if it turns out that bullet was *not* fired from the murder weapon, then it proves you switched guns right there in Garvin's office."

"Well, well," Mason said. "Under your reasoning I'm hooked either way."

"Well, what's wrong with that?"

"It seems unfair somehow," Mason said sarcastically. "I can't feel that it's fair to say that if the bullet came from the murder weapon I'm guilty of switching evidence and that if the bullet *didn't* come from the murder weapon I'm still guilty. It seems you're a little biased in your thinking, Sergeant."

Sgt. Holcomb said, "This is the same old razzle-dazzle. Every time we start working on a shooting case, you go drag in some extra guns and then start a sort of shell game trying to confuse the issues."

"Anything wrong with that?" Mason asked.

"It's illegal, that's all."

"Then I trust I'll be charged with whatever crime I've committed."

"You sure will in *this* case," Holcomb promised. "This time we have you dead to rights. You went too far out on a limb this time."

"You certainly credit me with a diabolical ingenuity," Mason said.

"I've simply learned your technique," Holcomb told him. "Now do you want to kick through and tell us what happened? Do you want to admit that that's what you did?

Mason shook his head.

"If you do," Holcomb said, "and if you come clean, we *may* be able to give you the breaks. If you don't, we'll take the bullet we recovered from the wall out there at Garvin's place, we'll match it up with the gun you had in your possession, and so help me, we'll crucify you. We'll throw the book at you!"

Della Street coughed significantly.

"That," Mason said, "would seem to be a very definite threat."

"That *is* a very definite threat," Holcomb told him.

"All right," Mason said, "I understand the point you've made, and I can't help you. All I can tell you is that I did not substitute any guns, that to the best of my knowledge the gun that young Garvin showed me out there, the gun which he took from the drawer of his desk, is exactly the same gun that he took up to Stephanie Falkner's apartment."

"By saying that," Sgt. Holcomb said, "you have made yourself an accessory after the fact. You're concealing evidence. You're acting the part of an accessory."

Mason shook his head and said, "I'm sorry, Sergeant. I'm telling you the truth."

"Okay, wise guy," Sgt. Holcomb said. "You asked for it."

He turned on his heel and walked out.

Mason waited until he was sure the sergeant was out of the office, then turned to Della and said, "Della, did you go out and get that bullet?"

"Why, Chief," she said, her eyes wide with surprise, "what in the *world* gave you any idea like that?"

"Did you? I gathered Holcomb was trying to scare me with a bluff."

"If I had swiped that bullet as a souvenir, would it be serious?"

"It *could* be very serious."

"Then if I had done it, and told you I had done it, that would put *you* in a very embarrassing position, would it not?"

Mason thought that over for a minute, then said, "Have it your own way, Della."

"Thank you," she said demurely.

CHAPTER THIRTEEN

Shortly after two-thirty Della Street entered Mason's private office and said apprehensively, "Junior is out there."

"Garvin?" Mason asked.

"That's right."

"He wants to see me?"

"He wants to see you very much indeed," Della Street said.

"How is his disposition?"

"His disposition as indicated by his manner is very, very bad. He has chips on both shoulders. He wants to fight."

"They you'd better send him in right away," Mason told her.

"Chief, let me have Paul Drake come down, or send a bodyguard, or..." Mason shook his head.

"Young Garvin is big and tough and strong," she said. "You know what it would do to the case if there was a knock-down-drag-out fist fight right here in your office."

"Send him in," Mason said. "I think he'll listen to reason."

"He doesn't act as though he would."

"Send him in anyway," Mason said, "and we'll get it over with. If he sees Paul Drake here, he'll know that I sent for him to act as bodyguard, and then he'll feel that I'm afraid of him. That wouldn't be good. Let's have it out man to man and straight from the shoulder right now. I'll see if I can clear up some things in Junior's mind."

"Well, here goes," Della Street said, "but I don't like it."

A moment later the door literally burst open and young Garvin came striding into the office.

"What the hell are *you* trying to do, Mason?" he shouted.

Mason said, "Sit down, Junior, take a load off your feet, and off your mind. Suppose you tell me what's the reason for all this outburst."

"I want to know what the hell you're trying to do dragging my wife's good name through all this muck and mire."

"I wasn't aware that I was dragging your wife's good name through the muck and mire."

"Well, everybody else is aware of it, even if you're not."

"Precisely what did I do?" Mason asked.

"You have made her the number one suspect in the killing of George Casselman."

"How?"

"By getting me to take that gun up to Stephanie Falkner. Damn it, Mason, I don't intend to stand for that. I'm going to hold you strictly responsible both as an attorney and as a man. You're going to account to me legally and unless you can give me some satisfactory explanation, I'm going to bust you in the puss before I get out of here."

Mason regarded the younger man with steely-eyed scorn. "So you think it would do some good to bust me in the puss, as you express it?"

"It would give me the greatest personal satisfaction," Garvin told him.

"It might also get you a broken jaw," Mason said. "The point is, however, would it do your wife any good? Would it do your case any good? You let the newspapers get the idea that you're having trouble with me over this thing and you'll *really* make a story of it."

"They've made a story out of it anyway."

"No, they haven't," Mason said. "They won't dare to publish the full implications with the full sensational embroidery unless you give them a peg on which they can hang a lot of innuendoes. Now either sit down and tell me calmly what this is all about, or else get the hell out of the office and let *me* try to figure the thing out."

Garvin took a couple of steps toward Mason's desk, paused uncertainly before the look in the lawyer's eyes, detoured a little to the side, and propped one hip against a corner of the big desk.

"Dawn worked in Las Vegas," he said angrily. "Casselman knew her and..."

"Now I take it Dawn is your wife?" Mason asked.

"Yes, Dawn Joyce. Casselman knew her and Casselman was always on the prowl. A girl in that kind of work gets hungry for real friendships. The tourists come and go. The transients make passes at her, and that's all they're thinking about.

"Casselman was a local man. He was friendly, and... well, Dawn liked him."

"They had dates?" Mason asked.

"Apparently so."

"Did she know he was here in town?" Mason asked.

"She knew he was here. After the write-up in the paper—well, Casselman called her, just a social call, just a matter of wishing her every happiness in the world."

"There's nothing wrong with that," Mason said.

"The hell of it is," Garvin said, "in the apartment where Casselman lived police found a notebook by the telephone with some numbers in it. He'd written down Dawn's telephone number, and she'd written down his unlisted number. It was on a pad by her phone."

"Anything else?" Mason asked tonelessly.

"Tuesday night, when Casselman was killed," Garvin said, "I had to go out to interview a car dealer about taking twenty used cars off his hands. He was stuck with them and he knew it. He wanted to get his money out of the old cars so he could put it into new merchandise. It looked like a good opportunity for me to make a deal."

"You had an appointment with him?"

"Yes."

"What time?"

"Don't bother about that," Garvin said angrily. "I can prove where I was every minute of the time."

"Carry a gun with you?" Mason asked.

"I did not. I left it in the desk drawer."

"I see. And where was your wife?"

"Where any wife would be at that time. She was home waiting for me, and she was just a little bit angry because I broke in on a honeymoon to go out and close a business deal."

"She was there when you got back?"

"Of course she was."

"And what time did you get back?"

"About nine-thirty or ten. I can't remember just what time. It was along in the latter part of the evening."

"And all this time your gun was in the drawer of the desk at your office?"

"During my conference it was. I got it after the conference and took it home."

"And your wife doesn't even have a key to the office?" Mason asked. Garvin hesitated.

"Well," Mason asked, "does she or doesn't she?"

"The unfortunate part of it was she did have a key. But she didn't use it. I— Hang it, Mason! I tell you she was home."

"All right, she was home," Mason said.

"But the point is, she can't *prove* it. She was home alone because I was out on this damned used-car deal. She's got no way of *proving* that she was home."

"She doesn't have to," Mason said. "If anybody wants to prove anything on her, let them prove that she *wasn't* home."

"Well, there's one unfortunate thing," Garvin said.

"What?"

"I tried to call her on the telephone and apparently I dialed the wrong number. She didn't answer, and..."

"You don't need to tell anybody about that," Mason said.

"It was in connection with this business deal. I talked with this fellow and I wanted to get some data about some of my accounts receivable. It was in a little notebook that I thought I had with me, but I'd left it on the dresser."

"And you telephoned your wife?"

"That's right."

"And got no answer?"

Garvin nodded, then added, "I apparently dialed the wrong number."

"You gave up after the one call?" Mason asked.

"No, I called her twice."

"No answer either time?"

"No answer."

"How far apart were the calls?"

"Five or ten minutes. But I tell you, Mason, I'd only moved into this new apartment about two weeks ago, and I had evidently transposed a couple of the figures in my mind. I dialed the wrong number. I must have, because she was there. And I mean she really *was* there. She isn't the sort of girl who would lie to you. That's one thing about Dawn, she'll hand it to you straight from the shoulder."

"The man with whom you were transacting the business knew you'd put through the calls?" Mason asked.

"Yes, that's the devil of it. He has no way of knowing that I dialed the wrong number. Even I wasn't aware of it at the time."

"But you did put through the calls and received no answer?"

"Yes."

"And as far as the man who was on the other side of the desk was concerned, you were dialing the right number and got no answer?"

"Yes."

"And because you were expecting your wife would be home, you probably made some remark to him about it being strange there was no answer?"

"I guess I did."

"What time did you put these calls through?"

"Around nine o'clock, I guess."

"What time did you leave your home?"

"I never got a chance to get around there during the evening, Mason. I was demonstrating a car and then we had a sales meeting, and then this deal came up on the block of used cars, and I dashed down to get to this used-car dealer before someone else beat me to it. I stopped for a hamburger on the way, and that's all I had to eat.

"I really didn't have any dinner, just that sandwich. I was intending to get back earlier than I did and take Dawn out for a good dinner someplace."

"You got back along in the latter part of the evening?"

"That's right."

"And had only had this sandwich?"

"Yes."

"Did you ask your wife to go out?"

"Yes."

"What happened?"

"She was angry because I hadn't been home for dinner, because I'd gone out to make a business deal so soon after we'd been married. We had a little argument."

"That's all you have to tell me?" Mason asked.

"That's all, except this boneheaded stunt of yours of shooting a bullet hole in my desk and—And now the officers claim that gun was the murder gun. It's absolutely impossible! It's utterly ridiculous! But if they keep messing around with it, they're going to drag Dawn's name into the newspapers."

"Not unless you do something that drags it in," Mason said. "The officers think that I had the murder gun in my possession, that I went out to see you, got you to produce your gun and fired your gun into the desk. Then I supposedly switched weapons on you in the confusion, so that the gun I gave you was the murder weapon, and I slipped the gun that was in your desk drawer in my pocket."

Garvin's face showed his surprise. "You say the *officers* think that?"

Mason nodded.

"But why?" Garvin said. "They're trying to sell me on the idea that my wife went down to the office, got the gun.... They've insinuated that Casselman was trying to blackmail her, and—How do *you* know what the officers are thinking?"

"Because," Mason said, "they've just been here and virtually threatened me with arrest for concealing evidence and a few other things."

Garvin slowly straightened away from the desk. "By George!" he said, "I never thought of that, but you *could* have done it. I thought I smelled a rat. You're not so dumb as to let a gun go off accidentally."

"Therefore," Mason said, "*if* I had the murder weapon in my possession, *if* I went out there and got you to produce your gun from your desk drawer and then *if* I fired your gun into the desk, I certainly made a sufficient commotion so that in the confusion I *could* have substituted the murder gun in place of your gun."

"You sure could at that," Garvin said.

"Now then," Mason said, "which gun was it that I fired? The gun that you took out of the desk, or the murder gun that I had with me?"

"You discharged my gun, the one that I took out of the desk," Garvin said unhesitatingly.

"You're certain of that?"

"Absolutely certain. I remember every move you made. I remember producing the gun and handing it to you. You took it in your right hand and swung it up and down two or three times getting the balance of it, and about the third time you tried it, you fired it right into the desk."

"The gun that you handed me?"

"The gun that I handed you," Garvin sad. "But you certainly could have switched guns afterwards, because everyone was dashing into the office. I remember you holding the gun in your hand, and then you— Good heavens, Mason! That's what you *did!*"

"The police seem to think so."

A grin spread over Garvin's features. "Now *that* puts a different aspect on the whole business. How are they going to make any trouble for Dawn if you had an opportunity to switch weapons? All right, Mason, they say all's fair in love and war. As far as I'm concerned, I'm going to play along with the police on the theory they have."

"Well," Mason said, "why the deuce do you think I gave you the tip in the first place?"

Garvin thought things over. Suddenly he moved over toward the lawyer, and shot out his hand. "Shake hands, Mason," he said. "You're... you're a gentleman! Wait till I get hold of Dawn and tell her about this!"

Garvin started for the door, closed his hand around the knob, then suddenly turned back to face the lawyer.

"Any time you want a good deal on a sports car, Mason, I'll make you a very extra special price on that x-60 job you were interested in."

"Thanks," Mason said, "but I wasn't interested in it."

"Well, I'll make you a mighty good price on it anyway."

"Just a moment," Mason said. "Can you tell me everyone who has keys to your office?"

Garvin seemed surprised. "The janitor, of course, my wife, my secretary."

"Your dad?"

"Oh sure. I have a key to his office, and he has a key to mine. We don't ever use ·them but we have them."

"I was just checking," Mason said.

"You don't want to sign an order for that sports job?"

Mason smiled and shook his head.

"Let me know when you change your mind."

Garvin whipped the door open and walked out into the corridor.

Mason returned to his desk.

Della Street said with admiration in her voice, "That was some exhibition of salesmanship, Mr. Perry Mason!"

Mason might not have heard her. "Get down to Paul Drake's office, Della. Ask him to get men on the job in Las Vegas and find out everything we can find out about Dawn Joyce."

CHAPTER FOURTEEN

Less than an hour after Junior Garvin had left the office, Della Street's telephone rang. She talked for a few moments, then said, "Just a moment. I'll see."

She placed her hand over the mouthpiece of the telephone, said, "Chief, it's Marie Barlow. She's uncovered some things that bother her."

"What?" Mason asked.

"Apparently some errors that are more serious than mere errors."

"Let me talk with her," Mason said.

Mason picked up his own telephone, said, "Connect me on Della Street's line, Gertie, and leave Della Street on there so we can both listen."

A moment later Mason heard the click of the connection and said, "Hello, Marie, this is Perry Mason. I'm on the line. What is it?"

"I didn't want to bother you, Mr. Mason," she said, "but I wanted you to know about it. There's something wrong here."

"What?"

"Checks have been made out on bills that have been received, but the firms to whom the checks were paid apparently didn't have any orders to do any work.

"For instance, I've uncovered several receipted bills from the Acme Electric and Plumbing Repair Company. The total of the different statements amounts to over six thousand dollars.

"Now there are cancelled checks showing that payments have been made in the exact amount of the respective statements. The statements aren't itemized. They're only general; such as, repairs and wiring on a certain building."

"Well, why not ring up the Acme Company and ask them what it's all about?" Mason said. "Tell them you're preparing a statement for property appraisers for income tax, and you want itemized bills and want to know how the orders were placed."

"I already thought of that," she said. "There's only one thing wrong with it."

"What?"

"There isn't any Acme Electric and Plumbing Repair Company listed in the book."

"What about the street address?"

"There's a street address," she said. "1397 Chatham Street, and apparently there isn't any such firm at that address."

"What about the bill?" Mason said. "The billhead—is it printed?"

"It's printed, and looks very imposing. It has a place for job numbers, ledger numbers, order numbers, and all of that. They're all filled in, in pen and ink, and look very fine, but there isn't any such company. Apparently no such job was performed and..."

"How about the checks?" Mason asked. "How were they endorsed?"

"With a rubber stamp and then cashed. The bank's closed, and I can't get any information on that until tomorrow morning."

"Well," Mason said, "let's start checking, Marie, but don't get stampeded into doing anything until we know a little more about it. What does it look like to you?"

She said, "It looks very much to me as though someone found out that Eva Elliott was green on the job and simply had billheads printed and sent in a bill to see what she would do. The first one was only three hundred and twenty-six dollars and eighty-five cents."

"What did she do?"

"She made a check."

"Then the check must have been mailed," Mason said.

"The check was mailed all right, and cashed."

"Go on," Mason said, his voice showing his interest. "What happened after that?"

"After that, nothing happened for a month, and then there was a bill for seven hundred and eighty-five dollars and fourteen cents. It was paid, and the next month bills came in for three jobs. They were in various amounts, but the total was twenty-nine hundred dollars and some odd cents."

"Found anything else?" Mason asked.

"The next month there were three more bills. That's all so far for the Acme Electric and Plumbing Repair Company, but if someone had found out it was that easy to get Eva Elliott to send out checks, I have a hunch it didn't stop there."

"How were the checks signed?" Mason asked.

"By Garvin. You know the way Mr. Garvin does. He'll have his secretary type out checks for bills that come in, and on the eighth of the month he'll sign all of the checks so as to get his cash discounts. Now that's another crazy thing. Eva Elliott made out checks for the bills and didn't take off the two per cent cash discount even when the billheads said right out in printing at the top: 'Two per cent cash discount if paid by the tenth.'"

"All right, Marie, I'll check into it. Thanks a lot for calling. What was that address again?"

"I have it, Chief," Della Street said. "1397 Chatham Street."

"We'll take a look," Mason said. "How's everything coming, Marie?"

"Oh, it's an unholy mess," she said, "but I'm getting it straightened out a little at a time."

"Don't overwork," Mason told her. "You'll be there tomorrow?"

"I'll be on the job tomorrow."

"I'll try to run in. I'd like to have a look at some of those statements."

"Okay, I'll be here."

"Bye now," Mason said, and hung up.

He looked at Della Street and frowned. "Now that's something," he said. "We'd better ask Paul Drake to take a look at this address on Chatham Street and see if he can find anything about the Acme Electric and Plumbing Repair Company."

"Well," Della Street said, "that's something for even a motion-picture secretary. Just open the letters, take out the bills, type out checks and send them in for the boss's signature, then mail out the disbursements."

Mason grinned. "Some system of bookkeeping, but it seems to have paid off all right."

"At least for one person," Della Street said.

Gertie opened the office door, said excitedly, "Here's the afternoon paper, Mr. Mason, with a photograph in it showing a bloody footprint in Casselman's apartment and there's someone from Las Vegas calling, a woman who says the only name you know her by is Lucille."

"Put Lucille on," Mason said, as Della Street took the newspaper from Gertie's hand and relayed it across the desk to him.

Gertie hurried back to the switchboard.

Mason picked up the telephone, waited until he heard the connection being made, then said, "Yes, hello. This is Mr. Mason talking."

The woman's voice was urgent with excitement. "Mr. Mason, I guess you know who I am. This is Lucille at the Double-O Motel."

"Go on, Lucille," Mason said.

"Mr. Garvin simply had to talk with his son about an urgent matter."

"Telephone?" Mason asked.

"No, personally. He chartered a plane."

"Go on."

"He took elaborate precautions to see that he wasn't followed to the airport."

"Go on."

"He told me that he would telephone me at three o'clock on the dot, at six o'clock on the dot, at eight o'clock on the dot, and at ten o'clock on the dot, that he'd be back by ten. He said if I didn't get any one of those calls, I was to call you and tell you. Otherwise, I wasn't to let you or anyone else know where he was."

"Okay," Mason said. "I gather that the three o'clock call didn't come through."

"That's right. I haven't heard from him at all. I wanted you to know."

Mason said, "Thanks. That means he's been picked up. There's nothing we can do until they book him. We'll stay on the job. Thanks for calling."

Mason hung up the phone, started studying the picture on the second page of the afternoon newspaper.

"Interesting?" Della Street asked.

"Very," Mason said. "You can see there's a man's footprint here, a footprint which has been made with a bloody shoe and there's a heel mark, the stamp of a fairly new rubber heel. Police have been able to make out the name: 'The Spring-Eze.'"

Mason pushed back the paper and started pacing the floor.

At length he paused and regarded Della Street quizzically.

"It's my contention, Della, that an attorney doesn't have to sit back and wait until a witness gets on the stand and then test his recollection simply by asking him questions. If facts can be shuffled in such a way that it will confuse a witness who isn't absolutely certain of his story, and if the attorney doesn't suppress, conceal, or distort any of the *actual evidence*, I claim the attorney is within his rights."

Della Street nodded.

"In this case," Mason went on, "the facts keep shuffling themselves. Usually the police get the main suspect, but have difficulty finding the murder weapon. Here they have the murder weapon and have so many main suspects, they don't know what to do."

Della Street said, "In this case you're one up on them. Knowing that you didn't switch weapons *you* know the murder weapon was in Junior's desk."

Mason nodded. "The only trouble, Della, is that I don't know who put it there, and I won't know until I can talk with Garvin, Sr."

"And if he *didn't* put it there?"

"Then the murderer did.

"We're going to have to work late tonight. Police are holding Stephanie Falkner. Now they've also picked up Garvin, Sr. He made the mistake of underestimating the police.

"We'll get Paul's men to check various job-printing establishments and see if we can find where these billheads of the phony repair company were printed. How's your headache?"

She looked at him, then slowly closed one eye. "*Much* better," she said.

CHAPTER FIFTEEN

Mason and Della Street entered the dimly lit interior of the cocktail lounge.

"Well," Della Street said with a sigh, "this is a welcome and relaxing atmosphere after the tense strain of working on a case."

Mason nodded. "We'll sit and relax, have a couple of cocktails, then get a nice steak dinner with baked potato and all the fixings. We can have a bottle of stout with the steak, and—However, Della, let's just check before we sit down. I'll give Paul Drake a ring to let him know where we are."

Mason stepped into the telephone booth, dialed Paul Drake's number, said,

"Perry Mason talking. Put Paul on, will you?"

Paul Drake said hello, and Mason said, "We're just letting you know where we are, Paul. We're going to take time out for a couple of cocktails, a good dinner..."

"Hold it!" Paul Drake interrupted.

"Not yet," Mason said. "A bottle of stout with the steak, perhaps a little garlic toast, and..."

"Hey! Whoa! Back up!" Drake shouted into the telephone. "You're wasting precious time."

"What is it?" Mason asked.

"Lt. Tragg of Homicide telephoned not over five minutes ago. They're frantically trying to reach you."

"Why?" Mason said.

"Homer Garvin, Sr. is being held for questioning in the office of the district attorney. He refuses to make any statement unless you are present. The D.A. is going to call in newspaper reporters and let them know of developments unless you show up and unless Garvin quote satisfactorily explains unquote certain evidence against him."

Mason hesitated for a moment.

"You there?" Drake asked.

"I'm here," Mason said. "I'm thinking. All right," he said, reaching a sudden decision, "where is Garvin now?"

"At the D.A.'s office."

"Tell them to expect me," Mason said. "I'm coming up." He slammed up the telephone, jerked the door open.

"Oh-oh," Della Street said, "here goes a perfectly good dinner."

"That's right," Mason told her. "It's postponed. Garvin, Sr. is in custody. They have him at the D.A.'s office. He refuses to make any statement unless I'm present, and demands that they notify me as his attorney."

"And they did?"

"They did."

"That means they're laying a trap for you too," Della Street warned.

"I know it," Mason told her. "However, I'm going to walk into it. Take my car, go to the office and wait. I'll get back there just as soon as I can and then we'll go to dinner. I'll take a taxi to the D.A.'s office. Okay, Della, be seeing you."

Mason thrust the keys to the car into her hand, dashed to the door, jumped into a waiting taxi and said, "You know where the district attorney's office is? I'm in something of a hurry."

The lawyer sat on the edge of the seat while the taxi driver twisted and wormed his way through traffic.

As the cab came to a stop against the curb, Mason handed the driver a five-dollar bill, said, "A good ride, keep the change," and sprinted for the elevators.

A uniformed officer sat at the reception desk in the district attorney's office.

Mason said, "I'm Mason. I think they're expecting me."

"Go on in," the officer said. "He's in Hamilton Burger's office. Last on the left."

Mason pushed open a swinging door, strode down a hallway flanked with officers, pushed open the door of an office marked "HAMILTON BURGER, DISTRICT ATTORNEY, PRIVATE," and said, "Good evening, gentlemen."

They were seated in shirt sleeves in a tight little group: Lt. Tragg of

Homicide, a uniformed officer, a shorthand reporter, Homer Garvin, and Hamilton Burger, the barrel-chested, grizzly bear of a district attorney.

The room was filled with a heavy aroma of cigarette smoke.

Hamilton Burger cleared his throat importantly, but first nodded to the shorthand reporter.

"Mr. Mason," he said. "Mr. Perry Mason. Please come in and be seated. Let the records show that Mr. Perry Mason has arrived. Now Mr. Garvin, you have stated that you would explain matters only when your attorney was present. I am now asking you to explain the bloodstained shoe, and the print of that bloodstained shoe in the apartment of George Casselman, who was murdered last Tuesday night."

Mason said, "Just a moment, gentlemen, if my client is going to make any statement, I want to talk with him first."

"We've waited long enough already," Hamilton Burger said.

"If I am denied an opportunity to confer with my client before this conference goes on," Mason said, "I will simply advise him not to answer *any* questions and you can keep right on waiting."

"In that event, we will not try to protect him as far as publicity is concerned," Hamilton Burger warned. "Mr. Garvin is a responsible businessman. I have explained to him that we don't want to work any injustice, that we don't want to drag his name into this case so that there will be any unfavorable publicity."

Mason said, "Let the record show that I have demanded an opportunity to confer with my client before the interrogation proceeds further, that I have been answered with a threat by the district attorney to call in reporters and crucify my client with publicity."

Hamilton Burger got to his feet, his face dark with anger.

Tragg said, "Just a minute." He arose, walked over and whispered in the district attorney's ear.

"We'll give you ten minutes," Hamilton Burger said after a moment. "There's an office in there on the left."

Mason nodded to Garvin. "This way, Garvin."

Garvin was out of his chair with alacrity. Mason opened the door and disclosed a secretarial office equipped with a typewriter desk, a machine, a cabinet of stationery, and several chairs.

Mason looked the place over quickly, then moved over to another door and opened it, disclosing a small coat and hat closet.

"In here," he said to Garvin.

Garvin entered the closet. Mason switched on a light. They stood close together within the narrow confines.

Mason said, "That room is probably bugged. I didn't like the expression on Burger's face. He gave in too easily. Keep your voice low. Now tell me what the devil this is all about and tell me fast."

Garvin said, "I should have told you before, I guess. I—Hang it, Mason! I was disappointed in my son."

"Lots of parents are disappointed in their children."

"Well, it's all right now. I thought for a while he was marrying the wrong girl, but now I think he married the right girl."

"By that, do you mean you think Stephanie Falkner is mixed up in this murder?"

"By that," Garvin said, "I mean that I'm in love with Stephanie Falkner. I guess I always have been in love with her ever since I met her. I wanted Junior to marry her. That is, I thought I did. But when he married someone else, I . . . I knew I should have been disappointed, but I wasn't. I was suddenly elated."

"Have you told her about it?" Mason asked.

"I'm afraid I hinted at it. That's all there'll ever be to it. I'm old enough to be her father."

"Barely," Mason said. "Some women prefer older men."

Garvin brushed the subject aside impatiently. "It's not in the cards, Mason, but I'm telling you that one fact so you can understand the situation."

Mason said, "We only have a minute. Give me facts, and give them to me just as fast as you can dish them out. You took that murder gun down to your son's office and planted it in his desk. I wanted to divert attention from the gun you had left with Stephanie, and thought I could do something smart. I loused things up, and—"

"Wait a minute. Wait a minute," Garvin said. "You're all wet. I didn't put any gun in my son's desk."

Mason said impatiently, "You went to Casselman's apartment before you went to your office. Did you kill him or not?"

Garvin said, "Don't be silly. Stephanie saw him after I did."

"Just what did you do?"

Garvin said, "I stopped in to see Casselman on the way to my office. I had just driven in from Las Vegas. It was around eight-fifteen. I had a key that worked the lock on the outer door of the apartment. I didn't want to tip him off by ringing his bell.

"You know how these street doors on apartment houses are, Perry. Almost any sort of key will work them. Well, I went up and knocked on Casselman's door. He opened it, but didn't invite me in. He seemed strangely disturbed when I told him who I was.

"He told me he had someone with him and was all tied up. He said I should return at eleven o'clock and he'd see me then. Then he all but slammed the door in my face. I took the stairs to the street.

"I don't know how you found out about this, Mason. I haven't told a soul."

"Never mind how I found out," Mason said. "You went to your office from Casselman's apartment?"

"Not directly. I stopped to get gas and called Las Vegas. Then I went to my office. I have a little emergency apartment fixed up in connection with my office. I had previously telephoned on ahead and asked Eva Elliott to wait for me. I wanted some information on some business matters, and wanted her to give it to me personally."

"All right," Mason said. "You went to your office. What happened?"

"I changed my clothes and took a shower. I told Miss Elliott to get the information for me while I was taking the shower and put it on my desk. After my shower, I asked Eva Elliott what the devil she meant by not telling you where I was. One thing led to another and I fired her. You know what happened after that."

"I'm not sure I do," Mason said.

"Well, I went to see you, and then we went down to see Stephanie Falkner, and . . ."

"And you were at Stephanie's when we left," Mason said.

"I stayed there for a short time. I tried to let Stephanie know how much I had wished to have her in my family."

"What about the gun?" Mason asked.

"I always carry a gun. I have a shoulder holster and my suits are tailored so I can carry the gun under my left arm without it showing. I took my gun out of the holster and gave it to her."

"Was that gun fully loaded when you gave it to her?"

"Of course."

"Had it been fired?"

"That gun hadn't been fired for months, Mason. I'm telling *you* this, but I'm not going to tell anyone else. Before I left Las Vegas I removed the shells in the gun and put in fresh shells. I intended to get rough with Casselman and I wanted to be armed when I called for a showdown. I felt I might need my gun."

"All right," Mason said. "Go ahead. What happened?"

"I keep another gun in my safe in the office. I was going to see Casselman at eleven, but I didn't tell anyone about that appointment. I wanted to be armed when I saw him, so after I left Stephanie's apartment I returned to my office, got the other gun out of my safe, put that gun in my shoulder holster, and then went to call on Casselman."

"That was at eleven o'clock?"

"Perhaps five or ten minutes either way."

"All right, what happened?"

"I used my key on the front door. I went up to Casselman's apartment. I knocked and got no answer. I tried the apartment door. It was unlocked. It had a key lock, not a night latch. I could walk right in, and I did.

"Casselman was in there, sprawled in a pool of blood. He was dead as a mackerel. I looked around. Some woman had stepped in the blood and there was the imprint of her foot and heel plate as plain as could be.

"I felt certain it was the print of Stephanie's shoe. I had to know for sure. So I left Casselman's apartment leaving the door unlocked.

"I went to Stephanie's apartment. She was in bed. She got up and let me in. I didn't tell her where I had been or what I had found. I told her I was terribly nervous and simply had to see her and talk with her for a while."

"All right. What happened?"

"I tried to tell her something about how I felt toward her without going too far. I told her to call on me if she ever needed a friend.

"I could see the gun I had given her was under the pillow. I made an excuse to handle it very briefly. When she had her back turned, I surreptitiously opened the cylinder and sure enough one shell had been fired since I had given her the gun.

"She was wearing a bathrobe, pajamas and slippers. I saw a pair of shoes. I managed to get a good look at them. One of them was still damp. Evidently it had recently been washed. There was a metal heel plate. It matched the imprint of the bloody shoe print I'd seen in Casselman's apartment."

"Did you ask her about it?" Mason asked.

"No. I stayed until around midnight. I told her I wanted her to know I'd be her friend if anything ever happened and she needed a friend, and then I left. I knew I had work to do."

Mason regarded him with level-lidded appraisal. "You went back to Casselman's apartment?"

"Yes. I went back and took time enough to eliminate all evidence that could point to Stephanie."

"What did you do?"

"I am kicking myself for overlooking the one real golden opportunity I had. I had that other gun of mine in my shoulder holster while I was in Stephanie's apartment that second time. I should have simply made a substitution, then and there. But I was too shocked to think clearly."

Mason, his face only a matter of inches from the other man's, regarded him with steady concentration. "You're not lying to me, Homer? You *didn't* switch guns?"

"Definitely not. I tell you, Mason, that gun had been fired between the time I left it with her and the time I returned."

"So what did you do in Casselman's apartment?" Mason asked.

"I did the only thing that could be done. The blood that outlined the print of Stephanie's shoe had dried. At first I thought of trying to scrub it up, but I was afraid there would still be traces they could find and I was afraid of being caught in there with the murdered man. I knew I had to work fast. I put my own foot in the puddle of blood and pressed down enough to get blood all over the sole of my shoe and particularly on my heel. The blood was thick and sticky by that time. I pressed my own bloodstained shoe directly over the print that had been made.

"I decided to take the heat off Stephanie in every way I could. I left several clues that would point to me. I wanted to be a red herring. Then I left the state, intending to keep out of the way of the police here so they couldn't question me. However, after this other matter came up, Junior was destroying your work. I felt I had to see him personally and tell him to sit tight.

"I thought I had eluded the detectives who were shadowing me in Las Vegas. Evidently, I played right into their hands. They waited until my chartered plane landed, and then they picked me up and brought me here for questioning. I refused to make any statement until you were present, and that's the story to date."

"All right," Mason said, "let's go back and face the situation. You follow my lead. I'll do most of the talking. Don't tell them anything unless I give you an okay. You're going to have to take the newspaper publicity. That's the weapon they're holding over you to make you talk. Under the circumstances, you can't avoid it. Come on. Let's go."

Mason opened the closet door, turned out the light, led the way across the secretarial office and back to Hamilton Burger's office.

"Well?" Hamilton Burger asked.

"What do you want to know?" Mason asked.

Burger said, "Mason, I'm calling your attention to a photograph. You've seen a reproduction of this photograph in the press. I want you to study a glossy print of the original photograph. You can see some things on there you can't see in the newspaper reproduction."

Burger handed Mason the glossy eight-by-ten print showing the pool of blood on the floor and, quite plainly, the print of a foot.

"Go ahead," Mason said. "What do you want to know?"

"Now this information," Burger said, "we would like to have come from your client rather than from you, Mr. Mason. We want to know if that is the print of your shoe, Garvin."

Garvin looked at Mason. Mason smiled and shook his head.

"Now wait a minute," Hamilton Burger said, his face coloring. "We're in this thing in good faith. Garvin at least intimated that he would tell us his story straight from the shoulder if we gave him an opportunity to get in touch with his attorney. Either you folks talk or you don't talk!"

"And suppose we don't talk?" Mason asked.

"Then you'd both be sorry."

Burger said, "I'm going to ask you, Garvin, if you went to a shoe shop at 918 Mowbray Street and had a pair of rubber heels put on a pair of new shoes about three weeks ago?"

"Answer that," Mason said.

"I did," Garvin admitted.

"I'm going to show you a pair of shoes and ask you if those are the shoes on which you had those rubber heels installed?"

Burger opened a drawer in his desk, took out a pair of shoes, and handed them to Garvin.

"Where did you get those?" Garvin asked with some surprise.

"Never mind," Burger said. "Are those yours?"

Garvin looked them over. There were several peculiar bluish stains on the sole of one of the shoes.

"Yes," he said.

"For your information," Burger went on, "those shoes have been given a benzidine test for blood. Those purplish stains you see are where there was a reaction indicating the presence of blood on that left shoe. Now in view of that, do you have any statement you want to make as to how that blood got on that shoe?"

"I don't think I care to make any statement on that at this time," Garvin said.

"All right," Hamilton Burger said with ponderous patience, "I'm now going to show you a color photograph," and handed it to Mason.

"Look that over carefully, Mason," he said. "Tell me what you see."

Mason said, "I see a footprint."

"Look it over *carefully*."

Mason studied the photograph.

Hamilton Burger said, "If you study that photograph carefully, you will see something quite plainly which you could only barely detect on the black and white photograph, but which nevertheless is shown here. It's another footprint, the print of a woman's shoe directly under the print of Homer Garvin's shoe. You can see the imprint of the heel plate on the very tip of the heel.

"Now then, Garvin, I'm asking you if you didn't go out to George Casselman's apartment *after* he had been killed, *knowing* he had been killed, for the purpose of leaving evidence there that would confuse the issues. I am asking if you didn't deliberately step in the puddle of blood and then place your own footprint over this woman's footprint with the deliberate intention of obliterating and concealing that footprint."

"Just a moment," Mason said. "As I understand it, that would be a crime."

"Permit me to congratulate you upon your knowledge of the law," Burger said sarcastically.

"Under those circumstances, I advise my client to refuse to answer the question," Mason said.

Burger took a deep breath, "Garvin, I am going to show you a fingerprint which was recovered from the knob of the back door. I may further state that someone had evidently wiped the knob of that back door clean of fingerprints. There was only one fingerprint on it, and that was a very plain, legible fingerprint of the ball of a thumb which had obviously been deliberately placed in the exact center of the knob after the surface had been wiped clean of any other fingerprints.

"That thumbprint is yours, Garvin. There can be no mistake about it. I am going to ask you the circumstances under which you made that print on the doorknob."

"Just a minute," Mason said, "if your contention is correct, and if Garvin was the one who wiped off the doorknob and then left his fingerprint on it, he would be guilty of a crime?"

"He would be guilty of a crime," Hamilton Burger said.

"Then I advise him not to answer," Mason said.

Hamilton Burger turned to Mason. "You yourself made an elaborate switch so you could juggle the murder weapon around in this case, Mason. I'm going to give you one chance to come clean. I want *you* to tell how that murder weapon came into your possession."

"And if I tell you the truth, you won't prosecute me?"

Hamilton Burger thought that over, looked at Mason with suppressed hatred in his eyes. "I'm trying to be fair about this thing, Mason. I'm not going to come out and make a lot of specific promises, but what you say now will greatly affect the attitude of the district attorney's office."

Mason said, "I went out to Homer Garvin, Jr.'s place. I asked him if he had a gun. He gave me a gun. I discharged the gun so that the bullet ploughed a furrow in Garvin's desk. I took Garvin, Jr. to Stephanie Falkner's apartment. He gave her the gun. Now I've told you the truth. What are *you* going to do?"

"I *know* that you switched guns out there, and that because of that switch young Garvin acted as your cat's-paw and took the murder weapon up to Stephanie Falkner."

Mason turned to his client. "There you are, Homer," he said. "That's a pretty good indication of what his promises are worth. If you tell him something that doesn't conform to his cockeyed theory of the case, he says it can't be the truth. He'll only believe the things he wants to hear."

Burger pushed back his chair, started to get to his feet, thought better of it, settled back again in the chair.

Tragg said, "May I ask a question, Mr. District Attorney?"

"Sure, go ahead. Ask all you want," Burger said.

Tragg said, "Mason, do I have your personal assurance, man to man, that you did not substitute any gun out there at young Garvin's place?"

"You have that assurance," Mason told him.

Tragg turned back to Hamilton Burger. "I tell you, Burger, there's something about this whole thing that is a lot deeper than we think at the present time. I personally can't conceive of any reason why Mason *would* have substituted weapons. I personally want to carry on this investigation on the theory that a weapon wasn't substituted, and that the gun Garvin, Jr., took out of his desk was the murder weapon."

"It couldn't have been," Hamilton Burger said flatly.

Lt. Tragg snapped, "Don't be silly!" then corrected himself quickly. "There are certain things about this case which don't fit together. Mason would have had no possible incentive for—"

"That'll do," Burger interrupted. "Watch yourself, Lieutenant. We're here to get information, not to give it. And I prefer to carry on our own arguments in privacy, not where Mr. Perry Mason can drink everything in with the idea that he can capitalize on the things we *don't* know."

Mason arose. "I take it then, the interview is at an end?" he said. "My client has refused to answer any more questions. I have answered your questions fully and frankly. I have given you every bit of information I could without violating my professional duty to safeguard the confidences of a client."

Hamilton Burger jerked a contemptuous thumb. "There's the door," he said.

"How about Garvin?"

Burger jerked his thumb upward. "Your client," he said, "is going to spend quite a little time in a hotel at the expense of the taxpayers."

"Gentlemen," Mason said, "I wish you a very good evening. Garvin, my instructions to you are to make no statement of any sort."

Hamilton Burger picked up the telephone, said to someone at the other end of the line, "Okay, send in the newspaper reporters."

Mason took the elevator down to the curb, caught a cab back to his office. Della Street, waiting apprehensively, said, "How did it go, Chief?"

Mason shook his head. "There's something in this case I don't understand as yet."

"How about the police?"

"There's a lot in the case they don't understand."

"And what about Homer Garvin?"

"Garvin," Mason said, "is going to be charged with being an accessory after the fact, and I'm afraid they've got the deadwood on him."

"And what else?"

"And Stephanie Falkner is being charged with murder, first-degree murder."

"And you?"

Mason grinned. "Garvin and I are being put on ice. The D.A. will get his murder firmly established and then he'll claim we're accessories."

"And how are you going to combat a situation of that sort?"

Mason said, "We're going to have to trust to a faith in human nature, a lot of mental agility and considerable ingenuity. Unless I'm greatly mistaken, the district attorney will have the grand jury indict Stephanie Falkner for the murder of George Casselman by noon tomorrow. He'll then hold Homer Garvin, Sr. as an accessory, and probably won't make any very serious objection to letting him out on bail. He'll hold that charge over him as a club, hoping that sooner or later the pressure will build up to such an extent that Garvin will cave in and help him."

"And in the meantime?" Della Street asked.

Mason grinned. "In the meantime, Della, we'd better get that dinner we were talking about. It may be the last good meal we'll thoroughly enjoy together."

"You mean they'll arrest you?" she asked.

"I doubt it," Mason said, "but somehow I have a feeling this may be the last meal we'll really *enjoy* for quite some time. Let's go.

CHAPTER SIXTEEN

Paul Drake slid into his favorite position, sitting crosswise in the big, overstuffed, leather chair, the small of his back propped against one big, rounded arm, his knees propped over the other, the legs dangling.

"Well, you've got a bear by the tail in one hand, and a tiger by the tail in the other, Perry," he said.

"Homer Garvin, Sr. was indicted for being an accessory in the murder of George Casselman. His bail was set at a hundred thousand dollars. He made bail almost immediately and will be out within an hour or two.

"Stephanie Falkner is held for first-degree murder without bail. The grand jury indicted her about an hour ago. There's an open trial date on the calendar and the district attorney is yelling for an immediate trial, pointing out that defense attorneys are always trying for delay, delay, delay, and he's making a great grandstand in the press."

"What have you found out about Dawn Joyce?" Mason asked.

"It's a little difficult to get a line on a girl like that," Drake said, "particularly after she's just married someone of family and means.

"You know how it is with any show girl or model. As a matter of fact, most models are steady-going, hard-working girls. A good many of them are married, have kids, make good mothers, and wonderful wives. But there's a provincial attitude on the part of the public. The fact that a girl is photographed in bathing suits or does kicks in front of an audience causes lots of people to get funny ideas.

"Over in Las Vegas, you can pick up gossip on Dawn Joyce. She lived in an apartment by herself. She worked part of the time as a show girl in a chorus. She worked part of the time as scenery, one of the girls who puts on a tight-fitting bathing suit and drapes herself around the pools in the various hotels. Then she'd act as a shill on the side, dolling herself out in low-cut, strapless dresses, circulating around the gambling tables, being easy to get acquainted with, and helping the suckers who wanted to gamble to make a little bigger bets and stay with the wheel a little longer than would otherwise be the case."

"Commission?" Mason asked.

"Apparently not," Drake said. "She was on a salary and all this was part of the job. There was nothing crude, no attempt to strong-arm a guy into playing; but you know how it is; a man will stay with the game and buy two or three more stacks of chips if there's an amiable, attractive, young woman standing alongside of him pouring chips across the board. He hates to have it appear that he's a piker when some young woman is giving him an appreciative eye, and at the same time is apparently plunging with her own money."

"And winning?" Mason said.

"Exactly," Drake observed. "You don't know just how they do it, but you watch them and they sure seem to win a lot more than the casual tourists. Of course, you can account for that in part, because they know the game. They know when to bet heavy and when to bet light. In the second place, it makes a lot of difference if you have an unlimited bankroll. Of course, they never cash in on their chips, and they know there's lots more where the last stack came from. Gamblers tell me that lots of people lose out at gambling because they don't have the guts to pile it on heavy enough when they're winning, or the prudence to tap it light when they're losing. Gamblers say luck comes in waves. You're hot and then you're cold. When you're hot you want to pour it on for all it's worth, and when you're cold you want to pull in your horns until you get hot again.

"I don't know whether there's anything to it or not. Personally I'm a poor gambler. Anyhow I'm just telling you about Dawn Joyce. She's easy on the eyes, and she showed as much scenery as the law allowed.

"Now she knew this fellow Casselman. There's no doubt about that. She went out with him on several occasions as a private date. She seemed to like him, or else they had some kind of a business deal hooked up. No one knows.

"Casselman was a blackmailer, but I can't *prove* that on him. No one knows just how he lived. He *was* a sharpshooter. He hung around the Strip in Las Vegas, and he managed to make a pretty good living doing nothing. He made it in cash. He didn't use bank accounts, and he didn't make income tax returns. He just drifted along on a hand-to-mouth basis.

"Lots of people come to Las Vegas. Some of them are tourists who are just passing through. Some of them are a café society set from Los Angeles and San Francisco.

"A man who had a good memory for faces and figures could make money by remembering things other people would like to forget. That would particularly be true if he had a few show girls giving him tips about who did what and when and where."

"Yes," Mason said, "I can see. And that might be hard to trace."

"It is hard to trace," Drake agreed. "Casselman had about fifteen hundred dollars in his wallet when he was shot. As far as anybody can tell, that's every cent he had in the world and yet you know damn well it wasn't. He's got money stashed away somewhere, either in a safety deposit box under another name or buried or hidden somewhere. In any event, he could have gone and put his hand on cash when he needed it. There were times when he paid out as much as ten or fifteen thousand dollars for options on property for a quick deal, and he's produced the cash every time, a nice assortment of hundred-dollar bills."

"And the income tax people have never looked him up?" Mason asked.

"Never made a pass at him as far as I can find out. The guy was a smooth operator. He kept in the background, and he had never made the mistake of making that first income tax return. As far as the records were concerned, no one knew he was alive.

"There's plenty of tie-in between Dawn Joyce who is now Homer Garvin, Jr.'s wife, and George Casselman who is now a corpse. For some reason, Mrs. Garvin, Jr. would like very, very much indeed to have the entire matter hushed up. Whatever her connections with Casselman and her Nevada activities were, she doesn't care about having them aired in the daily press, particularly in view of the fact that she'd like to be received into the upper crust as the wife of Junior Garvin."

"How does he rate?" Mason asked.

"That depends on the class of person you ask. He's a plunger and wild. But he may steady down, and his old man is well thought of, although the old man never goes in for any of the social stuff.

"The kid went into this used-car dealing and, believe me, he works it fast. He believes in quantity turnover and he'll take small profits if he can't make big profits. But he wants turnover and he gets turnover. He has evidently made quite a bit of money out of the car business, and he's plunging in real estate, taking options on various bits of property, and there again he makes quick turnovers. He managed to find out where some property was going to be condemned by the state. No one knows exactly how he found it out, but he showed up with a string of options, and naturally the state was anxious to do business with one man who had control of a big percentage of the property, and who was willing to make a fast buck and let it go at that."

"What did you find out about the Acme Electric and Plumbing Repair Company?"

"Both the Acme outfit and the Eureka Associated Renovators received mail at 1397 Chatham Street, a rooming house. Some man rented a room there and received all the mail. He seldom slept there, but kept his rent paid and dropped in from time to time."

"Description?" Mason asked.

"General," Drake said. "Fits almost anyone. Because he kept the rent paid in advance, no one paid much attention to him.

"I can give you one tip on this murder trial, Perry. Hamilton Burger is going to leave Dawn Joyce out of it just as much as he can. *His* idea is that you made a switch in murder weapons, and he thinks he can prove it. He thinks he's got the deadwood on Stephanie Falkner.

"Of course, you can try to bring in the idea that Dawn Joyce could have been the killer by introducing evidence about that gun, but the minute you do that, Burger is going to go all out with the contention that you went down there with the murder gun, that you pulled a fake accident in order to divert attention, and switched guns simply to drag in Dawn Joyce as a red herring."

"Well," Mason said, "I guess we'll give him all the chance he wants to make that claim. He can't prove I switched guns."

"Apparently he can't *prove* it," Drake said, "and that's burning him up. He can surmise and that's about all.... You're representing Stephanie Falkner?"

"I'm going to represent her."

"Look, Perry, just off the record, what does she say? What happened?"

"There," Mason said, "is the thing that bothers me. She won't say a word, except to assure me that she didn't shoot Casselman. She says she's innocent of any crime. She won't amplify that statement. She says that there is something she would have to disclose if I started cross-examining her that no one knows and she doesn't intend ever to let it come out."

"Something in her past?" Drake asked.

"I assume so," Mason said. "She'll break down her reserve and tell me her story eventually but right at the moment she's sitting tight.

"She says they are going to have to prove her guilty before they can convict her and she says they simply can't do anything more than direct suspicion toward her way with some very inconsequential circumstantial evidence.... And she may be right at that."

"Well," Drake said, "I wish you luck."

"There's just a chance I could need it," Mason told him grinning. "What about the place where those billheads were printed? Can you get any line on that?"

"Not so far. We're telephoning like mad, and we're covering all the more likely job-printing establishments with personal investigators. So far no luck."

"Keep after it," Mason said.

Drake lurched up out of the chair. "We'll sure do that, Perry, and we'll let you know anything that turns up."

CHAPTER SEVENTEEN

Hamilton Burger arose to make his opening address to the jury.

"In this case," he said, "I am going to be brief and factual. It is the intention of the prosecution to avoid all dramatics and to present the case with such mathematical certainty that there can be but one inescapable conclusion.

"On the seventh day of October of this year, George Casselman met his death. Medical evidence will show you ladies and gentlemen of the jury that a revolver was placed against Casselman's body just below the heart and slightly to the left of the median line. The trigger was pulled. The shot was what is known as a contact wound. That is, the muzzle of the revolver was firmly held directly against the body of the victim. In this way, the gases from the exploding shell as well as the bullet went into the victim's body. Under those circumstances, the sound of the report would have been greatly muffled.

"The prosecution intends to show that the defendant, Stephanie Falkner, had an appointment with George Casselman. She went to keep that appointment by entering the front door of Casselman's apartment. Sometime later she was seen surreptitiously leaving the apartment by way of the back door.

"We expect to show you that she stepped in the blood of her victim, that she went to the bathroom and tried to wash the blood from her shoe. She left a footprint etched in blood on the floor, and she left towels in the bathroom that bore traces of human blood and bits of material which came from her shoe.

"Her friend, Homer Garvin, tried to cover up the traces of her crime and did obliterate much of the evidence. For that he will in due time be tried, but enough evidence remains to convict this defendant.

"We expect to prove with mathematical certainty that the gun with which the murder was committed was in the possession of the defendant. An ingenious device was used by her attorney, Perry Mason, to confuse the issues on that point, but bear well in mind that the fatal weapon was found in her possession. Let her explain how that came about if she can.

"Mr. Perry Mason, the attorney who is representing both this defendant and Homer Garvin, has not been indicted as an accessory or an accomplice at this time. However, he has not been granted any immunity. We will ask you, ladies and gentlemen, to weigh the evidence and bring in a verdict of first-degree murder against this defendant. After that verdict is in, you may leave it to us to take such additional steps as will deal with the persons responsible for juggling evidence and obstructing the administration of justice. You are not to concern yourselves with that aspect of the case except as it shows certain things which explain the physical facts. Your sole concern is as to whether this defendant murdered George Casselman.

"We shall expect a just verdict and a fair verdict at your hands."

Hamilton Burger turned with dignity and walked back to his seat at the counsel table.

Judge Hilton Decker looked at Perry Mason.

"Does the defense wish to make an opening statement now, or wait until later?"

"We will wait," Mason said.

"Call your first witness, Mr. Prosecutor," Judge Decker said.

Hamilton Burger's chief trial assistant, Guy Hendrie, took charge and called as the prosecution's first witness one of the radio officers who had entered the Casselman apartment and who described briefly the body on the floor, the pool of blood, and the fact that the Homicide Squad had been promptly notified.

There was no cross-examination.

The prosecution's next witness was Sgt. Holcomb, who took the stand with an air of importance, testified to his connection with the Homicide Squad, the fact that he had arrived at the scene, had been in charge, had directed the taking of photographs, and eventually the removal of the body, that thereafter fingerprint men had been instructed to try to develop latent fingerprints.

Again there was no cross-examination.

The photographer who had taken the pictures was sworn and the various pictures were introduced in evidence, including a color picture of the bloodied footprint on the floor.

Again there was no cross-examination.

Judge Decker glanced sharply at Mason, started to say something, then changed his mind.

The autopsy surgeon testified to the nature of the wound and the course of the bullet. The wound, he explained, was what was known as a contact wound. He stated that the one shot had been almost instantly fatal, although there had been a brief period of unconsciousness during which there had been a very large internal and external hemorrhage. He identified the fatal bullet which had been recovered from the body of the decedent.

He fixed the time of death as being probably between seven o'clock in the evening of the seventh of October and midnight. He had performed an autopsy at noon of the eighth and he fixed the probable time of death as between twelve and seventeen hours prior to the autopsy, although he was inclined to consider fifteen to sixteen hours prior to the autopsy as being the most logical time.

Again Mason failed to ask any questions on cross-examination.

At that point, Guy Hendrie recalled Sgt. Holcomb to the witness stand.

"I am showing you herewith a certain Colt revolver of .38 caliber, and I will ask you if you have seen that gun before?"

"Yes, sir. I have."

"When did you first see it?"

"On the eighth of October, around eleven-forty-five o'clock of that day."

"Where did you first see it?"

"In the apartment of Stephanie Falkner, the defendant in this case."

"Where was it in that apartment?"

"Lying upon a table near the center of the room."

"Did you take or did you cause a photograph to be taken of the apartment?"

"I did, yes, sir."

"And does that photograph show where the gun was found?"

"Yes, sir."

"Do you have a print of that photograph with you?"

"Yes, sir." .

Sgt. Holcomb produced a photograph.

"We ask that it be received in evidence," Hendrie said.

"Just a moment," Mason said, "I would like to ask a question of the witness in connection with this photograph."

The jurors, impressed by the fact that this was the first attempt Mason had made to cross-examine a witness, turned to regard him with considerable interest.

"This photograph shows a weapon on the table, Sergeant," Mason said.

"Yes, sir."

"Is that the same weapon which you have identified?"

"Yes, sir."

"Is that weapon in the same position in which you found it?"

"Yes, sir."

"Then the photograph must have been taken before the weapon was moved?"

Sgt. Holcomb hesitated a moment, crossed his legs. "Well, the weapon was picked up, examined, and then returned to the same place where it had been found."

"Who examined it?"

"I did."

"Anyone else?"

"Lt. Tragg of Homicide was with me at the time."

"And of what did the examination consist?"

"We broke open the cylinder, we saw that there was an empty cartridge directly underneath the firing pin, we smelled the barrel."

"Did you dust it for fingerprints?"

"Yes."

"And then what?"

"Then the weapon was returned to the exact position in which it had been found so that it could be photographed."

"And then this photograph was taken?"

"Yes, sir. That is right."

"Now if you know," Mason asked, "was any attempt made to connect the fatal bullet in this case with this weapon?"

"Just a moment," Hamilton Burger said. "That is going to be proven by my next witness. I will have the ballistics expert on the stand, and he can be cross-examined."

"That's quite all right," Mason said. "All I am asking this witness is whether such an examination was made?"

"Yes, sir."

"When?" Mason asked.

"Shortly after the weapon was recovered. I don't know exactly the time, but it was within a few hours."

"What do you mean by a few hours?" Mason asked.

"Just a short time, a very brief interval."

"As much as twenty-four hours?" Mason asked.

The witness hesitated.

"As much as forty-eight hours?" Mason asked.

"No, it wasn't forty-eight hours."

"It could have been twenty-four hours?"

"It could have been. I think it was much less."

"Who put the weapon back on the table in the exact place where it was found?"

"I did."

"How did you know where that exact place was?"

"I remembered it."

"Did you mark it in any way?"

"No."

"Now when you entered the room," Mason asked, "and found this weapon, was the muzzle pointing toward the door or was it pointing away from the door?"

"It was on the table as shown in that photograph."

Mason, holding the photograph so the witness couldn't see it, repeated, "Was the muzzle pointed toward the door or away from the door?"

"At this moment, I can't remember. I knew at the time. The photograph will show its exact position. I replaced the gun within five minutes of the time I picked it up and while its position was fresh in my mind."

"Thank you," Mason said, "these are all the questions I have in regard to the photograph, if the Court please."

Hendrie said, "I now wish to offer the photograph in evidence."

"No objection," Mason said.

Hendrie turned to the witness. "Did the defendant make any statement to you with reference to the gun?"

"Yes, I asked her about the gun, and she said Mr. Homer Garvin had given it to her."

"Did you have any further conversation with her?"

"Yes, I asked her about the discharged shell in the gun and she said she knew nothing about it, that the weapon was in the same condition as when she had received it."

"We ask that the weapon be marked for identification."

"So ordered," the Court ruled. "It will be People's Exhibit Number 30, and the photograph is in evidence as People's Exhibit Number 29."

"You may inquire," Hendrie said.

"Did she say whether or not she had received the gun from Homer Garvin, Sr., or Homer Garvin, Jr.?" Mason asked.

"Just that she had received it from Homer Garvin. That was all she said."

"Did she say when she had received it?"

"No, sir. She didn't."

Hamilton Burger said, "If the Court please, we expect to connect up the time element. However, in that connection, I will ask Sgt. Holcomb one question. What time did you arrive at the defendant's apartment, Sergeant?"

"It was almost exactly eleven-forty-five."

"No further questions," Mason said.

"Call Alexander Redfield," Hendrie said.

Redfield, the ballistics expert, who had been cross-examined by Mason in several other cases and who had learned to be very wary indeed of Mason's ingenuity on cross-examination, took the oath and settled himself cautiously on the witness stand.

From Hendrie's manner, it was apparent that there was a certain feeling of exasperation on the part of the prosecuting attorneys toward Redfield, that Redfield, on the other hand, knowing Mason's ability as a cross-examiner and his knowledge of the subject of ballistics, was determined to give only such evidence as was completely unassailable.

"I show you People's Exhibit Number 30, the weapon which has just been received in evidence. Are you familiar with that weapon?"

Redfield took the exhibit in his hands, studied it carefully, checked the serial number, then said, "Yes, I am familiar with it."

"I show you a bullet which has previously been introduced in evidence as People's Exhibit Number 14, the fatal bullet. Are you familiar with that bullet?"

The witness took a magnifying glass from his pocket, carefully inspected the base of the bullet, then said, "Yes, sir. I am familiar with that bullet. It has my secret mark on it."

"That bullet has already been identified as the fatal bullet," Hendrie said. "Now can you tell us whether or not that bullet, Exhibit 14, was fired from the gun, Exhibit 30?"

"Yes, sir, that bullet was fired from this gun," the witness said.

"Could it have been fired from any other gun?"

"No, sir. It was fired from this gun."

"You may cross-examine," Hendrie said.

"No questions," Mason announced.

"Call Paul Clinton," Hendrie said.

Paul Clinton came forward, took the stand and identified himself as a scientific investigator in the employ of the police department. He qualified himself as an expert in the science of developing and comparing fingerprints, in making chemical tests for bloodstains, in the grouping of blood, in making various types of analysis.

"Did you have occasion to search the apartment occupied by the defendant in this case?" Hendrie asked.

"Yes, sir."

"When?"

"On the ninth day of October."

"Of this year?"

"Yes, sir."

"Did you find any wearing apparel in the apartment of the defendant which was stained with blood?"

"I did. Yes, sir."

"What article did you find?"

"I found a left shoe with blood on the sole and on the heel."

"Were you able to get enough blood to type the stain?"

"No, sir."

"Were you able to get enough blood to determine that it was human blood?"

"No, sir. The shoe had been carefully and thoroughly washed, but chemical tests gave a typical blood reaction."

"Do you have that shoe with you?"

"I do, yes, sir."

"Produce it, please. . . . This is the shoe which you found in the defendant's apartment?"

"Yes, sir."

"Is there anything distinctive about that shoe?"

"Yes, sir, the sole is of a certain patented composition."

"I will ask you if you found any soiled towels in the Casselman apartment?"

"I did, yes, sir. I produce herewith one towel which I consider especially significant."

"Why?"

"It had blood smears on it. It had been used to wipe off some bloodstained object. In addition to the bloodstains or smears, there was a very small bit of foreign matter adhering to the towel. Spectroscopic analysis showed that bit of foreign matter to have exactly the same component parts as the sole of this shoe."

Hendrie said, "I ask to have the shoe introducd in evidence as People's

Exhibit Number 31, the towel as People's Exhibit 32."

"No objection," Mason said.

"So ordered. They will be received in evidence," Judge Decker ruled.

"Now I'm going to call your attention to the photograph, Exhibit Number 12, which has been received in evidence. I am going to ask you if you have made a careful study of that photograph?"

"I have. Yes, sir."

"What did you find from your study?"

"I found that there are evidences in this color photograph of two footprints. There is the evidence of a shoe with a fairly high heel which has been covered with a metal plate held in place by four brads.

"Subsequent investigation convinced me that this heel plate bore the number 'thirty-three.' In part, the numbers which had been stamped into this plate are obliterated but in this photograph which I hold in my hand, it is possible to detect faint traces of the number thirty-three. This footprint made with the heel print bearing the number thirty-three has been almost obliterated by the footprint of a man wearing a much larger shoe and this footprint had been superimposed upon the other print at a time considerably later than the making of the first print."

"Can you tell how much later?"

"I would say probably two or three hours later."

"Referring now to the article of wearing apparel, the shoe which you found in the defendant's apartment, and which has been received in evidence as Exhibit Number 31, have you been able to determine whether this particular shoe which you hold in your hand made the bloody print which you have testified to finding underneath the print made by the larger shoe?"

"If the Court please," Mason said, "I object to that question as calling for a conclusion of the witness in a manner which invades the province of the jury. It is for the jury to determine whether this shoe made that print, if it should appear there is any print there, and the witness is not testifying purely to a figment of the imagination.

"This witness can testify as to what he has found. He can testify as to an opinion in connection with the legitimate field of expert evidence, but he cannot invade the province of the jury."

Judge Decker said, "Let me see that photograph and the shoe please."

The judge studied the photograph and the shoe for some seconds, then said, "The objection will be sustained. The jurors can and will draw their own conclusions. This witness can testify only as to the facts from which such conclusions can be drawn."

The prosecution took the ruling with poor grace. "If the Court please," Hamilton Burger said, ponderously getting to his feet and frowning with displeasure, "this witness has qualified himself as an expert."

"He may give his opinions as to collateral matters," Judge Decker ruled. "He may set forth the various factors in this case, but on the question of whether this identical shoe made this identical print which the witness claims he has been able to decipher from the photograph, the Court feels it would be invading the province of the jury to permit an answer to the question.

"The Court may point out that, while the witness contends there were two footprints visible in the photograph, that very point may be contested by the defense."

Hamilton Burger slowly sat down.

Hendrie resumed the examination. "You have testified that the second print, the one made with the man's shoe, and which covers the first print, was made some two hours later?"

"I would say approximately two or three or perhaps four hours later."

"How can you determine?"

"There are certain changes in blood which take place when the blood leaves the body. Blood will coagulate in some three minutes or less. After it has coagulated or clotted, it can be restored to liquid form by pressure or by certain types of agitation. In this case, it is my opinion that the person wearing the man's shoes stepped in the pool of blood after it had coagulated and that the track which was made thereafter shows distinctly certain characteristics which indicate the condition of the blood, a condition which, in my opinion, would probably indicate an interval of some time, probably two or three hours."

"Have you examined a man's shoe which could have made the covering track shown in this photograph?"

"I have."

"Do you have that shoe with you?"

"I do."

"Will you produce it please?"

The witness delved into his bag and produced a shoe.

"Is there something distinctive about this shoe?"

"There is."

"In what way?"

"There is a relatively new rubber heel on the shoe and there is a little defect in that rubber heel which can be noticed here and the same defect in exactly the same place can be seen in this photograph of the track."

"Have you tested this shoe for blood?"

"I have. Yes, sir."

"Did you find blood on it?"

"Yes, sir. My chemical tests showed the presence of blood."

"Those tests are responsible for the discoloration of the shoe?"

"That is right."

"Where may I ask did you get this shoe?"

"From a suitcase, the property of Homer Garvin, Sr."

Hendrie said, "May we have this shoe marked People's Exhibit Number 33 for identification. Now, Mr. Clinton, did you examine the Casselman apartment for latent fingerprints?"

"I did."

"What did you find?"

"The doorknobs of all doors had been carefully wiped by someone so that there were no latent fingerprints on any of the knobs with one exception."

"And that exception?"

"The back door. There was a left thumbprint on that back door without anything else in the line of a latent fingerprint appearing on it."

"Do you know whose fingerprint it was that was found on the door of this apartment?"

"Yes, sir."

"Whose was it?"

"The fingerprint of Mr. Homer Garvin."

"Cross-examine," Hendrie said turning to Perry Mason.

Mason said, "How do you know that the room had been wiped clean of fingerprints?"

"Because normally there are fingerprints in every room. There are latent fingerprints some of which are smudged, some of which can be developed so that they can be identified. But when one finds a complete absence of fingerprints, it indicates that someone has removed all fingerprints, particularly from objects like doorknobs."

"*When* was this done?" Mason asked.

"I can't tell you when it was done."

"You found a fingerprint on the knob of the back door?"

"Yes, sir. A left thumbprint."

"And you were able to identify that?"

"I did. Yes, sir. It was the left thumbprint of Homer Garvin."

"Senior or Junior?"

"Senior."

"When was it made?"

"I can't tell you."

"Was it made before the murder was committed?"

"*I don't know.* I *do* know that it was made after the knobs had been wiped clean of fingerprints, and since there was only the one fingerprint on all the doorknobs, I know that the cleaning of these objects for fingerprints must have been done while Mr. Garvin was in the room."

"How do you know that?"

"Because there were no other fingerprints. If he had entered the room after the knobs had been cleaned, there would have been fingerprints on the knobs where he had entered the room, where he had touched the doors, but, since there was only the one absolutely perfect fingerprint, which had been made by pressure of the thumb against the knob of the door, I know that the articles had been wiped clean at a time when he was in the room."

"This fingerprint was on the knob of the back door?"

"Yes, on the knob of the back door."

"Wasn't it possible that someone could have wiped the fingerprints from the inside of the knobs and that Mr. Garvin, coming up the back stairs of the apartment and finding the apartment door slightly open, had decided to close it, that he had reached in and, in doing so, had touched his thumb to the knob in this manner?"

"No, sir. That fingerprint was deliberately left on the doorknob. It was not in a position where a person would have normally placed his hand to close the door."

Mason said, "Someone could have reversed the doorknobs, could they not?"

"What do you mean?"

"The rounded doorknob is placed on a square spindle and held in place by a setscrew. The knob which you found on the inside of the door could at some previous time have been on the outside of the door, could it not?"

"It could have, yes," the witness reluctantly conceded.

"And the print of Mr. Garvin could have been made on the outside knob, and thereafter someone wearing gloves could have conceivabley transferred the outer knob to the inside?"

"Well, of course, if you want to engage in fanciful speculation as to the things which could conceivably have happened, it could have been done."

"That's all," Mason said.

"Now then, if the Court please," Hamilton Burger said, getting to his feet, "I am going to call a hostile witness. I am going to call Homer Garvin, Sr. to the witness stand."

"I take it," Judge Decker said, "you wish to be permitted to ask leading questions, on the ground that you are dealing with a hostile witness. I think, however, the better practice is to call the witness to the stand and proceed with the interrogation. Then if there are objections on the ground that the questions are leading, the Court will rule on those objections at the time they are made."

"Very well, Your Honor. Come forward, Mr. Garvin."

Garvin came forward, was sworn, and took his position on the witness stand.

"I am going to call your attention to a shoe which has previously been marked People's Exhibit 33 for identification. I am going to ask you if that is your shoe."

"That is my shoe."

"Did you wear that shoe on the night of October seventh of this year?"

"I did."

"Did you deliberately step into a pool of blood in the apartment of George Casselman in the Ambrose Apartments at number 948 Christine Drive, and thereafter place your foot over a footprint which you found etched in dried blood in that apartment?"

"Objected to as incompetent, irrelevant, and immaterial," Mason said.

"The objection will be overruled."

The witness said, "I refuse to answer."

"On what grounds?"

"On the grounds that the answer may tend to incriminate me."

"Your Honor, I now ask that the shoe previously marked People's Exhibit 33 for identification be received in evidence."

Judge Decker hesitated a moment, then said, "There appearing to be no objection, it is so ordered."

"Did you enter Apartment 211 of the Ambrose Apartments at 948 Christine Drive on the night of October seventh?" Burger asked the witness.

"Yes."

"At what time?"

"Perhaps about eleven or eleven-thirty in the evening."

"Did you at that time by the means of a cloth or some other manner deliberately remove fingerprints from certain objects in that apartment?"

"I refuse to answer on the grounds that the answer may incriminate me."

Hamilton Burger, seeing the rapt attention of the jurors, and knowing that the answers of the witness were the psychological equivalent of affirmative answers, smiled.

"On the seventh day of October, did you give or loan a weapon to the defendant in this case and tell her that you wanted her to have this weapon for her own protection?"

"I did."

"Was that weapon the revolver which I now hand you and which is marked People's Exhibit Number 30?"

Garvin examined the gun. "I believe that is the weapon. Yes."

"I will ask you to describe in detail your movements on the night of October seventh."

"I returned from Las Vegas. I went to my office where I have a shower, a wardrobe, and some clothes. I took a shower and changed my clothes."

"Then what did you do?"

Mason said, "Now, if the Court please, I object on the ground that the movements of this witness are incompetent, irrelevant, and immaterial, except as to the two matters on which the witness has already testified; to wit, that he was in the apartment of Casselman sometime in the vicinity of eleven o'clock, and that he loaned the defendant the weapon People's Exhibit Number 30. Aside from that, any other activities engaged in by this witness are incompetent, irrelevant and immaterial."

"They may be *very* pertinent," Hamilton Burger said.

"Then show that they are pertinent by showing what you want."

Judge Decker frowned. "This is a very peculiar situation," he said. "It is quite apparent to the Court what the prosecution seeks to prove by this witness, and, in view of the testimony, the time element is not too remote."

"However, if the Court please," Mason said, "it is quite possible that this witness may have done certain things that might be incompetent as far as the issues in this case are concerned."

"The Court is going to sustain the objection," Judge Decker said, "although it is apparently a close point. Quite evidently the witness has reached definite decisions in his own mind as to where he intends to exercise the privilege of his constitutional right not to incriminate himself. The Court can very readily understand that there is no statute of limitations which has run in the matter, and this witness is facing a very real danger in that after the conclusion of this case he is to be tried on certain matters concerning which he is now being interrogated.

"Under the circumstances and in view of the situation, I think the Court will narrow the examination, particularly in view of the fact that the testimony of this witness is being used to build up a case against the defendant. It is quite possible that certain things he might have done cannot be considered as being binding upon the defendant unless there was some unity of purpose or unless the actions were a part of some pact or design which had been mutually agreed upon."

"Very well," Hamilton Burger said, "we'll prove some of these activities by other witnesses."

Hamilton Burger engaged in a whispered conference with Hendrie, then said, "Where did you get this gun which has been introduced in evidence as People's Exhibit Number 30?"

"I owned a sporting-goods store among some of my other investments. While I was the owner of that sporting-goods store I withdrew three guns from the stock."

"And what did you do with those weapons?"

"I kept two for myself. I gave one to my son."

"And those you kept for yourself?"

"I customarily carried a gun with me. I also kept a spare gun in my office. When I was absent I locked this gun in the safe."

"Let's put it this way," Hamilton Burger said. "Let's call the gun which you gave your son the 'Junior Gun', let's call the gun you put in your safe the 'Safe Gun', and the gun which you carried in your holster the 'Holster Gun.'

"Now I will limit this question to certain specific activities. Isn't it a fact that after you gave the defendant the Holster Gun, you returned to your office, unlocked your safe and put the Safe Gun in your shoulder holster?"

"Is there any objection?" Judge Decker asked.

"No objection to that question," Mason said.

"Well," Judge Decker said, "it seems to me— However, if there is no objection, I will permit the answer."

"Did you do that?" Hamilton Burger asked.

"Yes, sir, I did."

"That very evening?"

"Yes, sir."

"When did you do that?"

"About...I would say about ten-fifty-five."

"Then did you return to the apartment of the defendant after that?"

"Yes, sir."

"Now then, after you had returned to the apartment of the defendant, did you have occasion to again see the Holster Gun, which is now Exhibit Number 30?"

"Yes, sir."

"Where was it?"

"It was on the bed of the defendant, under the pillow."

"Did you at that time examine the gun?"

"Yes, sir."

"Did you have it in your hands?"

"Yes, sir."

"And did you, at that time, notice that since the time you had given the gun to the defendant the gun had been fired?"

"Objected to as leading and suggestive, incompetent, irrelevant, and immaterial," Mason said.

"The objection is overruled."

"It is further objected to that it calls for the conclusion of the witness."

"On that ground," Judge Decker ruled, "I think perhaps there should be some further examination for the purpose of laying a foundation."

"I will put the question this way," Hamilton Burger said. "Was there something about the weapon when you saw it that second time at the defendant's apartment which caused you to make a detailed inspection of the cylinder of the weapon?"

The witness hesitated, crossed his legs.

"You're under oath," Hamilton Burger thundered at him, "and there's nothing in this question which calls for evidence which will incriminate you in any way. I am asking you if you, for some reason, made an examination of that weapon."

"Yes, sir. I did."

"What did you find?"

"I found that the cylinder contained an exploded cartridge."

"What was the condition of the gun when you gave it to the defendant earlier in the evening?"

The witness hesitated. "It was fully loaded," he said at length.

"You know that of your own knowledge?"

"Yes."

"*How* do you know it?"

"Because just prior to leaving Las Vegas, I had reloaded the gun with fresh ammunition. I had reason to believe that I might, later on in the day, be in a position of some danger."

"And the reason that you went to the apartment of George Casselman later on that evening was that you had reason to believe the defendant might have used the weapon which you gave her to kill George Casselman? Isn't that right?"

"Objected to, if the Court please," Mason said, "on the ground that the question is incompetent, irrelevant, and immaterial, and I assign the asking of that question as prejudicial misconduct on the part of the prosecution. This defendant is not bound by any reasoning or any ideas or any surmises or anything else which may have been in the *mind* of *this* witness."

"The objection is sustained," Judge Decker ruled. "The prosecution certainly should realize that the thoughts within the mind of this witness are not binding upon this defendant. This entire matter is being developed in an exceedingly unusual way. The Court is mindful of the fact that this is not a case against this witness, but is a case against this defendant, and that her guilt or innocence can only be established by certain pertinent rules of evidence. The jurors are instructed to completely disregard this question by the district attorney, and also any inference which may have been drawn from that question by the jurors. Proceed, Mr. District Attorney."

"That's all," Hamilton Burger said, smiling triumphantly.

"Just a moment," Mason said. "I have one question on cross-examination. Why did you give the defendant what the district attorney has referred to as the Holster Gun, the gun which is now Exhibit Number 30?"

"Because," Homer Garvin said, "she had at one time been engaged to my son, Homer Garvin, Jr. I had looked forward to having her in the family as a daughter-in-law, and then when it turned out that the engagement had been broken, I suddenly realized—I realized that I loved her."

Stephanie Falkner, sitting behind Mason at the bar, suddenly put a handkerchief to her eyes and started sobbing.

"Now then," Mason said, "I will ask you one more question. Prior to the evening of October seventh of this year, had you uncovered information which led you to believe that George Casselman had been the one who had murdered Glenn Falkner, the father of the defendant?"

The effect upon the jurors was electrical.

"Your Honor, Your Honor!" Hamilton Burger shouted, getting to his feet, gesticulating. "That question is absolutely incompetent, the asking of that question is misconduct on the part of the attorney for the defense. It is not proper cross-examination. It is no part of the case. It has no bearing in any way. The prosecution is not bound by anything this witness may have thought."

"The objection is sustained," Judge Decker said.

Mason smiled. "Now then, did you on the evening of October seventh *communicate to the defendant* in this case the fact that in your opinion George Casselman had killed her father?"

"The same objection," Hamilton Burger shouted.

"Same ruling," Judge Decker said.

"Just a minute," Mason said. "The prosecution called for part of a conversation which took place when this witness gave the defendant the gun. I am now asking this witness if something to this effect was not said when the gun was given to the defendant. In other words, when the prosecution calls for part of the conversation, I have a right to call for all of it."

"The witness may answer the question," Judge Decker ruled, "with the understanding that it will be limited to any statement which was made as part of the same conversation concerning which testimony was given on direct examination."

"Yes, sir," Garvin said. "I told her that I felt Casselman had killed her father, and that I was afraid he might try to kill her. I felt that she was in danger and I gave her this weapon so that she could protect herself. I told her to keep it in her possession at all times because I felt that I was in a position to develop a case against Casselman which would enable the authorities to arrest Casselman for the murder of her father and to prosecute him."

Mason said, "Thank you. That is all."

"No questions," Hamilton Burger snapped.

"Now, if the Court please," Mason said, "I move to strike out the entire testimony of the witness Garvin."

"On what grounds?" Judge Decker asked.

"On the grounds that there is no evidence whatsoever showing that the defendant knew of the things Garvin was doing or had any inkling of what he intended to do. She is not bound in any way by anything he might have done in the mistaken belief that he was aiding her.

"Let us suppose that for some reason this witness had decided in his own mind that I had killed George Casselman. In order to protect me, he went to the Casselman apartment. He found that Casselman had been murdered but there was no evidence to indicate that I had committed the murder. I had not communicated with him in any way. I had not asked him to do anything. He tried to protect me by removing certain evidence. I certainly am not bound by the fact that he removed that evidence."

Hamilton Burger on his feet said, "Just a moment, Your Honor. Just a moment! I want to be heard on this. There are certain peculiar conditions existing in that Casselman apartment. The doorknobs were wiped clean of fingerprints. The footprint of a woman's shoe, which the evidence now shows to be the defendant's shoe, was obliterated by this witness. We have a right to show the physical conditions in that apartment and how they occurred."

"You have a right to show the physical conditions," Judge Decker said. "You have the right to show that someone wiped the latent fingerprints from the doorknob. But that doesn't mean that you have a right to show that this was done by some friend of the defendant unless you can show that the defendant had some knowledge of the action and acquiesced therein, or suggested the action in some way."

"Exactly, Your Honor," Mason said, and sat down.

Judge Decker frowned. "This entire matter is highly unusual. It has been presented in a most unusual manner, and the Court is willing to confess that when the stock objections as to testimony being incompetent, irrelevant, and immaterial were made almost as a matter of routine, the Court didn't realize exactly what was in the mind of counsel. The Court feels that counsel should have elaborated upon this point at that time."

"If I had done so," Mason said, "and the Court had sustained the objection, the prosecution would have achieved a notable triumph in that the inference would have been plain to the jurors who would have felt that evidence was being withheld on a technicality."

"Well, there is certainly a part of this witness's evidence that is pertinent," Judge Decker said. "He gave the defendant the gun. He testified that, when he gave the defendant the gun, it was fully loaded. He has testified that later on that same evening he saw the gun for the second time, and that at that time it had one empty cartridge in the cylinder."

"We will not include that evidence in our motion to strike," Mason said. "Nor do we include evidence as to the shoe being that of the defendant. But we do object to all questions asked the witness as to his entering the apartment of George Casselman and we move that that portion of the evidence be stricken."

"The Court is inclined to go along with you on that point, Mr. Mason. However, it is now approaching the hour of the evening adjournment. The Court will take the matter under advisement until tomorrow morning. In the meantime, the Court will take a recess until ten o'clock tomorrow morning, during which the jurors are instructed not to form or express any opinion as to the merits of the case, not to discuss the evidence, or permit anyone to discuss it in their presence. The jurors will refrain from reaching any opinion until the case has been finally submitted. Court will take a recess until ten o'clock."

CHAPTER EIGHTEEN

Hamilton Burger saved his surprise witness for the morning.

"Call Homer Garvin, Jr.," he said as soon as court had reconvened and it was stipulated the defendant was in court and the jurors were all present.

Junior Garvin came forward, his lips a tight line of determination.

He was sworn, gave his name and address, and established his relationship as the son of the witness, Homer Garvin, who had previously testified.

"Now," Hamilton Burger said, holding an extended finger in front of the witness, "I am going to ask you to listen very carefully to my questions and to answer those questions, and not to volunteer any information. It has been established that your father purchased three guns, identical in appearance, caliber and make. For convenience in the testimony we have designated the gun which he gave you as the 'Junior Gun,' the one which he had in his holster early in the evening of October seventh of this year as the 'Holster Gun,' and the one which he had in his locked safe as the 'Safe Gun.' Do you understand those designations?"

"Yes, sir."

"It now appears without contradiction that during the evening of October seventh your father gave the defendant Stephanie Falkner the gun we have described as the Holster Gun, that he later on went to the safe and put the gun we have referred to as the Safe Gun in his holster.

"It also appears that one of these three guns was the murder weapon and it is now in court as Exhibit Number 30. You understand these facts?"

"Yes, sir."

"Very well. I now want to ask you about the weapon your father gave you which we will refer to as the Junior Gun. I am going to ask you whether on the eighth day of October of this year you gave Mr. Perry Mason this gun?"

"I did."

"Did Mr. Mason have it in his hands?"

"He did. Yes, sir."

"Did Mr. Mason do anything with that gun?"

"Yes."

"What?"

"Objected to as incompetent, irrelevant, and immaterial," Mason said.

"I propose to connect it up," Hamilton Burger said.

"I think we should have something more than the district attorney's statement that he proposes to connect it up," Mason said. "I would like to ask the witness a question simply on that phase of the case."

"Very well," Judge Decker said.

"Was that gun," Mason asked, "the one we are referring to as the Junior Gun, the same gun which I now show you and which has been introduced in evidence as People's Exhibit Number 30?"

The witness looked at the gun, said, "Definitely not. It was a gun exactly like this, in appearance, but it wasn't this gun."

"In that case, if the Court please," Mason said, "anything that the witness might have done with any other gun is certainly not binding on this defendant, and is entirely outside the issues of this case."

"I think that is correct," Judge Decker said. "The objection is sustained."

Hamilton Burger said angrily, "Well, I'll get at it another way. You see this gun People's Exhibit Number 30?"

"Yes, sir."

"Have you ever seen *that* gun before?"

"Yes, sir."

"When?"

"Perry Mason handed it to me."

"When?"

"On the eighth day of October of this year."

"And what did you do with *that* gun?"

"Objected to as incompetent, irrelevant, and immaterial," Mason said. "Whatever I did is not binding on the defendant."

"The Court is inclined to overrule that objection," Judge Decker said. "It now appears that the witness has identified the gun positively, the gun which is Exhibit Number 30."

"What did you do with that gun?" Hamilton Burger asked.

"I took it to the apartment of Stephanie Falkner."

"The defendant in this case?"

"Yes, sir."

"And then what did you do?"

"*I* didn't do very much. I stood there like a bump on a log, while Mr. Mason recited some rigmarole to the effect that the defendant was in danger of some sort and that I was bringing her a gun that she could use for defense."

"Now you say that Mr. Mason handed you this gun?" Hamilton Burger asked.

"Yes, sir."

"When?"

"On the eighth day of October of this year."

"Where?"

"Out at my place of business."

"Prior to that time had you handed Mr. Mason a gun?"

"Yes, sir."

"And what gun was that?"

"It was the gun we are referring to as the Junior Gun. It was identical in appearance with the one that I am now holding, which is the murder weapon, and which is marked People's Exhibit Number 30."

"You gave Mr. Mason that gun which we are calling the Junior Gun?"

"Yes, sir."

"And what did Mr. Mason do with *that* gun?"

"He discharged that gun."

"You mean he fired it?"

"Yes, sir. The bullet ploughed into my desk."

"I show you a photograph which purports to be a picture of a desk with a long furrow stretching along it, and ask you if you know what that picture represents?"

"That is the desk in my office approximately as it exists today. It is a picture of the desk immediately after Perry Mason had fired this shot into it."

"And then what happened?"

"Then during the confusion incident to firing that shot, Mr. Mason substituted this gun, which I hold in my hand, and which is People's Exhibit Number 30, in place of the gun I had handed him which we are calling the Junior Gun. He handed the murder gun back to me under such circumstances that I would think it was the Junior Gun and suggested that I give it to Stephanie Falkner."

"And by doing so apparently accounted for the discharged shell in the cylinder of the gun, and also at the same time sought to establish the fact that the murder gun, Exhibit 30, had been in your possession during the time the murder had been committed? Is that right?"

"Objected to as argumentative," Mason said, "and I assign the asking of the question as misconduct."

"The objection is well taken," Judge Decker said, "and the district attorney is admonished to refrain from such questions. That is purely argumentative and calls for a conclusion of the witness as to what happened. The jurors will disregard the question and will not draw any inference from it. Now proceed, Mr. District Attorney, and please ask questions which are within the scope of the issues and are proper."

Hamilton Burger flushed at the rebuke of the Court, turned to Perry Mason and said, "Cross-examine."

Mason said. "You have testified that I substituted this murder gun, Exhibit 30, for the Junior Gun which you had given me?"

"Yes, sir."

"Did you *see* me do that?"

"Certainly not. You did it when you had created so much excitement through the discharge of the Junior Gun that you were able to do it without anyone seeing you."

"Then how do you know I did it if you didn't see me do it?"

"It is a matter of simply putting two and two together."

"In other words, you have reached a conclusion in your own mind as to what must have happened?"

"Yes, sir."

"Then you are testifying not as to any fact concerning which you know, but only as to a conclusion which you have drawn from certain facts?"

"From certain inescapable facts," Garvin said.

"But nevertheless your testimony concerning the substitution of the gun is a conclusion?"

"A conclusion based on inescapable facts."

Mason smiled at the frowning judge and said, "Your Honor, I move to strike out the evidence of this witness in regard to the susbstitution of the guns on the ground that it is a conclusion."

"The motion is granted," Judge Decker snapped. "It should be quite apparent that the district attorney must have been familiar with the testimony of this witness and must have known that the witness's testimony was based on a conclusion."

"Just a moment, if the Court please," Hamilton Burger said. "I think the Court is being unduly harsh with the prosecution on this matter. If the Court will permit me, I will again examine the witness and establish facts which, as the witness has stated, are irrefutable. They lead to an inescapable conclusion."

"Let the jurors draw that conclusion then," Judge Decker said. "Don't put on witnesses who will testify as an absolute fact to conclusions which have been drawn."

Hamilton Burger, his face flushed, turned to the witness. "You have stated that Mr. Mason had a gun?"

"Yes, sir."

"You have stated that it was not this gun, the murder weapon, Exhibit Number 30, but the gun we are referring to as the Junior Gun, is that right?"

"Yes, sir."

"How do you know the Junior Gun which you gave him was not the murder weapon, Exhibit 30?"

"I know it was not because the evidence shows that this gun which I am holding in my hand was used to kill George Cassleman on the evening of October seventh of this year. It was absolutely impossible for the Junior Gun which I gave Mr. Mason to have been so used."

"Why was it impossible?"

"Objected to," Mason said, "as being an attempt to cross-examine the prosecution's own witness. I move to strike out the statement that it was impossible that the gun he handed me could have been the murder weapon on the ground that that is a conclusion of the witness and is not responsive to the question."

"The motion is granted, " Judge Decker snapped.

"But Your Honor," Hamilton Burger protested, "I certainly am entitled to show . . ."

"You are entitled to show facts, and nothing but facts."

"Very well," Hamilton Burger said. "You gave Mr. Mason a gun?"

"Yes, sir. I gave him the weapon we are designating as the Junior Gun."

"Where did you get that gun?"

"From a drawer in my desk."

"Where did you get the gun before that?"

"From my father. He gave it to me."

"When?"

"Sometime around last Christmas. I think it was a Christmas present."

"Where was that gun on October seventh?"

"In my possession."

"During all of the time on October seventh?"

"Yes, sir."

"What did you do with that gun?"

"I gave it to Perry Mason."

"And what did Perry Mason do with it?"

"He discharged it."

"And then what happened?"

"Then Mr. Mason handed me *a* gun and suggested I take that to Stephanie Falkner."

"Was that the same gun you handed Mr. Mason?"

"No."

"Now just a moment," Judge Decker said. "You have drawn the conclusion that it could not have been the gun? Isn't that correct?"

"Yes, sir."

"The answer will be stricken. The prosecution will kindly refrain from leading this witness into a position where an opinion or a conclusion is offered as evidence. Now just state the facts."

"Very well, I had this gun in my possession. I gave it to Mr. Mason, Mr. Mason fired the gun. Then he handed me back a gun, and asked me to deliver that gun to Stephanie Falkner. I did."

"What did she do with that gun?"

"She placed it on the table in the living room in her apartment."

"*Then* what did you do?"

"Then Mr. Mason and I left the apartment."

"Then what happened?"

"As we started across the lobby, we saw two officers entering the apartment house."

"Do you know those officers?"

"I do now. I didn't then."

"What were their names?"

"Sgt. Holcomb and Lt. Tragg."

"Now the gun that you gave Mr. Mason had been in your possession, you say, all during the seventh day of October of this year?"

"Yes, sir."

"Cross-examine," Hamilton Burger said triumphantly to Perry Mason.

Mason arose to his feet, faced the witness, "You say that the gun you gave me had been in your possession *all* of the seventh of October?"

"Yes, sir."

"You had been out to lunch?"

"Yes, sir."

"Did you take the gun with you?"

"No, sir."

"Where was it?"

"In my desk drawer."

"Was the desk locked?"

"No, sir."

"You consider that that was being in your possession?"

"Yes, sir."

"Where were you on the evening of October seventh?"

"I was calling on a customer about a car deal."

"Did you have the gun with you?"

"The gun was in my desk."

"When did you take it out of your desk?"

"After the conference was over. I returned to my office, took some cash out of the safe, and slipped the gun into my pocket."

"And you took it home?"

"Yes."

"What time was it that you took it home?"

"About nine-thirty or ten o'clock, as nearly as I can judge."

"You had recently been married?"

"Yes."

"Did you keep the gun in your pocket after you got home?"

"No, sir. I took it upstairs and put it on the dresser."

"What time did you go to bed that night?"

"About half an hour after I got home."

"What did you do with the gun?"

"I left it on the dresser."

"Was your office locked on the evening of the seventh of October?"

"Yes."

"Who has the key to that office?"

"I have a key. My father has a key, my secretary has a key, and the janitor has a key."

"Did your wife have a key?"

The witness hesitated, then said in a surly voice, "Yes, my wife had a key."

"And what did you do when you got up the next morning?"

"I dressed and had breakfast, I shaved, I cleaned my teeth," the witness all but shouted in anger.

"And then what?"

"Then I went to my office."

"And did you take the gun with you?"

The witness started to say something, then suddenly stopped, checked himself, thought for a moment, said, "I— As a matter of fact, I did not."

"What did you do with that gun, the one we have been referring to as the Junior Gun?"

"I left it on the dresser in my house."

"And then?" Mason asked.

"Then my wife telephoned and I asked her to bring the gun to me."

"So," Mason said, "you *assume* that the gun which you handed me was the same gun which you took home on the night of October seventh. Is that right?"

"There was only one gun. My wife took it off the dresser."

"How do you know she took it off the dresser?"

"Well, why...of course, I wasn't there."

"Exactly," Mason said. "So for all you know you may have handed me the murder weapon which could have been given you by your wife."

The witness jumped from the stand.

"That's a lie! I resent that!!!"

"Sit down," Judge Decker said. "The witness will sit down and remain in order."

Hamilton Burger said, "If the Court please, that last question was argumentative, it was not proper cross-examination, it contained a dastardly insinuation, it..."

"And as far as this witness knows," Judge Decker said, "it is true. The witness may resent it if he likes, but Mr. Mason is representing a defendant in a murder case. The objection is overruled."

"Now then, if the Court please," Mason said, "I again move to strike out all of the evidence in this case concerning the identity of the gun which was handed me by the defendant because it is now apparent that the entire testimony was based on hearsay testimony."

"I'll connect it up! I'll connect it up," Hamilton Burger shouted.

"How will you connect it up?" Judge Decker asked.

"By putting the wife on this witness stand."

Judge Decker shook his head. "The jurors will be permitted to consider the testimony of this witness insofar as it relates to what the witness did. But as far as the identity of the weapon which was handed Mr. Mason is concerned, it now appears that all testimony along that line was founded upon hearsay evidence and it will go out."

Judge Decker turned to the discomfited district attorney. "Now, Mr. Prosecutor," he said, "if the Court might make a suggestion, it would seem that a bullet was fired from whatever weapon Mr. Mason had in his hand. The bullet certainly didn't fade into thin air. You have a ballistics expert here who has testified, and test bullets have been fired from this gun which is Exhibit 30. It would certainly seem to the Court that there would be no great difficulty in demonstrating whether the weapon which was discharged either accidentally or otherwise by Mr. Perry Mason at that time was Exhibit 30, or was some other weapon."

"We can't prove it, Your Honor," Hamilton Burger said.

"Why not?" Judge Decker asked.

"Because someone took that bullet as a souvenir."

"Didn't the police take it?" Judge Decker asked sharply.

"No, Your Honor," Hamilton Burger said.

"Very well," Judge Decker snapped, "you can't penalize the defendant in this case because of the negligence of the police. The ruling of the Court will stand."

"I have no further questions of this witness," Mason said affably.

"You may leave the witness stand," Judge Decker said. "That's all, Mr. Garvin."

Garvin, his face livid, passed close to Perry Mason on his way from the courtroom. "I'll kill you for this," he said under his breath as he walked past the lawyer.

"Just a moment, Your Honor," Mason said. "I do have one more question of this witness. Will you please return to the stand, Mr. Garvin?"

Garvin hesitated.

"Return to the stand," Judge Decker ordered.

Garvin retraced his steps to the stand.

"As you were just about to leave the courtroom, and as you walked past me just now," Mason said, "you said something to me. What was it?"

"Oh, Your Honor," Hamilton Burger said. "I object. This is no part of the case. Whatever the witness's personal feelings toward Perry Mason may have been, they certainly can't affect the prosecution. I will confess that I have been and am very exasperated over the manner in which this entire hocus-pocus was handled."

"Your feelings don't enter into it," Judge Decker said. "You're not on the stand. The defense has every right to prove any bias on the part of the witness."

"What did you say?" Mason asked.

Garvin shouted, "I said I'll kill you for this, and, by God, I will!"

"That's a threat?" Mason asked.

"That's a promise," Garvin shouted. I'll..."

"You will spend twenty-four hours in jail for contempt of Court," Judge Decker snapped. "The courtroom is no place for threats such as you have just made. This witness has been repeatedly warned. I can realize that the witness is under an emotional strain, but the witness will spend twenty-four hours in jail for contempt of Court. Mr. Bailiff, will you please take the witness into custody."

The bailiff stepped forward, touched Garvin on the arm.

Garvin straightened, and for a moment it looked as though he would completely lose control of himself. Then with poor grace, he followed the bailiff from the courtroom.

"Call Eva Elliott," Hamilton Burger said.

Eva Elliott was obviously prepared to take full advantage of the dramatic aspects of the occasion. She had the appearance of a woman who had spent hours at a beauty salon as she walked with slow, deliberate grace to the witness stand.

"What is your occupation?" Hamilton Burger asked.

"I am a model and an actress."

"What was your occupation on October seventh of this year?"

"I was employed as a secretary by Homer Garvin, Sr."

"How long had you been so employed?"

"Nearly a year."

"Referring to the seventh of October, I will ask you if anything unusual happened in your office on that day?"

"Yes, sir."

"What?"

"Now just a minute," Judge Decker said. "There seems to be no objection by defense counsel, but it would seem that there should be some connection here. Anything which happened on the seventh of October outside of the presence of this defendant would have no bearing upon the case unless there is some evidence indicating that the defendant consented, acquiesced, or in some way profited therefrom or that it is part of the *res gestae.*"

Hamilton Burger said, "We want to show exactly what Mr. Garvin did on that day. We want to show that he knew of certain things and was in a position to communicate them to the defendant."

Judge Decker looked at Perry Mason. "Is there any objection from the defense?"

"No objection," Mason said smiling.

"Very well. Go ahead and answer the question," Judge Decker said, but his eyes, sharply accusing, regarded Perry Mason's bland countenance.

"Well, what happened?" Hamilton Burger asked.

"Mr. Garvin telephoned me from Las Vegas. He told me to wait at the office until he arrived."

"What time did he arrive at the office?"

"Around eight-forty-five, almost an hour prior to the time he said he would arrive. He was highly nervous and he refused to talk with me until after he vanished into his bathroom and took a shower."

"Now just a moment," Judge Decker said. "Mr. Garvin was called as a witness by the prosecution. Are you now attempting to impeach your own witness, Mr. Prosecutor?"

"The witness was a hostile witness," Hamilton Burger said. "He is quite definitely affiliated with the defendant, as was disclosed by his testimony."

"Nevertheless he was a witness called by the prosecution."

"There is no objection on the part of the defense," Mason said.

"Well, there should be," Judge Decker snapped.

Mason merely inclined his head out of deference to the Court, and continued to sit there saying nothing.

"Very well," Judge Decker said, controlling himself with a visible effort, "under the circumstances, there being no objection, the witness will be permitted to answer the question."

"You're certain of the time element?" Hamilton Burger asked.

"Absolutely certain," she said. "I resented being treated as a chattel. I felt that anything Mr. Garvin wanted to say to me could have been said before he—"

"Just a minute," Judge Decker interrupted. "Your thoughts are not important as far as this case is concerned. You are simply asked if you are sure of the time."

"I am sure of the time."

"Now did Mr. Garvin say anything to you about Mr. Casselman?" Hamilton Burger asked.

"Yes."

"Who was present?"

"Just Mr. Garvin and myself."

"What did he say?"

"He said, 'I have just talked with the man who I am certain killed Stephanie Falkner's father. I have made an appointment to see him at eleven o'clock tonight.' "

"Then what did he do, if anything?"

"He took off his coat. I noticed the revolver which was in his shoulder holster. He took off this shoulder holster and placed it on his desk, and then went into the shower room to take a bath."

"Can you identify the gun which was in that shoulder holster at that time?" Hamilton Burger asked.

"No, sir. I cannot. I am afraid of guns. I didn't go near it. However, it looked exactly like the gun marked People's Exhibit 30."

"You may inquire," Hamilton Burger said, turning to Perry Mason.

"Now what time was this?" Mason asked.

"When he arrived at the office, it was about a quarter to nine."

"He told you he had already seen Casselman?"

"His exact words were 'I have just talked with the man who I am certain killed Stephanie Falkner's father. I have made an appointment to see him at eleven o'clock tonight.' "

"You remember his exact words?"

"I do."

"But he didn't mention Casselman by name?"

"He meant Casselman all right. He said..."

"I am not asking whom he meant. I am asking if he used Casselman's name."

"He did not use Casselman's name."

Mason said, "I have no further questions."

Burger said, "I'll call Mrs. Garvin, Jr., to the witness stand."

Mrs. Garvin, a long-legged redhead, strode to the witness stand with every appearance of perfect composure. She smiled at the jurors, crossed her knees so as to display just the right amount of nylon, turned courteously and expectantly to the district attorney.

Hamilton Burger said, "You are the wife of the witness Homer Garvin, Jr., who has just testified in this case. I show you a weapon marked People's Exhibit Number 30, and ask you if you have ever seen that weapon before?"

"I can't say," she said smiling. "I have seen a gun which looked very much like that, but I am not an expert on firearms."

"Where did you see that gun?"

"My husband left it on the dresser."

"When?"

"On the night of the seventh of October."

"At what time?"

"At approximately ten-thirty o'clock."

"Did you see that gun on the eighth of October?"

"I did. Yes, sir."

"And what did you do with reference to it, if anything?"

"I telephoned my husband at his office that he had left a gun on the dresser."

"When did you telephone him?"

"When I got up and saw the gun there."

"That was after your husband had gone to his office?"

She smiled and said, "I am a newlywed, Mr. Burger. I am trying to train my husband right. I let him get his own breakfast, and I slept until about nine-thirty."

The audience laughed. Judge Decker smiled, and the jurors grinned. The good nature of the witness and her complete poise were making a terrific impression.

"What did you do with reference to that gun?"

"Following my husband's instructions, I took the gun to him at the office."

"When?"

"At about ten-thirty on the morning of the eighth of October of this year."

"Do you know whether that was the weapon we are referring to as the Junior Gun, or whether it was the People's Exhibit Number 30?"

"No, sir. I do not know. All I know is that I took the gun from the dresser to my husband. I can't even swear that there was no discharged cartridge in the gun at that time. I do know that my husband took a gun from his pocket when he was undressing at about ten-thirty on the night of October seventh. I do know that a gun similar in every way to that gun was still on the dresser at ten o'clock in the morning. I am quite certain no one entered the bedroom after we retired. I do know I took the gun which was on the dresser to my husband at his office on the morning of October eighth at about ten-thirty o'clock. I know nothing more than that."

"Cross-examine." Hamilton Burger said.

Mason said, "Mrs. Garvin, were you home all during the evening of October seventh?"

"Yes."

"Did you know your husband rang twice on the phone and received no answer?"

"He told me such was the case."

"You want the jury to believe you were there but didn't answer the phone?"

"I was sound asleep for about an hour, Mr. Mason."

"Did you tell your husband that?"

"No."

"Why?"

"It was our honeymoon. My husband went chasing off on a business deal. He didn't come home for dinner. I wanted him to realize I didn't like such conduct. I let him know I was hurt and a little angry. If he had known I had gone to sleep while I was waiting for him to return he wouldn't have been quite so concerned. I wanted him to be concerned. So I didn't tell him I was asleep. I think I convinced him he must have dialed the wrong number."

"Twice?"

"Twice."

"Didn't he require a lot of convincing?"

"Yes. A bride is in a position to convince her husband a little more easily than at any other time in her married life."

"Did you lie to him?"

"Heavens no! I suggested he had dialed the wrong number. He didn't ask me if I had been asleep, so I didn't tell him."

Mason said, "Getting back to this gun, Mrs. Garvin. For all *you* know that gun may have had one discharged shell in it when you took it to your husband's office."

She smiled sweetly and said, "Then, after you fired a shell into my husband's desk, there would have been two discharged shells, Mr. Mason."

"Assuming," Mason said, "that the gun which your husband gave me was the same gun which you had taken to his office."

"A bride must always assume that her husband is truthful, Mr. Mason."

"That's all," Mason said.

Burger's next witness was Lorraine Kettle, a spare-framed widow of fifty-six who testified that she lived in an apartment on the ground floor of the Ambrose Apartments. At about eight-forty-five on the evening of the seventh of October, she had seen a woman descending the service stairs from the back door of George Casselman's apartment.

She had, she said, felt the woman might have been a burglar, so she had left her own apartment by the back entrance and had followed this woman at what she referred to as "a discreet distance."

"Were you close enough to recognize her?" Burger asked.

"I was."

"Who was she?"

"That woman sitting right there, the defendant, Stephanie Falkner."

"What did she do?"

"She walked across to the sidewalk and then a man stopped his automobile and called to her. She got in that car. They drove away."

"Who was that man, if you know?"

"Mr. Perry Mason, the lawyer, sitting right there."

"Cross-examine," Burger snapped.

"How did you happen to be looking at the back stairs of the Casselman apartment?" Mason asked.

"I had seen young women go in there before. This time I was determined to complain."

"You mean you had seen this defendant go in there before?"

"I can't swear it was her."

"You mean prior to October seventh?"

"Yes."

"And had seen women leave by the back door?"

"I can't swear I'd seen more than one woman."

"You followed this woman who left on October seventh?"

"I followed the defendant, yes."

"Why did you follow her?"

"I wanted to see who she was."

"That was the only reason?"

"Yes."

"You intended to follow her only far enough to get a good look at her?"

"Yes."

"And then you were going to turn back?"

"Yes."

"You were still following her when she got into this automobile?"

"Yes."

"Then by your own testimony you hadn't got a good look at her by that time. Is that right?"

"I saw her all right."

"But you said you were going to turn back as soon as you had a good look at her, and you hadn't turned back at that time."

"Well....I'd like to have had a closer look but I'm pretty certain in my own mind."

"*Pretty* certain?"

"Yes."

"And if it hadn't been for her getting in the automobile, you'd have followed her farther?"

"Yes, I guess so."

"That's all," Mason said smiling.

"That's our case, Your Honor," Hamilton Burger said.

Judge Decker frowned.

"The defense moves that the Court instruct the jury to return a verdict of not guilty," Mason said. "The evidence at this time shows merely an inference, a suspicion."

Judge Decker said, "The Court does not wish to comment on the evidence other than to say that at this time the motion is denied. After the defense has put on its case, the question of proof will be in the hands of the jury. At the present time and for the purpose of this motion, the Court must accept all of the evidence in its strongest possible light as far as the prosecution is concerned. The Court makes no comment on that evidence other than to state that the motion is denied.

"The Court notices that it is approaching the hour of noon adjournment. The Court will take a recess until two o'clock, at which time the defense can put on its case.

"During that time, the jurors will remember the admonition of the Court not to converse about the case nor permit anyone to converse about it in your presence, and not to form or express any opinion until the case is finally submitted to you.

"Court is adjourned."

Mason turned to Stephanie Falkner. "Stephanie," he said, "you've got to go on the stand. You've got to deny that you killed George Casselman."

She shook her head. "I am not going on the witness stand."

"You have to," Mason said. "They'll convict you of murder if you don't. In view of the testimony we have managed to bring in about your father's death, the jurors won't bring in a death penalty, but they will find you guilty. The fact that your shoe had blood on it, the fact that there was an imprint made by a heel plate similar to yours—"

"I am sorry, Mr. Mason, I am *not* going on the witness stand."

"Why?" Mason asked. "Is there something in your past you're afraid they'll bring out? Have you been convicted of a felony?"

She shook her head. "Have you?" Mason asked.

"I am not going to make any statement to you, Mr. Mason, other than the fact that I am not going on the witness stand. They can do whatever they want, but they are not going to put me on the witness stand."

Mason said, "Stephanie, you can't do this. I'm going to call you to the stand as a witness."

"If you do," she said. "I will simply refuse to budge from my chair."

"All right," Mason told her, "that's better than nothing. It will at least give me something to argue about."

"Time for you to go now, Miss Falkner," the bailiff said.

CHAPTER NINETEEN

Mason, Della Street, and Paul Drake were eating a gloomy luncheon in the private dining room of a little restaurant near the courthouse.

They were half through when knuckles beat on the door in a rapid staccato, and a moment later Gertie, Perry Mason's receptionist, was in the room, all excited.

"Mr. Mason, Mr. Mason!" she said. "Marie Barlow came to the office. My heavens! Is that woman immense! I think she's going to have triplets at least. She shouldn't be out. I've told her...I've warned her..."

"Now wait a minute, Gertie," Mason said. "Calm down. What's this all about?"

"Marie was at Mr. Garvin's office. She had been trying to get the files cleaned out, you know, and she looked in the back of one of the file drawers of an old transfer case. Things in there are ten years old and older."

"All right," Mason said. "What did she find?"

Gertie lowered her voice. "Bloody towels that Mr. Garvin had left there the night of the murder."

"What?"

"That's right. Towels with dried, crusted blood on them. And they're stamped with the name of the Ambrose Apartments. They had been hidden there, and Marie was afraid—well, she didn't want anybody to know. She wanted me to find you and tell you and ask you what to do. She's loyal to Mr. Garvin but she simply can't sit still with anything like this on her mind and let Stephanie Falkner go to prison.

"She felt that perhaps she could wait and see how the case came out and then she could apparently find them for the first time and then you could move for a new trial on the ground of newly discovered evidence. But that wouldn't be right. She's all at sea, poor kid. She..."

Mason said, "All right, Gertie. Calm yourself. Now sit down and have some coffee."

"Heavens! I'm so terribly upset, Mr. Mason. You can see it all now. Homer Garvin really did kill George Casselman, and Stephanie Falkner knows it. Because she loves him she won't go on the witness stand and..."

"Hey! Wait a minute! Wait a minute!" Mason said. "That crazy, mixed up, romantic mind of yours has given me an idea."

Della Street looked warningly at Perry Mason. "She has lots of crazy ideas. Give her a button and she'll sew a romantic vest on it."

Perry Mason started pacing the floor. "Hang it!" he said. "It's corny. It's a grandstand. But it *will* catch the district attorney entirely by surprise, and it's the only thing I *can* do."

Gertie turned to Paul Drake. "And your office says for you to call *right* away. It's terribly important."

Paul Drake called for a phone to be plugged into an extension socket. Mason continued rapidly pacing the floor.

"What," Della Street asked, "do you have in mind?"

Mason said, "I'll call Stephanie Falkner to the stand as a defense witness. She will refuse to go. I'll argue with her. There'll be a scene in court. I'll order her to take the stand. She'll refuse to take the stand. Then I'll rest my case. I'll go to the jury with a whirlwind campaign that Stephanie Falkner knows the man she loved killed George Casselman, that— Wait a minute! Wait a minute, Della! I've got it. I've got it!" Mason said snapping his fingers rapidly.

"Got what?" Della Street asked.

Mason laughed. "They can't find the bullet I fired into the desk out at Junior's office. I've got it, Della! I've got it! We'll use those bloodstained towels."

"Go on," she said, his excitement communicating itself to her. "What are you going to do?"

Paul Drake, listening on the extension telephone which had been plugged in by the waiter, shoved his right index finger in his ear, said, "Don't make so much racket, you guys. My office is trying to reach me on something important."

Mason said, "Della, I'll claim that Junior Garvin actually did take the gun we've referred to as the Junior Gun up to Stephanie Falkner's apartment, that in the meantime Stephanie Falkner had noticed that the gun we've referred to as the Holster Gun, which was the gun Homer Garvin, Sr. had left with her, had an exploded shell in the chamber. That convinced her Homer Garvin, Sr. had killed Casselman. So instead of leaving the Junior Gun on the table where Homer Garvin, Jr. had put it, she grabbed that gun and concealed it in her apartment. Then she took the Holster Gun, the one which Homer Garvin, Sr. had given her the night before, the one with the exploded shell, and put it on the table in exactly the same position. And, by heaven, that's exactly what she *did* do!

"After all, Della, we're a gun short. Homer Garvin, Sr. gave Stephanie the Holster Gun on the night of the murder. Homer Garvin, Jr. gave her the Junior Gun at my suggestion the following day. The police searched her apartment *but they only found one gun*! As soon as they found that one gun, they quit searching.

"By George! I'll mix this case all up with the missing gun, bring in Gertie's romantic theory, make a whirlwind argument to the jury, demand that the

Court order my client to take the stand....Hang it! I'll throw on some courtroom fireworks that will make history!

"I'll recall Sgt. Holcomb to the stand. I'll point out that when he found that one gun in Stephanie's apartment, he had to rush to the ballistics department to have it tested. Then when he found it was the murder gun, he became so excited he never went back to search Stephanie's apartment until the ninth.

"We can see exactly what Stephanie did. As soon as Junior went out of the door, she put the Holster Gun on the table, and ditched the Junior Gun. By the time the police got back to search her apartment the second time, she'd had ample opportunity to put the Junior Gun where they'd never be able to find it.

"That's the only logical explanation. She felt Garvin, Sr. had killed Casselman so she switched guns.

"I know Garvin saw Casselman about a quarter past eight. He must have shot Casselman in self-defense. Then when Stephanie went in at eight-thirty she found Casselman dead. She stepped in the blood— She went out the back way— Hang it! Della, she saw Garvin when he was driving away from the apartment house. She knew he'd seen Casselman. It all hangs together. Police bungled the investigative work, and Stephanie was the one who switched guns!

"Della, I've been asleep at the switch! Why hasn't it occurred to me before? We've been running around in circles about that gun, and it has never occurred to anyone that the whole case lies in that missing gun that the police haven't found."

"Well," Della Street said thoughtfully, "if you can put that across to the jury with all the fire of white hot enthusiasm you have now, Chief, you'll get away with it."

"Get away with it!" Mason exclaimed. "Why the worst I'll get will be a hung jury. They won't convict her with that....Gertie, bless your romantic, daydreaming, exaggerating hide! I'm going to buy you five pounds of candy as soon as I get out of court this afternoon."

"Oh, Mr. Mason," she said. "Not candy, please! Anything else. I...I'm dieting this week."

"Five pounds of luscious chocolate creams!" Mason said. "A big, five-pound box of candy."

"Well," she sighed, "if you insist."

Paul Drake hung up the phone, said, "Hey! Wait a minute, Perry! I've been covering print shops all over the city trying to find the print shop that printed those billheads for the Acme Electric and Plumbing Repair Company and the Eureka Associated Renovators. Last night I started my men checking Las Vegas. We found a printing establishment in Las Vegas that printed the billheads all right. They were done at the order of a man who paid for them in cash and unfortunately we can't get any kind of a description of the man. It was done nearly a year ago. The people just can't remember him."

Mason snapped his fingers. "Never mind that, Paul, I'm going to put this crazy, romantic idea of Gertie's across. After all, why couldn't Stephanie have switched guns?"

Drake looked at his watch. "Well, I didn't hear all of that stuff. I was too busy on the phone. But you'd better finish eating if you're going to be in court at two o'clock."

Mason turned to Gertie. "Where is Marie now, Gertie?"

"Waiting in your private office."

"She has those towels with her?"

"Yes."

"On your way!" Mason said. "Tell her to wrap those towels in a package and bring them to me in court. I'll stall the case until she can get there."

"Oh, she wouldn't go into court with all that crowd, Mr. Mason. She's immense. It's going to happen any minute now."

"Marie will do anything that we tell her," Mason said. "Her appearance will make it all the better. The minute she walks in that courtroom, every eye will be on her. Tell her just to walk up to the table and hand me the package."

"But how are you going to stall things along until she can get there?" Della Street asked.

"Get started," Mason said to Gertie. "I'll stall along somehow. I'll recall the last witness for additional cross-examination. I'll think of something. Get started!"

Gertie hurried out of the restaurant.

Mason sat down to his lunch but was too excited to eat. "What a grandstand!" he said. "What a perfectly cockeyed theory! And the nice part of it is that the district attorney can't disprove it. After all, in a case of circumstantial evidence, the evidence has to be strong enough to exclude every reasonable hypothesis other than that of guilt."

"Is that hypothesis reasonable?" Drake asked skeptically.

"By the time Perry Mason gets done putting gilt paint on it," Della Street said, "it will look like fourteen carat gold!"

"Well," Drake said looking at his watch, "don't get so enthusiastic you forget to get to court at two o'clock. They say Judge Decker lowers the boom on guys who don't show up.

Mason nodded, left a bill which more than covered the luncheon check, started walking down the stairs to the street. "I'll recall Eva Elliott, Della. If I recall anyone else, it will look as though I'm stalling for time. Eva Elliott is the only witness I really have anything on. I'll come down on her like a thousand of brick about those bills she paid."

"But," Della Street asked, "is that proper cross-examination?"

"It isn't," Mason said, "but by the time I've asked a dozen questions, the jury will get the idea. Judge Decker will be mad as a wet hen. Burger will be yelling. Then with all the argument and all the objections and all of the hullabaloo, I can stall things along until Marie can get there with those towels. Then I'll spring this theory of the substituted guns on the jury and claim that it's a reasonable hypothesis other than that of guilt. We'll stampede that jury, Della. I'll put Marie on the stand. It'll be a circus!"

"You know," Della Street said, "you really do have something with that theory. Stephanie Falkner could have felt Homer Garvin killed him. She could have switched guns, concealed the gun they are calling the Junior Gun and substituted the one they are calling the Holster Gun, which was the murder weapon, putting it in exactly the same place on the table. She *must* have."

"Atta girl!" Mason said. "I'm getting *you* convinced, and you're skeptical, Della. If I can convince you, it's a certainty I can get at least one or two of the jurors looking at it my way."

"Remember," she warned, "Hamilton Burger has the closing argument."

"If he argues that point," Mason said, "he's simply floundering around in a legal quicksand. There *were* two guns. His own evidence shows there were two guns. He's never found that second gun. And since he hasn't found it, he can't refute the claim that Stephanie Falkner, desperately in love with Homer Garvin and trying to protect him, switched the guns and is willing to take the chance of being convicted in order to protect the man she loves."

"Well," Della Street said, "it's going to be quite some show and— Hang it, Chief! She *must* have done it!"

"Of course, she did," Mason said. "And that's why she won't go on the stand."

CHAPTER TWENTY

Judge Decker said, "It will be stipulated, I take it, gentlemen, that the jurors are all present, and the defendant in court."

"So stipulated," Mason said.

"The defense will proceed with its case."

"If the Court please," Mason said, "a certain matter has come to my attention which makes me wish to ask a few additional questions of one of the prosecution's witnesses."

"We object," Hamilton Burger said. "The prosecution has rested its case, the evidence is closed as far as the prosecution is concerned."

"Which witness?" Judge Decker asked Mason.

"Eva Elliott," Mason said.

"The defense motion will be granted. The case is reopened. Eva Elliott will return to the stand for further cross-examination," Judge Decker ruled.

Eva Elliott was called back to the stand. Mason, looking at his wrist watch, made a rapid calculation in regard to time.

Eva Elliott settled herself on the witness stand in the best tradition of the motion-picture witnesses.

Mason said, "Just one or two more questions on cross-examination, Miss Elliott. Did you have any secretarial experience before you started working for Mr. Garvin?"

"Objected to as incompetent, irrelevant, and immaterial, and not proper cross-examination," Hamilton Burger said.

"Sustained," Judge Decker said.

"It was part of your secretarial duties to make out vouchers in payment of bills which were incurred by the Garvin enterprises?"

"Yes."

"You habitually typed out checks covering those bills and Mr. Garvin would sign those checks?"

"Yes, sir."

"What audit did you make of those bills?" Mason asked.

"Objected to as incompetent, irrelevant and immaterial, and not proper cross-examination," Hamilton Burger said.

"Sustained," Judge Decker snapped.

"Isn't it a fact," Mason asked, "that during the time you were with Mr. Garvin, you made out and got his signature on several checks amounting to several thousand dollars payable to the Acme Electric and Plumbing Repair Company of 1397 Chatham Street, and the Eureka Associated Renovators of

1397 Chatham Street, when, as a matter of fact, there were no such firms, and no orders had ever been given to those firms?"

"Just a moment! Just a moment!" Hamilton Burger shouted. "Your Honor, this is completely outside the issues of this case. It is not proper cross-examination. It is incompetent, irrelevant and immaterial."

Judge Decker stroked his chin. "It would seem at first blush to be completely outside of the issues," he said, "unless counsel can assure the Court that he intends to connect it up in that it might show bias."

"My next question," Mason said, "will be to question the witness whether the person who was sending in these bills was not engaged in a conspiracy with her, and that this witness is therefore prejudiced and biased against Mr. Garvin, her former employer, because of fear that her defaultation will be discovered."

Judge Decker frowned. "I think I am going to permit the questions," he said. "It's rather a technical, legal point by which evidence which otherwise might well be extraneous is introduced into a case, but it needs only a glance at the face of this witness to tell that there is something here which is—'"

Eva Elliott interrupted. "Your Honor, I swear to you that I didn't get a penny of it. Mr. Casselman promised to—" She stopped.

"Go on," Judge Decker said.

"I don't think she should be permitted to volunteer a statement," Hamilton Burger said. "This is a very technical point. It is a matter which is being dragged in by the ears for the purpose of discrediting a witness whose actual testimony is not open to doubt and who has testified to a fact which is uncontradicted."

"It is uncontradicted as yet," Judge Decker said, "but the defense has not put on its case. The witness will kindly compose herself. You mentioned the name of Mr. Casselman, Miss Elliott."

Eva Elliott started to cry. "He promised to have me as his entertainer when the new motel went up. He lied. He couldn't make good. He promised me a floor show...."

The door of the courtroom opened. Marie Barlow, quite evidently in the last stages of pregnancy, carrying a paper package in her hand, moved with slow, measured steps down the aisle of the courtroom.

Judge Decker looked at her. The jurors looked, and spectators turned to look.

Marie Barlow approached the mahogany rail which divided the counsel tables from the courtroom, extended the paper parcel toward Perry Mason.

Mason took the parcel in his hand, turned to the witness.

Slowly, dramatically, he tore the paper from the package and brought out the bloodstained towels.

"Eva," he said, "after you shot George Casselman you wiped off some of the blood with towels and put those towels in your purse. You concealed them in the back of a filing cabinet in Mr. Garvin's office. Then you substituted the Safe Gun, which you had used in the killing, for the Holster Gun which you took from Mr. Garvin's holster while Mr. Garvin was in the shower. You put the Holster Gun back in the safe, didn't you?"

Eva Elliott got to her feet, then sank back into the witness chair.

"I did it in self-defense," she sobbed. "When I found out about what he had done, I...I..."

"Now just a minute! Just a minute!" Hamilton Burger shouted. "This whole matter now has the appearance of being a well rehearsed, carefully staged attempt to stampede the jurors."

Mason resumed his seat at the counsel table and grinned at Hamilton Burger.

"That's all, Mr. Burger," he said. "Rest your case, if you dare do so. The defense will put on no evidence."

"You have no further questions of this witness?" Judge Decker asked incredulously.

"None, Your Honor," Mason said.

Hamilton Burger sat undecisively for a minute. "I would like to ask the Court for a thirty-minute recess," he said. "It may be that the prosecution will..."

"Do you have any questions of this witness?" Judge Decker asked.

"No, Your Honor."

Judge Decker glanced at Perry Mason. "Does the defense oppose the motion for a thirty-minute recess made by the district attorney?"

"The defense opposes the motion," Mason said. "The defense does not intend to put on any evidence, and we would like to start the argument so that we can go to the jury this afternoon."

"Very well," Judge Decker said. "Proceed with your case, Mr. Prosecutor."

"That is all of our case. We had already rested."

"The defense does not intend to put on any evidence," Perry Mason said.

Judge Decker looked down at Eva Elliott. "Despite the fact that it is highly irregular, the Court is not satisfied to have the matter disposed of in this manner. Miss Elliott, did you kill George Casselman?"

"I shot him," she said. "I took the gun out of Mr. Garvin's safe to use as a bluff, to frighten him. Then he tried to choke me. He was trying to break my neck. Everything was going black, and I heard something go boom...and then I could breathe again."

"And with what gun did you try to bluff him?"

"The gun I had taken from Mr. Garvin's safe earlier that afternoon."

"And what did you do with that gun?"

"I put it in Mr. Garvin's shoulder holster while he was taking his shower. Then I put the other gun which had been in his shoulder holster in his safe."

Judge Decker gave the matter frowning consideration. "The Court is going to take a sixty-minute recess of its own motion," he said. "In view of the fact that this witness is one called by the prosecution, it would seem that the prosecution is bound by her testimony."

"Your Honor," Hamilton Burger said, "we don't want to be bound by the testimony of this witness until we can find out what happened during the noon hour, what inducements were made to this witness, what theatrical flimflam was arranged with those so-called bloodstained towels."

"The Court is not interested in your feelings in the matter," Judge Decker said. "The Court is interested in administering justice. This is a most peculiar situation. The Court will take an adjournment for one hour. At the end of that time, the Court will again entertain a motion to instruct the jury to return a verdict of acquittal in the case pending against this defendant."

CHAPTER TWENTY-ONE

Perry Mason, Della Street, Homer Garvin, Paul Drake, and Stephanie Falkner sat grouped about the table in Mason's law library. A bottle of whisky, a siphon of soda, a big jar of ice cubes and glasses were on the table.

Mason said to Stephanie Falkner, "You should have told me."

"I wasn't going to tell anyone, Mr. Mason. I saw Homer as he drove away from George Casselman's apartment house. He didn't see me. Later on, when he gave me that gun and I found there was an exploded cartridge in it, I felt I knew what had happened. Then when you arranged to have Junior give me a gun so that in case the police asked me to produce the gun they are calling the Holster Gun, the one that had been given me by Homer Garvin, I could give them the Junior Gun which his son had given me. I thought I would be smart in substituting guns, so that the police would find the murder weapon just where Junior would be forced to testify he had left the Junior Gun which he had given me. The Junior Gun I snatched from the table as soon as you folks left my apartment, and dropped it into a sack of flour in the kitchen. Later on I took it out of the flour sack, walked over to an adjacent lot where they were building a house and pushed the gun down into some wet cement that had just been poured into forms."

Homer Garvin said, "I didn't know you had seen me there at that apartment house, Stephanie. I went up to tell Casselman that I wanted a showdown. He told me he had an important appointment in ten minutes and that he simply couldn't see me. Eva Elliott must have been in there at the time. I told him I'd be back at eleven o'clock, and that I was going to call for a showdown."

Mason said, "Eva Elliott must have been the one who telephoned while I was in conference with Casselman, and said she was coming right up. It was that which disturbed him. He asked for a two-minute delay. That shows she was phoning from a nearby phone. I went out the front door and watched the front of the apartment house, but didn't see anyone come in. The fact that I knew someone was coming in, but didn't see anyone arrive, should have warned me that the person who entered the apartment must have gone up by the back stairs."

"Well, we know the whole story now," Garvin said. "She went in the back door. Casselman had persuaded her to put through checks on phony bills. He had promised her top billing in a floor show in the new motel. He'd promised her television contracts. She was willing to do anything to get in that floor show as the top actress. She wasn't the victim of her lack of secretarial experience. She was deliberately getting money for Casselman. Then she found out somehow he was double-crossing her."

Stephanie said, "A woman held the outer door open for me. I went up to Casselman's apartment and rang the bell. No one answered. I tried the knob of the door. The door was unlocked. I opened it and went in. George Casselman was lying there dead. I...I didn't know what to do. I suddenly realized I'd stepped in the pool of blood and then I became panic-stricken. I went into the bathroom and tried to wash the blood off my shoe. I had knelt over him to see if he was dead, and there was blood on my hands. I washed and washed and washed, and then I went down the back stairs.

"Because I felt certain Homer had killed him, I said nothing. I felt that it wasn't my duty to turn state's evidence."

Homer Garvin looked at her thoughtfully. "And you'd have taken a chance on being convicted of first-degree murder rather than implicate me?"

She said, "*You* should talk! After *you* thought I had committed the murder, you deliberately tried to put your neck in the noose so as to save mine."

Suddenly both of them started laughing.

"All right," Garvin said. "We'll discuss that later. In the meantime, Mason, I have something to say about your fee."

Garvin took out his checkbook, signed his name to a blank check, slid it across the table to Perry Mason, and said, "You fill it out and fill it out for plenty."

The phone rang. Della Street answered it, said, "Just a moment."

She turned to Mason. "Junior's on the line," she said. "He says he's sorry he lost his temper. He says he'll take six hundred dollars off that sports job you were driving when you took him to see Stephanie."

Mason grinned, picked up the blank check Garvin had signed.

"Tell him to call later, Della. I think we may make a deal."

THE CASE OF
THE FOOT-LOOSE DOLL

FOREWORD

Every once in a while a man comes along with a new idea. Unfortunately many of these men with new ideas are theorists. Their ideas may be sound but they are allowed to remain in the realm of theory for too long a period of incubation, and the egg spoils before the idea hatches.

Once in a blue moon a man comes along who combines a new idea with the executive ability to put it into execution before the period of incubation expires.

My friend, Theodore J. Curphey, M.D., Coroner of Los Angeles County, is such a man.

His idea is to get legal medicine put on a practical plane and made a part of the highly complex civilization of today so that it functions smoothly in a variety of fields.

Dr. Curphey points out that today over 80 per cent of law suits involve personal injuries in which the medical aspects of the cases are the deciding issue of the litigation; that in large centers of population there are far too many deaths involving criminal violence where the autopsies do not take advantage of all of the currently available scientific methods of crime detection. (The result of this is that not only do major crimes frequently escape detection, but in too many instances innocent persons are falsely charged with and convicted of crimes they did not commit.)

There is nothing startling about these basic ideas. The thing that furnishes the element of novelty is the manner in which Dr. Curphey proposes to put some of his plans into execution.

Space is not available to list these methods in detail. Suffice it to say that Dr. Curphey recognizes the swarming, teeming, heavily populated County of Los Angeles as being one of the best places in the country to demonstrate his ideas.

He accepted an appointment as Coroner of Los Angeles with the deliberate intention of getting the three medical schools in the district to unite with the law schools as well as with the police and sheriffs' departments in planning a constructive program; of bringing legal knowledge and medical knowledge into a practical partnership; establishing an Institute of Legal Medicine; forming advisory committees to study problems dealing with industrial deaths, maternal deaths, deaths from anesthesia, problems concerning the relationship between the coroner's office and the hospitals, and funeral directors and the coroner's office.

Dr. Curphey also wants to have practical training for undergraduate students in the joint field of law and medicine, a better understanding of the possibilities of legal medicine by the investigative officers and a better understanding of police methods and responsibilities by members of the medical profession.

These objectives are highly important, not only to the County of Los Angeles, but as part of a general public awakening to the importance of legal medicine.

There is something in the practical, two-fisted way Dr. Curphey has accepted the challenge of the problems at the Los Angeles Coroner's Office, has outlined his objectives, and gone about realizing those objectives, that indicates executive ability of a high order, added, of course, to highly professional competency in the intricate field of pathology and legal medicine.

So it is with great pleasure that I dedicate this book to my friend:

THEODORE J. CURPHEY, M.D.

Erle Stanley Gardner

CHAPTER ONE

At fifteen minutes past two o'clock that afternoon, Mildred Crest's world collapsed about her in a wreckage which left her so completely dazed that her mind became numb and her reasoning faculties simply failed to function.

At two o'clock that afternoon Mildred had been one of the happiest young women in the bustling town of Oceanside, California.

The expensive diamond which flashed from the ring finger of her left hand betokened her engagement to Robert Joiner, head accountant at the firm of Pillsbury & Maxwell, the big department store which had branches located in half a dozen southern California cities.

Joiner had arrived in Oceanside something over two years before. He had started in as bookkeeper and his advancement had been rapid. He had a quick, resourceful mind, was instantly adaptable to any new situation, and above all was not afraid of responsibility. He had complete confidence in his own judgment and soon his employers were sharing that confidence.

An entertaining conversationalist and a good hand at keeping the ball rolling at any party, Joiner was a social asset. He was considered by far the most eligible young bachelor in the community.

Mildred's engagement to him had had the effect of a bombshell in social circles, and for three months she had been veritably walking on air.

Then at two-fifteen Mildred had been summoned from her secretarial desk to take a personal call.

She felt certain it was from Robert, and was mildly annoyed because he knew the management frowned on employees accepting personal calls during business hours. Not only did it detract from their efficiency, but it tied up the lines on the switchboard. However, it was like Robert Joiner to push the rules to one side.

His voice held no hint of anything portentous. He sounded as casual and glib as ever.

"Hello, babe! How's the demon secretary?"

"Fine, Bob. Only—You know about calls here.... Only urgent matters.... I'm sorry—"

"Pay it no heed," Robert interrupted. "That is just an idea of the big brass to emphasize their own importance. And in a way this matter is urgent."

"Yes?" she asked.

"As of this moment," Bob said, "our engagement is annulled, canceled, discontinued, terminated, and rescinded. You are to keep the diamond ring and any other presents, and I trust, happy memories of a glorious three months."

"Bob, what on earth...? *What* are you saying? What's the matter? What—?"

"The ponies, babe, blame it on the ponies," he said. "You never guessed it, but I happen to be a gambler, and this was a nice gamble. I like to take chances even when they don't work out. Let the other man go through the humdrum routine of an ordinary existence with slow, painful, plodding steps up the ladder of success! I like skyrockets, baby. I like to shoot for the high places, and I like to work fast."

"Bob, but your family...."

"The myth of my wealthy family back East was simply a background to justify what otherwise would doubtless have been considered extravagances on the part of an accountant working on a salary. My system of playing the ponies furnished a lucrative sideline until suddenly something went sour and I'm damned if I know what it was.

"I started by borrowing from company funds and paid back when the system began to pay off. Then I got pretty deep into company funds again and suddenly realized I was up against an audit. There were a couple of suspicious circumstances, matters of sheer carelessness on my part. So I picked up all the loose cash that was lying around, threw the system out of the window and shot the works on a hot tip at Santa Anita today. A few moments ago the goat came in fourth!"

"Robert, is this some sort of a joke?" Mildred demanded. "Is this one of your psychological tests to get people's reactions? Because, if it is, you've upset me for the rest of the afternoon."

"Let's hope it won't be any worse than that," Joiner said jauntily. "I confess that I feel a twinge of conscience about you. You've been a sweet girl, Millie, and a wonderful pal. But realities are realities, and we may as well face them. Even if I am an embezzler with detection inevitable, I have no intention of putting on an act of tearful repentance, facing the contempt of all the dull clods who formerly looked up to me with envious admiration. I have no desire to throw myself on the mercy of the court, to ask for probation, and promise restitution.

"Since discovery is inevitable, I have decided to make my embezzlement worth while. I have taken everything around here that isn't nailed down. I started for the bank with the stated purpose of depositing funds, and from there I made several carefully thought out maneuvers which are going to make my trail very difficult to follow. Frankly, Millie, I'm willing to bet five to one that they can't *ever* put their hands on me.

"I'll be expected back at the office momentarily, and by three o'clock they will wonder what has happened to me. This is just to tell you that, if they should call you during the afternoon, you can tell them very curtly that our engagement has been broken; that you have no knowledge as to my whereabouts and no further interest in my actions.

"Of course, something like this was inevitable sooner or later. I can't see myself cast in the role of a dutiful husband or a fond parent making sacrifices to put brats through college. Frankly, even the last three weeks of our engagement have been a trifle irksome. You have been sweet and I have had a swell time, but essentially, I'm a roamer and I don't want to be tied down—to anyone. So, that's the story, and now, because the minions of the law will be barking on my trail at any moment, I have to hang up. Good-by and good luck!"

The phone clicked.

Somehow Mildred found her way back to her desk.

A sense of loyalty to her employers kept her hammering away at her typewriter until she had finished the important letter on which she was working. When she took the letter in for signature, her white face and trembling hands attracted attention. She said she felt ill and was told to go home for the rest of the day.

All she could think of was getting away for a time. She dreaded having to face the patronizing sympathy of the other girls in the office. She had a few friends who would stand by her loyally, but there were others whose noses had been put out of joint by the announcement of her engagement to Bob, and they would derive too much satisfaction from rubbing it in.

Mildred only wanted to crawl in a hole and pull the hole in after her.

Mildred went at once to the bank. She cashed the pay check she had received the day before, drew out every penny of her savings account, returned to her apartment, bathed, put on her newest traveling outfit.

At four-forty the phone rang. It was the general manager of Pillsbury & Maxwell. He was concerned about Robert Joiner.

Mildred said coldly that she knew nothing of Mr. Joiner's whereabouts, that her engagement had been broken, that she was no longer interested in Mr. Joiner, and then suddenly in the midst of the conversation, found herself crying. After a few choking attempts to carry on the conversation, she had slipped the receiver into place, hoping that the manager would think he had been cut off.

The manager showed his sympathetic understanding by not calling back.

Mildred had no desire for dinner. The thought of meeting someone whom she knew and to whom she might have to make explanations was intolerable.

Now that the blow had fallen, she realized that for the past few weeks there had been something wrong. Looking back, she could recall a hundred things that should have warned her, but she had been too happy, too willing to accept glib explanations at face value.

Robert had never been one to talk of himself. He always kept his association with her on a plane of jaunty superiority. From the beginning she had sensed that he had an intense aversion to having anyone pry into his private affairs. He would volunteer such information as he wished to give, but resented any questions seeking additional information.

She had been so dominated by the man, his poise, his self-assurance, his clever mind, that she had simply drifted along.

Mildred wished now that she had gone directly to her boss that afternoon and told him the whole story. She wished that she had called Pillsbury & Maxwell and told them what had happened.

Because she had not, she now found herself in an impossible situation. The thought of what was bound to happen the next day threw her into a tailspin.

Dimly she realized that her mind was going around in circles, that in her present emotional state she couldn't trust her own decisions. If she could just escape from everything. It was under such circumstances that the mind in a merciful attempt to escape too difficult problems resorted to the defense of amnesia. If she could just sink into amnesia, but she knew she couldn't deliberately induce amnesia.

Mildred slipped on her jacket, picked up her purse, and started for the parking lot. She found her car and started driving inland, driving somewhat aimlessly, not knowing where she was going or what she was going to do.

She remembered a story she had heard about two years before from a friend who liked to tell horror stories. It was about an earthquake he had seen in South America, and a beautiful young girl, the belle of the town, who yielded to panic. She had jumped in her new automobile and taken off down the road, trying to escape the crumbling walls of the buildings and the threat of a rocky avalanche from the mountainside.

A huge crack had opened up, cutting across the road as a gaping chasm. The screaming girl and the new, shiny automobile had plunged into this cleft in the earth. Then, as though it had only been waiting for its human prey, the crack had closed with a grinding, rumbling noise. The earthquake subsided. Where the crack had been was only a pressure ridge of earth and rocks and the crumbled blocks of the paved highway.

Now Mildred almost wished that some terrific earthquake would open up a chasm in the earth directly in front of her car so that she, too, could disappear. Her one desire was to sever all connections with the past, to vanish without a trace. When you had to work to live, however, in these days of social security numbers, driving licenses and income tax returns, vanishing into oblivion was no easy matter.

Then slowly she began to realize she dared not even try to escape from her past life or to disappear. A simple disappearance would only make it appear she had been Bob Joiner's accomplice in his embezzlements, and she must above all protect her reputation for honesty. She did not have to go back and face the music yet, however, and she needed time to build up her defenses against the sneers and laughter on the one hand and pity on the other that were surely awaiting her return to Oceanside.

After a few miles she glanced at her fuel gauge and realized she would need more gasoline. She stopped at a service station at Vista and while the attendant was filling the gas tank she noticed a young woman standing quietly by the side of the gas pumps.

At first Mildred thought she was the wife of the attendant. Then somehow she got the definite impression that something was very wrong. She felt the young woman's eyes on her, studying her discreetly. Then the figure came forward diffidently.

"May I ask where you're going?"

Mildred tried hard to bring her numbed mind to focus on the situation. "I don't know," she said absently. "I'm just—going."

"Could you give me a ride?"

Mildred said, "I'm, sorry, but I'm not going anywhere in particular."

"Neither am I."

Mildred saw a woman of twenty-three or twenty-four, with brown eyes, brown hair, and about her own build. And she fancied she saw desperation and abject misery which indicated a fellow sufferer.

"Get in," Mildred heard herself saying.

"I have a suitcase."

"Put it in."

The attendant filled up the tank, washed the windshield, checked the oil and water.

Mildred gave him her gasoline credit card, signed the charge slip, got in the car, started the motor, and said to the girl beside her, "I'm Mildred Crest."

"Fern Driscoll," the young woman said tonelessly.

Abruptly it occurred to Mildred that if she changed her mind again about returning to Oceanside, she might never receive the bill for the gasoline she had just purchased. She braked the car to a stop, put it in reverse and backed up to the service station.

Mildred said to the station attendant, "I'm Mildred Crest. I just signed a charge slip for gasoline. The amount was three dollars and forty cents. Here's the money. Please tear up the charge slip."

She handed the puzzled attendant three dollars and forty cents, stepped on the foot pedal and drove away.

After a few moments she turned to the young woman beside her.

"I'm not good company. I'm not certain where I'm going or what I'm doing. I may drive around awhile and then go back. I may never go back. You'd better get out and get a ride with someone else."

Fern Driscoll shook her head.

Mildred and the hitchhiker rode in silence for miles. Mildred came to the intersection with Highway 395, crossed it, taking the road to Pala.

Fern Driscoll turned and looked at her, her eyebrows raised in silent interrogation.

Mildred Crest, speeding up after the boulevard stop, at first said nothing, then feeling she might be taking undue advantage of the other's misery, turned to her abruptly.

"That's the main north-and-south road from San Diego to San Bernardino, then to Bishop and Reno. Want to get out?"

Fern Driscoll shook her head. "It's night. I'd prefer to go with you wherever you're going. If I do have to get out, I'd prefer to wait at a gasoline station where I can size up the people."

"I've told you I'm not going anywhere," Mildred said.

"That's good enough for me," Fern said.

"I live back there," Mildred ventured, "at Oceanside. I may decide to go back."

"Oceanside? Where's that?" Fern asked.

"On the coast road."

Fern said, "I'm a stranger in these parts. I arrived in San Diego late this afternoon, left within an hour. A nice-looking young man turned out to be a wolf. I was glad to get out of his car. I walked a mile before I came to the gasoline station."

"You live in Calfornia?"

"No—"

"In the West?"

"No. I'm just a foot-loose doll."

Silence settled between them. Not a relaxed silence of companionship and understanding, but a tense, uneasy silence.

Abruptly the young woman said bitterly, "I've made a mess of my life."

"Who hasn't?" Mildred commented.

Fern Driscoll shook her head. "You're just down in the dumps temporarily. You've had a jolt. *You* haven't burned your bridges. *I've* burned my bridges."

"I'd like to trade places with you," Mildred said.

"Sight unseen?" the other asked.

Mildred nodded.

Again there was a period of silence, then the other said, "Don't tempt me. It couldn't be done, but—well, it's an idea."

They came to Pala.

"Where does that road go?" Fern asked.

"Palomar Mountain," Mildred said. "That's where the big, two-hundred-inch telescope is."

She turned to the left.

"And this?" the hitchhiker asked.

"I don't know for certain," Mildred confessed. "I think it winds around and comes back to Highway 395."

Mildred gave her attention to piloting the car.

The road ran level for a while, then started climbing, and finally became a winding mountain grade.

On a sharp curve the lights penciled across the shoulder of the road and then were blotted out by the black void of a deep canyon.

Mildred heard the other girl's voice saying, "Wouldn't it be fine just to plunge into that blackness? Then nothing could ever catch up with us. We'd leave it all behind. Look, Mildred, are you game to do it?"

"Do what?"

"Drive off the road?"

"Heavens, no!" Mildred said. "You might be maimed, crippled for life. That wouldn't solve anything. That wouldn't—"

Mildred suddenly felt Fern Driscoll lunge against her. Strong hands grappled with the wheel and gave it a twist.

Mildred was caught by surprise. She threw her weight against the wheel, fighting to bring the car back onto the road.

Fern Driscoll gave a shrill, hysterical laugh, braced herself and ripped the wheel from Mildred's grasp.

In that last brief second, when the car seemed to hesitate, Mildred looked out into a terrifying black abyss. Then she felt the front of the car dip sharply downward. Her ears heard a grinding crash of steel on rocks, then she felt herself lifted into the air, felt the car turning over. Above all she could hear that wild, demoniacal laughter, the shrill cacophony of insane hysteria.

The car hit solidly, throwing Mildred against the steering wheel. Then the car rolled on in a crazy zigzag pattern. For a moment it was right side up. Then it keeled over sharply. Mildred heard a thud, like the sound of a ripe melon being smashed with an ax, then the scraping of metal. With a jolt the car came to a stop.

Mildred had a subconscious realizaton of groping for the ignition switch and then turning the headlights off, of lying there in the darkness, listening to the gurgle of water from the radiator, the trickling of oil from the crankcase. Then there was a permeating odor; the smell of raw gasoline seeping into the car.

Mildred tried the door. The car was all but upside down, the door was hopelessly jammed. But the window on her side had been lowered. By squirming and twisting she was finally able to extricate herself. The gurgling noises ceased. The quiet of the night descended around them. Overhead the stars were steady.

"Fern," Mildred said. "Fern, are you all right?"

There was no answer.

Mildred leaned over and looked down into the car. It was dark and she could not see much.

She felt for her purse and finally found it. There was a book of matches in the purse.

She scraped a match into flame.

She looked, and knew panic and nausea.

The hitchhiker had evidently got the door partially open and had been about halfway out when the car struck that last huge rock.

Mildred shook out the match, threw it away from her, leaned against the side of the wrecked car, and felt as though the last of her strength had drained out of her.

A car went by on the road high above them. Mildred screamed for help and her voice was swallowed up in the silent darkness as a speck of ink is absorbed by blotting paper.

The car whined onward, never pausing for so much as a moment in its snarling progress up the hill.

With a desperate effort Mildred pulled herself together and took stock of the situation. She had been badly shaken. There were one or two very sore places, but no bones were broken. She could feel her heart pounding, but her mind was beginning to function clearly.

She would have to scramble back up to the road, and stop some motorist. There would be authorities to notify.

She looked down at the dark shape of the girl and for a moment found herself wishing that the situation could have been reversed and that—

The idea struck Mildred with the force of a blow.

After all, why not?

Mildred could take Fern Driscoll's purse. There would be *some* identification in it. She could leave her own purse. The thing that had once been the other girl's head would now furnish no means of identification. Of course, Mildred thought calmly and coolly, there was the question of fingerprints. Would anyone have those, or would they take the prints of a corpse?

What if they did?

Mildred could try it. If it appeared the body was taken for that of Mildred Crest, Mildred could simply keep quiet. Otherwise she could come forward and state that she had found herself wandering around in a dazed condition, not knowing who she was. She knew that such things happened—retrograde amnesia, they called it.

She leaned down in the wreck, looking for Fern's purse. She found it and considered the problem of transferring what money there was in her own purse. If they found her purse without money—Well, why not? It was money for which she had worked hard. She certainly needed all the money she could get.... Swiftly she decided to take all the folding money from her purse.

Calmly competent now, her nausea overcome, Mildred made the change.

Again she struck a match as she leaned over to drop her purse by the steering post. The match flared up and burned her fingers. She dropped it, jerking back her hand with an exclamation of pain.

For the tenth part of a second there was a little flame, then a sudden flare of oily brilliance. As the gasoline ignited, Mildred had only time to jump back in horror before the rear end of the car became a blazing inferno.

Mildred clutched Fern Driscoll's purse, scrambled down the canyon out of the way of the flames. She heard tires scream on the road above as a speeding car skidded to a stop.

Mildred scrambled down the last few feet of the steep embankment, came to a rock-strewn stream bed, followed that blindly downhill, the fire lighting her way so she could see where she was going and avoid the branches which would have torn her clothes.

What followed was a nightmare compounded of many nightmares. There was the difficult terrain to be negotiated. As she put distance between herself and the wreck, the light from the fire was abruptly shut off by a jutting promontory. Finally she was stumbling along in darkness.

When she heard the sudden whir of a rattlesnake, it was impossible to place the noise in the darkness. Mildred knew it was only a few feet away, and the whirring was the dry, ominous rustle of death.

Mildred jumped wildly into the darkness, stumbled over a rock, fell face down in a bush, then extricated herself in the haste of blind panic and ran.

After a while, she heard sirens, saw a red glow indicating that the fire of the car had set off a brush fire. She heard fire-fighting apparatus, then finally found a place where she could scramble up to the road.

There were several cars standing there above the wreck. A man with a badge and flashlight was blocking all traffic. People were milling around in confusion.

Mildred picked a kindly-looking old couple, hastily straightened her clothes and smoothed her hair, and went up to them. "May I ride with you?" she asked. "I got out to look at the fire and my family turned back toward Pala. If I can only get to a phone—"

"Oh, but they'll miss you and come back," the woman said.

"I'm afraid not," Mildred observed, finding that her mind had powers of extemporaneous deceit which she hadn't realized. "You see, I was asleep in the back seat, all covered up with a blanket and my head on a pillow. They stopped the car and went up to look. I woke up, got out and they must have returned and passed me in the darkness. They think I'm still asleep on the back seat and won't know the difference until they get home.

"Where's home?" the woman asked.

"San Diego."

"Well, we're going the other way, to Riverside. Perhaps you'd better notify—"

"Oh, that will be quite all right," Mildred said. "I'll go to Riverside with you and then I can phone my folks. If they aren't home yet, I'll telephone the neighbor. I have friends in Riverside."

So Mildred had gone to Riverside. Then a bus had taken her into Los Angeles. She registered at a downtown hotel as F. Driscoll.

It was late that night when Mildred surveyed the contents of Fern Driscoll's oversized purse. It was then that she began to appreciate her predicament.

In a neat, compact bundle with heavy elastic bands she found forty, crisp, new hundred-dollar bills. In addition, there were some two hundred dollars in fives, tens and twenties. There was a driver's license giving Fern Driscoll's residence as Lansing, Michigan. There was a social security card, lipstick, a handkerchief, a compact, and there was a bundle of letters tightly tied up with waxed thread.

Mildred hesitated a moment, then untied the thread, looked through some of the letters. They were love letters signed by the name "Forrie." They were most affectionate, but they also indicated a family conflict, a father who was putting pressure to bear on his son to make him "come to his senses."

The letters only emphasized Mildred's own heartache. She did little more than skim through them, then tied them again into a compact bundle.

Mildred thought back to the dark eyes smoldering with emotion, the slightly sullen obstinacy of the beautiful features, the impulsive manner in which Fern had acted. Mildred realized that the hitchhiker could have done almost anything on sudden impulse. She was the type to act in haste, to repent, if at all, at leisure. On hysterical impulse, the girl had sent the car plunging down the canyon. Then at the last moment had regretted her impulse to destroy herself and had tried to escape.

However, there was no use trying to recall the past. Mildred found herself face to face with reality. Didn't the death of Fern Driscoll, tragic as it had been, give her the longed-for chance of escape from all that lay behind her at Oceanside? Mildred sat there thinking for a long time before she finally went to bed.

So Mildred Crest became Fern Driscoll. She changed the color of her hair, and adopted dark glasses.

Mildred knew that with her secretarial ability she could land jobs without the slightest difficulty. It would, of course, be necessary to work out a story that would account for a lack of references. But Mildred felt certain that once she was given a test she would have little difficulty in finding work, references or no references.

The money in the purse bothered her. There was too much of it. She decided to hold this money as a sort of trust until she found out more about the girl whose identity she was borrowing.

The newspaper stories were exactly what Mildred had expected. The Oceanside paper carried quite a story. Mildred Crest, popular secretary of a local manufacturer, had been instantly killed in an automobile accident. In some way the driver had lost control, the car had gone over the grade on the Pala highway. The unfortunate girl had apparently been half-in and half-out of the right-hand automobile door when it struck against a huge rock near the bottom of the canyon. Afterward, the car had caught fire and the body had been partially burned before prompt action on the part of a passing motorist, who had a fire extinguisher in his car, had put out the blaze. The flames had started a brush fire which had not been extinguished until some two hours later.

Mildred studied the newspaper accounts and decided she was safe. Within twenty-four hours she had a job with the Consolidated Sales and Distribution Company under the name of Fern Driscoll, and within forty-eight hours felt herself well-established.

Then almost immediately came the crushing blow.

Authorities were not "entirely satisfied." There had been a coroner's inquest. While much of the car had been consumed by fire, by a strange freak Mildred Crest's purse had not been consumed. The contents were quite recognizable. There were no bills in the purse, only change.

Authorities, moreover, found tracks indicating that someone had left the car after the wreck. Examination showed that the headlight and ignition switches had been turned off. Police felt it was quite possible that someone had crawled out of the window of the door on the driver's side of the car. There was to be a post-mortem examination of the burned body.

Mildred was in a panic. Would they discover the substitution of identities after that post-mortem?

Still going under the name of Fern Driscoll, because there was now nothing else for her to do, Mildred awaited the result of the autopsy.

She found it in a copy of the *San Diego Union*. The autopsy had shown that

"Mildred Crest" had been dead *before* the fire started. There was some evidence of possible foul play. A service-station man had come forward who remembered putting gasoline in Mildred Crest's car. She had signed her name to the charge ticket. Then she had returned, canceled the charge, and paid cash. This caused the service-station attendant to remember the transaction.

The attendant at the service station remembered, moreover, that Mildred Crest had picked up a hitchhiker who presumably had been in the car with her at the time of the accident. It was suggested that this hitchhiker had perhaps killed Mildred in an attempted holdup. In the ensuing struggle the car had gone off the road.

The authorities had a good description of the hitchhiker, about twenty-three or twenty-four, five-feet-four, weight a hundred and twelve to a hundred and fifteen pounds, chestnut hair, brown eyes, well dressed, apparently from the Middle West.

Then came the last sentence of the story, the last paralyzing sentence. The autopsy had shown that the body of "Mildred Crest" had been in the second month of pregnancy.

Mildred dropped the paper from nerveless fingers. She understood everything now. Fern Driscoll, a young woman, probably of good family, in the second month of pregnancy—the disappearance, the forty, new hundred-dollar bills in the purse, the emergency fund to "see her through," the misery in the girl's eyes, the desire to keep going, yet having no fixed destination in mind.

And now that Mildred Crest had taken the identity of Fern Driscoll, now that she dared not disclose her true identity, she knew that Fern Driscoll's pregnancy had been transferred to Mildred Crest.

How the tongues would be buzzing in Oceanside!

The newspaper account had mentioned that the authorities were making a "determined effort" to find and question the hitchhiker who had presumably been in Mildred Crest's car at the time it went off the road.

As though it were not enough to be branded by the stigma of another girl's pregnancy, she was now suspected of her own murder.

Mildred Crest was very glad she had started wearing dark glasses the day after she arrived in Los Angeles. She wore them all the time. The bright California sun, she said, hurt her eyes after living all her life in the Middle West.

CHAPTER TWO

The offices of the Consolidated Sales and Distribution Company where Mildred worked happened to be in the same building and on the same floor as offices occupied by Perry Mason, the famous lawyer. Mildred had noticed Mason's name on the door to his offices, and she had often heard stories of the daring exploits of the famous lawyer and his ingenious defense of innocent persons accused of crime.

Once she had ridden up in the elevator with the attorney and, as she stood beside him, looking up at the keen, piercing eyes, the rugged, granite-hard features, she experienced a strange feeling of confidence.

Almost without realizing that she had done so, Mildred had made up her mind that, if the worst ever came to the worst, she would turn to Perry Mason for help.

Twice she actually had been on the point of going to Mason's office, asking his secretary, Della Street, to arrange an appointment.

Each time she desisted because of a subconscious fear that Mason might tell her that what she was doing was wrong, insist that she go to the authorities and make a clean breast of the situation.

The more Mildred thought that possibility over, the more such a course seemed absolutely suicidal. She had reached a decision and she resolved never to turn back. She couldn't and wouldn't retreat.

Mildred Crest had no close relatives. Her father had died before she was born, her mother when she was five. She had been raised by an aunt who had died three years ago, so Mildred was on her own in every sense of the word.

Occasionally, there was a twinge of conscience as Mildred wondered about the background and connections of the dead girl whose name she had taken. But as day after day passed in a placid routine, she saw no reason for taking any radical step.

She practiced signing the name "Fern Driscoll," using the signature on the driving license as a pattern.

After repeated attempts, she was able to dash off a fairly good replica of Fern Driscoll's signature.

The forty one-hundred-dollar bills were still intact.

Mildred had secured a very satisfactory apartment. There was one long bus ride and then a short walk. The supermarket where she shopped was only two blocks away. Getting to and from the office and shopping represented Mildred's sole excursions into public life. She cooked her own meals in the apartment, kept to herself, formed no friendships at the office, but slowly and surely established her identity as Fern Driscoll.

Then one night out of a clear sky the blow fell.

It has been a hard day at the office. Mildred had worked overtime getting out some important letters. She had missed her regular bus. Dog-tired, she entered her apartment house. She had intended to stop by the supermarket, but she knew there were enough leftovers in the icebox to carry her through the evening, and there were eggs, bacon and toast for breakfast. She needed no more.

She hadn't even seen the man until she fitted her key to the door of the apartment. Then he materialized as from nowhere.

"Miss Driscoll?" he asked.

Something about the way in which he had been so inconspicuous as to defy notice and then the tense menace of his voice warned Mildred that this was no casual pickup.

She flashed him a quick look from behind her dark glasses.

"Well?" she asked.

The man nodded toward her key in the door of her apartment.

"Open the door," he said. "I'm coming in."

"Oh, no, you're not," she said, standing her ground. "Who are you? What do you want? How did you get in here?"

"The name wouldn't mean anything to you."

"Then you mean nothing to me."

"I think I do."

She shook her head angrily. "I'm not accustomed to being accosted by strangers in this manner. I'm going into my apartment and you're going to stay on the outside."

"I want to talk to you," he said, "about a certain automobile accident which took place near Pala; an accident where Mildred Crest met her death."

"I've never heard of Mildred Crest," she said. "I don't know about any accident."

He smiled condescendingly and said, "Listen, I don't want to make any trouble, but you and I have certain things to discuss and we'd better talk them over quietly."

"What is this, blackmail?"

His laugh showed genuine amusement. "Certainly not. I merely wanted to discuss the accident with you. I promise to be a gentleman, and if I'm not, you have the phone at your elbow. You can call the manager or the police—*if* you want the police."

"But I haven't the faintest idea what you're talking about."

"You will have, after you give me a chance to explain."

She remembered the woman who had the apartment across the hall, and Mildred had the uneasy feeling that she was listening. This woman was a thin, nervous busybody who had on several occasions tried to get acquainted, and the more reserved Mildred became, the more inordinate had been the other's curiosity.

She reached a swift decision.

"Very well. Come in," she said. "I'll listen to what you have to say and that's all. Then you're going out."

"Fair enough," the man said. "Just so you listen."

Mildred opened the door of the apartment.

Her visitor got down to brass tacks with a glib swiftness that indicated he had rehearsed the part he was to play.

"I'm Carl Harrod," he said, "an insurance investigator.

"We carried insurance on Mildred Crest's automobile. I was assigned to investigate the accident. The first thing I noticed was that Mildred had not been driving the automobile at the time it went over the bank. The next thing I noticed was that tracks indicated someone could well have walked away from the wreckage and gone down the canyon in the dark."

He paused and smiled apologetically. "I'm an investigator, I'm not a very good woodsman, and not a very good tracker, Miss Driscoll. But I did the best I could. I found tracks going down the canyon and finally I found what I was looking for; the place where you had climbed up out of the canyon.

"There was no money in Mildred's purse; that is, just a very small amount of change, yet I found she had gone to the bank and drawn out every cent she had on deposit, prior to the time she left Oceanside. There should have been more than five hundred dollars in the purse.

"For your information, Mildred Crest had received quite an emotional shock the day of her death. She had been keeping company with a young man who turned out to be an embezzler. He is now a fugitive from justice."

Carl Harrod settled back in the chair and smiled.

"Now then," he said, "it is quite apparent that Mildred Crest was dead before the fire was started. The trachea—the windpipe to you, Miss Driscoll—did not contain the faintest trace of the by-products of combustion. There were other things that the autopsy surgeon could tell, but I suppose you're not interested in the technical details. I think probably you know by this time that Mildred Crest was, unfortunately, in the second month of pregnancy.

"Putting these things together, it's possible to reach a very interesting and highly dramatic conclusion, a story which unfortunately is all too common."

Harrod smiled affably. "I'm not boring you, am I?"

"Go ahead," Mildred said.

"Our investigation was largely routine," Harrod said, "until I discovered the service station where Mildred had made her last purchase of gasoline. The attendant told me she had picked up a hitchhiker; that the hitchhiker had asked her where she was going and Mildred had said that she wasn't going anywhere.

"After I saw what had happened at the scene of the wreck, I naturally became interested in the hitchhiker. It really took only a slight effort to find you, Miss Driscoll. Your suitcase was in the car when it went off the road. The exterior was damaged by the fire, but I was able to trace the suitcase and finally to find the retailer who had sold it. His records disclosed your name.

"I felt perhaps you would come to the city and that you would look for work. It has taken me this long to locate you."

"What do you want?" Mildred asked.

"At the moment I want a signed statement from you," Harrod said.

"What sort of a statement?"

"I want a statement that you were driving the car at the time of the accident. I want a statement in your own handwriting as to just what happened and how it was that you left the automobile, stumbled down the canyon, finally climbed the bank and came here, all without reporting to the authorities anything that had happened.

"I would also like a signed statement from you that you took the money from Mildred's purse. This statement would also release the insurance carrier from any liability, since you would admit that the accident was your fault.

"Now then, we come to a rather sordid part of the entire affair. Since you had an opportunity to take the money from Mildred's purse, since you had the opportunity to retrieve your own purse from the wreck, it is quite apparent that the fire didn't break out until an appreciable interval after the car had gone over the bank. It is, therefore, quite apparent that the fire was deliberately set in order to conceal the evidence of the theft.

"I would like a statement from you to that effect."

"Do you think I'm crazy?" Mildred asked.

Harrod shrugged his shoulders. "After all, these things are self-evident, Miss Driscoll. Why shouldn't you sign such a statement?"

"Don't be silly," she said. "I never knew Mildred Crest in my life. I wasn't in any automobile. I didn't—"

Her voice trailed away into silence.

Harrod's smile was patronizing. "Just stopped to think, didn't you, Miss Driscoll? You felt the fire would destroy a great deal of evidence. It destroyed very little, if any. A passing motorist who carried a fire extinguisher put out the fire in the car. Most of the gasoline had been spilled out of the tank when the car hit a rock at the top of the hill. That fire got out of control, but thanks to the fire extinguisher, the flames in the back of Mildred's car were extinguished.

"So I found the suitcase was sold to you in Lansing, Michigan. I made a little investigation at Lansing. You had charge accounts and an excellent credit rating. You left a good position in Lansing overnight without telling anyone where you were going."

"What do you intend to do with this statement if I should give it to you?" Mildred asked.

"Well," Harrod said, "that's an interesting question. Quite frankly, Miss Driscoll, I don't know myself. Theoretically I'm supposed to make a complete report on the situation and append the statement to the report.... Actually I don't think I'll do it."

"Why not?"

"I find you quite intelligent. You are very good-looking. Someday you will marry. You may even marry money. In short, I see unlimited possibilities."

"Blackmail!" Mildred said.

"Now, blackmail is a very crude and a very ugly word. Please remember, Miss Driscoll, that I haven't asked you for anything except a signed statement."

"I have no intention of writing any such statement."

"That, of course, *would* be your first reaction," Harrod said. "Well, you just got back from the office. I know that you're tired. You probably want to get your dinner and I see you would prefer to be alone.

"I'll let you think things over for a day or two, and then I'll be in touch with you again."

Harrod walked to the door, turned and smiled at Mildred. "I'll be back, Miss Driscoll," he said, "and please, *please* remember that I have asked you for nothing except a signed statement as to the facts. I am making that request in my capacity as an investigator for an insurance company. It is a thoroughly legitimate request, particularly in view of the fact that you might try to make a claim against my employer, Mildred Crest's insurance carrier.

"I mention this in case you should consult with some private detective agency, a lawyer, or even, in fact, the police. All I am asking for is a signed statement as to what happened. I would like to have you tell me this in your words.

"Anyone will tell you that is a customary procedure in cases of this sort.

"Thank you very much, Miss Driscoll. I've enjoyed our little visit. I'll see you again. Good night."

Harrod eased himself out of the door.

Mildred stood watching the closed door with sickening apprehension.

She had, indeed, burned her bridges.

What Harrod evidently didn't know as yet, but would probably find out, was about the forty hundred-dollar bills in Fern Driscoll's purse.

In view of her actions, it would now be impossible to explain how the fire had started. Harrod quite naturally assumed she had rifled the other girl's purse and had then started the fire to conceal the theft.

Either in the identity of Mildred Crest, who had stolen four thousand dollars from Fern Driscoll, or in the borrowed identity of Fern Driscoll, who had stolen some five hundred dollars from Mildred Crest, she was between two fires.

And, in the background, was the possibility of her being charged with first-degree murder.

CHAPTER THREE

Della Street, Perry Mason's confidential secretary, said, "There is a young woman employed by the Consolidated Sales people down the hall who wants an appointment. She says it will only take a few moments and she'd like to run in and talk with you whenever it's convenient. She says she can get away for ten or fifteen minutes whenever we phone."

"Say what it's about?" Perry Mason asked.

"Only that it was a personal matter."

Mason looked at his watch, then at his appointment schedule, said, "These things that take only fifteen or twenty minutes quite frequently take an hour, and you don't like to throw a girl out right in the middle of her story. We have a half-hour, though.... Give her a ring, Della. Ask her if she can come in right away. What's her name?"

"Fern Driscoll."

"Do you know her?"

"I don't think so. She says she's seen me in the elevator. I think she's new with the company."

"Give her a buzz," Mason said, "tell her I can see her right away if she wants to come in now. Tell her that's with the understanding it will only take twenty minutes; that I have another appointment."

Della Street nodded and went to the telephone.

A few moments later she was back saying, "She's coming in right away. I'll go to the reception office and meet her."

"Skip the preliminaries," Mason said, "getting her name, address and all that. We'll get them when she comes in. I want to hear her story and rush things along as much as possible."

Della Street nodded, went to the reception office and within less than a minute was back. Turning to the young woman she had escorted into the office, Della Street said, "This is Mr. Mason, Miss Driscoll—Fern Driscoll, Mr. Mason."

"Sit down, Miss Driscoll," Mason said. "You're working for the Consolidated Sales and Distribution Company, I believe."

"Yes, sir."

"Where is your residence, Miss Driscoll?"

"309 Rexmore Apartments."

"What did you want to see me about?" Mason asked. And then added in a kindly manner, "I specialize mostly in trial work and a good deal of it is criminal work. I think perhaps you're in the wrong law office, but I may be able to help you get in touch with the right man."

She nodded briefly, said, "Thank you," then went on, "you'll have to pardon my dark glasses. Ever since I came to California some two weeks ago I've been having eye trouble—I hitchhiked and I feel as if the retina of my eyes became sunburned. Did you happen to read in the paper some two weeks ago about a Mildred Crest of Oceanside who was killed in an automobile accident?"

Mason smiled and shook his head. "These automobile accidents are a dime a dozen. They are usually all grouped together on an inside page. Was there something special about Mildred Crest's death?"

"I was riding with her when she was killed."

"I see," Mason said, eying her sharply. "Were you hurt?"

"Fortunately I was only bruised a little. I was sore for a day or two, but that was all."

Mason nodded.

"Mr. Mason," she said, "so that you can understand the situation, I have to tell you certain things.

"I lived in Lansing, Michigan. I wanted to disappear for reasons of my own. I can assure you I haven't violated any laws. I just wanted to get away where I could begin all over again. I was restless and nervous. I had sufficient funds to buy a ticket to any place I wanted to go, but the point was I didn't know where I wanted to go. I was drifting aimlessly. I was hitchhiking."

"Go on," Mason said.

"I went to Phoenix, stayed there for a few days, then went to San Diego, stayed there for only a few hours, got a ride out of San Diego and got as far as a little place called Vista and I was, for the moment, stranded there. It was about...oh, I don't know, seven-thirty or eight o'clock in the evening. It was dark and this Mildred Crest drove up."

"You knew her?" Mason asked.

"No, I was simply waiting there at the service station for a ride. You see, a young woman on the highway is a little different from a man. A man will stand out by a boulevard stop and try to thumb a ride. Anyone who stops is a good ride. But not many people stop.

"However, a young woman on the highway has plenty of rides. Almost every car stops and offers her a lift, but—Well, I don't care to play it that way. I like to be at a service station where I can size up the person and then ask if I may ride."

"So you asked Mildred Crest for a ride?"

"Yes."

"And what happened?"

"I sensed at the time that Mildred Crest was running away from something, that she was very much upset and—Well, for instance, I asked her where she was going and she said, 'Away.'"

"So what did you do?"

"Well, that was so exactly my own case, I asked her if I could go along with her, and she said, 'All right.' I don't know. I think we might have confided in each other after a while. I had troubles of my own and she certainly had plenty on *her* mind.

"However, we drove down to Pala and then turned on the road going up from Pala and there was an accident."

"What happened?"

"There was an accident. Another car met us right on a hairpin turn. I tried to avoid—I mean, it was impossible to avoid the other car entirely. It was going too fast. It just barely sideswiped us, just a little bit, but enough to put the car out of control and over the embankment. The car went down and Mildred, I guess, opened the door and tried to get out of the car before it went over, but she didn't have time. The door was unlatched and she was halfway out when the car went over. She struck her head against a rock and—Well, she died instantly."

Mason thought for a moment. "Who was driving the car?" he asked.

She took a deep breath. "At the time, I was."

"How did that happen?"

"Well, after we started out we talked a little bit and I could sense that Mildred was emotionally upset. She asked me if I drove and I said I did and she started to cry and tried to wipe the tears from her eyes while she was driving. So I offered to take the wheel and she said perhaps I'd better for a little while."

"Did you pick the roads or did she."

"She told me where to go."

Mason said, "If you went from Vista to Pala and then turned at Pala and started back up the grade, you were just doubling back on yourself and—"

"I know. I think eventually she intended to return to Oceanside, but—Well, as it afterward turned out, there were reasons why—"

"Oh, I remember the case now," Della Street interjected. She turned to Perry Mason and said, "You may remember it, Chief. We commented briefly about it. The girl had just learned her fiancé was wanted for embezzlement. The autopsy showed she was pregnant."

"Oh, yes," Mason said, looking at his visitor with renewed interest. "She didn't tell you anything about this?"

"No. I think she would have, but, as I say, there wasn't time. We were just getting acquainted when the accident happened."

"All right," Mason said, "why did you come to me?"

"Because I...I was trying to disappear. I certainly didn't want my name in the paper and I was afraid that, if the newspapers published that Fern Driscoll of Lansing, Michigan, was in the car, there would be an exchange item, or however it is they work those things, and the Lansing paper would get hold of it and—Well, you know the way they do, publish a little paragraph under headlines: 'LOCAL GIRL INVOLVED IN CALIFORNIA TRAFFIC ACCIDENT.' I just didn't want that. I wanted to keep out of the whole thing."

"So what did you do?" Mason asked.

She hesitated a moment, said, "I—Well, I'm afraid I was negligent. I am responsible for the car catching fire."

"How did it happen?"

"I found that I wasn't hurt. I squirmed out through the window on the left-hand side of the car. The door wouldn't open but the window was down. I was pretty badly shaken up and I guess pretty rattled. I struck a match and took stock of the situation. I wanted to see if I could help the other girl."

"Mildred?"

"Mildred."

"And what happened?"

"As soon as I saw the way she was lying, half-in and half-out of the door and her head—I...I just became terribly nauseated. It was frightful. She had been half-out of the car and her head had been—Well, it was smashed! Just a pulp!"

Mason nodded.

"After that it took me a little while to get myself together and, of course, all of that time gasoline was running out of the car. Apparently it was leaking out of the tank at the rear of the car and trickling down toward the front. I didn't know just what was happening and I'm afraid I'm responsible for not appreciating the danger. Anyhow, I struck a second match and that second match burned my fingers, so I dropped it. There was a flash and I jumped back and the whole thing started blazing into flame."

"You didn't have your hair or eyebrows singed?" Mason asked.

"No, I was holding the match down and—Well, that's the way it was."

"So then what did you do?"

"I had my purse with me, fortunately. I— My suitcase, with everything I own, was in the car. I started running from the fire and then I found myself at the bottom of a little canyon.... And then I guess I got in something of a panic. There was a rattlesnake that I almost stepped on and—Well, by the time I got up to the road, I just wanted to get away from there without having my name in the papers or anything, so—Well, that's what I did."

"You didn't report the accident to anyone?"

She shook her head.

"How long ago was that?"

"About two weeks, not quite. It was the twenty-second."

Mason's eyes narrowed.

"And some development has caused you to come to see me?"

"Yes."

"What?"

"A man by the name of Carl Harrod called on me last night. He's an investigator for the insurance company. From the position of the car and the manner in which the doors were jammed, it was apparent that only the person who was in the driver's seat could have squirmed out through the window. My suitcase was in the car, it wasn't entirely consumed by the fire. The fire burned uphill and some of the things in the front of the car weren't even damaged. A motorist with a fire extinguisher saved the car. Mildred's purse wasn't burned up.... Well, anyway, this man Harrod had put two and two together. He found out that Mildred had picked up a hitchhiker at Vista and then he traced the hitchhiker back from Vista, which wasn't too difficult to do.

"You see, a woman hitchhiker who is—" She broke off to smile at Mason and said, "All right, I'll use the term good-looking, naturally attracts some attention. I had given my right name to one of the people who picked me up and then there was the clue of the suitcase and—Well, that's the way it was."

"And what did Harrod want?" Mason asked.

"He wanted me to sign a statement."

"In regard to the accident?"

"Yes."

"Did you do it?"

"No."

"Why?"

"Because I...I have the feeling Mr. Harrod wants that statement not on behalf of the insurance company but—I think he wants to do something with it."

"Blackmail?" Mason asked.

"I wouldn't be too surprised."

"Did he make any overtures along that line?"

"He intimated something like that. Later on, he was very careful to point out that he actually had asked for nothing except a written statement."

Mason drummed with the tips of his fingers on the top of his desk. His eyes were squinted thoughtfully.

"So," she asked, "what do I do?"

Mason said, "You've gone this long without reporting an accident. That is bad. But sit tight and wait for another twenty-four or forty-eight hours. If Mr. Harrod calls to see you again, I want you to tell him only what I shall tell you to tell him.."

"What's that?"

"You have a pencil?"

She shook her head.

Mason nodded to Della Street.

Della Street handed the young woman a shorthand notebook and pencil. "You take shorthand?" Mason asked.

"Oh yes."

"All right, take this down," Mason said. "Here is what you tell Mr. Harrod. Simply say, quote, Mr. Harrod, I have consulted my attorney, Mr. Mason, about all matters in connection with your previous visit. Mr. Mason has advised me that, if you call on me again, I am to ask you to get in touch with him. So, therefore, I ask you to call Mr. Perry Mason, who is representng me in the matter. If his office doesn't answer or if it is night, call the Drake Detective Agency and leave word with Mr. Paul Drake. Mr. Mason is my lawyer. Aside from that, I have nothing to say. I don't care to discuss the matter with you. I don't care either to confirm or deny any deductions you may have made. I am, in short, referring you to Mr. Mason for all information concerning the matter under discussion."

Mason watched the pencil fly over the page of the notebok with deft, sure strokes.

"You're evidently a pretty good stenographer," Mason said.

She smiled. "I think I am. I'm fast and accurate."

Mason glanced at his watch. "All right. That's all *you* do. Just tear that page out of the notebook, read it over enough so you remember it, and if Mr. Harrod calls, refer him to me."

She detected the note of dismissal in his voice, got to her feet. "How much do I—?"

Mason waved his hand. "Forget it," he said. "You're employed on the same floor here in the building, which makes you something of a neighbor, and after all there's nothing—Wait a minute, do you have a nickel in your purse?"

"Why, yes."

"All right," Mason said, smiling, "give me the nickel. That means that I've been duly retained to protect your interests and anything you have told me is a privileged communication. Also, anything I have told you is entirely confidential. Now then, go back to work and quit worrying about Mr. Harrod. If he becomes a nuisance, we'll find some way to deal with him."

Impulsively she gave Mason her hand. "Thank you so much, Mr. Mason."

Mason held her hand for a moment, looked at her searchingly, said, "All right, Miss Driscoll....You're certain you've told me all of it?"

"Yes, yes. Of course."

"All right," Mason told her. "Run along back and get to work."

When she had left the office, Mason turned to Della Street.

"What do you think, Della?"

"She's really frightened. Why did you tell her not to report the accident? Didn't you take a risk doing that?"

"Probably," Mason said. "However, I didn't want her to get in any worse than she is now. Her story of what happened isn't true. I don't want her to make a false report."

"In what way isn't it true?"

"The other car didn't crowd her off the road. Notice she said, 'It was impossible to avoid the other car entirely.'

"No one on earth ever described an automobile accident of that sort in that way. A person would have said, 'Although we got way over on our side of the road, the other car hit us.'"

Della Street thought that over, then nodded thoughtfully.

Mason said, "Now that you know this Fern Driscoll, you'll be seeing her in the elevator and in the rest room. Keep an eye on her and see if she doesn't try to find some opportunity to confide in you. I have an idea the situation will change within the next forty-eight hours."

"And I'm to report to you?" Della Street asked.

"That's the idea," Mason said.

CHAPTER FOUR

That night after Mildred had cleaned away the dinner dishes, put the apartment in order, the chimes on the apartment door sounded.

She took a deep breath, set her face in the expression she wanted to use on Carl Harrod and opened the door.

The young woman who stood on the threshold was perhaps twenty-one or twenty-two. She had a dark complexion with finely chiseled features, a chin that was up in the air far enough to indicate pride, breeding a certain strength of character.

Gray eyes made an appraising study of Mildred.

"Well?" Mildred asked at length, breaking the silence.

"Oh, Fern," the young woman said, "I—It *is* Fern Driscoll, isn't it?"

Mildred nodded.

"I'm Kitty Baylor," the young woman said, as though that explained everything. And then she added, by way of explanation, "Forrie's sister."

"Oh," Mildred said, striving to get her mind adjusted so she could cope with this new complication.

"I know," her visitor said, the words rushing out rapidly, "I'm the last person in the world you expected to see, the last person on earth you *wanted* to see. However, there are certain things we're going to have to face. Running away from them doesn't help.

"I'm up at Stanford, you know, and when I found out about what had happened—Oh, Fern, please let me come in and talk things over. Let's see if we can't find *some* sort of a solution."

Mildred stood to one side. "Come in," she invited.

"I'd heard about you from Forrie," Kitty Baylor when on. "I...I don't know how to begin."

Mildred closed the door. "Won't you sit down?" she invited.

Mildred's visitor seated herself, said, "We've never met but you undoubtedly know about me and I know about you."

Kitty Baylor paused, and Mildred nodded dubiously, sparring for time.

"Now then," Kitty went on, "if it's a fair qustion, would you tell me just *why* you suddenly packed up and went away, why you left all of your friends, your contacts and simply disappeared?"

Mildred said with dignity, "I don't think I have to account to you for my actions."

"All right," Kitty said, "I'll put my cards on the table. This is going to hurt. I don't like to say some of the things I'm going to have to say, but I guess I've got to."

Mildred said nothing.

Kitty took a deep breath. "I'm interested in protecting your good name just as much as the good name of my family. I...I guess there's only one way of saying what I have to say and that's to be brutally frank. You and Forrie were friendly. You were *very* friendly. I *know* that."

Kitty paused and Mildred said nothing.

Kitty fidgeted for a moment, then pushing up her chin and looking Mildred in the eyes said, "A man whom Dad regards as a blackmailer has been trying to build up the facts for a scandal story. This man is going to publish a story in a slander magazine that makes a specialty of digging out dirt with a sex angle.

"That story concerns you. Are you interested?"

Mildred tried to say something, but couldn't.

"All right," Kitty went on, "I'll tell you what that story is. It's that you and Forrie were living together, that you became pregnant, that Forrie went to Dad, that Dad was furious, that he felt Forrie had jeopardized the good name of the family, that you were given a large sum of money to go away and have your baby, that you wanted Forrie to marry you, but that Dad wouldn't let Forrie even consider it and that Forrie was under Dad's domination."

Kitty paused and Mildred, not knowing what to say, maintained an embarrassed silence.

Kitty seemed to shrink within her clothes. "Well," she said, "I guess it's true. I'd have sworn it wasn't. I wouldn't have thought Dad would have done a thing like that. I *know* he wouldn't. He admits that he talked with Forrie about you and said in a general way that he hoped Forrie would marry in his social set. I guess it's no secret that Dad wanted and I guess he still wants Forrie to marry Carla Addis."

Kitty, suddenly weary, said, "I know I'm taking an awful lot on myself, but this *is* important. It's important to all of us. Do you want to say anything?"

Mildred shook her head.

"All right," Kitty went on, "here are my cards all face up, Fern. If the story is true, I'm on your side. If you are pregnant and were sent away like that, I'm going to do something about it.

"You're a woman. I'm a woman. I think you care for Forrie. I'm his sister and I love him. I know he has faults. I know, too, that Dad thinks altogether too much about family and social position and perhaps he's talked Forrie into his way of thinking."

Mildred remained silent.

"On the other hand," Kitty went on, her eyes boring diretly into Mildred's, "it may just be what Dad thinks, some sort of blackmail scheme by which you're planning to hold up the family, blast Forrie's future with a paternity suit, or team up with this man Harrod for a shakedown. If so, you're headed for trouble, and I mean big trouble. Dad is a fighter, and you just don't have any idea how hard he can fight. You're buying yourself a ticket to the penitentiary for blackmail.

"I came here to find out the truth."

Mildred met Kitty Baylor's eyes, said suddenly, "I'm sorry. I can't tell you what you want to know."

"Why not?"

"Because," Mildred said, "I don't know."

Kitty's eyes were suspicious. "You mean you don't know whether you're going to have a baby?"

"It isn't that," Mildred said. "It's...it's—"

"Is it a shakedown? Are you in need of money?"

"It isn't that. It's—I don't want to—"

Mildred rose abruptly, crossed to the window and absently watched the traffic in the street below. Then she turned suddenly. "All right, I guess I'm going to have to tell you.

"Will you promise not to interrupt and let me tell you the whole story in my own way?"

"Of course. Go ahead."

Mildred waited for a couple of seconds, then plunged ahead.

"I'm not Fern Driscoll!"

Then slowly, in detail, Mildred told Kitty exactly what happened the night she had picked up Fern Driscoll and about the visit she had had from Carl Harrod.

"So there probably *is* something to the claim this man Harrod is making," Mildred finished up. "*He* thinks I'm Fern Driscoll. I don't think he even suspects any switch in identity."

Kitty Baylor blinked her eyes as she tried to adjust herself to this new situation.

At length she asked, "Are you—? I mean...are you—?"

"No," Mildred said.

Kitty was silent for a few seconds, then she said thoughtfully, "I don't believe Harrod *really* does think you're Fern Driscoll. I think he's trying to get you to sign a statement as Fern Driscoll so he'll have you in his power. Then he can make you say or do almost anything he wants. He's on the track of a big story, something that he can make into a really sensational scandal feature. I'm terribly sorry about Fern. I never knew her, but I know that Forrie was fond of her and—Good Lord, things really *are* in a sweet mess, aren't they?

"This worm, Harrod, really has a story. Sordid sex, surreptitious trysts between a secretary and the son of a wealthy manufacturer, then the arrogant father with the power of wealth.... You haven't fooled Harrod a bit. The more I think of it, the plainer it becomes. You see, Harrod told Dad that Fern was two months preganant. He must have learned that from the autopsy."

"She could have told someone," Mildred said.

"I suppose so," Kitty said.

Mildred asked, "Why did she leave?"

"Probably because she was a darn decent kid," Kitty said. "She must have been in love with Forrie. She went away so she wouldn't bring any disgrace on Forrie. Even if they married, she knew that the child would come too soon and—No, Forrie wouldn't have let her go."

Mildred said, "No one knows this, Kitty, but there were four thousand dollars in Fern's purse, forty, new one-hundred-dollar bills."

Kitty looked at her with wide-eyed dismay. "Where's the money now?"

"I have it."

"Good Lord!" Kitty said. "That would make Harrod's story even better! The poor, little secretary finding herself pregnant tries to get the son of the wealthy manufacturer to marry her. The manufacturer kicks her out into the cold, cruel world giving her four thousand dollars to go and have her baby. Mildred, it *can't* be true!"

"Well, she had four thousand dollars in her purse," Mildred said flatly. "I don't know where she got it. And the autopsy showed she was two months pregnant."

Kitty put her hands to her temples. "What a mess! Did Harrod get anything out of you, Mildred?"

"I told him nothing," Mildred said. "I went to Perry Mason, the lawyer. If Harrod returns, I'm to tell him this." She read her shorthand notes.

Kitty Baylor's eyes showed sudden enthusiasm.

"That's it! That's the solution. We'll let Perry Mason deal with that dirty blackmailer."

"The hitch there is, he won't go to Perry Mason," Mildred said. "If, as you suspect, he knows that I'm masquerading as Fern Driscoll, he's just going to set a trap and—" She broke off at the sound of the door chimes.

"That may be Harrod now," Mildred said as she arose and started for the door.

Kitty motioned her back. "Wait a minute," she whispered.

Mildred paused.

"Look, if it's all right with you I'll go to the door and tell him that *I'm* Fern Driscoll, ask him what he means by saying that I'm pregnant, and slap his face. Is that okay by you?"

"He doesn't know you by sight?" Mildred asked, in a low voice.

Kitty shook her head.

"It's all right with me," Mildred said, "only I don't think you'll get away with it. I think he knows it was Fern Driscoll who was killed in the accident.... And when you slap his face, he'll punch you in the jaw. A character like Harrod isn't governed by the conventions about not striking a woman."

"Leave it to me," Kitty said, and strode into the little hallway.

Mildred heard the sound of the latch being thrown back on the door, then Kitty Baylor's voice saying, "I guess you don't know me. I'm—"

She was interrupted by Carl Harrod's voice. "Don't tell *me! I'll* tell *you!* You're Miss Katherine Baylor. Let me introduce myself. I'm Carl Harrod!"

Kitty Baylor's voice lost its assurance. "How—? How do you know who I am? I've never met you!"

Harrod's laugh was confident. "Just remember that I'm not an amateur at this game. Let's say that I've been casing the joint. I might even have followed you from the exclusive Vista del Camino Hotel, knowing that your family always stays there and feeling certain that some member of the family would be showing up to try and patch things up...."

"All right, Mr. Harrod," Kitty interrupted. "*I've* been looking for *you.* Now let *me* tell *you* a few things!

"In the first place, if you desire any further communication with the occupant of this apartment, you are to contact Mr. Perry Mason, her lawyer. If it's after office hours, and if it is urgent, call the Drake Detective Agency.

"In the second place, Mr. Carl Harrod, having delivered that message, let me give you a simple, forceful, personal message, indicative of the respect in which I hold you."

There was the smacking sound of a hard slap, a profane exclamation in a masculine voice, and then the slamming of the door and the rasp of a turning key.

Kitty Baylor was back, her face flushed, her eyes shining.

"Harrod!" she spat.... "Where do I wash my hands?"

Mildred indicated the bathroom.

While Kitty Baylor washed her hands, Mildred reached her decision. "Look, Kitty," she said as Kitty emerged, "I would like to continue as Fern Driscoll. After all, if Fern Driscoll is dead, I don't see what difference it's going to make. Harrod may suspect that I'm not Fern, but as long as I'm using Fern Driscoll's name and her identity, he may be a little cautious. It's one thing to print accusations about a dead girl who can't defend herself, and quite another to make charges like that against someone else.

"If it's all right with you, I'd like to keep on being Fern Driscoll, because I don't want to go back to being Mildred Crest. It would be good from your point of view, too. When it appears that there isn't going to be any illegitimate child, the magazine won't dare to go ahead with Harrod's story. What about it?"

Kitty thought things over. "When you opened Fern's purse, you found four thousand dollars?"

"Yes."

"Tell me, was there anything else? Anything that would help us?"

Mildred shook her head.

There was a silence during which Mildred was thinking furiously. She had no right to turn the letters in Fern's purse over to Kitty. Yet what was she to do with them? She must keep herself in the clear. Technically, she knew she was obligated to turn all Fern's property over to the coroner, or some public official, or someone.

"All right," Kitty said suddenly. "If you want to keep on being Fern Driscoll, go right ahead, but I warn you there will be some difficult problems."

Mildred said wearily, "There are problems either way....I'm afraid of Harrod."

"He's a slimy blackmailer."

"I'm afraid of him just the same."

Kitty Baylor said abruptly, "I want you to promise me one thing, Mildred. If you should hear from any of the other members of the family, don't mention the fact that I've been here. I'm not supposed to know anything about this, but if either my father or my brother gave Fern Driscoll money and told her to go away and have her baby—well, I want to know about it, that's all! I...I've had differences of opinion with them before, but this is very, very serious!"

Mildred remained thoughtful. "I wish you hadn't slapped Harrod."

"That trash!" Kitty said. "I'm going to show you how to deal with him."

"How?"

"You wait right here," Kitty said. "I'll be back in about fifteen minutes. I'll show you how you can handle him."

She slipped on her coat, started for the door.

"How did you find me, anyway?" Mildred asked.

With her hand on the knob, Kitty suddenly paused. "Now, that's something I should tell you about," she said. "Fern Driscoll wrote a letter to one of the girls in the accounting department, a girl whom she knew quite well. She said that the bottom had dropped out of things as far as she was concerned, and that she was leaving, she didn't want anyone to know where she was, that she was going to hitchhike to Los Angeles, to get a job and begin all over again.

"That girl knew that Fern was in love with Forrie, that there had been some trouble. She thought it was just a lover's spat and that Forrie might want to know where Fern was. In case he did, she wanted Forrie to be able to find her without too much trouble.

"So, this girl sent Fern's letter on to me, telling me not to say where I got the information but, in case Forrie confided in me, I could use my discretion and tell him where Fern was, if I thought that was the thing to do.

"Later on, Margaret—that's my younger sister—wrote me that the family was facing a possible scandal on account of Forrie's affair with Fern Driscoll, that Dad was terribly worried, and that a man named Harrod was trying to blackmail him.

"So I hired a detective agency and told them that Fern Driscoll was a secretary, a very competent secretary, that she had recently arrived in Los Angeles, and asked them to find her.

"I guess it was an easy job. They charged me thirty-five dollars, and gave me this address. I suppose you signed Fern's name to a utility application or something, didn't you?"

"To the telephone," Mildred said.

Kitty laughed. "Well, I guess it was *that* simple. I could probably simply have called information and got your number."

"Where are your father and your brother now?" Mildred asked.

"In Lansing, as far as I know.... You wait here, Mildred. I'm going out and get an ice pick for you."

"An ice pick!" Mildred exclaimed.

Kitty nodded. "It's a woman's best friend, the best weapon she can have. A sorority sister of mine tipped me off. Some police officer was the one who gave *her* the information.

"The hatpin used to be woman's traditonal weapon, and belive me, it was a good one. A man instinctively recoils from something long and needlepointed. This sorority sister of mine was in a community where they were having trouble with an exhibitionist. The police officer suggested that women who had to be out on the streets at night carry ice picks. You can put a cork over the point and slip it in a purse. Believe me, if you're ever out alone on a dark street, an ice pick can be worth its weight in gold!"

"You can't get an ice pick this time of night, and even if you could, I wouldn't want it," Mildred said.

"Oh, but I can! There's an arcade novelty store down a couple of blocks that's open and—You just try an ice pick on your friend Harrod and I can assure you, you won't have any more trouble with *him*."

CHAPTER FIVE

With Katherine Baylor gone, Mildred found herself in a panic. She feared Carl Harrod. She also realized now that Harrod must have discovered her impersonation and was playing with her as a cat plays with a mouse.

Why? He wanted something and the fact that Mildred wasn't quite sure what it was he wanted was disquieting.

"When the door chimes sounded again, Mildred's fear started her heart pounding. She went to stand by the door.

"Who is it?" she called in a thin, frightened voice.

"Kitty!" came from the other side of the door. "Open up...Fern!"

Mildred opened the door.

Kitty Baylor said, "I bring you weapons, my dear, the complete armory! Here you are! Three serviceable ice picks!"

"Three!" Mildred echoed.

"Three!" Kitty said, and laughed. "That's my bargain-hunting mind, I guess. They were priced at thirty-eight cents apiece, three for a dollar. I'm going to put one of them in *my* purse and carry it with me just in case.

"Harrod isn't going to lay a hand on me, not without getting an ice pick where he doesn't want it.

"Oh, don't look so horrified, Mildred. You don't have to *use* the things! It's simply the idea. A man can't stand having something like that jabbed at him.

"Now look, Mildred. I'm going to run on. I'm not going to say a thing to anybody about what you have told me. I want to find out for myself certain things. I want to find out if either Dad or Forrie did give Fern Driscoll four thousand dollars and tell her to get lost.

"Something happened, and I want to know what it was. I tighten up every time I start thinking of what happened to poor Fern. Even if she did kill herself, it was the result of hysteria and temporary insanity. All that was caused by what she'd had to go through.

"Don't tell anybody that I've been here, and I won't tell anybody. If anything happens, and you need me, I'll be at the Vista del Camino tonight. When Dad's in town, he has the presidential suite, but I'll be in a modest two-room suite. I haven't checked in yet, just stopped by to leave luggage. They all know me at the hotel. You won't have any trouble reaching me.

"Now are you going to be all right?"

"I guess so."

"I'm going to leave these two ice picks on this little table right here by the door. If Harrod should come back, don't be afraid of him. All blackmailers are cowards.

"All right, I'm on my way. Thanks for putting your cards on the table, and here's luck!"

Kitty Baylor thrust out her hand and grippd Mildred's with firm, strong fingers.

"You think I shouldn't have run away, don't you?" Mildred asked.

"I don't know," Kitty said after a moment's hesitation. "However, there's no use worrying about it. It's done now. And if you want to be Fern Driscoll, go ahead. But remember this: Dad may be looking for you, and Forrie may be looking for you. I certainly hope Forrie does come to try and help you and...and to stand by the girl he— Good-by, Mildred."

When Kitty had gone, Mildred felt a little guilty because she had not told Kitty about the letters. She had confided in Kitty as to her own secrets, but instinct had been to leave what little veil of privacy remained about the affairs of Fern Driscoll. More and more, Mildred was coming to sympathize with the girl who had wrenched the steering wheel from her hands and sent the automobile plunging down to destruction.

Kitty hadn't been gone more than five minutes when the telephone rang.

Feeling certain she would hear Carl Harrod's voice, Mildred picked up the receiver.

The voice which came over the telephone was richly resonant with authority.

"Miss Driscoll?"

Mildred hesitated a moment. "Yes?"

"I'm Harriman Baylor, Fern. Now, what the devil's this story about the family having given you money to go ahead and disappear for a while. I—"

"*You* should know," Mildred Crest said, suddenly filled with a desire to avenge Fern Driscoll's memory.

"Well, I don't know!" Baylor said impatiently. "And if my son has been putting his neck in that kind of noose, I want to find out about it. Now tell me, do you know a man by the name of Carl Harrod?"

She hesitated a moment, then said, "He was here earlier this evening."

"I understand that Harrod is going to sell a story about this whole affair to some scandal magazine," Baylor went on, "and he says that you have some letters Forrester wrote you that are definitely incriminating, that you've made arrangements to turn those letters over to him. Is that true?"

"No."

"Do you have such letters?"

There was something in the authoritative timbre of the voice that had Mildred on the defensive.

"I have the letters," she said. "I haven't told anyone about them, nor have I turned them over to anybody."

"All right," Baylor said, "I want to talk with you. It's been a job finding you. I don't know what you're trying to— Well, anyway, I want to come and talk with you. I'll be seeing you."

The phone clicked. He hadn't asked for permission to call. He had merely said he was coming. Mildred sensed the man did everything like that. He was accustomed to taking the right of way.

Mildred suddenly realized that she had unleashed forces that she couldn't control.

Did Harriman Baylor know Fern Driscoll by sight? Would he know as soon as he saw her that she was an impostor? Knowing that she was an impostor, what would he do? Would he expose her?

Did Kitty really not know that her father was in town?

And what to do with those letters?

Kitty Baylor was right. Harrod was going to get her to make a statement of the accident and the removal of money from the purse. She would sign this statement as Fern Driscoll. Once she had done that, she would be pretty much within his power. And Harrod was really after those letters that had been in Fern Driscoll's purse.

Mildred had no intention of giving Harrod those letters. Neither, on the other hand, did she intend to turn them over to Harriman Baylor, the father of the man who indirectly had been responsible for Fern Driscoll's death.

Suddenly Mildred Crest knew that she didn't want to face Harriman Baylor. She knew too much, and yet about some things she knew too little.

Mildred picked up the purse, dropped the little packet of letters in it, hastily switched out the lights in the apartment and hurried to the elevator.

Finding the elevator was in use on the way up, she didn't wait but turned swiftly to the stairs and went down to the street.

CHAPTER SIX

Perry Mason and Della Street were finishing dinner when the waiter said deferentially, "Excuse me, Mr. Mason, but the Drake Detective Agency asked you to call before you went out."

Mason nodded. "Anything important?"

"They didn't say, sir, just asked you to be sure and call before you left the restaurant."

Mason signed the check, nodded to Della Street, said, "Better give them a ring, Della. Find out what it is."

Della Street arose from the table and went over to the telephone booths.

Mason settled back in his chair, lit a cigarette, and surveyed the various people in the place with keen, observant eyes.

Della returned.

"What is it?" Mason asked.

"Well," she said, "we have two matters which would seem to require your attention."

"What are they?"

She said, "Fern Driscoll wants you to get in touch with her immediately. She says it's terribly important you see her. She seemed to be very upset, Drake's operator said. And you remember the blackmailer she told about, Carl Harrod?"

Mason nodded.

"He called up and asked you to get in touch with him about a matter of considerable importance to one of your clients. He left a number and an address, the Dixiecrat Apartments."

"He called the Drake Detective Agency?" Mason asked.

"That's right."

"Then he must have got that number from Fern Driscoll."

Della Street nodded.

"Well," Mason said, "let's make a couple of calls and see what it's all about. You have the numbers, Della?"

She nodded.

"First, we'll get Fern Driscoll at the Rexmore Apartments," Mason said.

He left the table, moved over to the telephone booths with Della Street.

Della's nimble fingers dialed the number. A moment later she said into the telephone, "Hello, Miss Driscoll. This is Della Street, Perry Mason's secretary. Mr. Mason will talk with you.... He's right here, Miss Driscoll."

Mason entered the telephone booth, said, "Hello, Miss Driscoll. What seems to be the trouble?"

Her voice came pouring over the wire. "Mr. Mason, a whole lot of things have happened. There were some things I didn't tell you about. I guess I held out a bit and— Well, there have been a lot of complications."

"Won't they keep until morning?" Mason asked.

"No. No. I— You see, there was someone, some intruder in my apartment, trying to get some things. He knocked me off my feet and I lashed out at him with an ice pick."

"Good work," Mason said. "Did you score?"

"I must have. The ice pick was jerked out of my hands and ... and I can't find it."

"Did you report all this to the police?" Mason asked sharply.

"No, and there are reasons I don't want to. I— You understand, I can't...."

Mason said, "Look, Fern, for a young woman who has a desire to remain obscure, you certainly do the damnedest things. Now, lock your door and try to keep out of trouble until I get there. You'd better tell me about this personally."

Mason hung up and said to Della, "Get this other number, Della. I'm afraid we're getting a lot of night work out of a five-cent fee."

"Aren't we," she laughed.

She called the number, said, "This is Miss Street, Mr. Mason's secretary. Mr. Perry Mason received a call from a Mr. Harrod....Oh yes, Well, just a minute, I'll put Mr. Mason on."

Della Street said, "Some feminine voice....Sounds attractive....She said she'll call Mr. Harrod."

Mason picked up the phone, said, "Hello."

A man's voice started to say hello, then was checked in a fit of coughing.

"Hello, hello," Mason said impatiently. "I am calling Carl Harrod."

The voice said, "This is Harrod....I wanted to talk with you...." Again there was a fit of coughing.

Mason, frowning impatiently, said, "Hello. Just what was it you wanted?"

Harrod's voice, sounding weak, said, "Your client stabbed me in the chest with an ice pick. We'd better talk it over right away."

"Where did this happen?"

"At Fern Driscoll's apartment."

"Did you report this to the police?"

"Of course not."

"Why?"

"That isn't the way to handle something of this sort."

"What is the way to handle it?"

"Come over here and I'll tell you."

"Shouldn't you have treatment?"

"It isn't that serious, medically. It's damned serious legally."

"Stay there," Mason told him. "I think it's about time we had a talk."

"You *bet* it is!"

"Where are you?" Mason asked.

"I'm in my apartment at the Dixiecrat Apartments. Apartment 218."

"All right," Mason said, "that's not far from where I'm talking. You wait there. I'm coming over."

Mason hung up the telephone and said, "Now, this is a real run-around. Fern Driscoll found someone in her apartment and stabbed him with an ice pick. Apparently, she doesn't know where she hit him, but it was a solid enough blow so he took the ice pick away with him. Carl Harrod says she stabbed him in the chest.

"Hang it, Della, I suppose we've got to go take a look-see. Let's run up and have a quick talk with Fern Driscoll first, and get the thing straightened out. Then we'll try to put this blackmailer, Harrod, in his place."

"But shouldn't Fern Driscoll notify the police if—?"

"That's the devil of it!" Mason said. "She's keeping under cover and— The Rexmore Apartments is only five minutes from her by cab."

They left the restaurant, found a taxicab and went at once to the Rexmore Apartments.

Mildred Crest was anxiously awaiting them. She unlocked her door, seemed almost hysterically relieved as she held onto Mason's hand.

"All right," Mason said, "let's find out *exactly* what happened."

Mildred, on the verge of panic, said, "I'm going to have to give you a little personal history."

"Go ahead," Mason said.

"I left Lansing, Michigan, because— Well, there was a man by the name of Baylor, Forrester Baylor. His family didn't approve of me and— Well, it's a long story."

"Shorten it, then," Mason said crisply. "Let's have it."

"He had a sister, Katherine, a wonderful girl. I had never met her. She came here tonight and met me for the first time. She told me she sympathized with me and she thought the family had been perfectly horrid in the way they had treated me."

"What about the ice pick?" Mason asked."

"She bought them for me."

"Who did?"

"Kitty—Katherine Baylor."

"Bought *them?* Was there more than one?"

"Yes."

"Why?"

"She said blackmailers were yellow and that if I pointed an ice pick at Harrod and threatened him, he'd leave me alone."

"And at the same time make you guilty of assault with a deadly weapon," Mason said drily. "How many ice picks did she buy?"

"Three."

"Where are they now?"

"One of them is on the little table by the door."

Mason moved over to the table.

"There's only one ice pick here."

She nodded.

Mason lifted the ice pick.

"There's a price tag on here underneath transparent Scotch tape," he said. "The price tag says thirty-eight cents, three for a dollar. There's some fine print—let me see—oh yes, the imprint of the Arcade Novelty."

"The Arcade Novelty," Mildred explained, "is down the street a short distance. It's an arcade with a lot of penny machines for amusement. They cater largely to sailors and people who are lonely and want cheap entertainment.

"They have everything from electric machine guns for shooting at images of airplanes to girl shows on film machines. They call it a penny arcade, but most of the shows are a nickel or a dime."

"And they sell ice picks?" Mason asked.

"Not there, but in connection with it. There's a novelty shop where they have bottle openers, bottled goods, novelties of all sorts, a machine that vends ice cubes and things of that sort."

Mason nodded. "Now, tell me exactly what happened."

"I came in from the street. I snapped on the light switch, and the lights didn't turn on. Everything was dark."

"Could you see anything?"

"Just here by the doorway. The light came in from the main hallway so I could see a little. Someone was in here, searching the apartment.

"What happened?"

"I snapped the light switch two or three times. The light wouldn't come on. Then I heard someone move."

"Did you scream?"

"There wasn't time. I just had that feeling of motion coming at me, and instinctively I grabbed up one of those ice picks just as someone hit me."

"With his fist?"

"No, no! I don't mean it that way. Someone hit me like a football player hits a line. It was just a rush. I was bowled over."

"And what happened?"

"Well, I had the ice pick pointed out toward whoever was coming at me, and...and..." She began to sob.

"Now, take it easy," Mason said. "Let's get this thing straight."

She said, "The ice pick stuck into this person and he or she ran on past me and that jerked the ice pick out of my hands."

"The pick didn't fall to the floor?"

"No. Whoever was in here—well, the ice pick was carried away with him."

Mason thought things over for a moment, said to Della Street, "Della, go down to the Arcade Novelty. Get three of these ice picks, make it as fast as you can. Then come back here. The cab is waiting downstairs. Take it."

Mason turned to Mildred Crest. "Your friend Harrod called up. He said he'd been stabbed in the chest with an ice pick."

Mildred raised her clenched knuckles to crush them tightly against her lips. Her eyes were wide with terror.

Mason said, "You must have something in this apartment, something someone wants. You're hiding something. What is it? Money? Letters?"

"I...I'm supposed to have some letters. I think Harrod wants them very badly."

"What do you mean, you're *supposed* to have them!" Mason said.

"Well, you see— The letters were addressed to Fern...to me."

Mason watched her narrowly. "You say you're *supposed* to have them. Do you have them or don't you?"

"I...I have them."

"Where are they?"

"In my purse. I had them with me."

"Then why did Harrod want them?"

"To sell to a magazine, I believe."

Mason said, "Look here, young lady, you're lying to me. Are you really Fern Driscoll?"

There was panic in her eyes.

"Are you?"

"I...I can't talk now. I can't, I can't, I can't!"

She dropped into a chair, started sobbing hysterically.

Mason said, "Cut it out! Listen, there's no time for all that stuff. I don't know what we're getting into. If anything should happen and the police should question you, say that you refuse to make any statement save in the presence of your attorney. Can you do that?"

"Yes."

"*Will* you do it?"

"If you say so."

"I say so. Now, where's that missing ice pick?" There were three. One's in Carl Harrod. Where's the other?"

"Kitty has it."

"What's her name?"

"Katherine Baylor."

"Where does she live?"

"She's at the Vista del Camino Hotel. She's from Lansing. Her family's rolling in money. Her father's Harriman Baylor, a big manufacturer. Her brother's Forrester Baylor. He's responsible for my condition—my pregnancy."

"How long have you been pregnant?"

"Two months.... No, no, Mr. Mason. I'm not really pregnant."

Again she started sobbing.

Mason looked at her with exasperation, then moved around the apartment looking at the drawers which had been pulled out and the contents dumped on the floor.

"We'll have to report this," he said.

"No, no! We can't! There are reasons. There isn't time to tell you everything now. I...I can't! I can't!"

Mason again turned away, looking around the apartment. He saw her purse on the chair, picked it up, opened it. "Are these the letters?"

She looked at the tightly tied packet. "Yes."

Mason put the letters in his pocket, looked again in the purse. Suddenly he said, "Where did you get all this money?"

She looked at him with tear-streaked eyes. "They're going to say I stole it—if they find it."

"Whose is it?"

"Fern Driscoll's."

"And you're not Fern Driscoll. You're Mildred Crest. Is that right?"

"Yes."

There was a knock at the door. Mason opened the door and Della said, "Well, here they are. Three ice picks, exactly the same as those others, but there's a different price tag on them."

"What do you mean?" Mason asked.

"They're forty-one cents straight now," she said, "but they were thirty-eight cents or three for a dollar."

"How come the price changed?"

"It's quite a story. The woman who rang up the sale dropped one, and when I picked it up I noticed the price for the first time. I inquired if the picks weren't three for a dollar. That's when she went into her long song and dance. It seems someone bought three picks earlier in the evening and this woman in charge went to replenish the stock in the display case and found there were only six left in stock. She says she orders them a gross at a time, so she made out an order for another gross and then found the price had gone up sharply since they had made their last order. So she tore the price tags off the others that were in stock and put the new price tags on them."

Mason turned to Mildred Crest. "Now look, Mildred, there isn't time to find out what this is all about now. I'm going to see Carl Harrod and find out about that ice-pick stabbing.

"Now, here are definite, positive instructions. If anybody comes and asks you about what happened, or about an intruder, or about stabbing anyone with an ice pick, you simply state that you have no comments to make. I am going to leave two of these ice picks here with you on the table. That will make a total of three.

"I want you to take all the price tags off all of these ice picks, flush them down the toilet and destroy them. You will then have three, identical ice picks. If the police start checking and find that one woman bought three ice picks, they'll find all three ice picks in your apartment. There won't be any missing."

"But won't they find out that—"

"Probably," Mason said, "if they start an investigation, but this will keep them from starting one unless they get a direct complaint. I'm taking these letters with me."

"Take the money, too."

Mason shook his head. "Keep that money right where it is. Put it in an envelope and mark it 'Property of Fern Driscoll.' Don't tell anyone anything about it. Don't answer questions about anything.

"Come on, Della."

Mason and Della Street left the apartment.

On the way down in the elevator, Della Street said, "What do I do with this extra ice pick?"

Mason said, "Harrod says my client stabbed him in the chest with an ice pick. Probably all he saw was a feminine figure silhouetted against light which was coming in from the corridor. He charged, doubtless intending to knock the woman over with the force of his charge and, while she was bowled over, make good his escape.

"That ice pick was invisible to him. It probably went in without any sensation of pain because the point was so fine and sharp. Later on, when he got out of the apartment house, he found an ice pick stuck in his chest. Harrod probably doesn't want to go to the police any more than our client wants to go to the police. So Harrod rang me up."

"And what does he want?" Della Street asked.

"That," Mason said, "is something we'll find out from Mr. Harrod himself. I have an idea that he wants to make a trade. I think he'll offer to trade his silence in return for some letters our client has.

"So," Mason went on, "the minute we get to Harrod's apartment, I'll do something to hold the attention of Harrod or whoever else is in the apartment. You plant this ice pick. Wear gloves, and be sure you don't leave any fingerprints."

"What about the price tag?"

"Leave it on."

"Why?" she asked. "If he was stabbed with an ice pick—"

"Exactly," Mason said. "I want it so *we* can tell the ice picks apart. The one that *you* planted and the one that someone stuck in his chest."

"If Harrod doesn't go to the police, we have simply presented him with an ice pick. If he does go to the police, the police will find two ice picks in his apartment. It will be up to Harrod to keep them straight so as to tell one from the other."

"Do I keep my gloves on all the time?" she asked.

"No," Mason said, "I have to explain your presence as my secretary. You plant the ice pick while I'm distracting their attention. As soon as you have the ice pick planted, take your gloves off and take out a notebook and pencil."

The cabdriver held the door open for them.

"Where to?" he asked.

Mason glanced significantly at Della Street.

"Drive straight down the street for three blocks," he said. "Then turn to the right and I'll tell you where we want to get out. We're meeting a person on a corner."

"Okay," driver said. "I take it you want me to drive slow."

"That's right," Mason said.

The driver closed the door and the cab moved off, went down to the designated corner, turned to the right and moved slowly along.

They passed the Dixiecrat Apartments, went for half a block, then Mason said suddenly, "This is where we're to meet the person. Stop right here."

The driver stopped and Mason handed him a five-dollar bill. "This will cover the meter and leave you a little over," he said.

As the man started to thank him, Mason handed him two more one-dollar bills. "And this will enable you to buy something for the kids when you go home."

"Gee, mister, thanks," the cabdriver said. "I sure won't forget this."

Mason said, "In that case, perhaps you'd better give me the two dollars back."

The cabdriver thought for a moment, then grinned. "I've got the poorest memory in the world," he said.

Mason handed him three more one-dollar bills. "In a cabdriver," he announced, "that's a wonderful asset."

He and Della got out on the corner. The cab drove away. Mason and Della walked the half block back to the Dixiecrat Apartments.

Mason consulted the directory. "Carl Harrod, 218," he said.

Mason pressed the button.

Almost instantly the buzzer sounded which released the outer door.

"We could probably have saved time on the stairs," Della Street said, as the elevator slowly and reluctantly slid to a stop.

Mason opened the outer door, pulled back the sliding metal grill. Della Street entered, Mason followed her and pressed the button for the second floor.

As the elevator came to a dispirited stop, Mason pulled back the sliding metallic grill, opened the hinged door, let Della precede him into the corridor, and stood for a moment looking which way to turn.

A woman stood in the corridor six doors to the right.

Mason strode past Della Street to take the lead.

"Mr. Harrod?" Mason asked the young woman as he approached.

"You're Mr. Mason?"

"Yes."

"This way," she said. "Carl is expecting you."

She held the apartment door open and Mason walked in, preceding Della Street.

The woman waited until Della Street had entered the apartment, then hurried forward and said to Mason, "He's had a chill."

She led the way over to an adjustable reclining chair in which a man was stretched, a blanket wrapped tightly around him.

The eyes were closed.

"Carl," she said, "this is Mr. Mason."

Harrod opened his eyes. "I'm glad you came, Mr. Mason."

"You're Harrod?" Mason asked.

"Yes."

Mason bent over him and the young woman half-turned toward Della Street to invite her to be seated.

Mason said, "Is this Mrs. Harrod?"

The woman whirled to face him. There was a moment's embarrassed silence.

Then the young woman said, "Answer him, Carl."

Harrod waited a moment, said, "Yes, this is Mrs. Harrod."

Mason held the young woman's eyes. "How long," he asked, "have you been married?"

"And what difference does that make?" she blazed.

"I wanted to know," Mason said. "I'm an attorney. I'm dealing with an injured man. I want to know how long you've been married."

"It's none of your business!"

Mason noticed out the corner of his eyes that Della Street was moving swiftly around the apartment, as though looking for a comfortable chair. Abruptly she gave an exclamation of annoyance. "That pesky fountain pen! The cap is full of ink. I'll go to the sink and—"

Della darted through the door to a kitchenette. No one paid any attention to her.

Harrod said, "Look, honey, this is Mr. Mason. He's a lawyer. I think he's going to help us."

"I don't care what *you* think!" the woman said. "My private affairs are my private affairs and I'm certainly not going to have some smart lawyer come in and start putting *me* on the pan."

"No offense," Mason said. "I just wanted to know what the situation was."

"Well, now you know," she said.

"I'm not certain I do," Mason told her.

Della Street returned to the room, removed her gloves and took a notebook from her purse. "Where do you want me, Chief?" she asked.

Mason said, "This is Miss Della Street, my secretary. I want her to make notes of this conversation. Now then, you're Carl Harrod?"

The man nodded and coughed.

"You say you've been stabbed with an ice pick?"

"Yes."

"Where's the ice pick?"

"We have it," the young woman announced.

"I'd like to see it."

"We're keeping it where it's safe," she said.

"And just why do you think I'd be interested in this stabbing?" Mason asked.

Harrod opened his eyes, shifted his position slightly, moved his hands under the blanket, then lay still again. "You're going to be very much interested," he announced.

"Why?"

"You're representing Fern Driscoll."

"Did she stab you?"

Harrod was silent for a long moment. He closed his eyes, opened them, then said, "Who do *you* think?"

Mason said sharply, "I'm not here to play guessing games. I came here because you said a client of mine had stabbed you. Now, if you have anything to tell me, start talking. If you haven't, I'm leaving."

Harrod said, "Fern Driscoll stabbed me. She's your client."

"How did it happen?" Mason asked.

"I wanted to have a talk with her. I was investigating an automobile accident in which she was involved. I went up to her apartment."

"Where?" Mason asked.

"Rexmore Apartments. 309."

"Go on."

"I found the door slightly ajar. I pushed the button. I could hear the bell chimes on the inside. Abruptly the door was flung open and Fern Driscoll said, 'Oh, it's you!' and with that she lashed out at me—I didn't see the ice pick at the moment. I felt a sharp, stinging sensation at the skin. I didn't feel deep pain at all."

"Then what happened?" Mason asked.

"She slammed the door in my face, and locked it. There was someone else in there with her. I could hear them talking."

"What did you do?"

"I rang the chimes again, rattled the doorknob. I saw she wasn't going to open up, so I made up my mind I'd make her regret it. Believe me, I have the goods on her. I decided to release everything I had on her, and that's a lot."

"Go on," Mason said.

"Well, I turned for the stairs and that was when I found there was an ice pick in my chest."

Harrod turned to the young woman, said, "Nellie, how about a drink?"

She went through the door into the kitchenette, came back with a bottle of whisky and a glass half-filled with water.

"Only about half that water," Harrod said.

She dutifully went back to the kitchen, returned with the tumbler about a quarter full.

She extended the bottle and the glass, but Harrod said, "Pour it and hold it to my lips."

Harrod drank the whiskey and water. The woman wiped his lips.

Harrod said, "It's funny but I've been cold ever since I got home."

"Have you had a doctor?" Mason asked.

"No."

"You'd better get one."

"I don't want one."

"Why?"

"Doctors ask too many questions."

"Did this ice pick go all the way in?" Mason asked.

"Clean to the hilt," Harrod said.

"Then you'd better have a doctor."

"I told you I don't want a doctor. Doctors go asking questions, and then they babble everything they know to the police."

"Well," Mason said, "it sounds to me as though the police should be notified."

Harrod shifted his eyes, said, "That would be bad for your client."

"I'll look out for the interests of my client," Mason said sharply.

"All right," Harrod said, "it wouldn't be good for me."

"Why not?"

"I am not the most exemplary citizen in the world, Mason," Harrod said. "I'm a— All right, I'm an opportunist."

"And a blackmailer?" Mason asked.

"He didn't say that," Nellie flared at Mason.

"I was trying to make it easier for him," Mason said.

"You don't have to!" Nellie snapped. "He can talk for himself."

Harrod said, "Fern Driscoll has some letters. I don't know how much you know about her history, but she was going with Forrester Baylor in Lansing, Michigan. Forrester is the only son of Harriman Baylor, a big manufacturer.

"Fern Driscoll was working as his secretary. She and Forrester got playing around and then all of a sudden all hell broke loose. I *think* perhaps someone found out Harriman Baylor was about to become a grandfather under circumstances that didn't appeal to the old bastard."

"Watch your language," Nellie said sharply.

Carl Harrod grinned, went on talking, "I started out trying to sharpshoot. I'm an investigator for an insurance company. That's the way I make my bread and butter. I'm also an undercover correspondent for a magazine entitled *The Real Low-down*.

"I wasn't sure about my story until after I'd interviewed Fern Driscoll. Then I was certain I was on the right track. The trouble was the story is too big. The magazine has to have proof. I understand there are some letters written by Forrester. It's also reported that Harriman Baylor gave her a big wad of dough to go bye-bye and have a baby very quietly, then release it for adoption to anyone that Harriman Baylor designated.

"That's the kind of a story that *The Real Low-down* would pay ten thousand smackeroos to get nailed down.

"I have everything I need execpt the letters," Harrod said. "That's why I went to Fern Driscoll's apartment."

"You're telling me all this?" Mason asked.

"I'm telling you all this," Harrod said.

"And that secretary of his is writing every word of it down," Nellie snapped.

"Let her," Harrod said. "Mason has got to play ball with me in this thing."

"Go on," Mason said.

"I'd been there earlier and tried to be nice," Harrod said. "Being nice didn't get me anywhere so I went back to try it again. This time I wasn't going to be so nice."

"Now, wait a minute," Mason said. "You went there the first time. What happened?"

"The door was opened by Katherine Baylor. I'd followed her to the place. You see, the Baylor family are out here quite often. Harriman Baylor has business interests in southern California. The family always stays at the Vista del Camino Hotel. I had a tip that Baylor himself had taken a tumble and was going to make a big try to get those letters.

"I felt certain some member of the family would show up. I had an idea they'd located Fern Driscoll. Katherine showed up, registered, left her baggage, and went right out to a cab.

"I followed in my car. She went direct to Fern Driscoll's apartment in the Rexmore.

"So I went up and rang the bell after she'd been there long enough to get the preliminaries over with."

"That was the first time you'd been to Miss Driscoll's apartment?" Mason asked.

"Actually it was the second time. . . . Suppose you let me tell it in my own way."

"All right," Mason said. "Go ahead."

"Well, Katherine came to the door, took a good look at me and after I'd introduced myself she used some strong language, then swung on me and cracked me on the nose."

"Then what happened?" Mason asked.

"I got a bloody nose. She slammed and locked the door before I could do a damned thing. I suppose she's accustomed to playing with people who are too gentlemanly to strike a woman. Believe me, if she hadn't got that door slammed and locked just when she did, I'd have broken her god-damned jaw."

"Your language, Carl!" Nellie admonished.

"Her god-damned jaw!" Harrod repeated, more emphatically and in a louder voice.

Nellie made clicking noises with her tongue against the roof of her mouth, indicating shocked disapproval.

"Go on," Mason said.

"All right. I went back after a while," Harrod said, "and knocked again. Believe me, if the door had opened and this Baylor bitch had been there, I'd—"

"Your language, Carl," Nellie said. "Mr. Mason's a lawyer."

"I mean, this Baylor girl," Harrod amended hastily, "if she'd been there, I'd have given her something to remember me by. That is, if she'd opened the door."

"She wasn't there?"

"I think she was," Harrod said. "*Someone* was in there with her. I could hear them talking. I don't know who it was."

"All right. What happened?"

"I've told you what happened. I rang the chimes. Fern Driscoll pushed open the door and lurched at me with this ice pick without so much as a word!"

"Not a single word?"

"Well, she said something like 'You again!' or something like that."

"Were the lights on in the apartment?" Mason asked.

"What do you mean, were the lights on?" Harrod countered.

"When the apartment door was opened," Mason said, "were lights on in the little reception hallway of the apartment?"

Harrod thought for a moment. "I don't remember. Why?"

"I was wondering why you didn't see the ice pick so you could avoid it," Mason explained. "You wouldn't have just stood there while someone made a pass at you with a weapon like that."

Again Harrod thought for a moment, then said, "I guess you're right. I sure as hell didn't see any ice pick. The lights *weren't* on in the apartment. That is, they may have been on in the apartment itself, but the door opens into a little hallway. When you go in the door, there's a little, narrow hallway, then you make a sharp, right-angle turn to the left and then you come into the main apartment."

"And you had no idea you had been stabbed with an ice pick until *after* the door closed?"

"That's right."

"And you didn't *see* the ice pick?"

"No."

"Then you couldn't have seen the face of the woman who wielded the ice pick clearly enough to be absolutely certain," Mason said. "As far as *you* know, it could have been Katherine Baylor who stabbed you instead of Fern Driscoll."

Harrod's face showed anger. "You've got no right to come up here and cross-examine me and— Damn it, I'm trying to be co-operative. Now I'll make you a proposition, Mason."

"What is it?"

"Your client can make a settlement with me. Your secretary there can type up a release and I'll sign it."

"What sort of a settlement?"

Harrod shook his head. "You go talk with your client, then *you* make *me* an offer. You've heard my story, now go get hers. Get it all. Don't take anything for granted. Ask her who she *really* is. *Then* you come back to me."

Mason said, "Not now, Harrod. First we're going to have a doctor look you over and see how serious the situation is."

"I don't want a doctor. I know exactly what I want."

Mason said, "I'm going to get my own personal physician on the job. He's going to give you a once-over. The idea is to keep any complications from developing."

"I told you I didn't want a doctor. He'll ask me questions and then go to the police. Once he does that, we're all in the soup."

"That," Mason interrupted, "is the beauty of having *my* doctor on the job instead of *yours*. He'll ask you how you feel, he'll take your blood pressure, he'll find your exact physical condition. He may ask you questions about how it happened, and, if he does, you're perfectly free to tell him that, for all you know, you were walking in your sleep, stumbled, and fell forward on an ice pick. Or you can simply refuse to answer questions, and tell him that you'll talk to your own doctor at the proper time."

"But what good is it going to do to have this doctor of yours see me?"

"It may save some complications," Mason said. "He'll be my doctor. Not yours. He'll be appraising the injury so as to assess damages."

"I don't need to tell him how it happened?"

"No."

"It won't cost me anything?"

"Nothing."

There was a moment's silence.

Mason went on, "There are some disadvantages. The doctor won't report to you. He'll report to me. But if he feels you should have any special treatment, he'll tell me. That will be to your protection.

"Because he's my doctor instead of yours, you won't have to answer any questions that you don't want to answer, and if he doesn't have any information from you that indicates you were the victim of a felonious stabbing, he won't have to make a report to the police."

Harrod grinned. "Particularly if I tell him that I was holding the ice pick in my hand when my wife pushed open the door carrying a bunch of dishes in from the kitchen, and that the door hit my hand and rammed the ice pick into my chest."

"Don't let him trap you," Nellie warned. "That's exactly what he wants you to do; make some contradictory story to a doctor and—"

Harrod's face showed anger "Shut up!" he said. "Keep your big bazzoo out of this!"

"Watch your language!" she said.

Harrod laughed. "Your bazzoo, I said, sweetheart. Your *bazzoo!*"

He turned to Mason, said wearily, "That's what comes of teaming up with an illiterate broad who tries to be refined."

Nellie sucked in a quick breath, started to say something, then changed her mind.

"How long will it take you to get your doctor here?"

"He should be here within an hour."

"What's his name?"

"The one I have in mind is Dr. Arlington."

"He's worked for you before?"

"Yes."

Harrod said to Nellie, "Get me another blanket, Nellie. I'm still cold." He turned to Mason, said, "Here's something you can be thinking about in the meantime. Your client can't stand an investigation. Don't let her pull the wool over your eyes. She isn't Fern Driscoll. She's Mildred Crest. She stole Fern Driscoll's purse, her identity and her money.

"You just let that broad of yours know that you know that, and that I know it.

Then you come back and we'll talk a little turkey.

"Now then, go get your doctor if that will make you feel any better."

CHAPTER SEVEN

Mason and Della Street called Dr. Arlington, then took a taxicab to the place where Mason's car was parked and drove back to the Dixiecrat Apartments.

They had waited some five minutes when Dr. Arlington drove up, parked his car ahead of Mason's, got out, shook hands, and said, "What's it all about, Perry?"

Mason said, "It's a damage claim. That is, it's going to be a damage claim. The man's name is Harrod. He's in Apartment 218. I told him I was sending my doctor. You ring the bell, go on up and take a look at him. Be sure you have it definitely understood that you are there as my physician, making an independent checkup. Explain to him that you are not his doctor, and that there is to be no confidential relationship of physician and patient. If he makes any statement to you about how he feels, I want you to be able to testify."

"All right," Dr. Arlington said. "What seems to be the trouble?"

"Something was stuck in his chest."

"A knife?" Dr. Arlington asked.

"No, no, not a knife," Mason said. "I think it was a much smaller pointed object."

"Not a nail?" Dr. Arlington said.

"Probably something about the size of an ice pick."

"I see."

"He probably won't give you any information about how it happened," Mason said, "although he may tell you that he was standing in front of the kitchen door when his wife came through with a big load of dishes, and kicked the door open. He was holding an ice pick in his hand, and the suddenly opened door jabbed it into his chest."

"Is that the way it happened?"

"He may tell you that's what happened."

"Did it happen that way?"

"How do I know?" Mason asked. "You go on up and find out what's wrong with the guy. He's having chills."

"The devil he is!"

"Uh-huh."

"That'd better be looked into," Dr. Arlington said. "An ice pick can be damned serious."

"All right," Mason told him. "Go look into it."

CHAPTER EIGHT

Dr. Arlington took his professional bag, walked up to the door of the apartment house and pressed the button on 218.

A few moments later the buzzer sounded and Dr. Arlington pushed the door open and went in.

"Well," Mason said to Della Street, "we'll soon find out just how much of a problem we have. You got that ice pick placed all right?"

"I'll say I did. I put it in the utility drawer in the kitchen."

"You were working pretty fast," Mason told her.

"You gave me a wonderful opportunity, inquiring about the woman's marital status. Wasn't that rather mean, Chief?"

"It was a good way to keep her attention occupied," Mason said.

"You didn't need to rub it in! She'll know what's in the apartment and, when she finds that extra ice pick, particularly since the price mark was left on it, she'll know it was planted and then she'll put two and two together."

Mason said, "And again she may feel that the ice pick with a price tag still on it *must* have been the one used in the stabbing."

Della Street thought that over for a moment, then smiled. "I think I begin to see a light," she said, "a very interesting and significant light."

Mason lit a cigarette. "We'll see what they tell Dr. Arlington."

"Don't you think you should have gone up with him?"

Mason said, "I don't want to be a witness. Let Dr. Arlington talk with the guy. Any court in the land will take Dr. Arlington's testimony at face value."

"I'll say," she agreed. "He makes a fine witness."

Della Street, who was standing by the side of Perry Mason's automobile, looking toward the back of the car, suddenly stiffened to attention, said, "Oh-oh, Chief! Here's trouble!"

"What?" Mason asked.

"A very official-looking car with a red spotlight."

"Coming here?" Mason asked.

"Looks like it."

"Jump in," Mason told her. "We'll get going. We don't dare to get caught—"

"There's not time," she interrupted. "They're right on us. Make up a good story."

"Get in," Mason said, sliding over so Della could get in behind the steering wheel. "They may not notice you."

Della Street, with quick, supple grace, twisted in behind the steering wheel, slammed the door shut, rolled the window down.

"Act as though you hadn't seen them," Mason said, "and be talking. They probably won't notice a parked car. They—"

He broke off as the interior of the car was flooded with red light from a police spotlight.

"Turn around," Mason said. "Look surprised! Otherwise they'll know we had seen them coming."

Mason turned quickly, then faced Della Street and said, "Look, look!" He pointed back toward the spotlight.

"How's that, Della?" he asked.

"Corny, but good," she said. "Here they are."

Sgt. Holcomb of Homicide Squad came walking up on the right side of the car. An officer moved up to the left-hand side.

"Well, well, well," Sgt. Holcomb said. "What are *you* doing here?"

"And what in the world are *you* doing here?" Mason asked. "We were just leaving."

"Were you really!" Holcomb said. "It didn't look like it to me. It looked as though you were waiting for someone. You know, Mason, you shouldn't have such an attractive secretary. When you get a girl with a figure like Miss America..."

"Miss Universe," Mason interrupted, grinning.

"All right, all right," Holcomb said with the easy good nature of one who has trumped all the aces in the deck. "When you get a good-looking secretary with a figure like Miss Universe, we naturally notice her when she slides in behind the steering wheel of an automobile. Now, suppose you tell me just *what* you're waiting for?"

Della Street, looking toward the door of the apartment house, nudged Perry Mason.

Dr. Arlington came hurrying out, took a step toward Mason's car, then seeing the officers, veered over toward his own car.

Holcomb watched him with smiling amusement.

"Oh, Doctor," he called.

Dr. Arlington stopped, looked back over his shoulder, said, "Yes?"

"You *are* a doctor, aren't you?" Sgt. Holcomb asked, staring pointedly at the medical bag.

"Yes."

"May I ask where you've been, Doctor?"

"In that apartment house," Dr. Arlington said.

"Wonderful!" Sgt. Holcomb observed. "Since we saw you come out of the apartment house, I have no reason to doubt your statment. Now, could you be a little more specific, Doctor, and tell us just what apartment you were in, in that house?"

"I fail to see that it concerns anyone," Dr. Arlington said.

"Oh, but I think it does," Sgt. Holcomb observed. "If you were up in Apartment 218, it would be of the greatest concern to the police. And if you were sent there by Mr. Perry Mason, then the situation would be more than interesting. It would be downright exciting.

"The fact that Mr. Mason was quite apparently waiting for you to come out indicates that he knew you were in there. If he knew you were in there, the probabilities are that he was responsible for you being there. The fact that you started to walk toward Mr. Mason's car as though to make a report to him, then saw the police car parked behind and made a sudden swing over to the car which, I take it, is your car, was quite a giveaway. What did you find, Doctor?"

Dr. Arlington reached a quick decision. He smiled and said, "I was making a checkup on a person who had been injured. I assumed it was a civil case with the possibility of malingering."

He looked past the officer standing by the side of the car to Perry Mason, raised his voice and said, "The man was dead by the time I got there. The woman who was with him, and who I assume is his wife, gives a history of an ice pick having been inserted in the man's chest. I made a quick examination and convinced myself that there had indeed been a small puncture wound in the chest. Under the circumstances, I felt that it was a case for the coroner and did nothing further."

"You called the police?" Sgt. Holcomb asked.

"The police has been called *before* I arrived," Dr. Arlington said. And then, with a meaning glance at Perry Mason, said, "I would, of course, have notified the coroner if the young woman hadn't already called the authorities."

"That's most interesting," Sgt. Holcomb said. "Now perhaps someone will tell us how it happened that Mr. Mason knew this man had been injured."

Mason said, "Just a moment, Doctor. Was there anyone in the apartment when you left?"

"Just the young woman."

"Do you know whether she's his wife?"

"I don't know. How should I? I didn't ask to see the marriage license."

"In other words, then, she's up there alone with the body and any evidence that may be in the apartment."

"That is correct," Dr. Arlington said.

Sgt. Holcomb sighed. "All right, Mason," he said, "you win. Much as I would like to interrogate you, I realize that my first duty is to get up there and investigate the homicide."

"Homicide?" Mason asked. "Wasn't it accidental?"

Sgt. Holcomb grinned. "The story we got over the telephone is that some woman pushed an ice pick right into his chest. However, we'll find out a lot more about it. Don't go away, Mason."

"Why not?" Mason asked.

"I'm going to want to talk with you."

"You can talk with me at my office."

"I don't want to waste the time," Sgt. Holcomb said. "I'm not going to detain you any longer than necessary, but you and the doctor stay right here. Now, let me ask you, have you been up in that apartment, Mason?"

"Yes," Mason said.

"That's what I thought."

"You want me with you, Sergeant?" the other officer asked.

"I want you with me," Holcomb said. "Another car with a deputy coroner and a fingerprint man will be here any minute."

He turned to Mason. "I'm giving you a lawful order from an officer in the performance of his duty. Don't leave here until I have a chance to talk with you."

Mason said, "All right, if it's a *reasonable* order, I'll obey it. But it has to be reasonable. I'll give you fifteen minutes. That's a reasonable length of time. If you have any questions you want to ask me or Dr. Arlington here, be back inside of fifteen minutes."

"I've a job of investigating to do up there."

"You can get the woman out of the apartment, seal up the apartment so that nothing will be touched," Mason said, "and you can do all that within two minutes. You'll have ten minutes for a first investigation and then you can come down here and talk with me. At the end of fifteen minutes I'm going to be on my way, and Dr. Arlington is going to be on his way."

Sgt. Holcomb hesitated a moment, then turned to the officer. "Come on, let's go!" he said.

When they had gone, Dr. Arlington said in a low voice to Perry Mason, "I didn't know what to do, Perry. The man was dead when I arrived. He evidently had been dead for about ten minutes."

"How about the woman with him. Hysterical?"

"Upset....But I wouldn't think he was irreplaceable in her life."

"Did she tell you anything I should know?" Mason asked.

"Only that she'd telephoned the officers. She said she told them Carl Harrod had been murdered."

"Murdered?"

"That's what she said: murdered. I was in a spot, Perry. I didn't know what you wanted; whether I should dash back down here and tell you that the man was dead and that she had called the authorities, or whether I should take a quick look at the body so I could see the nature and location of the wound.

"I decided you'd want to know something about the wound, so I pulled back the blankets and took a look. There was a small, livid puncture wound, and, unofficially, I have no doubt it was made with an ice pick and that it was the cause of death."

"Just the one wound?" Mason asked.

"Just the one wound. Of course, I didn't examine the entire body, but the man was naked from the waist up. I'm quite certain there was just that one puncture wound, at least in the chest cavity."

"All right," Mason said wearily. "We seem to be in a hell of a spot right now. Della, I think you'd better go telephone our client.... Hold it," Mason said sharply, as she placed her hand on the door latch, "here comes an officer to ride herd on us until it suits Sgt. Holcomb to come down and give us the third degree."

The officer who had gone up with Sgt. Holcomb came back from the apartment house, started across the sidewalk.

A second police car rounded the corner. The driver was unable to find a parking place, so double-parked with the red blinker on the top of the car flaring vivid flashes of warning light.

Men hurried from the car. A photographer carrying a heavy camera case by means of a shoulder strap, a smaller camera in one hand and a Strobe-light in the other hand, hurried across to the apartment house. He was followed by an officer carrying a fingerprint camera and a small, black case of the sort used to carry materials for developing latents.

The officer who had come down from the apartment moved over to confer with the newcomers briefly.

Two more men debouched from the second police automobile and entered the apartment house.

The officer came over to stand by Mason's car.

"Sgt. Holcomb says he doesn't want to detain you unduly, but he does want to question you and he doesn't want any of you to drive away."

"I'm a doctor," Dr. Arlington said. "I can't neglect my patients. I have to be where I can be available for phone calls and—"

"I know, I know," the officer interrupted. "It won't be long."

"Fifteen minutes from the time Sgt. Holcomb spoke to us," Mason said, "is a reasonable time. I advise you, Doctor, that if you are not interrogated and released within fifteen minutes, you are legally within your rights in leaving."

"Now, wait a minute," the officer said. "You can't pull that stuff. The law doesn't say anything about fifteen minutes."

"The law requires that any police order must be reasonable," Mason said. "Under the peculiar circumstances of this case, I feel that fifteen minutes is a reasonable time. I'm willing to accept that responsibility."

"Well, you may be accepting a hell of a lot of responsibility," the officer warned roughly.

"In my business I'm accustomed to accept a hell of a lot of responsibility," Mason told him.

The officer was plainly uneasy. He glanced anxiously at the door of the apartment house. "The sergeant said to hold you until he got here."

"I tell you I'm leaving in fifteen minutes."

"You're leaving when the sergeant says you can leave."

"I'm leaving in fifteen minutes from the time he told us to wait," Mason snapped.

The officer was trying to think of the answer to that, when the door opened and Sgt. Holcomb came striding across the sidewalk and out to the car.

"So," he said, "you and Miss Street got a statement from the guy and Della Street took it down in shorthand."

"Right," Mason said.

"He was stabbed by a client of yours."

"Wrong," Mason said.

"How the hell do you know?" Sgt. Holcomb asked.

"My clients don't stab people."

"Well," Sgt. Holcomb said, "it seems that the stabbing was done by a woman who was in the apartment occupied by Fern Driscoll, 309 at the Rexmore Apartments. Is Miss Katherine Baylor a client of yours, Mason?"

"I've never seen her in my life."

"How about Fern Driscoll?"

"Fern Driscoll is my client."

"All right. I'm going up to see her. What's more, I want to see her before you have a chance to do any telephoning."

Sgt. Holcomb looked at his watch. "You hold them here for ten minutes," he said to the officer, "and then you can let them go. However, I'm going to want to hear from you, Mason. I want a statement from you and I want a copy of the statement that this man Harrod made as to the circumstances surrounding the stabbing."

"How about the doctor?" the officer asked.

"Don't let anybody get to a phone for ten minutes," Sgt. Holcomb said. "I want to get up to that apartment and talk with this Driscoll woman before Mason has a chance to tip her off to clam up and say nothing. As I see it, she's the most valuable witness we are going to find."

Mason said, "I'm afraid, Sergeant, you don't understand how I work."

"I know all about how you work," Holcomb told him. "Keep them here, Ray. In exactly ten minutes you may let them go."

Sgt. Holcomb hurried away.

Mason looked at his wrist watch, stretched, yawned, lit a cigarette, put his head back against the cushion and closed his eyes.

Dr. Arlington, taking his cue from Perry Mason, went over to his car, opened the door and started to get in.

"Stay right here for ten minutes," the officer warned.

"Nine minutes now," Dr. Arlington said, climbing into his car and slamming the door shut.

Della Street, with an eye on her wrist watch, counted off the minutes.

"All right, Chief," she said, "nine and a half minutes."

At Mason's nod, she started the motor.

"Hold it," the officer said. "You have thirty seconds to go."

"Just warming the car up," Mason told him.

The officer seemed uneasy. "I'd like to get word from Sgt. Holcomb. He could communicate with us through communications and on the car radio."

"I know he could," Mason said, "but he said ten minutes, and ten minutes it is."

The officer seemed undecided.

"Okay, Della," Mason said.

Della Street, in the driver's seat, eased the car into gear.

Dr. Arlington's car slid out behind them.

"Now where?" Della asked.

"Drake Detective Agency," Mason said, "but first signal Dr. Arlington to come alongside."

Della Street drove for a block, then pulled off to the side of the road, motioned with her arm for Dr. Arlington to come alongside on the one-way street.

When Dr. Arlington was running abreast Mason said, "Go on home, Doctor, and don't answer questions."

Dr. Arlington nodded to show that he understood and shot ahead.

Della Street said, "I think Paul Drake is in the office tonight. He told me he was working on a case and expected to be there until nearly midnight."

"That's fine," Mason said. "We'll talk with Paul personally. Swing over to the right and turn a corner, Della. I presume that officer is still watching our taillight and it's quite possible Sgt. Holcomb might relay a radio message to him asking him to hold us for another inquiry."

CHAPTER NINE

The night switchboard operator at the Drake Detective Agency offices looked up as Mason held the office door open for Della Street.

She nodded and smiled.

"Anybody in with Paul?" Mason asked.

"No, Mr. Mason, he's alone."

"Tell him we're on our way," Mason said.

The operator nodded and plugged in a telephone line.

Mason opened the gate which led to a corridor lined with doors opening into small cubbyhole offices.

Paul Drake's private office was at the end of the corridor.

Mason opened the door.

"Hi, Perry!" the detective said. "Hi, Della. What brings you out at this time of night?—Oh-oh, I'll bet I don't want to know the answer."

Mason pulled up a chair for Della Street, then sat down next to Drake's desk. "Paul, we're mixed up in a case that I can't figure out. I want a lot of research work done and I want it done fast."

Drake picked up a pencil and moved a pad of paper toward him.

Tall, long-limbed, poker-faced, he moved with an easy, double-jointed rhythm which seemed awkward, yet eliminated all waste motion.

"Shoot!"

"A girl using the name of Fern Driscoll, 309 Rexmore Apartments. I want everything you can get on Fern Driscoll. She was working in Lansing,

Michigan, and left suddenly. Now, this girl who's using Fern Driscoll's name has a job with the Consolidated Sales and Distribution Company."

"This floor?" Drake asked, looking up.

"This floor."

"I know the head of that concern pretty well," Drake said. "I can get a line on her."

"She's only been here ten days or two weeks. I want to get her background."

"Okay, anything else?"

"Harriman Baylor of Lansing. A big-shot manufacturer. A daughter named Katherine and a son named Forrester. I want everything you can get on the family. Fern Driscoll worked for Baylor's company in Lansing."

"That's all?"

"Carl Harrod of the Dixiecrat Apartments, 218. I want to know everything about his past."

"How about the present?" Drake asked.

"There isn't any," Mason told him.

Drake looked up sharply. "What do you mean?"

"It's all in the past," Mason explained.

"Since when?"

"Probably about an hour ago."

"All of this is going to take lots of men and lots of time," Drake told him.

"It's going to take lots of men and probably lots of money, but it can't take lots of time."

"Why?"

"Because we don't have that much time."

"Do the police know about Harrod?"

"Yes."

"About your interest in him?"

"Hell yes!" Mason said. "I got caught standing in front of the apartment waiting for Dr. Arlington to come down and make a report."

"Report on what?"

"Nature and extent of the injuries. He was stabbed with an ice pick. The woman who was living with Harrod had already called headquarters before we got there and reported the death as a homicide. My friend, Sgt. Holcomb, caught me flat-footed."

"So what happens next?" Drake asked.

"I don't know," Mason said. "I want all the information I can get before the going begins to get tough."

"I take it there's some sort of a tie-in by which all of these people are joined together more or less?"

"There may be," Mason said.

"Okay. Where are you going now?"

"Down to my office," Mason told him. "You start getting information, relay it in as fast as you can get it. Minutes may be precious. We're probably one jump ahead of the police on certain phases of the case and I'd like to keep ahead of them as far as possible.

"The Baylor family use the Vista del Camino hotel as headquarters. They're very shy about the wrong sort of publicity. Carl Harrod was all set to see that they got lots of it.

"Katherine Baylor is in town. She may be implicated in some way. On the other hand, the girl using the name of Fern Driscoll says *she* did the stabbing."

"You don't think this girl really is Fern Driscoll?"

"I *know* she's Mildred Crest of Oceanside. Get busy and check everything."

"Okay," Drake said, "get down to your office and let me start pouring instructions into the telephone. I'll have ten men on the job within ten minutes and each one of those men will put out more men if he has to."

Mason nodded to Della Street and they left Drake's office, walked down the corridor to Mason's office.

Mason latchkeyed the door, switched on the lights.

"Well?" Della Street asked, as Mason hung up his hat and settled back into a swivel chair.

"We wait it out—for a while at least," Mason said. "If our client is telling the truth, she was entirely within her rights in protecting herself."

"And if she's lying?"

"Then," Mason admitted, "things could be in quite a mess."

"She seems to have lied before."

"Exactly. Those lies are going to put her in quite a spot if the breaks start going against her.

"As Mildred Crest, she *could* find herself charged with the murder of Fern Driscoll. All that background of deceit is going to make her a pushover in this Harrod case—if the authorities decide it's murder."

They waited twenty minutes, then the unlisted phone rang sharply.

"I'll take it," Mason said. "It must be Paul Drake."

Mason picked up the receiver, said, "Hello, Paul."

Drake's voice came over the wire. "Get either morning paper. You'll find a picture of Harriman Baylor, the famous manufacturer and financial wizard, just getting off an airplane. He arrived late this afternoon. Reporters met him at the airport."

"I'll take a look," Mason said. "You say there's a photograph?"

"A nice photograph. Mr. Baylor is not out here on business. Mr. Baylor is out here for a well-earned vacation and for his health. Mr. Baylor has been troubled with bursitis."

"Bursitis, huh?" Mason said.

"Uh-huh. An infection of a capsule of fluid or something in the shoulder that—"

Mason laughed and said, "I know all about bursitis, Paul. That is, I know enough about it to cross-examine doctors. It can be stubborn and painful. We don't have our morning papers at the moment. Tell me, how did Mr. Baylor look in the photos?"

"Influential," Drake said. "He has many million dollars, and he looks like many million dollars. The photograph shows him holding a brief case in his left hand, his right hand waving his hat in greeting, a beautiful hostess on each side and a caption about the manufacturing and financial wizard who believes that the Pacific Coast is on the eve of an unprecedented growth. Baylor says that what has happened so far is merely scratching the industrial surface."

"Radiating optimism, eh?" Mason asked.

"Radiating optimism."

"Could I call him at the Vista del Camino Hotel?" Mason asked.

"No dice," Drake said. "Trying to get a phone call through to him requires an Act of Congress and the unwinding of yards of red tape. But he's there and, as nearly as I can find out, he's in his suite."

"What about his background, Paul?"

"Big manufacturer. Big financier. Big investor. Boards of directors and all that stuff. *Who's Who* takes a whole column on him."

"Find out anything about Katherine Baylor?" Mason asked.

"Postgraduate work at Stanford. Nice kid. Popular. For herself and not for her money. Unostentatious. A good scout. Something of a crusader, imbued with the idea of improving the administration of justice, safeguarding justice for rich and poor alike. A nice kid."

"Entanglements?"

"Apparently not. Nothing formal. Very popular, therefore it's hard to tell whether she's playing the field or has her eye on some particular individual. Apparently, there was an affair back East, something that the folks were afraid might prove serious, and that's the reason for postgraduate work at Stanford.

"I'm just beginning to get the dirt, Perry, and I'll have more for you in a little while. But in the meantime I thought you'd like to know about Baylor."

"That's fine," Mason said. "Keep digging and keep in touch with us. I think I'll go to the Vista del Camino Hotel and try for an interview."

"No chance," Drake said. "He had a press interview at the plane, then he ordered everything shut off. No phone calls, no interviews. Nothing."

"Any exceptions?" Mason asked.

"I don't know. The house dick over there is a friend of mine. I might be able to find out."

"Find out and call me back," Mason said. "I'm interested."

The lawyer hung up the phone and Della Street drew a cup of coffee from the electric percolator.

"Listen in on the extension?" Mason asked.

She nodded.

"Take notes?"

Again she nodded.

Five minutes later Drake again called on the unlisted telephone.

"Now look, Perry," he said, "you're going to have to protect me on this. I got it from my close friend, the house detective. It would cost him his job if anyone knew there had been a leak coming from him."

"Go ahead," Mason said.

"Baylor has shut off all telephone calls. Everything. His suite is completely isolated. There's even a guard at the door. He has, however, left instructions that if a Mr. Howley tries to get in touch with him, the call is to be put through immediately, no matter what hour of the day or night."

"Howley, eh?" Mason asked.

"That's right."

"Who's Howley, do you know?"

"Can't find a thing in the world about him. All I know is Baylor is sewed up tight except for Howley. And Howley is to be put through the minute he picks up a phone."

"Is Howley arriving at the hotel?" Mason asked.

"I don't know. Instructions are for action the minute Howley shows up. I gather that he's probably coming in on a plane or something and Baylor is waiting for him."

"But you don't have anything definite on that? That's just a hunch?"

"Hunch, hell! It's a deduction," Drake said.

"All you have is the deduction?"

"That's right."

"Why should Baylor be taking all those precautions?" Mason asked. "It would seem to indicate that he expects to become the center of interest somehow."

"He *is* a center of interest," Drake said. "He's a big shot."

"But he doesn't ordinarily take all those precautions against disturbance?"

"He doesn't ordinarily have bursitis and—probably he's working on a big business deal. I don't know. All I can do is get the facts and relay them to you. You're going to have to do your own thinking."

"No more deductions?" Mason asked.

"Not after the cool reception I got on the other one."

Mason laughed. "Don't be so sensitive. Keep working, Paul."

Mason hung up the telephone, looked at Della Street thoughtfully, said, "Try to reach our client, Della. Perhaps the police haven't taken her out of circulation. In that event, they've probably completed their questioning and we might be able to get her on the line."

Della Street put through a call, got no answer, so called the manager of the apartment house, asked for Fern Driscoll in Apartment 309, said, "Just a moment, please," then turned to Mason. "The manager says Miss Driscoll left with two men and asked the manager to hold all mail."

"Okay," Mason said, "hang up."

Della Street said, "Thank you. I'll call later," and hung up.

Suddenly Mason turned to his secretary. "You sit here and hold the fort, Della. I'm going over to the Vista del Camino Hotel."

"Be careful," she warned.

Mason nodded.

Mason left the office and went directly to the Vista del Camino Hotel.

In the lobby the lawyer picked up one of the room phones, said, "Connect me with Mr. Harriman Baylor, please."

"I'm sorry, but Mr. Baylor's phone has been temporarily disconnected. He has left orders that he's not to be disturbed."

"Well, he'll talk with me," Mason said. "I'm supposed to call him."

"I'm very sorry, but there are to be absolutely no—Just a moment. What's the name, please?"

"Howley," Mason said.

Mason heard the sound of swift whispers, then the operator said, "Just a moment, Mr. Howley. If you'll hold on, I'll see if we can get Mr. Baylor."

A few moments later a rich baritone voice said cautiously, "Hello. This is Harriman Baylor speaking."

"Howley," Mason said.

Baylor's voice showed excitement. "Where are you now?"

"In the lobby."

"Well, it's about time," Baylor said. "They had the damnedest report that you'd been—Wait a minute. How do I know you're Howley?"

"As far as that's concerned," Mason said, "how do I know you're Baylor?"

"What's your other name, Howley?"

"Look," Mason said, "I'm not going to stand down here in the lobby where anyone can buttonhole me at any minute and have you give me a catechism. I'll come up there, then I'll answer your questions. I—"

"What's the other name I know you by?" Baylor interrupted.

Mason hesitated.

Suddenly the receiver clicked at the other end of the line and the line went dead.

Mason immediately left the room phone, sauntered across the lobby to the cigar stand and waited.

A house detective hurried to the bank of house phones, looked around, then made a survey of the lobby.

Mason lit a cigarette, strolled over to one of the reclining chairs, settled back and waited.

A bellboy, closely followed by the house detective, paged "Mr. Howley."

Mason made no move. He waited for five minutes, then went to the hotel drugstore, entered a phone booth and again called the number of the Vista del Camino Hotel.

"Will you please tell Mr. Harriman Baylor," Mason told the operator who answered, "that Mr. Howley is calling?"

The operator hesitated perceptibly, then after a moment a man's voice came on the line.

"Hello?" the voice asked.

"Mr. Baylor?" Mason asked.

"That's right," the voice said.

"Howley," Mason told him.

"Where are you now, Mr. Howley?"

"Not too far away," Mason said.

"If you tell me where you are, I'll—"

"Look here," Mason said indignantly, "this isn't Baylor. Who the hell is that?"

"Now, just a minute! Take it easy! Take it easy!" the man's voice said. "We're filtering Mr. Baylor's calls. Someone tried to get through to him by using your name. Just a minute, and I'll put Baylor on."

A moment later another voice came on the line. "Hello," the voice said cautiously.

"Baylor?" Mason asked.

"Yes."

"Howley."

Baylor said promptly, "What was the other name you gave me, Howley?"

"Why, hell! *You* know," Mason said.

"I know," Baylor retorted. "But I want to be sure that this is the man I think it is. What was the other name?"

"Carl Harrod," Mason said promptly.

"All right," Baylor told him, relief in his voice, "that's better! There was a report around that you were seriously incapacititated, that—Never mind, I'll discuss that with you. Now, I want you to come up to my suite. It's the presidential suite, Suite A. But you can't get near the door of the suite because it's guarded. Walk up to Room 428 and knock on the door. Knock twice, wait a moment, knock twice more, then wait a moment, and knock once. Do you understand that?"

"Perfectly!" Mason said.

"All right, I'll see you there. How long will it take you to get there?"

"About two minutes," Mason told him.

"Did everything go all right?"

"Everything went fine."

"All right. Come on up and we'll discuss arrangements."

Mason hung up the telephone, sauntered into the hotel, took the elevator to the fourth floor, walked down the corridor. Presidential Suite A was at the end of the corridor, and the entrance was blocked by a man who was over six feet tall, bullnecked, and built like a wrestler.

The man eyed Mason suspiciously. Mason paid no attention to him but turned sharply to the left to the door of 428 and knocked twice, waited a moment, knocked twice more, waited another moment, then knocked again.

The door was opened by a stocky, quick-moving individual in the early fifties, a man with a high forehead, bushy eyebrows, dark piercing eyes, and an assertative manner.

He recoiled as he saw Mason. His left hand holding the doorknob tried to slam the door shut.

Mason lowered his shoulder, pushed the door open and walked into the room.

"I'm Perry Mason, Mr. Baylor," he said. "I'm the attorney for the young woman in the Rexmore Apartments. I think you and I had better have a talk."

Baylor stepped back, said, "Perry Mason, the lawyer?"

"That's right."

Baylor said, "I'm sorry, but you can't come in, Mason. I can't see anyone!"

"Except Carl Harrod," Mason said. "For your information, Carl Harrod is dead."

"I . . . I . . ."

Mason kicked the door shut. "A great deal is going to depend on decisions you and I reach during the next few minutes, Mr. Baylor. I want to get some cards on the table."

"I don't want to talk with you. I've been warned about you."

Mason said, "I don't know how long you're going to have to discuss matters before the police get here. For your information, Mr. Baylor, I happen to know that Carl Harrod was blackmailing you. Carl Harrod was stabbed in the chest with an ice pick. He died a short time ago. He made a statement to me that Fern Driscoll had stabbed him with the ice pick, but under questioning admitted it could just as well have been your daughter Katherine that had pushed the ice pick into his chest.

"Now, I don't care how big you are or how powerful you are; Harrod's death is going to make complications. I don't know all the ramifications of what happened to Fern Driscoll, but it seems to me, you and I had better exchange a few facts before the newspapers come out with a sensational story."

"The newspapers!" Baylor exclaimed.

"Exactly," Mason said.

Baylor hesitated, suddenly said, "All right. You win!" He extended his left hand and shook hands with Mason. "You'll pardon the left hand," he said. "My bursitis has become suddenly worse. Come on in and we'll talk things over."

Baylor led the way across Room 428, which was fitted up as an ordinary hotel bedroom, through a connecting door and into the reception room of a luxurious suite.

"This is my daughter, Katherine," he said. "Katherine, this is Perry Mason, an attorney, who is representing Fern Driscoll."

Katherine Baylor jumped to her feet, her eyes wide with some emotion Mason was unable at the moment to classify. She moved over to give him her hand.

"Mr. Mason," she said.

"It's a pleasure to meet you," Mason said. And then added quietly, "My client has told me about you."

"Oh!" Kitty said.

"All right," Baylor said. "Sit down, Mason. Perhaps we'd better put some cards on the table."

Mason selected a chair, stretched his long legs out in front, crossed his ankles.

"Now, what's all this about Harrod having been killed?" Baylor asked.

"Stabbed with an ice pick," Mason said. "At first Harrod said Fern Driscoll had pushed the ice pick into his chest. Then it became clear that your daughter Katherine may have done it."

"What!" Katherine Baylor exclaimed. "Why, that's absolutely absurd! I slapped his face and—"

"Suppose you let Mr. Mason and me do the talking, Kitty," Harriman Baylor said. "I'd like to find out a little more about Mason's position in the matter, and exactly what it is he wants."

Mason said, "I want facts. I want to know exactly what your relations were with Harrod. I want to know why you came in here and closed off every means of communication providing that no one could reach you except Carl Harrod who was to call you under the name of Howley."

"And I want to know how *you* got *that* information," Baylor snapped.

Mason smiled. "I'm afraid there's some information I can't give you."

"Can't or won't?"

"Won't!"

"That's not a very good way to start playing your hands," Baylor said.

"It's my way," Mason told him.

Baylor colored. "I don't let men dictate to me, Mr. Mason."

"Probably not," Mason said. "However, we have one essential difference, Mr. Baylor."

"What's that?"

Mason grinned. "*I* don't care how often they put *my* name in the newspapers, and *I* don't care how large the type is."

Baylor's aggressive personality visibly collapsed.

"Precisely what do you want, Mason?"

"First," Mason said, "I want to know all about Fern Driscoll."

Baylor said, "There isn't any reason why you shouldn't know everything I know. Miss Driscoll was employed as my son's secretary. It is possible that some romantic attachment developed. It is even possible that Miss Driscoll was foolish enough to think a person in my son's position could have married her, and she may even have dared to think such an event would take place."

Mason regarded the man thoughtfully. "You say she *dared* to think that?"

"She may have."

"You consider such an event improbable?"

Baylor flushed and said, "I consider it utterly impossible!"

"May I ask why?"

"There are certain reasons that I don't think we need to go into at the present time, aside, of course, from the obvious difference in social status."

"You consider that important?" Mason asked.

"Quite important!" Baylor said drily.

The telephone rang. Evidently some sort of an agreed-upon signal: a long, two shorts and a long.

Katherine Baylor moved toward the phone, but her father shook his head, strode across the room, picked up the telephone, said impatiently, "Hello. Yes. What is it now?"

He listened for several seconds, then said, "Of course, I'll talk with him. Put him on!"

A moment later he said, "Hello, Sergeant. Yes, this is Harriman Baylor."

Again he listened for a few seconds, then said, "She is here with me. We will of course do everything in our power to co-operate, but any such charge as that is absolutely absurd! Now, I want to be certain of one thing: Are you positive that the man is dead?"

Baylor listened again for a few moments, then said: "I am exceedingly busy at the moment. If you could come within...oh, say, half an hour, that would be more convenient....I see....Well, make it twenty minutes then....I'm sorry, Sergeant, fifteen minutes is absolutely the best I can do for you...! I'm sorry, but that's final. Fifteen minutes! I don't give a damn if you subpoena me before a thousand grand juries, I'm tied up for fifteen minutes...! Very well. Goodby!"

Baylor slammed up the telephone, walked back to his chair, looked at his wrist watch, regarded Mason thoughtfully and said, "All right, Mason. We haven't time to do any more sparring for position.

"My son became involved with Fern Driscoll. She may be a most estimable young woman. I don't know. My son is also attached to a very nice young woman who is in his social set, a woman who would make him happy, and who would be unquestionably accepted into the social circle in which my son moves, something which would be exceedingly difficult for Miss Driscoll.

"Now then, the report seems to have spread in some way that there had been certain indiscretions; that Miss Driscoll was in trouble and that I had given her a large sum of money to leave town. That report is absolutely, unqualifiedly false."

"How about your son?" Mason asked.

"My son assures me that the report is false as far as he is concerned," Baylor said with dignity.

"Well," Kitty said, "I happen to know that—"

"That will do! Please keep out of this, Katherine," Baylor said. "The situation is rather delicate."

Kitty glanced indignantly at him. "What I was going to say might have been of some help...."

"Please!" her father commanded.

She remained silent.

"Now then," Baylor went on, "the situation became complicated because of this man Harrod. It seems that Fern Driscoll was involved in some way in an automobile accident, and Harrod was an investigator for an insurance company. He started backtracking and somehow or other found out a lot of garbled facts. Somebody gave him a lot of misinformation. The point is that he was dealing with a scandal magazine, which he felt would pay him ten thousand dollars for the story."

"You talked with him?" Mason asked.

Baylor thought things over some four or five seconds, then said in the manner of a man who is weighing his words carefully, "I admit that I talked with him. Harrod seemed to feel that perhaps I would be willing to pay him an amount at least equal to that which he could receive from the magazine for the story. However, he evidently had been advised in some detail concerning the law of extortion and it was very difficult to get him to say *exactly* what he had in mind.

"Moreover, Mason, I am not a man who submits to blackmail.

"The reason I am telling you all of this is that, according to Harrod, Fern Driscoll had some rather indiscreet letters which my son had written, and my son has admitted to me that there is the possibility Miss Driscoll saved some of his letters. He is not entirely clear as to the contents of those letters.

"In view of my name and position, a scandal magazine would regard a story involving the family as a very choice tidbit. It would undoubtedly pay a top price for such a story, and the publication of that story would cause a very great deal of unfavorable comment in the circles in which I move."

Mason nodded.

Baylor looked at his watch, and suddenly increased the tempo of his words. "I only have a minute or two, Mr. Mason. I don't want the officers to find you here. A Sgt. Holcomb wants to interview my daughter concerning the death of this man Harrod."

Again Mason nodded.

"I take it you must know something about that?"

"Yes," Mason said.

"Do you know Sgt. Holcomb?"

"Yes."

"Well, I don't want Sgt. Holcomb to find you here, and I'm not going to tell Sgt. Holcomb that you have been here. I'm telling you all this very frankly, Mr. Mason. I wouldn't submit to blackmail. However, certain circumstances which now exist put me in a very embarrassing position. I have every reason to believe that Miss Driscoll may need first-class legal services. I think that Miss Driscoll has certain letters which my son wrote. I want those letters. When those letters are delivered to me, I am prepared to pay you in cash for representing Miss Driscoll."

"I'm not a blackmailer," Mason said.

"I don't want you to be a blackmailer. You're representing Fern Driscoll. Now then, you're going to have to do a great deal of legal work for her. She doesn't have the money to pay you the sort of fees you customarily get. I know a great deal about you by reputation.

"On the other hand, Miss Driscoll isn't a blackmailer and you're not a blackmailer. You wouldn't think of using those letters in any adverse way. However, Mr. Mason, let me point out to you the extreme danger of the situation. If the police should search Miss Driscoll's apartment and should find those letters, it is almost certain that even if the letters themselves don't find their way into the public press, the existence of those letters would be established and that would be enough to give this scandal magazine all of the verification it needed so that it could go ahead and publish this dastardly story.

"Therefore, without in any way being guilty of any extortion, without you being guilty of any unprofessional conduct, you can assure your client that, if she will turn over those letters to you, and you can give them to me, she can have your services and they will be fully paid for. Do I make myself clear?"

Mason nodded.

"But, Dad," Kitty said, "she *isn't* Fern Driscoll!"

Her father turned on her angrily. "I asked you please to keep out of this!"

Mason regarded Harriman Baylor thoughtfully.

"All right," Baylor said, "suppose she isn't Fern Driscoll. Suppose your client should even be an impostor. The situation then becomes even more delicate. If it should appear that Fern Driscoll was the woman who was killed, if the autopsy showed that she was in the second month of pregnancy, if she left my employ suddenly, pulling up her roots and leaving without even pausing to say good-by to her friends—and then if it should appear that she had letters from my son—Damn it, Mason! I don't have to draw *you* a blueprint! I don't have to point out anything that's as obvious as the nose on your face. I want those letters!"

"And," Mason said, "the reason that you were not going to see anyone except

Harrod is that Harrod assured you he would have those letters and could deliver them to you in return for a cash payment. Is that right?"

"I don't propose to be cross-examined by you or anyone else," Baylor said, "and I want you out of here before the police come. I've said everything I care to say."

Baylor got up, strode across to the door, held it open.

Mason said, "I think I appreciate your position, Mr. Baylor."

"You'll consider my offer?"

"I'll consider the best interests of my client."

"You understand what I am trying to forestall?"

"Perfectly."

"If this magazine can't get *some* corroborating evidence, it won't dare to go ahead. If it can get the faintest bit of corroboration, it will come out with a story that will start a social scandal which will have a most disastrous effect.

"You need money for your services. I've told you how you can get an adequate fee."

"I understand you perfectly," Mason said. "I'll do whatever is best for my client."

He walked out.

CHAPTER TEN

Mason latchkeyed the door of his private office, grinned at Della Street, and said, "Well, we may as well go home."

"How did you come out?" Della Street asked.

"After making one false start, I got in to see Baylor. You may have one guess as to who Howley was."

"Howley?" she asked, puzzled. "Who was— Oh, I remember, Howley was the name that Baylor gave the hotel telephone operators and the house detectives, the one person whose calls were to be put through and who was to be admitted to see him no matter what hour he called."

"That's right," Mason said. "Guess who Howley really was?"

"I give up, Chief. Who *was* Howley?"

"Howley," Mason said, "was the alias for Carl Harrod."

"Oh-oh!" Della exclaimed. And then after a moment, "How in the world did you ever find that out?"

"I took a chance," Mason explained. "I made a shot in the dark. The first time I called up and said I was Howley, Baylor wanted to know under what other name he knew me, or words to that effect. He wasn't quite that crude, but he asked me what other name I had given him. I was hesitating, trying to think of some way out, when he slammed up the telephone.

"I thought things over for a while, came to the conclusion that Baylor was out here because of the Fern Driscoll situation, that Harrod had been in touch with him, that the situation was really crucial, that Harrod had probably given him some ultimatum and that Baylor was thinking it over.

"I had everything to gain and nothing to lose. So I went to another telephone, called once more, gave the name of Howley, and when Baylor again asked me under what other name he knew me, or words to that effect, I said 'Carl Harrod,' and that did the trick."

Della Street frowned. "Just what does that mean, Chief?"

"That," Mason said, "is something I'm trying to figure out. People should react to external stimuli in a manner consistent with their basic characteristics. Any time they don't *seem* to do so, it means that the external stimuli are being misconstrued by the investigator, or that the basic character of the person has been misconstrued or misinterpreted.

"Baylor puts up a bold front of being a man who will fight to the last ditch, a man who won't pay blackmail, a man who refuses to bow to anyone. Yet he flies out here from Michigan and, despite all of his bold protestations of independence, we find him making appointments with a blackmailer."

Mason started pacing the floor. He paced for several seconds, then spoke thoughtfully: "If it was part of the Fern Driscoll story, Harrod must have uncovered something new. He had approached Baylor in Michigan and intimated that he'd sell the story to Baylor for the same price that he could get from a magazine. Baylor threw him out."

Della Street said, "I can tell from the tone of your voice that, while you're thinking out loud, you have an idea what the answer is."

"The answer may be that Katherine Baylor has become involved in some way."

"How?" she asked.

"That," Mason said, "is one of the major mysteries of the case.

"And there again we run into inconsistent conduct. We know now that our client is actually Mildred Crest, that Fern Driscoll got in the car with Mildred and there was an accident. We know there's something phony about that accident. We know that Fern Driscoll died and Mildred took her identity, and yet the actions of Fern Driscoll aren't consistent."

"In what way?" Della Street asked.

"Fern Driscoll," Mason said, "was a pretty levelheaded young woman. She was an executive secretary for Baylor's son in a big organization. She must have had responsibilities and executive capabilities. Then all of a sudden she goes completely haywire and does a lot of things that simply don't make sense, no matter how you look at them."

"An unmarried woman who finds herself pregnant can go completely haywire," Della Street said. "Just realize the situation in which she found herself."

"I'm trying to," Mason said, "but it still doesn't account for her actions.... Call Paul Drake, Della. Tell him I'm back and that we're closing up shop. See if he knows anything new."

Della Street put through the call, then said, "Paul says he has some red-hot information. He's coming right down."

Mason moved over to the door of his private office, and as soon as he heard Drake's code knock, let the detective in.

"Well, how's it coming?" Mason asked.

"In bunches," Drake said. "I think your client's in one hell of a mess."

"Shoot!" Mason told him.

"According to Harrod's widow, Harrod made *another* statement after you left. This statement was when he realized death was imminent."

"Go ahead," Mason said, "what was the second statement?"

"The second statement was that your client is a complete impostor, that she's really Mildred Crest of Oceanside, that Mildred's boy friend embezzled some money and skipped out, that Mildred picked up Fern Driscoll as a hitchhiker, that either there was an accident, in which Fern Driscoll was killed and Mildred decided to take her identity, or that Mildred deliberately killed Fern Driscoll in order to have another identity."

"Go ahead," Mason said tonelessly. "What else?"

"Fern Driscoll had been engaged in a red-hot romance with Forrester Baylor. Young Baylor told her he was going to marry her. It wasn't until she found herself pregnant that she realized young Baylor was completely under the domination of his father. Then the old man moved in, told Fern Driscoll she could never hope to get into the sacred social precincts of the Baylor family, gave her a chunk of money, and told her to get out.

"She got out, but she had with her a bunch of torrid letters in the handwriting of Forrester Baylor. She never intended to use those letters, but when Harrod started investigating Mildred Crest's automobile accident on behalf of the insurance carrier, and tried to find out the identity of the hitchhiker Mildred had picked up, he did a good job of it and unearthed the scandal.

"Since that didn't have anything to do with Harrod's job as an insurance investigator, he was willing to play it on the side for what it was worth. He intended to sell the story to a scandal magazine. He evidently offered the story to the editors, who became terribly excited about it. They told Harrod that they'd pay him ten thousand bucks for the story but that they'd require some sort of proof. In order to get that proof, Harrod decided he needed the letters young Baylor had written.

"Harrod started out trying to make a deal with Mildred Crest, who was posing as Fern Driscoll, in order to get the letters. He went up to see her and came to the conclusion she wasn't Fern Driscoll. On his second visit, he ran into Katherine Baylor in the apartment.

"So Harrod waited and paid a third visit to the apartment. That time someone jabbed an ice pick into his chest.

"He came home, grinning from ear to ear. He telephoned Baylor and they had some mysterious conversation. Then he called you.

"Now, here's the funny thing. When Harrod *first* came home, he told his wife Katherine Baylor had stabbed him. After he had this conversation over the phone with Baylor, he told his wife it was Mildred Crest who had stabbed him. He told her to get you on the line and that he was going to make you jump through hoops.

"After he talked with you, he told his wife he had to set the stage and pretend the injury was very serious. So he covered up with blankets.

"He was in great spirits until just before you came. Then he began to complain of feeling cold. He said he was having a chill when you were there and his wife thought that was all part of the act. After you left she knew he really was feeling bad. She suggested he get up and get into a hot bath. He started to do that, then gave an exclamation of pain, fell back in the chair, and died within five minutes."

"Now then, Perry, here's something that's going to bother you: the police searched the apartment of your client and found four thousand bucks in nice, new hundred-dollar bills. According to police reasoning, that's the money that Fern Driscoll was given by either Harriman Baylor or by Forrester Baylor to go away and have her baby.

"In any event, it isn't money that Mildred Crest could have had legitimately. It's money that must have come from the purse of Fern Driscoll, the hitchhiker.

Taking it from the purse constitutes larceny.

"Police are going to build up a case on the theory that Mildred Crest either murdered Fern Driscoll in order to take over her identity, or that she stole her identity along with all the money that was in Fern Driscoll's purse, that when Carl Harrod got on the trail and found out what was happening, she decided to silence Carl Harrod by sticking an ice pick in his chest.

"That makes a nice, neat, first-degree murder case."

"They've taken my client into custody?" Mason asked.

"She's in custody. I think they already have her identified from the thumbprint on her driving license as Mildred Crest. It's going to make one hell of a story, and you're right in the middle of it."

"All right," Mason said, "they've hit us with everything in the bag now. There's nothing we can do at the moment except go home and go to bed.

"Keep your men working, Paul, trying to stay abreast of the situation. I'll talk with my client in the morning and see how much she's told them. The fat's in the fire by this time."

"Will they let you talk with her?" Drake asked.

"They'll have to," Mason said. "Once they've booked her for murder, she's entitled to counsel. They won't even *try* to stop me. If she's booked, they'll have a red carpet spread out for me. They'll be very, very careful to see that she has all of her rights."

"And if she isn't booked by morning?" Drake asked.

"Then it means the district attorney's office doesn't feel it has a case, and that it will be trying to tie up loose ends."

Drake said drily, "With Baylor's millions trying to keep his daughter's name out of it, I think you'll find they have a case."

"We'll know by ten o'clock in the morning," Mason said. "Go home and get some sleep, Paul."

CHAPTER ELEVEN

Foley Calvert, one of Hamilton Burger's more skillful trial deputies, arose to address Judge Marvin C. Bolton.

"Your Honor," he said, "this is the case of People vs. Mildred Crest, alias Fern Driscoll. She is charged with first-degree murder and this is the preliminary hearing. I wish to make a brief statement in order to explain the position of the prosecution and the reason for certain steps which will be taken by the prosecution. This statement is addressed to the Court solely for the purpose of showing the manner in which proof is to be submitted."

"Very well," Judge Bolton said. "You may make a statement and the defense may have an opportunity to reply to that statement if it desires."

"Thank you, Your Honor," Calvert said. "It is the theory of the prosecution that Mildred Crest, faced with social disgrace in Oceanside, decided to disappear; that, as a part of her scheme for disappearance, she intended to find some young woman of about her age and general appearance and substitute identities with that woman, killing the victim and leaving the body to be found under such circumstances that it would appear that Mildred Crest had died in an automobile accident."

"Just a moment," Judge Bolton interposed, "aren't you going rather far afield, Counselor? I am, of course, aware that this statement is addressed solely to the Court. However, if you rely upon that theory in *this* proceeding, then when you come to present your case before a jury, aren't you going to be faced with the fact that you are trying to introduce evidence of another crime, and that such evidence is based on surmise?"

"No, Your Honor," Calvert said. "We are prepared to argue the point. If the Court will bear with me a moment. It isn't the murder of Fern Driscoll, who was the young woman the defendant picked up as a victim, that furnishes the dominant motivation here. It is the fact that Carl Harrod, the decedent, was an investigator for an automobile insurance company and that his investigations disclosed the facts in the case which the defendant was trying to conceal. Therefore, it became necessary for the defendant to murder Carl Harrod, in order to carry out her scheme and keep from having the whole house of cards collapse.

"That, if the Court please, furnishes the motivation. The prosecution will show that motivation by competent evidence, of course."

"The defendant has not been charged with the murder of Fern Driscoll?" Judge Bolton asked.

"No, Your Honor."

"I take it that, if you had an airtight case—Well, the Court will make no comment on that. However, it is significant that she is not being prosecuted for *that* murder."

"She may well be prosecuted for that murder at a later date, Your Honor. I will state that she is already being charged with robbery in that she took four thousand dollars from the purse of Fern Driscoll."

"Four thousand dollars?" Judge Bolton asked.

"Yes, Your Honor."

"You didn't make that point in your original statement."

"Perhaps I overlooked that point, Your Honor. However, there is no question—that is, in the minds of the prosecution—there is no question but that this defendant took four thousand dollars from the purse of Fern Driscoll after the death of that young woman."

Judge Bolton looked at Mildred Crest with a complete lack of sympathy. "Evidence as to these matters will be introduced at this hearing?" he asked.

"Yes, Your Honor."

"Does the defense wish to make any statement?" Judge Bolton asked.

"No statement at this time, Your Honor," Perry Mason said.

"Very well, call your witnesses," Judge Bolton told the prosecutor. His voice had a note of cold finality.

Calvert put on a procession of minor witnesses: persons who had worked with Mildred Crest in Oceanside, who identified the defendant as being Mildred Crest; the chief of police of Oceanside who testified that Robert Joiner had been a fugitive from justice since the twenty-second day of the month, the day on which Mildred Crest had disappeared.

The manager of the bank testified as to the amount of money Mildred had drawn out of her account on the day of her disappearance.

Mildred's former employer testified as to the amount of salary she was receiving, the amount of the last pay check she had been given, the fact that she had announced her engagement to Robert Joiner, and that on the day of Robert Joiner's disappearance she had appeared in his office around two-thirty in the afternoon, white to the lips, and obviously ill, that he had commented on her personal appearance, and she had stated she was very sick, and he had sent her home.

Calvert's next witness was a member of the highway patrol, who testified as to the automobile accident. This witness identified photographs showing the position of the body. He testified as to all of the details concerning the accident, including tracks down the canyon showing that one person had left the overturned automobile.

"Cross-examine," Calvert said.

Mason said, "The automobile caught fire?"

"Someone set fire to the automobile," the officer said.

"How do you know the fire was set?" Mason asked.

"Because of the position and character of the fire."

"Just what do you mean by that?"

"When the car went off the road, it happened that a large, jagged rock caught the gasoline tank and wrenched it partially off. A big hole was torn in the tank and a large part of the gasoline was spilled at that point. When the car came to rest at the bottom of the steep incline, some of the gasoline from the tank had soaked the extreme rear of the car. It did not reach the front of the car. The ignition had been switched off. The lights had been switched off. Someone was alive and in the car at the time. The switches didn't turn themselves off. Since they were off, there was no way for the fire to have started other than through the agency of a match."

"Couldn't the impact of steel grinding against rocks have caused a series of sparks?" Mason asked.

"Well...yes, I suppose so."

"And couldn't one of those sparks have touched off the gasoline?"

"Perhaps," the officer conceded. "But in this case we *know* that the fire was set by a match and that it was set by a second match, because we found a first match at the scene of the wreck; a paper match which had been torn from a book of matches and had been used presumably for illumination."

"You found a paper match?" Mason asked.

"Yes, sir."

"You don't know when that paper match was placed there—of your own knowledge, do you?"

"Well, no. We assumed that it was—"

"Never mind your assumption," Mason said. "What do you *know*? Do you know that the match was struck at the time of the accident or immediately thereafter?"

"No, I don't know it of my own knowledge."

"It could have been left there from the day before, couldn't it?"

"Why would any person have struck a match at that particular place down at the bottom of that rocky canyon?"

"Don't question me," Mason said. "Answer *my* questions. For all you know, of your *own* knowledge, that match could have been left there from the day before the accident, couldn't it?"

The officer thought for a moment, then admitted reluctantly, "Yes, I suppose so."

"Now then," Mason said, "you have stated in your direct examination that the fire was put under control by the action of a passing motorist?"

"The fire in the car was controlled, yes, sir."

"Will you please tell me again just how that happened?"

"A motorist, coming along the road, saw the flames. He had a fire extinguisher in his car. As I have mentioned, the bulk of the gasoline had been spilled at a distance shortly after the car left the road where a big rock had partially wrenched the gasoline tank from the car and had torn a big hole in the tank. The motorist with his fire extinguisher, seeing a car at the bottom of the canyon, scrambled down to a point below the main part of the fire, directed his fire extinguisher on the fire in the automobile, and was able to bring that fire under control before the automobile had been completely consumed."

"Now, you mentioned in your direct examination that a suitcase was found which was the property of Fern Driscoll?"

"I didn't say it was the property of Fern Driscoll. I said that the initials 'F.D.' were on the suitcase and that subsequently we were able to trace it to the store which had sold it to Fern Driscoll, a store in Lansing, Michigan."

"If the Court please," Foley Calvert said, "I will stipulate that, as to the suitcase, the witness is testifying on hearsay evidence and it may go out."

"I'm making no objection," Mason said. "That, I take it, is a matter about which the authorities have satisfied themselves, and I see no reason for putting the state to the expense of proving this by showing the purchase itself. The witness, who is apparently somewhat biased but thoroughly competent, has stated what his investigation disclosed, and I have made no objection."

"We have the clerk who made the sale to Fern Driscoll here in court," Calvert said. "We have brought him from Lansing, Michigan."

"Very well, you may put him on later," Judge Bolton said. "There seems to be no objection on the part of the defense to the statement of this witness concerning the results of the police investigation. The Court will accept that statement for what it is worth. Proceed with your questioning."

"We have no further questions of this witness if the defense has finished its cross-examination," Calvert said.

"The defense is finished."

Calvert next put on the doctor who had performed the autopsy on the body, which he had at first assumed was that of Mildred Crest. He described the nature of the injuries, particularly an injury to the back of the head, a depressed skull fracture which, he said, could possibly have been made with a blunt instrument.

"Prior to the time of the automobile accident?" Calvert asked.

"Yes, sir."

"Immediately prior to the time of the automobile accident?"

"Yes, sir."

"Have you reached any conclusion as to the sequence of events leading to the death of the person whom you examined under the mistaken assumption that the body was that of Mildred Crest?"

"Yes, I have."

"What is that event sequence?"

"I believe that the injury to the back of the head was sustained *before* the wounds which were received on the front of the face and which made the face virtually unrecognizable. I believe that death ensued before the burns which were on the body of the deceased."

"Cross-examine," Calvert said.

Mason studied the witness for a moment, then asked, "You subsequently learned that the body was that of Fern Driscoll, and was not the body of Mildred Crest?"

"I did. Yes, sir."

"Now then, the depressed fracture in the back of the head, which you have mentioned and which you feel could have been an injury which was incurred before the automobile accident: do I understand you to mean that this injury could have been inflicted with a weapon?"

"It is *exactly* the type of injury which would have been inflicted with a round bar of some sort."

Mason said, "The photographs of the accident show the body on the right-hand side of the car with the head and shoulders partially protruding from the opened door?"

"Yes."

"Indicating that the person had opened the car door and started to jump out?" Mason asked.

"I wouldn't say as to that."

"How could the position of the body be accounted for otherwise?"

"The body could have been deliberately placed in that position."

"You mean," Mason said, "that some person, and I take it you have in mind the defendant, could have partially opened the door of the car, held the head and part of the shoulders of Fern Driscoll out of the car with one hand while driving over the bank with the other?"

"That could have been done. Yes, sir."

"Holding a body half-in and half-out of the car with the right hand, driving the car with the left hand?"

"It could have been done."

"It would have taken a great deal of strength?"

"It might have."

"And would have necessitated the driver of the car remaining in the car while it plunged down the deep canyon?"

"Yes."

"What assurance, then, did the driver have that she wouldn't be killed or seriously injured in the plunge?"

The witness hesitated. "Quite naturally, she couldn't have had any assurance at all."

"The bank was so steep that it was rather unusual for one of the persons in the car to be uninjured?"

"It was *very* unusual, almost miraculous."

"Then what would have been the motive for the defendant to have killed Fern Driscoll and held her body partially out of the car, if the probabilities were the defendant would also be killed?"

"If the Court please, that's argumentative," Calvert objected.

Judge Bolton smiled. "It *is* argumentative, but this witness, as an expert, has given reasons for his conclusions which give counsel the right to question his conclusions. The objection is overruled. Answer the question, Doctor."

The witness pursed his lips, shifted his position in the witness chair. "Of course, I can't duplicate the defendant's reasoning. She may well have contemplated suicide."

"Then the murder of Fern Driscoll would have done her no good?"

The witness squirmed uncomfortably. "That, I believe, is obvious."

"Now," Mason went on, "assuming that the decedent, whom you autopsied, had become panic-stricken when the car started to go over the grade and had jerked open the door on the right-hand side of the car trying to get out, would the position of the body, under those circumstances, have been the same as that of the body shown in this photograph?"

"Well...it could have been."

"And if the decedent had done that," Mason said, "isn't it possible that the doorpost of the automobile could have struck the back of her head at the first impact and left a depressed fracture exactly such as you have described?"

"Well...I don't know."

"Of course, you don't know," Mason said. "You've testified to a whole series of surmises. Now, I'm asking you if it isn't possible that the injury could have been sustained in that manner."

"It is possible, yes."

"And isn't it equally possible, as far as anything that *you* know of your *own* knowledge, from anything that you discovered at the autopsy, that the injury could just as well have been caused in that manner as by a blow inflicted with a round bar?"

"Well...perhaps."

"Yes or no?" Mason asked.

"Yes," the harassed witness blurted.

"Thank you," Mason said, smiling. "That's all."

Calvert put on the stand the manager of the Consolidated Sales and Distribution Company, who testified that the defendant had applied for a position with him and had given her name as Fern Driscoll; that she had given the social security number of Fern Driscoll; that she had stated her place of residence was Lansing, Michigan; and had further stated that she had recently arrived in the city and was looking for work.

Mason asked no questions on cross-examination.

The manager of the apartment house testified that the defendant rented an apartment, giving the name of Fern Driscoll and showing a driving license and social security card in the name of Fern Driscoll.

Again there was no cross-examination.

"Call George Kinney," Calvert said.

George Kinney held up his right hand, was sworn, gave his place of residence as Lansing, Michigan, and was, it turned out, the cashier of the Baylor Manufacturing and Development Company. George Kinney was also a shrewd individual who listened carefully to questions and had apparently been coached by some astute attorney as to exactly what he was to say, and exactly what he was to refrain from saying.

"Were you acquainted with an employee of the Baylor Manufacturing and Development Company named Fern Driscoll?"

"I was. Yes, sir."

"How long had she been in the employ of the corporation?"

"Two years, approximately."

"When did she sever her connections with the company?"

"On the ninth of last month."

"At the time she severed her connections, did you give her any money?"

"Yes, sir."

"How much?"

"I gave her a check covering the amount of her wages and severance pay."

"Did you give her anything else?"

"No, sir."

"During the period of her employment, had you come to know Fern Driscoll personally?"

"Yes, sir."

"At the time she terminated her employment, did you discuss with her the fact that her action was rather abrupt, and did she then and there make a statement to you as to the reason she was leaving the company?"

"Objected to," Mason said. "Incompetent, irrelevant, and immaterial. Hearsay as far as this defendant is concerned."

"Sustained!" Judge Bolton snapped.

"Did you notice her appearance at that time?"

"I did."

"Was there anything unusual in her appearance?"

"Objected to as incompetent, irrelevant, and immaterial. Not binding on the defendant," Mason said.

"I'll hear the testimony," Judge Bolton said. "I think that may be pertinent. In view of the contention of the prosecution, the objection is overruled."

Kinney said, "She was very shaken. She was very white. She undoubtedly had been crying. Her eyes were swollen and red."

"That's all," Calvert said.

"You say that you knew her rather intimately?" Mason asked.

"I knew her personally, yes."

"By the way," Mason asked, "did she own an automobile?"

"Yes, sir."

"Do you know what kind of car it was?"

"I'm not sure of the make of the car, but I think it was a Ford. It was, I believe, about three years old. She had recently purchased it secondhand."

"That car was registered in Michigan? It had Michigan license plates?"

"She lived in Michigan, purchased the car in Michigan, and drove the car in Michigan," Kinney said with polite sarcasm. "One would naturally assume it had Michigan license plates."

"Thank you," Mason said with elaborate politeness. "That's all."

"I have one further question which perhaps I should have asked on direct examination," Calvert said.

"Very well," Judge Bolton said. "Ask your question."

"Shortly prior to the time Miss Driscoll left your employ, did Mr. Forrester Baylor have you withdraw rather a large sum of money from the bank for him, and did you turn that money over to him in cash?"

"Objected to as incompetent, irrelevant, and immaterial," Mason said.

"If the Court please," Calvert said, "I would like to show that, at the time she left Michigan, Miss Driscoll had a rather large amount of money in her purse. I have shown that the defendant could not possibly have acquired some four thousand dollars in addition to her own bank account and salary check by any legitimate means. I would like to be permitted to show by inference that Fern Driscoll received rather a large sum of money from Forrester Baylor."

"You intend to show that by inference?"

"It is the only way I can show it, Your Honor."

Judge Bolton shook his head. "The objection is sustained."

"If the Court please," Calvert insisted, "I feel that we are entitled to resort to circumstantial evidence to prove motivation for the death of Fern Driscoll, particularly as we intend to show that Carl Harrod had acquired all this information."

"You may resort to circumstantial evidence," Judge Bolton said, "and draw logical inferences from it, but you can't establish the circumstantial evidence by inference."

"Very well," Calvert said, "I have no further questions of this witness."

"No further cross-examination," Mason said.

"Call your next witness," Judge Bolton said.

"Call Sgt. Holcomb," Calvert announced.

Holcomb took the witness stand, testified that he was a member of the Homicide Squad; that he had been so employed on the second of the month; that on that date he had been called to an apartment occupied by Carl Harrod; that the person who had called him had given her name as Nellie Harrod and had stated that she was the wife of Carl Harrod; that when he arrived there Carl Harrod was dead.

"Did you make a search of the apartment occupied by this defendant under the name of Fern Driscoll?"

"Yes."

"Did you find any money in that apartment?"

"I did."

"What did you find?"

"I found four hundred and thirty-six dollars in currency of various denominations, and then I found forty, new one-hundred-dollar bills."

"No other money?"

"No other money."

"I may wish to recall Sgt. Holcomb later for other aspects of the case," Calvert said, "but I have no further questions in regard to this matter. You may cross-examine, Mr. Mason."

Mason said, "I have no questions."

Sgt. Holcomb left the stand.

Foley Calvert said, "If the Court please, I have one more witness I would like to put on before the noon adjournment. This witness will give very brief testimony."

"Very well," Judge Bolton said, glancing at the clock.

"Miss Irma Karnes," Calvert called.

Irma Karnes, a rather thin, young woman with a prominent, pinched nose, small lips, and eyes which peered out through heavy-lensed glasses, came forward and took her seat on the witness stand.

"Your name is Irma Karnes? You reside here in this city?"

"Yes, sir."

"And were so residing on the second of this month?"

"Yes, sir."

"What was your occupation on the second of this month?"

"I was manager of the notions department in the Arcade Novelty Company."

"And where is the Arcade Novelty Company, with reference to the apartment occupied by the defendant, if you know?"

"About three and a half blocks."

"Are you open during the evening?"

"Yes, until eleven-thirty."

"Can you describe the nature of the business?"

"It is a varied business. There is a penny arcade, so called, with the peep-show type of entertainment. There are electric guns shooting at moving game and electric machine guns shooting at airplanes. In fact, there are a whole host of novelty machines. Then back in the arcade we keep a line of notions and novelties."

"Such as what?" Calvert asked.

"Bottle openers, ice picks, corkscrews, tumblers, plastic buckets for ice, thermal containers for ice cubes, needles, threads, buttons, neckties, shaving supplies, razor blades. In short, a whole list of notions and novelties of the kind persons might want to buy at night."

"You mentioned ice picks?"

"Yes, sir."

"Now, do you remember any transaction connected with ice picks on the second of this month?"

"Yes, sir. I do indeed."

"What was that transaction?"

"A young woman came in and bought three ice picks. As it happened, those were all of the ice picks we had on display in the little glass compartment where we keep the ice picks. After she had gone, I went to replace the stock and then found that we had only half a dozen ice picks left in stock."

"So what did you do then?" Calvert asked.

"Is this relevant to the case?" Judge Bolton asked.

"Quite relevant, Your Honor."

"Very well, go on. There seems to be no objection on the part of defense counsel. However, it would seem to me to be somewhat remote."

"It is simply for the purpose of making an identification, if the Court please."

"Very well. She may answer."

The witness said, "I put those six ice picks in the display stand. I took some Scotch tape and price tags, preparing to put price tags on the ice picks, but before I did so, I looked up the catalog number and put a gross of ice picks on our want list. It was then I discovered that there had been a paste-over in the catalog and that ice picks had gone up in price."

"So what did you do?"

"The other ice picks had been thirty-eight cents, three for a dollar. I found I would have to sell the new ice picks at forty-one cents straight, in order to keep our margin of profit, so I put the new price on those ice picks."

"And were some of those ice picks purchased that same evening while you were there in the store?"

"Yes, sir."

"Who purchased them?"

She pointed a long finger at Mildred Crest. "The defendant came in and purchased three ice picks."

"At the new price?"

"At the new price."

"And that new price was written on labels fastened to the ice picks and covered with transparent plastic tape?"

"Yes."

"And those were the three ice picks which were purchased by the defendant in this case?"

"Yes, sir."

"That is all. You may cross-examine," Calvert said.

"Just a moment," Judge Bolton announced. "It appears that it is time for the usual noon recess. Court will take a recess until two o'clock this afternoon. The defendant is remanded to custody."

CHAPTER TWELVE

Perry Mason, Della Street, and Paul Drake sat in the little, private dining room in the restaurant which they patronized so frequently when Mason was in court.

Mason, regarding his plate in frowning concentration, hardly touched his food. "They've got everything mixed up now," he said at length.

"You mean the ice pick?" Drake asked.

Mason nodded. "Their anxiety to force an identification of the defendant as the one who purchased the murder weapon means they got the wrong person, and if they did that, they must have the wrong ice pick."

"After all," Della Street said, "there is a certain superficial resemblance between Mildred Crest and me."

Mason nodded. "This is just another one of those cases of mistaken personal identification.

"In the mind of the average man, circumstantial evidence most frequently results in a miscarriage of justice. Actually, circumstantial evidence is the best evidence we have. It is only our interpretation of circumstantial evidence which makes for miscarriages of justice. The most deadly, dangerous evidence, the one which has resulted so many, many times in miscarriages of justice, is personal identification evidence."

"But how do you know they have the wrong ice pick?" Drake asked.

Mason said, "I planted one ice pick in Harrod's apartment at a time when I was satisfied he was trying to lay a foundation for blackmail. I hoped Harrod might become confused. Of course, at the time I had no idea he was fatally wounded."

"And now you think it was Nellie who became confused?" Drake asked.

"Not Nellie," Mason said. "The police were the ones who walked into the trap."

"What happened?"

"They found that some woman, whom they may or may not know was Katherine Baylor, had bought three ice picks; that thereafter some other woman had been in and bought three more, and that this second purchase could be differentiated from the first because there was a different price tag."

"So what happened?" Della Street asked.

"They talked to the girl who was running the place. She remembered the two transactions. Naturally, it occurred to the police that if they would prove that Mildred Crest was the one who bought the second batch of ice picks, and that those ice picks could be distinguished by the new price mark, they would have a perfect case against Mildred."

"And so they forced an identification?" Paul Drake asked.

"They probably forced the identification to this extent—they arranged for Irma Karnes to have an opportunity to see Mildred Crest when Mildred didn't know she was under observation. They didn't have a line-up. They simply gave the witness an opportunity for a surreptitious survey.

"And, of course, they used all their power of suggestion in telling Irma Karnes that they knew they had the girl in custody who had bought the ice picks; that it was simply a question of having her make the identification."

"So she made the identification?" Della Street asked.

Mason nodded.

"Just watch the expression on the face of that witness when she sees me!" Della said gleefully.

"Just how are you going to spring your trap?" Drake asked Mason.

"There," Mason said, "is the question. This is a case of mistaken identification. It's like any one of a thousand other cases. Only in this case we know the answer. *We* know the real purchaser and the police don't. When I confront this witness with Della Street, and the witness recognizes Della as the one who made the subsequent purchase of ice picks, there'll be a lot of commotion in court."

"But suppose she doesn't remember it was Della?" Drake asked.

"Then," Mason said thoughtfully, "my client might be in one hell of a jam, Paul. Of course, Della can always get on the stand and swear that she was the one who bought the ice picks, but in view of the fact she is working with me, her testimony would be taken with a grain of salt. . . . Judge Bolton will believe her, I think."

"The judge would," Drake said, "but how about a jury later on?"

"There, of course, is the rub," Mason admitted. "Judge Bolton knows me well enough to know that, if I put Della Street on the stand, it will be because I am absolutely convinced of the truth of her testimony. He doesn't know Della Street personally, but he knows she has been with me for a long while and is a trusted, confidential employee. He'll believe her.

"However, when Irma Karnes sees Della Street, it's almost certain that she will then realize she has made a mistake and will change her testimony."

"So what do you do?" Drake asked.

"So," Mason said, "I cross-examine this woman. I tie her up and get her so far out on a limb that when she is forced to back up she goes all to pieces."

"Then what happens?" Drake asked.

"Then," Mason said, "even if Judge Bolton binds the defendant over, I have a record on this witness so that when I get her in front of a jury later on, I'll mix her up like scrambled eggs. She'll be giving her entire testimony on the defensive."

"How about waiting until you do get her in front of a jury?" Drake asked. "Wouldn't it be better, since Judge Bolton will probably bind the defendant over anyway, to wait and pull this in front of a jury?"

"It would be better in many ways," Mason said, "but there's one thing against it."

"What?"

"The longer interval of time that elapses, the less likelihood there is that she'll change her testimony. By the time the case comes to trial in the superior court, she might even be so firmly convinced of her identification that she'll swear it was the defendant and that she had never seen Della Street in her life.

"No, I'm going to have to do it now in order to get the most good out of it. Even if she doesn't back up, the prosecutor will know that I wouldn't make a move of that sort unless it was true. They'll start hammering away at her between now and the time Mildred Crest goes to trial in the superior court. Then, by the time Irma Karnes gets on the stand in front of a jury, her entire attitude will be that of a woman who is very much on the defensive.

"However, the big thing is that, because of this fluke of identification, they *must have the wrong murder weapon.* Once the case gets to that point, there are infinite possibilities."

Drake said, "I'm going to be holding onto my chair watching what happens this afternoon."

"What do you want me to do?" Della Street asked.

"Keep out of sight," Mason said. "Irma Karnes probably saw you this morning, but I don't want her to see you any more until I call you to confront her. You can stay in one of the witness rooms and be available when I call you.

"When I do, that will show that you were the one who bought the new ice picks and then we've got the case on ice."

"But what will they say about the ethics of putting that ice pick in Harrod's apartment?"

"What *can* they say?" Mason asked. "We simply took an ice pick up to Harrod's apartment so I could ask Harrod if the ice pick with which he had been stabbed was identical to the one we had. Inadvertently, that ice pick was left in Harrod's apartment."

"But I can't swear to that," Della Street said.

"Bless your soul!" Mason told her. "*We* don't swear to anything except the truth. Your testimony is simply going to be that you bought three ice picks; that you took one of them up to Harrod's apartment, and that you left it there; that you were acting under my instructions."

"Will *you* then get on the stand?" Della Street asked apprehensively.

Mason shook his head. "I'll say to the Court that it's up to the prosecution to prove every step of its case. Everyone will know that I set a trap for Carl Harrod, and that the police walked into it. My justification will be that at the time I set the trap I thought I was dealing with a civil suit for damages. I had no idea of confusing the evidence in a murder case.... The main point is that the prosecution's entire case will turn out to be founded on incorrect evidence, an erroneous identification of the defendant, and the wrong ice pick as a murder weapon. That will leave the police and the deputy district attorney with very red faces."

"Well," Drake said, "it sounds all right the way you tell it, but somehow I have an idea that you're going to be walking on a tightrope over a very deep precipice."

Mason merely nodded.

"Well," Drake said, "you'd better be getting on up there. Then we'll see what's going to happen."

"On our way," Mason told him, glancing at his wrist watch. "This is where I'm going to have to ask just exactly the right questions in just exactly the right way. It's also a darned good lesson in the value of personal identification testimony. Here we have a case that's brought right home to us. And the worst of it is, Della, that mistaken identification could just as well have involved you in a murder if the circumstances had been different."

"How do you know it's not going to involve her in a murder the way it is?" Drake asked quietly.

Mason thought that over, then said, "Come on, Della. Let's go before Paul talks you into being guilty of killing Harrod."

"I wish I could sit in court this afternoon," Della Street ventured.

"Absolutely not," Mason told her firmly.

"Not even if I sat in the back row?"

"No, you might spring the trap too soon. I've got to play this *exactly* right."

"You can say *that* again," Paul Drake announced lugubriously.

"And in the meantime, Paul," Mason said, "I want to know where Fern Driscoll's car is."

"Why?"

"Because I want to search it for evidence. Call your office and start your bloodhounds baying."

"Okay," Drake said. "We'll get busy."

CHAPTER THIRTEEN

Judge Bolton said, "Let the record show the defendant is in court; that counsel for both sides are in attendance. I believe the witness, Irma Karnes, was on the stand and the direct examination had been concluded. Cross-examination on behalf of the defense was about to begin.

"Take the stand, Miss Karnes."

Irma Karnes walked to the stand with her long-legged, stiff-backed gait and looked at Perry Mason, blinking her eyes behind the thick-lensed glasses.

Mason said affably and casually, "I take it you wear those glasses all the time, Miss Karnes?"

"No, sir," she said.

"No?" Mason asked.

"No."

"When can you dispense with them?"

"When I'm asleep."

Laughter rippled through the courtroom. Irma Karnes held her face completely without expression so that it was impossible to tell whether she had deliberately set the stage for her remark or whether she was a literal-minded person who carefully took every statement at its face value.

"Do you," Mason asked, "know who the first young woman was who purchased three of the ice picks?"

"I do now. I didn't then."

"You know now?"

"Yes."

"Who was it?"

"Miss Katherine Baylor."

"And when did you learn that it was Miss Katherine Baylor?"

Calvert said, "Just a moment. Your Honor, I object on the ground that this is not proper cross-examination; that it is incompetent, irrelevant, and immaterial."

Judge Bolton shook his head. "The witness mentioned the first purchase. In fact, the witness made it an important part of her testimony. Therefore, counsel is entitled to go into it. Answer the question."

"It was...I don't know, rather recently."

"Who told you it was Katherine Baylor?"

"The police."

"The police told you Katherine Baylor was the young woman who purchased those first three ice picks?"

"Yes."

"Then the only knowledge that you have on this point is what the police told you?"

"No, sir. That's not right."

"Well, what *is* right?"

"They told me who it was, but they said they wanted me to take a look at her so I could be sure."

"In other words, *they* gave *you* the information, and then told you they wanted you to look so *you* could make an identification?"

"Well, yes."

"You knew you were expected to make the identification before you saw Miss Baylor?"

"Oh, Your Honor," Calvert said, "this is consuming the time of the Court and making a mountain out of a molehill. If counsel is at all concerned about the matter, *I'll* state that Katherine Baylor not only doesn't deny purchasing those first three ice picks, but presently I'm going to put her on the witness stand and she's going to testify to it."

"The fact remains, if the Court please," Mason said, "I am entitled to cross-examine this witness in my own way."

Judge Bolton nodded. "I think I see the point counsel is leading up to. Go right ahead."

"Isn't that a fact?" Mason asked the witness. "You knew that you were expected to make an identification of Miss Baylor as soon as you saw her?"

"I don't know what the police expected. I'm not a mind reader."

Mason said, "I'm not asking you what the police expected you to do. I'm asking you whether you knew what you were expected to do."

"I can't say."

"They told you that you were going to see Miss Baylor?"

"Yes."

"And they told you that she was the young woman who had made the first purchase of the three ice picks. Isn't that right?"

"Yes."

"So when you saw her, you knew that the police expected you to make the identification."

"Objected to as calling for a conclusion of the witness," Calvert said. "She can't testify as to what the police expected."

"The objection is sustained," Judge Bolton ruled.

"Well, the police *told* you that they expected you to make the identification, didn't they?"

"Not in so many words."

"At least by their actions and they also intimated that, didn't they?"

"Well, yes."

"Now then," Mason said, "when did you first know that it was Mildred Crest who made the second purchase of ice picks that night?"

"Just a short time after her arrest."

"What do you mean by the expression, a short time?"

"I mean it was only a short time."

"Two or three days?"

"Sooner."

"And did the police follow the same procedure in that instance? Did *they* tell *you* that Mildred Crest was the person who had purchased the second lot of three ice picks?"

"It was my understanding that she had."

"And did they tell you they expected you to make an identification?"

"Well, I knew that the police were certain she had made the purchase. Then when I saw her, *I* knew that she was the one who had made the purchase."

"You identified her to the police?"

"Yes."

"Did you meet her face to face?"

"I saw her clearly."

"Did you talk with her?"

"No."

"Did you hear her voice?"

"Yes."

"Where did this identification take place?"

"It was in a room—an interrogation room. There's a big mirror at one end of the room. That is, it's a mirror which shows a reflection to any person on the inside looking out, but it's a window to anyone who is in the adjoining room looking in. You see very distinctly, but the person in the other room can't see you at all."

"So you sat in this observation room and the defendant was ushered into the interrogation room and you looked at her through the one-way mirror, did you not?"

"Yes."

"And was there an officer with you at that time?"

"Yes."

"More than one?"

"Yes."

"How many?"

"Three."

"And did those officers make comments?"

"They were talking."

"To you?"

"Yes, and among themselves."

"And the gist of their conversation was that the defendant, Mildred Crest, was the girl who had purchased the ice picks, isn't that true?"

"They mentioned something to that effect. They were also discussing other things."

"Things which were calculated to prejudice you against the defendant, discussing the fact that she was supposed to have murdered Fern Driscoll?"

"They said something like that."

"Just what did they say?"

"I can't remember their exact words, but they said she had murdered Fern Driscoll, had stolen her money and, when Harrod found out about it, had stabbed him with an ice pick she bought from the store where I work."

"So *after* they said all that, you made the identification, did you?"

"Well, when I saw the defendant, I knew she was the one."

"Right away, the minute you saw her?"

"Yes."

"How long were you in this observation room?"

"About ten minutes, I guess."

"And how long were you in the observation room after the defendant was led into the interrogation room?"

"She was brought in within just a few seconds of the time I entered the observation room."

"And she was in the interrogation room all of the time you were in the observation room?"

"Yes."

"Which was a period of at least ten minutes?"

"I would say so."

"It could have been more?"

"Perhaps."

"But it couldn't have been less?"

"I think it was at least ten minutes."

"And during all of that time the officers were asking you to look the defendant over carefully?"

"Yes."

"Now then," Mason said, "if you made the identification as soon as the defendant walked in the room, what was the reason for the officers to keep you there for ten minutes, asking you to look the defendant over carefully?"

"Well, they said they wanted me to be sure."

"Weren't *you* sure?"

"I was, yes."

"You were sure when you left the room?"

"Yes."

"Were you sure before that?"

"I thought I was."

"Yet you kept looking at the defendant during all that ten-minute period?"

"Yes."

"Studying her features?"

"Yes."

"Why?"

"Well, the officers suggested—Am I at liberty to tell what they said?"

Calvert grinned. "Go right ahead. What *did* the officers say?"

"Well, they said that Mr. Mason was going to be representing the defendant, that he was noted for being tricky and that he might arrange to have some other young woman brought in and try to trick me that way. They said that I should study the defendant carefully so that Mr. Mason couldn't—Well, the way they expressed it was 'run in a ringer.'"

"And was that the reason you made such a careful study of the defendant?" Mason asked.

"Yes."

"For a period of ten minutes?"

"Yes."

"Now going back to the night of the second," Mason said, "what were your duties there at the Arcade Novelty Company?"

"Well, I acted as cashier."

"What were your duties as cashier?"

"To make change, giving out nickels, pennies and dimes as they were required."

"Anything else?"

"I sort of kept an eye on the various people to see what they were doing and see that everything was running in an orderly manner."

"Anything else?"

"No. That's about all."

"But you were also acting as saleslady?"

"Oh yes. I sold merchandise whenever anybody came in and wanted something."

"And wrapped the merchandise for them?"

"Usually I just dropped it in a paper bag."

"That took quite a bit of your time?"

"Not so much."

"Didn't quite a few people come in?"

"Well, it's a self-service place. That is, the people pick out what they want and bring it up to the cashier to be paid for and wrapped. About all I have to do is to ring up the money in the cash register and drop the articles in a paper bag. We keep an assortment of paper bags on a shelf right beneath the cash register."

"Then a big percentage of your time is put in making change for customers and watching what is going on in the Arcade?"

"Yes. Mostly watching, keeping an eye on things."

"You have quite a few customers?"

"Quite a few."

"And you try to keep an eye on what they're doing?"

"Yes. I have to make certain that things are run in an orderly manner; that the young men don't annoy the women who don't want to be annoyed."

"What do you mean by that?"

"Well, of course, if young women are sociably inclined and don't resent attention, why that's all right, but, if some young men become obnoxious or try to force their attentions on customers, then we do something about it."

"So you keep a sharp eye on what is going on?"

"Yes."

"I take it then that you're trained to see things that go on."

"Indeed I am, Mr. Mason. You have to have an eagle eye to run a place like that. You get so you're trained to see the faintest suspicion of a false motion."

"That is, you know what to look for?"

"Yes."

"And you keep looking?"

"Yes."

"Your spectacles have rather a heavy correction?"

"I'm blind as a bat without my spectacles, but with them I see very well."

"Directly in front of you?"

"Yes."

"Your vision to the side is somewhat impaired?"

"Yes, but I can see all right. That's my job, to see what's going on."

"You're also making change at the cash register?" Mason asked.

"Yes. I said I was. I told you that."

"And ringing up purchases?"

"Yes."

"Suppose there would be a shortage at the cash register?"

"There never is. Not when I'm on duty."

"You don't make mistakes?"

"No."

"How does it happen you have such a perfect record?"

"Concentration largely."

"By that I take it you mean that, when you're making change, you think about making change and nothing else."

"Exactly."

"And you don't make mistakes?"

"I never have. My cash has always balanced out to the penny."

"When you're ringing up a sale," Mason said, "you concentrate on making the correct change?"

"Yes."

"And putting the proper amount of money in the proper compartment in the cash register?"

"Yes."

"During that time your eyes necessarily are averted from what is going on in the Arcade, are they not?"

"That is true, Mr. Mason. But you learn to make the interval as brief as possible. And even during that interval you're sort of keeping an eye on things with an occasional quick glance."

"I take it then," Mason said, "that even while you're smiling at the customer you're actually looking over past the customer's shoulder to see that the place is being operated in an orderly manner."

"That's right."

"Now, just how clearly do you remember the transaction when the person you say was the defendant bought the three ice picks?"

"Quite clearly."

"Do you remember whether she paid you the exact purchase price or—"

"Certainly I remember. She put down a five-dollar bill. I gave her her change and I remember telling her that the ice picks had been three for a dollar earlier in the evening, but that when I replenished the stock in the display case I noticed that the price had gone up and so put a new price tag on the ice picks."

"The ice picks were then forty-one cents straight?"

"That's right."

"So three ice picks amounted to a dollar and twenty-three cents?"

"Yes."

"Plus sales tax?"

"Yes."

"How long do you suppose the person you state was the defendant was standing in front of you? How long did the transaction take place?"

"Just a few seconds."

"You didn't have any extended conversation?"

"No."

"The customer just handed you the ice picks, you rang up the money, took out the change, dropped the ice picks in a bag and handed them to her with the comment that they had been cheaper earlier in the evening?"

"That is right, yes, sir."

"Did you do all that within a period of ten seconds, would you say?"

"Let me see. Ten seconds." The witness closed her eyes. "Yes. I think so. I would say that ten seconds would probably be just about the right time interval."

"Now, during that ten seconds," Mason said, "you were making change of a dollar and twenty-three cents, plus sales tax, out of a five-dollar bill?"

"Yes, sir."

"And during that time, following your custom, you were concentrating on the operation of the cash register, on putting the five-dollar bill in the proper receptacle, taking out the change and being sure that you had the right amount?"

"Yes, sir."

"And during a part of that time, while you were smiling at the customer, you were looking over her shoulder into the Arcade to make certain that everything was being conducted in an orderly manner?"

"I suppose so."

"That is your usual custom?"

"Yes."

"So that out of the ten-second interval you were actually looking at the person who you claim was the defendant for only a small portion of that time, perhaps two or three seconds?"

"Well...I saw her well enough to recognize her."

"Perhaps two or three seconds out of the ten-second interval you were looking directly at the customer?" Mason asked.

"Perhaps."

"Could it have been more?"

"Well, let's see. I was looking at the cash register and—Well, perhaps half of the time I was looking directly at the customer."

"That would be five seconds?"

"Yes."

"But while you were looking at her you were also looking over her shoulder past her at the Arcade?"

"I guess I did."

"So that would cut down the five seconds' time?"

"Yes."

"Yet," Mason said, "when you looked at the defendant at police headquarters so that you could be sure I didn't run a ringer in on you, *it took you ten minutes, ten full minutes*, during which you were concentrating *entirely* on the features of the defendant. It took you ten, long minutes before you could be sure that you wouldn't be led into a trap and that you'd know her when you saw her again?"

"Well...it wasn't necessary for me to look at her that long."

"Then why did you do it?"

"I wanted to be *absolutely* certain."

"It took you ten minutes before you were *absolutely* certain?"

"Oh, I suppose so, if you insist."

"Ten full minutes of concentrated study," Mason said, "as opposed to two and a half seconds' casual observation."

"Well, I—Of course, at the time of the purchase, I—"

"Exactly," Mason said. "At that time you didn't have any particular reason for studying the features of your customer. Whereas when you were looking at the defendant, you knew you were going to be called on to make an identification and you had to be absolutely positive that someone didn't trick you. Isn't that right?"

"Yes."

"Thank you," Mason said with a smile. "That's all."

Calvert hesitated as though debating whether to try and salvage something from the testimony concerning the time element, then apparently decided against it. "That's all," he said.

"Your next witness," Judge Bolton said.

"Call Katherine Baylor," Calvert said.

Katherine Baylor came to the stand, took the oath, gave her name and residence to the court reporter, looked to Calvert for questioning.

"You are acquainted with the defendant, Mildred Crest?"

"Yes."

"When did you first meet her?"

"On the second of this month."

"Where did you first meet her?"

"At her apartment."

"Under what name was she going when you met her?"

"Well, she admitted to me—"

"Kindly listen to the question," Calvert interrupted. "Under what name was she going when you first met her?"

"The name of Fern Driscoll."

"Did you, on the evening of the second, purchase some ice picks from the Arcade Novelty Company?"

"I did."

"How many ice picks?"

"Three."

"What did you pay for them?"

"One dollar."

"Do you remember the price that was marked on the ice picks?"

"Yes, sir. I do."

"What was the price?"

"It was thirty-eight cents, three for a dollar."

"What did you do with those ice picks?"

"I took them to the apartment with me."

"You mean the apartment that the defendant was occupying under the name of Fern Driscoll?"

"Yes."

"And what did you do with them there?"

"I put one of them in my purse, and left the other two there on a table by the entranceway."

"And did you have some conversation with the defendant about them?"

"Yes."

"About using them?"

"Yes."

"About using them in what way?"

"As weapons."

"What did you tell her?"

"I told her an ice pick made a wonderful weapon; that if you needed to make a man keep his distance, an ice pick would do the trick."

"Did you say anything else about them?"

"I suggested putting a cork on the end of the ice pick so that it could be carried in a purse."

"And you put one of those ice picks in your purse?"

"Yes."

"Now, Miss Baylor, you are under oath. I want you to think carefully. Did you have any conversation with the defendant in which she told you she wanted these ice picks as weapons to use against Carl Harrod?"

"No."

"She didn't tell you that?"

"No."

"Or words to that effect?"

"No."

"You gave her these ice picks as weapons?"

"Yes."

"Did *you* suggest she use them, or one of them, as a weapon to intimidate Carl Harrod?"

The witness hesitated.

"Did you?"

"I told her if Carl Harrod tried any more blackmail, she could threaten him with an ice pick—to protect herself—in self-defense."

"And she accepted these ice picks from you after that conversation?"

"I just left them there in her apartment."

"Thank you. That's all. The defense may take the witness."

"Did you ever meet Carl Harrod in his lifetime?" Mason asked.

"I met him, yes."

"How did you happen to meet him?"

"He came to the defendant's apartment while I was there."

"What did you do?"

"I opened the door."

"He was standing there?"

"He was standing there."

"You recognized him?"

"He told me who he was."

"And what did you do?"

"I told him how I felt about blackmailers and then slapped his face."

"Did you, at that time, stab him with an ice pick?"

"Certainly not!"

"You say that you put one of these ice picks in your purse?"

"Yes."

"Why?"

"Because I wanted to carry it with me."

"Why?"

"To protect myself."

"Against whom?"

"Against anyone who might attack me."

"Did you feel that someone might attack you?"

"Yes."

"Who?"

"I have told you, Mr. Mason, I had slapped Carl Harrod's face. I was under no illusions about the character of Carl Harrod. He was a blackmailer who had—"

"Now, just a moment! Just a moment!" Calvert interrupted. "If the Court please, I feel that the witness should be admonished only to answer questions, not to volunteer any disparaging remarks concerning the character of the deceased."

Judge Bolton said, "I think, Mr. Prosecutor, the situation is obvious. The Court was not born yesterday. However, the law is the law, and the character of a decedent in a murder case is not in issue. However, the witness will refrain from making statements as to the character of the decedent."

"You felt you might have some trouble with Carl Harrod?" Mason asked.

"Yes."

"And for that reason put an ice pick in your purse?"

"Yes."

"Where is that ice pick now?"

"I don't know."

"You don't know?"

"No."

"Where was it when you saw it last?"

"I...I threw it away."

"And why did you do that?"

"Someone suggested that I should."

"Your father?"

"Yes."

"And why did your father make that suggestion?"

"We knew that Carl Harrod had been stabbed with an ice pick. My father knew that I had slapped his face. I told him about buying the ice picks. He suggested I had better get rid of the one that I had."

"When did this conversation take place?"

"On the second of this month, the day Harrod died."

"Do you remember that I visited your father on that date?"

"Yes."

"And while I was there, Sgt. Holcomb telephoned?"

"I believe so. Yes."

"Now then, when did you dispose of the ice pick with reference to my visit?"

"Immediately after you left and before Sgt. Holcomb came."

"And what did you do with it?"

"I took the elevator to the freight entrance. I went out in the alley where there were some trash cans. I raised the lid of one of the trash cans, put the ice pick in there, and then returned to the room."

"You were back in your suite at the hotel before Sgt. Holcomb arrived?"

"Yes."

"Did you tell him about what you had done with the ice pick?"

"No."

"Did you tell anyone?"

"No. I refused to discuss my testimony with anyone. I said that I would tell my story on the witness stand and that I wouldn't talk before I got on the witness stand."

"I see," Mason said. "You did, however, admit buying the three ice picks?"

"My father did, after Sgt. Holcomb told him that Carl Harrod had told his wife I had slapped his face, and that—"

"Just a moment," Calvert interrupted. "I object to the witness relating any conversation which took place with Sgt. Holcomb. That is hearsay."

"On the contrary, Your Honor," Mason said. "It is a fact in this case, so far as it concerns the motivation or bias of this witness. I am entitled to show the attitude of mind of this witness insofar as it may pertain to any bias either for or against the defense."

"The objection is overruled," Judge Bolton said. "Go on with your statement, Miss Baylor."

"Well, Sgt. Holcomb said that Mrs. Harrod, or the woman who was supposed to be Mrs. Harrod, had told the police that I had slapped Carl Harrod's face, and that, when Mr. Mason had been there getting a statement from Mr. Harrod, he had insinuated I was the one who had stabbed Harrod with an ice pick. Under the circumstances, Sgt. Holcomb suggested that a determined attempt might be made to have it appear I had done the stabbing and...and he didn't want to have that happen."

"Did you tell him about buying the ice picks?"

"No, *I* didn't tell him. My father told him. I made no statement whatever. I simply sat there."

"And Sgt. Holcomb didn't question you?"

"No."

"But talked with your father?"

"Yes."

Mason smiled. "Did Sgt. Holcomb say to your father that it might be better if he didn't question you at all until after he knew more of the facts, so that you wouldn't be a vulnerable witness in case I should take you on cross-examination?"

"Something like that."

"And your father told Sgt. Holcomb that you had purchased the three ice picks and given them to the defendant?"

"Yes."

"And did Sgt. Holcomb ask you or your father what had happened to the missing ice pick?"

"No, sir," she said. "He didn't know one was missing. They were all there in the apartment. That was the thing I couldn't understand; but I said nothing and my father said nothing. I don't think the officers knew about any other ice pick."

"Now then," Mason said, "you gave the defendant two of the ice picks?"

"Yes."

"To be used as weapons in case of necessity?"

"Yes."

"Can you suggest any reason why the defendant, having two ice picks which you had given her to be used as weapons, should go down to the Arcade Novelty Company and buy three more ice picks?"

"No, sir, I cannot. I have discussed that matter with my father, and we decided—"

"Just a moment!" Calvert interrupted. "We object to any statement as to what she said to her father or what her father said to her."

"The objection is sustained," Judge Bolton said. "In fact, the entire question asked by the defense counsel is argumentative."

"I have no objection to the question on that ground," Calvert said. "The prosecution has its own theory in the matter, and I think it is obvious. If Mr. Mason cross-examines this witness as to the reason the defendant might have had for purchasing those three ice picks, I intend to go into the matter on redirect examination."

"That's the vice of these questions which go far afield," Judge Bolton said. "The Court will of its own motion terminate this line of cross-examination. That question is argumentative, and the witness need not answer."

"The prosecution feels it is obvious, Your Honor," Calvert said, "that the defendant in this case wanted the crime blamed on Katherine Baylor. Knowing that Katherine Baylor had taken *one* of the ice picks away in her purse, the defendant purchased other ice picks so that the police would be led to believe that the two ice picks Katherine Baylor had given the defendant were still in the defendant's apartment, and therefore couldn't have been used in inflicting the fatal stabbing. This, if the Court please, is one of the strongest points in our case, because it shows premeditation. If it hadn't been for the peculiar quirk of fate by which there were different price tags on the ice picks, the defendant's ruse might have gone undetected."

"You can argue the case after the evidence is in," Judge Bolton said. "As far as this witness is concerned, I don't care to have her interrogated as to the possible motives of the defendant. I suggest, however, that it is significant that this witness disposed of the ice pick she had in the manner she did."

Calvert shrugged his shoulders. "Of course, Your. Honor, the witness was acting under the advice of her father, and her father knew that Mr. Perry Mason—Well, he knew his reputation and knew that Mr. Mason would confuse the issues if it was at all possible."

"They're confused now," Mason said.

"Not to the prosecution, they aren't," Calvert snapped.

"That will do," Judge Bolton ruled. "Are there any further questions of this witness?"

"None, Your Honor," Mason said.

"Your next witness?" Judge Bolton asked Calvert.

"My next witness," Calvert announced, "is Nellie Elliston."

The woman Mason had seen in Harrod's apartment came forward. She was dressed in a neat, new outfit, well shod, with lustrous, sheer stockings, and had evidently spent some time in a beauty shop.

After she had given her name and address, Calvert started questioning her and in questioning pulled no punches.

"Your name is Nellie Elliston?"

"Yes."

"Have you ever gone under any other name?"

"Yes."

"What?"

"Mrs. Carl Harrod."

"Were you married to Harrod?"

"No."

"You were, however, living with him as his wife?"

"Yes."

"In Apartment 218 at the Dixiecrat Apartments?"

"That's right."

"How long had you known Harrod?"

"About two years."

"Where did you meet him?"

"In a bar."

"How soon did you commence living with him after you first met him?"

"About a week."

"You assumed the name of Nellie Harrod purely as a matter of convenience?"

"Yes."

"Calling your attention to the second of this month, you were then living with Carl Harrod at the Dixiecrat Apartments as his wife?"

"I was using his name. We were going to be married. There were some legal complications. We didn't wait for those to be ironed out."

"Well," Calvert said, his voice radiating approval, "thank you for being so frank, Miss Elliston, even at the expense of your good name and reputation. I am sure the Court will appreciate it. Now, can you tell us exactly what happened on the night of the second?"

"Carl had been out. He came back about—Oh, I don't know, about eight-thirty or nine o'clock. He had had a nosebleed. He got some fresh handkerchiefs and changed his shirt. I asked him what had happened and he said a girl had smashed him; that she had taken him entirely by surprise."

"Then what?"

"I asked him what he did to her and he said nothing; that she had slammed the door before he had a chance."

"And then what?"

"Then he went out again. I had an idea he was going back—"

"Never mind your ideas," Calvert interrupted. "Just answer questions and give us the facts. The Court isn't interested in what you may have thought, only in the facts."

"Yes, sir."

"Now, he went out and then what happened? When did you see him again?"

"He came back in about—Oh, I don't know, about something over an hour, perhaps an hour and a half. I didn't check the time."

"And what was his condition at that time?"

"He was coughing. He coughed up a speck or two of blood. At first I thought it was from the—"

"Tut, tut," Calvert chided, holding up his finger and smiling. "Not your thoughts, Miss Elliston, just what you know."

"Yes, he came back and told me—"

"Now, just a moment. At that time, did he say anything to you about the fact that he thought he might be going to die?"

"No."

"Do you know from anything he said whether he thought any injury he might have had at that time was fatal?"

"He didn't think it was fatal. He was thinking only in terms of collecting damages. He actually was jubilant. He said we'd have some real money coming in and that then he could get the legal difficulties straightened out and then we could be married and go abroad on a honeymoon."

"Very well. Then I don't think it is proper for you to tell the Court anything he may have said at *that* time. You can tell us what happened and that's all."

"Well, he telephoned the Drake Detective Agency and said he wanted to get in touch with Mr. Perry Mason. Then when he got Perry Mason on the telephone he told him—"

"Now, there again, I doubt if that is pertinent," Calvert said. "And, of course, you don't know of your own knowledge that he had Mr. Mason on the other end of the telephone, do you? You simply heard one end of the conversation?"

"Yes."

"So you can't testify that Mr. Mason was on the other end of the line. After that, what happened?"

"Then Mr. Mason came and his secretary, Miss Della Street, was with him."

"And what happened at that time?"

"Well, Carl told Mr. Mason that he had been stabbed—"

"Now, just a minute. Did he expect to die at that time? That is, did he believe death was imminent because of some wound he had received?"

"No, sir, he did not. He was still trying to lay the foundation for collecting big damages."

"Then I feel that is not a proper statement. In other words, it was not a dying declaration within the meaning of the law. Just go ahead and tell us what happened. Did Mr. Mason and Miss Street leave?"

"They left."

"And then what happened?"

"Carl had been putting on an act to impress Mr. Mason. He said he was having a chill. At least, I thought it was an act, and—"

"Not your thoughts, *please*," Calvert interrupted. "We want the facts—only the facts."

"Well, after Mr. Mason left, he said he was cold and I suggested a hot bath. I drew the bath and told him it was ready.

"Then Carl started to get up out of the chair and then all of a sudden he began to feel worse. He almost collapsed. His face became pale as ashes and a look of the most horrible surprise came over his face and he said, 'Nellie, Nellie, I'm dying!'"

"Then at *that* time did he go on and make any statement to you as to what had happened at the time he had received the wound or injury?"

"Yes, sir."

"Now then, I believe that is a dying declaration within the meaning of the law. I believe that you are entitled to relate what he said, just tell us what he said had happened."

Judge Bolton looked down at Perry Mason. "Any objection from the defense?"

"No objection," Mason said, "but I would like to examine the witness for the purpose of laying the foundation as to a dying declaration."

"Proceed," Judge Bolton said.

"He told you he was going to die?" Mason asked.

"At that time, yes."

"And how long was that before he died?"

"Only a few minutes. I don't believe it was over ten minutes."

"There had then been a sudden change in his condition from the time I saw him?"

"Yes. It started when he tried to get up. He got partway up and then fell back. It was then that look of horrible consternation, surprise, and I think a little of terror, came over his face."

"He said he was dying?"

"He said, 'Nellie, that damned wound is—Something's happened. It's reached my heart, I guess. I'm...I'm dying.'"

"And then what?"

"Then he clutched his chest and said, 'Nellie, I don't want to die.'"

"And then what happened?"

"Then is when he made the statement."

Mason nodded to Calvert. "It would seem to be a dying declaration within the meaning of the law. I have no objection. Let her go ahead and tell what happened."

"Very well," Calvert said. "I am satisfied that it is a dying declaration. Just go ahead, Miss Elliston, and tell what happened. At this time you may relate what he said, use his exact words if you can remember them. If you can't, give your best recollection of what he said."

"He said that he had gone back to the defendant's apartment, that he had decided to show her who was boss, that if she would give him the letters she had, he wouldn't expose her."

"He said that she was using Fern Driscoll's name but she was really Mildred Crest. He said she had murdered Fern Driscoll and he felt he could prove it."

"Did he say anything about accusing her of murder?"

"Yes. He said that she came to the door; that she finally let him in; that he made his proposition to her."

"Then what?" Calvert asked.

"He said she laughed at him, that she told him he was a blackmailer, that she felt he had a police record, that if he didn't get out and stay out, she would claim she had found him burglarizing her apartment and shoot him.

"He said they had words and that she was holding the door open for him, telling him to get out. He said that suddenly, just as he was leaving, she swung her fist against his chest, then slammed and locked the door.

"He said that he didn't realize she had had an ice pick in her hand until he was almost to the elevator, that then he saw the ice pick sticking in his chest.

"He said that he didn't think he was badly hurt, but he felt he could use the girl's action as a lever to make her lawyer, Perry Mason, turn over the letters to him, that he could then get a large sum of money, either from the magazine, or from Mr. Baylor."

"What happened to the ice pick?"

"He brought it home with him."

"He told you that the pick he brought home was the one with which he had been stabbed?"

"Yes."

"Where is that ice pick now?"

"I gave it to the police."

"Did you mark that ice pick in some way so that you would know it again if you saw it?"

"Yes."

"What did you do?"

"I scratched my initials on the wooden handle."

"When?"

"Before it left the apartment."

"I now show you an ice pick and ask you if that is the ice pick you have been referring to?"

"That is the one."

"I will show that to counsel for the defense," Calvert said, "and then ask that it be introduced in evidence."

Calvert stepped over to the counsel table and handed the ice pick to Mason.

Mason studied the ice pick carefully. "May I ask a few questions on the exhibit, Your Honor?"

"Certainly," Judge Bolton said.

Mason turned to the witness. "I notice that this ice pick has a price mark on it, a price tag which is placed on with some sort of adhesive and covered with a piece of transparent tape. This price tag bears the label of the Arcade Novelty Company and the mark 'forty-one cents.' Was this price tag on the ice pick when you received it from Carl Harrod?"

"Yes."

"You are *positive* this is the ice pick that Carl Harrod gave you?"

"Yes."

"This is the ice pick Carl Harrod told you had been pushed into his chest?"

"Yes."

"He handed you this ice pick?"

"Yes."

"And you marked it?"

"Yes."

"When did you mark it?"

"When the police came."

"One of the officers suggested that you should mark this ice pick?"

"Yes, sir."

"So that you wouldn't be confused when it came time to give your testimony?"

"So that it could be identified."

"Were there any other ice picks in your apartment?"

"Yes, there was one other."

"Where?"

"In the kitchen drawer."

"By that you mean a utility drawer in the kitchen?"

"Yes."

"What else did that drawer contain?"

"Some cooking spoons, a bottle opener, a few little things of that sort."

"Very good," Mason said. "Now, I'm anxious to get this straight: were there *two* ice picks in this utility drawer?"

"Yes."

"Do you mean that you put the ice pick with which Carl Harrod had been stabbed in the utility drawer?"

"Yes."

"How did that happen? Didn't you realize that—?"

"Carl came home. He seemed to be high."

"What do you mean by being high?"

"I mean high! You know the way a person is when he's high."

"He'd been drinking?"

"No."

"Marijuana?"

"Yes."

"And what did he say?"

"He seemed very jubilant. He told me that he'd really hit the jackpot."

"And then what?"

"He told me that he was a good provider. He said he'd bought me an ice pick, and he tossed that ice pick in the sink."

"And then?"

"I asked him what on earth we wanted an ice pick for. I told him we used ice cubes and had no need for an ice pick."

"And then?"

"Then he went in the other room, sat down, and we talked for a while. Then I went back to the kitchen. I noticed there was a little pinkish stain in the sink where the point of the ice pick had rested in a drop of water, but I thought nothing of it. I picked the ice pick up, washed it, and put it in the drawer."

"You *washed* it?"

"Yes, I *washed* it?"

"Why?"

"I didn't know where Carl had secured it or anything, and he'd been carrying it around with him. I always wash dishes and utensils before putting them away."

"Did you at that time know there was an ice pick in the drawer?"

"Very frankly, Mr. Mason, I didn't. It came as a great surprise to me after the police had asked me to produce the ice pick, when I opened the kitchen drawer and found that there were two of them."

"Is there any chance—Now I want you to listen to this very carefully," Mason said, "and I want you to consider your answer very carefully—is there *any* chance, any *possible* chance that you got the ice picks confused?"

"Absolutely not!"

"How do you know you didn't?"

"Because the ice pick that I put in that drawer was put in at a certain place, right near the front of the drawer, and this second ice pick was way in the back of the drawer. Moreover, there was no price tag on the other ice pick. I remember distinctly that the ice pick that Carl brought home with him had this price tag on it."

"You're positive?"

"I'm absolutely positive."

Mason nodded to the prosecutor. "Under the circumstances, I have no further questions and no objection to the ice pick being received in evidence."

"The ice pick will be received," Judge Bolton said.

"That concludes my direct examination of the witness, Your Honor," Calvert said.

"Cross-examine," Judge Bolton said to Perry Mason.

Mason regarded the witness thoughtfully for a moment, then said, "While I was talking with Carl Harrod, didn't he admit that the light was dim and he couldn't be certain that it was the defendant who had stabbed him? Didn't he admit there was a possibility that Katherine Baylor had opened the door and stabbed him?"

"Just a moment! Just a moment!" Calvert shouted. "Don't answer that question, Miss Elliston. Now then, Your Honor, I wish to interpose an objection on the ground that this is incompetent, irrelevant, and immaterial, that it is not proper cross-examination.

"It appears now conclusively that, at the time Mr. Mason was talking with Carl Harrod, Carl Harrod was only putting on an act. He was trying to collect damages. He had no idea that he was about to die. The whole theory of the law under which dying declarations are permitted to be received in evidence is that the law presumes that a person who is about to die, knowing that nothing he can say or do will give him any material advantage, having been brought face to face with a situation where only spiritual assets can count, is going to tell the truth, at least to the same extent that he would if he were testifying under oath on the witness stand."

"I understand the theory of the law in regard to dying declarations," Judge Bolton said drily. "I think you may rest assured that the Court understands the elemental principles of law."

"Yes, Your Honor, I merely commented on it in order to show that there is a great difference between a true, dying declaration which is made when a person thinks he is going to die, and a spurious dying declaration which is a part of a fraudulent scheme by which a person is trying to get damages."

"I understand all that," Judge Bolton said, "but let us suppose that a dying declaration is given the force of testimony under oath. If Carl Harrod had testified under oath, Mr. Mason would have been permitted to ask him if he hadn't made some different statement at a different time, wouldn't he?"

"Certainly, Your Honor, but that's a different situation. Mr. Mason would then be asking Carl Harrod himself, and Carl Harrod would have the opportunity to explain any seeming inconsistencies. Now he is asking a third party about some so-called contradictory statement made by Harrod. It seems to me we are getting into the realm of hearsay."

"Nevertheless," Judge Bolton said, "I am interested in hearing the answer of the witness. I'd like to have the question answered. The objection if overruled."

"Very well," Calvert said, yielding with poor grace.

Judge Bolton turned to the witness. "Did he make some such statement, Miss Elliston?"

"I don't think so, Your Honor. I know that Mr. Mason was trying to mix him up and—"

"Now, never mind what you think Mr. Mason was trying to do," Judge Bolton said sternly. "I want to know what Carl Harrod said."

"Well, Mr. Mason brought out the fact that the light was rather poor, and then asked Carl how he could be certain it hadn't been Katherine Baylor who had stabbed him."

"And what did Mr. Harrod say?"

"Well, he became indignant and said he didn't intend to have Mr. Mason cross-examine him."

"Very well," Judge Bolton said to Mason. "Continue with your cross-examination, Counselor."

"Did Carl Harrod telephone Mr. Baylor after I left and in connection with the suggestion I had made?"

"He—"

"Just a minute!" Calvert interrupted. "Refrain from answering, if you will, until I have an opportunity to put in an objection. . . . If the Court please, I object to that question on the ground that it is incompetent, irrelevant, and immaterial, that it calls for hearsay evidence, that it calls for a conclusion of the witness, that it assumes a fact not in evidence, and that it is not proper cross-examination. I didn't go into any of these matters on direct examination. My direct examination was confined to the dying declaration with sufficient factual background of what had gone before to explain the situation."

"Well, let's consider this as part of the factual background," Judge Bolton said.

"Moreover, Your Honor, it calls for a conclusion of the witness, and it's argumentative. She doesn't know who was on the other end of the line."

"Do you know whether Carl Harrod called up Mr. Harriman Baylor after Mr. Mason left?" Judge Bolton asked the witness.

"No, sir."

"You don't know?"

"No, sir."

"Continue with your cross-examination, Mr. Mason," Judge Bolton said.

"Did he call up someone?"

"He used the telephone. Yes."

"Did you see the number he dialed?"

"No."

"Did you hear the person he asked for?"

She hesitated a moment, then said, "No."

"Did you hear him call the other party by name over the telephone? Did you hear him address that party as Mr. Baylor?"

"Just a moment! Just a moment!" Calvert said. "If the Court please, that is objected to on the ground that it isn't binding on the prosecution if a witness addresses someone by name over the telephone. I might call up Your Honor and say, 'Now listen, Mr. President . . .' and that wouldn't mean I was talking to the President of the United States."

"I understand," Judge Bolton said, "but that objection goes to the weight rather than to the admissibility of the evidence. I feel all this is part of the *res gestae*. I think I'll hear the answer. Did he telephone someone whom he addressed as Mr. Baylor?"

"Yes, he did."

"Thank you," Mason said smiling. "That's all!"

"Just a moment," Calvert said. "I have some redirect examination. You heard him use the name Baylor. You don't know whether he was talking with Mr. Baylor or Miss Baylor, do you?"

"I think he said, 'Mister.'"

"All right, then you don't *know* whether he was talking with Harriman Baylor or with Forrester Baylor, his son?"

"No, sir, that I don't know."

"And you don't even know whether the person he was addressing wasn't some stranger by the name of Baylor, some other Baylor altogether?"

"That's right. I don't."

"And you didn't hear him use the person's first name?"

"You mean at that conversation that took place after Mr. Mason left?"

"Yes."

"No, I didn't hear him use any given name."

"That's all," Calvert said.

"Just a minute," Mason said. "You referred specifically to the conversation he had after I left. Do you mean there were two conversations?"

"Yes, sir."

"When did the first conversation take place?"

"Very shortly after my husband returned to the apartment."

"And whom did he call then?"

"I don't know."

"Whom did he ask for?"

"He asked for Mr. Baylor."

"But you heard him call the person at the other end of the line 'Baylor' on both occasions?"

"Yes."

"He used the words 'Mr. Baylor'?"

"Yes."

"Then, as I understand it, he made one call immediately after returning home, and before you knew he had been stabbed with an ice pick, and the second call at a later time after I left. Is that right?"

"Yes."

"Thank you," Mason said, "I think that's all.

"However, in view of this testimony I do have one further question on cross-examination of the witness Irma Karnes."

"I object to having counsel conduct his cross-examination piecemeal," Calvert said. "He had an opportunity to cross-examine Miss Karnes, and he should have concluded his cross-examination. I don't think it is fair to the prosecution to have witnesses called back for further cross-examination from time to time."

"The conduct of the examination is entirely in the discretion of the Court," Judge Bolton said. "It appears to the Court, in view of the circumstances surrounding the testimony of this last witness, that we should attempt to get at the truth of the case."

Judge Bolton turned to the bailiff. "Summon Miss Karnes to the witness stand," he said.

A few moments later Miss Karnes returned to the witness stand.

Mason turned to the bailiff. "I would like to have the bailiff bring Miss Della Street, my secretary, from the witness room, please."

The bailiff left the courtroom, returned a moment later with Della Street.

"Miss Karnes," Mason said, "permit me to introduce Della Street, my secretary."

"How do you do?" Miss Karnes said.

"Please look at her closely," Mason said. "Have you ever seen her before?"

"I don't think so."

"As a matter of fact," Mason said, "Miss Street was the one who bought the three ice picks from you on the evening of the second. It was Miss Street with whom you had the conversation concerning the markup in price."

Irma Karnes vehemently shook her head. "No, it wasn't!" she said. And added gratuitously, "I was told that you'd try to confuse me by running in a ringer, and I'm all prepared for that, Mr. Mason. The person who bought those three ice picks is sitting right there beside you, the defendant in this case, Mildred Crest. It was *not* Della Street who purchased those ice picks. As far as I know, I have never sold Della Street anything in my life. I am not going to permit you to confuse me by any trick of substitution, Mr. Mason."

"You're absolutely positive that you never sold Miss Street anything in your life?"

"To my best recollection I have never seen her before. I am quite certain I have never sold her anything."

"And when you were making change for the ice picks which Miss Street had purchased," Mason said, "do you remember one of the ice picks rolled off the counter and fell to the floor and she stooped and picked it up?"

"That was when I was selling the ice picks to the *defendant*," the witness snapped. "She has told you about the incident, she has described it to you, and you are trying to rattle me on cross-examination. I am not going to be rattled, Mr. Mason. I know *exactly* what happened. I know that I sold these ice picks to the defendant in this case. I saw her. I recognized her, and I have studied her features too carefully to be confused."

Mason said angrily, "You've studied her features, all right, but that careful study took place when the police let you have her under observation for a full ten minutes. You didn't make that careful study of her features when she was buying the ice picks."

"I carefully studied her features when she was buying the ice picks."

"Why?" Mason asked.

"Well, because . . . because I don't intend to be confused on cross-examination, Mr. Mason."

"You didn't know you were going to be cross-examined when you were selling the ice picks," Mason said.

"Well, nevertheless, I am positive that it was the defendant who purchased the ice picks."

"And not Miss Street here?" Mason asked.

"Definitely, positively not!" Irma Karnes snapped in tones of finality. "I had been warned about you, Mr. Mason. I was prepared for this."

"Thank you," Mason said, "that's all."

"Any redirect?" Judge Bolton asked.

"No questions at all," Calvert said smiling. "You are excused from further testimony, Miss Karnes, and permit me to thank you for making an excellent witness."

Irma Karnes arose and strode from the witness stand, glowering at Mason as she passed by him.

"If the Court please," Calvert said, "that is my case. I have no further evidence which I care to put on at this time."

Mason, on his feet, said, "In that case, Your Honor, I move the Court dismiss the case against the defendant and discharge her from custody."

Judge Bolton shook his head. "The function of a preliminary examination is only to show that a crime has been committed and that there is reasonable ground for believing the defendant guilty of that crime. I think the prosecution has met that test.

"Frankly, the Court wants to hear from the defendant in this case if she wishes to avoid being bound over to the higher court for a jury trial. The testimony of the prosecution as to the actions of the defendant, if uncontradicted, discloses a background of motivation for the crime and there is at least *some* evidence tending to show the crime itself."

Mason said, "If the Court please, may I have a fifteen-minute recess? I am frank to state that I don't know whether to put the defendant on the stand and try to get the case dismissed at this time, or to sit tight, let this Court bind the defendant over for trial, and make my defense in front of a jury."

"That is a frank statement," Judge Bolton said, "and under the circumstances the Court will grant a fifteen-minute recess."

CHAPTER FOURTEEN

Mason, Della Street, and Paul Drake gathered for a brief conference in one of the unused witness rooms.

"Well, that's it," Mason said. "The witness Karnes saw Della Street briefly. She was led to believe that the person who bought the ice picks must have been Mildred Crest. She was given a ten-minute opportunity to study Mildred Crest. She was told that I would try to run in a ringer, her mind was conditioned against entertaining any doubt as to her opinion and—and there we are."

"So what do you do?" Drake asked.

Mason said, "I can put Della Street on the stand. She can swear that she was the one that bought the ice picks. Judge Bolton will be impressed, but in order to do any good I'm going to have to follow up by putting Mildred Crest on the stand."

"Then you'll be gambling your whole stack of chips," Paul Drake said.

Mason nodded.

"Can you afford to do that?" Paul Drake asked.

"No," Mason admitted. "However, Judge Bolton is interested now. If he has the right sort of reaction if I put Della on the stand, I'm going to go all the way. There are times when a lawyer *has* to gamble."

"Can you tell anything from Judge Bolton's facial expression?" Della Street asked.

"Not from his facial expression, but from the angle of his head. When he's interested, he leans forward. When he's decided the defendant is guilty, he leans back in his chair.

"During the examination of the last witnesses he's been leaning slightly forward. I think I'll put Della on the stand and watch the way he leans. If it's forward, I'll shoot the works.

"Come on. Let's go back to court. I want to prepare Mildred for what's to come."

They returned to court. Mason leaned over to whisper to Mildred Crest.

"Mildred," he said, "if I don't put you on the stand, the judge is going to bind you over. Then we're going to have to make our fight in front of a jury."

She nodded.

"If I put you on the stand," Mason said, "there's a chance, just a ghost of a chance, that you can convince him that there's something screwy about this case, and, while he may not turn you loose, he's pretty apt to hold that the evidence concerning deliberate first-degree murder is not sufficient to support that charge. Then he may bind you over for manslaughter."

"That will be an advantage?" she asked.

"That will be a tremendous advantage," Mason explained. "If we go to trial before a jury, some of the jurors will feel that the prosecution has proven a case of murder. One or two members will feel that you're innocent. They'll argue and discuss the case back and forth, and in the end someone will suggest a compromise verdict that they find you guilty of manslaughter and that's what they're very apt to do.

"But once we take the murder element out of the case, and you're on trial only for manslaughter, then there's not much chance of a compromise, and the jurors who think you are innocent may hold out and get a mistrial."

"You don't seem to think too much of my chances of acquittal," she said.

"I'm talking about the worst that can happen," Mason said. "I'm painting the gloomy side of the picture for you. Now then, what do you want to do?"

"Whatever you tell me to do."

"I'm inclined to put you on the witness stand," Mason said, "but I warn you that it's going to be something of an ordeal."

"I'll tell the truth," she said.

"All right," Mason said, "here's the judge coming into the courtroom. Sit tight. Hold onto your chair. Here we go!"

CHAPTER FIFTEEN

Judge Bolton called Court to order and said, "I note that the district attorney, Hamilton Burger, is now personally present in court."

Hamilton Burger, big-chested, arose with ponderous dignity. "May it please the Court," he said, "a situation has developed which has been communicated to me during the recess of court. It is a situation in which I take a professional as well as an official interest.

"I note that counsel, in the cross-examination of the People's witness, Irma Karnes, brought his secretary, Della Street, forward and tried to make it appear that Miss Street was the one who had bought the ice pick which is marked in evidence as People's Exhibit Number Seven.

"I am assuming that counsel does not intend to go any further with this insinuation. I have, however, talked with the witness, Miss Karnes, during the recess, and in the event Miss Street is put on the stand to testify that she bought that ice pick, I am going to conduct her cross-examination personally. I warn Miss Street and Perry Mason that I am then going to institute proceedings for perjury. It is one thing to try to confuse a witness by running in a ringer, but it is quite another thing to try to bolster up a weak case by perjured evidence. I feel that it is only fair that I should warn counsel."

Mason turned to Hamilton Burger. "Suppose it should appear that Irma Karnes was the one who was swearing falsely. Would you then prosecute *her* for perjury?"

"Irma Karnes," Hamilton Burger said with quiet emphasis, "is telling the truth. I have talked with her personally. There can be no question as to her positive identification."

Judge Bolton said, "I fail to see where this interchange between counsel affects the issue in any way as far as this Court is concerned. Mr. Mason, you will proceed to put on the defense, in case you care to introduce your defense at this time: otherwise the matter will be submitted to the Court and the Court will make its ruling, binding the defendant over."

"I am going to accept the challenge of the prosecution," Mason said. "Della Street will take the stand."

Della Street came forward and was sworn.

"I am directing your attention to the second of this month," Mason said, "and am directing your attention to the testimony of the witness Irma Karnes, as to the defendant having purchased three ice picks from her. Are you familiar, generally, with her testimony?"

"Yes," Della Street said.

"Will you describe any transaction which you had with Irma Karnes on the second of this month?"

Della Street said firmly, "I was in the apartment of Mildred Crest. I was with you. I was instructed by you to go to the Arcade Novelty and buy three ice picks identical in design and appearance with a certain ice pick which was there in the apartment.

"I went to the Arcade Novelty. I was waited on by Irma Karnes. I bought three ice picks. She told me that it had been necessary to raise the price during the evening; that if I had been earlier, I could have had them three for a dollar. While she was ringing up the sale, prior to putting them in the bag, one of the ice picks rolled and fell on the floor. I stooped and retrieved it."

"You may cross-examine," Perry Mason said.

Hamilton Burger arose ponderously. "Miss Street, you are in the employ of Perry Mason?"

"Yes, sir."

"And have been for some time?"

"Yes, sir."

"And as such are loyal and devoted to him?"

"Yes, sir."

"You have worked with him on many of his cases. It is part of your duties to be with Mr. Mason when he interviews witnesses, to take shorthand notes and keep Mr. Mason's records straight in regard to the various cases?"

"Yes, sir."

"You were with him when he interviewed Carl Harrod?"

"Yes, sir."

"I submit to you that, on the second day of this month, you did not purchase any ice picks at the Arcade Novelty Company, that you had never seen Irma Karnes until after the second of this month. I make that suggestion you, Miss Street, as a means of giving you a last opportunity to tell the truth. You have now testified under oath and testified falsely. A record has been made of your testimony. You have now committed perjury. I am giving you one last opportunity to retract."

"My testimony is correct," Della Street said.

"That is all," Hamilton Burger announced.

Della Street glanced up at Perry Mason.

"No more questions, Miss Street," Perry Mason said.

Della with her chin high left the witness stand, a dignity in her manner which added to her stature and subtracted from that of the discomfited, savagely angry Hamilton Burger.

Mason glanced at Judge Bolton, carefully surveying the jurist's position on the bench.

"I am going to call the defendant, Mildred Crest, to the witness stand," Mason said.

A sudden, tense hush swept the courtroom.

"All right," Mason whispered to Mildred Crest, "you're on your own now. Remember that your weapon isn't sex appeal but sincerity. Go to it!"

Mildred Crest walked slowly to the witness stand, held up her right hand, took the oath, then faced Perry Mason.

"Mildred," Perry said, "I want to get the story of what happened on the twenty-second day of last month, the telephone conversation you had with Robert Joiner. However, for the moment, before we go into that, I think you had better tell the Court about Robert Joiner. Who was he?"

"He was the man to whom I was engaged to be married," Mildred said.

"You were wearing his ring?"

"Yes."

"You had announced your engagement to your friends?"

"Yes."

"Very well. Go ahead and tell about the telephone conversation that you had on the afternoon of the twenty-second. After that, tell us everything you did on the twenty-second, as nearly as you can remember."

In a low, self-conscious voice, Mildred Crest started to talk. Gradually, as the sound of her own voice gave her a certain measure of reassurance, she raised her eyes to Judge Bolton, straightened herself somewhat, and talked more rapidly.

Mason's questions, searching and sympathetic, prompted her whenever she slowed down, until finally she had told the story of the phone call, the automobile accident, the determination to take the identity of Fern Driscoll and the resulting complications, the meeting with Carl Harrod, the ice picks which were purchased by Katherine Baylor, the subsequent visit of Mason and Della Street, and the replacement of the two missing ice picks by Della Street.

Mason turned to the prosecuting attorney.

"Cross-examine," he said.

Hamilton Burger arose with ponderous dignity. His voice seemed sympathetic, his manner restrained.

He said, "As I understand it, Miss Crest, you suffered a terrific emotional shock on the afternoon of the twenty-second."

"I did."

"You had no suspicion that your fiancé was embezzling money?"

"None whatever."

"Certainly you must have realized that he was living beyond the salary he was earning?"

"I did. Everyone in our set did. We all accepted his statement that he came from a wealthy family and was working only to learn the business."

"So when you found he was an embezzler, you didn't want to have any part of him. Is that right?"

"Yes."

"Yet," Hamilton Burger said, raising his voice slightly and introducing an element of sarcasm, "withing a few short hours after you had repudiated your boy friend because of *his* dishonesty, you yourself became a thief."

"I did not," she stormed.

"No?" Hamilton Burger asked in exaggerated surprise. "I perhaps misunderstood your testimony. I thought you said you took the purse of Fern Driscoll."

"I did. But I took it for a purpose."

"What purpose?"

"Simply so I could take over her identity until I had found myself."

"That was the only reason you had for taking her purse?"

"Yes."

"But there was four thousand dollars in her purse. Did you need that four thousand dollars in order to establish your identity as that of Fern Driscoll?"

"No."

"Yet you took that money?"

"It was in the purse."

"Oh! *It was in the purse*," Hamilton Burger said, mimicking her voice. "Is it in the purse now?"

"No."

"Who took it out?"

"I did."

"And what did you do with it after you removed it?"

"I put it in an envelope, and marked on the envelope, 'Property of Fern Driscoll.'"

"Indeed!" Hamilton Burger said. "And *when* did you do that?"

"That was before the police came to my apartment."

"Yes, yes," Hamilton Burger said smiling. "How long before?"

"Not long before."

"That was after Mr. Mason and Della Street had been there?"

"Yes."

"And didn't you write on the envelope 'Property of Fern Driscoll' at the suggestion of Mr. Mason?"

"Yes."

"That was when you knew that Carl Harrod had been stabbed in the chest with the ice pick?"

"Yes."

"In other words, all that was when you were expecting the police?"

"Yes."

"And at *that* time you put the words on the envelope, 'Property of Fern Driscoll'?"

"Yes."

"Simply as window dressing so you could assume a position of virtuous integrity when you got on the witness stand?"

"I wasn't thinking of getting on the witness stand."

"No, no, *you* weren't," Hamilton Burger said smiling, "but your attorney was, Miss Crest. You did this at the advice of your attorney."

"I don't know what my attorney was thinking of."

"No, no, of course not. But you couldn't say that he *wasn't* thinking of a little window dressing?"

"I tell you I don't know what he was thinking."

"You followed his advice?"

"Yes."

"And up to that time you had done nothing to mark this money as being the property of Fern Driscoll?"

"I had put it to one side as her property."

"You mean you hadn't as yet spent it?"

"I had no intention of spending it."

"Did you make any effort to find out who Fern Driscoll's heirs might be?"

"No."

"Did you communicate with the Public Administrator of San Diego County where the accident took place and tell him that you had some property belonging to Fern Driscoll?"

"No."

"You say you were holding the money as the property of Fern Driscoll?"

"Yes."

"Yet you yourself were taking over Fern Driscoll's identification as well as her property?"

"I went under the name of Fern Driscoll."

"Yes, yes. You found Fern Driscoll's signature on her driving license, and you practiced signing the name of Fern Driscoll so that it would look like the signature on that driving license, didn't you?"

"Yes."

"You wrote that name on the back of a check, didn't you?"

"A check?" she asked.

"A check made out to you for your first week's wages?"

"Yes," she said, "but that was money I had earned."

"Then why did you think it was necessary for you to try to copy the signature of Fern Driscoll as it appeared on the driving license?"

"Because sometime I thought I might have to produce that driving license as a means of identification."

"You didn't know anything about Fern Driscoll's background?"

"No."

"You didn't know that she didn't perhaps have loved ones who were anxiously awaiting some word from her?"

"I knew nothing about her."

"You didn't try to communicate with her loved ones? You didn't let them know that she was dead?"

"No."

"And you deliberately set fire to the automobile so as to aid you in your deception?"

"I did not."

"The fire started as the result of a match which you had struck?"

"Yes, but it was accidental."

"You had already struck one match?"

"Yes."

"And no fire resulted?"

"That's right."

"So you tried again. You struck another match and that time a fire did result."

"I tell you the fire was accidental."

"You knew there was gasoline in the car?"

"Yes."

"You could smell it?"

"Yes."

"Notwithstanding that, you struck a match and held it over the gasoline fumes?"

"I was trying to see down into the car."

"And when the fumes didn't ignite, *then* you managed to drop the match so that the gasoline did ignite."

"The match burned my fingers."

"You have struck matches before?"

"Naturally."

"You know that if you hold them too long the flame will burn your fingers?"

"Yes."

"Therefore, you ordinarily blow out the match before the flame gets to your fingers?"

"Yes."

"Why didn't you do that this time?"

"I had other things on my mind."

"I certainly agree with you on that," Hamilton Burger said sarcastically.

"Now then," Hamilton Burger went on, "after Katherine Baylor had left you ice picks so that you could defend yourself in case you were assaulted, you asked her where she had bought them, didn't you?"

"Yes."

"And she told you?"

"Yes."

"So you immediately went down and bought more ice picks so that, in case you stabbed Carl Harrod with an ice pick, you could establish your innocence in the eyes of the police by showing that you still had the ice picks in your apartment that had been there when Miss Baylor had left?"

"I did not!"

"You thought that you could call on your friend Katherine Baylor and say, 'Katherine Baylor left two ice picks here, didn't you, Katherine?' and Katherine would say, 'Why, of course. Those are the ice picks that I purchased.'"

"I did not purchase any ice picks!"

"You not only took the four thousand dollars which didn't belong to you, yet don't consider yourself a thief, but you also bought three ice picks from the witness Irma Karnes, and now lie about it and presumably don't consider that you're committing perjury!"

"I didn't buy the ice picks. Della Street bought those ice picks."

"How do you know?"

"I heard Mr. Mason instruct her to buy them."

"You have heard Irma Karnes state positively that *you* purchased those ice picks?"

"She is mistaken."

"You heard her make that statement?"

"Yes."

"You heard her state that she was positive?"

"Yes."

"And still in the face of that testimony, in the face of the fact that you stabbed Carl Harrod in the chest with an ice pick which you yourself had bought from Irma Karnes, you wish to adhere to this story of your innocence, this fairy tale of having entered your apartment, of having picked up an ice pick and having some man rush at you so that he impaled his chest upon the ice pick?"

"That is the truth."

Hamilton Burger looked at the clock. "If the Court please, I think I am about finished with the witness. However, it is approaching the hour of the evening adjournment and may I ask the Court for a recess at this time with the understanding that my questioning tomorrow morning will not exceed a very few minutes?"

"Very well," Judge Bolton said. "We will not continue the case until tomorrow morning at ten o'clock. The defendant is remanded to custody."

CHAPTER SIXTEEN

Perry Mason, Della Street, and Paul Drake stepped out of the elevator.

Drake said, "I'll go on to my office and see what's doing. I'll be down to your place after a while, Perry."

"Okay," Mason said. "Let me know if your men have uncovered anything important."

Mason and Della Street continued walking on down the corridor, rounded the turn and paused in front of the door marked PERRY MASON. PRIVATE.

Perry Mason fitted his latchkey, clicked back the lock, entered his private office, scaled his hat over to a chair, said, "Well, it's anybody's guess. What did you think of her, Della?"

"I think she's doing all right," Della Street said.

"Judge Bolton is watching her like a hawk."

"I know he is. He watches every move she makes, and he's leaning forward."

"And that," Mason said, "is a good sign. If he had made up his mind to bind her over, he'd simply sit there in judicial impassivity, waiting for her to get done with her testimony and then he'd announce that since there seemed to be sufficient evidence to indicate a murder had been committed, and that there was reasonable ground to believe the defendant was the guilty person, he was going to bind her over.

"You see, that mix-up on the ice picks has introduced a new note into the entire case. It means that he must consider that Mildred Crest is a deliberate, cold-blooded killer, if she did the things the prosecution claims she did."

"You mean purchasing those ice picks?" Della Street asked.

Mason nodded.

Della Street said, "I have a feeling that Judge Bolton believes me."

"I think he does, too," Mason said. "Well, I'll let Gertie know that we're back from court."

Mason picked up his telephone and, when he heard the click on the line at the switchboard, said, "We're back from court, Gertie. When you go home, fix the switchboard so outside calls come in on Della Street's telephone, will you? We're expecting—"

Gertie's voice interrupted him. She was so excited that she could hardly talk. "Just a minute! Please.... Hold on.... Just wait!" She hung up the telephone.

Mason turned to Della Street, said, "Something's got into Gertie. She's really steamed up about something."

Gertie, the incurable romanticist, came bursting into the private office, her eyes wide. "Mr. Mason, *he's* here!"

"Who?" Mason asked.

"He didn't want to give his name," Gertie went on. "He's terribly distinguished-looking, long, wavy, dark hair, that sweeps back from a beautiful forehead. Delicate features, and—"

"Who the devil are you talking about?" Mason interrupted.

"The man in the case," she said, in a hushed voice. "Forrester Baylor!"

"The devil!" Mason exclaimed.

"I don't care *what* they say, Mr. Mason. I know that he loved her. He's been living years during the past few days. The lines of suffering have etched character on his face, and—"

"Get your mind back out of the clouds," Mason said brusquely. "Send him in, Gertie, and don't go home. Stick on the switchboard. If any newspaper reporters call, lie like a trooper."

Gertie whirled with a swirl of skirts, showing a flash of well-rounded, nylon-clad legs.

"Well," Della Street said, as Gertie rushed from the office. "The plot thickens."

A moment later, Gertie was back. "Mr. Mason, Mr. Baylor," she said in a hushed voice.

The man who moved slowly past Gertie was tall, straight-backed, slim-waisted, and looked as though he hadn't slept for a week. The dark eyes seemed lackluster, although the face had breeding and character.

"Mr. Mason," he said in a low voice, and his long, strong fingers gripped the lawyer's hand. ,

"My confidential secretary, Miss Street," Mason said.

Forrester Baylor bowed.

"All right," Mason said, "sit down. Let's straighten out a few things. Who told you to come here?"

"No one."

"Who knows you're here?"

"No one."

"Your father?"

Forrester Baylor shook his head. "My father forbade me to leave Lansing."

"Your sister?"

"Kitty is a good egg. She'd help me out, but I don't want anyone to know I'm here."

"Where are you staying?" Mason asked. "At what hotel are you registered?"

"I'm not registered anywhere as yet. I checked my bag in a locker at the airport and took a taxi to the depot. Then I took another taxi here. I didn't want to be followed."

"You're traveling under your own name?"

"No, under an alias, and I've taken great pains to elude the newspaper reporters in Lansing."

"What do you want?"

"I want to tell you what I've found out."

"What have you found out?"

"That my father, doubtless with the best intentions in the world, was responsible for Fern's leaving. He manipulated things quietly behind the scenes so that life in the employ of his company became unbearable for her.

"I also want to tell you that Fern was a decent, straightforward, square-shooting girl. She wasn't pregnant."

"How do you know?"

"If she had been pregnant, she'd have told me. And she didn't tell me. She...she wasn't that kind."

Mason watched the man narrowly. "Sit down, Mr. Baylor. Make yourself comfortable. Unfortunately, it's easy to get fooled about women."

"But I'm *not* fooled about Fern Driscoll. I...I realize now how very, very much I loved her."

"It's a little late for that now."

"Mr. Mason, I want you to put my father on the stand."

"Why?"

"I want certain things brought out. He's the one who gave her four thousand dollars to leave Lansing."

"How do you know?"

"I know because I didn't give her that money. I know because I was getting ready to ask her to marry me, and my father knew it. My father bitterly dissaproved of Fern, not as an individual, but purely because of what he felt was her lack of social position. She was a working girl, a secretary. Dad wanted me to marry an heiress.

"My father came up the hard way. He had to work for everything he got. He has known poverty. He's known snubs. And now he's come to know snobs. In fact, he's in a fair way to become one himself.

"I was interested in Carla Addis. She's clever, in a brittle, highly artificial sort of way. She's a sophisticated product of modern wealth. I'll admit there was a fascination there, a glitter and a glamor, and it was easy to be swept along. There were times when *I* didn't know what *I* wanted. I was badly mixed up.

"When Fern left, I suddenly realized what she meant to me. I tried to find her. I searched in vain. I thought she was still in Lansing somewhere. Then my father told me about her death, and about the autopsy and I was...I was crushed! I can't believe it. I can't bring myself to believe anything like that about Fern."

"Autopsies don't lies," Mason said.

Baylor shook his head. "Things just don't add up. However, that's neither here nor there. It's too late to do anything now. But I do want you to know that my father must have given her that four thousand dollars, and heaven knows what he told her in order to get her to leave."

"You don't trust your father?"

"I admire him. I'm fond of him. I love him as a father and, in a matter of this sort, I wouldn't trust him for a minute."

"What do you want *me* to do?"

"I want you to put my father on the witness stand. I want you to make him admit that he is responsible for Fern's leaving."

"And what good would that do?"

"It would establish a lot of things."

"It wouldn't help my client," Mason said. "But I'm glad you came in. I wish you'd called several days earlier. As far as that's concerned, I wish—"

He broke off as Paul Drake's code knock sounded on the door.

Mason hesitated a moment, then said to Della Street, "Let Paul Drake in."

Della opened the door.

Mason said, "Mr. Drake, this is Forrester Baylor."

Paul Drake's face promptly became a smiling, wooden mask. His eyes completely concealed any emotion.

"How are you, Mr. Baylor? Pleased to meet you," he said, shaking hands, his manner that of one who has just met a person who means only a new face and a new name.

"I'm Forrester Baylor, the son of Harriman Baylor," the young man said, apparently stung by Paul Drake's casual attitude.

"Oh yes," Drake said. He nodded to Perry Mason. "Got some news for you, Perry."

"What about?"

"About the four thousand dollars."

"What about it?"

"It came from the Midfield National Bank in Midfield, Arkansas. The place was held up on the seventeenth by a slender, boyish-looking individual who stood in line and pushed the usual note through the cashier's window. The note said to turn over all of the hundred-dollar bills, keep the hands in sight, not press the alarm, and to wait five minutes before reporting anything. You know, the usual type of note.

"The cashier passed over forty hundred-dollar bills. At first he thought it was a young man. Now, the more he thinks of it, he believes it was a young woman in men's clothes. He never did hear the voice.

"The description matches that of Fern Driscoll."

Forrester Baylor lunged at Drake. "You lie!" he shouted. "You—"

Drake, with the ease of long practice, slipped Baylor's punch over his right shoulder.

Mason grabbed Baylor from behind, pinioned his arms to his waist. "Easy does it! Easy does it!" Mason said.

"That's a lie! That's a dirty, despicable lie! Fern Driscoll wouldn't do anything like that any more than...any more than you would!"

Mason swung Baylor to one side, sent him spinning down into the big, overstuffed chair by the desk.

"Sit there!" he said, his voice cracking like a whip. "Control your damned emotions! Use your head. Give us some help. I want to know about Fern Driscoll. I want a photograph."

Baylor, somewhat dazed, said, "She wouldn't! She didn't!"

"A picture!" Mason shouted at him. "Do you have a picture?"

Almost mechanically, Baylor reached in his pocket, took out a wallet and opened it. The smiling portrait of a girl peered up at them from behind a cellophane window.

Mason grabbed the wallet.

"And," Drake said, "we found Fern Driscoll's car."

"Where?" Mason asked.

"Wrecked at the bottom of a canyon between Prescott and Phoenix."

"Anyone in it?"

"No one."

"Baggage?"

"None."

"Anything else?"

"The car apparently just ran off the road, tumbled down the canyon. There's no sign anyone was injured. The driver evidently escaped."

Mason's eyes were hard. "So the car ran off the road and on the way down the driver not only escaped but dragged out her suitcase as well?"

Drake grinned. "The local authorities don't seem to have thought of that."

"What time was the bank held up at Midfield?" Mason asked.

"Ten-thirty in the morning."

Mason jerked the picture of Fern Driscoll out of Forrester Baylor's wallet. "Paul," he said, "I want you to have copies made of this picture. I want you to get a hundred men on the job. I want every newspaper to have a copy of this picture, and I want them to have the story of the bank stick-up in Midfield. You—"

Forrester Baylor came up out of the chair. Mason stiff-armed him back into the cushions.

"What's the big idea?" Drake asked.

"Never mind the idea," Mason said. "Get the hell out of here and get started before someone stops you. Cover every motel within a driving distance of three hours east and north of Midfield. Get rid of the lead and start moving! Show this picture. Get it in the press. Notify the F.B.I."

"You're playing right in the prosecution's hands," Drake protested. "You—"

Mason, still holding Forrester Baylor in the chair, half-turned toward Paul Drake. "Get started before I fire you," he said.

Forrester Baylor still struggling to get up said with low earnestness, "Mr. Mason, I'm going to kill you for this if it takes the rest of my life to do it!"

CHAPTER SEVENTEEN

Judge Bolton, sitting sternly upright, looked down upon the packed courtroom.

"The Court has seen the morning papers," he said. "I am going to ask the spectators to refrain from any demonstration of any sort.

"The defendant is in court; counsel are present. The defendant was on the stand being cross-examined by Hamilton Burger. Will the defendant please resume her position on the stand."

"Just a moment," Hamilton Burger said. "I find that I have no further questions on cross-examination."

"No redirect," Mason said.

"Very well, Mr. Mason. Call your next witness," Judge Bolton said.

"I will call Mr. Harriman Baylor as my next witness," Mason said.

"What?" Hamilton Burger shouted, in sheer surprise.

"Mr. Harriman Baylor!" Mason said, raising his voice. "Mr. Baylor, will you come forward and take the stand, please?"

Baylor jumped up and said, "I know nothing whatever about this case. I am only interested because—"

"You have been called as a witness," Judge Bolton said. "You will come forward and be sworn."

Hamilton Burger said, "If the Court please, I resent any attempt on the part of Mr. Mason to try and extricate himself by seeking to involve Mr. Baylor in a matter concerning which he knows nothing. I may state that I have personally interrogated Mr. Baylor in the greatest detail, and I am satisfied he knows nothing whatever concerning the facts of *this* case. I am satisfied that he does know certain matters concerning the background of Fern Driscoll, and it may be that the prosecution will want to bring out some of those facts when the case comes to trial in the superior court. But at this time, as part of the preliminary examination, there is nothing that Mr. Baylor knows which would be of the slightest value to the defense, and I feel that he should not be called as a witness."

"The district attorney should know," Judge Bolton said, "that the defense has it in his power to call any person he wishes as a witness. Mr. Baylor will come forward and take the stand. You will have an opportunity, Mr. District Attorney, to object to any specific question as it is asked."

Baylor reluctantly came forward.

"Hold up your right hand and be sworn," Judge Bolton said.

"If the Court please," Hamilton Burger said, "Mr. Baylor is suffering from bursitis. It will be necessary for him to hold up his left hand."

"Very well, hold up your left hand and be sworn," Judge Bolton said.

"Just a moment," Mason said. "If the Court please, I object to the district attorney giving testimony in this case."

Judge Bolton looked at Mason in surprise. "The district attorney has given no testimony in this case, Mr. Mason."

"I respectfully beg to differ with the Court. The district attorney is making statements which are evidentiary in their character and are of the highest importance."

"The district attorney said that Miss Street had committed perjury," Judge Bolton said. "The Court would have rebuked the district attorney if any objection had been made at the time. However, the Court feels that the district attorney is unquestionably sincere and that his statement was made for the purpose of saving a hard-working woman from being arrested on a charge of perjury."

"I am not referring to that," Mason said. "I am referring to Mr. Burger's statement that Mr. Baylor is suffering from bursitis and therefore cannot raise his right hand."

"Why," Hamilton Burger said angrily, "I'm not giving any testimony; I am merely explaining to the Court that such is the case."

"How do you know it's the case?" Mason asked.

"Why, Mr. Baylor...why, Mr. Baylor has been in my office. I have talked with him in detail. He has told me all about his trouble."

Mason grinned. "It now appears, Your Honor, that the district attorney is not only giving testimony before the Court, but that he is giving testimony which is founded purely on hearsay."

"Just what is all this leading up to?" Judge Bolton asked.

Mason said, "Under the law, a witness is required to raise his right hand and have the oath administered. If this witness refuses to raise his right hand, I demand to know why he can't raise his right hand."

Judge Bolton regarded Harriman Baylor. "You are unable to raise your right hand because of bursitis which is, I understand, a disease which affects the shoulder?"

There was a moment of silence.

"Or," Perry Mason said, "is Mr. Baylor unable to raise his right hand because of an infection in the right arm due to the wound of an ice pick?"

"An ice pick!" Judge Bolton exclaimed.

"An ice pick," Mr. Mason repeated firmly. "If the court will notice newspaper photographs of Mr. Baylor at the time he arrived in this city, the Court will notice he is coming down the stairs from an airplane carrying his brief case in his left hand, waving his right hand in a gesture of friendly salute, presumably at the cameraman who took the picture. At that time, according to the newspaper report, he claimed he had bursitis. If that was true, it must have been in his *left* shoulder. His right hand and his right arm were unaffected.

"Now, I would like to know why it is that he has had this sudden indisposition, in his *right* arm. I would like to have a physician examine Mr. Baylor to see whether or not there is bursitis in the *right* shoulder, and I would like to know the names of the physicians he has consulted since he has been here in this city so that we can subpoena them and find out whether the trouble with his right arm is not due to a wound inflicted by an ice pick."

Judge Bolton said, "Mr. Mason, that is a very serious charge, a very grave accusation. I trust that you have facts with which to back it up."

"It is no more grave than the statement made by the district attorney that Mr. Baylor was unable to raise his right hand because of bursitis," Mason said. "If you want to rebuke anybody, rebuke the district attorney."

Judge Bolton flushed. "Mr. Mason, that remark borders dangerously on contempt of Court."

"I didn't mean it that way," Mason said. "I simply felt a natural resentment that any statement I made as to the cause of Mr. Baylor's injury was accepted with the gravest doubt, whereas the district attorney was permitted to give the Court the benefit of his solemn assurance, an assurance which, as it turns out, was predicated entirely on hearsay testimony, and that *he* received *no* rebuke. I would suggest, with all due respect, that the Court examine Mr. Baylor and ask him for the names of the physicians who have treated him."

"That won't be necessary," Baylor said in a low voice. "I regret that the matter has reached this stage. I have carried on the deception long enough. My conscience is bothering me and now I am faced with complete ruination. I wish to make a statement to the Court. Mr. Mason is entirely correct. The bursitis is in my *left* shoulder. The trouble with my right shoulder is due to a wound from an ice pick which was at first painful but which now has become badly infected."

Judge Bolton banged furiously with his gavel. "Order!" he shouted. "Order! There will be order in the court or I will clear the courtroom! The spectators will refrain from making any disturbance! This is a court of justice. Now be silent."

When Judge Bolton had restored order somewhat, he looked at Baylor with a puzzled frown. "This is something," he said, "that I'm afraid I don't understand."

"It is simple enough," Baylor said. "I went to the apartment of Mildred Crest because I felt that I had to have certain letters my son had sent Fern Driscoll which could cause the greatest embarrassment to my family and to my social position. I felt that those letters were in danger of becoming public property through the activities of a scandal magazine. The defendant wasn't there when

I arrived. I entered her apartment by using a duplicate key which I obtained by bribing the janitor. I unscrewed the light bulbs so I could not be surprised and identified. I was searching for the letters with the aid of a flashlight, when the defendant unexpectedly returned.

"I suddenly realized the position in which I had placed myself. I felt that the only thing for me to do was to turn out my flashlight and in the dark rush past the young woman who blocked the doorway.

"I didn't want to hurt her, so I lowered my right shoulder and charged. What I didn't realize was that she had an ice pick in her hand. The ice pick was, by the momentum of my own charge, impaled in my arm near the shoulder and torn from her grasp. I ran down the stairs, and it was just as I was at the foot of the stairs, that I encountered Carl Harrod.

"Harrod apparently had been keeping an eye on the apartment house. He recognized me, turned and followed me.

"By that time I realized I was out of the frying pan and into the fire. Harrod had a camera. He got a flashlight picture as I ran to my car.

"The magazine with which Harrod had been negotiating for the story of my son's attachment would have paid many times as much for a story involving me as a housebreaker. I knew I was licked.

"Feeling that I might have a chance to buy my son's letters, I had arranged for a large sum of ready cash which I had on my person.

"I had withdrawn the ice pick and thrown it into the gutter before I made my arrangements with Harrod. I paid him ten thousand dollars in cash to help me out of my predicament. It was my only way out.

"Carl Harrod agreed to go to his apartment and call Perry Mason. He was to tell him that the defendant had stabbed *him* with the ice pick.

"Since I felt certain the defendant hadn't recognized me, and since we knew she'd call Mr. Mason and tell him she had stabbed someone, we felt Harrod's call to Mason would completely confuse the issues and give me a chance to keep out of it.

"I was to go to my suite in the hotel, shut off the telephone and refuse to see anyone. Harrod, however, was to report to me, using the name of Howley when he had performed his part of the bargain. I made arrangements so that any call from Howley would be put through at once.

"If Carl Harrod was able to convince Mr. Mason he was the one who had been stabbed, I was to give him another ten thousand dollars. I also realized there would be further payments, but at the moment I couldn't help myself.

"It was the only time in my life I had ever yielded to blackmail. This time I faced the pitiless publicity of a scandal magazine. I had no choice. Anything would have been better than that sort of publicity.

"We never expected Perry Mason would want to call a doctor to examine Harrod. We knew his client would have told him of the man who had rushed at her, of having stabbed him with the ice pick. It was my idea Harrod would claim the ice pick had penetrated his shoulder, but Harrod tried to put himself in a bargaining position by claiming he had been stabbed in the chest. That was so he could offer a settlement if Mr. Mason would turn over the letters we wanted. Harrod had my ten thousand dollars in cash, ten one-thousand-dollar bills. He knew that I would pay him another ten thousand dollars and that, if he could get those letters, I would pay him even more.

"Harrod knew that Mr. Mason would try at all costs to protect his client by keeping the matter from the police. Harrod, of course, was jubilant. He assured me he could handle Mr. Mason so Mason would, as he expressed it, be eating out of our hands. He said he had handled people of Mason's type before, that Mason couldn't be forced to do anything for himself, but that he could be made to do anything when it was a matter of protecting the interests of a client. Harrod assured me he was going to force Mr. Mason to turn over the letters we wanted. Harrod, of course, was expecting compensation for all of this, but he knew I would pay him more than the magazine would.

"I am sorry, Your Honor. I entered upon a scheme of deception and now I find myself trapped by my own chicanery."

Judge Bolton looked at the crestfallen, completely flabbergasted district attorney, then looked at Perry Mason.

"If this is the truth," Judge Bolton said, "*who* inflicted the fatal wound on Carl Harrod?"

"There was only one person, Your Honor," Mason said in a voice of quiet assurance, "who could possibly have done that. What Carl Harrod hadn't anticipated was that I would insist on calling a physician to make an independent examination.

"Harrod had no ice-pick wound, no wound of any nature when I was talking with him, but he knew after my interview that I had gone to summon a doctor. Carl Harrod, therefore, did the only thing he could. He told the young woman with whom he was living to insert an ice pick in his chest, not to insert it deep but to make a sufficient wound so that he could show a puncture mark to the doctor I was bringing, who was to make the examination.

"Nellie Elliston saw an opportunity to get the large sum of cash Carl Harrod had just acquired from Mr. Baylor. That is the only explanation that accounts for the facts. Harrod bared his chest. He instructed her to insert the ice pick an inch or two. She went to the utility drawer in the kitchen, took out an ice pick, returned to bend over Harrod, smiled down at him, and plunged the ice pick into his heart.

"Then she took the cash Harrod had acquired and fabricated an entirely spurious death scene and dying declaration. Because the district attorney was so anxious to get me involved in the case, he didn't have her submit to the rigorous tests which he would have imposed under other circumstances."

Judge Bolton looked around the courtroom, then turned back to Perry Mason. "How do you know all that, Mr. Mason?" he asked.

"Knowing that Irma Karnes was identifying the defendant, not because of the transaction at the Arcade Novelty, but because of mental suggestion and because of an image so firmly implanted in her mind by improper police methods, I knew there was only one thing that could have happened.

"And when I suddenly remembered the picture of Mr. Baylor arriving at the airport with his right hand waving a greeting, yet remembered that later on that same evening he had been forced to shake hands with his left hand, claiming a bursitis in his right shoulder, I knew what must have happened."

Judge Bolton said, "The Court noticed that, when Mr. Mason made his statement about the real reason Mr. Baylor could not raise his right hand, Miss Elliston slipped out of the courtroom. In order to dispose of the case at bar, the Court suggests that the district attorney instruct the officers to pick up Nellie Elliston for questioning. The Court might also suggest that it views with the greatest disapproval attempts to bolster the recollection of a witness who is making an identification so that she will not be shaken on cross-examination.

"The Court takes judicial cognizance of the fact that many of our miscarriages of justice are the result of mistaken identification, and suggests that, when a witness is making an identification, the witness be permitted to pick a person from a line-up under test conditions which are conducted with scrupulous fairness."

"And," Perry Mason said, "in order to keep the record straight, and in view of Mr. Baylor's statement, I now wish to call my last witness, Fern Driscoll."

"Who?" Judge Bolton snapped. And then added angrily, "Is this a trick, Mr. Mason?"

"This is not a trick," Mason said. "I wish to call Fern Driscoll as my next witness. She is waiting in the witness room. If the bailiff will please summon her, I will—"

"Order!" Judge Bolton shouted. "Order in the courtroom! I will have no more demonstrations. The spectators will remain orderly or I will clear the courtroom!"

Judge Bolton turned to Mason. "I trust, Mr. Mason," he said acidly, "that you are not attempting to impose upon the Court to obtain a dramatic effect. Having called Miss Driscoll as a witness, the Court is going to consider it as an abuse of the process of the Court unless you are able to produce that witness."

"Here she is now," Mason said.

Abruptly the courtroom became tensely quiet as a rather tall, dark-eyed, chestnut-haired, young woman walked slowly to the witness stand, held up her right hand, and was sworn.

"Your name?" Judge Bolton asked.

"Fern Driscoll," she said.

Judge Bolton glowered at Perry Mason. "Proceed!" he said.

"Would you kindly tell us what happened after you left the employ of the Baylor Manufacturing and Development Company in Lansing, Michigan?" Mason asked.

"I left there under circumstances that made me very despondent," she said. "I felt that I was no longer welcome in the organization. I started driving west with my car."

"And you picked up a hitchhiker?" Mason asked.

She nodded.

"And what happened?"

"The hitchhiker was a young woman who told me a story about being down on her luck. I guess she was. She told me she had listened to the importunities of a married man who told her that he loved her, that he was going to get a divorce and marry her. She found out that he was completely insincere, utterly ruthless, and, when she went to him and told him she was in trouble, he simply laughed at her. He threw her out. She had lost her friends. She had no money."

"Go on," Mason said.

"I think," Fern Driscoll said, "the young woman was temporarily insane. She was desperate. I had a little money. She watched for an opportunity, clubbed me over the head, grabbed my purse, knocked me unconscious, and rolled me out on the road. When I regained consciousness, I found that she had taken my car my suitcase, and all of my belongings. I reported the theft, but no one seemed particularly concerned.

"I felt certain my car would be recovered eventually. I even hoped nothing very serious would happen to the young woman who had stolen it. She was emotionally unstable and I believe temporarily insane. She had come to believe the world owed a living both to her and to her unborn child. It was quite in keeping with her emotional state for her to hold up a bank.

"No one paid any particular attention to me or made any effort to recover my property. It wasn't until the press announced that the identity of the bank robber was known and that Fern Driscoll had done the job, that the F.B.I. went into action. That organization located me within an hour.

"Needless to say, I knew nothing about the fact that I was supposed to have been murdered, or that this young woman was on trial, or that she had wound up with my purse and my identification."

"Was the defendant who is here in court the young woman hitchhiker who stole your car?" Mason asked.

"Absolutely not!"

Mason turned to the popeyed Hamilton Burger and smiled. "Your witness," he said.

Burger said, "No . . . no questions."

"That's my case, Your Honor," Mason said smiling.

"Do you have any further evidence?" Judge Bolton asked Hamilton Burger. The district attorney merely shook his head.

"The case against the defendant is dismissed," Judge Bolton said. "Court's adjourned."

Fern Driscoll started to leave the witness stand, then suddenly stopped, her eyes on the tall man who was hurrying toward her.

"Forrie!" she said quietly.

Forrester Baylor didn't waste time in conversation. He simply took her in his arms, held her close to him, and made no attempt to conceal the tears which were coursing down his cheeks.

"My darling!" he said at length. "My darling . . . ! Oh, my darling . . . !"

So intent were the newspaper photographers on catching the scene, that Mason and his client were able to slip out of the courtroom.

CHAPTER EIGHTEEN

Mason and Della Street entered the lawyer's private office.

Della Street moved close to Mason, held his arm, and he could feel her trembling.

"Chief," she said, "I'm so darned excited, and so . . . so . . . I want to cry."

Mason patted her shoulder. "Go ahead and cry."

"The look in his eyes—he really *did* love her, Chief! He really *did*! I mean he really *does!*"

"He shouldn't have let her get away," Mason said. "He was like so many men who take too much for granted."

She looked at him for a long, searching moment, then asked, "How in the world did you know she was alive?"

"When people start doing things that are definitely and decidedly out of character, you know that there's been a mistake somewhere," Mason said.

"Harriman Baylor *might* have paid money to Carl Harrod and started working with Carl Harrod, if Harrod had the letters his son had written to Fern Driscoll.

"However, Harrod didn't have those letters. I had them.

"We know that Harrod was stalemated. He couldn't sell his story without proof. He couldn't get proof until he got the letters, and he couldn't get the letters. Yet suddenly Harriman Baylor began to be very palsy-walsy with Carl Harrod.

"And as we gradually began to get the picture of Fern Driscoll, we learned that everything in connection with her as the hitchhiker was out of character. She wasn't the sort of girl who would have been in the second month of pregnancy, who would have tried to wreck Mildred Crest's automobile. The whole thing simply didn't add together into a total.

"Then when I learned that the money in Fern Driscoll's purse had come from a bank robbery, that Fern Driscoll's purse had come from a bank robbery, that Fern Driscoll's car had been found wrecked where it had evidently been driven off the road, it didn't take too much brainwork to realize that the woman who had wrecked Mildred Crest's car wasn't Fern Driscoll at all. After all, we only knew she had Fern Driscoll's purse and suitcase and was using Fern Driscoll's name.

"Therefore, I felt that if we could broadcast the fact that Fern Driscoll was wanted for the robbery of a national bank, we'd probably get some fast action. Fortunately we did. Paul Drake's correspondent was able to get Fern Driscoll on a midnight plane, giving a happy solution to an otherwise puzzling case. Then, by calling Harriman Baylor to the stand, we had the whole case really buttoned up."

"But you wouldn't have ever thought of calling him unless you had known—"

"I should have known a lot sooner than I did," Mason said savagely. "I made the mistake of looking at things from the police viewpoint instead of from an objective viewpoint. I *knew* that Mildred Crest couldn't possibly have stabbed him with that ice pick which was produced in court. Therefore, either the police had to have mixed up the ice picks, or Nellie Elliston was the only person who *could* have killed Carl Harrod."

"What about Mildred Crest?" Della Street asked. "What's going to become of her?"

Mason's face became granite-hard. "Mildred Crest," he said, "is going to have a very nice job with the Baylor Manufacturing and Development Company. And Mr. Harriman Baylor is going to see to it that she advances just as fast and just as far as her ability warrants."

Della Street looked up at him with misty eyes.

"Will you please bend over," she said, "so I can kiss you on the forehead?"

Mason regarded her with eyes that were tender. He said gently, "I'm afraid, Della, I can't bend quite that far. You won't mind if I'm a few inches short, will you?"

"Not at all," she told him.

THE CASE OF
THE WAYLAID WOLF

FOREWORD

For some years now I have been dedicating my Perry Mason books to outstanding figures in the field of legal medicine. Exceptional circumstances cause me to depart from this custom so that I can dedicate this book to a man who has done much to improve the administration of justice in this country.

Park Street, an attorney of San Antonio, Texas, is a member of the board of investigators and one of counsel of the Court of Last Resort.

On the occasion of writing this foreword Park Street is opening a "Perry Mason Room" in his suite of law offices. This room is dedicated not so much to Perry Mason but to the ideals Perry Mason stands for: unswerving loyalty to his clients, a devotion to the cause of justice, and an indomitable fighting spirit.

These are qualities that any good attorney has.

There are, of course, some attorneys whose definition of justice is measured in any given case by terms of expediency on the one hand and financial remuneration on the other.

These attorneys fortunately are in the minority. The overwhelming majority of lawyers in this country realize that they are officers of the court; that they are the high priests and priestesses in the temple of justice; that their duty is to their clients, to the courts and to the public. Having once embarked upon a case, they will fight to the last ditch with unswerving loyalty to their clients and to their ideals.

Perry Mason is, of course, a fictitious character. There are times when his loyalty to his clients and to the cause of justice leads him to take desperate chances. Attorneys who occasionally question his ethics still admire his loyalty and his sheer fighting ability. It is for these reasons that Park Street has dedicated a room to Perry Mason.

For some ten years now, in the Court of Last Resort, I have had the privilege of associating with a group of individuals who are devoting much of their time and energy trying to get the public to take a more active and understanding interest in the administration of justice. The bonds of friendship forged in the fires of fighting for a worthwhile objective are close indeed. During the years that I have been associated with Park Street, I have come to know him intimately. We have had many adventures together in the field of law and in investigating cases where innocent persons have been wrongfully convicted of crime.

And so, as the person who chronicles the adventures of Perry Mason, it gives me great pleasure to accede to Perry Mason's request to write this foreword as the first official document to be typed in Park Street's new Perry Mason Room, and to dedicate this book to a lawyer who has unswerving loyalty to his clients, who has for years cheerfully given both his time and money to advance the cause of justice, who is a loyal friend, an able attorney and a public-spirited citizen.

To my friend, PARK STREET.

Erle Stanley Gardner

CHAPTER ONE

I t had started to rain that morning when Arlene Ferris parked her car in the fenced-off parking lot reserved for employees in the executive offices of the Lamont Rolling, Casting and Engineering Company.

The precipitation was a cold, wintry rain, and Arlene rolled up the windows of her car, bundled her raincoat about her and walked briskly to the side entrance marked *Employees Only*.

It was still raining at noon, but there was no necessity for Arlene to leave the building since the employees of the executive officers were able to use the underground tunnel to the cafeteria in the main building.

At quitting time Arlene was in the midst of work on some specifications which she knew should go out in the night's mail. It would take her about thirty minutes to finish up, but since Arlene was never one to watch the clock on a secretarial job, she pounded away at the typewriter, heedless of the exodus of other employees.

When she handed in the work to George Albert, the office manager, he glanced at the clock and was gratefully surprised.

"Thank you very much, Miss Ferris," he said.

"Not at all. I realized these should be in the mail tonight."

"Not all of our girls are that considerate. We certainly appreciate your loyalty to the job. It surprised me you were willing to waive overtime."

"A good job is worth being loyal to," she said, and wished him good night.

The rain had turned into a cold drizzle. Reflected lights shimmered on the wet paving of the parking lot. Arlene hurried to her car, opened the door, got in, turned the key and stepped on the starter.

Sometimes the car took a little longer to start on cold, rainy nights, so she wasn't too concerned at first when the only sound which emanated from underneath the hood was the grind of the battery-driven starter with no explosive response from the motor.

After the first minute and a half, she became distinctly worried and looked around at the now all but deserted parking place. Only a few cars were spotted here and there, and Arlene suddenly realized that her battery was not turning the motor as fast as it had been. Her car seemed definitely stalled.

Suddenly a cheerfully competent voice said, "What's the matter? Having trouble?"

Arlene rolled down the left window to inspect the smiling, confident eyes of the tall, broad-shouldered man whose raincoat was belted about his trim waist.

"I seem to be having trouble with my motor," she said.

"Better let the battery rest for a minute," the man said. "You're not doing any good, just grinding away at it. Let me take a look."

He stepped to the side of the motor, raised the hood professionally, plunged his head and shoulders inside, then emerged after a moment and said, "Watch my right hand. When I wave it, press the starter. When I move it down sharply, stop. Be sure the ignition key is turned to the 'on' position. All ready?"

Arlene nodded gratefully.

Once more the head and shoulders vanished from sight. She watched the right hand. It waved gently, and Arlene pressed the starter. Almost at once the hand was plunged downward in a swiftly emphatic gesture, and Arlene took her foot off the starter.

The man lowered the hood of the car, walked around and shook his head. "No spark," he said.

"What does that mean?"

"Something's definitely wrong with your electrical system. There's no use running down your battery by using the starter. You're just not getting any current to the spark plugs. I'm afraid there's not much I can do in the rain. With the hood up, water keeps dripping down on the distributing system—that's probably what's the matter with it anyhow. I think you'd better leave it right here tonight. By tomorrow the rain will be over, the sun will be shining and the car will start right off."

"But," Arlene said, "I..."

The man's smile was engaging. "Exactly," he said. "I have my car right here. I'll be glad to take you home."

As Arlene hesitated, he added, "That is, if it isn't too far. If it is, I'll see that you get a bus or a cab."

Arlene took another long look at the face. The mouth was smiling. He had regular, even teeth. There was just the hint of something about the lips which indicated he was rather spoiled, but the eyes were expressive and there was a lean competence about him. Moreover, he wouldn't have been in the parking lot unless he was connected with the company, and if he was connected with the executive branch of the company he undoubtedly was all right.

"You're sure I won't be inconveniencing you?"

"Not at all," the man said, opening the door. "Roll up your window tight because it may rain some more tonight. I think it'll be clearing by midnight—at least that's the weather report. Here's my car, right over here."

When she saw the car she knew who he was. This was the son of old Jarvis P. Lamont, the owner of the company—Loring Lamont. He had been away on a tour of South America "surveying the business field" and had only recently returned. Arlene had, however, seen his car once when the elder Lamont had been chauffeured to the plant in it.

The young man held the door open for her with deferential courtesy. As she leaned back against the soft cushions, appreciating the rich leather upholstery, Loring Lamont jumped in the other side, and the motor, already running, purred into multi-cylindered response. A current of warm air flowed reassuringly about her chilled ankles. The big car glided into motion so gently she hardly realized it had started. Loring Lamont drove out past the watchman at the entrance to the parking lot.

"Right or left?" he asked.

"Left," she said.

"That's fine. That's the way I was going. How far?"

"My speedometer clocks it at two miles," she told him. And then added with a nervous laugh, "However, my car is not *quite* as late a model as this one."

"What's the address?" he asked.

She told him.

He frowned, said, "Say, look, I . . . what's your name?"

"Arlene Ferris."

"Mine's Lamont," he said. "Loring Lamont. Look, Miss Ferris, I suddenly remembered I've got some papers to deliver for the old man . . . gosh, I'm sorry. I heard your motor grinding away and realized you were running your battery down, and . . . well, you're pretty easy on the eyes and I guess I forgot my responsibilities for a minute."

"That's all right," she told him. "You can take me to where I can get a bus . . . or a cab."

"Now look," he said, "I can do better than that. If you aren't in a hurry, just settle back and relax. I'll have to deliver those papers, but the car is warm and comfortable. You can turn on the radio, get the latest news, music or anything you want. Then after I've delivered the papers I'll take you home. Or, if you'd like, we can stop for something to eat. I'm absolutely free after I deliver those confounded papers."

She hesitated for a moment, relaxing in the warm, dry comfort of the car. "All right," she said, "I'm in no hurry. If it won't inconvenience you . . ."

"No, no," he protested quickly. "I've got to come back to town anyway after I deliver the papers."

"Back to town?" she said quickly. "Is it far?"

"Not with this car," he said. "We'll get out of traffic and hit the freeway. Don't worry. Listen to the radio and . . . and I hope your acceptance includes dinner."

"We'll discuss that a little later," she said. And then, with a quick laugh, added, "After I get to know you better."

"Fair enough," he said.

The plant was within a mile of the freeway. Lamont turned on the freeway, drove for some fifteen minutes, then turned off, purred along a paved road for four or five miles, then turned off on a dirt road that wound its way among hills. They were now entirely out of traffic.

"How much farther is it?" Arlene asked, her voice sharpened with suspicion.

"Only a little way," he said. "We have a little country place up here, and my dad's associate is waiting for the papers there. Dad told him I'd be out."

"Oh," she said, and settled back again. She knew of the existence of the country place.

The dirt road was winding and twisting, a barbed-wire fence on each side. There were *No Trespassing* signs, then the car eased to a stop in front of a locked gate. Loring Lamont opened the gate, then drove along a graveled driveway, past a swimming pool, and finally stopped at a house which had a wide porch running around it, furnished with luxurious outdoor furniture.

"Well, what do you know!" Loring Lamont said. "The guy doesn't seem to be here."

"It's certainly all dark," she said, "and the gate was locked."

"We keep the gate locked, but he has a key," Loring said. "However, the place is dark, all right. You wait here and I'll run in and see if there's a note or something. My gosh, Miss Ferris, I certainly hate to have brought you all the way out here in case ... but the man *must* be here! He's to meet me here and wait for the papers ... he's staying here tonight and Dad's coming out later for a conference."

"Perhaps he went to sleep," she said, "and forgot to turn on the lights."

"You wait right here," he said. "I'll run in and see."

He left the motor idling, jumped out his side of the car and hurried into the house. She saw lights come on, on the porch, then lights in the interior of the house.

It was almost five minutes before he returned. His manner was apologetic. "Now," he said, "there *are* complications."

"What?"

"Dad's associate was delayed in town," he said. "He's on his way out here now. I got Dad on the phone and told him I'd leave the papers, but he says I'll have to wait, that those papers are classified and that I must deliver them personally and accept a receipt in person. It won't be long. Come on in and we'll wait. I don't think it will be over a few minutes."

She said, "I'll wait here in the car and ..."

He laughed. "Don't be so upstage. Anyhow, you can't wait in the car. I'm not too long on gas and I don't want to leave the motor idling. Without the motor running, the heater will be off, and ... come on in, I've turned up the thermostat and the house will warm quickly. You'll be very comfortable. If you'd like a drink we can fix up something that will put sunshine into the atmosphere."

He removed the keys from the car, then went around to her side of the car and held the door open invitingly, and after a moment's hesitation she gave him her hand, jumped to the ground and followed him into the house.

The interior was furnished with fine old Navaho rugs and mission furniture. It had an atmosphere of quiet luxury.

Loring Lamont crossed over to a sideboard, opened a door disclosing a sparkling array of glasses, opened another door to a compartment containing a stock of liquor.

"A drink while we wait?" he asked.

"No, thanks," she said. And then, looking at her wristwatch and for the first time having a vague feeling of apprehension, said, "I really *must* be getting home."

"Oh, come now," he said. "You're not in that much of a hurry. You're going to have dinner with me. Don't worry. Our man will be here in a few minutes, then all I have to do is give him the papers and we'll be on our way. I'm going to have a little drink. Come on, be sociable."

"Well," she said finally, "I'll take a Martini."

He mixed the drinks with a practiced hand. "Dry?" he asked.

"Rather dry, thank you."

He stirred the cocktails, poured them, handed her a glass, said, "Here's to getting better acquainted," and sipped the drink.

The telephone rang.

He frowned his annoyance, said, "*Now* what is it?" and crossed over to the telephone.

"Yes? Hello," he said.

He was silent for a moment, then said, "Oh, come now. I'm sorry but I've waited just as long as I can...where is he now? Where can I meet him? But I tell you, I *can't* wait any longer. I have a very important appointment and there's someone with me who has to...but look, Dad..."

He said "hello" several times, indicating that he had been cut off, then dropped the receiver into place and came across to frown moodily over the glass at Arlene. "This is the deuce of a note," he said. "That was Dad on the telehone. Old Jarvis P. himself, in one of his worst moods. He's opened up a brand new angle of discussion with this man, and I'm instructed to wait until he gets here. He says it may be as much as an hour."

Loring Lamont seemed genuinely concerned. "I'm terribly sorry," he said. "I got you into this. I should have told you right at the start...only I didn't know myself. The man was supposed to be waiting out here. When old Jarvis P. gets in one of those moods that's all there is to it. Finish your drink and I'll see if there is anything to eat in the refrigerator. We can at least have an appetizer."

Before she had a chance to protest, he tossed off the rest of his cocktail, went into the kitchen and she heard him rummaging around, opening the door of the refrigerator, closing it, opening and closing cupboard doors.

He came back and said, "How are you on biscuits?"

He said it so easily and naturally that, for the moment, she lost her suspicion and, emboldened by the warmth generated by her drink, said, "I'm pretty darn good on biscuits."

"Swell," he said. "If you'll make some biscuits, I'll fry some ham and eggs, and we can have dinner right here. I'm sorry I got you into this, but I simply must deliver those papers, and...it won't be as good a dinner as we could have had in a restaurant—except for the biscuits, of course. I have an idea *they'll* be out of this world."

"What do you have?" she asked. "Flour, milk, butter, shortening?"

"Everything," he said, "everything except fresh bread. There's no fresh bread here. There's fresh milk. We also have powdered milk, lots of canned goods, lots of ham, eggs, bacon, sausage, coffee, liquor. We keep the place provisioned because Dad likes to come out here occasionally for a conference, a more intimate type of conference than he can have in the office."

She unbuttoned her jacket, asked, "Where's the handwashing department?"

"Through that other room," he said. "First door to the left. You'll find everything—what do you want out here in the kitchen?"

"An apron mostly," she said.

She washed her hands, returned to the kitchen, and, feeling the effect of the cocktail, really began to enjoy herself. Loring Lamont turned on a hi-fi and the room was filled with music. Arlene mixed the biscuits and permitted herself a few dances with Loring Lamont while they were baking. To her delight, they turned out to be perfect—fluffy, flavorful biscuits which melted in her mouth when she tasted one.

Loring Lamont took a bite and was lavish in his praise.

He broke eggs in the frying pan, put ham on hot plates, lifted the percolator of coffee, smiled at her and said, "Now this is real cozy, real homelike."

At that moment the telephone sounded a strident summons.

Loring Lamont seemed for the moment genuinely surprised, then he excused himself, went to the phone, picked up the instrument, said cautiously, "Hello," then after a moment, "Oh, yes, hello...hello. All right. Okay. Now wait a minute let's not discuss it now. I'm...just a minute. Hold on. Okay."

Loring Lamont stepped out of the little alcove which housed the telephone, said to Arlene, "Will you take those eggs off the stove? Then go ahead and start eating—I won't be long. This is just an annoying interruption."

He went back, said into the telephone, "Okay. I'll take it on another line. Just hang on for a minute. Okay."

Loring Lamont left the phone off the hook, hurried back to another part of the lodge, picked up an extension phone and Arlene could hear a mumbled conversation.

She eased the eggs out of the frying pan to the plates, stood looking at the tempting array of ham, eggs and hot biscuits, thinking that this was homelike indeed, that someone always called on the telephone when hot food was on the table.

Then she heard Loring Lamont hurrying back.

He went to the telephone, picked up the receiver, slammed it into place and came toward her.

"Something serious?" she asked.

He kept on advancing toward her. For a moment she was puzzled. Then he had her in his arms, pulled her to him, kissed her hard on the lips.

She tried to push him away.

She was startled at the change in his face. There was no longer any mask of polite affability. There was savage, primitive passion, and a ruthlessness which frightened her.

Arlene pushed herself far enough back to aim a stinging slap at his face.

His eyes showed anger for a moment, then there was only a mocking smile. "Come on, baby," he said, "don't be a prude. Get off your high horse. We're stuck out here for a while and we may as well make the most of it. After all, I'm not exactly repulsive. At least I don't think I am. For your information, girls who have been nice to me have gone a long way in the company. Dad's private secretary, for instance, got *her* job through me. She was in a stenographic pool, and..."

"Well, I don't need to go a long way in the company," she blazed. "And *I* don't have to put up with anything like *your* tactics!"

Suddenly she realized a fatal discrepancy in his earlier remarks.

"You told me," she said, "that the man had already started, that he was on his way out here. Then after that telephone call you said your father was detaining him."

"I was mistaken the first time. They'd told me he'd started out so I wouldn't get too impatient. Then Dad called me and said he was holding him there for further conference."

"You know what I think?" she asked, looking at him contemptuously. "I think you had this thing planned from the very start. I don't think there's anyone coming out here. And, in case you want to know it, the reputation you have among the girls at the office isn't particularly flattering. I understand you think that anyone who works for the company has personal private obligations to you."

"It's an idea," he said, laughing. "Come off your high horse, Arlene. And you aren't going to gain anything, either now or later, by heaping abuse on me. You may as well face realities. Since you want to make something of it, I'll admit that I've been crazy about you ever since I got back from South America and saw you there in the office.

"If you want to know it, I lifted a part of the distributor out of your car so it wouldn't start. I 'happened' along at just the psychological moment. You're entirely correct in assuming that I made up this whole story. When I came in the first time I called a friend of mine and told him to call me back on the phone in exactly seven minutes. That was simply a decoy call.

"Now then, Sweetheart, I have the keys to the car. You're going to stay here until I get good and ready to let you go home. If you don't act up, we're going to have a pleasant evening. If you act up... well, that's all the good it's going to do you.

"Come on, Arlene, you may as well yield to the inevitable with good grace."

"It's not inevitable," she said. "I'm not yielding and I don't have any good grace. Now, you take me home at once or I'll lodge a criminal complaint against you, regardless of who you are."

He laughed and said, "Try it. See how far you get. Who do you think is going to believe a story about you coming out here with me, about having a drink with me and all that, and then suddenly becoming upstage?"

He dangled the car keys. "Here they are," he said. "Come and get them. I dare you."

Seething with indignation, she came at him in an avalanche of human fury, and was immediately shoved with brutal strength back through the dining room, into the living room. He pushed her back against a davenport until she collapsed. Then he was once more caressing her passionately.

She doubled her knees, got them against his chest, pressed her back against the davenport and gave a sudden push.

The push broke his hold. He staggered backwards. She was on her feet and picked up a chair. "You... you beast!" she said.

He laughed. "I like spitfires," he said. "Come on baby, you can't get anywhere with this stuff."

She realized that he must have done this many times before, that he knew exactly what he was doing.

"I'm going to have you arrested if you so much as put your hand on me again," she said.

"Let me tell you something about the law in this state," he replied calmly. "I happen to know what it is. If a woman presents a charge for criminal attack against a man, her own previous moral character can be inquired into. Dad's lawyers even gave me the California case that determined the point. It's People vs. Battilana. That means that with all the money at my command, I can put detectives on your back trail. I can turn you inside out on the witness stand. I can ask you names, dates, specific occasions, and..."

In an ecstasy of blind fury, she flung the chair.

He was hardly expecting this maneuver. The chair caught him low in the abdomen. For a moment there was a look of utter surprise on his face, then he doubled over in pain.

Arlene made for the door.

She grabbed her raincoat as she went through the reception hallway, then she was out on the porch, running down the gravel driveway, past the swimming pool, out to the dirt road.

She knew that he had the keys to the car, that it was no use to try and get transportation until she came to the main traveled highway, and even then it was doubtful if any cars would be along.

She didn't bother to put on the raincoat but held it bundled under her left arm. She ran pell-mell down the road until she found herself getting short of breath. Then she slowed to a walk and looked back over her shoulder.

She could see a blob of light from the house, then she saw a moving pencil of light, the beam of the headlights swinging around the driveway. Soon the headlights would be illuminating the road, cutting through the moist darkness.

She swung abruptly from the road, came to the barbed-wire fence, and crawled through. Then she hesitated a moment and turned back toward the house, keeping in the shadows cast by the trees.

The twin beams of the headlights swept down the road. The car was coming, but it was coming so slowly that for a moment she was completely fooled.

She stood there, protected by the trunk of an oak, watching the creeping lights moving slowly along the road.

The car came to the exact place where she had detoured to crawl through the fence and stopped.

Then as she saw Loring Lamont getting out of the car and walking to the front of the headlights, she saw the beam of a flashlight playing along the ground. The light switched abruptly and came toward the fence.

For the first time she realized the reason the car had been going so slowly. Lamont had known that she couldn't keep up a running pace down the mile or so of country road which was fenced on both sides. He had been following her tracks in the wet dirt, and when he came to the place where she had turned off, he was using the flashlight to track her.

For a moment she was cold with fear. This man knew exactly what he was doing. He was cold, ruthless and determined.

The beam of the flashlight following her tracks came to the fence.

Arlene Ferris wanted to scream and run, then suddenly her brain began to function smoothly. She moved quietly along the fence, then again crawled through the barbed wire and down into the roadway.

Lamont had come to the place now where she had been standing. It was a little more difficult tracking her in the terrain which had not been cleared into a roadway. But, nevertheless, he was following her steps. Her heels made unmistakable marks in the soft ground.

Loring Lamont had made one fatal error. He had left the headlights on, the motor running, the key in the ignition lock.

When she was within six or eight feet of the car, Lamont came to the place where she had gone through the fence for the second time. He evidently realized then what she had in mind.

The questing finger of the flashlight darted along the road, then suddenly caught her in its brilliance.

There was momentary panic in his voice. "You touch that car and you'll go to jail!" he shouted. Then he was scrambling through the fence, trying to get to the road in time to overtake her.

She jumped into the car, threw up her wet skirt in order to give her legs plenty of freedom, pushed the driving control lever and felt the car glide into motion.

He was in the roadway right behind her now. She could see the flashlight in the rearview mirror. Her toe found the throttle. She pressed down and the car leaped ahead as though it had been propelled by a rocket.

Surprised at the swift acceleration, she almost went into the ditch at the first turn. But she finally got control of the car. The power steering was new to her and bothered her for the first two hundred yards. After that, she had the car fairly well mastered, and by the time she had turned into the main highway she was handling the wheel like a veteran.

She drove to her apartment, left the car parked there, jumped into dry clothes, then, actuated by a bit of sardonic humor, looked up Loring Lamont's address in the telephone directory, drove the car to his apartment house, parked it in the street directly in front of a fireplug, walked four blocks to the main boulevard where there was a drugstore, phoned for a taxicab and went home.

CHAPTER TWO

The next day was bright and sunny, as Loring Lamont had predicted. Arlene Ferris had a repairman look at her car. Sure enough, he reported that a part had been taken from the electrical distributor. A new part was found and put into place, and the car ran perfectly.

Arlene typed mechanically, awaiting the summons which would bring her to the office of the office manager. She was grimly determined that this was one time Loring Lamont, spoiled son of a rich and powerful father, was not going to get away with it. Let them try to fire her. She'd show them she wasn't a chattel.

During the first part of the morning she debated whether or not to prosecute.

They would, of course, put detectives at work digging up every event in her past life. They would get the names of every boy with whom she had gone out. Every petting party would be turned into a major indiscretion. They would attempt to blacken her character, would doubtless claim that she had tried blackmail.

She knew that, for her own sake, it would be better to keep quiet, to say nothing. But she also felt that too many young women in Loring Lamont's life had decided to follow the line of least resistance, thereby making it doubly hard for the next young woman on whom Loring Lamont cast his predatory eyes.

Shortly before noon she made up her mind. She went to the women's lounge, looked up the telephone number of Perry Mason, attorney at law, and called his office.

Eventually she was connected with Della Street, Perry Mason's secretary.

"This is Arlene Ferris," she said. "I'm working at the Lamont Rolling, Casting and Engineering Company. I get off work at five o'clock. Would it be possible for me to see Mr. Mason tonight on a personal and very important matter? I can get away earlier, if it's necessary."

"Just a moment," Della Street said.

She was back on the line within a few minutes. "Do you think you could get excused so as to be here at two-thirty?" she asked.

"I'll be there," Arlene Ferris promised.

She felt as if a load had been lifted from her mind. She was going to go through with it. She'd show Loring Lamont she wasn't going to put up with that sort of treatment.

At one-thirty there was a ripple of excitement in the office. Jarvis P. Lamont, looking as though the world had caved in on him, hurried from the office. The second vice president emerged to run after Lamont.

There had been no sign of Loring Lamont.

A few minutes before two, Arlene Ferris went to the office manager. "I worked late last night," she said, "and now I have to be out for about an hour. You can dock me if you wish."

George Albert seemed somewhat nonplussed. "This is a *most* unusual request, Miss Ferris," he said.

"I know," Arlene said, "but it's an unusual situation."

"Well," he replied, hesitating, "of course, we are aware of the fact that you *have* put in overtime—I guess it's all right. You understand, Miss Ferris, the problem is that of creating a precedent—it sometimes happens that girls have dental or doctor appointments where they *have* to be excused, but if we are too liberal they'll be making beauty parlor appointments and we can't tell where things will stop."

"I understand," Arlene said briefly, and paused.

"Very well," Albert agreed reluctantly. "We'll expect you back in an hour."

"An hour and a half," Arlene said, firmly.

The man seemed puzzled by Arlene's manner. "Very well, Miss Ferris," he said, and let it go at that.

Arlene made no attempt to take her car, but took a cab so she wouldn't have to waste time finding a parking place. She wanted to get back within the designated period of an hour and a half because she had said she would, but she felt it really didn't make much difference. After all, she was quite certain that by this time tomorrow she would no longer be an employee of the company.

CHAPTER THREE

As Arlene Ferris finished her story, Della Street, Perry Mason's confidential secretary, looked up from her notebook. Her eyes were sympathetic as she waited for the lawyer's decision.

Mason, his face granite hard, his eyes shrewdly appraising the young woman, said, "Exactly what do you want to do, Miss Ferris?"

"I . . . I want to show him that women aren't chattels, that a working girl is entitled to consideration—just because I work for a company as a stenographer doesn't mean that I automatically have to become the plaything of the spoiled son of the owner of the business."

"You want to teach him a lesson, is that it?" Mason asked.

"Not exactly. I don't want to have to live my life feeling that women who work for an organization are . . . oh, all right, I *do* want to teach him a lesson."

"How?"

"That's what I wanted you to tell me."

"You can file a suit for damages," Mason said, "or you can go to the police and lodge a criminal complaint. But you can't do both."

"Why?"

"For practical reasons. The minute you file a suit for damages, the criminal case goes out the window. A shrewd defense attorney would make it appear that you were trying to capitalize on the experience."

"I see—and what if I file a suit and don't make a complaint to the police?"

"There, of course," Mason said, "you get to the ultimate question of what a jury will do, and, again, that depends on exactly what you want. If you want money to salve your injured feelings..."

"I don't. I just want to... it's hard to explain. I want to stand up for my rights. I want to stand up for my sex."

Mason nodded. "I think you measure up," he said. "If you want to put a stop to this sort of thing, we'll put a stop to it—but it isn't going to be easy. They'll throw mud, they'll claim blackmail, they'll have young Lamont testifying that you deliberately led him on, that *you* were the one who made passes at *him*, that when he was too bored to acquiesce you ran true to the old adage that hell hath no fury like a woman scorned."

Her face went suddenly white. "He'd do that?"

"Sure, he'd do that," Mason said. "You don't expect a man of that type to tell the truth, do you? Do you still want to go ahead with it?"

"Mr. Mason," she said, "I'll fight this thing through—if you'll stay with me I'll stay with the case. Once I start fighting I keep on fighting."

"Good girl," Mason told her.

He turned to Della Street. "Ring Paul Drake at the Drake Detective Agency. Ask him if he can come down here right away. Let's start getting evidence before young Lamont begins to realize what he's up against."

Mason turned to Arlene Ferris. "You say you left his car in front of a fireplug?"

"I parked it right smack-dab in front of a fireplug. I just hope they give him a dozen tickets for illegal parking."

Mason smiled, said, "That probably gives us our chance. He'll be making excuses for the illegal parking, and it will be interesting to see what story he tells."

"You don't think he'll tell the truth, do you?"

"No," Mason said, "I don't. But I do think that he'll tell a story to the effect that some angry girl was trying to get even with him. It may well differ from the story he'll tell when he gets into court.

"By the time he gets into court you will be described as the aggressor. You will have been literally throwing yourself at him, trying to advance yourself in the company by courting his favor. You say that he told you some other woman had got ahead through him?"

"Yes. The private secretary to Jarvis P. Lamont."

"Would you know her name?"

"Edith Bristol," she said.

"Have you met her?"

"I've seen her a number of times."

"Can you describe her?"

"A very good-looking girl—twenty-six or twenty-seven, really an outstanding figure, and... well, she'd stand out anywhere as a real beauty if it wasn't..."

"If it wasn't for what?" Mason asked.

"Her eyes," she said. "There's something about them, a defeated look... it's hard to describe. I never thought of it before, but now that you mention her in connection with..."

Paul Drake's code knock sounded on the door.

"That's Paul Drake," Mason said to Della Street. "Let him in."

By way of explanation, Mason said to Arlene Ferris, "The Drake Detective Agency does all of my investigative work. They have offices on the same floor here in the building. You'll like Paul Drake. He seems rather casual when you first meet him, but I can assure you he's thoroughly competent."

Della Street opened the door. Mason said, "Miss Ferris, this is Paul Drake, head of the Drake Detective Agency. Sit down, Paul."

Paul Drake acknowledged the introduction, seated himself across from Mason's desk.

Mason said, "Are you acquainted with the Lamont family, Paul? The Rolling, Casting and Engineering Company?"

Drake's eyes narrowed. "What about them, Perry?"

Mason said, "They have a country place up toward the hills—a real country lodge, I guess you'd call it, complete with swimming pool, Navaho rugs, barbecue, liquor closet, and the rest of it."

Drake nodded. "I know where it is."

"Loring Lamont's car was parked in front of a fireplug last night," Mason said. "I'd like to know what time it was moved and by whom. I'd like to know what Loring Lamont has to say about how it happened to be parked there, whether he accepts or disclaims responsibility, and, if possible, I'd like to find who some of his friends are, people in whom he would confide. I want to see if he has talked about where he was last night. I want to find out about all this before he knows any investigation is being made."

Drake's eyes met Mason's steadily. "Miss Ferris is the client?" he asked. Mason nodded.

Drake said, "I hate to do this, Perry. Probably I should get you to one side, but it may be that on account of the time element involved we don't have that much time to waste. Loring Lamont was murdered last night."

Mason's eyes snapped wide open. Arlene Ferris gave a dismayed gasp.

"Go on," Mason said, his face hard with expressionless concentration.

"I don't know too much about it," Drake said. "I heard a news broadcast over the radio. I was interested in developments in another case that we're working on, and I thought the police might have released some news this afternoon, so I tuned in on a broadcast about fifteen minutes before you called. All I heard was the bare announcement that Loring Lamont, son of Jarvis P. Lamont, the famed industrialist, had been murdered last night. His body was discovered in the rustic retreat maintained by the company as a place of recreation and for conferences. He had been stabbed in the back with a butcher knife."

"Any clues?" Mason asked.

"That was all the radio report said."

"Any statement about the guilty person?"

"Police were trying to find a young woman who had apparently been with him last night," Drake said.

Mason said, "All right, Paul, beat it."

Drake said, "Perhaps I..."

Mason interrupted. "Time is precious, Paul. I've got to give some advice to my client. I've got to give it to her fast. It has to be confidential. If you're here there's no privilege in connection with the communication. Conversations between an attorney and his client are privileged, provided he doesn't have outsiders present. Della Street isn't an outsider. She's included in the legal privilege. Get going."

Drake was out of the chair in one swift motion. He jerked open the door, smiled at Arlene Ferris, said, "You couldn't be in better hands," and shot out into the corridor.

Mason said, "All right now, let's get it fast. Did you kill him?"

She shook her head.

"What time was it when you left there?"

"I don't know. Perhaps—well, somewhere around seven o'clock."

"And you got your clothes pretty muddy?"

She nodded.

"Your clothes were torn?"

"My blouse was torn."

"Bra?" Mason asked.

"I was generally mussed up. I had to make emergency repairs after I got out on the main highway."

"You drove his car?"

She nodded.

"And you parked it directly in front of a fireplug?"

Again she nodded.

"The rearview mirror is the most sensitive place on a car for fingerprints," Mason said. "A person adjusting a rearview mirror will almost invariably leave prints of the third and fourth fingers. Do you remember if you adjusted the mirror? You must have if you were using it in driving."

"I adjusted it," she admitted.

"Gloves?"

"No."

Mason said, "Listen very, very carefully to what I have to say. Flight is an evidence of guilt. Failure to report a crime may also become a crime. On the other hand, a person is entitled to follow the advice of an attorney. If the attorney gives wrong advice that's his responsibility. If he advised a client to do something illegal he is subject to disbarment. Do you understand?"

She nodded.

"All right," Mason said. "I do *not* want you to resort to flight. Do you understand?"

She nodded.

"On the other hand, I don't dare have you tell your story to the police right at the present time. We'll need to get it corroborated with some sort of evidence. You took off your torn clothes and left them in your apartment?"

She nodded

"They're in your apartment now?"

"Yes."

"What about your outer garments?"

"I got mud on my skirt when I crawled through the barbed-wire fence."

"Now, think carefully," Mason said. "Were there any bloodstains?"

She hesitated for a moment, then wordlessly pulled up her skirt. On the thigh of her right leg was a long, red scratch. "I did that," she said. "when I plunged through the fence the second time—I was in a hurry. I wanted to get to his car before he realized that he'd left himself in a vulnerable position. As soon as I heard the sound of the idling motor I knew that if I could get to his car first . . . well, I guess I always do think in terms of a counteroffensive. I did *so* want to turn the tables on him. I threw discretion to the winds. I just shot under that fence and that's where I got the scratch."

"And it bled?"

"It bled."

"On the skirt?"

She nodded.

"The skirt was torn?" Mason asked.

"I don't think it was," she said. "I shot through under the fence feet first. My skirt was way up around my middle somewhere. My . . . my panties were stained from the mud. There was mud on the skirt."

"You washed your undergarment?" Mason asked.

She shook her head and said, "I left everything in my laundry basket."

"All right," Mason said, "we've got to concede certain trumps to the police. They're bound to take some tricks. Give me the key to your apartment. Authorize me to go there and do anything I see fit."

She opened her purse, handed him a key.

"Are you going to remove my clothes?"

"Heavens no! That would be tampering with evidence. I'm going to let the police do all the tampering with the evidence."

"I'm afraid I don't understand," she said.

"I don't want you to," Mason told her. "Now I want just as much time as I can get before you are questioned by the police. You'll have to co-operate on that."

"But I thought you told me you didn't want me to resort to flight."

"I don't," Mason said. "I want you to do exactly what any other young woman would do under the circumstances."

"What do you mean?" she asked. "Wouldn't it be normal to go to the police?"

"You're following *my* advice," Mason told her. "*I* will tell the police everything I feel that they need to know, at the time I think they should know it. Right at the moment I want you out of circulation, but I *don't* want you to resort to flight—now there's a difference. Do you understand?"

"I'm not certain that I do."

Mason said, "Do exactly as I tell you. If it comes to a showdown and you are absolutely forced to account for your actions, you can state you were following my advice. But I don't want you to make that statement until I tell you to.

"Now then, the first thing is to get yourself fired."

"That won't be difficult," she said. "Once it becomes known that I . . ."

Mason shook his head. "With Loring Lamont dead, there is no way that it's going to become known unless you left some evidence on the ground linking you to that country lodge."

"And if there isn't any such evidence?"

"They may not know that you were out there with him for some time," Mason said, "but we can't count on that. They may be looking for you any minute now. The first thing you've got to do is to get fired. Go back to your job and get discharged—at once."

She was thoughtful. "It might not be easy to . . ."

"I don't care whether it's easy or not," Mason snapped. "Get yourself fired."

"Then what?" she asked.

Mason said, "You have a girl friend somewhere here in the city?"

"Not right in the city."

"Close by?"

"Santa Monica."

"What's her name?"

"Madge Elwood."

"How old?"

"Twenty-seven."

"Blonde or brunette?"

"Brunette."

"What does she look like?"

"She's about my size. She has a wonderful figure. She was selected as a beauty queen a few years ago. I'm not as good-looking as she is, but there is quite a remarkable resemblance. Some people think we are related."

"What does she do now?"

"She's a secretary."

"Good job?" Mason asked.

"Yes. It's a responsible position."

"You've known her since you came here?"

"Long before that. We've been friends for years. It was through her that I came here—it was, in fact, through her that I got this job at the Lamont Company. She had some contact there, I don't know just who it was, but I know that she put through a telephone call and then told me to go in and things certainly were made easy for me. I just breezed into a position while some of the other applicants were still sitting around waiting."

Mason nodded. "Go get yourself fired. Then ring up Madge Elwood. Tell her that you've lost your job and that you just *have* to see her. Go down and stay with her in Santa Monica. Stay there overnight."

"And what do I tell her?"

"Tell her you got fired. Tell her you're satisfied you were discharged because Loring Lamont made a report to the boss, that he made a pass at you and you turned him down. Don't tell your friend any of the details. Simply say you're too upset to talk about it."

"She already knows about the trouble I had with Loring Lamont," Arlene said. "You see, since I got the job through her, I felt I owed her an explanation. I rang her up last night as soon as I got back and asked her why she hadn't warned me about the wolves in the company."

"And what did she say?" Mason asked.

She hesitated. "Madge is a good sport. Of course she's had people make passes at her. We all have. I guess it's just a question of how you handle them...I suppose I could have handled the situation last night if it hadn't been...well, he got this last telephone call and it seemed to do things to him. He just flung all tact and discretion to the winds...Well, you wanted to know about Madge...she asked me if I thought there were any jobs where the boss wouldn't make an occasional pass, so I described what happened—and when I told her about leaving his car in front of the fireplug I thought she'd die laughing."

Mason was thoughtful. "You'd better run down to visit your friend," he said. "Leave her telephone number and address with Miss Street here. And when Madge hears about the murder, tell her to keep quiet about everything you told her, and..."

"I'm not to tell her about the murder?"

"Not a word—not a word about that to anyone."

"Suppose she comes right out and asks me?"

"She won't," Mason said. "When you tell a friend about having a struggle with some man, the friend doesn't say, 'Oh, is he still alive?' Can you depend on this Madge Elwood?"

"Heavens, yes. She's a wonderful friend, very loyal."

"Get started," Mason said.

"But I'll need the key to go to my apartment and get..."

"You *don't* go to your apartment," Mason said. "You don't get a thing."

"Not even the clothes that..."

"There isn't that much time. Call up Madge Elwood as soon as you get yourself fired. Now leave her address and phone number with Miss Street and get started."

CHAPTER FOUR

It was five-forty when Paul Drake's code knock sounded on the exit door of the private office.

Mason nodded to Della Street, who opened the door.

"Hi, Della," Paul said, and nodded to Mason. "You want the latest on this Lamont murder?"

"What have you got, Paul?"

"Now, mind you, Perry, I don't know what you know, and I don't want to know what you know. I don't want to take that responsibility."

Mason nodded.

"I'm telling you what *I* know," Drake said.

"Go ahead."

"This rolling, casting and engineering company does some classified work. Not too much, but some. They have the place guarded. You need a clearance in order to get in. They have an executive parking lot reserved for people in the engineering office. There's a little cubbyhole office and a man stays on duty there. It's his job to see that cars that go in or out have the sticker of the company on them and are driven by authorized personnel. Actually, he doesn't pay too much attention to the cars going *out*, but the cars going *in* are different. He looks over the car and the driver. If he doesn't recognize the driver, or the car isn't properly fixed up with a sticker, he stops the car and makes a detailed check.

"He remembers that last night, about quarter to six, he saw Loring Lamont driving out. There was a young woman in the car with Loring. He's given the police a description of the woman. So far, it's more or less a general description—dark hair, rather young, somewhere in the twenties, good-looking. The police are acting on the theory that Loring Lamont had a date and went out to this country place the company maintains in the hills west of the city, that they had a drink, that Lamont cooked up a supper of ham and eggs, and that after supper there was an argument and the girl stabbed him.

"The police aren't releasing anything to the public as yet, but of course they're very anxious to find this girl and question her.

"The general gossip is that Lamont was inclined to be impulsive, as far as women were concerned."

Mason digested the information.

"I don't want to make any suggestions," Drake said, "but since the young woman was seen leaving the parking lot with Loring Lamont, the police have an idea that she was some woman who worked in the place. Since Lamont's car went out about five-forty-five, they have the idea that she was probably an employee who may have been working late, that Lamont had a date with her to go out after hours and had waited for her.

"You give the police that much to work with and it won't be long before they come up with an answer—now if that answer is going to involve your client, it's going to be a whole lot better to have her come out with her story first and claim that she was protecting herself against attack. If she waits until after the police pick her up, then it isn't going to look so good."

"She stabbed him in the back in self-defense, eh?" Mason asked.

"It *could* have happened," Drake said.

"Thanks a lot," Mason told him. "Keep your men on the job. Just where is this place, Paul?"

Drake took a map from his pocket. "Here's an automobile map, and here's a large-scale sketch map showing just how you get to the place. I understand the police are still out there, so don't let our mutual friend, Lieutenant Tragg, catch you snooping around or he'll immediately put another two and two together. I understand he's working on the job at the special request of Jarvis P. Lamont, who, as it happens, has a hell of a lot of influence."

Mason nodded, took the map, said, "Keep on the job, Paul. Della and I had planned to go out for dinner, and I was going to get in touch with you after dinner. As it is, we'll probably wait here a little while. I'm going to have to think this thing out."

Drake left the office. Della Street glanced apprehensively at Perry Mason.

Mason looked at his wrist watch. "Give them a couple of hours," he said, "and they'll have the answer."

"And then?" she asked.

"Then," Mason said, "they'll be looking for Arlene Ferris, and... Della, you have that Santa Monica number?"

Della Street nodded.

"Put through a call," Mason said.

"Ask for Arlene Ferris?"

"Heavens, no!" Mason said. "Ask for Madge Elwood."

Della Street gave him a quick glance, put through the call. A moment later she said, "Miss Elwood on the line."

Mason picked up the telephone. "Madge Elwood?"

"Yes."

"I'm Perry Mason, the lawyer, but please don't mention my name at your end of the line. Have you talked with Arlene Ferris?"

"Why yes... but good heavens! You! I'm a fan of yours... I... well, I'll hold it."

"Is Arlene there?"

"Yes."

"I want you to do something."

"Yes. What?"

"Confine yourself to noncommittal answers," Mason said, "that won't let Arlene Ferris know who is talking. I want you to do something that is for her best interests, but she may not approve of what I'm going to do."

"Very well."

"Are you willing to help?"

"Anything."

"Do you have a car?"

"Yes."

"You know where Arlene Ferris has her apartment?"

"Of course."

Mason said, "Make some excuse to Arlene. Tell her that you have a date with a boy friend, tell her to stay there in your apartment and not to go out until you get back."

"And then?"

"Then get in your car and drive at once to Arlene Ferris' apartment. Park your car about a block away—do you smoke?"

"Yes. Why?"

"When you get in front of the apartment house," Mason said, "light a cigarette."

"Isn't that rather—unusual?"

"You mean you don't smoke on the street?"

"Something like that."

"That's why I want you to do something that will tell me who you are. It has to be unusual but not suspiciously so. Light a cigarette when you're right in front of the apartment house."

"Yes. Go on."

"Now then," Mason said, "after you've struck the match and lit your cigarette, stand there for a minute. If the coast is clear, I'll come up to you. If I don't come up and speak to you within a matter of two or three seconds, just keep right on walking past the apartment house. Walk around the block, get into your car, drive back to Santa Monica and forget about the whole thing. Have you got that straight?"

"I think so."

"All right," Mason said. "How long will it take you to get there?"

"I can make it in...oh, I'd say twenty-five minutes from now."

"All right," Mason told her. "I'll be waiting. Remember, if I don't get in touch with you shortly after you've lit the cigarette, keep right on walking. Don't look at the apartment house or look around. Just walk on by as though you had stopped to light a cigarette and that was all. Get started now. That's a good girl."

Mason hung up.

Della Street raised her eyebrows in silent interrogation.

"I'm sorry," Mason said, "but you're going to have to wait this one out, Della. Stand by the telephone. Wait for me. Get me my miniature camera and the flashgun. I'll probably want some pictures. Get our photographer to stay on in his studio."

"How long will you be gone?" she asked.

"I don't know. I'm going to try to turn a red herring into a decoy."

"I'll wait," Della Street told him.

"Good girl," he said.

He went to his car, drove to a place where he could find a parking place within a couple of blocks of the building where Arlene Ferris had her apartment, smoked a cigarette, then took the camera case from the car and went to stand unobtrusively in the shadows in front of the building.

A few minutes later a young woman walking briskly along the sidewalk paused directly in front of the apartment house, took a cigarette from her purse, scraped a match into flame and held a light in her cupped hands.

She did a good job of acting, letting the match blow out, fumbling for another match, taking time to light the cigarette the second time.

Mason stepped up. "Madge Elwood?"

"Mr. Mason?"

"Yes. Let's go."

"Where?"

"At the moment, to Arlene Ferris' apartment. You're willing to help?"

"Heavens, yes! I'm willing to do everything I can. But will you tell me what this is all about, Mr. Mason? I had the news turned on, on the radio driving in, and I heard that Loring Lamont, son of Jarvis P. Lamont, had been killed. I knew that Arlene had been forced to fight him off . . . tell me, is there any . . . any possible connection?"

"You said you wanted to help Arlene," Mason interrupted.

"I do."

"All right then," Mason said. "Come on up to Arlene's apartment."

"You haven't answered my question, Mr. Mason."

"That's a very interesting observation on your part, and it's entirely accurate," Mason said. "I haven't. Come on, let's go."

They entered the apartment house, took the elevator to the fourth floor, and Mason said, "You know where Arlene's apartment is?"

"Yes, of course."

"Lead the way," Mason said. "Take this key. Open the door casually."

She looked at him questioningly, then took the key which he handed her, walked down the corridor, opened the door, went in, switched on the lights and held the door open for Mason.

"All right," she said, closing the door behind them. "Now what?"

Mason said, "You're going to have to take me on trust."

"I've done that long ago."

"Arlene says you're a good friend of hers."

"I am."

"That you're loyal to your friends."

"I try to be."

"How long have you known her?"

"Seven years."

"You knew her before she came here?"

"Yes. We were together in the East, and then I came out here and we didn't see each other for a couple of years—but we kept up a correspondence. Arlene is a wonderful girl. She'd do anything for me and I think I'd do anything for her."

Mason said, "You look very much like her. There's a striking resemblance."

"Isn't it weird? People always take us for sisters. Sometimes they get us mixed up; yet, as far as we can tell, there isn't any relationship."

Mason sized up the young woman, eying her speculatively until Madge stirred uneasily.

"Don't look at me like that. I feel you're mentally . . ."

"I am, but not the way you think. Where does Arlene keep her clothes?"

"In the closet."

"Find something you can wear," Mason said. "Go in the bathroom and put it on. Take off that skirt and give it to me."

"And then?" she asked.

Mason said, "Then, in case you are questioned, you are to say nothing—absolutely nothing. In the meantime, hold still. I want some pictures."

Mason took out the camera, focused it, took several snapshots, said, "Okay, now go change."

Madge Elwood hesitated. "Are you certain you know what you want? Perhaps I know some things you don't know, Mr. Mason."

"Look, we haven't time for a debate. Are you willing to help Arlene?"

"Yes."

"You buy your clothes in Santa Monica?"

"Yes."

"Your skirt has a Santa Monica label?"

"Yes."

Mason walked over to the window of the apartment, looked down at the street. Madge Elwood still hesitated, studying him thoughtfully.

Mason saw a police car glide around the corner, come to a stop in front of the building.

Mason whirled. "All right," he said, "it's too late. You haven't time to do it now. The police are here. Come on, we've got to go."

"This would help Arlene?" she asked.

"I think it would have helped. It's too late now."

She reached an instant decision, unfastened the belt on the skirt, pulled a zipper, dropped it to the floor and stepped out, clad in stockings and panties. "Throw me that skirt. The one on the first hanger," she said.

Mason shook his head. "I tell you there isn't time."

"Throw it, damn it!" she said. "I'll dress in the hall."

Mason looked at her long, graceful legs, said, "You'd start a riot, but..." He grabbed the skirt off the first hanger. "Okay, we'll try it. Whip into that skirt. Quick!"

While Madge Elwood was dropping the skirt over her head, Mason took out his pocketknife, made a cut in the skirt Madge Elwood had taken off, and ripped out a piece of the garment from the hem.

Madge Elwood, holding the skirt about her with one hand, pulled open the door.

"This way," Mason said.

They raced down the corridor to the stair door and were opening it just as the elevator came to a stop. Lt. Tragg and a plain-clothes officer stepped out into the corridor as the door slid shut behind Mason and Madge Elwood.

Madge Elwood twisted her hips into the skirt, hitched it around, pulled up the zipper, said, "Now what?"

"Now," Mason said, "we go down two flights, sit on the stairs and wait."

"And if one of the tenants uses the stairs?"

"We are engaged in low-voiced conversation," Mason said. "I am telling you that my divorce decree won't be final for another three months. You are telling me that if I am not in a position to marry you, you're going to break the whole thing off, that you're tired of being kept dangling on a string, that we can't go on living like this."

"It seems to me," she said smiling, "that I've read the lines somewhere. I may even have heard them."

"You might have," Mason said dryly. "How are you on acting?"

"We can try. And how long do we keep it up?"

"Thirty minutes anyway," Mason said. "Perhaps longer. We'll light a dozen cigarettes simultaneously and let them burn until they get down to stubs so we can have evidence that the conversation has been going for some time."

"I'm in your hands," she told him. "In your position you have to know what you're doing, and it has to be legal."

"Sometimes," Mason admitted, "I wish I had a greater margin of safety, but ... well, I can tell you this much. I try to give a client all the breaks. There's a popular belief that circumstantial evidence leads to injustices. Actually, circumstantial evidence is some of the best evidence we have, *if* it is properly interpreted.

"The evidence that is really responsible for more miscarriages of justice than anything else is personal identification."

"And I take it this has to do with personal identification."

"It does," Mason said. "I have reason to believe that a certain witness is going to identify anyone the officers point out to him as being the person he saw in a certain car with a certain party."

"How interesting. Don't you have the right to cross-examine such a person?"

"Sure, I have the *right*," Mason said, "and how much good does it do? According to my theory, you can cross-examine a man by putting him in a situation where his actions contradict his words a whole lot better than you can by trying to get his words to contradict his words."

"That," she said, "sounds very lawyer-like and very Perry Mason-like, if you don't mind my saying so. Shall we go down another flight of stairs and engage in our act?"

Mason nodded.

They walked down the stairs to the flight between the second and third floors. There Madge Elwood gathered her borrowed skirt tightly around her and made room for Mason to sit close to her.

Mason lit one cigarette after another, left them burning on the stairs until they got down to stubs, then ground them out.

"It really looks as though we've been here a long time," she said.

"I hope so," Mason told her.

"The arm, Mr. Mason."

"What about the arm?"

"It's out of place."

She gently took his left arm and put it around her waist. "Now then," she said, "I'll put my head on your shoulder and in this trusting, intimate position I'll ask you if you've read any good books lately."

"I don't have time to read," Mason said. "I keep too damned busy."

"It sounds like an interesting life," she murmured seductively.

"It is."

"I've followed your adventures, if that's the proper word, in the newspapers. You certainly seem to handle your cases in a spectacular way."

"I try to make them interesting," Mason said. "Jurors are human. They'll pay attention to something that interests them. If you start droning through the usual routine of handling a case they'll lose interest and you'll lose the case."

"You mean your client will," she muttered dreamily.

"With me it's the same thing," Mason said.

"With some lawyers it isn't," she told him, and snuggled closer.

Half an hour later Mason sighed, said, "This has been a perfectly delightful thirty minutes. Now run down to the door to the second floor, take the elevator down from there. Go through the lobby and walk out. If there's a police car at the curb, just keep on going. Don't come back. If the police car is gone, pretend that you forgot something, come running back to the elevator, take it to the second floor, then come to the stair door and beckon to me."

"If the police car's there, I'm to keep right on going?"

"Yes."

"Going where?"

"To Santa Monica."

"When will I see you again?"

"I don't know, but get tomorrow off if you can so you will be available for a phone call."

"On my way," she said.

Mason helped her to her feet. She shook out Arlene Ferris' skirt, tripped lightly down the stairs and through the stair door.

She did not return.

Mason sat there for another twenty minutes. His extravagant buildup with the cigarettes had consumed the entire supply in his cigarette case and he looked at his watch a dozen times in the last ten minutes of his wait. Then finally he arose, squared his shoulders, dusted off his clothes, walked down the stairs to the second floor, took the elevator to the lobby and walked out through the door.

The police car was no longer at the curb.

Mason walked to the place where he had parked his car and drove to his office building.

CHAPTER FIVE

Mason latchkeyed the door of his office.

Della Street had set up the electric percolator. The aroma of freshly brewed coffee filled the office.

"Smells good," Mason said. "How about a cup?"

"I made it for you," she said. "How did you come out?"

"Yes and no," Mason told her. "The police are on the trail of Arlene Ferris. They've got that far."

He took from his pocket the fragment he had cut from the hem of the skirt Madge Elwood had been wearing.

"What's that?"

Mason grinned and said, "I refuse to answer on the ground that it might incriminate me. Are you hungry?"

"I'm absolutely starved."

"All right," he said. "We have about an hour's nefarious activity to engage in, then we are going to eat."

"We can't eat first?"

Mason shook his head. "It's too close...heard anything from Paul?"

"Nothing more."

"Give him a ring," Mason said. "See if there's anything new. Tell him we'll call him again later on in the evening."

Della Street dialed Drakes's office, conveyed the message to the detective, put on her hat and coat.

"Do you have an extra pair of shoes in the office?" Mason asked.

"Yes. Why?"

"You're going to get those pretty muddy."

"I have a pair of rather flat heels and some higher heels."

"Wear the high heels," Mason instructed.

"You sound mysterious."

"I am."

"What are we going to do?"

Mason said, "We're going to skirt the outer periphery of illegality. It is a crime to suppress evidence. It is a crime to do certain things in connection with subtracting evidence. But as far as I know, it's not a crime to add, provided it is done in the proper manner. It is only a crime to subtract."

"What, may I ask, are we going to add?" Della Street asked.

"Nothing at all," Mason said, his face a mask of innocence. "We are going to examine. We are going to take some test photographs. And, of course, as we examine and photograph, I am afraid we will leave tracks. If the officers misinterpret those tracks we can't be held responsible for their lack of acumen in judging circumstantial evidence."

"Of course not," Della Street said, smiling.

"Particularly," Mason went on, "if our efforts result in directing the attention of the officers to bits of legitimate evidence which they might overlook otherwise."

She switched out the lights, they closed the office, went to Mason's car and drove out toward the hills. Mason handed Della Street the maps, said, "I want to go up the road toward the country place where the body was discovered."

"Drake told us the police are still there," Della Street warned.

"I know," Mason said, "but it's dark and I am assuming that the activities of the police are, at the moment, centered on the place itself and not on the approaches."

"And our activities will be centered on the approaches?" she asked.

Mason nodded.

They turned off the freeway onto a paved road which after a few miles gave place to a graded country road.

Mason switched off the driving lights, turned on the parking lights and eased the car along the road, letting the motor run quietly.

Ahead they could see the bright illumination of the lodge. To the left there was a sloping hill. To the right, a cut bank.

Mason stopped the car. "Here's our place, Della."

"What do we do?"

"We get out. You follow instructions implicitly and unquestioningly. If I don't have to make explanations you won't be sure about what's in my mind."

"I think whatever is in your mind is larcenous," she said, laughing nervously.

"Not necessarily," Mason told her. "There's a narrow line of demarcation and I want to keep on the right side of that line."

He led the way across the road, which by this time had dried out enough so that footprints would not be readily visible, to the bank which was still moist. Mason said, "I'm going to lift you up on the bank. Double up your knees, then when I've pressed your back against the barbed-wire fence, hold your skirt tightly around you so it doesn't get snagged on the barbed wire and then slide down the bank. I'll catch you—I want you to leave the imprints of heels as you slide down the bank. All ready now? Here we go."

Mason picked her up, raised her to his shoulder, then pushed her back against the barbed wire. "All ready?" he asked.

"All ready," she said. "Let me go and I'll slide."

Della Street, her skirt wrapped tightly around her legs, her knees doubled up, slid down the bank and into Mason's arms.

"How's that?" she asked.

"All right," Mason said.

"Now what?" she asked.

Mason said, "I'm simply testing to see what would have happened if a girl had slid under the fence. She would have left tracks like that, wouldn't she?"

"I'm quite sure she would have—under certain circumstances," Della said.

"And in that case," Mason said, "she would have been very apt to have left a part of her skirt on the barbed wire, wouldn't she?"

"She'd be lucky if she hadn't left part of her hide on the barbed wire," Della Street rejoined.

Mason nodded, reached up and impaled the fragment of cloth he had taken from his pocket on one of the barbs. "That," he said, "should indicate what might well have happened. Now we'll photograph the tracks and the fragment of cloth."

Mason held the camera and flash gun and took two pictures.

"*You've* left some footprints here in the soft soil," Della Street pointed out, "And so have I."

"I know," Mason said, "but I think those will be eliminated."

"By what?"

"Police psychology," Mason said. "The police will first observe this piece of cloth hanging from the barbed wire. They'll jump out of the car and crowd around to inspect it. After that, they'll begin to look for tracks. They'll find your heel tracks coming down the steep bank, and only after that will they begin to wonder where the person came from who left that piece of skirt on the barbed wire and where she went to. By that time the tracks down here at the foot of the bank will all have been trampled into a hopeless mess.

"So then the police will crawl through the barbed-wire fence to look on the other side. They'll fail to find any tracks leading to this particular place but then they will find the tracks made by Arlene Ferris last night."

"And what will they deduce from all that?" Della Street asked.

"Heaven knows!" Mason said. "I personally am only conducting a test. I wanted to see what sort of tracks a woman would have made in sliding down the hill, and to see whether a piece of cloth would readily impale on one of these barbs. Sometimes, you know, the barbs are dull and rusted and wouldn't be apt to catch a piece of cloth."

"You've made your test?" Della Street asked.

Mason nodded.

"And I take it, it would be embarrassing if a police car should come along the road and catch us here?"

Mason grinned. "Since I observe from your remark that you are hungry, I see no reason to delay getting the hell out of here and going to where we can eat."

"Those," Della Street said, "are welcome words to a woman's hungry ears. Let's go."

Mason backed the car down the road until he came to a wide place, turned the car, switched on his headlights and drove back to the city.

He and Della Street stopped at the photographer's studio, left films with specific instructions for development and enlargement, had dinner and then rang Paul Drake.

"Know anything new, Paul?" Mason asked.

"Very little," Drake said. "Police are checking evidence out at the place where the body was found. They're also following up the lead that Loring Lamont left the company parking place at about five-forty-five last night and that a young woman was in the car with him at that time."

"I want to talk with you about that," Mason said.

"What are *you* going to do?" Drake asked.

"I'm driving Della home, and then I'm going to bring you some pictures."

Drake said, "Your tone sounds suspiciously smug."

"Thanks for telling me," Mason said. "I'll un-smug it."

"Moreover, I can't tell," Drake said suspiciously, "whether your smugness is because you and Della have had a very satisfactory dinner, or whether you've been up to something."

"Food," Mason said, "always leaves me in an expansive mood."

"Now," Drake said, "I *know* it was something you two have been up to."

Mason drove Della Street home, then doubled back to the photographer's office and picked up an envelope containing enlargements of Madge Elwood. He drove at once to Drake's office.

"What's cooking?" Drake asked.

Mason said, "We're stealing a card from police procedure."

"How come?"

Mason regarded Paul Drake thoughtfully. "Paul," he asked, "what's the most dangerous evidence in the world?"

"Personal identification evidence," Drake said, "the so-called infallible evidence of eyewitnesses, but it's something we can't help. Some people have accurate memories for faces and some people don't."

Mason said, "It goes deeper than that, Paul. It's an inherent defect in police procedure as well as in the processes of human memory."

"How come?" Drake asked.

Mason said, "Suppose you should be the victim of a holdup. Police listen to your description of your assailant, they know that a certain ex-convict is in the neighborhood, they bring out mug shots of this ex-con and show them to you. They say, 'Mr. Drake, we have every reason to believe this is a picture of the man who held you up. Now don't make up your mind too hastily. Take your time. Look this picture over, study it carefully—no, no, don't shake your head—not yet. Remember that photographs sometimes look a little different from the way the individual appears—passport photographs, for instance. Sometimes you have to look several times to be sure. Now you just take your time and study that picture.'

"Then a couple of days later police ring you up and say, 'Mr. Drake, we think we have the man who held you up. We want you to come down and look at him in a police lineup.' You go down and look at the lineup. The ex-con is there. You suddenly realize he looks familiar to you. You're pretty apt to make an identification. Now, are you identifying him because you studied his picture so carefully in connection with the holdup, or are you making the identification because he's really the guy who held you up?"

"I know, I know," Drake said impatiently. "It's one of those things that happen. But what the hell—human nature is human nature and you can't change it, nor can you throw out all eyewitness evidence simply because *some* guys react to the power of suggestion more than others."

Mason grinned. "Exactly, Paul. We're going to steal a leaf from the police book. You say that the guard who was on duty at the parking lot saw Loring Lamont drive out about a quarter to six with a good-looking young woman in the car. Police think he can identify that woman. Now I want you to take this photograph, contact this fellow and ask him if that's the woman. Ask him to take a good look at the picure, to study it carefully and see if that isn't the woman."

"Now wait, a minute," Drake said. "You're getting out on a limb there, Perry. That's tampering with a witness."

"Where's the tampering?" Mason asked.

"Well...you're trying to force an identification."

"I'm doing nothing of the sort," Mason said. "I'm simply asking him if he can identify a picture."

"But the way you want him to do it," Drake said, "is putting ideas in his mind."

"Isn't that the way the police do it?" Mason asked.

"Well...I suppose so."

"All right. Would you say the police were tampering with evidence?"

Drake accepted the snapshot reluctantly. "I'll try it," he agreed. "It may be difficult to get in touch with this fellow. The police may have him sewed up. If I go out there in a rush, trying to contact him, I'm going to arouse suspicions, and once I arouse suspicions we're..."

"Don't do it that way," Mason said. "Don't arouse suspicions. Don't do this in too big a hurry. On the other hand, don't let a lot of grass grow under your feet. Just take it easy, but do it at the first good opportunity."

"All right," Drake agreed. "I'll get busy on it—provided I find the guy isn't being chaperoned by the police. But I'll do it my way. I won't go out to the plant where police can check me, and I won't try to force an identification."

"Okay," Mason said, "we'll button it up for tonight, Paul. But remember to get started early in the morning."

CHAPTER SIX

It was around eight-thirty the next morning when Perry Mason unlocked the door of his private office to find Della Street and Paul Drake studying the morning papers.

"How you coming with the photograph identification, Paul?" Mason asked.

"No dice," Paul said. "The guy works the evening shift and sleeps late in the morning. The police sent a car out there early this morning, woke him up and took him out with them somewhere."

Mason frowned.

"I did the best I could," Drake said: "I didn't want to wake him up for fear that would push us too far out in the open. Then the police moved in and took him in tow. I have a man planted out there at the house. As soon as the guy comes back I'll be notified, and my man will show him the picture and ask questions. Incidentally, Perry, you have your name in the papers, and the police have uncovered some new evidence."

"How come?"

"A little detective work on the part of our friend, Lieutenant Tragg, who is mighty efficient when you come right down to it."

"Go ahead," Mason said, seating himself on the rounded arm of the overstuffed leather chair in which clients were made to feel at ease. "What's the pitch?"

Drake said, "When they searched the body of Loring Lamont they found, in one of his pockets, a part of a car distributor."

Mason merely nodded.

"Yesterday it turned out that Arlene Ferris, a stenographer employed at the plant, telephoned for a repair service to come out and start her car. She said she had been unable to start it the night before and thought water had leaked into the distributor. The repairman found that someone had removed a part from the distributor. It was necessary for him to get a new part and replace it.

"The part that the police found in the pocket of Loring Lamont's clothes is identical with the part that was replaced in Arlene Ferris' car, and police have reason to believe it had been removed from the distributor on her car."

"Go ahead," Mason said. "How does my name enter into it?"

"In a rather peculiar way. Yesterday afternoon Arlene Ferris served notice that she must have time off. Mr. George Albert, the office manager, stated that Miss Ferris had a most unusual attitude, that she insisted on being excused. She was away from the office something over an hour.

"Naturally, by the time the investigation reached that point, police were interested in finding out where she went and what was so urgent. By checking with the gate guard, they found that her car hadn't been moved. So their next step was to start checking with the cab company that had a stand at the corner. They had struck pay dirt by six o'clock last night. They found that Arlene Ferris had asked the driver of a cab to get her to this address as quickly as possible, that she had an appointment with a lawyer. After she had left the cab the driver noticed she had left a piece of folded paper. He picked it up and unfolded it to see if it was anything important enough to turn in to the lost-and-found department. It was just a piece of stationery of the Lamont Company with your name, address and phone number on it. He shoved it in his coat pocket. It was still there when police questioned him. He gave it to them.

"So then police got a search warrant for the apartment of Arlene Ferris."

"I see," Mason said thoughtfully.

"Police couldn't find Arlene, but they searched her apartment and found a skirt with a peculiar rip in the hem. The skirt was of a soft, woven material. Police found that a small triangular piece had been torn out of the garment. Shortly after midnight they had a hunch about the skirt. They started examining the barbed-wire fence along the road leading to the lodge where the murder had been committed. They soon found the missing piece of the garment impaled on barbed wire, with tracks showing unmistakably that some woman more interested in speed than modesty had slid under the wire, going down the bank on her back, with her feet doubled under her.

"Search of the Ferris apartment had disclosed panties bearing mud stains so police came up with the theory that Miss Ferris had been the one who slid under the fence."

"That's a crime?" Mason asked.

"Murder is a crime," Drake said dryly.

"And police are drawing certain inferences?"

"Undoubtedly. But out of deference to the fact that Jarvis P. Lamont is a very powerful industrial tycoon, the police aren't promulgating those theories in print. They have simply stated that they are making an investigation, that they wish very much to talk with Arlene Ferris, that they wonder what caused Arlene Ferris to go to the office of Perry Mason in the middle of the afternoon and thereafter to be absent from her apartment.

"Also, police have uncovered a witness who saw a young woman park Loring Lamont's car directly in front of a fireplug. The description of that woman tallies with that of Arlene Ferris."

"Who's the witness?" Mason asked.

"A man named Jerome Henley. He lives in the apartment house where Loring Lamont has an apartment, and runs a music store—hi-fi, records, and things of that sort."

"What about the time?" Mason asked.

"Henley isn't certain of the time. His wrist watch was at the jeweler's for repair. He thought the time was ten or ten-thirty but he went to sleep right after dinner and admits he just doesn't know what time it was. He had been listening to some new records in his apartment, fell sound asleep, then wakened, went down to a lunch counter, got a cup of coffee, then went back to his apartment and to bed."

"What's the address of the place where Henley has his business?" Mason asked.

"1311 Broadside Avenue, according to the newspaper."

"All right, Paul," Mason said. "Be certain you aren't being followed. Go to see Henley. Show him the picture I gave you. Ask him if that's the young woman he saw getting out of the car."

Drake reluctantly got up out of his chair and started toward the door. "If they throw me in, you'll have to bail me out," he said, and walked out.

Mason glanced through the paper and the morning mail.

Twenty minutes later his unlisted desk phone rang and Paul Drake's excited voice came over the wire.

"It's going to work, Perry," Drake said. "At first the guy was dubious. I kept shoving the picture at him and then he began to weaken. He says she resembles the girl he saw getting out of the car and he thinks she's the one."

"Good work, Paul," Mason said.

"Here's something else," Drake said. "Lieutenant Tragg of Homicide has a stake-out on your car in the parking lot. He evidently has an idea you'll be going out and and leading him to the place where your client is hiding."

"You're sure?" Mason asked.

"Of course I'm sure. It's a police car parked in front of a fireplug across the street and I'll bet it's in telephone contact with Tragg himself."

"Okay," Mason said. "I'll give that matter some thought . . . they *may* have tapped my telephone . . . be seeing you, Paul."

Mason hung up the phone, turned to Della Street.

"Della," he said, "go down to a pay telephone. Don't use the office phones. Call Madge Elwood in Santa Monica. I told her to take the day off and be available for telephone calls. Tell her to drive in at once. Give her the address of the parking lot where I keep my car.

"Now, Della, this is important. I want her to stage things so that at *exactly* ten-forty-five she drives into that parking lot. Tell her to park her car. The attendant will give her a parking ticket—so far she won't have attracted any attention."

Della Street nodded.

"I will be waiting in my automobile with the motor running and car pointed toward the exit. As soon as she starts walking toward the exit I'll drive up alongside and open the door. At that time she is to jump in without hesitating."

"And then?" Della Street asked.

"Then," Mason said, "it depends on whether the astute Lieutenant Tragg tries to spring his trap before he finds out where we're going. I'm inclined to think that he'll give me quite a bit of rope in order to see whether I hang myself, but he may not."

"And just where *are* you going?" Della Street asked.

"Shopping," Mason sad, grinning. "Now synchronize your watch with mine and tell Madge Elwood to synchronize hers with yours over the telephone. We want to do this on a split-second timing."

"Shall I tell her anything about Arlene Ferris?" Della Street asked.

"Tell her to convey a message to Arlene. Tell Arlene to sit tight for the moment, but it won't be for very long."

"Ten-forty-five on the dot," Della Street said.

"That's right. Come over here now and synchronize your watch with mine."

Della Street moved over to Perry Mason, said, "There's less than thirty seconds difference between our watches."

"Mine is right," Mason said. "I keep it right on the button. Set your watch up thirty seconds. This calls for precision timing. I want to have it click right to the second."

"But with traffic and everything," Della Street said, "she may be delayed a few seconds, even in driving around the block. It's pretty difficult to have her drive into a parking lot at exactly a certain time."

"I want it just as close to that time as she can make it," Mason said. "We have a little margin but not a great deal. Tell her that it's *exceedingly* important that she do just as I suggest."

Della Street nodded and left the office.

CHAPTER SEVEN

Promptly at ten-thirty-nine Mason left his office, went down in the elevator, turned into the parking lot, nodded to the attendant, went to the stall where his car was kept, entered the car, started the motor and backed out into the lane reserved for exit, the maneuver taking him to within a few feet of the lane of incoming traffic.

At that point Mason seemed to have some trouble with his gas feed. He frowned, put his head on one side, listening to the motor, raced the throttle a few times, then let the car idle.

The time was precisely twenty seconds past ten-forty-five.

A car swung into the parking lot. The attendant stepped out of his cage, gave the driver a ticket and Madge Elwood emerged from the door shaking out her skirt.

Mason raised his hat. "Ride?" he called.

She flashed him a smile, said, "Sure," crossed around in front of the car and jumped in beside Mason.

The lawyer eased the car out of the parking lot and into the stream of traffic. "Any trouble?" he asked.

"Not at all. I was a few seconds late. I . . . well, I was terribly nervous. I guess I misjudged the time a little."

"That's all right," Mason said. "You did very well."

"Why so particular about the time?" she asked.

Mason said, "I wanted to make my exit look natural and I would prefer not to be followed if we can avoid it."

"Why should we be followed?"

"Have you seen the papers?"

"Not the late editions."

"It's probably just as well," Mason said.

They made a right turn at the corner, then a left turn at the next corner. Mason eased his way past two signals just as they were changing, then settled down to steady driving.

"Can't you circle around two or three blocks in a figure eight?" she asked. "If you think you're being followed that will enable you to find out. I read somewhere that . . ."

"Sure," Mason interrupted, "that's all right under certain circumstances but I don't want anyone to think that I'm at all suspicious. I don't want to give the impression that I'm worried about being followed. That's part of the game."

"And just what is the game?"

Mason smiled and said, "Act perfectly natural. That's all you need to do."

Mason drove conservatively, turned into Broadside Avenue, found a parking lot in the 1200 block and said to Madge Elwood, "We walk a block. How's Arlene getting along?"

"All right," she said. "She had trouble sleeping but I gave her some sleeping pills I had and they worked all right."

"And this morning?"

"She's feeling better. She is, of course, bursting with curiosity, but I told her to leave everything to you. She's dying to know what you wanted with me but I couldn't help her very much there because I didn't know myself."

"That's right," Mason said, offering no further explanation.

Abruptly the lawyer said, "Are you interested in music? In the new records?"

"I'm crazy about the new stereophonic gadgets," she said.

"Well, let's go in and look around," Mason told her, and taking her elbow in his hand, piloted her through the door of a store which featured hi-fi equipment and records in the window.

A salesman came forward and Mason said, "I'd like to discuss a deal for a complete hi-fi installation."

"Yes, indeed," the salesman bowed.

"You are the manager here?"

"I'm the head salesman."

"There is, I believe, a Mr. Henley here."

"He owns the place."

"Is he available?"

"That's the man there, in the office."

"The one behind the glass partition?"

"That's right."

"I think I'd like to talk with him," Mason said, "about the installation. Would you mind?"

"I know he'll be glad to come over," the salesman said.

"Well, we can walk over there," Mason said. "I don't want to bother him and I don't want to do anything that would interfere with any commission or bonus arrangement you might have. Would you mind asking him a question for me?"

"Certainly not."

"Ask him if he knows Jim Billings," Mason said. "I think Mr. Billings got his equipment here."

"Very well," the salesman said, and walked toward the glass-enclosed office.

Mason followed him, to stand just outside the glassed-in office.

The salesman approached Henley, who listened, looked up, frowned, then following the nod of the salesman's head, looked toward Mason and Madge Elwood.

Henley hesitated a moment, then arose from his chair and walked to the door of the office.

"Good morning," he said. "There was some question about a Mr. Billings? I don't believe I recall the name but I can assure you that we're prepared to give you the best service, the best prices and..."

"Just a minute," a dry voice cut in from behind Mason. "We'll take charge here now."

Mason turned. "Why, Lieutenant Tragg! What are *you* doing here?"

"I just happened to be in the neighborhood," Lt. Tragg said. "You see, we talked with Jerome Henley earlier in the day—in fact, quite early this morning. Mr. Henley and I are by way of being old friends."

Tragg turned to Henley and said, "Do you know this man, Henley?"

The manager shook his head.

"All right," Tragg said. "For your information, this is Mr. Perry Mason, the famous attorney who specializes in trial work and primarily in defending persons accused of murder. I don't know who this young woman is. That doesn't make any difference. I want you to look at her carefully before you answer my next question.

"I don't like to impugn Mr. Mason's motives but I am very much afraid the astute lawyer is trying one of his tricks by which he confuses a witness whom he expects to cross-examine. This is something he's done before. If a witness is going to identify someone...if there is any possibility *you*, for instance, might be called on to identify this young woman as the person you saw getting out of Loring Lamont's car when it was parked in front of the fireplug a couple of nights ago, Mr. Mason could bring her into your store where you'd see her casually.

"Then later on, when you get on the witness stand and identify her as the woman who got out of Lamont's car, Mr. Mason could smile fiendishly at you and say on cross-examination, Aren't you mistaken? Isn't *this* the young woman who was in your store with me when I was asking you about hi-fi equipment?'

"Now, Henley, I don't want you to get trapped. I don't want you to speak up until you're certain. Have you ever seen this young woman before? Is this the woman who got out of Loring Lamont's car?"

Mason said, "And don't let *him* confuse you, Henley. This is no way to make an identification. If this young woman is..."

"She is!" Henley interrupted. "*That's* the woman I saw get out of the car. She was dressed a little differently but that's the woman."

"Now be sure. Be absolutely sure," Lt. Tragg said.

"I'm sure that's the woman."

Tragg turned to Mason with a smile. "Won't you introduce me, Mason?" he said. "Or perhaps there's no need for you to do it. Miss Arlene Ferris, I am Lieutenant Tragg of Homicide and I'd like to ask you a few questions about where you were on the night Loring Lamont was murdered."

Madge Elwood stepped back with an exclamation of dismay so well done that even Mason was fooled. Her face actually seemed to go white to the lips.

"Come, come, now," Tragg said. "If you're innocent there's nothing to be afraid of, and..."

Mason interrupted. "I'm afraid you have made a slight mistake, Lieutenant. Miss Elwood, permit me to present Lieutenant Tragg. Lieutenant Tragg, this is Madge Elwood, a secretary from Santa Monica. She also happens to be interested in hi-fi equipment so I brought her in here to listen to some of the latest equipment."

Tragg's voice suddenly was edged with sharp authority. "You're sure?" he asked Henley.

"I'm absolutely certain, Lieutenant. That's the woman."

"I thought it would be," Tragg said. "We'll unscramble the names later. That's Mason for you! You can see the trap he was setting for you. He'd have asked you a question or two, then walked out. You are busy. There is no reason for you to remember two customers who make a casual inquiry.

"Later on, when you identified this girl, Mason would have convinced the jury your subconscious had played a trick on you, that you remembered her as the girl who had been in here with him."

"I see," Henley said. He leaned slightly forward, looking at Madge Elwood. His forehead creased with a frown.

Tragg said harshly, "You've raised hell if this isn't the girl."

"Tut-tut, such language," Mason said reproachfully.

"It's the girl," Henley said at length.

Tragg turned to Perry Mason. "We can dispense with your company, Counselor. Miss Elwood and I are going to take a little ride."

"You've got a warrant?" Mason asked.

"I don't need one," Tragg said.

"You need one in order to take her into custody and dispense with my company," Mason said. "If you're going to take a ride I'm going with you. You can't take Miss Elwood away from me simply on your say-so."

"She has just been identified as..."

"I have good ears," Mason said. "I heard the identification. I heard how positive it was. Just remember that when we get to court."

"I don't know what kind of a razzle-dazzle you're trying at the moment," Tragg said, "but I'm going to find out. Come on, Miss Elwood, you're coming with me."

"And I'm coming along," Mason said.

Tragg hesitated a moment, then yielded the point. "Very well," he said, "but you're not going to interfere in any way. You're going to keep quiet. I'm going to do the talking. If you try to confuse the witness, I'm going to dust off a few sections of the Penal Code which you may have forgotten."

Mason's smile was urbane. "Come, come, Lieutenant," he said, "I never *forget* any of the sections of the Penal Code. I can't afford to."

Tragg said to Madge Elwood, "We're going in a police car. Come on."

He led the way outside to where the police car with a driver was waiting at the curb.

Tragg held the rear door open for Madge Elwood and the lawyer.

Mason, catching her eye, made a gesture for silence.

They entered the car. Tragg said something in a low voice to the driver, and the car eased out into traffic, then purred into swift speed.

The car veered off into a residential district of rather modest houses. Tragg and the driver held a low-voiced conversation. Tragg indicated a street, the driver turned to the left and stopped in front of a small bungalow.

Tragg said, "You folks wait here."

He went to the house, rang the bell and after the door was opened, went inside. He was in for about five minutes, then came out accompanied by a man who walked with him to the automobile.

Tragg stood with his back to the car, the man facing him. They said nothing for a few moments, then Tragg said, "We'll try not to detain you. Look at the other side."

They walked around the automobile. The man apparently was inspecting the police car.

After a moment Tragg led the way back into the house. He was in there for another five minutes, then came out and said to the driver, "All right. Take them back to the music store."

"May I ask what this is all about?" Mason asked.

"Sure you can ask," Tragg said.

"Will you tell me?"

"I'll let you guess."

Mason said, "I suppose this car was in an accident somewhere and you wanted the man to identify it."

Tragg grinned. "Could be."

"Or perhaps the city is thinking of selling police cars as surplus and this man wants to buy," Mason went on.

"Could be," Tragg said in a tone of voice which didn't invite further speculation or conversation.

They rode in silence back to the music store. "All right," Tragg said, "this is where we picked you up, this is where we let you out."

"Thanks," Mason told him. "Any time we can be of service, just let us know—how did it happen you located me in that music store, Lieutenant?"

"I just happened to be in the neighborhood," Tragg said, "and saw you in there, so I thought I'd keep you from sabotaging the People's case by putting Henley in a spot where he'd be vulnerable on cross-examination."

"He's vulnerable now," Mason said.

"I'm not arguing," Tragg said. "They pay me to investigate cases, not to argue with lawyers. Come on, Frank, let's go."

The car moved away from the curb.

"Mr. Mason," Madge Elwood said in a panic, "you can't let them do that to me! This man in the music store, he has no right to say that he saw me getting out of a car. I was in Santa Monica and..."

"Take it easy," Mason said, "take it easy. I think Lieutenant Tragg didn't seem too happy as he drove off. Let's see if we can find out the cause of his unhappiness."

"What are you going to do?" she asked.

"Take a ride," Mason said. "Come on, let's go."

He went to the parking lot, got out his car and started driving.

"But this is the same way that the police officers went," she said at length.

"I know," Mason said.

"You're going back to that same house?"

Mason nodded.

"Why?"

"Just to check up," Mason said.

She started to protest, then lapsed into silence. Mason drove the car back to the bungalow, parked it, went up to the house and rang the bell.

The same man who had walked out to look at the car answered the door, started to say something, then said, "You're the man who was out here with the police a short time ago?"

"That's right," Mason told him.

"I told the Lieutenant all I know," the man said. "I can't be sure. It looks something like the girl, but I can't be sure it's the same one. A man was out here with a picture. He asked me if I could identify the picture. I told him I couldn't. I think the girl with the police was the one whose picture I saw.

"I only had a quick glimpse as Loring Lamont drove his car out of the parking lot. There was a girl with him. I'm not certain this is the one."

"Thank you very much," Mason said. "I'm sorry I bothered you."

"Not at all. The police woke me up early this morning. I can't go back to sleep. I'd like to help, but I'm not going to say I'm sure if I'm not sure, and that's that."

"I know exactly how you feel," Mason told him, "and I respect your feelings. What's your name again?"

"Tom Grimes."

"Thanks a lot," Mason said, shaking hands. "I'll try not to bother you again."

He walked back to the car.

"Now, let's not misunderstand each other," he said to Madge Elwood. "You're willing to do anything you can to help Arlene?"

"That's right."

"I'm going to mix you up in this thing," Mason said.

"How deep?" she asked apprehensively.

"Not so deep that you can't get out," Mason told her. "They're going to drop you like a hot potato but I want to be sure they get their fingers pretty badly burned before they do it. All right with you?"

"Anything you say is all right with me, Mr. Mason. The main thing I want to do is to help Arlene. I'll...I'll do anything—absolutely anything to help her."

"All right," Mason said. "I'll take you back to the parking lot. Get your car and drive to your apartment. Newspaper reporters will be there shortly after you arrive. Go home now and fix yourself up for the photographers. I want you to take good pictures."

"Cheesecake?" she asked.

"Within moderate limits," Mason said. "Don't let them overdo it."

CHAPTER EIGHT

Mason returned to his office to find Paul Drake waiting for him.

"The police have picked up Arlene Ferris," Drake said.

"Where did they find her?" Mason asked.

"Down at Santa Monica, in the apartment of a friend."

"How did they get the lead?" Mason asked. "What started them down there searching for her?"

"I don't know. They probably started checking on all of her friends."

Mason said to Della Street, "Get me Hamilton Burger on the phone. I'd like to talk with him personally, but if I can't do that I'll talk with his chief deputy."

"Going right to the top, eh?" Drake asked.

"Going right to the top," Mason said.

He watched while Della Street relayed the call through the switchboard in the outer office, then, after a moment when she nodded and said, "The district attorney is coming on the phone," Mason took the phone.

"Hello, Burger," Mason said.

Hamilton Burger's voice was cautious. "Hello, Mr. Mason, what can I do for you?"

"The police are picking up one of my clients, an Arlene Ferris."

"Yes," Hamilton Burger said. "They want to question her in connection with the murder of Loring Lamont."

"All right," Mason said. "She's my client. If you question her I want to be there."

"I have no intention of questioning her. Someone in my office may be present, but the police will probably conduct the interrogation."

"That's just dandy," Mason said. "Now, as soon as she's brought in I want to have it understood that I talk with her."

Burger said, "Well, don't complain to me about it, Mason. Take it up with the police. You know how they work as well as I do. They've probably questioned her at some length, and by the time they bring her in and book her the questioning will have been completed."

Mason said, "A word from your office to the police might save us both a lot of trouble. I want to have the privilege of visiting her as her attorney as soon as she is brought into detention, whether she's booked or not."

"Well, why not take it up with the police?"

"I'm taking it up with you," Mason said. "With your assistance, I can do it the easy way. Without your assistance I'll have to do it the hard way."

"What's the hard way?" Burger asked.

"Habeas corpus," Mason said. "That will put us both to a bit of trouble."

Hamilton Burger thought for a moment, then said, "I'm quite certain you won't have any trouble visiting her as soon as she's brought in—provided, of course, you are her attorney."

"I'm her attorney."

"All right. Let me ask you a couple of questions. I happen to know something about this case personally. When she heard Loring Lamont had been murdered why didn't she come to the police and say that she had been out with Lamont at the scene of the murder the night that it occurred—that is, of course, assuming that she's innocent?"

"Well," Mason said, "that brings up a nice question. When did she learn that he had been murdered?"

"You're asking me questions in answer to my questions," Burger said.

"I don't know any other way to handle the situation."

Burger said, "I'll tell you this much frankly, Mason. If she's innocent we don't want to drag her through a lot of publicity. If she's guilty, naturally we want to prosecute her—unless, of course, you'd like to consider entering a guilty plea. And if it was self-defense, she'd better come out and say so right now."

Mason said, "I'll discuss the matter with my client."

"You've already discussed it with her probably half a dozen times," Burger said.

"You might be surprised," Mason told him.

"All right, all right," Burger said testily. "You won't need to file a habeas corpus, you get to talk with her as soon as she's brought in. But I don't think the police are going to bring her in until after they've asked her a lot of questions."

"Quite all right with me," Mason said. "I take it you're personally familiar with the details of the case?"

"I'm getting familiar with them. The Lamont family is rather prominent. This is hardly a run-of-the-mill murder case."

"Okay," Mason told him, "I'll rely on your promise to fix things up so I can see my client as soon as she's brought in. Thanks a lot."

Mason hung up, turned to Paul Drake. "Know anything else, Paul?"

"This much," Drake said. "Loring Lamont went out to that lodge. He had a young woman with him. They cooked ham and eggs and a plate of hot biscuits, and then sat down and ate. Lamont was killed within a matter of minutes after the meal."

"Both of them ate?" Mason asked.

"Both of them ate."

Mason frowned thoughtfully.

"What have you found out about that place out there, Paul?"

"Well, it's maintained by the company as a place of entertainment."

"Any caretaker or anybody in charge?"

"Yes. There's a woman who lives abut five miles down the road, who keeps the place clean."

"What's her name?"

"Sadie Richmond, a widow."

"What else?"

"The place is completely surrounded by a woven-mesh, heavy-wire fence, ten feet high, with strings of barbed wire across the top. You either get in through the gate or you don't get in at all. The gate is kept locked. They're very careful to keep it locked at all times because there's a swimming pool there and they don't want to be responsible for anybody who might blunder into the swimming pool and get drowned."

"There's no way a person could drive in except along that road through the gate?"

"That's right."

"No back gate, no back entrance to the property?"

"Nothing."

"What about Sadie Richmond?"

"She goes in every day, usually between ten o'clock and noon. She straightens the place up. Sometimes people will be out there and leave dirty glasses, dirty dishes and generally mess the place up. She keeps it clean.

"There are a couple of bedrooms in the place and sometimes executives of the company or their friends will sleep out there. Sadie keeps the beds changed with fresh linen. A man comes in, in the afternoons, and keeps the yard in condition. A pool company services the swimming pool, and their representative has a key to the gate. It's a heated swimming pool with a thermostat and it's kept at an even temperature all year round."

Mason glanced at his watch. "How long ago did the police pick up Arlene Ferris, Paul?"

"I can't tell for certain, but it must have been nearly an hour."

Mason frowned. "They evidently got there soon after Madge Elwood left the apartment. Come on, Paul, we're going to take a run out and look the property over—the scene of the crime."

"We can't get in," Drake said.

"What'll you bet?" Mason askd.

"Now, wait a minute, Perry, let's not try anything that's going to make trouble."

"The police are finished out there?"

"The police have finished, the newspaper reporters have been admitted and given an opportunity to take photographs, and now the place is closed up tight as a drum."

"That suits me fine," Mason said. "Let's go hunt up Sadie Richmond. You have her address?"

Drake nodded.

"Okay," Mason said. "Let's go."

"Want me?" Della Street asked.

Mason hesitated a moment, then nodded his head. "Come on," he said, "a woman's eye may detect certain things that would escape a man."

"What are you looking for?" Paul Drake asked.

"If I knew," Mason told him, "I wouldn't have to go out. Come on, let's go."

The three of them went down to the parking lot, got in Mason's car, drove out along the freeway, then turned off at the point Drake designated. After a short distance they turned from the pavement to a dirt road.

"Sadie Richmond lives along in here," Drake said.

Mason slowed the car.

"This is the place. Turn in here," Drake said.

Mason turned in to a neat little bungalow, stopped the car, said, "Now let's see if we get this straight, Paul. You can't get in without a key?"

"That's right."

"But there are several keys—the executives of the company have them, Sadie Richmond has one, the swimming-pool people have one, the man who takes care of the place has one."

"That's right."

"What's his name?"

"Otto Keswick."

"Where does he live?"

"About half a mile up the road here."

"All right," Mason said, "Let's go see Sadie Richmond."

They left the car, walked up the steps of the bungalow and Mason rang the bell.

The woman who came to the door was in her early thirties, a rather large woman, but a woman who carried no extra weight and moved with lithe grace. She had a well-modeled figure.

Mason introduced himself.

"I'm interested in the Loring Lamont case," he said.

"Who isn't?" Sadie Richmond asked, with a ghost of a smile.

"Have you been in the place this morning to clean up?"

"The police don't want it cleaned up, not for a while."

"Have you been out there this morning?"

"No, I haven't been out there yet. Police asked me to wait until they telephoned that it was all right to go in. They removed quite a few articles, I understand."

"You haven't been notified yet?"

"Yes, they notified me about half an hour ago and said it was all right, that they were finished with the place."

"So you're going in to clean up?"

"That's right."

"How would you like some help?" Mason asked.

She smiled and shook her head.

Mason opened his wallet, took out a twenty-dollar bill.

Sadie Richmond looked at the bill. Her face became wooden. She said nothing.

Mason took out a second twenty-dollar bill, then another and another. He smoothed them out, then folded them and folded them once more, making them into a compact packet.

"We wouldn't get in the way at all," he promised.

Sadie Richmond smiled and shook her head.

Mason said, "Look here, a young woman is accused of that murder. I'm representing her. The police are finished with the place. There's no more evidence out there. I'd like to get familiar with the place so I can represent this young woman intelligently.

"I don't know how much you know about Loring Lamont's personal life, but this young woman was lured out there and...and now she's charged with murder. I'm representing her. I want to see the place. I can get a court order letting me in, but that's going to take time. My time is worth money."

He handed Sadie Richmond the eighty dollars. She hesitated a moment, then closed her hand over the money. "I don't know about what happened the night of the murder," she said dryly, "but I've seen things sometimes when I was cleaning up that... well..."

"Yes?" Mason asked, as she hesitated.

"I'm not saying anything," she said.

"Nothing?" Mason asked.

"Nothing. But you can come along. I guess there's no law against that, is there?"

Mason said, "I told you I thought I could get a court order to let me in if I had to."

"You wouldn't need to tell anyone that I let you in."

"I'm the soul of discretion," Mason said.

"All right," Sadie Richmond said. "I'll go in my car, you go in yours. I'll go first and unlock the gate. I guess I've got a lot of work to do out there this morning."

"Dirty dishes?" Mason asked.

"The police took the dishes."

"All of them?"

"All of the dirty ones."

"Well," Mason told her, "that'll simplify the job. All right, we'll get in our car and drive out to the road. You go right ahead and we'll follow."

Sadie Richmond, driving a rather beaten-up, old-model car, came out of the driveway, turned into the dirt road and sent her car into speed. The roadway had now dried out sufficiently so that there was a faint trace of dust behind the wheels, and Mason, following closely, had fine particles of dirt thrown up against his car by the speeding rear wheels.

Drake said dryly, "I guess they don't pay her portal-to-portal. She believes in getting on the job once she starts... my gosh, Perry, that woman drives like the devil."

Mason, concentrating on his driving to keep reasonably close to the car ahead, grinned and said nothing.

At length the woman braked her car to a stop, jumped out and unlocked the big padlock, left the chain dangling on the gate, threw the gate open and drove through.

Mason followed, stopped his car behind hers. She jumped out, closed the gate and locked it.

We're supposed to keep it locked—always," she said.

"You have good brakes on that car," Drake observed.

She looked at him blankly.

"Otherwise you'd have wound up in the swimming pool."

There was no expression on her face. "We're not allowed to use the swimming pool," she said. She got in her car and swung around the driveway to stop at the back of the house.

"That, for you and your wisecracks," Della Street said, laughing.

"Now there's a woman for you," Drake said. "She looks innocent enough on the surface, but—well, I'd hate to sit in a poker game with her."

"She might take the pot with a pair of deuces," Mason said, as he emerged from the car and walked around to open the door for Della Street.

Della slid to the ground with a quick flash of shapely legs. "Want me to bring a book?" she asked.

"I don't think so," Mason said. "Just a small notebook."

"I have one in my purse. There are some big notebooks in the glove compartment."

"The small one will be all right," Mason said.

They followed Sadie Richmond into the house.

"Well, here it is," she said.

Mason looked around at the sumptuous rustic furnishings, the Navaho rugs, the kitchen with its electric stove, garbage disposal, dishwashing machine, the array of copper-bottomed pots and pans hanging above the stove.

"Fixed up for cooking," he observed.

"Occasionally they have barbecues out here. Mr. J. P. Loring is a very fine cook. When they have barbecues they have me out here to serve and wash the dishes."

"A walk-in icebox?" Mason asked.

"No, just that one refrigerator there. They bring out steaks when they're having a barbecue. They don't keep much here except some ham and a lot of eggs. Occasionally they have a few pounds of bacon. They want it so if they get stuck out here on some kind of a conference they can fix themselves up a snack. But they don't go in for cooking out here except when they have the barbecues. Then they bring out all the food."

"Mr. Lamont is a good cook?" Mason asked.

She sighed and said, "Like all men cooks, he can dirty more damn dishes than anybody you ever saw."

Della Street laughed.

Mason looked at the chalked outline on the floor and the sinister reddish tinge. "I take it this is where the body was."

"I guess that's right," she said. "They told me to clean it up. I don't know whether old J. P. intends to give me a bonus or not, but my job certainly isn't supposed to include cleaning up the blood from dead bodies."

"I take it you've worked on parties given by Loring Lamont," Mason said.

"*His* parties were just for two," she said, and turned abruptly away.

Mason nodded to Paul Drake. They started looking through the house, and when Sadie Richmond made no objection, began opening and closing drawers, looking in closets.

"No clothes out here?" Mason asked.

"No. J. P. Lamont keeps some coveralls that he uses when he's putting on a barbecue, and there are a couple of cook aprons up there on the shelf, but they don't keep any clothes out here except playclothes—shorts, swimsuits, things like that. Down by the pool they have a few dressing rooms where they keep a supply of swimsuits for guests."

Mason moved over to a writing desk.

"Why the writing desk?" he asked.

"I don't know," she said. "It's always been here."

"Anybody ever use it?"

"I use it."

"What for?"

"I keep my bills in there, things that I pay out for running the house—laundry bills and things of that sort."

Mason opened the desk, the door of which swung down to make a writing shelf, and looked casually through the pigeonholes.

"Hello," he said. "What's this?"

Mrs. Richmond looked over Mason's shoulder.

"A checkbook," she said.

"Yours?"

"Heavens, no. I don't use a checkbook."

Mason said, "There are only four or five checks used out of it. It's on the California Second National."

Mason looked at the check stubs. "One a week ago to an automobile agency for seventy-eight dollars and fifty cents. One to the Endicott Arms Holding Corporation for six hundred and twenty-five dollars. One for five hundred to Orval Kingman. That was dated...that was dated on the day of the murder. Here's another one for five hundred—the last one in the book. The stub says simply 'O.K.'"

Mason looked at the figures on the side of the stub. "There's a balance of twenty-five hundred seventeen dollars and thirty cents."

"Where was it?" Mrs. Richmond asked.

"In this pigeonhole, with all these papers," Mason said, spreading out some receipted bills and some bills which hadn't been receipted: one from the company which serviced the pool marked "O.K.," another from the laundry marked "O.K."

"What are these?"

"Bills that are to be picked up and paid," she said.

"Whenever anyone comes out here they pick up the bills."

"And the O.K.?" Mason asked.

"That's what I put on them when they're to be paid."

"What about this check stub?" Mason asked. "Did you put the O.K. on there?"

She shook her head and said, "I wouldn't okay check stubs. Why would I?"

"That," Mason said, "is a fair question."

"What do you mean by that?"

"I was just wondering why you would okay it."

"Well, then, why did you ask?"

"Simply because you had marked 'O.K.' on bills and I wanted to see if you had put the 'O.K.' on this."

"Well, I told you," she said. And then suddenly, with her manner changing, said, "You wanted to get in here in order to see the premises. You've seen them—nothing was said about you going around opening drawers and desks and looking at papers."

"We'd like to look around," Mason said, "just to familiarize ourselves with..."

"Well, you've done it now. You're acquainted with what the place looks like."

Mason said suavely, "As I understand it, Loring Lamont was stabbed with a butcher knife. I wonder if you could tell us where that knife came from, if there's one short here in the kitchen, or..."

"I couldn't tell you a thing," she said. "You wanted to get in and you've got in. The more I think of it, the more I think it might be worth my job if anyone knew about this. Come on, you're going out."

She marched determinedly toward the door.

As she had her back turned, Mason slipped the checkbook into his inside coat pocket. "All right," he said, "if you feel it might jeopardize your job, we certainly don't want to do that."

"I'll let you out the gate," she said, "and lock the gate behind you when you go out. I don't think Mr. Lamont would like the idea of me letting you in here...in fact, I know he wouldn't."

She marched out through the door, left her car where it was, walked down to the gate, took out a key, unlocked the big padlock, swung the gate back and stood waiting.

"Well," Mason said, as they got in the car, "there seems to have been an abrupt change in her manner."

"The soul of cordiality, isn't she," Drake said.

"You can't blame her," Della Street said. "Personally, I think you swept her off her feet with that eighty dollars and she decided to take a chance. But the more she thinks of it, the more she realizes she can get into trouble, and..."

Mason started the car. "It was that checkbook that changed her manner," he said.

"Sure," Della Street told him. "She suddenly realized that you were uncovering evidence and that you might use it, and then people would want to know how you happened to know about it."

"Where's my camera?" Mason asked.

"The little 35 mm. is in the glove compartment."

"We've got an adjustment on there for closeups?"

"There's one in the case," Della Street said. "Do you want it?"

"Maybe we'd better have it," Mason said.

Della Street opened the glove compartment, took out the camera. Mason held the checkbook up in the sun. "Put on the closeup attachment, Della. We can take a picture at a hundredth of a second, and ... just be sure it's in focus."

Della Street adjusted the camera.

"Come on, come on, hurry up," Sadie Richmond called from the gate. "I can't stay here all day."

Mason held the checkbook in the sunlight. Della Street, holding the camera only a few inches from the checkbook, snapped one picture after another as Mason turned the check stubs.

"Got it?" Mason asked.

"Got it," Della Street said.

Abruptly Sadie Richmond left her position at the gate and came striding toward them. "Now look," she said, "I told you to get out. I don't want anyone to catch you here. You've been here long enough."

Mason said, "We appreciate your position, Mrs. Richmond. Here, incidentally, is the checkbook, which I held onto because I wanted to study it. You'd better put it back in the desk where it was."

"You didn't have any right to take that."

"We didn't take it," Mason said. "Now, may I suggest, Mrs. Richmond, that you call this checkbook to the attention of the police. I think it's evidence."

"Evidence of what?"

"I don't know."

"Neither do I," Sadie Richmond said, literally snatching the checkbook out of Mason's hand. "Now, will you please get going."

Mason raised his hat. "Thank you very much," he said.

"Don't mention it," she snapped.

The lawyer started the car and they drove out. Behind him, Sadie Richmond swung the gate shut and clicked the padlock into place.

"Now, Paul," Mason said, "it's up to you to find out whether that checkbook was the property of Loring Lamont and who Orval Kingman is."

"You think it's his checkbook?" Drake asked. "The way she acted, it looked as though she might have something to do with it. It might be that she's got an account she doesn't want anyone to know about."

"It could be," Mason said, "but whoever wrote that last check wrote it after the check to Orval Kingman, dated the day of the murder, was written. The check may well have been payable to cash and—well, it's a strange thing that Sadie Richmond puts 'O.K.' on the bills that are to be paid and that someone put 'O.K.' on the stub of a check made for five hundred dollars. If that checkbook should turn out to be Loring Lamont's checkbook it's a valuable piece of evidence."

"How come?" Drake asked. "Perhaps he keeps it there in the desk and ..."

"He couldn't, Paul—that is, I don't think he did. It was taken from his pocket. The checks were checks that had been made over a period of four or five days and included a check for a garage bill and apparently a check for the rent on his apartment. Now, he wouldn't have kept his checkbook in the desk out there in that rustic retreat and driven out there in order to have picked up the checkbook, written the check to the car agency that serviced his car, then written a check for his apartment rental."

"Suppose it's somebody else's checkbook."

"Then," Mason said, "it's the checkbook of someone who lives in the Endicott Arms Apartments."

"Well, anyhow," Della Street said, "we've got a clue."

"To what?" Drake asked.

"That," Mason said, "is the thing which interests me. You get to work on that, Paul. I'm going to talk with my client and see if *she* can give us any information that will be of any help."

CHAPTER NINE

Mason sat in the conference room reserved for attorneys and regarded Arlene Ferris thoughtfully. "Now you've told me everything?" he asked.

"Every single blessed thing," she said.

Mason said, "They're filing charges against you. They seem to be very confident. I'm satisfied they have some hidden evidence that I don't know anything about."

"Well, I don't know what it could be. I didn't kill him, I know that." And then, after a moment, she said savagely, "Sometimes I wish I had. If I'd got hold of that knife I..."

"Tut-tut," Mason interrupted. "None of that. Now, you did tell your story to the police?"

"I did. I probably shouldn't have, but this Lieutenant Tragg of Homicide was so nice and fatherly, and he seemed—well, it seemed as though he really didn't *want* to take me into custody. He wanted me to explain, if I could."

"Yes, I know," Mason said. "That's part of the police technique. And you told him?"

"I told him."

"Everything?"

"Everything."

Mason frowned thoughtfully. "Now look," he said "we'll be in court within a few days on a preliminary hearing. The purpose of that hearing is to find out if there's sufficient cause to hold you on a criminal charge. But we have the right to ask questions and we have the right to call witnesses. It usually doesn't do any good to call witnesses, but it does give us an opportunity to size up the prosecution's case.

"There are certain things that we know happened. Loring Lamont must have walked back to the cabin, and he must have eaten the ham and eggs almost immediately."

"Why do you say almost immediately?"

"Because," Mason said, "cold ham and eggs wouldn't be very palatable. Now, you're certain there were two plates of ham and eggs?"

"Yes. I had just placed the eggs on the plates."

"Then someone was there to eat that other plate of ham and eggs and some of the biscuits," Mason said. "Now, that someone must have been there within a matter of minutes of the time you left—how many cars did you meet on the road?"

"Not a one, not until after I had left the graveled road and got to the highway."

"Think carefully," Mason said. "Are you sure? There must have been *some* car that came along and..."

She shook her head vehemently. "No, I know there wasn't any other car."

Mason frowned thoughtfully. After a moment, he said, "Now, as you tell the story, there was a remarkable change in his tactics after he got that last telephone call. He was playing it for a long, cozy evening prior to that time, then suddenly he got rough."

"I'll say he did!"

"Something in that conversation changed his entire plan of operation," Mason said. "He knew he had to speed up his approach. Someone was coming. Was there any clue as to who it was?"

She shook her head. "I didn't pay too much attention to the conversation. He wasn't doing much talking—at least until after he left the one telephone and went back to the extension line."

"He was doing *some* talking, all right," Mason said. "The fact that he went to the extension line indicates that he was going to say something that he didn't want you to hear. What did he say when he picked up the telephone? Wasn't there anything that would give you a clue as to the person he was talking with?"

She shook her head.

"No names?"

"I'm quite sure he didn't mention any names."

"You don't know whether it was a man or a woman from the nature of the conversation, from what he said?"

"No, I don't...he seemed to be agreeing with this person, though. It wasn't anyone he was arguing with."

"What makes you say that?"

"Well, he kept saying, 'All right, all right.'"

"Was that what he said, 'All right?'"

"Yes, and I remember he kept saying, 'Okay.' He said something about..."

Mason came bolt upright. "Wait a minute!" he snapped. "Try and remember just what he said about okay."

"Well, he said, 'Hello,' and then he said, 'Hi.' You know, the way you would talk to someone you knew intimately, and then he said something about okay, and I think he said, 'All right,' or something. I just can't remember, Mr. Mason, but I do remember he said, 'Okay,' and I think at one time he said, 'All right, okay.' I remember it sounded just a little strange for him to agree twice."

"Then okay could have been his nickname for the person he was talking with," Mason said excitedly. "Someone whose initials were O.K."

"Yes, that could have been the case, all right. That would have accounted for it."

"All right," Mason said. "Don't say anything about this to anyone. Keep a stiff upper lip and we'll do the best we can. You've done your talking. Don't talk any more and don't tell anyone about this telephone conversation, about this O.K. Just keep quiet from now on."

Mason got to his feet.

"I wish I could have remembered a little more, Mr. Mason. I ... well, I have always been trained *not* to listen in on other people's conversations—you know how it is, I just ... well, I probably wouldn't have noticed it at all if it hadn't been for the fact that the food was hot and I ... I was proud of those biscuits and I wanted him to eat them while they were hot. Biscuits can get soggy rather quickly, and ..."

"I know," Mason said. "Don't worry about it. I'll do the worrying from now on. I probably won't see you again until after you're brought into court. Just sit tight and keep a stiff upper lip."

Mason left the visiting room and hurried to his office.

"Anything new?" Della Street asked.

"Lots," Mason said. "I want to find out about Orval Kingman. Have we heard anything from Paul?"

"Not yet. He said ... here he is now," she said, as Drake's code knock sounded on the locked exit door of Mason's office.

"All right, Paul," Mason said, as Della opened the door, "I've got something for you. This check that was made to 'O.K.' may be damned important. O.K. may not mean what we think it means. It may be the initials of the person to whom the check was payable. Now, there's one check to Orval Kingman and ..."

"I've got the dope on Orval Kingman," Drake said. "He's a bookie."

Mason raised his eyebrows.

"A high-class bookie," Drake said, "and I wouldn't be too surprised if Loring Lamont didn't give him quite a bit of business."

"Now that," Mason said thoughtfully, "would account for a lot of things."

"Wait a minute," Della Street said, opening her notebook. "We've got one more O.K."

"What do you mean?" Mason asked.

"Otto Keswick, the gardener who takes care of the yard."

Mason became suddenly thoughtful. "Darned if we haven't," he said. "What do you know about Otto Keswick, Drake? Have you found anything on him?"

"I have a report on him," Drake said. "I haven't met him. I can tell you one thing about him—he's a parolee."

"The devil!" Mason said. "What was he in for?"

"Blackmail," Drake said.

Mason turned to Della Street. "Get those films of the checkbook developed right away, and ..."

"They're already being developed," she said. "I've left word for enlargements and I have an appointment with a handwriting expert who will perhaps be able to tell whether the O.K. is in the handwriting of Loring Lamont."

"What are the chances?" Mason asked.

"Pretty good," she said, "if we have any other O.K. written by Loring Lamont to use as an exemplar. Otherwise, the chances aren't quite so good. He can probably tell whether the other writing on the check stubs was written by Loring Lamont, but just two letters that way are going to be pretty difficult unless we have some other places where Loring Lamont has written O.K."

Mason nodded, said, "And we can probably produce some bills with an O.K. written by Sadie Richmond and see if she wrote that O.K. on the check stub.

However, if it's Loring Lamont's checkbook, the chances are a hundred to one it's Loring Lamont's writing."

Mason was thoughtful for a moment, then said, "Paul, get in touch with the tellers at the bank on which that check was drawn. I want to find out who presents that five-hundred-dollar check to be cashed."

"They won't pay it?"

"Not unless it was paid before banking hours on the night Loring Lamont was killed. They won't cash any checks after a man is dead—but, of course, the check *could* have been presented and cashed the morning of the next day. As I understand it, they didn't find Lamont's body until after noon. Get busy there at the bank. If someone showed up with the five-hundred dollar check and they turned it down because Loring Lamont was dead, they'll remember the occasion and remember the person. If the check was cashed in the morning before they were notified of Loring Lamont's death, the canceled check will be in Lamont's account."

Drake nodded. "I'll get on it right away, Perry."

"And in the meantime," Mason said, "probably before we get all this information, we'll have a chance to go into court and question the witnesses for the prosecution. At least we'll find out what they know about it and what hole card Hamilton Burger, the district attorney, is holding."

"You think he has an ace in the hole?" Drake asked.

"He has something," Mason said. "He's altogether too confident and he's moving altogether too rapidly. There's some bit of evidence in the case that we don't know about, and you can be pretty certain it's evidence that isn't going to do Arlene Ferris any good."

Drake said, "You know, Perry, my idea is that her best bet is to show that she was deliberately enticed out there, to use that distributor part to show that the whole thing was deliberately planned by Loring Lamont, and then claim self-defense and..."

"Self-defense with a knife wound in the back?" Mason asked.

"Oh-oh, I stubbed my toe on that one before—" Drake said.

"The trouble is," Mason told him, "that she's already told her story."

"She could change it," Drake pointed out, "particularly if she said that she didn't tell the *whole* truth because some of the details would be embarrassing."

Mason's face was granite hard. "Whenever she tells her story on the witness stand, Paul, it'll be the truth. It won't be the story that's the most expedient. I think that the truth is not only the most powerful weapon, but as far as I'm concerned it's the only weapon."

"Have it your way," Drake said, "but she *could* show a little cheesecake and breeze through this case in a walk if she told a story of enticement and used that part from the distributor to back up her claim."

"Don't worry," Mason said, "we'll use that part from the distributor."

"But it won't have a real kick unless—well, you know, a girl fighting for her honor and all that."

"I know," Mason said, "but also don't forget that she told the police they left the ham and eggs untouched and the autopsy shows that Loring Lamont was killed within a matter of minutes after he had eaten those ham and eggs."

Drake heaved a long sigh. "Damn it," he said, "someone is always taking the joy out of life."

CHAPTER TEN

Donald Enders Carson, a young, aggressive trial deputy of the district attorney's office, said, "If the Court please, this is the preliminary hearing of the People of the State of California against Arlene Ferris. The People are ready. The defendant, represented by Perry Mason, is in court, and this is the time heretofore fixed for the preliminary hearing."

"The defendant is ready," Perry Mason said.

"Call your first witness," Judge Carleton Bayton said to the prosecuting attorney.

"Dr. Harmon C. Draper, the autopsy surgeon, will be my first witness," Carson said.

Draper came forward, was sworn, qualified himself, and testified that he had examined the body of Loring Lamont, that death had been caused by a stab wound in the back with a knife which still protruded from the back at the time the body was delivered to the autopsy room; that he could not definitely fix the time of death with reference to the hour of the day, but he could definitely fix death as having occurred within a very few minutes of the time a meal consisting of ham and eggs had been ingested, probably within much less than twenty minutes of the time of the meal, certainly no more than twenty minutes. That death might have taken place at any time after seven or before midnight on the evening of the fifth of the month, but was within twenty minutes of the time the food had been ingested, probably within five to ten minutes of the time the decedent had started to eat the meal.

"Cross-examine," Carson said to Mason.

"*You* have no information as to when the meal was ingested?" Mason asked.

"No."

"Death was instantaneous?"

"Virtually instantaneous."

"Despite the fact that the knife was in the back, Doctor, would it have been possible for the wound to have been inflicted by someone standing in front of the decedent?"

"I think not."

"Thank you," Mason said. "That's all, Doctor."

Carson said to the Court, "I apologize for putting on Dr. Draper out of order. He is, however, exceedingly busy and I told him I would call him as my first witness. I will now proceed with the regular groundwork of showing the location of the crime and the identification of the corpse."

Carson called a surveyor and a photographer, introduced maps, diagrams, sketches and photographs. He then said, "Call Mr. George Quincy Albert."

George Albert took the witness stand.

"If the Court please," Carson said, "I desire to use Mr. Albert as a general witness in this case, and, therefore, in order to save time, I am also going to use him as the witness who will identify the corpse."

"Very well," Judge Bayton said, "let's move along as rapidly as possible, gentlemen. I understand this is a case which has attracted considerable public interest, but, after all, this is simply a preliminary hearing."

"What is your occupation, Mr. Albert?" Carson asked.

"I am now, and for several years have been, an office manager in the executive offices of the Lamont Rolling, Casting and Engineering Company."

"Your age?"

"Thirty-two."

"Were you acquainted with Loring Lamont in his life-time?"

"I was."

"Where is he now?"

"He is dead."

"How do you know he is dead?"

"I identified his body in the morgue."

"Who asked you to do that?"

"The police. They wanted someone to make an identification and it was agreed that since Mr. Jarvis P. Lamont, the father, was quite broken up..."

"Never mind that," Carson interrupted. "You made the identification at the request of the police?"

"Yes, sir."

"And that identification was made while you were conferring with the police and the district attorney on the evening of the sixth?"

"Yes, sir."

"The police had sent for you to get information concerning certain phases of the case, and while you were there you volunteered to make the identification of the body at the morgue?"

"Yes, sir."

"You are acquainted with the defendant in this case?"

"Yes, sir."

"How long have you known her?"

"Since she started work at the Lamont Company."

"How long ago was that?"

"A period of a little more than two months."

"Now, directing your attention to the evening of the fifth, which was on Monday, did you have any conversation with the defendant on that day?"

"Yes, sir."

"When?"

"In the evening, after the regular quitting time."

"And what was the conversation? What did she say?"

"There were matters to be taken care of which called for overtime work—that is, it was not a necessity that she work overtime—I very seldom request that of any employee, particularly in view of what might be called a general trend of the times. Stenographers are not as interested now as..."

"Never mind that," Carson interrupted. "I am simply asking you if there was a conversation about her working overtime."

"Well, it came time for the office to be closed, that is, for the stenographers to leave and..."

"What time is that?"

"Five o'clock."

"And what happened?"

"The defendant kept right on working."

"Did you have a conversation with her?"

"I did later."

"When was that? That is, about what time?"

"About five-thirty. I thanked her for staying to finish the work and she told me that she knew the specifications on which she was working should go in the night's mail, that it was important that they go out and that she had decided to stay and finish them."

"What time did she leave?"

"A little after five-thirty."

"Was anyone else in the office at that time?"

"No, sir. Just the defendant and myself."

"Do you know what the weather was on that night?"

"It was raining. It had been raining during the day."

"You may cross-examine," Carson said.

Mason studied the witness thoughtfully. "You say the defendant had been working for the company for about two months?"

"Yes."

"Had you known her prior to the time she started work?"

"I had not."

"There is a personnel placement department in the corporation?"

"There is."

"And stenographic staff usually comes from this personnel placement?"

"It does."

"Do you have anything to do with hiring the people?"

"I do not."

"But you have authority to discharge them?"

"I do."

"You remember when the defendant started working for you?"

"Very well."

"Did she come to you through the regular placement channels?"

"She did not."

"She was not hired in the ordinary course of employment?"

"She was not. She was placed on the payroll because of specific instructions from Loring Lamont."

Mason straightened in his chair. "You mean that her employment did not go through the regular channels?"

"That is exactly what I mean."

"When did the defendant cease working?"

"I discharged her on the sixth because..."

"Answer the questions," Mason interrupted. "I am only interested in the date she ceased working for the company."

"The sixth."

"Very well," Mason said. "That concludes my cross-examination."

"No questions on redirect," Carson said.

"Call your next witness," Judge Bayton said to Carson.

"Jerome Henley," Carson announced.

Henley came forward, took the oath, and testified as to his name, residence and occupation.

"Directing your attention to the late evening of the fifth of this month, a Monday evening," Carson said, "I will ask you where you were on that evening."

"In my apartment."

"What is the address of your apartment?"

"9612 Endicott Way."

"That is an apartment house?"

"It is."

"You have an apartment there?"

"I do."

"Are you married or single?"

"Single."

"You live alone in this apartment?"

"I do."

"Are you acquainted with Mr. Loring Lamont, or, rather, were you acquainted with him in his lifetime?"

"I was...that is, I'd seen him often enough to know who he was."

"Were you acquainted with the automobile that he drove?"

"I was."

"And I believe he had an apartment in the same apartment house in which you reside?"

"That is right."

"Now, on the evening of the fifth, sometime during the night, did you see someone in Loring Lamont's automobile?"

"I did."

"Do you know who that person was?"

"Yes."

"Who was it?"

"Miss Arlene Ferris, the defendant in this case."

"And what did she do at that date and at that time, that you noticed in particular?"

"She had just driven Mr. Loring Lamont's car up to the curb and parked it in front of a fireplug...now, just a moment, I will retract that. I *assume* that she drove it up. I walked along just as she was getting out of the car."

"Where was the car parked?"

"Directly in front of a fireplug."

"Did you recognize the car?"

"I did."

"And you recognized the defendant?"

"I did."

"Is there any question in your mind as to the indentification?"

"There is none."

"You may inquire," Carson said to Mason.

"You remember the occasion when I entered your store on the seventh?" Mason asked.

"I do, very well indeed, Mr. Mason."

"I was accompanied by a young woman on that occasion?"

"You were."

"And Lieutenant Tragg of Homicide entered your place of business while I was there?"

"He did."

"And he asked you if you had ever seen the young woman who accompanied me on that occasion?"

"That is right."

"And did you not, at that time and place in the presence of Lieutenant Tragg and myself and this other woman, state definitely and positively that this other woman was the woman you had seen getting out of the car that night in front of the apartment house?"

"That is correct, I did. I was mistaken."

"The matter was more fresh in your recollection at that time than it is now?"

"No. The contrary is the case—I have had an opportunity to think the entire situation over and I realize now that I was tricked."

"Tricked by whom?"

"By you and by a private detective who showed me a photograph of the young woman who was with you, a woman named Madge Elwood. The circumstances were such that I was forced to associate the photograph with the person I had seen getting out of the car. The power of suggestion was such that when I saw the person who had posed for the picture I made a mistake."

"But you did identify Madge Elwood at that time as the person you had seen parking the car?"

"I repeat, I was tricked into..."

"The question is, Did you or did you not make such identification?"

"I did, but it was the result of trickery."

"You did make such identification?"

"Well...yes."

"A positive identification?"

"I'm not certain I know what you mean by a positive identification."

"You said you were positive?"

"I may have."

"*Were* you positive of the identification?"

"I thought I was at the time."

"Positive?"

"Mistakenly positive."

"But positive?"

"Well, yes."

"And what date was this that you saw someone parking Lamont's car?"

"It was on the evening of the fifth."

"At what time?"

"I can't tell the exact time."

"Can you tell the approximate time?"

"No, sir, I can't. It was prior to midnight. That's all I know."

"How are you certain it was prior to midnight."

"Because the place where I got a cup of coffee closes at midnight. I can't be certain as to the time. My watch was at the jeweler's. I had been listening to records and reading. I went sound asleep on the couch. I don't know how long I slept. I wakened and went down to get a cup of coffee. I came back and got into bed. I am not going to testify as to the *exact* time because I don't know. All I can say is that it was some time during the evening of the fifth. I have an impression it was around ten o'clock, but I don't *know*. I just had a sort of ten o'clock feeling, as though I had been sound asleep for three hours. That, of course, is not any evidence, any satisfactory criterion. I must have gone to sleep right after supper. I simply don't know the time."

"What did the defendant do after she got out of the car?"

"She stood at the curb for a minute, turned around and slammed the door shut on the right-hand side of the car. Then she walked down toward the corner."

"Which corner?"

"The corner to the north."

"No further questions," Mason said.

"No redirect examination," Carson said. "My next witness is Thomas Grimes."

Grimes came forward and was sworn, gave his name and address.

"You are employed as a guard in the parking lot at the executive division of the Lamont Rolling, Casting and Engineering Company?"

"I am."

"And is it your duty to check the cars that go in and out?"

"Principally to check the cars that go in, but we keep an eye on things."

"You were so employed on the evening of the fifth of this month?"

"I was."

"Were you acquainted with Loring Lamont during his lifetime?"

"Yes, sir. I knew him by sight."

"You were acquainted with his automobile?"

"Yes, sir."

"I will ask you if, on the evening of the fifth, you saw Mr. Loring Lamont leave the parking place in question."

"I did."

"At what time?"

"At approximately five-forty-five."

"Was he alone?"

"He was not."

"Who was with him?"

"A young woman."

"Could you identify that young woman?"

"Yes."

"Is she in court?"

"She is."

"Where?"

"She is the defendant, Arlene Ferris, sitting next to Mr. Perry Mason."

"You may inquire," Carson said, with a slight bow at Mason.

"You're certain this woman was the defendant?" Mason asked.

"I am."

"Do you remember being asked to look at another young woman on the seventh of this month?"

"I do."

"And didn't you identify her as being the woman you saw in Loring Lamont's automobile?"

"I did not," the witness said vehemently. "I did absolutely no such thing. I told Lieutenant Tragg and I told you that I couldn't be sure she was the same one—she wasn't."

"When did you find out she wasn't?"

"After I saw the right young woman."

"Meaning the defendant?"

"Yes."

"And prior to that time you didn't identify this other person as being the one you had seen?"

"I definitely did not. I refused to make the identification. I refused to do so for you and I refused to do so for Lieutenant Tragg."

"Quite right," Mason said. "Did you tell Lieutenant Tragg you weren't certain?"

"I told him I wasn't certain."

"And you weren't certain?"

"Not when I saw Miss Elwood—not that time."

"For how long did you see this woman who was in the car with Loring Lamont?"

"While he was driving through the gate."

"At what speed was he driving?"

"Oh, perhaps ten or twelve miles an hour."

"It was raining?"

"Yes."

"You were under shelter?"

"Yes."

"You were looking through a window in that shelter?"

"Yes."

"So you only saw this young woman while Loring Lamont was driving past that window. That window is how wide?"

"Oh, perhaps thirty inches."

"So you got a glimpse of this young woman while she was moving past a window thirty inches wide at a speed of ten miles an hour?"

"Yes."

"Was this young woman sitting on the left-hand side of the car?"

"Certainly not. Mr. Lamont was driving the car. She was seated on his right."

"You saw Mr. Lamont?"

"Yes."

"You are positive he was driving the car?"

"Positive."

"You didn't look at his face?"

"Of course I looked at his face."

"For how long?"

"Long enough to recognize him."

"While he was driving by?"

"Yes."

"And did you look at the woman before you recognized Loring Lamont or afterwards?"

"Afterwards."

"Then you looked at Loring Lamont first?"

"Yes, sir."

"Now, let's see," Mason said. "If Lamont was driving past a thirty-inch window at ten miles an hour he was going approximately fourteen feet a second, so he drove past the window in approximately one-fifth of a second."

"I haven't figured it out."

"Well, take a pencil and paper and figure it out for yourself," Mason said. "We'll wait."

The witness took a notebook from his pocket, started multiplying, dividing, then nodded his head.

"So you saw the people in the car for approximately one-fifth of a second."

"Yes, sir."

"And in that time you first looked at Loring Lamont long enough to recognize him?"

"Yes, sir."

"Then after that you looked at the person who was with him?"

"Well, I guess so."

"So you looked at this person for less than one-fifth of a second."

"All right."

"And when you saw this other woman on the seventh you said you weren't certain. Isn't that right?"

"That's right."

"You weren't certain that she *was* the woman?"

"That's right."

"And you weren't certain that she *wasn't* the woman?"

"I didn't say that she wasn't. However, I didn't think..."

"What did you say?"

"I said I wasn't certain."

"That she wasn't the woman?"

"I said I wasn't certain that she *was* the woman."

"You weren't certain that she was *not* the woman?"

"No."

"You simply said you weren't certain?"

"Yes. That's the general effect of it."

"Then after you saw a photograph of the defendant, and after Lieutenant Tragg or some other person on the police force had told you that that picture was one of the woman you saw on the seventh, you became certain?"

"I am now absolutely certain in my own mind that this defendant was the young woman I saw in the car," the witness said.

"Then," Mason said, smiling, "you are certain *now* but you weren't certain on the seventh?"

"I didn't see the defendant on the seventh."

"But you saw another young woman and said you weren't certain that she was not the woman?"

"I wasn't certain."

"Thank you," Mason said. "That's all."

"No questions on redirect," Carson said. "My next witness is Otto Keswick."

Keswick, in his early forties, alert, broad-shouldered, powerful in build, took the stand, was sworn and testified that he lived in a rented room in a house about two miles from the lodge where the murder had been committed, that he was employed as gardener and general handy man, that he had what he described as a somewhat ancient and battered automobile with which he went back and forth to work, that he had no particular hours of employment but was, rather, obligated simply to keep the premises in shape; that sometimes he worked as much as ten or twelve hours a day and other times he worked only a few hours a day.

He further testified that at a little after one o'clock the afternoon of the sixth he had driven to the lodge, that he had found the outer gate locked with a padlock to which he had the key, that he had inserted the key, unlocked the padlock, driven his car into the grounds, locking the gate behind him in accordance with his instructions, and had started doing some watering and trimming some trees; that he had noticed the side door of the house was slightly ajar, that he had gone to the door to close it, had looked inside and had seen a man's feet lying on the floor, that he had therefore stepped inside to see what was the trouble and had found the body of Loring Lamont.

The witness testified that he had been careful to touch nothing, that he had carefully backed out of the room—had, however, taken the precaution of closing the door; that he had then gone directly to his car, had driven to the gate, unlocked the padlock, gone out, locked the gate behind him and had driven to the home of Sadie Richmond; that he had reported what he had found there and that Mrs. Richmond had telephoned the authorities.

"Your witness," Carson said to Mason.

"How long had you been employed as a caretaker and general handy man prior to the murder?" Mason asked.

"For about two years."

"You knew the various persons who used the lodge and they were acquainted with you—I am referring now to the executives of the company?"

"Yes, sir."

"You knew J. P. Lamont?"

"Yes, sir."

"And he knew you?"

"Of course."

"And you knew Loring Lamont?"

"Certainly."

"Quite well?" Mason asked.

"I knew him as well as could be expected, and he knew me."

"When Mr. J. P. Lamont called you to do anything, what did he call you? How did he address you?"

"Otto."

"When Loring Lamont called you, what did he call you?"

"Otto."

"Did Mr. Loring Lamont ever refer to you by your initials of O.K.?"

The witness hesitated for an all but imperceptible moment, then said, "Not to my knowledge. He called me Otto."

"Where were you the night of the fifth?" Mason asked.

"I was at home."

"And where is at home?"

"At the residence I mentioned, where I rent a room."

"Was anyone else with you?"

"Not with me, but I was with someone."

"Who?"

"Mrs. Arthur Sparks."

"And who is Mrs. Sparks?"

"She is a widowed woman of about sixty-five. She owns the place where I rent a room. I was with her in the living room at her request, watching television."

"During what time?"

"From about seven o'clock in the evening until ten-thirty."

"About ten-thirty?"

"Exactly ten-thirty," the witness said. "The television show I as watching was over at ten-thirty and as soon as the show was over I went to bed."

"What time did you get up in the morning?"

"About seven-thirty."

"But you didnt go to the lodge until a little after one o'clock?"

"That's right. I did some odd jobs around the house for Mrs. Sparks. I don't pay cash rental for my room, but keep the house and grounds in order."

"Are you paid a salary for taking care of the lodge?"

"No, sir. I am paid by the hour. I put in the time I think necessary and keep track of my time and am paid by the hour."

"Who checks on your time—anyone? Do they simply put you on your honor?"

"Not exactly. I keep an account of my time and give Sadie Richmond my time slips. She marks them 'O.K.' and puts them in the desk. Then someone from the company picks them up, figures the total of hours and the total I have coming and they send out a check."

"You're certain the gate was locked when you went to the place on the sixth?"

"Quite certain."

"Was there anything at all about the premises that indicated anything unusual had taken place there?"

"Only the door which was standing slightly ajar."

"Nothing else?"

"Nothing else."

"Thank you," Mason said. "That's all."

Keswick left the stand, quite evidently relieved that his cross-examination had been so perfunctory.

Carson said, "My next witness, if the Court please, is Peter Lyons. I think his testimony will be rather brief."

Judge Bayton glanced at the clock. "Let us hope so," he said. "This is only a preliminary hearing, yet it has consumed the entire morning. I'm afraid it will be necessary to take the usual noon adjournment. I had hoped to have the afternoon free for another case."

"Perhaps," the prosecutor said, "counsel will be willing to stipulate to Mr. Lyons' testimony."

"What do you expect to prove by him?" Mason asked.

"Mr. Lyons," Carson said, "is a police officer who was on duty until midnight on the night of the fifth. He will testify that he found the automobile of Loring Lamont parked in front of a fireplug, that he issued a ticket for illegal parking. The location of the illegally parked car was exactly where the witness, Jerome Henley, saw it when the young woman emerged from it."

"Only one ticket was issued?" Mason asked.

"That's all that this particular officer issued."

"What eventually became of the car?"

"Other officers who came on duty after midnight tagged the car for illegal parking and eventually, at three o'clock in the morning, it was towed away. Ordinarily these officers do not enforce traffic regulations but there had been trouble with illegal parking in the vicinity and an order had gone out to watch for illegal parking. All officers patrolling this district had been instructed to tag cars, and, after the second or third tag, to have the offending car towed away."

"And I take it," Mason said, "that you have talked with all these officers yourself and understand the facts?"

"I have."

"Upon that statement by counsel," Mason said, "I will stipulate that Officer Lyons, if called, would so testify on direct examination that he gave one tag for illegal parking. At what time was it?"

"About nine. He gave one parking ticket at about nine P.M.," Carson said.

"You know that to be the fact?" Mason asked.

"I do."

"Then I will stipulate that would be his testimony on direct examination."

Carson went on. "And will you stipulate that the other officers who came on duty at midnight gave two additional parking tickets and the car was towed away about three o'clock?"

"You state that as a fact?" Mason asked.

"I do," Carson said. "Not, of course, of my own knowledge but based upon my conversation with the officers."

"I will stipulate that these officers would so testify on direct examination," Mason said.

"Does that conclude your case?" the judge asked.

Carson glanced at the clock and said, "Unfortunately, it does not. I have one other witness I intend to put on the stand."

"His testimony will be brief?" Judge Bayton asked.

"I don't know. That depends quite largely on cross-examination. The witness is Lieutenant Tragg, who will testify to some very significant facts."

"Can they be stipulated?" Judge Bayton asked.

"I am afraid not, Your Honor. These facts are quite—well, I dislike to comment on the evidence in advance, but these facts are quite conclusive, and perhaps may come as a surprise to the defense."

"After all, this is only a preliminary hearing," Judge Bayton said. "There's no jury present. Go ahead and state what you expect to prove."

Carson said, "This witness will testify not only to circumstantial evidence but to conversations with the defendant and admissions made by her. I would prefer to let the witness disclose the circumstantial evidence."

"Very well," Judge Bayton said with obvious reluctance, "we will have to continue the case apparently through the afternoon. Court will adjourn until two o'clock P.M. The defendant is in custody and is remanded to custody."

Arlene Ferris glanced apprehensively at Perry Mason. "How is it coming?" she asked, as the judge retired to his chambers.

"Better than I had expected," Mason said. "Those witnesses are so mixed up in their identification now that by the time we get them in the Superior Court in front of a jury they'll have testified to two different things."

"But that means you expect I'll be bound over for trial in the Superior Court?" she asked apprehensively.

"I'm afraid so," Mason said. "Attorneys seldom expect to have a defendant released at a preliminary hearing—and, after all, young lady, circumstances have conspired to put you behind the legal eight ball."

"I hadn't realized what a nightmare this would be," she said, "being shut up in jail and...it's horrible."

"No one ever realizes what it means until it happens," Mason told her. "I'm sorry, Arlene, but right now I don't care to try to play things any differently. If I tried to get you released now I might wind up doing your case a lot more harm than good. I'd have to put you on the stand and you'd have to convince the judge you were telling the truth. You can't do that with Judge Bayton. He adopts the position that it's not up to him to judge a conflict in the evidence, that as long as there's evidence indicating a crime and connecting the defendant with the commission of that crime, he binds the defendant over to the Superior Court and lets the jury decide—I think we can get you a quick trial and..."

"And then what?" she interrupted.

"And prompt acquittal," Mason said, "if you do *exactly* as I say."

"I'll do it," she promised.

Mason patted her shoulder. "All right, chin up," Mason told her.

She hesitated. "Is it true that Jarvis P. Lamont has said I'm a liar and an adventuress, that he's going to go through my past with a fine-tooth comb?"

"That's true," Mason said. "And it's a wonderful thing in your favor. I'm going to encourage the press to exploit it as much as possible. It's wonderful publicity for you. The picture of a young, vitually penniless woman fighting for her freedom and her honor, and, pitted against her, a ruthless tycoon who is trying to prop up the reputation of a profligate son by damning the woman whom the son wronged, is going to make a background that will arouse public sympathy and the sympathy of a jury. You'll have to go now. Keep a stiff upper lip."

Mason watched Arlene Ferris being led out of the courtroom, then went to the back of the courtroom where Paul Drake and Della Street were chatting with Madge Elwood.

"How does it look?" Madge Elwood asked.

"About the way I expected—perhaps a little better," Mason said. "This Jerome Henley was so mad that he had been tricked, he blurted out some admissions that we can use later."

"Won't he deny he said them?" Madge Elwood asked. "I think he's capable of it."

Mason shook his head. "There's a court reporter taking everything down. What he said is in the record and it's going to stay in the record. We're going out to lunch. Better come along."

"No, thanks. I...I have a date with a friend."

"You'll be in court this afternoon?"

"Of course."

"At two o'clock," Mason said. "Be sure to be there."

Mason turned to Paul Drake. "Paul," he said, "there's something peculiar about that car being parked in front of the fireplug."

"What do you mean?"

"This officer, Peter Lyons, tagged the car around nine. He put the first tag on it. Now, Henley saw Arlene Ferris getting out of the car. He can't fix the time but because of that parking ticket we know it must have been before nine.

"Now then, we run into a sort of hiatus. The officers were instructed to watch for illegal parking, to put on two or three tags and then radio for a tow-car. Lyons went off duty at twelve o'clock, he put the first tag on the car at nine o'clock. The other two officers came on at midnight. They found the car illegally parked and put two or three tags on it, and then had it towed away. But what happened between nine o'clock and midnight? Why didn't Lyons tag it again?"

Drake shrugged his shoulders. "Those things can happen."

"Well," Mason said, 'I've offered to stipulate, but there's a string to my offer Carson may not have noticed. Get a couple of operatives checking the records at police headquarters. Let's see what happened to that car—just how many tags were on it and when they were put on it."

Drake said, "Why didn't you bring out the fact that Otto Keswick had a criminal record, Perry? You could have shown him up on cross-examination."

"Sure," Mason said. "I could have done that all right, and it would have harmed Keswick, but wouldn't have done our case a darned bit of good. There's no use dragging out a man's dead past unless you expect to accomplish something by doing it.

"Incidentally, Paul, just check his alibi. Ask this Mrs. Sparks if he's correct on his time of watching the television—better send a man out there to talk with her and have him phone in a report."

"Okay," Drake said, moving toward the phone booth. "You and Della have lunch and I'll get busy on the phone and try to line up the information you want."

As Drake entered the phone booth, a short, heavy-set man of about forty-five came pushing purposefully through the last of the spectators who were straggling from the courtroom.

Cold gray eyes beneath black eyebrows surveyed Mason. "Perry Mason?"

Mason nodded.

The man's hands were pushed down in the side pockets of his coat. He kept them there. "Orval Kingman," he said.

"Oh, yes," Mason observed.

"In my business," Kingman said, "a man keeps an eye on his back trail. If anyone starts sniffing around he wants to know why. He also wants to know who and then he may want to do something about it."

Mason stood looking down at the man, at the hands thrust in the side pockets, the belligerent set of the shoulders.

"And so?" Mason asked.

"And so," Kingman said, "I get the word that private eyes are sniffing around on my trail. Then I get the word that these private eyes are employed by Perry Mason and that you might have the idea of dragging my name into this Lamont murder case."

"And so?" Mason asked.

"And so I came to tell you not to do it."

Mason said, "When I'm trying a case nobody tells me what to do and what not to do. I do the thing that's for the best interests of my client. You're a bookmaker. Loring Lamont played the horses with you. You evidently had some kind of an understanding with him by which he played on the cuff until the amount reached five hundred dollars, then you collected."

"All right," Kingman said. "That still doesn't mean you can make me a Patsy in order to get your client out of a jam."

"I'm not trying to make you a Patsy," Mason said. "I'm trying to get at the facts. If I find the facts will benefit my client I'll bring them out in court."

"Now that just might not be healthy," Kingman said.

"For you or for me?"

"For you, Mr. Mason."

"I'll watch out for my health," Mason said. "It's excellent, thank you. You can watch out for yours. Now, suppose you tell me what you were doing on the night of the fifth."

"That I'll do," Kingman said. "That's one of the things I came to tell you."

"It might have helped the situation if you'd told me first," Mason said, "instead of discussing my health."

Kingman shrugged his shoulders, set his thick neck, looked up at Mason and said, "I was in a poker game."

"From when until when?"

"From seven o'clock until nearly midnight."

"That can be established?" Mason asked.

"That can be established," Kingman said, "but the people who were playing with me wouldn't want to have their names brought into it."

"You got a check from Loring Lamont on the fifth?"

"On the morning of the fifth."

"What time?"

"About ten o'clock, I guess."

"To cover past bets?"

"Let's put it this way, it kept his credit up."

"You didn't trust him for more than five hundred dollars?"

"Look, Mr. Mason, I don't trust anyone for more than five hundred dollars. That's my limit."

"He made bets on the fifth?"

"That's right."

"On the afternoon of the fifth?"

"On the afternoon of the fifth."

"And won or lost?"

"Does that make any difference?"

"I think it does, because I think perhaps he lost rather heavily and you wanted five hundred dollars more from him before you got in that poker game."

"Aren't you funny!" Kingman said sarcastically.

"And," Mason said, "you telephoned him and told him he'd been plunging and had gone over the five hundred credit limit, that you wanted five hundred and that you were coming out to collect it. You probably told him you were going to sit in a poker game that night and you wanted cash."

"That would be a nice idea," Kingman said. "Go ahead, follow it up. What happened after that?"

"You went out to the lodge."

"All the way out there to collect a lousy five hundred bucks?"

"You may have needed it. You were going to be sitting in a poker game. I don't imagine they took IOU's in that poker game."

"Okay," Kingman said. "Keep talking, Counselor. Let's get this idea of yours out in the open and look it over. You think I went out there to collect the five hundred bucks."

"You could have."

"And then what?"

"You could have had an argument and stuck a knife in his back."

"You mean I took a knife out there with me?"

"There were knives in the kitchen."

"So I went out there, had a talk with him about five hundred bucks and stuck a knife into him?"

"I'm simply investigating the possibilities," Mason said.

"All right. Let's look at it this way," Kingman said. "Why would I stick a knife in him? He was a customer."

"Perhaps because he didn't pay the five hundred bucks."

The black bushy eyebrows went up. "Loring Lamont didn't pay the five hundred? Come, come, Counselor, you're going to have to do better than that. Loring Lamont wanted to keep his credit good with me. He liked to play the horses and I was his bookie. He knew he could trust me. I paid off when he won. I kept my mouth shut. The old man was never going to learn anything about what was going on through me. Loring Lamont knew that. Why should he refuse to pay me the five hundred bucks?"

"Perhaps he gave you a check," Mason said, watching the man closely.

"All right, go on. What happened?"

"And then you got in an argument—perhaps over a woman."

"How you talk," Kingman said. "Look, Mr. Mason, in my type of business women grow on bushes."

"This may have been a particular woman."

"Not with me. There aren't any particular women. In my racket a broad is a broad. Now let's get this thing straight," Kingman said. "You think I went out there to collect five hundred bucks because I was going to get in a poker game. You think I was in a hurry for the five hundred smackeroos."

"It could be," Mason said.

"Sure, it could be," Kingman said, with a twisted smile which emphasized the line of his broken nose. "So I went out to get the five hundred. Then, in place of hurrying back to a poker game, Loring Lamont said, 'Look, Orval, I had a date with a babe who ran out on me. We were just getting ready to sit down and eat some ham and eggs. They're getting a little cold now, but why don't you sit down here with me and have some ham and eggs?'

"So I sat down at the table with him and had some cold ham and eggs, notwithstanding the fact I was in a hurry to get back to this poker game."

"You seem to know a lot about what happened," Mason said.

"In my business, when someone tries to frame me for something, I find out the facts."

"All right," Mason said. "You find out the facts. Now I'll tell you what might have happened. Lamont might have told you, 'Look, Orval, I'm hungry. This food is on the table. I was just sitting down to eat when a babe ran out on me. You wait until I've finished eating and I'll make you out a check. If you're hungry you can eat that plate of ham and eggs. If you aren't, you can throw them out.'

"Okay," Kingman said. "We'll ride along with it your way, Counselor. Then what happened?"

"Then you ate the ham and eggs and then you had an argument."

"Did I get a check or didn't I?"

"You got a check," Mason said.

"For five hundred bucks?"

"For five hundred bucks."

"And then I got in an argument with him?"

"That's the part I'm investigating."

"Go ahead and investigate all you damn please," Kingman said. "For your information, Mr. Mason, I didn't go out to that country place. I didn't call him on the telephone. I only got the one check from him and that was in the morning. You'll find that I cashed it at the bank before two o'clock. That was on the fifth. I don't hound my customers and when I want to play poker I don't have to go dashing around getting money to put up for an ante. Now, you have a theory. You'd better get some facts to back up your theory before you start making it public."

"Don't tell me how to practice law," Mason said. And then added quietly, "Now you've been telling me things. I'm going to tell you something. I'm investigating this case. I have no desire to try to push anyone around. I don't want to invade anyone's private life. I want to know what happened, that's all. You say you were in a poker game from seven until nearly midnight. Give me the names of the people you were playing with. I'll check. It will be a quiet check. If you check out, that's all there is to it. If you don't, I'll do some more checking."

"I've told you some of the people wouldn't want to be brought into it."

"That may be," Mason said, "but there are certain facts which lead me to believe you may have talked on the telephone with Loring Lamont."

"What facts?"

"Let me ask you this," Mason said. "How did he refer to you? Did he call you by your first name or by your initials?"

"By my first name, whenever he used names. If he called me anything he'd call me Orval."

"He never called you O.K.?"

"He never called me O.K.," the man said, the gray eyes holding Mason's.

"All right," Mason said. "Give me a list of the persons who were in the game with you and I'll check. I'll do it quietly."

Kingman shook his head. "I tell you, I don't do business that way. I'm telling you what the facts are for your own guidance, just so you don't lead with your chin and so you keep healthy."

Mason reached to an inside pocket, pulled out a folded legal document, took out his fountain pen, wrote the name "Orval Kingman" in a blank and handed the document to Kingman.

"What's this?" the man asked, unfolding the paper to look at it.

"That," Mason said, "is a subpoena duly issued under the seal of the court, ordering you to apear at two o'clock this afternoon as a witness on behalf of the defense."

Kingman's face darkened. "I've tried to tell you and tell you nice," he said.

"And I've tried to tell you and tell you nice," Mason told him. "You give me a list of the men who were in that poker game with you and I'll check. Otherwise, you'll go on the stand and tell where you were on the night of the fifth."

"You're bluffing," Kingman said. "You aren't going to put on any evidence. No smart lawyer ever puts on evidence on behalf of the defense at a preliminary hearing."

Mason shrugged his shoulders. You've got your subpoena. Be there at two o'clock this afternoon. If you think I'm bluffing this will be a good way to find out."

"Now, wait a minute," Kingman said. "Let's not get each other wrong. I...."

"You have your subpoena," Mason said. "If you want to get out of testifying temporarily you can give me a list of those names."

Kingman's face darkened, then abruptly he pulled a notebook from his pocket, started writing.

"There are five names," he said, tearing the sheet from the notebook and handing it to Mason. "Those people wouldn't like it if they thought I'd given you the information. But if you want to check with them quietly and confidentially you'll find out where I was on the night of the fifth.

"There are two men whose names I've marked with a little check mark. I'd prefer to have you start with them. They're regular poker players and it wouldn't mean so much to them. The other three men are businessmen who think they're pretty good poker players."

"They lost?" Mason asked.

"As it happens, they lost."

"And you won and these two men whose names you have checked, won?"

"If it's any of your business, we won."

"I can see why you might not care to have the situation publicized," Mason said.

"That doesn't make me guilty of murder, Mr. Mason."

"Now there," Mason told him, "is where you're using words that I'll listen to. I don't want to abuse my position or the power of the law. All I'm interested in is finding out what happened. If you were in that poker game and didn't leave it, that's enough for me. Even if you can't prove an alibi I'll still do some checking before I put you on the stand or bring your name into it—assuming, of course, that you don't start calling my hand. If you want to call my hand we'll start putting cards on the table."

Kingman said, "Okay, Counselor, that's good enough for me. They told me you were a square shooter. Get your men doing a little investigating and you'll find I'm clean."

Abruptly the man's right hand shot out of his pocket and was extended toward Mason.

Mason shook hands.

"They told me you were on the up and up," Kingman said. "I just had to be sure, that's all."

"You only got the one check that day?" Mason asked.

"So help me, Counselor, that's the truth. I got the one check. I saw him about ten o'clock in the morning when he stopped by to give me the check and he picked some horses for the afternoon. And since we're putting cards on the table, I'll tell you something else. He won. Not too heavy, but he won. If he'd lived he would have had money coming to him.

"And as it is?"

"As it is, he gets nothing," Kingman said. "That's one of the chances a man takes. If I give him credit and he bets with me, loses and then drops dead I can't present a bill against his estate. If he bets with me and wins and drops dead his estate doesn't get anything. I can't come in and say, 'I'm a bookie. I owe the guy fifteen hundred bucks.'"

"Was it that much?" Mason asked.

"Just about," Kingman said.

He turned to Della Street. "I'm sorry I had to strut my stuff in front of you, Miss Street," he said, "but with a man like Mason you have to talk to him when you can get him. I didn't know what he was planning to do this afternoon and I wanted to talk with him—I'm glad I did."

He bowed, swung on his heel and pounded his way back down the corridor toward the elevators.

Mason glanced at Della Street.

"Well," she said.

"What's the reaction of your feminine intuition?" Mason asked.

"I believe him," she said. "That last touch was the thing that sold me. When he said that Loring Lamont had won and if he lived he'd have had some money coming to him."

Mason nodded thoughtfully. "Just the same," he said, "we'll get hold of Paul Drake and do a little checking on that poker game. That five-hundred-dollar check to a person listed simply as 'O.K.' assumes even greater importance as we go on."

"Of course," Della Street pointed out, "the initials 'O.K.' wouldn't necessarily be those of the person receiving the check. It could be some sort of a code."

"In which event," Mason said, "it's up to us to crack the code. Come on, Della, let's eat."

CHAPTER ELEVEN

At five minutes before two o'clock, as Mason was entering the courtroom, Paul Drake, hurrying from a telephone booth, tapped the lawyer on the shoulder.

"What is it, Paul?"

"Everything checks on that car in front of the fireplug," Drake said. "Peter Lyons, who went off duty about midnight, gave the first ticket. After midnight there were two more tickets. Police had been ordered to keep a watch on that street. They'd been troubled with a lot of illegal parking there and had had lots of complaints about blocked driveways, so orders had gone out to keep an eye on cars in the district, tag on the first illegal parking, then keep an eye on the car and order a tow-away after the third ticket.

"The Lamont car was handled as routine until police found out about its importance. By that time the car had been towed away. Of course, after the murder there was a frantic scramble to look the car over for fingerprints. I think they have some."

Mason thought that statement over.

"Well?" Drake asked. "Does that hit you too hard?"

"I don't know," Mason said. "We'll see what develops."

The lawyer walked on into the courtroom.

When Judge Bayton had called court to order, Mason said, "If the Court please, I was asked to stipulate to the testimony of the officers about the parked car.

"I am, of course, willing to make any stipulations which will save time and which do not affect the substantial rights of the defendant. However, in regard to the testimony of Peter Lyons, the officer who put the first tag on the car at nine o'clock, I feel that the interests of the defendant require I should cross-examine the officer. I am therefore serving notice on the prosecution at this time that, while I was willing to stipulate as to what Lyons' testimony would have been on direct examination, I now wish to exercise my right of cross-examination."

"Very well," Judge Bayton said. "That was the stipulation, and I presume the prosecution will have Officer Lyons here for cross-examination, although the Court doesn't see that the testimony in regard to the parked car has any great significance."

Donald Carson arose with smiling urbanity. "Not only do I agree with Your Honor, but since it now appears his testimony would necessitate a delay in the case, I will withdraw my stipulation and we won't use the testimony of Officer Lyons at all."

"Then you withdraw your stipulation as to Lyons' testimony and it will be considered he was not a witness?" Judge Bayton asked.

"Yes, Your Honor."

"Just a minute, if the Court please," Mason said, getting to his feet. "We object to such procedure. Officer Lyons, having been brought into the case, can't be taken out of it now. The understanding was that I would stipulate as to his testimony on direct examination. The defense has the right of cross-examination."

"But the prosecution has now withdrawn the witness," Judge Bayton said.

"The prosecution can't do it," Mason said, "after I accepted the stipulation Officer Lyons was deemed to have testified on direct examination that certain things happened. This was subject to my right of cross-examination in the event I desired to use that right. The stipulation was offered, was accepted and I now desire to use the right of cross-examination."

Judge Bayton frowned. "Is it *that* important, Mr. Mason?"

"I don't know," Mason admitted frankly, "but I intend to find out."

"Very well," Judge Bayton said, smiling. "I think Mr. Mason is correct, Mr. Prosecutor. The stipulation was offered and was accepted. The defense has the right to cross-examine any witnesses he so chooses. You will have Mr. Lyons in court."

"I don't know that we can get him in court on such short notice," Carson said.

"But you must have realized that the stipulation was so worded that the defense could cross-examine him if it so desired," Judge Bayton said with some indication of impatience.

"But I didn't have any faintest idea that the defense would want to cross-examine the officer."

"Well, you evidently guessed wrong," Judge Bayton snapped. "The Court trusts you will arrange to have Officer Lyons here for cross-examination so that the case will not be delayed. Now who's your next witness?"

"Lieutenant Tragg of Homicide," Carson said.

"Very well. Put Lieutenant Tragg on the stand and arrange to get Officer Lyons here so he can be cross-examined."

"If I may have the indulgence of the Court for a moment," Carson said with poor grace, "I'll see what can be done about getting Officer Lyons here."

Carson glared at Perry Mason, tiptoed over to an officer, whispered briefly to him, then straightened and said, "Lieutenant Tragg to the stand, please."

Lt. Tragg, broad-shouldered, grizzled, lumbered up to the witness stand, was sworn, gave his name, address and occupation and faced Carson expectantly.

"You were called to the Chatsworth property of the Lamont Rolling, Casting and Engineering Company on the evening of the sixth?"

"I was."

"And the body of Loring Lamont, which had been previously discovered, was still there at that time?"

"No. The body had been removed before I got there."

"Now, Lieutenant, I don't want to take up a lot of time going over details which are already in evidence, so I will therefore, with the permission of counsel, ask questions which are sufficiently leading to designate the particular evidence I want to elicit. Were you present at the morgue when a search was made of the pockets of the clothing of Loring Lamont?"

"I was."

"Was anything particularly unusual found in those pockets?"

"Yes."

"What?"

"A rotating part for the electrical distributing system on an automobile."

"Do you have that part in your possession at the present time?"

"I do."

"Will you produce it, please?"

Lt. Tragg reached in his pocket, took out a sealed envelope, took a knife from his pocket, cut through the edge of the envelope, took out a small object and handed it to the deputy district attorney, who, in turn, submitted it to Mason for his inspection, then turned back to the witness.

"What is the function of this part in the distributing system of an automobile, Lieutenant—if you know?"

"It distributes the electrical charge in rotation to the different spark plugs so that the cylinders will fire in order."

"And if this part is removed from a car, what is the effect on the ignition system?"

"The ignition system fails. You can't get any current to the spark plugs."

"And it is, therefore, impossible for the car to operate?"

"That's right. You can't start the motor."

"And this was found in the pocket of the decedent?"

"It was."

"Are you familiar with the automobile of the defendant in this case?"

"I am, yes, sir."

"Can you state whether or not this part, which I now hand to you, fits the electrical system in the car of the defendant?"

"It does."

Carson turned to Perry Mason and said, "Strictly speaking, the questions I am now going to ask Lieutenant Tragg can be objected to as hearsay, but in the interests of saving time and simply in order to present a complete picture to the Court, I am going to ask these questions, realizing that if counsel for the defense wishes he can object and I will then be forced to put a mechanic on the stand. However, I think we all wish to save time on matters about which there can be no dispute."

Carson turned back to Lt. Tragg. "Did you make any investigation as to whether the car of the defendant had been in a condition to be operated on the night of the fifth?"

"I did."

"What did you find?"

"The car had remained on the parking lot all the night of the fifth and the morning of the sixth. On the morning of the sixth, a mechanic came to the lot, tested the car and repaired it so it would start."

"Do you know what the mechanic found to be wrong with the car?"

"I do."

"What?"

"This part was missing from the distributor."

"This part?"

"Either this part or a part identical with it."

Carson said, "I will now ask that this rotating part be placed in evidence as People's Exhibit—whatever the next designation may be."

"I think it's Exhibit B-7," Judge Bayton said.

"Very well. Let it be marked as Exhibit B-7 for identification."

"Now then, Lieutenant Tragg," Carson went on, turning once more to the witness, "you interrogated the defendant concerning her whereabouts on the evening of the fifth of this month?"

"I did."

"When did that interrogation take place?"

"On the seventh, after the defendant had been picked up by the police."

"Who was present at the time of that conversation?"

"I was and Ralph Grave, a member of the police force."

"And were any inducements, threats or promises made to the defendant in order to get her to make a statement?"

"There were none."

"Was she advised as to her rights and the fact that she did not need to make a statement?"

"She was told that any statement she might make could be used against her. I asked her if she cared to explain where she had been on the night of the fifth and whether she had been with Loring Lamont."

"And what did the defendant say?"

"Briefly, she stated that she had tried to start her car in the parking lot, that it would not start, that Loring Lamont had come along and offered her a ride, that he had taken her to the rural lodge maintained by the Lamont Company, that there he had attempted to force his attentions upon her, that this came at a time when he had cooked up a supper of ham and eggs and she had baked biscuits, that she repulsed his advances and ran out of the cabin, down the road; that he had started to follow her in his automobile, so she had detoured to the side of the road and crawled through the barbed wire, that she had then realized he was following her tracks in the wet ground on the surface of the dirt road, that when he came to the place where she had crawled through the wire, he had stopped and left the car with the motor running while he crawled through the fence after her, that she had managed to double back, get through the fence, race down the road and had jumped into the car and taken off in his automobile before he could catch up with the car.

"She further said that she had driven the car back to town and then, feeling that she would add what she called a touch of sardonic humor to the situation, had deliberately parked it in front of a fireplug and had gone off and left it."

"Did she say what time this was?"

"She said she thought it was about eight-fifteen to eight-thirty."

"And she had deliberately parked the car in front of the fireplug?"

"Directly in front of the fireplug."

"Had left the keys in it?"

"Yes."

"Now, to go back a moment, she stated to you that the deceased had cooked ham and eggs?"

"That is right."

"Did she state that they had partaken of the ham and eggs?"

"She specifically stated that the altercation had taken place and she had run away prior to the time the ham and eggs were consumed."

"Did you," Carson asked, "make any attempt to verify certain aspects of this statement by physical examination of the evidence and any objects which might tend to furnish corroboration?"

"I did, yes, sir."

"What did you do and what did you find?"

"First we dusted Loring Lamont's car for fingerprints. We found two of the defendant's fingerprints on the back of the rearview mirror. We also searched the road trying to find tracks which would corroborate the statement made by the defendant."

"And what, if anything, did you find?"

"We found that there had been so much travel over the dirt road that it was impossible to detect footprints on the road. Following the discovery of the body, there was an enormous amount of travel due to the nature of the crime and public interest because of the social and financial prominence of the victim."

"That was on the road itself?"

"Yes, sir, that was on the road itself."

"Now, what about the place adjoining the road—the bank?"

Lt. Tragg squared his shoulders as though bracing himself for an attack. "We found," he said, choosing his words carefully, "where the defendant had planted evidence in an attempt to corroborate her story."

Judge Bayton looked up quickly, snapping to attention at the answer. He glanced at Perry Mason, then at Donald Carson, then at the witness.

"Is there any objection to that question or any motion to strike," he asked, "on the ground the witness has testified to a conclusion?"

Mason said, "Rather than object, I would like to cross-examine the witness on the point."

"You can't sit idly by and let extraneous matter be brought into a case, hoping to cross-examine," Judge Bayton said.

"I don't think it's extraneous," Mason said. "If the defendant did plant this evidence it's a very material and a very convincing fact."

"But the witness doesn't *know* she planted it," Judge Bayton snapped. "I think it's your duty to object and move to strike."

"If the Court please," Carson said, "I think the witness *does* know it. I think the circumstantial evidence on the point is damning. We would welcome cross-examination; both the witness and the prosecution would welcome it."

"Well, it isn't up to the Court to tell counsel how to try his case," Judge Bayton said. "The witness has certainly testified to a conclusion, however."

"A conclusion which I think this witness, by reason of his training as an expert and his peculiar aptitude in such matters, is quite competent to draw," Perry Mason said urbanely. "There is no objection by the defense."

Carson swung back to the question of the witness. "Just what did you find?"

"At first, and on the morning of the seventh, prior to the time we had questioned the defendant, we found that someone had cut a piece from the hem of the defendant's skirt. This piece had been cut with a knife. Then this fragment or segment had been taken out to the barbed-wire fence near the scene of the crime. Someone had impaled it on the barbed-wire fence in such a position that it would be certain to attract attention.

"We then found that some woman, wearing high-heeled shoes, had been lifted against the bank and had been lowered down the soft soil, leaving tracks made by high-heeled shoes in an apparent attempt to make it appear this person had slid through the lower wire of the fence."

"Are you prepared to state definitely, Lieutenant Tragg, that this person who had left those tracks did *not* slide through under the wire of the fence?"

"Definitely."

"And how can you tell that?"

"Because the ground was sufficiently soft back of the fence to have retained the imprint of heel tracks, and there were no tracks on the other side of the fence—that is, the side away from the road."

"Did you subsequently find the skirt from which that piece had been cut?"

"We did."

"Where?"

"It was one of the defendant's skirts and had been left temptingly displayed in her apartment where it would be virtually impossible to miss it."

"Do you have that skirt with you?"

"I do."

"Will you produce it, please?"

Tragg opened a brief case and produced the skirt Madge Elwood had been wearing when she and Perry Mason visited the apartment of Arlene Ferris.

"You have the piece which was cut from the garment with you?"

"I have."

"Will you produce it, please?"

Tragg produced the torn piece.

"This triangular piece fits in the hem of the garment?"

"It does."

"Will you please demonstrate to the Court?"

Tragg spread the skirt out over his knee, took the triangular piece of cloth which Mason had cut from the garment and fitted it into place.

Judge Bayton, frowning, leaned over from the bench to study the piece of cloth and the skirt with the cut hem, then glanced ominously at Perry Mason.

"Please let the Court inspect that, Lieutenant," he said.

Tragg spread the garment and the torn piece on the bench. Judge Bayton carefully fitted them together.

"We now ask that the skirt and the fragment be introduced in evidence as People's Exhibits, appropriate numbers—B-8 for the skirt, B-9 for the fragment," Carson said.

Judge Bayton said, "Counsel is, of course, entitled to examine this witness on *voir dire* before the articles are introduced in evidence. Does counsel wish to do so?"

"Counsel does," Mason said.

"Very well. You may examine the witness on *voir dire*," Judge Bayton said.

Mason smiled at Lt. Tragg. "You have said that the evidence was designed to substantiate the story of the defendant?"

"There can be no other possible explanation," Tragg said crisply.

Mason smiled. "Then the attempt was rather clumsy, Lieutenant. A person trying to substantiate a story of the defendant would, at least, have had the young woman who was leaving the tracks go on the other side of the fence and run along the soft ground."

"There may not have been time."

"And," Mason when on calmly, "you have stated that the skirt from which this fragment was cut was a skirt belonging to the defendant."

"It was her size and found in her apartment. I consider that sufficient evidence of ownership."

"Did you make any attempt to find where the defendant had purchased this skirt, Lieutenant?"

"No."

"Why?"

"Because I didn't think it was necessary."

"Did you make any attempt to find cleaning marks on the skirt? That is, the identification marks made by cleaners?"

"Yes. We found the code number on the skirt."

"Did you make any attempt to trace that cleaning mark?"

"Not as yet."

"You are aware that different cleaners use different code marks and that those marks are sometimes stamped in indelible inks, sometimes in invisible ink which is only visible under ultraviolet light, and that it is possible to trace the ownership of a garment through these figures?"

"That is a technique which is used by the police many times a month."

"But you didn't use it in this case?"

"Not as yet."

"Yet you have testified that this skirt is the property of the defendant?"

"On the evidence we have I still say it is hers. It is her size and it was found in the defendant's apartment."

"Now then," Mason said, "this little bit of cloth hanging from the barbed-wire fence attracted your attention, did it not?"

"It did."

"And caused you to study the tracks carefully?"

"That is right."

"And from that careful study you came to the conclusion that an attempt had been made to furnish what we might call a synthetic corroboration for the story of the defendant?"

Tragg said, "That question calls for my opinion. I will give that opinion. I believe the defendant killed Loring Lamont. There may have been extenuating circumstances, but rather than tell the truth about these circumstances the defendant decided to concoct a story about having been pursued through a barbed-wire fence and deliberately sought to plant evidence which would support her story."

"That's a conclusion of the witness," Judge Bayton pointed out.

"It's his opinion as an expert," Carson insisted. "The question called for it, and his answer was responsive."

"After all," Judge Bayton said, "This is all on *voir dire*, and defense counsel apparently has some plan in view, but the Court doesn't care to have its time taken up with opinions and conclusions regardless of whether there are objections. Let's get along with the case."

"Did this evidence cause you to make a further search of the premises in the vicinity of the place where this piece of cloth was found?"

Tragg hesitated a moment, then said, "Well, yes."

"And if it hadn't been for that piece of cloth there on the fence, it is quite probable that you wouldn't have searched the surrounding country?"

Tragg permitted himself a frosty smile. "Anything is possible, Mr. Mason."

"And did your search of the surrounding country disclose other evidence which *did* substantiate the defendant's story?"

"There were tracks," Lt. Tragg said, "but these tracks were all a part of fabricated evidence."

"How do you know?"

"The ground was in two general classifications, or perhaps I should say three. First, there was the surface of the road. This was a dirt road which had been rained on and which showed tracks which could have been followed on the night of the fifth, but which were pretty well obliterated by the rain which came afterward, and which definitely were not visible on the sixth or the seventh. The second class of soil was the soft soil on the side of the road. There were depressions on the side of the road in which surplus water from the road had drained. That soil remained soft for some time. The same was true of the bank leading down to the westerly side of the road. On the other side of the fence, on the west of the road, we came to a third classification of soil. This was soil covered with grass and other vegetation, and the ordinary footprint would have been invisible here. However, marks made by high heels were visible here and there. We did find some marks made by high heels but there was not enough of a pattern to enable us to make an accurate interpretation of the tracks, but we knew the whole evidence had been fabricated because the closest heel prints on the other side of the fence were found twenty-seven feet from the place where the piece of cloth was found."

"These tracks would have gone unnoticed if it hadn't been for the cloth on the fence?"

"As to that I can't say."

Mason turned to the deputy district attorney. "Do you wish to introduce this garment in evidence?"

Carson said, "I want the garment introduced in evidence."

"Then I am going to insist that the cleaning mark be traced," Mason said. "There is no evidence of ownership other than that the skirt was found in the defendant's apartment. Any evidence of ownership so far is a mere conclusion of the witness."

"There is plenty of circumstantial evidence of ownership," Carson said. "It was found in the defendant's apartment. It is her size. It was used in a hurried and futile attempt to substantiate a fabricated story."

Judge Bayton said, "Under the circumstances, the garment will be marked for identification only at this time. We will wait to admit it until the ownership has been proven. That concludes Mr. Mason's *voir dire* examination and you may continue with your direct examination of this witness, Mr. Prosecutor."

Carson turned to Tragg, "Did you find any physical evidence which negatived the defendant's story?"

"Lots of it," Lt. Tragg said dryly.

"Will you please tell the Court what it was?"

"In the first place, the shoes worn by the decedent had not been worn on a muddy road. They were entirely free from mud. The trousers worn by the decedent had not been out in any wet brush. The clothes worn by the decedent did not have any mud on them, as would have been the case if he had slid under a barbed-wire fence. The dinner of ham and eggs which the defendant stated had not been touched had actually been eaten."

Carson turned triumphantly to Mason. "You may cross-examine."

Mason frowned thoughtfully. "You examined the shoes worn by the decedent?"

"We did."

"And found no traces of mud?"

"None whatever."

"The cuffs of the trousers?"

"No traces of mud, no indications that they had been in any wet vegetation. If the decedent had been running around through the grass on the other side of the fence, or if he had been splashing around through the mud on the road, his garments would have so indicated. There would have been unmistakable traces of soil and mud on the shoes, and the lower part of the trousers would have been soaked."

"Directing your attention to the apartment of the defendant," Mason said, "did you find underwear which was stained with mud?"

"We did."

"Did you make an attempt to find out whether that soil was the same as that in the vicinity of the Lamont lodge?"

"We did not."

"May I ask why?"

"We considered the garments a plant, just the same as the torn skirt which we found."

"It is always dangerous," Mason said, "to jump to conclusions, Lieutenant. I suggest that the police endeavor to check the stained garments with the soil at the scene of the crime, and I have no further questions."

"Are there any further questions?" Judge Bayton asked Carson.

"I have a further question of Lieutenant Tragg, in view of the situation which has developed."

"Very well, go ahead."

Carson turned to Lt. Tragg. "Did you mark for identification the shoes and trousers which the decedent was wearing?"

"I did."

"And do you have those garments with you?"

"They are available. It would take me a few moments to get them."

"Could you have them here within ten minutes?"

"I'm quite sure I could."

"May we ask the Court for a ten-minute recess," Carson asked, "in order to get these garments here?"

"Very well," Judge Bayton said. "We will take a ten-minute recess. However, it would certainly seem that the prosecution should have anticipated the necessity for introducing these garments. The Court will take this ten-minute recess, but that will be the last indulgence which will be given. If there are any other items of evidence which the prosecution wishes to introduce, be sure that they are here, Mr. Prosecutor."

Judge Bayton arose and walked into his chambers.

Mason turned to Arlene Ferris. "Look here, Arlene," he said, "I'm going to be brutally frank with you. The most expensive luxury that you can indulge in is that of lying to your lawyer."

She nodded.

"If you have lied to me," Mason went on, "you're in a mess and I don't think I can get you out. But in any event, if you *have* lied, I want to know it now."

"I've told you the absolute truth, Mr. Mason."

Mason shook his head. "If they produce those shoes and those trousers, and the shoes don't show mud stains, the bottom of the trouser legs don't show indications of having been wet, as would be the case where a person ran through wet brush, you're either going to prison for life or to the gas chamber."

"I can't help it, Mr. Mason. I've told you the absolute truth."

Mason became thoughtfully silent.

She said, "Couldn't the murderer have changed clothes on the corpse after..."

"Oh, sure," Mason said sarcastically, "just try selling that idea to a jury. The murderer knows that you're going to have a fight with Loring Lamont and run out on him in Lamont's own car. The murderer goes out there with an extra pair of trousers, socks and shoes. He waits until Loring Lamont comes back to the lodge, then he stabs him, then he opens the man's mouth and shoves ham and eggs down his throat, then he takes off his pants and socks and shoes and dresses the corpse—just try to stand up in front of a jury of twelve reasonably intelligent individuals and sell them an idea of that sort."

Arlene Ferris was near tears. "But that's what *must* have happened."

Mason shook his head and turned away.

Tragg returned to court carrying a bag.

Judge Bayton again came to the bench. Court was called to order, and Carson resumed his questioning.

"You now have the clothes the decedent was wearing when his body was found?"

"Yes, sir."

"I would like to have you first produce the shoes."

"Yes, sir," Tragg said, and, opening the bag, took out a pair of shoes.

"These are the shoes the decedent was wearing?"

"They are."

"What is their condition now, with reference to the condition when they were found on the body?"

"The shoes are in *exactly* the same condition except for chalk marks which have been placed upon the soles."

"What was the purpose of those chalk marks?"

"Identifying marks, so we could identify the shoes later on."

Carson walked over to the witness, took the two shoes, came back and handed them to Mason for the lawyer's inspection.

Mason turned the shoes over in his hands, carefully keeping his face without expression.

"We move that these shoes be introduced in evidence," Donald Carson said.

Mason arose. "Once more, Your Honor, I wish to examine the witness on *voir dire*."

"Very well."

Mason turned to Lt. Tragg. "Have you," he asked, "any way of knowing that these were the shoes the decedent was wearing at the time he was killed?"

"Only that they were on the feet of the corpse when I first saw it."

"Did you make any effort to search the cabin or lodge to see whether there were other garments?"

Tragg's voice showed a certain amount of indignation. "Of course we did. We searched that lodge from one end to the other, Mr. Mason."

"Did the decedent have *any* clothing there?"

"The decedent had no clothing there, no clothing of any sort other than the following exceptions—one pair of tennis shoes, the same size as those worn by the decedent, one pair of Bermuda shorts, two short-sleeved sports jackets, two pairs of swimming trunks, one terrycloth robe, one pair of sandals, one linen golf cap."

"Were there other clothes there?" Mason asked.

"None that would possibly fit the decedent. The decedent's shoes were size ten and a half."

"But you did find other clothing on the premises?"

"The decedent's father, Jarvis P. Lamont, had some coveralls, cook aprons and shoes there but the shoes of Jarvis P. Lamont were eight and a half. Loring Lamont could not possibly have worn his father's clothes."

"You examined the place thoroughly?"

"We virtually took the place to pieces," Lt. Tragg said, "and that includes the dressing rooms at the pool."

"The place was provisioned with liquor and food?" Mason asked.

"Well provisioned with liquor, with frozen food and canned food. There were very few perishables. There was a supply of linen for the beds, plenty of blankets, a frozen-food locker well filled with frozen food, but, for instance, there wasn't any fresh bread in the place. There was, however, a bowl in which biscuit dough had been mixed, a pan containing biscuits which had been baked in the electric oven. Six biscuits had been eaten from the pan. There were six left in the pan. There was a frying pan with grease in it, in which cooking had been done recently. The grease was ham grease. There was a smaller pan in which eggs had apparently been fried because there were bits of the cooked egg white adhering to the pan near the outer edges. There were plates from which food had been eaten..." Tragg turned to Donald Carson and said, "Do you want all of this now, or am I supposed to answer only about the clothing?"

"Tell about it now if the defense has no objection," Carson said.

Lt. Tragg nodded. "Two plates which contained portions of egg yolk, particles of ham grease, a can of butter which had been opened and from which some butter had been taken, a jar of jam, small bread and butter plates on which there were biscuit crumbs and remnants of jam. There were cups and saucers."

"How many cups and saucers?" Mason asked.

"Two. These contained small amounts of coffee. There was a percolator with coffee in it, and there were two water glasses. The dirty dishes were found on a table in the dining room, the pans and cooking utensils on the stove in the kitchen."

"I have no further questions at this time," Mason said.

"You mean that concludes your *voir dire* examination?" Judge Bayton asked.

"Yes, Your Honor. I have no further questions at this time on the *voir dire* examination in regard to the shoes. This does not mean that I waive my right to cross-examine the witness about these articles, nor do I waive my right to question the witness on *voir dire* regarding any other garments which may be produced."

"Very well," Judge Bayton said. "The prosecutor will proceed."

Carson said, "Now what about the trousers, Lieutenant?"

Lt. Tragg produced a pair of neatly creased trousers.

"These were the ones the decedent was wearing when the body was found?" Carson asked.

"Yes."

"I call your attention to certain stains near the top of the trousers and ask you if you know what those stains are."

"Yes, sir. They're bloodstains."

"They were on the trousers when the body was found?"

"Yes, sir."

"And the trousers were on the body?"

"Yes, sir."

"I offer these trousers in evidence," Carson said, "together with the shoes as People's appropriate exhibits."

"No objections," Mason said.

"Do you have any *voir dire* examination on the trousers?" Judge Bayton asked.

"None, Your Honor."

"I think that concludes my examination of Lieutenant Tragg," Carson said.

"Cross-examination?" Judge Bayton asked.

"You said that you searched the place thoroughly. Is that correct, Lieutenant?" Mason asked.

"We searched the place thoroughly," Tragg said. "We all but tore it apart."

"You looked in the writing desk?"

"We looked in the writing desk."

"Did you find some papers in there?"

"We did."

"Did you find a checkbook on the California Second National?"

"We did."

"With check stubs?"

"Yes, sir."

"Do you know whose checkbook that was?"

"We know that the writing on some of the check stubs was that of Loring Lamont and the checks which matched those stubs had been cashed and they were signed by Loring Lamont."

"All of the checks?"

"One of them was missing."

"What one was that?"

"A stub which purported to show that a five-hundred-dollar check had been issued."

"To whom was that check issued?"

"To no one."

"What do you mean by that?"

"The check had evidently been made out and for some reason had been torn from the checkbook *after* the amount had been written on the check stub. The stub had then been marked O.K. to show that it was all right to have a check stub there for five hundred dollars without the name of the payee."

"That's a conclusion?" Mason asked.

"For what it's worth," Tragg said, "that's a conclusion. If you want the bare facts I will state that there was a check stub in the book showing the amount of five hundred dollars. The stub had nothing else on it except the letters O.K."

"And were those letters in the handwriting of Loring Lamont?"

"I don't know."

"The check, of which this was the stub, had been torn off on the day of the murder?"

"I don't know that."

"You don't?" Mason asked.

"No."

"There was another check stub immediately in front of that check stub payable to Orval Kingman, was there not?"

"That's right."

"And this other check would naturally have been torn off after that first check?"

"I object on the ground that the question is argumentative and calls for a conclusion of the witness," Carson said.

Judge Bayton nodded his head.

"Just a moment," Carson said suddenly. "I will withdraw the objection. I'd like to have Lieutenant Tragg answer that question."

"The question is argumentative and calls for a conclusion of the witness," Judge Bayton pointed out wearily. "The Court doesn't need the opinions of witnesses. The Court wants facts."

"Nevertheless, Your Honor, I would like to have Lieutenant Tragg give the answer so that we can have it in the record."

"Well, if you withdraw the objection I'll let the witness answer this one question," Judge Bayton said, "but I don't want to take up time having a lot of argumentative questions even if they aren't objected to. You may answer this one question, Lieutenant."

"The answer," Lt. Tragg said, "is that in my opinion, for what it is worth, Loring Lamont started to make Orval Kingman a check for five hundred dollars on the wrong check. Then, realizing his mistake, he tore off that check and destroyed it, marked O.K. on the stub to show that it was all right to have a blank stub at that point and then made the check to Orval Kingman on the check which he should have used."

Mason smiled. "It is your opinion then that this was done inadvertently and that Loring Lamont, running through the check stubs, inadvertently turned over a check stub to which the check itself was attached without noticing what he was doing?"

"I think he must have," Tragg said.

"That's rather unlikely, isn't it?" Mason asked. "A man running through check stubs would certainly know when he came to a stub to which the check was attached."

"That's what I think happened," Lt. Tragg said.

"You didn't impound this checkbook as evidence?"

"Evidence of what?"

"Evidence of the activities of the decedent on the last day of his life."

"We did not. We made a list of the checks and that's all."

"Where is this checkbook now?"

"As far as I know it's still in the desk. I will state that Sadie Richmond telephoned me that you had instructed her to turn the checkbook over to the police but..."

"Now just a moment," Judge Bayton interrupted, "this inquiry is going altogether too far afield. We're now getting hearsay evidence. If the defense wishes, it certainly is entitled to bring that checkbook into court. However I don't know what bearing it could have on the case."

"If the Court please," Mason said, "it indicates that Loring Lamont had the checkbook with him when he went to the lodge. It indicates that he took the checkbook out of his pocket and, in my opinion, made a check for five hundred dollars to someone whose initials were O.K. That he was in a hurry and so simply put the initials of the payee on the stub."

"Was the stub dated?" Judge Bayton asked.

"It was not. Just the figure five hundred dollars and the initials were on it."

"But what if your assumption is correct?" Judge Bayton asked. "What would you expect to prove by that?"

"It would prove that someone else had been out at that lodge that evening."

"You may introduce the checkbook in evidence as part of your case if you want to," Judge Bayton said, "but I can assure you, Mr. Mason, it would take more persuasive evidence than that for the Court to feel that someone else had been out there. Do you have any further questions on cross-examination?"

"No further questions," Mason said.

"Very well," Judge Bayton said to Lt. Tragg. "You may stand down."

"If the Court please," Carson said, "the People have no further witnesses we care to call, at least at this time. We may have rebuttal evidence."

Mason was on his feet. "Just a moment," he said. "We have a right to cross-examine Peter Lyons."

"Oh, yes," Carson said. "I have sent for Lyons. Just a moment. I will call him."

Carson turned to an officer who sat beside him and engaged in a whispered conversation.

Abruptly the deputy district attorney frowned and became vehement. The officer shook his head.

Carson bent closer. There was a whispered conference again, then Carson straightened and said, "Your Honor, a most embarrassing situation has developed. It seems that this is Peter Lyons' day off. He is out somewhere, and can't be reached. I am afraid that perhaps I am partially to blame in the matter. I told Lyons that I would need him as a witness unless the defense was willing to stipulate as to his testimony. I told him further that if the defense would stipulate as to his testimony, he would not be needed. When Mr. Mason made his stipulation I so advised my office. Someone in my office advised Mr. Lyons that there had been a stipulation as to his testimony. I am afraid there was a misunderstanding all around. In fact, I am free to confess to the Court that I, myself, did not appreciate the full technical significance of Mr. Mason's stipulation until he raised the point that he was entitled to cross-examine the officer.

"Under the circumstances, if Mr. Mason will state the points he expects to bring out on cross-examination, I may be able to stipulate that under cross-examination Peter Lyons would so testify."

Mason shook his head. "I want the privilege of cross-examining this witness," he said. "That was the understanding."

Judge Bayton frowned with annoyance. "Surely, Mr. Mason, you must know the type of cross-examination you expect to make and the points you expect to bring out on cross-examination."

"Frankly, Your Honor, I am at the moment working on a theory of the case that I do not care to disclose until after I first have asked certain questions of the witness—after all, this witness is a police officer, he is a witness for the prosecution, and I fail to see why I should be required to tell the deputy district attorney my entire plan of attack on cross-examination."

"Do you question his testimony?" Judge Bayton asked.

"I may question his testimony and his credibility," Mason said.

"But that is absurd!" Carson protested. "This man is a police officer. At the time he tagged the car of Loring Lamont for illegal parking he had absolutely no idea that he was doing anything other than performing a routine act. The tag which he issued was a so-called non-fixable tag, and the records are there. They speak for themselves. I have talked with Peter Lyons personally and at some length. All Peter Lyons knows about the situation is what is disclosed by the records. At the time, the Loring Lamont car was simply another car parked in front of a fireplug. He sees hundreds of them every month."

Judge Bayton glanced inquiringly at Perry Mason.

"I still want to cross-examine this witness," Mason said doggedly.

"Well," Judge Bayton said irritably, "the law gives you the right to be confronted with witnesses and to cross-examine them. If you insist upon that right, I suppose the Court has no alternative except to continue the case until tomorrow morning at ten o'clock. However, I wish to point out to both counsel that there is a backlog of cases, that under instructions from the Judicial Council we are trying to get caught up, that in the opinion of the Court this case shouldn't have taken more than half a day. It was continued into the afternoon, and now apparently the Court will be forced to waste a large part of the afternoon and again resume the case tomorrow morning."

"I'm sorry," Mason said. "The mistake wasn't mine. I specifically stated in my stipulation that I would stipulate Lyons would so testify on direct examination."

"The prosecutor should have noticed the obligation which was placed upon him to have the witness available for cross-examination," Judge Bayton snapped. "Court will adjourn until ten o'clock tomorrow morning. The defendant is remanded to the custody of the sheriff. I will point out, however, to defense counsel that unless there is some cross-examination of the officer, Peter Lyons, which indicates that the defense has some pertinent theory which it is following up, the Court will feel that it has been imposed upon.

"That is all. Court is adjourned until ten o'clock tomorrow morning."

Mason turned to Arlene Ferris. "Have you," he asked, "anything else to tell me?"

She was almost in tears as she shook her head in tight-lipped negation.

"Very well," Mason said. "I'll see you tomorrow morning."

CHAPTER TWELVE

Mason sat at his office desk, drumming silently with his finger tips on the blotter. In an ash tray by his right hand, a neglected cigarette was slowing being consumed to ash, a wisp of smoke moving steadily upward in a straight line, then turning into a spiral before dispersing in little wisps of faint blue smoke.

Della Street, knowing his moods, sat on the other side of the desk, pencil poised over a shorthand book, remaining absolutely motionless so that she would not interfere with his concentration.

Mason, his eyes level-lidded with thought, said at length, "Take this down, Della. Let us start out with the supposition that Arlene has lied to us. The physical evidence is directly opposed to her story. Why did she lie? Dash-dash. Was it because she's guilty? Dash-dash. If that is the case, she would have made up a lie that would have fitted the facts. The girl is reasonably intelligent. Why does she tell a lie which doesn't fit the facts?"

Della Street completed taking down Mason's comments, then waited.

After a few minutes, Mason said, "She must be protecting someone. But how would such a story protect anyone, and who is that someone? Dash-dash. Who could it be?"

Slowly, almost imperceptibly, Mason shook his head.

He pushed back his chair from the desk, ground out the cigarette in the ash tray, got up and started pacing the floor.

Suddenly Mason stopped mid-stride, whirled, said to Della Street, "All right, Della, take this. Suppose client is not lying? Dash-dash. Then why don't the physical facts agree with her story? Dash-dash. The only possible solution is, we have an incomplete story."

Mason smacked his fist against the desk. "Hang it, Della," he exclaimed, "make a note! I want a sign made and I want it hung on the wall just back of my desk. *Try to have confidence in your clients.*"

"You think she's telling the truth?" Della Street asked.

"She's telling the truth," Mason said, "and I have fallen into the worst trap a defense attorney can ever fall into."

"What's that?" Della Street asked apprehensively.

"Letting myself get hypnotized by the reasoning of the prosecution and thinking that things happened the way the prosecution says they happened just because the evidence seems to support them."

Della Street, knowing that in moments like this, Mason wanted someone to help him clarify his thinking, said, "You mean the evidence is open to two interpretations."

"It has to be," Mason said. "The key witness is Peter Lyons, that police officer they were so reluctant to produce."

"You feel they were reluctant?" she asked.

"Of course they were," Mason said. "They tried every way in the world to keep me from cross-examining Peter Lyons. Now, what the devil does Peter Lyons have to say that is going to upset their applecart?"

"They make him sound like a very unimportant witness," Della Street said.

"That's the point," Mason said. "They're deliberately playing him down because they're afraid I'm going to play him up. Now why?"

"What reason *could* there be?" Della Street asked.

"Because," Mason said, "Peter Lyons is going to testify to something that will help my case. They've tried their damnedest to keep me from cross-examining him. This business of Lyons being where he can't be located is sheer nonsense. It's a stall."

"Why?" Della Street asked.

"Let's analyze why," Mason said. "A lawyer always has to look at things logically and from an independent viewpoint. Any time he gets off on the wrong track because of taking something for granted, he's lost. Now then, we know what Peter Lyons is going to testify to, because Donald Carson told us."

"But did the deputy district attorney state the truth?" Della Street asked.

"Sure, he did," Mason said. "He wouldn't dare do otherwise. He would be guilty of unprofessional conduct, of misleading the Court, of prejudical misconduct in the case...no, he *had* to tell the truth. But he didn't have to tell *all* the truth.

"Now, as I remember the statement made by the deputy district attorney, Peter Lyons would testify that he found Loring Lamont's car in front of a fireplug at nine o'clock, that he gave a citation for illegal parking which presumably he would have tied on the steering wheel of the car—now, why don't they want me to cross-examine him about that?"

Della Street shook her head in puzzled contemplation, while Mason once more resumed pacing the floor.

"Arlene Ferris tells me she left the car in front of the fireplug, so Peter Lyons' testimony would agree with hers. Now then, remember that Peter Lyons only gave one citation. He..."

Mason stopped abruptly, turned to face Della Street, said in a low voice, "Well, I'll be damned!"

"What's the matter?" Della Street asked.

"The matter is," Mason said, "I've been unspeakably naïve. I've been a babe in the woods. Of course, they don't want me to cross-examine Peter Lyons! Peter Lyons is going to testify to something that will be diametrically opposed to the facts as they understand them, and...that's it! That has to be it!"

"What?" Della Street asked.

"Peter Lyons is going to testify that he came back later on before he went off duty, some time between nine o'clock and midnight, *and the car was gone.*"

"Gone?" Della Street asked. "How could it have been gone? It was there in front of the fireplug all night."

"It was gone," Mason said, "because Arlene Ferris left the keys in the ignition. Somebody came along, took that car away and then brought it back and parked it again right in front of the fireplug so the other two officers who came on duty at midnight found the car there and proceeded to issue citations for parking violations, and then, toward morning, had the car towed away."

"But why should anyone take it and then bring it back?" Della Street asked.

"That," Mason said, "is what we're going to find out, and we're going to begin looking in the place where we should have looked right at the start."

"Where?"

"We're going to talk with Edith Bristol, private secretary of J. P. Lamont, and George Albert, the office manager."

"How come?" Della Street asked.

"We're going to get the evidence in order this time," Mason said. "Remember what Arlene Ferris told us. There were lots of people wanting to go to work for the Lamont Company. The company had a waiting list of persons applying for secretarial positions, but Arlene Ferris simply told Madge Elwood she wanted a job. Madge Elwood spoke to somebody and immediately and forthwith Arlene Ferris was given a job. George Albert said that Loring Lamont issued some sort of an executive order just before he left for South America. Thereafter the whole personnel department was brushed aside and Arlene was put to work."

Della Street's eyes widened. "That's right, Chief!"

"And the devil of it is," Mason said angrily, "the whole evidence was right there in front of me all the time and I damn near muffed it. Come on, Della, let's go."

"Just what are we after?" Della Street asked.

"The truth," Mason told her.

They hurried down to the parking lot, got Mason's car and drove to the executive offices of the Lamont Company.

Mason told the receptionist, "I want to see Edith Bristol, J. P. Lamont's secretary, and I also want to see George Albert, the office manager. I'm Perry Mason, the attorney, and it's important."

"Just a minute," the receptionist said.

She put through a telephone call, said, "Very well, hold on," and turned to Perry Mason. "Miss Bristol says that she doesn't think the district attorney would want her to talk with you."

Mason said grimly, "All right, then I'll subpoena her as a witness and I'll show bias by showing that she wouldn't talk with anyone because she was afraid she'd hurt the district attorney's feelings."

"Just a minute," the receptionist said, and again turned to the telephone, talking rapidly.

After a few moments she said, "Very well. She'll see you. Take the elevator to the third floor. Miss Bristol will be waiting at the elevator for you."

Mason and Della Street entered the elevator. At the third floor, as the elevator door opened, a young woman stepped forward. "I'm Edith Bristol," she said. "Will you come to my office, please?"

She led the way down a corridor, past stenographers who were clacking away at typewriters and who looked up with surreptitious curiosity as the trio walked past.

In the office Edith Bristol closed the door, indicated seats and said, "Just what is it you want, Mr. Mason?"

Mason surveyed her in thoughtful appraisal. "I had hardly expected one so young in so important a position," he said.

"What is it you want, please?" she asked once more, her tone cold with formality.

Mason said, "I want to know just why it was that Arlene Ferris asked her friend, Madge Elwood, to get her a job here, and within a couple of days Arlene Ferris was at work, apparently by some order that was issued directly from Loring Lamont."

Edith Bristol lowered her eyes. "I'm sure I couldn't tell you," she said. "You said you wanted to see the office manager."

Mason nodded.

"Perhaps he can tell you."

"He was on the witness stand," Mason said, "and he didn't seem to have any idea except that she had been put to work on direct orders of Loring Lamont. I think someone else can tell me why Loring Lamont took the trouble to intervene. Can you tell me that?"

She slowly shook her head. "I'm afraid there's not very much I can tell you, Mr. Mason. I know that occasionally persons were employed because of certain personal contacts. Miss Elwood, I believe, worked here for some two years and her work was very highly thought of. Did you intend to ask the office manager?"

"I did," Mason said.

"Perhaps we'd better get him in here."

Edith Bristol picked up a telephone and said, "Connect me with George Albert, please."

After a moment, she said, "Mr. Albert, Mr. Perry Mason, the attorney, is here in the office. He is accompanied by Miss Della Street, his secretary, who is apparently prepared to take notes. Mr. Mason wants to know how it happened that Arlene Ferris was employed without going through the usual channels in the personnel department, and wants to know how it happened that Madge Elwood was able to bring to bear enough influence to have Miss Ferris put on ahead of the waiting list. Would you mind coming to my office and answering Mr. Mason's questions? Yes, right away, please."

She hung up the phone, smiled at Mason and said, "Perhaps we can get the matter clarified, Mr. Mason. I'm quite certain that no directive came through this office. In other words, Mr. Jarvis P. Lamont knew nothing about it, therefore I know nothing about it. You will understand that Mr. Lamont, Senior, has not been in the office since he learned of his son's murder. However, I have been his secretary for some two years and I can assure you that any preferential treatment given Miss Ferris was not because of any directive issued by him."

Mason, frowning thoughtfully, nodded. His manner was completely preoccupied.

They sat silently for a few moments, waiting for George Albert. Mason stirred uneasily, looked toward the door, then back at Edith Bristol.

"I'd like to know a little about how Loring Lamont lived," he said. "He didn't live with his father?"

"No."

"He had an apartment of his own?"

"Yes."

"That was at 9612 Endicott Way?"

"Yes."

"He had perhaps a cook, a housekeeper, a Filipino boy?"

"No."

"Then he must have eaten out a good deal of the time."

"I wouldn't know."

"He took an active part in the business here?"

"Yes."

"Did he have any particular position in the firm?"

"Vice president."

"He traveled quite a bit?"

"Yes."

"And I take it, he and his father were fond of each other?"

"Yes."

Mason smiled. "You don't seem to volunteer much in the way of information."

"I'm not being paid to volunteer information, Mr. Mason. I don't even know whether Mr. Jarvis P. Lamont is going to approve of this meeting."

The door of the office was pushed open. George Albert entered the room, smiled a greeting at Perry Mason, then glanced quickly at Edith Bristol.

"You know Mr. Albert," Edith Bristol said.

"I've met him in court," Perry Mason said. "This is Della Street, my secretary. I want to get some information about Arlene Ferris and how she got her job."

"I'm afraid I can't tell you very much more than I told you on the witness stand."

"I think you can," Mason said. "It certainly wasn't the custom for Loring Lamont to intercede personally in connection with jobs in the business. There was a personnel department, and I take it the hiring was in the hands of the personnel department."

"Yes."

"Yet in the case of Arlene Ferris, Loring Lamont issued a directive."

"That's right."

"Now then," Mason said, "it seems that Arlene Ferris went to her friend, Madge Elwood, that Madge had worked here at one time and Madge was the point of contact."

"That could well be," Albert said.

"What do you mean by that?"

"I mean that Miss Elwood could very well have telephoned Loring Lamont and asked him to put Arlene Ferris on the payroll."

"And Loring Lamont would have done it?"

"He did it, didn't he?"

"Do you know that Madge Elwood telephoned him?"

"I don't *know* it, no. I'm only drawing conclusions from what you yourself have said. After all, you're Arlene Ferris' atorney. She must have told you how she got the job."

"Perhaps she doesn't know," Mason said.

Albert shrugged his shoulders.

"Yet," Mason said, "knowing that Arlene Ferris was, so to speak, under the protection of one of the big executives of the company, you had no hesitancy about firing her."

"I try to keep efficiency in the office, Mr. Mason. That's my job. I can't let some young woman indulge in impudence simply because she may be friendly with one of the Lamonts. They don't pay me to run an office that way."

"When did you first know Arlene Ferris was coming to work?"

"Loring Lamont told me."

"What did he say?"

"He handed me a folded slip of paper. That was before he left for South America. The name Arlene Ferris was on it. He said, 'Put her to work as an expert stenographer at the top salary we pay.'"

"So Arlene went to work without any test, as far as you know, and started drawing top pay right at the start?"

"I believe those are the facts."

"And you don't know any more about the situation than that?"

"That's all."

"Had that ever happened before with anyone else?" Mason asked. "In other words, had anyone else ever been put to work in exactly that way?"

"The applications are regularly channeled through personnel."

"I'm not asking about regular applicants. I'm asking if this particular thing had ever happened before."

Albert said, "I would have to consult the records, and..."

"Quit hedging," Mason said. "I'm going to call you back to the witness stand if I have to. Now, there's something funny going on here."

"What do you mean?" Albert asked, drawing himself up belligerently.

"You know what I mean," Mason said. "You're stalling around. You're covering up, both of you. When Miss Bristol asked you to come in here, she didn't pick up the phone and say to the operator, 'Ask George Albert to come in here.' Instead, she asked for you personally on the phone, then when she got you she didn't say, 'Can you come into my office for a minute,' but she went on to tell you all about Mr. Perry Mason, the attorney, being in the office, all about what I wanted, all about my secretary being with me. Even then you didn't come in here right away. You stopped to think things over and have the answers ready.

"Now let's quit stalling around on this thing. How many other people came to work in this office because of directives of Loring Lamont?"

"I only know of one," Albert said.

"Who?"

"Madge Elwood."

"George!" Edith Bristol exclaimed, her voice a whiplash of sharp rebuke.

"I can't help it," Albert said. "What's the use of stalling? You haven't seen him in court. I have. He'd do exactly what he said. He'd get me in court and bring it out on the witness stand."

"What I want to know," Mason said, turning to Edith Bristol, "is why *you* were trying to keep *that* under cover."

Edith Bristol said coldly, "I think, Mr. Mason, we are going to terminate this interview. You now have the information you want. I may state that you have all the information we can give you."

"All right," Mason said, "if you want to put it that way, we'll put it that way."

He whipped two documents from his pocket, handed one to Edith Bristol, one to George Albert.

"What are those?" Edith Bristol asked.

"Subpoenas to appear in court at ten o'clock tomorrow morning in the case of People versus Arlene Ferris, and testify on behalf of the defendant as defense witnesses," Mason said.

"I'll expect to see you there. I'll resume my interrogations at that time. Good afternoon."

Mason and Della Street left the office.

"Now what?" Della Street asked.

"First we telephone Paul Drake and see what he's learned," Mason said. "There's a telephone booth there on the sidewalk."

Della Street put through the call, got Paul Drake on the line, then motioned excitedly to Perry Mason.

"Paul has something on Otto Keswick," she said. "He's checked on Keswick's alibi."

She extended the receiver to Mason, who entered the telephone booth. "Hello Paul. What is it?" Mason asked.

"A couple of things," Drake said. "I checked up with Mrs. Arthur Sparks, who has the house where Otto Keswick rooms. Keswick was correct in saying he does odd jobs around the place in order to earn his room rent.

"On the night of the fifth they were watching televison all right, but Mrs. Sparks wasn't with him after seven-thirty. She sat and watched television with him until then. But she had a splitting headache and went to bed. She says that Keswick *could* have gone out, although she doesn't think so. She knows that he kept the television on because she couldn't get into a really sound sleep. She would doze off for a while, then snap wide awake. She heard the television every time she wakened. Finally it was turned off at ten-thirty, because she remembers the program finishing. But that doesn't mean that she can testify Keswick was there between seven-thirty and ten-thirty."

"I see," Mason said thoughtfully.

"Now then," Drake went on, "here's something else. A fellow who has the adjoining piece of property on the north has a nice little cabin on the property. He works as a bookkeeper and the Lamonts don't consider him in their social class at all. In other words, they aren't neighborly. He may have a slight resentment on account of that. It's hard to tell. Anyway, he had cut a road on the south side of this property. That side adjoins the Lamont property on the north. Last year some storm water ran down this new road and washed a ditch. That ditch had thrown water on the Lamont property and they threatened to sue him.

"On the night of the fifth, knowing that it had started to rain, this fellow was a little concerned about whether the embankments he had thrown up would keep the water out of the road and off the Lamont property. He went out just to make certain. He says that shortly after he turned into his property and had switched out the lights on his car, another car came along the road and went through the gate at the Lamont property. Now, *he* says that the gate was open—that the car drove slowly through and came to a stop, that he knows the car driven by Otto Keswick, that it has a peculiar piston slap, and he's positive this was Keswick's car. He says he heard voices, and he thinks he heard the voice of Sadie Richmond, but he can't swear to it."

"What's his name?" Mason asked.

"George Banning."

"Now, that's terribly important," Mason said. "I want to talk with Banning and I want to have him subpoenaed as a witness for the defense. I want him in court tomorrow morning."

"I've already served a subpoena on him," Drake said, "and I've made arrangements for him to attend. I've fixed it up so he doesn't feel sore at all, but is going to testify to what he knows. I think he's a little bit peeved at the Lamonts."

"How long did this car stay on the place?" Mason asked.

"He doesn't know. Banning just looked around enough to make sure that his new drainage system was keeping the water out of the road and sending it on down to the east, so that it would miss the Lamont property entirely. The water had already begun to wash a channel. He stayed only long enough to check on that and then drove back to the city.

"He says lights were on in the Lamont lodge the entire time he was there, and that lights were on when he left. He also says the gate must have been open, because the car didn't stop at the gate, and he knows that an automobile was in there when he drove out."

"What time was it?" Mason asked.

"He can't fix the time exactly. It was right around seven-thirty to seven-forty-five."

Mason said, "Okay, Paul, I think we've hit pay dirt. That indicates Otto Keswick was lying. That last check for five hundred dollars must have been made to Keswick. I think he failed to present it at the bank because he knew Loring Lamont was dead and therefore the check was valueless."

"And why did Lamont do such a hurried job on the check stub?"

"Because," Mason said, "he ... damn it, Paul, there's only one reason for him to do such a hurried job on that check stub and that's because he *was* in a hurry."

"I'll keep digging," Drake said.

"Do that," Mason told him. "Now, here's something else, Paul. I told Madge Elwood to be in court this afternoon. She didn't show up. I'm going to run down to Santa Monica and see if I can contact her at her apartment, but I wish you'd start looking around a bit and see if you can pick her up."

"And if I do?" Drake asked.

"Throw a tail on her."

"Okay, will do," Drake said, and hung up.

CHAPTER THIRTEEN

Mason and Della Street drove in silence until they reached the Kelsington Apartments.

Mason rang Madge Elwood's apartment repeatedly, got no answer. He then went to the manager. She was a middle-aged, capable-looking woman. "I'm trying to get in touch with Madge Elwood," he said. "It's very important. She doesn't seem to be in, but I would like to check and make certain."

"I don't think she's in," the manager said. "I saw her leaving this afternoon. She had two suitcases. Apparently she's going someplace and intending to be away for some time. Have you inquired at the place where she works?"

"Do you know the place where she works?" Mason asked.

"No. She has a secretarial job here somewhere with an advertising firm—anyway, they'd be closed now. I'm sorry I can't give you any help."

"Would it be possible for you to use your passkey and just take a quick look in the apartment to see if she's..."

The manager shook her head. "I'm sorry. We don't pry into the affairs of tenants. They pay their rent. They come and they go as they please. We try not to take an undue interest in what they do, and we are very careful not to give out information. I may have told you too much already, but—I recognized you, of course, from your photographs and I know you're interested in a case in which Miss Elwood is involved in some way, so I thought it would be all right to tell you that she took two suitcases and left."

"Thanks a lot," Mason said. "Do you know whether she drove off in her car or whether she took a taxicab?"

"I'm sure I couldn't tell you that. I just happened to see her coming out of the elevator with these two suitcases. They were too heavy for her to carry both at once, so she took them out one at a time. I guess that must mean she went somewhere in her own car. If she had gone in a cab, the cabdriver would have picked up one of the suitcases."

Mason said, "Do me one more favor. Does she pay her rent by check or with cash?"

"By check."

"And do you remember the bank?"

She said, "There's no reason why I shouldn't tell you that, I guess. Her account is in the neighborhood bank right around the corner. It caters to office workers and stays open until seven-thirty every night except Saturday."

"You say it's around the corner?"

"Go to the right as you leave the apartment, turn right again at the first corner and it's midway in the block."

"Thanks a lot," Mason said.

He and Della Street left the apartment and went to the bank.

"I want to talk with the manager," Perry Mason said. "It's a matter of some importance. My name is Perry Mason, I'm a lawyer, and..."

"Oh, yes. Just a minute. If you'll step right this way, please, and wait for just a few minutes."

Mason followed the young woman into an office, waited some two minutes and was then introduced to the manager of the bank as he came bustling in.

"What can I do for you, Mr. Mason?" the manager asked.

Mason said, "This is perhaps a little irregular, but I can assure you that it's highly important. I want to know something about the status of Madge Elwood's account."

The manager shook his head. "I'm sorry. We can't give out any information of that sort."

Mason said, "I'm very much concerned because I have reason to believe she cashed a check this afternoon and I think the check may have been a forgery."

"Well, of course, *that's* different," the manager said. "We're always interested in detecting forgeries."

"If you'll consult your records," Mason said, "I think you'll find that the check she cashed this afternoon is worthless. I'd like to get in touch with her before she draws on the account."

"Just a moment," the manager said, his voice showing great concern. "You wait right here, Mr. Mason."

When the manager had left, Della Street glanced quizzically at the lawyer. "What makes you think she cashed a check this afternoon?"

"If she's going someplace she needs cash," Mason said.

"Then why wouldn't she simply make a withdrawal from her account?"

"She would. In that case, the bank manager will let us know, either by telling us so, or else by inadvertently letting the cat out of the bag. He'll come back and say, 'You're mistaken, Mr. Mason. The only check which went through her account this afternoon was her own check.'"

Della Street nodded.

"On the other hand," Mason said, "if someone has financed her flight, there's just a chance we'll find out who that someone is."

Della Street thought the situation over and smiled. "It's what you call a daring approach and a direct approach."

"Those approaches sometimes pay off," Mason said. "Bear in mind that in this case we're dealing with a branch bank that caters to payroll deposits. It probably has very few large transactions and the manager would be particularly embarrassed if he sustained any loss through a forgery. He..."

Mason broke off abruptly as the manager, looking very disturbed, re-entered the office.

"Mr. Mason," he said, "this is highly unusual and highly irregular. Can you tell me what makes you believe that the check was forged?"

"Frankly, I cannot," Mason said. "I have reason to believe, however, that she, in all innocence, may have cashed a check which was a forgery. If there was such a transaction, I suggest you take steps to verify the check."

The manager said, "Just a minute." He once more left the office, then came back and seated himself at the desk. His face was very plainly worried.

After a moment, the phone rang.

The manager picked up the phone, gave his name and position, said, "I am inquiring about a check which was cashed this afternoon by Madge Elwood. The transaction is a little out of the ordinary. The check is rather large and I would like to verify it. Is it possible for me to reach Mr. Jarvis P. Lamont?"

The banker was silent, listening for a few minutes, then abruptly the look of worry left his face. "Well, thank you very much," he said. "I was just checking, that's all... no, thank you... no, not at all. You see, we're rather a small branch bank here and the transaction was unusual... yes, thank you very much. I'm sorry I bothered you, Good-by."

He hung up the phone and smiled at Mason. "No, Mr. Mason," he said, "the check was quite all right, so there's nothing for either of us to worry about."

Mason let his face break into a big smile of relief. "Well," he said, "that's something! I'm very glad to learn that. I..."

"Could you tell me what caused you to believe the check might be forged?" the banker asked.

"I'm sorry," Mason said. "It evidently was a misunderstanding all around. You know how annoying these anonymous tips can be. I'm sure you must have had experience with them."

"I understand," the banker said. "It's quite all right. I talked with the personal secretary of the man who signed the check and it's good as gold. She knows all about it."

"Thanks a lot," Mason said, shaking hands. "I'm sorry I bothered you, and, under the circumstances, I'd appreciate it if you didn't mention this to anyone."

"Indeed I won't," the banker said. "We keep all of our transactions entirely confidential. Good afternoon, Mr. Mason."

The banker escorted them to the door of his office.

Outside in the street, Della Street and Perry Mason exchanged glances.

"Well," Mason said, as he walked back to the place where he had parked his car, "the plot begins to thicken."

"I'll say it thickens," Della Street said. "That double-crossing Edith Bristol! She knew all along about that check and...but why was it given?"

"The answer to that is obvious," Mason said. "The check was given to Madge Elwood because Jarvis P. Lamont wanted her out of town—so now we ask ourselves why he wanted her out of town. And the answer is that, in all probability, he was afraid I was going to put her on the witness stand.

"So now we have a beautiful puzzle, Della. Let's try to reason it out."

"Where do we begin?" Della Street asked.

"We start where we should have started in the first place," Mason said, "with Loring Lamont."

Della Street regarded him with a puzzled expression. "I don't get it."

"In order to know what happened, we have to find out what forces were at work. Now, let's for the moment assume that Arlene Ferris is telling the truth. Now, what would have happened after she left?"

"What do you mean?"

"What would Loring Lamont have done?"

"If she is telling the truth," Della Street said thoughtfully, "there is only one thing he could have done. He turned around and walked back to the rustic lodge. He went in and ate the ham and eggs, and..."

"Two plates?" Mason asked.

"Well," Della Street said, "he *could* have thrown one down the garbage disposal."

"Exactly," Mason said. "Why not two? He was hardly in a mood for cold ham and eggs. But he was in the mood for a number of other things."

Della Street nodded. "Go on."

"He wanted a drink, he wanted dry clothes, he wanted feminine companionship, and, naturally, he wanted transportation back to town."

"So he called someone who could give him the things he wanted?"

Mason nodded.

"Who?" she asked.

"Take a guess," Mason said.

She shook her head.

"There was only one person it could have been," Mason said. "The facts are plain as day."

"Who?"

"Madge Elwood."

Della Street looked at him, started to say something, caught herself. Slowly her eyes widened. "Then," she said, "then it was...it really *was* Madge Elwood that Jerome Henley saw getting out of the car?"

"Sure, it was Madge Elwood," Mason said. "Notice that Madge Elwood had pull. All she had to do was pick up the phone and say, 'I want a job for my friend, Arlene Ferris.' Immediately Loring Lamont went to George Albert and said, 'We're putting a new stenographer to work. Her name is Arlene Ferris and she's to draw top salary. She won't come to you through the personnel department. She'll come to you through me. That's all the authorization you need. Put her to work.'

"That happened in Madge Elwood's case and it happened in Arlene Ferris' case.

"So," Mason went on, "after Loring Lamont got back to the lodge he picked up the telephone and called Madge Elwood. He said, 'Madge, your friend turned out to be a nasty-tempered prude. What the devil did you mean by getting me mixed up with a girl of that sort? Now she's stolen my car and made off with it. Go to my apartment, get me some dry clothes, some shoes and get out here fast."

Della Street nodded. "So Madge Elwood took his car and drove out there with the dry things and...wait a minute, Chief. There's something wrong with that."

"What?"

"How could Madge Elwood have known his car was parked in front of his apartment? How could Loring Lamont have told her where it was?"

"Remember," Mason said, "that as soon as Arlene got back to her apartment she called Madge and told her all about how Loring Lamont had turned into a rapacious wolf and that she'd taken his car, left him stranded, and had parked his car in front of a fireplug where he could pay some fines on it."

"That's right!" Della Street exclaimed, "But isn't there a conflict in the time element?"

Mason gave the matter some thought. "Madge probably got the call from Loring Lamont, then decided to doll herself up before going to the lodge. She probably was putting on the finishing touches when she received Arlene's call."

"That would make it work out just about right," Della Street said, "but it presupposes a very intimate relationship between Madge and Loring Lamont."

"Such things have been known to happen," Mason said.

"Then that would explain a lot of things," Della Street said.

Mason nodded. "And that's why they're so anxious to keep Peter Lyons off the witness stand. He'll testify that he put a tag on the car, all right, at perhaps around nine o'clock. But he'll also testify that later on he looked for the car and didn't see it. Now, that doesn't fit in with the prosecution's theory of the case, so they don't want to bring that fact out. They're perfectly willing to state to the Court that he would testify that he found the car parked in front of a fireplug at nine o'clock and he tagged it. They want his testimony to stop right there. They don't want him stating that after that he looked for the car and couldn't find it."

"Then what happened?" Della Street asked. "Madge Elwood must have gone on out to the lodge."

"She went out there," Mason said. "She gave him his dry clothes, and then, for some reason or other, they got into quite an argument, and in the course of that argument, Madge grabbed a knife and plunged it into his back.

"Prior to that time, he had probably sought to solace his injured masculine feelings and he'd cooked up a fresh batch of ham and eggs. He and Madge Elwood had eaten the ham and eggs, and then the fight started.

"So then Madge Elwood found herself with a corpse on her hands and suddenly decided to play it smart. She knew that Arlene Ferris had been out there and had had a fight with him. She knew exactly what had happened because she had the story both from Loring Lamont's lips and from Arlene's phone call. So all she had to do was to take the car back and leave it exactly where Arlene Ferris had parked it and go on back to her apartment and pretend to be innocent.

"How she must have laughed at me when I came to her and tried to get her co-operation in clearing Arlene. She was smart enough to play right into my hands, keep a poker face and keep her mouth shut."

"And Jerome Henley saw her when she was getting out of the car. But the police talked him out of that identification," Della Street said.

Mason nodded.

"And it wasn't at ten."

"Of course not," Mason said. "Everything about it indicates that it was later, but I made the mistake of not questioning the time element the way I should have because I knew that Arlene Ferris had driven the car up to the curb and parked it in front of the fireplug prior to nine o'clock—it had to be prior to nine because Peter Lyons put a tag on the car then."

"And now?" Della Street asked.

"Now," Mason said, "we're going to find Madge Elwood. We're going to force her to make a confession."

"How are we going to do that?"

"By lowering the boom on her," Mason said. "We'll show that we know exactly what happened. We'll tell her that Jerome Henley actually saw her."

"But what about Henley? Will he co-operate?"

Mason said, "He's angry and embarrassed. No man likes to have someone make a fool of him. He thought that I had made a fool of him. Police convinced him that I had rung a ringer in on him, that I had substituted Madge Elwood for Arlene Ferris, that Arlene was the girl he had actually seen. They showed him pictures, they gave him a buildup and finally convinced Henley. Actually, his first impression was the correct one. It had been Madge Elwood he had seen. He *may* be too confused now to remember anything clearly."

"Can we expect anything from him?" Della Street asked.

"I don't know," Mason said. "I can go out and put my cards on the table. I can tell him what happened and then we'll see if he'll co-operate."

"Do we do that next?"

"No," Mason said. "We try to get some physical evidence next."

"Such as what?"

Mason said, "Madge Elwood took some dry clothes and shoes out to the lodge. Loring Lamont put them on. The trousers he had taken off, which were soaking wet, the shoes he had taken off, which were wet and muddy, were not left at the lodge. Therefore, someone must have put them in a car and taken them away— probably it was Madge Elwood. Yet they weren't in the car when she parked it."

"Therefore?" Della Street asked.

"Therefore," Mason said, "she took the things out and did something with them. Probably she transferred them to her own car. Now, what would she have done with them?"

"They may still be in her car."

"They may be in her car," Mason said, "and they may be in her garage. She probably drove her car into the garage. She may have taken out the trousers and the shoes. There's just one chance in ten that she did. Perhaps the chances are better than that. It may be an even-money chance."

"Do you suppose we can get in?"

"We may be able to," Mason said. "If her car is out of the garage, the garage may well be unlocked."

"And what about J.P. Lamont?"

"J.P. has a pretty good idea what happened," Mason said. "He doesn't want Arlene to tell her story, and he doesn't want to have that story corroborated by Madge Elwood. Therefore, he's given Madge Elwood some sort of a bonus to get out of circulation and keep out of circulation until the case is finished."

"But what about Otto Keswick and Sadie Richmond?"

"Now there," Mason said, "we have an interesting situation. Bear in mind the phone call that Loring Lamont received there at the lodge just after the biscuits had been taken out of the oven and he and Arlene were ready to sit down to eat. It was a call which caused him to change his entire plan of operations.

"That call was probably from Otto Keswick. Keswick and Sadie Richmond must have some sort of a partnership. It would be strange if, with Loring's nature, they didn't have some sort of a hold on him, something that would enable them to shake him down for a little blackmail when they needed the money.

"So Keswick telephoned and said, 'Look, Loring, Sadie and I need some money. We want five hundred bucks. We want it tonight. We're coming over to get it. I'll be there in half or three-quarters of an hour.'"

"Couldn't Lamont have told him to wait an hour or so?" Della Street asked.

"He may have tried to," Mason said. "We don't know what he said over the telephone, but we have a pretty good idea that Keswick and Sadie Richmond went out there. Loring Lamont knew they were coming, and so Lamont forgot all about the supper and the waltzing to the hi-fi and the seductive approach he had planned. He became crisply businesslike and efficient. He wanted what he wanted, and he wanted it before Keswick and Sadie Richmond got out there."

"And then they came out?"

"They came out after Arlene Ferris had gone home," Mason said. "They got a check from Loring Lamont, but by that time Loring Lamont was anxious to get rid of them because Madge Elwood was on her way out, and he wanted to get Otto Keswick and Sadie Richmond off the place before Madge arrived."

"Darned if it doesn't sound logical," Della Street said, excitement in her voice.

"So," Mason said, "we have three people who know that Loring Lamont was alive after Arlene Ferris left. We have Madge Elwood, we have Otto Keswick and we have Sadie Richmond."

"And none of them will want to involve themselves by testifying."

"None of them will want to become involved," Mason said.

"Look here, did Sadie and Otto get into a fight with him and . . . ?"

Mason shook his head. "Remember the fresh clothes. He didn't get those fresh clothes until after Madge Elwood arrived with his car."

Della Street thought it over, then became suddenly jubilant. "Chief," she said, "it all adds together! It fits into a perfect picture. You can blow the case into smithereens tomorrow morning and get Arlene Ferris acquitted."

"I can, if I can get the testimony," Mason said. "But remember this: Every one of those witnesses has lied or will lie. We can count on no co-operation from the authorities. We're going to have to dig up the evidence ourselves, and we don't have very much time to do it."

"And we start with Madge Elwood's garage?"

Mason nodded.

"Illegal?" she asked.

"That depends," Mason said. "If there's no lock on the door and we can simply open the door and walk in, we may be guilty of trespass, but we won't be guilty of burglary. We won't enter the place with felonious intent. We'll enter it for the purpose of discovering evidence."

"You don't think we could ring up Lieutenant Tragg and . . . ?"

Mason interrupted her by shaking his head. "Tragg would laugh at us."

"All right," she said, "let's go. I'm game."

"There's no reason for you to go in," Mason said. "You can sit in the car."

She said angrily, "What do you take me for? If you're going to take risks, I'm going to take them right along with you. In case you do find anything, you're going to need a witness, someone to corroborate your testimony. As a matter of fact, because you're the attorney for Arlene Ferris, you won't want to get on the stand yourself. You'd prefer to call me as witness and then corroborate my testimony if circumstances made it necessary to do so."

"You win," Mason said. "Let's go."

They drove back to the apartment house. Mason turned at the entrance to the garages.

"The garages are numbered," Della Street said, "and there are cards to the right of each door."

They found Madge Elwood's garage.

Mason tried the door. It was unlocked.

"I think we'd better drive our car in here, Della," he said. "If we leave it outside and are prowling around it may attract attention. I'll drive in and then we'll close the door behind us and turn on the lights."

Mason drove the car into the garage. They closed the door.

Mason found the light switch and turned it on.

Della Street said, "I'll take this side of the garage. You take the other side and we'll see what we can find—there's certainly a collection of junk here, a couple of old battered suitcases, a steamer trunk and a couple of tires."

Mason said, "The things we want may be in the trunk or the suitcase. How about that trunk, Della? Is it locked?"

Della Street tried the trunk and nodded. "It's locked," she said.

Mason said speculatively, "I don't know whether we dare to go and ask for a search warrant or not—you see, Della, so far we're working on surmise. We may have a pretty good idea what happened, but I'd like to get something positive to go on."

Mason paused to sniff the atmosphere in the garage. "It has that musty, mildewed smell beach places have that have been kept closed up," he said. "I wonder if..."

He broke off abruptly.

Della Street said, with alarm in her voice, "Chief!"

Mason put his finger to his lips for silence.

A car came to a stop just outside the garage door.

Mason and Della Street stood perfectly still. Abruptly the door was flung open. George Albert started to walk in, then recoiled with sheer surprise as he saw the car in the garage, saw Mason and Della Street standing there.

Lt. Tragg, who had been riding in Albert's car, opened the door and got out.

"Well, well," he said, "we seem to have stumbled on something of a jackpot, Albert."

George Albert said indignantly, "I told you they'd be trying to plant evidence. I want these people arrested, Lieutenant."

"On what grounds?" Mason asked.

"You know what grounds," Albert said. "You've been trying to plant evidence here. You've got some incriminating articles which were given you by Arlene Ferris, and you're trying to frame this thing on Madge Elwood. You've been trying to frame her right from the start. You got one of her skirts and tore it and left a piece out on the barbed wire. You left the skirt in Arlene Ferris' apartment. You've done everything you could to plant evidence that would drag Madge Elwood into this thing.

"You had your detective take pictures of her and go to Jerome Henley and try to bamboozle him into thinking that it was Madge he saw getting out of the car in front of the fireplug. You are now engaged in breaking into private property and planting evidence."

"We may be trespassing," Mason said, "but we aren't breaking in and we aren't planting anything. We're investigating."

"It's just as I told you, Lieutenant," George Albert said. "They're trying to drag Madge into this thing. I want this garage searched, and I want it searched now, for the purpose of finding whatever articles these people have planted here. Arlene Ferris went to Mason almost immediately after she killed Loring Lamont, and Mason has been planning to use Madge Elwood as a fall guy ever since. Now we've caught him redhanded."

Lt. Tragg regarded Perry Mason, slowly nodded. "We've caught him redhanded, Albert," he said. "I don't know just what the offense is that we've caught him at—we'll let the district attorney unscramble that one."

Mason said, "Tragg, can I talk with you for a moment in private?"

Tragg shook his head. "The only talking you're going to do is to the district attorney."

The officer turned to Albert. "Now look, Albert," he said, "I would advise you not to demand that we make an arrest. We've caught them here. That's enough. You and I will search the garage. We'll go through it from stem to stern. If we find any articles that they've planted we'll turn those articles over to the district attorney."

"Well," Albert said reluctantly, "I'm going to follow your advice—as soon as I knew they'd been around making inquiries I felt certain they'd try to plant something. I'm glad I got you on the job."

"I'm glad you got me on the job," Lt. Tragg said. "The district attorney is going to be glad you got me on the job. But let's use our heads a little bit."

"Whatever you say, Lieutenant."

Tragg said to Mason, "Albert will back his car out of the way. You and Miss Street can leave, Perry."

Mason said, "Tragg, I have reason to believe there are some articles of evidence in this garage. Don't let anyone give you any false notions. Go ahead and find them."

"And if you find them," Albert said, "you'll know who put them here."

"Never mind the argument," Tragg said to Albert. "Back your car up so they can get their car out. We'll start searching."

Albert got in his car, backed it out of the way.

Mason held his car door open for Della Street, walked around, got in beside her, backed the car out, turned it and drove out to the highway.

"Well?" Della Street asked.

Mason, his face grim, said, "There was a break that went against us."

"How bad a break?" she asked.

"Just about the worst break we could possibly get," Mason said. "If they find anything they'll swear that I planted it. You can rest assured that Hamilton Burger, the district attorney, will take personal charge of the case if they find anything."

"And it won't count against Madge Elwood?" she asked.

"Not now," Mason said. "It will count against Arlene Ferris."

"But look, Chief, you and I can both testify that..."

"You and I can both shout until we're black in the face," Mason said. "Our protestations will do no good. That's the trouble with being a citizen who has no authority and trying to shortcut the law."

"But it wouldn't have done a particle of good if you'd gone to Lieutenant Tragg or the district attorney or the police or anyone else," Della Street said, almost crying. "You could have told them your suspicions and they'd have laughed at you. They wouldn't have done a thing."

"I know," Mason said, "but right now we're caught, and caught redhanded."

"Doing what?" she asked.

"That," he said, "is where we have a chance. We'll go to court tomorrow. If Hamilton Burger, the district attorney, walks in to take charge of the case personally we'll know that our deductions were correct, that they have found some evidence and that we're in just about the worst predicament we've ever been caught in."

Her hand moved out to rest on his. "All right, Chief," she said, "I'm in it with you. We're together in the thing."

Mason said grimly, "You're in it with me. We're both in the soup. But we aren't going to stay there. We're going to fight our way out."

CHAPTER FOURTEEN

Precisely thirty seconds before ten o'clock, Hamilton Burger, the district attorney, came striding into the courtroom, and, with a perfunctory nod to Perry Mason, seated himself beside his deputy, Donald Carson.

A few seconds later, Judge Carleton Bayton took his place on the bench. Court was called to order, and the judge looked down at District Attorney Burger. "Was there something you wanted, Mr. Burger?" he asked.

Burger arose. "No, Your Honor. I am merely sitting in on the case of the People versus Arlene Ferris."

Despite himself, Judge Bayton couldn't control the expression of surprise. "I'm afraid I don't understand, Mr. District Attorney. This is a routine preliminary examination which is all but concluded. There remains only a few minutes of testimony this morning."

"Nevertheless," Burger said, "I am sitting in on the case. I may state to the Court that I think there will be developments this morning which will change the entire complexion of the case. A matter has arisen since the adjournment of court which my office feels calls for the most thorough investigation, and in view of the fact that I may be called upon to take action in the matter, I wish to conduct that investigation personally."

Judge Bayton, plainly puzzled, said, "Very well. We will proceed with the case. Now, as I understand it, Mr. Prosecutor, the case had been continued to this morning with the idea that Peter Lyons, the officer whose testimony on direct examination had been stipulated by counsel, could be cross-examined by the defense."

"May I put it this way, Your Honor," Donald Carson said. "The People had not actually rested their case, but had announced their desire to do so. However, we are still putting on our case and we are not bound as to the witnesses we will call. However, the Court is quite right in stating that yesterday afternoon it was agreed that Peter Lyons, a police officer who had placed the first illegal parking ticket on Loring Lamont's automobile, would be present in court so that he could be cross-examined by the defense attorney.

"Mr. Peter Lyons is here, and I now ask him to take the stand—come forward and be sworn, Mr. Lyons."

Peter Lyons, a man in his early thirties, with high cheekbones, a crew haircut and lip set in a firm line of determination, came forward, held up his hand, was sworn and took his place on the witness stand.

Donald Carson said, "Mr. Lyons, you are a police officer on the metropolitan force. You were on duty during the evening of the fifth of this month, and you had occasion to put a tag for illegal parking on the automobile registered in the name of Loring Lamont, who is now deceased. Your testimony on direct examination was stipulated to, and this is the time fixed for cross-examination. Mr. Mason will now cross-examine you."

Mason arose and approached the witness. "Mr. Lyons, you put a tag on the Lamont automobile for illegal parking at about what time?"

"At about nine o'clock, according to my report."

"Where was the car parked?"

"Right in front of the fireplug near the apartment house at 9612 Endicott."

"What time did you go on duty?"

"At five o'clock."

"You were in a radio patrol car?"

"I was."

"Ordinarily do you pay attention to illegal parking?"

"At times, but... well, yes. In case of what we might call a flagrant violation, we issue a ticket. For instance, if a car is parked for a long time in front of a fireplug or perhaps if it is parked in front of a driveway we put on a ticket, then make it a point to swing back around within the next half hour or so, and if the car is still there, we radio in to the dispatcher to have a tow car come and tow it away."

"Your district comprises the territory within which the Lamont car was parked?"

"Yes, of course."

"And you had been patrolling it since five o'clock in the afternoon?"

"Yes, sir."

"Did you get past this number on Endicott on an average of once an hour?"

"Now as to that, it's difficult to say. Sometimes we'd come down Endicott Way, sometimes one of the other streets. We were patrolling the district."

"But you did drive along Endicott Way several times between five o'clock, when you went on duty, and approximately nine o'clock, when you tagged the Lamont car?"

"Yes."

"During that time, on any of those trips, did you notice the Lamont car parked in front of the fire hydrant?"

"Of course," Lyons said, shifting his position on the witness stand, "we aren't primarily interested in parking violations, Mr. Mason. Therefore, I wouldn't be absolutely positive that..."

"That's not my question," Mason said. "I asked you if you noticed the Lamont car parked in front of the fireplug *prior* to the time you gave it the ticket."

"No, sir, I did not."

"The first time you noticed it parked in front of the fireplug you issued a ticket?"

"Yes, sir."

"Now, was there some reason why you were particularly interested in cars that were illegally parked in the territory?"

"There had been some complaint about illegal parking, and... well, yes, we had been instructed to keep an eye open for cars which were parked illegally. There was something of a drive on to stop illegal parking in that district."

"So that prior to nine o'clock on the evening of the fifth, during all of the times you had driven along Endicott Way, you had been on the alert for cars that were illegally parked?"

The witness hesitated for several seconds, then said, "Yes."

"Do you remember how many other automobiles you tagged that night for illegal parking?"

"I think there were two."

"Other than the Lamont car?"

"Yes."

"Now, you say there had been a problem in regard to illegal parking in the vicinity?"

"Yes."

"Do you know anything of the nature of that problem?"

"There are three apartment houses within three blocks. They are rather large apartment houses which do not have garages. There is a double vacant lot near one, which is used as a parking for automobiles. As for the rest, cars are parked along the street, and after about six or seven o'clock in the evening the parking problem becomes very acute. As a result, many cars have been illegally parked and we have received complaints."

"You mean in front of fire hydrants?"

"Some of them were in front of fire hydrants. Most of the complaints, however, were for obstructing a driveway. Some complaints were from the owners of cars parked in the lot where another car was parked so that it was impossible to move the car because of the other car. There were numerous complaints and we were asked to try and clear up the situation."

"After nine o'clock you were on duty until how late?"

"Midnight."

"And you had occasion to drive through the district several times after nine?"

"Yes."

"Was the Lamont car still parked in front of the fireplug?"

"I don't know."

"Why don't you know?"

"Because I didn't actually see it, although I assume that it..."

"Never mind what you assume," Mason interrupted. "Let's talk about what you *know*."

"Yes, sir."

"Do you *know* that the Lamont car was parked in front of the fireplug between nine o'clock and midnight?"

"I don't know it, no, sir."

"Do you know that it wasn't?"

The witness hesitated.

"Yes or no," Mason said.

Lyons scratched his head, finally blurted, "I don't think it was."

"You're not certain?"

"Yes, I'm certain—that is, I'm as near certain as can be."

"What makes you certain?"

"I drove past there shortly before eleven o'clock, and I remember that just prior to making that swing around I made up my mind that if the cars I had tagged hadn't been moved I was going to phone in for a tow car and have them towed away before I went off duty."

"So you looked for the Lamont car then?"

"Now, Mr. Mason, I want to be absolutely fair. I remember that I had made up my mind that *if* I saw these cars illegally parked after I had ticketed them, I was going to call in for a tow car."

"And you didn't see the Lamont car illegally parked?"

"No."

"Did you look to see if it was still there?"

"Frankly, Mr. Mason, I have forgotten the exact sequence of events. I know that about the time we got to the address on Endicott Way a report came in of a prowler at the other end of my district, and we put on speed and went to take that call. Now, whether that call came in before we had passed the location of the Lamont car or afterwards I don't know. Of course, if that call had come in before, there is a possibility that I wouldn't have been as alert in regard to the illegal parking problem. I am now trying to recall certain things that happened. At the time, there was nothing particularly unusual about what was taking place. It is, therefore, simply a problem of trying to recall routine after a period of time. I'm sorry that I can't be more specific. I have tried to be fair. I have discussed this matter with the deputy district attorney and with my superiors. I have consulted my notes. I have done the best I can, and I'm sorry that that is the most definite answer I can make. However, it is my considered opinion that, at about eleven o'clock, the Lamont car had been moved and was no longer in front of the fireplug."

"That's your best judgment?"

"That's my best judgment."

"Now then," Mason said, "what can you tell us about the other cars you tagged for illegal parking?"

Lyons made a gesture of throwing up his hands. "Nothing," he said. "All I know is, I issued tickets for illegal parking and turned the tickets in, in the usual course of routine. The cars were moved before I made my final checkup.

Therefore, I can't tell you very much about them now. There has been no occasion for me to remember *them* or to refresh my recollection concerning them."

"Do you know where they were parked or what the nature of the violation was?"

"I remember that one of them was parked in front of a fireplug, but I think the other was parked so it was partially blocking a driveway. I can't be certain...no, wait a minute. There was one car that was double-parked. I remember now, the motor was running and the lights were on. Apparently the driver had just stepped out for a minute. I waited—oh, perhaps thirty seconds, and he didn't show up, so I tagged the car."

"And then what?"

"I drove down as far as the corner, then stopped my car and waited while I looked in my rearview mirror to see if the car that was double-parked was being driven away. It was, so I didn't pay any further attention to it."

"You went on around the corner and on about your business?"

"That's right."

Mason said, "If it hadn't been for the fact that this Lamont car was owned by a man who had been murdered on the date you tagged the car for illegal parking; if it hadn't been that your brother officers, who came on duty after you went off duty, assured you that the car was illegally parked all during the night in exactly the same place where you had tagged it; you wouldn't have had any question in your mind but what the car had been moved before you went off duty. Isn't that right?"

"I think that is right," Lyons said.

"And your best present judgment is that the car was moved between nine and eleven?"

The witness again shifted his position. "I don't think I can tell you any more than what I have told you already, Mr. Mason."

"Thank you," Mason said. "That's all."

"I have no questions on redirect," Donald Carson said.

"Does that conclude the People's case?" Judge Bayton asked.

Hamilton Burger got to his feet. "Your Honor," he said, "it does not. A matter has come up which concerns me, not only as a prosecutor but as a member of the legal profession. Something has happened which I feel must be investigated in detail. I feel that an attempt has been made to fabricate evidence in this case, and I feel the facts should be so well established that proper steps may be taken. I wish to prepare a record at this preliminary hearing so that in case any of the witnesses should be spirited out of the country and not be available at the time of trial in the Superior Court, I can read the testimony of those witnesses into the record in accordance with the provisions of Section 686 of the Penal Code."

"Isn't this rather an unusual procedure under the circumstances?" Judge Bayton asked.

"It is an unusual case, Your Honor, and is a case in which I wish to prepare a record which can be used either under the provisions of Section 686, or for the purpose of impeachment."

"Very well," Judge Bayton said, "go ahead."

"I wish to recall Lieutenant Tragg to the stand," Carson said.

Lt. Tragg, evidently carefully rehearsed as to the part he was to play, stepped briskly forward.

"You have already been sworn," Judge Bayton said to the witness. "Go ahead, Mr. Prosecutor."

"Directing your attention to yesterday evening," Carson asked, "did you have occasion to go to an apartment house where one Madge Elwood has her residence? An apartment house known as the Kelsington Apartments in Santa Monica?"

"Yes, sir."

"Now, prior to that time had you taken any steps to identify the garment which has heretofore been marked for identification, the skirt with the cut in it?"

"I did. Yes, sir."

"What did you do?"

"I ascertained the store where the garment had been sold. I found that it was sold at a store in Santa Monica. I traced the code number of the cleaning establishment that was on the garment and found that number had been issued to one Madge Elwood, living at the Kelsington Apartments in Santa Monica. I may incidentally mention that when we arrested the defendant in this case she was living with Madge Elwood in this apartment; that is, she said she was visiting there, but she was actually living there with Madge Elwood at the time."

"So what did you do yesterday afternoon?" Carson asked.

"In the latter part of the afternoon, around five o'clock, I guess, I went to the Kelsington Apartments to investigate."

"Were you alone?"

"No, sir."

"Who was with you?"

"Mr. George Quincy Albert."

"Mr. Albert has previously been a witness in this case?"

"Yes, sir."

"And what did you do?"

"Mr. Albert had pointed out to me that..."

"Never mind any statements which were made outside of the presence of the defendant," Carson interrupted. "Those would be hearsay."

"I understand," Lt. Tragg said. "I didn't intend to state anything other than an incidental matter. However, I appreciate the point and will confine myself to what happened."

"And what did happen?"

"We went to the Kelsington Apartments. We first decided to look in the garage."

"You mean the garage that was rented to Madge Elwood along with the apartment?"

"That's right. The apartment house has a driveway which leads into a rather large area in the back. This area is in the form of a square, and three sides of that square are occupied by garages. Each garage is numbered for the apartment that goes with it, and names are put on the garages."

"And you went to the garage which had the name of Madge Elwood?"

"Yes, sir."

"What did you do?"

"Mr. Albert was driving the car. We came to a stop in front of the garage. Mr. Albert got out to try the garage door to see if it was locked."

"Was it locked?"

"No, sir."

"And Mr. Albert opened the garage door?"

"He did."

"What did you find inside of the garage?"

"We found an automobile in the garage, an automobile which was registered in the name of Mr. Perry Mason, the attorney for the defendant. We found Mr. Perry Mason and his secretary, Della Street, in the garage. They were out of the car at the time."

"Did you ask them what they were doing in there?"

"Mr. Albert accused them of planting evidence."

"And what did Mr. Mason say, if anything?"

"Objected to, if the Court please," Mason said. "This is hearsay. This conversation took place outside of the presence of the defendant. It is incompetent, irrelevant and immaterial."

"Mr. Mason, if the Court please," Carson said, "is the accredited representative of the defendant. The accusation was made in his presence, and his statement was in reply to that accusation."

Judge Bayton frowned, then shook his head. "It may be that counsel for the defendant has been indiscreet. It may be that he has been unwise, but the Court sees no reason why a conversation held in the presence of the attorney for the defendant, but without the defendant being aware of that conversation, should be binding upon her. The objection is sustained."

"Very well. What did you do?" Carson asked.

"Well," Tragg said, "we first got rid of Mr. Mason and Della Street, and then we went to work in the garage."

"Doing what?"

"Searching it."

"For what?"

"For any evidence which might have been left there—*by anyone*."

"What did you find?"

"We found a pair of mud-stained shoes. We found a pair of trousers with a rip down one seam of the trousers."

"Do you know who owned those articles?"

"I do now. I didn't then."

"You made an investigation?"

"I did."

"Take the shoes, for instance, Lieutenant. What did you do with reference to them?"

"I wired the factory, asking for the names of firms handling those shoes in the Los Angeles area. I may state that they were a very exclusive and expensive shoe. There were five shops which handled that shoe in Los Angeles. I finally located the name of the purchaser."

"Who was that purchaser?"

"Just a minute," Mason said. "Quite obviously that's hearsay evidence. He is relying upon what some shopowner told him."

Judge Bayton said, "Quite evidently it calls for hearsay evidence. However, can't we make certain stipulations here?"

"I am willing to stipulate as to statements which were made to Lieutenant Tragg by various persons, upon being assured that those statements *were* made," Mason said, "and subject to my right to bring the witnesses into court and cross-examine them if I so desire. I am willing to stipulate that certain witnesses would have so testified on direct examination."

"Very well," Carson said. "Will you stipulate that the owner of one of the stores stated that he had Loring Lamont as one of his regular customers, that Loring Lamont customarily bought shoes of this style and make, and that these shoes were in his size? That is, they were the size purchased and worn by Loring Lamont?"

"That is a fact?" Mason asked.

"That is a fact."

"I will so stipulate."

"Will you stipulate that Mr. Loring Lamont's tailor identified these trousers as being part of the suit he had made for Mr. Loring Lamont, of identical material, and that the label in the waistband furnished a means of identification and that this tailor identified these trousers as being trousers which he had made for Mr. Loring Lamont in his lifetime?"

"That is a fact, is it?" Mason asked.

"That is a fact."

"I will so stipulate that the tailor would so testify, with the understanding that at any time I have the right of cross-examination if I so desire. I am simply stipulating as to what the testimony of these gentlemen would have been on direct examination."

"Very well," Carson said, and turned to Lt. Tragg. "Where were these articles found, Lieutenant Tragg?"

"In a locked trunk in the garage where we found Perry Mason and his secretary."

"You may cross-examine," Carson said to Mason.

"You stated," Mason said, "that you were looking for evidence which might have been planted by anyone, and, as I noticed the way you testified, you made a rather significant pause before saying the words *by anyone* and then you emphasized those words."

"That may be correct," Lt. Tragg said.

"When you said by anyone, I take it you meant what you said?"

"Exactly."

"The evidence could have been planted by me?"

"It certainly could have."

"And the evidence could have been planted by the defendant in this case?"

"It could have, although she was in jail at the time and...well, she could have, yes."

"And the evidence could have been planted by Madge Elwood?"

Lt. Tragg hesitated and then said, "I suppose it could have been."

"Thank you," Mason said. "That's all. No further questions."

"Now then, if the Court please," Carson said, "we are trying desperately to get in touch with Madge Elwood. It seems to be difficult to find her. However, with reference to the skirt which was identified by Lieutenant Tragg as being the property of Madge Elwood, I wish to call Bertha Anderson to the stand."

Bertha Anderson came forward and was sworn. Mason recognized her as the manager of the apartment house at Santa Monica.

"What is your occupation?" Carson asked.

"I am the manager of the Kelsington Apartments at Santa Monica."

"Do you know Madge Elwood?"

"I do."

"Does she live there?"

"She does."

"Do you know Mr. Perry Mason?"

"Yes. I have met him."

"When did you meet him?"

"I met him yesterday afternoon."

"And did you have a conversation with Mr. Mason?"

"I did."

"About Madge Elwood's apartment?"

"Yes."

"And did Mr. Mason ask if he could get in that apartment? If you would let him in with a passkey?"

"Objected to, if the Court please," Mason said, "on the ground that the question is incompetent, irrelevant and immaterial; that it is leading and suggestive, and further on the ground that counsel, well knowing the ruling of the Court in regard to conversations had with me outside the presence of the defendant, has deliberately tried by this leading question to prejudice the Court against the defendant's case."

"The objection is sustained," Judge Bayton said, "and counsel is admonished. In fact, I wish to state, Mr. Prosecutor, that I consider the nature of this question was such as to constitute an attempt on your part to void and nullify the ruling of the Court. The Court has ruled, at least temporarily, that anything Mr. Mason may have said or done outside of the presence of the defendant is not binding upon the defendant."

"He's her legal representative. He was acting on her behalf," Carson said angrily.

"The Court understands that, Mr. Carson, but the Court has ruled. You are familiar with the Court's ruling."

Hamilton Burger arose ponderously. "If the Court please, may I be heard?"

"You may be heard, Mr. Burger."

"We wish to state," Burger said, "that this is rather a serious matter, that it has come up out of a clear sky, so to speak. We have not had time to look up the authorities but I wish to state to the Court that I feel positive that we can find authorities indicating that as long as the defendant is represented by Mr. Perry Mason and as long as he is her duly constituted agent and attorney that the things he has done on her behalf are binding upon her. Furthermore, I feel that we should have an opportunity to show what these things are so that under the doctrine of agency we will force the defendant either to ratify the acts of her agent or to take steps to disaffirm those acts."

"The Court has ruled. The Court's position is that the acts of Perry Mason and conversations which he has had outside the presence of the defendant are not binding upon her. Now, the Court can be in error in this matter and if you have any authorities which you wish to present, the Court will be glad to consider those authorities. In the meantime, however, the Court is going to adopt the position that you can only show acts of the defendant and can only show conversations which occurred within the presence of the defendant. Otherwise they would be hearsay."

"But, if the Court please," Hamilton Burger said, "here is a plain case, if I may speak frankly, where evidence which is exceedingly vital to the issues in this case has been planted by someone in a garage at the Kelsington Apartments. Mr. Mason, as the attorney for the defendant, was caught redhanded in that garage. It is at least a reasonable assumption that the only person who could have given those garments to him was the defendant in this case."

"That's looking at it from the prosecution's viewpoint," Judge Bayton snapped. "On the other hand, you haven't as yet negatived the possibility that those garments were placed there by the most logical person of all, the person who rented that garage, Madge Elwood."

"But where could she possibly have secured those garments?' Hamilton Burger asked. "She wasn't out at the lodge the night of the murder. She..."

"How does counsel know she wasn't?" Mason interrupted.

Hamilton Burger flushed angrily. "I don't choose to be interrupted," he said.

"And the Court would very much prefer not to have you interrupted," Judge Bayton said, "but since the interruption has been made, I will state that the question propounded by counsel for the defense is one which the Court intended to ask. How do you know she wasn't out there?"

"We'll prove it," Hamilton Burger said.

"Go ahead and prove it, then," Judge Bayton said, "and after your evidence has been concluded, if you then have sufficient circumstantial evidence to indicate that the articles in question *must* have been placed at the spot where they were found by any person acting under the direction and control of the defendant, you will have an opportunity to renew your offers of testimony. The Court will then permit you to recall these witnesses and ask these questions, provided you have in the meantime found some authorities to support your position.

"At the present time you are working only on an inference. The circumstances are not, in the opinion of the Court, strong enough to indicate a chain of circumstantial evidence necessarily connecting this defendant with the articles in question. However, the Court is very much interested in this phase of the inquiry and intends to cooperate in any way it can."

"Thank you," Hamilton Burger said, and sat down.

Carson turned to the manager of the apartment house. "Were you the manager of the Kelsington Apartments on the fifth and the sixth of this month?"

"I was."

"Were you acquainted with Madge Elwood on that date?"

"I was."

"Now, I am going to ask you if you saw Madge Elwood on the sixth of the month."

"I did."

"At what time?"

"I saw her several times."

"Did you see her in the evening? Early in the evening?"

"Yes."

"Did you have a conversation with her at that time?"

"Yes."

"Did you see the defendant on the sixth?"

"I did. Yes."

"And what happened at that time?"

"On the afternoon of the sixth Madge brought the defendant, Arlene Ferris, in with her. She was on her way to the elevator. She introduced me to Arlene Ferris and said Arlene was going to be visiting with her for perhaps a few days."

"Now, that was on the afternoon of the sixth?"

"Yes."

"And this conversation took place in the presence of the defendant?"

"Yes."

"Now, I show you a skirt, which has heretofore been marked for identification as People's Exhibit B-8, and I will ask you if you recognize that skirt."

"I do."

"Where did you see it?"

"I saw it on Madge Elwood on the sixth of the month."

"She was wearing that skirt?"

"She was wearing that skirt," Bertha Anderson said with positive finality.

"Now then, did you see her later on after that, on the sixth?"

"I did."

"At about what time?"

"It was early in the evening."

"What was Madge Elwood wearing at that time?"

"She was wearing that skirt."

"When you say that skirt, you are referring to the People's Exhibit B-8, the skirt which I am now holding in my hand?"

"Yes, sir."

"And where was she when you saw her?"

"She was in the lobby, going out of the apartment."

"Now, did you see her when she returned?"

"Yes."

"And what time was that?"

"That was quite a bit later—two or three hours later."

"And what was Madge Elwood wearing at that time?"

"She was wearing a different skirt. I remember noticing that she had gone out in one skirt and had returned in another. I started to say something and then held my tongue. After all, it was none of my business."

"Now, that was on the sixth of the month?"

"Yes."

"You may cross-examine," Carson said.

Mason turned to the witness. "Do you see people when they go and when they come out?"

"Quite frequently. I have an apartment which is back of the office, but I try to stay in the office so that I can see the lobby, particularly during the hours when the street door is kept unlocked."

"There's a desk there?"

"A sort of counter, yes."

"Any switchboard?"

"No. Tenants have their own phones or else use the phone booth in the corridor."

"Did you see Madge Elwood on the fifth of the month?"

"Yes, I saw her."

"In the evening?"

"I saw her when she came back from work in the early evening or late afternoon, and then I saw her again."

"When did you see her last on the fifth?"

"Objected to as incompetent, irrelevant and immaterial—not proper cross-examination," Carson said. "We have asked no questions about the fifth."

"I certainly have a right to test the recollection of the witness," Mason said.

"The objection is overruled. Proceed," Judge Bayton ruled.

"I saw her on the evening of the fifth about...oh, I guess it was about nine o'clock."

"And what, if anything was she doing when you saw her?"

"She was going out."

"Did you see her come back that evening?"

"No."

"She came back after you had locked up for the evening?"

"Yes."

"And what time did you leave the lobby and lock up?"

"It was...I would say it was about eleven o'clock."

"Now, was Madge wearing this skirt which you have referred to, on the fifth?"

"No, she wasn't."

"How do you happen to remember this skirt so clearly?"

"Because I have one almost exactly like it. It is almost exactly the same pattern. Madge and I have commented on that from time to time."

"Madge left the apartment yesterday?"

"Yes."

"Carrying two suitcases?"

"Yes."

"Did you see her?"

"Yes."

"Did she tell you where she was going?"

"No."

"Did she tell you how long she expected to be away?"

"No."

"Wasn't that rather unusual?"

"Well, I don't inquire about a tenant's business as long as the rent is paid and..."

"That isn't the question," Mason said. "Wasn't that rather unusual?"

"Well, yes, it was."

"Now then, since she left have you entered her apartment with a passkey?"

"Objected to as incompetent, irrelevant and immaterial and not proper cross-examination," Carson said.

"I think it goes to show the bias of the witness," Mason said.

Judge Bayton hesitated. "I will permit the question."

"Did you enter the apartment?"

"Yes."

"With a passkey?"

"Yes."

"Were you alone?" Mason asked.

"Lieutenant Tragg was with me," she said.

"And what did you find in the apartment?" Mason asked.

"Now, if the Court please," Carson said, "that is definitely objected to as incompetent, irrelevant and immaterial and not proper cross-examination. We have not asked this witness anything about that at all on direct examination. This is going into an entirely different matter which will take the inquiry far afield."

"The Court is inclined to sustain that objection," Judge Bayton said. "I think perhaps the latitude on cross-examination has been ample to test the credibility of the witness."

"That's all," Mason said. "No further questions."

"If the Court please," Carson said, "I wish to introduce these trousers and the shoes as People's Exhibits, and at this time to renew our motion to show conversations with Mr. Perry Mason at the place where the articles were found. We feel that there has been sufficient circumstantial evidence to show that these articles were planted by Mr. Mason acting on behalf of the defendant."

Judge Bayton slowly shook his head. "You haven't connected it up yet," he said.

"But if the Court please," Carson said, "these articles were the property of the decedent. It is quite evident that the defendant planned a story which would be well calculated to arouse the most sympathy on the part of a jury. She wanted to show that she had been attacked, that she had tried to defend her virtue, that she had been pursued through wet brush along a muddy road, that she had plunged through a barbed-wire fence.

"We have now shown, at least by inference, that Mr. Mason had Madge Elwood furnish a skirt which was deliberately left in the defendant's apartment after having been taken to the scene of the crime and a part of the skirt left on the barbed-wire fence. We have shown that this evidence could only have been planted on the evening of the sixth, some time after the murder had been committed, probably nearly twenty-four hours after the murder. That was for the purpose of substantiating the defendant's story.

"Now, we are also in a position to show that counsel secured possession of some of Loring Lamont's shoes and a pair of his trousers, that the shoes were deliberately muddied up and the trousers were dragged through wet brush and then ripped as though on a piece of barbed wire, and that counsel was actually caught redhanded in the act of planting those articles. We feel that under the circumstances there is every reason to believe that this was done as the result of a conspiracy between the defendant and her counsel and that the defendant is bound by his acts, that this attempt to fabricate evidence is an indication of guilt."

"That's all very well," Judge Bayton said, "but how do you connect it up with the defendant? In the first place, how do you connect it up with Mr. Mason?"

"Mr. Mason and his secretary were caught redhanded," Carson said grimly.

"No, they weren't," Judge Bayton contradicted. "Their hands weren't red at all. For all you know they hadn't been in that garage more than a matter of seconds. For all you know they were in there looking for evidence. Lieutenant Tragg has stated that he and George Albert went to the garage looking for evidence. Now suppose the sequence had been reversed? Suppose Perry Mason and Della Street had driven up a few seconds *after* Lieutenant Tragg and George Albert had entered the garage? Would you say that that was evidence that Lieutenant Tragg and George Albert were caught redhanded planting these articles in the garage?"

Carson's face flushed. "Certainly not."

"Well, it's exactly the same type of evidence that you have against Perry Mason," Judge Bayton said.

"But Perry Mason had reason to plant these articles. It was to his advantage —to the advantage of his client to have them discovered there."

"For all you know," Judge Bayton said, "it was to the advantage of George Albert to have the articles discovered there. It was to the advantage of the police to have the articles discovered there. I don't say that is was, I'm simply stating that for all you know it was. For all the Court knows, it was."

"Well, we're practical men," Carson said. "We know what happened."

"You know what you think happened," Judge Bayton said, "but what you think happened isn't binding upon the Court."

"Of course," Carson said with a trace of irritation in his voice, "if the Court expects us to produce eyewitnesses who will swear that they actually *saw* Perry Mason and Della Street open the trunk and put the garments in, we can't do it. Persons who commit a crime, particularly persons of intelligence, usually select a time when there are no witnesses."

Judge Bayton's face colored slightly. "The Court can well appreciate all that. The Court readily understands that usually crimes have to be established by inference, by circumstantial evidence. But the fact remains that the accused is entitled to certain presumptions. That's the function of a Court, to keep a sane perspective on the evidence.

"The Court feels that the evidence as it is now before the Court is capable of several interpretations, one of the most logical being that the person who rented that garage is the one who put the garments in the trunk. The Court is not unmindful of the fact that the witness, Jerome Henley, first identified Madge Elwood as being the person who was seen parking that automobile. Now I'm going to state frankly that the Court wants to get at the bottom of this. The Court would like to have Mr. Henley recalled to be questioned, not by counsel, but by the Court."

"Mr. Henley has returned to his place of business," Carson said. "Trying to get him back here would cause a delay. We understand and appreciate the desire of the Court to get this case disposed of."

"The Court has a very great desire to get this case disposed of," Judge Bayton said, "but the Court has an even greater desire to see that justice is done. I don't think it will take long to get Mr. Henley here and we can continue the case until he arrives."

"Perhaps," Mason said, "it will help clear this matter up if, while the Court is waiting for Mr. Henley to arrive, I can recall Lieutenant Tragg to the stand for further cross-examination."

"Very well," Judge Bayton said.

"Of course," Hamilton Burger said irritably, "this is only a preliminary examination. We only have to show that a crime was committed and that there are reasonable grounds to believe the defendant committed the crime."

"That's all you need to show at a preliminary examination," Judge Bayton said, "but this case has gone beyond that point. The good faith and the ethics of Mr. Perry Mason and his secretary have been questioned. The Court has no doubt but what the public press will make considerable capital out of this situation. Having gone this far, we're going to go the rest of the way.

"Lieutenant Tragg, will you return to the stand, please. I suggest to the bailiff that Mr. Henley be reached on the telephone and instructed to attend this Court."

Tragg came forward and took his place on the witness stand.

"Dirty dishes were found in the lodge by the police?" Mason asked.

"They were."

"They were taken to the police laboratory?"

"Yes, sir."

"They were processed for fingerprints?"

"Yes, sir."

"Did you find any fingerprints of the defendant on those dishes?"

"We did."

"Why did you fail to mention that fact in your direct testimony?"

"I wasn't asked."

"*Where* did you find the fingerprints?"

"On several of the dishes—particularly on the bowl which had been used for mixing the biscuit dough."

"On the coffee cups?"

"Well, no."

"On the plates?"

"We found one fingerprint on one of the plates."

"And, of course, you found fingerprints of the decedent?"

"Yes."

"Now then," Mason said, "isn't it a fact that you found fingerprints of at least one other person?"

Tragg hesitated a moment, then slowly nodded. "Yes, there were the fingerprints of at least one other person."

"Have you identified those prints?"

"Not as yet."

"And did you fail to mention the fingerprints of the defendant because the prosecutor had instructed you not to say anything about them for fear that my cross-examination would bring out the fact that another person's fingerprints were there?"

"I was told not to volunteer any information."

"Do you have the fingerprints of Madge Elwood?"

"No."

"Then you don't know that those other fingerprints were not those of Madge Elwood, do you?"

"We don't know whose they were. We do know they were not the prints of Sadie Richmond. We had thought that when she was putting the dishes away after they had been washed from the last time they were used, she might perhaps have left fingerprints. We therefore took her prints and compared them. They aren't her prints."

"Now then," Mason said, "when the defendant was telling you her story, did she tell you that the decedent had admitted to her that he had made a dummy telephone call? In other words, that he had gone into the lodge while she was still in the car, that he had called someone and asked that someone to call him back within a given number of minutes?"

"She told me that."

"Did you make an attempt to trace that call?"

"We made a check of all calls placed from the lodge on the night in question."

"And there again," Mason said, "you refrained from mentioning certain facts on your direct examination."

"There again," Lt. Tragg said, "I wasn't asked."

"You're being asked now," Mason said. "To whom did Loring Lamont place that call?"

"We don't know," Tragg said. "It was a station-to-station call. He simply called the number of the executive offices of the Lamont Company."

"The call wasn't placed to any particular person?" Mason asked, puzzled. "Just to the office."

"All right," Mason said desperately, "what *other* calls were placed? After Loring Lamont found that he needed dry clothes and a new pair of shoes, whom did he call?"

"Now, just a moment before you answer that question," Carson said. "If the Court please, we object to that question as being argumentative, as assuming facts not in evidence, and not being proper cross-examination."

"The objection is sustained as to the last part of the question," Judge Bayton said. "The first part of the question will stand. Whom else did Loring Lamont call from the lodge?"

"No one," Tragg said.

"What!" Mason exclaimed in surprise.

"There were no calls," Tragg said. "No long-distance calls. Of course, we can't tell about incoming calls, but on the calls which were placed from that telephone there was only the one call and that was a station-to-station call to the office of the Lamont Rolling, Casting and Engineering Company—the executive offices."

"And the time of that call?" Mason asked.

"The time was six-twenty-two, approximately the time when the defendant and the decedent arrived at the lodge, according to the story the defendant told us."

Mason half-closed his eyes in thoughtful concentration.

"Any further questions?" Judge Bayton asked.

"No further questions," Mason said.

"No questions," Carson said.

"We will take a ten-minute recess," Judge Bayton said. "We will reconvene just as soon as Jerome Henley arrives in court."

Judge Bayton left the bench. Hamilton Burger arose and, pointedly ignoring Perry Mason, strode into an anteroom.

Mason turned to Paul Drake and Della Street. "All right," the lawyer said, "we've got ten minutes to solve this case. Now what the hell happened? Loring Lamont *must* have made some arrangements to get dry trousers and shoes out to the lodge. How in the world could he have done it unless he telephoned?

"In view of the evidence they have now produced, we know that Arlene's story must be true. We know that he pursued her through the wet brush, that he slid down through the barbed-wire fence and tore his trousers when he did it. We know that he ran through the mud in the road, that his shoes were all muddy. Yet by the time he was killed someone else had appeared at the lodge. We are pretty certain now that that someone must have been Madge Elwood. But how did Madge Elwood get the dry clothes to him unless he telephoned her? How did she get into his apartment?"

Drake shrugged his shoulders. "He couldn't have contacted her by mental telepathy."

"There's only one answer," Mason said after a moment. "Madge Elwood must have called *him*."

"But why would she call him?"

"Because," Mason said, "she was close to him. She knew what Arlene had done. She had the number of the lodge and she called Loring Lamont at the lodge. We're fighting minutes on this thing, Paul. Get on the telephone. Call the telephone company. Tell them it's a matter of the greatest importance. Find out if Madge Elwood didn't place a call to that lodge on the evening of the fifth."

Drake said, "I'll try. I don't hope for much luck."

"Explain the circumstances to the manager of the telephone company," Mason said. "It's really a matter of life or death. Let's get at the bottom of this thing. See if you can get all the calls Madge Elwood placed from her apartment at about... now, let's see. Let's assume that Arlene left the lodge at about seven o'clock, that she drove back to her apartment, that she cleaned up, that she took Loring Lamont's car and put it in front of the fireplug, that she went to her apartment, that she called Madge Elwood. That probably would be somewhere between—well, let's see, let us say around eight-thirty. Also, Paul, try and trace that call to the Lamont Company that was made at six-twenty-two. Let's see what happened on that."

"I'll try," Drake promised. "You haven't given me much time."

"That's because I haven't got it to give," Mason said.

Mason started pacing the floor of the courtroom, head thrust slightly forward, forehead creased in concentration.

After several minutes Mason whirled. "Della!" he said.

"Yes, Chief?"

"Go hunt up Paul Drake. He's telephoning. We've overlooked the vital point in the case."

"What is it?"

"Get the license number of the car that Peter Lyons tagged for double parking. Then get Paul to start his men running down the registration of that car, or it probably will be on the traffic ticket itself since the officer would take the owner's name from the Certificate of Registration which the law requires to be either on the steering post or on some portion of the automobile that is clearly visible."

Della Street nodded, arose and left the courtroom.

Another five minutes passed.

Jerome Henley entered the courtroom, his manner that of a man who has been hurrying and is considerably exasperated.

Word was conveyed to Judge Bayton, and the judge once more took the bench.

Della Street came hurrying into the courtroom, seated herself beside Mason, and, as Jerome Henley was being called to the stand, said in an excited whisper, "Chief, he struck pay dirt. Madge Elwood placed a long-distance call to the lodge. Then after that she called two Los Angeles numbers. Paul Drake is running down those numbers now. He had to go to another phone to contact his office and they're getting all the information on that traffic ticket issued by Peter Lyons on the car that was double-parked."

Mason settled back in his chair. Slowly a smile came over his face. He turned to Arlene Ferris and gave her a reassuring wink just as Jerome Henley seated himself on the witness stand and Judge Bayton said, "Mr. Henley, the Court wants to ask you some questions."

"Yes, Your Honor."

"Now," Judge Bayton said, "I don't want counsel for either side to interrupt. The Court is going to ask this witness some questions. Mr. Henley, try and put aside all prejudice from your mind. I am going to ask you to try and do something that perhaps may be more than human nature can readily do. I'm going to ask you to think back to the time when Perry Mason came into your store accompanied by a young woman whose name we now know was Madge Elwood. At that time you identified Madge Elwood as the woman you had seen getting out of the car."

"I had been tricked by a previous..."

"Just a minute," Judge Bayton interrupted. "Forget all this about having been tricked. You were *subsequently* convinced that you had been tricked and you resented it. You thought Mr. Mason had tried to trap you and tried to make a fool of you. Now, I am going to ask you to get that entire thought out of your mind. I want you to think back to the occasion when Mr. Mason entered your store with Madge Elwood. How positive were you *at that time* that Madge Elwood was the woman you had seen getting out of the car?"

"I wasn't positive, I was tricked..."

"You said you were positive at that time. Now what caused you to say that?"

"Trickery."

"Mr. Henley," Judge Bayton said, "the Court is not entirely convinced that you *were* tricked. An *attempt* may have been made to trick you, but the Court is beginning to believe that it is quite possible that Madge Elwood actually was the person you saw getting out of that automobile."

Both Hamilton Burger and Carson jumped to their feet in protest. Judge Bayton motioned them to silence. "Now just a minute," he said. "The Court is doing this. I asked not to be interrupted by counsel for either side. I want you gentlemen to sit down and be quiet."

Judge Bayton turned to the witness. "The Court is here for the purpose of doing justice, Mr. Henley. The Court wants you to think back to purge your mind of all prejudice against anyone."

Judge Bayton waited. There was a tense silence in the courtroom.

"Well," Jerome Henley said at length, "of course, Your Honor, I was convinced at the time that she was the person I saw getting out of the car. However, I had previously been shown her photograph and asked to identify that photograph. I had identified it, and that's where the trouble came in."

"But why did you identify the photograph?" Judge Bayton asked.

Jerome Henley stroked the angle of his chin thoughtfully. "Well, now, as to that," he said, "of course... well, the photograph looked something like that... looked exactly like the face of the person I had seen getting out of the car. That's because Madge Elwood and the defendant look a great deal alike and the photograph had been very cunningly taken..."

"It was a photograph of Madge Elwood?"

"Yes, there's no question about that."

"And it looked like the person you saw getting out of the car?"

"Very much."

"And then when you saw Madge Elwood you felt certain she was the person whose photograph you had seen?"

"That's the reason I made the identification."

"But are you prepared now to state on your oath to this Court that it was *not* Madge Elwood whom you saw getting out of the car? Now, think carefully, Mr. Henley. This isn't an attempt to trap you. This is simply an attempt on the part of the Court to get at the truth of the matter."

Henley closed his eyes, trying to concentrate. He continued to stroke the angle of his jaw with the tips of his fingers. "Well," he said at length, "they told me not to let Perry Mason make a fool of me, and I didn't intend to have him do so. But, of course, Your Honor, when you come right down to it, when I saw that picture of Madge Elwood... well, at the time I *thought* that was the young woman I saw getting out of the car. Then when I saw Madge Elwood, of course there had been a certain amount of suggestion and... well, when I saw her I thought she was the woman, all right."

"You don't think so now?"

"Well, now," Henley said, "the situation is different. I look at the defendant and I think she's the woman, but of course I've been shown *her* picture, too."

"Forget all the picture business," Judge Bayton said. "Try and think back. Try and visualize the young woman who got out of the car. Was it Madge Elwood or was it the defendant in this case?"

Jerome Henley looked up at the judge and finally blurted out, "When you put it that way, Your Honor, I don't know. When I first saw Madge Elwood I was pretty certain that was the young woman. Then I became certain it was the defendant, but when you put the thing that way—when you put it up to me in just that way, I just don't know."

"That's all," Judge Bayton said. "Now, if counsel for either side wants to question the witness, they can. But as far as the Court is concerned this witness made a positive identification of Madge Elwood. He made it under circumstances that impress the Court. He now says he doesn't know. Does counsel for either side want to question him?"

"No questions," Mason said.

Hamilton Burger and Carson engaged in a whispered conference, then Hamilton Burger said, "No, Your Honor, no questions."

Mason said, "I have one more question of Lieutenant Tragg. You don't need to resume the stand, Lieutenant. You can answer it from right where you are in the courtroom. Among other things that you didn't mention in your testimony, was there anything about the blood alcohol of the body of Loring Lamont?"

Tragg said, "I didn't run that test myself. That was done by the autopsy surgeon, Dr. Draper."

"But you know what the results were," Mason said. "What were they?"

"Well," Tragg said, "I understand the blood alcohol percentage was point one nine."

"That," Mason said, "would indicate a considerable degree of intoxication, would it not?"

Tragg said dryly, "It would."

"Considerably more than a man of his size could get from ingesting one cocktail or two or three?"

"Probably four, five or six," Lt. Tragg said.

"I'll ask the prosecution to stipulate that Dr. Draper would so testify if he had been asked," Mason said.

Again Carson and Hamilton Burger had a whispered conference.

"Don't you know?" Judge Bayton asked.

"Yes, Your Honor," Carson said with poor grace. "We know. We will so stipulate."

"But obviously," Judge Bayton said, "this is changing the complexion of the case materially."

"I don't see why," Hamilton Burger said. "The Court is acting on what I think is an erroneous assumption."

"What's that?"

"That the defendant is telling the truth. We don't feel she is telling the truth. We feel she went out there deliberately and was there for a long time with the decedent, that they had drinks, that this defendant wasn't at all averse to any familiarities, that she led the decedent on, that she didn't object to his getting drunk and she didn't object to his taking liberties."

"Then how did it happen the decedent had in his clothing a part of the distributor from the defendant's car?"

"Because she placed it there after his death. *She* was the one who deliberately disabled her car so Loring Lamont would offer her a ride. From that point, she led him on."

"Then why did she run away, dash down the road and plunge through the barbed-wire fence?"

"I don't know that she did, Your Honor."

"Well, the clothes belonging to the decedent indicate that she did."

"After all," Hamilton Burger interposed irritably, "the Court doesn't need to go into all this. The function of the Court is only to find out *at this time* if there is reasonable ground to believe the defendant was connected with the commission of a crime."

"That's all very true from a standpoint of abstract law," Judge Bayton snapped, "but here we have a young woman whose reputation is at stake, whose liberty is at stake. A lot of evidence has been introduced and you have now made it a point to question the integrity of Mr. Perry Mason, an officer of this court.

"If the defendant is guilty, if Mr. Mason was guilty of planting evidence, the Court wants to find it out. If they are innocent, the Court wants to establish that fact. The function of a court of law, Mr. District Attorney, is to see that justice is done. In the opinion of this Court, that is far more of an obligation on the Court than to comply with the letter of the law in regard to a preliminary examination."

Paul Drake hurried into the courtroom, pushed a piece of paper in front of Mason. "All right, Perry, here it is," he whispered. "Madge Elwood called the lodge. Then she called two numbers. One of them was the number of George Quincy Albert and the other was the number of the apartment of Edith Bristol. I've traced the call from the lodge to the executive offices of the Lamont Company. Lamont simply called up the switchboard operator and told her to call him back in exactly seven minutes and as soon as he answered to hang up the phone without staying on the line to listen to what was being said."

Judge Bayton said, "Are there any further witnesses?"

"We have none, Your Honor," Hamilton Burger snapped. "That's the prosecution's case. We rest, and regardless of what may happen in the Superior Court, we wish to point out that there is more than ample evidence to bind this defendant over for trial."

"Does the defense have any evidence?" Judge Bayton asked.

Mason got to his feet. "We have some evidence, Your Honor. It will take us a little time to produce it unless the district attorney's office wishes to stipulate. However, it is a matter of record, and the records can be verified by the Court or by the prosecution."

Paul Drake whispered to Della Street, left the courtroom.

"What is this evidence?" Judge Bayton asked.

"Let us assume," Mason said, "that the story of the defendant is true. Loring Lamont found himself marooned out at the lodge. He was wearing wet clothes. He had torn the trousers. He had been repulsed in his advances. He was angry, he was wet, he was frustrated, and he had been outwitted. His automobile had been—well, borrowed.

"We only need to put ourselves in his position to find out what he would do."

"Just a moment, Your Honor," Hamilton Burger interrupted. "We object to any argument at this time. If the defense has any evidence, let them put it on. After the evidence is in, counsel can use his eloquence all he wants—and then *we'll* have an opportunity to point out our interpretation of the facts."

Judge Bayton nodded. "I think as a matter of procedure the prosecutor is correct, Mr. Mason. I think argument as such should come at the close of your evidence. However, the Court will state that the Court will welcome such argument at that time."

"I was merely trying to show the background, Your Honor," Mason said. "I think the Court understands the background. What's your evidence?"

"Simply this," Mason said. "I had thought that Loring Lamont would call someone to bring him clothes and a car and I was very frankly surprised when the record of long-distance calls showed he hadn't done so. The reason for that is now..."

"Here we go again," Hamilton Burger shouted. "Counsel is continuing with this same type of argument after the Court has admonished him. We assign this as misconduct and an attempt to circumvent the ruling of the Court."

"The Court agrees with the district attorney," Judge Bayton said sternly. "Mr. Mason, if you have any evidence, present it. Save your argument until after your evidence has been presented and please comply with the rulings of the Court."

"Yes, Your Honor," Mason said. "The evidence is simply this. The records of the telephone company show that Madge Elwood called Loring Lamont at the lodge from her apartment on the evening of the fifth. It shows that immediately after she'd finished talking with the lodge she made two calls. One of them was to the number of George Albert and the other one was to the number of the apartment of Edith Bristol, the personal secretary of J.P. Lamont."

Paul Drake again came hurrying into the courtroom.

"If I may have the indulgence of the Court for just a moment," Mason said. Drake handed Mason a paper. Mason looked at the paper, then smiled at the Court and said, "And the records also show that the car which was tagged by Peter Lyons for being double-parked was a car that was registered in the name of Edith Bristol. Those are matters of record and we ask the prosecution to so stipulate in order to save time."

"Will the prosecution so stipulate?" Judge Bayton asked.

"The prosecution will so stipulate only on the assurance of counsel for the defendant that he knows such facts to be true."

"I know such facts to be true," Mason said, "only because of telephone conversations had by Paul Drake, the detective, with the officials of the telephone company and a hasty investigation of the parking ticket issued by Officer Lyons. However, I am assured that such are the facts and if there is to any question about them I would like to have a continuance until they can be verified."

"We object to such a continuance," Hamilton Burger said, "and we don't feel that we should stipulate in view of the situation."

"You will stipulate, will you not," Judge Bayton asked, "subject to the proviso that if any of the facts should turn out to be incorrect those facts can be called to the attention of the Court?"

"We'll make that stipulation," Hamilton Burger said with poor grace, "however we can't see the relevancy of all this."

"You object to the evidence on the ground that it's incompetent, irrelevant and immaterial?" Judge Bayton asked.

"We do," Hamilton Burger said.

"The objection is noted," Judge Bayton ruled. "Now, Mr. Mason, the Court would very much like to hear argument upon the objection of the prosecution. This will be an opportunity to present your theory of the case."

Judge Bayton sat back, the ghost of a smile on his lips, his hands across his stomach, the fingers interlaced.

Hamilton Burger, realizing the trap into which he had walked, arose as though to make some objection, then slowly sat down.

"Mr. Mason will proceed," Judge Bayton said.

Mason said, "If the Court please, the situation is simply this. Looking at it from a logical standpoint, Loring Lamont must have returned to the lodge after his car had been taken by the defendant. He angrily dumped the ham and the eggs down the garbage disposal, he probably didn't care for coffee at that time. He poured himself several drinks. He didn't know exactly what to do. He was debating how to proceed. He didn't know where his car was. He didn't know whether the defendant had gone to lodge a criminal complaint against him or not.

"The defendant in the meantime drove back to town, parked Loring Lamont's car in front of a fireplug and telephoned her friend, Madge Elwood, telling her what she had done. Madge Elwood knew Loring Lamont. There is no purpose at this time in exploring the intimacy of that relationship. Madge Elwood was a modern young woman with a certain amount of independence and a tolerant outlook on life. She probably telephoned Loring Lamont at the lodge and said, in effect, 'Arlene Ferris telephoned me. You certainly went at her pretty rough. She took your automobile and left it parked in front of a fireplug. What do you want me to do?'

"And at that time Loring Lamont told her, 'What I want you to do is to bring the car out to me, contact someone who can go to my apartment and get me a clean pair of slacks, a dry pair of shoes, and you can bring them out here.'

"Thereupon," Mason said, " Madge Elwood made two calls. One of them was to a person whom she wanted to accompany her out to the lodge because in Loring Lamont's mood she didn't care to go out there alone. The other one was to the person who was to go to Loring Lamont's apartment and get him the articles of wearing apparel he had requested. Obviously that would be a person who had a key to the apartment, a person who was sufficiently intimate with Loring Lamont to be able to go to his apartment at will, and quite apparently that person was either George Albert or Edith Bristol.

"One of those persons accompanied Madge Elwood to the lodge. The other person went to the apartment and got the wearing apparel.

"We have to use inference to determine which was which.

"We know that parking space was at a premium around the apartment. We know that cars were parked at such times in front of driveways and in front of fireplugs. The person who went to the apartment of Loring Lamont to get the articles in question was in a hurry and didn't have time to park the car a long distance from the apartment and walk. That person took a chance on double-parking. The car that was double-parked in front of the apartment was tagged by Officer Lyons, at the same time he tagged the Loring Lamont car. That car belonged to Edith Bristol.

"If, therefore, my surmise is correct, Edith Bristol was the one who took out the garments to Loring Lamont, and George Albert was the one Madge Elwood telephoned when she wanted someone to escort her out there."

Edith Bristol, arising, came stalking forward. "May I make a statement to the Court?" she asked.

"This is out of order," Hamilton Burger protested.

"The district attorney will please be seated," Judge Bayton said. "What sort of a statement did you wish to make, young woman?"

"I am Edith Bristol, the private secretary to Jarvis P. Lamont," she said. "I am tired of deception. I am tired of intrigue. I probably would have confessed anyway, but there's no use trying to carry on the deception any more. I killed him."

"Come forward and take the witness stand," Judge Bayton said. "Now, young woman, I want you to understand that anything you say can be used against you. You are entitled to the benefit of counsel. You don't have to make any statement at this time. Do you wish the Court to appoint an attorney to represent you, or do you wish to call on..."

She shook her head. "I only want to get it over with, Your Honor."

"Very well," Judge Bayton said, "go on. Get it over with. Tell us what happened."

She said, "Loring Lamont was a fascinating and influential man. He swept me off my feet when I came to work for the Lamont Company and I suppose the fact that he was influential had something to do with it. I became intimate with him. I thought he was going to marry me. He assured me that he would as soon as he could condition his father's thinking. In the meantime he told me that he would manipulate things so I could get in his father's office as a private secretary and that would give me a chance to, as he put it, 'soften up the old man.' I soon found that Loring Lamont was either having an affair or preparing to have an affair with another young woman in the office, Madge Elwood. Madge Elwood was a very broadminded, modern young woman. I went to her and put the cards on the table. Madge Elwood told me that up to that point she and Loring Lamont were good friends, that that was all. She assured me the situation hadn't progressed beyond that point, and that she didn't intend to let it progress beyond that point. She told me that she actually was becoming interested in George Albert, the office manager. She told me that in order to simplify the problem as far as I was concerned, she would leave the employ of the Lamont Company. She did so.

"She pointed out to me, however, that an attractive young woman who dressed in the modern style in order to accentuate her sexual charms or at least disclose them enough to attract the masculine eye, certainly shouldn't resent masculine attention. She was, as I state, very tolerant and very broadminded.

"I happen to know that Loring Lamont continued to try and date her, that she became more and more interested in George Albert and that Loring's attempts to date her were fruitless, although she did like him. She wanted to be friends with him but there was nothing platonic about Loring Lamont's relationships with the opposite sex. More and more I was forced to close my eyes to his affairs with women.

"On the night of the fifth Madge Elwood telephoned me. She seemed rather amused. She said that Loring Lamont had taken Arlene Ferris out to the lodge and had become a little impetuous, that Arlene had grabbed his automobile and gone off in it, leaving Loring Lamont on foot. Loring was terribly afraid that his father would find out about the situation. It seems that his father had taken Loring to task on several occasions about his immoral conduct and particularly had ordered him not to use the lodge under any circumstances for any of his affairs.

"Madge told me that Loring Lamont had asked her to instruct me to go to his apartment and get trousers and shoes. I had a key to his apartment. I think I was the only person besides himself who did.

"I drove at once to his apartment. I double-parked and ran up and got the shoes and trousers. When I came down there was a tag for parking violation on my car. I hurried out at once to the lodge.

"Loring Lamont was there. He was offensively, obnoxiously drunk. I gave him the trousers and shoes. He changed into dry clothes. I fixed some coffee in an attempt to sober him up. I also cooked ham and eggs in order to induce him to eat. There was a pan of cold biscuits. I warmed them up. We had ham and eggs together.

"He became exceedingly obnoxious. He taunted me with the fact that I had been, as he called it, a pushover. He said I had a nice figure but no glamour. I remember he said that the newness had worn off his affair with me, and that he was tired of having to try to deceive me whenever he saw a new person who appealed to him. He then boldly and brazenly announced his determination to get in his car and go to the apartment of Arlene Ferris and force her to apologize for stealing his car. He said if she wasn't 'nice' to him he'd have her arrested for car stealing. He said that he liked women who were difficult, that he was really going to make her pay for what she had done.

"I was terribly upset and he was in a beastly mood. I finally slapped him. Then he started to choke me. I ran into the kitchen and tried to get out the kitchen door. It was bolted and locked. There was no way out. He was between me and the door back to the living room. I kept a table between us. By that time he was in a murderous rage. I grabbed a butcher knife. He lunged toward me, stubbed his toe and missed. As he went by me, half falling, I lashed out with the butcher knife. I didn't know I had killed him. I did know the knife had gone into his back. I had no idea it would go in so easily. I was frightened at what I had done, but I had no idea he was even seriously wounded. I only hoped the knife thrust would slow him down enough so I could escape further abuse. I ran into the living room.

"He tried to chase me but stumbled and fell by the table. I dashed out, got in my car and drove away."

There was silence in the courtroom.

Mason said quietly and with consideration in his voice, "Miss Bristol, did he tell you anything about a check for five hundred dollars?"

She nodded. "That was why he became so impetuous with Arlene Ferris. He said that he had intended to play it slow and easy for a while but that Otto Keswick, who with Sadie Richmond had been blackmailing him for some time over certain of his affairs he didn't dare have come to the attention of his father, had called him and said they needed five hundred dollars at once and would be out within half an hour."

Mason turned to the back of the courtroom. "Now perhaps we'll hear from you, Mr. Albert," he said.

Albert arose and said with dignity, "As it happens, Madge Elwood is my wife. We were married last night in Las Vegas. I flew back here in order to be present in court. As the husband of Madge Elwood I cannot be called upon to testify against her, nor can she be called upon to testify against me."

Albert sat down.

Judge Bayton looked at the district attorney, then at Carson, then at Mason. "Does the defense have any further evidence?"

"None, Your Honor."

"The case against the defendant is dismissed," Judge Bayton said. "The Court orders Edith Bristol into custody. The Court does so with reluctance. The Court feels that this young woman has told her story with great sincerity. It is a story which has made a deep impression upon the Court. The Court has every reason to believe that a jury will believe the story and that Loring Lamont was killed in self-defense. Court is now adjourned."

CHAPTER FIFTEEN

Perry Mason, Della Street, Paul Drake and Arlene Ferris sat in Mason's office.

Arlene Ferris, almost hysterical with joy, was red-eyed from crying, and Della Street sat beside her holding her hand, patting it reassuringly from time to time.

"Well," Mason said, tossing his brief case on the desk, "there's another case out of the way."

"It's just a case to you," Arlene Ferris said, "but it's my whole life."

Mason looked at her sympathetically.

"It's his whole life, too," Della Street said. "His life's work is to see that justice is done, not only in one case, but in *all* his cases."

"Come on, Perry," Paul Drake said, "just what happened?"

"It's simple," Mason said. "Loring Lamont was a wolf. He deliberately planned a conquest of Arlene. He would do it nicely if he could. He would do it the hard way if he couldn't do it the easy way. Apparently he had had quite a bit of experience and he knew the California law, that a woman who becomes the complaining witness in a rape case can be questioned about past indiscretions.

"That gives an unscrupulous man with unlimited money to hire detectives a very considerable leeway.

"However, Otto Keswick put the bite on Loring, told him he would be out in half an hour. Loring decided to speed up operations. We know what happened.

"Sometime later, Madge Elwood had telephoned and told him she'd bring his car out. She also told him she'd arrange to get dry clothes for him, but Madge Elwood didn't have any intention of being placed in the same predicament Arlene had. So she called for her fiancé, George Albert, to go with her. In the meantime she called Edith Bristol. Edith went to the apartment, got the things Lamont wanted and went out to the lodge. Madge deliberately gave Edith a head start."

"Why didn't Edith leave her car and drive Loring Lamont's car out to the lodge?" Drake asked.

Mason said, "Nothing was said about that. Lamont didn't want either to drive Edith home or be saddled with her for the rest of the evening. Remember the evidence shows he had been drinking heavily. When Madge telephoned him he told her to have Edith, who lived close to his apartment and had the only other key, go and get some dry clothes and bring them out. Then Madge was to bring his car out and he planned to have Edith drive Madge back. Loring Lamont didn't intend to let Arlene get away with her coup. He probably planned to drive to her apartment and surprise her. This time he didn't intend to let her throw a chair."

"And the clothes?" Drake asked.

"By the time Madge and George Albert got out there," Mason said, "Loring Lamont was dead. I'm satisfied that they found the body and simply decided to say nothing about it. They felt that the police would be without any clues, and they wanted to keep out of it. So they decided to take Lamont's discarded clothes and hide them. In that way they felt they could keep anything from coming out about what had really happened. Madge was saving Edith's good name, Arlene from publicity, and protecting herself at the same time. So Madge simply returned Lamont's car to the place where Arlene had parked it. She and George Albert felt no one would ever know what had happened after Arlene left."

"Isn't that a crime?" Drake asked, "failing to report a murdered man? Can't they be hooked on that?"

"Sure, it's a crime," Mason said grinning, "provided the D.A. can prove it."

"He can't prove it?"

Mason shook his head. "They're married. Burger can prove Madge Elwood phoned Edith to go out to the lodge, but he can't prove Madge Elwood ever went out there. Thanks to the way the police tried to brainwash Jerome Henley, there's no way of proving Madge was the young woman who parked Loring Lamont's car. At first Henley said she was, then he said she wasn't, then he swore he didn't know. It's a case of the prosecution kicking its own case out of the window by trying to influence a witness."

"How about the check Loring Lamont wrote out there at the lodge?" Della asked. "If Otto and Sadie were so anxious to get it why didn't they cash it?"

"It's almost a sure bet," Mason explained, "that they wanted this check to finance some gambling activities of their own. I'd be willing to wager that when the facts are known we'll find that pair turned the check over to some bookmaker that night. The next day before the check was presented at the bank this person learned of the death of Loring Lamont and knew the check was worthless. A bank can't pay any check drawn on the account of a depositor once the bank knows the man is dead. So the holder of the worthless check tore it up rather than get mixed up in a situation where he'd have explanations to make."

"How about the other check, the one from Jarvis P. Lamont?" Della Street asked. "The one he gave Madge Elwood?"

Mason said, "He did that so she could get married and so neither she nor Albert could be called as a witness. Jarvis P. Lamont wanted to protect the so-called good name of his son if he could. Apparently he was willing to sacrifice Arlene in order to do it."

"But," Della Street asked, "how in the world did Jarvis P. Lamont know all that had happened?"

Mason grinned. "I think we have to concede, Della, that Madge Elwood is a very astute young woman as well as a good-looking one."

"Yes," Paul Drake chimed in, "that makes me wonder what you were talking about all the time she was changing her skirt in Arlene's apartment. It seems to me you were gone quite a spell on that trip. What *were* you talking about?"

Mason winked at Della Street. "Books, Paul," he said.

"Next time," Drake observed, "you'd better use me to do your leg work."

"It was brain work," Mason corrected.